Shih-shuo Hsin-yü
A New Account of Tales of the World

Shih-shuo Hsin-yü

A New Account of Tales of the World

by Liu I-ch'ing
with commentary by Liu Chün

translated with introduction and notes
by Richard B. Mather

University of Minnesota Press, Minneapolis

Copyright © 1976 by the University of Minnesota.
All rights reserved. Printed in the United States of America.

Published in Canada by Burns & MacEachern Limited,
Don Mills, Ontario

Library of Congress Catalog Card Number 75-22650

ISBN 0-8166-0760-5

In memory of
Peter Alexis Boodberg
(1903-1972)

Contents

        Preface   ix
        Introduction   xiii
        Translator's Note   xxxi
   I   Virtuous Conduct   3
  II   Speech and Conversation   25
 III   Affairs of State   81
  IV   Letters and Scholarship   92
   V   The Square and the Proper   146
  VI   Cultivated Tolerance   179
 VII   Insight and Judgment   196
VIII   Appreciation and Praise   210
  IX   Classification According to Excellence   248
   X   Admonitions and Warnings   274
  XI   Quick Perception   292
 XII   Precocious Intelligence   297
XIII   Virile Vigor   301
 XIV   Appearance and Behavior   308
  XV   Self-renewal   318
 XVI   Admiration and Emulation   321
XVII   Grieving for the Departed   323
XVIII   Living in Retirement   331

XIX	Worthy Beauties	340
XX	Technical Understanding	357
XXI	Skill and Art	363
XXII	Favors and Gifts	369
XXIII	The Free and Unrestrained	371
XXIV	Rudeness and Contempt	392
XXV	Taunting and Teasing	400
XXVI	Contempt and Insults	428
XXVII	Guile and Chicanery	441
XXVIII	Dismissal from Office	450
XXIX	Stinginess and Meanness	455
XXX	Extravagance and Ostentation	458
XXXI	Anger and Irascibility	465
XXXII	Slander and Treachery	468
XXXIII	Blameworthiness and Remorse	470
XXXIV	Crudities and Slips of the Tongue	479
XXXV	Blind Infatuations	484
XXXVI	Hostility and Alienation	489
	Biographical Notices	499
	Glossary of Terms and Official Titles	613
	Abbreviations	665
	Bibliography	679
	Index	695

Preface

In a footnote to an important essay on Six Dynasties thought written in 1948, the late Etienne Balazs related an exchange between two intellectuals in postwar Italy involving an ironic interpretation of a quotation from the Gospel of Matthew. He went on to say, "A moment's reflection on how difficult it would be to translate [such an exchange] into Chinese makes it easy to understand why the *Shih-shuo hsin-yü* will remain untranslated for a long time to come."

Professor Balazs' prediction has remained unchallenged in the West for twenty years or more because it rests on a very sound assumption. Since we do not know the exact situations in which some of the conversations in this collection took place, to say nothing of the broader social and cultural milieu, their point often eludes us completely, and even when the point seems within our grasp, its interpretation remains ultimately ambiguous. The fact that I am now offering a complete translation therefore requires some justification. The most obvious argument at hand is that we are not quite so much in the dark as we were twenty-five years ago. Numerous studies and research tools devoted to this text have appeared in both China and Japan, and at least three complete, or nearly complete, translations have been published in Japanese. The time is ripe for a Western-language translation of a work so crucial to the understanding of medieval Chinese culture to be attempted, even if it succeeds only in focusing attention on where further work needs to be done to make later efforts succeed better.

In acknowledging the kindness of the many persons who have assisted in this undertaking over the long period since its inception in the spring of 1957, I am aware that some names have been inadvertantly left out, and some persons may, on the other hand, be embarrassed to discover their complicity in the venture. In either case I wish to stress the arbitrariness of my decision to use or neglect the assistance they provided. I alone am responsible for what has finally resulted.

x   TALES OF THE WORLD

To begin with, I owe an incalculable debt to Professors Fukunaga Mitsuji, Kawakatsu Yoshio, and Tanaka Kenji of the Research Institute of Humanistic Sciences at Kyoto, to Professor Murakami Yoshimi of the History Department of Kansei Gakuin University, and to Mr. Yoshikawa Tadao, lecturer in the History Department of Kyoto University, some of whom had begun weekly seminars on this text as early as 1953, when Donald Holzman temporarily joined their group. I myself was invited to participate while I was at the Research Institute during two sabbatical leaves from the University of Minnesota, the first in 1956-57, when Galen Eugene Sargent was also working with them, and again in 1963-64 when they were completing their project.

A great deal of bibliographical assistance was provided me by Dr. Kaiming Ch'iu, director emeritus of the Harvard-Yenching Institute Library in Cambridge, while he was serving as consultant for the University of Minnesota Library during 1965-66, and by Mr. Paul Cheng, the university's East Asian Librarian from 1965 to 1971. I wish also to record my appreciation for the personal interest and encouragement of Professor Yoshikawa Kōjirō, now retired from the Department of Literature of Kyoto University, who introduced me to the section of the T'ang manuscript fragment of the *Shih-shuo* in the Ogawa Collection in Kyoto. To the Ogawa family itself, for permitting me to handle and photograph that most valuable treasure, and to Professor Fujieda Akira of the Research Institute, for taking such a lively interest in the manuscript's style and provenance, I wish also to express special thanks.

Other persons whose counsel on particular points has been deeply appreciated include Professor Richard Ch'i of the Department of East Asian Languages and Literatures of Indiana University, who kindly read the draft of Chapter II; Professor Nathan Sivin of the Humanities Department of the Massachusetts Institute of Technology, whose advice on technical and scientific matters has been extremely valuable; and Professors K'un Chang and Michael Rogers of the Department of Oriental Languages of the University of California at Berkeley, both of whom have provided useful information and corrections. Always present in my mind, though we were not often in direct communication, has been the influence of my teacher, the late Professor Peter Boodberg, also of Berkeley, to whose memory the book is dedicated.

Grateful acknowledgment is hereby made to the editors of the *Journal of the American Oriental Society* for permission to reprint, with revisions, the two chapters "Speech and Conversation" (II) and "Letters and Scholarship" (IV), which appeared in Volumes 91.2 (1971) and 84.4 (1964) respectively. I am likewise grateful for the two periods of sabbatical leave from the University of Minnesota mentioned above, during which a large portion of the work was accomplished. These were generously supported by grants from the American Educational Commission in Japan, the Guggenheim Foundation, and the American Council of Learned Societies. The Graduate School and the Office of International Programs of the University of Minnesota have also made it possible through smaller grants to pursue aspects of this study in the United States.

The large characters on the title page and chapter headings, written in the style of the fifth century with a brush reconstructed after a T'ang model in the Shōsōin collection in Nara, as well as the smaller characters in the appendices, were penned by my research assistant, Mr. Liao Ling-te, whose expert help in other substantive

matters I would also like to acknowledge here. The painstaking and
genuinely helpful editing of Anne Hage of the University of Minnesota
Press, and the miraculously versatile typing of Sandra Hyvare have
improved the readability of the book beyond telling, and both of them
have my undying gratitude. I cannot close this catalogue without mentioning the moral support provided by my wife, Virginia Temple Mather,
whose well informed and helpful criticisms and encouragement have
sustained my frequently sagging enthusiasm through all the years of
preparing this book.

                                                            Richard B. Mather

St. Paul, Minnesota
Fall 1975

Introduction

The World of the Shih-shuo hsin-yü

If the stories, conversations, and short characterizations which make up this book of "Tales of the World" describe an actual world, we might well ask what kind of world it is. Is it a real world or an imaginary one? Is it the whole world of its particular place and time (China in the second to fourth centuries) or only a narrow segment of that world? And finally, is it an objective portrayal of that world or a highly subjective tract pleading a special point of view? Questions such as these are surely not easily answered, if for no other reason than that the alternatives they pose are in most cases not mutually exclusive. Yet some attempt to face them should prove helpful at the beginning of our study.

Let us start with the problem of reality. A scholar writing in Hong Kong in 1955 noted that the period most thoroughly covered by this book--the Chin Dynasty (265-420)--is ill served by its official history, the *Chin-shu*, because of the latter's hasty compilation three hundred years or so later and because of the "tampering" of the T'ang official historians. By contrast, he observed, the treatment of the Chin period in the "Tales of the World," which was compiled only a decade after the dynasty's close, within the actual lifetime of some of the protagonists, has preserved the sayings and events of these times "as they originally were."[1] This is an important observation, but its conclusion would be extremely difficult to prove. In fact even a casual reading of the biographies in the *Chin-shu* reveals the considerable dependence of that work on the "Tales of the World" itself as a source, and few if any cases of significant tampering could be demonstrated beyond dispute.

What *is* clear is that nearly all of the 626 characters appearing in the pages of the "Tales of the World" are otherwise attested in the histories and other sources. Furthermore, for most incidents and remarks, allowing for literary embellishment and dramatic exaggeration, there is no good reason to doubt their reality. Only a small minority pose problems of anachronism, contradition of known facts, gross supernatural intrusions, or apparent inconsistencies. Among the verifiable facts, for example, in Chapter II, 59, there is a record of the planet Mars (Ying-huo) reentering the "heavenly enclosure" T'ai-wei (parts of the constellations Virgo and Leo) in retrograde motion on a date corresponding to February 17, 372. This can be checked against accurate modern projections for the planetary motions of the fourth century and found to be absolutely correct.[2]

Similarly, when we are told that the Eastern Chin general Huan Wen (312-373) was engaged in military expeditions against the Taoist rebel state of Ch'eng-Han in Szechwan between 346 and 347 (Chapter II, 58), and against the proto-Tibetan state of Former Ch'in in Shensi in 354 (II, 55), and against the proto-Tungusic state of Former Yen in Honan and Hopei in 356 (IV, 96), we need not look for any tampering with facts, since these events are all well documented elsewhere. What actually happened or what actually was said on these occasions may not have been exactly as reported in the "Tales of the World," but the same accusation can be leveled at Ssu-ma Ch'ien's (145-90 B.C.) narration and dialogue in the "Records of the Grand Historian" (Shih-chi) and at most Chinese historiography after him. A certain amount of local color and fictionalization was more or less expected even in the standard histories.

Yet the writing of history seems not to have been the intention of the author of the "Tales of the World." Certainly the compilers of the bibliographical monographs of the Sui dynastic history (Sui-shu 34) and the two T'ang histories (Chiu T'ang-shu 47 and Hsin T'ang-shu 60) did not place the work under the Division of History (shih-pu), but rather in the Division of Philosophers (tzu-pu), under Minor Tales (hsiao-shuo). There, tucked between technical treatises on agriculture and war, it enjoyed the company of fictionalized biographies like the story of "Crown Prince Tan of Yen" (Yen Tan-tzu), which elaborates the already fictionalized account of Ching K'o's attempted assassination of the First Emperor in 227 B.C. recounted in the "Intrigues of the Warring States" (Chan-kuo ts'e 31) and again in the "Records of the Grand Historian" (Shih-chi 86). Under the same heading are also listed source books for advisers to the throne, such as the "Forest of Arguments" (Pien-lin) or "Formulae for Those to the Right of the Throne" (Tso-yu fang); jokebooks for court jesters, like Han-tan Ch'un's (third cent.) "Forest of Laughs" (Hsiao-lin); and general enliveners of conversation, like the "Essential and Usable Answers for Repartee" (Yao-yung yü-tui). Another work in this category very close in form to the "Tales of the World" itself was P'ei Ch'i's "Forest of Conversations" (Yü-lin), which first appeared in 362 and, if we can believe the story in Chapter XXVI, 24, of the "Tales," after a lightning popularity, quickly dropped from sight because of false or unflattering references to living persons.

The association of such heterogeneous works under the same rubric helps to clarify what the "Tales of the World" itself was considered to be in its own times. It was partly an aid to conversation, and certainly one of its aims was to provide enjoyable reading. This is perhaps its strongest link with the later "novels," also called hsiao-shuo, one of the earliest of which, the "Romance of the Three Kingdoms" (San-kuo yen-i), actually includes a few of the same anecdotes, suitably enriched and expanded, especially those concerning

Ts'ao Ts'ao (155-220), the founder of the Wei Kingdom. Ts'ao's personality as it appears in the official biography by Ch'en Shou (233-297) in the *Wei-chih* (*SKWei* 1) is somewhat colorless. He is depicted as a man of action, a military genius, who in his youth was "quick-witted and alert, skilled in adapting to circumstances." The greatest flaws in his character were his love of knight-errantry and his "recklessness." But within a generation or two of his death a legend had grown up about him as a cold-blooded villain who would kill a faithful slave merely as a warning to any would-be assassins, or murder the man who had given him shelter, with all the members of his household, simply to cover a cruel mistake.

The "Tales of the World" includes nineteen stories about Ts'ao Ts'ao, most of which already show the influence of the legend. The sources were undoubtedly the same ones quoted by P'ei Sung-chih (372-451) in his commentary to the *Wei-chih*, published in 429, just one year before the "Tales" itself: the anonymous "Biography of Ts'ao Man" (*Ts'ao Man chuan*), Wang Ch'en's "Wei History" (*Wei-shu*, late third cent.), Kuo Pan's "Stories of the World" (*Shih-yü*, ca. 300), and Sun Sheng's "Miscellaneous Accounts of Things Unfamiliar and Familiar" (*I-t'ung tsa-yü*, mid-fourth cent.). In different ways the stories about Wang Tao (276-339) and his cousin Wang Tun (226-324), and of Hsieh An (320-385) and Ku K'ai-chih (ca. 345-406), also reflect the legends which had grown up around these names.

By linking the tales of this collection and its numerous sources with the storytelling tradition which produced the later "novels," I do not mean to suggest a direct lineage between the early *hsiao-shuo* and the later productions of the same name. Obviously there were many layers of influence intervening. I wish merely to stress the entertainment factor which was common to both--the telling of a good tale or a particularly witty remark, and the recording of eccentricities and curiosities--which was by no means least among the intentions of the author of the "Tales of the World."

If the book was, at least in part, a fictionalization rather than sober history, we might go on to ask, Does it attempt to depict the *whole* of the Chinese world of the second to fourth centuries A.D.? Looking at the chapter headings one might get a first impression of some sort of universal encyclopedia or "book of categories" (*lei-shu*). The stories in the first parts of the book are classified according to civic and moral virtues (Chapters I-VIII) and cultivated and intellectual accomplishments (IX-XVII). The next chapters are devoted to recluses (XVIII) and women (XIX). There is a fascinating pair on technology and art (XX and XXI). From Chapter XXII to the end (XXXVI) is one of the most exhaustive lists of human frailty one could find in any literature. Yet somehow these "Tales of the World" fall far short of providing a whole picture of the times. There are occasional references to slaves and serfs, but they are incidental objects decorating the homes and estates of the great. One or two incidents involve palace guards and soldiers on campaign, but these are mentioned only to illustrate some trait of their commanding officers, most of whom were not career army men who had risen from the ranks, but gentlemen. Tantalizing references are also made to merchants plying their trade along the waterways near the southern capital in Chien-k'ang (modern Nanking), but they are merely stage props for the escapades of some of the more colorful members of the gentry. Even the subjects mentioned in the chapters on technology and art are drawn not from the artisan class but from the aristocracy. The world of these tales is consequently a very narrow world indeed: of emperors and princes, courtiers, officials, generals, genteel hermits, and urbane monks. But though they live in a rarefied atmosphere of great refinement and sensitivity, they are, nevertheless, for the most part involved in a very earthly, and often bloody, world of war and factional intrigue. It is a dark world against which the occasional flashes of wit and insight shine the more brightly.

In the three centuries spanned by the lives and events of the tales (roughly 120-420 A.D.) a series of cataclysms occurred in close succession: (1) In 184 a revolt of desperate peasants in the eastern provinces (the Yellow Turbans) precipitated four decades of civil war ending in the fall of Han. (2) In 249, by a coup d'etat, the Ssu-ma family seized power in the new Kingdom of Wei, initiating a bloody purge of all persons opposing their reactionary retreat to a pre-Wei ideology, and eventually founding the Chin Dynasty in 265. (3) In 300 one of the Chin princes, seeking to replace the imbecile Emperor Hui (r. 290-306), started a fratricidal war among his rivals, the so-called War of the Eight Princes, which lasted six years and brought the state to utter exhaustion, leaving the door open for non-Chinese peoples living in the north to destroy both the capitals at Lo-yang (Honan) in 309 and Ch'ang-an (Shensi) in 316, and to set up a succession of non-Chinese states in north China. (4) After mass migrations between 307 and 312 of those gentry families who could afford to escape, an exile regime, the Eastern Chin, was set up with its capital in Chien-k'ang, where it maintained a precarious existence until 420, protected from northern incursions only by its natural defenses. (5) In 383 one of the northern rulers, Fu Chien (337-384), who then controlled all of north and west China, made a bid to conquer Eastern Chin as well, but failed only because of problems of logistics. (6) Between 401 and 403, again in desperate economic straits, the peasants of the lower Yangtze delta revolted under the Taoist leaders Sun En (d. 402) and his successor Lu Hsün (d. 411), and in the following year the ambitious general Huan Hsüan (369-404) usurped the throne for three months before being cut down by another general, Liu Yü (356-422), who himself founded the Sung Dynasty in 420.

In view of the uncertainty of life against such a background and the ever-present tensions of clan and factional partisanship, it is relevant to ask not only whether the tales are real, or whether they depict the whole world of the time, but also whether they are told objectively, or if they might perhaps reflect the bias of some particular faction. There were, of course, many factions struggling against each other during the period covered by this book. In Later Han there were the Yellow Turbans, mostly peasants, and their leaders, men from impoverished gentry families, versus the Han government, represented by the commanders of the counterinsurgent forces. There were the literati at court versus the eunuchs and upstart consort families. Later there were the loyalists of Wei--supporters of the Ts'ao royal family--versus the reaction led by the Ssu-ma family, who later founded the Chin.

During Western Chin there were the factions loyal to the old consort family of Yang versus those who supported the new consort family of Chia, whose struggle ended in the bloody War of the Eight Princes mentioned above. At the same time a bloodless feud, which occasionally erupted in searing verbal exchanges, was going on between the "libertines" under the leadership of the grand marshal Wang Yen (256-311), versus the moral and ritual conformists, whose spokesman was the vice-president of the Imperial Secretariat, P'ei Wei (267-300). After the exile to the Yangtze delta and the founding of Eastern Chin in 317 a succession of family hegemonies dominated the court at Chien-k'ang--the Wangs of Lang-yeh, the Yüs, the Hos, the Huans, the Hsiehs--terminating in the rise of the Lius of Sung in 420. Underlying this court intrigue, which was largely an affair of the exiles from the north, was the fierce regional animosity of the older settlers of the Yangtze region, the natives of Wu and Ch'u, whose leading families did not relish this sudden overshadowing by intruders from the north after 307.

But whatever other factors complicated the relations between these factions throughout this period--political, social, economic, or even religious, they seem to have boiled down by the third century to two fundamentally opposed points of view, which for convenience I shall designate by the terms most often used by contemporaries: those who favored naturalness (*tzu-jan*) versus those who insisted on conformity to the Moral Teaching (*ming-chiao*). In each succeeding period the issues were slightly different, but basically upholders of naturalness were inclined toward Taoism in their philosophy, unconventionality in their morals, and non-engagement in their politics, while upholders of conformity favored the Confucian tradition, fortified with a generous admixture of Legalism, conventionality in morals, and a definite commitment to public life. Though it is not blatantly obvious from a first reading of these tales, it is at least arguable that some characters appearing in them are more admirable than others. It is even possible to suggest that the admirable ones seem to hold certain characteristics in common. For example, they all seem to be lovers of good conversation and literature, they tend to prefer the regressive virtues of peace, tranquillity, withdrawal, freedom, and unconventionality, and to despise aggressive qualities in the less admirable characters, such as martial prowess, virility, excitability, and rigid conformity to moral and ritual norms. In short the first group are adherents of naturalness and the latter of conformity, and whoever put these tales together seems to have had a preference for the former over the latter.

A few examples may help to make the point clear. By far the strongest character to emerge in the whole work is Hsieh An (320-385), who figures in over a hundred anecdotes. His prowess in "pure conversation" (*ch'ing-yen* or *ch'ing-t'an*) was acknowledged even by his enemies, and, characteristically, he remained a recluse in the Chekiang hills until he was forty before finally answering the desperate need of the realm for his talents. He faced many grave crises in the course of his rise to supreme power at court, but always with total tranquillity, a quality named "cultivated tolerance" (*ya-liang*) in the "Tales," which devotes an entire chapter (VI) to examples of its exercise. Cultivated tolerance includes the ability to conceal the slightest hint of anxiety, fear, excitement, or joy in either facial, verbal, or bodily expression. It is very much like the quality of "imperturbability" (*ataraxia*) so highly prized in the late Hellenistic world, another highly civilized society living under the imminent threat of extinction. In Hsieh An's case, whether he was caught in a sudden squall on a boating excursion, or facing ambush and certain death at a banquet served by his mortal enemy, or receiving the victory announcement of the Eastern Chin forces over vastly superior odds at the Fei River, in each situation he simply went on chanting poems or playing encirclement chess as if nothing had happened.

More aggressive men, by contrast, are certainly held up to no great honor in the "Tales." Beside Huan Wen (312-373), the military dictator and near usurper who serves as the perfect foil for Hsieh An, there is the bold adventurer Wang Tun (266-324). This man's "virile vigor" was able to support a seraglio of "several tens" of female slaves and concubines, and on the occasion of a banquet at the home of the wealthy and ostentatious Shih Ch'ung (249-300) he adamantly refused to drink, just to test his host, who had sworn that the beautiful girls serving the wine would be decapitated on the spot whenever the guests they served did not drain their cups. After three girls in a row had lost their heads, Wang continued with flintlike unconcern to refuse to drink, in spite of the agonized pleading of his cousin, Wang Tao (276-339), later chancellor in Eastern Chin, whose sensitivity and humanity are set off by the cold inhumanity of Wang Tun in the same way that Hsieh An's imperturbability is emphasized by Huan Wen's irascibility a generation later.

Thus, though it cannot be demonstrated conclusively, it seems probable that the author of the "Tales," whoever he was, was a partisan of naturalness and a foe of conformity. But what then are we to do with the traditional authorship, which has always been attributed to Liu I-ch'ing (403-444), the very conservative and conventional nephew of Liu Yü (356-422), the military founder of the Sung Dynasty? To side with the critics of strong military action and strict ritual conformity would hardly befit a man in his station. The theory, therefore, first advanced in 1924 by Lu Hsün in his "Short History of Chinese Fiction" (*Chung-kuo hsiao-shuo shih-lüeh*),[3] that Liu had only sponsored the work of subordinates on his staff is given considerable credence, especially in the light of a recent article by Kawakatsu Yoshio, entitled "On the Compilation and Editing of the *Shih-shuo hsin-yü*" ("*Sesetsu shingo* no hensan o megutte").[4]

Kawakatsu argues persuasively that since the general viewpoint I have hinted at prevails in the work, and especially since Liu's contemporary and one-time staff member, Hsieh Ling-yün (385-433), who was executed in 433 as a rebel against the Sung court, is depicted in Chapter II, 108, with complete sympathy, there is good reason to believe the actual compilation and editing may have been done by Hsieh's close friend and colleague on Liu's staff, Ho Ch'ang-yü, whose stated views match those of the book. Of course it is only a hypothesis, and there is still the problem of why the prince should have permitted his name to be attached to a potentially subversive work. But with still other oblique confirmations, such as the shocked disbelief of the commentator, Liu Chün (462-521), whenever he came upon what he felt to be a particularly flagrant example of moral laxity or distortion of the facts in the "Tales," it makes a good deal of sense to suppose that Liu I-ch'ing was not the actual author.

Since the generalized polarity between naturalness and conformity offers a convenient touchstone by which the characters of the book may be roughly separated, let us move on to examine these two ideologies in their various cultural ramifications, for in a sense the whole direction of literary, intellectual, and religious history in this period may be viewed from this dual perspective. The naturalistic poets and essayists extolled the recessive virtues of withdrawal and tranquillity and laid the foundation for the growth of nature poetry in the following period. To some extent they were even liberated from the formal stylistic restrictions beloved by the conformist writers of the same period. They strongly favored the five-word line with its greater spontaneity over the archaizing tendency of poets like P'an Yüeh (247-300) whose "Songs on the Family Tradition" (Chia-feng shih), alluded to in Chapter IV, 71, in heavy four-word meter are replete with Confucian admonitions.

In the mid-third century the greatest exponents of naturalness in their literary compositions were Hsi K'ang (223-262) and Juan Chi (210-263). Hsi K'ang's bitter enmity against Chung Hui (225-262) is well documented in the "Tales" and was the ultimate cause of Hsi's death. In his "Letter Breaking off Friendship with Shan T'ao" (Yü Shan Chü-yüan chüeh-chiao shu) Hsi had written: "My taste for independence was aggravated by my reading of Chuang-tzu and Lao-tzu; as a result any desire for fame or success grew daily weaker, and my commitment to freedom increasingly firmer . . . Of late I have been studying the techniques of prolonging one's life, casting out all ideas of fame and glory, eliminating tastes, and letting my mind wander in stillness: what is most worthwhile to me is Inaction (wu-wei) . . .[5]

In his poem "Sequestered Grief" (Yu-fen), attributed to the time of his incarceration before his execution, Hsi was still stressing the same theme, using the images found in his favorite philosophers:

> Committed affectionately to Lao-tzu and
>   Chuang-tzu,
> I have devalued things and valued my own person.
> My ambition has consisted in guarding the
>   Uncarved Block,
> In nourishing the Undyed Silk, and preserving
>   Reality whole.[6]

His friend and contemporary Juan Chi was less abrasive as a person and more skillful in adapting to hostile circumstance, but his sentiments were no less committed to naturalness. In his celebrated satire "The Biography of Mr. Greatman" (Ta-jen hsien-sheng chuan), he did not hesitate to compare the conformists, who, he said, "like to think that their actions set a permanent example . . . and that their words are everlasting models," to the "lice that inhabit a pair of trousers" ready for the bonfire, so obsessed with the cocoon-like comfort of their narrow world that they are oblivious of its imminent destruction.[7] In one of his many poems found under the title "Poems from My Heart" (Yung-huai shih), he makes a similar contrast:

> Amid the clouds there is a dark-hued crane;
> With high resolve it lifts its mournful sound.
> Once flown from sight into the blue-green sky,
> In all the world it will not cry again.
> What has it to do with quails and sparrows
> Flapping their wings in play within the
>   central court?[8]

After Hsi K'ang's execution as a perverter of public morals by Ssu-ma Shih in 262, the admirers of naturalness had to seek more subtle ways of expressing their ideals. One of those associated with Hsi K'ang and Juan Chi, Hsiang Hsiu (ca. 221-300), while ostensibly joining the conformists by accepting office under the Chin, managed to maintain a delicately balanced compromise whereby he outwardly conformed to all their moral and ritual demands while inwardly remaining natural and free. If the commentary on *Chuang-tzu* by Kuo Hsiang (d. 312) is, as some maintain, heavily dependent on Hsiang Hsiu's lost original, the statement there that "the sage constantly roams beyond the world in order to expand what is *within* it," summarizes his mystical union of the two.[9]

A younger writer, Yü Ai (262-311), resolved the problem by a more thoroughgoing escape from time and space into the world of thought. In his "Poetic Essay on Thought" (*I-fu*) he wrote:

> The Realized Man abandons all defiling bonds,
> His nature boundless, free, and without shores.
> Unchecked, he roams in spacious courts,
> Commits his body to quiescent halls.
> Heaven and earth for him are briefer than the
>   morning glory,
> A million ages fleeter than the early dawn.
> He looks back on the universe, a tiny speck,
> Slender as but half a tip of down.
> He drifts through subtle and untrammeled realms;
> There are no depths he leaves untried.
> Obliviously identified with the
>   Naturally-so (*tzu-jan*),
> He melts and flows away and is dispersed.[10]

After the exile to Eastern Chin in 307-312 this compromise of inward or mental naturalness amid outward conformity became the right wing of the new naturalness, standing between the conformists and certain radicals whose pose of pure disengagement may have camouflaged other motives for staying out of politics. Spokesmen for the mediating position were Sun Ch'o (active mid-fourth cent.) and Yuan Hung (328-376), both of whom were deeply involved in public life. Sun once remarked, "For those who embody the Mysterious (*hsüan*) and understand the Remote (*yüan*), public life or retirement amounts to the same thing."[11] So it is not surprising to read in his "Poetic Essay on Roaming in the T'ien-t'ai Mountains" (*Yu T'ien-t'ai-shan fu*) the account of a purely mystical ascent into perfect union with the Naturally-so while carrying on his mundane official duties. His debt to Yü Ai's essay is evident in the closing passage:

> Aware that dismissal of the Actual (*yu*)
>   is incomplete,
> And realizing that experience of the
>   Non-actual (*wu*) is subject to interruptions,
> I mingle with the Emptiness of Matter, uniting it
>   with my (worldly) traces,
> And fuse with Actuality itself to gain
>   the Mysterious.
> Blending the myriad signs in mystic contemplation,
> I am obliviously identified with the
>   Naturally-so.[12]

What is new in Sun Ch'o's mysticism is the accommodation of Mahayana Buddhist ideas like Emptiness (k'ung = śūnyatā), properly meaning "absence of self-nature or independent existence," though still understood by the Chinese as more or less the equivalent of the Taoist term, wu, Nothing, or Non-actuality.

Yüan Hung was primarily a historian, working within the proper domain of the conformists, but he managed to develop a quasi-naturalist theory of history in his "Annals of Later Han" (Hou-Han chi): "The relation between ruler and subject and between father and son is the basis of the Moral Teaching (ming-chiao). This being the case, what is the origin of this Teaching? In my view it has determined the meaning of names (ming) by complying with the nature of Heaven and Earth, and by seeking the principles of the Naturally-so (tzu-jan)."[13] In other words, human relations, which are the essence of historical events, are basically determined by the *nature* of the universe. The Moral Teaching is really based on naturalness after all. It is only the artificial perversions of some moralists which create any tension between the two.

Yüan Hung served for several years as an aide on Huan Wen's staff, and it is obvious that some of his animus for Huan sprang from the mere fact of being a subordinate. But it is also clear that Yüan had no use for Huan's type--the vigorous military activist, full of patriotic and moral platitudes. During one of his northern campaigns Huan Wen climbed to the observation tower of his ship and, observing the devastation about him, declared with a sigh, "For letting the Sacred Provinces of the Central Plain be overrun and lie waste for a hundred years, Wang Yen and his gang (the "libertines" of Western Chin) must bear the blame!"

He was immediately contradicted by Yüan Hung, who remonstrated, "How can the rise or fall of human destiny depend on the faults of any particular group?" Flushing with anger, Huan thereupon hinted none too subtly that Yüan had outlived his usefulness.[14]

Though there are reasons to suspect the following two stories, preserved in the text and Commentary at Chapter IV, 97, about Yüan Hung's lost magnum opus, the "Poetic Essay on the Eastern Expedition" (Tung-cheng fu), a euphemism for the debacle ending in the founding of Eastern Chin, it is significant, I believe, that both have to do with military men of strong anti-naturalist sentiments--Huan Wen's father, Huan I (276-328), and T'ao K'an (259-334). In the first account Yüan is said to have omitted all reference to T'ao K'an in the essay. Since T'ao was conspicuous in the founding of Eastern Chin, it was indeed a large omission, and Yüan was narrowly saved from the exploding resentment of the slighted general's son, T'ao Fan (fl. ca. 376), only by his quick wit in improvising six lines of acclaim for T'ao K'an on the spot. The Commentary, citing T'an Tao-luan's (fifth cent.) "Continued Chronicle of Chin" (Hsü Chin yang-ch'iu), carries a similar story about another six lines hastily pulled from Yüan's fertile brain when Huan Wen discovered the omission of *his* father's name. In view of Huan's already stated opinion of "Wang Yen and his gang," and T'ao K'an's stern denunciation of his underlings when he came upon them gambling, these omissions could hardly have been fortuitous. At the very least they were a "Freudian slip." T'ao K'an had once harangued his gambling officers as follows: "The frivolities of Lao-tzu and Chuang-tzu have nothing in common with the model sayings of the Former Kings, and one dare not practice them. [T'ao believed

that Lao-tzu invented dicing and later taught it to the Western
barbarians.] A gentleman ought to straighten his robe and cap and
conduct himself with dignity and decorum. What business has anyone
cultivating a reputation by his disheveled hair and calling himself
great and untrammeled?"[15]

Though Sun Ch'o and Yüan Hung stood on middle ground, there were
others who took a far more radical stance. Such were certain aristocratic
recluses who made a point of spurning the world and its affairs
and who lived in their well-appointed hermitages in the
Chekiang hills and wrote about the beauties of unspoiled nature. The
most celebrated of these in his own day was Hsü Hsün (d. ca. 358),
whose five-word poems the future Emperor Chien-wen (r. 371-2) acclaimed
as surpassing in subtlety those of all his contemporaries.
Unfortunately, almost nothing of Hsü's work remains. An imitation by
Chiang Yen (444-505) appears in Wen-hsüan 31.13b-14a.[16] But it is
their ideological difference which explains to a large degree the
rivalry between Hsü Hsün and Sun Ch'o in the "Tales." In Chapter IX,
61, it is claimed that "those who honored Hsü for his exalted
feelings would correspondingly despise Sun for his corrupt conduct,
and those who loved Sun for his literary ability and style would conversely
have no use for Hsü." As is explained in the Commentary, citing
the "Literary Chronicle" (Wen-chang chih), both Hsü and Sun
talked about "turning their backs on the world," but it was only Hsü
who never "compromised his determination."

When asked by the monk Chih Tun (314-366) how he would rate himself
in comparison to Hsü Hsün, Sun Ch'o answered, "As far as exalted
feelings and remoteness are concerned, your disciple has long since
inwardly conceded Hsü's superiority. But in the matter of a single
humming or a single intoning of poetry, Hsü will have to sit facing
north [i.e., take the student's position]" (IX, 54). The latter
remark may have referred primarily to Sun's self-assumed superiority
over Hsü in letters, but in the light of the earlier reference to
Sun's "corrupt conduct," I think Sun was implying, "Hsü Hsün may be
'exalted' and 'remote,' but since he never sullies himself with
worldly matters, how can he be qualified to write any poem worth humming
or intoning?" The two represented, in fact, two distinct points
of view, even though both were opposed to the straight conformists.

The intellectual climate in which these ideological differences
developed is usually covered by the blanket term "Mysterious Learning"
or "Study of the Mystery" (hsüan-hsüeh), which is by some taken to be
a resurgence of philosophical Taoism, i.e., "Neo-Taoism," eclipsing
the old Han Confucianism.[17] Others have pointed out, however, that
any identification of the Mysterious Learning with Taoism fails to
take account of its close association with the official class and the
effort to provide a new metaphysics to replace that of the discredited
New Text School of classical exegesis.[18] The principal forms in which
the Mysterious Learning manifested itself were determined by the primary
needs of each succeeding period. At the end of Han and after the
establishment of the Wei Kingdom, finding suitable men of talent for
administrative posts seemed to be a dominant concern, and hence the
art of "pure criticism," or "criticism by the pure" (ch'ing-i), arose,
in which incumbents or candidates for office were succinctly characterized
in terms of matching ability with function. Liu Shao's (fl.
ca. 190-265) "Study of Human Abilities" (Jen-wu chih)[19] is an early
example; Chung Hui's (225-264) "Treatise on the Four Basic Relations

between Natural Ability and Human Nature" (*Ssu-pen lun*) became the classic statement during the third and fourth centuries. Chapters VII through IX of the "Tales of the World," especially the last, on "Classification According to Excellence" (*P'in-tsao*), incorporate further instances of its application.

This is thought by some to have been the origin of the art of "pure conversation" (*ch'ing-yen* or *ch'ing-t'an*),[20] but other developments of the art were bound to appear in which the originally practical application all but disappeared and purely metaphysical problems were discussed, such as the relation of Nothing, or Non-actuality (*wu*), to Something, or Actuality (*yu*).[21] Ho Yen (ca. 190-249?), the adopted son of Ts'ao Ts'ao, seems to have set the tone of these discussions with his twin discourses on the *Lao-tzu*, the "Discourse on the Way" (*Tao-lun*) and "On the Power" (*Te-lun*), surviving only in quotations. These were soon followed by the brilliant commentaries of his younger contemporary, Wang Pi (226-249), on the "Book of Changes" (*Chou-i lüeh-i*) and the *Lao-tzu* (*Lao-tzu chu*), both of which are extant. In the latter Wang explained the relation between Actuality and Non-actuality as follows:

"All that is Actual takes its origin from the Non-actual. Therefore, before anything possesses form or has a name, (the Tao) becomes the origin of all things. At the moment things have form or names, then (the Tao) makes them grow, nourishes them . . . and becomes their mother. That is to say, the Tao by means of the formless and nameless originates and completes all things. Because it originates and completes, yet no one knows how it does so, it is more mysterious than the Mysterious (*hsüan*). All things originate from the infinitesimal (*wei*) and later reach perfection. They originate from the Non-actual and later come to birth" (*Lao-tzu chu* 1).

Though this may sound rather unrelated to the events following the downfall of Han civilization, it seems that by making the Non-actual, or the as-yet "unformed" and "unnamed," the philosophical substratum of all actual events the Wei rulers and their advisers were laying the groundwork for massive innovations, unprejudiced by the rigid forms and correct names of the old Han orthodoxy. In their place Wang Pi and the others substituted the normative principle of Naturalness, or the Naturally-so (*tzu-jan*): "Heaven and Earth comply with the Naturally-so, not contriving (*wu-wei*) and not creating (*wu-tsao*). All things of themselves control and order each other. . . . The Naturally-so is a word without qualifications, a term of infinite applicability" (*Lao-tzu chu* 5, 25).

It was, at least in part, a shocked reaction against the unimaginable chaos toward which this philosophy might lead which brought about the downfall of the faction led by the regent, Ts'ao Shuang, to which both Ho Yen and Wang Pi belonged, and all of them perished in the coup d'etat of Ssu-ma I in 249. Thereafter the art of pure conversation took another turn. While the Cheng-shih era (240-249), the age of Ho Yen and Wang Pi, because of its freshness and creativity is called the "Golden Age" of pure conversation by Miyazaki Ichisada,[22] the next fifteen years of transition before the formal establishment of Chin, from 250 to 265, he calls the "Silver Age." Here the controversy over naturalness and conformity, which had up to now been only latent, became explicit. The lines were sharply drawn between the supporters of the reactionary Ssu-ma faction, who held the positions of power, and the Wei loyalists, who were for the most part out of office. While Hsi K'ang, Juan Chi, and the others associated with the group later known as the "Seven Worthies of the Bamboo Grove," were exalting naturalness and disengagement[23] and demonstrating it in their behavior, Chung Hui and his collaborators in the "Treatise on the Four Basic Relations between Natural Ability and Human Nature" were busy demonstrating that whether nature and ability are identical (*t'ung*), different (*i*), combined (*ho*), or distinct (*li*), they do in some way bear a relation to what a man can contribute to society by putting his talents to work in a political office.[24] According to a charming story in the "Tales of the World," Chung wanted very much to discuss this "Treatise" face to face with Hsi K'ang, but lost his nerve at the last minute and never drew it from his bosom until he had left and was a safe distance from the door, after which he turned and hurled it back (Chapter IV, 5).

After Hsi's death in 262, as I have already indicated, the philosophical climate became a great deal chillier. The open controversy ceased with the open cessation of resistance to government service, but a new philosophy of "untrammeled freedom" (*k'uang-ta*) gained currency, especially among those wealthy aristocrats who could afford to assume a detached view of their sinecures at the Lo-yang court. A group of these came to be known later as the "Eight Free Spirits" (*pa-ta*). Among their number was Yü Ai, whose "Poetic Essay on Thought" has already been mentioned. The line, "Unchecked, he roams in spacious courts," expresses the philosophical and moral posture of this group, which, according to rumors which circulated at the time, went in for all-night drunken orgies and even nudism, both of which were a kind of symbolic protest against the confinement of ritual conventions.[25]

But of course the official ideology of the Chin court was always more sedate than this, and probably their most vigorous spokesman before the fall of Lo-yang in 311 was P'ei Wei (267-300). His "Treatise in Praise of Actuality" (*Ch'ung-yu lun*) provides a strongly worded apologia for positive action in the face of the paralyzing wave of nihilism which was presumed to underlie the libertinism of people like the "Eight Free Spirits." In the early-fourth-century work "Eulogies of Chin Nobles" (*Chin chu-kung tsan*), quoted in the Commentary of Chapter IV, 12, the circumstances of P'ei Wei's writing of the "Treatise" are set forth: "In the younger generation people like Yü Ai all admired unceremoniousness and unconventionality. P'ei Wei was distressed by the morals of his age and by the exaltation of the principle of Nothingness (*hsü-wu*), so he composed the two treatises, 'In Praise of Actuality' (*Ch'ung-yu*) and 'In Honor of Non-actuality' (*Kuei-wu*), to refute them."

The text was said to be so profound that contemporary scholars were unable to appreciate its meaning.[26] If even *they* had trouble, we may perhaps be forgiven if some of it is still beyond our grasp today. But the general tenor of the essay is clear. The cult of "Non-actuality," claimed P'ei, leads directly to irresponsibility in both public and private life: "If one devalues Actuality (*yu*) he is sure to consider the body extraneous; and if he considers the body extraneous he will surely neglect controls; and if he neglects controls he will surely be remiss about preventive measures; and if he is remiss about preventive measures he is sure to forget the rites. If rites and controls are not preserved, then there is nothing left with which to carry on government."[27]

Philosophically P'ei Wei's position was very close to the "Neo-Taoist" compromise of his contemporary, Kuo Hsiang, whose commentary on the *Chuang-tzu* has already been noted. P'ei said, "The Ultimate Nothing (*chih-wu*) has no means of being able to produce anything, so whatever begins to be produced is self-produced. If it is self-produced it must embody Something (*t'i-yu*)."[28] This is almost verbatim what Kuo Hsiang said about "Nothing" in commenting on *Chuang-tzu* 22:

"What could have existed before all things? We might suppose Yin and Yang to have existed before all things, but Yin and Yang are themselves merely things. So what existed before Yin and Yang? We might suppose the Naturally-so (*tzu-jan*) to have existed before them, but the Naturally-so is merely things being what they are. We might suppose the Ultimate Way (*chih-Tao*) to have existed before this, but the Ultimate Way is none other than the Ultimate Nothing (*chih-wu*). Since it is Nothing, how then can it have existed before anything? If that is the case, what is it which existed before things? The fact that there is always something else ad infinitum makes clear that things are so of themselves; it is not something else which makes them so."[29]

The contrast represented by debates on Actuality versus Non-actuality, or Something versus Nothing, with their corresponding life-styles of conformity versus naturalness, persisted into the fourth century in the exile dynasties at Chien-k'ang, but the only significant new directions came from an unexpected source--Buddhism. Buddhism had, of course, existed on Chinese soil since its first importation from India and Central Asia about the time of Christ, but few members of the lettered classes seemed greatly attracted to its doctrines, which had developed in a very different social and philosophical climate from China's own, until the downfall of Western Chin in the second decade of the fourth century. The reasons for the gradualness of this receptivity have been discussed at length in other easily accessible works[30] and need not detain us here. For an understanding of the role of Buddhism in the world of these "Tales" it is only necessary to be aware that Chinese intellectuals of the fourth century, somewhat jaded with the clichés of the Mysterious Learning, felt they had discovered a new dimension in facing the old problems.

It was not just Actuality versus Non-actuality, or Something versus Nothing, but Samsara versus Nirvana; not falsehood versus truth, but delusion versus enlightenment; not mundane affairs versus transcendence over them, but life of the worldling versus that of the monk or devoted layman, which now occupied their thinking. They felt they had now found the cause and cure of suffering--a problem simply glossed over by China's sages--and a new sense of compassion for all living beings. To be sure, this was the period in Chinese Buddhist history of the "Six Schools," in which the Mahayana doctrine of the "emptiness of self-being" (*svabhāva-śūnyatā*) proclaimed in the newly translated *Prajñāpāramitā-sūtras* was still being understood largely in terms of the "Neo-Taoist" concept of Non-actuality.[31] The syncretistic instinct, always strong in Chinese converts, continued to find harmonies with Confucian and Taoist ideals in the face of apparent contraditions, even after the lucid translations and exegesis of Kumārajīva (d. 409) had revealed the unique character of Buddhist thought. But the transfusion of the new terminology and new insights into the old art of pure conversation prolonged its life at least another two centuries.

One of the most sought-after conversationalists at the Eastern Chin capital, and the most popular lecturer at public expositions and debates in Buddhist temples both in the capital and at K'uai-chi to the southeast, was Chih Tun (314-366). His new interpretation of Chuang-tzu's "Free Wandering" (*Hsiao-yao yu*) chapter (*Chuang-tzu* 1) in terms of Buddhahood, free of the confining bonds of the Self and transcending the stultifying effects of self-satisfaction with one's "lot" (*fen*) advocated in Kuo Hsiang's commentary, created something of a sensation in his day. According to the "Tales," "thereafter the chapter was always interpreted with Chih's principles."[32] Chih Tun is credited with being the first to use the term *li*, "principles within the natural order," in an absolute sense—"*the* Principle" or "Truth"—comparable to the Buddhist notion of "Suchness" (*tathatā*). In later philosophical discussions it was always to have overtones of this new meaning.[33]

Chih Tun managed to remain aloof from politics and the ideological tensions separating the opposing champions of comformity versus naturalness. However, he counted among his lay disciples spokesmen for both sides. Ch'ih Ch'ao (336-377), the powerful minion of the warlord Huan Wen, was devoted to him, and even composed a manual for Buddhist laymen, the "Essentials of Religion" (*Feng-fa yao*), which preserves a strong Confucian moral tone.[34] Sun Ch'o, the poet whose compromise of inner naturalness and outward conformity has already been noted, was also a faithful follower. Even Hsü Hsün, whose front of nonconformity may have been largely a pose, professed to be Chih's disciple, though the latter on at least one occasion rebuked him for loving mere argument more than Truth (*li*).[35] Pure conversation among such lay disciples turned not infrequently to Buddhist themes, such as the Three Vehicles (*san-sheng* = *triyāna*),[36] the *Prajñāpāramitā*- and *Vimalakirti-sūtras*,[37] or the Six Faculties (*liu-t'ung* = *saḍabhijñā*) and Three Insights (*san-ming* = *trividya*).[38]

The role of religious Taoism in the "Tales" is not so conspicuous as that of Buddhism, since it seems only to have figured as part of the unrecorded private lives of some of the main actors. But enough glimpses are afforded to make it very plain that this religion was not merely a movement among illiterate farmers. Some very important families, like those of the calligrapher Wang Hsi-chih (309-ca. 365) and Ch'ih Yin (313-384), the father of Ch'ih Ch'ao, were "for generations" devotees of the Heavenly Master Sect (*T'ien-shih tao*). This meant, among other things, that they probably supported and participated in the periodic philanthropic feasts (*ch'u-hui*) of this sect, and in times of crisis would call in a Taoist physician or confessor, as did Wang Hsi-chih's son, Hsien-chih (344-388), who on his deathbed confessed his lifelong regret at having divorced his first wife, Ch'ih Tao-mao.[39] There is nothing to indicate whether adherence to the Heavenly Master Sect affected in any way a person's posture vis-à-vis the current ideological polarity. Wang Hsi-chih, for all his free spontaneity as a calligrapher, was definitely committed to official service, and once rebuked the youthful Hsieh An for shirking his patriotic duty by trying to be a recluse,[40] while the poet T'ao Ch'ien (d. 427), a relative of the stern general T'ao K'an and also described as an adherent of the Heavenly Master Sect, became the classic exemplar of disengagement and naturalness for the entire age.

Leaving aside any further attempt to piece together the multicolored fragments making up the world of these "Tales," let us turn to examine the document itself.

The History of the Text

It seems that the original title of the book was simply "Tales of the World" (*Shih-shuo*), the name by which it appears in the bibliographical sections of the Sui and T'ang dynastic histories, as well as in citations in the early-seventh-century encyclopedias *Pei-t'ang shu-ch'ao*, *Ch'u-hsüeh chi*, and *I-wen lei-chü*. But to distinguish it from an earlier work of the same name, now lost, by Liu Hsiang (80-9 B.C.), it soon acquired the added words "*New Writing* of Tales of the World" (*Shih-shuo hsin-shu*), the title by which it is cited in the ninth-century miscellany *Yu-yang tsa-tsu* (IV, 7a) by Tuan Ch'eng-shih. This title is confirmed by the oldest surviving manuscript fragment of the work, the so-called "T'ang fragment," written in the calligraphic style of the eighth century and covering most of the sixth *chüan* of the ten-*chüan* version (Chapters X through XIII). The present title, "*New Account* of Tales of the World" (*Shih-shuo hsin-yü*), seems to appear for the first time in Liu Chih-chi's "Compendium of History" (*Shih-t'ung*), which was first published in 710.[41] It is indiscriminately mixed with the other two titles in citations appearing in the early Sung encyclopedias, *T'ai-p'ing kuang-chi* and *T'ai-p'ing yü-lan*, of 983, but thereafter the work is consistently referred to by its present title.

When Liu I-ch'ing's staff first put the work together around 430[42] it was apparently completely contained within eight scrolls (*chüan*), but with the addition of Liu Chün's commentary in the early sixth century it was expanded to ten.[43] Although Tung Fen in his colophon to the 1138 block-print edition, which is the ancestor of all modern texts, states explicitly that Yen Shu (991-1055), whose version he followed, had reduced an original forty-five chapters (*p'ien*) to the present thirty-six by "completely eliminating all redundancies," I find it difficult to believe that he actually disturbed the order of Liu I-ch'ing's text, since the chapter titles and numbers in the T'ang fragment correspond exactly to those of the modern text. What Yen did do, and what can be documented by a comparison with the T'ang fragment, was to make extensive cuts in Liu Chün's commentary, so that the whole could be encompassed within its present three *chüan*.

The wood blocks for Tung Fen's edition, which were stored in Yen-chou (Chekiang) where Tung had served as grand warden, were later destroyed by fire, and a successor to the wardenship fifty years later, the poet Lu Yu (1125-1209), had them recut exactly following the earlier edition. This is essentially our present text, as it was faithfully reproduced in Yüan Chiung's edition of 1535 and again, with minor modifications, in the Han-feng lou edition, now reproduced in the modern corpus, *Ssu-pu ts'ung-k'an*. The present translation is based, however, on the Sung wood-block edition (known alternately as the Sonkei Kaku or Kanazawa Bunkō edition, preserved in the Maeda family library in Japan), as collated with the T'ang fragment and later editions by Wang Li-ch'i. Wang's collation is appended to the Peking edition of 1956, which reproduced both the Sonkei Kaku text and the T'ang fragment.

The T'ang fragment has a fascinating history of its own, related by Sugimura Hōgen in the photographic halftone reproduction which appears under the title *Tōshōhon Sesetsu shinsho*, No. 176, in the calligraphic series *Shoseki meihin sōkan*, edited by Nishikawa Yasushi and Kanda Kiichirō and published by Nigensha in 1972. It seems that at least one Chinese manuscript of the ten-scroll edition, containing

Liu Chun's commentary, was already in Japan around the end of the
ninth century when the earliest catalogue of Chinese books in Japan,
the *Nihon-koku genzai sho mokuroku* ("Catalogue of Current Books in
the Kingdom of Japan"), was compiled, for it is listed there.[44] By
the middle of the fourteenth century one scroll--the sixth--containing
chapters X through XIII, either of that manuscript or of another of
equal antiquity, was in the possession of a Shingon monk named Kōbō
(d. 1362), who was living in the Kanchi-in of the Tōji Monastery in
Kyoto. By that time also the manuscript already had a Tantric text
written on its reverse side: the *Chin-kang-ting i-ch'ieh ju-lai chen-
shih she ta-sheng ta-chiao-wang ching* (*Vajraśekkhara-sarva-tathāgata-
mahātantra-rāja-sūtra*),[45] with the mantras in Siddham characters and
the text in Chinese characters of Heian (794-1185) style.[46]

After Kōbō's death the manuscript remained among the Tōji's numerous treasures until around 1877, when the monastery called in the
paleographer Nishimura Kenbun to sort out the large collection of
manuscripts in the treasure house. In return for his services
Nishimura was presented with several scrolls, including the present
fragment. In the course of time Nishimura showed the fragment to four
of his antiquarian friends living in Kyoto, all of whom expressed an
excited interest in it. Finally, in an unselfish gesture he divided
the scroll into five equal parts so that each friend could have one.
It was the first of these segments, then in the possession of the
Ogawa family of Kyoto, which the Chinese scholar Yang Shou-ching
(1839-1915) saw during a short sojourn in Japan early in the present
century and described in his travelogue, "Account of Looking Up Books
in Japan" (*Jih-pen fang-shu chih*). In 1916 the Chinese paleographer
Lo Chen-yü managed to get all the segments back together for reproduction and produced the photolithographed volume, *T'ang-hsieh-pen
Shih-shuo hsin-shu ts'an-chüan*, which served as the source for all
later reproductions before the appearance of the halftone volume
published by Nigensha in 1972.

There is, however, still another tradition of *Shih-shuo hsin-yü*
texts, which might conveniently be overlooked except for the important role it played in the revival of interest in this work during
the sixteenth and seventeenth centuries in China and the eighteenth
and nineteenth centuries in Japan. In the early years of the
sixteenth century Ho Liang-chün, following the fashion of his day,
attempted an enlarged edition; this incorporated a reconstruction of
P'ei Ch'i's lost "Forest of Conversations" (*Yü-lin*) of 362 culled
from quotations from the T'ang and Sung encyclopedias as well as from
Liu Chün's commentary to the "Tales of the World" itself. Since the
"Tales" had apparently faded in popularity, two brothers, Wang Shih-
chen (1526-1590) and Wang Shih-mao, felt they could revive an interest in it by refining Ho's "abridged and supplemented" edition. This
new work, under the title "Supplement to the 'New Account of Tales of
the World'" (*Shih-shuo hsin-yü pu*), was published in 1556 and became
an immediate success. The revival of interest in the work in Tokugawa
Japan was through the Wang "Supplement," and until very recent times
all Japanese versions and commentaries were based on this edition.
Revival of interest in the original, pre-Ming version in both China
and Japan seems to be a phenomenon of only the last fifty years. Two
modern works which gather together the major contributions of Chinese
and Japanese scholars, especially work done in the last two decades,
are the complete annotated Japanese translation of Murakami Yoshimi,

Kawakatsu Yoshio, and others of the Research Institute of Humanistic Sciences of Kyoto University, published in 1964, and the truly definitive edition of Yang Yung of the New Asia College in Hong Kong, *Shih-shuo hsin-yü chiao-chien*, published in 1969. Needless to say the present translation is heavily indebted to both these works, as well as to the extremely helpful research tools published by the Department of Chinese Literature of Hiroshima University, especially the "Table of Text Criticism to *Shih-shuo hsin-yü*" (*Sesetsu shingo kōkanbyō*), compiled by Furuta Keiichi in 1957, and the "Concordance to *Shih-shuo hsin-yü*" (*Sesetsu shingo sakuin*), compiled by Takahashi Kiyoshi in 1959.

Notes to Introduction

[1] V. T. Yang, "About *Shih-shuo hsin-yü*," *Journal of Oriental Studies* 2.2 (1955), 313.

[2] See below, Chapter II, 59.

[3] Lu Hsün, *Chung-kuo hsiao-shuo shih-lüeh*, Peking, 1958 (based on revision of 1930), p. 44.

[4] *Tōhō gakuhō* 41 (1970), 217-234.

[5] Lu Hsün, ed., *Hsi K'ang chi*, Peking, 1956 (autograph reproduction), 2.6b, 8a; trans. J. R. Hightower in Cyril Birch, ed., *Anthology of Chinese Literature* (Vol. I), New York, 1965, pp. 163, 165.

[6] *Hsi K'ang chi* 1.5a.

[7] *Chin-shu* 49.2a; trans. in Balazs, *Chinese Civilization and Bureaucracy*, ed. Arthur F. Wright, New Haven, 1964, p. 238. See also Donald Holzman, "Une conception chinoise du héros," *Diogène* 36 (1961), 37-55.

[8] Ting Fu-pao, ed., *Ch'üan Han san-kuo Chin nan-pei-ch'ao shih*, Taipei, 1962 (reprint of 1916 ed.) I, 217.

[9] *Chuang-tzu* VI, 13a.

[10] *CS* 51.7b.

[11] *SSHY* IV, 91, commentary (citing *CHS*).

[12] *Wen-hsüan* 11.6b (Hu-shih tsang-pen ed.).

[13] *Hou Han chi* 36; quoted in Ch'en Yin-k'o, *T'ao Yüan-ming chih ssu-hsiang yü ch'ing-t'an chih kuan-hsi*, Chungking, 1945, p. 21.

[14] *CS* 98.20b-21a.

[15] *SSHY* III, 16, Commentary, citing *CYC*.

[16] Trans. in J. D. Frodsham, "The Origins of Chinese Nature Poetry," *Asia Major* (n.s.) 8.1 (1960), 81.

[17] This is basically the view of Fung Yu-lan in his *History of Chinese Philosophy*, Princeton, 1953, II, 168.

[18] See e.g., Erik Zürcher, *The Buddhist Conquest of China*, Leiden, 1959, I, 87.

[19] Trans. J. R. Shryock, *The Study of Human Abilities*, New Haven, 1937 (American Oriental Series, Vol. II).

[20] See, e.g., Miyazaki Ichisada, "Seidan," *Shirin* 31 (1946), 1-17. A classic treatment of the whole range of "pure conversation" is Ho Ch'ang-ch'ün's *Wei-Chin ch'ing-t'an ssu-hsiang ch'u-lun*, Shanghai, 1947.

[21] The meaning of *wu* and *yu* varies according to whether they are in the relation of opposites, as is usually the case in *Chuang-tzu*, or in a generative relation where *wu* is the substratum of *yu*, as is often the case in *Lao-tzu*. For the first meaning I use the terms "Something" and "Nothing," and for the latter, "Actuality" and

"Non-actuality." I am indebted to my student, Mr. Un-chol Shin, for helping to clarify this distinction in an unpublished paper.

[22]"Seidan," pp. 6-7.

[23]See Hsi K'ang's "Discourse on Release from Self-interest" (*Shih-ssu lun*), *Hsi K'ang chi*, 6.1a; trans. Donald Holzman in *La vie et la pensée de Hi K'ang*, Leiden, 1957, pp. 122-30.

[24]See Hou Wai-lu et al., *Chung-kuo ssu-hsiang t'ung-shih* (2nd edition), Peking, 1957, III, 59.

[25]See, e.g., the biography of Kuang I (fl. ca. 312), one of the "Eight," in *CS* 49.26ab.

[26]*CCKT*.

[27]*CS* 35.10b.

[28]*CS* 12b.

[29]*Chuang-tzu* XXII, 32b.

[30]E.g. Arthur F. Wright, *Buddhism in Chinese History*, Stanford, 1959, esp. pp. 21-64; Zürcher, *Conquest*, Vol. I, esp. pp. 18-80; Kenneth Ch'en, *Buddhism in China*, Princeton, 1964, esp. pp. 21-53.

[31]See Arthur E. Link, "The Taoist Antecedents of Tao-an's Prajñā Ontology," *History of Religions* 9.2-3 (1969-1970), 181-215.

[32]*SSHY* IV, 32. See Fukunaga Mitsuji, "Shi Ton to sono shūi: Tō-Shin no Rō-Sō shisō" (Chih Tun and His Environment: Lao-Chuang Philosophy in the Eastern Chin), *Bukkyō shigaku* 5.2 (1956), 12-34; Ch'en Yin-k'o, "Hsiao-yao-yu Hsiang-Kuo i chi Chih Tun i t'an-yüan" (An Investigation into the Source of the Interpretations of the Hsiang-Kuo [Commentary] and That of Chih Tun), *Ch'ing-hua hsüeh-pao* 12 (1937), 309-314.

[33]See Paul Demiéville, "La pénétration du Bouddhisme dans la tradition philosophique chinoise," *Cahiers d'histoire mondiale* 3.1 (1956), 28ff; Zürcher, *Conquest*, I, 125-126.

[34]*Hung-ming chi* 13 (*Taishō* 52.86a; trans. in Zürcher, *Conquest*, I, 164-176). See also Fukunaga Mitsuji, "Chi Chō no Bukkyō shisō: Tō-Shin Bukkyō no ichi seikaku" (Ch'ih Ch'ao's Buddhist Thought: A Characteristic of Eastern Chin Buddhism), in *Tsukamoto hakase shōju kinen Bukkyōshigaku ronsō*, Kyoto, 1961, pp. 631-646.

[35]*SSHY* IV, 38.

[36]*SSHY* IV, 37.

[37]*SSHY* IV, 45.

[38]*SSHY* IV, 54.

[39]*SSHY* I, 39. See also Yoshikawa Tadao's recent biography of Wang Hsi-chih and characterization of Six Dynasties aristocratic society, *Ō Gishi: rikuchō kizoku no shakai*, Tokyo, 1972; Hsü Shih-ying, "Wang Hsi-chih fu-tzu ho T'ien-shih-tao ti kuan-hsi" (The Relation between Wang Hsi-chih and his Sons and the Heavenly Master Sect), *K'un-lun* 4.2 (1960), 5-6.

[40]*SSHY* II, 70.

[41]*Shih-t'ung* 17.2b (SPTK ed.).

[42]See Kawakatsu Yoshio, "*Sesetsu shingo* no hensan o megutte," *Tōhō gakuhō* 41 (1970), 226-232.

[43]*Sui-shu* 34.10b.

[44]*Nihon-koku genzai sho mokuroku* 32; see Ohase Keikichi, *Nihon-koku genzai sho mokuroku kaisetsukō*, Tokyo, 1936, appendix, p. 14.

[45]*Taishō* 18.319b (with many divergencies).

[46]For the identification of the styles of writing I am indebted to the trained eye of Professor Fujieda Akira of the Research Institute of Humanistic Science of Kyoto University. Professor Sugimura ventures the opinion that the Tantric text may be Kamakura (1185-1333) in date; see *Tōshōhon Sesetsu shinsho*, Tokyo, 1972, p. 73.

Translator's Note

Nothing in the *Shih-shuo hsin-yü* is really so esoteric as to be inaccessible to those who are not native to Chinese culture. The anecdotes, conversations, and characterizations gathered here are mostly of a kind which, given a few substitutions, could occur in any society. For this reason I have tried to retell them as nearly as possible in their original form, even when this results in some "barbarization" of normal English idiom, feeling as I do that preserving the verbal images and conceits of the original text is better than finding the English equivalent which comes nearest to the "intention" of the author but changes his images in the process.

In spite of the relative accessibility of most of the anecdotes, however, there is still considerable need for annotation. If even Liu Chün, the original commentator, who lived only two or three generations after the *Shih-shuo* was first published, found it necessary to increase the bulk of the original text from eight scrolls to ten with his Commentary, it is no wonder that modern readers from a different culture would need not only his, but still further elucidations. Liu Chün's Commentary consists almost entirely of parallel or supplementary anecdotes quoted from earlier sources now no longer extant. Occasionally he has added a few laconic observations of his own. Because of the light this supplementary material sheds on the text, and also because of its intrinsic interest, I have attempted to incorporate as much of it as possible in the notes.

The reader should know, however, that Liu Chün's Commentary has undergone a twofold abridgement: the first imposed by the eleventh-century editor, Yen Shu, who found Liu's lengthy citations far too prolix for the readers of his day, and the second by the present translator's perception of the tastes of twentieth-century readers who, I daresay, would find even Yen Shu's surgery not radical enough. In addition to this, biographical material of a purely factual nature from Liu Chün's sources has for the most part been transferred to the "Biographical Notices" in the Appendix.

In the translation and notes I have tried with more or less consistency to observe the following conventions:

1. Enclosed in parentheses after each translated anecdote are the acronymic titles of works where variant versions of the same incident may be found--works such as the dynastic histories and the early encyclopedic collections of quotations, where many of the *Shih-shuo* stories are repeated. The full titles represented by the acronyms may be found in the list of Abbreviations in the Appendix, together with their editors and dates. In identifying these variant versions I have relied upon Furuta Keiichi's excellent tables, *Sesetsu shingo kōkanbyō* (Hiroshima, 1957), where they are collated in parallel columns.

2. The annotations, as stated earlier, consist largely of Liu Chün's citations from lost works of the third to fifth centuries, together with a few laconic observations of his own, plus occasional supplementary explanations by the translator; they follow immediately after each anecdote. They are distinguished from each other in the following manner: Liu Chün's citations, except when he is quoting well-known works, are prefaced by the acronymic titles of their sources; these acronyms too may be found in the list of Abbreviations. Unless they are unusually brief, the citations are not enclosed in quotation marks. Liu Chün's personal comments, as distinct from his citations, are always introduced as such. Translator's notes appear in two forms: at the beginning of a note they are not introduced, but when they follow Liu Chün's Commentary they are set apart in a separate paragraph enclosed in parentheses.

3. Wherever the translator has interpolated material into the text or Commentary for clarity's sake it is enclosed in parentheses. If the interpolation is translated directly from a parallel source it is placed in square brackets and the source identified. Deletions in the text are usually marked with suspension points, and paraphrases are identified as such.

Following the translated text are four appendixes designed to supplement the somewhat eliptical comments in the notes.

1. The brief Biographical Notices of the six hundred-odd persons named in the text are listed alphabetically and serve also as an index of the occurrences of each name in the *Shih-shuo* text.

2. The Glossary of Terms and Official Titles gives laconic definitions of key terms occurring in the text, and the Chinese characters for all romanized words. It also identifies the Chinese titles which appear only in translated form in the text, including a very general indication of the functions of each office listed.

3. The list of Abbreviations consists of the acronymic titles of works cited in Liu Chün's Commentary, with their full titles and Chinese characters, together with their authors or compilers and dates, when these are known. It also includes the acronymic titles of other reference works mentioned in the notes but not cited in the Commentary. These latter are marked with an asterisk.

4. The Bibliography is in three parts: The first lists the texts of the *Shih-shuo* itself in chronological order. The second includes special studies and reference tools devoted exclusively to the *Shih-shuo*. The third gives background works of a broader frame of reference, concentrating on the Six Dynasties period, but including other works mentioned in the notes.

It is my hope that this somewhat unwieldy apparatus will quickly become unobtrusive while at the same time enhancing the intelligibility and enjoyment of the text.

Shih-shuo Hsin-yü
A New Account of Tales of the World

CHAPTER I

Virtuous Conduct

1. Ch'en Fan's[1] words became a rule for gentlemen and his acts a model for the world. Whenever he mounted his carriage and grasped the reins it was with a determination to purify the whole realm. When he became grand warden of Yü-chang (Kiangsi), the moment he arrived he immediately inquired where Hsü Chih[2] was living, wishing to see him first of all. His superintendent of records reported, "The members of your staff would like you first to enter the commandery office, sir." Ch'en replied, "King Wu (1122-1116 B.C.) bowed in his carriage before Shang Jung's[3] village gate, and had no leisure to keep the seat in his office warm. What is improper in my paying respects to a worthy man?" (*HHS* 83.4b; *TPYL* 474)

[1] *JNHHC*: Ch'en Fan had a house whose courtyard was overgrown and littered and which he never swept out. He explained, "When a great man serves in the government he should sweep the *whole realm* clean." (Cf. *HHS* 96.1a.)
 In the biography of Teng Ai (*SKWei* 28, 16b-17a) the statement, "His words and writings were a model for the world and his acts a rule for gentlemen," is ascribed to Ch'en Shih's (*sic*) gravestone in Ying-ch'uan (Honan). Ai himself for a time took the personal name Fan (Model) and the courtesy name Shih-tse (Rule for Gentlemen), but later changed them to avoid confusion with another member of his clan with the same name. The passage "mounted his carriage . . . to purify the whole realm" was originally applied to Fan P'ang (137-169); see *HHS* 97.16b.

[2] *HCHHS*: Hsü Chih's purity and loftiness transcended the world and abrogated all custom. Many times he was summoned to office by various nobles, but even though he never accepted a post, whenever the summoner died he would travel 10,000 *li* to express his condolences. Once (on the occasion of Huang Chiung's death in 164) he prepared a roast chicken, took silk and steeped it in wine, dried

it in the sun and wrapped the chicken in it, went directly to a spot outside the crowd who had come for the burial, steeped the silk in water, took a *tou*-measure of cooked rice and some white rushes for a mat, and placed the chicken before it. After pouring a libation he left his card and immediately departed without seeing the host.

YHHC: While Ch'en Fan was in Yü-chang he kept a couch (*t'a*) for the sole use of Hsü Chih, and each time after the latter had left he would hang it up. Thus was Chih treated with deference.

³For Shang Jung see *SC* 3.11b. Liu Chün's commentary cites Hsü Shen, author of the *SW*: "Shang Jung was a worthy man of the Yin era (trad. 1766-1122 B.C.) who was the teacher of Lao-tzu." The same statement may be found in Kao Yu*'s second cent. A.D. commentary at *LSCC* 15.3a.

2. Chou Ch'eng frequently said, "If for two or three months I do not see Huang Hsien, then a mean and stingy mind has already sprung up again within me."¹ (*HHS* 83.4b)

¹TL: Some of Huang Hsien's contemporaries said that Yen Hui (Confucius' favorite disciple) had been reborn. But his family emerged out of obscurity; his father was a cow-doctor.

Hsün Shu grasped Huang Hsien's hand and said, "Sir, you are my teacher and model." Later he saw Yüan Lang and said, "In your state there is a Yen Hui. Did you know it?"

Lang replied, "Have you by any chance been visiting our Huang Hsien?"

Tai Liang in his youth was condescending toward Huang Hsien, but after he had seen him he lowered his opinion of himself and appeared disheartened, as though he had lost something. His mother asked, "Why are you unhappy? Have you come again from that son of a cow-doctor?"

Liang replied, "'I looked up at him in front of me and suddenly he was behind me' ("Analects" IX, 11). He's the one who should be called my teacher."

3. When Kuo T'ai¹ arrived in Ju-nan (Honan) and went to pay his respects to Yüan Lang,² his carriage hardly stopped in its tracks, nor did the bells cease ringing on the harness. But when he went to visit Huang Hsien he spent a full day and two nights. When someone asked his reason, T'ai replied, "Huang Hsien is vast and deep, like a reservoir of ten thousand *ch'ing*; clarify him and he grows no purer, stir him and he grows no muddier. His capacity is profound and wide and difficult to fathom or measure."³ (*HHS* 83.4b; *TPKC* 169; *SWLC*, pieh 27)

¹HSHS: As soon as Li Ying had seen Kuo T'ai he praised him, saying, "I've seen gentlemen aplenty, but never any like T'ai."

When Kuo T'ai died Ts'ai Yung wrote his epitaph with the remark, "I never write an inscription for anyone without a feeling of embarrassment. It's only in the case of Kuo T'ai that I can compose a eulogy for his epitaph without shame." (*HHS* 98.2b)

Earlier when he had been recommended as Gentleman with Principles (*yu-tao chün-tzu*), T'ai said, "I have observed heavenly signs and human affairs. 'What Heaven has abandoned' cannot be propped up." (*Tso-chuan*, Hsiang 23.7) Whereupon he declined, claiming illness.

²The Yüan Hung (Hsia-fu) of the text is an error.

³*Kuo T'ai PC*: When Hsüeh Kung-tsu asked, T'ai replied, "Yüan Lang's capacity is like overflowing waves; though they are pure, it is still easy to draw from them. Huang Hsien is vast and deep, etc."

4. Li Ying's manner and style were outstanding and proper, and he maintained a haughty dignity. He wished to take on himself the responsibility for the Moral Teaching (*ming-chiao*) and right and wrong for the whole realm. Among the gentlemen who later progressed in office, if any succeeded in "ascending to his hall,"[1] they all felt they had climbed through the Dragon Gate (Lung-men).[2]

[1]"Analects" XI, 15.

[2]A famous rapids on the Yellow River near the border of Shansi and Shensi.

SCC: Lung-men, the Dragon Gate, is also called Ho-ching, the River Ford. It is 900 *li* east of Ch'ang-an. The waters plunge down an infinite distance, so that turtles and fish and the like cannot ascend it. If any do ascend, they are forthwith transformed into dragons.

5. Li Ying once praised Hsün Shu[1] and Chung Hao,[2] saying, "Master Hsün in his pure understanding would be hard to surpass, while Master Chung in his supreme virtue may be taken as a teacher."[3] (*HHS* 92.12b)

[1]*HHHC*: The clerks who wielded the tablets, erasing knives, and styluses in Hsün Shu's office, whom he had selected from among leather-and-wool-clad herdsmen, were all heroic and outstanding men.

[2]*HHHC*: Chung Hao's lofty style was continued for generations . . . Though deficient in "man-made status," he had enough and to spare of "heaven-bestowed nobility." (*Mencius* VI.16; Legge II, 418-419)

[3]*HNHHC*: Of the former generation in Ying-ch'uan (Honan), the ones who were taken as teachers by all within the Four Seas were Ch'en Chih-shu, Hsün Shu, and Chung Hao. Li Ying honored these three gentlemen and used to say, "Master Hsün in his pure understanding, etc., Ch'en and Chung in their supreme virtue, etc."

6. Ch'en Shih once went to visit Hsün Shu. As he was poor and frugal and had no servants or attendants, he had his eldest son, Chi, lead the carriage, and his second son, Ch'en, follow along behind with a staff in his hand. His grandson, Ch'ün, who was still tiny, he had ride inside the carriage.

After they arrived, Hsün Shu had his third son, Ching, receive them at the gate, and his sixth son, Shuang, serve the wine. The other six "dragons"[1] he had wait on table. His grandson, Yü, who was also tiny, he had sit before his knees.

At the time the grand astrologer reported to the Throne, "A Realized Man (*chen-jen*)[2] is traveling eastward."[3] (*PSLT* 6; *TPYL* 849; *SWLC*, hou 3, pieh 27)

¹*CFHC*: Hsün Shu had eight sons: Chien, Kun, Ching, Tao, Wang, Shuang, Su, and Fu. While Shu was living in the village of Hsi-hao (Honan), the prefectural magistrate, Yüan K'ang, said, "In antiquity the Lord of Kao-yang (Chuan Hsü, trad. 2513-2435 B.C.) had eight talented sons." Accordingly he renamed their village Kao-yang Village, and contemporaries called them the "eight dragons."

²"Chen-jen" here appears to have the double meaning of the name of a star and the Taoist term for one who realizes the Tao within himself. See *Chuang-tzu* VI, 2a; Watson, 77.

³*HCYC*: When Ch'en Shih accompanied his sons to visit Hsün Shu and his sons, there was at the time a confluence of powerful stars, and the grand astrologer reported to the Throne, "Worthies from a distance of 500 *li* are gathering."

7. A guest once asked Ch'en Ch'en, "What achievements and virtues does your father, Ch'en Shih, have that he enjoys such an honorable reputation throughout the realm?"

Ch'en replied, "My father is like a cassia (*kuei*) tree growing on the slopes of Mt. T'ai (Shantung). Above there is a height of ten thousand *jen*, and below, an unfathomable depth. From above it is sprinkled with sweet dew, and from below it is watered by hidden springs. Yet while this is going on, how can the cassia tree know the height of Mt. T'ai or the depth of the hidden springs? I wouldn't know if he has any achievements and virtues or not." (*IWLC* 89; *TPYL* 518, 957; *TPKC* 169)

8. Ch'en Chi's son, Ch'ün, possessed outstanding ability. Once he and his cousin, Chung (the son of Chi's younger brother, Ch'en), were each discussing his father's relative achievements and virtues, and, after getting into an argument over it, could not reach a solution. They referred the matter to their grandfather Ch'en Shih, who replied, "It's hard to regard either Chi as the older brother or Ch'en as the younger." (*SWLC*, hou 8)

9. Hsün Chü-po had come from a distance to visit a sick friend. It happened just then that Hu¹ bandits attacked the commandery. The friend said to Chü-po, "I'm going to die now, anyhow. You may as well leave."

Chü-po replied, "I came a long distance to see you, and now you are telling me to leave. Is destroying morality to save his own life something Hsün Chü-po would do?"

After the bandits arrived they said to Chü-po, "A large army has arrived and the entire commandery is deserted. What sort of man are you that you dare to remain here alone?"

Chü-po replied, "My friend is sick and I can't bear to abandon him. I would rather give myself up for my friend's life."

The bandits talked it over among themselves and said, "We are people without morality who have entered a state where morality prevails." And forthwith they withdrew their army and returned home, and the entire commandery was preserved intact. (*IWLC* 21; *TPYL* 409)

¹Hu is a general term for non-Chinese peoples of the North and Northwest, especially Hsiung-nu, Hsien-pei, and inhabitants of Turkestan. Several uprisings and raids by such groups, mostly in

border areas, are recorded between the years 155 and 166, when
Hsün Chü-po was active (*HSCC*). See *TCTC* 53.1731-55 and 1796.

10. Hua Hsin in his treatment of his sons and younger brothers was
extremely strict: even at leisure within the bosom of the family he
maintained a rigid formality as though attending a court ceremony.
Ch'en Chi and his younger brother (Ch'en), on the other hand, were
very free in their expression of tenderness and affection. Yet within
the two households neither one on this account ever strayed from the
path of harmony and peace.[1] (*TPYL* 511; *HTC* 4)

[1]*WeiL*: During the reign of Emperor Ling (168-189) Hua Hsin accompanied Ping Yüan and Kuan Ning of Pei-hai (Shantung) in their
travels and study and was friendly with them. At the time people
used to say, "The three of them make one dragon," meaning that
Hsin was the dragon's head, Ning the belly, and Yüan the tail.

11. Kuan Ning and Hua Hsin were together in the garden hoeing vegetables when they spied a piece of gold in the earth. Kuan went on
plying his hoe as though it were no different from a tile or a stone.
Hua, seizing it, threw it away.
    On another occasion they were sharing a mat reading when someone
riding a splendid carriage and wearing a ceremonial cap passed by the
gate. Kuan continued to read as before; Hua, putting down his book,
went out to look. Kuan cut the mat in two and sat apart, saying,
"You're no friend of mine."[1] (*IWLC* 65, 69, 83; *SLF* 9; *TPYL* 409, 611,
709, 764, 811, 824; *TPKC* 235; *SWLC*, hsü 9; *PTSC* 97, 133)

[1]*WeiL*: When Kuan Ning was young he was quiet and dispassionate and
used to laugh at Ping Yüan and Hua Hsin for having the ambition to
become officials. When Hua was appointed director of instruction,
he sent up a letter to the throne deferring to Kuan. But when the
latter heard of it he laughed and said, "Hua always wanted to be
an old bureaucrat, so let him have the glory of it and be done
with it."

12. Wang Lang often praised Hua Hsin for his understanding and capacity. On the day of the Year-end Sacrifice (*cha*)[1] Hua used to gather
his sons and nephews for feasting and drinking, so Wang also imitated
his example. When someone told Chang Hua of this affair, Chang remarked, "Whenever Wang imitates Hua it's always the externals of the
form only, and that's why he ends up farther away from him than
ever." (*YCPT* 12; *IWLC* 5; *PTSC* 155; *SLF* 5; *TPYL* 33; *HTC* 4)

[1]"Record of Rites" XI, 21 (Legge, *Li Ki* I, 431): The Son of Heaven's Great Year-end Sacrifice (*ta-cha*) consisted of eight
parts . . . (The legendary ruler) I-ch'i was the first to perform
it. *Cha* means "to search." In the twelfth month of the year he
gathers all things and searches for the spirits and offers them food.
    WCYI: During the Three Dynasties the Year-end Sacrifice was
called La: the Hsia (trad. 2205-1766 B.C.) called it Chia-p'ing,
Auspicious Leveling; the Yin (1766-1122) called it Ch'ing-chi,
Pure Sacrifice; the Chou (1122-256) called it the Ta-cha. The general term for all three is La.
    LCI: The Year-end Sacrifice is a time when "the Son of Heaven
gathers all things and searches for the spirits and offers them

food." It is a time at the year's end when he rests the aged and
eases the people. The La are the five sacrifices offered in the
ancestral temple. According to tradition *la* means "to join." At
the sacrifice the new and old years are joined together. Ever
since Ch'in and Han times the day following the La sacrifice has
been the first day of the new year. It is a traditional term from
the past. (*IWLC* 5; *TPYL* 33)

13. Hua Hsin and Wang Lang were sailing together in a boat fleeing
the troubles of war[1] when someone wanted to join them. Hua, for his
part, disapproved, but Wang said, "Fortunately we still have room.
Why isn't it all right?"
  Later, when the rebels were overtaking them, Wang wanted to get
rid of the man they had taken along, but Hua said, "This was precisely the reason I hesitated in the first place. But since we've already accepted his request, how can we abandon him in an emergency?"
So they took him along as before to safety.
  The world by this incident has determined the relative merits of
Hua and Wang.

[1] I.e., during Tung Cho's removal of the Later Han capital from Lo-
yang (Honan) to Ch'ang-an (Shensi) in 190.
  PH: While Hua Hsin was magistrate of Hsia-kuei Prefecture
(Shensi) the House of Han was in the midst of upheaval, and Hua
took flight together with six or seven like-minded gentlemen,
Cheng T'ai and others. As they emerged from the Wu Pass (E. Shensi), along the way they came upon a man traveling alone who wanted
to join them. Every one took pity on him and wanted to let him do
so. Hua alone said, "It won't do. Right now we're already in danger, and the chances of good or evil fortune are about equal. But
if we take him with us now without sufficient reason, there's no
telling what the chances will be. If we have to hurry on or retreat, could we then abandon him midway?"
  But the others could not bear to leave him, so in the end he
accompanied them. Along the way this man fell in a well and everyone was in favor of abandoning him. But Hua said, "Since he's already in our company, it's not right to abandon him." So they went
back together and pulled him out, and after that he parted from
them. (Cf. *SKWei* 13.10b, comm.)

14. Wang Hsiang in serving his stepmother, Mme. Chu, was extremely
conscientious.[1] There was a plum tree (*li*)[2] in their home whose fruit
was exceptionally good, and his stepmother always had him protect it.
Once when a storm of wind and rain came up suddenly, Hsiang embraced
the tree, weeping.
  On another occasion Hsiang was sleeping on a separate bed when his
stepmother herself came over and slashed at him in the dark. As it
happened, Hsiang had gotten up to relieve himself, and her vain
slashing struck only the bedclothes. After Hsiang returned to the
room he realized his stepmother bore him an implacable resentment,
and kneeling before her he begged her to end his life. His stepmother
then for the first time came to her senses and loved him ever afterward as her own son.[3] (*CS* 33.1b; *TPYL* 413)

[1] Wang Hsiang lost his own mother, Mme. Hsüeh of Kao-p'ing (Shantung), at an early age. His father, Wang Jung*, later married

Mme. Chu of Lu-chiang (Anhwei). See *SSHY* Comm., citing (*Wang*) *Hsiang shih-chia*.

[2] In *CS* 33.1b and *TPYL* 413 the tree is identified as a crab apple (*nai*).

[3] *HTC*: In Wang Hsiang's stepmother's courtyard there was a plum tree. When it began to bear fruit she had Hsiang watch it by day for crows and sparrows, and by night to drive away rats. One night a heavy storm of wind and rain came up, and Hsiang embraced the tree, weeping. When dawn came and his stepmother saw him she felt sorry for him . . .

Once in midwinter, when the ice was solid, his stepmother suddenly had a craving for fresh fish. Hsiang unfastened his clothes and was about to break the ice to get some when it happened that a place in the ice opened slightly and a fish came out . . .

Hsiang's stepmother had a sudden craving for roast sparrow (*huang-ch'üeh*), and Hsiang thought to himself that it would be difficult to accomplish in a hurry. But in a matter of moments forty or fifty sparrows flew into his net.

Whatever his stepmother required he was sure to rush off in person to find, and he never failed to get it. Such was the extent of his sincerity (*ch'eng*).

CYC: Hsiang's stepmother frequently slandered him, but whenever she treated him unreasonably, his half brother, Lan (her own son), would always take Hsiang's part. Furthermore, whenever she abused Hsiang's wife, Lan's wife would also rush to her support, all of which his stepmother resented.

YYCS: Because of his stepmother Hsiang slowly wasted away and never took office. When he was well on toward sixty the governor of Hsü Province (N. Kiangsu and Anhwei), Lü Ch'ien, summoned him to serve as lieutenant-governor. His contemporaries used to sing the following song about him:

> "The sea and River I's repose
> Are truly due to our Wang Hsiang.
> That land and state do not lie waste—
> All credit to the governor's aide."

He was eventually promoted to become grand protector.

15. Ssu-ma Chao once exclaimed in admiration, "Juan Chi is the most prudent of men. Whenever I talk with him, all his talk is about the abstruse and remote. I have never yet heard him pass any judgment on personalities."[1] (*TPYL* 390)

[1] *WSCC*: Juan Chi was free and unrestrained and would not be bound by rites or custom. The governor of Yen Province (N. Anhwei), Wang Ch'ang, requested an interview with him, but never got to speak with him the whole day. Ch'ang was humiliated and resentful, feeling that he himself was unable to fathom Chi. Chi for his part never talked about worldly affairs; he remained spontaneous and transcendent.

CC: Long ago I (Li Ping) was once seated in the presence of the former "Emperor" (Ssu-ma Chao). At the time there were three senior administrators who had come to see him together. As they were about to excuse themselves and leave, His Majesty said, "To be an official or chief one should be incorruptible, prudent, and diligent. If you cultivate these three you need never worry that order will not prevail."

They all accepted the imperial advice. His Majesty then turned and said to us, "If you had to make a choice, which of the three should be paramount?"

Someone replied, "Of course, incorruptibility is the root of the others."

Then he asked me, and I replied, "The ways of incorruptibility and prudence require each other to be complete. But if I had to make a choice, then prudence would be the greatest."

His Majesty said, "Your words have got to the root of the matter. Could you give me an example from recent times of someone who has been able to be prudent?"

I then gave as examples the former grand marshal, Hsün I, and President Tung Chung-ta, and Vice-president Wang Kung-chung.

His Majesty said, "All these men, inasmuch as they are warm and respectful from morning till night, and are models in their management of affairs, are also, each in his own way, prudent. However, the most prudent man in the realm-- wouldn't it be Juan Chi? Whenever I talk with him, etc. He has never yet criticized or discussed current affairs or passed any judgment, etc. Might he not be called the most prudent?"

16. Wang Jung said, "I have lived with Hsi K'ang[1] for twenty years[2] and never saw an expression of either pleasure or irritation on his face." (CS 49.12a)

> [1]*WYCS*: Hsi K'ang's surname was originally Hsi*. His ancestors moved from Shang-yü Prefecture (Chekiang) to escape a grievance and settled in Chih Prefecture of Chiao Principality (S. Honan). Since his family had come from K'uai-chi (Chekiang), he took one part of the name of the principality (-*chi*), and pronounced it like his original name, Hsi.
>
> *YYCS*: In Chih Prefecture there is a Mt. Chi*. Since his home was on its slope, he took his name from it.
>
> (*Hsi*) *K'ang PC*: K'ang's nature was to swallow insults and hide his resentment. Love and hate did not contend within his breast, nor were pleasure and anger expressed in his face. His friend, Wang Jung, while he was living in Hsiang-ch'eng (Honan), saw him face to face several hundred times, but never heard his voice raised or saw his face flushed in anger. This was indeed an excellent model for the realm, as well as a superb achievement in human relations.
>
> [2]Wang Jung met Juan Chi when he was fifteen (ca. 250) and presumably did not begin his acquaintance with Hsi K'ang or the other "Worthies of the Bamboo Grove" before that time. Since Hsi K'ang was executed in 262, Wang could in that case have known him only about twelve years.

17. Wang Jung[1] and Ho Ch'iao experienced the loss of a parent at the same time, and both were praised for their filial devotion. Wang, reduced to a skeleton,[2] kept to his bed; while Ho, wailing and weeping, performed all the rites.[3] Emperor Wu (Ssu-ma Yen, r. 265-290),

remarked to Liu I, "Have you ever observed Wang Jung and Ho Ch'iao? I hear that Ho's grief and suffering go beyond what is required by propriety, and it makes me worry about him."

Liu I replied, "Ho Ch'iao, even though performing all the rites, has suffered no loss in his spirit or health. Wang Jung, even though not performing the rites, is nonetheless so emaciated with grief that his bones stand out. Your servant is of the opinion that Ho Ch'iao's is the filial devotion of life, while Wang Jung's is the filial devotion of death. Your Majesty should not worry about Ch'iao, but rather about Jung." (CS 43.11a)

[1]*CCKT*: While "Emperor Wen" (Ssu-ma Chao) was in control of the (Wei) government (255-265) Chung Hui recommended Wang Jung to him with the words, "P'ei K'ai is pure and perceptive; Wang Jung is unceremonious and concentrates on the essential."

[2]Literally, "chicken-boned."

[3]*CYC*: While Jung was serving as governor of Yü Province (Honan) he experienced the loss of his mother. He was by nature extremely filial but was not bound by the ritual code. Even though he drank wine and ate meat as usual, or watched games of draughts and chess, his facial appearance became emaciated and downcast, and he could rise only with the aid of a staff. At the same time Ho Ch'iao of Ju-nan (Honan) was also a famous gentleman. He held himself rigidly to the ritual code. While he was mourning the loss of a parent (CS 43.7a specifies his father) he measured his rice before eating, but his sorrow and emaciation did not approach Jung's.

18. The Prince of Liang (Ssu-ma T'ung) and the Prince of Chao (Ssu-ma Lun), being close relatives of the emperor, were most noble and honored in their time. P'ei K'ai[1] each year requested from their principalities a tax of several million cash (*ch'ien*) in order to relieve the needy members on his mother's and father's sides of the family. Someone ridiculed him, saying, "How can you beg from others to perform an act of private charity?"

P'ei replied, "To diminish excesses and supplement deficiencies is the Way of Heaven."[2] (CS 35.14b)

[1]*MSC*: Once P'ei K'ai had chosen a course of action, he moved in complete compliance with his own mind. Even though slanderous remarks came his way, he held his ground calmly.

[2]*Lao-tzu* 77.

19. Wang Jung said, "Although Wang Hsiang lived in the Cheng-shih era (240-249), he did not belong to the group of able conversationalists.[1] Yet whenever anyone talked with him, the effect of his reasoning[2] was pure and remote. Isn't it a case of his virtue having overshadowed his speech?" (CS 33.4a)

[1]I.e., Ho Yen, Wang Pi, Teng Yang, and others of the coterie of Ts'ao Shuang, whose brilliance as conversationalists gave the Cheng-shih era its luster as the "Golden Age" of "pure conversation" (*ch'ing-t'an*).

[2]Emending *li-chung* of the Sung edition to *li-chih* after CS 33.4a.

20. When Wang Jung experienced the loss of his mother, his extreme grief went beyond that of other men. P'ei K'ai, after going to offer his condolences, said, "If a single sorrow could actually hurt a person, Wang Jung could not escape the charge of 'extinguishing his nature.'"[1] (CS 43.11a, where P'ei Wei is credited with the statement)

[1]*Ch'ü-li* ("Record of Rites" I, 33; Legge I, 87-88): The rites for one in mourning are: though emaciated and lean, he should not show it, nor let his sight and hearing be dimmed. . . . If he becomes unable to perform the mourning, it is comparable to being uncompassionate or unfilial.

Hsiao-ching (18): To become emaciated, but not to the point of extinguishing the nature -- this is the teaching of the sages.

21. Wang Jung's father, Wang Hun*, had an honorable reputation, and in his official career had reached the governorship of Liang Province (Kansu). When Hun* died, loyal friends in the nine commanderies where he had successively served, cherishing the memory of his virtues and favors, got together and contributed several million cash. But Jung accepted none of it.[1] (CS 43.9b; TPYL 550)

[1]*YYCS*: It was on the strength of this that Wang Jung got his reputation.

22. Liu Pao was once sentenced to penal servitude, and the Prince of Fu-feng (Ch'ang-an), Ssu-ma Chün,[1] ransomed him for five hundred bolts (*p'i*) of cloth. Later he employed him as a junior administrator. At the time it was considered to be an exemplary act.

[1]*CCKT*: When Ssu-ma Chün was in his eighth year (239) he became cavalier attendant-in-ordinary and attendant-explicator to the Wei Prince of Ch'i, Ts'ao Fang. After the Chin received the mandate (265) he was enfeoffed Prince of Fu-feng and stationed in Kuan-chung (Ch'ang-an). His administration was considered the best the region ever had. After his death he was given the posthumous title, Prince Wu. The people of the West missed him sorely, and those who merely saw the inscription on his tombstone all did obeisance and wept. Such was the legacy of affection he had left.

23. Wang Ch'eng, Hu-wu Fu-chih, and their circle all considered giving rein to their impulses to be "freedom" (*ta*),[1] and there were even some among them who went naked.

Yüeh Kuang laughed about it and said, "In the Moral Teaching (*ming-chiao*) itself there are also enjoyable places. Why go to such lengths?" (CS 43.23b; WHLSC 38, 39, 40)

[1]*WYCS*: Toward the end of the Wei Kingdom, Juan Chi in his fondness for wine let himself go completely. Baring his head and letting his hair loose, he would sit with his legs sprawled apart, completely naked. After him his disciples who valued "free wandering" -- people like Juan Chan, Wang Ch'eng, Hsieh K'un, and Hu-wu Fu-chih -- all carried on the tradition founded by Juan Chi, claiming they had attained the root of the Great Way. So they doffed kerchief and cap, stripped off their clothes and exposed their foul ugliness like so many birds or beasts. Those who went to extremes were called "unimpeded" (*t'ung*), and those in the next

category were called "free" (ta). (Cf. also the biography of Kuang I, CS 49.14b-15a, and Zürcher, Conquest, 78-79; Fung, History, II, 190-191.)

24. When Ch'ih Chien met with the devastation and upheavals of the Yung-chia era (307-312),[1] he was living in his home village (Chin-hsiang, in Shantung) in extreme poverty and hunger. The villagers, because of his reputation and virtue, took turns sharing their food with him. At first Ch'ih always took along his elder brother's son, Ch'ih Mai, and his sister's son, Chou I*, whenever he went to eat. But the villagers said, "All of us are hungry and hard-pressed ourselves. It's only because you're an important, worthy person that we want to share in helping you. But we're afraid we can't survive if we feed the children too."

Ch'ih thereafter went alone to eat, but each time would hold the rice in his mouth tucked against the sides of his two cheeks. When he got home he would spit it out and give it to the two boys. Afterward they all survived and crossed the Yangtze River together.

When Ch'ih Chien died (339), Chou I* was serving as magistrate of Shan Prefecture (Chekiang). Resigning from his post, he returned home and sat on a straw mat at the head of Ch'ih's spirit bed (ling-ch'uang) in heart-mourning for a full three years.[2] (CS 67.19a; MCYC, hsia; PSLT 6; TPYL 367, 486, 512)

[1] I.e., the invasions and destruction of Western Chin by the Hsiung-nu.

[2] The mourning prescribed for teachers, without outward signs, but in the heart. (See "Record of Rites" III, 2; Legge I, 121.)

25. While Ku Jung was living in Lo-yang (Honan), he once accepted someone's invitation to a meal. Sensing that the man who was serving the roasts had the appearance of wanting some himself, he stopped eating his own and gave it to him. Those who were seated with him laughed at him, but Jung replied, "Should the one who holds meat in his hands all day never know its flavor?"

Later on when he encountered the disorders[1] and was fleeing south across the Yangtze River, whenever he was passing through danger or an emergency, he always found a man on his left or his right protecting him. After inquiring into the reason, it turned out that it was the man who had received the roast.[2] (CS 68.1b; PTSC 145; TPYL 477, 863; SWLC, hsü 10)

[1] Of 307-312; see the preceding anecdote.

[2] WSC: Once while Ku Jung was in the Department of Punishments, he was feasting with his colleagues when he observed that the man serving the roasts was different from an ordinary servant, so he cut off some of his own and gave it to him to eat. Later when the Prince of Chao, Ssu-ma Lun, usurped the throne (300), his son, Ssu-ma Ch'ien*, who was serving as central commander coerced Jung to serve as his senior administrator. When Lun was executed (301), Jung was also taken into custody and over ten persons of his group were killed. But there was someone who saved Jung's life. When asked for his reason, the man replied, "I am the servant from such-and-such a department who received the roast from you."

Jung then realized who he was and, sighing, said, "The proverb 'Yesterday's kind favor of a single meal today is not forgotten,' is no empty saying of the ancients!"

26. When Tsu Na was young, though orphaned and impoverished, he was by nature extremely filial, and would always personally tend the stove and prepare the food for his mother. Wang I, hearing of his excellent reputation, made a present to him of two female slaves and took him on as a junior administrator. Someone teased him, saying, "So the price of a male slave is twice that of a female slave!"

Tsu replied, "Was Po-li Hsi[1] necessarily less valuable than the five ram skins with which he was ransomed?"[2] (*CS* 62.20a, where Wang I is mistakenly identified as Wang Tun; *IWLC* 35; *TPKC* 246)

[1] Po-li Hsi was a grandee of the seventh century B.C. who, after wandering from state to state offering his services, fell into the hands of brigands, and was ransomed by King Mu of Ch'in (r. 659-621 B.C.) for five ram skins and raised to high honors. (*CKHHC*)

[2] There may be a pun intended between Hsi's name and *nu*, both of which mean "male slave," and between *pei*, "female slave," and *p'i*, "skin," both of which in Middle Chinese were pronounced *b'jie.

27. Chou Chen had resigned his post as grand warden of Lin-ch'uan (Kiangsi) and was returning to the capital. Before he went up to court he stopped and moored his boat by the bank of the Ch'ing Creek (south of Chien-k'ang), where Chancellor Wang Tao went to visit him. It was during the summer months and a violent rainstorm suddenly came up. The boat was extremely small and in addition leaked profusely, so that there was scarcely any place to sit down. Wang said, "In what respect did Hu Wei's incorruptibility surpass this?"[1] Accordingly he memorialized to have Chou employed as grand warden of Wu-hsing Commandery (Chekiang). (*PTSC* 38; *MCYC*, hsia; *TPYL* 21, 262; the first and fourth quotations substitute Chou I for Chou Chen)

[1] *CYC*: Hu Wei's father, Chih, was famous for his loyalty and incorruptibility. When Chih was governor of Ching Province (Hunan-Hupei) Wei went from the capital (Lo-yang) to visit him. When he announced that he was returning, Chih presented him with a bolt of silk. Kneeling, Wei said, "Father, with your incorruptibility and eminence, where did you get this?"

Chih replied, "This was left over from my salary, so I'm using it for your provisions on the trip, that's all."

Wei accepted it and departed. Whenever he arrived at an inn, he would personally put out his donkey to graze, then gather firewood and cook his own meals. When he was finished eating he would resume his travels.

The director-general from Chih's staff had been secretly laying aside provisions and wanted the silk. Accordingly he accompanied Wei as a traveling companion, and in all matters helped make the arrangements, and furthermore ate very little rice himself. Wei became suspicious of him and, confidentially drawing him out with questions, discovered he was none other than the director-general. Wei therefore [taking the silk he had previously been given] repaid and thanked him and sent him on his way. Later [in a separate letter] he reported the matter to Chih, and Chih had the director-general beaten with one hundred strokes and his name removed from the official register. Such was the incorruptibility and prudence of father and son.

When Wei became governor of Hsü Province (northern Kiangsu and Anhui), Emperor Wu (Ssu-ma Yen, r. 265-290) granted him an interview and talked with him about affairs at the frontier. When the conversation touched upon everyday life, the emperor sighed in admiration over his father's incorruptibility, and took the occasion to ask Wei, "How does your incorruptibility compare with your father's?"

Wei replied, "Mine falls short of his."

The emperor asked, "In what way did his surpass yours?"

Wei replied, "In the case of my father's incorruptibility, he was afraid other people would know about it. In my case, I'm afraid other people *won't* know about it. In this respect mine falls far short of his."

(Portions in square brackets have been interpolated from *SKWei* 27.5a, comm., which cites the same source.)

28. When Teng Yu began his flight from the troubles of war,[1] he abandoned his own son along the way to save the son of his deceased younger brother.[2] After crossing the Yangtze River he took a concubine whom he loved devotedly. Some years later he inquired about her origins, and the concubine told him her whole story -- she was a northerner who had emigrated after meeting with the disorders. When she recalled the names of her parents, it appeared she was Yu's niece on his mother's side. Yu had always led a virtuous life, and his speech and conduct were above reproach. When he heard this he was stricken with grief and remorse. To the end of his life he never again kept a concubine.[3] (*CS* 90. 13ab, 14b)

[1]I.e., during the Hsiung-nu invasions of the North between 307 and 312.

[2]Yu's younger brother's name is unknown; the brother's son was Teng Sui (Li-min; see below, n. 3, end).

[3]*TTCC*: During the Yung-chia Period (307-312) Yu was captured by the Hsiung-nu chieftain Shih Lo, who summoned him for an interview, keeping him standing beneath the tent. After talking with him, Lo took a liking to Yu and had him sit down and eat with him.

The place where Yu's carriage was parked was hub-to-hub with that of a Hu barbarian. The Hu neglected his fire and burned down the whole carriage encampment. One of Lo's petty officers interrogated the Hu, who falsely accused Yu. Yu estimated that it would be impossible to argue with him, so he said, "A while ago I was cooking gruel for my old woman and I neglected the fire, which spread out of control. My crime deserves ten thousand deaths."

When Lo learned of it he pursued him. But the Hu who had falsely accused him generously repaid Yu's kindness and gave him his own donkey and horse and convoyed him out of the camp so that he was able to make his escape.

WYCS: Because of the length of the journey, Yu hacked his carriage to pieces and had the ox and horse carry his wife and the children on their backs to make their escape. Bandits later robbed them of the ox and horse. Yu said to his wife, "My younger brother died early and there is only his son, Sui, left to carry on his name. Now that we have to travel on foot, to carry both boys on our backs and have all of us die would not be as good as abandoning our own son and carrying Sui in our arms. Afterwards we may still have another son." His wife consented.

CHS: Yu abandoned his own son in the grass. The boy followed, sobbing and calling after them, finally catching up with them at nightfall. The next morning Yu bound his son to a tree and departed, and so they got across the Yangtze River . . . When Yu died, this younger brother's son, Sui, wore the coarse hempen mourning garments of the second degree for him for three years.

29.[1] Wang Yüeh as a person was respectful and agreeable, and in serving his parents completely discharged his filial duty of "care with a cheerful countenance."[2] Each time his father, Chancellor Wang Tao, saw him he was always glad, whereas each time he saw Yüeh's younger half-brother, T'ien, he was always angry. When Yüeh talked with the chancellor he always made a discreet intimacy his first principle. As the chancellor returned to his office, when it came time to go, Yüeh never failed to escort him to the rear of the carriage, and he would always arrange the boxes and cases for his mother, Mme. Ts'ao (Ts'ao Shu).

After Yüeh died, when the chancellor returned to his office, from the time he mounted the carriage he continued to weep until he reached the office gate. Mme. Ts'ao placed a seal on the boxes and could not bring herself to reopen them. (CS 65.11a and 10a)

[1] In KI, this item is prefaced by the following anecdote: Chancellor Wang Tao once dreamed that a man wished to buy his elder son, Wang Yüeh, for a million cash. The chancellor was very upset over it and secretly made elaborate arrangements for someone to pray for him. Later, while he was building a room, he inadvertantly unearthed and discovered a vault of cash, estimated at ten million. Very unhappy, he hid the whole treasure away and locked it up. Without warning, Yüeh died.

[2] Cf. "Analects" II, 8.

30. Each time Huan I heard anyone characterize Chu Fa-shen, he would always say, "Since this gentleman had a reputation in the past, and in addition enjoyed the praise of the former generation, and furthermore had the most cordial relations with my deceased father (Huan Hao), it's not proper to talk about him."

31. Among the horses which Yü Liang used to ride there was a White Forehead (ti-lu).[1] When someone[2] suggested that he sell it, Yü replied, "If I sell it, there has to be a buyer, and so I will be harming the new owner. I would far rather inconvenience myself than shift the risk to someone else. Long ago Sun Shu-ao[3] killed a two-headed snake for the benefit of those who might come after him. Isn't it a mark of understanding to imitate the excellent stories of antiquity?" (CS 73.10b)

[1] HMC: Horses with a white forehead extending to their mouths as far as the front teeth are called Elm Geese (yü-yen), or White Foreheads (ti-lu). If a slave rides one, he will die in a strange

land, and if the owner rides, he will be executed in the marketplace. It is an ill-omened horse.

(SKShu 2.6a, comm., quoting WCSY, describes Liu Pei's escape on a White Forehead which could "leap thirty feet in one bound.")

[2]YL (so also CS 73.10b): Yin Hao urged him to sell the horse.

[3]CIHS (Ch'un-ch'iu p'ien): When Sun Shu-ao (fl. 600 B.C.) was a boy he went out on the road and saw a two-headed snake, which he killed and buried. When he came home and saw his mother he was crying. She asked the reason, and he answered, "The person who sees a two-headed snake is sure to die. Today I went out and saw one, and that's why I'm crying."

His mother asked, "Where is the snake now?"

He answered, "I was afraid people coming after me would see it, so I killed and buried it."

His mother said, "Whoever does good in secret will surely be rewarded openly. You have nothing to worry about."

Subsequently he rose to favor at court in Ch'u, and when he was grown he became prime minister.

32. While Juan Yü was living in Shan (Chekiang) he owned a fine carriage. For anyone who asked to borrow it he never failed to make it available. There was one man who was burying his mother who had in mind to borrow it but did not dare speak to him. Juan, hearing of it later, sighed and said, "If I own a carriage and make people not dare to borrow it, what's the use of having a carriage?" Whereupon he burned it. (CS 49.10b)

33. While Hsieh I was serving as magistrate of Shan Prefecture (Chekiang) there was an old man who had violated the law. Hsieh penalized him by making him drink unmixed wine. Even after the man had become excessively drunk, he still did not stop.

I's younger brother, Hsieh An, was in his seventh or eighth year at the time, and was seated by his elder brother's knee wearing blue cloth trousers. He rebuked I, saying, "Big brother, the old man is to be pitied; how can you do this to him?"

I at this point changed his expression and said, "Do you want me to let him go?" Whereupon he dismissed him. (CS 79.12a; TPYL 516)

34. Hsieh An[1] was an absolute admirer of Ch'u P'ou, and often praised him, saying, "Although Ch'u P'ou doesn't speak, the working of the four seasons is nonetheless complete."[2] (CS 93.6b)

[1]WTC: When Huan I saw Hsieh An in his fourth year, he praised him, saying, "This boy's manner and spirit are outstandingly perceptive. He will carry on the tradition of Wang Ch'eng*."

[2]Cf. "Analects" XVII, 17: The Master said, "Does Heaven speak? The four seasons make their rounds by it; the hundred living things grow by it. But does Heaven speak?"

35. While Liu T'an was residing in Tan-yang Commandery (Chien-k'ang), as he approached his end and was breathing his last, he heard below his room the drumming and dancing of sacrifices to the spirits, and stated with a solemn expression, "Let us have no obscene offerings."

Someone outside asked permission to kill the ox which drew his carriage as a sacrifice to the spirits, but T'an replied, "'I have already been praying for a long time';[1] don't trouble yourselves any further." (CS 75.34a)

[1] Cf. "Analects" VII, 35. Liu quoted Confucius directly, using the latter's personal name, Ch'iu, rather than the first-person pronoun.

36. Hsieh An's wife (Mme. Liu) was once instructing her sons (Hsieh Yao and Hsieh Yen), when she asked An, "How comes it that from the start I've never once seen you instructing your sons?"
An replied, "I'm always naturally instructing my sons."[1]

[1] SSHY Comm. (cf. CS 41.12a): The grand marshal, Liu Shih (219-309), was incorruptible and possessed determination and integrity. He conducted himself according to the rites, but his two sons (Chi and Hsia) were incompetent, and both were convicted of accepting bribes. Shih (as their father) was implicated in their crime and relieved of his post.
A stranger asked him, "Why didn't you instruct them and lead them in the right way?"
Shih replied, "My own conduct of affairs was what their ears and eyes continually heard and saw, yet they did not imitate me. Would they have been changed by severe admonitions?"

37. When the Chin Emperor Chien-wen (Ssu-ma Yü) was serving as General Controlling the Army (345-361), he would not permit the dust to be brushed off the dais on which he sat. When he saw the tracks where rats had run he looked on them as a thing of beauty. One of his aides saw a rat running in broad daylight and struck and killed him with his baton. The general was displeased in both mind and expression. But when one of his underlings raised an accusation against the aide, he rebuked him, saying, "Even when a rat comes to grief I can't get it out of my mind; so now isn't it out of the question to harm a man on account of a rat?" (SWLC, hou 41)

38. When Fan Hsüan was in his eighth year he was cutting vegetables in the back garden when he accidentally injured his finger and started to cry loudly.
Someone asked, "Does it hurt?"
He replied, "It's not because it hurts, but 'even the hair and skin of the body I dare not destroy or injure'[1] -- that's the reason I'm crying."
Hsüan was incorruptible in behavior as well as modest and frugal. When Han Po once left him a hundred bolts (p'i) of silk, he would not accept them. Han reduced them to fifty, but still he would not accept them. In this way Han kept reducing the amount by half until there was only one bolt left, but in the end Hsüan would not even accept that.
Later Han and Fan were riding together, and while they were in the carriage Han tore off two *chang* (about twenty feet) and presented it to Fan with the words, "Would you have your wife go without trousers?"
Fan, laughing, accepted it.[2] (CS 91.15a; TPYL 370, 426, 696, 817; SWLC, hsü 21)

¹*Hsiao-ching* 1.

²*CHS* (cf. *CS* 91.15b): Hsüan's family was extremely poor, and he seldom took part in ordinary human affairs. When the grand warden of his home commandery, Yü-chang (Kiangsi), Yin Hsien, observed that Hsüan's thatched cottage was unfinished, he wanted to rebuild his house for him, but Hsüan adamantly refused. Hsien was very fond of him, and since Hsüan was poor, and, moreover, the year was famine-stricken and an epidemic was raging, he provided him with generous portions of food, but again Hsüan would accept none of it.

39. Wang Hsien-chih was critically ill. Taoists, when they offer up a petition (*shang-chang*), must make a confession of their faults (*shou-kuo*).¹ The master in attendance² asked Hsien-chih what unusual events or successes and failures there had been in the course of his life.

Hsien-chih replied, "I'm not aware of anything else, except only that I remember being divorced from my wife of the Ch'ih family (Ch'ih Tao-mao)."³ (*CS* 80.14a)

¹The petition was written out on paper and burned with incense. It was addressed to the Celestial Ruler (T'ien-ti) and usually requested an extension of life. It was accompanied by a confession, on the assumption that all sickness is the result of wrongdoing. See Holmes Welch, *The Parting of the Way*, Boston, 1957, p. 115.

²Cf. below, *SSHY* XVII, 16, n. 3: An unknown Taoist master came a distance to attend the two Wang brothers, Hui-chih and Hsien-chih, who were ill at the same time. They both died in the same year (388), only a month apart.

³In the version of this story quoted from *TPYL* 641, Hsien-chih says, "I have nothing to confess. It's only my having sent away the daughter of the Ch'ih family which causes me regret."

40. After Yin Chung-k'an had become governor of Ching Province (Hunan-Hupei), he encountered a shortage of food due to floods. His meals always consisted of five bowls, and there was no extra food beyond what was in the dishes. If a grain of rice fell between the dishes and the mat, he would always pick it up and devour it. Although in doing so he wished to set an example for others, he was also following the true simplicity of his nature. He would often say to his sons and younger brothers, "Don't imagine, because I have accepted office in the present province, that I have given up my usual attitude of earlier days. At present the situation in which we are living is not easy, but 'poverty is the gentleman's normal state.'¹ Why should he climb out on the branches and lose contact with his roots? You all should preserve this principle!" (*CS* 84.15b)

¹*Lieh-tzu* 1.6 (Graham, p. 24).

41. Earlier Huan Hsüan and Yang Kuang had both advised Yin Chung-k'an to deprive Yin Chi of his post as Commandant of Southern Barbarians in order to establish their own power. Chi himself was also aware of their intentions. One day, on the pretext of walking after taking a powder,¹ he went directly to his private residence and never returned. No one either inside or outside his headquarters had any foreknowledge that he would do so, for his mood and expression were

serene, resembling from afar Tou Ku-yü-t'u's lack of resentment.[2] Contemporary discussions lauded him for this.[3] (CS 83.16ab)

[1]*Hsing-san*, literally, "to walk a powder," was a therapeutic practice adopted from Hsien-Taoism, the "Immortality Cult" of the late Han period, and popularized in the third century by Ho Yen (see below, SSHY II, 14). The powder was a blend of five mineral substances (*wu-shih*): stalactite (*shih-chung-ju*), sulphur (*shih-liu-huang*), milky quartz (*pai-shih-ying*), amethyst (*tzu-shih-ying*), and red bole or ochre (*ch'ih-shih-chih*). Taken with warm wine and cold food (the alternate name was cold-food powder, *han-shih-san*), it was circulated through the body by walking and was supposed to have simultaneously tranquilizing and exhilarating properties. See *Pao-p'u-tzu* 4.11a; Murakami Yoshimi, *Chūkoku no sennin*, Kyoto, 1956, p.57; Masutomi Junosuke, "Shōsōin yakubutsu o chūshin to suru kodai sekiyaku no kenkyū," *Shōsōin no kōbutsu*, Kyoto, 1958, I, p. 21-22, and Yü Chia-hsi, "Han-shih san k'ao," in *Yü Chia-hsi lun-hsüeh tsa-chu*, Peking, 1963, pp. 181-226.

[2]Cf. "Analects" V, 19: The prime minister of Ch'u, Tzu-wen (Tou Ku-yü-t'u, 7th cent. B.C.), served three times as prime minister, but never looked pleased. Three times he was dismissed, but never looked resentful.

[3]*CHS*: Earlier Yin Chung-k'an wanted to raise men-at-arms to attack Ssu-ma Tao-tzu and secretly sought help from Yin Chi, but Chi would not join him. Yang Kuang and his younger brother, Yang Ch'üan-ch'i, urged Chung-k'an to kill Chi, but he would not consent. (See below, SSHY X, 23, for the background of this incident.)

42. (In 397) when Wang Yü was governor in Chiang Province (Hupei and Kiangsi), and was being pursued by Yin Chung-k'an and Huan Hsüan,[1] he fled for refuge to Yü-chang (Kiangsi), and it was not known whether he was alive or dead. His son, Wang Sui, was in the capital (Chien-k'ang), and since anxiety and grief showed in his face, whether in his daily acts or in eating and drinking, in everything he suffered a decline. His contemporaries called him a "son who is tasting the mourning of his parents." (CS 75.15b)

[1]*HKCC*: Wang Yü had barely arrived at his post in Wu-ch'ang as governor of Ching Province when Huan Hsüan and Yang Ch'üan-ch'i began raising men-at-arms in response to the call of Wang Kung to punish Ssu-ma Tao-tzu (in 397). Coming downstream from Chiang-ling, they arrived unexpectedly. Yü was undefended and in panic took refuge in Lin-ch'uan (Kiangsi), where he was captured by Huan Hsüan. When Hsüan usurped the throne (in 404), Yü was transferred to be vice-president of the Court Secretariat.

43. After Huan Hsüan had defeated the governor of Ching Province, Yin Chung-k'an (in 399), he apprehended ten or more of Yin's generals and aides, including the advisory aide, Lo Ch'i-sheng.[1] In the past Huan had treated Ch'i-sheng generously, so just before he was to be executed, Huan first sent a man to tell him, "If you apologize to me, I will remit your sentence."

Ch'i-sheng replied, "I am a petty officer on the staff of the governor of Ching Province. At present the governor has fled and disappeared and there is no telling if he is dead or alive. How should I have the face to apologize to Lord Huan?"

After he came out into the marketplace for execution Huan again sent someone to ask if he wanted to say anything. He replied, "In the past Prince Wen of Chin (Ssu-ma Chao) killed Hsi K'ang, but Hsi's son, Shao, became a loyal minister of the Chin.[2] I beg of you to spare my one younger brother (Lo Tsun-sheng) to take care of my aged mother."

Huan did spare the brother as requested.

On an earlier occasion Huan had presented Ch'i-sheng's mother, Lady Hu, with a lambskin coat. Lady Hu was living at the time in Yü-chang Commandery (Kiangsi). When news of Ch'i-sheng's execution arrived, she burned the coat the very same day. (CS 89.26b)

[1] *(Huan) Hsüan PC*: When Hsüan conquered Ching Province, he killed Yin Tao-hu (son of Yin Chung-k'an's younger brother) and Chung-k'an's aides, Lo Ch'i-sheng and Pao Chi-li, all of whom had been intimately relied upon by Chung-k'an.

CHS (cf. *CS* 89.26ab): Yin Chung-k'an had at first requested Lo Ch'i-sheng to serve as work-detail officer in his headquarters, but when Huan Hsüan came to attack, he transferred him to advisory aide. Chung-k'an was frequently in doubt and seldom decisive, which was a source of deep concern to Ch'i-sheng. He said to his younger brother, Tsun-sheng, "Lord Yin is a good man, but indecisive, and his affairs are certain not to succeed. But whether they succeed or fail is with Heaven. I will stick with him dead or alive."

When Chung-k'an fled, none of his civil or military staff saw him off. Only Ch'i-sheng accompanied him. Their route passed Ch'i-sheng's house, where Tsun-sheng tricked him by saying, "If we're going to part like this, can't you at least shake hands?"

Ch'i-sheng turned his horse about and extended his hand, whereupon Tsun-sheng pulled him down and said, "You have an aged mother at home; what will she do?"

Ch'i-sheng brushed away his tears and said, "In today's affair I am sure to die. All of you take care of her, and don't neglect the way of sons. If in a single family there are both loyal and filial sons, then what regrets can there be?"

Tsun-sheng held him even more tightly in his arms, while Chung-k'an waited for him in the road. Ch'i-sheng shouted at a distance to him, "Today it's all the same if I live or die. Please don't wait any longer!"

Chung-k'an saw there was no possibility of Ch'i-sheng's getting away, so, goading his horse, he departed.

In a very short time Huan Hsüan arrived. Men and officers all flocked to Hsüan. Ch'i-sheng alone did not go, but stayed to put Chung-k'an's house in order. Someone said to him, "Hsüan's nature is suspicious and impetuous; he'll never be able to comprehend your sincerity or integrity. If you don't go to visit him, calamity will surely come to you."

Ch'i-sheng replied with a solemn expression, "I am a petty officer of Lord Yin, who has treated me like a gentleman of the state. Since I haven't been able to join him in rooting out the wicked and rebellious, but he has instead ended in flight and defeat, with what countenance would I approach Huan to plead for my life?"

When Hsüan heard of it he was furious and apprehended him, saying, "After I have treated you so well as this, why have you turned your back on me?"

Ch'i-sheng replied, "Sir, the blood of your sworn alliance with Yin is not yet dry on your mouth, yet you have hatched this treacherous plot. For myself I am distressed that my strength has been too weak to cut down the evil and rebellious. I only regret that I'm so late dying!"

Huan forthwith decapitated him. He was at the time in his thirty-seventh year.

[2]*WYCS*: When Emperor Hui (Ssu-ma Chung, r. 290-306) was defeated (in 304) at Tang-yin (Honan), all his officers and attendants fled and dispersed. Only Hsi Shao, with perfect dignity and unruffled cap, defended the emperor with his own person. Armed men clashed by the imperial palanquin, and flying arrows gathered like rain, and thus he was killed.

44. When Wang Kung returned to the capital from K'uai-chi (Chekiang), Wang Ch'en went to see him. He observed that Kung was sitting on a six-foot bamboo mat, and accordingly said to him, "You've just come from the east and of course have plenty of these things; how about letting me have one?"

Kung said nothing, but after Ch'en had left he took up the one he had been sitting on and sent it along with him. Since he had no other mats, he sat thereafter on the coarse floor matting.

Later Ch'en heard of it and in extreme astonishment said, "I originally thought you had a lot of them, and that's the reason I asked for one."

Kung replied, "You don't know me very well. I'm the sort of person who has no extra things." (*CS* 84.1a)

45. Ch'en I of Wu Commandery (Soochow) was extremely filial in his family relations. His mother was fond of eating scorched rice from the bottom of the pot. While I was superintendent of records for the commandery he always kept a sack ready, and every time he cooked a meal he would always put aside some of the scorched rice in it. On the occasions when he returned home he would give it to his mother.

Later (in 401) it happened that Sun En's rebellion broke out in Wu Commandery. The grand warden, Yüan Shan-sung, started punitive action against them the very same day. I had already collected several dipperfuls (*tou*) of scorched rice, but as he had not yet had leave to return home, he carried it with him on the campaign. They fought at Hu-tu (northwest of Shanghai) and were defeated. The men in the ranks scattered and absconded among the hills and swamps, and most of them died of starvation. I alone, because of the scorched rice, managed to live. His contemporaries considered that this was the reward of his "unmixed filial devotion."[1] (Cf. *Nan-shih* 73.7b, under biog. of P'an Tsung)

[1]Cf. *Tso-chuan*, Yin 1.4.

46. While K'ung An-kuo served as personal attendant to Emperor Hsiao-wu (Ssu-ma Yao, r. 373-396), he was treated with fond regard. When the emperor was buried at Shan-ling (the imperial mausoleum near Chien-k'ang), K'ung was at the time serving as grand ordinary. His frame had always been emaciated, and now he wore heavy mourning garments, weeping and wailing all day long. Those who saw him thought he was a true filial son (mourning his father). (*CS* 78.3b-4a)

47. The two brothers, Wu T'an-chih and Wu Yin-chih, were living in Tan-yang Commandery (Chien-k'ang). Sometime thereafter they experienced the loss of their mother, Mme. T'ung (T'ung Ch'in-i), and from morning to evening they wept as they approached her coffin. Whenever their longing became extreme, or when guests came to offer condolences, they would wail and leap, and their grief would know no bounds; even those passing by on the road would shed tears for them.

At the time Han Po was serving as intendant of Tan-yang, and his mother, Lady Yin, was living with him in the commandery next door to the Wu residence. Every time she heard the two Wu brothers weeping she felt sorry for them and would say to Po, "If you are ever in a position to select officials, you should treat these men well." Po himself also was well aware of the situation.

Afterwards Han Po actually became president of the Board of Civil Office, and although the elder Wu never survived the period of mourning,[1] the younger Wu subsequently attained great honor.[2] (*CS* 90.15a)

[1]*THHTC* (quoted, *IWLC* 20): On the evening in which Wu T'an-chih's mother was buried they set up nine food offerings. Each time T'an-chih approached for one of the offerings he would always cry out in grief until he lost his breath. At the seventh offering he spit up blood and died.

[2]*HTC*: When Yin-chih encountered the loss of his mother, his grief and emaciation surpassed what was required by the rites. At the time he was living as a neighbor with the grand ordinary, Han Po. Po's mother, the younger sister of Yin Hao, was an intelligent and enlightened woman. Every time Yin-chih wept, Po's mother would always stop whatever she was doing to shed tears, her sympathy being beyond control. Till the end of the funeral it was like this. She said to Po, "If later you ever occupy the office of weighing and selecting officials, always use this kind of person!"

Later after Po became president of the Board of Civil Office, he promoted and employed Yin-chih.

CATC: Wu Yin-chih was already extremely filial by nature, but in addition was frugal and incorruptible. Whatever he received in salary he shared with all nine branches of his family, though he himself went without bedclothes even in winter.

(Ca. 400) Huan Hsüan, wishing to clean up the corruption in Ling-nan, appointed him governor of Kuang Province (Kwangtung-Kwangsi). Twenty *li* from the provincial headquarters there was a river called the Avarice (T'an-shui). For generations there had been a tradition that whoever drank from it, his heart would never know satiety. Accordingly, when Yin-chih came to the bank of the river he poured himself a cupful and drank it, and proceeded to compose a poem, which went:

> In Stone Gate is the Avarice Spring,
> One whetting of the lips and there's a craving
>   for a thousand gold.
> But try and make Po I or Shu Ch'i take a drink;
> Till death they'd never change their minds.

CHS: According to an old saying, anyone going to Kuang Province who drinks from the Avarice Spring looses his frugality and incorruptibility. But when Wu Yin-chih became governor, he poured himself a cup from Avarice Spring and drank it, and then wrote an inscription on the Stone Gate in the form of a poem, which went, etc.

(Previous governors of Kuang Province, succumbing to the soft life of the tropics and the profitable exploitation of the pearl industry along the southern coast, had made the post notorious. See CS 90.15b-16a; E. H. Schafer, "The Pearl Fisheries of Ho-p'u," JAOS 72, 1952, 155-168.)

CHAPTER II

Speech and Conversation

1. When Pien Jang came for an interview with Yüan Lang he got the order of precedence backward. Yüan remarked, "When the Sage-king Yao summoned the recluse Hsü Yu for an interview, Hsü showed no sign of embarrassment in his face.[1] Why are you 'putting your clothes on topsy-turvy'?"[2]

Pien replied, "Your Excellency has only just arrived at his post, and the moral power of Yao has not yet been displayed. It's only for this reason that your humble servant has 'put his clothes on topsy-turvy.'"[3]

[1] *HFMKSC*: Yao and Shun both had Hsü Yu for a teacher and studied with him and served him. Later he retired in P'ei Swamp (Anhui), where Yao subsequently offered to yield him the throne.

As a person Hsü Yu based himself on moral principle and trod a straight path. He refused to sit on an improper mat or to eat improper food, and when he heard of Yao's offer he departed. His friend Ch'ao Fu, on learning that Yu had been made an offer by Yao, considered it a defilement of his own person and immediately went down to a pool to wash his ears. The owner of the pool became angry and cried, "Why are you defiling my water?"

After this Yu went into hiding and worked on a farm near the Central Peak (Mt. Sung, in Honan), on the northern bank of the Ying River, at the foot of Chi Mountain. Throughout his life he had never involved himself in the affairs of the realm, but died and was buried on the summit of Chi Mountain, ten *li* south of Yang-ch'eng.

On the occasion of his death Yao visited his grave and named him the God of Chi Mountain and made an offering of food equivalent to that for the Five Sacred Peaks. For generations the offerings have continued to be made, nor have they stopped to this day.

²See "Songs," No. 100:

> The east is not yet bright;
> He puts his clothes on topsy-turvy.
> Topsy-turvy he wears them;
> From the court they summon him.

³In his commentary Liu Chün points out that Yüan Lang never held any office higher than assistant to the grand marshal and could not have been grand warden of Pien Jang's home commandery of Ch'en-liu (the "Ju-nan" of the text must be an error?). In *HHS* 86.5b, however, we find that Yüan did serve on Wang Kung's staff while the latter was grand warden of Ju-nan.

2. When Hsü Chih was in his ninth year he was once playing in the moonlight. Someone asked him, "If there weren't any objects in the moon, wouldn't it be a lot brighter?"

Hsü replied, "Not at all. It's like the pupil in a man's eye. If he didn't have this, his eye certainly wouldn't be bright." (*SLF* 1; *TPYL* 385; *TPKC* 164)

3. When K'ung Jung was in his tenth year he accompanied his father to Lo-yang. At the time Li Ying was at the height of his reputation there as commandant of the Capital Province. Those who came to his gate gained admittance only if they were men of exceptional talent and unblemished reputation, or if they were relatives on their father's or mother's side. Jung arrived at Li's gate and announced to the gatekeeper, "I'm a relative of Commandant Li." After he was let in and seated before his host, Li Ying asked him, "And what relationship have you with me?"

He answered, "Long ago my ancestor K'ung Chung-ni (Confucius) had the respectful relationship of student to teacher with your ancestor Li Po-yang (Lao-tzu),¹ which means that you and I have carried on friendly relations for generations."

Li Ying and all the guests marveled at him.

The Great Officer of the Center, Ch'en Wei, arrived later. Someone reported what Jung had said, and Wei remarked, "If a lad is clever when he's small it doesn't necessarily mean he'll be superior when he grows up."

Jung retorted, "I suppose when you were small you must have been clever?"²

Wei was greatly discomfited. (*HHS* 100.4b; *SKWei* 12.4b, comm.)

¹See *SC* 63.2a: Confucius went to Chou (Lo-yang) to inquire about the rites from Lao-tzu. Lao-tzu said, "The ones you are talking about--both the men and their bones have long since rotted away . . ."

²*K'ung Jung PC*: When Jung was in his fourth year, whenever he ate pears in company with his elder brothers he always took the smallest one. When someone asked the reason, he replied, "The smallest boy ought to take the smallest."

4. K'ung Jung had two children.¹ Once when the older one was in his sixth year and the younger one in his fifth their father was taking a siesta, and the younger one, stealing some wine from the head of the

bed, drank it. The older one said to him, "Why didn't you perform the proper ceremony?"

He replied, "When it's stolen, who performs rites?" (*TPYL* 385; *SWLC*, ch'ien 46)

[1] The names of the children are unknown and reports of their sex and relative ages differ. According to *HHS* 100, the older was a boy and the younger a girl two years his junior; all other accounts state they were both boys, one year apart.

5. When K'ung Jung was apprehended[1] those both inside and outside the court were panic-stricken. At the time Jung's older son was in his ninth year, and the younger in his eighth. The two boys continued as before their game of throwing spikes (*cho-ting*)[2] without the slightest agitation showing in their faces.

Jung said to the officer who had come for him, "I trust the punishment ceases with my own person. May my two sons be spared?"

The sons came forward gravely and said, "Father, would you expect to find any unbroken eggs under an overturned nest?"

In a short while officers came to apprehend them as well.[3] (*HHS* 100.17a; *SKWei* 12.6ab, comm., quoting *WSCC*)

[1] *WSCC*: Having spoken slanderous words against Ts'ao Ts'ao to the emissary of Sun Ch'üan, Jung was convicted and sentenced to public execution . . .

WCSY: Because it was a lean year, Ts'ao Ts'ao placed a prohibition on drinking. K'ung Jung remonstrated, "Wine is necessary for fulfilling the rites; it's improper to prohibit its use." In this way he misled the people, and Ts'ao Ts'ao had him arrested and punished for it . . .

[2] It seems to have resembled the modern game of mumblety-peg. According to the seventeenth-century miscellany of Chou Liang-kung, *Yin-shu wu shu-ying (tse-lu)*, quoted in the Japanese commentary, *Sesetsu sembon* (XII, 16b-17a), the ground was first marked in squares. The first spike was thrown into one of the squares, and a second scored if it lodged in the same square. If it missed the square or struck the first spike, it was disqualified. All other accounts of this incident, probably based on the *WSCC*, identify the game as *i-ch'i*, or *go*. See the following note.

[3] *WSCC*: When Jung was arrested the two boys were playing *i-ch'i*. They remained calmly seated without getting up. The attendants said, "Your father is being arrested!"

The boys replied, "When was there ever a nest destroyed where the eggs weren't broken?" And subsequently they were both killed.

WCSY: When Jung was arrested he looked back and said to his two boys, "Why don't you run away?" They replied, "As long as you have come to this pass, Father, what is left to run away from?"

SSHY Comm.: P'ei Sung-chih (5th cent., in his commentary at *SKWei* 12.6b) noted that the *WCSY*, in stating that the boys did not escape because they knew they would surely die together, seems a trustworthy account. Sun Sheng's (d. 373) account in the *WSCC*, on the other hand, is really without parallel. If a little boy in his eighth year were able to transcend the calamity that had struck, and with intelligence and exceptional understanding keep a majestic distance from it all, then his control over feelings of sorrow or joy would surely surpass that of any adult. Where is there any little boy who would not turn pale on seeing his father arrested, but who would, on the contrary, keep on playing *go* without ever getting up, just as if he were enjoying himself at leisure?

Long ago when Shen Sheng (the deposed and condemned heir of Duke Hsien of Chin, r. 676-652 B.C., who, when urged to kill his father to avenge the wrong done to himself, committed suicide instead) went to his fate, he did not forget his father in what he said, nor did he cast away feelings of remembrance of his father because of his own imminent death. If, when his father was perfectly safe, he could still act like this, how much more would he have done so if his father had fallen upon misfortune!

In considering this to be a fine remark on the part of the boys, was not Sun Sheng discrediting the role of a son? He would seem to have been overfond of bizarre feelings, unaware of how his words do injury to right principles.

6. The grand warden of Ying-ch'uan (Honan) had penalized Ch'en Shih by shaving his head.[1] A guest once asked Ch'en's son, Chi, "What sort of man is the grand warden?"

Chi replied, "A high-minded and enlightened ruler."

"And what sort of man is your father?"

"A loyal minister and filial son."

The guest then asked, "In the 'Book of Changes' it says,

> 'When two men are agreed in mind
> Their keenness cuts through metal.
> Words of the agreed in mind
> Are fragrant as the orchid.'[2]

How can there be a high-minded and enlightened ruler who would punish a loyal minister and filial son?"

Chi replied, "How mistaken your words are!" Whereupon he made no further reply.

The guest said, "You're just like a man who feigns respectfulness because he's hunchbacked, but in reality you're unable to answer."

Chi replied, "Long ago the Shang ruler, Wu-ting, banished his filial son, Hsiao-chi;[3] the Chou minister, Yin Chi-fu, banished his filial son, Po-ch'i;[4] and the Han minister, Tung Chung-shu, banished his filial son, Fu-ch'i.[5] Surely these three rulers were all high-minded and enlightened, and these three sons all loyal and filial?"

The guest retreated in shame.

[1] *SSHY* Comm.: When Ch'en Shih was in his home village (Ying-ch'uan) all who had any doubtful cases which they could not settle would bring them to him. Some would confess after they arrived; some would change their terms en route; others would plead madness or panic. But all said, "I would rather suffer the pain of punishment than be denounced by Lord Ch'en." Could he have possessed such abundant virtue to move others without being able to keep himself out of trouble, bringing punishment on himself instead? Hardly! This story is so much "nonsense from the eastern wilderness" and nothing more.

[2] Cf. "Book of Changes" (*Hsi-tz'u*, shang; Wilhelm I, 329).

³*TWSC*: Wu-ting of Yin (r. 1324-1264 B.C.) had a worthy son, Hsiao-chi, whose mother died early. Wu-ting, incited by his second wife's nagging, sent him away to his death, while all the realm mourned for him.

⁴*CT*: Yin Chi-fu (fl. ca. 800 B.C.) was a minister under the Chou. His wife bore him a son named Po-ch'i. When Po-ch'i's mother died, Chi-fu remarried. His second wife, after bearing him a son named Po-kuei, proceeded to slander Po-ch'i to Chi-fu, who forthwith banished him to the wilds.

King Hsüan (r. 827-782) happened to be on an outing in company with Chi-fu, when Po-ch'i, catching sight of them, composed a song, hoping to move him by its words. King Hsüan, hearing it, remarked, "These are the words of a filial son!" Chi-fu then sought for Po-ch'i in the wilds, and later shot and killed his second wife.

⁵There is no mention in Tung Chung-shu's (ca. 179-104 B.C.) biography, *HS* 56.1a-23a, of any son named Fu-ch'i.

7. Hsün Shuang¹ once had an interview with Yüan Lang of Ju-nan (Honan), who inquired about the gentlemen of Shuang's native place, Ying-ch'uan (Honan). Shuang first mentioned his elder brothers,² whereupon Lang said, laughing, "Is it permissible for a gentleman only to think of his own relatives and old acquaintances?"

Shuang replied, "Your Excellency objects?"

Lang said, "Just now I inquired about the gentlemen of your principality, and you mentioned your elder brothers. It's only for this reason that I'm complaining."

Shuang said, "Long ago Ch'i Hsi (6th cent. B.C.) in recommending insiders did not neglect his own son, Wu, and in recommending outsiders did not neglect his enemy, Chieh Hu, for which he is considered extremely fair.³ Chi Tan, the Duke of Chou, in the song 'King Wen,'⁴ did not discuss the virtues of the Sage-kings Yao and Shun, but sang instead the praises of his father, King Wen, and his brother, King Wu. This is what is meant by the phrase, 'Treat relatives as relatives.'⁵ The whole purport of the 'Spring and Autumn Annals' is to 'treat those of one's own state as insiders and all the other feudal lords as outsiders.'⁶ Furthermore, 'If a person does not love his own relatives, but loves those of other people instead, is it not a perversion of virtue?'⁷ (*TPKC* 173; *SSYW*, shang)

¹*HNC*: There was not any piece of writing or classical text which Hsün Shuang had not read through. His contemporaries had a saying, "Among the 'Eight Dragons' of the Hsün family Shuang is without peer." He lived in retirement with steadfast purpose, and though summoned to office, never accepted.

CFHC: While Tung Cho was in control of the government (189-192) he again summoned Shuang, and Shuang attempted to abscond, but the officer only held him the more urgently. Within ninety-five days, from the time he was still out of office until his final promotion, he rose from obscurity to one of the Three Ducal Offices (i.e., director of works).

²I.e., Chien, Kun, Ching, Tao, and Wang.

[3] *Tso-chuan*, Ch'eng 18 (Legge V, 410): Ch'i Hsi was serving as Commander of the Central Army.

Ibid., Hsiang 3 (Legge V, 419-420): He requested retirement on account of old age. When the Marquis of Chin inquired about who should succeed him, he proposed Chieh Hu, his enemy. When they were about to install Chieh in office he died. The marquis again inquired of Ch'i, who replied, "Wu will do." Wu was his son.

SSHY Comm.: Gentlemen say that Ch'i Hsi might be considered capable of recommending the good. He proposed his enemy without currying favor, and established his own son without showing partiality. (See also *Tso-chuan*, Hsiang 21; Legge V, 491.)

[4] "Songs," No. 235, traditionally attributed to the Duke of Chou.

[5] "Record of Rites" 32.14 (Legge, *Li Ki* II, 312).

[6] *Kung-yang chuan*, Ch'eng 15.

[7] *Hsiao-ching* 9.

8. Ni Heng[1] was once degraded by Ts'ao Ts'ao to become a drummer. In the middle of the first month, at the time of reviewing the drums, Heng lifted his drumstick and played the "Yü-yang Drum-roll."[2] *Yüan-yüan*! it rang with the sound of metal and stone, and those seated 'round about were all deeply affected by it.

K'ung Jung said to Ts'ao Ts'ao, "Ni Heng's punishment is like that of the chain-gang slave Fu Yüeh, but unlike Fu he has not been able to appear in Your Highness's dreams."[3] Ts'ao Ts'ao was ashamed, and pardoned him. (*HHS* 110B.20b-21a; *PTSC* 108; *TPYL* 30)

[1] *WSC*: It is not known where Ni Heng's ancestors originated, but he himself was of outstanding talent, and from his youth he had a "thee-thou" relationship with K'ung Jung. At the time he was not yet twenty, while Jung was already fifty. (According to *HHS* 110B, the age differential was only twenty years.) Jung respected Heng's superior talent, and the two were bound intimately together in an inseparable friendship.

At the beginning of the Chien-an Era (196) Heng traveled north. Someone urged him to visit the nobles in the capital. Heng carried a calling card in his bosom, but when he arrived the card had disappeared and in the end he never visited anyone.

K'ung Jung frequently sent memoranda to Ts'ao Ts'ao praising Heng's talents, so that Ts'ao was eager to see him. But Heng would always claim illness and was unwilling to go, though he often talked about it. Ts'ao Ts'ao became very angry with him, but because of his talent and reputation did not kill him. Instead, wishing to humiliate him, he had him registered with the drummers.

Later, at the time of the eighth month (*sic*) court assembly, there was a grand review of drum rhythms. They erected a three-tiered pavilion in which the guests were seated in ranks, and they made clothes for the drummers of silk and pongee. For each drummer they made one high-peaked hat (*ts'en-mou*) and one single robe of yellow-green silk (*tan-chiao*) and a small pair of underpants (*kun*). As each drummer finished, he was to take off his old clothes and put on the new. When it came Ni Heng's turn, he beat the drum in the "Yü-yang Drum-roll," stamping the ground as he rushed forward, rapidly mincing with his legs and feet, his expression and manner quite out of the ordinary, and the sound of the drum exceedingly poignant. Both timbre and rhythm were unusual and strange, and no one present was not deeply affected, as everyone realized it must be Ni Heng.

After he was finished, he was unwilling to change his clothes. The other drummers taunted him, saying, "Drummer, how comes it you're the only one not changing your clothes?"

Thereupon Heng took his stand directly in front of Ts'ao Ts'ao. First he removed his underpants, following with the rest of his clothes, and stood there stark naked. Then, slowly and deliberately, he proceeded to put on the high-peaked hat, followed by the single robe of yellow-green silk, and last of all by the underpants. When he was all through he beat the drum another roll and departed, his facial expression not the least embarrassed.

Ts'ao Ts'ao laughed and remarked to those around him, "I originally intended to humiliate Heng, but he has humiliated me instead!" To this day there is still the "Yü-yang Drum-roll," which originated with Ni Heng . . .

[2] Yü-yang was a border town in the north.

[3] *TWSC*: The Yin ruler Wu-ting dreamed that Heaven had bestowed on him a worthy man. When he awoke he had his artists draw the man's likeness and then made a search for him throughout the realm. They finally discovered him among construction workers in a chain gang, wearing coarse homespun, in the wilds of Fu-yen (Shansi). The man was called Fu Yüeh. (Cf. *SC* 3.8b)

9. P'ang T'ung of Nan Commandery (Hupei) heard that Ssu-ma Hui[1] was living in Ying-ch'uan (Honan), so he traveled two thousand *li* to visit him. When he arrived he found Hui gathering mulberry leaves. T'ung called out to him from inside his carriage, "I've heard that when a great man lives in the world he should be wearing the gold seal and purple ribbon at his girdle.[2] Who ever heard of a man repressing his vast overflowing capacities merely to take up the occupation of a silkworm girl?"

Hui replied, "If you'll just get down from your carriage, I'll explain. You happen to know that a shortcut saves time, without realizing that you've missed the way and are lost. Long ago Po Ch'eng (Tzu-kao)[3] plowed in tandem with his wife and didn't hanker after the glory of the feudal lords. Yüan Hsien (Tzu-ssu)[4] with his mulberry doorpost wouldn't change it for the mansion of a man in office. Why must a man sit in splendid rooms and travel with sleek horses and possess several tens of female slaves before he can be considered remarkable? This is the reason why Hsü Yu and Ch'ao Fu were roused to indignation and why Po I and Shu Ch'i heaved long sighs.[5] Even if a man might possess noble rank unlawfully seized from Ch'in,[6] or the wealth of a thousand four-horse teams,[7] it still wouldn't be sufficient cause for honor."

T'ung said, "I was born and bred on the frontier and have seldom seen persons of great principle. But if I don't strike the great bell or pound the thunderous drum, I'll never know their sound." (*SKShu* 7.1a)

[1] *(Ssu-ma) Hui PC*: While Hui was living in Ching Province he realized that the governor, Liu Piao, was of a dark, secretive

disposition, and that he would surely do injury to good men, so he kept his mouth shut and engaged in no discussions or consultations. If any of his contemporaries inquired of him about any person, he would not make any distinction whatever between the man's high or low qualities, but would uniformly say, "The man's excellent."

His wife remonstrated with him, saying, "People consult you when they're in doubt, and you ought to discuss the matter with them. But if you always say, 'The man's excellent,' how is anybody going to find out your opinion?"

Hui replied, "What you say is also excellent." Such was his ambiguity and evasiveness.

Once someone mistakenly recognized Hui's pig as his own, so Hui yielded and gave it to him. Later the man found his own pig, and, kowtowing with embarrassment, brought Hui's pig back. Hui for his part declined and thanked him profusely.

Liu Piao's son, Tsung, once went to visit Hui and sent someone to inquire if he were home. It happened that Hui was in the garden doing his own hoeing. Tsung's servant asked, "Is Lord Ssu-ma at home?"

Hui replied, "That would be me."

Tsung's servant, observing how homely and low-class he looked, reviled him, saying, "You stupid hired hand! The general's son wishes to see Lord Ssu-ma. What class of slave are you, claiming to be him?"

Hui went back into the house, combed his hair and put on a cap, and came out for an interview. When Tsung's servant saw that it was, after all, the same old man he had just seen, he was afraid to report it to Tsung, so, waiting until Tsung got up to go, he kowtowed profusely to Hui and apologized.

Hui said to him, "Really, you shouldn't do that. Otherwise I'll be terribly ashamed over it. This business of doing my own hoeing in the garden . . . you're the only one who knows about it."

Once when the silkworms were about to spin, a neighbor came and asked for a spinning frame (*ts'u-po*). Hui abandoned his own silkworms and gave him his.

Someone remarked, "Usually when a person takes from his own supply to help someone else, it's because the other person is destitute and he himself is well off. But in this case both of you are in exactly the same circumstances. Why should you give him your frame?"

Hui replied, "The man never asked anything from me before. If I had refused him, then he would have been embarrassed. How could I embarrass him just over some material thing?"

Someone once said to Liu Piao, "Ssu-ma Hui is an unusual gentleman. It's only that he's never met with good fortune, that's all."

Later Piao had an interview with him and remarked afterward, "This man's really nothing but a small-time bookworm." Such were the instances of his being really wise, yet able to appear stupid.

[2] See the commentary of Li Hsien (7th cent.) at HHS 40.11b: The highest officers, including the chancellor, grand marshal, and director of works, are distinguished by wearing the gold seal and purple ribbon at their girdles.

[3] Cf. *Chuang-tzu* XII, 5b (Watson, p. 131): While Yao ruled the realm Po-ch'eng Tzu-kao resigned his post as a feudal lord and

took up plowing in the wilds. Yü went to see him, hastening forward with a self-demeaning air, and asked him about his decision.

Tzu-kao replied, "Formerly, while Yao ruled the realm, he offered no rewards, yet the people urged each other on to their work. He imposed no punishments, yet the people feared him. Today you offer rewards and impose punishments, yet the people are still not good. For this reason your moral power has declined and penalties have correspondingly risen. Why don't you run along and stop interfering with my work?"

[4] *(K'ung-tzu) chia-yü* (not in present text of *KTCY*; cf. *Chuang-tzu* XXVIII, 14ab, Watson, pp. 315-316): Yüan Hsien (Tzu-ssu, one of Confucius' disciples) lived in Lu (Shantung) in a hut with mud walls 'round about, thatched with green grass, with a mat door which was unfinished, a mulberry doorpost, and broken jars for windows. The roof leaked, and the floor was damp, but he sat upright in it and played his zither and sang.

Tzu-kung (another disciple), whose high carriage could not be accommodated in the alley, went to see him, and said, "Master, what ails you?"

Hsien replied, "I've heard that when a man has no property he is said to be poor, and that when he studies but can't put what he's learned into practice, he's said to be ailing. Right now I'm poor, but not ailing. To act only with a view to the world's praise, to make friends only with partisans, to study only for the purpose of impressing others, and to teach only for private profit, to hide behind 'goodness and morality' in making a grand display of chariots and horses . . . all these are things I cannot bring myself to do."

[5] Cf. *Mencius* II, i, 9, 1 (Legge II, 206): Po I and Shu Ch'i (recluses at the end of the Shang, ca. 1122 B.C.) would not look on evil sights with their eyes, nor listen to evil sounds with their ears. Living with their fellow villagers, they considered them so much mud and ashes. Such was the purity of the sages.

(This citation from Liu Chün's Commentary differs considerably from the present Mencius text, q.v.)

[6] *KSK*: Lü Pu-wei (d. 235 B.C.), acting on behalf of the Ch'in prince, Tzu-ch'u, son of King Hsiao-wen (r. three days in 250), brought gold and merchandise to the King's concubine Lady Huayang, requesting that Tzu-ch'u be established as heir. When Tzu-ch'u mounted the throne as King Chuang-hsiang (r. 250-247), he enfeoffed Pu-wei Marquis Wen-hsin with income from the 100,000 households of Lo-yang.

[7] "Analects" XVI, 12 (Legge I, 315): Duke Ching of Ch'i (r. 546-489) possessed a thousand four-horse teams, but the people found no virtue in that for which to praise him.

10. Liu Chen, having failed to pay the proper respect to Lady Chen, was sentenced to hard labor.[1] "Emperor Wen" (Ts'ao P'ei)[2] asked him, "Why were you so careless about the laws and regulations?"

Chen replied, "Your servant is sincerely sorry for his shortcomings, but my plight is also due to the fact that the meshes of Your Majesty's net of laws are not wide-set."[3] (*HTC* 4)

[1]*TL*: In the sixteenth year of the Chien-an Era (211) Ts'ao P'ei became Commandant of the Five Offices, and since Ts'ao Ts'ao was subtle in his literary tastes, he had Liu Chen accompany P'ei everywhere and wait on him. Once at a drinking party, when everyone was merry, P'ei had his wife, Lady Chen, come out and greet the company. Nearly all the seated guests prostrated themselves on the floor; Chen alone remained seated and looked at her face to face. Some days later Ts'ao Ts'ao heard of it and had Chen arrested, but commuted his sentence from death to hard labor.

WSC: Liu Chen was by nature quick-witted in argument, and whatever was said to him he answered on the rebound. After he was sentenced for looking at Lady Chen face to face, his sentence was commuted to hard labor, and he was set to polishing rocks. When Ts'ao Ts'ao came to the workhouse to inspect the workers, he found Chen sitting bolt upright with a solemn expression polishing rocks.

Ts'ao asked him, "How are the rocks coming along?"

Taking the opportunity to illustrate his own case, Chen kneeled and replied, "The rock came from the mountains of Ching (Hupei), from the summit of beetling cliffs. Outside are five-colored patterns; inside the Jewel of Pien Ho (see *Han-fei-tzu* XIII, 66-67). Polish it and no luster is added; carve it and the pattern is not enhanced. The spirit with which it is endowed is firm and true (*chen*, a pun on his own name), for it was received from the Naturally-so. Regard the injustice of its plight, as it submits to this twisting and turning, with none to plead its cause!"

Looking back at his attendants, Ts'ao laughed aloud, and pardoned him that very day.

[2]*SSHY* Comm.: All accounts agree that Liu Chen was punished during the lifetime of Ts'ao Ts'ao (d. 220), and that he died of an illness in the twentieth year of the Chien-an Era (215). It was not until the seventh (*sic*) year after that (221) that Ts'ao P'ei ascended the throne. So the claim that Chen committed his offense during the Huang-ch'u Era (220-226) is mistaken.

(If "Emperor Wu"--Ts'ao Ts'ao--is substituted for "Emperor Wen" in the text, the anachronism could be avoided.)

[3]See *Lao-tzu* 73.

11. Chung Yü and his younger brother Chung Hui both enjoyed excellent reputations in their youth. When they were around thirteen years old, Emperor Wen of Wei heard of them and said to their father, Chung Yu, "You may bring your two sons to see me sometime."

Accordingly an imperial audience was arranged for them. Yü's face was covered with sweat, and the emperor asked, "Why is your face sweating?"

Yü replied,

> "Tremble, tremble, flutter, flutter;
> My sweat pours out like so much water."

Turning to Hui, the emperor asked, "And why are you *not* sweating?" Hui replied,

> "Tremble, tremble, flutter, fall;
> My sweat can't even come at all."

(*TPYL* 385, 387; *SWLC*, hou 18)

II SPEECH AND CONVERSATION   35

12. When Chung Yü and his younger brother Chung Hui were small, it happened once that their father, Chung Yu, was taking a siesta, and availing themselves of the opportunity, they both stole a draught of medicinal wine.[1] Their father, who was awake at the time, feigned sleep in order to observe them. Yü drank only after performing the proper ceremony; Hui drank without performing any ceremony at all.

Afterward the father asked Yü, "Why did you perform the ceremony?"
Yü replied, "'It's right to drink in order to fulfill the rites.'[2] I wouldn't dare not perform the ceremony."

Yu then asked Hui, "And why did you *not* perform the ceremony?"
Hui replied, "Theft is basically contrary to the rites, so I didn't perform any ceremony." (*PTSC* 85; *SLF* 17; *TPYL* 845)

[1]This anecdote appears to be a variation of No. 4, above.

[2]*Tso-chuan*, Chuang 22 (Legge V, 103): It is right to drink in order to fulfill the rites, but not to continue to the point of wantonness.

13. Emperor Ming of Wei (Ts'ao Jui, r. 227-239)[1] built a mansion for his maternal grandmother, Lady Chang,[2] on the estate of his mother, Lady Chen. After it was completed he went in person to see it and asked those in attendance, "What name ought we to use for the mansion?"

The personal attendant, Mu Hsi, replied, "Your Majesty's sage solicitude is equal to that of the wise kings of antiquity, and your 'boundless devotion'[3] surpasses that of Tseng Ts'an and Min Tzu-ch'ien.[4] Since in building this mansion your feelings gather about your 'maternal uncle,' it would be fitting to name it Wei-yang, the 'North Bank of the Wei River.'"[5] (*SKWei* 5.8b; *IWLC* 63; *TPYL* 194, 521)

[1]*WMC*: Ts'ao Jui was Emperor Wen's crown prince, but because his mother (Empress Chen) had been rejected (in 221), he had not yet been confirmed as successor. Emperor Wen was once hunting with him when they spied a doe with her fawn. The emperor shot the doe, who fell instantly with the twang of the bowstring. He then commanded Jui to shoot the fawn. But Jui laid down his bow and wept, saying, "Father, you've already killed the dam; I can't bear to kill the fawn as well."

Emperor Wen replied, "You've spoken good words that move the heart." Whereupon he confirmed Jui as his successor, and later he became Emperor Ming.

[2]The family relationships appear in the following chart:

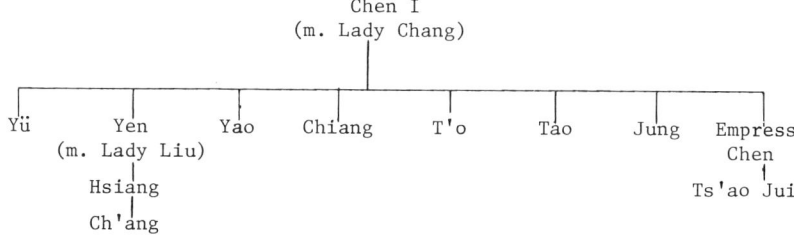

36 TALES OF THE WORLD

SKWei 5.8b (cf. WeiS, cited in the SSHY Comm.) records that in the last year of the Ching-ch'u Era (239) a large mansion was erected for Empress Chen's grandnephew, Chen Ch'ang, and that in its rear garden Ch'ang built an observation shrine for *his* grandmother, Chen Yen's wife, Lady Liu, and named the district Wei-yang District. As Liu Chün points out, it was neither the *emperor's* grandmother for whom the shrine was built, nor was it the *mansion* which was named Wei-yang.

[3] See "Songs," No. 202: I wished to requite your kindness/ *Boundless* as Great Heaven.

[4] Disciples of Confucius noted for their filial devotion.

[5] See "Songs," No. 134: I escorted my *maternal uncle*/ As far as Wei-yang.

SSHY Comm.: The song "Wei-yang" (No. 134) was written by Duke K'ang of Ch'in (r. 620-608 B.C.) in memory of his mother (cf. Legge IV, 203), who was the daughter of Duke Hsien of Chin (r. 676-652). When her brother, Duke Wen of Chin (r. 635-628), encountered the troubles over their mother, Lady Li (killed in a palace intrigue in 651), he fled to Ch'in, where he remained an exile for nineteen years. Before he returned to Chin, the consort of Duke Mu of Ch'in, his sister, Duke K'ang's mother, died. Duke Mu (r. 659-621) had sheltered Duke Wen. Duke K'ang, who was then heir apparent, escorted his maternal uncle Duke Wen as far as the north bank of Wei River (Wei-yang), and there remembering his mother whom he would never see again, he sang the lines (not in the present text of the "Songs"): "When I look at my maternal uncle,/ It is as if my mother were still here."

14. Ho Yen once said, "Whenever I take a five-mineral powder (*wu-shih san*),[1] not only does it heal any illness I may have, but I am also aware of my spirit and intelligence becoming receptive and lucid."

[1] See SSHY I, 14, n. 1, above.

HSSL: Although the prescription for the cold-food powder (*han-shih san*) originated during the Han period, its users were few and there are no accounts handed down concerning them. It was the Wei president of the Board of Civil Office, Ho Yen, who first discovered its divine properties, and from his time on it enjoyed a wide currency in the world, and those who used it sought each other out.

15. Hsi K'ang once said to Chao Chih,[1] "In the clear delineation between the whites and blacks of your eyes you have the manner of Po Ch'i.[2] What a pity your frame is so small and slight!"

Chao replied, "With an eight-foot gnomon one can measure the degrees of the celestial sphere (*chi-heng*),[3] and with an inch-wide pipe one can determine the ebbing and flowing seasonal forces (*ch'i*).[4] Why must their usefulness consist in bigness? Simply ask how sensitive they are and let it go at that." (CS 92.9b; IWLC 22; PSLT 12; TPYL 446)

[1] CCHs (cf. CS 92.9a-11b): At the end of the Han, Chih's ancestor, fleeing as a refugee, had settled in Kou-shih Prefecture (Honan). When the prefectural magistrate first arrived at his post, Chih

was in his twelfth year and was standing with his mother by the side of the road looking on. His mother said to him, "Your ancestor came from a family of no mean status (CS adds: but because the times were confused and he had drifted far from home, he simply became a military colonist [shih-wu]). Some day could you too be an official like this?"

Chih replied, "I might do that, but nothing more."

When he got home he went immediately to a teacher and began to study reading and writing. Early one morning he heard the sound of his father's voice shouting at the ox as he plowed, and putting down his books he wept. When his teacher asked why, he replied, "I'm grieving for myself that I'm not rich and famous, so that I could free my father from this toil and drudgery."

(When not needed for fighting, military colonists were farmers.)

In his fourteenth year he entered the Grand Academy (in Lo-yang). At the time (ca. 260) my father (Hsi K'ang) was at the academy writing ancient-style characters for the stone-engraved classics. (Ts'ai Yung did this work between 172 and 177, and Han-tan Ch'un again between 240 and 249, but no other reference to Hsi K'ang doing it around 260 has been found.) When the work was completed and my father was leaving, Chih followed his carriage and asked, "Master, what is your name?"

My father answered, "You're quite young; why do you ask?"

Chih said, "I've observed that your manner and ability are outstanding. That's the only reason I asked."

My father then told him his full name.

When Chih was in his fifteenth year, he feigned madness and ran distractedly this way and that, having to be pursued and brought back by his family, sometimes as far as five *li*. At other times he burned his body in ten or more places.

(Chih would automatically have become a soldier in his sixteenth year. Reprisals against the families of deserters from the military colonies were severe; hence Chih's extreme measures to obscure his real motives.)

In his sixteenth year he disappeared altogether. He traveled till he reached Lo-yang, where he looked for my father but could not find him, so he went on to Yeh (S. Hopei).

Shih Chung-ho of P'ei Principality (N. Anhui) was the grandson of the Wei Commander, Shih Yü. Chih placed himself under his guardianship and changed his name to I and his courtesy name to Yang-ho. (The CS account gives different names.) When my father came to Yeh, Chih reminded him about the incident in the Grand Academy, and he accompanied my father back to Shan-yang (near Lo-yang), where he spent several years.

Chih was seven feet (*ch'ih*) three inches (*ts'un*) in height, with black hair streaked with white, vermilion lips, and bright eyes. His sideburns were not heavy. In his capacity as a judge he would examine cases calmly and pass sentence with composure, his body looking all the while as if it were too frail to bear the weight of his clothes. My father once said to him, "Your head is small and pointed, and the whites of your eyes clearly delineated. In examining a case or passing judgment you have the manner of Po Ch'i."

Chih would argue lucidly in any discussion or consultation, and he had ability as a political adviser, but in this matter, too, he never considered himself very skilled. Meng Yüan-chi summoned him to serve as an administrator in Liao-tung Commandery (S. Manchuria), where he settled nine lawsuits in the commandery and won praise for his incorruptibility and fairness. But he blamed himself for abandoning his parents to travel so far, and his mother died without his seeing her. Weeping until he spit blood, he became ill, and before the mourning period was over, he died.

[2]*SCH*: Po-Ch'i (3rd cent. B.C.) was the Lord of Wu-an, in Ch'in . . . The Lord of P'ing-yüan (Shantung) urged King Hsiao-ch'eng of Chao (r. 265-245) to accept the offer of Feng T'ing (who had proffered his commandery of Shang-tang in Han in return for Chao's assistance against Ch'in).

The king said, "If I accept his offer, the Ch'in armies will surely come, and the Lord of Wu-an (Po Ch'i) will surely be at the head of them. Who can stand against *him*?"

The Lord of P'ing-yüan replied, "At the meeting of Ch'in and Chao (in 279 B.C.) at Min-ch'ih (Honan) I got a close look at the Lord of Wu-an. He has a small head and his face is pointed. The whites and blacks of his eyes are clearly delineated. In looking forward or up his eyes do not turn. One whose head is small and whose face is pointed dares to make bold decisions. One the whites and blacks of whose eyes are clearly delineated is perceptive in judging events. One whose eyes do not turn when he is looking forward or up is firm in holding to his purpose. You may fight a long war of attrition with him, but it would be difficult to contend with him in a pitched battle. He is modest and frugal as a person, bold as a bird of prey, but affectionate toward his men. He understands adversity and can endure disgrace. If you fight with him in wild terrain you will be no match for him, but if you hold out where you are, you will be able to withstand him." The king followed his advice.

[3]See "Book of Documents" II, 5 (Legge III, 33), where the terms *hsüan-chi* and *yü-heng*, astronomical instruments of uncertain function, appear. A discussion of these instruments may be found in Needham, *Science and Civilisation*, III, 332-339, where Michel's hypothesis that the *hsüan-chi* was a circumpolar template, identified with certain serrated jade discs discovered in Western Chou sites, appears. In this context *chi-heng* appears to be metonymy for the dome of heaven scanned by these instruments, specifically the path of the sun between the solstices.

CPSC (cf. *Chou-pei suan ching*, SPTK ed., I, 35ab): At the summer solstice the sun is 16,000 *li* south (emending the "26,000 *li* north" of the text, after *CPSC*), and at the winter solstice it is 135,000 *li* south. When the sun is at the meridian the gnomon is erected and the shadow measured (again emending the text's "if the gnomon is erected it casts no shadow," after *CPSC*). The Chou gnomon (*Chou-pei*) is eight feet (*ch'ih*) in length. At the summer solstice the shadow (*kuei*) cast by the sun is one foot six inches (*ts'un*) in length . . . One thousand *li* due south of Yang-ch'eng (in Honan), the Chou observatory, the shadow is one foot five inches, and one thousand *li* due north it is one foot seven inches.

(Using the simple rule of one inch of shadow to every thousand
li of solar distance, one arrives at a distance of 16,000 *li* for
the sixteen-inch shadow at the summer solstice, and 135,000 *li* for
the 135-inch shadow at the winter solstice. See Needham, *Science
and Civilisation*, III, 284-294, and Ho Peng-yoke (Ho Ping-yü), *The
Astronomical Chapters of the Chin Shu*, Paris, 1966, pp. 49-51.)

[4]*LSCC* (V, 5, 51): The Yellow Emperor had Ling Lun gather bamboos
growing in the Chieh-ku Valley on the northern slope of the K'un-
lun Mountains west of Ta-hsia (Bactria?). Those whose interior di-
ameter was even, he cut between the joints and blew on them, getting the pitch *huang-chung*. He then cut the bamboos into twelve
graduated pipes, tuned to the call of the phoenix: six for the
male and six for the female, and these became the twelve pitch
pipes (*lü-lü*).

HsHS, Lü-li chih: The permutations of the twelve pitch pipes
reach sixty (a five-note scale for each pitch). The pipes were
used to observe the seasonal forces (*hou-ch'i*). The method of observing the seasonal forces is to build a room with concentric
walls, with the doors closed and all cracks plastered to make sure
it is tightly sealed all around. Orange curtains are spread about
and wood is used for stands on which the pipes are mounted (one at
each of the twelve directions). Ashes of the inner membranes of
reeds are deposited within the pipes, and whichever pipe is moved
by the appropriate seasonal force, its ashes will be scattered.
This is the method of observation.

(Cf. Needham, *Science and Civilisation*, IV.1, 186-190, and Derk
Bodde, "The Chinese Cosmic Magic known as 'Watching for the
Ethers' [*hou-ch'i*]," in S. Egerod and E. Glahn, eds., *Studia Seri-
ca Bernhard Karlgren Dedicata*, Copenhagen, 1959, pp. 14-35.)

16. When Prince Ching (Ssu-ma Shih) made his eastward expedition he
selected Li Hsi of Shang-tang (Shansi) to be his junior administrator.
On this occasion he asked Hsi, "Some time ago when Our father (Ssu-ma
I) summoned you, you didn't respond. Now when We have summoned you,
how is it you've come?"

Hsi replied, "In the case of Your Highness's father, since I was
treated with propriety, I could with propriety either accept or decline. But in the case of Your Highness I was compelled by law. It's
only because I fear the law that I've come." (*CS* 41.4b)

17. Teng Ai had a speech impediment, and when talking would refer to
himself as "Ai-Ai."

Prince Wen of Chin (Ssu-ma Chao), teasing him, said, "How many Ais
are there, anyhow?"[1]

He replied, "When Chieh Yü sang, 'Phoenix! phoenix!' naturally
there was only one phoenix."[2] (*IWLC* 25; *TPYL* 466, 740; *SWLC*, pieh 20)

[1]Since Teng Ai's name, Ai, meant the lowly mugwort, there was a
double edge to this jibe, which Teng neatly parried by comparing
himself to the phoenix, king of all mythical birds.

[2]"Analects" XVIII, 5. Cf. *LHC*: Lu T'ung was the madman of Ch'u,
Chieh Yü. He was fond of cherishing his nature and wandering among
famous mountains. Once he met Confucius and sang,

"Phoenix! phoenix!
How has your virtue fallen!
What is past cannot be remedied;
What is to come may still be pursued."

Later he went into Shu (Szechwan) and lived on O-mei Mountain.

18. After Hsi K'ang had been executed (262), Hsiang Hsiu was recommended for office in the quota for his commandery and went to Lo-yang. Prince Wen (Ssu-ma Chao) had him brought in and asked him, "I heard you had the ambition of retiring to Chi Mountain;[1] what are you doing here?"

Hsiu replied, "Ch'ao Fu and Hsü Yu were timid, pusillanimous men, not worthy of much emulation."

The prince heaved a great sigh of admiration.[2] (CS 49.16b; WH 16.7b, Li Shan's comm.)

[1]Chi Mountain in Honan was the hermitage of the ancient recluses Ch'ao Fu and Hsü Yu.

[2]*Hsiang Hsiu PC*: When Hsiang Hsiu was about twenty he composed a "Treatise on Juism and Taoism" (*Ju-Tao lun*), which he later abandoned and never copied. Some practical joker got possession of it and claimed it was the work of one of his kinsmen, but later, distressed over its lack of popularity, he reported the matter to Hsiu, hoping to borrow his name to promote its circulation. Laughing, Hsiu said, "What? Just that thing?"

(There follows the incident recorded in the *SSHY* text, but with a variant of Hsiu's reply: "I've always thought that those fellows [Ch'ao Fu and Hsü Yu] never comprehended Yao's meaning when he offered the throne. They're basically not the sort I would emulate.")

(The Kuo Hsiang commentary, which is thought by some to incorporate Hsiang Hsiu's ideas, at *Chuang-tzu* I, 6b, makes clear that Yao maintained Non-action [*wu-wei*] even while occupying the throne, and that Hsü Yu, in declining because he did not wish to become involved in Action, was totally mistaken.)

19. When Emperor Wu (Ssu-ma Yen) first ascended the throne, he drew a divining straw and obtained the number "one" (*te-i*). The number of reigns in a dynasty depends upon whether the number drawn is large or small. Since the emperor was plainly dismayed, all his ministers turned pale, and there was no one who had anything to say. The personal attendant, P'ei K'ai, then stepped forward and said, "Your servant has heard that 'Heaven by attaining the One (*te-i*) is limpid; earth by attaining the One is calm . . . and nobles and kings by attaining the One become the standard for the realm.'"[1]

The emperor was pleased, and all the ministers sighed with relief. (CS 35.14a)

[1]See Wang Pi's (d. 249) commentary at *Lao-tzu* 39: One is the beginning of numbers, the smallest unit of any object. Everything is produced from one object, and for this reason one is paramount . . . Each thing by its "attainment of the One" achieves such a "limpidity," "calmness," or "standard."

20. Man Fen was afraid of drafts. Once he was present at a gathering with the Chin Emperor Wu. The north window was made of a screen (*p'ing-feng*) of colored glass (*liu-li*).[1] In reality it was tightly sealed, but appeared to be open. Fen was looking uncomfortable and the emperor laughed at him.

Fen answered, "Your servant is like the water buffaloes of Wu which pant when they see the moon."[2] (*IWLC* 84; *CHC* 1; *PSLT* 1; *SLF* 2; *TPYL* 4, 808; *SWLC*, ch'ien 3)

[1]*Liu-li* (Skt. vaiḍurya) was glass, usually greenish or bluish in color. Though it had been locally produced in China since Chou times, it continued to be imported as a luxury item from Iran even as late as the eighth or ninth century because the import was more durable than the local product. See E. H. Schafer, *The Golden Peaches of Samarkand*, Berkeley, 1963, pp. 235-237, and Needham, *Science and Civilisation*, IV.1, pp. 101-111. Glass panes are mentioned in the *Hsi-ching tsa-chi* 1, which purports to tell of matters in the Han court during the second century B.C. However, since the composition of the *HCTC* cannot safely be assigned to a date earlier than the sixth century A.D., this cannot be cited as prior evidence for the use of glass in windows. The present story seems to imply that it was still a novelty in the third century.

[2]*SSHY* Comm.: The modern water buffalo is only raised in the area between the Yangtze and Huai rivers, so it is called the "buffalo of Wu." In the south it is hot most of the year, and these buffaloes are afraid of the heat, so when they see the moon, suspecting it to be the sun, they start panting.

21. When Chu-ko Ching was in Wu he was present at a grand assembly in the audience hall. The Wu king, Sun Hao, asked him, "Your courtesy name is Chung-ssu, 'Think.' Just what is it you think about?"

He replied, "At home I think about filial devotion, in serving my ruler I think about loyalty, and among friends and associates I think about trustworthiness[1]--that's all." (*TPKC* 173)

[1]"Analects" I, 7 (Legge I, pp. 140-141).

22. Ts'ai Hung had just come to Lo-yang (ca. 285).[1] A resident of Lo-yang[2] asked him, "The government headquarters has recently opened and the high officials are making appointments. They are seeking the brilliant and rare from obscure and lowly places, and selecting the worthy and outstanding from among the recluses of the crags and caves. You're a gentleman of Wu and Ch'u, a remnant from a defeated state. What unusual talent do you have that you've responded to this summons?"

Ts'ai replied, "The night-shining Pearl of Sui[3] didn't necessarily come from the Yellow River at Meng-ching (near Lo-yang), nor was the hand-filling jade of Pien Ho[4] found on the slopes of the K'un-lun Mountains (in Central Asia). The great Yü was born among the Eastern I barbarians, and King Wen among the Western Ch'iang.[5] Why must you always look for sages and worthies in the usual places? Long ago when King Wu punished the last Shang ruler, Chou Hsin, he resettled the insubordinate Shang people in Lo-yang.[6] Are you gentlemen by any chance their descendants?" (*TPYL* 464, quoting *WSC*; *PTSC* 79, quoting *KPCC*; *CS* 52.14b-15a)

¹Liu Chün points out that the story is incorrectly attributed to Ts'ai Hung, all sources agreeing that the subject was Hua T'an (d. ca. 322), and the place Chien-k'ang.) See CS 52.14b-15a.

²In the Hua T'an story, the interlocutor is Wang Chi.

³CShuo: The Marquis of Sui set out on a journey and found a serpent which had been cut in half. The marquis joined the halves together so that the serpent came to life and went on its way. Later it returned holding a luminous moon pearl in its mouth to requite his kindness. The pearl's radiance shone at night as bright as day, and ever after it was known as the Pearl of Sui.

(Cf. also Tso Ssu's "Poetic Essay on the Shu Capital" [Shu-tu fu], WH 4.1b, Li Shan's commentary, and the Huai-nan-tzu 6.91, commentary of Kao Yu*; also E. H. Schafer, The Vermilion Bird, Berkeley, 1967, p. 160.)

⁴Though the source of true jade (nephrite) was principally along the Southern Silk Road, on the slopes of the K'un-lun range, examples purporting to be jade are also cited from China proper. See Han-fei-tzu 13.66-67, the story of the uncut jade of Pien Ho, presumably found in Ch'u.

⁵Liu Chün, citing Mencius IV, 2 (Legge II, p. 316), points out that it was Shun and not Yü who was born among the Eastern I, and that King Wen was born among the Western Jung, not the Ch'iang.

⁶"Book of Documents" IV, 26 (Legge III, p. 571).

23. All the famous gentlemen of the Western Chin court once went together to the Lo River on a pleasure excursion.¹ On their return Yüeh Kuang asked Wang Yen, "Did you enjoy today's excursion?"

Wang replied, "P'ei Wei is good at conversing on Names and Principles (ming-li); his words gushed forth in a torrent, but with an air of refinement. Chang Hua² discussed the 'Records of the Grand Historian' (Shih-chi) and the 'History of the Han Dynasty' (Han-shu); his words were slow and deliberate, well worth the listening. Wang Jung and I talked about Chi Cha and Chang Liang;³ our words, too, were totally transcendent, abstruse but lucid." (CS 43.10a; TPYL 446, 390)

¹CLCHL: Wang Chi and the others once went to the Lo River for the spring purification rites (chieh-hsi). The following day someone asked Chi, "On yesterday's excursion what conversations and discussions were there?" Chi replied, etc. (Cf. CS 43.10a.)

²CYC: Chang Hua was widely read and informed about everything, and there was no subject he had not thoroughly investigated. Emperor Wu once inquired about the affairs of the Han Dynasty, and when he mentioned the "thousand gates and ten thousand doors" of the Chien-chang Palace, Hua drew a plan of it on the ground, responding to questions in a steady stream. Even the encyclopedic genius Chang An-shih (first cent. B.C.) could not have surpassed him.

³Chi Cha (sixth cent. B.C.) was a worthy of the Wu state; see Tso-chuan, Hsiang 29, Chao 27; Legge V, pp. 549 and 721. Chang Liang (third and early second cent. B.C.) was the recluse-turned-adviser who served Liu Pang, the founder of the Han Dynasty.

24. Wang Chi and Sun Ch'u were each boasting about the beauties of his native place and the people there. Wang said,

> "Our land is level and plain,
> The rivers limpid and clear,
> The people modest and true."

Sun responded,

> "Our mountains are tall-towering and crag-crested,
> The rivers mud-roiled with tossing waves,
> The people rock-rugged, with heroes aplenty."[1]

(TPYL 390)

[1] The maximum contrast suggested by the bland adjectives in double rhyme (*t'an, bi̯wɒng/ d'am, ts'i̯äng/ liäm, t̂i̯äng) of Wang's description against the rough-textured binomes (dz'uai-nguei, ts'â-ngâ/ γap-iäp, i̯ang-puâ/ luâi-luâ, i̯ɒng-tâ) used by Sun could hardly have applied to the two prefectures in T'ai-yüan Commandery (Shansi) from which Wang and Sun respectively hailed--Wang was from Chin-yang and Sun from Chung-tu, only a few li distant. As Liu Chün points out, the original story, as it appears in the earlier sources YL and SCC, is told of one I Chi, an emissary of Shu (Szechwan) to Wu (Kiangu-Chekiang) in the third century, who is contrasting the rugged terrain of his native Shu with the lush lowlands of Wu. The attribution to Wang Chi and Sun Ch'u is purely facetious.

25. Yüeh Kuang's daughter was married to the generalissimo, the Prince of Ch'eng-tu, Ssu-ma Ying. The prince's elder brother, the Prince of Ch'ang-sha (Ssu-ma I), who wielded the power in Lo-yang, subsequently attempted to conquer Ying by force of arms.[1] Ssu-ma I was friendly and intimate with petty men, but distant and aloof toward gentlemen, so that everyone at court harbored a sense of danger and fear. Since Yüeh Kuang enjoyed the respect of the court, and was in addition related by marriage to Ying, all the petty men slandered him to I, charging collusion with Ying.

When Ssu-ma I asked him about it, Yüeh's spirit and expression remained self-composed, and he replied mildly, "Would I exchange five sons for one daughter?"[2]

From then on the prince was relieved and no longer felt suspicious or anxious.[3]

[1] The brothers Ssu-ma I and Ssu-ma Ying were rivals for the control of Lo-yang. The former, as grand marshal, defended the city against numerous assaults by the latter in the winter of 303. The rivalry was only settled by the death of both brothers shortly thereafter. See TCTC 85.2692-3.

[2] If Yüeh had sided with his son-in-law, Ssu-ma Ying, he would surely have been executed with all three (sic) of his sons: K'ai, Chao, and Mo. The reference to five sons seems to be an allusion to Hex. 43, Kuai, "Resoluteness," of the "Book of Changes," which is composed of five "male" lines, topped with one "female." To be "resolute" one must preserve the five strong and dispense with the one weak line. Cf. Wilhelm I, pp. 177-181; II, 249-255.

[3]Yüeh Kuang's biography (CS 43.24a) and CYC, quoted in Liu Chün's Commentary, both state that the prince was unconvinced and continued to be suspicious, and this is given as the cause of Yüeh's "death by mortification" the following year (304).

26. When Lu Chi went to visit Wang Chi, Wang set before him several *hu*-measures of goat curd (*yang-lao*). Pointing them out to Lu, he asked, "What do you have east of the Yangtze River to match this?"
Lu replied, "We only have water-lily soup (*ch'un-keng*) from Thousand-li Lake (Kiangsu), and salted legumes (*yen-shih*) from Mo-hsia (Chien-yeh), that's all."[1] (CS 54.7a; TPKC 234)

[1]Emending *wei-hsia* to *Mo-hsia*, after CS 54.7a.

27. In the days of the Central Court (Western Chin) there was once a small boy whose father was sick and who went to a neighbor's to ask for some medicine. The host asked what kind of sickness it was.
"He's suffering from malaria (*nüeh*)," the boy replied.
"Your honorable father is an enlightened and virtuous gentleman. How could he be suffering from malaria?"[1]
"It came and made a gentleman sick; that's precisely why it's called 'cruel' (*nüeh*)." (TPYL 743)

[1]SSHY Comm.: Popular tradition has it that the evil spirit which causes malaria is small, and for the most part does not attack great men. It was for this reason that the Later Han Emperor Kuang-wu (r. 25-57) once said to the Generalissimo Ching Tan*, "I've heard that a mighty warrior never gets malaria; now do you mean to tell me you've got malaria?"

28. Ts'ui Pao once went to visit the Capital Commandery (in Lo-yang). The capital intendant, whose name was Ch'en, asked Ts'ui, "Sir, how many generations are you removed from Ts'ui Shu?"[1]
"Your servant is about as many generations removed from Ts'ui Shu as Your Excellency is from Ch'en Heng,"[2] came the reply.

[1]Ts'ui Shu was a nobleman of Ch'i (Shantung) who killed his ruler, Duke Chuang (r. 553-548 B.C.), and set up Duke Ching (r. 547-490) in his place. See SC 32.17a-19b.

[2]Ch'en Heng (alias T'ien Ch'ang), another nobleman of Ch'i, killed his ruler, Duke Chien (r. 484-481), and set up Duke P'ing (r. 480-456) in his place. See SC 32.24b.

29. When Emperor Yüan (Ssu-ma Jui) first crossed the Yangtze River (in 307), he said to Ku Jung, "A sojourner in your native land, I feel a continual sense of shame in my heart."
Kneeling, Jung replied, "Your servant has heard that those who rule have all-under-heaven for their home. It was for this reason that the Shang kings set up their capitals now at Keng (Shansi) and now at Po (Honan), with no fixed location, and that during the Chou the nine tripods were moved to Lo-yang.[1] I pray Your Majesty not to be distressed over having moved the capital." (TPYL 98)

[1]TWSC: The Shang-Yin king, Tsu-i (r. 1525-1506 B.C.), moved the capital to Keng, which was later inundated by the Yellow River . . . P'an Keng (r. 1401-1374), after moving the capital five times, finally went south to live at Po.

Tso-chuan, Huan 2 (Legge V, p. 39): When the Chou king, Wu (r. 1122-1116), conquered Shang, he moved the nine tripods (originally cast by Yü with metal from each of the nine provinces of his empire) to Lo-yang.

30. Yü Liang once went to visit Chou I. Chou asked him, "What are you so happy about that you've grown suddenly fat?"
Yü countered, "And what are you so *sad* about that you've grown suddenly thin?"[1]
Chou replied, "I'm not sad about anything. It's just that purity and emptiness are daily increasing, and foulness and pollution are daily on the wane, that's all."[2] (*TPYL* 378; *SWLC*, hou 18)

[1] This is facetious, since Chou was enormously fat. See below, *SSHY* XXV, 18.

[2] *CYC*: Chou I possessed both urbanity (*feng-liu*) and ability, for which he gained a reputation in his youth. With his formal bearing and lofty air, none of his peers dared take any liberties with him. Pen T'ai of Ju-nan (Honan), a gentleman of perspicuity and probity, once praised him, saying, "Ju-nan and Ying-ch'uan commanderies are undoubtedly full of worthy gentlemen, but ever since the times have been in decline, the way of refinement has almost disappeared. But now, at last, I've seen Chou I, who will rid us of old habits and purge our land and people."

31. Whenever the day was fair, those who had crossed the Yangtze River[1] would always gather at Hsin-t'ing (a southern suburb of Chien-k'ang) to drink and feast on the grass. On one occasion Chou I, who was among the company, sighed and said, "The scene is not dissimilar to the old days in the North; it's just that naturally there's a difference between these mountains and rivers and those."[2]
All those present looked at each other and wept. It was only Chancellor Wang Tao, who, looking very grave, remarked with deep emotion, "We should all unite our strength around the royal house and recover the sacred provinces. To what end do we sit here facing each other like so many 'captives of Ch'u'?"[3] (*CS* 65.3ab; *IWLC* 28, 39; *TPYL* 194, 539)

[1] I.e., the refugees from the Western Chin court at Lo-yang who had emigrated to the Yangtze Delta during the barbarian invasions of the North between 307 and 312. In *TCTC* 87.2771 this incident is assigned to the year 311.

[2] Parallel accounts in *CS* 65.3ab, *CTCKC* 22, and *TCTC* 87.2771, as well as quotations from the *SSHY* in *IWLC* 28 and 39 and *TPYL* 194 and 539 all read: *chü-mu yu Chiang-Ho chih i*, "When I lift my eyes, there is the difference between the Yangtze and the Yellow rivers." All editions of the *SSHY*, however, have: *cheng tzu yu shan-ho chih i*, which I have followed.

[3] *Tso-chuan*, Ch'eng 9 (Legge V, p. 371): Ch'u (Hupei) had attacked Cheng (Honan), and all the feudal lords had come to Cheng's rescue. Cheng held captive the Duke of Yün (Hupei), Chung I, and presented him to Chin (Shansi) in return for their assistance. Duke Ching of Chin (r. 599-581 B.C.) saw him during an inspection of army headquarters and asked, "Who's the fellow with the southern cap tied up over there?"

The officer in command answered, "A captive of Ch'u, sir." Duke Ching ordered him to be untied and asked him about his family.

He replied, "We are musicians."

"Can you play?"

"It was my father's profession. Could I have presumed to take up another?"

They gave him a zither, and he performed airs of the South . . .

Fan Wen-tzu remarked, "The captive of Ch'u is obviously a gentleman. In playing he performed native airs, not forgetting his former roots. Your Excellency should return him to his home in order to reinforce the solidarity of Chin and Ch'u."

32. When Wei Chieh was about to cross the Yangtze River (in 311)[1] his body and spirit were emaciated and depressed, and he remarked to his attendants, "As I view this desolate expanse of water, somehow without my being aware of it a hundred thoughts come crowding together. But as long as we can't avoid having feelings, who indeed can be free of this?"

[1] *(Wei) Chieh PC*: When Wei married the daughter of Yüeh Kuang, P'ei Hsia said, "The wife and her father have the beauty of the transparency of water; the son-in-law has the nobility of the luster of jade. It's like the equal matching of Ch'in and Chin." (See *Tso-chuan*, Hsi 23; Legge V, p. 187.)

In the fourth year of the Yung-chia era (311) he arrived at Chiang-hsia (Hupei). When he parted from his elder brother (Wei Ts'ao, d. 312) at Liang-li Creek, he said to him, "Among the three obligations (to parents, teacher, and ruler) which are honored by men, can we fail to strive for the fate of the loyal minister who gives his life for his ruler?" He traveled on as far as Yü-chang (Kiangsi), and there he passed away.

33. Before Ku Ho had become famous he once went to visit Chancellor Wang Tao. The chancellor was slightly indisposed and sat opposite him looking tired and sleepy. Ku thought of some means to rouse him, so he said to those seated with him, "I often used to hear my kinsman Ku Jung tell how His Excellency the Chancellor aided Emperor Yüan[1] in preserving the territory beyond the Yangtze River. The way his body didn't rest even for a moment made me gasp for breath!"

On hearing this, the chancellor came wide awake and said to Ku, "This fellow 'stands out conspicuously like a jade dagger-ax (*kuei*) or scepter (*chang*)';[2] his wit startles with a sharp point!" (*CS* 83.1b)

[1] *CSCC* 83.1b notes that since both the *SSHY* and *CS* have Ku refer to Emperor Yüan by his posthumous temple name, Chung-tsung, this incident should be dated after 322.

TTCC: Wang Tao had been friendly with Emperor Yüan while both were in obscurity. When he realized that the Central States (Western Chin) were on the verge of collapse (in 307), he urged the emperor to cross the Yangtze River. The emperor (then Prince of Lang-yeh, with the title, General Pacifying the East) sought him for his sergeant-at-arms, and all policies were decided by Wang. The emperor called him "Uncle" (Chung-fu, as Duke Huan of Ch'i had called his adviser, Kuan Chung). Among those who earned merit in the restoration of Eastern Chin, Wang Tao occupies the first place.

²Cf. "Record of Rites" 49.11; Legge, *Li Ki* II, 464.

34. Ho Hsün of K'uai-chi (Chekiang), both physically and intellectually, was pure and remote; his every word and act accorded with propriety. Wang Tao once said to him, "Not only are you 'one of the local excellencies of the Southeast,'¹ indeed you're the most outstanding man within the Four Seas!"² (*CS* 83.1b)

¹Cf. *Erh-ya* 9.4a: Among the local excellencies of the Southeast are the bamboo arrow shafts of K'uai-chi.

²The text has somehow become scrambled with the preceeding item. In *CS* 83.1b, Wang says to Ku Ho (*sic*), "You stand out like a jade dagger or scepter; your wit startles with a sharp point. Not only are you 'one of the local excellencies,' etc."

35. Although Liu K'un had been isolated by the invading barbarians, his loyalty remained with the Chin court. He said to Wen Ch'iao, "Pan Piao¹ recognized that the (Han) House of Liu would rise again, and Ma Yüan² knew that the Later Han Emperor Kuang-wu (r. A.D. 25-57) was worthy of support. Today, although the Chin rule is in decline, the mandate of Heaven has not yet been changed. I would like to establish my merit here north of the Yellow River, and have you extend my reputation south of the Yangtze River. Will you do it?"

Wen replied, "Even though I'm not clever, and my ability isn't up to that of the ancients, nevertheless, since Your Excellency is establishing his merit after the pattern of Dukes Huan and Wen³ as a restorer of the dynasty, how could I presume to refuse your command?"⁴ (*CS* 67.1b)

¹Pan Piao (A.D. 3-54), father of the Han historian Pan Ku, in his "Discourse on the Royal Mandate" (*Wang-ming lun*, *WH* 52.1a-4a), written during the attempted usurpation of Wei Hsiao in A.D. 22, predicted that the rule would return to the Han royal house of Liu. See also *HS* 100, and H. H. Dubs, *History of the Former Han Dynasty*, Baltimore, 1938, I, p. 23.

²Ma Yüan (14 B.C.-A.D. 49), originally a follower of Wei Hsiao and Kung-sun Shu, remarked after seeing Emperor Kuang-wu, "The realm is topsy-turvy and the names of rebels beyond numbering, but today, after seeing Your Majesty's overwhelmingly great capacity, equal to that of our founder, Emperor Kao (r. 206-195 B.C.), I know at last that the former rulers now have someone to carry on their line after all." See *HHS* 54.3b; *TKHC*.

³Duke Huan of Ch'i (r. 685-643 B.C.) and Duke Wen of Chin (r. 635-628), the two most powerful hegemons of the Spring and Autumn Era.

⁴*YYCS*: At this time (317) the two capitals (Lo-yang and Ch'ang-an) were overturned and the realm was in great disorder. Liu K'un, hearing that Emperor Yüan had received the mandate to restore the Chin Dynasty, was deeply moved where he was in the far north, and his loyalty remained with the Chin court. As he sent Wen Ch'iao on a mission to Chien-k'ang, Ch'iao said with a sigh, "Although I lack the ability of a Kuan Chung or a Chang Liang (advisers, respectively, to Duke Huan of Ch'i and the Han Emperor Kao), nevertheless, since Your Excellency possesses the determination of a

Duke Huan or Wen, could I presume to refuse on the grounds of my stupidity and thus disobey your high commands?"

Whereupon he became K'un's assistant administrator and undertook the mission to urge the emperor to ascend the throne of Eastern Chin.

36. Wen Ch'iao had just crossed the Yangtze River as an emissary of Liu K'un. At the time construction south of the river was barely beginning and the lines of government had not yet been raised up. Since Wen was a newcomer, he was deeply troubled by numerous anxieties, so he went to have an interview with Chancellor Wang Tao. His recitation of the bitter tale of the emperor's cruel abduction,[1] of the burning of the gods of soil and grain, of the leveling of the imperial tombs, had all the pathos of the song "The Millet Bends Down" (*Shu-li*).[2] Wen's loyalty and grief were deep and intense, and his words welled up with his tears, so that the chancellor, too, wept with him as he listened. After he had finished recounting his tale, he solemnly declared his allegiance, and the chancellor for his part warmly reciprocated and accepted him.

When Wen emerged from the interview he exclaimed with delight, "Since there is, after all, a Kuan Chung south of the river, from now on what cause is there for worry?"[3] (*CS* 67.2a)

[1] Emperor Huai (Ssu-ma Chih, r. 307-313) was captured by the Hsiung-nu general, Liu Yao, as he fled from the assault on the palace in Lo-yang in 311, and was sent off to the Hsiung-nu capital at P'ing-yang (Shansi), where he served wine at banquets. For details, see *TCTC* 87.2763 and A. Waley, "Lo-yang and Its Fall," *History Today* April, 1951, reprinted in Waley, *The Secret History of the Mongols*, London, 1963, pp. 54-55.

[2] "Songs," No. 65:

> That millet bends down,
> The sprouts of that grain!
> I, too, walk with hanging head,
> In my midmost heart I am shaken.
> Those who know me say my heart grieves;
> Those who know me not ask what I am seeking.
> O distant blue heaven,
> What men are these?

[3] *YL*: When Wen Ch'iao had just arrived in Chien-k'ang on his mission to urge Emperor Yüan to mount the throne, Emperor Yüan invited a large number of guests to meet him. As Wen first entered the room his manner and appearance were extraordinarily unprepossessing, so much so that the whole company was dismayed. But after he had been seated and began his recital of how the imperial household was weakened and cut off, the emperor and all his ministers were shaken with sobbing. And when he declared that the realm must not be left without a lord, all of his hearers leaped for joy, and their hair stood straight up against their ceremonial caps.

Chancellor Wang Tao had profound confidence in him, and Wen, for his part, after seeing the chancellor, was immediately encouraged and exclaimed, "Now that I've seen Kuan Chung, the troubles of the realm no longer worry me."

II SPEECH AND CONVERSATION   49

37. Wang Tun's elder brother, Han, had been in the palace as Great Officer of Brilliant Favor. After Tun plotted rebellion and encamped with his base at Nan-chou (i.e., Ku-shu, in Anhui), Han left his post and fled to Ku-shu. Their cousin, Chancellor Wang Tao, went to the court to offer his apologies. The various officials who had served under him while he was director of instruction, chancellor, and governor of Yang Province,[1] wanted to write a letter expressing their concern, but in their distress did not know how to phrase it. Ku Ho, who at the time was lieutenant-governor of Yang Province, seized a brush and wrote, "Since Wang Han has fled far from 'baseless rumors,'[2] and Your Excellency has been 'covered with dust'[3] along the road, all your underlings are uneasy, not having ascertained how matters stand with your honorable person."[4]

[1]Wang Tao became chancellor and governor of Yang Province with the founding of Eastern Chin in 317 (TCTC 90.2844), but was not named director of instruction until 323 (TCTC 92.2911). At the time of Wang Tun's revolt (322) he was still director of works.

[2]A reference to the Duke of Chou's moving east to escape rumors that he would kill the crown prince. See "Book of Documents" IV, 8; Legge III, pp. 357-359.

[3]The original reference is to King Hsiang's (r. 651-619 B.C.) flight from Lo-yang and temporary residence in Cheng (Honan) to escape trouble from his brother, Tai. Thereafter, to be "covered with dust" (meng-ch'en) became a euphemism for the flight of any important person. See Tso-chuan, Hsi 24; Legge V, p. 193.

[4]TTCC: Earlier when Wang Tao aided Emperor Yüan in restoring the dynasty, Wang Tun won merit for his campaign in the provinces. Tun, feeling that Liu K'uei was alienating him from the throne, raised an army to punish him. It was for this reason that Wang Han fled south to Wu-ch'ang (Hupei), and that the court began to be alarmed and to build its defenses.

CHS: When Wang Tao's cousin, Tun, raised an army to punish Liu K'uei, Tao, at the head of over twenty of the younger members of his family, went each morning to the palace gate (kung-ch'e) with mud on his head to apologize for his family's crimes.

38. When Ch'ih Chien was appointed director of works (329), he said to those seated with him, "All my life my ambitions have never consisted of much. It just happens the world is now in such disorder that I've finally arrived at one of the Three Ducal Offices. But the 'bird-cry of Chu Po'[1] really makes me ashamed in my heart."

[1]See "Book of Changes," Hex. 61, Chung-fu, "Inner Truth" (Wilhelm I, 254): "The bird-cry mounts to heaven;/ Augury: inauspicious." Wang Pi's third-century commentary explains, "The cry soars up, but the reality (the bird) does not accompany it."

Han-shu (cf. HS 83.19b and 27B3.18b-19a): When Chu Po . . . became chancellor (5 B.C.), as he was about to be invested and was received into the hall and mounted the steps to accept his investiture, there was a great sound like the tolling of a bell . . . The emperor (An-ti, r. 6-1 B.C.) asked his attendants, Yang Hsiung (53 B.C.-A.D. 18) and Li Hsün about it. They replied, "This is what (Fu Sheng's 'Great Commentary' on) the Hung-fan chapter of the "Book of Documents" (see *Shang-shu ta-chuan* 3.11a) means by "the portent of tolling" (*ku-yao*). When a ruler of men is not perceptive and those with empty reputations get promoted, there is a sound without physical basis."

SSHY Comm.: Po was later involved in a plot and committed suicide (see *HS* 27B3.19a). Therefore in his preface to the *Han-shu* (*HS* 100B.20b) Pan Ku says, "As for Chu Po's 'bird-cry,' the 'portent of tolling' occurred first."

39. The monk Kao-tso (Śrīmitra)[1] did not speak Chinese. Someone inquired about the significance of this, and the future Emperor Chien-wen (Ssu-ma Yü) replied, "It's to save himself the trouble of answering questions."

[1]*Kao-tso PC*: His Reverence (*ho-shang*) was of a godlike appearance, lofty and luminous, and his style and manner were vigorous and forthright. The moment Wang Tao saw him he admired him and declared, "I am his disciple."

While Chou I was serving on the Board of Civil Office, he once patted Kao-tso on the back, remarking with a sigh, "If in my selections for civil office I could get someone as worthy as this, I'd have no regrets." Very soon after that (322) Chou met his death at the hands of Wang Tun, and His Reverence sat opposite his coffin reciting several thousand words of Sanskrit mantras, his voice shrill and penetrating, while he kept brushing away his tears and repressing his sobs . . .

He was by nature haughty and unceremonious, and never learned the Chinese language. Whenever any gentleman spoke with him it was always through an interpreter. In spite of this fact, he understood intuitively and immediately before any words were uttered.

TSC: Śrīmitra's tomb is called Kao-tso, the High Seat, and is located in Shih-tzu kang (south of Chien-k'ang). He used to practice ascetic exercises (*dhūta*). He died in Mei-kang and was buried there. Emperor Yüan of Chin (? error for Emperor Ch'eng, r. 326–342?) erected a monastery at the site of the tomb, which was known thereafter as Kao-tso.

40. Chou I was courteous and affable and of a fine, prepossessing figure. When he went to visit Wang Tao, as he first got down from his carriage he was supported by several men.[1] Wang watched him with suppressed amusement. After they had been seated, Chou, completely self-assured, began whistling and intoning poems.

Wang asked him, "Are you trying to imitate Hsi K'ang and Juan Chi?"[2]

Chou replied, "How could I presume to discard a close model like Your Excellency to imitate such distant ones as Hsi K'ang and Juan Chi?"

[1]*TTCC*: Chou I's manner was liberal and magnanimous, and he was skilled at adapting himself to every situation. His quick wit in repartee was enough to overshadow several other people. He maintained such profound self-assurance that he could attract other people without ever himself going to them.

[2]For Juan Chi's reputation as a whistler, see below, *SSHY* XVIII, 1.

II SPEECH AND CONVERSATION   51

41. Yu Liang once entered a stupa, and seeing there a representation of the reclining Buddha,[1] remarked, "This man's tired after all the ferrying and bridging of sentient beings to salvation."
At the time it was considered a famous remark. (*TPYL* 653)

[1] To my knowledge this is the earliest literary reference to the parinirvāṇa scene in Chinese art; see also No. 51, below. Examples of this subject in sculpture or wall painting are relatively rare from the Six Dynasties period in North China, only one case being noted from the Yün-kang caves in Shansi. See A. Soper, *Literary Evidence for Early Buddhist Art in China*, Ascona, Switzerland, 1959, p. 192. However, perhaps through the influence of Fa-hsien's translation of the *Mahāparinirvāṇa-sūtra* (*Taishō* No. 376) in 417-418 at Chien-k'ang, it was more common in the South, at least after that date.

Liu Chün cites the *Nieh-p'an ching* (cf. the *Ta nieh-p'an ching*, *Taishō* 1.198c-199b, based on the Pāli *Mahānibbāna-sutta*, whose translation is wrongly attributed to Fa-hsien): "The Tathāgata, bearing his pain, lay between the twin Sāla trees, with his head to the north."

42. Chih Chan[1] had been grand warden of four commanderies and census aide to the generalissimo (Wang Tun). On top of that he was sent off to be governor of Sui Principality (Hupei). He was barely in his twenty-ninth year.
As he was taking leave of Wang Tun, Tun said to him, "You're not yet thirty years old, yet you've already reached a salary of ten thousand piculs,[2] which is entirely too soon."
Chan replied, "In comparison with you, sir, it may be a bit too soon, but compared with Kan Lo[3] I'm already old."

[1] *CSSP*: Once Chih Chan observed Wang Tun take an old fur coat and give it to an aged and sick director of the external department of his headquarters. Chan admonished Tun, saying, "Even though Your Excellency's fur coat is old, you oughtn't to give it to a petty officer."
Tun asked, "And why not?"
Chan, who was drunk at the time, said, "If the clothes of a superior may be used as gifts to his underlings, then might your cap of office decorated with cicada patterns and sable tails also be given to an underling?"
Tun replied, "It's an inappropriate analogy you've cited. Under the circumstances you don't deserve a post with a salary of two thousand piculs (i.e., a grand wardenship)."
Chan said, "I look on taking leave of Hsi-yang Commandery as I would on taking off my sandals."
Tun countered by demoting Chan to become Governor of Sui Principality . . .
Chan was high-minded and straightforward and possessed spirit and integrity, and therefore he answered Tun (as related above). Later, realizing that Tun had disloyal ambitions, in the fourth year of the Chien-hsing era (316) he held out against Tun in Ching Province together with its governor, Ti-wu I, but in the end was killed by him.
(*TCTC* 89.2824 carries a notice of Wang Tun's appointment of his cousin, Wang I*, to be governor of Ching Province only a few months

after the court had appointed Ti-wu I to that post in A.D. 315. This was evidently the primary cause of Ti-wu's resistance.)

[2] Ten thousand piculs of grain was the salary of someone in one of the Three Ducal Offices. Adding together the four grand wardenships and the new governorship, all at two thousand piculs, the cumulative figure would reach ten thousand.

[3] Kan Lo (third cent. B.C.) was a grandson of the Ch'in minister, Kan Mao. At the tender age of twelve, Lo made a diplomatic mission on behalf of Ch'in (Shensi) to Chao (Shansi), and for his pains was ennobled a high dignitary and endowed with his grandfather's estate. See *SC* 71.9a-11a.

43. The son of the Yang[1] family of Liang Principality (Kaifeng) in his ninth year was extremely quick-witted and intelligent. K'ung T'an once came to visit his father. Not finding the father at home, he called out, announcing his presence. The son came out and set some fruit before him, among which were some *yang-mei*, or arbutus berries. K'ung pointed them out to the boy, saying, "This is your family fruit."

The boy quickly rejoined, "I never heard, sir, that the peacock (*k'ung-ch'üeh*) was your family bird!"

[1] Most of the persons named Yang in the *SSHY* were from the Yang family of Hung-nung (W. Honan).

44. K'ung T'an once presented his fur coat to his cousin, K'ung Ch'en. Ch'en declined and would not accept it. T'an said, "Yen Ying (sixth cent. B.C.) was so frugal that 'in sacrificing to his ancestors the shoulders of the suckling pig did not cover the sacrificial dish.'[1] Moreover, 'he wore the same fox-skin coat for several decades.'[2] So who are you to decline this one?"

At this point Ch'en accepted the coat and put it on. (*CS* 78.12a)

[1] "Record of Rites" X, 19; Legge, *Li Ki* I, p. 402.

[2] Ibid. IV, 23 (Legge, *Li Ki* I, p. 174).

45. The monk Fo-t'u-teng used to roam about in company with the Shihs (Shih Lo and Shih Hu). Of this the monk Chih Tun observed, "Teng treats Shih Hu like the sea gulls."[1]

[1] Liu Chün cites *Chuang-tzu* (now only in *Lieh-tzu* II, 21; A. C. Graham, *The Book of Lieh-tzu*, London, 1960, p. 45): A man who lived by the sea was fond of sea gulls, and went every morning to the seashore where he accompanied the gulls in their play. The gulls that came to him numbered in the hundreds.

The man's father said, "I hear the gulls accompany you in your play. Bring one home so I can play with it, too."

The next day when the man went to the seashore, the gulls hovered above him, but would not come down.

46. When Hsieh Shang was in his eighth year his father, Hsieh K'un, was holding a farewell party to speed a guest on his way. At the time Shang's speech already gave indication of a divine perceptiveness, and he himself participated in the conversation with the best of them.

Everybody was gushing in admiration over him, and saying, "The young man is the Yen Hui[1] of the entire company!"

Shang replied, "Since there's no Confucius present, how can you single out any Yen Hui?" (*CS* 79.1a)

[1] Yen Hui (fifth cent. B.C.) was the indigent, but very intelligent and receptive disciple of Confucius whose death in his thirty-second year left the Master desolate.

47. During T'ao K'an's last illness (334) he left no word whatever either of approval or disapproval concerning a successor.[1] The gentlemen of the court all thought this to be regrettable. But when Hsieh Shang heard of it he said, "At present, since there's no Shu Tiao around,[2] naturally we don't have T'ao K'an's last instructions."

Worthies of those times considered this to be the remark of a virtuous man.

[1] *WYCS*: As T'ao K'an approached his end (in 334), he sent up a memorial to Emperor Ch'eng (r. 326-342), which stated: "When I was young I was continually alone and impoverished, and my early desires were limited. But after receiving the favor of the former court (Western Chin), in the course of time I changed my mind. Now I am approaching eighty and my status surpasses that of all other ministers. 'Uncover my hands and my feet' and observe that they are intact as I received them from my parents ("Analects" VIII, 3). What is left to regret? Only this: that the remaining rebels have not yet been executed, and the imperial tombs (in Lo-yang) not yet restored. The reason that I feel indignation and sorrow together in my breast is this, and this alone. I had hoped that my teeth, like those of a dog or horse, might last a little longer, so that they might for the sake of Your Majesty gulp down Shih Hu (the Hsiung-nu conqueror) in the North and kill Li Hsiung (the rebel warlord of Shu) in the West.

"But alas! my strength is not sufficient to act, and the good plan will remain forever at rest. As I bend over this document I grasp my wrist (a gesture of determination), and the tears flow in a flood. I humbly pray that Your Majesty might choose out a man to take my place. If, indeed, you find one of good talent, sufficient to carry out the plan of 'Emperor Hsüan' (Ssu-ma I, d. 251), who will respectfully fulfill his purpose and patrimony, then, even though it be the day of my death, it will yet be a year of life."

SSHY Comm.: Since there was such a memorial as this, it is hardly true to say "he left no word whatever either of approval or disapproval."

[2] *LSCC* (XVI, 184-185): When Kuan Chung was dying (645 B.C.), Duke Huan of Ch'i (r. 685-643) asked him, "If you're not averse to discussing it, who should take your place as minister? Would the eunuch Shu Tiao do?"

Kuan Chung replied, "To take a man from the palace apartments to serve his ruler is contrary to human sensibilities. He's certainly not to be used."

Later Shu Tiao was duly installed as minister, and as predicted, he rebelled against Ch'i.

48. Once when the monk Chu Tao-ch'ien was present at a gathering at the villa of the future Emperor Chien-wen (Ssu-ma Yü), Liu T'an asked him, "How is it that you, a monk, are enjoying yourself within the vermilion gate?"

Chu replied, "You naturally see it as a vermilion gate; to this indigent monk it's as if he were enjoying himself within a mat door."[1]

According to some, it was Pien K'un who asked the question. (KSC 4, Taishō 50.348a)

[1]KISMC: While the dharma master was living in K'uai-chi (Chekiang), the Emperor (Ssu-ma I**, r. 366-371), in deference to his refined manner and moral power, sent a message to invite him to the capital. The dharma master emerged for a short while from his retreat to respond to this invitation. The chancellor-prince of K'uai-chi (Ssu-ma Yü) was by nature humble and free from desire, and joined himself to the dharma master in a pleasant friendship of mutual solicitude. Although the dharma master tread upon cinnabar courtyards and frequented vermilion halls, he was oblivious of them, free and unrestrained, just as if they were a mat shed.

49. Once when Sun Sheng was serving as secretarial aide to Yü Liang[1] he accompanied Yü on a hunting trip, taking along his two sons (Sun Ch'ien and Sun Fang). Yü was unaware of this, and suddenly caught sight of the younger son, Fang, on the hunting grounds. At the time the boy was in his seventh or eighth year. Yü called out to him, "Did you come along, too?"

Fang quickly rejoined, "As it says in the 'Songs,'

> 'There are no small and no great:
> All follow the duke in his travels.'"[2]

(CS 82.12b; TPYL 385, 833; IWLC 66)

[1]Sun Sheng became Yü Liang's superintendent of records when the latter was appointed General Chastizing the West, stationed in Wuch'ang (Hupei) in 334. See SSHY Comm., citing CHS, and TCTC 95.2996.

[2]"Songs," No. 299.

50. When the two brothers Sun Ch'ien and Sun Fang were small, they once paid a visit to Yü Liang. Yü asked Ch'ien, "What is your courtesy name?"

Ch'ien replied, "Ch'i-yu."

"Who is it with whom you wish to be equal (ch'i)?"

"With Hsü Yu."

Turning to Sun Fang, Yü asked, "And what is *your* courtesy name?"

Fang replied, "Ch'i-chuang."

"With whom do *you* wish to be equal?"

"With Chuang Chou."[1]

"Why don't you emulate Confucius instead of Chuang Chou?"

"Since the Sage was 'wise at birth,'[2] he'd be difficult to try to emulate."

Yü was most delighted with the small boys' replies.[3] (CS 82.12b; TPKC 174)

[1]The philosopher Chuang-tzu (4th cent. B.C.).

[2]"Analects" XVI, 9 (Legge I, 313).

[3]*Sun Fang PC*: When Fang was in his eighth year the grand marshal, Yü Liang, summoned him for an interview. Since Fang had a reputation for purity and outstanding ability, Yü wished to observe and test him, so he handed him paper and brush and ordered him to write. Fang accordingly wrote his own name and courtesy name. After Yü had appraised it, he asked, "Is it that you wish to emulate Chuang Chou?"
Fang wrote in reply, "My intention is to emulate him."
"Why don't you emulate Confucius instead of Chuang Chou?"
"Since Confucius was 'wise at birth,' he's not the sort I could hope to try to approach. But since Chuang Chou was his inferior, I'm emulating him, that's all."
Yü said to the other guests, "Even Wang Pi's answer (see below, SSHY IV, 8), I daresay, couldn't beat this."

51. Chang Hsüan-chih and Ku Fu were both grandsons of Ku Ho, the latter on his son's, and the former on his daughter's side. Both were clever and intelligent when they were young. Ho recognized the talents of both, but always thought Ku was superior, and in affection and honor was partial in the extreme, which made Chang somewhat unhappy.
When Chang was in his ninth year and Ku in his seventh,[1] Ho once accompanied them both to a Buddhist monastery where they saw a representation of the Buddha's parinirvāṇa, in which some of the disciples were weeping and some were not. Ho asked his two grandsons about this, and Hsüan-chih replied, "Those over there were loved by him, and that's why they're weeping. Those over here weren't loved, and that's why they're not weeping."
Fu said, "No, that's not it. It must be because those over here have 'forgotten their feelings,'[2] and that's why they're not weeping. Those over there can't 'forget their feelings,' and that's why they *are* weeping." (*TPKC* 170)

[1]*SSHY* XII, 4, states they were the same age.

[2]Cf. *Chuang-tzu* V, 28b (Watson, p. 75). Liu Chün quotes the "*Ta chih-tu lun*" (the passage is not comparable to anything found in Taishō, No. 1509): While the Buddha was in the shady Amra Grove between the twin Sāla trees, he entered Nirvāṇa, lying with his head to the north. There was a great earthquake, and the disciples of the three learning stages (*san-hsüeh*) were all unhappy and shedding tears of grief. But the disciples of the non-learning stage (*wu-hsüeh*) were only remembering how all the dharmas are impermanent.
(An example of a stone relief from the second century A.D. from Gandhāra, now in the Victoria and Albert Museum, depicts exactly this contrast. See John M. Rosenfield, *The Dynastic Arts of the Kushans*, Berkeley and Los Angeles, 1967, fig. 85.)

52. The monk K'ang Fa-ch'ang[1] once went to visit Yü Liang holding in his hand a sambar-tail chowry (*chu-wei*)[2] which was extremely beautiful. Yü said to him, "This is extremely beautiful; how did you get possession of it?"

Fa-ch'ang replied, "An unacquisitive man doesn't seek such things, and an avaricious man doesn't give them away, so I just got possession of it, that's all." (*IWLC* 69; *KSC* 4, *Taishō* 50.347a)

[1] All texts agree in giving his surname as Yü, an obvious scribal error influenced by the next item. See *KSC* 4 (*Taishō* 50.347a); *FYCL* 66; *TPYL* 703 (citing *YL*); and *IWLC* 69.

[2] Examples of the *chu-wei* may be seen in the eighth-century Japanese imperial collection, Shōsōin, at Nara, and in the wall paintings and bas-reliefs of Tun-huang, Yün-kang, and Lung-men. It became an inseparable accouterment of the "pure conversationalist," in which function it seems to have been derived from the popular iconography of Vimalakīrti's spirited conversation with the bodhisattva, Mañjuśrī, recorded in chapters five through nine of the *Vimalakīrtinirdeśa*. See *Taishō* 14.525b-532a. See also E. H. Schafer, *The Vermilion Bird*, p. 230; Ho Ch'ang-ch'ün, "Shih-shuo hsin-yü cha-chi (chu-wei k'ao)," *Kuo-li chung-yang t'u-shu-kuan kuan-k'an (fu-k'an)*, No. 1 (March 1947), 1-5, and Fujieda Akira, "Yuima-hen no keifu," *Tōhō gakuhō* 36 (1964), 287-303.

53. When Yü I[1] became governor of Ching Province (Hunan-Hupei), he presented a feather fan (*mao-shan*)[2] to Emperor Ch'eng (Ssu-ma Yen*).[3] The emperor suspected that it was a secondhand article, but his personal attendant, Liu Shao, said, "When the Cypress Beam Terrace (Po-liang t'ai)[4] was constructed high as the clouds, the workmen and artisans first lived beneath it; and before the intricate performances on pipes and strings, both Chung Tzu-ch'i[5] and the music master, K'uei,[6] first listened to the sounds. In presenting the fan, Yü I had in mind only its excellence, not its newness."
Hearing of this later, Yü remarked, "This man is well suited to be in attendance on the emperor." (*CS* 73.12b)

[1] Liu Chün points out that since this anecdote appears in the biography of Yü I's elder brother, I*, it is wrongly attributed here. See *CS* 73.22b.

[2] See Fu Hsien (fl. ca. 300), preface to "Poetic Essay on a Feather Fan" (*Yü-shan fu*), cited in *SSHY* Comm.: In antiquity the people of Wu used to cut off the wings of birds and fan with them just as they were, the breeze thus generated being no less than that of square or round fans, and the effort no more. However, in the Central States no one made a business of them. After the suppression of Wu (in 280) everybody started to value them so much that everybody used them.

[3] The *SSHY* text identifies the emperor anachronistically as Wu-ti (r. 265-289). I have emended to the graphically similar Ch'eng-ti (r. 326-342), following *CS* 73.12b.

[4] One of the projects of Emperor Wu of Han, built around 115 B.C. See *HS* 6.16b.

[5] Chung Tzu-ch'i (sixth cent. B.C.), a native of Ch'u (Hupei) who listened appreciatively to the zither playing of Po-ya.

[6] K'uei was the music master of Shun (r. 2255-2208 B.C.). See "Book of Documents" II, 1 (Legge II, 47-48).

54. After the death of Ho Ch'ung, Ch'u P'ou was summoned to court.¹ When he arrived at Shih-t'ou (west of Chien-k'ang), Wang Meng and Liu T'an both came to visit him. Ch'u said to Liu, "Why do you need me?"

Liu, looking back at Wang, replied, "This man can tell you."

Ch'u then looked at Wang, who said, "The state has its own Duke of Chou."²

¹Ch'u P'ou's daughter, Ho-tzu, was Emperor K'ang's legal consort, and after the emperor's death and the accession of the infant Emperor Mu (r. 345-357), she became empress dowager and regent. Ho Ch'ung, as president of the Central Secretariat, out of deference to her, invited Ch'u to take his place as president, but Ch'u, fearing the rivalry of the Yü clan at court, asked for a provincial assignment instead, and was given a military governorship with headquarters at Ching-k'ou (Kiangsu). When Ho died two years later, in 346, Ch'u was again summoned to court, but was easily persuaded to withdraw in favor of Ssu-ma Yü. See *TCTC* 97.3061-3070.

CYC: When Ho Ch'ung died, advisers said that Ch'u P'ou, as father of the empress dowager, should hold the principal power at court. P'ou came in from Tan-t'u (Kiangsu), but the president of the Board of Civil Office, Liu Hsia*, urged him, saying, "The Prince of K'uai-chi, Ssu-ma Yü, is a man of excellent virtue and is the state's Duke of Chou. Your Excellency should entrust the major power to him." P'ou's senior administrator, Wang Hu-chih, also urged him to return to the provinces, whereupon P'ou adamantly declined to serve at court and returned to Ching-k'ou.

²I.e., Ssu-ma Yü, then Prince of K'uai-chi, who, upon Ch'u P'ou's withdrawal, became Generalissimo Controlling the Army, with high responsibility in the Central Secretariat. The original Duke of Chou--Tan, brother of King Wu (r. 1122-1116 B.C.)--assumed the regency for the young King Ch'eng in 1115, and ruled the Chou state until his death in 1104.

55. When Huan Wen went on his northern expedition (369), as he passed by Chin-ch'eng (Kiangsu) he observed that the willows he had planted there earlier (in 341) while governing Lang-yeh Principality had all of them already reached a girth of ten double spans (*wei*).

With deep feeling he said, "If mere trees have changed like this, how can a man endure it?" And pulling a branch toward him, he plucked a wand, while his tears fell in a flood. (*CS* 98.20b; *IWLC* 89; *CHC* 28, bis)

56. When Emperor Chien-wen (Ssu-ma Yü) was serving as Generalissimo Controlling the Army (345-361), he once came into the audience hall with Huan Wen. After the two had repeatedly yielded precedence to each other, Huan finally had no recourse but to go first.¹ In so doing he said,

> "The earl grasps his spear
> And goes ahead as the king's forerider."²

Chien-wen countered with,

> "There are no small and no great;
> All follow the duke in his travels."³

¹Ssu-ma Yü was of higher status, Huan of superior age. Before 361, however, Huan's power was not yet a factor, so the story may reflect their later relationship; see No. 59, below. For a very different solution to the same dilemma, see below, SSHY XXV, 46.

²"Songs," No. 62.

³Ibid., No. 299; cf. No. 49, above.

57. Ku Yüeh was the same age as Emperor Chien-wen, but his hair had turned white earlier. Chien-wen asked him, "How is it you've turned white first?"

Ku replied, "The character of rushes and willows is to drop their leaves as they approach the autumn, while the nature of pines and cypresses is to be still more luxuriant amid the ice and frost."¹ (CS 77.27a; IWLC 18; SLF 25; TPYL 283, 957; SWLC, ch'ien 44)

¹"Analects" IX, 27 (Legge I, 225). Liu Chün cites Ku K'ai-chih's biography of his father, KYC: Because of his policy of honesty, my father suffered considerable bodily deterioration in the world. He once went to court to have an interview with the prince (Ssu-ma Yü). The prince's hair had not yet turned color at all, while my father's was already quite gray.

The prince asked about my father's age, and then said, "Why is it that only you have turned white so early?"

My father replied, "The nature of pines, etc. It's only the difference in the fate we've each received."

The prince complimented him on the remark for a long time.

58. On entering the Yangtze Gorges¹ where sheer cliffs hang suspended and dashing waves rush headlong, Huan Wen sighed and said, "Since being a loyal minister means I can't be a filial son, what shall I do?"²

¹The "Three Gorges" of the Yangtze River in the upper, mountainous reaches between Feng-chieh in Szechwan and I-ch'ang in Hupei are, in the usual listing, the Chü-t'ang, the Wu, and the Hsi-ling. At these points the cliffs rise perpendicularly on each side to nearly a thousand feet, and navigation through the boulder-strewn rapids between them is extremely hazardous. In 346 Huan Wen set out upstream from Wu-ch'ang with 70,000 men to conquer the secessionist regime of Li Shih in Shu (Szechwan). See SSHY Comm., citing CYC.

²HS 76.23b: When Wang Yang (first cent. B.C.) became governor of I Province (W. Szechwan), as he was traveling to take up his assignment, he arrived at Chiu-che pan, the Slope of Nine Turns, in Ch'iung-lai Commandery (Szechwan). Sighing, he said, "I received my body as a bequest from my parents; how can I continually subject it to such danger?" And using the pretext of ill health, he resigned from his post.

Later Wang Tsun became governor, and when he arrived at the slope he asked his officers, "Isn't this the road Wang Yang was afraid of?"

They replied, "This is it."

Wang shouted to his driver, "Take it at full speed!"

Wang Yang was a filial son; Wang Tsun a loyal minister.

II SPEECH AND CONVERSATION   59

59. Some time earlier (between Nov. 24 and Dec. 22, A.D. 371) the planet Mars (Ying-huo) had entered the celestial enclosure T'ai-wei,[1] and shortly thereafter (between Dec. 23, 371, and Jan. 21, 372) Huan Wen had deposed the Duke of Hai-hsi (Ssu-ma I**). (About Feb. 17, 372), after Emperor Chien-wen had succeeded him to the throne, the planet had reentered T'ai-wei, and the emperor was very upset over it.[2]

At the time Ch'ih Ch'ao was working in the Central Secretariat and was in attendance. The emperor called Ch'ao in for an audience and said, "The length or shortness of the heavenly mandate is basically not within human control. Surely there will not be a repetition of recent events?"

Ch'ao replied, "The grand marshal (Huan Wen) has newly strengthened the frontiers without and pacified the gods of soil and grain within. There is surely no cause for any such anxiety. I guarantee it for Your Majesty with all the mouths of my household."

On hearing this, the emperor chanted the words of Yü Ch'an's poem,

> "The determined knight is pained when the court is in peril;
> The loyal minister grieves when his lord is disgraced."[3]

As he chanted his voice became intensely poignant and piercing.

When Ch'ih obtained leave to return east to K'uai-chi, the emperor said to him, "Inform your honored father (Ch'ih Yin) that since the affairs of family and kingdom have come to this pass, from now on We are unable personally to rescue or defend them according to the Way, and Our thoughts are plagued with foreboding. How can words describe the depths of Our shame and sighing?" As he spoke, the tears coursed down his lapel. (CS 9.5b)

[1] The celestial enclosure (yüan), T'ai-wei, corresponds to the court of the Son of Heaven on earth, hence invasions into it by certain planets were taken to be ominous. See CS 11.16a; Ho Peng-yoke, *Astronomical Chapters*, p. 76. It includes stars in the constellations Virgo and Leo and Coma Berenices and is now centered at about longitude 190°. Taking account of the precession of the equinoxes, it should have been centered at about 165 to 170 at the end of the fourth century, but according to present data appears to have been nearer 160. See Gustave Schlegel, *Uranographie chinoise*, The Hague, 1875. The dates inserted in parentheses in the translation follow the CYC, quoted in Liu Chün's Commentary, and CS 13.20ab (trans. in Ho Pen-yoke, *Astronomical Chapters*, p. 214), and accord perfectly with the positions of Mars for these dates calculated by Bryant Tuckerman in his *Planetary, Lunar, and Solar Positions . . . at Five Day and Ten Day Intervals*, Vol. II: A.D. 2 to A.D. 1649, Philadelphia, 1964. I am indebted to Nathan Sivin for most of the information in this note. For a chart plotting the course of Mars between November 15, A.D. 371, and May 29, 372, based on Tuckerman's tables, see *Journal of the American Oriental Society* 91.2 (1971), 251.

[2] CATC: When Huan Wen was routed by the Yen general, Mu-jung Ch'ui at Fang-t'ou (Honan, in 369), he knew that the expectations of the people would desert him, so he made a scapegoat of a subordinate, and killed Yüan Chen at Shou-yang (Anhui). Afterward he said to Ch'ih Ch'ao, "Will that be enough to wipe out the disgrace of Fang-t'ou?"

Ch'ao replied, "It still won't satisfy the feelings of those who know what happened. Your Excellency is now sixty years old, and you've been defeated in a major undertaking. If you don't establish the kind of merit which transcends the world, you'll never be able to satisfy the people's expectations." Accordingly he recommended to Wen the tactic of deposing one emperor and setting up another. At the time Wen himself had long since been toying with the same idea, and eagerly accepting Ch'ao's advice, he deposed the Duke of Hai-hsi.

HKCC: On the *hsin-mao* day of the twelfth month of the first year of the Hsien-an era (Feb. 17, 372), the planet Mars, having reversed its orbit, reentered the enclosure T'ai-wei, and even as late as the third month of the second year (April 20 to May 18, 372) was still there. The emperor, taking a warning from the deposing of the Duke of Hai-hsi, was extremely troubled in his heart over it. (Cf. *CS* 13.20b, trans. in Ho Peng-yoke, *Astronomical Chapters*, p. 214.)

HCYC: The Emperor Chien-wen, oppressed from without by a powerful minister (Huan Wen), became anxious and frustrated and was unable to accomplish his aims. After reigning for two years he passed away.

[3]Liu Chün identifies the title of the poem as "Accompanying the Expedition" (*Ts'ung-cheng shih*).

60. Emperor Chien-wen was once sitting in a dark room when he summoned Huan Wen. Huan arrived and asked, "Sire, where are you?"
Chien-wen replied, "So-and-so is over here."[1]
His contemporaries considered it an able reply.

[1]"Analects" XV, 16 (Legge I, 305-306): The blind music master, Mien, came for an interview. When he reached the steps the Master said, "Here are the steps." When he reached the mat the Master said, "Here is the mat." When everyone was seated, the Master informed him, "So-and-so is over here, and so-and-so is over here."

61. On entering the Flowery Grove Park (Hua-lin yüan)[1] Emperor Chien-wen looked around and remarked to his attendants, "The spot which suits the mind isn't necessarily far away. By any shady grove or stream one may quite naturally have such thoughts as Chuang-tzu had by the Rivers Hao and P'u,[2] where unselfconsciously birds and animals, fowls and fish, come of their own accord to be intimate with men."[3] (*IWLC* 65; *PTSC* 12; *WH* 50.6b, Li Shan's comm.; *TPYL* 376, 824; *SWLC*, hou 20, hsü 9)

[1]Traces of the wall foundations of this royal preserve, originally laid out in the Wu period (221-280), can still be found to the northeast of Nanking.

[2]See *Chuang-tzu* XVII, 19b (Watson, pp. 188-189): Chuang-tzu and Hui Shih were once strolling on the bridge over the River Hao (Anhui), when Chuang-tzu remarked, "See how the minnows dart in and out so free and unconcerned. Such is the pleasure that fish enjoy." Hui-tzu replied, "You aren't a fish. How do you know what pleasures fish enjoy?"

Chuang-tzu said, "You aren't me. How do you know I don't know what pleasures fish enjoy? . . ."

Ibid., 18b-19a (Watson, pp. 187-188): Chuang-tzu was once angling in the River P'u (Shantung), when the King of Ch'u sent two great officers to visit him there, hoping to tie Chuang-tzu down with responsibility for his entire realm. Chuang-tzu, still holding his rod without looking around, answered them, "I hear that in Ch'u you've got a sacred tortoise who's been dead for three thousand years and is wrapped in a napkin preserved in the ancestral temple. Would this tortoise rather be dragging his tail in the mud, or would he rather have his bones preserved and honored?"

The two great officers replied, "He'd rather be dragging his tail in the mud."

"Then be off with you! I'd rather drag my tail in the mud, too."

[3] Ibid., IX, 8b-9a (Watson, p. 105): In an age of perfect virtue men live together with birds and animals.

62. Hsieh An once said to Wang Hsi-chih, "In my middle years I'm so affected by grief or joy that whenever I part with a relative or friend I'm always indisposed for several days."

Wang replied, "Since our years are at the 'mulberry and elm' stage,[1] it's natural we should come to this; it's precisely the time to depend on stringed instruments and pipes to dispel our melancholy. But the continual fear lest the younger generation will find out about it has spoiled my zest for this pleasure." (CS 80.9b)

[1] I.e., old age. One interpretation is that these are two stars between which the sun sets; another states that as the sun sets its last rays are seen in the tops of these trees. Both explanations seem to imply that the real explanation is unknown.

63. The monk Chih Tun always kept several horses. Someone remarked, "A holy man and raising horses don't go together."

Chih replied, "This humble monk values them for their divine swiftness."[1] (SWLC, hou 38; KSC 4, Taishō 50.349b)

[1] Like that of the human mind.

64. Liu T'an and Huan Wen were once listening together to an exposition of the "Record of Rites" (Li-chi). Huan remarked, "At times there are things he says which enter the recesses of the mind, and it's then that I feel within a few inches of the 'Gate of Mysteries.'"

Liu replied, "This hasn't anything to do yet with ultimate matters; it's just naturally the kind of talk you might hear in the Hall of Golden Splendor (Chin-hua tien)."[1]

[1] Liu Chün, citing Pan Ku's preface to the Han-shu (HS 100A.2a), identifies this hall, located on the grounds of the Wei-yang Palace in Ch'ang-an, as the place where the youthful Han Emperor Ch'eng (r. 32-7 B.C.) was taught by imperial tutors at the beginning of his studies.

65. Yang Ping had been aide-de-camp to the General Controlling the Army, but died young (before 291) with an excellent reputation. Hsia-hou Chan wrote a preface for his collected works[1] which was extremely laudatory and sad. Later while Ping's nephew Yang Ch'üan was serving as imperial attendant and was waiting by Emperor Chien-wen's seat, the emperor asked him, "Hsia-hou Chan once wrote a preface for Yang Ping's works which was most memorable. What relation was Yang Ping to you? Did he have any descendants?"

Ch'üan replied, weeping, "My late uncle's excellent reputation was well known when he was still young, but he has had no one to continue his line. His name was proclaimed as far as Heaven's (i.e., Your Majesty's) hearing, yet his line was cut off from the present sage-like era."

The emperor sighed with deep feeling for a long while.

[1]*YPH*: The wife of Yang Ping's uncle (Yang Chih), Lady Cheng, being childless, adopted Ping. He was handsome from childhood, painstaking, respectful, and full of tact. In his tenth year Lady Cheng passed away, and Ping's thoughts and facial expression were completely grief-stricken. Later unexpectedly his father (Yang Yu) and mother (Lady Yüeh; see below, *SSHY* VIII, 11, n. 1) both died. Ping followed the tradition of his father implicitly, performing all the proper observances. "Others did not disagree with his parents' report of him" ("Analects" XI, 4), so mild and affable was his nature.

When he took up his post as aide to the General Controlling the Army, he was on the verge of striding forth with thousand-*li* legs and flying up with heaven-soaring wings, but, alas, when his springs and autumns were but thirty and two, he died.

Long ago when Han Hu died (528 B.C.), Tzu-ch'an felt there was no one left with whom he could practice virtue (*Tso-chuan*, Chao 13; Legge V, 652), and now that the Master (Yang Ping) has died, I feel the same melancholy that Tzu-ch'an did. After his death there was a male heir, but he, too, did not grow to maturity. What kind of reward was this for doing good, that his misfortunes only multiplied instead? Was not this the lament of Ssu-ma Ch'ien regarding Po I? (Cf. *SC* 61.3b-6b.)

66. Wang Meng and Liu T'an met after having been separated for some time. Wang said to Liu, "You've progressed higher in rank than ever."

Liu replied, "This is just like 'heaven's being naturally high,'[1] that's all."[2]

[1]*Chuang-tzu* XXI, 20b (Watson, p. 226): It's like Heaven's being naturally high, earth naturally thick, and the sun and moon naturally bright. Do they cultivate these qualities?

[2]Liu Chün cites the earlier version of the *YL*: *Wang*: You've made great progress lately. *Liu*: Do you look up? *Wang*: What do you mean? *Liu*: If you didn't look up, how could you estimate the height of heaven?

67. Liu T'an said, "Everybody thinks that Wang Hui[1] is outstanding. But I rather think that under a tall pine tree there is apt to be a refreshing breeze, that's all."[2]

¹Emending the "Wei" of the text to "Hui," following CS 43.20a and the *Wang-shih p'u* in the *Shih-shuo jen-ming p'u*.

²I.e., he is basking in the reputation of his father, Wang Ch'eng. See also below, SSHY VIII, 52.

68. On hearing the Man language¹ without understanding it, Wang Meng observed dryly, "If Ko Lu of Chieh were to come for an audience,² no doubt we wouldn't be in the dark about this language."

¹The name "Man" in classical times referred broadly to all non-Chinese peoples to the south of the Central States of the Yellow River valley. During the Six Dynasties it seems to have been limited to the non-Chinese (Miao-Yao and T'ai) tribes in the area of Ching Province (Hunan-Hupei). See also below, SSHY XXV, 35.

²*Tso-chuan*, Hsi 29 (Legge V, 214): Ko Lu, ruler of Chieh (in Shantung), came for an audience with Duke Hsi (r. 658-626 B.C.) of Lu. On hearing the lowing of a cow, he said, "She has borne three calves, all of whom have been used for sacrifice. Her lowing says so." Upon inquiry, it turned out to be true.

Cf. also *Lieh-tzu* II, 27 (Graham, p. 55): The people of the state of Chieh in the East understand the languages of the six domesticated animals (oxen, horses, sheep, dogs, chickens, and pigs): no doubt such a skill may be gained even by those of limited knowledge.

69. While Liu T'an was intendant of Tan-yang (between 345 and 347), Hsü Hsün came out of retirement to the capital and spent the night with him. The bed curtains were new and beautiful, the food and drink plentiful and sweet. Hsü remarked, "If a person could keep a place like this intact, it would far surpass living in retirement in the Eastern Mountains (Chekiang)."

Liu replied, "If you figure that 'fortune and misfortune proceed from men,'¹ why shouldn't I keep this place intact?"

Wang Hsi-chih, who was among the company, said, "If it had been Ch'ao Fu or Hsü Yü² meeting with Hou Chi or Hsieh,³ there certainly wouldn't have been any exchange like this!"

The two men looked ashamed.

¹*Tso-chuan*, Hsi 16 (Legge V, 171).

²See above, Nos. 1 and 9.

³Hou Chi served under Yao; Hsieh under Shun and Yü.

70. Wang Hsi-chih and Hsieh An went up together to Yeh-ch'eng (east of Chien-k'ang).¹ Hsieh was bemused, with his thoughts far away, for he had the determination to transcend the world (i.e., to be a recluse).

Wang said to Hsieh, "Yü of Hsia ruled with such diligence that his hands and feet were worn and calloused.² King Wen of Chou didn't even allow leisure in the day for his evening meal.³ And today, when 'the four suburbs are filled with fortifications,'⁴ every man should be exerting himself. But if instead people neglect their duty for empty talk, and hinder the essential tasks with frivolous writing, I'm afraid that's not what is needed right now."

Hsieh replied, "The Ch'in state followed the principles of Wei Yang, Lord of Shang,⁵ and perished with the Second Emperor (Erh-shih, r. 209-207 B.C.). Was it 'pure conversation' which brought them to disaster?" (CS 79.6a)

¹*YangCC*: During the Wu Kingdom (221-280) Yeh-ch'eng, Foundry City, was a place for forging metal, and even after the pacification of Wu it was not abandoned. It was rebuilt by Wang Tao.

²*TWSC*: In controlling the flood waters Yü worked so hard his hands and feet were worn and calloused.

SSHY Comm.: There is a tradition in the world that Yü suffered a stroke and was half paralyzed, so that one foot could not pass the other. This is what is meant nowadays by the expression "Yü's walk" (*Yü-pu*).

³"Book of Documents" V, 15.10 (Legge III, 469): From dawn till sunset King Wen allowed no leisure to eat.

⁴"Record of Rites" I, 39 (Legge, *Li Ki* I, 92): When the four suburbs are filled with fortifications, it is the shame of the ministers and great officers.

⁵A minister under Duke Hsiao of Ch'in (r. 362-338) who specialized in law and public administration, whose name is attached to the Legalist work, "The Book of Lord Shang" (*Shang-chün shu*), translated by J. J. L. Duyvendak, London, 1928. The Ch'in chancellor Li Ssu (d. 208 B.C.) put his ideas into practice when he came to power in 214.

71. On a cold snowy day Hsieh An gathered his family indoors and was discussing with them the meaning of literature, when suddenly there was a violent flurry of snow. Delighted, Hsieh began,

"The white snow fluttering and flurrying--what is it like (*zi)?"

His nephew, Lang, came back with,

"Scatter salt in midair--nearly to be compared (*ngji)."

His niece, Tao-yün, chimed in,

"More like the willow catkins on the wind rising (*k'ji)."¹

Hsieh laughed aloud with delight. She was the daughter of his eldest brother, Hsieh I, and the wife of Wang Ning-chih.² (CS 96.9ab; IWLC 2; CHC 2; TPYL 512; SWLC, ch'ien 4)

¹This is an example of the parlor game of "sequences" (*yü-tz'u*) in which the host establishes a topic and rhyme with a single line, usually of seven words, and every other member of the company follows with a rhyming line of the same length on the same topic. For a longer example, see below, *SSHY* XXV, 61.

²*CATC*: Ning-chih was a devotee of the "Five-Pecks-of-Rice" sect of Taoism (*Wu-tou-mi tao*). When the Taoist magician-rebel Sun En threatened K'uai-chi (in 399), Ning-chih said to his people and lower officers, "There's no necessity to prepare any defense; I've already requested the Great Way to exorcise all the devil men-at-arms and come to our rescue. The rebels will simply destroy themselves." Inasmuch as he had made no preparations, he was killed by Sun En.

72. Wang T'an-chih had the historians Fu T'ao and Hsi Tso-ch'ih write discourses on the great personalities of their respective localities, Ch'ing (Shantung) and Ch'u (Hunan-Hupei). When the discourses were nearly completed, he showed them to Han Po, requesting a judgment, but Han said nothing one way or the other.
Wang asked, "Why don't you say something?"
Han replied, "There's no 'may' nor 'may not.'"[1]

[1]"Analects" XVIII, 8 (Legge I, 337). In his Commentary Liu Chün has condensed the substance of the two discourses from the "Collected Works of (Fu) T'ao" (*T'ao chi*), of which I offer here a still further abridgement: Beginning with the Spring and Autumn era (722-481 B.C.) and moving methodically through to the Wei Kingdom (A.D. 220-265), Fu listed all the great men of the North: Kuan Chung, Yen Ying, Mencius, Hsün-tzu, Lu Chung-lien, T'ien Kuang, Tung-fang Shuo, Kuan Yu-an, Hua Tzu-yü, etc. At the same time he did not fail to include at least three of his own illustrious ancestors. Hsi responded by noting that the mythical heroes of antiquity--Shen Nung, Fu Hsi, Shao Hao, and Shun--were all either born or buried in the South. The "Shao-nan" section of the "Book of Songs" describes the southern scene, and the "Spring and Autumn Annals" has words of praise for many a talented southerner. The northern advisers, Kuan Chung and Yen Ying, were beneath comparison with their southern counterparts, Tzu-wen and Shu Ao. The recluse Chieh Yü and the Fisherman of Ch'u were both from the South. Lu Chung-lien was no match for Lao Lai-tzu when the latter lived with his wife south of the Yangtze. T'ien Kuang of Ch'i could not hold a candle to Ch'ü Yüan of Ch'u, while the southern statesmen, Teng Yü and Cho Mao, had no peers in the North. In more recent times, Kuan Yu-an did not surpass his southern contemporary P'ang Te-kung, and Te-kung's nephew, P'ang T'ung, was in no way inferior to Hua Tzu-yü, etc., etc. "Comparing their persons, one finds their relative levels as I have described them; discussing their territory, one finds all the sages buried there (i.e., in the South). Investigating their songs, one finds it was the South the poets were singing about; researching their history, one discovers no rebels in the South like the Red Eyebrows or the Yellow Turbans. How can there really be any comparison with the North?"
Fu then countered with similar claims for the North, to which Hsi was unable to respond, and the discussion ended.

73. Liu T'an said, "In a fresh breeze under a bright moon I always think of Hsü Hsün."[1]

[1]*CHS*: Hsü Hsün was an able conversationalist, and his contemporaries all admired and loved him.

74. While Hsün Hsien was stationed at Ching-k'ou[1] he climbed North Fortress Mountain (Pei-ku shan)[2] and looked out over the sea and said, "Although I can't see the Three Isles of the Transcendents,[3] still it quite naturally makes me want to soar up to the clouds, and, like the lords of Ch'in and Han,[4] to feel that I must surely 'lift up my skirts' and get my feet wet."[5]

[1]Ching-k'ou was northeast of Chien-k'ang on the northern bank of the Yangtze River. It was the headquarters of the General Chastizing the North, as well as of the governor of Yen and Hui provinces.

²*NHCC*: Northwest of the city walls of Ching-k'ou there is a separate ridge jutting into the Yangtze River, overlooking the water on three sides, and several hundred feet in elevation. It is called North Fortress.

³*SC* 28.11a: These three mountains--P'eng-lai, Fang-chang, and Ying-chou--according to tradition are located in the sea, not far from the habitation of men. Those who have been there say the elixir of immortality of the transcendent ones (*hsien-jen*) is found there. Gold and silver form their palaces and towers, and all the flora and fauna are white. When one gazes at them from a distance they are like clouds, but when one comes close to them it turns out they are under water, and when one tries to reach them, immediately the boat is drawn away by the wind, so that in the end no one has ever been able to set foot on them.

⁴Ibid., 11b: When Emperor Shih-huang of Ch'in (r. 246-210 B.C.) climbed a mountain in K'uai-chi (Chekiang), he looked out over the sea and hoped to find the wonderful elixir of the above-mentioned three divine mountains.

Ibid., 25a: After Emperor Wu of Han (r. 140-87 B.C.) had performed the *feng*-sacrifice to Heaven on Mt. T'ai (Shangtung), there was no change in the wind or rain, but the moment the Taoist magician changed his pronouncement to say that the various elixirs of P'eng-lai were obtainable, the emperor then cheerfully went eastward to the sea, hoping he could get possession of P'eng-lai.

⁵Cf. "Songs," No. 87: "If you lovingly think of me,/ Then lift your skirts and wade the Chen."

75. Hsieh An said, "Though worthies and sages are set apart from other men, the distance between is also slight."
His sons and nephews would not agree to this. Sighing, Hsieh went on to say, "If Ch'ih Ch'ao had heard this remark, *he* certainly wouldn't have considered it 'as limitless as the Milky Way.'"¹

¹Cf. *Chuang-tzu* I, 7b (Watson, p. 33): Chien Wu said to Lien Shu, "I heard something Chieh Yü (the madman of Ch'u) said, big and baseless, going forth but not coming back, and I was frightened by his words, limitless as the Milky Way."

Ch'ih Ch'ao PC: Ch'ao was very subtle in discussions of Principles and Meanings. The monk Chih Tun considered him the most outstanding man of his age.

76. The monk Chih Tun was fond of cranes. While he was living on Yang Mountain in the eastern part of Shan Prefecture (Chekiang), someone sent him a pair of cranes. After a short time their wings grew out and they were on the point of flying away. Reluctant to let them go, Chih clipped their pinions. The cranes spread their wings to soar aloft, but found they could no longer fly, and turning back to observe their wings, hung their heads and looked at Chih as if with reproach and disappointment.
Chih said, "Since they look as if they would soar up to the clouds, how could they be willing to perform vulgar tricks of the ear and eye for humans?" Whereupon he cared for them until their pinions had grown out again and then set them free so they could fly away. (*KSC* 4, *Taishō* 50.349b; *IWLC* 90; *SLF* 19; *TPYL* 389, 916)

77. Hsieh Wan was once passing the Posterior Lake of Ch'ü-o (near Chien-k'ang), and asked his attendants, "What body of water is this?" They replied, "Ch'ü-o,¹ the Lake of Crooked Banks."
Hsieh said, "Undoubtedly it is profoundly filled and quietly limpid, receptive but not flowing on."²

¹*TKTC*: Ch'ü-o was originally named Yün-yang, but Emperor Shih-huang of Ch'in, supposing that the place had the quality of a rival royal seat, gouged out the earth and leveled the mountains in order to destroy its efficacy, intercepting its straight course and making its banks crooked; therefore it was called Ch'ü-o, the Lake of Crooked Banks. During the Wu Kingdom the name was changed back to Yün-yang, but today it is again known as Ch'ü-o.

²Kawakatsu *et al*. in their Japanese translation in *Chūgoku koshōsetsu shū*, Tokyo, 1964, p. 70, suggest that there are cryptic allusions in this remark to *Lao-tzu* 22 and 4.

78. Whenever the Chin Emperor Wu (Ssu-ma Yen, r. 265-290) had sent gifts to Shan T'ao they were always meager. Hsieh An inquired about this of the young people of his family, and Hsieh Hsüan replied, "It's probably because the recipient's desires were few, which made the giver forget about the meagerness of the gift."¹

¹Cf. *Chuang-tzu* XXV, 23a (Watson, p. 281): The perfect man . . . can make kings and nobles forget their rank and emoluments and act as if they were lowly.
Hsieh Ch'e-chi chia-chuan: Hsieh Hsüan's uncle (Hsieh An) was once at a gathering of his nephews and nieces at a banquet, where he asked, "Emperor Wu entrusted Shan T'ao with one of the Three Ducal Offices (i.e., director of instruction), and with the presidency of the Board of Civil Office. But when it came to bestowing gifts, it was never more than a catty (*chin*) or a tenth of a pint (*ko*). Would he have had a purpose in doing so or not?"
Hsüan answered, etc.

79. Hsieh Lang said to Yü Ho, "Everybody's coming to your place this evening for conversation; you'd better strengthen your walls and ramparts!"
Yü replied, "If Wang T'an-chih is coming, we'll wait for him 'with a single division.'¹ But if Han Po is coming, we'd better 'cross the river and burn our boats behind us!'"²

¹Cf. *Tso-chuan*, Hsüan 12 (Legge V, 317): Chih-tzu broke through the enemy lines with a single division.

²Ibid., Wen 3 (Legge V, 236): When the Earl of Ch'in attacked Chin, he crossed the Yellow River and burned his boats behind him.
(Liu Chün quotes Tu Yü's third-century commentary to explain this was to demonstrate they would fight to the death.)

80. Li Ch'ung continually sighed over not being met with an offer of a post. The governor of Yang Province, Yin Hao,¹ knowing that Li's family was poor, asked him, "Are you able to cramp your ambition within the confines of one hundred square *li* (i.e., a prefecture)?"
Li replied, "The sighs of the Song, 'The Northern Gate' (*Pei-men*),² have long been heard on high. Does a hard-pressed monkey fleeing through the forest have the leisure to pick his tree?"

68 TALES OF THE WORLD

Yin accordingly offered him Shan Prefecture (Chekiang). (CS 92.22ab; TPYL 414, 485)

[1]In his biography (CS 92.22ab), it is Ch'u P'ou who offers him the post.

[2]"Songs," No. 40:

> I go out at the Northern Gate,
> My sad heart grieving.
> I am in want and poor;
> No one knows my trouble.

Liu Chün explains that the song is a satire on the plight of an official who has not achieved his ambition.

81. When Wang Hu-chih arrived at Yin Islet in Wu-hsing Commandery (Chekiang)[1] and looked about, he remarked, "It's not just that it makes a man's feelings more open and clean, but one is also aware that even the sun and moon shine brighter here."

[1]WHC: Seventy li east of Yü-ch'ien Prefecture is Yin Islet. To one side of the islet is White Rock Mountain (Pai-shih shan), whose sheer cliffs rise upward four hundred feet. Yin Islet is situated in the lower waters of the numerous mountain streams. From Yin Islet upstream as far as the prefectural seat is a dangerous passage entirely made up of rocks and rapids and not navigable by boat. But from Yin Islet downstream the water course is without danger, so travelers congregate there.

82. Hsieh Wan was made governor of Yü Province (N. Anhui) and inspector-general of military affairs for the four provinces of Ssu, Yü, Chi, and Ping.[1] When he was newly appointed and about to go westward to his post, people at the capital entertained him at farewell parties for several days in succession, so that Hsieh was exhausted and his head nodded. At this point Kao Sung went directly over to his seat and took the occasion to ask, "Now that you have an imperial commission as a provincial governor, you will have to keep order on the western frontier.[2] How do you propose to administer your government?"

Hsieh spoke in a general way of his intentions, and Kao proceeded to read him a lecture on administration and the use of power which went on for several hundred words. After that Hsieh finally rose from his seat.

When Kao had left, Hsieh, running after him, called out, "A-ling! (Kao's baby-name) you really have talent of a sort!" By this means he was able at last to quit his seat.[3] (CS 71.16a)

[1]See TCTC 100.3168. The designation of these northern provinces (properly in Honan and Shansi) as Hsieh's domain of operation was a kind of "government in exile," since Eastern Chin territory at the time (358) did not actually extend north of Shou-ch'un in northern Anhui, where Hsieh was to be stationed.

[2]I.e., the frontier along the borders of the non-Chinese states of Former Yen (307-370) to the north and Former Ch'in (351-394) to the northwest. Since Chien-k'ang was east of the Yangtze River, everything on the opposite bank was "west."

[3] In Kao Sung's biography (CS 71.16a) Kao finds Hsieh lying down in his room resting from his strenuous farewell parties and lectures him on the art of administration. Hsieh then gets up and shouts at Sung, "A-ling, are you *sure* you have any talent or capacity?"

83. When Yüan Hung became sergeant-at-arms to the General Pacifying the South, Hsieh Feng (stationed in Kwangtung), his friends in the capital escorted him as far as Lai Village (south of Chien-k'ang). As he was about to part from them, since he himself felt sad and hesitant, he sighed and said, "The hills along the Yangtze River are so far off, they actually have the appearance of already being ten thousand *li* away!" (WH 38.11b., Li Shan's comm.)

84. Sun Ch'o wrote a poetic essay on "Fulfilling My Original Resolve" (*Sui-ch'u*),[1] and built a house in Ch'üan-ch'uan (Chekiang), claiming he had experienced the lot of one who "stops when he has had enough."[2] In front of his study he planted a pine tree, which he constantly banked up and tended with his own hands.

Kao Jou, who at the time was living in the neighborhood, said to Sun, "It's not that your pine tree isn't elegant, but just that it's eternally useless for pillars and beams, that's all."

Sun retorted, "Even though maples and willows are large enough to fill your embraces, what are *they* good for, either?"[3] (CS 56.16a; SLF 24; TPYL 953)

[1] SSHY Comm. quotes the preface of the poetic essay from SCFH: When I was young I admired the Way of Lao-tzu and Chuang-tzu, and have looked up to their free and elegant manner (*feng-liu*) for a long time. But moved by the words of the worthy wife of Tzu-chung of Wu-ling (during the Warring States period she persuaded her husband not to accept a ministry in Ch'u, but to flee with her instead to another state to become a gardener), I have become disillusioned and have come to my senses. I have built a house on five *mou* of land on the slope of Long Mountain (Ch'ang-fu) in the Eastern Mountains (Chekiang), surrounded by dense woods. Compared with sitting amid decorated curtains or listening to the playing of bells and drums (i.e., court ceremonial), how could these pleasures be mentioned in the same year?

[2] *Lao-tzu* 44: The one who knows when he has had enough will never be disgraced, and he who knows when to stop will never be in danger.

[3] To get the full cutting edges of this exchange, one has to be aware that Sun's posture as a recluse, symbolized by the pine, was taken by Kao to be shirking his duty as a "pillar of state." See, however, the ironic turn in SSHY XXVI, 16, below. Kao Jou's presumably genuine withdrawal from the world, on the other hand, was known by all to have been motivated by the very worldly attachment he felt for his lovely wife (symbolized by maples and willows), from whose embraces he is said not to have been able to part. See below, SSHY XXVI, 13.

85. Huan Wen rebuilt the walls of Chiang-ling (Hupei) so that they were exceedingly beautiful.[1] Assembling a group of guests and underlings, he took them out to the ford of the Yangtze River to gaze at

the walls from a distance, and said, "If there's anyone here who can describe these walls, he shall have a reward."

Ku K'ai-chih, who at the time was a guest and among the company, described them thus:

> "From a distance I gaze at the storied walls,
> Their vermilion towers like sunset clouds."[2]

Huan immediately rewarded him with two female slaves. (*TPYL* 176)

[1]In 345 Huan Wen was appointed General Pacifying the West and governor of Ching Province, with headquarters in Chiang-ling, on the northern bank of the Yangtze, west of Wu-ch'ang (Hupei).

ChingCC: The walls of the administrative seat of Ching Province (i.e., Chiang-ling), overlooking the Han (*sic*) River, were built by the Prince of Lin-chiang (Liu Jung, d. ca. 156 B.C.). The prince was summoned to court, and as he was going out by the North Gate, the axle of his carriage broke. An old man wept and said, "My prince is departing never to return." From that time on they never opened the North Gate again. (The prince later committed suicide; see *HS* 53.3a.)

[2]An allusion to the storied palaces of the transcendents in the mythical K'un-lun Mountains of the far West. See *Huai-nan-tzu* IV, 56.

86. Wang Hsien-chih once said to Wang Kung, "Yang Hu was a fine man just for himself, and for no other reason. What, after all, had he to do with other men's affairs? In that respect he wasn't even the equal of the dancing girls who performed for Ts'ao Ts'ao's spirit on the Bronze Sparrow Terrace (T'ung-ch'üeh t'ai)."[1]

[1]See Liu Chün's Comm., citing the "Last Will and Testament of Ts'ao Ts'ao" (*WWIL*): Let my concubines and dancing girls all gather on the Bronze Sparrow Terrace (in Yeh, No. Honan), and let them set up there a six-foot bed with gauze curtains, and on the first and fifteenth of the month let them perform facing the curtains.

87. When the monk Chih Tun first saw Ch'ang-shan, Long Mountain, in Tung-yang Commandery (Chekiang),[1] he remarked, "How level and gently sloping!"

[1]*KCTTC*: The mountain is gently sloping and long, so the prefecture takes its name from the mountain.

88. When Ku K'ai-chih returned to Chiang-ling from K'uai-chi (Chekiang),[1] people asked him about the beauty of its hills and streams. Ku replied,

> "A thousand cliffs competed to stand tall,
> Ten thousand torrents vied in flowing.
> Grasses and trees obscured the heights,
> Like vapors raising misty shrouds."

(*CS* 92.35a; *CHC* 5)

[1]Ku had asked for a leave of absence to return to his native K'uai-chi while serving as an aide in Yin Chung-k'an's administration of Ching Province about 392. See below, *SSHY* XXV, 56.

II SPEECH AND CONVERSATION 71

89. When Emperor Chien-wen died, his son, Emperor Hsiao-wu (Ssu-ma Yao, r. 373-396),[1] who was ten or so years old, succeeded him. Even up until evening of the funeral day he had not gone up to the coffin to weep. His attendants informed him, "According to the usual practice, Your Majesty should go up to weep."
The emperor replied, "When grief comes, then I'll weep. Who cares about 'the usual practice'?" (CS 9.18a)

[1]SMTWCC: Before Hsiao-wu's birth Emperor Chien-wen had consulted a book of omens which said, "The rule of the House of Chin will be utterly brilliant (ch'ang-ming)." When Emperor Hsiao-wu was born (362), it was just beginning to grow bright in the east, therefore they took the time of his birth for his given name, Yao (Brilliance, Dawn), but at the time those in attendance forgot to report it. When the emperor asked about it, they responded with his given name. Moved to tears, the emperor exclaimed, "I never dreamed that the "Brilliance" (Ch'ang-ming, Yao's courtesy name) of our house would appear immediately!"

90. Emperor Hsiao-wu was about to have an exposition of "The Book of Filial Piety" (Hsiao-ching), and the elder and younger Hsieh brothers (Hsieh An and Hsieh Shih), together with several other persons, were rehearsing the exposition in a private room.[1] Ch'e Yin was diffident about asking too many questions of the Hsiehs, and remarked to Yüan Hung,[2] "If I don't ask any questions, then the 'virtuous sound' of the answers will go to waste, but if I ask too many questions, then I'll be overburdening the two Hsiehs."
Yüan replied, "When did you ever see a bright mirror wearied by frequent reflections, or a clear stream roiled by a gentle breeze?" (CS 83.15a; IWLC 55; PTSC 97; TPYL 617, 717)

[1]HCYC: On the ninth day of the ninth month of the third year of the Ning-k'ang era (375), the emperor (then in his thirteenth year) was having an exposition of the "Book of Filial Piety." The vice-president of the Court Secretariat, Hsieh An, was presiding. The president of the Board of Civil Office, Lu Na, together with the personal attendant, Pien Tan, were reading. The imperial attendant, Hsieh Shih, and the clerk of the Board of Civil Office, Yüan Hung, were both holding the text (i.e., making the explanations). The clerk of the Central Secretariat, Ch'e Yin, and the capital intendant, Wang Hun**, were selecting the passages (i.e., asking questions).

[2]The Yüan Yang (= Ch'iao) of the text is an inadvertence, since Ch'iao died in 347, twenty-eight years earlier. I have emended to agree with HCYC; see the preceding note.

91. Wang Hsien-chih said, "Whenever I travel by the Shan-yin road (in K'uai-chi Commandery),[1] the hills and streams naturally complement each other in such a way that I can't begin to describe them. And especially if it's at the turning point between autumn and winter, I find it all the harder to express what's in my heart." (SLF 5; TPYL 25)

[1]KCTTC: The town of Shan-yin lies on the shady (yin = north) side of the mountains (shan), hence the name.

72   TALES OF THE WORLD

> *KCCC*: In the K'uai-chi area there is an especially large number of famous mountains and streams, where peaks tower upward, lofty and precipitous, disgorging and swallowing clouds and mist; where pines and junipers, maples, and cypresses rise with mighty trunks and gaunt branches; and where lakes and pools lie mirror-like and clear. After seeing it, Wang Hsien-chih exclaimed, "The beauty of the hills and streams is such that, etc."

92. Hsieh An once asked his sons and nephews, "Young people, after all I have nothing to do with your affairs, yet why am I just now wanting you to become fine people?"[1]

No one had anything to say except Hsieh Hsüan, who replied, "It's just like wanting to have fragrant orchids or jade trees growing by the steps or courtyard, that's all." (*CS* 79.12b; *TPYL* 961)

[1] In *CS* 79.12b the story is prefaced with the statement that Hsieh An had just been teaching and admonishing the young people.

93. The monk Chu Tao-i[1] was fond of manipulating and adorning sounds and expressions. When he was returning from the capital (Chien-k'ang) to the Eastern Mountains (Chekiang), after he had passed through Wu-chung (Soochow) it chanced that snow began falling, though it was not very cold.

On his arrival the monks asked about what had befallen him along the road, and Tao-i replied,

> "The wind and frost, of course, need not be told,
> But snow 'first gathering'[2]—how dark and dense!
> Villages and towns seemed of themselves to whirl and dance
> While wooded hills then naturally turned white."

[1] *MTSMTM*: Tao-i's biography (cf. *KSC* 5, *Taishō* 50.357b):

> With galloping speed he freely speaks
> In words that surely are not vain.
> Only one like Master I
> Is generous to overflowing,
> Like an orchard in spring
> Bearing fragrance and blossoms;
> Stems and branches, pliant and lush,
> With boughs and trunk, luxuriantly leafed.

[2] See "Songs," No. 217: "Just as that falling snow,/ First gathering, becomes sleet . . ."

94. While Chang T'ien-hsi was governor of Liang Province (Kansu) he claimed independent rule over the western frontier.[1] Subsequently (376) he was taken captive by Fu Chien and was employed by him as personal attendant. Later (383) at Shou-yang (Anhui)[2] they were both defeated by Eastern Chin, and Chang came to the capital where he was much valued by Emperor Hsiao-wu for his ability. Whenever he came into the emperor's presence for conversation it would always be for the entire day.

Someone who was rather jealous of him and was present on one of these occasions[3] asked Chang, "What is there in the North that's valuable?" Chang replied,

"Fruit of the mulberry, sweet and fragrant,
Mellowing the *ch'ih-hsiao* bird's[4] astringent voice;
Pure curds of milk (*lao*)[5] to nourish human nature,
Releasing it from jealous thoughts."

(CS 86.34b; TPYL 973; IWLC 87)

[1] Actually it was T'ien-hsi's father, Chang Chün, who had founded the Former Liang state. T'ien-hsi ruled it from 364-376.

[2] The battle site is usually located on the Fei River, a tributary of the Huai. See, however, a provocative challenge to the traditional importance attached to this battle in Michael Rogers, "The Myth of the Battle of the Fei River (A.D. 383)," *T'oung Pao* 54 (1968), 50-72.

[3] In Chang's biography (CS 86.34b) the questioner is identified as Ssu-ma Tao-tzu, Prince of K'uai-chi. In IWLC 87 it is the emperor who asks the question. In any case, the tone is condescending.

[4] See "Songs," No. 299:

> Fluttering are those flying *hsiao*
> Gathering in the grove by the pool.
> After eating our mulberry fruit,
> They soothe us with lovely cries.

[5] *HHCS*: In Ho-hsi (Shensi-Kansu) the cattle and sheep are fat, and the curds (*lao*) produced there are exceptionally fine and good. They merely pour out the curds and place them on a piece of rawhide, where they do not break up or scatter at all.

95. While paying homage at Huan Wen's grave (at Ku-shu, in Kiangsu), Ku K'ai-chih composed the following verse:

"The mountain has crumbled, the boundless sea
   run dry;
The fishes and birds--on what will they rely?"

Someone asked him, "Since you were dependent on Huan Wen and held him in such high esteem,[1] may we have a glimpse of your manner of mourning him?" Ku replied,

"My nose was like the long wind (*kuang-mo*)[2] over the
   northern steppe;
My eyes like the bursting forth of a dammed-up river."

According to another account he said,

"My voice was like reverberating thunder smashing
   the mountains;
My tears like an overturned river flooding the sea."

(CS 92.34b)

[1] *SMTWCC*: While Ku K'ai-chih was serving as Huan Wen's aide he was treated with great affection and intimacy.

[2] Literally, the "broad and boundless" wind. Cf. *Tso-chuan*, Chuang 28 (Legge V, 114), "The broad and boundless territory of the Ti barbarians will serve as a capital for Chin (Shansi)." Liu Chün cites a subcommentary on the above passage, the *CCKIY*: "Separated by forty-five days from the Non-surrounding (*pu-chou*) Wind (i.e., the northwest wind, the Broad and Boundless Wind arrives. 'Broad

74 TALES OF THE WORLD

and boundless' means very great and full, namely, the north wind. Some call it the Cold Wind (han-feng)." See SW, under feng, "wind."

96. Since Mao Hsüan was confident of his talents and prowess, he frequently used to say, "I'd rather be an orchid plucked, or jade broken, than artemisia in profusion, or mugwort in full bloom."[1]

[1]Cf. Yen Yen-chih's fifth century "Commemorative Essay Offered to Ch'ü Yüan (Chi Ch'ü Yüan wen) in WH 60.16a: Orchids are plucked for fragrance; jade broken for its fine grain." Li Shan's comment alludes to an earlier version of this remark of Mao Hsüan in the YL. Ch'ü Yüan's original remark, to which all these allude, is found in Li-sao, vv. 155-156 (Hawkes, Songs of the South, p. 32):

When orchids and iris fade, they are no longer fragrant;
When the ch'üan and hui wilt, they become mere rushes.
How have yesterday's fragrant grasses
Today become artemisia and mugwort!

97. When Fan Ning became grand warden of Yü-chang Commandery (Kiangsi), on the eighth day of the fourth month "invitation of the Buddha,"[1] he sent congratulatory placards (pan) to the local monasteries. All the monks were in doubt whether or not to make a reply. But a young novice in the last seat of the assembly said, "When the Bhagavān was silent, it signified approval."[2]
The congregation followed his counsel.

[1]Ch'ing-Fo, The ceremony of bathing the infant Buddha, symbolizing the invitation to return to earth, is celebrated in most northern Buddhist communities on the eighth day of the fourth lunar month, which is designated as the Buddha's birthday.

[2]See also Vimalakīrti-nirdeśa 3, 9 (Taishō 14.539c, 14.551c) for precedents of silence. Apparently some response was normally expected on the reverse side of such placards. See below, SSHY IV, 103. The monks' dilemma was that, although they were flattered, their vows forbade direct contact with officials. See Leon Hurvitz, "'Render unto Caesar' in Early Chinese Buddhism," Sino-Indian Studies 5 (1957), 2-36.

98. There was an evening gathering in the studio of the grand tutor, Ssu-ma Tao-tzu. At the time the sky and the moon were bright and clear, without even a slender trace of mist. The grand tutor, sighing, declared it to be a beautiful sight.
Hsieh Chung, who was among those present, remarked, "In my opinion, it's not as beautiful as it would be with a wisp of cloud to touch it up."
The grand tutor thereupon teased Hsieh, saying, "Are the thoughts you harbor in your heart so impure that now you insist on wanting to pollute the Great Purity of Heaven (t'ai-ch'ing)?"[1] (CS 79.20b; IWLC 25)

[1]For a discussion of this Taoist term, see Pao-p'u'tzu XV, 70, and Fukui Kōjun, Dōkyō no kiso-teki kenkyū, Tokyo, 1952, p. 154.

99. Commander Wang[1] was extremely fond of Chang T'ien-hsi, and once asked him, "As you have observed the various people who have crossed the Yangtze River and are now settled here and there throughout the area southeast of that river, what would you say is great or outstanding about the traces they have left? How would you say these latter-day gentlemen compare with those of the old days in the Central Plain?"

Chang replied, "Those who study and probe into matters obscure and remote are carrying on the tradition of Wang Pi and Ho Yen. Those who are complying with the times and revising the system of laws do so in the manner of Hsün I and Hsün Hsü and Yüeh (?Kuang).

Wang then asked, "Your experience was ample; why did you allow yourself to come under the control of Fu Chien?"[2]

Chang replied, "The Positive Force (Yang) was dissipated, and the Negative Force (Yin) had come to rest; therefore 'Heaven's course'[3] became 'Difficulty at the Beginning' (Chun) and 'Obstruction' (Chien).[4] 'Stagnation' (P'i) and 'Ruin' (Po)[5] became its signs. Was that sufficient cause for blame?"

[1] The Wang Chung-lang of the text cannot be either Wang T'an-chih (d. 375), who is usually identified by that title, or Wang Shu* (d. ca. 330), whom Yang Yung suggests, since Chang T'ien-hsi did not come south until 383.

[2] Fu Chien annexed Former Liang in 376.

[3] I.e., the destiny of the state. See "Songs," No. 229: "Heaven's course is trouble and distress."

[4] "Book of Changes," Hex. 3, Chun, "Difficulty at the Beginning." The T'uan Commentary explains: "The hard (Yang) and the soft (Yin) begin to interact: a difficult birth." (Wilhelm II, 33.) Hex. 39, Chien, "Obstruction." The T'uan explains: "Chien means trouble: danger lies ahead." (Wilhelm II, 226.)

[5] Ibid., Hex. 12, P'i (Ch'ien above and K'un below), "Stagnation." T'uan: "Heaven and earth do not interact: the myriad creatures are blocked." (Wilhelm II, 85.) Hex. 23, Po, "Ruin." T'uan: "Po means ruin. The soft is transforming the hard: misfortune." (Wilhelm II, 141.)

100. Hsieh Chung's daughter, Yüeh-ching, was married to Wang Kung's son, Yin-chih, and the heads of the two households were extremely fond of each other. When Hsieh, who had been serving as the grand tutor's (Ssu-ma Tao-tzu) senior administrator, was dismissed, Wang immediately took him on as his own senior administrator with concurrent responsibility for Chin-ling Commandery (Kiangsu). Since the grand tutor already resented Wang Kung, and did not want to let him have Hsieh, he took the latter back as consulting aide. Outwardly he made a pretense of retaining him for his talents, but in reality he did it to alienate him from Wang.

After Wang's defeat (398),[1] the grand tutor was walking around the walls of the Eastern Villa[2] after having taken a five-mineral powder. All his underlings were by the south gate in anticipation, waiting to greet him. After he arrived he said to Hsieh, "In the case of Wang Kung's plot, they say it was you who laid his plans for him."

Hsieh, without ever showing the slightest expression of fear, adjusted his tablet (*hu*) and replied, "Yüeh Kuang once said in a similar situation, 'Would I exchange five sons for one daughter?'"³

The grand tutor, satisfied with his answer, raised his cup and urged him to drink with the words, "Ver-ry fine! Ver-ry fine!"

¹In 397 Wang Kung, in collaboration with Huan Hsüan and Yin Chung-k'an, accomplished a coup d'etat in which the faction of Ssu-ma Tao-tzu was temporarily overthrown, and Tao-tzu's favorite, Wang Kuo-pao, was executed. In the autumn of the following year, however, Wang was captured by loyalist troops and killed, together with his younger brother and five sons.

²*TYC*: West of the wall of the Eastern Villa was the mansion of Emperor Chien-wen (Ssu-ma Yü), which he had occupied while he was Prince of K'uai-chi. To the east of this was the villa of Prince Hsiao-wen (i.e., Ssu-ma Tao-tzu; it was built in 395, see *TCTC* 108.3420). When Tao-tzu became governor of Yang Province (in 396), he continued to live in his former residence, so it was popularly called the "Eastern Villa."

³See above, No. 25. Hsieh's five sons were Hsün, Chan, Hui, Chüeh, and Tun.

101. After Huan Hsüan had returned to the capital on his way home from I-hsing (Kiangsu),¹ he had an interview with the grand tutor, Ssu-ma Tao-tzu. The grand tutor was already drunk, and as there were many guests at the party, he asked somebody, "Huan Wen recently wanted to start a rebellion! What about it?"²

Huan Hsuan prostrated himself and was not able to rise. Hsieh Chung, who at the time was serving as Tao-tzu's senior administrator, raised his tablet and replied, "Of course Lord Hsüan-wu (Huan Wen's posthumous title), in deposing a stupid and benighted emperor and establishing a sage and enlightened one,³ surpassed in merit both I Yin and Huo Kuang. All the various and assorted proposals will be decided upon by the sage judgment of the emperor."⁵

The grand tutor said, "I understand, I understand." And immediately raising his cup, he said, "Grand Warden Huan, a toast to you!"

As Huan went out, Ssu-ma Tao-tzu apologized for his intemperate remark. (*CS* 64.14ab)

¹He had been grand warden there in 396 and in disappointment soon retired to his native Chiang-ling (Hupei).

²Huan Wen, Hsüan's father, had attempted to usurp the throne before his death in 373. Ssu-ma Tao-tzu was not only accusing Hsüan's father of treason but used the taboo name of the deceased--a gross impropriety.

CATC: When Huan Wen was in Ku-shu (Anhui, 373), he ridiculed the court, demanding the Nine Bestowals. Hsieh An had the clerk of the Board of Civil Office, Yüan Hung, prepare the draft, and showed it to the vice-president, Wang Piao-chih. Piao-chih, the color rising to his face, cried, "Sir, how can you talk to me about a matter like this!"

An calmly asked if he had a plan.

Piao-chih said, "I hear his illness is already quite serious. Just delay the matter a bit longer." An followed his advice and therefore did not carry out the Bestowals.

II SPEECH AND CONVERSATION   77

³Huan Wen had deposed the Duke of Hai-hsi (Ssu-ma I**, r. 366-371) and replaced him with Emperor Chien-wen (Ssu-ma Yü, r. 371-372). See above, No. 59.

⁴I Yin was a minister under the Hsia who assisted the first Shang king, T'ang (r. 1766-1754 B.C.) in overthrowing the Hsia state. Later he also exiled T'ang's unworthy grandson, T'ai-chia (r. 1753-1721 B.C.). Huo Kuang was the younger brother of the illustrious Han general, Huo Ch'ü-ping. Following the dying wish of Emperor Wu (r. 140-87 B.C.), Kuang helped place Emperor Wu's son, Emperor Chao (r. 86-74), on the throne. After Emperor Chao's death, observing the misrule of another of Emperor Wu's sons, the Prince of Ch'ang-i, Kuang deposed him in favor of Emperor Hsüan (r. 73-49).

⁵A reminder that the reigning emperor, Hsiao-wu (Ssu-ma Yao, r. 373-396), being the son of Emperor Chien-wen, whom Huan Wen had established, would not be inclined to welcome aspersions against Huan Wen's loyalty.

102. When Huan Wen moved his headquarters to Nan-chou (i.e., Ku-shu, in Anhui, A.D. 371), he ordered the streets and crossroads laid out level and straight. Someone said to Wang Hsün, "When your grandfather, Chancellor Wang Tao, was first rebuilding Chien-k'ang (Nanking),¹ not having any model to follow, he ordered it laid out all twisted and turning—quite inferior to this."
Wang Hsün replied, "It was precisely in this that the chancellor was astute, for the land southeast of the Yangtze River is cramped, not at all like the Central States of the North. If he'd had the streets and crossroads laid out long and straight, then in a single glance one could see everything. Therefore he had them 'twisting and turning, zigging and zagging,'² as though to make them impenetrable."

¹CYC: After Su Chün had been executed and his rebellion crushed (329), the capital was in ruins. Wen Ch'iao proposed moving the capital to Yü-chang (Kiangsi), in order to get back to prosperity and normalcy immediately. The gentlemen of the court and the powerful families of the three Wu cities (K'uai-chi, Wu-hsing, and Tan-yang, in Chekiang and Kiangsu), felt that the capital should be moved to K'uai-chi. Wang Tao alone maintained, "The capital should not be moved. Chien-yeh (the name during the Wu period), and its predecessor, Mo-ling (the name during Ch'in and Han), and the ancient site before that, all had memorials proposing them as suitable seats for imperial or royal rule. Furthermore, Sun Ch'üan (first ruler of Wu, r. 222-252) and Liu Pei (first ruler of Shu, r. 221-223) both maintained it to be the home of kings. Even though today it is in ruins, we should cultivate the principle of 'putting the people to work and letting them come; returning them to their homes and resettling them' ("Songs," No. 181, and preface), thus calming the feelings of the masses. The 'walls a hundred *tu* high will all rise again' (ibid). Why should we be distressed, supposing that we can't restore it?" In the end it became a prosperous and peaceful city, thanks to Wang Tao's policy.

²Cf. Ssu-ma Hsiang-ju (d. 117 B.C.), "Poetic Essay on the Upper Grove Hunting Preserve" (*Shang-lin fu*), WH 8.1b.

78 TALES OF THE WORLD

103. Huan Hsüan once went to call on Yin Chung-k'an while the latter was taking a siesta in the apartment of a concubine. Yin's servants made excuses for him but did not notify him. Huan later mentioned this incident to Yin, who replied, "I wasn't sleeping at all; and even if I had been, how do you know I wasn't 'honoring worthiness more than sex'?"[1]

[1] See "Analects" I, 7 (Legge I, 140). K'ung An-kuo*'s (ca. 154 B.C.) comment, quoted by Liu Chün, explains, "If a man were fond of worthiness with the same passion that he is fond of sex it would be a good thing."

104. Huan Hsüan asked Yang Fu, "Why does everybody prize the speech of Wu?"[1]
Yang replied, "It must be because of its seductiveness and frivolity."[2]

[1] I.e., the artificial court language used in the southern capital (Chien-k'ang) during the period of division (317-589), which attempted to preserve the old pronunciation of the Western Chin court at Lo-yang before its fall in 311. It is usually contrasted with its northern counterpart as being "lighter" and "clearer." See below, SSHY VI, 29, and R. Mather, "A Note on the Dialects of Lo-yang and Nanking during the Six Dynasties," in Chow Ts'e-tsung, ed., Wen-lin, Madison, 1968, esp. pp. 250-251.

[2] There may be an intentional pun involved, since an alternative reading might be: "Everybody gives weight (chung) to Wu speech because it's insubstantial (yao) and floating (fu)."

105. Hsieh Hun asked Yang Fu, "Why is it that Confucius in calling Tzu-kung a 'vessel,' specified the hu-lien?"[1]
Yang replied, "No doubt because it was a vessel used for making contact with the spirits."[2]

[1] "Analects" V, 3 (Legge I, 173). The sacrificial vessel, hu-lien, is defined in SW and Li-chi XII, 2, as well as in Cheng Hsüan's second-century A.D. comment on this passage, as a vessel used in the ancestral temple to hold offerings of millet, called hu in Hsia times and lien in Shang. It was originally made of wood, the "jade" classifier having been added later. In Chou times it was replaced by a bamboo vessel called fu-kuei. Old Chinese **g'o-lian and **piwo-kiwəg are probably binomes whose etymology was no longer understood in Han times; even the identity of the vessels was probably unknown by then.

[2] Tzu-kung was the disciple who complained, "The Master's discourses on moral cultivation may be heard, but we never get to hear what he has to say about human nature or the Way of Heaven." See "Analects" V, 12; Legge I, 177. Perhaps it was this side of his nature to which Yang Fu was alluding.

106. After Huan Hsüan had usurped the throne (early in 404), the imperial couch sank down slightly into the ground, and all the ministers turned pale. But the personal attendant, Yin Chung-wen, came forward

and said, "It must be because Your Majesty's sage virtue is so profound and weighty that even the massive earth is unable to carry it."¹
His contemporaries applauded him for this. (CS 99.21b)

¹This is a parody of *Chuang-tzu* V, 23b (Watson, p. 71), "There is nothing heaven does not cover, or that earth does not carry."

107. After Huan Hsüan had usurped the throne he was about to reassign the quarters of the palace staff, and asked his attendants, "Where should the department of the Tiger-swift Commander of the crown prince's guard be located?"
Someone¹ answered, "There's no such department."
At the time such an answer was deemed an exceptionally flagrant case of lèse majesté.
Hsüan asked, "How do you know there isn't?"
The man replied, "P'an Yüeh stated in the preface to his 'Poetic Essay on the Mood of Autumn' (*Ch'iu-hsing fu*): 'Holding simultaneously with the office of assistant to the grand marshal the office of Tiger-swift Commander, I lived in the palace in the department of the cavalier attendant-in-ordinary.'"²
Hsüan, sighing with admiration, gave his approval. (WH 13.3a, Li Shan's comm.)

¹*LCCCC*, cited in the *SSHY* Comm., identifies the nameless interlocutor as the author's (Liu Ch'ien-chih) own elder brother, Liu Chien-chih, who merely suggested it would be proper for the Tiger-swift Commander to follow the precedent of P'an Yüeh. There was no question of lèse majesté.

²For the preface, see *WH* 13.3a (trans. in von Zach, *Die Chinesischen Anthologie*, Cambridge, 1958, I, 193): In the fourteenth year of the Chin (278), when I was in my thirty-second year and just starting to turn gray, I was serving as assistant to the grand marshal (Chia Ch'ung), holding simultaneously the office of Tiger-swift Commander, and living in the department of the cavalier attendant-in-ordinary, etc.

108. Hsieh Ling-yün was fond of wearing a straw hat mounted on a bent shaft.¹ The recluse K'ung Ch'un-chih said to him, "Since you wish to still your mind and be lofty and remote from the world, why can't you avoid the appearance of a bent-shaft canopy?"
Hsieh replied, "Isn't it the man who's afraid of his shadow who's not yet able to forget his anxieties?"² (*MCYC*, chung)

¹Reconstructions of this hat are conjectural. From this context it would appear to have been attached somehow to the shoulders by a bent shaft without touching the head, like the bent-shaft canopy used on the chariots of the great. See the reconstruction in Morohashi, *Dai Kan-Wa jiten* V, 953c.

²*Chuang-tzu* XXXI (Watson, pp. 348-349): The Old Fisherman said to Confucius . . . "There was a man who was afraid of his shadow (a Taoist image for fame) and who hated his footprints (an image for overt acts in the world), who kept running away from them. But the more often he lifted his feet, the more footprints there were, and the faster he ran, the more his shadow never left him. Supposing

that he was still too slow, he ran faster and faster and never rested, and in the end he used up his strength and died. For him not to have understood that by staying in the shade he could have put an end to his shadow, or that by staying still he could have eliminated his footprints, was foolish indeed . . .

"If you would cultivate your heart-mind and preserve your reality and turn back from external objects and from reliance on others, then you will never be bound by them. But if you don't cultivate your own person, but look instead for something from other people, aren't you, too, just another one of those who are preoccupied with externals?"

CHAPTER III

Affairs of State 政事

1. While Ch'en Shih was magistrate of T'ai-ch'iu Prefecture (Honan), one of his clerks once fraudulently claimed that his mother was ill in order to get a leave of absence. When the truth was discovered Ch'en arrested the clerk and sentenced him to death for it. His superintendent of records requested permission to visit the jail and investigate the man's numerous other crimes, but Ch'en replied, "To deceive one's superior is disloyal, and to make one's mother ill is unfilial. There aren't any greater crimes than disloyalty and unfilialness. Even if you were to investigate the man's numerous other crimes, would you find anything worse than these?"

2. While Ch'en Shih was magistrate of T'ai-ch'iu Prefecture, there was a thief who had killed a rich man and had been caught by members of the rich man's household. Ch'en had not yet arrived at the scene of the crime when on the way he heard that among the common people there was a mother who had abandoned her child on the grass receiving mat and had not picked it up. Turning his carriage around, he immediately went to take care of the case. His superintendent of records remonstrated with him, saying, "But the thief is more important; he should be the first to be tried and punished."

Ch'en replied, "So a robber killed a rich man. How can that be compared to harming one's own flesh and bone?"[1]

[1] In the Commentary Liu Chün observes that this story is told about Chia Piao (fl. ca. 158 A.D.; see *HHS* 97.25b). He never heard it attributed to Ch'en Shih.

3. When Ch'en Chi was in his eleventh year he went to call on a certain Master Yüan.[1] Master Yüan asked him, "While the worthy head of your family (Ch'en Shih) was magistrate of T'ai-ch'iu Prefecture, he was praised by everyone far and near. How did he conduct himself?"

Chi replied, "While my father was magistrate of T'ai-ch'iu he curbed the strong with rectitude and fortified the weak with goodness. Since he was accommodating to what was most comfortable for each, as time went on he became more and more respected."[2]

Master Yüan said, "I myself in the past was once magistrate of Yeh Prefecture (Honan) and did precisely these things. I don't know whether your father was imitating me or whether I was imitating him."

Chi replied, "The Duke of Chou and Confucius appeared in different generations, yet in their dealings, in activity as well as in repose, they were in all respects the same. The Duke of Chou had never studied under Confucius, nor had Confucius studied under the Duke of Chou."

[1] Liu Chün, after consulting numerous histories of the Later Han, was unable to identify anyone named Yüan who had ever been magistrate of Yeh.

[2] *YHHC*: While Ch'en Shih was magistrate of T'ai-ch'iu Prefecture, his administration was orderly without being severe, for which the common people respected him.

4. When Ho Shao became grand warden of Wu Commandery (Soochow), at first he did not go outside the gate, and the various clans in Wu-chung held him in contempt. They put an inscription on the gate of his headquarters which read,

> "The K'uai-chi cock[1]
> Can't even croak."

When he got word of it, Ho purposely went out. Walking as far as the gate, he turned back to look. Then he asked for a brush and added the following lines,

> "I may not croak,
> Lest I kill Wu folk."

Thereupon he went to their various castles and made an investigation of all the officials and soldiers privately employed by the Ku and Lu clans, and of the escaped criminals sheltered by them, and reported the matter in detail to the throne. The guilty thus exposed were extremely numerous. Lu K'ang was serving at the time as inspector-general of Chiang-ling (Hupei). It was only after he had made a special trip down to the capital (Chien-yeh, modern Nanking) to plead with Sun Hao (r. 264-280) that he was able to get them pardoned.

[1] Ho was a native of K'uai-chi (Chekiang).

5. Because his capacities were ample, Shan T'ao was looked up to by the court, and though his years were past seventy, he was still entrusted with temporal responsibilities.[1] Youths from noble families like Ho Ch'iao, P'ei K'ai, and Wang Chi all sang his praises. Someone wrote on a pillar in Shan T'ao's offices,

> "East of the office there is a large ox;
> Ho Ch'iao at the halter,
> P'ei K'ai at the hocks,
> Wang Chi scratching and tickling--it can't
>   relax."[2]

Some say it was P'an Ni who wrote it.

[1]He was appointed vice-president of the Imperial Secretariat between 272 and 279, when he was 67 to 74 years old, and concurrently held the post of president of the Board of Civil Office.

YYCS: When Shan T'ao was in his seventeenth year (221), one of his kinsmen said to Ssu-ma I, "Shan T'ao will be one of those who will rule the realm with your sons, Shih and Chao."

Ssu-ma I asked him in jest, "How did your insignificant clan get possession of this keen-witted fellow?"

T'ao was fond of *Chuang-tzu* and *Lao-tzu*, and was on good terms with Hsi K'ang. Once (ca. 247) while he was serving as an administrator in Ho-nei Commandery (Honan), he was doing night duty at the palace with Shih Chien (d. ca. 291). T'ao got up in the night and kicked Chien, saying, "What a time to be sleeping! If you knew the grand tutor (Ssu-ma I) were lying abed, what would you think?"

Chien replied, "When a chief minister doesn't attend the dawn audience for three days, they hand him an order telling him to go back to his mansion to nurse his illness. Why are you worried about it?"

T'ao said, "Ha! Is Master Shih so safe between the horses' hooves?" and resigning his duty, he departed.

Eventually (249) there occurred the Ts'ao Shuang affair (when Ts'ao and his clique fell), and T'ao thereafter went into hiding and made no contact with worldly affairs. Later he moved successively through the offices of president of the Board of Civil Office, vice-president of the Imperial Secretariat, junior tutor to the crown prince, and director of instruction. He died in his seventy-ninth year and was given the posthumous title, Marquis K'ang.

[2]*WYCS*: At first when Shan T'ao became president of the Board of Civil Office, P'an Yüeh (*sic*), who was a member of the board, opposed him, and secretly composed a ditty about him which went,

> "East of the office there is a large ox,
> Wang Chi at the halter,
> P'ei K'ai at the hocks,
> Ho Ch'iao pricking and goading--it can't relax."

CLCHL: When Shan T'ao occupied the presidency of the Board of Selection, he was disappointed and frustrated, so this saying was handed down about him.

6. When Chia Ch'ung was first codifying the laws and ordinances (in 264), he went in company with Yang Hu to consult the grand tutor, Cheng Ch'ung. Cheng told them, "The stern, bright precepts of Kao Yao[1] are not to be fathomed by one of my dim stupidity."

Yang replied, "His Highness's (Ssu-ma Chao)[2] wish was to have you make them a bit more liberal and generous."

Thereupon Cheng set down in a general way his ideas.

[1]The traditional founder of laws and penalties under the Sage-king Shun. See "Book of Documents" I, 2.20 (Legge III, 44-45), and *Tso-chuan*, Chao 14 (Legge V, 656); cf. also No. 26, below.

[2]*HCYC*: Some time earlier Ssu-ma Chao had commissioned Hsün Hsü, Chia Ch'ung, P'ei Hsiu, and others to sort out and establish the rites and ceremonies, laws and ordinances. In all cases they first consulted Cheng Ch'ung before putting them into operation.

7. Shan T'ao's selections for public office which he had made throughout his career had practically run the gamut of the various offices, and of those he had recommended none had ever fallen short in ability. In every case where he had written an estimate of a candidate's ability it proved to be exactly as he had stated. It was only in the case of the appointment of Lu Liang, who had been appointed by imperial command, that exception was taken to Shan's advice. He had contested it, but his advice was not followed. Liang was indeed eventually ruined through taking bribes.[1]

[1]*CCKT*: Lu Liang was treated with intimacy by Chia Ch'ung. While Shan T'ao was left vice-president of the Imperial Secretariat (between 272 and 279), he was also in charge of selections. T'ao's own conduct of affairs differed from Ch'ung's; nevertheless, since Ch'ung was respected by Emperor Wu (Ssu-ma Yen, r. 265-290), in all matters of selection and recommendation he would consult Ch'ung, but Ch'ung never got what he wanted. Some busybody advised Ch'ung, "You ought to put in one of your own men as president of the Board of Civil Office to participate with Shan T'ao in the selection and recommendation of the candidates. If the opinions of the two don't agree and a compromise can't be worked out, then you could simply not call in Shan T'ao in making selections, and thus really get to state what's in your heart."

Ch'ung felt this to be good advice, and accordingly recommended Liang as "just, loyal, and without self-interest."

T'ao felt that Liang would disagree with his own opinions, and in addition feared that his assistance would be unsatisfactory, so he repeatedly recommended Liang as "fit to be left assistant chancellor, but not capable of selecting officials."

Emperor Wu would not consent to this, whereupon T'ao resigned on the pretext of illness and returned home. After Liang was in office, as predicted, he proved incapable of making satisfactory selections, and after becoming involved in a scandal, was relieved of his post.

8. After Hsi K'ang had been executed, Shan T'ao recommended K'ang's son, Shao, for curator of the palace library.[1] Shao consulted Shan T'ao on whether he should take the post or remain in retirement, and Shan replied, "I've been thinking about it on your behalf for a long while. 'If even heaven and earth and the four seasons have their periods of decrease and increase, how much more do men!'"[2]

[1]*SKCS*: Emperor Wu ordered the selection of a curator of the palace library. Shen T'ao wrote in his recommendation, "Hsi Shao is just and unceremonious, warmhearted and intelligent. He has a cultivated mind, and in addition understands phonology. In time he will become a great asset, but for now he should first serve as a clerk in the library." The emperor replied, "If Shao is as you say, then he can be curator. It's not appropriate anymore having him be a clerk."

CCKT: Twenty years after Hsi K'ang met his end (i.e., in 282), Shao was recommended for office by Shan T'ao.

WYCS: At the time, because Shao's father, K'ang, had been sentenced to death, the officials in charge of selection dared not recommend him. But in his twenty-eighth year (i.e., 280, *sic*) Shan T'ao recommended his employment. Emperor Wu issued a special order making him curator of the palace library.

CLCHL: Shao was afraid he might not be tolerated if he were to remove the coarse garments of his retirement, and therefore consulted with Shan T'ao about it.

[2] See "Book of Changes," Hex. 55, Feng, T'uan comm. (Wilhelm II, 321): The sun at midday begins to set; the moon at the full begins to wane. If heaven and earth are now full, now empty, and decrease or increase with the seasons, how much more do men!

9. While Wang Ch'eng was grand warden of Tung-hai Commandery (Shantung), a petty official stole some fish from a pond. When the superintendent of records pressed charges against him, Wang replied, "The parks of King Wen (twelfth cent. B.C.) were shared with the masses.[1] Are the fish in the pond after all really worth grudging?" (*MCYC*, chung; *PSLT* 28; *CS* 75.2b)

[1] See *Mencius* I, 2.2 (Legge II, 153ff.).

10. While Wang Ch'eng was grand warden of Tung-hai Commandery a petty official seized and brought in a man who had violated the curfew. Wang asked the man, "Where were you coming from?"

He replied, "I was coming home from taking instruction at my teacher's house and wasn't aware of how late it was."

Wang said, "To flog a Ning Yüeh[1] in order to establish an awesome reputation is, I'm afraid, no basis for the administration of government." Whereupon he ordered the petty official to escort the man and enable him to get home. (*MCYC*, chung; *CS* 75.2b-3a)

[1] *LSCC* (XXIV, 5, p. 314): Ning Yüeh was a peasant of Chung-mou (Honan) who toiled bitterly at his plowing and planting. Once he remarked to his friend, "What can I do to escape from this bitter toil?"

His friend replied, "There's nothing so good as study. Study thirty years, and you'll make it."

Ning Yüeh said, "I'd like to do it in fifteen. While others are resting, I'll not dare rest; while others are sleeping, I'll not dare sleep."

So he studied fifteen years and became the tutor to Duke Wei of Chou (r. 425-404 B.C.).

11. (In 328) when the boy-emperor Ch'eng (Ssu-ma Yen* r. 326-342) was in Shih-t'ou (west of Chien-k'ang),[1] Jen Jang, in the emperor's presence, seized the personal attendant, Chung Ya, and the general of the right guard, Liu Ch'ao. The emperor cried out in tears, "Give me back my personal attendant!"

Jang, disregarding the imperial command, decapitated Ch'ao and Ya.

After the uprising had been suppressed, T'ao K'an, who had a longstanding friendship with Jang, wanted to have him pardoned. Now Hsü Liu's son, Yung (who had been involved in Su Chün's revolt through his father), was an exceedingly fine man, and all the court dignitaries wanted to spare him. But if they spared Yung, then they had no recourse but to spare Jang as well, for T'ao K'an's sake, so they

asked to have both men pardoned. But when the matter was presented to
the throne the emperor said, "Jang is the one who killed my personal
attendant; he may not be pardoned."
All the dignitaries felt the young ruler could not be disobeyed,
so they decapitated both men. (CS 70.21b)

> [1] It seems that during Su Chün's occupation of Chien-k'ang in 328,
> the emperor, who was then seven years old, was removed to the port
> of Shih-t'ou, west of the capital, where he was held a virtual
> prisoner. Early in the following year, after Su Chün's death, mem-
> bers of the emperor's bodyguard, Chung Ya and Liu Ch'ao, planned
> to spirit the young emperor out of Shih-t'ou to join the loyalist
> forces to the west, but were caught and killed by the rebel gener-
> al Jen Jang before they could accomplish their mission. (Chung Ya
> PC; TCTC 94.2956-2966)

12. When Chancellor Wang Tao was appointed governor of Yang Province
(Kiangsu-Anhui-Chekiang), several hundred guests gathered to give him
a warm welcome. Everyone looked happy except a guest from Lin-hai
(Chekiang) named Jen[1] and several Central Asiatics (Hu), who were not
fully at ease. For this reason the chancellor came over, and as he
passed by Jen remarked, "When you came to the capital, Lin-hai then
was left without any people!"
Jen was greatly cheered by this, whereupon Wang passed by in front
of the Central Asiatics, and, snapping his fingers,[2] said, "Lân-dźi̯a,
lân-dźi̯a!"[3] All the Central Asiatics laughed together, and the whole
company was delighted.

> [1] YL: Jen, whose given name was Yü, was serving at the time as an
> official at the capital (Chien-k'ang), and was among Wang Tao's
> guests.
>   CYC: Wang Tao was attractive and responsive in his personal re-
> lations, and there were few who were ever put off by him. Even
> casual acquaintances or ordinary guests, the moment they saw him,
> would for the most part find themselves becoming completely open
> and sincere with him, and stated themselves that they were treated
> by Tao just as if they were old friends.
>
> [2] Cf. Ta pi-ch'iu san-ch'ien wei-i ching ("Sutra of Three-thousand
> Regulations for Bhikṣus"), Taishō 24.915c: There are five things
> to be observed on entering the door at night: (1) on the point of
> entering one should stand still, snap his fingers three times, and
> enter without letting the door make any sound . . . etc.
>
> [3] This is evidently a Chinese approximation for some Central Asian
> or Prakrit version of the Buddhist Sanskrit greeting, Rañjanī
> meaning something like "Good cheer." Jao Tsung-i's suggestion in
> Yang Yung, SSHY chiao-chien, Hong Kong, 1969, p. 136, that it
> stands for araṇya, "Peace!" is less plausible, since the accented
> first syllable would not normally be lost in transcription, and
> Chinese *dź'i̯a would not normally transcribe Sanskrit ṇya.

13. Grand Marshal Lu Wan once went to see Chancellor Wang Tao to consult about some matter, and later without warning took a different
course of action. Wang thought it odd that he should have acted like
this, and later asked Lu about it. Lu explained, "Your ability is

superior and mine deficient, so at the time I didn't know what to
say. But afterward I realized what you advised was impracticable,
that's all."

14. Chancellor Wang Tao came once (in 326) during the summer months
to Shih-t'ou (the port of Chien-k'ang) to call on Yü Liang. Yü was
just then busily engaged in his affairs, so the chancellor said,
"Surely during the hot season it's permissible to reduce your work a
little?"
  Yü replied, "If *you* were to neglect *your* affairs, the whole realm
would also find it unsatisfactory."

15. During Chancellor Wang Tao's last years he was somewhat less attentive to his affairs. He merely gave his approval to all petitions
and memoranda that came to him. He himself said with a sigh, "People
say I'm too lax; but those that come after me will miss this laxity."[1]

[1]*HKLC*: Wang Tao held office during three reigns (Emperor Yüan, r.
317-322; Emperor Ming, r. 323-325; and Emperor Ch'eng, r. 326-
342), and kept a continuity through both peaceful and perilous
times. His administration of the government was liberal and mild,
and in all matters followed a simple and easy course. For this
reason he left behind him an amiable reputation.

16. T'ao K'an was by nature frugal and strict and conscientious in
his work.[1] While he was governor of Ching Province (Huan-Hupei) he
ordered the shipbuilding officers to save all the sawdust regardless
of whether there was much or little. At the time nobody understood
the purpose of this. Later at a New Year's assembly, it happened that
the skies had just cleared after a heavy snowfall. On the front steps
of the audience hall it was still wet after the snow had been removed, so they used all the sawdust to cover them, yet T'ao offered
no objection whatsoever.
  Whenever the shipbuilding officers used bamboo, he always ordered
them to save the butt ends, piling them up like mountains. Later,
when Huan Wen led an expedition against Shu (in 347) and was outfit-
ting the ships, they used them all to make nails.
  It is also told how on one occasion he was issuing bamboo punting
poles when one of the foremen took the poles, roots and all, to serve
just as they were for pole ends. After that T'ao employed him at an
advance of two ranks. (*TPYL* 29; *TCTC* 93.2935)

[1]*CYC*: T'ao K'an was scrupulous in everyday affairs and conscien-
tiously devoted himself to agriculture. Even men in the army ranks
would all be encouraged and urged by him to work in the fields.
Whenever anyone brought a gift of food he would always ask where
it came from. If it had been produced by the man's own labor he
would thank him cheerfully and give him gifts in return, but if it
had been gotten from someone else he would reprimand the man and
give it back. In this way soldiers and peasants were encouraged to
work in the fields, and every family supplied enough for men's
needs.
  He was by nature meticulous and fond of interrogations, somewhat like the honest judge, Chao Kuang-han (fl. 86-74 B.C.). Once

he ordered the setting out of some willow trees. The inspector-general, Hsia Shih, stealthily removed the ones he had set out by the West Gate of Wu-ch'ang (Hupei). K'an later went out of the city in person and stopped his carriage at Shih's gate. He asked Shih, "These are the willows from the West Gate of Wu-ch'ang. Why did you steal them?"

Shih in fear and trembling confessed his crime. The three armies under K'an's command acclaimed his enlightened judgment.

K'an was conscientious and proper and exerted himself unstintingly. He was in addition fond of supervising and offering encouragement to others. He once said, "Life for the people means being conscientious. If even the great sage Yü begrudged an inch of shadow on the sundial, when it comes to ordinary people, they ought to begrudge a tenth of an inch! How can they afford to take their ease? If while living a man is of no benefit to his own times, and after his death leaves no reputation for posterity, this man has repudiated himself. Furthermore, the frivolities of Lao-tzu and Chuang-tzu have nothing in common with the model sayings of the Former Kings, and one dare not practice them. A gentleman ought to straighten his robe and cap and conduct himself with dignity and decorum. What business has anyone cultivating a reputation by his disheveled hair and calling himself great and untrammeled?"

CHS: T'ao K'an often checked up on his assistants and underlings. If he found any playing pieces for the gambling games *chaupar* or *po-i*, he would throw them away, crying, "*Chaupar* was created by Lao-tzu when he entered the land of the Western barbarians. It's nothing but a foreign game. And as for *go* (*wei-ch'i*), it was used by Yao and Shun to teach their imbecile sons. *Po-i* was invented by the tyrant Chou. You gentlemen are the vessels of the state. How can you act like this? If when the king's business is slack you're worried about being bored, why don't the civil officers among you read books, and the military practice archery?" Those who discussed it had no means of altering T'ao's injunctions. (Cf. *CS* 66.12b-13a; *TCTC* 93.2935.)

17. While Ho Ch'ung was serving as governor of K'uai-chi Commandery (before 341), Yü Ts'un's younger brother, Chien, was superintendent of records for the commandery. Observing that Ho was becoming worn out from interviewing visitors, Chien wanted to petition to refuse ordinary visitors and to have a member of the household staff exercise his discretion in selecting the ones who might be admitted. When he had finished writing the petition he showed it to Ts'un. Ts'un, who at the time was Ho's senior assistant, was just then having his meal with Chien, and said to him, "Your petition is extremely good. Wait till I'm through eating and I'll make some suggestions."

When the meal was over he took a brush and signed the petition. Afterward he said, "If you could get a keeper of the gate like Kuo T'ai,[1] it should be as petitioned, but where will you get a man like him?"

Chien accordingly refrained from sending it up.

[1] *(Kuo) T'ai PC*: Kuo T'ai had a perspicuous understanding of human abilities. All the gentlemen within the realm whom he had recommended or ranked, some as youths and some in his home village,

later became outstanding and accomplished men--more than sixty persons in all. He himself wrote a book in which he discussed the basis of selecting officials; but before it had gained currency it encountered the disorders (i.e., the Yellow Turban Revolt) and was lost.

18. Wang Meng, Liu T'an, and the monk Chih Tun[1] came in a body to visit Ho Ch'ung. Ho was reading documents and letters and paid no attention to them. Wang said to him, "We've come today along with Chih Tun for a visit, hoping you would lay aside ordinary duties and join us in some abstruse conversation. How does it happen that we find you just now with bowed head reading this stuff?"
Ho replied, "If I didn't read 'this stuff,' how would you fellows manage to survive?"[2]
Everyone considered this a fine answer.

[1] Ch'eng Tu-yüan, "SSHY chien-cheng" (quoted in Yang, SSHY chiao-chien, p. 141), notes that the monk must have been Fa Shen, since Chih Tun had not yet come to the capital when Ho Ch'ung was active at court (ca. 343). Chih Tun remained in the K'uai-chi area until 362, before taking up residence in the capital. However, there is no pressing reason to assume either that this incident took place at the capital or in 343.

[2] CYC: What Ho Ch'ung, on the one hand, and what Wang Meng and Liu T'an, on the other, liked and esteemed, were poles apart. For this reason Ho was ridiculed by his contemporaries. (Cf. the similar anecdote below, SSHY XXV, 24.)

19. While Huan Wen was governing Ching Province (ca. 345) he wanted very much to have his virtue extend throughout all the area of the Yangtze and Han rivers, and he was therefore ashamed to employ harsh punishments to intimidate his subjects.[1] On one occasion a clerk was being flogged and the rod merely passed over his vermilion robe of office. Wen's son Huan Hsin, who was young at the time, came in from outside and said, "Just now I passed by the courtroom and saw a clerk being flogged. They were clearing away the cloud roots above and sweeping off the earth footings below." He meant to make fun of the fact that the rod made no contact.
Huan Wen replied, "I'm still sorry it was so severe." (PTSC 45; TPYL 65; SWLC, pieh 16, 22)

[1] (Huan) Wen PC: In the first year of the Yung-ho era (345) Huan Wen was moved from Hsü Province (N. Anhui and Kiangsu) to become governor of Ching Province. While he was in the province he was liberal and mild, and the common people were content with him.

20. While Emperor Chien-wen (Ssu-ma Yü) was chancellor (between 361 and 371), affairs moved so slowly it took years before anything got done. Huan Wen was extremely upset over his dilatoriness and continually prodded him. The emperor replied, "'In one day ten thousand decisions';[1] how can I hurry?"

[1] See "Book of Documents" I, 4.5 (Legge III, 73).

21. After Shan Hsia quit his post as grand warden of Tung-yang (Chekiang),¹ Wang Meng approached Emperor Chien-wen (then Prince of K'uai-chi) with a request for the commandery,² saying, "Since I will be succeeding a 'ferocious administration,'³ I may achieve order with 'harmonious calm.'"⁴

¹According to his biography in CS 43.8b, Shan Hsia died in office as grand warden of Tung-yang.

²Wang Meng's biography (CS 93.10b) mentions that late in his life (he died in 347) he sought the post of grand warden of Tung-yang but did not get it.

³Cf. "Record of Rites" IV, 56 (Legge, Li Ki I, 191): "An oppressive administration is more ferocious than tigers."

⁴Cf. Chuang-tzu XVI, 4b-5a (Watson, p. 172): At this time the Yin and Yang were harmonious and calm, ghosts and spirits were undisturbed, and the four seasons attained their proper spacing . . . This is called "achieving unity."

22. (In 346) when Yin Hao had just begun his term as governor of Yang Province (Kiangsu-Anhui-Chekiang),¹ Liu T'an went on a journey. The day was barely growing late when he had his servants get out his bedding. When someone asked his reason he replied, "The governor is strict; I don't dare travel at night."

¹CHS: At the beginning of the Chien-yüan era (343), Yü Liang (d. 340) and his younger brother (Ping, d. 344) and Ho Ch'ung (d. 346) and others had died, and Emperor Chien-wen, in his capacity as General Controlling the Army and Regent (i.e., in 346; see TCTC 97.3070) summoned Yin Hao to replace Ho Ch'ung as governor of Yang Province, in compliance with his reputation among the common people.

23. In the time of Hsieh An¹ (373-385) many soldiers and camp followers who had deserted or become vagrants had come near the capital and had sneaked in among the boats moored below the southern bank (of the Ch'in-huai River).² Someone wished to make a simultaneous search to round them up, but Hsieh would not permit it. He said, "If we didn't make room to accommodate this crowd, how could this be the capital?" (TPYL 156)

¹I.e., after Huan Wen's death in 373, when Hsieh became president of the Court Secretariat and held the principal power at court until his death in 385.

²HCYC: After the Central Plain was lost and in disorder, the people became separated from their native localities. During the restoration south of the Yangtze River, where powerful families were monopolizing the land, some displaced persons drifted and became separated from their families, and the registry of their names was lost. Midway in the T'ai-yüan era (ca. 383), because they were defending the border against a powerful Ti barbarian (i.e., Fu Chien), they rounded up the people, and in the three Wu commanderies (Tan-yang = Nanking, K'uai-chi, and Wu-hsing = Soochow) a thorough investigation was made with a view to straightening out their proper places of registry. Among those so rounded up from

time to time were recluses who had been living in retirement among mountains and lakes and had come to the capital.

The General of the Rear, Hsieh An, was at the time entertaining some guests, when someone in the company remarked, "We ought to apprehend those missing persons who have been given shelter or are in hiding."

An always governed his subjects with generosity and kindness, overlooking petty details. Furthermore, since a powerful bandit was invading the realm, he felt it inappropriate to increase the people's perturbation, so he replied, "What you're worried about is merely the large number of vagrants. But if it were otherwise, how could this be the capital?" The questioner looked ashamed.

24. When Wang Ch'en was a clerk in the Board of Civil Office he was once writing a draft of the selections for office. Just as he was about to present it, Wang Min came in, and Ch'en briefly took it out to show him. After Min got hold of it he proceeded on his own to change nearly half of those selected. Wang Ch'en, himself strongly convinced that Min's choices were good, rewrote the draft and presented it forthwith.

25. Wang Hsün and Chang Hsüan-chih were good friends. After Wang became grand warden of Wu Commandery (Soochow), someone asked his younger brother, Wang Min, "Now that Hsün is grand warden of the commandery, what are the morals and administration like?"

Min replied, "I don't know what his administration or his moral influence is like; only that his fondness for Chang Hsüan-chih is more flourishing every day, that's all."

26. When Yin Chung-k'an was about to go to Ching Province (Hunan-Hupei) as governor (in 392), Wang Hsün asked him, "The virtuous consider preserving themselves whole to be praiseworthy,[1] and the good take not harming others to be reputable. But nowadays anyone who governs the Chinese people occupies an office of killing and slaughter. Doesn't this go against your basic principles?"

Yin replied, "When Kao Yao created a system of punishments and penalties,[2] he did nothing unworthy, and when Confucius occupied the office of minister of crime,[3] he never did anything unkind."

[1]See "Record of Rites" XXV, 36 (Legge, Li Ki II, 229): Our parents gave birth to us with our limbs intact. If a son returns his body to them intact he may be called filial.

[2]See above, No. 6, n. 1.

KSK: The chief justice was called Kao Yao, an advisor to the Sage-king Shun. Shun recommended him to Yao, and Yao made him an official in charge of punishments.

[3]KTCY (II, 4b-5a): Confucius proceeded from minister of works in Lu to become minister of crime. In his seventh day in office he executed the rebellious great officer, Shao-cheng-Mao. (Cf. also SC 47.9b.)

CHAPTER IV

Letters and Scholarship 文學

1. While Cheng Hsüan was among the disciples of Ma Jung, he did not get a personal interview with the master for three years. Jung's top disciple merely passed on to him the master's instruction, and nothing more. Once while Jung was calculating the degrees of the celestial sphere,[1] it did not come out correctly, nor could any of his disciples resolve the problem.

Someone remarked, "The one who can do it is Cheng Hsüan." Jung thereupon summoned Hsüan and had him do the calculation. With a single turn Hsüan solved the problem and the whole company acknowledged his superiority with amazement.

When Hsüan's term of study was completed, he asked leave to return home. As he did so, Jung heaved a sigh and said, "The 'Rites' and 'Music' are both going eastward with you."[2]

Fearing lest Hsüan would overshadow his own reputation, Jung was jealous in his heart. Hsüan, for his part, also suspected that he would be pursued, so he sat beneath a bridge, above the water and resting on a pair of wooden clogs. As anticipated, Jung spun the divining board (*shih*)[3] to track him down, and announced to those about him, "Hsüan is beneath earth and above water, resting on wood. This surely means he is dead." Whereupon he called off the pursuit, and Hsüan thereby eventually managed to make his escape.[4] (*HHS* 65.3ab; *PTSC* 97)

[1] The theory of the "celestial sphere" (*hun-t'ien*) is fully discussed in Needham, *Science and Civilisation*, III, 210-224.

[2] (*Cheng*) *Hsüan PC*: When Hsüan was young he was fond of studying calligraphy and mathematics. By his thirteenth year he was reciting the Five Classics and was fond of astrology and divination and the secret art of *feng-chüeh* (divining by the direction of the wind). In his seventeenth year he observed a great wind rising, and going to the prefectural office, reported, "At such-and-such a

time there will be a conflagration." At the stated time it happened as predicted. Wise men marveled at him.

By his twenty-first year he had thoroughly mastered a host of books and had made a detailed study of the words of numerous charts and apocrypha, at the same time gaining a detailed knowledge of mathematics. He therefore quit his post and went to study under the former governor of Yen Province (S. Shantung), Ti-wu Yüan-hsien. From there he went to Chang Kung-tsu of Tung Commandery (Hopei) to take instruction in the "Rites of Chou" (*Chou-li*), the "Record of Rites" (*Li-chi*), and the "Spring and Autumn Annals" (*Ch'un-ch'iu*) with its commentaries. He had traveled everywhere and observed widely. Whenever he passed any mountain or stream he would take in its aspect in a single glance, never forgetting any of it to the end of his life.

Ma Jung of Fu-feng (Shantung) was famous as a literatus, so Hsüan went to study with him to check their agreements and differences. Since Jung was a relative of the empress (Empress Ma, consort of Emperor Ming, r. 58-75), he was arrogant in his treatment of other gentlemen, and Hsüan did not get to see him. He lived nearby and built himself a study. Later, through an intermediary, he made contact with Jung. At the time Lu Tzu-han of Cho Commandery (Hopei) was the top disciple, but whereas Hsüan by thinking solved five out of seven problems whose answers Jung did not know, Tzu-han only solved three. Jung said to Tzu-han, "You and I are no match for him."

On the eve of Hsüan's departure, Jung grasped his hand and said, "The Great Way is going eastward; do all you can for it!"

[3]For a careful reconstruction and explanation of the *shih* and its function, see Needham, *Science and Civilisation*, IV.1, 261-271.

[4]*SSHY* Comm.: Ma Jung was one of the greatest literati within the Four Seas, and clung to morality and goodness as to his bedding and clothes. Cheng Hsüan's name is listed among his disciples and he personally transmitted his teaching. Why would Jung have been jealous or acted out of deadly spitefulness? This is another case of the gossip of back alleys despoiling a great man.

2. Cheng Hsüan had wanted to write a sub-commentary on the "Tso Commentary" of the "Spring and Autumn Annals" (*Ch'un-ch'iu chuan*), but had not yet completed it. At the time, while on a trip, he met by chance with Fu Ch'ien, and they spent the night at the same inn. Neither one had known the other before. Fu was outside on his carriage explaining to someone the ideas of his own sub-commentary on the "Tso Commentary."

Hsüan listened to him for a long time, and found that for the most part Fu's ideas agreed with his own. Approaching his carriage, Hsüan said to him, "I myself have long wanted to write a sub-commentary, but haven't finished it yet. After listening to what you've just said, I find that for the most part it agrees with my own ideas, so now let me present all that I've so far commented on to you."

Thereafter it became known as "Fu's Sub-commentary" (*Fu-shih chu*).[1]

[1] In Late Han times this commentary shared equal distinction with one by Chia K'uei (30-101), and in the fourth century was commonly mentioned together with that of Tu Yü (222-284), but later fell into disuse. It was still in existence in Sui times, as it appears in the *Sui-shu* bibliographic monograph (*SuiS* 32.20b, 21a), but is now known only in quotations.

3. In Cheng Hsüan's household even the male and female slaves (*nu-pei*) were literate. Once while Hsüan was being waited on by a female slave, she failed to satisfy his wishes. He was on the point of flogging her, when she began making excuses for herself. In a rage, Hsüan had her dragged through the mire. A moment later another female slave came by and asked in the words of the Song, *Shih-wei*,

"What are you doing in the mire?"[1]

She replied, from the Song, *Po-chou*,

"I went to him and pled my cause,
But there met only with his wrath."[2]

(*IWLC* 35; *PTSC* 98; *CHC* 19; *PSLT* 6; *TPYL* 500)

[1] "Songs," No. 36.
[2] Ibid., No. 26.

4. Since Fu Ch'ien was well versed in the "Spring and Autumn Annals" and its commentaries, he was on the point of making a sub-commentary, but wanted to compare points of agreement and difference with other experts. Hearing that Ts'ui Lieh had gathered his disciples to lecture on the "Tso Commentary," he took an assumed name and hired himself out as a cook for Lieh's disciples. Whenever it came time for them to attend a lecture, he would always listen surreptitiously at a crack between the door and the wall. After he was satisfied that Lieh's interpretation could not improve upon his own, he briefly assembled the disciples and reviewed its short and long points.

Lieh, on hearing of this incident, could not guess who it might be. However, since he had long heard of Ch'ien's reputation, he suspected in his heart that it was he. Early the next morning he went to Ch'ien's room, and before the latter had awakened, called out his courtesy name, "Tzu-shen! Tzu-shen!"

Without realizing it, Ch'ien made a startled response. After that the two became fast friends. (*PTSC* 98, fragment)

5. When Chung Hui had barely finished editing his "Treatise on the Four Basic Relations between Natural Ability and Human Nature" (*Ssu-pen lun*),[1] he wanted very much to have Hsi K'ang look it over. Putting the manuscript in his bosom, [he went to the latter's house].[2] But after he had entered and was seated, he became apprehensive of Hsi's objections and kept it in his bosom, not daring to bring it out.

After he was outside the door he threw it back from a distance, then turned around and walked hastily away. (*TPYL* 365, 394; *HTC* 4)

[1] See below, Nos. 34, 51. According to *WC*, cited in the Commentary, the treatise consisted of four essays: one by Fu Chia, maintaining

that natural ability (ts'ai) and human nature (hsing) are identical (t'ung); one by Li Feng, maintaining that they are different (i); one by Chung Hui himself, maintaining that they are combined (ho); and one by Wang Kuang, maintaining that they are separate (li). The texts have been lost.

[2] The clause in square brackets is interpolated from quotations of this incident in TPYL 394 and HTC 4.

6. While Ho Yen was serving as president of the Board of Civil Office (240-249) he enjoyed both status and acclaim. Conversationalists of the time thronged the seats of his home. Wang Pi, who was then not yet twenty, also went to visit him. Since Yen had heard of Pi's reputation, he culled some of the best arguments from past conversations and said to Pi, "These arguments I consider to be ultimate. Do you care to raise any objections?"
Pi proceeded to raise objections, and after he was finished the whole company considered that Yen had been defeated. Pi then went on, himself acting as both "host" (chu) and "guest" (k'o) for several bouts (fan).[1] In every case he was unequaled by anyone else in the whole company. (IWLC 55; PTSC 98, 136; TPYL 474, 617, 698)

[1] WCHL: Ho Yen was capable in pure conversation and occupied a position of power in his time. Most of the conversationalists of the realm looked up to him as their ideal.
WSCC: When Ho Yen was young he possessed unusual talent and was skilled in discussions of the "Book of Changes" and Lao-tzu.
(Wang) Pi PC: When Wang Pi was in his teens he was already fond of Chuang-tzu and Lao-tzu, and was a competent debater and able conversationalist. He was befriended by Fu Chia, and Ho Yen admired him greatly, characterizing him in the words of Confucius, "'Those born after us are to be held in awe.' With such a person one may discuss the frontier between Heaven and Man."
Ho appointed him acting court attendant, but for Pi the conduct of affairs was basically not his forte, and he paid less and less attention to his work. Furthermore, he was inclined to use what was his forte (conversation) to ridicule others, so that he was cordially hated by his contemporaries. In addition he was, as a person, shallow and insensitive to the feelings of others . . .
During the Cheng-shih era (249) he was dismissed in a public scandal (the fall of Ts'ao Shuang's clique), and in the fall of the same year, falling prey to a pestilence, died in his twenty-fourth year. Ssu-ma Shih sighed over him for days, crying, as Confucius did at the death of Yen Hui, "Heaven is destroying me!" Thus was his loss lamented by the eminent and wise.

7. When Ho Yen's commentary on the Lao-tzu was barely completed, he went to visit Wang Pi. After observing how thorough and remarkable Wang's commentary was, he yielded to Wang's superiority, saying, "With such a person one may discuss the frontier between Heaven and Man!"
For this reason he converted what he himself had commented on into two treatises, one on the Way (tao), and one on the Power (te).[1] (SKWei 28.37a, comm.)

¹*WSCC*: In his discussion of the Way (*tao*) Wang Pi was inferior to Ho Yen in conciseness and beauty of style, but in naturalness (*tzu-jan*) he far outstripped him.

The *Sui-shu* bibliographical monograph (*SuiS* 34.3b) lists a *Tao-te lun* in two chüan by Ho Yen, and his *Tao-lun* is quoted by Chang Chan (fl. ca. 320) in his commentary on the *Chung-ni* and *T'ien-tuan* chapters of *Lieh-tzu* (IV and I).

8. When Wang Pi was barely twenty he went to visit P'ei Hui. Hui asked him, "Non-actuality (*wu*) is indeed that by which all things are sustained, yet the Sage (Confucius) was unwilling to vouchsafe any words on the subject.¹ Lao-tzu, on the other hand, expatiated on it endlessly.² Why?"

Wang Pi replied, "The Sage *embodied* Non-actuality. Furthermore, Non-actuality may not be the subject of instruction. Therefore of necessity his words applied to Actuality (*yu*). Lao-tzu and Chuang-tzu, not yet free of Actuality, were continually giving instruction about that in which they felt a deficiency." (*SKWei* 28.37a, comm.; *MCYC*, hsia)

¹"Analects" V, 13: The Master's words on culture we are vouchsafed to hear, but his words on human nature (*hsing*) and the Way (*tao*) of Heaven we are not vouchsafed to hear.

²E.g., *Lao-tzu* 11: Thirty spokes make up a wheel; but it is at the point where there is *nothing* (*wu*) where its usefulness to the carriage lies."

9. Fu Chia was skilled in talking about the Empty and Transcendent (*hsü-sheng*),¹ while Hsün Ts'an in his conversations favored the Mysterious and Remote (*hsüan-yüan*). Whenever during their conversations there was conflict due to mutual misunderstanding, P'ei Hui would arbitrate the views of both parties. Since he was familiar with the inner thoughts of both of them, he never failed to bring it about that the feelings of each were satisfied.

¹In other versions of this incident (see below), the "Empty and Transcendent" (*hsü-sheng*) is replaced by "Names and Principles" (*ming-li*).

FT: Fu Chia was already conversant with government and fond of what was proper, and moreover possessed pure principles and understood essentials. If he discussed ability and human nature, his original premises were meticulous and subtle, and few were able to equal him. Chung Hui was extremely young when Chia befriended him.

(*Hsün*) *Ts'an PC*: Hsün Ts'an was a capable conversationalist on the subject of the Mysterious and Remote (*hsüan-yüan*), and once maintained that since Confucius' disciple, Tzu-kung, had complained, "The Master's words on human nature and the Way of Heaven we are not vouchsafed to hear" ("Analects" V, 13), therefore, even though the Six Classics have survived, they are certainly nothing but the chaff and leavings of the sages. Capable conversationalists could not refute him. At the beginning of the T'ai-ho era (227) Hsün Ts'an came to the capital (Lo-yang) and conversed with Fu Chia. Chia was skilled in Names and Principles (*ming-li*), while Ts'an favored the Mysterious and Remote. Although their ultimate ideals were the same, in the heat of debate there were times when

they would be at odds and did not get each other's meaning. P'ei
Hui understood the inner thoughts of both of them and would act as
moderator between the two. In a short while Ts'an and Chia became
fast friends.

  KLC: Commissioner P'ei Hui had lofty ability and outstanding
capacity. He was skilled in conversing on the Mysterious and
Subtle (hsüan-miao).

10. Ho Yen had been writing a commentary on the Lao-tzu and had not
yet finished when he went to visit Wang Pi. Wang explained for him
the gist of his own commentary on the Lao-tzu. Ho's ideas for the
most part were inferior to Wang's, so he never got to make a sound,
except only to answer, "Quite so, quite so."
  After that he did not go on with his commentary, but composed separate treatises on the Way (tao) and the Power (te) instead.[1]

[1] See above, No. 7.

  WCHL: According to the treatises of the Juists ("Confucians"),
Lao-tzu denigrated the sages and recommended "Putting an end to
the rites and discarding learning" (Lao-tzu 19, 20). Ho Yen explained that Lao-tzu is, after all, in agreement with the sages,
and therefore composed the treatises on the Way and the Power,
which have been circulated in the world.

11. During the time of the Central Court (Western Chin, 265-316), a
certain person of the Taoist persuasion went to visit Wang Yen to
consult him on a doubtful point. It happened that on the previous day
Wang had already overextended himself, and, feeling slightly fatigued,
was not inclined to answer his question. So he said to the guest,
"Today I'm somewhat indisposed. P'ei Wei lives near here. Why don't
you go over and ask him?"[1]

[1] CCKT: When P'ei Wei conversed on a topic, he and Wang Yen never
yielded to each other.
  (Since P'ei represented the activists and Wang the quietists,
Wang's sending an inquirer to see P'ei would be like Lao-tzu sending someone to see Confucius.)

12. When P'ei Wei composed his "Treatise in Praise of Actuality"
(Ch'ung-yu lun),[1] his contemporaries joined in attacking it and raising objections, but no one could refute it. It was only when Wang Yen
came to converse with him that his arguments seemed to yield slightly.
Thereafter the others tried using Wang's arguments in raising objections, but P'ei's arguments only returned with renewed vigor.

[1] Extensive quotations from P'ei's treatise may be found in his biography (CS 35.10-13a), partially translated by Etienne Balazs in
"Entre révolte nihiliste et évasion mystique," Etudes Asiatiques 2
(1948), 27-55; trans. in Balazs, Chinese Civilization and Bureaucracy, ed. A. F. Wright, New Haven, 1964, pp. 226-254.

  CCKT: Beginning with Hsia-hou Hsüan (209-254) of Wei, Juan Chi
(210-263) and others had all composed treatises on the Way and the
Power. At a later time Yüeh Kuang (252-304) and Liu Mo (emending
the "Liu Han" of the Sung text after Yang Yung, SSHY chiao-chien,
p. 155) also embodied the Way and talked about simplicity. But
Wang Yen, while expounding on topics, was void of ability, and

Tai Ao made studying the Way his sole occupation. In the younger generation people like Yü Ai (262-311) all admired unceremoniousness and unconventionality. P'ei Wei was distressed by the morals of his age and by the exaltation of the principle of Nothingness, so he composed the two treatises, "In Praise of Actuality" and "In Honor of Non-actuality," to refute them. His ability was so vast and his allusions so wide that scholars could not trace them all.

Later Yüeh Kuang found himself at leisure with P'ei and wanted to discuss a topic with him, but P'ei's terminology and allusions were so rich and wide ranging, that Kuang, who considered that he himself embodied Non-actuality, merely laughed and did not respond.

HTCCC: P'ei Wei composed the two (above-named) treatises in order to set right the abuses of nihilism and libertinism (hsü-tan). The style and terminology were meticulous and rich, and they became famous treatises in the world.

13. When Chu-ko Hung was young he was unwilling to pursue his studies. The first time he conversed with Wang Yen he already revealed a transcendent perceptiveness. Wang commented with a sigh, "Your natural ability is most outstanding. If in addition you would only apply a little study and research, there wouldn't be a single person in whose presence you would need to feel ashamed."

Hung later read the Chuang-tzu and Lao-tzu, and when he conversed with Wang again, he was able to match wits with him on equal terms. (PTSC 98, of Chu-ko Hui)

14. When Wei Chieh was a young lad with his hair in tufts, he asked Yüeh Kuang about dreams.[1]

Yüeh said, "They're thoughts (hsiang)."

Wei continued, "But dreams occur when body and spirit aren't in contact. How can they be thoughts?"

Yüeh replied, "They're the result of causes (yin). No one's ever dreamed of entering a rat hole riding in a carriage, or of eating an iron pestle after pulverizing it, because in both cases there have never been any such thoughts or causes."

Wei pondered over what was meant by "causes" for days without coming to any understanding, and eventually became ill. Yüeh, hearing of it, made a point of ordering his carriage and going to visit him, and thereupon proceeded to make a detailed explanation of "causes" for Wei's benefit. Wei immediately began to recover a little.

Sighing, Yueh remarked, "In this lad's breast there will never be any incurable sickness."[2] (CS 43.22b-23a; TPYL 397, 739)

[1] Chou-li 6.28 (including Cheng Hsüan's comm. in parentheses): There are six kinds of dreams: 1--regular dreams (i.e., when we dream in peace, undisturbed by anything); 2--nightmares (i.e., when we dream after being frightened); 3--yearning dreams (i.e., dreams about what we yearn for while awake); 4--daydreams (i.e., dreams induced while we are still awake); 5--dreams when we are happy; and 6--fearful dreams (i.e., dreams when we are afraid).

SSHY Comm.: What Yüeh Kuang meant by "thoughts" were probably "yearning dreams" (ssu-meng); and his "causes" are probably "regular dreams" (cheng-meng).

[2] Tso-chuan, Ch'eng 10 (Legge V, 374): Duke Ching of Chin (r. 599-581 B.C.) was ill and sought a physician in Ch'in (Shensi). The

Earl of Ch'in sent the physician Huan to cure him. Before he arrived the duke dreamed that his sickness took the form of two boys, one of whom said, "That's a good physician; I'm afraid he'll hurt us."

The other one replied, "If we stay above the diaphragm and below the heart, what can he do to us?"

When the physician arrived he announced, "Your illness is incurable. It's above the diaphragm and below the heart. If I attack it directly I can't touch it; if I puncture, I can't reach it; medicine won't get to it either."

The duke replied, "You're a good physician."

15. When Yü Ai started to read the *Chuang-tzu* he opened the scroll a foot or so, then put it down, saying, "It's not the least bit different from what I've thought all along."[1] (*CS* 50.7a)

[1]*CYC*: Yü Ai himself claimed to be a follower of Lao-tzu and Chuang-tzu, saying, "I never read these books before, but in my mind I always imagined that the Ultimate Principle (*chih-li*) was like this. Now that I've seen the books, they're exactly in secret agreement with my own mind."

16. A questioner once asked Yüeh Kuang about the statement "Meanings do not reach" (*chih pu chih*).[1]

Yüeh for his part made no further detailed analysis of the words or sentence. Instead, he directly seized the handle of his sambar-tail chowry (*chu-wei*) and struck it against the table, asking, "Does it reach or not?"

The questioner said, "It reaches."

Yüeh then lifted the chowry and said, "If it reaches, then how can it be removed?"

At this point the questioner realized what he meant and accepted it. The brevity of Yüeh's statements and the perceptiveness of his ideas were all of this sort. (*TPYL* 703)

[1]*Chuang-tzu* XXXIII, 23a (Watson, p. 375). Cf. also *Lieh-tzu* IV, 48 (A. C. Graham, *The Book of Lieh-tzu*, London, 1960, p. 88) where this argument of Kung-sun Lung-tzu (ca. 320-250 B.C.) in his "Essay on Meanings and Things" (*Chih-wu lun*) is recapitulated. See also Fung Yu-lan, *History of Chinese Philosophy*, II (Princeton, 1953), 176-178, and A. C. Graham, "Kung-sun Lung's Essay on Meanings and Things," *Journal of Oriental Studies* 2 (1955), esp. 287-289.

SSHY Comm.: A hidden boat moves imperceptibly; persons passing shoulder-to-shoulder are forever parted. A single moment does not remain; in a sudden flash it comes into being and disappears. Thus the shadow of a flying bird is never seen to move; the wheel of a rolling chariot never touches the ground. Therefore, since removing the chowry did not really remove it, how could there have been any reaching? Since reaching the table did not actually reach it, how could there have been any removal? Thus, since the former reaching did not differ from the later one, the term "reaching" came into existence. And since the former removal did not differ from the later one, the term "removal" was established. But now that it has been proved that there is no removal in the world, is not removal a falsehood? And since *it* is false, can reaching be real either?

17. Previously none of the several tens of commentators on the *Chuang-tzu*[1] had ever been able to get the full essence of its ideas. Hsiang Hsiu, going beyond the earlier commentators, wrote an "Explanatory Interpretation" (*Chieh-i*) which made a subtle analysis of its marvelous contents and gave great impetus to the vogue of the Mysterious (*hsüan-feng*). His comments on the two chapters "Autumn Waters" (*Ch'iu-shui*) and "Supreme Joy" (*Chih-lo*)[2] were the only ones not completed when Hsiu died (ca. 300). Since Hsiu's sons were still in their infancy, his "Interpretation" fell into oblivion, but a separate copy still survived.

Now Kuo Hsiang was a person of mean behavior who nevertheless possessed outstanding ability. Observing that Hsiang Hsiu's "Interpretation" had not been transmitted to the world, he proceeded surreptitiously to pass it off as his own commentary, while he himself commented on the two chapters "Autumn Waters" and "Supreme Joy," and made, in addition, some alterations in the chapter "Horses' Hooves" (*Ma-t'i*).[3] For the remaining chapters he merely established the punctuation for the sentences of the text, and nothing more.

Later the separate copy of Hsiang Hsiu's original "Interpretation" was published, so today there are two versions of the *Chuang-tzu*, the Hsiang and the Kuo, whose interpretations are identical.[4] (*CS* 50.8b-9a; *WH* 21.12a, Li Shan comm.; *SWLC*, pieh)

[1]The *Sui-shu* bibliographical monograph (*SuiS* 34.36ab) lists the following commentators on *Chuang-tzu* who might have antedated Hsiang Hsiu: Ts'ui Chuan (3rd cent.), Ssu-ma Piao (240-305), Li I (late 3rd cent.), a Mr. Meng, and Li Kuei (also late 3rd cent.).

(Hsiang) Hsiu PC: Hsiang Hsiu was a friend of Hsi K'ang and Lü An, but their likes and dislikes were not the same. Hsi K'ang despised the world, remaining unfettered; Lü An was free and untrammeled, defying convention. Hsiang Hsiu, on the other hand, was basically fond of reading, for which the other two twitted him from time to time. Later, when Hsiu was about to write his commentary on the *Chuang-tzu*, he first announced his intention to Hsi K'ang and Lü An. They both said, "Does this book require another commentary? You'll only be forsaking the company of other people to do what you enjoy, that's all."

When the commentary was finished, Hsiu showed it to the two. K'ang remarked, "Have you actually beat us again?"

An cried out in surprise, "Chuang Chou isn't dead!"

Later he wrote a commentary on the "Book of Changes" (*Chou-i*). The general interpretation was acceptable, but there were discrepancies with that of the Han literati. It was not as good as the unprecedented achievement of his interpretation of the hidden meaning of *Chuang-tzu*.

HHPC: Hsiang Hsiu rambled through the works of numerous worthies, but remained disdainful of them all to the end of his life, never writing commentaries on any of them. It was only the *Chuang-tzu* which he loved. More or less following the commentary of Ts'ui Chuan, he wrote one to fortify himself against forgetting it.

CLCHL: After Hsiang Hsiu had written this interpretation, everyone who read it felt released, as if he had emerged beyond the dust of the world to peer into Absolute Mystery (*chüeh-ming*). For the first time such a one understood that beyond sight and hearing there is a divine power and abstruse wisdom which enables one to leave the world behind and pass beyond all external things. Even though such a one might again be made to become an agitated and competitive man, he would look back to view all he had traversed, and in every case with a sense of revulsion would of his own accord feel a desire to be rescued.

²*Chuang-tzu* XVII, XVIII.

³Ibid., IX.

⁴On the basis of separate quotations in Lu Te-ming's (7th cent.) *CTSW* and Li Shan's (also 7th cent.) commentary to the *WH*, Shou P'u-hsüan convincingly refutes the allegation of plagiarism on Kuo Hsiang's part. See "An Investigation of the Ancient Text of *Chuang-tzu* through the *Ching-tien shih-wen*" (*Yu Ching-tien shih-wen shih-t'an Chuang-tzu ku-pen*), *Yen-ching hsüeh-pao* 28 (1940), 95.

WSC: When Kuo Hsiang wrote his commentary on the *Chuang-tzu*, it had the greatest clarity and the most compelling ideas of any.

18. Since Juan Hsiu had an excellent reputation, the grand marshal, Wang Yen, went to visit him, and asked, "The *Lao-tzu* and *Chuang-tzu* on the one hand, and the teaching of the Sage (Confucius) on the other--are they the same or different?"

Juan replied, "Aren't they the same?" (*chiang-wu t'ung*)

The grand marshal liked his answer and appointed him his aide, so in his day he was known as "the Three-word Aide."

Wei Chieh teased him about this, saying, "For only *one* word you still would have been appointed. Why bother with three?"

Juan replied, "If this is what people in the world are looking for, then even for no words at all I would have been appointed. Why bother with one?"

Whereupon they became fast friends.¹ (*CS* 49.5b)

¹In *CS* 49.5b, the incident is attributed to Juan Chan and Wang Jung.

MSC: Juan Hsiu was fond of *Lao-tzu* and *Chuang-tzu* and was able to converse on a topic, but did not enjoy seeing vulgar people. If at times by mistake he encountered any, he would immediately remove himself and haughtily disregard them. Though his household might be without a single picul (*shih*) of rice, he was perfectly content.

When Wang Tun became minister of court ceremony, he said to Hsiu, "The assistant (*ch'eng*) to the minister of court ceremony is a post with a somewhat low salary, but you're always without food. Can you take it?"

Hsiu replied, "It's all right, I guess." Whereupon he became assistant to the minister of court ceremony and equestrian forerunner to the crown prince.

19. P'ei Hsia married the daughter of the grand marshal, Wang Yen. Three days after the wedding all the sons-in-law of the Wang family were gathered in large numbers at the P'ei home. Famous gentlemen of the day, as well as the younger members of the Wang and P'ei families, were all assembled.

Kuo Hsiang, who was among those present, challenged P'ei to a bout of conversation. Kuo's ability was extremely great, but for the first few exchanges he was not yet in stride. His marshaling of arguments was also extremely vigorous, but P'ei calmly analyzed everything Kuo had said, and the effect of his reasoning was extremely subtle, so that everyone present sighed with admiration and delight.[1] Wang Yen himself also thought it was marvelous, and said to everyone, "You fellows had better not try it, or you'll get into trouble with Our son-in-law!"[2]

[1] *TTCC*: P'ei Hsia made argumentation his sole occupation, and was skilled at expounding Names and Principles (*ming-li*). His terminology and manner were clear and incisive, cold as the notes of the zither. All who heard him speak, whether they knew him or not, would sigh in acquiescence.

[2] The term translated "Our" (*kua-jen*) was originally affected by heads of feudal states in the Chou period. Apparently aristocrats of the Six Dynasties also used it on occasions when they wished to be facetious.

20. When Wei Chieh had newly crossed the Yangtze River, he went for an audience with the generalissimo, Wang Tun. Since it was an evening session, the generalissimo had also summoned his senior administrator, Hsieh K'un. When Chieh met Hsieh he liked him immensely, and, paying no more attention whatsoever to Wang, continued a subtle conversation with Hsieh until dawn. The whole night long Wang never got a chance to get in a word.

Chieh's body had been sickly since childhood, and in the past he had always been restrained from overexertion by his mother, but that evening he was heedless in the extreme, so that afterward his illness took a turn for the worse, and he never rose again from his bed.[1] (*CS* 49.19b)

[1] *(Wei) Chieh PC*: When Wei Chieh was young he possessed prowess in Names and Principles and was conversant with the "Book of Changes" and *Lao-tzu*. Since he himself was afflicted with an emaciating illness, at first he never dared hold any debates with outsiders. At the time his friends used to sigh and say, "Lord Wei doesn't speak, yet his words always enter into Mystery" (*hsüan*; the Sung text has the synonym *ming*). In Wu-ch'ang (Hupei) he had an interview with the generalissimo, Wang Tun. As Tun conversed with him he kept sighing in admiration in spite of himself.

21. According to an old tradition, when Chancellor Wang Tao emigrated south of the Yangtze River, he conversed on only three topics: "Musical Sounds Are Without Sorrow or Joy" (*Sheng wu ai-lo*),[1] "Nourishment of Life" (*Yang-sheng*),[2] and "Words Fully Express Meanings" (*Yen chin-i*),[3] and nothing else. However, in the devious turns of conversation, whenever their relevance came up, he never failed to bring them in.

[1] I.e., Hsi K'ang's (223-262) essay on this topic. Liu Chün gives the following excerpt in the Commentary (cf. *HKC* V, 1b, Lu Hsün ed.): In different places with their separate customs, singing and lamentation are not carried on in the same way. If one were to use

them for the wrong occasions, some, on hearing the lamentation, would rejoice; others, listening to the singing, would grieve. Thus the feelings of grief or joy are undifferentiated. So now if with undifferentiated and identical feelings we produce sounds of infinite variety, is not this evidence of the relativity of meanings and sounds?

[2] I.e., Hsi K'ang's essay on this topic. Liu Chün gives the following abridgement (cf. HKC III, 4a; trans. Holzman, La vie et la pensée, 86-91): When lice attach themselves to the head they are black; when the musk deer eats the cypress he exudes fragrance. The throats of those living in precipitous places develop goiters (ying); the teeth of those living in Chin (where there are many jujubes) turn yellow . . . Are there only vapors which cause heaviness, and none which cause lightness? Or fragrances which perfume but do not prolong life? . . .

If a person could truly be impregnated with the vapor of magic mushrooms (ling-chih) and bathed in sweet springs . . . he would become self-possessed and actionless, his body subtle, his mind abstruse . . . Peradventure he could match his age with the ancient adept, Hsien-men, or compete in years with the magician, Wang Ch'iao. Why should it be impossible to nourish life?

[3] I.e., Ou-yang Chien's (ca. 265-300) essay on this topic. Liu Chün gives the following abridgement in the Commentary: When a principle is perceived in the mind, if it were not for words, it would not be clear; when objects are determined in the external world, if it were not for names, they would not be distinguished. Names change according to objects; words are transformed in dependence on principles. They may not be polarized into two. So if name and object, word and principle, are not two, then there is no word which is not fully expressive.

22. When Yin Hao was appointed senior administrator for Yü Liang,[1] as he was about to set out from the capital (Chien-k'ang), Chancellor Wang Tao held a gathering in his honor. Huan Wen, Wang Meng, Wang Shu, and Hsieh Shang were all present. The chancellor, personally rising and pushing aside the curtains, took his sambar-tail chowry from his girdle and said to Yin, "Today you and I will converse together and analyze principles."

Once they had become engrossed in pure conversation (ch'ing-t'an) together, they continued until the third watch (midnight). The chancellor and Yin both talked back and forth, while the other worthies hardly participated at all. When the two had exhausted their arguments, the chancellor said with a sigh, "In previous conversations we never knew the point toward which the source of Truth (li-yüan) would lead us back, and as far as words and analogies not being at odds is concerned, the voices of the Cheng-shih era (i.e., of Ho Yen and Wang Pi) must have been like this and nothing else."

The next morning Huan Wen said to the others, "Last night listening to Yin's and Wang's pure conversation was most excellent. Not only was Hsieh Shang far from bored; even I was mentally stimulated from time to time. But when I turned around to look at the two Wangs (Wang Meng and Wang Shu), they were as startled (*tiep-ṣap) as unfamiliar bitches."

¹The Commentary, citing YLLSM and CHS, points out that Yin was Yü's sergeant-at-arms, not his senior administrator. To add to the confusion, TCTC 95.299b records that when Yü Liang became governor of Ching Province (Hunan-Hupei) in 334, he summoned Yin Hao to serve as *secretarial aide*.

23. Once when Yin Hao saw a Buddhist sutra, he remarked, "The Truth (*li*)¹ should be in this (*a-che*)."² (TPYL 653)

¹For a discussion of the meaning of this term during the fourth century, see Demiéville, "La pénétration du Bouddhisme dans la tradition philosophique chinoise," Cahiers de l'histoire mondiale 3 (1956) 28-35.

²SSHY Comm.: The currency of Buddhist sutras in China is of high antiquity; no one knows exactly what its origins were.

MT (abridged; cf. Taishō 52.4c-5a): The Han Emperor Ming (r. 58-75) dreamed one night of a divine man whose body had the radiance of the sun . . . The next day he inquired widely of his ministers . . . and the savant Fu I replied, "Your servant has heard that in T'ien-chu (north India) there is a man of the Way, named Buddha (Fo), who can levitate and fly, and whose body has the radiance of the sun. It probably would be this god."
Whereupon the emperor . . . dispatched the general, Ch'in Ching, and the erudite, Wang Tsun*, and others, twelve in all, to the country of the Greater Yüeh-chih (Kushāna), where they copied and brought forty-two Buddhist sutras (i.e., the "Sutra in Forty-two Sections"; see below), and stored them in the Lan-t'ai Stone Chamber (of the palace library).

LHC: If we scan the works of the hundred schools, investigating and testing them all, we find that of the one hundred forty-six who became transcendent beings (*hsien*), seventy-four were already mentioned in the Buddhist sutras, therefore I (Liu Hsiang, putative author of the LHC) have edited the lives of the remaining seventy, so that the learned and broadly knowledgeable may emulate them.

SSHY Comm.: If this is so, then already during the reigns of the Han emperors Ch'eng (r. 32-7 B.C.) and Ai (r. 6-1 B.C.), there were sutras, which differs from the tradition recorded in MT.

WeiL, "Section on Western Barbarians" (*Hsi-Jung chuan*; cf. SKWei 30.29b, comm.): Within the domain of T'ien-chu is the country of Lin-erh (*Li̯əm-ńźi̯e = Lumbinī). The Buddhist sutras say that the king of this country begot the Buddha, who was his crown prince. The father was called Śuddhodana and the mother Māya. The Buddha's body and clothing were yellow in color, his hair like blue silk, his nails like bronze. His mother became pregnant while dreaming of a white elephant, and when the Buddha was born, he came out of her right side with a protuberance on his head. As he touched the ground he was able to walk seven paces. In T'ien-chu there was another divine person called Sha-lü (*Ṣa-li̯uet). Long ago, in the first year of the Yüan-shou era of the Han Emperor Ai (2 B.C.), the erudite, Ching Lü, received oral instruction in the Buddhist sutras from the I-ts'un, ambassador from the king of the Greater Yüeh-chih, who said that Buddha is this person.

(For an illuminating discussion of this passage, see Zürcher, Conquest, pp. 24-25.)

HWKS: The Hsiung-nu king, K'un-yeh, killed the king of Hsiu-ch'u, and came with his horde to surrender to Han. Emperor Wu (r. 140-87 B.C.) took his gods in the form of golden men and set them up in the Kan-ch'üan Palace. The golden men were all over ten feet tall, and since for their sacrifices the Hsiung-nu do not use oxen or sheep, but only the burning of incense and doing obeisance, His Majesty worshipped them according to the custom of their original country.

SSHY Comm.: These gods were entirely in the same category as buddhas; could it be that in the time of the Han Emperor Wu, their sutras had not yet gained currency in China, but only their gods were worshipped? On the contrary, using the evidence of Liu Hsiang's and Yü Huan's statements (in LHC and WeiL), the arrival of Buddhism by the time of Emperors Ch'eng and Ai is plain. On the other hand, the text of the "Sutra in Forty-two Sections" has survived to this day and is not spurious (see Taishō No. 784, Vol. 55, 42c-43c). Probably Emperor Ming sent to search broadly for other reports. It was not a case of their being no sutras at that time. (See also Zürcher, Conquest, pp. 21-22.)

24. When Hsieh An was young he requested Juan Yü to talk about Kung-sun Lung-tzu's "Discourse on the White Horse" (Pai-ma lun).[1] Juan discussed it for him in order to show what it meant. At the time Hsieh did not immediately understand what Juan was saying and repeatedly questioned him until he was satisfied.

At the end Juan said with a sigh, "It's not just the man who can talk who's hard to find, but precisely the man who probes for explanations who's equally hard to find."

[1]Chap. II of the Kung-sun Lung-tzu. For a brilliant reinterpretation and editing of this difficult text, see A. C. Graham, "Two Dialogues in the Kung-sun Lung-tzu: 'White Horse' and 'Left and Right,'" Asia Major (n.s.) XI, No. 2 (1965), esp. pp. 128-150.

KTT: The man of Chao, Kung-sun Lung, said, "A white horse is not a horse. 'Horse' is that whereby we designate a shape; 'white' is that whereby we designate a color. The designation of a color is not the designation of a shape. Therefore I say, a white horse is not a horse."

CHS: Juan Yü was extremely meticulous in dealing with objections.

25. Ch'u P'ou remarked to Sun Sheng, "The erudition of the Northerners[1] is profound and comprehensive, broad and all-embracing."

Sun replied, "The erudition of the Southerners is clear and penetrating, concise and essential."

Chih Tun, hearing of this, added, "Sages and worthies, of course, are those who 'forget speech,'[2] but if we're talking about people from the middle range on down, the reading of the Northerners is like viewing the moon in a bright place, while the erudition of the Southerners is like peering at the sun through a window." (TPYL 607)

[1] Though it is tempting to take the "Northerners" here as the courtiers and scholars of Western Chin (265-316), and the "Southerners" as those of Eastern Chin (317-420), I believe T'ang Ch'ang-ju is correct in identifying them as Han literati of north of the Yellow River (e.g., Cheng Hsüan), and the Hsüan-hsüeh experts of Honan to the south of it (e.g., Wang Pi). Ch'u P'ou's origins were north of the Yellow River; Sun Sheng, though from T'ai-yüan (Shansi), appears to have considered himself a "Southerner." See *Wei-Chin Nan-pei-ch'ao shih lun-ts'ung*, Peking, 1955, pp. 361-364.

[2] *Chuang-tzu* XXVI, 6a (Watson p. 302): Speech exists for its meaning. Get the meaning and forget speech.

SSHY Comm.: What Chih Tun is saying merely illustrates and completes the arguments of Sun and Ch'u. Thus if a man's erudition is broad, then it is hard for him to be comprehensive, and if it is hard to be comprehensive, his knowledge will be dim, like viewing the moon in a bright place. But if a man's erudition is narrow, then it is easy to be thorough; therefore his wisdom is bright, just like peering at the sun through a window.

26. Once while Liu T'an was conversing with Yin Hao, Liu's arguments seemed to be weakening slightly. Yin said to him, "Hey! Don't you want to be the general who was good at rising to the attack on his cloud-scaling ladders?"[1]

[1] *Mo-tzu* 50 (abridged; cf. *Mo-tzu hsien-ku*, CTCC, IV, 292-295): "Kung-shu Pan made high cloud-scaling ladders for the King of Ch'u, desiring to use them to attack Sung (Honan). When Mo-tzu heard about it, he set out from Lu (Shantung) with torn robes and bare feet, resting neither night nor day, and after ten days and ten nights arrived at Ying (the Ch'u capital in northern Anhui) . . .

He had an interview with the king of Ch'u and asked, "I hear Your Majesty is about to attack Sung. Is it true?" The king replied, "It is."

Mo-tzu said, I request that you have Kung-shu Pan construct his weapons for a mock attack upon Sung, and that I be allowed to try and defend it."

Thereupon Kung-shu Pan set up his plan for attacking Sung, and Mo-tzu encircled it with his girdle to defend it. Nine times Shu attacked, and nine times Mo-tzu repulsed him. Finding himself unable to penetrate the defenses, the king called off his men-at-arms.

27. Yin Hao once remarked, "My nephew, Han Po, has never received my verbal favors (*ya-hou hui*)."[1]

[1] Literally, "my ultramolar favors," i.e., verbal recommendations.

28. When Hsieh Shang was young he heard that Yin Hao was skilled in pure conversation, and made a special trip to visit him. Yin, who had never before clarified anything for Hsieh, outlined several topics for him in a few hundred words. Since they had excellent content and at the same time the terminology was rich and complex, Hsieh found it quite enough to stir his imagination and tax his powers of listening.

He was pouring out his spirit and overturning his mind, unaware that streaming sweat was crossing and recrossing his face.

Yin calmly said to those in attendance, "Fetch a hand towel and give it to Master Hsieh[1] to wipe his face."

[1] Liu Chün is puzzled by Yin's condescending treatment of Hsieh, and by his calling him, "Master Hsieh" (*Hsieh-lang*), a term of address usually appropriate for young boys, when actually the two were very close in age. He writes in the Commentary: "Yin Hao was older than Hsieh Shang by only three years, and belonged to the same generation. Perhaps he wished to honor his superior accomplishment, and for this reason wiped his sweat for him?"

29. Huan Wen was assembling the famous and outstanding men of the time for lectures on the "Book of Changes" (*I*),[1] and was planning to do one hexagram a day. Emperor Chien-wen (Ssu-ma Yü) was at first planning to listen, but when he heard this he turned back, saying, "Some of the interpretations will naturally be difficult and some easy. How can each lecture be limited to one hexagram?"

[1] *ICTT*: Confucius said, "The 'Changes' (*I*) means: 'simplicity' (*i*), 'transformation' (*pien-i*), and 'unchangingness' (*pu-i*). These three, after fulfilling their virtue, become the repository of the Way. 'Simplicity' is each thing's virtue. Light pervades everywhere; sun, moon, stars, and constellations are spread throughout the heavens; the Eight Trigrams follow in order; the four seasons are in harmony. 'Transformation' means that if heaven and earth are not transformed, they cannot produce the dawn; if husband and wife are not transformed, they cannot produce a family. 'Unchangingness' refers to one's proper station. Heaven is above and earth below; the ruler faces south and the subject north; the father sits while the son prostrates himself. These are their unchanging aspects. Therefore the 'Changes' represents the Way of Heaven, Earth, and Man."

IH: The name "Changes" in one word comprehends three meanings: (1) "simplicity," (2) "transformation," and (3) "unchangingness."

In the *Hsi-tz'u* of the "Book of Changes" (A12, B5; Wilhelm I, 347, 369) it says: "Ch'ien and K'un, the Creative and Receptive, are the repository of the 'Changes' . . . the gateway of the 'Changes.'"

And again (B1, A1; Wilhelm II, 351, 307-308), it says: "Ch'ien, the Creative, firmly demonstrates to men the easy. K'un, the Receptive, pliantly demonstrates to men the simple . . . Since it is easy, it is easy to know; since it is simple, it is easy to follow." This refers to the model of its simplicity and ease.

Again (B7; Wilhelm II, 374), it says: "The Way of the 'Changes' is to make frequent shifts; transforming and changing without staying still; flowing all around through the six empty spaces of the hexagrams; rising or sinking without constancy; firm and yielding alternating with each other. It may not be cast in fixed rules, but is only applicable through transformation."

This refers to the transformations of its seasonal outs and ins. Still further (A1; Wilhelm II, 301), it says: "Heaven is honorable, earth base; thus are the Creative and Receptive determined. According to their baseness or loftiness the noble or ignoble stations of

men are disposed. Movement and quiescence have their constant
times; firm and yielding are predetermined." This refers to the
unchangingness of its establishments and dispositions. If we explain the Way of the "Changes" according to these three meanings,
how broad it is! How great!

30. There was a monk who had just arrived from the North who was fond
of virtuoso discussion. He encountered Chih Tun at the Wa-kuan Temple
(in Chien-k'ang) while the latter was lecturing on the "Smaller Version" of the *Prajñāpāramitā-sūtra*.[1] At the time the monk Chu Tao-
ch'ien and the layman Sun Ch'o were also present listening to what
this monk had to say. The monk frequently posed doubts and objections,
but Chih Tun's arguments and replies were always clear and analytical,
and both his terminology and manner were so forthright that this monk
was outargued and defeated every time.

Afterwards Sun asked Tao-ch'ien, "Your Reverence (*shang-jen*) should
be a person whose fragrance may be smelled upwind.[2] How is it that
just now you didn't say anything at all?"

Tao-ch'ien smiled, but made no reply.

Chih Tun said, "It's not that white *candana* (sandalwood) isn't
fragrant, but how can it send its fragrance upwind."[3]

Tao-ch'ien caught his meaning, but maintaining his composure, did
not deign to answer.

[1]There were three versions of this sutra current during the fourth
century: (1) *Tao-hsing po-jo ching*, in 8000 ślokas, translated by
Lokaksema between 168 and 188 (*Taishō*, No. 224), and known as the
"Smaller Version" (*Hsiao-p'in*); (2) *Fang-kuang ching*, in 25,000
ślokas, translated by Moksala between 291 and 304 (*Taishō*, No.
221), known as the "Larger Version" (*Ta-p'in*), and (3) *Kuang-tsan
ching*, another translation of the "Larger Version" by Dharmaraksa
in 286 (*Taishō*, No. 222), unknown in the South until around 376.

According to Zürcher, *Conquest*, p. 140, this debate took place
between 364 and 365, when both Chih Tun and Chu Tao-ch'ien were in
Chien-k'ang.

[2]Cf. *Dhammapada* 12 (*Fa-chü ching, Taishō* 4.563b):

> Aromatic grasses, perfumed flowers,
> Breathe not their fragrance up the wind.
> But now the Way has been proclaimed abroad,
> And virtuous men (i.e., monks) send their fragrance
>   in every direction (*pien-hsiang*).
>
> The *candana* of many fragrances,
> The blue-green lotus and the perfumed flowers;
> Their fragrance, though indeed called real,
> Cannot compare with that of taking vows.

For a discussion of sandalwood, see Schafer, *Golden Peaches*, pp.
136-138.

[3]*Satyasiddhi-śāstra* 51 (*Ch'eng-shih lun, Taishō* 32.271b): Again,
some fragrances may be smelled upwind, such as that of the heavenly
paricitra tree."

31. Sun Sheng once went to Yin Hao's house, where they conversed together. Their exchanges back and forth were both hairsplitting and

insistent, and arguments of host and guest followed each other without interruption. The servants brought in food which grew cold and was rewarmed three or four times. Both men were gesticulating and pounding their sambar-tail chowries until the hairs had worn off completely and fallen all over the food, but guest and host continued until nightfall, forgetting to eat.

Finally Yin said to Sun, "Don't be a stubborn-mouthed horse, or I'll pierce your nose!" To which Sun retorted, "Don't act like a noseless ox, or I'll pierce your cheeks!"[1] (CS 82.11a; SWLC, hsü 16)

[1]HCYC: Sun Sheng was skilled in conversing on Principles and Meanings (li-i). At one time Yin Hao had monopolized the reputation as greatest conversationalist of the age; the only one who could oppose him in spirited debate was Sun Sheng, and no one else.

32. The "Free Wandering" (Hsiao-yao) chapter of the Chuang-tzu[1] had in the past always been a problem spot, where famous and worthy commentators had only been able to bore for the flavor, but from which they had never been able to extract any principles beyond those of Kuo Hsiang and Hsiang Hsiu.[2]

While Chih Tun was at the White Horse Temple (in Chien-k'ang), he held a debate with Feng Huai, in the course of which they discussed the "Free Wandering." Chih boldly marked out new principles beyond any proposed by the two above-named commentators, and established an interpretation unlike that of any of the previous worthies, entirely beyond the reach of those famous worthies in their groping for the flavor. Thereafter the chapter was always interpreted with Chih's principles.[3] (KSC 4; Taishō 50.348b)

[1]Chuang-tzu I.

[2]HYI (Chuang-tzu I, 5b-6a, comm.): Whether the P'eng-bird soars to 90,000 li, or the quail rises only to the elm and sapanwood, regardless of the difference in size, each is complying with its own nature. Since each is fulfilling its lot (fen), the free roaming of each is one and the same. However, different creatures, each in its own way, are equally dependent on something outside of themselves, and only after they get what they depend on are they free. It is the sage alone who unites mystically with other creatures and complies with the Great Transformation, who can be independent and continually unimpeded. Is he himself the only one who is unimpeded? On the contrary, he allows those who are dependent not to lose what they depend on. And if they do not lose it, then they have become identified with the Great Way.

[3]HYL: Free roaming (hsiao-yao) means the heart-mind of the Perfect Man (chih-jen). When Chuang-tzu talked about the Great Way, he used the analogy of the P'eng-bird and the quail. Because the P'eng-bird's way of life is untrammeled, it loses all particular direction in the realm beyond the body (t'i-wai). But because the quail, on the other hand, lives in the near and scoffs at the far, there is a certain complacency in the realm within its mind (hsin-nei). The Perfect Man, riding upon the correctness of Heaven, soars aloft, wandering infinitely in unfettered freedom. Since he treats

objects as objects, without being treated as an object by other objects, therefore in his roaming he is not self-satisfied. Being mystically in communion with the universe, he does not act purposefully. He is not hurried, yet he moves swiftly. Therefore in his freedom he goes everywhere. This is how it becomes "free roaming."

But if, on the other hand, one has a desire to fulfill one's own contentment, and to be content with one's own contentment, such a person in his happiness has something like natural simplicity, like a hungry man once he is satiated, or a thirsty man once his thirst is quenched. But would such a man forthwith forget all about cooking and eating in the presence of grains and cereals, or put an end to all further toasting and pledging in the presence of wines and liquors? Unless it is *perfect* contentment (*chih-tsu*), how can it be a means to free roaming?

(Liu Chün concludes that this narrow and easily gained "complacency" is the point where the interpretations of Hsiang Hsiu and Kuo Hsiang were inadequate. The interpretation of Chih Tun, on the other hand, giving a Buddhist tinge to Chuang-tzu's original concept of emancipation, was felt to be genuinely transcendent. Chih Tun's treatise, quoted above, is listed in *CSTCC* 12, *Taishō* 55.83a, with the title *Hsiao-yao yu-hsüan lun*. See Fukunaga Mitsuji, "Shi Ton to sono shūi: Tō-Shin no Rō-Sō shisō," *Bukkyō shigaku* 5, 1956, 102-104, and Ch'en Yin-k'o, "*Hsiao-yao-yu*: Hsiang Kuo i chi Chih Tun i t'an-yüan," *Ch'ing-hua hsüeh-pao* 12, 1937, 309-314.)

33. Yin Hao once went to Liu T'an's place, where the two engaged in pure conversation for a long time. Yin's argument was already slightly sagging, but his wandering verbiage never came to an end. Liu, for his part, was no longer answering him.

After Yin had left, Liu finally said, "A country bumpkin forcing himself to imitate someone else talks just like that." (*TPYL* 390)

34. Although Yin Hao's thought and study were excellent in all subjects, it was on the subject of "Natural Ability and Human Nature" (*ts'ai-hsing*) that he was uniquely expert. If someone inadvertently mentioned the "Treatise on the Four Basic Relations between Natural Ability and Human Nature" (*Ssu-pen lun*),[1] it was like having to face an impregnable stronghold with scalding moats and iron battlements.[2]

[1] See No. 5, above.

[2] *SNS*: Even though a city possessed stone walls ten *jen* (eighty feet) in height, with a scalding moat one hundred paces across, ringed with armed men one million strong; if there were no grain, it would not be able to preserve itself.

35. Chih Tun composed a "Treatise on Matter-as-such" (*Chi-se lun*).[1] When the treatise was completed he showed it to Wang T'an-chih. Wang looked it over without saying anything whatever.

Chih asked, "Are you 'understanding in silence'?[2]

Wang replied, "Since no Mañjuśrī is present, who can be appreciated?"[3]

[1] This treatise, and others quoted under different titles though possibly the same work, was the basic text for the "School of Matter as Such" (Chi-se tsung), associated with Chih Tun, which was one of six "schools" during this period of Buddhism in China. For a full discussion of these schools, see T'ang Yung-t'ung, *Han-Wei liang-Chin nan-pei-ch'ao Fo-chiao-shih* (Shanghai, 1938; reprinted, Peking, 1955), I, 254-263; Zürcher, *Conquest*, pp. 123-124; Walter Liebenthal, *The Book of Chao*, Monumenta Serica Monograph XIII, (Peking, 1948), pp. 152-157.

MKC: Now as for the nature of matter (*rūpa*), it does not exist by itself. If matter does not exist by itself, then, even though it be matter, it is nevertheless empty (*śūnya*). Therefore it is said (*Fang-kuang ching* 3; *Taishō* 8.6a; cf. *Kuang-tsan ching* 3A; *Taishō* 8.153c): "Matter itself is Emptiness; at the same time Matter differs from Emptiness." (See also Zürcher, *Conquest*, p. 123.)

[2] "Analects" VII, 2.

[3] *Wei-mo-chieh ching* (*Vimalakīrti-nirdeśa* 9; *Taishō* 14.542, footnote): Mañjuśrī asked Vimalakīrti . . . "What is the bodhisattva's entrance into the dharma gate of nonduality?"

Then Vimalakīrti was silent and said nothing.

Mañjuśrī sighed in admiration, crying, ". . . This is the *real* entrance into the dharma gate of nonduality!"

(While Chih Tun must have known only Chih Ch'ien's third-century version, translated above, Liu Chün has quoted from Kumārajīva's, which appeared in the year 406; *Taishō* 14.551c.)

36. When Wang Hsi-chih was appointed governor of K'uai-chi Principality (Chekiang), at the time of his arrival (353) Chih Tun was still living there. Sun Ch'o said to Wang, "Chih Tun is original and different, and whatever he sets his mind to, he is always excellent. Would you like to meet him?"

Now Wang himself had always possessed a forthright and uncompromising spirit and was especially contemptuous of Chih. Later, when Sun and Chih rode together to Wang's place, Wang was completely reserved and did not exchange a single word with Chih, who, after a short while, withdrew.

Later, just as Wang was on the point of setting out from his house, and his carriage was ready at the gate, Chih arrived and said to Wang, "Your Lordship, pray do not leave yet. This poor monk would have a small conversation with you." Whereupon he discoursed on the "Free Wandering" chapter of the *Chuang-tzu*,[1] in several thousand words. His eloquence and style were fresh and wonderful, like the blooming of flowers or a burst of sunlight. In the end Wang threw open his lapels and unfastened his girdle and lingered, unable to tear himself away.[2] (*KSC* 4; *Taishō* 50.348c)

[1] See No. 32, above.

[2] *CFSC*: After studying the ten stages (*ti* = *bhūmi*) in the bodhisattva's career, the dharma master Chih Tun understood sudden enlightenment (*tun-wu*) in the seventh state (*chu* = *sthiti*). After searching through the *Chuang-tzu*, he distinguished the free wandering (*hsiao-yao*) of the Sage (*sheng* = Buddha). All the famous gentlemen of the age savored the meaning of his teaching.

THL (in which Sun Ch'o compared seven monks of the fourth century to the Seven Worthies of the Bamboo Grove):

> Tun may be likened to Hsiang Hsiu
> In his refined admiration for Lao and Chuang.
> These two, though of different times,
> In spirit are mystically one.

37. On the distinctions among the "Three Vehicles" (*san-sheng*)[1] the Buddhists are confused in their interpretations, but Chih Tun's division and definition made all three brilliantly distinct. Listeners sitting below in the lecture hall all said they could explain them, but after Chih had descended from the platform and sat down and they discussed it together among themselves, it appeared they could barely get through the first two. When they entered the third they became confused.[2]

Even today, though Chih Tun's disciples have transmitted his interpretation, they still do not entirely comprehend it.

[1] *Fa-hua ching* (*Saddharmapuṇḍarīka-sūtra* 3; *Taishō* 9.13b--Liu Chün seems to be quoting from a commentary): The Three Vehicles are: (1) Sheng-wen sheng (*śrāvaka-yāna*), the Vehicle of Hearers, or Disciples; (2) Yüan-chüeh sheng (*pratyeka-buddha-yāna*), the Vehicle of the Self-enlightened; and (3) P'u-sa sheng (*bodhisattva-yāna*), the Vehicle of the Bodhisattvas, or Saviors of Others. The Hearers find the Way by being awakened to the Four Truths (*ssu-ti* = *āryasatyāni*). The Self-enlightened find the Way by being awakened to the Twelvefold Cycle of Dependent Origination (*yin-yüan* = *pratītyasamutpāda*). Bodhisattvas find the Way by practicing the Six Perfections (*liu-tu* = *pāramitā*). Thus the Arhat (*lo-han*), or Hinayānist Saint, finds the Way entirely through the Buddha's teaching. That is why he is called a Hearer. The Pratyekabuddha (*pi-chih*) finds the Way, either by understanding after hearing about Dependent Origination, or by becoming enlightened after listening to tinkling jade pendants. His spirit is able to perceive the Truth unaided. That is why he is called Self-enlightened. The Bodhisattva is a man of the Great Way. Through Expedience (*fang-pien* = *upāya*) he carries out the Six Perfections. Because of the True Teaching, he thoroughly cultivates a myriad good acts, whose merit is not for himself, but all of it for the universal salvation of others. That is why his is called the Great Way.

[2] On the analogy of a similar story in *KSC* 4 (*Taishō* 50.348c), Zürcher translates this passage as follows: ". . . they could just reach two turns to speak, but at the third turn they became confused and could not go on." *Conquest*, p. 118; see also p. 358, n. 168.

38. When Hsü Hsün was young people compared him to Wang Hsiu, which Hsü felt was very unfair. At the time all the noteworthy gentlemen, including the dharma master, Chih Tun, were gathered at the Western Temple (Hsi-ssu) in K'uai-chi (Chekiang) for an exposition of the sutras, Wang also being among them. Hsü, his mood very angry, proceeded to the Western Temple to marshal arguments with Wang, and settle with him once and for all who was superior and who inferior.

Bitterly they crushed and ground each other in debate, until Wang finally suffered a severe defeat. Hsü then took Wang's argument, while Wang took Hsü's argument, and once more they debated back and forth. Again Wang was defeated.

Afterward Hsü said to Chih Tun, "What did you think of your disciple's discussion just now?"

Chih calmly replied, "Your discussion was fine, I guess, but to what purpose was the mutual bitterness? Was it a conversation in which you were seeking the heart of Truth?"[1]

[1]*WTC*: Previously Wang Pi (226-249) had been the same age as Wang Hsiu (ca. 335-358) when he died. Therefore Hsiu's nephew (the "younger brother" of the text is an error) Hsi said with a sigh, "He has nothing to be ashamed of before his predecessor, though his age was the same."

(In *CS* 93.11a this remark is credited to Hsiu himself, on his deathbed.)

39. The monk Chih Tun once went to visit Hsieh An. An's nephew, Hsieh Lang, at the time was just a young lad with his hair in tufts. He had recently gotten up from an illness, and his body was not yet able to endure any strain. As he expounded his ideas and discussed them with Chih Tun, the debate eventually became intense on both sides. Lang's mother, Lady Wang (Wang Sui §), was behind the wall listening to them, and twice sent messengers ordering him to come back, but Hsieh An detained them both.

Lady Wang therefore came out in person and said, "This bride encountered family difficulties in her youth, and all she has to rely on for the rest of her life is bound up in this son." So saying, with tears flowing she gathered her son into her arms and took him back with her.

Hsieh An said to those seated with him, "The words and feelings of my elder brother's wife are deeply moving, and their sentiment worthy of being handed down. What a pity the court gentleman[1] wasn't here to witness them." (*CS* 79.20a; *SWLC*, hou 6)

[1]I.e., Liu Hsiang (80-9 B.C.), author of the "Lives of Virtuous Women" (*Lieh-nü chuan*).

40. Chih Tun, Hsü Hsün, and other persons were once gathered at the villa of the Prince of K'uai-chi, Ssu-ma Yü. Chih acted as dharma master (*fa-shih*) and Hsü as discussant (*tu-chiang*).[1] Whenever Chih explained an interpretation there was no one present who was not completely satisfied, and whenever Hsü delivered an objection everyone applauded and danced with delight. But in every case they were filled with admiration for the forensic skill of the two performers, without the slightest discrimination regarding the content of their respective arguments. (*KSC* 4; *Taishō* 50.348c)

[1]See above, *SSHY* II, 90.

KISMC: Chih Tun at the time was lecturing on the *Vimalakīrti-nirdeśa* (*Wei-mo chieh ching*).

41. While Hsieh Hsüan was still in mourning for his father, Hsieh I (d. 358), the monk Chih Tun went to his house to converse with him,

not leaving until nearly nightfall. Someone on the road saw him and
asked, "Sir, where are you coming from?"

Chih replied, "Today I'm coming from a bout (*ch'u*) of spirited debate with Hsieh the Mourner."

42. When Chih Tun first came out to the capital (in 362) from the East
(K'uai-chi), he lived at the Tung-an Temple.¹ Wang Meng, having worked
out beforehand his choicest arguments, and in addition having selected
the finest examples of his eloquence, went to converse with Chih,
but the latter did not offer much response. Wang set forth his ideas
in several hundred words, thinking to himself that they were the most
elegant and wonderful of all Names and Principles (*ming-li*).

Chih Tun said to him very calmly and deliberately, "You and I have
been separated many years, but your interpretations and terminology
haven't made any progress whatever."

Wang withdrew in great embarrassment. (*KSC* 4; *Taishō* 50.349a)

¹*KISMC*: While Chih Tun was living in K'uai-chi Commandery, the
Chin Emperor Ai (r. 362-365), attracted by his manner and flavor,
sent an emissary to the east to invite him to the capital. Tun
thereupon bade farewell to hills and canyons, and took the high
road to the City of the Son of Heaven.

(He remained in Chien-k'ang at the Tung-an Temple from 362 to
365. See Zürcher, *Conquest*, pp. 119-120, 149.)

43. When Yin Hao was reading the "Smaller Version" of the Prajñāpāramitā-sūtra,¹ he jotted down two hundred notations, all of them intricate subtleties and obscure problems of the age. He often wished he
might debate them with Chih Tun, but in the end he never got a chance
to do so.²

To this day (his annotated copy of) the "Smaller Version" still
survives.

¹*SSHY* Comm.: Of the Buddhist sutras which discuss Emptiness
(*śūnyatā*, i.e., the *Prajñāpāramitā-sūtras*), there is a detailed
one, and an abridged one. The detailed one is called "The Larger
Version" (*Ta-p'in*), and the abridged, "The Smaller Version"
(*Hsiao-p'in*).

(See above, No. 30, n. 1.)

²*KISMC*: Yin Hao was capable in conversing on Names and Principles.
But since he himself realized there were points he did not comprehend, he wanted to consult about them with Chih Tun. Subsequently,
to his disappointment, they never met, for which he felt profound
regret. Such was the extent of Chih Tun's appreciation and honor
among famous savants.

YL: Yin Hao found some passages in the Buddhist sutras which he
did not understand, so he sent someone to invite Chih Tun to discuss them with him. Tun, in his humble innocence, was on the point
of going, but Wang Hsi-chih restrained him, saying, "The extent of
Yin Hao's thought is profound and varied. This being the case, it
won't be easy to stand up to him. Moreover, what he himself
doesn't understand, Your Reverence may not necessarily be able to
clarify. On the other hand, even if he should submit and follow
you, your reputation still wouldn't be enhanced because of it. But

if you should make a careless blunder and disagree with him, then
you'd lose what you've managed to preserve for the past ten years.
It's surely not necessary to go."
  Chih Tun also felt this to be the case, and in the end refrained from going.
  (See Zürcher, *Conquest*, pp. 131, 364 n. 254.)

44. The Buddhist sutras hold that by purifying and refining the spirit
and intelligence one may become a Sage (*sheng* = Buddha).[1] Emperor
Chien-wen (Ssu-ma Yü) once remarked, "I don't know whether a man may
scale the peak and arrive at the Ultimate or not, but even if he
doesn't achieve this, the merit of shaping and refining is still not
to be despised."

[1]*SSHY* Comm. (quoting loosely from the "Buddhist sutras"): All sentient beings possess the buddha nature (*fo-hsing*), but it is only those who are able to cultivate wisdom and put an end to the defilements, in whom the myriad practices are all complete, who actually become buddhas.
  (For the first statement, cf. *Mahāparinirvāna-sūtra* 10; *Taishō* 12.881b.)

45. Yü Fa-k'ai's reputation at the beginning competed with Chih
Tun's. Later public sentiment gradually came to favor Chih, which
left Fa-k'ai exceedingly discontented, and in the end he went to live
in seclusion beneath the Shan Mountains (Chekiang).
  Fa-K'ai once dispatched a disciple[1] to the capital, instructing
him to go by way of K'uai-chi (Chekiang), where at the time Chih Tun
was in the midst of lecturing on the "Smaller Version" of the *Prajñā-pāramitā-sūtra*.[2] Fa-k'ai forewarned his disciple, saying, "Chih Tun's
exposition at the time of your arrival should be in the middle of
such-and-such a chapter." Whereupon he demonstrated what Chih would
say, and then attacked it with objections through several tens of
bouts. He concluded, "In the past it was always this passage where
Chih could no longer clarify his interpretation."
  The disciple went as directed to visit Chih Tun, who, as it happened, was just in the midst of lecturing on the passage in question.
Accordingly, the disciple respectfully repeated Fa-k'ai's ideas, and
the debate went back and forth for a long time.
  In the end Chih Tun was defeated. With an edge in his voice, he
complained, "Sir, what right have you to come in here freeloading on
another man's ideas?"[3] (*KSC* 4; *Taishō* 50.350b)

[1]In *KSC* 4 (*Taishō* 50.350b), the disciple is identified as Fa-wei,
a good debater in his own right.

[2]See above, No. 30, n. 1.

[3]*MTSMTM*: Fa-k'ai's eloquence in debate was known far and wide, and
he propagated the Teaching by means of divination techniques (*shu-shu*).
  KISMC: Fa-k'ai at first was famous as an exegete, but later
found himself in competition with Chih Tun, and consequently withdrew to live in Shan Prefecture (Chekiang), where he changed to
the study of medical arts (*i-shu*).

116 TALES OF THE WORLD

46. Yin Hao once asked, "If Nature (*tzu-jan*)¹ is without conscious intention in the matter of human endowment, then how does it happen that it is precisely the good men who are few and the evil many?"

No one among those present had anything to say. Finally Liu T'an replied, "It's like pouring water over the ground. Just of its own accord it flows and spreads this way and that, but almost never in exactly square or round shapes."

All his contemporaries sighed with the highest admiration, considering it an illustrious clarification.

¹*Chuang-tzu* II, 3b (Watson, p. 37): As for the piping of Heaven, it blows through the myriad openings, each in a different way, letting each be itself.

KHCTC: Since Nothing (*wu*) is nonexistent, it cannot produce Something (*yu*), and if Something has not yet been produced, it, in turn, cannot produce anything either. This being the case, who is it who produces production? Clod-like it produces itself, that's all. It is not produced by a Self (*wo*), and if a Self does not produce other objects (*wu*), and objects do not produce a Self, then they are just so of themselves (*tzu-jan*), that's all. We call this the "naturally-so" (*t'ien-jan*). The naturally-so is not created; that's why we use the word "nature" (*t'ien*) in speaking of it, because this is a means of clarifying its self-so-ness.

47. When the monk K'ang Seng-yüan first crossed the Yangtze River, he was as yet unknown, and continually made the rounds of the markets and shops in Chien-k'ang begging alms to support himself.

In the course of his rounds, quite unintentionally, he went to the house of Yin Hao, which happened at the time to be filled with guests. Yin bade him be seated, and started to chat with him casually about the weather, and eventually the conversation got around to interpretations and principles (*i-li*). K'ang's choice of words and his basic ideas showed not the slightest trace of embarrassment; on the contrary he arrived at a general grasp of the main essentials in a single stride.

From then on he was known.

48. Yin Hao, Hsieh An, and the others were once gathered together, and Hsieh took the occasion to ask Yin, "Do the eyes go out and come in contact with the myriad shapes, or do the myriad shapes come in and enter the eyes?"¹

¹Nathan Sivin has brought to my attention the similarity of this discussion to debates by the pre-Socratics on theories of vision.

Liu Chün feels the conversation lacks an answer, and supplies one from the Sarvāstivādin treatise, *Satyasiddhi-śāstra* 49 (*Ch'eng-shih lun*; *Taishō* 32.268a), though this work was unknown to any of the persons in the discussion, having first been translated in 405. The passage states: "Visual consciousness does not require making contact with its object to perceive its unreal qualities . . . but through the medium of space and light it can perceive shapes-and-colors. If the eye were to make contact with shapes-and-colors directly, then there would be no intervening space and light, just as when the eyelid is pressing against the eye, the eye is unable to see. Therefore you should understand that visual consciousness does not make contact with its object directly in order to perceive it." Liu Chün adds, "According to this theory the eyes neither go out, nor do shapes enter, but perception takes place through being related at a distance."

49. Someone once asked Yin Hao, "Why is it that

> About to get office,
> One dreams of coffins;
> About to get wealth,
> One dreams of filth?"

Yin replied,

> "Office (*kuân) is basically 'stinking decay,'[1]
> So someone about to get it
> Dreams of coffins (*kuân) and corpses.
> Wealth is basically 'feces and clay,'[2]
> So someone about to get it
> Dreams of foul disarray."

[1]*Chuang-tzu* XVII, 19a (Watson p. 188): Chuang-tzu said to Hui-tzu, "An owl had caught a decayed rat, and as the *yüan-ch'u* (a mythical bird which eats only bamboo fruit) passed overhead, the owl looked up and cried, 'Shoo!' Now *you* are wanting to shoo me off from your precious Liang ministry!"

[2]*Kuo-yü*, Chin 4: Jades, silks, wines, and viands are like so much feces and clay. (Cf. also *Tso-chuan*, Hsi 28; Legge V, 210.)

50. When Yin Hao was dismissed to Tung-yang (western Chekiang),[1] he began to read the Buddhist sutras. At first, after seeing the *Vimalakīrti-nirdeśa*,[2] he suspected that the "Larger Version" of the *Prajñāpāramitā-sūtra*[3] was too prolix. Later, when he saw the "Smaller Version," he complained that the words of this were too few.

[1]After Yin's debacle in the North in 353, he was divested of noble rank and banished to Hsin-an in western Chekiang. The last three years of his life were spent in deep study of Buddhist sutras. See No. 59, below.

[2]Concerning the popularity of this sutra during the fourth century in the translation of Chih Ch'ien (*Taishō*, No. 474), see Paul Demiéville's "Vimalakīrti en Chine" in E. Lamotte, *L'enseignement de Vimalakīrti*, Vol. 51 of Bibliothèque de Muséon, Louvain, 1962, pp. 438-355.

CWMC: In the Chinese language Vimalakīrti is Ching-ming, "Pure Reputation." It seems he was a great gentleman of the Dharmakāya (i.e., a bodhisattva), who manifested himself and lived on this earth in order to propagate the Way.

[3]See No. 30, n. 1, above.

SSHY Comm.: *Pāramitā* in our language means "arriving at the other shore." The sutras state that there are six means of arriving there: (1) *dāna*, almsgiving, (2) *śīlā*, keeping the commandments, (3) *kṣānti*, patient endurance, (4) *vīrya*, zealous progress, (5) *dhyāna*, meditation, and (6) *prajñā*, transcendental insight.

Thus the first five are the boat and *prajñā* is the pilot. It pilots across the stream of Being (*yu*), to disembark on the other shore of Non-being (*wu*). That is why it is called *pāramitā*.

Before Yin Hao was clear about the meaning of the sutras, even though their words were few, he suspected they were too many. But after he had thoroughly studied their meaning, even though the words were many, he regretted they were so few.

(Zürcher, *Conquest*, p. 131, understands the anecdote to mean that Yin Hao found the *Vimalakīrti-nirdeśa* a happy medium between the prolixity of the "Larger Version" and the conciseness of the "Smaller." Liu Chün's explanation that even the "Larger Version" was too short, however, is probably the correct one.)

51. Chih Tun and Yin Hao were both present at the villa of the chancellor-prince (Ssu-ma Yü). The chancellor-prince said to the two men, "You may try an exchange of conversation, but the topic, 'Natural Ability and Human Nature' (*ts'ai-hsing*),[1] happens to be Yin Hao's 'stronghold of the Yao Mountains and Han-ku Pass.'[2] You'd better be careful!"

At first Chih kept changing direction to keep a safe distance from that topic, but after three or four exchanges he inadvertently walked right into Yin's trap.

The chancellor-prince patted his shoulder and smiled, saying, "This is naturally his victorious battlefield. How can you match sword points with him?"

[1] See above, Nos. 5 and 34.

[2] *SSHY* Comm.: Yao refers to the area of the two Yao mountain ranges (between Honan and Shensi); Han is the Han-ku Pass (running between these ranges). Both were the precipitous frontiers of Ch'in, the dwelling place of those who ruled the world. As Tso Ssu (fl. ca. 300) wrote in his "Poetic Essay on the Shu Capital" (*Shu-tu fu*; *WH* 4.9a), "Yao and Han, the abode of emperors and kings . . ."

52. On the occasion of a gathering of the young people of his family, Hsieh An once asked, "What is the finest passage in the Mao edition of the 'Songs'?"[1]

An's nephew, Hsüan, answered,

> "Then, when we departed,
> Poplars and willows were waving;
> Now, as we're returning,
> Sleet and snow are flying."[2]

An said,

> "With mighty counsels he determines
>   the Mandate;
> With farsighted plans he makes
>   timely announcements."[3]

He went on to say, "This passage uniquely contains the profoundest sentiments of the cultivated man."

[1] In Han times there were four recensions of the "Book of Songs," but only that of Mao Ch'ang (second cent. B.C.) survived in its entirety.

²"Songs," No. 167.

³Ibid., No. 256. Liu Chün cites the commentary of Cheng Hsüan (127-200 A.D.) on this song: This means that in the first month when the weather begins to moderate, he extends his administration throughout the cities and hamlets of the various states.

53. After Chang P'ing had been recommended for the degree Filial and Incorrupt, and was on his way to the capital, he boasted of his ability and prowess, claiming he was sure to mingle freely with the great men of the day, and that he was going to visit Liu T'an. His fellow villagers, including those recommended with him, all laughed at him.

Subsequently Chang actually did visit Liu T'an, who was washing, and setting his affairs in order. After showing him to an inferior seat, Liu only made a few remarks about the weather, and there was no meeting of their spirits or minds. Chang longed for a chance to express himself, but there was no opportunity.

A little later Wang Meng and the other worthies arrived for pure conversation. Whenever guest and host had a point of misunderstanding, Chang, from his distant post in the lowest seat, would arbitrate it. His words were concise and his ideas far-reaching, adequate to express the sentiments of both sides, so that everyone present was astonished. Liu T'an invited him to a higher seat, where they engaged in pure conversation all day, and Chang for this reason remained overnight.

The following morning, as Chang was about to leave, Liu said to him, "You may go for the present, but I was just about to take you with me to see the general controlling the army (Ssu-ma Yü)."

Chang returned to his boat, where his companions asked him where he had spent the night. Chang smiled without answering. In a short while Liu T'an sent a messenger with instructions to look for the boat of Chang the Filial and Incorrupt. His companions were completely taken by surprise.

Immediately thereafter Liu and Chang rode together to visit Ssu-ma Yü. When they reached the gate, Liu went in first and announced to the general, "Today I've secured for Your Excellency a marvelous choice for the post of grand ordinary erudite."

After Chang had come forward, Ssu-ma Yü conversed with him. Heaving a sigh of admiration, he praised him with the words, "Chang P'ing, short as he is (*b'uət-suət), is a storage cave of Truth!" and immediately employed him as grand ordinary erudite. (CS 75.34ab)

54. The dharma master Chu Fa-t'ai said, "The Six Supernatural Faculties" (liu-t'ung) and the Three Insights (san-ming)¹ are ultimately the same. They're just different names, that's all."

¹SSHY Comm., citing "a sutra": The Six Faculties are the meritorious powers of the Three Vehicles (san-sheng): (1) the faculty of divine sight (t'ien-yen), which sees shapes-and-colors at a distance; (2) the faculty of divine hearing (t'ien-erh), which hears through barriers; (3) the body faculty (shen-t'ung), which enables one to fly about and make oneself invisible or manifest at will; (4) the faculty of knowing the minds of others (t'a-hsin), which mirrors like water their myriad thoughts; (5) the faculty of

knowing past existences (*su-ming*), which divinely knows what is already past; and (6) the faculty of knowing the cessation of defilement (*lou-chin*), which is enlightenment and deliverance after successive ages. . . . The Three Insights are what one gets when deliverance takes place in the mind and shines brightly through the three times (past, present, future).

On the basis of the above citations Liu Chün concludes: That being the case, the five faculties--divine sight, divine hearing, the body faculty, knowing the minds of others, and knowing the cessation of defilement--are all equivalent to the insight into present thoughts (*hsien-tsai hsin*). The faculty of remembering past existences is equivalent to the insight into past thoughts (*kuo-ch'ü hsin*). Through divine sight there comes into being a knowledge of the future, which is equivalent to the insight into future thoughts (*wei-lai hsin*). The significance of the statement that they are "ultimately the same," but "different names," resides in this.

(For a different interpretation, see *Ta chih-tu lun* 4 [*Taishō* 25.71c]: Knowledge of former existences, divine sight, and knowledge of the cessation of defilement are called the Three Insights. Q: What is the difference between the Faculties and the Insights? A: Merely to know events of past existences is called a *faculty*; to know the dependently originated karma of the past is called an *insight*. Merely to know that one dies here and is reborn there is called a *faculty*; to know the point of contact between karma and its dependent origination without error is called an *insight*. Merely to know the binding and working of the defilements, but not to know that at rebirth they will not be reborn, is called a *faculty*; to know that after the cessation of the defilements they will never again be reborn is called an *insight*.)

55. Chih Tun, Hsü Hsün, Hsieh An, and others of outstanding virtue were gathered together at the home of Wang Meng. Hsieh, looking all around, said to everyone, "Today's is what might be called a distinguished assembly. Since time may not be made to stand still, and this assembly as well, no doubt, would be hard to prolong, we should all speak, or intone poems, to express our feelings."

Hsü then asked the host, "Have you a copy of the *Chuang-tzu*?"

It so happened that he had the one chapter, "The Old Fisherman" (*Yü-fu*).[1] Hsieh looked at the title and then asked everyone present to make an exposition of it. Chih Tun was the first to do so, using seven hundred or more words. The ideas of his exposition were intricate and graceful, the style of his eloquence wonderful and unique, and the whole company voiced his praises.

After him each of those present told what was in his mind. When they had finished, Hsieh asked them, "Have you gentlemen fully expressed yourselves?"

They all answered, "What we've said today still seems not quite to have exhausted what we feel."

Hsieh then raised a few general objections, and on the basis of these set forth his own ideas in more than ten thousand words. The peak of his eloquence was far and away superior to any of the others.

Not only was he unquestionably beyond comparison, but in addition he put his heart and soul into it, forthright and self-assured. There was no one present who was not satisfied in his mind.

Chih Tun said to Hsieh, "From beginning to end you rushed straight on; without any doubt you were the best."

[1] *Chuang-tzu* XXXI.

56. (In 345) Yin Hao, Sun Sheng, Wang Meng, Hsieh Wan,[1] and other capable conversationalists were all at the villa of the Prince of K'uai-chi (Ssu-ma Yü). Yin and Sun were discussing together the topic "The Symbols of the 'Book of Changes' Are More Subtle Than the Visible Shapes of Nature" (*I-hsiang miao yü hsien-hsing*).[2] Sun's words were logical and his enthusiasm reached the clouds. The whole company felt uneasy about Sun's argument, yet his words could not be refuted. The Prince of K'uai-chi sighed with deep feeling, and said, "If only Liu T'an were to come, then we'd have a means of putting that fellow in his place!" Whereupon he immediately sent for Liu T'an.

Sun's ideas already began to be less assured than before. After Liu T'an arrived, he first had Sun state his own basic argument. Sun made a rough restatement of what he had said before, all the time feeling it was not up to its previous level. Liu then spoke for two hundred or more words, stating his objections concisely and trenchantly, and thus Sun's argument was finally refuted.

The whole company applauded and laughed together, praising Liu for a long time. (*CS* 75.32b-33a)

[1] In Liu T'an's biography (*CS* 75.324b) this incident is dated at the beginning of Ssu-ma Yü's term as chancellor (*hsiang*). Although he did not formally hold that office until 361, his appointment to generalissimo controlling the army in 345 usually marks the beginning of his duties as "chancellor-prince" (*hsiang-wang*). At that time, Wang Mang and Hsieh Wan were both members of his staff. Hsieh An was still in obscurity in K'uai-chi.

[2] *IHMYHHL* (as abridged by Liu Chün): The sages realized that the observational instruments for divining were inadequate to gain a thorough understanding of natural change. Therefore they externalized the universal correspondence of seen and unseen worlds by means of the milfoil stalks and tortoise shells. The universal correspondence (because it is constantly changing) could not be made into a regular pattern, therefore they committed its subtle traces to the six lines of the hexagrams. The six lines have universal application, but become appropriate to particular situations only through change. Therefore, even though it be only one line, both auspicious and inauspicious may be alternately manifested through it, whereas if it were limited to only one interpretation, then its usefulness would be lost. By checking the divining instruments (milfoil and tortoise shells) against the symbols (the hexagrams), both lucky and unlucky are revealed, whereas if one were bound to the instruments alone, then their usefulness would be lost.

Therefore by setting up the eight trigrams, these become the reflected traces which follow the changes; while all under heaven remains a single shape (i.e., a particular situation) which is visible to the eyes. These universal reflections (the trigrams) complete the yet uncompleted symbols; the "single shape" includes the yet unshaped shapes. Therefore the direct examination of the Two Modes (the actual heavens and the actual earth) is not equal in subtlety to an examination of the hexagrams Ch'ien, Heaven (No. 1), and K'un, Earth (No. 2); nor in the case of the alternations of actual wind and rain, are these identical in substance with the hexagrams Sun, Wind (No. 57), and K'an, Water (No. 29).

57. While the monk Seng-i was living at the Wa-kuan Temple (in Chien-K'ang), Wang Hsiu came to converse with him, and on this occasion had Seng-i propose the topic. Seng-i said to Wang, "Does the sage have emotions, or not?"
Wang replied, "He does not."
Seng-i asked again, "Is the sage like a pillar, then?"
Wang said, "He's like counting rods (*ch'ou-suan*).[1] Even though they themselves have no emotions, the one manipulating them does."
[Seng-i said, "Then who manipulates the sage?" Wang, unable to reply, departed.][2]

[1]For a discussion of counting rods in Chinese mathematics, see Needham, *Science and Civilisation*, III, pp. 70-72.

[2]I have bracketed the last two lines, since Liu Chün admits he supplied them from only one text (all others he consulted being without them), but he felt the meaning required some interpolation. "However," he concludes, "Wang Hsiu was skilled in conversing on a topic, but a conversation of this sort is extraordinarily remote from human sensibilities. I still conclude this text to be corrupt."

For possible light on Wang Hsiu's thesis, see SKWei 28.37b, comm.: Ho Yen maintained that the sage does not have either pleasure, anger, grief, or happiness, and his discussions on the subject were extremely meticulous. Chung Hui and others transmitted his ideas. But Wang Pi disagreed with them, maintaining that what makes the sage superior to other men is his *intelligence* (*shen-ming*), whereas the thing that makes him equal with other men is precisely the five emotions. Because his intelligence is superior, he is able to embody an agreeable moderation (*ch'ung-ho*) in comprehending the Non-actual (*wu*). And because his emotions are equal with other men, he cannot be without grief and joy in responding to other beings. Thus the sage's emotions enable him to respond to other beings, without becoming *attached* to other beings. So now when people maintain that since he is without attachment, therefore he no longer responds to other beings, they are grossly mistaken.

58. The grand tutor, Ssu-ma Tao-tzu, once asked Hsieh Hsüan, "In Hui-tzu's 'five cartloads of books,'[1] why was there not one word which entered the realm of the Mysterious (*hsüan*)?"
Hsieh replied, "Undoubtedly it must be that his subtler points were never transmitted."

[1]*Chuang-tzu* XXXIII, 22b-23b (Watson, pp. 374-376): Hui Shih was full of formulas, and his books filled five cartloads, but his Way

was paradoxical and contradictory, and his words wide of the mark . . . He claimed, "An egg has feathers; a chicken three legs; horses lay eggs; a dog may be a sheep; . . . fire doesn't burn; . . . eyes don't see; . . . a tortoise is longer than a snake; frogs have tails; a white dog is black; linked rings may be separated; . . ." He could outtalk other men's mouths, but could not get the consent of their minds. This, it seems, was the limitation of the debaters.

59. When Yin Hao was dismissed and transferred to Tung-yang[1] he read a large number of Buddhist sutras, gaining a detailed understanding of them all. It was only when he came to places where items were enumerated,[2] that he did not understand. Whenever he chanced to see a monk he would ask about the items he had noted down, and then they would become clear.

[1] See above, No. 50.

[2] *Shih-shu*; see the Glossary. Liu Chün cites several examples in the Commentary: The Five Personality-components (*wu-yin*), the Twelve Entrances (*shih-erh ju*), the Four Truths (*ssu-ti*), the Twelvefold Cycle of Dependent Origination (*yin-yüan*), the Five Sense-organs (*wu-ken*), the Five Powers (*wu-li*), the Seven Degrees of Enlightenment (*ch'i-chüeh*), etc. A convenient handbook for these innumerable and troublesome schematizations is the *Mahāvyutpatti*, edited by Sakaki Ryōsaburō, Kyoto, 1916.

60. Yin Chung-k'an studied in great detail the treatises dealing with the Mysterious (*hsüan*), and people claimed there was not one of them he had not investigated thoroughly. Yin, for his part, sighed and said, "If only I understood the 'Treatise on the Four Basic Relations between Natural Ability and Human Nature,'[1] then I could converse forever!"

[1] See above, Nos. 5, 34, and 51.

61. Yin Chung-k'an once asked the monk Shih Hui-yüan, "What is the substance of the 'Book of Changes'?"
Hui-yüan replied, "Stimulus-response (*kan*) is the substance of the 'Changes.'"
Yin continued, "When the bronze mountain collapsed in the west and the magic bell responded in the east, was *that* the 'Book of Changes'?"[1]
Hui-yüan smiled without answering. (*TPYL* 609)

[1] *TFSC*: In the time of the Han Emperor Wu (r. 140-87 B.C.) the bell in the foremost hall of the Wei-yang Palace (in Ch'ang-an) sounded by itself without being rung. For three days and three nights it did not stop. The emperor inquired of the grand astrologer, who referred the inquiry to Wang Shuo. Shuo said, "I fear there is a portent of armed conflict."
They then asked Tung-fang Shuo, who replied, "Your servant has heard that bronze is the child of the mountains, and mountains the mother of bronze. Speaking in terms of the Yin and Yang, the child and mother are responding to each other. I'm afraid some mountain

124   TALES OF THE WORLD

is about to collapse, and that's why the bell is first crying out. The 'Book of Changes' says (Hex. 61; Wilhelm I, 252), "A crying crane in the shade; its young cries in harmony with it.' News of details should arrive within the next five days." After three days the grand warden of Nan Commandery (Hupei) sent up a letter reporting, "A mountain has collapsed over a distance of more than twenty *li*."

Fan Ying PC (cf. HHS 112A.14b-17a): During the reign of the Later Han Emperor Shun (r. 126-144) the bell below the hall sounded, and the emperor asked Yin about it. Ying replied, "Min Mountain in Shu (Szechwan) has collapsed. Mountains are mothers in relation to bronze. When the mother collapses the child cries. It is not a calamity for this sagelike dynasty." Later, Shu, as predicted, sent up a report of the mountain collapsing. Both the day and the month matched exactly the time the bell had sounded.

62. Yang Fu's younger brother, Fu*, had married Wang Seng-shou, the daughter of Wang Na-chih.¹ After the Wang family had called on their new son-in-law, Yang Fu escorted them back home, and the younger brother, Fu*, went along. At the time Wang Na-chih's father, Wang Lin-chih, was still living, and his son-in-law, Yin Chung-k'an, was also among the company at the Wang home.

Yang Fu had always been skillful in the interpretation of principles, and accordingly discussed the "Discourse on the Equalization of Things" (*Ch'i-wu lun*) of the *Chuang-tzu*² with Yin Chung-k'an. Yin started to raise objections, but Yang said, "Sir, after four bouts you'll find yourself agreeing with me."

Yin laughed and said, "So long as we may get to exhaust the subject, why is it necessary to agree with each other?"

But when they had gotten as far as the last clarification of the fourth bout, Yin heaved a sigh and said, "Indeed, I have nothing with which to disagree," and he praised the novelty and uniqueness of Yang's interpretation for a long while.

¹The following chart may help to clarify the relations of the persons mentioned in this narrative:

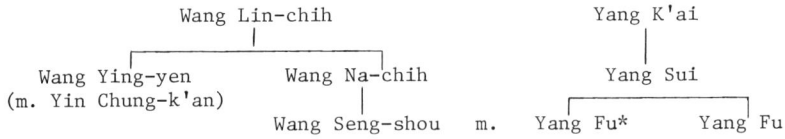

²*Chuang-tzu* II.

63. Yin Chung-k'an said, "If for three days I don't read the 'Book of the Way and its Power' (*Tao-te ching*),¹ I begin to feel the base of my tongue growing stiff." (CS 84.11a)

¹Cf. No. 7, above.

64. (In 397) when Saṅghadeva first arrived (in Chien-k'ang), he lectured on the "Abhidharma" (*A-p'i-t'an*)¹ for the benefit of Wang Hsün

and Wang Mi.² He had just started his lecture, and the session was barely at the halfway point, when Wang Mi announced, "It's completely clear to me already," and forthwith, taking from among those present three or four monks who were willing to accompany him, he proceeded to another room to lecture himself.

After Saṅghadeva's lecture was finished, Wang Hsün asked the monk Fa-kang, "We disciples haven't understood anything at all so far. How has A-mi (Wang Mi) managed to understand already? Incidentally, what do you think of his grasp of the subject?"

Fa-kang replied, "The general outline is entirely correct. Of course there are still some small points he hasn't studied in detail yet, that's all." (CS 65.13b; KSC 1, Taishō 50.329a)

¹APTH (cf. Taishō 55.72b-73a): The Abhidharma represents the essential tenets of the Tripiṭaka (Sutras, Śastras, and Vinaya), the subtle words of its intonation and chanting. It brings together all the sutras, culling from them a collection of the finest passages. That is why the author of the Abhidharmahṛdaya-śāstra gave it the name Hṛdaya, Heart. There was a monk-bodhisattva named Fa-sheng (Dharmajina?) . . . who, in view of the fact that the sources of the Abhidharma were very broad and in the last resort difficult to trace . . . separately edited this work . . . with two hundred fifty gāthas in all. Considering it to be an essential exegesis, he called it Hṛdaya . . . The Kashmiri monk, Saṅghadeva, had been familiar with this text from his youth, and I (Hui-yüan) therefore requested him to translate it . . .

SSHY Comm.: Abhidharma, in the Chinese language, means "Great Teaching" (ta-fa). The dharma master Tao-piao (fifth cent.) says, "Abhidharma in Chinese means 'Matchless Teaching' (wu-pi fa)."

CCH: In the first year of the Lung-an era (397) Saṅghadeva traveled to the capital (Chien-k'ang), where the Marquis of Tung-t'ing, Wang Hsün, welcomed him to his vihāra to lecture on the "Abhidharma." Since Saṅghadeva's grasp of essential doctrine was lucid, he opened up the obscurities of the meaning, so that Wang Min (sic), after one hearing, was then able to lecture himself. Such was the ease with which his clarification of the meaning enlightened the minds of others. It is not known in what year Saṅghadeva died.

(Saṅghadeva on his arrival in Ch'ang-an around 381 introduced the highly scholastic doctrines of the Sarvāstivāda, or "Realistic" School of Hinayana Buddhism, translating its monumental text, the Jñānaprasthāna-abhidharma-śāstra--Taishō, No. 1543--in 383. The following year he did an abridgement of the former, the Abhidharma-hṛdaya-śāstra, whose text was later lost. In 391, at the request of Hui-yüan at Lu-shan--Kiangsi--he retranslated the latter text, for which Hui-yüan wrote the preface, partially quoted above.)

²KSC (Taishō 50.329a) gives the name, Wang Mi (Wang Seng-chen), instead of the Wang Seng-mi (= Wang Min) of both the CS and SSHY texts. The graphic similarity of chen and mi and the accidental identity of the character mi in both names account for the confusion. But since Wang Min died in 388, nine years before Saṅghadeva's arrival in Chien-k'ang, it cannot have been Hsün's younger brother, Min, who is meant.

65. Whenever Huan Hsüan conversed with Yin Chung-k'an, they would always attack each other with objections. After more than a year, their conversations lasted only one or two bouts.

Hsüan sighed to himself, "My eloquence and thinking are going more and more into a decline."

"On the contrary," said Yin, "this simply means your understanding is getting better and better."

66. Emperor Wen of Wei (T'ao P'ei, r. 220-226) once ordered the Prince of Tung-o (Ts'ao Chih) to compose a poem in the time it would take to walk seven paces. If it was not completed, the maximum penalty was to be inflicted. On the spur of the moment Chih then composed the following poem:

> "Boiled beans are taken to make a soup,
> Strained lentils utilized for stock.
> While stalks beneath the pot are blazing up,
> The beans within the pot are shedding tears.
> Originally from the same root grown,
> For one to cook the other, why such haste?"[1]

The emperor looked profoundly ashamed. (WH 60.2a, Li Shan's comm.; CHC 10; MCYC, hsia; TPYL 841; TPKC, huang 173; SSYW, shang)

[1] This poem, generally considered spurious, appears for the first time in the SSHY. Jen Fang (460-508) alludes to it briefly in his "Memoir of Hsiao Tzu-liang" (d. 494) in WH 60.2a.

WC: When Ts'ao Chih was in his teens . . . he was skilled in composing literary pieces. His father, Ts'ao Ts'ao, once looked at one of his compositions and said, "So, you're a plagiarist, eh?"

Falling on his knees, Chih replied, "When I utter words, they become a treatise; when I set brush to paper, it turns into an essay. Look for yourself, and try me to my face; why should I be a plagiarist?"

At the time the Bronze Sparrow Terrace had just been completed in Yeh (northern Honan). Ts'ao Ts'ao took all of his sons to the top of it and had them each compose a poetic essay (fu). Chih seized a brush and completed his instantly, in a form which was readable.

He was by nature unceremonious and easygoing, and paid no attention to etiquette. In the matter of decorations for his carriage and horses, he had no regard for luxury or fine ornament. Whenever he was faced with a problem or a question, he would always answer on the spur of the moment. Ts'ao Ts'ao favored and loved him above his other sons, and was on the point of declaring him his heir on several occasions.

When his elder brother, P'ei, came to the throne (in 220), Chih was enfeoffed Marquis of Chüan-ch'eng (Shantung), later (223) being transferred to Prince of Yung-ch'iu (Honan), and again (229) to Prince of Tung-o (Shantung).

Chih continually sought to prove himself, but never got an opportunity. Moreover, since his principalities were frequently shifted, he became frustrated and unhappy, and died in his forty-first year.

IV LETTERS AND SCHOLARSHIP   127

67. When the Wei court enfeoffed Ssu-ma Chao Duke of Chin (264), they did so with full ceremony including the Nine Bestowals (*chiu-hsi*). Chao adamantly declined, and would not accept them. Dukes, nobles, generals, and commanders were about to visit his headquarters to urge him to announce his acceptance, and the director of works, Cheng Ch'ung, dispatched a messenger posthaste to Juan Chi, requesting the appropriate document.

Chi was at the home of Yüan Chun at the time. Though he had been drunk since the day before, and had to be supported to get up, writing directly on a wooden slip, without any blots or corrections, he simply inscribed it and handed it to the messenger. His contemporaries considered it an inspired piece of writing.[1] (*CS* 49.2b)

[1] *CWCC*: Juan Chi's document urging accession to the throne (*JCCCW*) poured forth in a torrent with mighty effect. By extremely devious arguments, slowly he sought to bring Ssu-ma Chao around.

For the text of the *JCCCW* see *WH* 40.14a-15b (von Zach, *Die Chinesischen Anthologie*, II, 760-762). *SSHY* Comm. gives the following abridgement: It has come to our attention that Your Excellency has adamantly refused the Bestowals. Cheng Ch'ung and the rest of us, filled with fond regard, while cherishing stupid thoughts in our bosoms, consider that when the sage-kings created government, and throughout the hundred generations in which the same tradition has been kept, the practice of praising the virtuous and rewarding the meritorious has been of long standing indeed . . .

The Duke of Chou, availing himself of King Wen's already completed work, and resting upon a fully settled power, "made his glorious home" in Ch'ü-fou (Shantung), and "completely possessed Mounts Kuei and Meng" (also Shantung) . . .

Your Excellency should obey the sage will (of the abdicating ruler, Ts'ao Huan), and accept this mighty blessing . . .

68. (Ca. 282) when Tso Ssu first completed his "Poetic Essays on the Three Capitals" (*San-tu fu*),[1] contemporaries joined in ridiculing and belittling them,[2] and Tso Ssu was quite unhappy about it. Later he showed them to Chang Hua, and Chang remarked, "From now on, instead of 'The Two Capitals,'[3] people may talk about 'The Three.' However, since your writings haven't yet found recognition in the world, you should have them introduced by some gentleman of eminent reputation."

Tso Ssu accordingly sought help from Huang-fu Mi. When Mi saw the essays he sighed in admiration, and proceeded to write a preface for them.[4] After this all who had at first attacked and belittled the essays now "pulled in their lapels" (in a gesture of obsequiousness) and sang their praises. (*CS* 92.7b-8a; *TPYL* 586, 599)

[1] *WH* 4-6. The first described the Shu capital at I-chou (Szechwan); the second, the Wu capital at Chien-yeh (Nanking); and the third, the early Wei capital at Yeh (northern Honan). Translations of all three may be found in von Zach, *Die Chinesischen Anthologie*, I, 44-92.

[2] *Tso Ssu PC*: At that time (302) the "Poetic Essays on the Three Capitals" were not yet completed, and some years later Tso Ssu took sick and died. The revisions of his essays only stopped at

128   TALES OF THE WORLD

his death. When he first composed the "Poetic Essay on the Shu Capital," he had written:

> "Golden horses flash like lightning on the high ridge;
> Jade cocks flap their wings as the clouds part.
> Devil crossbowmen let fly their pellets, forming
>   heaped boulders;
> Fiery wells (of natural gas) shoot out rays in a blaze
>   of sunlight."

The present (fourth-century?) text lacks the line beginning, "Devil crossbowmen," and in consequence various versions of the essay appeared from time to time which differed from each other. (The existing text in WH 4.10a differs considerably.)

As a person, Tso Ssu had no administrative ability, though he did possess literary talent. Furthermore, because of his sister's presence in the imperial harem, he became somewhat conceited, and consequently his peers did not respect him . . .

As for Tso Ssu's alleged visit to Chang Tsai to inquire about matters in Min and Shu (Szechwan), their relationship was also a distant one. Huang-fu Mi was an eminent gentleman of Hsi Province (Kansu), Chih Yü was famous as an old-time literatus, but was not among Ssu's associates (the two both were, however, members of the "Twenty-four Friends" of Chia Mi, as was Tso Ssu). Both Liu K'uei* (fl. ca. 295) and Wei Ch'üan (d. ca. 291; and who, according to CS 92.8a, wrote commentaries and prefaces for the essays) died early, and neither one wrote any prefaces or commentaries for Tso Ssu. All the comments and explanations were written by Tso Ssu himself. To enhance his own reputation, he borrowed the names of his contemporaries.

(CSCC 92.10ab finds this bilious attack on Tso Ssu's integrity totally unjustified, and gives rather convincing reasons for accepting the CS tradition.)

[3]I.e., the poetic essays on the Western and Eastern Han capitals at Ch'ang-an and Lo-yang, the earlier set (Liang-tu fu) by Pan Ku (d. A.D. 92), and the later (Hsi-ching fu and Tung-ching fu) by Chang Heng (78-139), in WH 1-4; von Zach, Die Chinesischen Anthologie, I, 1-44. The first two are also translated in Georges Margouliès, Le "Fou" dans le Wen siuan, Paris, 1926. See also E. R. Hughes, Two Chinese Poets: Vignettes of Han Life, Princeton, 1960, for an abridged translation with commentary.

[4]See WH 45.18a-19b.

69. When Liu Ling[1] composed his "Hymn to the Virtue of Wine" (Chiu-te sung),[2] it was the document to which he committed his whole heart and soul.

[1]MSC: Liu Ling was reckless and dissolute, and considered the universe too confining. He used to ride in a deer-drawn cart carrying a pot of wine. He had a man carrying a spade on his shoulder following behind, so that when he died the man could dig in the earth and bury him on the spot. He treated his body like so much earth and wood, and roamed about his whole life.

CLCHL: Ling's habitation between heaven and earth was vague and boundless, and there was nothing to which he set his mind. Once he got into an altercation with a ruffian, who pulled up his sleeves and started up, fully intending to attack him. Ling, composing his expression, said, "Are mere chicken ribs strong enough to withstand your honorable fists?" The ruffian, completely nonplussed, called off the attack and went home.

He never committed his thoughts to written form, and ended his days having composed only one piece, "Hymn to the Virtue of Wine," and nothing else.

[2] The text appears both in Liu's biography, CS 49.18ab, and in WH 47.5b-6a. In the Commentary Liu Chün quotes from what appears to be the earliest source, the CLCHL of Tai K'uei (fourth cent.):

There was a certain Mr. Great Man, for whom
>   Heaven and earth were but a morning's span,
>   A myriad ages but a flash of time;
>   The sun and moon, a door and window's eye,
>   The eight directions like a country lane.
>
>   He traveled without leaving track or trace,
>   And domiciled in neither room nor hut;
>   For curtain--sky, and for a mat--the earth;
>   He let his fancy wander where it would.
>   At rest he grasped a goblet or a cup,
>   And moving, always carried jug or pot.
>   For wine, and wine alone, was all his lot.
>   How should he know about the rest?

Now there was
>   A certain noble duke, Lord High-and-Great,
>   And a retired scholar, Sir Silk Sash,
>   Who, hearing rumors of our hero's ways,
>   Came to discuss with him the hows and whys.
>   Waving their sleeves and baring wide
>   their breasts,
>   With wildly glaring eyes and gnashing teeth,
>   They lectured loud and long on rites and laws,
>   While rights and wrongs rose up like spears.

At this the Great Man
>   Took the jar and filled it at the vat,
>   Put cup to mouth and quaffed the lees;
>   Shook out his beard and sat, legs sprawled apart,
>   Pillowed on barm and cushioned on the dregs.
>   Without a thought, without anxiety,
>   His happiness lighthearted and carefree.
>
>   Now utterly bemused with wine,
>   Now absently awake,
>   He calmly listened, deaf to thunder's
>   crashing roar,
>   Or fixed his gaze, unseeing of Mt. T'ai's
>   great hulk.
>   Of cold or heat he felt no fleshly pangs,
>   Of profit or desire no sensual stir;

> He looked down on the myriad things, with all
>   their fuss,
> As on the Chiang or Han with floating weeds.
> And those two stalwarts, waiting by his side—
> How like to blacktail flies their busy buzz!

70. Yüeh Kuang was skilled in pure conversation, but not outstanding with a writing brush. When he was about to resign from the intendancy of Ho-nan (Lo-yang), he requested P'an Yüeh to write the memorial for him.

P'an said, "I can do it, I guess, but I'll need to get your ideas."

Yüeh thereupon stated for him his own reasons for resigning, setting forth the items in two hundred or more words. Using what he had said directly, P'an sorted and rearranged the words, and in this way it became a famous document.

Contemporaries all said, "If Yüeh hadn't borrowed P'an's literary skill, or if P'an hadn't used Yüeh's ideas, it never would have turned out as it did." (CS 43.22b)

71. When Hsia-hou Chan's reconstructions of the lost "Songs of Chou" (Chou-shih)[1] were completed, he showed them to P'an Yüeh. P'an said of them, "These are no vain rewarmings of the 'Court Songs' (Ya), but in their own right reveal the quality of filial devotion and brotherly submission.

Inspired by these, P'an proceeded to compose his own "Songs on the Family Tradition" (Chia-feng shih).[2] (CS 55.9a; IWLC 56; TPYL 586; HTC 4)

[1] I.e., the six titles without text in the "Book of Songs": Nan-kai, Pai-hua, Hua-shu, Yu-keng, Ch'ung-ch'iu, and Yu-i. The first three follow No. 170, and the last three No. 172. A fragment of Hsia-hou's "reconstruction" of one of the six (no title is given) is quoted by Liu Chün:

> With diligence and modesty
> Look up and tell their whelming grace.
> At eve resolved, at dawn self-searching,
> Serving by day, and waiting by night.
>
> At midnight visit, then retire,
> Until the cock crows at the gate.
> Respectfully receive instructions;
> Day and night remain sincere.

[2] The text may be found in Ting Fu-pao, Ch'üan Han san-kuo nan-pei-ch'ao shih, Shanghai, 1916 (reprinted, Taipei, 1962), I, 373:

> Bind the hair, oh bind the hair,
> Hair upon the temples.
> Daily heed, oh daily heed,
> Reverent be and cautious.
>
> Nothing owned, and naught possessed,
> But that received from father, mother.

> The "crying crane" hears no response,
> The riven fuel has not been borne.
>
> Oh hidden grief, and whelming shame--
> Our ritual hall remains unbuilt.
>
> By rules of right I have been taught;
> Our family's way is excellent--
> How dare I shirk or take my ease?
> "In one day three self-searchings!"

72. When Sun Ch'u removed the mourning clothes after the death of his wife (Lady Hu-wu),[1] he composed a poem and showed it to Wang Chi. Wang said, "I don't know whether the text is born of the feeling, or the feeling of the text, but as I read it I am sad, and feel the increased weight of the conjugal relation."[2] (CS 56.15b; IWLC 32; PSLT 6; TPYL 586; HTC 4)

[1] The "Record of Rites" (Li-chi 13.2.21; Legge, Li Ki II, 52) prescribes one year of mourning for a wife.

[2] SSHY Comm. quotes the text from Sun Ch'u's "Collected Works" in Sun Ch'u chuan:

> Time hastens on and does not stay,
> Days, months flow by like lightning.
> Since your spirit rose on high,
> Already a full year has passed.
>
> By ritual rule, as I am taught,
> I state the end of mourning at your tomb,
> But at the altar suffer pain,
> As if my inmost heart were drawn.

73. T'ai-shu Kuang was extremely good in the give-and-take of argument, while Chih Yü excelled with brush and ink. Both were of ministerial rank. Whenever they attended a noble gathering, T'ai-shu would converse, and Chih would be unable to reply. Chih would then withdraw and compose an essay objecting to T'ai-shu's arguments, to which T'ai-shu, in his turn, would then be unable to respond.[1] (CS 51.19b)

[1] WYCS: Chih Yü and T'ai-shu Kuang were about equal in reputation and status, but Kuang excelled in speaking ability and Yü in writing ability. When both were young and serving in the government, whenever a group was seated and Kuang would converse, Yü would be unable to respond, . . . etc. Therefore they ridiculed each other more than ever, and there was some confusion among their contemporaries as to which one was really superior. But Kuang left nothing by which he might be remembered, whereas Yü was commemorated in many works, and it was because of this that he came out the victor.

74. After their migration east of the Yangtze River, Yin Jung and his nephew, Yin Hao, were both capable in conversation on a topic, but they differed in their relative eloquence. Whenever Yin Hao became too formidable in an oral debate, Jung would always say, "You'd better rethink what I've written in my treatises!"[1]

¹*CHS*: Huan I had clear judgment in human relations, and when he saw Yin Jung he praised him extravagantly. Jung composed the treatises "The Symbols of the 'Book of Changes' Do Not Fully Express Thought" (*Hsiang pu-chin i*) and "Great Worthies Need the 'Changes'" (*Ta-hsien hsü I*), whose subject and argumentation were intricate and subtle, and for which he was acclaimed by the conversationalists.

Jung's elder brother's son, Hao, was also able in pure conversation, and whenever Jung conversed with Hao and was defeated, he would retire and compose a treatise, after which Jung would again emerge the victor.

While he was serving on the staff of the director of instruction, after a few drinks he used to like to dance, whistling and intoning poems all day, never allowing himself to be bound by worldly responsibilities . . .

75. After Yü Ai had completed the "Poetic Essay on Thought" (*I-fu*),¹ his cousin, Yü Liang, saw it and asked, "Do you have thoughts? If so, they're not going to be fully expressed in a poetic essay. Or don't you have thoughts? Because if you don't, then what is there to write a poetic essay about?"

Ai replied, "I'm just between having thoughts and not having any."² (*CS* 50.7b)

¹The text appears in Yü Ai's biography, *CS* 50.7ab: Ai saw the numerous difficulties of the royal house, and understood that in the end he himself would be engulfed in disaster. Therefore he composed the "Poetic Essay on Thought" in order to give vent to his feelings, and to amplify the sentiment of Chia I's (201-169 B.C.) "Poetic Essay on the Owl" (*Fu-niao*; see *WH* 13.10b-13a, trans. J. R. Hightower, in Cyril Birch, ed., *Anthology of Chinese Literature*, New York, 1965, I, 138-140).

> The Ultimate Principle reverts to the
>   Blended Whole;
> Glory and disgrace in turn are bound by
>   the same cord.
> Survival and perdition are already leveled;
> Merely to cease and die--what need for
>   further sighs?
>
> Things are all determined ere they begin;
> We wait their time to happen, then
>   experience them.
> And like the fourfold seasons' customed round,
> How can the present moment then be made to last?

Moreover,

> Where are they now--the long-lived or
>   the early dead--
> Of whom some, in their passions wild, were
>   full of longing?
> In the whole scheme at the first they were
>   not separate,
> And yet the greatly virtuous lose their
>   heartfelt wish.

> The insects' wrigglings all are spirit acts;
> The fool and sage both of one stuff are formed.
>
> The Realized Man abandons all defiling bonds,
> His nature boundless, free, and without shores.
> Unchecked, he roams in spacious courts,
> Commits his body to quiescent halls.
>
> Heaven and Earth for him are briefer than
>   the morning glory,
> A million ages fleeter than the early dawn.
> He looks back on the universe, a tiny speck,
> More slender than a gossamer's half-tip.
>
> He drifts and floats through subtle and
>   untrammeled realms;
> There are no depths he leaves untried.
> Obliviously one with the Self-so,
> He melts and flows away and is dispersed.

[2]Cf. *Chuang-tzu* XX, 9ab (Watson, p. 209): Chuang-tzu, laughing, said, "I might take a position *between* being useful and being useless. Such a position seems to be the right one, but really isn't, so a person taking it will still not be free of trouble."

76. There is a poem by Kuo P'u[1] which goes,

> "In the forest are no silent trees,
> Of streams no stagnant flow."

Juan Fu once said of it, "The babbling of waters and rustling of mountain tops are truly ineffable, but every time I read this passage I always feel my spirit transported and my body far removed." (*IWLC* 56)

[1]*Kuo P'u PC*: Kuo P'u had an impediment in his speech and was inferior at chanting poems, and ordinary people did not think him outstanding. In addition, he never observed the rules of etiquette, his body was sickly and stooped, he often gave way to his passions, and he was arrogant and lazy. Occasionally he had lapses of gluttony and drunkenness as well. His friend, Kan Pao, admonished him (in the words of Mei Ch'eng's "Seven Incitements," *Ch'i-fa*, *WH* 34.2a), "These are the axes that fell human nature."

  P'u replied, "What I've received has been rationed. I'm always afraid I won't use it up. How can wine or women do me any harm?"

77. When Yü Ch'an first composed his "Poetic Essay on the Yang Capital" (*Yang-tu fu*),[1] he made the following reference to Wen Ch'iao and Yü Liang:

> Wen lifted the righteous banner,
> Yü was the people's hope.
> If one were to match their fame, it would be
>   with "metal's sound,"[2]
> Or compare their virtue, it would be
>   to "jade's brightness."[3]

When Yü Liang heard the essay was completed, he asked to see it, and made lavish presents to Ch'an of gifts and money. Ch'an thereupon changed "hope" (wang) to "paragon" (chün), and the rhyming word, "brightness" (liang), to "luster" (jun), and so on through the rhyming section.⁴ (IWLC 61)

   ¹The Yang capital was Chien-k'ang (modern Nanking). The complete essay has not survived.

   ²Mencius X, 1 (Legge II, 372): The great corpus of the teaching of the sages is like the sound of metal or jade (i.e., of bells and stone chimes).

   ³"Record of Rites" XLV, 13 (Legge, Li Ki II, 464): Anciently the gentleman likened his virtues to jade: its softness and luster was like goodness, etc.

   ⁴It seems incredible that Yü Ch'an would originally have used his kinsman's taboo name, Liang, in a poetic essay, and the suspicion lingers that, as in all the other stories of last-minute textual changes, the "final" form was actually the original one.

78. When Sun Ch'o composed his "Obituary for Yü Liang" (Yü-kung lei), Yüan Ch'iao said of it, "To read this is to tighten one's slackness."¹ At the time it was considered a famous appreciation.

   ¹This appears to be an allusion to the second line of the third stanza of the obituary, which is given below, SSHY V, 48, n. 1.

79. After Yü Ch'an had completed the "Poetic Essay on the Yang Capital," he presented it to Yü Liang, who, through feelings of kinship, greatly enhanced its reputation and value by remarking, "It may serve as a third with Pan Ku's 'Poetic Essays on the Two Capitals,' and as a fourth with Tso Ssu's on 'The Three.'"

After this people all vied with each other in copying it, and as a consequence the price of paper in the capital soared out of sight. Of this Hsieh An said, "It won't do. This is merely 'building a house under a house that's already there,'¹ and nothing more. Item by item is imitated from its predecessors; how can it avoid being narrow and cramped?" (TPYL 181, 599; SSYW, shang)

   ¹Liu Chün cites Wang Yin's fourth-century "Treatise on Yang Hsiung's (53 B.C.-A.D. 18) 'Book of the Great Mystery'" (T'ai-hsüan ching): The Hsüan-ching is wonderful, but adds nothing to knowledge. For this reason the ancients referred to it as "building a house under a house that's already there."

80. Hsi Tso-ch'ih's ability as a historian was extraordinary. Huan Wen valued him highly, and even before Hsi was thirty employed him as keeper of central documents in his administration of Ching Province (between 345 and 363). In his letter of thanks on receiving the appointment, Hsi wrote, "If I had never met Your Excellency, I should have remained in Ching Province a perpetual clerk, and nothing more."¹

Later Hsi came to the capital (Chien-k'ang) where he met Ssu-ma Yü. When he returned to report, Huan asked him, "So you met the chancellor-prince. What did you think of him?"

Hsi replied, "Never in my whole life have I seen such a man!"

From this point on Hsi was in Huan's bad graces. He was sent out to be grand warden of Heng-yang Commandery (Hunan), where his health became impaired.[2] But during his illness he still managed to write the "Annals of the Han and Chin" (Han-Chin ch'un-ch'iu),[3] whose critical evaluations are outstanding and untrammeled. (CS 82.17a; TPYL 263; SWLC, pieh 28, wai 12)

[1]HCYC: Beginning as a clerk in the provincial office, within one year he was transferred three times, until he reached the post of keeper of central documents.

[2]The illness seems to have involved his feet and legs, as in his biography it is called "foot trouble" and "limping."

[3]This work, originally in fifty-four scrolls, no longer survives, but is frequently quoted by Ssu-ma Kuang in the TCTC, published ca. 1086. Hsi's purpose in writing the work, according to his biography (CS 82.18a), was to oppose the ambitions of Huan Wen, who before his death in 373 was planning to accept the abdication of Emperor Chien-wen (r. 371-372) and found a new dynasty. Hsi contended that forced abdication did not lay the foundation for legitimate succession. The text of his concluding essay is quoted in full in CS 82.18b-21b, of which Liu Chün offers a brief abridgement in the Commentary, taken from Hsi's collected works (HTCC).

81. Sun Ch'o said, "Tso Ssu's 'Poetic Essays on the Three Capitals' and Pan Ku's on the 'Two Capitals' are the drumming and piping for the Five Classics."[1] (CS 56.16b; CHC 21)

[1]SSHY Comm.: These five poetic essays are the "wings and pinions" of the classics.

82. Hsieh An once asked his superintendent of records, Lu T'ui, "Why is it that your father-in-law, Chang P'ing, composed an obituary for his mother, but not for his father?"

T'ui replied, "Surely it must be because a man's virtue is displayed in his conduct of affairs, while a woman's excellence, unless it be the subject of an obituary, would never be made public." (TPYL 596)

83. When Wang Hsiu was in his thirteenth year he wrote a "Treatise on Worthy Men" (Hsien-jen lun).[1] His father, Wang Meng, took it to show to Liu T'an.

Liu read it over and remarked, "After seeing the treatise which your son Hsiu has written, I find it worthy to join other works of 'subtle speech' (wei-yen)."[2] (CS 93.11a)

[1]CS 93.11a gives his age as "the twelfth year," and the title, "Treatise on the Perfection of Worthiness" (Hsien-ch'üan lun).

WHsC: Q: The 'Book of Changes" (Hex. 2; Wilhelm I, 14) says of the worthy man, "The wearer of the yellow skirt (i.e., the loyal minister) will have supreme good fortune." But if he is not yet able intuitively to identify himself with Truth, what can he do but "seek for success"? (Chuang-tzu XVII, 16a; Watson, p. 184).

But if he "is seeking for success," then he lacks something, and
if he lacks something, then is not the claim that he "will have
supreme good fortune" specious?

A: Indeed the worthy man (unlike the sage) is not yet able intuitively to be identified with Truth, and therefore he should, of course, try to conform to it. However, if you compare him to one whose identity with Truth is complete (i.e., a sage), it's like comparing a gossamer to a beam. If a gossamer is compared to a beam, even though in relation to Truth it may lack something, this is not enough to disturb the beam. The worthy man is the most passionless of all sentient beings, just as the gossamer is the smallest of all physical shapes. And if the gossamer does not reach the point of disturbing the beam, in the case of the worthy man, how can he really lack anything?

[2]*HS* 30.1a: In antiquity, after Confucius passed away, subtle speech (*wei-yen*) was cut off; and after his seventy disciples died, great morality was perverted.

84. Sun Ch'o said, "P'an Yüeh's writings are sumptuous; reading them is like draping brocade--there's no place in them which isn't good. Reading Lu Chi's writings, on the other hand, is like spreading sand and picking out gold--every now and then you see a treasure."[1]

[1]See also No. 89, below. In Chung Hung's (d. 552) "Critique of Poetry" (*Shih-p'in*), under the section on P'an Yüeh, this remark is attributed to Hsieh Hun.

HWCC: In P'an Yüeh's writings he selected his words and simplified his paragraphs, so that their limpid delicacy was beyond comparison.

WSC: Lu Chi was skilled in writing, When Chang Hua saw his work, he praised section after section, but at the same time criticized his style for being too contrived. He said, "When other people write compositions, I'm distressed at their lack of ability; but in your case it's the fact that your ability is excessive that distresses me!"

(A very different judgment was expressed by the Taoist writer, Ko Hung [ca. 250-330], in Lu Chi's biography at *CS* 54.15b, where Ko is quoted as saying, "Lu Chi's writings are like heaped jade in the Hanging Orchards of the K'un-lun Mountains; there is not one piece among them which is not a night-gleaming jewel, or a spring of water feeding five rivers. Their vast gracefulness, fresh vigor, bold trenchancy, and untrammeled freedom are also the despair of the entire age!")

85. Ssu-ma Yü praised Hsü Hsün, saying, "Hsün's five-word poems may be said to surpass in subtlety those of all his contemporaries."[1]

[1]*HCYC*: Hsü Hsün possessed ability and style and was skilled in literary composition. Ever since such worthies as Ssu-ma Hsiang-ju (ca. 179-117 B.C.), Wang Pao (d. 61 B.C.), and Yang Hsiung (53 B.C.-A.D. 18), the world had esteemed the poetic essay (*fu*) and hymn (*sung*), and everyone imitated the "Songs" (*Shih*) and "Elegies" (*Sao*), gathering from every quarter the words of a hundred authors.

During the Chien-an era (196-219), lyric poems (*shih*) and essays (*chang*) enjoyed a great florescence, and even as late as the end of the Western Chin (265-316) people like P'an Yüeh (247-300) and Lu Chi (261-303), although from time to time they produced substantial writings, never departed from the old models and sources.

During the Cheng-shih era (240-249), Wang Pi (226-249) and Ho Yen (ca. 190-249) had favored mysterious and transcendent (*hsüan-sheng*) conversations about *Chuang-tzu* and *Lao-tzu*, and after that the world set great store by them. But at the time of the crossing of the Yangtze River (307-312) Buddhist doctrines became especially flourishing. So Kuo P'u (276-324), in his five-word poems, began gathering together the words of Taoist masters and setting them to rhyme. And Hsü Hsün and Sun Ch'o (active between 330 and 365), each in turn, were taken as models and admired, and moreover, they used Buddhist terms like "the three times" (past, present, future), and thus the imitation of the "Songs" and "Elegies" came to an end. Hsün and Ch'o both became literary models for the entire age, and from their time onward all writers imitated them. It was not until the I-hsi era (405-418) that Hsieh Hun (d. ca. 412) initiated a change.

86. When Sun Ch'o had finished writing his "Poetic Essay on Roaming in the T'ien-t'ai Mountains" (*T'ien-t'ai shan fu*),[1] he showed it to Fan Ch'i, and said, "Try throwing it on the ground; it will surely resound like metal bells and stone chimes."

Fan said, "I'm afraid the sounds of your metal bells and stone chimes won't be found in the *kung-shang* scale."

However, every time he came to a felicitous passage, he would invariably cry out, "This ought to be our kind of language!" (*CS* 56.16b; *IWLC* 56; *PTSC* 102; *TPYL* 599)

[1]The text is preserved in *WH* 11.2b-6b; trans. by von Zach, *Die Chinesischen Anthologie*, I, 159-162, and Mather, "The Mystical Ascent of the T'ien-t'ai Mountains: Sun Ch'o's *Yu-T'ien-t'ai-shan fu*," *Monumenta Serica* 20 (1961), 226-245.

87. When Huan Wen saw the "Proposal for the Posthumous Title Chien-wen" (*Chien-wen shih-i*) for Ssu-ma Yü (d. 373),[1] composed by Hsieh An, he read it through, then tossed it to the guests who were present, saying, "Here's a piece of Hsieh An's splintered gold (*sui-chin*)."[2]

[1]*LCCCC* (Hsieh An's "Proposal"): I note respectfully that in the terminology of posthumous titles, one who has never neglected a single virtue is called Chien, "Uncomplicated," and one who is broadly informed on the Way and its Power is called Wen, "Cultivated." As it is stated in the 'Book of Changes' (*Hsi-tz'u* A; Wilhelm I, 308), "Simple and *uncomplicated* (*chien*), the principles of the realm are attained," and again (ibid., Hex. 22; Wilhelm II, 135), "Observing human *cultivation* (*wen*), he transforms and perfects the realm." The 'great conduct' of his life is still comparable to these statements in the "Changes," so he should be called T'ai-tsung, Grand Ancestor, with the posthumous title, Chien-wen, "Uncomplicated and Cultivated."

²"Splintered gold" is usually used in a complimentary sense. It seems obviously sarcastic in this context, and Michael Rogers, in his very stimulating article, "The Myth of the Battle of the Fei River (A.D. 383)," *T'oung Pao* 54 (1968), 70, goes so far as to suggest that it is a "*double-entendre* with sinister political implications. It might be rendered, 'smashing the metal,' and since metal was the elemental virtue assigned to the Chin . . . Huan in using it was surely accusing Hsieh An of planning usurpation at that critical juncture following the death of Chien-wen-ti in 372."

88. When Yüan Hung was young he was poor, and used to work as a hired hand for boatmen transporting tax grain to the capital. Hsieh Shang was once on a boating excursion,[1] and on that particular night there was a fresh breeze and a bright moon. He heard on one of the merchant ships moored along the river shore the sound of someone chanting poems with very deep feeling. The five-word poems which were being intoned were, moreover, some he had never heard before, and he sighed endlessly in admiration over their excellence.

Immediately dispatching someone to make more detailed inquiries, he discovered it was none other than Yüan Hung chanting his own "Chanted History Poems" (*Yung-shih shih*).[2] Because of this Yüan was invited to join the party, and thereafter achieved great recognition. (*CS* 92.22b-23a; *TPYL* 444)

[1] According to *CS* 79.3a, Hsieh Shang was governor of Yü Province (northern Anhui) between 350 and 354, stationed at Li-yang, across the Yangtze from Niu-chu, where this incident took place. See also *CS* 92.23a.

[2] The genre of "Chanted History Poems" was popular in this period, as is plain from the numerous examples in *WH* 21, though Yüan Hung is not represented there. The two Yüan Hung examples included in Ting Fu-pao, "Poems," p. 449, reveal an extremely compressed, allusive form.

89. Sun Ch'o said, "P'an Yüeh's writings are shallow, but limpid. Lu Chi's are deep, but weed-choked."[1]

[1] See above, No. 84.

90. When P'ei Ch'i's "Forest of Conversations" (*Yü-lin*)[1] first appeared (362), it was widely circulated by people far and near. All young people who were au courant passed it along and copied it, so that everyone owned a copy. It included Wang Hsün's "Poetic Essay on Passing Beneath Master Huang's Wineshop" (*Ching Huang-kung chiu-lu-hsia fu*),[2] which showed great ability and feeling.

[1] See below, *SSHY* XXVI, 24, for a contemporary discussion of this earlier anecdotal collection which supplied Liu I-ch'ing with a large proportion of his material.

[2] Concerning the topic of this lost essay, see below, *SSHY* XVII,2.

91. When Hsieh Wan wrote his "Discourse on Eight Worthies" (*Pa-hsien lun*),[1] he discussed it back and forth with Sun Ch'o, and there was some disagreement between them.

Hsieh later went out and showed it to Ku I, who said, "I, too, am writing such a discourse, and I know you will not be named in it." (CS 79.18b)

[1]*CHS*: Hsieh Wan's "Collected Works" carries an account of four recluses and the four men of affairs whom they counseled to leave the world, which he called the "Discourse on Eight Worthies." The eight were: (1) the Old Fisherman and (2) Ch'ü Yüan (332-295 B.C.); (3) Ssu-ma Chi-chu (a diviner of Ch'u) and (4) Chia I (201-196 B.C.); (5) the mysterious "Old Man of Ch'u" and (6) Kung Sheng (71 B.C.-A.D. 9); (7) Sun Teng and (8) Hsi K'ang (223-262).

Hsieh Wan's general idea was that recluses were superior and men of affairs inferior. Sun Ch'o objected to this, saying, "For those who embody the Mysterious and understand the Remote, public life or retirement amounts to the same thing."

92. Huan Wen commissioned Yüan Hung to write the "Poetic Essay on the Northern Expedition" (*Pei-cheng fu*).[1] After it was completed, Huan and several other worthies of the time were reading it together, and everyone was sighing in admiration over it.

At the time Wang Hsün was among the company, and said, "It's a pity it lacks one sentence. If it could have one ending with the word (*hsieh*), 'pour forth,' to fill out the rhyme, then it would be just right."

Right then and there in the presence of the company Yüan seized a brush and added the words,

> "Emotions do not cease within the heart;
> Against the flowing wind, alone, I pour them forth."

Huan turned to Wang Hsün and said, "Now we can't help recommending Yüan because of this!"[2] (CS 92.28b-29a)

[1]*HCYC*: Yüan Hung accompanied Huan Wen on his expedition (in 369) against the Hsien-pei Kingdom of Former Yen (352-370), and on this occasion composed the "Poetic Essay on the Northern Expedition." It was the most exalted of all his works.

In the Commentary Liu Chün quotes a portion of the essay from YHC:

> I've heard the tale as it was handed down:
> 'Tis said a *lin* ("unicorn") was taken in this field.
> Such a portentous beast with lucky power—
> Why should they hand his body to the guard?
>
> I grieve for Master Chung-ni's heartfelt tears,
> Tears that seemed truly heartfelt and not false.
> Was it, the one beast only, worth his grief?
> Indeed, he meant his grief for the whole realm. (*hsia*)
>
> Emotions do not cease within my heart;
> Against the flowing wind, alone, I pour them forth. (*hsieh*)

[2]*CYC*: Yüan Hung was once in attendance together with Wang Hsün and Fu T'ao at the seat of Huan Wen. Wen ordered T'ao to read aloud Hung's poetic essay "On the Northern Expedition." When he reached the passage "Indeed, he meant his grief for the whole realm," it was at this point that the rhyme changed.

Huan said, "What you've chanted so far is moving and profound to a thousand years. But now, after the words 'the whole realm' (*t'ien-hsia*), there's a change of rhyme, and the impact of the written message of the preceding passage seems somehow incomplete."

T'ao then suggested, "If you could write an extra sentence continuing the old rhyme, perhaps there would be a slight improvement."

Huan Wen said to Hung, "Try putting your mind to extending it." Hung, writing completely extempore, made the extension, and Wang and Fu both acclaimed its excellence.

93. Sun Ch'o characterized Ts'ao P'i's literary style, saying, "It's like bright luminary brocade (*ming-kuang chin*)[1] with a white ground, cut to make breeches for a lowly census-board bearer.[2] Not that there's any lack of pattern or color, but there's definitely no cut or shape."

[1] See *YehCC* (*Shuo-fu* 59), where several varieties of brocade are listed, including "bright luminary."

[2] "Analects" X, 16: Whenever Confucius saw someone in mourning, he bowed to him; he even bowed to census-board bearers.

94. After Yüan Hung had finished writing his "Lives of Famous Gentlemen" (*Ming-shih chuan*)[1] he went to see Hsieh An. Hsieh, laughing, said, "I used to characterize the people and events of the North in the company of others, just for amusement and nothing more. Now you've come along and written a book about it!"

[1] The *MSC* was divided into three parts: (a) *CSMSC*, "Famous Gentlemen of the Cheng-shih Era" (240-249), viz., Hsia-hou Hsüan, Ho Yen, and Wang Pi; (b) *CLMSC*, "Famous Gentlemen of the Bamboo Grove" (ca. 250-265), viz., Juan Chi, Hsi K'ang, Shan T'ao, Hsiang Hsiu, Liu Ling, Juan Hsien, and Wang Jung; (c) *CCMSC*, "Famous Gentlemen of the Central Court" (Western Chin, 265-316), viz., P'ei K'ai, Yüeh Kuang, Wang Yen, Yü Ai, Wang Ch'eng*, Juan Chan, Wei Chieh, and Hsieh K'un.

95. Wang Hsün arrived at Huan Wen's headquarters (363) to serve as a petty official.[1] After he had prostrated himself below the side gate (*ko-hsia*), Huan had someone surreptitiously remove his letter of introduction. But right then and there, where he was below the gate, Wang rewrote it, without repeating a single character from the original document. (*PTSC* 69)

[1] Hsün became Huan Wen's superintendent of records when the latter was named grand marshal in 363, according to *TCTC* 101.3192. Hsün would have been barely thirteen years old; hence the practical joke.

96. When Huan Wen went on his northern expedition (in 369), Yüan Hung was at the time accompanying him, but after being reprimanded for some fault had been relieved of his post. It happened that Huan needed a conspicuous sign proclaiming his victory. Summoning Yüan, he ordered him to write one, propped against the front of his horse.

Yüan's hand did not leave off writing until in one dash he had filled seven sheets of paper, all extremely beautiful to behold.

Wang Hsün, who was by his side, sighed with the greatest admiration for his ability. Yüan said to him, "This ought to let us win a verbal victory, anyway."[1] (*PTSC* 98; *TPYL* 597; *SWLC*, pieh 7)

[1] I am grateful to Michael Rogers, "Fei River," p. 70, for correcting my earlier translation of this remark in *JAOS* 84 (1964), 385, and for pointing out the importance of this incident in the "propaganda war" of the late fourth century.

Huan Wen's first campaign in 354 had been directed against Former Ch'in (351-394), whose capital was in Ch'ang-an (Shensi). A second campaign, in 356, against Former Yen (352-370) in the northeast, succeeded temporarily in recovering the old Chin capital at Lo-yang, but Huan was unsuccessful in persuading the Eastern Chin court at Chien-k'ang to return north on the strength of it. In 369, acting on his own initiative, Huan launched a second attack on Former Yen, and needed to record a victory in sending a memorial to the throne justifying his action. Very soon after this event, however, he suffered a disastrous defeat at Fang-t'ou (Honan), and was forced to return in disgrace.

97. When Yüan Hung first composed his "Poetic Essay on the Eastern Expedition" (*Tung-cheng fu*),[1] he made no mention whatever in it of T'ao K'an. K'an's son, T'ao Fan, enticed Yüan into a narrow room, and menacing him with a drawn sword, demanded, "In view of the fact that my late father's merit and accomplishments were so great, what did you mean, when you wrote your 'Poetic Essay on the Eastern Expedition,' by disregarding and slighting him?"

Hard pressed and without recourse, Hung replied, "But I made generous mention of your father; how can you say I didn't?" Whereupon he intoned the words,

> "Finest metal, hundred-tempered,
>   In every cutting able to sever;
> Worthy of a lord of men,
>   In office, queller of disorder.
> The Duke of Ch'ang-sha's glorious name
>   In history be praised forever!"

(*CS* 92.23b; *TPYL* 587)

[1] *HCYC* (cf. *CS* 92.23ab): Yüan Hung had served as secretarial aide to the grand marshal, Huan Wen. Later he composed the "Poetic Essay on the Eastern Expedition" (i.e., on the founding of Eastern Chin), in which he praised all the celebrities who had crossed the Yangtze River (ca. 307-312). At the time Huan Wen was in Nan-chou (= Ku-shu).

Hung announced to everyone, "I made no mention whatever in the essay of Huan's father, Huan I (276-328)." At the time Fu T'ao was also attached to Huan's staff, and, being on friendly terms with Hung, strenuously admonished him. Hung laughed and made no reply.

T'ao privately informed Wen, who flew into a rage. But since Hung was the literary paragon of the entire age, and furthermore, since Wen had heard this particular essay already had some reputation, he did not wish to make any public inquiries about it.

Later Wen went on an outing to Ch'ing Mountain (Anhui) where there was much drinking and toasting. When it came time to return, Wen ordered Hung to ride with him, and everyone was apprehensive and frightened. They had traveled in silence several *li*, when Wen suddenly asked Hung, "I hear that when you composed the 'Poetic Essay on the Eastern Expedition' you praised many former worthies. Why did you fail to mention my father?"

Hung replied, "Praise and acclaim for your honored father was naturally not something a minor official like me would presume to attempt on his own, so, inasmuch as I hadn't yet submitted the draft for your approval, I haven't presumed to make it public, that's all."

"What had you intended to write?" asked Wen. Hung immediately replied,

> "His elegant judgment's diffused light
> By some was gathered, by others quoted.
> Although his body may have perished,
> His Way can never fall from sight.
> Thus Huan Hsüan-ch'eng's integrity
> In truth for all time is assured."

Moved to tears, Huan Wen dropped the subject.

98. Someone asked Ku K'ai-chih, "How does your 'Poetic Essay on the Twelve-stringed Zither' (*Cheng-fu*)[1] compare with Hsi K'ang's 'Poetic Essay on the Seven-stringed Zither' (*Ch'in-fu*)?"[2]

Ku replied, "An unappreciative person might dismiss it as a derivative piece, but those of profound understanding will value it, as well as its predecessor, for its loftiness and wonder."[3] (*CS* 92.34b)

[1] A small fragment is quoted in *IWLC* 44 (cf. also *CHC* 16): As an instrument, it has

> Squared corners, long and straight;
> Heaven-arched above, earth-flat below.
> Ornate designs on a plain ground;
> Sparkling and luxuriant, like waves forming.
> The gentleman takes pleasure in its rich decor;
> The musician magnifies its harbored feelings.
> Empty at the core, it exalts virtue;
> Correctly tuned, it shows the norm.
>
> The skillful craftsman adds his art:
> Light colors, shimmering and glimmering.
> Black lacquer seals its resonance;
> An auspicious cloud enfolds its body.

[2] The text is preserved in *WH* 18.8a-14a; trans. R. H. van Gulik, *Hsi K'ang and His Poetical Essay on the Lute*, Tokyo, 1941.

[3] *CHS*: Ku K'ai-chih was broadly learned and possessed talent. As a person he was slow-witted and dull, yet he thought very highly of himself, and for this he was ridiculed by his contemporaries.

SMTWCC: Huan Wen once said, "In Ku K'ai-chih's body folly and genius each occupies one half. Taken together, they are exactly in balance." His contemporaries used to say, "There are three things in which he excels: painting, writing, and folly."

HCYC: Ku K'ai-chih was boastful far beyond the facts, and young people on this account used to flatter him, just for the fun of it. While he was serving as cavalier attendant-in-ordinary, his office adjoined that of Hsieh Chan (387-421). One night he was intoning poems under the moon, for he claimed that he caught the style and form of the ancients. After each poem Chan would applaud him from a distance. On the strength of this K'ai-chih put his whole soul into it, forgetful of fatigue. Chan, about to fall asleep, told someone who was tapping time with his feet to take over the applause, and K'ai-chih, unaware of any difference, kept going until dawn before stopping.

(See also the excellent monograph, by S. H. Chen, *Biography of Ku K'ai-chih*, Chinese Dynastic Histories Translations, No. 2, Berkeley, 1953.)

99. Yin Chung-wen's natural ability was universally admired, but his reading was not very wide. Fu Liang sighed and said, "If Chung-wen's reading were only half that of Yüan Pao,[1] his ability would be no less than that of Pan Ku."[2] (*CS* 99.23b, where the speaker is Hsieh Ling-yün)

[1] Nothing is said in the brief notices of Yüan Pao (d. 413; *CS* 83.9a and *WCH*) about the extent of his reading. Since he once held the post of historian, a slot usually filled by scholars, he must have been considered such in his day.

[2] Pan Ku (d. A.D. 92), author of the *HS* and editor of the encyclopedic work *Po-hu t'ung-i*, was the classical paradigm of the educated man.

100. Yang Fu composed an "Ode to Snow" (*Hsüeh-tsan*), which went:

> "In substance pure, it is transformed;
> Riding the ethers, flurries down.
> On meeting forms, it makes them new;
> Instantly cleansed, they turn to light."

Huan Yin subsequently wrote it on a fan. (*PTSC* 134; *SLF* 14; *TPYL* 588, 702)

101. While Wang Kung was living in the capital (396), he was once walking after having taken a powder (*hsing-san*). Arriving in front of the gate of his younger brother, Shuang, he asked him, "Which passage in 'The Old Poems' (*Ku-shih*)[1] is the best?"

Shuang was still thinking and had not yet answered, when Kung chanted,

> "'In all I meet is no familiar thing;
> What else, but quickly to grow old?'

This passage is the finest."

[1] I.e., the "Nineteen Old Poems" (*Ku-shih shih-chiu shou*). See *WH* 29.1b-5b; partially trans. A. Waley, *170 Chinese Poems*, New York, 1938, pp. 59-68. The anonymous poems are usually dated in the Later Han period. Wang Kung has quoted from the beginning of the second stanza of No. 10.

102. (In the autumn of 398) climbing the Southern Tower of the walls of Chiang-ling (Hupei), Huan Hsüan said, "Now I will compose an obituary (*lei*) for Wang Kung." Whereupon he hummed and whistled for a long while, then immediately set brush to paper. In one sitting the obituary was completed.[1]

> [1] *HHC* ("Preface to the Obituary for Wang Kung"): On the seventeenth day of the ninth month of the second year of Lung-an (Oct. 13, 398) the general of the front, governor of the two provinces of Ch'ing and Yen (Anhui-Kiangsu), Wang Kung, deceased.
>
>> To streams and hills came down a god;
>> A worthy man was nurtured here.
>> But since his spirit has gone hence,
>> No longer does he leave his blessing.
>>
>> The way of Heaven is dark and hidden,
>> Who can plumb the depths of weal or woe?
>> Horses and dogs turn back to bite,
>> While jackals and wolves kick up their paws.
>>
>> The ridge is shorn of its tall tree;
>> The forest bare of old bamboo.
>> The people--ah! they are bereaved,
>> The state has lost its herding hand.
>>
>> With this I now lament his loss,
>> And blazon forth his fragrant grace . . .

103. (In 400) when Huan Hsüan first annexed Western Hsia (Hupei), he was invested simultaneously with the governorships of the two provinces of Ching and Chiang (Hunan-Hupei-Kiangsi), two military commands,[1] and one principality.[2] At the time it was the first snowfall of the year. The officials of the five separate offices all sent congratulations,[3] and the five congratulatory placards (*pan*) all arrived together.

Hsüan was in his reception hall, and as each placard arrived, he immediately wrote a reply on the reverse side. All of them were brilliant and perfectly composed, with no admixture or confusion among them.

> [1] *Huan Hsüan PC*: After Huan Hsüan had conquered Yin Chung-k'an and Yang Ch'üan-ch'i (399/400), he dispatched an emissary to taunt the court, and the court appointed Hsüan governor-general of military affairs in eight provinces (Ching, Hsiang, Yung, Liang, Ch'in, I, Ning, and Chiang; or nearly all of Eastern Chin territory west of the capital), in addition to governor of the two provinces of Ching and Chiang.
>
> [2] This apparently refers to Hsüan's inherited estate as Duke of Nan Commandery (the area of Chiang-ling), which he received on the death of his father, Huan Wen, in 373.
>
> [3] I.e., on the occasion of the first snowfall of the year, an augury of Heaven's approval.

104. When Huan Hsüan was descending on the capital (in 402),[1] Yang Fu was at the time lieutenant-governor of Yen Province (N. Kiangsu).

Coming by way of the capital to visit Huan, Yang sent in a note with the words, "Lately the affairs of the world have gone awry, and the thoughts of our hearts have sunk into despondency. Your Excellency has now opened a dawning light amid the gathering gloom, and clarified the hundred streams with a single source."

When Huan saw the note, he hastened to summon Yang in, crying, "Tzu-tao, Tzu-tao! (Yang's courtesy name) how late you have come!" and immediately employed him as his secretarial aide.

Meng Ch'ang, who was then serving as Liu Lao-chih's superintendent of records, went to visit Yang to pay his respects, saying, "Lord Yang, Lord Yang, all of us are depending on you!"

[1] In the spring of 402 Huan Hsüan, on the pretext of suppressing the rebellion of the Taoist magician, Sun En, which had already been put down by Liu Lao-chih, proceeded down the Yangtze from Chiang-ling. He was welcomed by all in the capital who had, like him, opposed the party of Ssu-ma Tao-tzu.

CHAPTER V

The Square and the Proper

1. Ch'en Shih had made an appointment with a friend to travel, setting the time at midday. When it was past midday, and the friend had not arrived, Ch'en left without him. After he had left, the friend finally arrived. Ch'en's son Chi, who at the time was in his seventh year, was playing outside the gate. The guest asked Chi, "Is your father at home?"

He replied, "He waited for you a long time, and since you didn't come, he's already left."

The friend, becoming angry, said, "He's no man, to make an appointment with someone to travel, and then leave without him!"

Chi said, "If you made an appointment with my father for midday, and at midday you hadn't shown up, that was a lack of trustworthiness. And if in the presence of the son you revile the father, that is a lack of courtesy."

The friend, feeling ashamed, got down from his carriage and beckoned the boy, but Chi went in the gate without looking back.

2. Tsung Ch'eng of Nan-yang (Honan) was a contemporary of Ts'ao Ts'ao, but utterly despised him as a person and would not have anything to do with him. When Ts'ao became director of works (in 196) and controlled the court administration, he asked Tsung very affably, "Now may we be friends?" He replied, "The integrity of the pine and cypress still remains."[1]

Since Tsung Ch'eng had offended Ts'ao Ts'ao's feelings, he was treated distantly, and his rank never matched his virtue. But every time Ts'ao's sons, Ts'ao P'ei and Ts'ao Chih, visited his house they would both individually do obeisance as disciples to a teacher below his couch. Such was the courtesy he received.[2] (*TPYL* 410; *TPKC* 235)

[1]"Analects" IX, 28: It is after the year turns cold that one realizes the pine and cypress are the last to shed their leaves.

²*CKHHC*: When Ts'ao Ts'ao was a young man of around twenty he went frequently to Tsung Ch'eng's gate, but it always happened that because of the large number of visitors he never got to speak to him. So he waited until Ch'eng got up, and went over to ask him for an interview, extending his hand and requesting his friendship. Ch'eng refused and would not accept him.

Later when Ts'ao became director of works and held the power in the Han court, he said to Ch'eng, "In the past you never had any use for me; now may we be friends?"

Ch'eng replied, "The integrity of the pine and cypress still remains."

Ts'ao Ts'ao was displeased, but because Ch'eng had a reputation as a worthy, he continued to treat him with respect and courtesy, and commanded his son, P'ei, to cultivate him with the rites of a disciple.

3. When Emperor Wen of Wei (Ts'ao P'ei, r. 220-226) accepted the abdication of the last Han ruler (Emperor Hsien, r. 190-220), Ch'en Ch'ün had a grieved look on his face. The emperor asked him, "We received the mandate in response to Heaven. Why are you unhappy?"

Ch'ün replied, "Your servant and Hua Hsin cherish the former dynasty in our hearts, and today, though we rejoice in your sage rule, still the old loyalty shows in our faces."[1] (*MCYC*, shang)

[1]*PH*: When Wei accepted the abdication of Han, all the court ministers from the Three Ducal Offices (director of works, etc.) on down received noble rank. Hua Hsin, because he showed an expression deemed offensive to the occasion, was transferred to director of works, but not promoted in rank.

Emperor Wen was displeased for a long time, and on this account once asked the president of the Imperial Secretariat, Ch'en Ch'ün, "We received the mandate in response to Heaven, and of the hundred appointments to office everyone was delighted, and showed it in his expression and in what he said, except for the chancellor (Hua Hsin) and you. Why?"

Ch'en Ch'ün, rising and leaving his mat, knelt for a long time, and then said, "Your servant and the chancellor once served the Han court, and even though in our hearts we were delighted for Your Majesty, our old loyalty showed in our faces. We were also apprehensive that we might be resented by Your Majesty." The emperor, greatly pleased, sighed for a long while, and thereafter doubly honored them.

4. While Kuo Huai was governor-general of Kuan-chung (Shensi, 220-250), he completely won the sympathies of the populace, and in addition frequently gained merit in battle.[1] Huai's wife was the younger sister of the grand marshal, Wang Ling, and, being implicated by blood in Ling's revolt (in 251),[2] was to be executed with him. The messenger who came on orders to arrest her was exceedingly insistent. Huai made preparations for the journey, and set the date when she should start. Both civil and military officials in the provincial headquarters, as well as commoners, urged Huai to raise an armed revolt, but Huai would not permit it.

When the date arrived he sent his wife off. Several tens of thousands of commoners, wailing and weeping, followed with a great clamor for several tens of *li*. Huai then finally ordered his attendants to pursue the lady and bring her back, whereupon both civil and military officials rushed headlong, as urgently as if they were saving their own heads.

After she arrived back home Huai wrote a letter to Ssu-ma I, saying, "My five sons are grief-stricken and pining, longing for and remembering their mother. If their mother is no more, there will be no more five sons, and if my five sons are no more, there will be no more Kuo Huai either."

Ssu-ma I thereupon sent up a memorial requesting a special pardon for Huai's wife.[3] (*SKWei* 26.16b, comm., citing *SY*)

[1] *WC*: In the first year of the Huang-ch'u era (220) Kuo Huai sent a messenger congratulating Emperor Wen (Ts'ao P'ei, r. 220-226) upon ascending the throne, but he himself was detained and could not get there in time for the coronation. Later at a festive banquet where all the ministers were gathered, the emperor, assuming a solemn expression, rebuked him for being late, saying, "In antiquity, when the sage-king Yü feasted the feudal lords at T'u-shan (Chekiang), the people of Fang-feng (Chekiang) arrived late, and Yü had them slaughtered on a large scale. Today the whole realm is offering congratulations together, and you're the most dilatory of them all. Why?"

Huai replied, "Your servant has heard that when the Five Sovereigns (trad. 2698-2358 B.C.) initiated their rule, they led the people with their moral power. During the reign of Yü (2205-2198) the government declined, and they began using punishment and coercion. But today we have come to the era of Yao and Shun (2357-2206), so I knew I would avoid the fate of the people of Fang-feng." The emperor was pleased.

[2] *WeiL*: While Wang Ling made his eastern expedition against Wu (in 251), he secretly desired to set up the Prince of Ch'u, Ts'ao Piao (in a move to reclaim power from the Ssu-ma clan). Ssu-ma I came out from the capital personally to punish him. Ling, putting himself in bonds, came to I confessing his crimes. When still at a distance he cried out to I, "Even if you were to summon me with a half-summons (*che-chien*), how would I dare not come?"

Ssu-ma I replied, "I figured you'd be unwilling to obey a half-summons," whereupon he sent someone to escort him back west to Loyang.

Ling himself realized that his crime was serious, so he tried asking for a coffin and nails to test Ssu-ma I's intentions. Ssu-ma I supplied them.

Ling traveled as far as Hsiang-ch'eng (Honan). In the night he called together all his underlings and bade them farewell, saying, "I've lived eighty years, and my person and reputation are both ruined. It's fate!" So saying, he (swallowed poison and) took his own life.

[3] *WCSY*: When Kuo Huai's wife was about to become engulfed (in her brother's downfall), a messenger from court came to arrest her. Several thousand commanders, generals, and chieftains of the Ch'iang and Hu (western tribes), kowtowing, requested Huai to

send up a memorial to let his wife remain, but Huai would not consent.

After his wife was on her way, everyone was shedding tears and grasping their wrists in a resolve to detain her by force. Huai's five sons, kowtowing till the blood flowed, pleaded with Huai, until Huai, unable to endure the sight of them, gave the order to pursue her. Thereupon several thousand horsemen rode out in pursuit of her and brought her back.

Huai wrote in a letter to Ssu-ma I, "My five sons are mourning their mother, etc. So now I have pursued her and brought her back. If there is anything illegal in my action, I will accept the appropriate punishment from my Lord." When the letter arrived, Ssu-ma I memorialized to have her pardoned.

5. When the Shu general Chu-ko Liang camped on the bank of the Wei River (in 234), all of Kuan-chung (Shensi) was in upheaval. Emperor Ming of Wei (Ts'ao Jui, r. 227-239), deeply apprehensive lest Ssu-ma I would do battle, dispatched Hsin P'i to serve as his sergeant-at-arms. Since Ssu-ma I was stationed directly across the Wei from Liang, Liang set up decoying devices on every hand. I, as expected, was violently aroused, and was on the point of going out to meet him with heavy armor. Liang dispatched spies to observe what he would do, and these returned and reported, "There's an old man impassively leaning on a yellow battle-ax,[1] standing squarely in the gate of the encampment, and the army can't get out."

Liang said, "That would be Hsin P'i."[2] (*CS* 1.7ab; *IWLC* 68; *PTSC* 130)

[1] An emblem of imperial authority.

[2] *CYC*: Chu-ko Liang had invaded Wei territory at Mei (Shensi) and occupied the southern bank of the Wei River. Emperor Ming ordered Ssu-ma I to stop him. Liang was skilled in tactics and brilliant in military maneuvers. Moreover, since he was deploying his troops on a distant campaign away from their native soil, with all the attendant hazards of grain transport, his advantage lay in guerrilla warfare (*yeh-chan*). Each time the Wei court heard of his forays, they hoped to frustrate him by not fighting. Ssu-ma I was also of this mind and kept his large armies tightly confined, protecting them from insults from the outside. But since he felt it improper to give the impression from a distance of any cowardice or weakness, therefore, even while feeding the horses, the men rode them fully armed, always giving the appearance of awesome conquest.

Liang often challenged them to battle, sometimes sending Ssu-ma I a kerchief or a headpiece. Now kerchiefs and headpieces are ornaments worn by women, and Liang hoped thereby to arouse their anger, so he might get the "advantage of Ts'ao Chiu" (the jailer who released Hsiang Liang, see *SC* 7.1b-2a; i.e., break them out of confinement). The court was worried lest Ssu-ma I would be unable to control his temper, and since the commander of the Palace Guard, Hsin P'i, was a blunt and unyielding minister, the emperor sent him with a staff of authority to serve as Ssu-ma I's sergeant-at-arms.

As predicted, Liang challenged them to battle again, and, as feared, Ssu-ma I flew into a rage and was on the point of going out to meet him. But P'i stood with his staff of authority in the middle of the gate, whereupon Ssu-ma I desisted.

6. When Hsia-hou Hsüan had been fettered and manacled (in 254),[1] Chung Yü was serving as director of punishments. Yü's younger brother, Chung Hui, had not formerly been among Hsüan's friends, and took occasion to make fun of him.

Hsüan said, "Even though I'm a man maimed by punishment, I'll still not presume to take orders from you."

During his interrogation and arrest, at first he uttered not a single word, and just before his execution in the Eastern Marketplace (in Lo-yang) his facial expression remained unchanged.[2] (SKWei 9.33b, end)

[1]WSCC: At the time of Ssu-ma I's decease (251), Hsü Yün said to Hsia-hou Hsüan, "Now you've got nothing to worry about any more."

Hsüan, sighing, said, "Shih-tsung (Yün's courtesy name), why don't you look at the facts? This man can still deal with me through the younger members of his family. Ssu-ma Shih and Ssu-ma Chao will not tolerate me."

Later the president of the Central Secretariat, Li Feng, disliked the way Ssu-ma Shih was assuming doctatorial powers, and plotted to have Hsüan replace him. Shih, hearing of this plot, executed Feng, and arrested Hsüan and handed him over to the director of punishments.

[2]WCSY: When Hsüan arrived at the place of the director of punishments, he was unwilling to make any statement. The director of punishments, Chung Yü, personally tried Hsüan's case. Hsüan said with a solemn expression, "What statement should I make for a petty clerk like you to incriminate myself? You (ch'ing) go ahead and make one for me."

Yü, realizing that Hsüan was a famous gentleman, whose integrity was lofty and unbendable, and that his trial had somehow to be ended, made a statement in the night, claiming that he was implicated in the plot, and with tears in his eyes, showed it to Hsüan. Hsüan looked it over and remarked, "It shouldn't be like this!"

Chung Hui was younger than Hsüan, and Hsüan had never been friendly with him. But on this day he was beside Chung Yü's seat, making fun of Hsüan. With a solemn expression, Hsüan said, "Master Chung, where did you get the right to act like this?"

MSC: Earlier, since Hsüan felt that Chung Yü's ambitions and inclinations were different from his own, he never became friendly with him. When Hsüan was arrested, Yü was director of punishments. Grasping Hsüan's hand, he cried, "T'ai-ch'u (Hsüan's courtesy name), how have you come to this!" Hsüan, looking solemn, replied, "Even though I'm now a man maimed by punishment, I still can't be friends with you."

SSHY Comm.: Kuo Pan (author of the WCSY) was a man of Western Chin (265-316), and nearer in time to the events described. When he wrote the WCSY his facts were for the most part detailed and thorough. People like Sun Sheng (author of WSCC, ca. 340?) likewise all state in their accounts that Hsüan rejected Chung Hui. But Yüan Hung's MSC was the last to be published (ca. 360?), and does not depend on the earlier histories. His insistence that it was Chung Yü (and not Chung Hui) is surely mistaken.

7. Hsia-hou Hsüan was a good friend of Ch'en Pen of Kuang-ling (Kiangsu). Pen and Hsüan were feasting and drinking in the company of Pen's mother, when Pen's younger brother, Ch'ien,[1] came back from a trip, and on his way entered the door of the hall. Hsüan thereupon got up and said, "You may stay in the same room, but you may not mingle with us."[2]

[1]CYC: Ch'en Ch'ien did not have the manner of a man of forthright speech, but was slippery and devious and full of sophisticated connivings.

[2]MSC: Hsia-hou Hsüan, because of the honor accorded him for his age and nobility in his own village and party, was basically uninterested in other people's virtue or status. Anyone older than himself he would always treat with deference. But while he was drinking with Ch'en Pen in the company of Pen's mother, when Ch'ien entered, he made an exception. Ch'ien was one who might stay in the same room, but not mingle (in the conversation).

(A different interpretation appears in Ch'en Ch'ien's biography, CS 35.1a: While Ch'ien was still young he was once insulted by Hsia-hou Hsüan, but his mood and expression remained self-composed, for which Hsüan marveled at him.)

8. Duke Kao-kuei (Ts'ao Mao, r. 254-260) had just deceased,[1] and those inside and outside the court were in an uproar. Ssu-ma Chao asked the personal attendant, Ch'en T'ai, "By what means shall we quiet them down?"

T'ai said, "The only way would be to kill Chia Ch'ung,[2] and thus make amends to the people of the realm."

Chao said, "Might we not take someone less important?"

He replied, "I only see taking someone *more* important, not less."[3] (SKWei 22.12a, comm., citing KPCC).

[1]I.e., he had been murdered.

[2]Who had given the order for his death.

[3]HCCC: After the incident of Ts'ao Fang (i.e., his dethronement by Ssu-ma Shih in 254), the Wei court reduced the number of palace guards and did not replace their worn-out armor, so the guards at all the gates were only aged and sickly men. Ts'ao Mao observed the majesty and power of Wei daily departing, and could not contain his anger. Calling his personal attendant, Wang Ch'en*, President Wang Ching, and the cavalier attendant-in-ordinary, Wang Yeh, he said to them, "Ssu-ma Chao's ambitions are known to everybody in the streets. I'm no longer able to sit by and take the ignominy of another dethronement. Today I'm going out there with you in person to punish him."

Wang Ching admonished him, but he would not listen, and forthwith drew out from his bosom a written order and hurled it to the ground, crying, "Our action has been decided! Even if we are forced to die, what is there to lose? But how much less so if we don't have to die?" So saying, he went in to announce his plan to his mother, the empress dowager. Ch'en and Yeh ran in panic to report to Ssu-ma Chao, who prepared for his attack.

Mao then led several hundred young boys and servants, who came out clamoring and shouting. Ssu-ma Chao's younger brother, Chou, who was a cavalry commandant in the Palace Guard, entered the palace and met Mao at the Eastern Gate, where courtiers were wont to park their carriages. Shouted at from left and right, Chou's forces ran in panic.

The commander of the Central Guard, Chia Ch'ung, was the next to resist Mao, fighting beneath the Southern Watchtower. Mao himself was brandishing a sword, and his hosts were about to retreat. The crown prince's bodyguard, Ch'eng Chi, asked Ch'ung, "The situation is critical; what shall we do?"

Ch'ung replied, "His Lordship (Ssu-ma Chao) has been keeping you fellows on for just such an emergency as today's. There's no need to ask questions." Chi went immediately forward and thrust Mao through. The blade came out at his back.

WSCC: The emperor, Ts'ao Mao, wanted to execute the generalissimo, Ssu-ma Chao. He issued an order to the authorities that they again promote Chao to chancellor, and offer him the Nine Bestowals (*chiu-hsi*). That night the emperor personally led his officers, Vice-president Li Chao, Palace Attendant Chiao Po, and others, down to the Ling-yün Terrace, where he issued arms. The plan was to take advantage of the investiture ceremony to send them as his agents, and to go out himself to carry out the punishment. It happened that it rained and the ceremony was called off.

The following day the emperor saw Wang Ching and others, and drawing out a yellow-and-white order from his bosom, cried, "If this man can be endured, then who can't be endured? Today I'm going to settle this matter!"

Drawing his sword, the emperor mounted his chariot and led a host of white-headed officers and young boys of the Palace Guard, pounding the war drums and swarming out of the Cloud Dragon Gate.

Chia Ch'ung entered from outside. The emperor's host scattered in confusion, but the emperor still had the title "Son of Heaven," and continued with sword in hand to strike out furiously, and of Ch'ung's host none dared to oppose him. Ch'ung's doughty commander, Ch'eng Chi, came forward with a spear, and the emperor fell in the midst of his troops. At the time there was a blinding rainstorm with thunder and lightning, and the sky was darkened.

KPCC: After Duke Kao-kuei was killed, Ssu-ma Chao called together the courtiers to plan what to do. The grand ordinary, Ch'en T'ai, did not come, so they dispatched his uncle, Hsün I, to fetch him and report back if he would come or not.

T'ai said to him, "People in the world say I'm more square than you, and now you are proving that you're not my equal."

The young people both inside and outside his family all put pressure on him, and finally, his tears falling, he came in to court. Ssu-ma Chao was waiting for him in a secluded room, and said to him, "Hsüan-po (T'ai's courtesy name), how would you advise me?"

"You might execute Chia Ch'ung to make amends to the people of the realm."

"For my sake, think of another plan."

T'ai said, "I can only go this far. I know no other plan." Ssu-ma Chao thereupon desisted.

HCCC: When Ts'ao Mao deceased, Ssu-ma Chao, on hearing the news, hurled himself on the ground and cried, "What will the people of the realm think of me?" Whereupon he called together his officials to consult about the situation. Chao, his tears streaming, asked Ch'en T'ai, "How would you advise me?"

T'ai replied, "Your Excellency's brilliance reaches through many generations, your merit covers the realm. I think you should unite your tracks with the ancients and extend your excellence to posterity. If someday there were the record of an incident involving the murder of a ruler, wouldn't it be indeed regrettable? Quickly have Chia Ch'ung beheaded, and you might even yet preserve your own brightness."

Chao said, "But Ch'ung simply *can't* be killed. Think of another plan."

T'ai replied in a stern voice, "My thoughts only go this far, and no further. The others are not worth recommending." After returning home, he took his own life.

WSCC: When Ch'en T'ai urged the generalissimo to execute Chia Ch'ung, the latter replied, "Think of something else." T'ai responded, "Are you trying to make Ch'en T'ai make a second statement?" Whereupon he spit blood and died.

9. Ho Ch'iao was intimately loved and respected by Emperor Wu (Ssu-ma Yen, r. 265-290), who said to Ch'iao, "The crown prince (Ssu-ma Chung)[1] lately seems to have grown more mature than before. I suggest you try going to see him."

After Ch'iao had returned, the emperor asked, "How was he?"

He replied, "His Imperial Highness's sage nature is as it was before." (*CS* 45.13b)

[1]*KPCC*: The crown prince (Ssu-ma Chung) had a simple-minded, old-fashioned manner, and was trusting and gullible to a fault. The personal attendant, Ho Ch'iao, frequently said to the emperor (Ssu-ma Yen), "This age is full of deceitfulness, yet the crown prince is still trusting. He's not the type for a ruler of all within the Four Seas. I'm worried that the crown prince doesn't really understand Your Majesty's family affairs, and I wish you would think back to the succession of King Wen (d. 1135 B.C.) and King Wu (r. 1122-1115 B.C.)." (King Wen passed by his eldest son, I-k'ao, in favor of King Wu.)

But since the emperor honored the succession of the eldest legal son, and furthermore, since he harbored fears of those who talked about the faction of the Prince of Ch'i (Ssu-ma Yu) taking power, he did not accept Ch'iao's advice.

Later the emperor said to Ch'iao, "Recently, when the crown prince came to court, I thought he showed a little more maturity than before. Why don't you and Hsün I go together and talk with him?"

After Hsün I had carried out the emperor's command, he came back and reported, "The crown prince's enlightened intelligence is vastly renewed, just as Your Majesty said."

When the emperor asked Ch'iao, Ch'iao replied, "His sage nature, etc." The emperor was silent.

CYC: Emperor Wu was doubtful whether the crown prince would be able to carry on the Great Inheritance, and dispatched Ho Ch'iao and Hsün Hsü (sic) to go and observe him. After they had seen him, Hsü praised him, saying, "The crown prince's virtue is more flourishing than ever, not at all like what it has been in the past."

Ch'iao said, "The crown prince's sage nature, etc. . . . This is a family matter for Your Majesty to decide, and is not something your servant can really deal with." When people in the realm heard of it, everyone praised Ch'iao for his loyalty and wanted to get rid of Hsü.

SSHY Comm.: Hsün I was incorruptible and cultivated, and not obsequious by nature. If we compare the two accounts, Sun Sheng's (CYC) is the one which rings true.

(Since, as P'ei Sung-chih points out--SKWei 10.13a, comm.--Hsün I [d. 274] died long before Ho Ch'iao became personal attendant [285?] and could have taken part in this consultation, Liu Chün's note in the Commentary seems justified.)

10. Chu-ko Ching submitted to Chin rule late.[1] When he was appointed grand marshal, he did not answer the summons. Because of his enmity with the house of Chin, he always sat with his back to the Lo River. But since he had an old-time friendship with the Chin Emperor Wu (Ssu-ma Yen), the emperor wanted to see him. Finding no occasion, he finally requested the consort of the Chu-ko family (the wife of Ssu-ma Chou and older sister of Chu-ko Ching) to call Ching. After he had come, the emperor went to her apartment to see him. The formalities having ended, when the wine had begun to take effect, the emperor said, "Do you still remember our old friendship of the days when we used to ride our bamboo horses together?"

Ching said, "It's only because your servant is unable to 'swallow charcoal and lacquer his body'[2] that today I look upon your sage face." And with that the tears coursed down in a flood. The emperor, ashamed and remorseful, left the room. (CS 77.20a)

[1]CCKT: When Wu was conquered (in 280), Chu-ko Ching came to Lo-yang. Because his father, Chu-ko Tan, had been killed by Ssu-ma Chao (in 257), he had sworn never again to see Chao's son, Emperor Wu (Ssu-ma Yen). The emperor's maternal aunt, the consort of the Prince of Lang-yeh (Ssu-ma Chou), was Ching's older sister. Later, taking advantage of Ching's presence in his sister's apartment, the emperor went to see him there, whereupon Ching hid from him in the toilet. After that he gained a reputation for extreme filial devotion.

Earlier (262), Hsi K'ang had also been killed (by Ssu-ma Chao), but K'ang's son, Shao, died in the campaign of Tang-yin (Honan, in 304) defending Chao's grandson, Emperor Hui (Ssu-ma Chung).

Conversationalists all agreed: "Only after observing the two men, Hsi Shao and Chu-ko Ching, may one know how to distinguish between the way of loyalty and the way of filial devotion."

[2]An allusion to Yü Jang of the Chin state during the Warring States period (403-256 B.C.), who, when his lord, Chih Po, was

killed by Chao Hsiang-tzu, fled into the hills, changed his name, and sought revenge. After one failure, he lacquered his body to cause his skin to break out in ulcers, swallowed charcoal to disguise his voice, and lay in wait for Hsiang-tzu under a bridge. He was eventually recognized and caught by Hsiang-tzu, and took his own life.

11. Emperor Wu (Ssu-ma Yen) said to Ho Ch'iao, "I wish to give Wang Chi a painful scolding before I confer a noble title on him."[1]

Ch'iao said, "Wang Chi is bold and forthright; I'm afraid he's not to be intimidated."

The emperor thereupon summoned Chi and bitterly reprimanded him. Then he said, "Are you ashamed, or not?"

Chi replied, "The folk song 'A foot of cloth and a peck of millet'[2] continually makes me ashamed on behalf of Your Majesty. Others can make the distant intimate, but your servant can't even make the *intimate* intimate.[3] This is why I'm ashamed for Your Majesty." (*CS* 42.5b)

[1] *CCKT*: When the Prince of Ch'i (Ssu-ma Yu) was about to be banished to the frontier (in 283), Wang Chi remonstrated and pleaded many times, and kept sending his wife, the Princess of Ch'ang-shan (elder sister of Emperor Wu), together with the wife of Chen Te, the Princess of Ch'ang-kuang (younger sister of the emperor), to see the emperor to kowtow and set forth their plea to keep the prince at the capital.

The emperor became extremely angry, and said to Wang Jung, "I and my brothers are extremely close. Today's banishment of the Prince of Ch'i is my own private family problem, yet Chen Te and Wang Chi have been continually sending over their wives, like mourners for the living. If Chi and his crowd are acting like this, how much worse will it be with the others!" After this Wang Chi was reprimanded and degraded to the rank of libationer.

[2] *HS* (cf. *HS* 44.1a-7b and *SC* 118.1a-5b): Prince Li of Huai-nan, Liu Ch'ang, was the youngest son of Emperor Kao (Liu Pang, r. 206-195 B.C.) . . . After committing an offense, he was banished by his older brother, Emperor Wen (r. 179-157 B.C.), to Shu (Szechwan), where, after refusing to eat, he died. The common people sang a song about it:

> A foot of cloth may still be sewn,
> A peck of millet still be hulled.
> But as for older and younger brother--
> Neither can tolerate the other.

[3] Emending *ch'in-su* to *ch'in-ch'in*, after *CS* 42.5b.

12. When Tu Yü set out for Ching Province (Hupei, in 278), he stayed overnight at Seven-li Bridge (Ch'i-li ch'iao, east of Lo-yang), where the gentlemen of the court all gathered for a farewell party. Earlier, while Yü was a young man of low station, he had been fond of the company of bravos and knights-errant, and hence was not accepted by others. Since Yang Chi belonged to a famous family, and was of a bold

and forthright disposition, he could not tolerate Yü, and left the party without sitting down.

A moment later Ho Ch'iao arrived, and asked, "Where's Yang Chi?" One of the guests answered, "A while ago he left without sitting down."

Ch'iao said, "He must be below the Ta-hsia Gate (in the north wall of Lo-yang) riding his horse around." Proceeding to the Ta-hsia Gate, he found, as expected, a grand review of cavalry. Ho Ch'iao seized Chi with both arms and took him into his carriage, and together they rode back and sat down at the party as before. (*TPYL* 489)

13. When Tu Yü was appointed General Governing the South (in 278), the gentlemen of the court all came to offer congratulations, and everyone sat on adjoining couches (*lien-t'a*). At the time P'ei K'ai was also there. Yang Hsiu, arriving later, said, "Hmm, I see Tu Yü is seating his guests on adjoining couches,"[1] and immediately left without sitting down.

Tu requested P'ei to chase after him. Yang, who had by then gone several *li*, halted his horse, and afterward they returned together to Tu's house. (*CS* 93.2b)

[1] *YL*: Persons of the Central Court at the time of his returning to his post (in Hsiang-yang, as General Governing the South, in 278) refused to sit beside Tu Yü. So when Yü returned from the campaign against Wu (in 280), he (also) sat on a seat by himself, and would not share it with his guests.

14. During the reign of Emperor Wu of Chin (265-290) Hsün Hsü[1] was director of the Central Secretariat and Ho Ch'iao was president. According to ancient custom, director and president shared the same carriage in coming to, or leaving, the court. Ch'iao was by nature cultivated and proper, and he was continually annoyed by Hsü's obsequiousness and flattery.

Later, when the official carriage arrived, Ch'iao immediately mounted and sat facing directly forward, not allowing any more room for Hsü. Hsü then had to look for another carriage before he could leave. The practice of director and president each being provided with a separate carriage began from this incident.[2] (*CS* 45.13b)

[1] *WYCS*: Hsü's nature was insinuating and flattering. He praised the crown prince (Ssu-ma Chung; see No. 9, above), and agreed to the banishing of the Prince of Ch'i (Ssu-ma Yu; see No. 11, above). At the time, he was privately plotting to destroy the state and harm the people, like Sun Tzu or Liu Fang (rebels during the reign of Emperor Ming of Wei, 227-239). In later ages, if a good historiographer should arise, he should include his biography among the "Insinuating and Self-interested."

[2] *TCCCC*: The director and president of the Central Secretariat always came to court in the same carriage. But when Ho Ch'iao became president and Hsün Hsü was director, Ch'iao, his mind unyielding and protesting, rode in the carriage alone. And so it was that the practice of director and president riding in separate carriages began from this.

15. Shan T'ao's eldest son (Shan Kai)[1] was short in stature. Wearing a silk cap (*ch'ia*), he was once sitting inside the carriage, when Emperor Wu (Ssu-ma Yen) wished to see him. Shan T'ao dared not decline, so he asked the boy, but the boy was unwilling to go. For this reason contemporary evaluators of character claimed he was superior to his father. (CS 43.6b)

> [1] This is probably a case of mistaken identity. CS 43.6b carries the story, attributed to Shan's third son, Yün, who had "suffered in childhood from a debilitating disease and was puny in stature, but exceptionally intelligent."

16. While Hsiang Hsiung was serving as superintendent of records for the grand warden of Ho-nei (northern Honan), there was a public incident which did not involve Hsiung, but the grand warden, Liu Chun,[1] flew into a blind rage, and, after administering the rod, dismissed him.

Hsiung later served as a palace attendant while Liu was personal attendant. At first they did not speak to each other. Emperor Wu (Ssu-ma Yen), hearing of it, admonished Hsiung to restore the friendly relation between superior and subordinate, so Hsiung had no recourse but to visit Liu. Bowing twice, he said, "I've come after receiving an imperial order. But if the loyal relation between superior and subordinate is already broken, what can be done about it?" With this he immediately departed.

When Emperor Wu heard that they were still unreconciled, he became angry, and asked Hsiung, "I ordered you to restore the friendly relation between superior and subordinate. Why is it still broken?"

Hsiung replied, "'The superiors of antiquity promoted people with propriety and demoted people with propriety. Superiors today promote people as if they were about to take them on their knees, and demote them as if they were about to drop them into an abyss.' The fact that your servant, as far as Liu Chun is concerned, has never been the 'leader of an armed revolt,'[2] has, after all, only been a matter of luck. How can there still be any 'friendly relation between superior and subordinate'?" (CS 48.1b-2a; PSLT 12)

> [1] In the Commentary Liu Chün cites a discussion between Wang Yin and Sun Sheng on "Not Being on Speaking Terms with a Former Superior" (*Pu yü ku-chün hsiang-wen i*): Earlier, at the beginning of the Chin (ca. 265), the commandant of Wen Prefecture in Ho-nei Commandery, Hsiang Hsiung, while delivering some imperial sacrificial oxen to the court, failed to present them first at the commandery office, but delivered them directly to Lo-yang. Just at that time the weather was very hot and most of the oxen delivered from the commandery perished from the heat. The laws governing lower officials were extremely severe, and the grand warden, Wu Fen (*sic*), called Hsiung in to administer the rod. Hsiung refused to take the flogging, saying, "Whether I had brought the oxen to the commandery office or presented them directly, in either case they would have died anyway."
>
> Fen was furious, and sending Hsiung down to prison, was on the point of inflicting a heavier penalty. But it happened that just then the Capital Province (Honan) summoned Hsiung to serve as a functionary in the capital administration.

After several years he became a palace attendant, and Fen a personal attendant. Though they were in the same department, they avoided each other and never saw each other. When Emperor Wu got word of it, he provided Hsiung with a present of wine and had him visit Fen to resolve their quarrel, so Hsiung complied with the order.

(CS 48.1b-2a indicates that Hsiang Hsiung tangled with at least two grand wardens of Ho-nei: Wu Fen, and Liu I [sic] both of whom later became personal attendants.)

[2]"Record of Rites" IV, 20 (Legge, *Li Ki* I, 173): Tzu-ssu said, "The superiors of antiquity promoted people with propriety, etc. If (the victims of injustice) do not become leaders of an armed revolt, is it not, after all, a lucky thing?"

17. While the Prince of Ch'i, Ssu-ma Chiung, was serving as grand marshal and was in control of the government (in 301), Hsi Shao was a personal attendant, and went to visit Chiung to consult about some matter. Chiung had prepared a feast and had invited Ko Yü, Teng Ai, and others, and they were discussing together matters appropriate to the times. Yü and the others said to Chiung, "Personal Attendant Hsi here is a skilled musician. Your Highness may command him to play for us." Whereupon they handed him a musical instrument.

Shao declined and would not take it. Chiung said, "Today we're enjoying ourselves together. Why do you decline?"

Shao replied, "Your Highness's aid and management of the imperial house makes your 'conduct of affairs something to be imitated.'[1] Although my office is humble, I'm fulfilling the duties of a palace attendant. To play a stringed instrument, or tune the bamboo pipes, is properly the business of the music officers. I shouldn't be wearing the 'prescribed attire of the Former Kings'[2] while performing the duties of an entertainer. But now that I'm constrained by your exalted command, I dare not decline, so I'll remove my official cap and put on my own clothes. These are my sentiments."

Yü and the others, feeling ill at ease, withdrew. (CS 89.3b-4a; TPYL 689)

[1]*Hsiao-ching* 9: The ruler is not like other men. His words are something to be repeated, his acts something to be enjoyed, his virtue something to be revered, his conduct of affairs something to be imitated.

[2]Ibid. 4: Were it not the prescribed attire of the Former Kings, I would not presume to wear it.

18. Lu Chih, as he was sitting among a company of guests, once asked Lu Chi, "Sir, what is your relation to Lu Hsün and Lu K'ang?"

Chi replied, "The same as yours to Lu Yü and Lu T'ing."

At this Chi's younger brother, Lu Yün, turned pale.[1] After they had gone out the door, he said to his older brother, "Why did you go so far as to say that? Maybe he really didn't know about our family."

Chi said, "Our father's and grandfather's reputations have been proclaimed everywhere within the Four Seas; how could there be anyone who doesn't know them? Only the son of a ghost[2] would presume to speak as he did."

When those who discussed personalities wondered which of the two Lus (Lu Chi or Lu Yün) was superior and which inferior, Hsieh An settled it with this incident. (CS 54.7a)

[1] Lu K'ang and Lu Hsün were, respectively, father and grandfather of Lu Chi and Lu Yün, as were Lu T'ing and Lu Yü of Lu Chih. Since Lu Chih, whether intentionally or not, had referred to Lu Chi's immediate forebears by their taboo names, Lu Chi, with definite malice aforethought, reciprocated in kind. Another nuance, lost in translation, is the fact that whereas Lu Chih had used the deferential pronoun "sir" (chün), Lu Chi replies with the familiar, or condescending, "you" (ch'ing). See No. 20, below.

[2] The Commentary includes a lengthy tale from the KSCK about Lu Chih's presumed great-great-grandfather, the issue of a ghostly alliance (cf. also TPKC 316, quoting SSC; MCYC, shang): Lu Ch'ung was a man from Fan-yang (Shensi). Thirty li west of his home was the tomb of a certain master of the wardrobe, Ts'ui (Ts'ui Shao-fu). One day before the arrival of winter Ch'ung went out of his home toward the west to hunt. He saw a musk deer (chang), and raising his bow, shot and wounded it. The deer fell, then got to its feet again. Ch'ung kept pursuing it, unconscious of the distance, until suddenly he saw a village gate, like that of a mansion. Inside the gate was a majordomo, who called out, "There's a guest before the gate!"

Ch'ung asked, "Whose mansion is this?"

He replied, "It belongs to the master of the wardrobe."

Ch'ung said, "My clothes are a mess. How am I fit to see an honorable person?"

Immediately someone welcomed him, holding out a robe and a new suit of clothes. Ch'ung put them on and found they fit his body perfectly. Then he went in to see the master of the wardrobe and revealed his name.

After the wine and meats had made several rounds, Ts'ui said, "I recently received a letter from your late father contracting a marriage for you with my little daughter, and I've only been waiting for you to show up." Whereupon he held up the letter to show Ch'ung. Although Ch'ung was small when his father had died, nevertheless, when he saw his father's handwriting, he heaved a sigh and was speechless.

Ts'ui then gave orders inside to have his daughter decked out in wedding finery, and had Ch'ung proceed to the eastern apartment. When Ch'ung arrived, his wife had already alighted from her carriage and was standing at the head of the mat. They bowed to each other.

When three days had passed, Ch'ung returned to see Ts'ui, who said, "You may go home now. My daughter shows signs of having conceived. If she bears a son, she'll return him to you. If she bears a daughter, she'll keep her and raise her herself."

He then gave orders to those outside to prepare the carriage and escort the guest on his way. Ts'ui himself escorted him to the gate, held his hands, and wept. The feelings at parting were no different from those of living men. He provided him with another change of clothes and a set of bedding. Ch'ung then mounted the carriage and departed with the speed of lightning.

In a flash he had arrived home. When the members of his family saw him, they had mixed feelings of sorrow and joy. As they questioned him about what had happened, he realized that Ts'ui was a deceased person, and that he had entered his tomb. As he thought back on it, he was filled with remorse.

Four years after that, on the third day of the third month, as he was amusing himself beside the shore of a river, suddenly he saw two calf-drawn carriages, now floating, now submerged. After they had come up on the bank, Ch'ung went and opened the rear door of the first carriage and saw Ts'ui's daughter with her three-year-old son riding with her. When Ch'ung saw her he was overjoyed and wanted to grasp her hand, but the girl raised her hand and pointed to the rear carriage, saying, "My father wants to see you."

Ch'ung went over to give his greetings to the master of the wardrobe, and returned to ask for news. The girl, carrying the child in her arms, returned him to Ch'ung. In addition she gave him a golden bowl. As they parted she also presented a poem, which went:

> Brilliantly shining, the magic mushroom's substance,
> Radiant and fair, how flourishing it grows!
> The flower's beauty, soon to be revealed,
> By goodly portents showed a divine wonder.
>
> Harboring her splendor, not yet in full bloom,
> In midsummer she suffered the frosty blast.
> Her glory, now forever dark and quenched,
> Her path on earth eternally undone.
>
> Oblivious of Yin and Yang's succession,
> Till the wise one's sudden-coming rite.
> The meeting superficial; the parting all too swift!
> Both wrought through spirits of heaven and earth.
>
> With what can I endow my dearest love?
> This golden bowl may wean our son.
> With love and kindness, from henceforth we part,
> Severed and cut, my liver and my spleen!

Ch'ung took the child and the bowl, along with the poem, and suddenly no longer saw the place where the two carriages had been. He led the child back home, where everyone, thinking he was the issue of a ghostly liaison, spit at him from a distance, but his form remained as before. They asked the child, "Who is your father?" and the child went directly and clung to Ch'ung's bosom.

At first everyone thought the situation unnatural and evil, but after reading and circulating the poem, they sighed with wonder at the mysterious communication between the dead and the living.

Ch'ung went to the market to sell the bowl, raising the price high to prevent a quick sale, in hopes there might be someone who would recognize it. Out of nowhere there came an old slave woman who asked Ch'ung where he had gotten the bowl. He rushed home and reported to the entire household that she was the girl's aunt. When they sent someone (*SSC* specifies "the child") to see her, it turned out to be actually so.

She said to Ch'ung,"My niece, the daughter of master of the wardrobe Ts'ui, died before she was married, and her family and kin grieved for her and presented her with a golden bowl, which was placed inside her coffin. Today when I saw your bowl, it resembled it very closely. May I hear how you got the bowl, from beginning to end?"

Ch'ung replied with the entire story, and she immediately went to visit Ch'ung's home and greeted the child. The child had the Ts'ui family likeness and resembled Ch'ung as well.

The aunt said, "My niece was born at the end of the third month, and her father said, 'Spring is warm and mild (wen). May the child grow up happy (hsiu) and strong.' Whereupon he gave her the courtesy name, Wen-hsiu, Warmth and Happiness. Wen-hsiu (*˙uən-xiəu) with finals reversed is yu-hun (*ieu-xuən), posthumous marriage. The portent of her posthumous marriage was thus prefigured in her name.

The child subsequently became an honorable personage and was successively appointed grand warden of several commanderies, at a salary of two thousand piculs. In all his appointments he left a brilliant record. Later he fathered Lu Chih* (d. ca. 192), who became president of the Imperial Secretariat under the Later Han. Chih's son, Yü (d. 257), became director of works under the Wei, and top offices have come down in the family to the present day.

19. Yang Ch'en's disposition was extremely incorruptible and unbending. When the Prince of Chao, Ssu-ma Lun, became chancellor (in 300), Ch'en was serving as chief administrator for the grand tutor (Ssu-ma Yüeh), and was summoned to become the chancellor's military aide. When the messenger arrived in great haste, Ch'en was genuinely alarmed, sensing some impending disaster. Without taking time to saddle his horse, he fled instantly, riding bareback. The messenger pursued him, but Ch'en, who was a skillful archer, shot left and right, so that the messenger dared not approach, and thus he made his escape.

20. Although Grand Marshal Wang Yen was not on particularly friendly terms with Yü Ai, Yü continually addressed him with the familiar pronoun, "you" (ch'ing).
Wang objected, "Sir (chün), you shouldn't call me that."
Yü replied, "You naturally 'sir' me, and I naturally 'you' you. I naturally use my method, and you naturally use yours." (CS 50.8ab)

21. Juan Hsiu was once chopping down a sacred tree (she-shu)[1] when someone stopped him. Hsiu said, "If the sacred thing (she) is a tree, then if I chop down the tree the sacred thing is no more. Or if the tree is a sacred thing, then if I chop down the tree, its sacredness will have moved elsewhere." (CS 49.8a; TPYL 532)

[1] *Tso-chuan*, Chao 29 (Legge V, 731): Kung Kung had a son named Kou Lung who became Hou T'u, Ruler of the Soil . . . Hou T'u was sacrificed to at the she, or sacred mounds.

(T'u [*t'o] and she [*d'o] are both graphically and phonetically cognate, and, as Bernhard Karlgren has shown in "Some Fecundity Symbols in Ancient China," *Bulletin of the Museum of Far Eastern Antiquities* 2 [1930], the graphs represent a phallic-shaped mound of earth, symbolizing the fertility of the soil.)

> FSTI (cf. ch. 8, under *she-shen*): The "Book of Filial Devotion" (not in the present text of the *Hsiao-ching*) states: "*She*, mound, is *t'u*, soil. In broadcasting seed it is impossible to show reverence everywhere; hence the heaping up of soil into sacred mounds, and sacrificing to them in requital for the soil's productivity."
> SSHY Comm.: Thus the sacred mounds are naturally for sacrifice to Kou Lung, and not for offerings to the soil.

22. Juan Hsiu was once discussing the existence or nonexistence of ghosts and spirits. Some maintained that when a man dies he has a ghost. Hsiu alone maintained that he has not. He said, "Nowadays when someone sees a 'ghost' he says, 'He was wearing the clothes he wore when he was alive.' But if when a man dies he has a ghost, then do his clothes have ghosts too?"[1] (*TPYL* 884)

> [1] The SSHY Commentary cites the similar argument of Wang Ch'ung (27-ca. 100) in the *Lun-heng* (cf. ch. 61, pp. 202-203, *CTCC* ed.): People in the world say, "When a man dies he becomes a ghost." This is false. When a man dies he does not become a ghost. What has no consciousness cannot harm people. If it were to be proved on examination that ghosts are the vital spirits of people, then, if a man were to see one, it should have a naked body. It would not be seen to have clothes or girdle, or to be covered with outer garments. Why is this so? Because clothes have no vital spirit. Speaking from this point of view, if clothes and outer garments have the *appearance* of a person, then the form and body also have the *appearance* of a person. And we know that if they have the *appearance* of a person, they are not the vital spirit of a dead man. In all cases where there have been ghosts in heaven or earth, they have never been the vital spirits of men who have died.

23. After Emperor Yüan (Ssu-ma Jui, r. 317-322) had ascended the throne, because of his favoritism toward Empress Cheng, he wanted to put aside his eldest son, Shao, and establish Empress Cheng's son, Yü, in his place. At the time the counselors all said, "To set aside the elder and establish the younger is already immoral in principle. Besides, Shao, being intelligent and bright as well as brave and decisive, is better fitted to carry on the succession."

Chou I and Wang Tao and the other courtiers all fought bitterly and earnestly against it. It was Tiao Hsieh alone who wanted to accept the younger prince in order to humor the emperor's wishes. Emperor Yüan then wished to put his intention into operation, but feared lest the courtiers might not obey the order. Therefore he first called in Chou I and Wang Tao, intending after that to issue the order, entrusting it to Tiao Hsieh.

After Chou I and Wang Tao had come in and had barely reached the head of the steps, the emperor sent back a counterorder for them to stop, instructing them to go instead to the eastern apartment. Chou I, not fully aware of what had happened, immediately turned around and made his way hastily back down the steps. But Chancellor Wang Tao, brushing aside the counterorder, strode directly in before the imperial dais and said, "It's not clear why Your Majesty wishes to see your servant."

The emperor remained silent and said nothing. Finally he took from his bosom the yellow paper order, tore it up, and threw it away. After this the imperial succession was finally settled.

It was only then that Chou I, feeling a deep sense of shame, sighed and said, "I've always said of myself that I surpassed Wang Tao, but today for the first time I realize that I'm not his equal."[1] (CS 65.6a)

[1]CHS: Emperor Yüan felt that since his sons by Lady Hsün, Shao and P'ou, were not the sons of Empress Ching (née Yü), and further, since P'ou had the capacity for great accomplishment, he was superior to Emperor Ming. Therefore very casually he asked Wang Tao, "In establishing an heir the important thing is virtue, not age. Today which of my two sons is more worthy?"

Tao replied, "The heir presumptive (Shao) and the Duke of Hsüan-ch'eng (P'ou) both possess a lively and brilliant virtue. It's impossible to determine which is superior and which inferior. This being the case, of course you should go by age." The emperor accordingly re-enfeoffed P'ou Prince of Lang-yeh.

SSHY Comm.: (The above citation from the CHS) differs from the account given in the Shih-shuo. However, Ho Fa-sheng (author of the CHS) was careful to discern what was true in the documents he selected. Moreover, his account of the casual consultation (between the emperor and Wang Tao) seems the more reliable one. How could the emperor have changed his plans merely on the basis of one word spoken while ascending the steps, without any noteworthy statement before that?

24. When Chancellor Wang Tao had newly arrived in the area east of the Yangtze River (in 307), hoping to make an advantageous alliance with the people of Wu, he requested a marriage contract between his family and that of his aide, Lu Wan. Lu responded with the words, "'On small mounds (pu-lou) there are no pines or cypresses';[1] 'nor does one put fragrant grasses (hsün) and foul-smelling caryopteris (yu) in the same container.'[2] Although I'm untalented, I don't intend to be the first to confound the rules of right relationships." (CS 77.2b; TPYL 541)

[1]Tso-chuan, Hsiang 24 (Legge V, 508).

[2]KTCY 8.1b.

25. Chu-ko Hui's eldest daughter, Wen-piao, was given in marriage to Yü Hui, the son of Grand Marshal Yü Liang. His second daughter was given to Yang K'ai, the son of the governor of Hsü Province (northern Kiangsu and Anhui), Yang Ch'en. Later, after Yü Liang's son was killed by Su Chün (in 328), the eldest daughter was remarried to Chiang Pin. Chu-ko Hui's son, Heng, was married to Teng Yu's daughter. At the time Hsieh P'ou also sought Hui's youngest daughter, Wen-hsiung, for a marriage with his son, Hsieh Shih.

On this occasion Hui said to him, "In the case of the Yangs and Tengs, they were equal marriages.[1] In the case of the Chiangs, we were accommodating them, and in that of the Yü's, they were accommodating us. I can't under the circumstances contract a marriage with your son."

After Hui's death (in 345), however, the marriage was eventually contracted. On this occasion Wang Hsi-chih went to the Hsieh home to see their new daughter-in-law. She still had the good breeding bequeathed by her father, Chu-ko Hui: her manners were correct and fastidious, her appearance and dress shining and neat.

Wang, sighing in admiration, exclaimed, "If it were *my* daughter, I'd have to be still living at the time she was given in marriage for her to be like this!" (*TPYL* 541; *SWLC*, hou 13)

[1] Emending *shih-hun* to *p'ing-hun*, after *TPYL* and *SWLC*.

26. When Chou Mo was appointed grand warden of Chin-ling (Kiangsu), his older brothers, Chou I and Chou Sung, went to bid him farewell. Because he was about to part from them, Chou Mo wept and cried without stopping. The middle brother, Chou Sung, said in disgust, "This man acts for all the world like a woman. When he parts from somebody he does nothing but yammer and blubber!" Whereupon he removed himself and left.[1]

The eldest brother, Chou I, alone remained behind to drink wine with him and talk. As he was about to part from him, with tears flowing he patted his back and said, "Little brother (A-nu), take good care of yourself!"

[1] *TTCC*: Chou Sung's nature was impatient, blunt, decisive, and forthright, and he frequently insulted other people with his ability and spirit. When his older brother, I, was killed by Wang Tun (in 322), Tun sent a messenger to offer his condolences. Sung retorted, "My late elder brother, who was the most moral man in the realm, was murdered by the most immoral man in the realm. What is there to offer condolences about?" Tun harbored a deep resentment over this, but still took Sung on his staff as a commander. Because of some incident he later executed him (ca. 324).

CYC: Chou Sung was a devotee of Buddhism, and even at his execution continued to intone sutras.

27. While Chou I was serving as president of the Board of Civil Office (317) and living in that department, one night he became critically ill. At the time, Tiao Hsieh was president of the Imperial Secretariat, and in his efforts to save Chou's life became very intimate and affectionate.

After a while the illness abated somewhat, and the next morning he reported it to I's younger brother, Chou Sung. Sung came in great haste, and as he started to enter the door, Tiao got down from the bed and wept profusely in front of him as he recounted I's critical condition of the night before. Sung struck him with his hand. Tiao retreated in alarm to the side of the door, whereupon Sung strode directly in. Without so much as a question about his illness, he said bluntly to I, "When you were in the Central Court (in Lo-yang) your reputation was on a par with that of Ho Ch'iao. How can you now have any friendly relations with that obsequious flatterer, Tiao Hsieh?" And with that he strode directly out again.

28. Wang Han's administration of Lu-chiang Commandery (Anhui) was corrupt and disorderly. His younger brother, Wang Tun, used to cover up for his older brother, and therefore at a gathering he once praised him, saying, "My older brother has certainly been excellent in his

commandery post. The people and gentlemen of Lu-chiang are all singing his praises."

At the time Ho Ch'ung was Tun's superintendent of records and was present among the company. With a solemn expression he said, "I'm a Lu-chiang man myself; what I've heard is different from this."

Tun was silent. The people on either side squirmed uneasily on Ch'ung's behalf, but Ch'ung himself was at ease, his spirit and mood completely self-possessed.[1] (CS 77.6a)

[1] *CHS*: Wang Tun, through his prestige as a powerful leader, gathered worthy and outstanding men into his employ, and thus it was that he summoned Ho Ch'ung to be his superintendent of records. Ch'ung, realizing that Tun had disloyal intentions, kept his distance from him. When Tun praised Han for his benign administration, the whole company, out of fear of Tun, merely beat time to his tune, and nothing more. Ch'ung alone stood up to him. At the time everyone turned pale on his behalf, and from then on he was in Tun's bad graces, and was dismissed to become literary erudite for the Prince of Tung-hai (Ssu-ma Ch'ung, d. 341).

29. Ku Hsien once urged Chou I to drink with him, but Chou refused. Ku then shifted his position and started urging a pillar to drink. Addressing the pillar, he said, "How do you suppose he considers himself to be a pillar of state?"

Chou got the point and broke into a laugh, whereupon they became fast friends.

30. Emperor Ming (Ssu-ma Shao, r. 323-325)[1] had assembled all the courtiers in the Western Hall of the palace. They had been drinking, but were not yet very drunk, when the emperor asked, "How does today's gathering of illustrious ministers compare with those of the sage-kings, Yao and Shun?"

At the time Chou I was serving as vice-president of the Imperial Secretariat, and on this occasion said with a severe tone, "Today, although Your Majesty is, like them, a ruler of men, how could this possibly be considered equal to the rule of the sages?"

The emperor became very angry. Retiring to an inner apartment, he composed an order written in his own hand and filling an entire sheet of yellow paper, which he then entrusted to the director of punishments, with orders to arrest Chou, his intention being to have him killed.

Several days later the emperor issued another order to have Chou released. As the various ministers went to visit him, Chou said, "I knew all the time I wasn't going to die; after all, my crime wasn't serious enough for that." (CS 69.17b)

[1] *SSHY* Comm.: Chou I had already been killed by Wang Tun (in 322) before Emperor Ming ever ascended the throne. This story is untrue.
 (In *CS* 69.17b it is clearly Emperor Yüan who called the gathering; Chou's remark is also attributed in that source to intoxication.)

31. When Wang Tun was about to descend on the capital (in 322), at the time everybody said there was no significance in this. But Chou I said, "Unless our present ruler were a Yao or a Shun, how could he be

free of faults? Moreover, what right has any minister of his to levy an army and march on the court? Whenever his greed is aroused, Wang Tun is hard and stubborn. Where is Wang Ch'eng now?"[1] (CS 69.18b)

[1] (Chou) I PC: When Wang Tun made his punitive expedition against Liu Wei (in 322), Wen Ch'iao was serving as attendant to the crown prince, and was outside the Gate of Inherited Splendor. Catching sight of Chou I, he said, "This action by Wang Tun is within the bounds of right, and doesn't transgress them." Chou I replied, "You're young and inexperienced. There has never yet been a minister who acted like this who wasn't starting a rebellion. After everybody has promoted and supported him for the past several years, does he still have the right to act like this? When his greed is aroused, Wang Tun is strong and ruthless. Where is Wang Ch'eng now?"

CYC: While Wang Ch'eng was governor of Ching Province (Hunan-Hupei, in 312) hosts of rebels rose up simultaneously, and he fled to Yü-chang (Kiangsi). Still relying on his past reputation he hurled insults at Wang Tun. Tun suborned some ruffians, Lu Jung and others, to seize and kill him.

PT: As Wang Ch'eng came down (the Yangtze) from Ching Province, Wang Tun lay in wait to kill him. Ch'eng had in his retinue twenty men who were very strong. All of them were carrying iron shields and horsewhips, while Ch'eng himself always carried a jade pillow.

Wang Tun proceeded to give a feast to all the civil and military officials in Ching Province. The twenty men, having been plied with food and drink, were all unable to move. Tun then borrowed Ch'eng's pillow, and holding it in his hand, got down from the couch. Ch'eng tugged at Tun's girdle with his hand and snapped it. Then, after struggling furiously with the powerful warriors, he fought his way up to the roof of the house, where, after a long while, he died.

32. When Wang Tun made his descent on the capital, he halted his ships at Shih-t'ou (west of Chien-k'ang). Among his desires was the intention of deposing the crown prince (Ssu-ma Shao).

Tun had called a large gathering and guests filled the seats. Since Tun realized the crown prince was intelligent, he wanted to use "unfilial behavior" as the excuse for deposing him. Every time he mentioned the circumstances of the crown prince's unfilial behavior, he would always say, "This is what Wen Ch'iao says. Ch'iao was once a commander of the Eastern Palace guard (the crown prince's bodyguard), and later served as my sergeant-at-arms, and knows him very well."

After a while Wen Ch'iao himself arrived, and Tun, assuming his most majestic manner, asked him, "What is the crown prince like as a person?"

Wen replied, "A petty man like me has no means of fathoming a gentleman."

Tun's voice and expression both grew more severe. He wanted, through the force of his majesty, to make Wen agree with him. Finally he asked Wen gravely, "For what reason is the crown prince praised as good?"

Wen said, "One who 'plumbs the depths and reaches afar'[1] certainly can't be fathomed by persons of superficial understanding, but, since he serves his parents according to the prescribed rites, he may be praised as filial."[2]

¹"Book of Changes," *Hsi-tz'u* A (Wilhelm I, 343).

²*LCCCC*: Wang Tun, wishing to depose the crown prince, said to those assembled, "The crown prince's carrying out of his duties as a son leaves something to be desired. My sergeant-at-arms, Wen Ch'iao, used to be in the Eastern Palace and knew all about his affairs." But after Ch'iao himself had corrected his statement, Tun was angry and humiliated over it.

33. After Wang Tun had rebelled and arrived at Shih-t'ou, Chou I went to see him. Wang said to Chou, "Why did you betray me?"¹
Chou replied, "Your Excellency's soldiers and chariots were violating the right. This petty official was filling in as a commander of the Six Armies (the loyalist forces), but the royal army did not succeed. In this I 'betrayed' Your Excellency."² (*CS* 69.18b)

¹Chou I had once been a protégé of Wang Tun in 313, when he was fleeing for his life; see *TCTC* 88.2802.

²*CYC*: After Wang Tun had descended on the capital, the Six Armies were badly routed. Chou I's senior administrator, Ho Chia, together with the civil and military officers in his entourage, urged I to escape from the troubles.
I replied, "While I fill the position of a great officer, and the court is tottering and in peril, how can I seek to save my own life in the wilderness, or cast my lot among the Hu caitiffs (the barbarian dynasties of the north)?" Whereupon, in company with other warriors of the court, he went to see Tun.
Tun said, "After the battles of the past few days, have you any strength to spare?" I replied, "I only regret my strength hasn't been sufficient. How could there be any to spare?"

34. After Su Chün had arrived at Shih-t'ou (in 328), all the officials in the capital scattered and fled. Only the personal attendant, Chung Ya, remained by the emperor's side (Emperor Ch'eng, r. 326-342). Someone said to Chung, "'To advance when you see the possibilities, and retreat when you know the difficulties'¹ is the way of antiquity. Since your nature, sir, is transparent and straightforward, you'll certainly not be spared in the rebels' vengeance. Why don't you use the expedient of following what's appropriate to the time, instead of sitting here waiting for death?"
Chung replied, "I 'couldn't correct the state when it was in disorder, or save the ruler when he was in danger,'² yet now everyone is running away to hide, seeking to avoid trouble. I'm just afraid a Tung Hu³ will 'come forward, holding the bamboo slips in his hand.'"⁴ (*CS* 70.23ab)

¹*Tso-chuan*, Hsüan 12 (Legge V, 317).

²Ibid., Hsiang 25 (Legge V, 515).

³Ibid., Hsüan 2 (Legge V, 290-291).
(Tung Hu was a chronicler for the Chin state during the seventh and sixth centuries B.C. For his recording that Chao Tun "murdered" his sovereign, Duke Ling [r. 620-607], when he failed to punish the actual murderer, he won the admiration of Confucius as a "good historiographer.")

⁴Ibid., Hsiang 25 (Legge V, 514-515).

(After Ts'ui Shu of the Ch'i state [sixth cent. B.C.] had murdered his sovereign, Duke Chuang [r. 553-548], the court chronicler made a record of it, and was promptly executed. His brother proceeded to record this fact, and was in turn executed, and so on through several intrepid chroniclers, until the deed was finally recorded. A chronicler from the south, hearing of the problem, "came forward holding the bamboo slips in his hand," ready to record his own death, but returned, after learning the record had already been made.)

35. As he was about to leave the capital (during Su Chün's revolt in 327), Yü Liang turned back and said to Chung Ya, "All subsequent affairs I completely entrust to your care."
  Chung said, "'When the central pillar is broken and the rafters cave in,'¹ who will be to blame?"
  Yü said, "Of today's events there's nothing more to say. You should just hope for success some day in reconquest and restoration, that's all."
  Chung said, "I hope Your Excellency wouldn't be ashamed of me if I were merely a Hsün Lin-fu,² and nothing more." (CS 70.23b)

¹*Tso-chuan*, Hsiang 31 (Legge V, 566).

²Ibid., Hsüan 12, 15 (Legge V, 316-321, 328-329).
  (Hsün Lin-fu was a general of the Chin state under Duke P'ing [r. 557-532 B.C.], who was sent to rescue the state of Cheng after it was threatened by Ch'u. He fought the Ch'u army and was defeated, whereupon he requested death from his lord, but, through the intervention of a friend, was pardoned. Later he defeated a raid by the Red Ti [northern barbarians], and was rewarded.)

36. During the rebellion of Su Chün, K'ung Ch'ün had been threatened by one of Su's officers, K'uang Shu, in Heng-t'ang (southwest of Chien-k'ang).¹ After the rebellion had been suppressed, Chancellor Wang Tao spared Shu's life, and on the occasion of a feast, as a joke, he ordered Shu to urge Ch'ün to drink with him, to resolve their animosity at Heng-t'ang.
  Ch'ün responded, "I'm no match for my ancestor, Confucius, but I've got this in common with him: I was harassed by a man of K'uang.² Even though the warmth of spring spreads its vapors abroad, and 'the hawk transforms himself into a dove,'³ those who understand still dislike the look of his eyes." (CS 78.11b)

¹The incident is told in No. 38, below.

²"Analects" IX, 5: The Master was imperiled in K'uang.
  KTCY 22.12b: When Confucius went to Sung, Chien-tzu of K'uang ambushed him with armed warriors. The disciple Tzu-lu angrily brandished a spear and was about to do battle, but Confucius restrained him, saying, "If the 'Songs' and 'Documents' aren't expounded, or the 'Rites' and 'Music' practiced here, that would be my fault. But if it's wrong to transmit the Way of the Former Kings, then it's not my crime, but Fate. Sing, and I'll sing in

harmony with you." Whereupon Tzu-lu strummed his sword, and Confucius sang in harmony with him. By the end of the third song the people of K'uang unbuckled their armor and called off the ambush.

³"Record of Rites" VI, 13, 14 (Legge, *Li Ki* I, 258): In the second month of spring the hawk transforms himself into a dove.

37. After the Su Chün affair had been suppressed (in 328),¹ Wang Tao, Yü Liang, and the other courtiers wanted to employ the director of punishments, K'ung T'an, as capital intendant. After the separations caused by the rebellion, the common people were suffering and in distress. K'ung said with deep feeling, "Formerly when Emperor Ming (r. 323-325) lay dying, and the nobles went up in person to the imperial bed, and all were favored with his loving recognition and together received his last will and testament, I, K'ung T'an, being distant of kin and mean of rank, was not included in his parting command. Since the people are beset by hardship and distress, to put an insignificant minister at the head of the capital administration would be for all the world like putting spoiled meat on the sacrificial stand for the people to chop into shreds, and nothing more." Whereupon he shook out his clothes and departed.

The courtiers, for their part, also refrained from making the appointment.² (*CS* 78.6b-7a)

¹*LKC, Yao-ch'eng*: At the beginning of the reign of Emperor Ming (323) there was a folk saying (*yao*) which went, "When the high mountain (*kao-shan*) crumbles, the rock (*shih*) will break of its own accord." "High mountain" is "lofty" (*chün*, i.e., Su Chün), and "rock" is "boulder" (*shih*, i.e., Su Shih), Chün's younger brother. Later the courtiers executed Su Chün. Su Shih, who was still holding Shih-t'ou (west of the capital), fled in panic, and they pursued and beheaded him.

²*WYCS*: After the Su Chün affair had been suppressed, T'ao K'an wished to promote K'ung T'an to become grand warden of Yü-chang (Kiangsi). K'ung declined on account of his mother's old age, and did not take up the post. The court then offered him Wu Commandery (Soochow), but since Wu was full of famous families and K'ung was young, they finally gave him the governorship of Wu-hsing Principality (Chekiang).

SSHY Comm.: There is no record of any offer of the capital intendancy.

38. K'ung Yü and his cousin, K'ung Ch'ün, were once traveling together. On the imperial highway (going south from the palace) they met K'uang Shu. Since his entourage was exceedingly numerous, Shu took the occasion to go over and talk with K'ung Yü. K'ung Ch'ün from the first never looked at him, but blurted out, "'Though the hawk transforms himself into a dove,'¹ all the other birds still dislike the look of his eyes."

Shu, becoming very angry, was about to cut off his head on the spot. It was only after K'ung Yü jumped down from the carriage and held Shu in both arms, crying, "My younger cousin is out of his mind, please, for my sake, be lenient with him!" that Ch'ün managed to preserve his head intact. (*CS* 78.11b)

[1]See above, No. 36, n. 3.

39. Mei I had once done a favor for T'ao K'an.[1] Later, when he was serving as grand warden of Yü-chang Commandery (Kiangsi), he became involved in an incident, and Chancellor Wang Tao dispatched someone to arrest him.

K'an said, "The Son of Heaven (Emperor Ch'eng, r. 326-342) is still rich in springs and autumns (i.e., still young), and all critical decisions are made by the courtiers. Since Wang Tao got to imprison him, why may T'ao K'an not release him?" Whereupon he dispatched someone to Chiang-k'ou (Kiangsi) to take Mei forcibly out of custody.

Later when Mei I saw T'ao K'an he did obeisance, but K'an stopped him. Mei said, "If I don't do so now, tomorrow how could my knees ever bend again?"

> [1]*TTCC*: Earlier someone had slandered T'ao K'an to Wang Tun, so that Tun had replaced K'an in his post as governor of Ching Province (Hunan-Hupei) with his own cousin, Wang I*, and had demoted K'an to be governor of Kuang Province (Kwangtung-Kwangsi). Both civil and military members of K'an's staff opposed Wang I* and sought to have K'an reinstated. When Tun learned of it he became very angry. After he had issued the order, and K'an was about to go to his post in Kuang Province, Tun had him pass by his own place, where he had deployed armed men with the intention of harming K'an. But Tun's advisory aide, Mei T'ao (*sic*), admonished Tun against it, so Tun desisted and sent him off with generous presents.
>
> (The Commentary cites a similar account from *WYCS*, then concludes on the basis of these sources [*TTCC* and *WYCS*] that the man who did the favor for T'ao K'an was Mei I's younger brother, Mei T'ao, and not Mei I.)

40. Chancellor Wang Tao once arranged an entertainment with female performers, and had provided couches and mats for his guests. Ts'ai Mo was at first among the company, but became displeased and left. Wang, for his part, did not detain him. (*CS* 77.19b; *TPYL* 568)

41. Ho Ch'ung and Yü Ping were both serving as principal ministers in the government. At the time, immediately after Emperor Ch'eng's decease (342), his successor had not yet been determined. Ho wished to establish the legitimate heir (Ssu-ma P'ei), while Yü and the rest of the court counseled that the enemies without were just then at their strongest, and the legitimate heir was weak and still in infancy, so in the end they established Emperor K'ang (Ssu-ma Yueh*, r. 342-344).

When Emperor K'ang ascended the throne, he assembled all the ministers, and addressing Ho, asked, "Through whose counsel was it that today We have received the great inheritance?"

Ho replied, "Your Majesty's dragon flight is the accomplishment of Yü Ping; it was not the result of any efforts on the part of your servant. At the time, if they had used your insignificant servant's counsel, we would not today be looking upon this prosperous and enlightened age."

The emperor appeared embarrassed.[1] (*CS* 77.7ab; *TPYL* 99)

¹*CYC*: Earlier, when Emperor Ch'eng was on his deathbed, Yü Ping counseled setting up an adult ruler as his successor, while Ho Ch'ung maintained that it was proper to accept the imperial heir. After arguing the point and not getting his wish, Ch'ung became uneasy about his situation, and requested a post outside the capital.

When Ping was about to leave for his post (as governor of Chiang Province) in Wu-ch'ang (in 343), Ch'ung hastened back from Ching-k'ou (Kiangsu), and said to Emperor K'ang, "It's improper for Ping to leave the capital. Last year (342), when Your majesty made his dragon flight, causing the virtue of Chin to prosper once again, it was all through Ping's merit. Your servant had no part in it."

42. When Chiang Pin was young, Chancellor Wang Tao once invited him to play a game of encirclement chess (*wei-ch'i*) with him.¹ Although Wang usually played with a handicap of two lines or so, on this occasion he wanted an equally matched game as an experiment, in order to observe Chiang.

Chiang did not immediately put down any pieces, and Wang asked, "Why don't you move?"

Chiang said, "I'm afraid it won't do this way."

One of the bystanders said, "This young man's game isn't bad, eh?"

Wang, slowly lifting his head, said, "As far as this young man is concerned, it's not only chess at which he excels."

¹*FWCP*: Chiang Pin and Wang Tao's son, Wang T'ien, tied for first class (as chess players). Wang Tao himself was fifth class.

43. When K'ung T'an was critically ill (336), Yü Ping, who was then serving as governor of K'uai-chi Principality (Chekiang), went to visit him, inquiring about his condition with extreme solicitude, and weeping over him.

After Yü had gotten down from the bed, K'ung said with deep feeling, "A great man is about to die, and instead of asking about a policy for keeping the state at peace, here you are asking the kinds of questions women and children ask!"

On hearing this, Yü turned back to apologize, and requested his last words of counsel. (*CS* 78.8b)

44. Huan Wen once went to visit Liu T'an. Liu was lying in bed and did not get up. Drawing his crossbow, Huan shot it at Liu's (ceramic) pillow, and the (clay) pellet shattered all over the bedclothes.

Liu, flushing with anger, got up and said, "Governor,¹ are you trying to win a battle in a place like this?"

Huan looked extremely contrite.

¹*CHS*: Huan Wen at one time served as governor of Hsü Province (northern Kiangsu and Anhui).

SSHY Comm.: P'ei Principality (Liu T'an's native place) belonged to Hsü Province, so T'an addressed Wen as "Governor." The reference to "winning a battle" was because Wen was also a general.

45. There were many young people of the later generation who used to characterize the monk Chu Ch'ien. Ch'ien said to them, "You yellow-

billed fledglings, don't criticize or discuss the gentlemen of the past. In the old days I used to travel about with the two emperors, Yüan (r. 317-323) and Ming (r. 323-326), and the two courtiers, Wang Tao and Yü Liang."[1]

[1]*KISMC*: The two Chin emperors, Yüan and Ming, let their minds wander freely in the Mysterious and Empty (*hsüan-hsü*), and committed their feelings to the flavor of the Way. They treated the dharma master Chu Ch'ien as they would have entertained a friend. Wang Tao and Yü Liang sat in rapt attention beside his mat, enjoying the same tastes as his own.

46. When Wang T'an-chih was young, Chiang Pin, who was doubling as vice-president of the Board of Civil Office in charge of the selection of officials, was on the point of picking Wang for clerk of the Imperial Secretariat.

When someone informed Wang, Wang said, "Ever since the crossing of the Yangtze River (307-312) they have used nothing but second-rate men as clerks of the Imperial Secretariat. Why did they have to pick me?"

Chiang, hearing of this, desisted.[1] (*CS* 75.6b)

[1]*Wang Piao-chih PC*: Piao-chih's (305-377) paternal uncle, Wang Tao, once said to him, "If the selection board picks you for clerk of the Imperial Secretariat, with luck you might become an assistant to one of the imperial princes."

SSHY Comm.: From this we know that the office of clerk was in the poor and humble category.

47. When Wang Shu was transferred to become president of the Imperial Secretariat (in 364), as soon as his affairs were in order, he immediately took up his new post. His son, Wang T'an-chih, said, "Surely you ought to have declined and dissembled a few times?"[1]

Shu rejoined, "Would you say I'm fit for this post, or not?"

T'an-chih said, "Why wouldn't you be fit for it? It's only that 'being able to decline'[2] is in itself an excellent thing, and I daresay not to be neglected."

Sighing, Shu said, "Since you've said I'm fit for the post, why should I still decline? People say you're superior to me, but it turns out you're not even my equal."[3] (*CS* 75.5a)

[1]*Ku ying jang tu hsü*. Kawakatsu et al., *Chūgoku koshōsetsushū*, p. 107, translate, "Couldn't you have yielded in favor of Tu or Hsü?" I feel, however, that since the identity of these persons is not readily apparent, it is preferable to take *tu* as a verb, "to dissemble," and *hsü* as a verbal complement, "a few times."

[2]See "Book of Documents," *Yao-tien* I, 1 (Legge III, 15): Yao was respectful and able to decline.

[3]*Wang Shu PC*: Wang Shu always maintained that in occupying an office a man ought first to estimate his own capacity and then act accordingly. He meant there should be no specious declining. Therefore, if he ought to refuse a post, he should steadfastly stay by his refusal. Shu's integrity and honesty in not violating this rule were always of this sort.

48. When Sun Ch'o composed his "Obituary for Yü Liang" (*Yü-kung lei*), the text was full of expressions of mutual intimacy.¹ After it was completed, he had someone show it to Liang's son, Yü Hsi. Hsi read it and with a sigh sent it back with the message, "My late father's relation with you, sir, hardly reached this degree of intimacy!"

¹Cf. *SSHY* IV, 78, above.
SunCC:

> Alas for me and you--
> Our refined manners reverted to a common source!
> Like in degree our mutual love;
> I looked upon you as my mentor.
>
> Friendship between gentlemen
> Gives mutually, is free of self;
> In humbleness accepts the right,
> Speaks forth sincerity, rebukes the wrong.
>
> Although, indeed, I am not bright,
> Respectfully I gird "bowstring and thong,"
> Forever cherishing your words,
> My mouth intoning my heart's grief.

(See *Han-fei-tzu* 24.146: Hsi-men Pao's disposition was hasty, so he girded himself with a thong to restrain himself; Tung An-yü's mind was slothful, so he girded himself with a bowstring to urge himself on.)

49. (About 345) when Wang Meng had requested the post of grand warden of Tung-yang (Chekiang), the General Governing the Army (Ssu-ma Yü) had not used him. Later, after he became critically ill and was about to die (347), the general, sighing with grief, said, "I'm obligated to Wang Meng in this matter," and issued an order to employ him.
Wang Meng said, "People say the Prince of K'uai-chi (Ssu-ma Yü) is an idiot. He really *is* an idiot!" (*CS* 93.10b)

50. Liu Chien had served as Huan Wen's lieutenant-governor of Hsü Province. Later (after Huan became grand marshal in 363) he served as his eastern office aide, but because he was unbending and straightforward, he became somewhat estranged from Huan.
Once while they were listening to a lawsuit, Chien said absolutely nothing. Huan asked, "Liu, why don't you hand down an opinion?"
He replied, "It happens to be one you can't use."
Huan, for his part, showed no surprise.

51. Liu T'an and Wang Meng were once traveling together. The day was far spent and they had not yet eaten. A certain commoner (*hsiao-jen*) of their acquaintance offered them his own dinner, placing rich foods in great abundance on the table, but Liu declined to eat any of it.
Wang said, "It's only to 'satisfy hunger';¹ why insist on declining?"
Liu said, "With petty persons (*hsiao-jen*) one simply may not have any dealings whatever."² (*TPYL* 849)

¹*Mo-tzu* 21.102: In the rule of the sage-kings of antiquity, the laws for eating and drinking were: to stop after having had enough to satisfy hunger, etc.

[2]"Analects" XVII, 23: It's only women and petty persons who are hard to deal with. If one is too intimate, they become unruly; if too distant, they are resentful.

52. Wang Hu-chih was once living in the Eastern Mountains (Chekiang) in extreme poverty and want. T'ao Fan, who was serving as magistrate of Wu-ch'eng Prefecture (Chekiang), sent him a boatload of rice as a present, but he declined and would not accept it, responding bluntly, "If Wang Hu-chih were hungry, naturally he'd go to Hsieh Shang to ask for food. He has no need of T'ao Fan's rice."[1] (SWLC 22)

[1]No explanation is offered for this snub. It may be because the Wangs of Lang-yeh and the T'ao's were not of the same faction, or, more likely, because T'ao Fan's father, K'an, was a military man and therefore socially inferior.

53. When Juan Yü went (from K'uai-chi) to attend the funeral of Emperor Ch'eng (r. 326-342) at the imperial mausoleum (outside of Chien-k'ang), after arriving in the capital, he did not visit the homes of either Yin Hao or Liu T'an, but when his business was completed promptly returned home. Everybody followed after him in a body, but since he also was aware that the fashionable crowd would surely pursue him, he departed with all possible dispatch, and reached Square Mountain (Fang-shan, forty-five li southeast of Chien-k'ang) before they caught up with him.

At the time Liu T'an was visiting K'uai-chi, and sighed, saying, "When I came here I was just on the point of mooring my boat below An-shih Island (near Juan Yü's hermitage), but didn't dare get any closer than that to Juan Yü himself. If I had, he could have seized a staff and beaten me, which would have been no laughing matter!"[1] (CS 49.10a)

[1]CHS: Juan Yü would lie around listlessly all day. He did nothing to bring it about, yet other people would spontaneously honor him. (Cf. SSHY IX, 30, n. 1, below.)

54. Wang Meng, Liu T'an, and Huan Wen went together to Overturned Boat Mountain (Fu-chou shan, northeast of Chien-k'ang) for an outing. After the wine had begun to take effect, Liu drew his foot up and placed it on Huan's neck. Huan did not tolerate this at all, and raising his hand, brushed it away.

After they had returned, Wang Meng said to Liu, "Do you mean to say he can overawe other people by his physical appearance?"[1]

[1]Huan Wen PC: Wen had a heroic and overbearing manner.

55. Huan Wen once asked Huan I*, "Since Hsieh An knew in advance that his younger brother, Hsieh Wan, would surely be defeated (in 359),[1] why didn't he warn him?"

Huan I* replied, "Probably because Wan is a difficult man to cross, that's all."

Flushing with anger, Wen said, "Hsieh Wan is pliant and weak, with only average ability. What kind of severe countenance has he, that makes him so difficult to cross?"

[1]In Huan Wen's northern campaign of 359, Hsieh Wan had suffered a disastrous rout at Hsia-ts'ai (northern Anhui) at the hands of the

Former Yen ruler, Mu-jung Chün (r. 349-360), for which he was temporarily divested of noble rank.

56. Lo Han was once in a certain person's home, when the host asked him to converse with the other guests who were seated there.
He replied, "The people I know already are too many; don't bother to introduce me to any more."

57. While Han Po was ill, he used to wander about his front courtyard leaning on a staff. Seeing the various members of the Hsieh family,[1] all wealthy and honorable, thundering past pompously in their carriages up and down the street, he sighed and said, "How does this differ from the days of Wang Mang?"[2]

[1] The Hsieh faction, represented by Hsieh An, his cousin, Hsieh Shang, and his younger brother, Hsieh Wan, dominated the Eastern Chin court during most of the reign of Emperor Hsiao-wu (373-397), after which they were replaced by Hsieh An's son-in-law, Wang Kuo-pao, and his cousin, Ssu-ma Tao-tzu, in 385. The Hsieh's greatest moment was the victory over Fu Chien at the Fei River in 383.

[2] Wang Mang, ruler of the short-lived Hsin Dynasty (A.D. 9-23), was the nephew of the consort of the Former Han Emperor Yüan (r. 48-33 B.C.), who came to power through his aunt's connections.
HS 99A.1a: Of the members of Wang Mang's family and clan there were in all ten marquises and five grand marshals. No consort family had ever been more flourishing than they.

58. While Wang T'an-chih was serving as Huan Wen's senior administrator (363), Huan sought Wang's daughter for a marriage with his son. Wang promised to talk it over with his father, Wang Shu.
Later he returned home. Now Wang Shu was very fond of T'an-chih, and even though he was fully grown, he still used to hold him on his knees. T'an-chih then told him of Huan's suit for his own daughter in marriage. In a great rage Shu thrust T'an-chih down from his knees, crying, "Are you also such a fool as to be intimidated by Huan Wen's face? A military man, eh? How could you ever give your daughter in marriage to *him*!"
T'an-chih returned and reported to Huan, "In this humble official's family we had previously arranged a marriage contract for our daughter."
Huan said, "I understand. This simply means your esteemed father is unwilling, that's all."
Later Huan's second daughter (Huan Po-tzu) eventually was given in marriage to T'an-chih's second son (Wang Yü).[1] (CS 75.5a; TPYL 541)

[1] The Commentary, citing the *Wang SP*, identifies the son as Wang K'ai, T'an-chih's eldest. The CSCC 75.15a, however, points out that it is Yü, not K'ai, who is called Huan Wen's "son-in-law" (*hsü*), and Yü's son, Sui, Huan Hsüan's "cousin" (*sheng*).

59. When Wang Hsien-chih was only a few years of age, he was once watching his father's pupils playing *chaupar* (*shu-p'u*). Seeing in advance who was going to win or lose, he said, "'The southern airs can't compete (with the northern).'"[1]

The pupils, belittling him because he was a small boy, then said, "This lad's another case of someone 'peeping at a leopard through a tube';[2] every now and then he sees a spot."

With an angry glare Hsien-chih snapped, "From the more distant past, I'm ashamed for you in the presence of Hsün Ts'an (d. 240), and from the recent past, I blush for you in the presence of Liu T'an (d. ca. 347)."[3] With that he dusted off his clothes and departed. (CS 80.12ab)

[1] *Tso-chuan*, Hsiang 18 (Legge V, 479): The people of Ch'u were attacking Cheng. Shih K'uang (a blind musician of the Chin court) said, "No harm will come of it . . . I have just now sung sourthern airs, and the southern airs cannot compete (with the northern), but are full of the sounds of death. Ch'u (a southern state) will surely not succeed.

[2] Cf. *Chuang-tzu* XVII, 18ab (Watson, 187): Is this not like peeping at the heavens through a tube?

[3] I.e., Hsün and Liu would have appreciated his perceptiveness.

60. Hsieh An, having heard of Yang Sui's excellence, sent a message inviting him to come, but to the end Yang was unwilling to visit him. Later, while Sui was an erudite in the Grand Academy, he went to see Hsieh about some matter, and Hsieh immediately secured him for his superintendent of records.

61. Wang Hsi-chih once accompanied Hsieh An to visit Juan Yü. When they reached the gate, Wang said to Hsieh, "Of course we ought both to recommend our host (as foremost conversationalist)."

Hsieh said, "Recommending people is exactly the thing that is naturally difficult."

62. When the Hall of the Grand Ultimate (*T'ai-chi tien*) was newly completed (in 378),[1] Wang Hsien-chih was at the time serving as Hsieh An's senior administrator. Hsieh sent a placard with an order for Wang to inscribe the title of the hall on it.

Wang, looking as if he had been insulted, said to the messenger, "You may throw it outside the gate."

Later Hsieh saw Wang and asked, "How are things going with inscribing the placard and mounting it on the hall? Formerly, during the Wei Dynasty (220-265), Wei Tan and others also did the same thing themselves."[2]

Wang quipped, "That's why the Wei mandate didn't last."

Hsieh considered this a famous remark.[3] (CS 80.13ab)

[1] *HKCC*: In the second year of the Ning-k'ang era of Emperor Hsiao-wu (374) the president of the Imperial Secretariat, Wang Piao-chih, and others, memorialized the throne to build a new palace.

In the second month of the third year of the T'ai-yüan era (378), six thousand men of the Palace Guard and the army began the work of construction, completing it by the seventh month. The Hall of the Grand Ultimate was eighty feet (*ch'ih*) high, two hundred seventy feet long, and one hundred feet wide. Hsieh Wan supervised the project, for which he was granted noble rank as Marquis Within the Passes. The chief architect, Mao An-chih, was granted the rank of Marquis Amid the Passes.

[2] See *SSHY* XXI, 3, below.

[3] *SMTWCC*: In the T'ai-yüan era (376-396) the new palace was completed, and the advisers for the project wanted to impress Wang Hsien-chih into inscribing the signboard, so that it would be a treasure for ten thousand generations. During the verbal exchange between Hsieh An and Wang on the subject, Hsieh took the occasion to mention the time during the Wei Kingdom when they were building the Ling-yün Pavilion (see *SSHY* XXI, 3, below) and had forgotten to inscribe the signboard, and consequently had made Wei Tan inscribe it while sitting on a suspended bench. By the time Wei had gotten back down, his beard and hair had turned completely white, and he was gasping for breath. After returning home, he said to the young people of his family, "You should all stop studying how to write formal script (*k'ai-fa*)."

Hsieh An had hoped by this recital to influence Wang's thinking, but Wang, seeing through his intentions, said with a solemn expression, "That was a strange business. Wei Tan was a great minister of the Wei court. How could they make him do a thing like that? Now I can understand why the virtue of Wei didn't last." Hsieh An understood his thoughts and put no further pressure on him.

63. Wang Kung wanted to ask Chiang Ai to serve as his senior administrator. Early one morning he set out to visit Chiang, but Chiang was still inside the bed curtains. Wang sat down, not daring to speak immediately about his mission. After a long while he finally got an opportunity to mention it, but Chiang did not answer. Directly calling a servant to bring wine, he drank a bowlful by himself, without offering any at all to Wang.

Laughing as he spoke, Wang said, "Who ever heard of drinking alone?"

Chiang said, "Do you want some, too?" Whereupon he called the servant again and drank a toast with Wang. Wang finished drinking the wine, and thus got to excuse himself and leave.

Before he went out the door, Chiang heaved a sigh and said, "A man's evaluation of his own capacities is certainly a difficult thing."

64. Emperor Hsiao-wu (Ssu-ma Yao, r. 373-396) asked Wang Shuang, "How would you rate yourself in comparison with your older brother, Wang Kung?"

Shuang replied, "As far as being outstanding for cultivated manners (*feng-liu*) is concerned, your servant is no match for Kung, but in loyalty and filial devotion, in what respect am I inferior to him?"[1]

[1] *CHS*: Wang Shuang was loyal and filial, square and blunt. When Emperor Hsiao-wu deceased, Wang Kuo-pao opened the palace gate by night and entered to receive the emperor's last bequest. Shuang, who was serving as a palace attendant, blocked his way, saying, "His Majesty has just deceased; the crown prince has not yet been determined. Whoever presumes to enter first will be beheaded." Terrified, Kuo-pao stopped in his tracks.

65. Wang Shuang was drinking with the grand tutor (Ssu-ma Tao-tzu). The grand tutor, who was quite drunk, kept addressing Wang as "my little boy" (*hsiao-tzu*).

Wang said, "My late grandfather, the senior administrator (Wang Meng), was a friend of Emperor Chien-wen (Ssu-ma Yü, r. 371-372), when the latter was still wearing cotton clothing (i.e., in obscurity). My late aunt (Wang Mu-chih), and my late elder sister (Wang Fa-hui), were both devoted consorts in the palaces of the two emperors Ai (Ssu-ma P'ei, r. 362-364) and Hsiao-wu (Ssu-ma Yao, r. 373-396). Where do you get that 'little boy' stuff?" (*CS* 93.12b-13a)

66. Chang Hsüan and Wang Ch'en had previously not been acquainted with each other. Eventually they met at the home of Fan Ning, and Fan had the two men converse together. Chang accordingly straightened his seat and pulled in his lapels in anticipation. Wang stared fixedly at him for a long while and said nothing. Greatly disappointed, Chang prepared to leave, but Fan kept making explanations in an effort to detain him. In the end he was unwilling to stay.

Since Fan was Wang's uncle, he chided him, saying, "Chang Hsüan is the most outstanding of all the gentlemen of Wu, and moreover is treated with respect by all his contemporaries, yet you have brought things to this pass! I can't understand you at all."

Wang, laughing, said, "If Chang Hsüan wants to make my acquaintance, he should come himself to see me."

Fan sent someone posthaste to inform Chang of this, and Chang immediately tied his girdle and went to visit him. After that they raised their cups and conversed together without any feelings of awkwardness on the part of either guest or host. (*CS* 75.14b)

CHAPTER VI

Cultivated Tolerance

1. The grand warden of Yü-chang Commandery (Kiangsi), Ku Shao, was the son of Ku Yung. Shao died while still in the commandery. Yung had called a large gathering of his officials and subordinates, and was himself in the midst of a game of encirclement chess (wei-ch'i). Reports from the outer (commanderies) arrived, but there was no letter from his son. Although he showed no change in his spirit and manner, in his heart he divined the reason, and with his fingernails he dug into the palm of his hand until the blood flowed, soaking the mat.

Only after his guests had dispersed did he finally heave a sigh and say, "Since I don't possess the lofty aloofness of a Chi Cha,[1] at least let me not be reproached for 'losing my eyesight' (from weeping)."[2] So saying, he gave vent to his emotions and dissipated his grief, after which his facial expression again became self-possessed. (TPYL 518; SWLC, hou 7)

[1] See "Record of Rites" IV, 59 (Legge, Li Ki I, 192-193): Chi Cha of Yen-ling (Kiangsu) went to Ch'i (Shantung). On his return his eldest son died, and he buried him between Ying and Po (Shantung). Confucius said, "Chi Cha is the most versed in ritual practice in the state of Wu. I went and observed the burial. The pit was deep, but did not reach water level. The corpse was dressed in the clothes of the times. After the burial a mound was raised, broad enough to cover the pit and high enough to lean on. After the mound was raised, with his left arm bare, he proceeded toward the right around the mound, crying out three times, 'The fact that his bones and flesh return again to the soil is fate, but his soul and vital breath are everywhere!' And with this he went on his way." Confucius continued, "How in agreement Chi Cha was with the 'Rites'!"

[2] Ibid. III, 36 (Legge, Li Ki I, 135-136): When Confucius' disciple Tzu-hsia was mourning his son, he lost his eyesight (from weeping and malnutrition). Tseng-tzu (another disciple) went to console

him with the words, "When a friend or companion loses his eyesight, one weeps for him."

As Tseng-tzu wept, Tzu-hsia also wept, crying, "O Heaven! I am innocent!"

Tseng-tzu replied in anger, "Shang (Tzu-hsia's given name), in what way are you innocent? You and I served the Master between the Chu and Ssu rivers (Shantung), and now you have retired and grown old in Hsi-ho (Shansi), and have made the people of the area confuse you with the Master. This was your first offense. When you mourned for your parents, you did so in such a way that the people never heard of it. This was your second offense. Now in mourning for your son, you've lost your eyesight. This is your third offense."

Tzu-hsia threw down his staff and did obeisance, crying, "I've done wrong! I've done wrong!"

2. On the eve of Hsi K'ang's execution in the Eastern Marketplace of Lo-yang (in 262),[1] his spirit and manner showed no change. Taking out his seven-stringed zither (*ch'in*), he plucked the strings and played the "Melody of Kuang-ling" (*Kuang-ling san*). When the song was ended, he said, "Yüan Chun once asked to learn this melody, but I remained firm in my stubbornness, and never gave it to him. From now on the 'Melody of Kuang-ling' is no more!"

Three thousand scholars of the Grand Academy sent up a petition requesting Hsi's release to become their teacher, but it was not granted. Ssu-ma Chao (who had ordered the execution) himself later repented of it. (*CS* 49.16)

[1]The location of the Ox and Horse Market where Hsi K'ang was executed is described in *LYCLC* II.

CYC: Earlier Hsi K'ang and Lü An of Tung-p'ing (Shantung) were intimate friends. An's own elder brother, Lü Hsün, committed adultery with An's wife, Lady Hsü. An, wishing to make a public accusation of Hsün and to divorce his wife, consulted with Hsi K'ang about it. K'ang advised him to desist. Meanwhile, Hsün, ill at ease with himself, surreptitiously spread rumors accusing An of beating his mother, and sent up a memorial requesting that he be exiled to the border. As An was about to go into exile, he made a plea in his own defense in the text of which he mentioned Hsi K'ang.

WSC: When Lü An got into trouble, Hsi K'ang visited the prison to get a clarification of the circumstances. Chung Hui wrote a public accusation against K'ang, which said, "Today the imperial way is clear and enlightened, and the winds of its morality are wafted to all within the Four Seas. Along the frontiers are no speciously subservient peoples, and in the streets and alleys no dissident counsels. But Hsi K'ang does not subject himself to the Son of Heaven above, nor does he serve the princes and nobles below. He despises the times, is arrogant toward the world, and is of no use to his fellows. Unprofitable to the present age, he is a baneful influence on its morals. In antiquity T'ai-kung Wang (adviser to King Wen, eleventh cent. B.C.) executed Hua Shih, and Confucius put to death Shao-cheng Mao (see *SC* 47.9b), because they boasted of their talent while inciting the people to rebellion and deluding the masses. Today, if Hsi K'ang is not executed, there will be no means of purifying the Royal Way."

Thereupon Hsi K'ang was convicted and imprisoned. On the eve of his death, his elder and younger brothers and his nearest of kin went together to bid him farewell. K'ang's facial expression showed no change. He asked his elder brother, "Have you brought my zither?" His brother said, "Yes, I've brought it." K'ang took and tuned it and played the "Melody of the Grand Peace" (*T'ai-p'ing yin*). After the song ended, he sighed and said, "The 'Melody of the Grand Peace' from now on is no more!"

WYCS: On the occasion of Hsi K'ang's imprisonment, several thousand scholars of the Grand Academy made a petition on his behalf, and all the great and powerful figures of the time followed K'ang into prison. All of them sought to obtain his release, but were simultaneously dispersed and sent away. In the end K'ang was executed together with Lü An.

3. Hsia-hou Hsüan was once writing propped against a tree trunk. At the time a heavy rainstorm came up, and a crashing thunderbolt split the trunk against which he was propped, leaving his clothes singed and burned. His spirit and facial expression showed no change, and he went on writing as before. The guests who were in attendance all fell into a panic and were unable to stay.[1] (*SLF* 3; *TPYL* 13, 187; *SWLC*, ch'ien 4)

[1]*YL*: Hsia-hou Hsüan had accompanied the Wei emperor to sacrifice at the imperial tombs, and was among the company under the pines and cypresses. At the time a heavy rainstorm came up, and a crashing thunderbolt made a direct hit on the tree under which he was standing, leaving his cap singed and torn. Those in attendance who saw it fell on their faces, but Hsüan's facial expression did not change.

(Liu Chün's Commentary points out that the account of this incident in *TJHCS* substitutes Chu-ko Tan for Hsia-hou Hsüan. So also *PTSC* 152, citing *TCCCC*.)

4. When Wang Jung was in his seventh year, he was once playing with the other little boys when they spied a plum tree by the side of the road with so much fruit the weight was breaking the branches. All the boys raced over to pick the plums. Jung alone remained unmoved. When someone asked him about it, he replied, "If the tree is by the side of the road and still has so much fruit, this means they must be bitter plums." When they picked them, they found it indeed to be the case.[1] (*CS* 43.9b; *IWLC* 68; *PSLT* 30; *TPYL* 385; *SWLC*, hou 25)

[1]*MSC*: Because of this incident Wang Jung was acclaimed for his divine intelligence even in his youth.

5. Emperor Ming of Wei (Ts'ao Jui, r. 227-239) was having a tiger's claws and teeth cut off on the Hsüan-wu Review Grounds (north of Lo-yang), and had permitted the common people to watch. Wang Jung, then in his seventh year, had also gone to look. The tiger, taking advantage of an unguarded moment, climbed up on the railing and roared, his voice shaking the earth. The spectators all fled wildly in every direction, falling headlong in their excitement, but Jung remained placid and motionless, without the slightest appearance of being afraid.[1] (*CS* 43.9b)

¹*CLCHL*: Emperor Ming was himself watching from a pavilion and witnessed Jung's behavior. He sent a man to ask Jung's surname and given name and marveled at him.

6. When Wang Jung was serving as personal attendant, the grand warden of Nan Commandery (Hupei), Liu Chao, sent a bribe of fifty[1] bolts (*tuan*) of sheer cloth (*chien-pu*) in bamboo tubes. Although Jung did not accept it, he responded cordially to his letter.[2] (*CS* 43.10b-11a)

¹Emending *wu* to *wu-shih*, after both *CS* 43.10b and *CYC*.

²*CYC*: The commandant of the Capital Province (Honan), Liu I, sent up a memorial reporting that the grand warden of Nan Commandery, Liu Chao, had sent a bribe of fifty bolts (*p'i*) of cloth and other miscellaneous objects to the former governor of Yü Province (southern Honan), Wang Jung, and requested that Liu Chao be sent to the capital in a caged van and delivered to the director of punishments to be dealt with for his offense, and that his name be removed from the register of officials for the rest of his life. Since Jung in his letter of response had not agreed to the bribe, he was not implicated.

CLCHL: Because Wang Jung had responded to Liu Chao's letter, the counselors at court all considered him deserving of censure. But Emperor Wu (Ssu-ma Yen, r. 265-299) was displeased with this, and issued an oral statement, saying, "As far as Wang Jung in his capacity as a gentleman is concerned, how could his intentions ever include self-interest?" Thereafter the counselors desisted, and Jung for his part did not offer any apology.

7. When P'ei K'ai was arrested (in 291),[1] his spirit and manner showed no change, and his demeanor remained self-possessed. Requesting paper and brush, he proceeded to write letters. After the letters were completed and delivered, those who came to his rescue were many, and thus he gained his release. Later he was given rank with ceremony equal to the Three Ducal Offices. (*CS* 35.15a)

¹*CCKT*: P'ei K'ai's son, Tsan, had married the daughter of Yang Chün (father of the consort of Emperor Wu). When Chün was executed (in 291), K'ai, because he was related to Chün by marriage, was arrested and handed over to the director of punishments. The personal attendant, Fu Chih (a recipient of one of the letters), gave evidence of K'ai's past loyalty, and thereby he gained his release.

MSC: During the troubles over the Prince of Ch'u (Ssu-ma Wei, who was also killed by Empress Chia in 291), Li Chao, resenting the fact that K'ai's reputation was weightier than his own, arrested him and was on the point of putting him to death. K'ai's spirit and facial expression showed no change, and his every movement was self-possessed. Everyone requested that he be spared, and thus he gained his release.

8. Wang Yen had once entrusted some business to a kinsman, who had let the time go by without doing it. Meeting the kinsman by chance at a banquet in a certain place, Wang took the occasion to say, "In regard to that piece of business I recently entrusted to you, how is it you haven't done it yet?"

The kinsman, becoming very angry, raised his wine cup and flung it in Wang's face. Wang said absolutely nothing. After he had finished washing his face and hands, he led Chancellor Wang Tao out by the arm and left in the same carriage with him. In the carriage he looked in a mirror and said to the chancellor, "Look at the luster of my eyes, how it gleams even brighter than the back of the carriage ox!"[1] (CS 43.14a; TPYL 759)

[1] SSHY Comm.: Wang Yen evidently thought of himself as dignified and outstanding in manner and spirit, not stooping to pick quarrels with others.

9. P'ei Hsia was at Chou Fu's place, where Fu had arranged to be host for a party. Hsia was playing encirclement chess with someone, when Fu's sergeant-at-arms wanted to drink a toast with him. Since Hsia was in the midst of the game, he did not immediately drink. The sergeant-at-arms became furious and dragged Hsia backward so that he fell on the floor. Hsia returned to his seat, his demeanor and facial expression unchanged, and resumed the game where he had left off.

Wang Yen later asked Hsia, "At the time, how was it that your facial expression showed nothing unusual?"

He replied, "Because he was just trying to pick a private quarrel,[1] that's all." (CS 35.18b-19a)

[1] I have accepted Yang Yung's suggestion that the obviously garbled text (an-tang/ an-ku/ tou-chiang) should be tou-pien, "a private quarrel."

10. While Liu Yü was senior administrator on the staff of the grand tutor (Ssu-ma Yüeh), many gentlemen of the time were implicated by him in various offenses. Yü Ai alone, by setting his mind free beyond the affairs of the world, left no traces by which he might be incriminated.

Later, because Yü's nature was frugal, though his family was wealthy, Liu spoke to the grand tutor, asking him to have Yü change one hundred thousand cash, in the expectation that Yü would short-change him, and thus become vulnerable.

In the midst of a large gathering the grand tutor asked Yü about it. At the time Yü was slumped down, already quite drunk, his cap having fallen onto the table. Pushing forward with his head, he put it back on, and with deliberation answered, "In this petty official's home of course there should be two or three hundred thousand cash. Let His Excellency take as much as he wants." At this Liu gave up his quest.

Afterward, someone mentioned this incident to Yü, who said, "It's what you might call trying to measure the mind of a gentleman by the scheming of a petty man."[1] (CS 50.8a)

[1] Tso-chuan, Ai 11 (Legge V, 824): If a gentleman has long-range schemes, what would a petty man know about them?
(In CS 50.8a the last remark is made by Ssu-ma Yüeh.)

11. Wang Yen and P'ei Mo disagreed in their ambitions and tastes. P'ei resented this, and wanted to provoke Wang into an argument, but in the end could not get any response. Finally he went deliberately

to visit Wang, and let his words fly in a torrent of extreme abuse, hoping to make Wang answer him, so that they would "share the reproach"[1] evenly.

Wang showed no sign of anger, but said calmly, "So now the white-eyed boy (*pai-yen erh*) has started in."

[1] *Tso-chuan*, Hsüan 12 (Legge V, 320): Sui Chi said, "The Ch'u army is just now at its strongest. If they join battle with us, our army will surely be decimated. It would be better to gather our forces and retreat, and share the reproach with the living. Wouldn't that, in its way, be permissible?"

12. Wang Yen was older than P'ei Wei by four years[1] but had not previously made his acquaintance. Once when all of the famous gentlemen of the time were together in one place, someone said to Wang, "In what way is P'ei worthy of respect?" So after that Wang always addressed P'ei with the familiar pronoun "you" (*ch'ing*).

P'ei remarked, "Sir (*chün*), of course you may fulfill your well-bred ambitions (by calling me 'you')."

[1] According to information derived from their biographies, Wang was born in 256 and P'ei in 267, which makes an actual differential of ten or eleven years.

13. (In 338) there were those who traveled back and forth (along the Yangtze River) who reported, "Yü Liang has intentions of coming east (for a coup d'etat)."[1] Someone said to Wang Tao, "You'd better take some slight precautions in secret to guard against any mishap."

Wang replied, "In my relations with Yü Liang, in spite of the fact that we're both His Majesty's ministers, I've always cherished our friendship from the time we were both wearing cotton clothes. If he should actually wish to come, I'd don the cornered cap (*chüeh-chin*) of a retired gentleman and go straight back home to Black Clothing Street (Wu-i, southeast of Chien-k'ang).[2] What is there to take any 'slight precautions' about?" (*CS* 65.9a)

[1] In 339 Yü Liang, who was then governor-general of military affairs in six provinces, with headquarters in Wu-ch'ang (Hupei), did actually contemplate a coup against Wang, who was still chancellor, though his faction was no longer dominant at court. However, Yü won no support for his plan. Wang died the same year, and Yü the year following.

[2] The street followed along the south bank of the Ch'in-huai River near the Vermilion Sparrow Bridge.

TYC: Black Clothing Street originated in Wu times (223-280) as a place where black clothes were manufactured. When the Chin was newly restored east of the Yangtze River (in 317), it became the site where the Wangs of Lang-yeh lived.

CHS: Thereupon (i.e., after Wang Tao's remark) the wind and dust were dissipated of themselves, and affairs inside and outside the court grew orderly and peaceful.

14. Chancellor Wang Tao's superintendent of records was about to make an investigation of all the personnel under Wang's jurisdiction. Wang said to him, "I'd better make the rounds with you, to make sure you don't try to find out about other people's legal cases."

15. Tsu Yüeh loved money, while Juan Fu loved wooden clogs (*chi*). Both of them constantly devoted themselves to their obsessions. Both were continually tired out by their labors, so that it was never settled which was the superior and which inferior.

Someone once went to visit Tsu, and found him counting and checking over his money and possessions. When the guest arrived, the process of putting them away had not yet been completed, and two leftover small round baskets (*lu*) had been placed hastily behind Tsu's back, while he bent his body to screen them, his mind unable to rest at ease.

Someone also went to visit Juan, and found him blowing the fire himself to wax his clogs. His guest on this occasion sighed and said, "I never knew how many pairs of clogs one would wear in one lifetime!"

Juan's spirit and facial expression remained perfectly relaxed and cheerful, and it was only then that it became apparent who was the winner and who the loser. (*CS* 49.7ab; *PTSC* 136)

16. Hsü Tsao and Ku Ho both served as administrators for Chancellor Wang Tao. At that time they had already met, and whether at banquets or other gatherings they were almost never separated. One evening they came to the chancellor's home for recreation. After the two had enjoyed themselves to the full, the chancellor invited them to retire inside his own bed curtains to sleep. Ku tossed and turned until dawn, unable to get comfortable, while Hsü was snoring with might and main the moment he touched the bed.

Looking back at the other guests, the chancellor said, "It's mighty hard to find a place to sleep in here!" (*SWLC*, hou 21)

17. Yü Liang was imposing and tall in manner and bearing, and never made an undignified movement. His contemporaries all considered him a poseur. Liang's firstborn son, Yü Hui,[1] was well-bred and dignified when he was only a few years of age. He was quite naturally like this, and everyone knew it was his native disposition.

Wen Ch'iao once hid behind a curtain and startled Hui. The boy's spirit and expression remained unruffled. Calmly kneeling down, he said, "Your Excellency, how could you do such a thing?" Those who discussed personalities agreed that he was in no way inferior to Liang.

During the rebellion of Su Chün (328) Hui was killed. Someone remarked, "After seeing the son, I knew that the father was no poseur." (*CS* 73.10b, of Yü Pin; *IWLC* 69; *PTSC* 133; *TPYL* 699)

[1] According to *CS* 73.10b, it was Liang's second son, Pin (also d. 328), not Hui.

18. (In 323) when Ch'u P'ou was transferred from being magistrate of Chang-an Prefecture (Kiangsi) to become secretarial aide[1] to the grand marshal (Yü Liang), his name was already well known, though his status was slight, and not many persons recognized him when they saw him. When Ch'u set out toward the east (to take up his new post in the capital), he boarded a merchant ship, and several of his fellow officials escorted him on his way, stopping for the night at the Ch'ient'ang Inn (Chekiang).[2]

186   TALES OF THE WORLD

At the time Shen Ch'ung of Wu-hsing (Chekiang) was magistrate of Ch'ien-t'ang Prefecture, and was just then escorting a guest across the Che River. When he and his guest appeared, the innkeeper evacuated Ch'u, and moved him down to the ox shed.

When the tidal bore came in,[3] Shen got up and was strolling back and forth. He asked, "Who's the fellow down in the ox shed?"

The innkeeper replied, "Yesterday there was this northerner (*ts'ang-fu*)[4] who came to stay in the inn. Since you had an honorable and noble guest, I temporarily moved him."

Shen, who was slightly tipsy, therefore called out from a distance, "Hey! you northerner! Would you like to eat some rice cakes (*ping*)? Let's get together and talk!"

Ch'u thereupon raised his hand and replied, "I'm Ch'u P'ou from Ho-nan."

Now everyone far and near had long since heard of Ch'u's name, and the magistrate, on hearing this, became greatly alarmed. Not daring to have Ch'u moved a second time, he went down personally to the ox shed and presented his card for a visit. In addition he ordered animals slaughtered for a sumptuous feast, and had the innkeeper horsewhipped in front of Ch'u, in hopes thereby of expiating his shame. Ch'u, for his part, drank and ate with him, neither his words nor facial expression showing anything unusual, and his manner appearing as if he were unaware of anything amiss. The magistrate escorted Ch'u on his way as far as the border of the prefecture.

[1]The *SSHY* Comm., citing the *YLCTTM*, states that Ch'u P'ou was only an aide, without secretarial duties. Yü Liang was keeper of central documents from 323 to 325, and since Shen Ch'ung died in 324, Ch'u must have been going to join the staff of that office. "Grand marshal" was Yü's posthumous title.

[2]*CTHC*: Ch'ien-t'ang Prefecture, being near the sea, is frequently inundated by the tides, so all the prominent families of the prefecture collected cash (*ch'ien*) and hired men to heap up the earth into dikes (*t'ang*).

[3]The famous Hangchow Bore, as the tide breaks into the estuary of the Ch'ien-t'ang River, is said to be at its peak at the full moon of the eighth lunar month, and has been the theme of poems and an attraction for tourists down to the present day.

[4]For a discussion of this term, see Hsü Shih-ying, "Chin-shih nan-pei jen hsiang-ch'ing," *Ta-lu tsa-chih* 1.6 (1950), 17.

19. While Ch'ih Chien was in Ching-k'ou (Kiangsu), he dispatched a retainer with a letter to Chancellor Wang Tao, requesting a son-in-law from among Wang's nephews for his daughter, Ch'ih Hsüan. The chancellor said to Ch'ih's messenger, "Go to the eastern apartment and follow your own wishes in making a choice."

After the retainer had returned, he reported to Ch'ih, "The sons of the Wang family are all of them admirable, each in his own way. When they heard that someone had come to spy out a son-in-law, they all conducted themselves with circumspection. There was just one son who was lying[1] sprawled out on the eastern bed as though he hadn't heard about it."

Ch'ih said, "He's just the one I want."
When he went to visit him, it turned out to be Wang Hsi-chih. So he gave his daughter to him in marriage. (CS 80.1b; TPYL 371, 444)

[1] Both CS 80.1b and TPYL say he was eating.

20. In the early days after the crossing of the Yangtze River, whenever an official was appointed, he would celebrate by holding a feast. When Yang Man was appointed capital intendant (in 324), the guests who came early all received fine entertainment, but as the day wore on, the provisions became exhausted, and were no longer up to their original excellence. It was entirely a matter of whether the guests came early or late, with no questions asked about high or low rank.
But when Yang Ku was appointed grand warden of Lin-hai Commandery (Chekiang), throughout the day it was all excellent entertainment. Even the latecomers received a sumptuous feast.
Contemporary critics considered that Yang Ku's plenty and grandeur were not as good as Yang Man's honesty and straightforwardness. (CS 49.24ab; TPYL 849; PTSC 143)

21. Chou Sung had been drinking and was drunk. With angry eyes he turned his face toward his elder brother, Chou I, and said, "Your ability isn't as good as mine, and yet, by some perversity, you've got a weightier reputation." A moment later he picked up a lighted candle and hurled it at I.
I, laughing, replied, "Little brother (A-nu), your 'attack by fire' certainly proceeds from an inferior strategy,[1] that's all I can say." (CS 69.18a)

[1] STPF XII, 216-222 (CTCC ed; trans. S. B. Griffith, Sun-tzu, the Art of War, Oxford, 1963, pp. 141-142): There are five kinds of attack by fire: (1) burning personnel, (2) burning supplies, (3) burning transport equipment, (4) burning arsenals, and (5) burning encampments . . . In general, the troops surely understand the variations of attack by fire . . . So he who uses attack by fire has to be intelligent.
Ibid. III, 35 (Griffith, p. 77): Generally, in the art of war, to take a state intact is best; to destroy a state is less desirable . . . To subdue the enemy without a battle is the best strategy of all.

22. While Ku Ho was first serving as an administrator in Wang Tao's government of Yang Province (Kiangsu-Anhui-Chekiang, ca. 318), the first morning of the month, at the time of the dawn audience, before entering, he stopped his carriage outside the provincial office gate. Chou I also arrived to see Chancellor Wang Tao and passed by the side of Ho's carriage. Ho was searching his clothes for lice and remained where he was impassively without budging. After Chou had passed by, he turned around and came back, and with his finger pointed at Ku's heart, asked, "What's inside here?"[1]
Ku, continuing to pick lice as before, calmly answered, "What's inside here is the most difficult place of all to fathom."
After Chou had entered, he said to the chancellor, "Among the officers in your provincial administration there's one with the ability

of a president or vice-president of the Imperial Secretariat." (CS 83.1ab; TPYL 265,444)

[1]SSHY Comm., citing the YL: Chou I had been drinking and was already drunk. Wearing a white lined garment (chia) and supported by two persons, he came to visit the chancellor.

23. Yü Liang had joined battle with Su Chün and been defeated (in 328). With ten or so attendants he boarded a small boat and fled westward (up the Yangtze toward Wu-ch'ang). When rebel soldiers came raiding and looting, one of Liang's attendants shot at them and accidentally hit Liang's own helmsman, who fell instantaneously with the twang of the bowstring. Everyone on board turned pale and scattered in confusion. Without changing his expression Liang calmly said, "How could a marksman as poor as this be used to hit the rebels?" Whereupon everyone became calm. (CS 73.4b)

24. Yü I had once gone out, and had not yet returned. His mother-in-law, Lady Juan (Juan Yu-o), who was the wife of Liu Sui, together with her daughter (Yü's wife, Liu Ching-nü), climbed the tower of the wall of An-lu (Hupei)[1] to watch for him. Very shortly I returned, whipping "a fine horse" complete with "chariot and defense."[2] Lady Juan said to her daughter, "I've heard that I is an able rider. How might I get to see him in action?"

His wife reported this to I, who, for her benefit, opened a space in the procession right where he was on the road. Mounting his horse, he started to wheel about in a double turn, but slipped from the horse and fell to the ground. His mood and facial expression remained completely self-possessed.

[1]The text reads An-ling, but the only towns of that name which are well known are in Honan and Shensi, and Yü I would have emigrated from the north when he was only six or seven. Since Yü I was temporarily stationed at An-lu Prefecture during his abortive northern campaign of 343 (see CS 73.19b and TCTC 97.3056), I suspect the ling of the text to be a scribal error for the similar lu, and have emended accordingly.

[2]"Book of Changes," Hex. 26, Ta-ch'u (Wilhelm I, 112): Nine in the third place: when a fine horse proceeds, it is advantageous to be aware of any difficulty. To practice chariot and defense, it is advantageous to have a destination.

25. Huan Wen was once riding in the same carriage with Emperor Chien-wen (Ssu-ma Yü) and the grand minister (Prince of Wu-ling, Ssu-ma Hsi). He had secretly ordered persons before and behind the carriage to blow horns and beat drums and make a great outcry. Pandemonium broke loose in the procession. In a blind panic the grand minister attempted to get down from the carriage. But when Huan looked around to observe Emperor Chien-wen, the latter was at ease and limpidly calm.

Huan said to the others, "To think that in the court there is such a worthy man as this!" (CS 9.5a)

26. Wang Shao and his younger brother, Wang Hui, went together to visit Huan Wen. It happened to be just at the time of the arrest of

Yü Hsi's entire family (in 372).¹ Hui, uneasy within himself, was fidgeting nervously and wanted to leave. But Shao sat stolidly without moving, waiting until word of the arrest was brought back. It was only after he had ascertained that the matter had been settled that he went out. Critics considered Shao the superior of the two.

¹*CHS*: Yü Hsi and his brothers (Ch'ien, Jou, Yün, Yu, and Mo) were all honorable and prosperous, and Huan Wen was jealous of them. (In 366) after criticizing Hsi, Huan relieved him of his post (as governor of Hsü and Yen provinces), after which Hsi took refuge in Chi-yang Prefecture (Kiangsu).

Earlier Kuo P'u had divined that Yü Ping's sons and grandsons would surely get into serious trouble, and only if they fortified themselves in the "three Yang" might they have any prosperity. Therefore Hsi requested to be stationed in Shan-yang (Honan), his younger brother, Yu, became grand warden of Tung-yang (Chekiang), and Hsi himself made his home at Chi-yang.

When Huan Wen executed Hsi (in 372), his younger brothers, Jou and Ch'ien, hearing of Hsi's troubles, fled to Hai-ling (Kiangsu), later returning to Ching-k'ou (northeast of Chien-k'ang), where they gathered together a host. But the plan failed, and they were executed by Huan Wen.

27. (In 372) Huan Wen and Ch'ih Ch'ao were deliberating over the weeding out and purging of the court ministers.¹ After it had been determined which names should be entered on the document, that night they slept in the same room. Early next morning Huan got up and called in Hsieh An and Wang T'an-chih. He tossed them the memorandum to look over, while Ch'ih was still inside the bed curtains.

Hsieh said absolutely nothing. Wang immediately tossed it back, stating that there were too many names.

Huan Wen took a brush and was on the point of crossing off some, when Ch'ih, without thinking, started to talk privately with Huan from inside the curtains.

Hsieh, repressing his laughter, said, "Master Ch'ih is what you might call the 'guest within the curtains.'"² (*CS* 67.20b; *TPYL* 699)

¹*HCYC*: Ch'ih Ch'ao felt that Huan Wen was a bold warrior, fit for the destiny of a leader, so he placed himself deeply in his confidence. Wen, for his part, also held him in deep trust and esteem. Therefore in his secret planning there was nothing in which Ch'ao was not first consulted.

²In the *CS* 67.20b version, the wind blew open the curtain and revealed Ch'ih.

28. While Hsieh An was in retirement in the Eastern Mountains (Chekiang, before 360), he was once boating on a lake for pleasure with Sun Ch'o, Wang Hsi-chih, and others.¹ When the wind rose and the waves tossed, Sun and Wang and the others all showed alarm in their faces and urged having the boat brought back to shore. But Hsieh An's spirit and feelings were just beginning to be exhilarated, and humming poems and whistling he said nothing. The boatman, seeing that Hsieh's manner was relaxed and his mood happy, continued to move on without stopping. But after the wind had become more and more violent

and the waves tempestuous, everyone was shouting and moving about and not remaining seated.

Hsieh calmly said, "If it's like this, let's go back."

Everyone immediately responded to his voice, and they turned back. After this it was realized that his tolerance was adequate for a governing post, either at court or in the provinces. (CS 79.4b; TPYL 392)

   [1]CHS: While Hsieh An was originally living in K'uai-chi Commandery he used to wander about in company with the monk Chih Tun, Wang Hsi-chih, and Hsü Hsün. Outdoors they would fish and hunt in the hills and streams, and indoors they would hold discussions on compositions and essays, without ever having the slightest intention of living in the world.

29. Huan Wen held a feast with armed men concealed about the premises, and extended invitations widely to the gentlemen of the court, with the intention of killing Hsieh An and Wang T'an-chih.[1] Wang was extremely apprehensive, and asked Hsieh, "What plan should we make?"

Hsieh, his spirit and mood showing no change, said to Wang, "Whether the Chin mandate survives or perishes will be determined by this one move."

As they went in together Wang's fears grew more and more apparent in his face, while Hsieh's cultivated tolerance became more and more evident in his manner. Gazing up the stairs, he proceeded to his seat, then started to hum a poem in the manner of the scholars of Lo-yang,[2] reciting the lines by Hsi K'ang, "Flowing, flowing mighty streams."[3] Huan, in awe of his untrammeled remoteness, thereupon hastened to disband the armed men.

Wang and Hsieh had hitherto been of equal reputation; it was only after this that they were distinguished as superior and inferior. (CS 79.5b; TPYL 302)

   [1]CATC: When Emperor Chien-wen deceased (in the summer of 372), he left a last bequest to Huan Wen that he should follow the precedent of Chu-ko Liang (whom Liu Pei had requested to serve as regent in 223) and Wang Tao (of whom Emperor Yüan had made a similar request in 322). Wen was greatly incensed, and considered it a detraction from his authority, instigated by Hsieh An and Wang T'an-chih. As they went to visit the imperial mausoleum (early in 373), the hundred officials along the road were paying their respects (to Hsieh and Wang, while Huan), looking on from his seat, trembled with dread and turned pale. Some said it was from this moment that Huan wished to kill Wang and Hsieh.

   SMTWCC: Huan Wen halted at Hsin-t'ing (south of Chien-k'ang). He had made a large-scale deployment of armed men and guards, and had invited Hsieh An and Wang T'an-chih (to a feast), intending to do them harm while they were seated. When Wang entered, he lost his composure, and was holding his hand tablet (shou-pan) upside down. Sweat was pouring down and soaking his clothes.

   On the other hand, Hsieh's spirit and appearance as well as his demeanor were no different from usual. Raising his eyes, he looked around at the guards on Wen's left and right and said to Wen, "I've heard that the feudal lords who were virtuous were protected by their neighbors on all sides. Why is it necessary for Your Excellency to place all these fellows inside the walls of this room?"

Huan, laughing, said, "Just because I can't do otherwise." With that his haughty, overbearing attitude was quickly dissipated, and he ordered the attendants withdrawn, and urged on the feast and the making of toasts, and with laughter and conversation they continued far into the night.

[2] For a discussion of this manner of chanting and the pronunciations it sought to preserve, see R. Mather, "A Note on the Dialects of Lo-yang and Nanking during the Six Dynasties," in T. T. Chow, ed., *Wen Lin*, Madison, 1968, pp. 247-256.

SMTWCC: Hsieh An was able to chant in the manner of the scholars of Lo-yang, but when he was young he had suffered from a nasal ailment which made the sound of his voice turgid (*cho*). Later, famous poetry reciters for the most part imitated his style, but none could approach it, except by reciting with the hand cupped over the nose.

[3] The poem, the thirteenth of nineteen written by Hsi K'ang to his elder brother, Hsi, on the occasion of the latter's entrance into the army, is included in *WH* 24.6a (tr. von Zach, *Die Chinesischen Anthologie*, I, 388, and D. Holzman, *La vie et la pensée*, p. 20).

30. Hsieh An and Wang T'an-chih went together to visit Ch'ih Ch'ao. The day was growing late and they had not yet gotten an opportunity to go in. Wang was on the point of leaving, when Hsieh said, "Aren't you able, for the sake of your life, to be patient a few moments?" (*CS* 67.21b)

31. When the monk Chih Tun was about to return east to K'uai-chi (in 365),[1] the worthies of the time all gave him a farewell party in the Pavilion of the General Chastizing Caitiffs (Cheng-lu t'ing, east of Chien-k'ang).[2] Ts'ai Hsi, being the first to arrive, sat near to Tun, while Hsieh Wan came later, and sat a little farther away. Ts'ai got up temporarily and Hsieh moved into his place. When Ts'ai returned and saw Hsieh there, lifting him up together with his mat, he threw him on the floor and resumed his own seat. Hsieh's cap went awry and fell off, but he calmly picked himself up, and adjusting his clothes returned to his seat. His spirit and mood were extremely tranquil, and he felt no trace of anger, but after he was seated he said to Ts'ai, "You're a strange man. You almost ruined my face."

Ts'ai replied, "Basically I had no designs on your face." And from then on neither of them paid any more attention to the incident. (*CS* 79.19a; *KSC* 4, *Taishō* 50.349b)

[1] *KISMC*: Chih Tun had been invited to the capital by Emperor Ai (in 362) and had moved about the capital for a long time, but his heart was still in his old hermitage in the Eastern Mountains (Chekiang). Accordingly (in 365) he shook out his clothes in farewell to the royal capital and returned to his crags and caves.

[2] *TYC*: During the T'ai-an era (302-303) the General Chastizing Caitiffs, Hsieh An* (not the grand tutor, who was born in 320) erected this pavilion, and it was named after him.

32. Ch'ih Ch'ao, out of respect and reverence for the virtuous reputation of the monk Shih Tao-an, made him a present of a thousand *hu* of rice, and composed a letter of many pages in which his sentiments were expressed with great solicitude.

Tao-an in his reply merely said, "As I am the recipient of your gift of rice, I am made more than ever aware of the vexations of 'being dependent.'"[1] (*KSC* 5, *Taishō* 50.352c; *CSTCC* 15, *Taishō* 55.108b; *IWLC* 72)

[1]Cf. *Chuang-tzu* I, 5b (Watson, p. 32): Even though Lieh-tzu avoided walking (by riding the wind), he still was dependent on something.

33. Hsieh Feng had been dismissed as president of the Board of Civil Office (in 360), and was returning to the east (Chekiang). Hsieh An was on his way (from Ku'ai-chi to the capital) to take up his post as sergeant-at-arms for Huan Wen. They met at P'o-kang (southeast of Chien-k'ang), and since they were going to be far separated, they lingered for three days, conversing together. An wanted to console him on the loss of his post, but Feng would always steer the conversation away to another topic. Although they spent two nights together in mid-journey, to the end they never mentioned this matter.

An's deep regret over this lingered in his heart unresolved, and he said to those traveling with him in the boat, "Hsieh Feng is certainly a strange gentleman!"

34. When Tai K'uei came out to the capital from the east (Chekiang), Hsieh An went to see him. Hsieh had always been contemptuous of Tai, and when he saw him he only talked with him about the seven-stringed zither (*ch'in*) and calligraphy. Since Tai showed no sign of reluctance to talk, but conversed about the zither and calligraphy with more and more subtlety, Hsieh came at last to realize the measure of his tolerance. (*LTMHC* 5; *PTSC* 109)

35. Hsieh An was playing encirclement chess (*wei-ch'i*) with someone, when suddenly a messenger arrived from Hsieh Hsüan (who was leading the defense against Fu Chien) at the Huai River (in 383).[1] An read the letter to the end in silence, and without saying a word, calmly turned back to the playing board. When his guests asked whether the news from the Huai was good or bad, he replied, "My little boys (his nephew, Hsüan, and his younger brother, Shih) have inflicted a crushing defeat on the invader." As he spoke his mood and expression and demeanor were no different from usual.[2] (*CS* 79.7a)

[1]*HCYC*: At first when the Former Ch'in ruler Fu Chien (r. 358-385) invaded the south (in 383), those in the capital were greatly alarmed, but Hsieh An showed no sign of fear. He gave orders to be driven out to his country estate, where he played encirclement chess with his elder brother's son, Hsüan. That night he returned to the capital and proceeded to lay out and apportion the Chin defenses. In a few days, everything had been arranged. After the Chin forces had defeated the invader, again he showed no sign of joy. Such was his lofty tolerance.

HsCCC: The Ti (Proto-Tibetan) invader, Fu Chien, emptied his state's resources in a massive expedition, with a host of a million men. The Chin court dispatched its armies to resist him, eighty-thousand men in all. Fu Chien advanced and pitched camp at Shou-yang (Anhui). Hsieh Hsüan was the commander-general of the Chin spearhead. With his cousin, Hsieh Yen, and others, he selected the finest and keenest of the troops for a decisive battle. An archer wounded Fu Chien. The capitives were numbered in the ten thousands, and they took Chien's pseudo-imperial carriage, together with a carriage enclosed in mica (yün-mu) and a mountainous heap of jeweled paraphernalia, ten thousand bolts (tuan) of brocaded wool (chin-chi), and a hundred thousand head of oxen, horses, donkeys, mules, and camels.

[2]*CS* 79.7a: After Hsieh An had finished the game and returned to his inner quarters, the joy in his heart was so great as he crossed the threshold he did not even realize he had broken the teeth on his clogs.

36. Wang Hui-chih and his younger brother, Hsien-chih, were once seated together in the same room. A fire suddenly broke out above them, and Hui-chih fled from the room in terror, not even taking time to pick up his clogs. Hsien-chih's spirit and expression remained tranquil. Calmly calling for his attendants, he went out leaning on them for support, as if nothing were different from usual.

It was this incident by which the world determined the relative spiritual tolerance of the two Wangs. (*CS* 80.12b)

37. When the Fu Chien threat was approaching the Chin domain (in 378),[1] Hsieh An said to his senior administrator, Wang Hsien-chih, "Let's take those who occupy the enemy's pivotal positions and put an end to this venture of theirs."

[1]Fu Chien began his southern campaign in 378 by threatening Hsiang-yang (northern Hupei), which fell the following year. A second spearhead set out for the Huai River valley in 382, culminating in the battle of the Fei River the following year.

38. Wang Min and Hsieh Hsüan were both at a gathering at Wang Hui's place. Wang Min, raising his cup, urged Hsieh to drink with him, saying, "A toast to the governor!"[1]

Hsieh replied, "It's all right, I guess."

Wang sprang impetuously to his feet, livid with anger, and cried, "You're (*ju*) basically nothing but a low-class fisherman from the streams of Wu-hsing (Chekiang).[2] How dare you make a fool of me?"

Hsieh, unperturbed, clapped his hands and laughed, saying to his host, Wang Hui, "Seng-mi (Min's baby name) is extraordinarily reckless to go so far as to invade a 'superior state.'"

[1]Liu Chün notes in the Commentary that Hsieh Hsüan was then governor of Hsü Province (northern Anhui). According to *TCTC* 104.3291, his appointment to this post was made in 379.

[2]*SSHY* Comm.: Hsieh Hsüan's uncle, Hsieh An, had once been grand warden of Wu-hsing, and when Hsüan was young he used to wander about there with him.

39. Wang Hsün served as Huan Wen's superintendent of records. Since for generations Wang's family had had an excellent reputation, Huan

was extremely desirous of having someone of his prestige and status as the cynosure of his entire administrative staff. When Wang first came to see Huan to offer his thanks, he committed some breach of etiquette, but his spirit and expression remained self-possessed. All the guests who were present started to laugh in derision, but Huan said, "You're wrong. If you had observed his mood and manner, you would have seen they were by no means those of an ordinary man. I'm going to try him out."

Later, on the occasion of the monthly dawn audience, while Wang was waiting prostrate below the side gate (ko-hsia), Huan, galloping on horseback from inside, charged out directly toward him. Everyone on his left and right scattered headlong, but Wang did not move. From this point on his reputation and worth were greatly enhanced, and everyone said, "This is top ministerial caliber."

40. Toward the end of the T'ai-yüan era (276-396) a comet (ch'ang-hsing) appeared,[1] and Emperor Hsiao-wu (Ssu-ma Yao, r. 373-396), was extremely distressed about it in his heart. One night while he was drinking in the Hua-lin Park (northeast of Chien-k'ang) he raised his cup and addressed the comet, saying, "Comet, I toast you with a cup of wine! From all antiquity, when was there ever a Son of Heaven who lived ten thousand years?" (CS 9.18ab)

[1] HKCC (cf. CS 13.40a; trans. in Ho Peng-Yoke, Astronomical Chapters, p. 243): In the ninth month of the twentieth year of the T'ai-yüan era (Sept. 30 to Oct. 29, 395) there was a tangle-star (p'eng-hsing, a tailless comet?) like loose cotton wool traveling toward the southeast. It passed the stars Hsü and Nü (lunar mansions 10 and 11 = ε and β of Aquarius) traveling as far as Yang (μ of Capricorn).

SSHY Comm.: At the end of the T'ai-yüan era there was only this portent (i.e., of a tangle-star) noted; nothing was ever heard of any comet (ch'ang-hsing). Moreover, in the eighth year of the Han Emperor Wen (172 B.C.) a comet had appeared in the east. Wen Ying's (second cent. A.D.) commentary (at HS 4.12b) states: "Comets have a luminous tail . . . sometimes stretching the full length of the sky, sometimes thirty feet, and sometimes only twenty feet. There is no constant length . . . When these comets appear, for the most part they portend armed uprising." It was sixteen years after this (156 B.C.) before Emperor Wen deceased. Thus we know that comets have no connection with the Son of Heaven. The Shih-shuo account is specious.

(John Williams's Observations of Comets from B.C. 611 to A.D. 1640, Extracted from the Chinese Annals, London, 1871, also confirms that there is no record of a comet in the years 376-396, though Halley's Comet appeared in 370 and again in 446.)

41. Yin Chung-k'an had a friend who had composed a poetic essay in the playful tradition of Shu Hsi.[1] Yin was strongly convinced that the man had ability, and said to Wang Kung, "I just happened to see a new piece of writing which is extremely readable." Whereupon he brought it out from its handkerchief wrapping.

All the while Wang was reading, Yin was laughing uncontrollably. Wang read to the end without laughing once, nor did he say whether he liked it or disliked it. He merely tapped it with his baton (*ju-i*), and nothing more. Yin was miserably disappointed. (*TPYL* 391, 703)

[1] An example of one of Shu Hsi's "playful" pieces is his "Poetic Essay on Rice Cakes" (*Ping-fu*), a fragment of which is preserved in *IWLC* 72:

> In darkest winter, when it's bitter cold,
> There is an early morning feast.
> Tears freeze inside the nose;
> Frost cakes outside the mouth.
> To fill the void and ease the shivers
> Hot rice cakes are the best of all.
>
> Soft as spring down,
> White as autumn silk.
> Steam rises thick and spreads abroad;
> Its fragrance scatters far and wide.
> The traveler wastes saliva down the wind;
> The slave boy chews thin air and looks askance.
> The bearer of the vessel licks his lips,
> And he who serves it swallows dry.

42. When Yang Sui's second son,[1] Yang Fu, was young he possessed outstanding ability. Since he was on friendly terms with Hsieh Hun, he went early one day to Hsieh's house. They had not eaten yet, when unexpectedly Wang Hsi and his brother Shuang arrived. They had not previously been acquainted with Yang, so when the Wangs faced his seat they looked displeased, as if they would have liked to have him leave.

Yang, for his part, paid no attention to them whatever, but merely propped his feet on the low table, chanting poems and staring straight ahead, completely self-composed. It was only after Hsieh had finished exchanging a few words with the Wangs about the weather, and had turned back to converse appreciatively with Yang, that the Wangs became aware of his unusual qualities, and started to converse with him.

In a short while food was brought in. The two Wangs did not get to eat anything, but only addressed themselves to Yang incessantly. Yang hardly responded to them at all, but kept plying himself with food. When he had finished eating he immediately excused himself. They insistently tried to detain him, but Yang was unwilling to stay. He said bluntly, "Earlier the reason I didn't get to comply with your wish to have me leave, was because my 'Central States' (i.e., my stomach) were still empty."

The two Wangs were the younger brothers of Wang Kung.

[1] *Shih-shuo jen-ming p'u* 64b lists Fu as Sui's eldest surviving son.

CHAPTER VII

Insight and Judgment

1. When Ts'ao Ts'ao was young he had an interview with Ch'iao Hsüan. Hsüan told him, "The whole realm is now in disorder, and all the warriors are struggling like tigers. Aren't you the one who will control the situation and set it in order? However, you're really a brave warrior in an age of disorder, but a treacherous rebel in an age of order.[1] I regret that I'm old now and won't live to see you come to wealth and honor, but I'll entrust my sons and grandsons to your care." (*SKWei* 1.2ab)

   [1] *HsHS*: Earlier, while Ts'ao Ts'ao was still a student and had not yet made his reputation, Ch'iao Hsüan admired him greatly.
   WeiS: When Ch'iao Hsüan saw Ts'ao Ts'ao he said, "I've seen a lot of warriors, but never one like you. The realm is on the verge of disorder; unless someone comes forward with the ability to control the world, it can't be saved. Wouldn't you be the one to pacify it?"
   WCSY: Ch'iao Hsüan said to Ts'ao Ts'ao, "You're still without reputation; you should make friends with Hsü Shao." So Ts'ao Ts'ao went to see Shao, and the latter accepted him.
   SSTY (cf. *SKWei* 1.2b): Ts'ao Ts'ao once asked Hsü Shao, "What sort of person am I?" After he had asked insistently, Shao finally answered, "An able minister in an age of order, and a treacherous warrior in an age of disorder." Ts'ao Ts'ao laughed aloud.
   (In the Commentary Liu Chün concludes, on the basis of the above passages from *WCSY* and *SSTY*, that the *Shih-Shuo* account is "mistaken.")

2. Ts'ao Ts'ao once asked P'ei Ch'ien, "You were formerly with Liu Pei in Ching Province (Hupei). What do you think of Pei's ability?"
   Ch'ien said, "If he were living in the Central States, he could stir up the people to revolt, but he couldn't conduct a stable government. If, on the other hand, he were to take advantage of the

natural defenses of a border area to maintain himself in a mountain fastness, he would be adequate as the ruler of a single locality."[1] (SKWei 23.17a)

[1] WC (cf. SKWei 23.17a): P'ei Ch'ien said privately to Wang Ts'an and Ssu-ma Chih, "Liu Pei isn't the caliber to become a hegemon or a king. If (like King Wen of Chou) he should wish to maintain himself as 'Earl of the West' (Hsi-po), his fall would come in less than a day."

3. Ho Yen, Teng Yang, and Hsia-hou Hsüan all sought the friendship of Fu Chia, but to the end Chia would not accept any of them. The three finally prevailed on Hsün Ts'an to speak to Chia about a rapprochement. Ts'an said to Chia, "Hsia-hou Hsüan is the outstanding gentleman of the entire age, and has no ulterior motives in relation to you, yet in your mind you feel he's unacceptable. If you do get together with him, your friendship will mature, but if you don't, then it will end in a feud. In the case of the two other worthies, to be friendly toward them would be a good thing for the state. This, after all, was the reason why Lin Hsiang-ju demeaned himself before Lien P'o."[1]

Fu said, "As for Hsia-hou Hsüan, his ambition is great and his mind is very busy. He's been quite capable in gathering together an empty reputation, and is truly what (Confucius) was talking about when he spoke of 'those who through clever speech will overthrow the state.'[2] As far as Ho Yen and Teng Yang are concerned, they're active but impetuous, 'widely read but lacking in what is essential.'[3] Externally they're addicted to profit, and internally they lack the restraints of bolt and key. They honor those who agree with them and hate those who differ. They talk a great deal and are jealous of any who are ahead of them. One who talks much offends much, and one who is jealous of those who are ahead of him will have no intimate friends. As I see it, these three worthies are all merely persons who will ruin the virtuous, and nothing more. Even keeping my distance from them, I'm still afraid of becoming involved in their downfall. How much worse would it be if I were ever intimate with them?"

Later, in all three cases, it turned out to be as he had said.[4] (SKWei 21.23a, comm., citing FT; TPYL 410)

[1] SC (81.4b-5b): Lin Hsiang-ju (third cent. B.C.), because his merit was great, was appointed a high minister in the state of Chao (Shansi) with rank higher than that of Lien P'o. P'o was incensed over this and wanted to humiliate him. But (for the dawn audiences) Hsiang-ju would always claim illness and stay home, and whenever he saw P'o approaching on the road, he would draw his carriage to the side to let him pass. Hsiang-ju's retainers wanted to put P'o out of the way, but Hsiang-ju said, "Even in the case of one with the majesty of the king of Ch'in (Shih-huang-ti), I still scoff at him. Why should I be afraid of General Lien? But it so happens that Ch'in is strong and Chao is weak, and it is only because of us two, Lien P'o and myself, that Ch'in dares not take arms against Chao. Today if the two tigers should fight against each other, it is unlikely we would both survive. I consider the public weal urgent, and put private quarrels second." Lien P'o, hearing of this, apologized for his offense.

[2]"Analects" XVII, 16: The Master said, "I hate the way purple diminishes vermilion, and I hate the way the airs of Cheng confound the music of the Court Songs. I hate those who through clever speech will overthrow the state."

[3]*SC* (130.4b): The Juists (literati) are widely read, but lacking in what is essential. They are busy, but accomplish little.

[4]Ho Yen and Teng Yang were executed with Ts'ao Shuang in 249, Hsia-hou Hsüan in 254.

FT: At this time Ho Yen, because of his ability and eloquence, was conspicuous among the nobility and imperial relatives. Teng Yang was fond of making connections and joined his faction, and thus developed a reputation among the people. Since Hsia-hou Hsüan was the son of a noble minister, even in his youth he had a weighty reputation. They all sought friendly relations with Fu Chia, but Chia would not accept them. Chia's friend, Hsün Ts'an, had an understanding of ultramundane matters and a determination to live remote from the world. In spite of this he still urged Chia to enter into friendship with them.

4. (In 280) Emperor Wu of Chin (Ssu-ma Yen, r. 265-299) held a military review (in celebration of demobilization) on the Hsüan-wu review grounds (north of Lo-yang).[1] The emperor, wishing to "put an end to warfare and cultivate the civil arts,"[2] went out in person to attend the review, and had summoned all his ministers to do the same.

Shan T'ao felt it was inappropriate (to disarm), and accordingly talked with all the presidents of the various boards on the fundamental ideas in the military classics by Sun Wu and Wu Ch'i[3] concerning the use of arms, after which they discussed the matter exhaustively. The entire company sighed in admiration, and everyone said, "Shan T'ao is the most famous conversationalist in the realm."

Later, the various princes, taking matters into their own hands, plunged recklessly into war and disaster,[4] and after that brigands and bandits gathered like ants from every quarter.[5] Since the commandaries and principalities were for the most part unarmed, they could not curb or stop them, and eventually the bandits became gradually stronger and stronger. Everything happened just as Shan T'ao had predicted.

Contemporaries felt that even though Shan T'ao had never studied Sun Wu or Wu Ch'i, intuitively his principles agreed with theirs. Wang Yen also sighed and said, "Intuitively he's in harmony with the Way."[6]

[1]*CLCHL*: After Wu had been pacified in the Hsien-ning era (275-279), Emperor Wu was about to reenact the "T'ao-lin and Mt. Hua affair" (i.e., to imitate King Wu of Chou, after the conquest of Yin in the eleventh cent. B.C.), and to call an end to military campaigns and armaments, to demonstrate to the realm that there would be a grand peace. At the time all provinces and commanderies dismissed their men-at-arms. In the large commanderies they stationed one hundred military officers, and in the small, fifty men. At the same time in the capital they held a (demobilization) review. It was on this account that Shan T'ao discussed the fundamental ideas of Su Wu and Wu Ch'i on the use of arms. As a person,

Shan T'ao was unceremonious and taciturn, but it seems he felt that those who rule the state cannot afford to forget how to fight, so he brought the matter up.

MSC: Shan T'ao lived through the transition from Wei to Chin and had never had a conspicuous reputation as a conversationalist. But once, while conversing with Lu Ch'in (d. 278, *sic*), he brought up the fundamental ideas on the use of arms. Emperor Wu, hearing of it, remarked, "So Shan T'ao is a famous conversationalist!"

[2]"Book of Documents" IV, 5 (Legge III, 308): When King Wu came from Shang to Feng (Shensi), he put an end to warfare and cultivated the civil arts. He returned his horses to the southern slopes of Mt. Hua, and grazed his oxen in the fields of T'ao-lin, to demonstrate to the realm that he would not use them again in warfare.

[3]"Sun Wu" (ca. 400-320 B.C.), *Ping-fa*, also known as *Sun-tzu*; and Wu Ch'i (d. 381 B.C.), *Wu-tzu*. The former has been translated by S. B. Griffith under the title, *Sun-tzu, the Art of War*, Oxford, 1963.

[4]I.e., the "War of the Eight Princes" (300-306), a bloody struggle among the imperial princes to replace the imbecile Emperor Hui (Ssu-ma Chung, r. 290-306).

[5]Especially the Hsiung-nu invasions of Liu Yüan in 309 and the sack of Lo-yang by Shih Lo in 311.

[6]*MSC*: Wang Yen recommended the praised Shan T'ao, saying, "Intuitively he acts in harmony with the Way. His depths are unfathomable."

5. While Wang Yen's father, Wang I, was serving as General Pacifying the North (272), he was involved in a public incident, concerning which he had dispatched a messenger to the court to plead his cause, but without result. Wang Yen was at the capital at the time, and, ordering his carriage, he went to see his uncle, the vice-president of the Imperial Secretariat, Yang Hu, and the president of the Board of Civil Office, Shan T'ao. At the time Yen was only a young lad with his hair in tufts,[1] but his appearance and ability were outstanding and unusual, and, since the impact of his presentation was refreshing, and the content, moreover, reasonable, Shan T'ao was greatly impressed with him. After he had left, T'ao gazed after him without taking his eyes away. At last he sighed and said, "If one were to have a son, oughtn't he to be like Wang Yen?"

Yang Hu rejoined, "The one who will confound the morals of the realm is certainly this boy."[2] (*CS* 34.5b)

[1]He was actually sixteen (see note 2).

[2]*CYC* (cf. *CS* 43.13b-14a): Wang Yen's father, Wang I, had a notification of censure and was about to be dismissed from his post. Yen was in his seventeenth (*CS* 43.14a has "fourteenth") year at the time, and went to see his uncle, Yang Hu, to plead his father's cause. His words were unusually impressive, but Hu did not grant his request. Yen thereupon shook out his clothes and rose to depart. Hu, looking back, said to the other guests, "This man will certainly have a flourishing reputation and occupy a great posi-

200   TALES OF THE WORLD

tion in his own age, but at the same time, the one who will destroy the morals and harm the good influences of his age will also certainly be this man."

HCCC: Earlier, Yang Hu, because of military regulations, was about to have Wang Yen's cousin, Wang Jung, beheaded. Furthermore, Wang Yen was angry because Hu had said that Yen would certainly come to a bad end, and because Hu did not treat him with honor or respect. Everyone in the realm said of him, "As long as the two Wangs (Jung and Yen) hold power at court, nobody in the world dares to say anything good about Yang Hu."

6. P'an T'ao, on seeing Wang Tun when the latter was young, said to him, "Sir, your 'waspish eyes' are already showing, but your 'wolfish voice' hasn't reverberated yet, that's all.[1] You'll surely be capable of devouring others, but you'll also be devoured by others."[2] (*CS* 98.1b)

[1] Cf. *Tso-chuan*, Wen 1 (Legge V, 230): The chief minister Tzu-shang said of the proposed Ch'u heir apparent, Shang Ch'en, " . . . This man has waspish eyes and a wolfish voice. There's nothing he wouldn't do. He may not be established as heir apparent."

[2] *HCCC*: Earlier (ca. 307), Wang Yen had spoken to the Prince of Tung-hai, Ssu-ma Yüeh, to have Wang Tun transferred to be governor of Yang Province (Kiangsu-Anhui-Chekiang). At the time P'an T'ao was serving as Yüeh's senior administrator, and said to Yüeh, "Wang Tun's 'waspish eyes,' etc. . . . Now if you set him up beyond the Yangtze River, and give free reign to his overweening ambition, this is simply making a rebel out of him."

CYC: While Wang Tun was an attendant of the crown prince (ca. 300), he was a fellow officer of P'an T'ao, and that is why P'an made this statement.

7. Shih Lo did not know how to read or write.[1] He once had someone read aloud to him from the "History of the Former Han Dynasty" (*Hanshu*). When he heard the part where Li Shih-ch'i urged the establishment of the descendants of the rulers of the six pre-Ch'in states, and about the carving of the seals, and how Liu Pang was on the point of handing them over to them,[2] he became greatly alarmed, and cried out, "This method will fail! If he does that, how will he ever get possession of the realm?"

But when he came to the part where Chang Liang[3] warned against it, he said, "It's a good thing this man was there, that's all I can say!" (*CS* 105.7a)

[1] *TTCC*: Shih Lo did not know how to read or write, nor did his eyes recognize any characters. But often while on campaign he would have someone read aloud to him, and in every case he would understand the meaning.

[2] *HS* (1.27b-28a): While Hsiang Yü was critically besieging the king of Han (Liu Pang) at Ying-yang (in 205/204 B.C.), the king consulted with Li Shih-ch'i on how to break the power of Ch'u. Shih-ch'i urged him to establish the descendants of the rulers of the six pre-Ch'in states (Yen, Chao, Han, Wei, Ch'i, and Lu), and the king gave the order to hasten and carve the appropriate royal

seals. Chang Liang came in and warned him that it was ill-advised.
The king, who had been eating, stopped and spewed out a mouthful
of food and cursed Li Shih-ch'i, crying, "That bastard of a literatus nearly ruined our cause!" Whereupon he hastened to give the
order to melt down the seals.

[3]Chang Liang (d. 187 B.C.) was a hermit-turned-adviser who aided
the first Han emperor (Liu Pang, r. 206-195 B.C.).

8. When Wei Chieh was in his fifth year, his spirit and manner were
most lovable. His grandfather, the grand protector, Wei Kuan, said,
"There's something different about this child. I'm only sorry I'm old
and won't live to see him grow up, that's all." (CS 36.13a)

9. Liu K'un said, "Hua I is short on insight and ability, but he's
got stubborness and determination to spare."[1]

[1]HCCC: Liu K'un, knowing that Hua I would fail, said it would be
his own choice.

10. Chang Han was summoned to serve as an aide in the administration
of the Prince of Ch'i, Ssu-ma Chiung (in 301). While he was in Lo-
yang, and saw the autumn winds rising, it was then that he longed for
the wild rice (ku-ts'ai), the water-lily soup (ch'un-keng), and the
sliced perch (lu-yü kuai) of his old home in Wu (Soochow). He said,
"What a man values in life is just to find what suits his fancy, and
nothing more. How can he tie himself down to an official post several
thousand li from home, in pursuit of fame and rank?" Whereupon he ordered his carriage and proceeded to return home. Shortly thereafter
the Prince of Ch'i was defeated and killed (302). His contemporaries
all claimed Chang was clairvoyant.[1] (CS 92.16a; IWLC 3; PTSC 145;
PSLT 12; SLF 5, 29; TPYL 25, 862, 937)

[1]WSC: Chang Han said to his fellow townsman, Ku Jung, "The turmoil
in the realm (i.e., the "War of the Eight Princes") has not yet
subsided, and for anybody who has a reputation within the Four
Seas to seek to retire from public life is very difficult. By nature I'm a man of hills and forests, and for a long time have had
no expectation of recognition by my contemporaries. But you're
skilled at defending against repeating mistakes of the past
through intelligence, and being foresighted against mistakes of
the future through wisdom."
Jung, grasping his hand, said with deep feeling, "I, too, will
just pluck the ferns of the southern hills with you, and drink the
waters of the three rivers of Wu (i.e., the Sung, the Tung, and
the Lou, all flowing into Lake T'ai)."

11. When Chu-ko Hui first crossed over to the area east of the Yangtze River (ca. 317), he used to refer to himself by his courtesy
name, Tao-ming,[1] though his reputation was below that of Wang Tao and
Yü Liang in honor. His first post was magistrate of Lin-i Prefecture
(Kiangsu), at which time Chancellor Wang Tao said to him, "Someday
Your Excellency will become a black-haired ducal minister."[2] (CS
77.20a; TPYL 364)

¹*CHS:* When Chu-ko Hui (Chu-ko Tao-ming) crossed the Yangtze River to escape the troubles, he had an equal reputation with Hsün K'ai (Hsün Tao-ming) and Ts'ai Mo (Ts'ai Tao-ming). They were known as the "Three Mings of the Chin Restoration." Their contemporaries made up a ditty about them which ran:

> "In the capital are Three Mings; (*$m_i̯wɒng$*)
> Each of which has fame. (*$mi̯ang$*)
> Ts'ai is learned and cultured;
> Hsün and Ko without blame."

²I.e., you'll reach the top while you're still young.

YL: After Chancellor Wang Tao had been appointed director of works (in 321), Chu-ko Hui was once seated next to him. Wang, pointing to his cap of office, said, "You, too, one day will be wearing this."

12. Wang Ch'eng, never having been acquainted in the past with his nephew, Wang Hsüan, said of him, "His ambition is greater than his capacity; in the end he'll die within the walls of a fort."[1]

¹*CCKT:* (In 313) in his administration of Ch'en-liu Commandery (Honan), Wang Hsüan carried out repression and punishments on a large scale, and was eventually killed by someone in a fort.

13. When Generalissimo Wang Tun was beginning his descent on the capital (in 322), Yang Lang warned him insistently against it, but the generalissimo did not follow his advice. Eventually Yang exerted all his efforts on Wang's behalf. Mounting the observation-and-command chariot (*chung-ming yün-lu ch'e*), he drove directly up before Wang Tun and said, "When you hear the sound of this petty officer's drumming, the moment you advance you'll be victorious!"

At that time Wang grasped his hand and said, "If this venture is successful, I'll surely use you as governor of Ching Province (Hunan-Hupei)."

Later, however, he forgot about it, and used him instead as grand warden of Nan Commandery (within the province).

After Wang Tun had been defeated (in 324), Emperor Ming (Ssu-ma Shao, r. 323-325) arrested Yang Lang and was on the point of having him put to death, but shortly after that the emperor deceased, and thus he managed to escape with his life.

Later he held the Three Ducal Offices (director of instruction, director of works, and grand marshal) simultaneously,[1] and appointed several tens of men as his subordinate officials. These men were all unknown at the time of appointment, but later all were accorded fame and recognition. Contemporaries praised Yang for his knowledge of men.

¹According to the meager information available in the citations from *WYCS*, Yang never held any office above governor of Yung Province (northern Hupei).

14. Chou I's mother, on the occasion of the winter solstice, raised her wine cup and toasted her three sons with the words, "I always used to think that after crossing the Yangtze River, I'd have no place to set my feet, but now your families are well-connected, and with all of you here in a row before me, what further worries do I have?"

Her second son, Chou Sung, rose and, kneeling for a long time, said with tears in his eyes, "Mother, things aren't quite as you say. As far as your firstborn, Chou I, is concerned, as a person his ambition is great but his ability is in short supply. His reputation is weighty but his insight is dim, and he's fond of taking advantage of other people's weaknesses. This is no way to preserve himself. As for me, your second-born, my nature is wolfish and brusque, and I, too, won't be tolerated long in the world. It's only Little Brother A-nu here (Chou Mo), who's easygoing and muddles along, who has any certainty of remaining in your presence."[1] (CS 96.8a)

[1]Chou I and Chou Sung were killed by Wang Tun in 322 and 324 respectively. Chou Mo's date and cause of death are unknown.

15. After Generalissimo Wang Tun had met his end (in 324), his nephew, Wang Ying, wished to take refuge with Tun's cousin, Wang Pin,[1] who was governor of Chiang Province (eastern Hupei and Kiangsi). Ying's father (Tun's elder brother), Wang Han, on the other hand, wished to take refuge with another cousin, Wang Shu*, who was governor of Ching Province (Hunan-Hupei). Han said to Ying, "What connection did the generalissimo ever have in his life with Wang Pin, that you want to join forces with him?"

Ying said, "This is precisely the reason we should go to him. Whenever a person is strong and influential Wang Pin is capable of standing up to him, whether he agrees with him or not, which is not what ordinary people would do. And when he sees a person in weakness or danger, it's sure to arouse his sympathy. Wang Shu*, on the other hand, sticks to the letter of the law and is totally incapable of doing anything beyond what is expected."[2]

Wang Han did not follow this advice, and consequently they both took refuge with Wang Shu*. As predicted, Shu* had both father and son drowned in the Yangtze River.[3]

When Wang Pin learned that Ying was going to come, he secretly provided a boat to take care of him, and in the end, when Ying failed to come, it was a matter of deep regret to him. (CS 76.8a)

[1]*Wang Pin PC*: When Pin's cousin, Wang Tun, descended the Yangtze to Shih-t'ou, he killed Chou I. Pin had been a longtime friend of I's, and went to weep by his corpse with extreme anguish. Later he saw Tun, who thought it odd he should have such a grieved expression, and asked him about it.

Pin replied, "I've just been weeping for Chou I, and my feelings can't stop."

Tun said, "Chou I brought about his own punishment and death. Why are you still carrying on?"

Pin replied, "Chou I was a gentleman of incorruptible reputation. What crime is there in weeping for him?" Whereupon he reprimanded Tun, saying, "You have raised the banner of revolt against your sovereign, and have killed and butchered loyal and good subjects!" As he spoke, his voice and words, thick with emotion, fell with his tears.

Tun was extremely angry. Chancellor Wang Tao, who was also present, was repeatedly alarmed on Pin's behalf, and commanded Pin to do obeisance and apologize.

204   TALES OF THE WORLD

Pin said, "I've got foot trouble. Even if I'd come for an audience with the Son of Heaven, I still wouldn't want to do obeisance. What's all this nonsense about kneeling down!"

Tun said, "Which is worse: foot trouble or neck trouble?" But because he was a relative, he did not harm him.

²The "expected" would be that since Tun was a rebel, his brother and nephew should be killed. The following example of Shu*'s literalness comes from his biography, *Wang Shu* chuan*, cited in the Commentary: When Shu* was appointed grand warden of K'uai-chi (Chekiang), inasmuch as his father's taboo name was Hui (the same character as the K'uai of K'uai-chi), he repeatedly memorialized the throne explaining his situation and requesting a transfer to another commandery, whereupon the emperor changed the first character of K'uai-chi to K'uai* (adding radical 163). Shu* then had no recourse but to go to his post.

³*SSHY* Comm.: When Wang Han took refuge with Wang Shu*, Shu* sent troops to oppose him. Both Han and his son Ying drowned in the water of the Yangtze River. Long ago Li Chi (second cent. B.C.) sold his friend Lü Lu and was criticized for it. How much worse when someone betrays his blood cousins to insure his own safety? Wang Shu* was inhuman!

16. When Meng Chia of Wu-ch'ang (Hupei) became an administrator in the Chiang provincial headquarters of the grand marshal, Yü Liang (ca. 334), his reputation was already well known. The grand tutor Ch'u P'ou, had a good capacity in judging men, and on his return to the capital after quitting his post as grand warden of Yü-chang Commandery (Kiangsi), he passed through Wu-ch'ang. (At the New Year's gathering of the staff) Ch'u asked Yü, "I hear the administrator Meng Chia is excellent. Is he here today?"

Yü said, "Try by yourself to find him."

Ch'u looked all around for a good while, then, pointing to Chia, he said, "This gentleman is a little different from the others; wouldn't he be the one?"

Yü, laughing aloud, said, "Right!" At the time he not only sighed in admiration over Ch'u's "understanding in silence,"¹ but was also delighted that Chia had been appreciated.² (*CS* 98.30a)

¹"Analects" VII, 2.

²The source of Meng's biography in both *CS* and *Meng Chia PC* seems to have been T'ao Ch'ien's (365-427) "Biography of My Ancestor Meng, Senior Administrator for the Chin Generalissimo Chastizing the West, Huan Wen" (*Chin ku cheng-hsi ta-chiang-chün chang-shih Meng Fu-chün chuan*; see Kao Ming, ed., *Liang Chin nan-pei-ch'ao wen-hui*, Hong Kong, 1960, pp. 1936-37). T'ao was descended from Meng's fourth daughter.

Meng Chia PC: When the grand marshal, Yü Liang, took on the governorship of Chiang Province, he summoned Chia to take charge of the administrators of Lu-ling Commandery (Kiangsi). Chia had gone down to the commandery and returned to Wu-ch'ang, and Liang, drawing him aside, questioned him about the state of morals in the commandery.

Chia replied, "Wait until I go back and find out; I should ask the administrators."

Liang, raising his sambar-tail chowry (*chu-wei*) to cover his mouth, laughed aloud. He said to his younger brother, Yü I, "Meng Chia certainly is a man of overflowing virtue!" and transferred him to educational administrator.

The grand tutor, Chu P'ou, possessed insight into human capabilities. At the New Year's gathering of Liang's staff P'ou asked Liang, "I hear that in Chiang Province there is a certain Meng Chia. Where is he?"

Liang said, "He's here. Just spy him out for yourself."

P'ou observed each in turn for a long time, then, pointing to Chia, asked, "Wouldn't this be the one?"

Liang laughed delightedly. He was happy that P'ou had discovered Chia, and at the same time amazed that Chia had been discovered by P'ou. After that he entrusted Chia with greater responsibility.

Later (in 345), Chia became an aide to the General Chastizing the West, Huan Wen. On the ninth day of the ninth month (the Double Ninth Festival), Wen went for an outing to Lung Mountain (Hupei), and all his aides and officers were gathered together. At the time it was customary for assistants and officers to wear military uniforms. The wind blew Chia's hat off and it fell to the ground. Wen warned his attendants to say nothing about it, to observe what he would do. At first Chia was unaware of it, but after a good while, when he left to relieve himself, Huan ordered someone to pick it up and give it back to him. He then had Sun Sheng compose a literary piece making fun of him. When it was completed he attached it to Chia's seat. On returning, Chia immediately composed a reply, and everyone present sighed in admiration.

Chia was fond of drinking, and even when he had had too much, he was never disorderly. Wen asked him, "What good is there in wine, that you're so addicted to it?" Chia replied, "Your Excellency has never discovered the pleasure to be found in wine, that's all."

On another occasion he asked him, "When I'm listening to performers, stringed instruments don't sound as good as bamboo, and bamboo instruments don't sound as good as flesh (i.e., the human voice). Why would that be?" He replied, "Because you're getting closer with each one to what is natural (*tzu-jan*)."

17. When Tai K'uei was ten or so years old, he was painting a picture in the Wa-kuan Temple (in Chien-k'ang). The senior administrator, Wang Meng, seeing him, said, "This lad's not only able to paint; someday also he'll end up being famous. My only regret is that I'm too old to see the time of his full flowering." (*LTMHC* 5; *TPKC* 210)

18. Wang Meng, Hsieh Shang, and Liu T'an went together to visit Yin Hao at his graveyard hermitage (336-346) in Tan-yang (Chien-k'ang). Yin remained adamant in his unshakable determination to live in retirement. After they had returned, Wang and Hsieh were saying to each other, "If Yin Hao won't come up out of retirement, what effect will it have on the *people*?" And they were deeply distressed over it.

Liu said, "Are you two *really* worried that Yin Hao won't come up?"[1] (*CS* 77.22b)

[1] Yin became the rallying point for the opposition to Huan Wen's rise between 343 and Yin's debacle in 353. For nearly ten years

prior to this he had remained out of politics ostensibly mourning his mother, who died ca. 336.

19. As he was approaching his end (in 345), Yü I personally memorialized the throne to have his son, Yü Yüan-chih, succeed him as governor of Ching Province (Hunan-Hupei). The court,[1] worried lest Yüan-chih might not obey orders, did not quite know whom to send in his stead, and after consultation, the consensus was to use Huan Wen.

Liu T'an said, "If *that* man goes, he's certain to be able to conquer and rule all of Western Ch'u (Hunan-Hupei-Szechwan), but when that happens, I'm afraid he can no longer be controlled himself." (*CS* 75.32ab)

[1]*T'ao K'an PC*: Before Yü I deceased (in 345), he had memorialized the throne to have his son, Yüan-chih, succeed him as governor of Ching Province. Ho Ch'ung said, "T'ao K'an was a man of weighty merit, yet on the eve of his death he high-mindedly yielded in favor of another. Before Chancellor Wang Tao had deceased (in 339), his second son, Wang T'ien, was only a fourth-grade general, and even up to the present his status has remained unchanged. If we're talking about relatives, then Yü Hsi*, who is a cavalier attendant without duties, never received any outstanding offer of this sort, either. So let's make the governor of Hsü Province, Huan Wen, General Pacifying the West and governor of Ching Province."

SMTWCC: When Yü I memorialized the throne to have his son succeed him, the court was alarmed over it, and some counselors wanted to give the post to Huan Wen. At the time (the future) Emperor Chien-wen (Ssu-ma Yü) was in control of the government, and consented to this. But Liu T'an said, "If Wen goes, he's certain to be able, etc. . . . I would rather Your Highness yourself were stationed at the upper reaches of the Yangtze (i.e., in Wu-ch'ang), and that I be allowed to serve as your administrative sergeant-at-arms." Emperor Chien-wen would not agree to it, so Huan Wen was appointed, and afterward things turned out exactly as predicted.

20. When Huan Wen was about to start his punitive expedition against the kingdom of Ch'eng-Han in Shu (Szechwan, in 347),[1] all the worthies in his administration of Ching Province argued that the family of the Ch'eng-Han ruler, Li Shih, had lived in Shu a long time, and Li had inherited his patrimony through successive generations. Moreover, his territory was situated at the upper reaches of the Yangtze River, and the Three Gorges[2] had never yet been easy to conquer.

It was only Liu T'an who said, "That man's certain to be able to conquer Shu. I've observed his gambling habits, and if he's not certain of winning, he won't play."[3]

[1]This independent satrapy in the mountain fastnesses of Szechwan had been founded by a Taoist popular leader named Li T'e in 302, during the distractions of the "War of the Eight Princes" (300-306).

[2]See *SSHY* II, 58, above.

[3]*YL*: Liu T'an, observing that whenever Huan Wen played a game, he had to be sure of winning, said to him, "If you're so fond of coming out on top, why don't you (take a chance now and then and) 'scorch your head'?"

(The "scorched head" is an allusion to *HS* 68.19b, where the story is told of a man whose stove had a straight flue and who kept his firewood piled against the stove. A neighbor advised him to use a crooked flue and move the firewood farther away, but the advice went unheeded. As expected, the house burned down and the man had to be rescued by his neighbors. Afterward, to show his gratitude, he gave a feast. Those with scorched heads got the top seats, and the man who advised precautionary measures sat at the bottom.)

21. While Hsieh An was living in retirement in the Eastern Mountains (Chekiang, before 360), he kept a female entertainer on the premises.[1] (The future) Emperor Chien-wen (Ssu-ma Yü) said, "An is sure to come out of retirement. As long as he shares the same pleasures as other men, he can't help sharing their anxieties as well." (*CS* 79.4b)

[1]*SMTWCC*: Hsieh An let his mind wander freely beyond the affairs of the world, and was careless of the ordinary restraints. He always kept a female entertainer about the premises, and, hand in hand, they would wander about freely enjoying themselves.

22. Ch'ih Ch'ao was not on good terms with Hsieh Hsüan. (In 377) when Fu Chien was about to "inquire after the Chin mandate," he had already devoured like a wolf the areas of Liang and Ch'i (i.e., Former Yen, in Shansi and Hopei, in 370), and was now eyeing like a tiger the southern shores of the Huai River (Anhui and Kiangsu). It was at this point that the court at Chien-k'ang was deliberating over whether to dispatch Hsieh Hsüan northward on a punitive expedition. Among those present several argued against it.

It was Ch'ih Ch'ao alone who said, "This man is sure to save the situation. I used to serve with him on Huan Wen's staff, and observed that he always made the utmost use of people's abilities. Even if they were only menials wearing sandals or clogs, he always picked the right man for every job. Drawing inferences from this, I feel he'll surely be able to establish his merit in this undertaking."

After Hsüan's great victory at the Fei River had been won (in 383), his contemporaries all sighed in admiration over Ch'ao's foresight. In particular they honored the way in which he had not let his personal likes or dislikes conceal the good qualities of another.[1] (*CS* 79.12b-13a)

[1]*CHS*: At the time (377) the Ti (Proto-Tibetan) bandits were at their strongest, and the court deliberated about looking for a good general with both civil and military qualifications who might pacify the north. The generalissimo of the Palace Guard, Hsieh An, said, "The only man who may be entrusted with this undertaking is my older brother's son, Hsüan."

The clerk of the Central Secretariat, Ch'ih Ch'ao, hearing this, sighed and said, "In opposing the majority and proposing his own relative, Hsieh An is being intelligent. Hsüan is certain not to betray his trust."

23. Han Po had no deep friendship with Hsieh Hsüan. After Hsüan had set out on his northern expedition (in 383), people discussing it in the streets were speculating that he would not succeed. Han Po said, "This man loves fame. He's sure to be able to fight."

When Hsüan learned of this, he was extremely angry, and whenever he was in a crowd, he would say with a severe expression, "When a great man leads a thousand men-at-arms into the place of death, he does it as a service to his ruler and his parents. You can hardly say it's for fame!"

24. When Ch'u Shuang was young, Hsieh An understood him very well. He always said of him, "If Ch'u Shuang is not a fine fellow, I'll make no more characterizations of gentlemen." (CS 93.13a)

25. Ch'ih Ch'ao used to go about in company with Fu Yüan. Yüan showed him his two sons, who were both young with their hair in tufts.[1] Ch'ao looked at them a long while, and then said to Yüan, "The younger one, in both ability and reputation, will surpass the older.[2] But the preservation of your family will in the end rest with the older brother."
They were Fu Liang and his older brother, Fu Ti. (SS 43.8a; NS 15.19b)

[1] According to the ascertainable dates, Fu Liang, the younger of the two brothers, could not have been more than three or four years old when Ch'ih Ch'ao died in 377. SS 43.8a and NS 15.19b record that he was "in his fourth or fifth year."

[2] In the SS and NS accounts Ch'ih Ch'ao, as a test, had someone remove Fu Liang's jacket and carry it off. Liang showed no sign of being unwilling to part with it.

26. Wang Kung had accompanied his father, Wang Yün, to live in K'uai-chi Commandery (Chekiang, ca. 375-376). Wang Ch'en[1] arrived from the capital to do obeisance at the grave of his father, Wang T'an-chih (d. 375). Kung went briefly to where Ch'en was staying by the base of the grave to visit him. The two had been friendly from their youth, and consequently it was more than ten days before Kung returned.
His father asked him, "Why did you stay so many days?"
He replied, "Whenever I start talking with A-ta (Wang Ch'en), it goes on like the continuous song of the cicada, so I couldn't get back."
Thereupon his father said to him, "I'm afraid A-ta is no friend of yours." In the end the two became estranged, just as Wang Yün had predicted.[2] (CS 93.12b; IWLC 21; SWLC, ch'ien 24)

[1] In CS 93.12b it is not Wang Ch'en, but Wang Yüeh, the eldest son of Wang Tao (d. 339), who is visiting his father's grave. But since Yüeh had died before his father, it must be a clerical error for the similar character, Ch'en.

[2] Since Wang Ch'en was the younger brother of Wang Kuo-pao, the favorite of the grand tutor, Ssu-ma Tao-tzu, he found himself in the opposite clique from Wang Kung and Yin Chung-k'an during the power struggle of 389-390. Their dramatic break is recorded in SSHY XXXI, 7, below.

27. While Ch'e Yin's father (Ch'e Yü) was serving as work-detail officer[1] in the administration of Nan-p'ing Commandery (Hupei, ca. 345), the grand warden of the commandery, Wang Hu-chih, relocated the commandery office on the south side of the Feng River (northern

Hupei), in order to avoid trouble from Ssu-ma Wu-chi.[2] At this time Yin was ten or so years of age, and every time Hu-chih came out of the office he would always see Yin through the fence and wonder at him. He said to Yin's father, "This boy will achieve an eminent reputation one day."

Afterward, whenever there was a festive occasion, people always invited Yin, and after he was fully grown he was also recognized by Huan Wen. His reputation for incorruptibility was known throughout the official world, and his rank rose as high as president of the Board of Civil Office. (CS 83.14b)

[1] *HCYC* states he was "superintendent of records."

[2] Ssu-ma Wu-chi's father, Ssu-ma Ch'eng, had been killed by Wang Hu-chih's father, Wang I*, during Wang Tun's rebellion in 322, on orders from Wang Tun (see below, *SSHY* XXXVI, 3 and 4). Wu-chi was appointed grand warden of Nan Commandery (Chiang-ling, near Tso-t'ang, the seat of Nan-p'ing Commandery) about 345.

28. When Wang Ch'en died (in 392), the person to succeed him in the western command (Ching Province, Hunan-Hupei) had not yet been determined, and the court nobles were all hoping it might be one of themselves. At the time, Yin Chung-k'an was among the palace attendants. Although he occupied a critical and influential position, his qualifications and reputation were slight, and public sentiment had not yet granted his capability as a pillar of state. But the Chin Emperor Hsiao-wu (Ssu-ma Yao, r. 373-396), desiring to single out his close relatives and bosom friends for special favor, proceeded to appoint Yin governor of Ching Province.

Though the matter had been settled, the decree had not yet been made public when Wang Ch'en's son, Hsün, asked Yin, "Why is it there hasn't been any appointment made for Shan-hsi (Ching Province) yet?"

Yin replied, "There already is someone."

Hsün thereupon made successive inquiries among the nobles and courtiers, and they all said this was not so. Hsün himself felt that his own ability and status were such that the post surely ought to be conferred on himself, so he asked again, "Am I not the one?"

Yin replied, "It seems not."

That night the decree was made public that Yin would be used for the post. Hsün said to his intimates, "When has there ever been an imperial attendant who was given a responsibility like this? This appointment of Chung-k'an is simply a portent of the state's doom."[1]

[1] *CATC*: Emperor Hsiao-wu, deeply concerned over what might happen after his own decease, selected Yin Chung-k'an to succeed Wang Ch'en as governor of Ching Province. Although Chung-k'an had an excellent reputation, the counselors had not yet granted his capability as a pillar of state. After having given him such a critically important responsibility, occupying the strategic area of the upper reaches of the Yangtze River, the counselors then felt that it had been a dangerous mistake. In the end Yin was killed by Huan Hsüan (399/400).

(According to *PCNC* [*Taishō* 50.936c-937a], Emperor Hsiao-wu originally intended to replace Wang Ch'en with Wang Kung, but Huan Hsüan, fearing that Kung would thwart his own ambitions, prevailed on the influential nun, Miao-yin, to persuade the emperor to appoint the ineffectual Yin Chung-k'an instead.)

CHAPTER VIII

Appreciation and Praise

1. Ch'en Fan once said with a sigh of admiration, "A person like Chou Ch'eng is truly capable of governing the state. If I were to compare him to a valuable sword, he'd be the Kan-chiang[1] of the age." (*TPKC* 169)

[1]*WYCC*: King Ho-lü of Wu (r. 514-496 B.C.) requested Kan-chiang to make him a sword. Kan-chiang was a native of Wu. His wife was called Mo-yeh. Kan-chiang selected the finest of the six metals from the essence of the Five Mountains, worshipped Heaven and Earth, and sacrificed to the Yin and Yang forces and to the hundred spirits. When he approached the forge to look, the essence of the metal and iron would not fuse together. Husband and wife then cut off their hair and nails and threw them into the furnace, and the metal and iron fused. Thereupon he made it into two swords; the Yang one he called Kan-chiang, and marked it with a tortoise pattern. The Yin one he called Mo-yeh, and marked it with a flowing water design. Kan-chiang hid the Yang one and brought out the Yin one to present to Ho-lü. Ho-lü valued it highly.

2. Contemporaries characterized Li Ying as "brisk and bracing (**siuk-siuk*) like the wind beneath sturdy pines."[1] (*SLF* 24; *TPYL* 53)

[1]*LiSCC*: Li Ying was lofty as a mountain and pure as a deep pool. His eminent manner was highly honored. Everyone in the realm praised him saying, "Grand Warden Li of Ying-ch'uan (Honan) towers high like a jade mountain. Ch'en Fan of Ju-nan (Honan) surpasses all others like a thousand-*li* horse, and Chu Mu of Nan-yang (Honan) is cool and breezy, as when one walks beneath pines and cypresses."

3. When Hsieh Chen saw Hsü Shao and his brother, Hsü Ch'ien, he said, "In the deep waters of P'ing-yü (Honan) there are two dragons."
   Once when he saw Hsü Ch'ien before the latter was of age, he said,

with a sigh, "A person like Hsü Ch'ien has the capacity to occupy a key position in the state. In his correct expression and loyal speech he'll be the equal of Ch'en Fan,[1] and in his prosecution of evil doers and expulsion of the unorthodox he'll have the manner of Fan P'ang."[2]

[1] Ch'en Fan's "words became a rule for gentlemen." See above, SSHY I, 1.

[2] Fan P'ang was one of the most formidable enemies of the eunuchs, whose rising influence in the latter half of the second century signaled the downfall of Later Han.

4. Kung-sun Tu characterized Ping Yüan as follows: "He's what might be called a white crane among the clouds; not to be caught in a net set for swallows and sparrows."[1] (SKWei 11.19b, comm.)

[1] Ping Yüan PC (cf. SKWei 11.18a-19b): When Yüan was only a few years old (SKWei comm. has "eleven"), he once passed a school crying. The teacher asked him, "Little boy, why are you crying?"

Yüan replied, "Usually a person who gets to study has relatives who in the first place won't let him be an orphan, and in the second place help him get to study. Deep in my heart I feel the pain (of being orphaned); that's the only reason I'm crying."

The teacher took pity on him and said, "If you want to study, you wouldn't have to pay for it." Whereupon Yüan started going there for instruction . . .

Knowing that the world was on the verge of disorder (on the eve of the Yellow Turban Revolt in 184), Yüan fled to Liao-tung (Manchuria), where Kung-sun Tu treated him generously.

After the Central States had been pacified, Yüan wanted to return to his home village, but was forbidden to do so by Tu. Yüan surreptitiously packed his belongings and said to his underlings, "I'm moving north, nearer the commandery," to observe their reaction. They all said they would be glad to move.

From his previous flight Yüan still possessed a large fishing boat. That day he invited everybody in the village for a feast and got them all dead drunk. Then in the night he left them. After several days Tu found out about it. A petty officer wanted to give pursuit, but Tu said, "Ping Yüan is what might be called a white crane among the clouds, etc."

5. Chung Hui characterized Wang Jung as follows: "A-jung is quick and perceptive (*lieu-lieu) and understands the thoughts of others."

He said of P'ei K'ai's[1] conversation: "He goes on for days without being talked out."

When the post of secretary of the Board of Civil Office became vacant, Ssu-ma Chao asked Chung Hui which man should fill it, and Hui said, "P'ei K'ai is pure and comprehensive; Wang Jung is unceremonious and keeps to the essential. They're both good choices for the job." Whereupon he employed P'ei. (CS 35.13b-14a; IWLC 48; PTSC 33, 60, 98)

[1] The text reads merely, "Lord P'ei" (P'ei-kung), which Liu Chün in the Commentary mistakenly identifies as P'ei Wei, who lived a generation later.

6. When the two men Wang Jung and P'ei K'ai were young boys with their hair in tufts, they went to visit Chung Hui.[1] A short time later, after they had left, a guest asked Chung, "What do you think of the two boys who were here just now?"

Chung replied, "P'ei K'ai is pure and perceptive; Wang Jung is unceremonious and keeps to the essential. Twenty years hence these two worthies should be presidents of the Board of Civil Office.[2] Let's hope that at that time there will be no unused men of ability in the realm." (CS 35.13b-14a; IWLC 22, 48; SWLC, hsin 11; PTSC 60; CHC 11; TPYL 214, 385, 444)

[1]This story is obviously a variant of the preceding one and virtually identical with No. 14, below.

[2]Chung was approximately ten years older than the two boys, who must have been around fifteen at the time of the story. Wang Jung was first appointed president of the Board of Civil Office early in 289 (about forty years later) and transferred in the autumn of the following year to grand tutor. In the spring of 291 he resumed the presidency and remained there until the fall of 297, when he became director of works. Although P'ei K'ai is known to have become personal attendant and president of the Central Secretariat, there is no record of his having held the presidency of the Board of Civil Office.

7. The saying goes:

> "Among the leaders of the new
> There is P'ei Hsiu."

(CS 35.3b)

8. P'ei K'ai characterized Hsia-hou Hsüan as follows: "He is sedate and dignified (*$si̯uk$-$si̯uk$), as if entering the court or ancestral temple; there is no cultivation of reverence, yet the people naturally revere him."[1] Another version is: "As if entering the ancestral temple; in clear tones (*$lâng$-$lâng$) one perceives nothing but the sound of ceremonial instruments.

"When I look at Chung Hui, it's like looking into an armory and seeing nothing but spears and halberds in dense profusion (*$si̯əm$-$si̯əm$).[2]

"When I look at Fu Chia, he's vast and limitless (*·$wâng$-$zi̯ang$) containing everything.

"When I look at Shan T'ao, it's like climbing a mountain and looking down, far, far from the world." (CS 35.16a)

[1]"Record of Rites" (IV, 57; Legge, Li Ki I, 191): Chou Feng said to Duke Ai of Lu (r. 494-467 B.C.), "Among the altars of the spirits of the land and grain and the ancestral temples there is never any cultivation of reverence, yet the people naturally revere them."

[2]The binome *$si̯əm$-$si̯əm$ is interpolated, following CS 35.16a, to match those in the other characterizations.

9. Once when Yang Hu was returning to Lo-yang (ca. 260), Kuo I was serving as magistrate of Yeh-wang Prefecture (Honan). As Yang reached

his territory, Kuo dispatched a man to invite him to stay in the area, while Kuo himself went out to meet him. After Kuo had seen Yang, he sighed in admiration, saying, "Why is Yang Hu necessarily inferior to me?"

Later he went again to Yang's place, and returned after getting to know him slightly. Again he sighed in admiration, saying, "Yang Hu surpasses me by far!"

When Yang left the area, Kuo escorted him on his way for several days, traveling a hundred *li* before returning. Then, since he had gone beyond the bounds of his own territory, he was dismissed from his post. Once more sighing in admiration he said, "Why is Yang Hu necessarily inferior to Yen Hui?"[1] (*CS* 45.18b-19a)

[1] Yen Hui (Tzu-yüan), 514-483 B.C., the favorite disciple of Confucius.

10. Wang Jung characterized Shan T'ao as follows: "He's like unpolished jade or unrefined gold. Everyone delights in his great value, but no one knows how to name what kind of vessel he is."[1] (*CS* 43.13a)

[1] *HT*: Shan T'ao could not be described or named. Pure, deep, mysterious and silent--no one saw his limits, yet all agreed that he had, indeed, entered upon the Way. Therefore no one who saw him could say what he was, but bowed nevertheless before his greatness.

11. Yang Ch'en's father, Yang Yu, being a first cousin of Yang Hu, was on friendly terms with the latter. He held office as high as assistant to the General of Chariots and Horsemen, but died young. Yang Ch'en and his four elder brothers[1] were thus orphaned in their childhood. When Yang Hu came to weep at Yu's bier, he observed that Yang Ch'en's expression of grief and his every movement were plainly like those of an adult. Sighing admiringly, he said, "My cousin is not dead."

[1] Yang Yu's five sons, in order of birth, were Ping, Chi, Shih, Liang, and Ch'en.

12. When Shan T'ao recommended Juan Hsien for clerk in the Board of Civil Office, he characterized him as follows: "Incorruptible and honest, with few desires; the myriad things of the world cannot budge him."[1] (*CS* 49.46; *IWLC* 48; *PTSC* 33, 60; *TPYL* 216; *SWLC*, hsin 11)

[1] For the text of his recommendation see *STCS* (cf. *CS* 49.4b): Honest and plain, with few desires, he is profoundly acquainted with the difference between the incorruptible and the venal. The myriad things of the world cannot budge him. If he occupies an official post, he will surely surpass all his contemporaries.

CYC: Since Juan Hsien personally made many violations of the ritual code in his conduct, when Shan T'ao recommended him for clerk in the Board of Civil Office Emperor Wu (Ssu-ma Yen, r. 265-290) did not permit the appointment to go through.

CLCHL: When Shan T'ao recommended Juan Hsien he definitely knew that the emperor would not be able to use him. It seems he simply did it because he admired the strength of his freedom from the world, and no one understood his ideas. In consideration of Hsien's violations and his ultramundane ideas, when Shan praised him as incorruptible and honest, with few desires, his implication that Juan was beyond the world of actual events becomes self-evident.

13. Wang Jung characterized Juan Wu as follows: "He has a perceptive understanding of pure human relations. Ever since the beginning of Han[1] there has never been such a man as this."

[1] An allusion to Chang Liang, adviser to the first Han emperor.

14. Wu Kai characterized P'ei K'ai and Wang Jung as follows: "Jung honors brevity; K'ai is pure and comprehensive."

15. Yü Ai characterized Ho Ch'iao as follows: "In dense profusion (*siəm-siəm), like a pine tree at a height of a thousand *chang*. Though gnarled (*luâi-luâ) and full of knots, if used for a large building, it may serve as a beam or pillar."[1] (*CS* 45.13a; 50.8a, of Wen Ch'iao; *SLF*, hua 24, said by P'ei Wei)

[1] *CCKT*: Ho Ch'iao always admired his maternal uncle, Hsia-hou Hsüan, as a person, and therefore he was like a lone peak among the courtiers and did not mingle with the crowd. Those of his own age and class were in awe of the rigor of his manner.

16. Wang Jung said, "The spirit and manner of the grand marshal, Wang Yen, are lofty and transcendent, like a jade forest or a jasper tree. He's naturally a being who lives beyond the reach of the wind and dust of the world."[1] (*CS* 43.13a)

[1] *MSC*: Wang Yen's natural physique was wonderfully unique, brilliantly outstanding, like a god's.

PWKS: When the Hsiung-nu leader Shih Lo saw Wang Yen (in 311), he said to his senior administrator, K'ung Ch'ang, "I've traveled much throughout the realm, but I've never seen a man like this. Oughtn't we to let him live?"

Ch'ang replied, "Those in the Three Ducal Offices of Chin (Wang Yen was grand marshal) are of no use to us."

Lo said, "Even so, I perfer not to put him to the sword." That night he had someone push the wall (so that is collapsed on him) and killed him.

17. After Wang Chan had completed the period of mourning for his father (Wang Ch'ang, d. 259), he continued to live by the tomb. Whenever his older brother's son, Wang Chi, came to do obeisance at the tomb, he almost never stopped by his uncle's place to pay his respects, and his uncle, for his part, also did not greet him.[1] When on rare occasions Chi did stop by, he only talked about the weather and nothing more.

Later when he made a slight attempt to bring his inquiries around to recent events, Chan's replies were exceedingly eloquent and well phrased, far beyond anything Chi had anticipated, and he was extremely surprised. As Chi continued talking with him, their conversation grew more and more refined and subtle.[2]

At first Chi had been casual, and had shown none of the respect proper to a nephew, but after hearing his uncle speak, without realizing it he was deeply impressed, and his mind and body both became reverent. After that he stayed on and they conversed together for several days and nights.

Although Chi was a bold and forthright person, he began now to "view himself as inadequate."[3] Heaving a deep sigh, he said, "Our family has all along had a famous gentleman in it, and for thirty years I've been unaware of it!"

As Chi was leaving, his uncle escorted him as far as the gate. Now in Chi's entourage there was a horse which was extremely difficult to mount, and there were few who could ride it. On the spur of the moment Chi asked his uncle, "Do you enjoy riding?"

His uncle said, "I enjoy that, too."

Chi then had him ride the horse which was difficult to mount. Not only were his uncle's bearing and form wonderful to behold, but he twirled his whip like a reel. There was not a famous horseman anywhere who could have surpassed him.[4] Chi sighed more than ever over his unfathomability, which was by no means limited to one thing.

After Chi had returned home, his father, Wang Hun, asked him, "How does it happen that for so short a journey you've taken several days?"

Chi replied, "At last I've discovered my uncle!"

Hun asked what he meant, and Chi related everything in detail, with sighs of admiration, just as it has been told.

Hun said, "How does he compare with us?"

Chi replied, "He's superior to me."

Whenever Chi's father-in-law, Emperor Wu (Ssu-ma Yen, r. 265-290), saw Chi, he always used to tease him about Wang Chan, saying, "Has your family's half-witted uncle died yet?"

Chi usually had nothing to say in reply, but after he had "discovered" his uncle, when Emperor Wu asked again as he used to do, Chi said, "Your servant's uncle is no half-wit." Whereupon he waxed eloquent over Wang Chan's real excellence.

The emperor asked, "With whom would you compare him?"

Chi replied, "He comes somewhere below Shan T'ao, and above Wei Shu."[5] After this Chan's reputation became well known, and in his twenty-eighth year (276) he entered for the first time upon an official career. (CS 75.1b)

[1] Wang Chi, though belonging to the next generation, was actually nine years older than his uncle.

[2] *TTCC* (cf. CS 75.1b): Chi observed that by Chan's bed there was a copy of the "Book of Changes" (*Chou-i*), so he said to Chan, "Uncle, what are you doing with this? Do you ever look at it?"

Chan laughed and said, "When I'm in fine health (CS reads: 'not in fine health'), on rare occasions I look at it, that's all. Today I'll talk with you about it."

Accordingly Chan talked with him about the "Changes," analyzing its principles and entering into its subtleties. His marvelous words and their unusual interest were such as Chi had never heard before, and he sighed with admiration over his uncle's unfathomability.

[3] Cf. *Chuang-tzu* I, 6b (Watson, p. 32): (The sage-king said to the recluse Hsü Yu), "I view myself as inadequate (to rule)."

[4] *TTCC*: Chi was by nature fond of horses. The horse he rode was

spirited and swift and he loved it dearly. Chan said, "Although it's fairly swift, its strength is slight, and it can't endure hardship. Recently I saw the inspector-general's horse, which should be superior to this one. It's only that his care of it doesn't come up to yours."

Chi took the inspector-general's horse and fed it on grain for thirty or forty days, then tried it out with Chan. Chan had never ridden a horse before in his life, but in a flash he immediately galloped off, his riding form, whether pacing or trotting, no different from Chi's, but neither horse beat the other.

Chan said, "Now if we go straight along the chariot road, how can we find out which of the two horses is superior? Let's just go as far as the anthill, yonder." Whereupon they went as far as the anthill and wheeled their horses around, and at last Chan fell to the ground. Such was his outstanding knowledge and natural genius.

[5]*CYC*: Wang Chi possessed judgment and insight into human relations, and even when he was young he had a fine understanding of the difference between the cultivated and the vulgar, the true and the false. When he saw Chan, he sighed in admiration over his virtuous capacity.

Contemporaries said to Chan, "You don't quite measure up to Shan T'ao, but are a little better than Wei Shu."

When Chan heard this he said, "Do you mean to place me between the eldest and the youngest brothers?"

18. Contemporaries called P'ei Wei "the wooded swampland of conversation."[1] (*CS* 35.8a; *PTSC* 98, 100; *TPYL* 390)

[1]*HTCCC*: P'ei Wei's topics were exceedingly profound and broad. To match him in discussion was difficult.

19. When Chang Hua had seen Ch'u T'ao, he said to Lu Chi, "With you and your younger brother, Yün, cavorting like dragons through the Milky Way (*yün-ching*),[1] and with Ku Jung singing like a phoenix on the eastern slope (*chao-yang*),[2] I began to think the treasure of the southeast had already been exhausted, but now unexpectedly I've seen it once more in Ch'u T'ao."[3]

Lu Chi replied, "Sir, you haven't yet seen the ones who aren't cavorting or singing, that's all." (*CS* 92.12b-13a)

[1] The Lu brothers and Ku Jung had come to Lo-yang from Wu in 289. The "Milky Way"-- literally, the "Cloudy Ford" (*yün-ching*)--while serving as an image for the court at Lo-yang, is also a pun on Lu Yün's name, and the image of dragons a pun on his courtesy name, Shih-lung, "Dragon among Gentlemen." Cf. also the "Book of Changes." Hex. 1 (Wilhelm I, 7-8): "Nine in the fourth place: something cavorting in the abyss . . . Nine in the fifth place: a flying dragon in the heavens."

[2] I.e., in Lo-yang. "Songs," No. 252:

> The phoenix sings
> On yon high hill.
> The paulownia grows
> On the eastern slope.

³*CSCC*: Chang Hua wrote a letter to Ch'u T'ao, saying, "The two Lus are cavorting like dragons in the Milky Way (*Han-chiang*), and Ku Jung is singing like a phoenix on the eastern slope. Nowadays I am continually afraid that the gold of the south has already been exhausted, but once more I find it in you, my child. So I know for certain that the virtue of Yen-chou (i.e., Chi Cha, a southern aristocrat who served a northern lord in the sixth century B.C.) is not alone, nor is the treasure of (southern) streams and mountains lost."

20. Someone asked Ts'ai Hung, "How would you describe the members of the principal old families of Wu?"[1]

He replied, "Wu Chan is an aged and accomplished man out of the era of the sage kings, a forceful and able man from an enlightened age.

"Chu Tan represents the supreme virtue in ruling the people, the highest hope in the selection of the incorrupt.

"Yen Yin is the 'crying crane in the ninefold swamp,'[2] the 'pure white colt in the empty vale.'[3]

"Ku Jung is a seven-stringed zither (*ch'in*), or twenty-stringed zither (*se*) among the eight timbres (*pa-yin*); a dragon shape of five colors.[4]

"Chang Ch'ang is a luxuriant pine in the cold of the year,[5] a surpassing radiance in the lonely night.

"[Lu Chi and][6] Lu Yün are the flying-to-and-fro of the wild goose and swan, the waiting-to-be-struck of a suspended drum.

"All these gentlemen

> Used their mighty pens for hoe and plow,
> Their paper and bamboo for fertile field.
> They used mysterious silence for their crops;
> Meanings and principles were the abundant yield.
>
> Conversation was their glory,
> 'Loyalty and reciprocity'[7] their treasure.
> Composing essays was their embroidery,
> Weaving the five colors[8] their brocade.
>
> They sat on humble modesty for mats,
> And hung complaisance up for curtains,
> Practiced goodness for a dwelling place,
> And cultivated virtue as their home."[9]

[1] See No. 142, below.

[2] "Songs," No. 184:

> A crane is crying in the ninefold swamp;
> Its voice is heard in the wild.

[3] "Songs," No. 186:

> Dazzling is the pure white colt
> In yonder empty vale.

[4] See *SC* 7.13a: Fan Tseng said to Hsiang Yü (d. 202 B.C.), "I had someone look at the emanations (*ch'i*) from the face of the Duke of P'ei (the future Emperor Kao of Han, r. 206-195 B.C.); they are

218   TALES OF THE WORLD

all dragons and tigers turning into the five colors. These are the emanations of a Son of Heaven."

[5] Cf. "Analects" IX, 28.

[6] Lu Chi's name is omitted in the Sung texts and in the Commentary.

[7] "Analects" IV, 15.

[8] All but the Sung text have "Five Classics," i.e., the "Book of Changes," the "Book of Documents," the "Book of Songs," the lost "Book of Rites," and the "Spring and Autumn Annals."

[9] The source of this anecdote seems to have been a "Letter to Governor Chou Chün" (Yü tz'u-shih Chou Chün shu), included in Ts'ai Hung's "Collected Works" (THC): One day I was in attendance at the emperor's seat, and the conversation touched on the gentlemen of Wu. (As it says in the "Songs,") "Inquire of grass cutters and wood gatherers," so His Majesty condescended to ask each of those present in turn. What was said I will not record, but His Majesty commanded us to write up brief biographical sketches for each name, and after withdrawing and thinking about it, I herewith acclaim those I have some slight knowledge of: Wu Chan, etc.

SSHY Comm.: The gentlemen discussed by Ts'ai Hung, sixteen in all, did not include the Lu brothers (Chi and Yün), nor did his discussion contain the passage beginning, "All these gentlemen . . ." I suspect someone has added it.

21. Someone asked Wang Yen, "What was Shan T'ao like as far as his Meanings and Principles were concerned? In which category did he belong?"

Wang replied, "This man at first was unwilling to occupy himself with conversation. However, without even reading the *Lao-tzu* or the *Chuang-tzu*, from time to time he heard them being recited, and frequently agreed with their ideas."

22.   In Lo-yang, tra-la-la,
           There were three men named Chia:

Liu Ts'ui (Ch'un-chia), Liu Hung (Chung-chia), and Liu Mo (Ch'ung-chia). Brothers they were; sons of the same mother, nephews of Wang Jung,[1] and all sons-in-law of Wang Jung as well. Liu Hung was Liu T'an's grandfather.

           In Lo-yang, sound ding-ding!
           There was one Feng Hui-ch'ing.

His given name was Sun, and he was the son of Feng Po. Feng Sun and Hsing Ch'iao were both grandchildren on their mother's side of the director of instruction, Li Yin, and together with Yin's son, Li Shun, all three were well known. Their contemporaries said of them:

           Feng's ability is clean,
           And Li's is bright;
           But the pure and undefiled is Hsing.

(CS 35.32ab)

[1] In the Commentary Liu Chün cites the *Liu SP* as evidence that the

mother of the three Liu brothers was a daughter of Wu Chou, *not* a sister of Wang Jung, as claimed.

23. While Wei Kuan was serving as president of the Imperial Secretariat, he observed Yüeh Kuang conversing with the famous gentlemen of the central court (in Lo-yang), and admired him, saying, "Ever since the former generation has passed on, I've been constantly afraid lest the art of subtle words might come to an end. But now at last I'm hearing such words again from you, sir."[1]

He commanded the younger members of his family to go and visit Yüeh, saying, "This man is a water mirror to other men. Seeing him is like rolling away the clouds and mist and gazing at the blue sky." (*CS* 43.21a)

[1]*CYC*: The president of the Imperial Secretariat, Wei Kuan, saw Yüeh Kuang, and said, "In the old days, after Ho Yen and the others died (in 249), I always used to think that pure conversation had come to an end. But now again I'm hearing it from you, sir."

WYCS: Wei Kuan was skilled in Names and Principles (*ming-li*), and used to converse with Ho Yen, Teng Yang, and the others. When he saw Yüeh Kuang, he said admiringly, "Every time I see this man I feel purified, as when the clouds and mists have cleared away and I'm gazing at the blue sky."

24. The grand marshal, Wang Yen, said, "I observed P'ei K'ai's (d. 302) pure radiance shining abroad, overarching all other men; his was no ordinary understanding! If the dead might rise again, I'd throw in my lot with him."[1]

Some say it was Wang Jung who said this.

[1]"Record of Rites" IV, 70 (Legge, *Li Ki* I, 199): Chao Wen-tzu said, "If the dead might rise again, with whom would I throw in my lot?"

25. Wang Yen sighed to himself, saying, "Whenever I converse with Yüeh Kuang, I never fail to be aware that my own speech is verbose."[1] (*CS* 43.21a)

[1]*CYC*: Yüeh Kuang was skilled at satisfying people's minds with few words, and in the case of matters about which he was ignorant, he kept silent. The grand marshal, Wang Yen, and the Great Officer of Brilliant Favor, P'ei K'ai, were both capable in pure conversation, but they frequently said, "Whenever we converse with Yüeh Kuang, we're aware that his brevity is ultimate, while we're all being verbose."

26. Kuo Hsiang possessed outstanding ability, and conversed capably on the *Lao-tzu* and *Chuang-tzu*.[1] Yü Ai frequently praised him, each time saying, "Why is Kuo Hsiang necessarily inferior to me?"[2]

[1]Concerning Kuo Hsiang's commentary on the *Chuang-tzu*, see above, *SSHY* IV, 17.

[2]*MSC*: Yü Ai said to Kuo Hsiang, "You're undoubtedly the most able person in the present age. All that I've ever thought about in the past you've already mastered.

27. Wang Ch'eng characterized his older brother, Grand Marshal Wang Yen, saying, "Brother, your physical appearance bears some resemblance to the Way, but the point of your spirit is too sharp."[1]
The grand marshal replied, "Well, I'm certainly not as lackadaisical and easygoing (*lâk-lâk m̯iuk-m̯iuk) as you are!"[2] (CS 43.17b)

[1] I.e., he was physically non-active (wu-wei), but temperamentally had not sufficiently "blunted his sharpness"; see Lao-tzu 2.

[2] WYCS: Wang Ch'eng was perceptive and transparent, and fond of human relationships, yet his own feelings were never involved.

28. In the administration of the grand tutor, Ssu-ma Yüeh, there were three geniuses: Liu Yü was the long genius;[1] P'an T'ao the great genius; and P'ei Mo the pure genius.[2] (CS 62.15a)

[1] CYC: When the grand tutor was about to summon Liu Yü, someone said, "Yü is like grease; get near him and he'll get you dirty." The grand tutor became suspicious and dropped him. Yü then secretly spied out the number of men-at-arms in the entire realm, silently ascertaining the position of all encampments and storehouses, the amount of personnel and supplies, the oxen and horses, equipment and machines, and the topography of their water and land positions. At this time there were many affairs involving the army and the state, but every time the officials discussed them in conference, from P'an T'ao on down no one knew how to meet the situation. Yü then proceeded to count off statistics on his fingers: how many troops and arms had been deployed, together with their location, the amount of grain and transport. There was no matter in which he was at a loss for figures. Thereafter the grand tutor entrusted him with heavy responsibility.

[2] PWKS: Liu Yü's genius was long on general investigations, P'an T'ao was famous for his wide learning, P'ei Mo stood firm on the square and correct. All were intimately befriended by the Prince of Tung-hai (Ssu-ma Yüeh), and appeared together in the same administration. Therefore their contemporaries praised them, saying, "Liu Yü is the long genius, etc."

29. The Seven Worthies beneath the Bamboo Grove each had sons of outstanding ability.
Juan Chi's son, Hun, had a capacity and tolerance which were vast and untrammeled.
Hsi K'ang's son, Shao, was pure and remote from the world, cultivated and correct.
Shan T'ao's son, Chien, was detached yet perceptive, high-minded yet simple.
Juan Hsien's son, Chan, was disinterested and relaxed, with a determination to keep himself remote from the world.
Chan's younger brother, Fu, was forthright and brilliant, and careless of most things.
Hsiang Hsiu's sons, Ch'un and T'i, were both fine and virtuous, in the purest tradition.
Wang Jung's son, Sui, had the promise of great accomplishment, but was "cut off as a sprout before it is full grown."[1]
It was only Liu Ling's sons of whom nothing was ever heard.

Of all these sons Juan Chan alone was the crown. But Hsi Shao and Shan Chien were also honored in their time.

[1] "Analects" IX, 22.

30. Yü Tsung suffered from a crippling ailment, but was extremely well known. Since his house was located west of the city of Lo-yang, people called him "His Lordship from west of the city."[1]

[1] Though "Your Lordship" (*kung-fu*) was the usual term of address for a person in one of the Three Ducal Offices, Yü himself never rose above a minor post on the grand marshal's staff.

31. Wang Yen said to Yüeh Kuang, "There aren't many famous gentlemen. Of course we may leave it to Wang Ch'eng to know who they are."[1]

[1] *Wang Ch'eng PC*: Wang Ch'eng's elegant manner and reputation reached everywhere, and his determination and spirit set him above the crowd. The reputations of his cousin, Jung (president of the Board of Civil Office from 293 to 297), and brother, Yen (president from 305 to 306, and grand marshal till his death in 311), crowned the age. Once any gentleman within the Four Seas had been characterized by Wang Ch'eng, then his cousin and brother paid no further attention to the matter. They would say, "It's already been cleared by Ch'eng." Such was the importance attached to his judgments. For this reason his reputation became more and more flourishing, and whether a person was known or unknown in the realm depended entirely upon him.

Ch'eng's later conduct did not come up to expectations, and both those at court and in the provinces became disappointed in him. However, all who had known him from past associations continued to say, "He's the most famous gentleman of the present age."

32. The grand marshal, Wang Yen, said, "When Kuo Hsiang converses, it's as if he were tilting the Yellow River to drain its waters; it pours and pours, but is never exhausted." (*CS* 50.8b; *TPYL* 464)

33. In the headquarters of the grand tutor, Ssu-ma Yüeh, were many famous gentlemen, the outstanding and unique men of the entire age. Yü Liang once said, "Whenever I saw my father's cousin, Yü Ai,[1] in their midst, he was always naturally exhilarated in spirit."[2] (*CS* 50.7b)

[1] Yü Ai served as Ssu-ma Yüeh's administrative clerk.

[2] In *CS* 50.7b "exhilarated in spirit" (*shen-wang*) is replaced by the graphically similar expression "putting his hands in his sleeves" (*hsiu-shou*). The unmistakable allusion, however, to *Chuang-tzu* III, 3b (Watson, p. 52; cf. also *SSHY* VI, 28, above), makes the former reading preferable.

34. When the grand tutor and Prince of Tung-hai, Ssu-ma Yüeh, was stationed in Hsü-ch'ang Prefecture (Honan, in 307), he had Wang Ch'eng as his secretarial aide, and always treated him with recognition and respect.

In instructing his heir, Ssu-ma P'i, Yüeh wrote: "What is to be gained through study is superficial, but what is to be secured through personal experience is profound. Therefore a desultory memorization of the rules of etiquette can't compare with emulating a living model of proper behavior, nor can chanting and savoring the words handed down from the past compare with personally receiving a living man's spoken instruction. Take the expression of proper human relations exemplified by my aide, Wang Ch'eng, as your teacher!"

Some accounts state that he said, "Take the expression of proper human relations exemplified by my *three* aides, Wang Ch'eng, Chao Mu, and Teng Yu, as your teachers!"

When Yüan Hung composed the "Lives of Famous Gentlemen" (*Ming-shih chuan*), he merely had Yüeh say, "my aide, Wang Ch'eng." According to others, however, the Chao family formerly was still in possession of a copy of this letter (by Ssu-ma Yüeh, which was addressed to all three aides).[1] (*CS* 75.2b; *TPKC* 235)

[1] *CWCHC*: Ssu-ma Yüeh addressed a letter to Chao Mu, Wang Ch'eng, Juan Chan (*sic*), and Teng Yu, stating, "The Rites require that a boy in his eighth year should go to study with an outside teacher. The tenth year is called 'Studies for the Young,' which makes clear that he may be gradually introduced to the teaching of the Former Kings. However, what is to be gained through study is superficial, etc. Inasmuch as my little boy, P'i, does not have any good qualities to begin with, and has never heard of the manner of those who follow the Way and its Virtue, I would like to presume upon you gentlemen in your leisure excursions to keep him company and gently instruct him."

35. When Yü Liang was young, he was recognized by Wang Hsüan. After Yü had crossed the Yangtze River, he praised Wang, saying, "Just to take shelter under his eaves enabled a person to forget the heat or cold."

36. Hsieh K'un said, "My friend Wang Hsüan is pure and comprehensive, unceremonious and cheerful. Hsi Shao is magnanimous and cultivated, noble and outstanding. Tung Yang is majestic and distinguished, with supreme tolerance."[1]

[1] *WYCS*: During the Yung-chia era (307-312), within the northeast corner of the walls of Lo-yang, the ground of the Pu-kuang Ward collapsed, and there appeared two geese. The speckled one flew away, but the white one could not fly. When inquiries were made, even those of broad erudition could not explain it.

When Tung Yang heard about it, he sighed and said, "This is the spot where long ago during Chou times (631 B.C.) they made the covenant at Ti-ch'üan (see *Tso-chuan*, Hsi 29; Legge V, 214). As for the sudden appearance of the two geese, speckled ones are the sign of the Hu barbarians. Later the Hu will enter Lo-yang. The fact that the white one couldn't fly is a portent of doom for this state." (White, being the color of the element metal, represented the virtue of Chin.)

YHLH: When Tung Yang of Ch'en-liu Commandery (Honan) witnessed Emperor Hui's (r. 290-306) deposing of his mother's cousin, Empress Yang Tao, during the Yüan-k'ang era (291), he mounted the hall of the Grand Academy and cried, "Why did they build this hall? Every time I see letters of amnesty in this state, those who plot rebellion and insubordination are all granted amnesty. But when grandsons murder their grandparents, or sons murder their parents, they are never granted amnesty, on the supposition that the royal laws will not allow it. What can be done when nobles and ministers give counsel, and so twist and embellish the rites and laws that we have come to this? Since the principles of both heaven and man have come to an end, great disorder will now arise!"

Looking back, he said to Hsieh K'un and Juan Fu, "In the 'Book of Changes' (*Hsi-tz'u* B: Wilhelm I, 367) it says: 'How divine to know the springs of action!' May you, good sirs, take it deeply to heart!" So saying, he went with his wife, bearing his belongings on his back, into Shu (Szechwan), and no one knows where he died.

37. Wang Tao characterized the grand marshal, Wang Yen, as follows: "High-towering (**ngam-ngam*) the unsullied peak, standing like a cliff a thousand *jen* high."[1]

[1] This characterization is almost identical with one written by Ku K'ai-chih on a portrait of Wang Yen, the *(Wang) I-fu hua-tsan*, cited in the Commentary.

38. While Yü Liang was still in Lo-yang (before 307), he once went to pay a call on his father's cousin, Yü Ai. Ai invited him to stay awhile, saying, "Everyone will soon be here (for conversation)."

Shortly thereafter Wen Chi, Liu Ch'ou, and P'ei K'ai all arrived, and proceeded to drink and converse back and forth all day. Long afterward Yü Liang still remembered the ability and forcefulness of Liu Ch'ou and P'ei K'ai, and the disinterested moderation of Wen Chi.

39. While Ts'ai Mo was still living in Lo-yang (in 301), he met Lu Chi and his younger brother, Yün, who were then occupying a three-bay tile-roofed house in the aide-de-camp's quarters (of the Prince of Chao, Ssu-ma Lun). Lu Yün occupied the eastern end, and Lu Chi the western. (Ts'ai recalled that) Lu Yün as a person was lovable, while Lu Chi, over seven feet (*ch'ih*) tall, had a voice that boomed like a bell, his words for the most part uttered with deep feeling.[1] (*TPYL* 181, 388)

[1] *WSC*: Lu Yün's nature was magnanimous and placid, and he was admired by other gentlemen and friends. Lu Chi was frank and critical, with an imposing manner, and was feared by his fellow townsmen.

40. Wang Meng was Yü Tsung's grandson on his mother's (Yü San-shou) side. Chancellor Wang Tao once characterized Yü Tsung, saying, "He has entered deeply into the realm of Truth (*li*)--a man superior to me."

41. Yü Liang characterized Yü Ai, saying, "My father's cousin just chatted about things."[1]

[1] *T'an-t'an chih hsü* (*hsü* is a final particle). Since Liu Chün offers several variant readings, the text may be corrupt.

MSC: Yü Ai never conversed discursively or analytically on any topic, but always selected the essential idea. Wang Yen often honored him.

42. Yü Liang characterized Yü Ai, saying, "His spirit and manner were pleasant and relaxed, almost as if he had gained a higher level of existence."[1]

[1] *CYC:* Yü Ai was relaxed and profoundly uninhibited. Nothing that he heard ever disturbed him.

43. Liu K'un praised Tsu T'i for his transparent purposefulness, saying, "In his youth he was admired by Wang Tun."[1]

[1] *CYC:* Tsu T'i and the director of works, Liu K'un, were both famous as brave warriors. When T'i was in his twenty-fourth year (289), he and K'un were both summoned to be superintendent of records for the commandant of the Capital Province (Honan). Their affections were tightly knit together, and they slept together under the same coverlet. In the middle of the night, when they heard the cock crow, they would rise together and say, "It's not such an unpleasant sound!"

Often they would talk about the affairs of the world, or at midnight would rise and tell each other, "If all the world is boiling like a cauldron and heroic warriors are rising up together, you and I will both just flee from the Central Plain, that's all."

44. Contemporaries characterized Yü Ai as follows: "Skillful in great undertakings; excelling in self-concealment."[1]

[1] *MSC:* Although Yü Ai occupied offices and assumed responsibilities, he never let himself become involved in the affairs of the world, but remained tranquilly free and aloof. At the time the realm was filled with turmoil, and crises were arising in rapid succession, while the activists were advocating strange and unusual solutions; yet disaster followed upon disaster. Yü Ai kept silent through it all, and consequently neither grief nor joy came his way.

45. Wang Ch'eng despised the world, and, since he possessed outstanding ability himself, there were few persons whom he deigned to admire. But whenever he listened to Wei Chieh conversing, he would always sigh so deeply with admiration that he fell over.[1] (*CS* 36.13b)

[1] See No. 51, below.

Wei Chieh PC: Whenever Wang Ch'eng listened to Wei Chieh's conversations, as they reached the point where Truth is understood (*li-hui*), the boundary of the Essential and Subtle (*yao-miao*), he would always sigh so deeply that he fell over in his seat. He listened to him three times in succession, and fell over for him three times. So his contemporaries used to say,

"When Wei Chieh talked about the Way,
Wang Ch'eng took his tumbles three."

46. The generalissimo Wang Tun once sent a memorial to Emperor Yüan (Ssu-ma Jui, r. 317-322), in which he said, "My cousin, Wang Shu*, in his manner and bearing is unceremonious and correct--indeed a cultivated man--much more so than his younger brother, Wang Sui**. He's the one whom your servant has recognized and singled out from his

youth more than any other. Recently my cousins, Wang Yen and Wang
Ch'eng, said to me, 'You've recognized both cousins, Wang Shu* and
Wang Tao. Of the two Wang Tao already has a fine reputation, and has
truly confirmed your critical judgment. Wang Shu*, on the other hand,
has never been recognized by anyone else, either by a relative or a
nonrelative. We often recall what you said about him, and so far
there has been absolutely no confirmation. Perhaps you have already
come to repent of your judgment?'

"Your servant said to them with deep feeling, 'You can see for
yourselves by this memorial that now at last there is someone who is
praising him.' What I mean to say is that ordinary men are precisely
the ones about whom people complain that to recognize them is going
too far, and not to recognize them is disregarding the facts."

47. After Chou I's defeat in Ching Province (in 313),[1] he returned to
Chien-k'ang, but had not as yet received any appointment. In a letter
to a friend, Chancellor Wang Tao wrote: "How could a man of such cultivation and vast capacity be overlooked?" (CS 69.16b)

[1] TTCC: When Chou I was appointed governor of Ching Province (Hunan-Hupei), he had barely arrived at his post when the people of Chien-p'ing (Szechwan)--Fu Mi and others--revolted, joining forces with other rebels of Shu (i.e., Tu T'ao). Chou I, his affairs in disorder, lost control of the province. T'ao K'an rescued him, and he was able to escape alive. When he reached Wu-ch'ang (an error for Yü-chang, Kiangsi), he threw in his lot with Wang Tun. Tun at that point chose T'ao K'an to replace I, while I returned to Chien-k'ang, where as yet he had not been able to be employed.

48. Contemporaries attempted to characterize the monk Śrīmitra, but
were not quite able to do so. When Huan I asked Chou I about it, Chou
said, "He might be called majestically transparent."

Huan Wen said, "His essence and spirit are manifested out of the
depths."[1] (KSC 1, Taishō 50.327c)

[1] KTC: Yü Liang, Chou I, Huan I, and their whole generation of famous gentlemen, as soon as they saw His Reverence (Śrīmitra), opened their collars and gave him their full attention. Once while characterizing His Reverence, they tried a long time without success. Someone said, "Śrīmitra might be called majestically transparent." Only then did Huan I begin to sigh with approval, feeling it was the ultimate in describing him.

Huan Wen once said, "When I was young I saw His Reverence and remarked that his essence and spirit were manifested out of the depths; he was the outstanding man of the year." Thus was he praised by famous gentlemen.

49. Wang Tun once praised his (adopted) son, Wang Ying, with the
words, "The condition of his spirit seems to be on the point of being
all right."

50. Pien K'un characterized the ancient worthy, Yang-she Hsi,[1] as
"bright and airy as a room with a hundred bays."

[1] Yang-she Hsi (Shu-hsiang), sixth century B.C., was a noble of the

226   TALES OF THE WORLD

Chin state who won the plaudits of Confucius for his honesty. See
Tso-chuan, Chao 14; Legge V, 656.

51. When Wang Tun became generalissimo,[1] he was stationed at Yü-chang
(Kiangsi). Wei Chieh, fleeing from the disorders (in 312), arrived
from Lo-yang and placed himself under Tun's protection. The moment
they met they were delighted with each other and conversed together
for days on end. At the time Hsieh K'un was Tun's senior administrator. Tun said to K'un, "Whoever would have thought that in the Yung-chia era (307-312) we'd hear again the sounds of the Cheng-shih era
(240-249)?[2] If Wang Ch'eng were here, he'd fall over again with a
sigh!"[3] (*CS* 36.14a; *TPYL* 446)

[1] Wang Tun was not appointed generalissimo until the spring of 317,
when he was stationed at Chiang-ling (*TCTC* 90.2844). When Wei
Chieh reached Yü-chang in the summer of 312, only a short while
before his death, Tun was there as governor of Yang Province (*TCTC*
88.2789-90; see also *SSHY* IV, 20, above).

[2] I.e., the "golden age" of pure conversation of Ho Yen and Wang
Pi.

[3] See No. 45, above.

52. Wang Ch'eng, in a letter to a friend, once praised his son Wang
Hui, saying, "His style and manner improve daily, and this is enough
to dispel my anxieties."

53. (In the same letter Wang Ch'eng also wrote): "Hu-wu Fu-chih spits
out fine words like sawdust;[1] he's the leader of the younger generation." (*CS* 49.21a)

[1] *SSHY* Comm.: The conversationalists set words flurrying (*$p'jwei$-$p'jwei$*; emending the graphically similar *mi-mi*, "slowly," or "lasciviously," of the text to agree with *CS* 49.21a) like a saw putting out sawdust.

54. Chancellor Wang Tao once exclaimed about Tiao Hsieh's pristine
purity (*$ts'ăt-ts'ăt$*), Tai Yüan's crag-like loftiness (*$ngâm-ngâm$*),
and Pien K'un's mountaintop majesty (*feng-chü*).[1] (*CS* 70.16a)

[1] *YL* K'ung T'an, who was serving as personal attendant, secretly
admonished Emperor Ch'eng (Ssu-ma Yen*, r. 326-342) that it was
not proper for him to make personal calls on Wang Tao's wife, Lady
Ts'ao. When Wang Tao learned of it, he exclaimed, "I'm in my dotage, that's all! If it had been someone with Pien K'un's crag-like
loftiness, etc., would His Majesty have had the audacity to do
such a thing?"

SSHY Comm.: This remark of Wang Tao had a very special motivation, and just for this reason I have recorded (the context from
the *YL*).

(Though the *YL* version reverses Pien K'un and Tai Yüan and
their respective epithets, the *Shih-shuo* version seems preferable,
since it preserves a pun on Tai's alternate name, Yen, matched
with the doublet, *yen-yen* [*$ngâm-ngâm$*], "crag-like loftiness."
Pien's courtesy name, Wang-chih, "Gazing afar," of course, goes

equally well with either *yen-yen* or *feng-chü,* "mountaintop majesty.")

55. The generalissimo Wang Tun said to his cousin's son, Wang Hsi-chih, "You're the promising young person of our family. You'll be no less distinguished than my superintendent of records, Juan Yü."[1] (*CS* 80.1b)

[1] *CHS*: When Juan Yü was young, he was known for his virtuous conduct. Wang Tun, hearing of his reputation, summoned him to be his superintendent of records. But Yü, knowing that Tun had disloyal ambitions, remained in a continuous drunken stupor, and paid no attention to his duties.

56. Contemporaries characterized Chou I as: "Unscalable as a sheer cliff."[1] (*MCYC*, shang)

[1] *CYC*: Chou I was rigidly correct in his personal relations, and unapproachable. Even in the case of companions of the same age, no one dared take liberties, or be familiar with him.

57. Chancellor Wang Tao was once entertaining Tsu Yüeh, and they conversed all night until dawn without sleeping. Early next morning a guest arrived. The chancellor had not yet dressed his hair, and was also a little tired. The guest said, "Your Excellency appears to have lost some sleep last night."
  Wang Tao replied, "Last night I was talking with Tsu Yüeh, and as a result he made me completely forget my fatigue."

58. Generalissimo Wang Tun wrote a letter to his cousin, Chancellor Wang Tao, in which he praised Yang Lang, saying, "Yang Lang has a capacity for knowing men and an understanding of Truth, and his ability rests on enlightened judgment. Not only is he of statesman caliber in his own right, but he is, in addition, the son of Marquis Yang Chun. Lately the status and prestige of the Yang family have been rather much on the decline,[1] so that even *you* are good enough to occupy the same place with him!"

[1] A reference to the downfall of the Yang consort family in 291.

59. Ho Ch'ung once paid a call at the home of Chancellor Wang Tao. The chancellor, indicating his own mat with his sambar-tail chowry (*chu-wei*), invited Ho to sit with him, saying, "Come, come. This is your seat, sir."[1] (*CS* 77.6ab)

[1] Before Wang's death in 339, when the chancellorship (at that time combined with the office of director of instruction) passed to his powerful rival, Yü Liang, he had attempted to have his nephew and protégé, Ho Ch'ung, made chancellor; see *CS* 77.4a and *TCTC* 96.3031. Ho Ch'ung did actually achieve tremendous influence after the death of Yü Liang's younger brother, Yü I, in 345, by getting the court to appoint his own protégé, Huan Wen, as Yü's successor, but Ho died the following year, never having served himself in the highest office.

60. Chancellor Wang Tao was having the administrative offices of Yang

Province (Kiangsu-Anhui-Chekiang) repaired. As he went about inspecting the work, he said, "I'm having these repairs made just for Ho Ch'ung's sake, and for no other reason."

When Ho was young he was highly respected by Wang Tao, and for this reason Wang often expressed admiration of this sort.[1] (CS 77.6b)

[1] CYC: Ho Ch'ung was the son of the elder sister of Wang Tao's wife (Lady Ts'ao), and the husband of the younger sister of Empress Mu (Yü Wen-chün), consort of Emperor Ming (Ssu-ma Shao, r. 323-325). The resonance of his thought was profound and far-reaching, and he possessed both literary talent and moral sensibility. Wang Tao valued him profoundly, and for this reason even in his youth he had an excellent reputation. As he became more conspicuous and higher in rank, Tao had intentions of making him his assistant and successor, so he often made references to this in the presence of his superiors and inferiors.

61. When Chancellor Wang Tao was appointed director of instruction (in 323), he sighed and said, "If Liu Ch'ou had also come south across the Yangtze River, I wouldn't be the sole appointee to this Ducal Office."[1]

[1] TCCCC: Liu Ch'ou had a weighty reputation, but was killed by Yen Ting during the Yung-chia era (307-312). The director of instruction, Ts'ai Mo, often sighed and said, "If Liu Ch'ou had gotten to cross the Yangtze River, he would have been an excellent choice for director of instruction.

62. Wang Shu as a person was late in maturing, and consequently his contemporaries called him an idiot. But since he was the son of Wang Ch'eng, Chancellor Wang Tao employed him as his aide.

One time at a gathering of Wang's staff, every time the chancellor made a remark, everybody competed with each other in praising it. Wang Shu, who was sitting in the lowest place, said, "Our host is no Yao or Shun, why should every single thing he says be so?"

The chancellor sighed deeply in appreciation. (CS 75.3b)

63. Contemporaries characterized Yang Lang as follows: "Thorough in investigation; expeditious in judgment."

The director of instruction, Ts'ai Mo, said of him: "If only the Central Court (Western Chin, 265-316), had not been in turmoil, the Yang family would never have ceased to occupy the Ducal Offices."[1]

Hsieh An said, "Yang Lang is a great genius."

[1] See above, No. 58, n. 1.
PWKS: Yang Chun had six sons—Ch'iao, Mao, Lang, Lin, Chün*, and Shen—all of whom achieved an excellent reputation. Those who discussed personalities therefore said they all had expectations of reaching the Ducal Offices. Yü Liang often sighed saying, "If only the Central Court had not been in turmoil, etc."

64. Liu Sui was Liu Pao's nephew, and was once called "dazzling and preeminent as jade" by Yü Liang.[1]

Yü also said of him, "Whether among a thousand people, or among a hundred, he'd still be conspicuous." (TPYL 446)

¹The Commentary, for reasons unexplained, identifies the "Lord Yü" of the text as Liang's uncle, Yü Tsung. However, since the latter never attained ducal rank, and since "Lord Yü" in nearly every other reference is Yü Liang, I have identified him accordingly.

65. When Yü Liang became General Protecting the Army (324), he commissioned Huan I to be on the lookout for a good officer for his staff. Finally, several years later, Huan accidentally met Hsü Ning and got to know him, whereupon he recommended him to Yü Liang with the words, "What other people ought to have, he doesn't necessarily have, but what other people ought not to have, he himself definitely does not have.¹ He's truly an incorruptible gentleman from the area between the sea and Mt. T'ai" (i.e., Tung-hai Commandery, in Shantung). (CS 74.1b)

¹I have emended pu-pi wu to pi wu, on the analogy of No. 84, below.

66. Huan I said, "Ch'u P'ou is the 'Spring and Autumn Annals' in a human skin." He meant that his judgments hit the mark.¹ (CS 93.6b)

¹CS 93.6b: He meant that even though outwardly he said neither "yea" nor "nay," inwardly there was, nevertheless, either approval or disapproval.

67. Ho Ch'ung was once escorting a man from the east (Chekiang) on his way home. Looking into the distance and seeing Chia Ning riding in the carriage behind them, he said, "Unless this man dies, in the end he'll become the supreme figure among the courtiers."¹

¹CYC: At first Chia Ning allied himself with Wang Ying and Chu-ko Yao (partisans of Wang Tun), but after Ying was defeated (in 324), he wandered through Wu and K'uai-chi (Chekiang), where the people of Wu all insulted and humiliated him. Hearing that the capital was suffering a rebellion (in 327), he rushed to throw in his lot with Su Chün. Chün became very intimate with him and made him chief strategist. When Chün heard that the loyalist army was being mobilized, and accordingly moved his camp from Ku-shu to Shih-t'ou (west of Chien-k'ang), this was Ning's plan. Before Chün was defeated (328) Ning first surrendered. Later his rank reached grand warden of Hsin-an (Chekiang).

68. When the ancestral tomb of Tu I's family collapsed in ruins, Tu's expression of grief did not come up to expectations. Yü Liang, looking back at Tu during a party, said to the other guests, "Tu I is extremely frail; he shouldn't give way completely to his grief."

On another occasion he said, "When Tu I weeps, he shouldn't feel any grief."

69. Contemporaries praised Yü Liang as "the jade of prosperous years." and his younger brother, I, as "the grain of lean years."¹

According to the "Discourse on the Yü Family" (Yü-chia lun), it was Yü Liang who praised his younger brother, I, as "the grain of lean years," and his nephew, Yü T'ung, as "the jade of prosperous years." (IWLC 22)

¹SSHY Comm.: This means that Yü Liang had the capacity for service

in palace portico and ancestral temple (in times of peace), while Yü I had the ability to set the world to rights (in times of disorder)."

70. Contemporaries characterized Tu I as "unique and refreshing," and Ch'u P'ou as "mild and laconic."

71. Someone characterized Tu I as follows: "Unique and refreshing, pure and delightful, his abundantly virtuous airs may be sung to a musical accompaniment."[1]

[1] YL: Someone characterized Tu I as: "Unique and refreshing, extremely pure and delightful. From the start, if pleased or happy, his expression never fails to respond in kind. His abundantly virtuous airs may be sung to a musical accompaniment."

72. Yü Liang once said, "Wang Hsi-chih is the choice of the state." So when Yü Ch'ien composed the stele inscription for Wang (d. ca. 365),[1] he wrote: "He was outstanding among the crowd, the choice of the state."

[1] The traditional date of 379, usually given for Wang Hsi-chih's death, is certainly an error, as the execution of Yü Ch'ien, who composed his stele inscription, is attested for 371 (TCTC 103.3251).

73. Yü I once wrote a letter to Huan Wen in which he commended Liu Hui in the following terms: "From morn till night he is busy at his work, and whether it is a large or a small matter he is extraordinarily quick in handling it. He cherishes the idea of sharing his pleasures, and is not only a fine man himself, but worthy to be a friend. He is really and truly a man of excellent capacities, and I recommend him as one who will work together with you to save us from Trouble and Stagnation (chien-p'i)."[1]

[1] Following Kawakatsu et al., I read chien-pu as chien-p'i, "Trouble and Stagnation." P'i, being Hex. 12 of the "Book of Changes," represents a stalemate between the Yin and Yang forces. Yang Yung takes pu here, and in SSHY VI, 26, above, as a "meaningless particle."

74. When Yang Shu was appointed governor of Yang Province (Kiangsu-Anhui-Chekiang, in 354), his superintendent of records requested to know the taboo names (hui) of the members of his family.[1] Wang instructed him: "The personal names (ming) of my late grandfather (Wang Chan) and of my father (Wang Ch'en) were broadcast everywhere within the Four Seas, and known by everyone far and near. 'The taboo names of their wives are not to be uttered outside the gate.'[2] As far as the rest are concerned, there are no taboos."

[1] See "Record of Rites" I, 41 (Legge, Li Ki I, 93): On entering the door, ask what names are taboo (so as to avoid using them accidentally).

[2] Ibid.: The taboo name of one's wife is not to be uttered outside the gate.

VIII APPRECIATION AND PRAISE

75. Hsiao Lun was Sun Ts'ung's father-in-law. Liu T'an was present once at a gathering in the home of the General Controlling the Army (Ssu-ma Yü), and at the time (between 345 and 347) proposed Hsiao Lun for the post of grand ordinary. In doing so, Liu said, "I don't know whether or not Hsiao Lun might serve in one of the Three Ducal Offices, but there is no office below these which he couldn't fill." (CS 56.16a)

76. Before Hsieh An had reached his twentieth year (ca. 339), he made his first trip west (from K'uai-chi to Chien-k'ang), where he visited Wang Meng, and engaged in pure conversation for a long time.
  After he had left, Wang Meng's son, Hsiu, asked his father, "How would you rate the guest who was just here in comparison with yourself?"
  Meng replied, "The guest who was just here is absolutely indefatigable (*$mjwei-mjwei$) and gave me some very close competition." (CS 79.4a)

77. Wang Hsi-chih said to Liu T'an, "We should certainly both recommend Hsieh An for office."
  Liu T'an replied, "If Hsieh An's determination to remain in retirement in the Eastern Mountains (Chekiang) is definitely established, we should then by all means join with everyone in the whole realm in recommending him."[1]

  [1] Cf. *Chuang-tzu* XI, 19a (Watson, p. 116): If a man values his own person more than ruling the realm, then he may be entrusted with the realm; if he cherishes his own person more than ruling the realm, he may be given the realm. (Cf. also *Lao-tzu* 13.)
  HCYC: Earlier, while Hsieh An made his home in Shang-yü Prefecture of K'uai-chi Commandery (Chekiang), he wandered carefree amid the mountains and forests for a space of six or seven years (ca. 354-360). When summoned to office, he did not go. Even though summonses and memorials came in swift succession, followed by threats of imprisonment, he was blissfully disdainful of them all.

78. Hsieh An once praised Wang Shu, saying, "Lift up his skin, and underneath it's all real."[1]

  [1] Cf. *Chuang-tzu* XXXI, 7a (Watson, p. 350): The real is what we are endowed with by Heaven; it is what it is, and may not be changed.
  HKCC: In Wang Shu's case, whenever anyone examined into his real intentions, they were never obvious.

79. Huan Wen, traveling past the tomb of Wang Tun (d. 324), gazed up at it and said, "You were an all-right fellow!"[1] (CS 98.25a)

  [1] *YYLC*: The characterization of Wang Tun as an "all-right person" has persisted through several decades.

80. Yin Hao once characterized Wang Hsi-chih, saying, "Wang Hsi-chih is a pure and noble man. My own relation to him is extremely close. In this I fall behind no one else in the entire age."

81. Wang Meng once praised Yin Hao, saying, "It's not because he's in a senior position that he surpasses other men; on the contrary, in

spite of his occupying a senior position, he still surpasses other men."[1]

[1] *CYC*: Yin Hao was good at accepting other persons with openness and kindness.

82. Wang Hu-chih, after conversing with Yin Hao, sighed in admiration, saying, "The mysteries stored in my own treasury have long since been all poured out and manifested to view, but Yin's marshalled forces are like a vast (*hao*) and boundless sea, whose multitudinous sources (*yüan*)[1] have never yet been fathomable."[2]

[1] There is a conscious punning here on Yin's given name, Hao, "Vast," and on his courtesy name, Yüan-yüan, "Abysmal Source."

[2] *HKCC*: Yin Hao's "pure conversation" and subtle argumentation had a mysterious impact. All the famous gentlemen of the age acknowledged his excellent reputation.

83. Wang Meng once said to Chih Tun, "Liu T'an is the sort of person of whom it might be said that 'gold and jade fill up his hall.'"[1]

Chih Tun replied, "If 'gold and jade fill up his hall,' then why does he make such a reduction and selection in what he says?"

Wang said, "It's not that he makes any reduction or selection, but only that when he does utter any words, they're just naturally few, that's all."[2]

[1] Cf. *Lao-tzu* 9: When gold and jade fill up the hall, no one can keep them safe.

[2] Cf. "Book of Changes," *Hsi-tz'u* B9 (Wilhelm I, 381): The words of fortunate men are few; those of excitable men, many.

84. Wang Meng characterized Chiang Kuan as follows: "What other people ought to have, he doesn't necessarily have, but what other people ought not to have, he definitely does not have."[1]

[1] Cf. No. 65, above.

85. K'ung Ch'en, Wei I, Yü Ch'iu, Yü Ts'un, and Hsieh Feng of K'uai-chi Commandery (Chekiang) were all outstanding members of the four principal clans of K'uai-chi, and great men of their time. Sun Ch'o characterized them as follows:

> "Ch'en is the K'ung family's gold,
> And I the Wei family's jade.
> The Yüs honor Ts'un and Ch'iu,
> The Hsiehs for Feng bow down."

(*CS* 78.12a)

86. Wang Meng and Liu T'an went to visit Yin Hao to converse. When their conversation was ended, they rode away together. Liu said to Wang, "Yin Hao is really all right."

Wang replied, "You've certainly fallen head over heels into his clouds and mist!"[1]

[1] *CHS*: Yin Hao was very capable in conversing on a topic, and his discussions were intricate and subtle. He was especially expert in

the *Lao-tzu* and "Book of Changes." Therefore the elegant set (*feng-liu*) all accorded him their honor and allegiance.

87. Liu T'an often praised Wang Meng, saying, "By nature he's extremely uninhibited (*t'ung*), and yet, quite spontaneously, there are restraints."[1] (CS 93.10a)

[1] *Wang Meng PC*: In his relations with others Wang Meng emptied himself and accepted the good of others, and always put himself in the place of others before acting. Rarely did anyone see any signs of pleasure or dislike in his face. In most cases, after the first meeting with him, everyone respected and loved him. However, since he had lost his father in his youth, his care of his mother was extremely attentive. With her he was warmly affectionate, and disregarded picayune rules of etiquette. He was praised for his purity and poverty.

88. Wang Hsi-chih characterized Hsieh Wan as follows: "Living as he does among woods and lakes, he's naturally on a more vital and a higher plane."
   In praise of Chih Tun he said, "His capacity is brilliant, his spirit keen."[1]
   Characterizing Tsu Yüeh, he said, "A man of his manner and physical appearance I'm afraid I'll never see again till my dying day."
   Of Liu T'an he said, "He's a tree whose top reaches the clouds, yet whose leaves are not densely overgrown."[2]

[1] *Chih Tun PC*: Setting his mind free, Tun walked alone; his manner was lofty and radiant.

[2] *Liu Yin PC*: Liu, because of his eminent status as a relative of the imperial house (he was married to the daughter of Emperor Ming), of course found himself frequently in important posts. However, his nature was not wedded to worldly affairs, and his mind was indifferent to glory and gain. Although he had himself climbed to conspicuous positions, nevertheless he would always withdraw and step down, and merely keep himself in leisurely calm, nothing more.

89. Emperor Chien-wen (Ssu-ma Yü) characterized Yü T'ung as follows: "Uncomplicated and forthright, he's well-ordered and free of impediments."
   Hsieh Shang said of him, "In Yü T'ung's breast are no extraneous objects."

90. Yin Hao characterized his nephew, Han Po, saying, "Even in his youth Po was always in an exemplary position, and, as it's turned out, he is of a caliber that stands above the crowd. Whenever he utters a word or a phrase, it always carries a weight of feeling."[1]

[1] *CYC*: Han Po was pure and gentle, with a thoughtful reasonableness. In his youth he was praised by his uncle, Yin Hao.

91. Emperor Chien-wen (Ssu-ma Yü) characterized Wang Shu, saying, "His ability isn't particularly outstanding to begin with, and even in the case of glory and gain, he's not entirely indifferent toward

them. It's only that with a small amount of genuine forthrightness he's capable of matching other people's abundance on equal terms."[1]

[1] *CYC:* When Wang Shu was young he was poor and destitute, "living with basket and gourd in a lowly alley," and never seeking fame or success. For this he was honored by those with understanding.

92. Chih Tun once said to Wang Hsi-chih, "Whenever Wang Meng utters a few hundred words, there's not one which is not well spoken, as if he hated not to be exhaustive (*k'u*)."[1]

Wang replied, "Wang Meng naturally doesn't want to exhaust other people."

[1] *SSHY* Comm.: The word "*k'u*" (literally, "to be bitter") means exhausting other people with words.

93. Yin Hao wrote a letter to a friend in which he characterized Hsieh Wan as follows: "The reasoning in his writings grows more and more vigorous. To accomplish such a thing is far from easy."[1]

[1] *CHS:* Hsieh Wan's ability and capacity were outstanding, and he loved to show off his prowess, so it came about that he had a reputation in his own day. Since he combined skill in literary composition with his ability in conversation, his contemporaries praised him.

94. Wang Meng said, "The subjects comprehended by Chiang Tun's thought are not confined to the area covered by the Juists (i.e., the literati)."[1]

[1] *HKCC:* Chiang Tun was by nature a dedicated scholar and was never without a book in his hand. He had read widely in the ancient classical texts, and combined a mastery of both the Juist and Taoist traditions.

95. When Hsü Hsün first came out of retirement to the capital to escort his mother home,[1] someone asked Liu T'an, "Does Hsü Hsün really measure up to what we hear about him?"

Liu replied, "His ability and feelings *surpass* anything you've heard."

[1] *HsHsC:* Hsün came out of retirement to the capital to meet his elder sister. On the road he composed poems.

SSHY Comm.: The *HCYC* says the same thing (see below, No. 144, n. 1); so the statement here that he was escorting his mother is probably mistaken.

96. Juan Yü once said, "The Wang family (of Lang-yeh) has three young men: Wang Hsi-chih, Wang Ying,[1] and Wang Yüeh." (*CS* 80.1b)

[1] In *CS* 80.1b, Wang Ch'eng* is wrongly substituted for Wang Ying. Both had the courtesy name An-ch'i, but Ch'eng* belonged to the T'ai-yüan Wang family, and hence was not related to the others.

97. Hsieh An once characterized Hsieh K'un, saying, "If he should ever meet the Seven Worthies, they would undoubtedly seize him by the arm and lead him into the Bamboo Grove."[1]

¹*CTMSC*: Hsieh K'un was uninhibited and unceremonious and possessed understanding. He did not bother with the rules of decorum or the amenities. His actions were free yet his mind was correct, his appearance turgid but his speech clear. He occupied his physical body as if it were impure, and his movements were unfettered by his high status.

In the neighboring household there was a girl whom K'un once tried to seduce. The girl was just then at her weaving, and, seizing the shuttle, threw it at him and broke his two front teeth. After he returned home he started whistling a tune with a self-satisfied air, saying, "Anyway, she didn't ruin my whistle!" Such was his unconcern for his physical body. (See below, *SSHY* IX, 17, n. 3)

98. Wang Meng once sighed in admiration over Chih Tun, saying, "His accomplishment in searching after subtleties is in no way inferior to that of Wang Pi."¹ (*KSC* 4, *Taishō* 50.348b)

¹Wang Pi was the great conversationalist of the Cheng-shih era (240-249).

Chih Tun PC: Tun's spirit and mind were alert and perceptive, and he had a pure understanding of the Mysterious and Remote (*hsüan-yüan*). Once, after he arrived in the capital, Wang Meng praised his accomplishment in reaching subtleties, claiming it was no different from that of Wang Pi.

99. Yin Hao had been living in his graveyard hermitage (in Tan-yang, a section of Chien-k'ang) for nearly ten years (336-346). At the time both those at court and in the provinces compared him to Kuan Chung and Chu-ko Liang.¹ His decision whether or not to come up out of retirement they took to be an augury of the rise or fall of the whole area east of the Yangtze River.² (*CS* 77.22b)

¹Kuan Chung (d. B.C. 645), the able minister of Duke Huan of Ch'i, and Chu-ko Liang (181-234), the chief minister of Liu Pei, had both been called to office out of retirement.

²*HCYC*: At that time Emperor Mu (r. 345-361) was a child, and the empress-mother was acting as regent, while (the future) Emperor Chien-wen (Ssu-ma Yü), being the most worthy of the imperial relatives and the hope of the people, had assumed the reins of government as General Controlling the Army. Huan Wen had won merit for pacifying Shu (Szechwan, in 347) and Lo-yang (356, *sic*), and was exercising independent power in Hsi-shan (Hunan-Hupei). Emperor Chien-wen estimated that he himself was too literary and effete and had no means of resisting him. Yin Hao had in the past had a flourishing reputation, and contemporary discussions compared him to Kuan Chung and Chu-ko Liang. So they summoned Hao to be governor of Yang Province (346). Huan Wen realized that the intention was to resist his own rise and was extremely angry over it.

100. Yin Hao once characterized Wang Hsi-chih as follows: "With incorruptible judgment he values what is essential."¹

¹*CATC*: Wang Hsi-chih's manner and style were pure and exalted.

101. Hsieh An became Huan Wen's sergeant-at-arms (ca. 360). When Huan went to visit him it happened that Hsieh was combing his hair, and in great haste he put on his clothes and hat. Huan said, "Why bother with all this?" Whereupon he got down from his carriage, and they conversed together until dark. After Huan had departed, he said to his attendants, "Have you ever in your life seen such a man?"[1] (CS 79.5a)

[1] HCYC: Earlier Hsieh An had roamed carefree among hills and streams, amusing himself writing and analyzing principles. Huan Wen was on the eastern frontier (in Wu-ch'ang, Hupei), and respected (Hsieh's) flourishing reputation. By way of taunting the court, he requested him for his sergeant-at-arms. Hsieh, realizing that the world was not at peace, and determined furthermore to help set it to rights, left his home (in K'uai-chi) in his fortieth year (360) to answer the call of duty.

102. On becoming Huan Wen's sergeant-at-arms, Hsieh An entrusted several tens of his own protégés (*men-sheng*) to Huan's field-work officer, Chao Yüeh. When Chao reported it to Huan, Huan replied, "For the time being employ half of them."

Chao unexpectedly proceeded to employ them all, explaining, "Even in the past, while Hsieh An was living in retirement in the Eastern Mountains, the nobles and upper gentry kept solicitously importuning him, fearing lest he might never become involved in public affairs. How much more, now, in the case of candidates he has personally chosen from his home village, should we avoid going against his wishes?"

103. (In 356) in his "Memorial (on the Pacification of Lo-yang)" Huan Wen wrote: "Hsieh Shang's spirit and thought stand out above the crowd, and from his youth he has enjoyed an excellent reputation among the people."[1]

[1] HWC (*P'ing-Lo piao*): Today, since the central provinces have already been pacified, the time has come to restore peace. The General Governing the West and governor of Yü Province (So. Honan and Shantung), Hsieh Shang, whose spirit and thought stand out above the crowd, has enjoyed an excellent reputation among the people from his youth. Therefore he is worthy to discuss the hundred counsels in court, or to be a local governor on the frontier. He should advance (from his present station in Shou-ch'un) to occupy Lo-yang, and govern and pacify the black-haired common people. I feel that he might do so on the basis of his current office as governor-general of military affairs in Ssu Province (Honan).

(Huan Wen sent up this memorial after his successful northern campaign of 356. Hsieh Shang, who was in poor health, died the following year without taking up the new post.)

104. Contemporaries characterized Hsieh Shang as "transcendently free (*ling-ta*)."

Juan Fu once said of him, "He's pure and cheerful, seemingly free (*ssu-ta*)."

Someone else said, "Hsieh Shang is naturally on a transcendently higher level of existence (*ling-shang*)."[1]

¹*CYC*: Hsieh Shang was relaxed and free, enlightened and on a transcendently higher level of existence.

105. When the grand marshal, Huan Wen was ill (in Ku-shu, west of Chien-k'ang, in 373), Hsieh An went to pay a sick call, and entered by the east gate.
  Huan, gazing at him from a distance, sighed, saying, "It's been a long time since I've seen such a man in my gate."

106. Emperor Chien-wen (Ssu-ma Yü) characterized Wang T'ien as "transparently tranquil (*lang-yü*)".[1]

  [1] A pun on Wang's courtesy name, Ching-yü, "Reverently Tranquil," as well as on his personal name, T'ien, "Calm."
  WTC: Wang T'ien's understanding of Truth (*li*) was enlightened and noble; he was the crown of the later generation.

107. While Sun Ch'o was serving as Yü Liang's aide-de-camp, they went together on an outing to White Rock Mountain (Pai-shih shan, near Chien-k'ang). Wei Yung was also among the company. Sun said of Wei, "This man's spirit and feelings have nothing in common with mountains and streams (*shan-shui*), yet he can write."
  Yü replied, "Although Wei Yung's style (*feng-yün*) is not equal to that of people like yourself, still the places where he's fully poured out his feelings are by no means superficial."
  Sun bathed luxuriantly in these words.

108. Wang Hsi-chih once characterized Ch'en T'ai (d. 260) as "rough and rugged (*luâi-k'uâi*)[1] with a square bony structure." (*TPYL* 375)

  [1] Cf. *SSHY* XXIII, 51, below.

109. Wang Meng said, "Liu T'an knows me better than I know myself!"[1] (*CS* 93.10a)

  [1] In *CS* 93.10a this remark is joined to Liu's appreciation of Wang recorded in No. 87, above.
  Wang Meng PC: Wang Meng and Liu T'an had equal reputations. Contemporaries compared Meng to Yüan Huan, and T'an to Hsün Ts'an (both of the early third century), because of their common friendship and close mutual understanding and appreciation.

110. Wang Meng and Liu T'an were once listening to Chih Tun lecturing. Wang said to Liu, "The one over there on the elevated seat is certainly a malevolent person."
  But as he kept listening, Wang said again, "Without doubt, this man's a Wang Pi or a Ho Yen behind an almsbowl" (*puât-jiu*).[1] (*KSC* 4, Taishō 50.349a)

  [1] *KISMC*: Wang Meng once sought out Chih Tun, and came upon him lecturing at the Jetavana Temple (Chih-yüan ssu, in Chien-k'ang) just as he was in the elevated seat. With every lifting of his sambar-tail chowry (*chu-wei*) he would discourse for several hundred words, and both his sentiments and reasoning were exhilarating. The hundred or more persons who were sitting to hear him were all holding their tongues and concentrating their attention. Meng remarked to

238   TALES OF THE WORLD

the monks who were listening to the lecture, "The one over there on the elevated seat is a Wang Pi behind an almsbowl." (Cf. No. 98, above.)

111. Hsü Hsün said, "The one meant by the line in Hsi K'ang's 'Poetic Essay on the Seven-stringed Zither' (Ch'in-fu), 'Except with the most highly refined, one cannot analyze its principles,'[1] is Liu T'an. And the one meant by the line, 'Except with the profoundly tranquil, one cannot remain at leisure,'[2] is Emperor Chien-wen (Ssu-ma Yü)."

[1] WH 18.13a (trans. van Gulik, Hsi K'ang and his Poetical Essay on the Lute, Tokyo, 1941, p. 66).

[2] WH 18.12b-13a.

112. Wei Yin and his younger brother, T'i, even in their youth had a taste for learning. When they were still young lads with their hair in tufts they once went to visit Hsieh Feng. After Hsieh had conversed with them he was greatly pleased, and said, "Although the clan as a whole has suffered a decline, there already are men again in the Wei family!"[1]

[1] The Wei was one of the four clans of K'uai-chi; see above, No. 85.

113. Emperor Chien-wen (Ssu-ma Yü) once said, "Although Yin Hao's conversations don't reach in one leap the ultimate of simplicity, nevertheless, in those places where he is weaving the strands of his argument and searching with his thoughts, there certainly is a chess-board-like order."

114. At first when Chu Fa-t'ai came to Chien-k'ang (ca. 365) from the north, his name was as yet unknown, and Wang Ch'ia personally undertook to provide for his needs.[1] Whenever Wang went about visiting the homes of the famous and outstanding men of the day, he would always take Fa-t'ai along with him, and if for any reason Fa-t'ai was not available, then he would stop his carriage and not go on. For this reason Fa-t'ai's name was eventually honored.

[1] Fa-t'ai came to Chien-k'ang to live in the Wa-kuan Temple shortly after 365 (see Zürcher, Conquest, p. 148), seven years after Wang Ch'ia's death. The mention of Ch'ia's name here and in Fa-t'ai's biography (KSC 5, Taishō 50.355a), is perhaps due to a confusion with one of his sons, Hsün or Min.

CPCS: Shih Tao-an was captured by the former Yen ruler, Mu-jung Chün (r. 349-360). Wishing to take refuge in Hsiang-yang (northern Hupei), he traveled as far as Hsin-yeh (so. Honan). Gathering together his disciples, he counseled them, saying, "Right now we've run into a bad year. Unless we have the support of a ruler, the work of our religion will be hard to accomplish." Whereupon he divided up his disciples, and sent Chu Fa-t'ai to Yang Province (Kiangsu-Anhui-Chekiang), saying, "Those people are mostly nobles. Throw in your lot with the top level." Fa-t'ai accordingly crossed the Yangtze River and arrived in the territory of Yang Province.

MTSMTM: Fa-t'ai was lofty and radiant, open and free.

FTT:	An icy wind sweeps through the forest;
Shining springs gleam in the vale.
Bold and forthright, Chu Fa-t'ai,
Matches virtue without shame.
Beyond the world, he's fancy-free;
Within his spirit, limitless.
Truth from his past arises,
Fame with his future will leap up.

TYCCC: Fa-t'ai died in the twelfth year of the T'ai-yüan era (387, emending the "fifteenth year" of the text to agree with KSC 5; Taishō 50.354b). Emperor Hsiao-wu (r. 373-396) issued a rescript, saying, "Master Fa-t'ai has passed away; grief and pain wound my heart. Let there be an offering of 100,000 cash."

115. Wang Meng wrote a letter to Huan Wen in which he characterized Yin Hao as follows: "His understanding provides a peaceful abode; he is worthy to take part in the conversations of the times."

116. Hsieh An once said, "Liu T'an's conversations are thorough and meticulous."[1]

[1]LTL:	His spirit like a mirror in the depths,
His every word a pearl or jade.

117. Huan Wen once said to Ch'ih Ch'ao, "A-yüan (Yin Hao, d. 356) possessed both virtuous conduct and conversational ability.[1] If he'd been utilized as a president or vice-president of the Imperial Secretariat, he'd have been worthy to serve as a model of behavior for all the other ministers. As it was, the court's actual use of him (in military commands) was merely a violation of his abilities, and nothing more."

[1]Cf. "Analects" XI, 13.

118. Emperor Chien-wen (Ssu-ma Yü) once said to Ch'ih Ch'ao, "Toward the end, Liu T'an's (d. 346) conversations were, to tell the truth, a little below his usual standard. But as I recall what he said, there was, even at that, nothing amiss."

119. Sun Ch'o and Hsü Hsün were both in the White Tower Pavilion (Pai-lou t'ing)[1] discussing together and briefly characterizing famous uninhibited personalities of the past.
    Chih Tun, who had not participated in their conversation, listened to the end, and then remarked, "You two gentlemen, too, in your own right, clearly possess ability and feeling."

[1]KCCC: The pavilion is located in Shan-yin Prefecture (Chekiang) overlooking a stream and reflected in the water.

120. Wang Hsi-chih once characterized his cousin, Wang Lin-chih, saying, "Our family's A-lin, in his dazzling purity, far exceeds the rest of us."

121. Wang Meng wrote a letter to Liu T'an in which he characterized

Yin Hao as follows: "Whatever situation he encounters, he always extends the 'Book of Changes' (to encompass it)."[1]

[1] Cf. "Book of Changes," *Hsi-tz'u* A8 (Wilhelm I, 336): Extending (the sixty-four hexagrams) to every category encountered, all possible situations under heaven are encompassed.

122. Hsieh Wan once said, "Wang Ch'i-chih's wild and unbridled (*lâk-t'âk) disposition comes straight out of his own family tradition."

123. Chih Tun once said, "Wang Hsiu is a man of transcendent perceptiveness (*ch'ao-wu*)."[1]

[1] *WTC*: When Wang Hsiu was young he was acclaimed for his outstanding excellence.

124. Liu T'an at first deferred to Hsieh Shang, but Hsieh considered Liu the more well-bred and honorable, saying, "From the beginning I've always been the one who faced north."[1]

[1] I.e., like a subject before his ruler.
   SSHY Comm.: Hsieh Shang (b. 308) was older than Liu T'an (b. ca. 310), and his spiritual precociousness was manifested very early. To say that he "faced north" before Liu T'an is unbelievable.

125. Hsieh An praised Wang Hu-chih, saying, "Wang Hu-chih is a person with whom one may wander amid forests and lakes."[1]

[1] *Wang Hu-chih PC*: Hu-chih frequently left worldly duties behind and made high-minded retirement his ideal. He was a good friend of Hsieh An.

126. An old ditty (*yen*) goes:

> In Yang Province who walks alone?
> Wang T'an-chih.
> Of those come lately who stands out?
> Ch'ih Ch'ao.[1]

[1] *HCYC*: Ch'ih Ch'ao in his youth possessed ability and spirit, transcending the world and outstripping the common. He did not conform to ordinary rules, and his contemporaries considered him the one with the most flourishing reputation of his generation. A saying (*yü*) went:

> Who has talent great and grand?
> Hsieh An.
> East of the river who walks alone?
> Wang T'an-chih.
> With flourishing virtue daily new--
> Ch'ih Ch'ao.

127. Someone asked Wang Meng about Chiang Pin and his younger brother Tun, and their numerous cousins.
   Wang replied, "The Chiangs are all entirely capable of living their own lives."

128. Hsieh An characterized Wang T'an-chih as follows: "When I see him, he doesn't make me feel satiated. Yet when I go out the door and leave him, he doesn't make me miss him either."[1]

[1] *HCYC*: Hsieh An used to walk hand in hand with the young boys who were his friends, and they would nourish their ambitions by the seashore. The sentiments in their bosoms were transcendent and exhilarating; they were especially fond of music (*sheng-lü*). However, he would restrain them by ritual, so that in grief they might be able to reach (the proper balance).

After his younger brother, Wan, died (361), he listened to no stringed instruments or flutes for ten years. But when he came into control of the government (after 373), he built a mansion with gardens and halls, with splendid carriages and wardrobe. Even in cases of mourning for near relatives he never went without female entertainers and music. For this Wang T'an-chih bitterly chided him.

SSHY Comm.: It seems Hsieh An felt that Wang T'an-chih was too fond of straight speech, and for this reason did not miss him, that's all.

(I prefer to interpret Hsieh's remark in the spirit of the "Record of Rites" XXXII, 30, Legge, *Li Ki* II, 328: "The way of the gentleman is flavorless [*tan*], not producing satiety.")

129. Hsieh An said, "Wang Hu-chih has attained the supreme vantage point from which he solves all problems universally."[1]

[1] *Chuang-tzu* II, 18a (Watson, p. 40): Only at the axis of the Way (*tao-shu*) does one attain the center of the circle (*huan-chung*), from which one may respond to an infinite variety of situations.

SMTWCC: Hu-chih's nature was unceremonious, and he was fond of freedom (*ta*) and conversation about the Mysterious (*hsüan-yen*).

130. Liu T'an said, "Whenever I see Ho Ch'ung drinking, it makes me want to pour out my whole wine cellar for him."[1] (*CS* 77.9a; *MCYC*, hsia; *SLF* 17)

[1] *SSHY* Comm.: When Ho Ch'ung drank, he was able to maintain a genteel control.

131. Hsieh An said to Liu T'an, "A-ling (Wang Hu-chih) certainly wants to become well sharpened at this business (of being a gentleman)."

Liu[1] replied, "He's also the one with the highest integrity of all the famous gentlemen."

[1] The Sung text reads "Hsieh" for "Liu."

132. Wang Hui-chih said, "Contemporaries characterized Tsu Yüeh (d. 330) as transparent, and my family (i.e., my father, Wang Hsi-chih) also considered him pellucidly transparent."

133. Hsieh An said, "Wang Meng's conversations are by no means verbose, but you might say they have an excellent sound."[1] (*CS* 93.10b-11a)

¹*Wang Meng PC*: Meng's nature was pleasant and affable, and he was capable in pure conversation. When talking about the Way, or honoring the Heart of Truth (*li-chung*), his speech was simple, yet to the point. When he was discussing the personalities of ancient worthies, or the border between expression and silence, his words and ideas were both excellent, and always carried a lofty impact."

134. Hsieh Shang characterized Wang Hsiu as follows: "Both in letters and scholarship he is strictly avant-garde (**tsuk-tsuk*); he's incapable of being unoriginal."¹

¹*YL*: Wang Hsiu had unusual ability, and the worthies of the time all honored him. While Wang Hsi-chih was grand warden of K'uai-chi Commandery, whenever he went to visit Wang Hsiu, Hsiu's younger brother, Yün, would always ride along in the same carriage. But Hsi-chih was constantly annoyed at his dilatoriness, and afterward went to meet Hsiu on horseback. Even if there were wind and rain, he still would not use the carriage.

135. Liu T'an characterized Chiang Kuan as follows: "Not an able speaker, yet able to speak."

136. Chih Tun said, "Whenever I see Wang Hu-chih, his flashes of intuition keep coming in rapid succession, not giving a person time to pause. But at the same time I can talk with him all day long, oblivious of fatigue."

137. Contemporaries acclaimed Wang Hsiu as "extraordinary and outstanding," and his younger brother Yün as "pure and affable."

138. Emperor Chien-wen (Ssu-ma Yü) said, "Even when Liu T'an is tipsy (**miäng-tieng*),¹ he's still in possession of the principle of Truth."

¹The *ming-k'o*, "a branch of the tea plant," of the text is a copyist's error.

139. After Hsieh Lang became historian, he was once writing the biography of Wang K'an, but since he was not familiar with what sort of person Wang K'an was, he consulted his uncle, Hsieh An.

An replied, "Wang K'an was in his time well treated by the court. He was the son of Wang Lieh, the brother-in-law (*i-hsiung-ti*) of Juan Chan, and the cousin (*chung-wai*) of P'an Yüeh.¹ He's the one referred to in P'an Yüeh's poem:

> 'Your mother was my paternal aunt (*ku*);
> My father your maternal uncle (*chiu*).'

He was also Hsü Yün's son-in-law (*hsü*)."

¹I.e., Wang K'an and Juan Chan were married to sisters, and Wang K'an's father's sister was P'an Yüeh's mother.

PYC: When Wang K'an became sergeant-at-arms to the Prince of Ch'eng-tu (Ssu-ma Ying), P'an Yüeh escorted him as far as Pei-mang Mountain (north of Lo-yang), and as they parted, he composed the following poem:

> "Fine, fine, the hair and skin
> Received from father and mother.
> Lofty, lofty, the princely nobles
> Who were my cousin's forebears.
> Your mother was my paternal aunt;
> My father your maternal uncle."

140. Hsieh An held Teng Yu (d. 326) in high esteem and often said, "There's no sense in heaven or earth that Teng Yu should have been left without a son!"[1] (CS 90.14b)

[1]Teng had abandoned his own son to save the only son of his deceased brother, while fleeing south ca. 307-312; see above, SSHY I, 28.
CYC: After Teng Yu had abandoned his son, he never had another heir, which was a source of tragic regret to all people of understanding.

141. Hsieh An wrote a letter to Wang Hsi-chih, saying, "Your cousin, Wang Ch'ia, has committed his whole being to the lovely and the excellent."

142. The four principal surnames of Wu Commandery (Soochow)[1] used to be characterized as follows: "The Changs are cultured, the Chus martial, the Lus loyal, and the Kus hospitable."

[1]Cf. No. 20, above.
WL (Shih-lin): In Wu Commandery there are the Kus, the Lus, the Chus, and the Changs, who make up the "Four Surnames." During the Three Kingdoms (222-280) these four were very flourishing.

143. Hsieh An once said to Wang Kung, "In the whole body of your family's Wang Shu there's nothing of the ordinary man."[1]

[1]SSHY Comm.: Although Wang Shu was unceremonious, his nature was not liberal or patient. For "throwing himself into the fire" (like Duke Chuang of Chu in the fifth century B.C., who did so in anger when someone urinated in his courtyard), or "bursting into a rage over a fly" (as Wang Ssu of the third century A.D. did when flies gathered on the point of his writing brush), there was no one who could compare with him. Either Hsieh An was just making an empty characterization with complimentary embellishments, or else the Shih-shuo is just fabricating this tale out of whole cloth.
(For some examples of Wang Shu's tantrums, see above, SSHY V, 58; and below, XXXI, 2.)

144. Hsü Hsün once went to visit Emperor Chien-wen (Ssu-ma Yü). That night the wind was calm and the moon clear, and together they held a heart-to-heart conversation. The lyrical expression of inner feelings was something at which Hsü especially excelled, but now the limpid grace of his use of language surpassed even his usual performance. Although Emperor Chien-wen had been a close friend of long standing, on this occasion he sighed more deeply than ever in admiration, and without realizing it, they were knee to knee and hand in hand as they talked, continuing on until nearly daybreak.

Afterward Emperor Chien-wen said, "Talent and feeling such as Hsü Hsün has are surely not easy to find in great quantity."[1]

[1] *HCYC*: Hsü Hsün was capable in conversing on a topic. He once came out of retirement to the capital to meet his older sister (see above, No. 95, n. 1). Whenever Emperor Chien-wen and Liu T'an discussed the emotional content and lyrical expression of inner feelings in Hsü's poems, they always exchanged appreciations knee to knee, extending the night far into the day.

145. When Yin Yün set out westward from the capital (to join Huan Wen's staff, ca. 348), Ch'ih Ch'ao wrote a letter of introduction to Huan's aide, Yüan Hung, saying, "Yin Yün is looking for a good friend and would like to have friendly relations with you, but don't try to appeal to him by 'bringing out his excellence (*k'ai-mei*)'."

Contemporaries had characterized Yüan Hung as one who "brings out the excellence (of others)." This is why Wang Hsien-chih wrote in a poem: "Yüan Hung has a capacity for bringing out excellence."

146. Hsieh Hsüan once asked his uncle, Hsieh An, "Liu T'an's (d. ca. 347) disposition was extremely harsh; why, after all, was he worthy of so much honor?"

Hsieh An replied, "It's only that you never met him, that's all. Even when I meet Wang Hsien-chih, he still makes me unable to tear myself away."[1]

[1] *YL*: Yang Lin*, who was drunk at the time, patted Hsieh Hsüan and said to Hsüan's uncle, Hsieh An, "In what way does this fellow fall behind your cousin, Hsieh Shang (d. 357)?"

An replied, "Even when I (deleting *ju*, after Liu P'an-sui, quoted by Yang Yung) meet Wang Hsien-chih, I bathe luxuriantly in his presence, as if having a discussion with someone from the older generation!" (I.e., you just have never met Hsieh Shang; that's why you think Hsüan is so great.)

SSHY Comm.: Making inferences from this remark, then An felt it was only because Hsüan had never met Liu T'an that he did not honor him, that's all. If even when An met Wang Hsien-chih (who was over twenty years his junior), he still honored him, how much more Liu T'an (who was nearly ten years his senior)!

147. When Hsieh An was serving as director of the Central Secretariat (in 374) Wang Hsün had some business to attend to and they were due to go up together to the departmental office. Wang arrived after Hsieh, and the seats were crowded. Although the Wangs and Hsiehs were not on speaking terms,[1] Hsieh An nevertheless drew in his knees to make room for him. Wang's spirit and mood were relaxed and cheerful, and Hsieh fixed his eyes on him in fascination.

After Hsieh had returned home he said to his wife, Lady Liu, "Just now I saw A-chao.[2] He certainly is a person not easily come by. Even though we've nothing to do with each other, he just naturally makes me unable to tear myself away."

[1] For the rift between the Hsieh and Wang families, see below, *SSHY* XVII, 15. Wang Hsün had divorced Hsieh An's niece, and his younger brother, Wang Min, had divorced Hsieh's own daughter.

²*SSHY* Comm.: Wang Hsün's baby name was Fa-hu, yet here he is called A-chao, which is inexplicable, unless he had two baby names.

148. Wang Hsien-chih said to Hsieh An, "You're certainly lighthearted and carefree (*sieu-sie̯*)."
   Hsieh replied, "I'm not really lighthearted and carefree, but your characterization is so extremely apt that just naturally, in spite of myself, I feel pleasantly cheerful."[1]

   [1]*HCYC*: Hsieh An was a sincere and cultivated man with great capacity. His manner and spirit were pleasantly cheerful.

149. After Hsieh Hsüan had met Wang T'an-chih for the first time, he said, "When I met T'an-chih, even though I treated him with a lighthearted and carefree air, he, for his part, remained amiable and relaxed (*ˑi̯əm-ˑi̯əm*) all evening."[1]

   [1]Wang T'an-chih evidently had a reputation for solemnity. See above, No. 128, n. 1.

150. Fan Ning said to his nephew, Wang Ch'en, "Your elegant manner (*feng-liu*) is the cynosure of all eyes; truly, you're the most outstanding of the whole younger generation."
   Wang replied, "If I didn't have an uncle like you, how could you have a nephew like me?"[1] (*CS* 75.14b)

   [1]Fan Ning was a conservative Confucian scholar who felt it his mission to stamp out the nihilistic morals of the time, which he traced to Ho Yen and Wang Pi. Since his younger sister's son, Wang Ch'en, was an ardent admirer of the "Eight Free Spirits" (*pa-ta*) of the late third century, it is plain that this exchange was purely sarcastic.

151. Wang Hsien-chih wrote a letter to his elder brother, Wang Hui-chih, characterizing their eldest brother (*hsiung-po*)[1] as follows: "When he's feeling lonely (*sieu-sâk*), and there's little that takes his fancy, if he comes upon any wine, then, drunk and carefree, he forgets to return home, which, naturally, is admirable."

   [1]Perhaps Wang Hsi-chih's eldest son, Hsüan-chih, who died at an early age, is meant, but more probably the second son, Ning-chih, who became governor of K'uai-chi Principality.

152. Chang T'ien-hsi's family for generations had been chieftains in Liang Province (Kansu), but because their strength had grown weak, T'ien-hsi went (as a captive of war) to the capital (Chien-k'ang, in 383). Although he was from a distant place and different from others, nevertheless he was a chieftain of the border peoples. He had heard that there were many men of ability in the imperial capital, and had come full of respectful admiration.
   While Chang was still staying (in his boat) on the river flats (south of Chien-k'ang) before entering the city, a certain historian named Ssu-ma went to visit him. His speech and appearance were homely and crude, and there was nothing particularly pleasant-looking or sounding about him. T'ien-hsi began to feel extremely sorry in his heart that he had come, and was thinking how he might fortify himself in some distant place beyond the border.

Wang Min had outstanding ability and an excellent reputation.¹ At
the time he heard of Chang's arrival and went to visit him. After he
had come, T'ien-hsi observed the purity and refinement of his manner
and spirit, and the way his speech flowed like a stream, and how in
his narration of things past and present there was nothing which he
did not know thoroughly. He observed, furthermore, that in his recitation of facts about various personalities and families, everything he
cited was well attested. T'ien-hsi was surprised and completely cap-
tivated.

¹HCYC: Wang Min's style and feelings were outstandingly expressed,
his talents and manner of speech richly endowed.

153. Wang Kung was at first extremely fond of Wang Ch'en, but later,
encountering the alienation of Yüan Yüeh, the two eventually became
mutually suspicious and estranged.¹ However, whenever either of them
came upon any exhilarating experience, there would unavoidably be
times when they missed each other.

Kung was once walking after having taken a powder (*hsing-san*), on
the way to the archery hall at Ching-k'ou (near Chien-k'ang). At the
time the clear dewdrops were gleaming in the early morning light, and
the new leaves of the paulownia were just beginning to unfold. Kung
looked at them and said, "Wang Ch'en is surely and unmistakably as
clear and shining (*ȃ'ǎk-ȃ'ǎk*) as these!"

¹CATC: At first Wang Ch'en had been on friendly terms from his
youth with his fellow clansman, Wang Kung, and they were both acclaimed with equal reputations. But after the two came to court,
and Kung was well treated by Emperor Hsiao-wu (r. 373-396), and
Ch'en by the minister, Ssu-ma Tao-tzu (leader of the opposition
clique), there began to be rumors inside and outside the court of
disharmony between them. Kung, for his part, was deeply disturbed
over it, and finally said to Ch'en, "The rumors that have been going around indicate that there are some differences between us. It
must spring from the fact that the General of Hardy Horsemen (Ssu-
ma Tao-tzu) has been disrespectful at the imperial audiences.
Shouldn't you calmly remonstrate with him about it? If only lord
and minister become reconciled, then the rest of us may strive toward creating an enlightened regime. What further cause would
there then be for worry?"

Ch'en agreed with him, but was worried that his counsel would
not be heeded, and finally asked Yüan Yüeh (a favorite of Ssu-ma
Tao-tzu) to state the whole case for him. Yüeh had always wanted
to alienate Kung from Ch'en, and accordingly denounced Kung angrily
in the presence of Ssu-ma Tao-tzu, saying to Kung, "Why are you
falsely fabricating differences and creating suspicion and misunderstanding in the court and in the provinces?" His tone was extremely harsh and severe.

Kung was startled and disappointed, thinking Ch'en had betrayed
him, while Ch'en, even though not disloyal to Kung at heart, had
no way of clearing himself. Thereafter their friendship suffered a
serious rift, and their mutual resentment and estrangment became
complete.

154. The grand tutor, Ssu-ma Tao-tzu, made a characterization of the

two Wangs (Wang Kung and Wang Ch'en) as follows: "Kung, towering aloft (*d'ieng-d'ieng), rises straight up; Ch'en, loosely spreading out (*lâ-lâ), is pure and relaxed."[1]

[1] *SSHY* Comm.: Kung was correct and honest and overbearingly zealous; Ch'en was uninhibited and transparent and permissively relaxed.

155. Wang Kung used clear terminology and uncomplicated ideas. He was very capable in oral expression, but his reading was limited, and he used a good many redundancies.
Someone characterized him by saying, "Wang Kung has such original ideas one isn't aware of his repetitions."[1]

[1] *CHS*: Even though Wang Kung's eloquence was not great, in his lucid argumentation he surpassed others.

156. After Yin Chung-k'an's death (in 399/400), Huan Hsüan asked Chung-k'an's cousin Yin Chung-wen, "When all's said and done, what kind of man was your family's Yin Chung-k'an?"
Chung-wen replied, "Although he was unable to 'bring prosperity and enlightenment'[1] to the age in which he lived, he is worthy to shine through the Nine Springs of the underworld."[2]

[1] Cf. *Tso-chuan*, Hsüan 3 (Legge V, 293): When the ruler's virtue brings prosperity and enlightenment, though the tripods are small, they are heavy.

[2] I.e., his goodness will be vindicated after his death. There is a certain irony in this dialogue, as Huan Hsüan had attacked Yin Chung-k'an and forced him to commit suicide in the winter of 399/400, and afterward took his place as governor of Ching Province (Hunan-Hupei). Yin Chung-wen is saying, in effect, "You may have beaten him in this round, but he'll beat you in the next, when history judges between you."

CHAPTER IX

Classification According to Excellence

1. In general discussions of the relative merits of the two men, Ch'en Fan of Ju-nan, and Li Ying of Ying-ch'uan, no one was able to determine which was superior and which inferior. Ts'ai Yung criticized them as follows: "Ch'en Fan is stubborn in crossing the will of his superiors, while Li Ying is strict in the management of his inferiors.¹ Crossing the will of superiors is difficult; managing inferiors is easy."

Ch'en Fan was accordingly classified at the foot of the "Three Gentlemen" (san-chün),² and Li Ying at the head of the "Eight Heroes" (pa-chün).³ (TPKC 169)

   ¹*CFHC*: Contemporaries made up a saying about (Ch'en Fan and Li Ying) as follows: "The one unafraid of powerful opponents is Ch'en Fan; the model for the realm is Li Ying."

   ²*HCHS*: The "Three Gentlemen" were honored by their whole generation. Tou Wu, Liu Shu, and Ch'en Fan (all three killed in their struggle against eunuch domination in 168) possessed high integrity in their youth; everyone within the Four Seas revered and praised them, and for this reason they received this designation.

   ³*HYHHS*: Li Ying, Wang Ch'ang*, Hsün Yü, Chu Yü, Wei Lang, Liu Yu, Tu Mi, and Chao Tien were the "Eight Heroes." (The names of these second-century personalities have been emended to agree with *HHS* 97.4b.)

   WTYHC: Before this, Chang Chien (fl. ca. 196) and others got together and made a list of officials to be impeached. Those who were among the impeached teased each other, saying, "Among us who have been impeached there are indeed 'Eight Heroes' and 'Eight Attainers'" (pa-chi, emending to agree with *HHS* 97.4b), just like the "Eight Paragons" (pa-yüan) and "Eight Victors" (pa-k'ai) of antiquity." (See *Tso-chuan*, Wen 18; Legge V, 282.)

HCHS: The "Eight Heroes" were those of greatly outstanding reputation.

YHSW: Ch'en Fan, with superior spirit and lofty zeal, possessed the restraint proper to a minister in relation to his sovereign. Li Ying--loyal, strong, correct, and honest--possessed the ability required for government. Discussions about these two within the Four Seas had never resolved (which was superior), but when Ts'ai Yung laid down his single dictum to shift (the deadlock), the doubtful discussions were finally settled.

2. When P'ang T'ung arrived in Wu (in 210),[1] the people of Wu all befriended him. After he had seen Lu Chi*, Ku Shao, and Ch'üan Tsung, he made characterizations for them as follows: "Lu Chi* might be called an old horse who has the capability for swiftness of foot; Ku Shao might be called an old ox who can carry heavy burdens and travel long distances."

Someone asked P'ang, "According to your characterization, then, is Lu the better of the two?"

P'ang replied, "An old horse, though he be the finest and swiftest, can carry no more than one man. As for an old ox, though in one day he might travel but a hundred *li*, is his load limited to one man?"

Since no one of the people of Wu raised any objections, (P'ang continued,) "Ch'üan Tsung is a lover of fame and reputation, something like Fan Tzu-chao of Ju-nan."[2] (*SKShu* 7.1b-2a; *TPKC* 169)

[1] This event took place, according to *SKShu* 7.1b, after the death of the Wu general, Chou Yü, hero of the Battle of the Red Cliff against Ts'ao Ts'ao two years before (208). P'ang accompanied Chou's remains back from Nan Commandery (Hupei) to Wu for burial, and on his return to Shu was escorted by the three worthies whom he here characterizes.

[2] According to *SKShu* 7.2a, P'ang's characterization of Ch'üan was: "In your fondness for giving away your possessions and your desire for fame, you're somewhat like Fan Tzu-chao of Ju-nan. Although your wisdom and strength are not great, you are, nevertheless, one of the finest men of the present age."

CCWCL (also quoted in P'ei Sung-chih's comm. at *SKShu* 7.2a): Hsü Shao considered that this appraisal (of the three worthies) was unjust, in that it upgraded Fan Tzu-chao and downgraded (Hsü's cousin), Hsü Ching. Liu Hua countered by saying, "Tzu-chao rose from the status of a merchant, and even after he had reached the age of seventy (*SKShu* has *erh-shun*, i.e., sixty), he was able to maintain his serenity, and in business he never competed unfairly."

Chiang Chi (fl. ca. 250, author of *CCWCL*) replied, "Tzu-chao, indeed, from youth to maturity, was completely pure in his demeanor. However, if you ever observed the way he bared his teeth and set his jaws and protruded his lips (in an argument), he was naturally no match for Hsü Ching."

3. Ku Shao once stayed overnight conversing with P'ang T'ung. Ku asked, "I hear you're famous as a knower of men. Between the two of us, which is better?"

P'ang replied, "In forming and fashioning the morals of the age, or 'floating or sinking with the times,' I'm no match for you. But in

discoursing on policies handed down by the ancients for the rule of kings and hegemons, or reviewing the strategic moments (of history) when 'prosperity or calamity hung in the balance (*i-fu*)' I would seem to be a day or so older than you."
Ku Shao, for his part, was also content with this statement. (*SKShu* 7.2a, comm.; *TPKC* 169)

4. Chu-ko Chin, his younger brother Liang, and his cousin Tan all had flourishing reputations, but each lived in a different one of the Three Kingdoms. At the time people said that Shu had gotten the dragon of the family, Wu its tiger, and Wei its cub (*kou*).[1]
Chu-ko Tan lived in Wei and shared an equal reputation with Hsiahou Hsüan. Chu-ko Chin lived in Wu, where the Wu court respectfully acknowledged his vast tolerance.[2] (*IWLC* 22; *PTSC* 115; *PSLT* 12; *TPYL* 446, 516; *TPKC* 169)

[1]Chu-ko Liang's friend, Hsü Shu, had introduced him to Liu Pei, founder of the Shu Kingdom, as a "reclining dragon" (*wo-lung*; *SKWu* 5.2a), a nickname by which he is still known. The term *kou*, which in modern Chinese means "dog," in earlier times referred to the young of animals. Chu-ko T'an was the youngest of the three.

[2]*WuS*: Chu-ko Chin, fleeing the disorders (of the Yellow Turban Revolt in 184), crossed the Yangtze River. Sun Ch'üan took him on as his senior administrator and sent him on a mission to Shu, where he came face to face with his younger brother, Chu-ko Liang. But he withdrew from the interview without betraying any private feelings in his face. Moreover, he maintained a proper expression and full powers of judgment, for which his contemporaries acknowledged his vast tolerance.

5. Ssu-ma Chao once asked Wu Kai,[1] "How would you compare Ch'en T'ai with his father, Ch'en Ch'ün?"
Kai replied, "In regard to being able to make teaching and influencing everyone in the realm his own responsibility with uninhibited urbanity and broad cheerfulness, T'ai is not the equal of his father. But when it comes to establishing his merit and getting things done with enlightened discipline and utmost simplicity, he surpasses his father." (*SKWei* 22.11b; *TPKC* 169)

[1]*WC*: Wu Kai was a close friend of Ch'en T'ai; that is why Ssu-ma Chao addressed the question to him.

6. During the Cheng-shih era (240-249), whenever gentlemen were being discussed in pairs, the "Five Hsüns" were compared to the "Five Ch'ens": Hsün Shu was compared to Ch'en Shih; Hsün Ching[1] to Ch'en Ch'en; Hsün Shuang to Ch'en Chi; Hsün Yü to Ch'en Ch'ün; and Hsün I to Ch'en T'ai.
In addition the "Eight P'eis" were compared to the "Eight Wangs": P'ei Hui was compared to Wang Hsiang; P'ei K'ai to Wang Yen; P'ei K'ang to Wang Sui; P'ei Ch'o to Wang Ch'eng; P'ei Tsan to Wang Tun; P'ei Hsia to Wang Tao; P'ei Wei to Wang Jung; and P'ei Mo to Wang Hsüan.

[1]*ISC*: Hsün Ching lived in retirement and pursued his studies, and in all he did, acted in harmony with the rites. His younger

brother, Shuang, also possessed literary ability and learning, and was well known in his own generation. Someone asked Hsü Chang of Ju-nan, "Between Shuang and Ching, which is the more worthy?" Chang replied, "The two men are both pieces of jade. But Shuang gleams on the surface, while Ching glows from within".

7. The two sons of Yang Chun, the governor of Chi Province (Hopei), Yang Ch'iao and Yang Mao, were both of mature capacity while they were still young lads with their hair in tufts. Since Chun was on friendly terms with both P'ei Wei and Yüeh Kuang, he sent the two lads to see them.

P'ei Wei's nature was magnanimous but proper, and, being fond of Ch'iao for his possession of a lofty manner, he reported to Chun, "Ch'iao will come up to you some day; Mao will fall a little behind."

Yüeh Kuang's nature on the other hand was pure and unmixed, and, being fond of Mao for his possession of a spiritual discipline, he reported, "Ch'iao will undoubtedly come up to you, but Mao will become even more refined than you are."

Chun laughed and said, "The superiority and inferiority of my two sons turns out to be nothing more or less than the superiority and inferiority of P'ei Wei and Yüeh Kuang!"

Thereafter, when those who discussed personalities evaluated the two, they considered that although Yang Ch'iao possessed a lofty manner, his spiritual discipline was not as well-rounded as his brother's, and that Yüeh Kuang's appraisal had hit upon the truth. However, both Ch'iao and Mao became outstanding members of the younger generation. (CS 43.23ab; TPKC 169)

8. When Liu Na first came to Lo-yang (from the south) and met all the famous gentlemen, he sighed and said, "Wang Yen is completely fresh and scintillating; Yüeh Kuang is the one I respect; Chang Hua is the one I don't understand; Chou Hui is clever at utilizing his shortcomings; Tu Yü is clumsy at utilizing his strong points."[1] (SWLC, pieh 19)

[1]Cf. the statement attributed to Wang Jung in CS 43.13a: "(My son-in-law), P'ei Wei, is clumsy at utilizing his strong points; Hsü Hsün is skillful at utilizing his shortcomings."

9. Wang Yen said, "Lü-ch'iu Ch'ung is better than Man Fen and Hsi Lung. These three men are all of high ability, but Ch'ung should have the foremost rating."[1]

[1]YenCC: At the time, the gentlemen of Kao-p'ing Commandery (Shantung) happened to be numerous, and Man Fen and Hsi Lung were rated ahead of Lü-ch'iu Ch'ung. Their reputations and status were well known. But Liu Pao and Wang Yen still considered that because of Ch'ung's modesty and nobility, he was worthy to precede the other two men.

10. Wang Yen once compared Wang Ch'eng* to Yüeh Kuang. For this reason, when Ch'eng*'s grandson, Wang T'an-chih, was composing a stele inscription for his grandfather, he wrote, "In contemporary ratings he was paired with Yüeh Kuang."[1] (CS 75.2ab)

[1]CTMSC: When Wang Ch'eng* conversed on a topic or made distinctions

among personalities, he only clarified the main essentials, with
no superfluous verbiage. Those who possessed understanding acknowledged his ability to clarify his point with brevity. The
grand marshal, Wang Yen, was the most authoritative figure of his
age. After he had met Ch'eng* he praised and honored him, comparing him with Yüeh Kuang of Nan-yang (Honan).

11. Yü Ai walked slightly behind and to the side (*yen-hsing*) with
Wang Ch'eng.[1]

[1]*CYC*: At first Wang Ch'eng was acclaimed for his perspicuity and
brilliance, but he made light of it and produced no actions to
match the acclaim. His elder brother, Wang Yen, had a flourishing
reputation, and his contemporaries attributed to him a sound
understanding of human character. (Yen) once made the following
characterization for the gentlemen of the realm: "Wang Ch'eng is
number one; Yü Ai number two; and Wang Tun number three."
  Ai felt that Ch'eng and Tun were not his equals. When Wang
Ch'eng was killed (in 323, by Wang Tun; see above, *SSHY* V, 31) and
Tun himself defeated (in 324), Yü Ai's reputation in the world returned to where it had been in the beginning.

12. While Wang Tun was still at the Western Chin court (in Lo-yang,
before 309), whenever he met Chou I he would always fan[1] his face
without being able to stop.[2]
  Later, after they had both crossed the Yangtze River, he could no
longer do so. With many a sigh Wang said, "I don't know whether it's
I who have progressed, or Chou who has retrogressed." (*SLF* 14; *TPYL*
702)

[1]Deleting *chang*, "to screen," after *KI*.

[2]*SYCS*: Where Chou was concerned, Wang Tun had from the beginning
been afraid of him, and whenever he met him his face would always
flush hotly. Even in midwinter he would still keep fanning his
face without stopping, so great was his fright.
  SSHY Comm.: Tun's nature was like a sturdy beam from youth to
maturity. When Shih Ch'ung beheaded the female entertainer (see
below, *SSHY* XXX, 1), he never flinched. How could a man as brazen
as this be frightened in the presence of Chou I? This statement is
untrue.

13. During the reign of Emperor Yüan (Ssu-ma Jui, r. 307-322), Yü Fei
of K'uai-chi Commandery (Chekiang), was employed in the same department with Huan I.[1] As a person he possessed eloquence and reasoning
powers and an excellent prestige.
  Chancellor Wang Tao once said to Fei, "K'ung Yü has the ability
for one of the Three Ducal Offices, but not the prestige; while Ting
T'an has the prestige for it, but not the ability.[2] Wouldn't the one
in whom the two are combined be you?" But Fei died before he had
reached this eminence. (*CS* 76.17a, 78.14b)

[1]Emending *Hsüan-wu* (= Huan Wen) of the text to the graphically
similar *Hsüan-ch'eng* (= Huan I), since Huan Wen would have been
only a boy. Huan I and Yü Fei were clerks together in the Board of
Civil Office.

²*CYC*: K'ung Yü (Ching-k'ang), Ting T'an (Shih-k'ang), and Chang Mao (Wei-k'ang) all had conspicuous reputations, and in their time were called the "Three K'angs of K'uai-chi Commandery."

Chang Mao once dreamed he received a large elephant, and asked Wang Ya about it. Ya replied, "You're about to become grand warden of a large commandery, but it won't be a good thing. The elephant is a large animal (*$d'\hat{a}i$-$\acute{s}i\partial u$), which takes the same sound as grand warden (*$t'\hat{a}i$-$\acute{s}i\partial u$). That's how I know you'll be grand warden of a large commandery. However, the elephant loses its life because of its tusks. [Later you'll be killed by someone who will take your commandery.]" (Bracketed sentence added from *KI*.) Later Chang did become grand warden of Wu Commandery (Soochow), and, as predicted, was killed by Shen Ch'ung.

14. Emperor Ming (Ssu-ma Shao, r. 323-325) asked Chou I, "How do you think of yourself in comparison with Ch'ih Chien?"

Chou replied, "Chien would seem to be more conscientious than I am."

The emperor then asked the same thing of Ch'ih Chien.

Ch'ih replied, "Chou I has more of the family tradition of a statesman than I have."

15. When Wang Tun descended the Yangtze River (in his coup against the capital in 322), Yü Liang asked him, "I've heard that you have 'Four Friends.' Who are they?"

Wang replied, "The commander from your family (Yü Ai), the grand marshal from my family (Wang Yen), A-p'ing (Wang Ch'eng), and Hu-wu Fu-chih. A-p'ing, of course, should be considered the least of the four."[1]

Yü said, "It seems he may not quite be the least." Yü then went on to ask, "And who is at the head of the list?"

Wang replied, "Naturally there's someone."

Yü asked again, "Who is it?"

Wang said, "Well, of course, there are public estimates of who it is."

At this point one of Liang's attendants stepped on his foot, and he finally stopped asking questions. (*TPKC* 235)

[1]*PWKS*: Hu-wu Fu-chih from his youth had recognition from both the cultivated and the common. Together with Wang Ch'eng, Yü Ai, Wang Tun, and Wang Yen, he was one of the "Four Friends."

16. Someone asked Chancellor Wang Tao, "How would you rate Chou I (d. 322) in comparison with Ho Ch'iao (d. 292)?"

The chancellor replied, "Ho Ch'iao was craggier (*$ts'\hat{a}$-$ng\hat{a}t$)."[1]

[1]For a discussion of the numerous variants of this binome, see P. A. Boodberg, "Proleptical Remarks on the Evolution of Archaic Chinese," *Harvard Journal of Asiatic Studies* 2 (1937), esp. pp. 362-364. There is probably a mild play on Ho's personal name, Ch'iao, "Mountain Peak."

17. Emperor Ming once asked Hsieh K'un, "How would you rate yourself in comparison with Yü Liang?"

Hsieh replied, "As for 'sitting in ceremonial attire'[1] in temple or hall, and making the hundred officials keep to the rules, I'm no match for Liang. But when it comes to '(living in seclusion on) a single hill,' or '(fishing in) a single stream,'[2] I consider myself superior to him."[3] (CS 49.19b; TPKC 169)

[1] See *Tso-chuan*, Chao 1 (Legge V, 578).

[2] Cf. HS 100A.6 b: "If the ruler fishes in a single stream, then the myriad beings will not be disloyal to his will; and if he lives in seclusion on a single hill, the whole realm will not alter his delight." See also *SSHY* XXL, 12, below.

[3] CYC: Hsieh K'un accompanied Wang Tun in his descent on the capital (in 322). Entering the court, he had an interview with the crown prince (Ssu-ma Shao) in the Eastern Palace, where they talked until nightfall. The crown prince casually asked K'un, "Those who discuss personalities compare you with Yü Liang. Which of you do you yourself consider to be superior?" K'un replied, "In the beauties of temple and hall, or the opulence of the hundred officials, I'm no match for Liang. But when it comes to letting the mind go free among hills and streams, I consider myself superior to him."

TTCC: Hsieh K'un and the other companions of Wang Ch'eng emulated the "Seven Worthies of the Bamboo Grove," and with their heads disheveled and hair falling loose, would sit around naked, their legs sprawled apart. They called themselves the "Eight Free Spirits" (*pa-ta*). This was why the girl next door broke Hsieh's two front teeth (see above, *SSHY* VIII, 97, n. 1). Contemporaries made up a ditty, which went,

> "Dissolute without relief,
> Hsieh K'un broke his two front teeth."

18. Chancellor Wang Tao's two younger brothers, Ying and Ch'ang, never crossed the Yangtze River. Contemporary evaluations compared Wang Ying to Teng Yu, and Wang Ch'ang to Ho Ch'iao. Ying had been a consultant, and Ch'ang summoned to be a libationer. (CS 65.10a)

19. Emperor Ming asked Chou I, "How do you feel about the way those who evaluate personalities compare you with Ch'ih Chien?"
   Chou replied, "It's not necessary for Your Majesty[1] to involve me in comparisons."

[1] *SSHY* Comm.: Chou I (d. 322) had been dead a full year before Emperor Ming ascended the throne. The *Shih-shuo* is therefore mistaken in this account.

20. Chancellor Wang Tao said, "Recent evaluations compare me with Wang Ch'eng* and Juan Chan, and at the same time promote the claims of these two men.[1] And they, in their turn, both promoted the claims of the grand marshal, Wang Yen. So *this* gentleman must have been extraordinarily outstanding."[2]

[1] Both Wang Ch'eng* and Juan Chan served as secretarial aides to the Prince of Tung-hai, Ssu-ma Yüeh, and were highly regarded by the gentlemen of Eastern Chin. See CS 75.3a.

[2] CCKT: Wang Yen's nature was dignified and lofty, and from his youth he was recommended by his peers.

IX CLASSIFICATION ACCORDING TO EXCELLENCE   255

21. Sung Wei[1] was at one time the concubine of Wang Tun, but afterward came into the household of Hsieh Shang. Shang asked her, "How do I compare with Wang?"

Wei replied, "Wang Tun is to you as a peasant is to a nobleman, that's all." She said this because Hsieh Shang was charming and handsome.

[1] Although Liu Chün claims in the Commentary to know nothing about this musician-beauty, her checkered career is recounted in *IWLC* 44, under "Flutes" (*ti*).

22. Emperor Ming once asked Chou I, "How would you rate yourself in comparison with Yü Liang?"

Chou replied, "As for living in quietude beyond the cares of the world, Liang is no match for me; but when it comes to maintaining a calm dignity in hall or temple, I'm no match for Liang."[1]

[1] *SSHY* Comm.: All accounts compare Hsieh K'un with Yü Liang (see No. 17, above). I have never heard of any comparisons with Chou I.

23. After Chancellor Wang Tao had summoned Wang Shu to serve as his aide, Yü Liang asked the chancellor, "What sort of person is Wang Shu?"

Wang Tao replied, "In honesty, independence, simplicity, and nobility, he's no less qualified than either his grandfather Wang Ch'eng*, or his father Wang Chan. But when it comes to living an untrammeled and dispassionate existence, of course, he'd be no match for you."[1] (*CS* 75.3b)

[1] *SSHY* Comm.: He said this because Wang Shu was an irascible, narrow-minded man.

24. Pien K'un said, "In Ch'ih Yin's person there are three contradictions: (1) he's rigidly correct in serving his superiors, yet loves to have his subordinates flatter him; (2) in his private life he's pure and incorruptible, yet he's always working on grand schemes and intrigues; (3) he himself loves to read, yet he hates the learning of others."[1] (*TPYL* 446)

[1] *SSHY* Comm.: The grand marshal, Liu Shih (d. 312), said of Wang Su (d. 256; editor of the *KTCY*): "He's rigidly correct in serving his superiors, yet loves to have his subordinates flatter him; by nature he's addicted to glory and honor, yet he'd never seek any improper connections; in his private life he's not corrupt, yet he's extraordinarily stingy with his money and property." Could it be that in both ambition and nature Wang Su and Ch'ih Yin were fortuitously identical?

25. In contemporary evaluations Wen Ch'iao[1] was rated the highest of all the second-class persons who had crossed the Yangtze River. When famous gentlemen of the time got together to discuss personalities, as the list of first-class persons drew to a close, Wen would always turn pale.

[1] *WenSP*, hsü: The great officer of Chin, Ch'üeh Chih (sixth cent. B.C.) was enfeoffed at Wen (Honan), and his sons and grandsons

were surnamed accordingly. They settled in Ch'i Prefecture of T'ai-yüan Commandery (Shansi) and became one of the illustrious surnames of the commandery.

26. Chancellor Wang Tao said, "Whenever I meet Hsieh Shang, he always enables me to reach a higher level of existence, but when I converse with Ho Ch'ung"--Wang simply raised his hand and pointed toward the ground--"it's just exactly like this."[1]

[1]*SSHY* Comm.: The preceding chapter (*SSHY* VIII, 59 and 60) and other sources all state that Wang Tao held Ho Ch'ung in high regard, and felt that he would surely succeed himself as chancellor. Yet in this chapter he points to the ground, as though he meant to belittle or demean him. Perhaps in pure conversation or analyzing principles Ho could not come up to Hsieh Shang?

27. When Ho Ch'ung became a minister of state (in 344),[1] there were some who complained that the office with which he had been entrusted had not been filled with the right man.[2] Juan Yü said with deep feeling, "Ho Ch'ung should never have come this far. For one who is still 'in cotton clothes' (i.e., in obscurity) to leap over the heads of others into the position of minister of state is regrettable--just this one point and nothing else."[3]

[1]I.e., when he became director of the Central Secretariat.

[2]*CYC*: The persons with whom Ho Ch'ung was intimate were a common and motley crew. For this reason his reputation suffered.

[3]*YL*: When Juan Yü heard that Ho Ch'ung had become minister of state, he sighed and said, "Where am I going to live now?"
    SSHY Comm.: This meant Juan never conceded Ho to be of statesman caliber. The two accounts, therefore, are in agreement.

28. When Wang Hsi-chih was young, Chancellor Wang Tao said of him, "Why should Hsi-chih any longer be considered inferior to Liu Sui?"

29. In Ch'ih Yin's household there was a northern (*ts'ang*) slave who knew something about literature and had ideas on every subject. Wang Hsi-chih once praised him to Liu T'an.
    Liu asked, "How would you rate him in comparison with his master, Ch'ih Yin?"
    Wang replied, "Oh well, he's just a low-class person who has a few ideas, that's all. How can he be compared with Ch'ih Yin?"
    Liu said, "If he's not comparable to Ch'ih Yin, he really *is* an ordinary slave!" (*CS* 75.32a)

30. Contemporaries characterized Juan Yü as follows: "In style and manner he doesn't approach Wang Hsi-chih; in simplicity and preeminence he's not the equal of Liu T'an; in graciousness and charm he's no match for Wang Meng; in intellectual power he's not equal to Yin Hao; but he combines in his person the excellent qualities of them all."[1] (*CS* 49.10a)

[1]*CHS*: Juan Yü considered that a man has no need for extensive learning, but should simply make etiquette and deference to others

his first concern. For this reason he would lie around listlessly
all day. He did nothing to cultivate it, yet other people would
spontaneously honor him. (Cf. above, SSHY V, 53, n. 1.)

31. Emperor Chien-wen (Ssu-ma Yü) said, "Ho Yen's (d. 249) cleverness
got in the way of the Truth (*li*), and Hsi K'ang's (d. 262) outstanding ability did injury to the Way."[1]

[1]SSHY Comm.: The Truth is basically sincere and straightforward;
to be clever is to do violence to its contents. The Way is simply
empty and flavorless; to be outstandingly able is to violate its
essence. Therefore Ho Yen and Hsi K'ang did not escape (i.e., they
were both executed).

32. Contemporaries were discussing together which was the greater
mistake of Emperor Wu of Chin (Ssu-ma Yen, r. 265-290): his banishment of his younger brother, the Prince of Ch'i (Ssu-ma Yu),[1] or his
establishment of his son, Emperor Hui (Ssu-ma Chung, r. 290-306) as
crown prince.[2]

The majority held that the establishment of Emperor Hui was the
graver mistake. But Huan Wen said, "You're wrong. He had his son continue his father's work, and younger brother carry on the family sacrifices. What was improper about that?"[3]

[1]See above, SSHY V, 11, n. 1.

CYC: Earlier, Hsün Hsü and Feng To had been intimate favorites
of Emperor Wu. Ssu-ma Yu hated Hsü's obsequiousness, and Hsü was
terrified that in the event of Yu's accession to the throne, he
would surely execute him. Moreover, Yu had found great favor in
the hearts of the people, and all the court worthies looked up to
him. It happened that the emperor was ill, and when Yu and the
crown prince (Ssu-ma Chung) entered to inquire after his health,
the court gentlemen all fixed their eyes on Yu, and paid no attention to the crown prince. At this point Hsü said casually, "After
Your Majesty's ten thousand years of rule, the crown prince will
not get to be established."

The emperor asked, "Why?" Hsü replied, "Since the hundred officials at court and in the provinces are all loyal to the Prince of
Ch'i in their hearts, how could the crown prince get to be established? If Your Majesty should attempt to order the Prince of Ch'i
to return to his principality, the entire court would surely think
it improper. And that being the case, your servant's words will
have been proved true."

The personal attendant, Feng To, said further, "Your Majesty
will surely want to establish all the nobles and complete the five
ranks (duke, marquis, earl, viscount, baron). You should begin
with the nearest of kin, and none is nearer than the Prince of
Ch'i."

The emperor followed his advice and issued an order sending Yu
to his principality in Ch'i (modern Shantung). When Yu learned
that Hsü and To had alienated him from the emperor, he was sorrow-
ful and angry and did not know what to do. He entered to bid farewell, then went out, spit blood, and died.

The emperor wept for him bitterly, but Feng To said, "The reputation of the Prince of Ch'i exceeded his real worth, and thus the

whole realm gave him their loyalty. But now that he himself is dead and gone, why does Your Majesty grieve so sorely?"

After that the emperor finally stopped weeping. When Liu I learned of it, for the rest of his life he claimed illness because of it.

[2] See above, SSHY V, 9, n. 1.

[3] SSHY Comm.: Emperor Wu's provocation of disaster and rebellion, and the overthrow of the Sacred Provinces, consisted in this and nothing else. If even the humblest clerk understands that this was the case, how much more would someone of the vast ability of Huan Wen? This story is untrue!

33. Someone asked Yin Hao, "The princes and the nobles of the present age are comparing you with P'ei Hsia (fl. ca. 300). What do you say to that?"

Yin replied, "Of course it's because I have a perceptive understanding of obscure points."[1]

[1] SSHY Comm.: Both Hsia and Hao were capable in pure conversation.

34. The General Controlling the Army (Ssu-ma Yü) once asked Yin Hao, "When all's said and done, how do you compare with P'ei Wei (d. 300)?"

After a long while Yin answered, "Of course I'm just better than he was, that's all."

35. When Huan Wen was young, he and Yin Hao were of equal reputation, and they constantly felt a spirit of mutual rivalry. Huan once asked Yin, "How do you compare with me?"

Yin replied, "I've been keeping company with myself[1] a long time; I'd rather just be me." (CS 77.25b)

[1] CS 77.25b has "with you."

36. The General Controlling the Army (Ssu-ma Yü) once asked Sun Ch'o, "How would you evaluate Liu T'an?"

Sun replied, "Pure, yet luxuriant; unceremonious, yet genteel."
"What about Wang Meng?"
"Warm and gracious; placid and affable."[1]
"And Huan Wen?"
"Haughty and forthright; aggressively outstanding."
"And Hsieh Shang?"
"Pure, yet easygoing; genteel, yet uninhibited."
"What about Juan Yü?"
"Magnificently gracious; universally excelling."
"And Yüan Ch'iao?"
"Washed and scoured; pure and alert."
"And Yin Jung?"
"Remote from the world, yet deep in thought."

Ssu-ma Yü then asked, "How would you evaluate yourself?"

Sun replied, "What my own talents and abilities are concerned with is in no case comparable to these worthies. And as far as deliberating on policies suited to the times, or ways of ruling the present world, are concerned, in these matters, too, for the most part, I don't approach them. On the other hand, precisely because I'm untalented, I set my thoughts from time to time on the Mysterious and Transcendent (hsüan-sheng) and intone from afar the words of Lao-tzu and Chuang-tzu. Lonely and aloof in lofty retirement, I don't concern my thoughts with temporal duties. I myself feel that in this attitude I yield to none." (CS 93.10b)

[1]HKCC: Whenever people praised the cultivated set (feng-liu che), they would always cite Wang Meng and Liu T'an as the ideal examples of it.

37. When the grand marshal, Huan Wen, descended the Yangtze River to the capital (in 365),[1] he asked Liu T'an, "I hear the conversations of the Prince of K'uai-chi (Ssu-ma Yü) are notably advanced. Is it true?"

Liu replied, "He's *extremely* advanced. However, he's definitely only among those of the second class."

Huan said, "Oh? And who are in the first class?"

Liu replied, "Just people like me, that's all." (CS 75.33a)

[1]Huan Wen PC: In the first year of the Hsing-ning era (363; the "ninth year" of the text is a copyist's error), because Huan had reconquered the old capital (Lo-yang) and pacified all of China (Hua-hsia), he was promoted to governor-general of military affairs inside and outside the court, personal attendant, and grand marshal, and given the imperial yellow halberd, authorizing him to participate in the court administration.

(Since Huan did not actually reach Chien-k'ang until early in 365, this is the probable date of the present incident.)

38. After Yin Hao had been dismissed (early in 354),[1] Huan Wen said to the others, "When I was young I used to play at riding bamboo horses with Yin Hao, but after I gave it up, he immediately seized upon it. Of course, he's turned out to be less skillful at it than I was."[2] (CS 77.26a; TPKC 169; SWLC A, 29)

[1]I.e., after his fiasco in the north.

[2]HCYC: While Emperor Chien-wen (Ssu-ma Yü) was in control of the court administration (in 346) he selected Yin Hao to be governor of Yang Province (Kiangsu-Anhui-Chekiang), wishing thereby to thwart the ambitions of Huan Wen. But Huan had always despised Hao, and was never afraid of him.

39. Someone asked the General Controlling the Army (Ssu-ma Yü), "In the last analysis, how would you rate Yin Hao as a conversationalist?"

Yü replied, "He's unable to beat anyone in an argument, but quite adequate at the art of give-and-take in a crowd."

40. Emperor Chien-wen (Ssu-ma Yü) said, "In purity and gentility Hsieh Feng isn't the equal of his younger brother, Hsieh P'in, nor in the pursuit of learning does he come up to K'ung Yen. But just as he is, by himself, he's superb."[1]

[1]SSHY Comm.: This means that Hsieh Feng followed his natural simplicity (t'ien-chen).

41. In the period before the Duke of Hai-hsi (Ssu-ma I**, r. 365-371) was deposed, Wang Hsün asked Huan Wen, "In the case of the Viscount of Chi and Pi Kan,¹ though their actions differed, their intentions were the same. May I ask Your Excellency's opinion as to which was right and which wrong?"

Huan replied, "In their praise as good men, there's no difference between them, but I'd rather be a Kuan Chung."²

¹"Analects" XVIII, 1: The Viscount of Wei deserted his half brother, Chou Hsin (trad. r. 1154-1122 B.C.); the Viscount of Chi, Chou's uncle, became his slave; Pi Kan, another uncle, remonstrated with him and died. Confucius said, "In these, Yin (= Shang) had three good men."

Ho Yen's commentary (*Lun-yü chi-chieh*) explains: Though the three men's actions differed, they were equally praised for their goodness, because they all grieved over the disorder of the state and cherished peace for the people.

²Ibid. *XIV*, 17: The disciple Tzu-lu said, "When Duke Huan of Ch'i (r. 685-643 B.C.) killed his brother and rival for the succession, Prince Chiu (in 686), Shao Hu died fighting for him, while Kuan Chung (who requested to be taken prisoner) did not. Was Kuan not a good man?"

The Master replied, "The fact that Duke Huan brought together the feudal lords without the use of arms or chariots was solely due to the efforts of Kuan Chung. But as for his goodness, as for his goodness . . ."

42. Liu T'an and Wang Meng were once (ca. 346) at a gathering at the Wa-kuan Temple (in Chien-k'ang) where Huan I* was also among the company. They were discussing together and evaluating personalities of the Western Chin court (265-316) in comparison with those of east of the River (Eastern Chin, 317-420).

Someone asked, "How would Tu I compare with Wei Chieh?"¹

Huan I* replied, "Tu I had a purity of the complexion; Wei Chieh, radiantly shining, had a gentility of the spirit."

Wang and Liu applauded his words.² (*CS* 93.5b, attrib. to Huan I; also 36.14b)

¹Tu I was extremely frail, and died young. Wang Hsi-chih described his complexion as being like "solidified ointment" (*CS* 93.5b). Wei Chieh was also of delicate health and died young. He was described as a "man of jade."

²*Wei Chieh PC*: During the Yung-ho period (345-354) Liu T'an and Hsieh Shang were discussing together and evaluating the personalities of the Central Court (Western Chin, 265-316). Someone asked, "Might Tu I be compared with Wei Chieh?" Hsieh replied, "How can he be compared with him? Between these two there would be room for several persons."

CTMSC: Liu T'an said, "I would like to evaluate Tu I and Wei Chieh. Tu I had purity of the complexion; Wei Chieh purity of spirit." Those who discussed personalities considered this to be an understanding remark.

43. Liu T'an once patted Wang Meng on the back and said, "Meng, old

chap (A-nu), compared to the chancellor (Wang Tao) you simply have the greater endowment of elegance."[1]

[1]*YL*: Liu T'an and Chancellor Wang Tao were not mutually congenial. Liu often said, "Compared with the chancellor, Wang Meng is more straightforward and uninhibited, more endowed with purity."

44. Liu T'an and Wang Meng were once both present at a banquet. Wang, slightly in his cups, got up and performed a dance.
Liu said to him, "Meng, old chap, today you're not a whit behind Hsiang Hsiu!"[1]

[1]*SSHY* Comm.: His action was in the same class with Hsiang Hsiu's ability to let himself go.

45. Huan Wen once asked K'ung Yin, "How would you rate Hsieh An in comparison with Yin Chung-wen?" K'ung thought awhile but had not yet answered, when he returned the question to Huan, saying, "How would *you* rate him?"
Huan replied, "Hsieh An, as one would expect, is inviolable; his very position is naturally superior."

46. Hsieh An was once appraising and discussing personalities together with other worthies of the time while Hsieh Hsüan and Hsieh Lang were also present. An asked Li Ch'ung, "How would you rate Li Chung (d. 300) of your family in comparison with Yüeh Kuang (d. 304)?"
At this Li Ch'ung burst into tears and said, "When the Prince of Chao (Ssu-ma Lun) usurped the throne in open revolt (in 301), Yüeh Kuang personally handed over to him the imperial seal.[1] My late uncle (Li Chung) was a cultivated and a proper man; he was ashamed to remain in a rebellious court, and accordingly was driven to taking his own life by swallowing poison. I'm afraid it's difficult to compare the two. But these matters are self-evident in the facts of the case; they're not merely the words of a prejudiced relative."[2]
Hsieh An, turning to Hsieh Lang, said, "The opinion of one who has an understanding of the case is, as expected, no different from my own."

[1]*CYC*: When the Prince of Chao, Ssu-ma Lun, usurped the throne, Yüeh Kuang, Man Fen, and Ts'ui Sui brought forward the imperial seal.

[2]*CCKT*: When the Prince of Chao was serving as chancellor, he picked Li Chung for his left sergeant-at-arms. Chung, realizing Lun was about to usurp the throne, declined on the excuse of illness and did not take up his post, but after Lun had strongly urged him, Chung could no longer help himself. When his illness became extremely critical, leaning on a staff, he dragged himself to Lun's headquarters to receive his appointment, and a few days later he died. His contemporaries mourned his loss, and he was given the posthumous title of cavalier attendant-in-ordinary.

47. Wang Hu-chih (of the Lang-yeh Wangs) once asked Wang Meng (of the T'ai-yüan Wangs), "How would you compare my family's Wang Hsi-chih with your family's Wang Shu?"
Wang Meng had not yet answered when Hu-chih added, "Wang Hsi-chih's reputation and nobility are greater."
Wang Meng rejoined, "But Wang Shu is not exactly ignoble, either."[1]

[1]CHS: Since Wang Hsi-chih was a personal friend of the Prince of K'uai-chi (Ssu-ma Yü), he was transferred to become grand warden of Lin-ch'uan (Kiangsi), while Wang Shu left his post as work-detail officer in the administration of the General of Spirited Cavalry to become magistrate of Wan-ling Prefecture (Anhui). While Shu was magistrate of Wan-ling, he had for the most part to make his own household furniture, and at the beginning there were rumors of his living in drudgery and want. Chancellor Wang Tao sent someone to tell him, "For the son of a famous father (Wang Ch'eng*) to demean himself in a tiny prefecture is extremely improper."

Shu replied, "If I'm content, then naturally I should stop where I am" (cf. Lao-tzu 44). Nobody understood him at the time, but later, after he had been frequently summoned to govern provinces and commanderies but never took up the posts, the world began to appreciate him.

48. Liu T'an once went to Wang Meng's house for pure conversation. At the time Wang Meng's son, Hsiu, was in his thirteenth year and was listening by the side of the couch. After Liu had left, Hsiu asked his father, "How does Intendant Liu's conversation compare with yours, Father?"

Wang Meng replied, "For sheer musical effect and elegant terminology, he's not equal to me; but when it comes to speaking out directly and hitting the mark, he surpasses me."[1]

[1]Liu T'an PC: Liu T'an possessed outstanding ability, and his conversations and expositions on the Empty and Transcendent (hsü-sheng) were the result of a thorough understanding of the Truth. Wang Meng was, in a rough way, equal to him in this, but surpassed him in his powers of expression. His terminology was apt.

49. After Hsieh Wan's defeat at Shou-ch'un (Anhui, in 359), the future Emperor Chien-wen (Ssu-ma Yü) asked Ch'ih Ch'ao, "Of course Hsieh Wan should have been defeated, but why on earth did he have to alienate the affections of his men to such a great extent?"[1]

Ch'ih Ch'ao replied, "Because he's of a frank and uninhibited nature, he wanted to make a distinction between wisdom and courage."[2]

[1]An example of Wan's contemptuous treatment of his men is found in SSHY XXIV, 14, below.

[2]I.e., he wanted to prove he was a gentleman, and his men mere soldiers. Cf. the argument between Lü An and Hsi K'ang, recorded in K'ang's "Discourse on Intelligence and Daring" (Ming-tan lun), in Lu Hsün, ed., Hsi K'ang chi (Peking, 1956), pp. 124-128; Holzman, La vie et la pensée, pp. 73-74.

CHS: While Hsieh Wan was governing Yü Province (Anhui, in 359) the Ti and Ch'iang (Former Ch'in) were ravaging Ssu and Yü provinces (Honan), and the Hsien-pei (Former Yen) were uniting their forces in Ping (Shansi) and Chi (Hopei) provinces. Since Wan had been given responsibility for that area, he himself led a host to Ying (Honan) to relieve the Chin forces at Lo-yang. Wan was boastful and arrogant toward others, and lost the good will of both officers and men. When the Commandant of the North, Ch'ih T'an, returned to P'eng-ch'eng (N. Kiangsu) on account of illness, Wan, supposing he had retreated because of superior enemy forces, proceeded himself to turn back southward, whereupon his army broke spontaneously into confusion. With great hardship Wan returned home alone. Emperor Mu (r. 345-361) reprimanded him and degraded him to a commoner.

50. Liu T'an once said to Hsieh Shang (quoting Confucius), "'Ever since I've had (Yen Hui, the first of my) four friends, my disciples have become increasingly close to me.'"

To Hsü Hsün he said, "'And ever since I've had Tzu-lu, evil words no longer reach my ears.'"[1]

The two men accepted these remarks without resentment.[2]

[1] *SSTC*: Confucius said: "King Wen (eleventh cent. B.C.) had 'four friends' ('Bringer-near of the Distant,' etc.; see below). Ever since I've had Yen Hui, my disciples have become increasingly close to me. Isn't he my 'Bringer-near of the Distant' (*hsü-fu*)? Ever since I've had Tzu-kung, gentlemen from distant places have arrived. Isn't he my 'Headlong Runner' (*pen-tsou*)? Ever since I've had Tzu-chang, I've had light before and radiance behind. Isn't he my 'Attendant Before and Behind' (*hsien-hou*)? Ever since I've had Tzu-lu, evil words have no longer entered my ears. Isn't he my 'Guard against Insults' (*yü-wu*)?"

(For the names in quotation marks, see "Songs," No. 237.9. Another passage in *SSTC*, cited in *IS* 59, reads: King Wen of Chou called "Bringer-near of the Distant," "Headlong Runner," "Attendant Before and Behind," and "Guard against Insults"--the *four neighbors* by which he escaped harm in Yu-li [where he was imprisoned by Chou Hsin].)

[2] Kawakatsu *et al.* in their translation suggest that by praising the mild and attractive Yen Hui to the more bold and aggressive Hsieh Shang, Liu T'an was comparing Hsieh negatively to Hsü Hsün, who resembled Yen Hui. And by praising the bold and aggressive Tzu-lu to Hsü Hsün, he was in turn, comparing him negatively to Hsieh Shang.

51. Contemporaries characterized Yin Hao as follows: "In the thorough perceptiveness of his thought processes, he's comparable to Yang Hu (d. 278)."[1]

[1] *SSHY* Comm.: Yang Hu's virtue towered above his entire generation, and his ability was equal to the requirements both of peace and of danger. How could the glow from Yin Hao's smoking candle be compared to the brilliance of the sun and moon?

52. Someone asked Huan Wen for a comparison of the good and bad points of Hsieh An and Wang T'an-chih. Huan hesitated a moment and was about to speak, then in mid-course thought better of it and said, "Since you enjoy broadcasting what other people say, I can't go on and tell you."[1]

[1] Huan's opinions of both Hsieh and Wang were doubtless unrepeatable. See above, *SSHY* VI, 29.

53. Wang T'an-chih once asked Liu Shih, "How am I compared with Wang Hsiu?"

Liu replied, "As far as your ability is concerned, it's probably no better than Hsiu's, but the places where it matches your reputation are more numerous."
Wang laughed and said, "Stupid!"

54. Chih Tun once asked Sun Ch'o, "How would you rate yourself in comparison with Hsü Hsün?"
Sun replied, "As far as exalted feelings and remoteness are concerned, your disciple has long since inwardly conceded Hsü's superiority. But in the matter of a single humming or a single intoning of poetry, Hsü will have to sit facing north."[1] (CS 56.16b)

[1] I.e., as a student before his teacher.

55. Wang Hsi-chih once asked Hsü Hsün, "How would you rate yourself in comparison with Hsieh An and Hsieh Wan?"
Hsü had not yet answered when Wang continued, "Of course Hsieh An is superior to you. But Hsieh Wan would burst his eyeballs trying to compete with you."[1]

[1] CHS: Hsieh Wan's capacity and tolerance were not equal to those of his elder brother, Hsieh An, and even though Wan occupied a post on the frontier (as governor of Yü Province) while An was still living at home (as a private citizen), An's reputation and acclaim were higher than Wan's. (See also No. 60, below.)

56. Liu T'an said, "People say that Chiang Pin is a peasant (t'ien-she). Chiang does, to be sure, live in a house in the fields (t'ien)."[1]

[1] SSHY Comm.: He meant that his capabilities far exceeded his possessions.

57. Hsieh An said, "Among those present at the Chin-ku gathering (at the villa of Shih Ch'ung in 296)[1] Su Shao was the most outstanding."
Shao was Shih Ch'ung's elder sister's husband, the grandson of Su Tse, and the son of Su Yü.

[1] CKSH (cf. WH 20.22a): In the sixth year of the Yüan-k'ang era (296), in company with the grand master of chariots, I set out from Lo-yang as commissioner of military affairs in Ch'ing and Hsü provinces (Shantung and northern Anhui and Kiangsu). I own a villa on the outskirts of Ho-nan Prefecture, by Chin-ku Creek (near Lo-yang), with some high and some low ground. There are clear springs and verdant woods, fruit trees, bamboos, cypresses, and various kinds of medicinal herbs, all in great abundance. In addition there are water mills, fish ponds, caves in the earth, and all things to please the eye and delight the heart. The libationer and General Chastizing the West, Wang Hsü*, was due to return to Ch'ang-an (Shensi), so I and the other worthies escorted him as far as the creek. Day and night we roamed about and feasted, each time moving to a different place, sometimes climbing to a height and looking down, sometimes sitting by the water's edge. At times seven- or twenty-five-stringed zithers (ch'in-se), mouth organs (sheng), and bamboo zithers (chu) accompanied us in the carriages, and were played in concert along the road. When we stopped, I had

each person perform in turn with the orchestra. Then each one composed a poem to express the sentiments in his heart. Whenever anyone could not do so, he had to pay a forfeit by drinking three dipperfuls (*tou*) of wine. Moved by the impermanence of our lives, and dreading the unappointed hour of falling leaves, I have duly recorded below the offices, names, and ages of those who were present. In addition I have copied their poems and appended them after the names, in hopes some curiosity-seeker of later times may read them.

SSHY Comm.: There were in all thirty persons; the tutor to the Prince of Wu (Ssu-ma Yen**), consultant, Marquis within the Passes, Duke Wu of Shih-p'ing (Shensi), Su Shao, who was in his fiftieth year at the time, was at the head of the list.

(For other references to this historic gathering, see below, SSHY XVI, 3, and XXXVI, 1. P'an Yüeh's contribution, the only one to survive, is recorded in WH 20.22ab. See also H. Wilhelm, "Shih Ch'ung and his *Chin-ku-yüan*," Monumenta Serica 18, 1959, 315-327.)

58. Liu T'an characterized Yü Ai (d. 311) as follows: "Although they say he didn't resemble the Way in his calm serenity (*·iəm-·iəm), in his towering height (*t'uət-nguət) he might almost be compared to the Way."[1]

[1]*MSC*: Yü Ai was listless and profoundly relaxed; there was nothing which aroused his attention.

59. Sun T'ung once said, "Hsieh An is purer than his older brother Hsieh I, and more gracious than Ch'en K'uei."

60. Someone asked Chih Tun, "How does Wang Hu-chih compare with the two Hsiehs (An and Wan)?"

Chih Tun replied, "Unquestionably he would have to climb up to reach An, but he could dangle Wan from his hand."[1]

[1]*Wang Hu-chih PC*: Hu-chih was fond of conversations and explications, and skilled in both writing and speaking, for which he was honored by his own generation.

61. Sun Ch'o and Hsü Hsün were both famous men of their age. Those who honored Hsü for his exalted feelings would correspondingly despise Sun for his corrupt conduct, and those who loved Sun for his literary ability and style would conversely have no use for Hsü.[1] (*CS* 56.16b)

[1]*SMTWCC*: Ch'o was widely read in the Classics and histories, and excelled in literary composition. He and Hsü Hsün both talked in terms of turning their backs on the world, but while Hsün, to the day of his death, never compromised his determination, Ch'o became deeply enmeshed in worldly affairs.

HCYC: Although Sun Ch'o had literary ability, he was dissolute and full of corruption in his conduct, for which his contemporaries despised him. (See SSHY XXVI, 9, 22, and XXVII, 11, below.)

62. Ch'ih Chao characterized Hsieh An as follows: "In an intimate knee-to-knee discussion, even though he's not profoundly penetrating

(ch'e), still the winding thread of his argument finally reaches the point."

Someone[1] remarked, "But Wang Hsi-chih goes directly to the point (i)!"

Ch'ih Ch'ao,[2] hearing of this, said, "No, he can't be said to go directly either. You can just call them companions, that's all."[3]

Hsieh An felt that Ch'ih Ch'ao's statement was apt.

[1] Reading yu, "someone," for yù, "further."

[2] Through a copyist's error, Ch'ih Ch'ao's courtesy name, Chia-pin, is repeated in the text.

[3] SSHY Comm.: In general, the terms "penetrating" (ch'e) and "going directly to the point" (i) signify profound thoroughness. Hsieh was not penetrating, and Wang, also, did not go directly to the point. Hsieh and Wang, in their relation to Truth, were therefore keeping each other company.

63. Yü Ho once said, "As far as orderliness of thinking and harmony of human relations are concerned, I'm ashamed before my cousin, Han Po, and in the matter of the strength and correctness of my determination, I'm ashamed before Wang T'an-chih. But as for any others besides these two, I'm a hundred times better than them all!" (CS 75.34b)

64. Wang Wei-chih despised Chih Tun. His father, Wang Shu, said to him, "Don't imitate your older brother, T'an-chih.[1] Without any question, your older brother is no match for Chih Tun."

[1] An example of the strained relations between Wang T'an-chih and Chih Tun may be found in SSHY XXVI, 21, below.

65. Emperor Chien-wen (Ssu-ma Yü) once asked Sun Ch'o, "How would you characterize Yüan Ch'iao?"

Sun replied, "Those who don't know him don't recognize his ability, and of those who do know him no one has any use for him as a person."[1]

[1] SSHY Comm.: That is, he had ability, but lacked virtue.
(It is difficult to match this characterization of Yüan Ch'iao with Sun's earlier one in No. 36, above.)

66. Ts'ai Hsi[1] once said, "Although Han Po has no bones to hold him up, nevertheless, for all that, he stands up by his skin."[2]

[1] Through a copyist's error, Ts'ai's courtesy name, Tzu-shu, is reversed.

[2] Han was evidently extremely fat and was said by one person to look like a "boned duck." See SSHY XXVI, 28, below.

67. Ch'ih Ch'ao once asked Hsieh An, "How does Chih Tun's conversational ability compare with Hsi K'ang's (d. 262)?"

Hsieh replied, "Only by laborious plodding could Hsi K'ang manage to move."

Ch'ao asked again, "And how does Yin Hao compare with Chih?"

Hsieh replied, "If you're just referring to his possession of a transcendent preeminence, then of course Chih surpasses Yin, but for sheer indefatigable discussion and debate, in an oral encounter Yin would probably get the better of Chih."[1] (KSC 4, Taishō 50.349a)

[1] CTC: The quick release of Chih Tun's divine perceptiveness and the effect of his fame and prestige were spontaneous and transcendent.

(For an example of an exchange between Yin and Chih, see above, SSHY IV, 51.)

68. Yü Ho said, "Lien P'o and Lin Hsiang-ju,[1] though dead for more than a thousand years, trembling with excitement, will always have the breath of life. But Ts'ao Mao-chih and Li Chih, though still alive, tranquil and complacent, are like departed souls beneath the Nine Springs. If everyone were like them, then 'order would prevail by knotting cords.'[2] Only I'm afraid the foxes and wild boars would eat them up!"[3]

[1] See above, SSHY VII, 3, n. 1.
SC (81.1a-4b): Lien P'o (third cent. B.C.) was a good general of Chao (Shansi), and had a reputation for bravery among the feudal lords . . . Lin Hsiang-ju was also a man of Chao. During the reign of King Hui-wen of Chao (r. 298-245 B.C.), the king got possession of the jade of Pien Ho. King Chao of Ch'in (r. 306-251 B.C.) requested to have it in exchange for fifteen walled cities. Chao dispatched Hsiang-ju with the jade, and Ch'in accepted it, but with no intention of handing over the cities. Hsiang-ju asked for the jade in order to point out its flaws, whereupon he took the jade in his hands and stepped back against a pillar. Angrily, with his hair bristling against his cap, he cried, "If Your Majesty insists on harrassing your servant, your servant's head will be smashed together with this jade!" The King of Ch'in apologized to him . . .
Later the King of Ch'in had the King of Chao strum the twenty-five-stringed zither (se), and Hsiang-ju requested the King of Ch'in to pluck the bamboo zither (chu) . . . Because Hsiang-ju's merit was great, Chao appointed him a high minister with rank above that of Lien P'o.

[2] See "Book of Changes," Hsi-tz'u B2 (Wilhelm I, 360): In early antiquity order prevailed by knotting cords. Later generations exchanged the cords for written documents.

[3] SSHY Comm.: If all people were like Ts'ao and Li, then in their simpleminded ignorance and artless innocence everyone under heaven would be free of treacherous folk and they could achieve order by knotting cords. However, ability and wisdom would never be heard of, and all traces of human accomplishment would disappear. People's bodies would be completely devoured by foxes, and they would leave no names to startle the world.

69. Wei Yung was the elder brother of Hsiao Lun's wife. Hsieh An once asked Sun T'eng,[1] "How does your family characterize Wei Yung?"
Sun replied, "We say he's a man of worldy occupation."

Hsieh said, "That's not so at all! Without any question he's a man of principle and morality."

At the time he was compared to Yin Jung.

¹Sun T'eng was Hsiao Lun's grandson on his mother's side; hence Wei Yung was his mother's uncle (*chiu*).

70. Wang Hsien-chih once asked Hsieh An, "How did Chih Tun (d. 366) compare with Yü Liang (d. 340)?"

Hsieh would not accept the comparison at all, replying, "The older generation never used to discuss them, but Yü Liang was undoubtedly capable of overwhelming Chih Tun."¹

¹*YHYH*: At the time, someone praised Yü Liang as a man of principle. Yin Hsien replied, "This gentleman loves to be preeminent. Using the basic and fundamental (for a club) he bludgeons other people."

71. Hsieh Hsüan and the others were all together discussing who was superior and who inferior among the Seven Worthies of the Bamboo Grove.¹ Hsieh An said, "The older generation never used to praise or criticize the Seven Worthies."²

¹For the "Seven Worthies" see above, *SSHY* VIII, 29.

²*WSCC*: Shan T'ao was perceptive and unceremonious as well as virtuous. Hsiang Hsiu, Juan Hsien, Wang Jung, and Liu Ling were transparently free, as well as exceptionally talented. Contemporary conversations ranked Juan at the head, with Wang Jung next to him. Shan T'ao, Hsiang Hsiu, and the rest followed, each in order.

SSHY Comm.: If things were as Sun Sheng says (in the *WSCC*), then it was by no means the case that there was no praise or criticism. This statement (of Hsieh An) is mistaken.

72. Someone compared Wang T'an-chih to Hsieh Hsüan. When Hsieh heard of it, he said, "Digging by slow degrees (*k'uət-k'uət*) he finally made it!"¹

¹*HCYC*: Wang T'an-chih was cultivated and noble with wide knowledge and liberality. His style and manner were lofty and correct.

73. Hsieh An once said to Wang Kung, "Liu T'an is also marvelous in self-knowledge. However, I wouldn't say he surpasses Wang Meng in this."¹

¹Cf. *SSHY* VIII, 109, above.

74. Wang Hui-chih and his two brothers (Ts'ao-chih and Hsien-chih) went together to visit Hsieh An. Hui-chih and Ts'ao-chih talked volubly of worldy matters, but Hsien-chih only remarked about the weather, and nothing more.

After they had gone out, the guests who remained asked Hsieh An, "Of the three worthies who were here just now, which is the best?"

Hsieh replied, "The youngest (Hsien-chih) is the most excellent."

A guest asked, "How did you know it?"

Hsieh replied, "'The words of fortunate men are few; those of excitable men many.'¹ It was by inference from this that I knew it." (*CS* 80.12a)

¹See "Book of Changes," *Hsi-tz'u* B9 (Wilhelm I, 381), and *SSHY* VIII, 83, n. 2, above.

75. Hsieh An asked Wang Hsien-chih, "How would you rate your own calligraphy in comparison with that of your father (Wang Hsi-chih)?"
Hsien-chih replied, "Of course mine isn't the same as his."
Hsien An said, "According to the discussions of outsiders that isn't at all the case."
Wang replied, "How could outsiders know?"[1]

¹*SMTWCC*: Wang Hsien-chih was skilled at writing in the clerical script (*li-shu*), and changed the style of his father, Wang Hsi-chih, into the modern form. The strokes of his characters were outstandingly graceful, utterly surpassing the writing of all his contemporaries. He and his father both achieved fame, but his draft script (*chang-ts'ao*) was loose and weak, not at all the equal of his father's. Someone asked Hsien-chih, "Is your father's calligraphy superior?" Hsien-chih was unable to decide between them.
  Someone then asked Hsi-chih, "According to contemporary discussions, your calligraphy doesn't come up to that of Hsien-chih." Hsi-chih replied, "That's not so at all."
  On another day this person saw Hsien-chih and asked, "How does your father's calligraphy compare with yours?" Hsien-chih did not reply. He asked again, "Those who discuss it say that of course yours isn't as good as his." Hsien-chih, laughing, replied, "How could other people know that?"

76. Wang Kung asked Hsieh An, "How would you rate Chih Tun in comparison with my grandfather, Wang Meng?"
Hsieh An said, "Wang Meng was magnificently flourishing."[1]
"And how would you rate him in comparison with Liu T'an?"
Hsieh replied, "Ah! Liu T'an was outstanding!"
Wang said, "If things are as you say, then he wasn't the equal of either of these two men?"
Hsieh replied, "My meaning is precisely this."

¹Cf. *SSHY* XIV, 29, below.

77. Someone asked Hsieh An, "With which of the former generation might Wang Hsien-chih be compared?"
Hsieh replied, "Hsien-chih comes near to combining the fine points of Wang Meng and Liu T'an."[1]

¹*HCYC*: Wang Hsien-chih's skills in letters and discussion were by no means his strongest points, yet he was able to combine all his superior qualities in such a way as to monopolize a reputation in his day as the crown of all cultivated gentlemen.

78. Hsieh An once said to Wang Kung, "If I were to compare your grandfather, Wang Meng, with Liu T'an, of course (Liu) could measure up to him."
Wang Kung replied, "It wasn't that Liu T'an *couldn't* measure up to my grandfather: he simply *didn't* measure up."[1]

¹*SSHY* Comm.: That is, Wang Meng was natural (*chih*) and Liu T'an cultivated (*wen*).

79. When Yüan Hung became a clerk in the Board of Civil Office, Wang Hsien-chih wrote a letter to Ch'ih Ch'ao in which he said, "Now that Yüan Hung has already entered the court, it should certainly be enough to repress his exuberant airs. He'll surely understand that one who beats and flogs his way is, naturally, hardly a human being. Let's hope that if he retreats a little, he'll improve, that's all."

80. Wang Hui-chih and his younger brother, Hsien-chih, were both praising the men together with their eulogies in (Hsi K'ang's) "Lives of Eminent Gentlemen" (*HKKSC*). Hsien-chih praised Ching Tan's[1] "lofty purity."
  Hui-chih rejoined, "It still wasn't the equal of Ssu-ma Hsiang-ju's[2] 'contempt of the world.'" (*CS* 80.11b)

[1]*HKKSC*: Ching Tan (first cent. A.D.) was a man of wide learning and lofty discourse. In the capital (Lo-yang) there was a saying about him which went,

> "Amid the Five Classics hither and yon
> Sits Ching Ta-ch'un.
> Never yet with letter or card
> Has he called on anyone."

All the Five Princes of the Northern Palace (i.e., the sons of Emperor Kuang-wu, r. 25-57) repeatedly invited him, but none could succeed in getting him to come. The Marquis of Hsin-yang, Yin Chiu (younger brother of Empress Yin), sent someone to demand his presence. Unable to help himself, he went. The marquis set before him some wheat and rice, and some leeks and vegetables, to observe what he would do. Tan pushed them away, saying, "I supposed that princes and lords were able to offer excellent viands, and that's the only reason I came over here. What's the idea of treating me like this?" Whereupon they brought out a sumptuous repast.
  When the marquis rose from the table, his attendants brought forward a palanquin (*nien*). Tan, laughing, said, "I've heard that the ancient tyrants Chieh and Chou rode on human carriages. Is this by any chance what's meant by a human carriage?" The marquis immediately had the palanquin removed.
  The foremost cavalier, Liang Sung (son-in-law of Emperor Kuang-wu), because of his ability, inspired the court with awe. He attempted to be friendly with Tan, but the latter was unwilling to see him. Later Tan fell ill in an epidemic, and Sung himself took a physician to see him. Some time after Tan's illness was cured, Sung lost his eldest son, Lei. Tan went immediately to offer his condolences. At the time guests were crowding the hall. Tan, his fur and coarse woolen coat in tatters, entered the door. Those who were seated there all gazed in awe at the appearance of his face. Tan made long bows with his hands pressed together to those all around him, then went forward to speak with Sung. After the etiquette for guest and host had been completed, he made another long bow and went directly to his seat. No one got a chance to speak with him. Unwilling to play the part of a petty official, he went directly out, and thereafter hid in retirement. His eulogy is as follows.

> Ching Tan, *lofty and pure*,
> Hankered not for fame or rank;

> Held off five princes of the blood,
> Refused their friendship as non-peers;
>
> Openly scoffed at palanquins—
> Attendants lost their haughty airs.
> Coarsely attired, he made long bows,
> Insulting the assembled crowd.

²*HKKSC*: Ssu-ma Hsiang-ju (d. 117 B.C.) was at first an attendant in the service of Emperor Ching (r. 156-141 B.C.). When Prince Hsiao of Liang (Liu Wu) came to court (in Ch'ang-an) in the company of the intinerant adviser, Tsou Yang, and others, Hsiang-ju was delighted with him, and on the pretense of illness resigned from his post and traveled to Liang (Honan). Later, as he passed by Lin-ch'iung (Szechwan), the daughter of the rich man Cho Wang-sun, Wen-chün by name, had recently been widowed, and as she was fond of music, Hsiang-ju wooed her with his zither. Wen-chün eloped with him, and together they returned to his native Ch'eng-tu. Later they came upon hard times and moved back to Lin-ch'iung, where they purchased a wine shop. Wen-chün tended the vats (*lu*) while Hsiang-ju, clad only in short calf-nosed pants (*tu-pi kun*), washed the utensils in the marketplace.

As a person, Hsiang-ju suffered from an impediment in his speech, but he was skilled in literary composition. While he was in public office he did not hanker after eminence or noble rank, but frequently, on the pretense of illness, would fail to participate in the grand events of the lords and nobles, and ended his days quietly at home. His eulogy is as follows:

> Hsiang-ju, *contemptuous of the world*,
> Dispensed with rites, cast off restraint;
> Wore calf-nosed pants in the marketplace,
> Quite unashamed of how he looked.
>
> Feigning illness, he fled his post,
> Despising lords and ministers;
> Instead, composed the *fu*, "Great Man,"
> Transcendently without a peer.

81. Someone asked Yüan K'o-chih, "How would you rate Yin Chung-k'an in comparison with Han Po?"

Yüan replied, "As far as a comparison of their understanding of principles and interpretations is concerned, there's really no distinction between them. However, in the matter of the peace and quiet of their households, even though naturally he possessed the cultivated air of a famous gentleman, Yin was not the equal of Han. That's why, when Yin wrote (Han's) obituary he stated,

> 'His rustic gate by day is closed,
> The idle courtyard is at rest.'"

82. Wang Hsien-chih asked Hsieh An, "How would you rate Ch'ih Ch'ao in comparison with Yü Ho?"

Hsieh replied, "Yü Ho does, to be sure, combine in his person all that is pure and perceptive, but Ch'ih Ch'ao is unquestionably his superior."

83. When Wang Hsün's illness was approaching a crisis (in 401), he asked his cousin, Wang Mi, "In contemporary discussions, with whom do they compare my father, Wang Ch'ia (d. 358)?"

Wang Mi replied, "Contemporaries compare him with Wang T'an-chih (d. 375)."

Hsün turned over and lay facing the wall. With a sigh he said, "People surely have no right to do so simply because he didn't have as many years to live."[1]

[1] *SSHY* Comm.: Wang Ch'ia died in his twenty-sixth year. Wang Hsün's meaning is that his father's reputation and virtue would have surpassed those of Wang T'an-chih, but he did not have as many years (Wang T'an-chih died in his *forty*-sixth year), and only for this reason got the same rating.

(Liu P'an-sui in *SSHY chiao-chien*, quoted by Yang Yung, finds the identification of the text's "Northern Commander Wang" as Wang T'an-chih to be unbelievable, and suggests the less celebrated holder of the same title, Wang Shu*, as more plausible.)

84. Wang Kung characterized Hsieh An as follows: "He's the ultimate of richness."

On another occasion he said, "Wang Meng was empty, Liu T'an outstanding, and Hsieh An perspicuous."

85. Wang Kung asked Hsieh An, "How would you rate Chih Tun in comparison with Wang Hsi-chih?"

Hsieh replied, "Wang Hsi-chih surpassed Chih Tun, but Chih Tun was ahead of Wang Hu-chih, and, in his own right, noble and discerning."[1]

[1] *SSHY* Comm.: He did not say he was the equal of Hsi-chih, but only that he surpassed Hu-chih.

86. When Huan Hsüan became grand marshal (in 402)[1] he called together a large assembly. It was not until the court ministers were fully gathered and settled in their seats that Huan asked Wang Chen-chih, "How do I compare with your seventh uncle, Wang Hsien-chih?"

At the time all the guests gasped in alarm for him, but with calm deliberation Wang replied, "My late uncle was a paradigm of a single age, while Your Excellency is the hero of a thousand years."

The whole company felt relieved. (*CS* 80.12a)

[1] The *SSHY* text reads "grand tutor" (*t'ai-fu*), but since Huan Hsüan never held that office, I have emended to agree with the parallel account in *CS* 80.12a. Hsüan became grand marshal in the spring of 402 (*TCTC* 112.3541).

87. Huan Hsüan asked Liu Chin, "How do I compare with the grand tutor, Hsieh An?"

Liu replied, "Your Excellency is high; the grand tutor is deep."

"How do I compare with your maternal uncle, Wang Hsien-chih?"

"The haw (*cha*) and the pear (*li*), the tangerine (*chü*) and the pomelo (*yu*), each has its own excellence."[1]

[1] Cf. *Chuang-tzu* XIV, 29a (Watson, p. 160): The rites and laws of the Three August Ones and the Five Rulers (sage-kings of mythical antiquity)--are they not like haws and pears, tangerines and

pomelos? Their flavors are mutually opposite, yet all of them are palatable.

88. In the old days people used to compare Huan Ch'ien with Yin Chung-wen. During the reign of Huan Hsüan (404) Chung-wen once entered the court. Huan, gazing at him from the middle of the hall, said to those seated with him, "How could Our family's Huan Ch'ien ever come up to this man?"

CHAPTER X

Admonitions and Warnings

1. Tung-wu Hou-mu, the wet nurse of the Han Emperor Wu (r. 140-87 B.C.), once committed some offense outside the palace, and the emperor was on the point of inflicting a penalty. The wet nurse sought help from Tung-fang Shuo. Shuo told her, "This isn't something to be argued with lips and tongue, but if you really hope to be saved, then when it comes time to leave the emperor's presence, just look back at him a few times, only be careful not to say anything. This might, by one chance in ten thousand, be a way of hope for you."

When the wet nurse had come into the emperor's presence Shuo was also in attendance at his side and took the occasion to say, "You fool! Do you expect the emperor to remember the tenderness of the days you suckled him?"

Now although the emperor was a talented and brave man whose heart was inured to suffering, he was at the same time deeply affectionate. Touched to the quick, he took pity on her and immediately forgave her offense.[1] (SC 126.6b-7a)

[1] SC (126.6b-7a): When Emperor Wu of Han was young, Tung-wu Hou-mu once served as his nurse. Later she was known as the Great Wet Nurse. Her sons and grandsons and the slaves who accompanied them ran amok in Ch'ang-an (the Han capital, Shensi), snatching people's clothing and belongings along the streets. The authorities requested that the wet nurse be banished to the borders, and the emperor gave his consent. The wet nurse came in to bid farewell.

Now one of the emperor's favorite ladies-in-waiting was Mistress Kuo. Whenever she said anything or made excuses, even if it were not always in agreement with the Great Way, she could, nevertheless, make the Lord of men agree with her. So the wet nurse went first to see her, and, falling down before her, wept.

Mistress Kuo said, "Go in right away and say good-bye, but don't leave immediately. Look back several times."

The wet nurse did as she was told, and Mistress Kuo reviled her in a harsh voice, saying, "Shoo, you old hag! Why aren't you moving faster? His Majesty is grown up now. Do you think he still needs a wet nurse to keep him alive? Why do you keep looking back?"

At this point the Lord of men took pity on her and gave the order to stay her exile, punishing those who requested it instead.

2. Ching Fang was once holding a discussion with the Han Emperor Yüan (r. 48-33 B.C.), and in the course of it asked the emperor, "Why did the Chou rulers, Yu (r. 781-771 B.C.) and Li (r. 878-842 B.C.),[1] perish? To what sort of people did they entrust responsibility?"

The emperor replied, "The men they entrusted with responsibility were disloyal."

Fang went on to ask, "Even knowing they were disloyal, they still trusted them. Why?"

The emperor replied, "Every ruler of a perishing state considers his ministers worthy. How could he entrust them with responsibility if he knew they were disloyal?"

Kowtowing, Fang said, "I'm just afraid those who today look back at antiquity are like those of later times who will look back at today."[2] (*HS* 75.7a-8a)

---

[1] Barbarians from the west invaded the Western Chou capital at Hao (Shensi) in 843 B.C., and the following year King Li's subjects removed him and made the Dukes of Chou* and Shao regents in his stead. King Yu was killed by the "Dog Barbarians" (Ch'üan-Jung) in 771 B.C., after seven years of "baneful influence" from the harem favorite, Pao Ssu.

[2] *HS* (75.7a-8b): Once during a banquet Ching Fang asked the emperor, "Why did the Chou rulers, Yu and Li, perish? To what sort of people did they entrust responsibility?"

The emperor replied, "The rulers, for their part, weren't enlightened, and their ministers were glib-tongued and obsequious."

Fang asked, "Did they entrust them with responsibility, knowing they were glib-tongued and obsequious, or did they consider them to be worthy?"

"They considered them worthy."

"In that case, how do we know that they were unworthy?"

"We know it because their times were disorderly and they, the rulers, were in danger."

Fang then said, "This means that when a ruler entrusts the incompetent with responsibility and there is disorder, it's simply the way of nature. Why didn't King Yu and King Li come to their senses and receive the counsels of the worthy long before that? Why, in the end, did they entrust the incompetent with responsibility and so perish?"

At this point the emperor said, "Every ruler of a disorderly and perishing age considers his ministers worthy. If you have them all coming to their senses, how could they get to be rulers of a disorderly and perishing age?"

Fang asked, "Why didn't Duke Huan of Ch'i (r. 685-643 B.C.) and the Second Emperor of Ch'in (r. 209-207 B.C.) take warning from King Yu and King Li, instead of entrusting responsibility to scoundrels like Shu Tiao (seventh cent. B.C.) and Chao Kao (d. 207 B.C.), and having their rule grow daily more disorderly?"

The emperor replied, "Only one who possesses the Way can understand the future by the past."

Fang said, "Since Your Majesty ascended the throne robbers and brigands have gone unchecked, mutilated ex-criminals have thronged the marketplaces, etc., etc. I ask Your Majesty, is the present age orderly or disorderly?"

The emperor replied, "All the same, it's better than those times were."

Fang said, "Those two rulers of the past both felt the same way you do. I'm just afraid those of later times looking back at today will be like those of today looking back at the past."

The emperor asked, "Who are the ones causing disorder today?"

Fang replied, "Those with whom Your Majesty is intimate, with whom you plan affairs within the inner curtains." Pointing, Fang continued, "I mean Shih Hsien and Ch'ung Tsung!"

After that Shih Hsien and the others memorialized the throne, suggesting that it would be appropriate to try Ching Fang out as warden of a commandery away from the capital. So the emperor made Fang grand warden of Tung Commandery (Hopei). Shih Hsien then exposed Fang's private implication in a plot and had him executed in the marketplace.

3. When Ch'en Chi encountered the loss of his father, Ch'en Shih, he wept and wailed with grief and affliction until his body was emaciated and his bones stood out. His mother, feeling sorry for him, surreptitiously covered him with an embroidered coverlet. On a visit of condolence, Kuo T'ai caught sight of it and said to him, "You're the man with the most outstanding ability within the Four Seas; in all the four quarters you're the paragon. How does it happen that during mourning you're covered with an embroidered coverlet? Confucius once asked Tsai Wo, 'Is it comfortable for you to be clothed with embroidery and fed with rice?'[1] *I* wouldn't choose to do so!" So saying, he shook out his clothes and left.

From then on guests stopped coming to visit for a hundred days or more. (*TPYL* 511)

[1]"Analects" XVII, 19: Confucius asked Tsai Wo, "Is it comfortable for you to be clothed with embroidery and fed with rice during the three years of mourning?"
"Quite comfortable."
"If you're comfortable, then go ahead and do it."

4. Sun Hsiu (Emperor Ching of Wu, r. 258-264) loved to shoot pheasants. When their season arrived (i.e., between spring and summer), he would set forth at dawn and return at nightfall. His numerous ministers all remonstrated with him, saying, "They're only small creatures. Why are they worth wasting so much time?"

Hsiu replied, "Even though they're only small creatures, their 'resolute integrity' (*keng-chieh*)[1] surpasses that of men. That's why I love them." (*SKWu* 3.10a)

[1]*I-li* III, 1: Etiquette between gentlemen visiting each other requires that for a gift in winter one use a pheasant . . .
Cheng Hsüan's (127-200) commentary explains: "One chooses the pheasant for its resolute integrity."

HCWC: Sun Hsiu was keenly interested in canonical books and documents, and wanted to read all about the matters discussed in the writings of the "Hundred Schools." He was also rather fond of shooting pheasants, and when spring arrived (*SKWu* 3.10a reads, "the time between spring and summer") he would go forth at dawn and return at nightfall. It was only at this season that he neglected his books.

TLWS: While Sun Hsiu was on the throne he was very conscientious, and there were few untoward incidents. It was only in the matter of shooting pheasants that he could be criticized.

(From the beginning of this anecdote through the end of Chapter XIII the text has been collated with the T'ang manuscript fragment, described above in the Preface. Passages included in the fragment but excised from the Sung text, are inserted in square brackets; other significant differences are noted as they occur.)

5. Sun Hao (last ruler of Wu, r. 264-280) asked Chancellor Lu K'ai, "How many members of your family have served in the court?"

Lu replied, "Two chancellors, five marquises, and over ten generals."

Sun Hao replied, "That's great!"

Lu replied, "When the ruler is worthy and his ministers loyal, this is the greatness of the state, and when the father is kind and his sons filial, this is the greatness of the family. At present the government is corrupt and the people in distress. I live in dread that we shall all be overthrown and perish. How can your servant speak of greatness?"[1] (*TPYL* 470)

[1]*WuL*: At the time the last ruler, Sun Hao, was cruel and tyrannical. Lu K'ai, being proper and honest, reprimanded him severely, but because Lu's family was powerful and great, Hao did not dare execute him.

6. Ho Yen and Teng Yang had Kuan Lu make a hexagram for prognostication, saying to him, "We don't know if our status will reach the Three Ducal Offices or not."

When the hexagram was completed, Lu quoted the ancient interpretations, warning them gravely. Teng Yang said, "This is the usual talk of an old scholar."

But Ho Yen said, "'To know the springs of action--how divine!'[1] This is what the ancients considered difficult. Though distant in friendship--yet still sincere in what one says. This is what men of today consider difficult. Today in one stroke you have satisfied the requirements of both difficulties. This is what is meant by the statement, 'Illustrious virtue is a far-reaching fragrance.'[2] Isn't there a line in the 'Book of Songs' which goes,

>'In my midmost heart I've hid it,
>What day could I forget it'"[3]

(*SKWei* 29.20a)

[1]"Book of Changes," *Hsi-tz'u* B4 (Wilhelm I, 367).

[2]"Book of Documents" IV, 23 (Legge III, 539).

[3]"Songs" No. 228.

Kuan Lu PC (cf. *SKWei* 29.19b-21a, comm.): [When Lu was in his eighth year he was fond of observing the stars to tell people's fortunes, and was therefore frequently consulted. When he became an adult, as one might expect,] he understood the 'Book of Changes' (Chou-i) [and the method of divination by the direction of the wind (feng-chüeh), and by physiognomy (chan-hsiang)]. His reputation spread throughout Hsü Province (northern Anhui and Kiangsu). The governor of Chi Province (Hopei), P'ei Hui [summoned him to fill a vacancy as Literary Erudite. The first time they met they began a "pure conversation" and talked all day. At the second meeting he was transferred to be divisional administrator for Chü-lu Commandery (Hopei). At the third meeting he was transferred to central administrator. At the fourth meeting he was transferred to lieutenant-governor. In the tenth month (of 248)] he was recommended for the hsiu-ts'ai degree. [On the eve of his departure for the capital, Hui] said to him, "The two presidents of the Board of Civil Office, Ho Yen (SKWei 29.19b, comm., citing the same source, reads, "Ting Mi") and Teng Yang, have ability to rule the state, but in the matter of the principles of things they're not well versed. President Ho's divine intelligence is pure and penetrating, almost to the point of splitting the tip of a strand of autumn down. Be wary of him. He himself admits that he doesn't understand the 'nines' (the lines of the hexagrams for which all three tosses of the milfoil are Yang) in the 'Book of Changes' and will certainly consult you about them and compare notes. When you get to Lo-yang you should be well versed in their principles."

Lu replied, "If the 'nines' are all explained according to [Wang Pi's interpretation (i.e., stressing "the Mysterious" rather than Yin and Yang; emending chih-i, "ultimate principle," to Wang-i, after the T'ang text)], then they are not worth troubling one's thoughts over, but if it's a matter of Yin and Yang, I've been well versed in that for a long time."

When Lu arrived in Lo-yang, he was, as predicted, requested by President Ho to discuss the "nines." [When the "nines"] were all clearly understood, Ho said, "Your discussion of Yin and Yang is unmatched in this generation."

At the time President Teng Yang was also present in the company and said, "This gentleman is expert in the 'Book of Changes,' yet from the beginning of his discussion he never mentioned the interpretation of any of the terms in the 'Book of Changes.' Why?"

Lu replied [on the instant], "An expert in the 'Book of Changes' doesn't discuss the 'Book of Changes.'"

President Ho, smiling, praised him, saying, "It's what you might call a case where 'Essential words are never wordy,' eh?" Whereupon he said to Lu, "I hear you're not only expert in discussing the 'Book of Changes,' but in the matter of dividing the milfoil stalks and thinking about the separate lines of the hexagrams, you're also divinely subtle. Would you try making a hexagram, to find out whether or not I'll reach one of the Three Ducal Offices? And another thing: I've had [successive] dreams that thirty or forty blue flies came and gathered on the tip of my nose. When I drove them away, they wouldn't leave. What did it mean?"

Lu said, "The ch'ih-[hsiao] (see above, SSHY II, 94, n. 4) are the basest birds in all the realm, yet when they're in the grove,

'After eating our mulberry fruit,
They soothe us with their lovely cries.'
("Songs," No. 299)

How much greater is my heart than grass and trees? Yet in pouring out my feelings like the sunflower and the bean plant (which turn upward to the sun), how would I dare be less than completely loyal? Please think it over.

"Long ago, when the "Eight Paragons" (*yüan*) and "Eight Victors" (*K'ai*) served the Sage-king Yao, their proclamation of compassion and their kindly affability were the ultimate in goodness and morality. And when the Duke of Chou held the regency for King Ch'eng (1115-1097 B.C.), his waiting for the dawn (i.e., for the king to come of age) was the ultimate in respect and circumspection. It was for this reason that they were able to flood their radiance to the six directions, and that the myriad states were all at peace. After that, they seized the legs of the Tripod (Ting = Hexagram 50) and mounted it on the metal carrying pole (i.e., they brought the kingdom to prosperity), and harmonized the Yin and Yang, and aided the thronging multitudes. This was a case of resting and responding to the way of Treading, or Ritual Conduct (Lü = Hexagram 10). It's not something that can be understood by divination with milfoil stalks. Today Your Lordship's status is more honorable than the Five Sacred Peaks, and your power like thunder and lightning. People flock to your shadow like those who gaze at the clouds (waiting for rain). Over an area of ten thousand miles your reputation has sped in every direction. Yet those who cherish you for your virtue are few, and those who fear you for your awesomeness are many. Almost none are 'careful and reverent' (*iək-iək), or gentlemen of ample felicity.

"Now, about your nose. Nose is Mountain (Ken = Hexagram 52). This is the 'mountain in the middle of the heavens' (*SKWei* 29.19b, comm., cites the "Book of Physiognomy," *HsS*). It's high, but not steep, and thereby continually maintains its honored position' ("Book of Filial Piety" 3). Now blue flies, which are foul and evil creatures, have gathered and alighted on it. The inevitable fate of one whose position is high is to be overthrown, and that of one who despises the powerful is to perish. Though changes and transformations produce each other, push either to its extreme and harm will result. Though empty and full contain each other, if one overflows, the other will run dry. The sage, observing the nature of Yin and Yang, understands the principles underlying survival or perdition. He diminishes his gains, turning them into losses; he holds back his advances, turning them into retreats. For this reason,

if Mountain ☶ is in the middle of Earth ☷,
it's called Modesty (Ch'ien ䷎ = Hexagram 15);
and if Thunder ☳ is above Heaven ☰,
it's called Power of the Great (Ta-chuang ䷡ = Hexagram 34).

Modesty means 'taking from the excessive to make up the deficient.' Power of the Great means 'not treading on any path contrary to correct ritual.'

"It's my humble wish that on the upper level Your Lordship should search out the main idea of the six individual lines (*yao*) of each hexagram as given by King Wen, and on the lower level think over the interpretations of the judgments (*t'uan*) and images (*hsiang*) as given by Confucius. Then the problem of whether or not you'll reach one of the Three Ducal Offices may be solved, and the blue flies driven away."

[President] Teng Yang said, "This is the usual talk of an old scholar."

[Lu] rejoined, "This 'old scholar' (*lao-sheng*) perceives that someone will not live (*pu-sheng*); as for the 'usual talk' (*ch'ang-t'an*), he perceives that someone will not talk (*pu-t'an*)."

MSC: At this time (240-249) Ts'ao Shuang was in control of the government, and those who understood were worried that a crisis would occur. Ho Yen had a weighty reputation and was related by marriage to the Wei imperial house. Although inwardly tormented by anxiety, he nevertheless did not resign from his position. He composed the following five-word poem to express his feelings:

"The wild swans, wing to wing, pass on;
Flying in flocks, they play in heaven's Grand Purity,
Yet ever fearful of the sky-spread net,
They worry lest some sudden woe engulf them.

How can this be compared with gathering by Five Lakes,
Adrift with currents, nibbling floating plants?
Eternal peace pervades their inmost thoughts;
Why should they ever tremble with alarm?"

He composed the poem because he was afraid after hearing what Kuan Lu had said.

(Ho Yen and Teng Yang were executed with other members of Ts'ao Shuang's faction early in 249; see *TCTC* 75.2378.)

7. Since Emperor Wu of Chin (Ssu-ma Yen, r. 265-299) was not fully aware of the feebleness of the crown prince, Ssu-ma Chung, he held tenaciously to his intention of having him carry on the succession. The prominent ministers, for their part, mostly offered up honest counsels against it. The emperor was once at a gathering on the Ling-yün Terrace (on the palace grounds at Lo-yang) when Wei Kuan was in attendance by his side. Wishing somehow to state what was in his heart, Wei took the occasion to kneel before the emperor as though he were drunk, stroking the dais on which he was sitting, and crying, "Alas for this seat!"

The emperor, although aware of what he meant, laughed and said, "Are you drunk?"[1] (*CS* 36.4b-5a)

[1]*CYC*: Earlier, while Emperor Hui (Ssu-ma Chung) was still crown prince, [all the officials at court] said [the crown prince] would be unable to take part personally in the government. Wei Kuan often wished to propose that he be set aside, but so far had not dared to do so. Later, on the occasion of a party, while drunk he knelt before the emperor's dais and said, "Your servant wishes to make a proposal." The emperor said, "What is it you wish to say?" Kuan was on the point of speaking and then stopped, three times in succession. Thereupon, stroking the dais, he cried, "Alas for this

seat!" The emperor's thoughts finally became aware of what he
meant, and therefore, dissimulating, he said, "You're *really* dead
drunk!"

The emperor later ordered all the functionaries of the Eastern
Palace (i.e., the crown prince's entourage) to attend a large
gathering, at which he had the attendants request the president of
the Board of Civil Office to perform some business as a demonstration for the benefit of the crown prince, to have him make a judgment, but the crown prince did not know what to answer. The
prince's consort, Lady Chia, thereupon asked an outsider to answer
for the crown prince, but he started quoting ancient terms and expressions. The clerk, Chang Hung, said to her, "The crown prince
hasn't any education, as His Majesty very well knows. The prince
should simply see a case and judge accordingly, and not quote from
books."

Lady Chia agreed, and Hung prepared a draft and had the crown
prince copy it and present it [to the emperor]. The emperor [read
it and] was very pleased, and showed it to Wei Kuan. After that
Lady Chia's father, Chia Ch'ung, said to her, "That old rascal Wei
Kuan nearly ruined your family!" From this point on Lady Chia was
resentful of Kuan and subsequently had him executed.

8. Wang Yen's wife was the daughter of Kuo Yü. Her natural abilities
were dull and her nature stubborn. Insatiable in her acquisitiveness,
she was also constantly interfering in other people's affairs. Yen
was distressed about it, but was unable to stop her. At the time a
fellow townsman of his, the governor of Yu Province (northern Hopei),
Li Yang,[1] was a great knight-errant (*hsia*) in the capital (Lo-yang),
just like Lou Hu[2] of Han times, and Lady Kuo was afraid of him. Yen
repeatedly warned her, saying, "I'm not the only one who says you may
not do it; Li Yang also says you may not!"

Lady Kuo was slightly restrained by this. (*CS* 43.15a)

[1]*YL*: Li Yang was by nature a knight-errant. [After his appointment
as governor of Yu Province (northern Hopei)], one day in midsummer
he visited several hundred families to say good-bye, and guests
who came to say good-bye to him continuously thronged his gate;
later he died under a low table (? *chi*; the T'ang manuscript reads
fan, "generally," which suggests the text may be corrupt); therefore they feared him. (The last phrase is missing in the T'ang
text.)

[2]*HS* (92.7b-9b): Lou Hu (fl. ca. A.D. 1) studied the classics and
commentaries (or: the "Spring and Autumn Annals" and "Tso-commen-
tary") and gained a large reputation. When his mother died, three
thousand carriages accompanied her funeral procession . . .

9. Wang Yen had always esteemed the Mysterious and Remote (*hsüan-
yüan*), and, being continually vexed by the avarice of his wife, Lady
Kuo, and by her worldly contamination, he never let the word "cash"
(*ch'ien*) pass his lips. Desiring to test him, his wife had a female
slave surround his bed with cash, so that he could not walk past it.
When Yen awoke in the morning and saw the cash obstructing the way,
he called in the slave and said, "Get these objects (*a-che wu*) out of
here!"[1] (*CS* 43.15a)

¹*CYC*: Wang Yen was fond of giving alms. His father occasionally had debtors, and for these Yen would always burn the notes, without ever calculating the interest.

WYCS: Wang Yen sought wealth and honor and achieved wealth and honor. His riches were piled mountain-high, so that he was unable to use them up. What need had he to ask about cash? Yet the world considered his not asking to be "lofty." Were they not after all, deluded?

10. When Wang Ch'eng was in his fourteenth or fifteenth year, he observed that Lady Kuo, the wife of his older brother Wang Yen, was so avaricious that she was going to have a female slave pick up the manure along the road and carry it home suspended from a pole (to be used for fuel). Ch'eng reprimanded her, and moreover told her it was not to be done.

Lady Kuo flew into a violent rage and said to Ch'eng, "Some time ago, when your mother, Lady Jen,¹ was on her deathbed, she put you, little boy, under the care of me, the new bride. She didn't put the new bride under the care of the little boy!" And with that she quickly seized the lapel of his coat and was about to administer a beating.

Ch'eng, exerting all his strength, struggled to get free, and, leaping through the window, ran away. (*CS* 43.17ab)

¹*YCLJM*: Ch'eng's father, Wang I, in his third marriage, took the daughter of the Jen family of Lo-an (Shantung) to wife, who bore him Ch'eng.

11. When Emperor Yüan (Ssu-ma Jui, r. 317-322) crossed the Yangtze River (in 307), he was still fond of drinking. Wang Tao had a long-standing friendship with the emperor and often admonished him with tears about it. The emperor promised him he would quit and ordered pledges of wine for one moistening of the lips (*ch'a*),¹ after which he put an end to his drinking.² (*CS* 6.14a; *TPYL* 387)

¹Emending *t'o*, "spit out," of the T'ang text to the graphically similar *ch'a*, after KI. The Sung and later texts read *han*, "spree."

²*TTCC*: The emperor personally lived a simple and austere life in order to put his temporal duties first. By nature he had always loved wine, and as he was about to cross the Yangtze River, Wang Tao gravely admonished him for it. The emperor thereupon ordered his attendants each to pledge a toast. He drank and then turned his cup upside down, and from that time on never drank again. Because he thus "conquered himself and restored the rites," his officials all attended to their offices, and the work of restoration prospered accordingly.

12. While Hsieh K'un was serving as grand warden of Yü-chang (Kiangsi, in 322), he accompanied the generalissimo, Wang Tun, down the Yangtze River as far as Shih-t'ou (in the latter's assault on Chien-k'ang). Tun said to K'un, "Never again will I be able to do such a glorious and virtuous thing!"

K'un answered, "Why so? Only let it be that from this day forward the 'glorious and virtuous thing' might daily perish and daily depart, that's all!"¹

Tun on another occasion claimed illness and failed to attend the dawn audience. K'un remonstrated with him, "Recently in the matter of Your Excellency's coup d'etat, though you meant it for the greater preservation of the gods of soil and grain, within the Four Seas in reality men's hearts don't yet fully understand your intentions. If you could only have an audience with the Son of Heaven, you'd enable the various ministers to rest more easily, and the hearts of all beings would then be reconciled. You'd then be catering to the people's expectations and complying with the feelings of the masses, and at the same time you'd be fulfilling the rites of humble deference in service to the Lord Above. If you should do this, your merit would equal the 'one rule' (secured by Kuan Chung for Duke Huan of Ch'i),[2] and your reputation would be handed down for a thousand years."

Contemporaries considered this to be a famous remark.[3] (CS 49.20a)

[1] A parody on the "Book of Changes," *Hsi-tz'u* A5 (Wilhelm I, 321-322): The glorious and virtuous great undertaking of the ruler is ultimate! Because it possesses all things in abundance, it is called the great undertaking. Because it is daily renewed, it is called glorious and virtuous.

[2] "Analects" XIV, 17: When Kuan Chung became minister to Duke Huan of Ch'i (r. 685-643 B.C.), he made him hegemon over all the feudal lords and put the realm under one rule.

[3] *CYC*: While Hsieh K'un was grand warden of Yü-chang, Wang Tun was on the point of starting a rebellion and, seeing that K'un had the confidence of his contemporaries, Tun compelled him to accompany him. After he had conquered the capital and was about to return to Wu-ch'ang (Hupei), K'un said to him, "If you fail to go for an audience and pay your respects to the emperor, I'm afraid of the private discussions which will go on in the realm." Tun asked, "Can you guarantee that there would be no incident?"

K'un replied, "Recently I went in to pay my respects and the Lord Above was keeping an empty seat by his side, waiting for a chance to see Your Excellency. All departments of the palace are friendly. You should certainly have no untoward anxieties. If Your Excellency does go in for an audience, I request to accompany you." Tun said, "If I just killed a few hundred fellows like you, what loss would there be to the times?" So saying, he left without having an audience.

13. During the reign of Emperor Yüan (Ssu-ma Jui, r. 317-322), the director of punishments, Chang K'ai, was living in a small marketplace (in Chien-k'ang) and privately built a general-access gate (at the head of his alley).[1] Since he closed the gate early and opened it late, all the commoners living in the area were annoyed over it and went to the provincial headquarters to lodge a complaint. When they failed to get a judgment, they proceeded to beat the drum outside the audience hall which summons magistrates to a hearing, but still their suit remained unsettled. Hearing that the director of works, Ho Hsün, was on his way to the capital and had reached P'o-kang (southeast of Chien-k'ang), a succession of persons went to Ho with their complaints.

Ho said, "I was summoned to serve as a ceremonial official and have no jurisdiction over these matters." All the commoners kowtowed and said, "If Your Lordship will not see to a settlement, then we have no one to whom to complain."

Ho did not say anything at the time, but ordered them to leave for the time being, thinking that if he should see Director Chang he would say something to him about it.

When Chang heard of it, he immediately destroyed the gate and went himself to Fang-shan (southeast of Chien-k'ang) to meet Ho. Ho came out to see him, and, after greeting him, said, "I'm not necessarily concerned with this, but in the matter of the feelings aroused over your gate, I feel sorry about it on your behalf."

Chang, ashamed, apologized, saying, "I had no idea before that the commoners felt this way, or I'd have destroyed the gate long ago!" (CS 68.17b-18a)

[1] According to CS 68.17b, Chang had confiscated the houses on either side of his own in order to enlarge his premises, and had built the gate to keep the whole alley to himself.

14. Ch'ih Chien in later life was fond of conversation. Even when, as was frequently the case, the topic was a subject on which he was not well informed, he was still extremely boastful of his prowess.[1] Later at the dawn audiences, feeling that Chancellor Wang Tao's behavior was mostly contemptible, whenever he saw him he would always confront him with some bitter remonstrance. Wang, for his part, understood his intention and would always divert the conversation to another topic.

On the eve of Ch'ih's return to his command,[2] he made a point of ordering his carriage and going to visit the chancellor. His beard bristling, Ch'ih assumed a stern air. Mounting his seat, he then said that since he was about to take [permanent][3] leave, he had to talk about what he had observed. His mind was full, but his mouth heavy, and his words extraordinarily unfluent.

Wang seized the opportunity right after he spoke to say, "Since we've not made any appointment to meet again, I too would like to state all that's in my heart: namely, I wish you wouldn't talk anymore."

After that Ch'ih glared at him in anger; icy-bosomed, he left without getting to say another word.

[1] CHS: When Ch'ih Chien was young he was fond of study and had read widely [in all books and studies]. Although he never attained a detailed knowledge of the chapters and verses, nevertheless, for the most part he got a general aperçu.

[2] I.e., as governor-general of military affairs in Hsü and Yen provinces (southern Shantung and northern Kiangsu) and governor of Yen Province, with headquarters in Kuang-ling (Kiangsu). The date may have been close to 338, when he was named grand marshal.

[3] Emending *kuai*, "turn aside," to the graphically similar *yung*, "permanent," after the T'ang text.

15. When Chancellor Wang Tao was serving as governor of Yang Province (Kiangsu-Anhui-Chekiang, ca. 318), he sent the divisional administrators for the eight commanderies[1] to their posts. Ku Ho was at the time a humble messenger. When they returned they all had audience at the same time with the governor. Each administrator reported on the

merits and failings of the officials who received salaries of two thousand piculs (i.e., the grand wardens). When it came Ku Ho's turn to report, he alone had nothing to say.

Wang asked, "And what did *you* hear?"

Ku replied, "In Your Excellency's governance it would be better to have the 'net of laws allow to escape fish big enough to swallow a boat.'² Why should you choose to listen to rumors and institute a spotlessly white (*$ts'ăt-ts'ăt$) regime?"³

The chancellor heaved a sigh and praised the excellence of his remark, while all the other administrators "looked upon themselves as deficient."⁴ (CS 83.1b)

¹The eight commanderies of Yang Province were Tan-yang (Kiangsu), Hsüan-ch'eng (Anhui), K'uai-chi, Wu, Wu-hsing, Tung-yang, Lin-hai, and Hsin-an (Chekiang).

²SC 122.1b: At the beginning of Han (206 B.C.) the net of laws allowed to escape fish big enough to swallow a boat, yet the rule of the officials was humane, and they did not become treacherous.

³*$Ts'ăt-ts'ăt$ may also have the double entendre of "petty investigation" from the meaning of *$ts'ăt$ when used alone.

⁴*Chuang-tzu* I, 6b (Watson, p. 32).

16. When Su Chün made his eastward expedition against Shen Ch'ung (in 324),¹ he requested the clerk of the Board of Civil Office, Lu Mai, to accompany him. As they were about to arrive in Wu Commandery (Soochow), Chün secretly ordered his attendants to enter Ch'ang Gate and set fires as a demonstration of his might. Lu Mai, realizing what Chün intended, said to him, "Since Wu has been orderly and peaceful for a long time,² you're sure to have a revolt on your hands. As long as you're building steps toward revolt, you may as well start your fire at my house!"³ Chün accordingly desisted.

¹*CYC*: When Ch'ung was young he was fond of warfare and through flattery entered the service of Wang Tun. When Tun subdued the capital (in 324) he made Ch'ung General of Chariots and Horsemen and governor of Wu Principality. When Emperor Ming went out to punish Wang Tun, Ch'ung led his army to join Wang Han, saying to his wife, "If I don't set up a leopard-tail standard (i.e., make my mark as a warrior), I'll never return." After Tun's death, the court had Su Chün go after Ch'ung. Ch'ung's general, Wu Ju, cut off his head and sent it to the capital.

²Reading *lai-chiu* for *wei-chiu*, after the T'ang text.

³Lu was a resident of Wu.

17. When Lu Wan was appointed director of works (in 340), someone came to see him and asked for a soup-ladle¹ of wine. When he had received it, he then personally got up and poured out a libation on the ground between the central pillars and prayed, saying, "At present, because there is a shortage of talented men, they have used you for a plinth-stone (*chu-shih*) office. I pray you, don't go upsetting other people's pillars and beams!"

Wan laughed and said, "I'll take your good warning to heart!"² (CS 77.4a; TPYL 187)

¹Reading *keng-pei*, with the T'ang text, for the *lectio facilior*, *mei*, "excellent," of the other texts.

²*Lu Wan PC*: At this time Wang Tao (d. 339), Ch'ih Chien (d. 339), and Yü Liang (d. 340) had died one after the other, and those at court and in the provinces were anxious and afraid. Because Lu Wan possessed virtue and prestige, the emperor appointed him director of works. Wan declined and refused to accept it. Finally, [after he was appointed], he sighed and said to his friends and acquaintances, "The fact that they are putting me in one of the Three Ducal Offices means that there's no one in the whole realm to do it." His contemporaries considered this to be an understanding remark. (See *SSHY* II, 38, above.)

18. While Yü I was stationed in Ching Province (Hupei-Hunan, ca. 343), at a large gathering of his official staff he asked his various officers and assistants, "How would it be if I were to become another Emperor Kao of Han (Liu Pang, founder of Han, 206 B.C.) or 'Emperor' Wu of Wei (Ts'ao Ts'ao, actual founder of Wei, A.D. 220)?"¹

No one in the entire company answered except the senior administrator, Chiang Pin, who said, "Far better that Your Excellency did the work of Duke Huan of Ch'i (hegemon between 685 and 643 B.C.) or Duke Wen of Chin (hegemon between 635 and 628 B.C.), than become another Emperor Kao of Han or 'Emperor' Wu of Wei!"

¹*SMTWCC*: How could someone of the reputation of Yü I have been so insane as this! If there ever was such a remark, it is certainly the error of the one who transmitted the report.

19. While Lo Han was serving as an administrator under Huan Wen (in 345),¹ Hsieh Shang became grand warden of Chiang-hsia Commandery, and Lo went on a mission to investigate him.

After Lo arrived, he asked no questions whatsoever about affairs in the commandery, but went directly to visit Hsieh, and returned after spending several days drinking with him.

Huan Wen asked, "What affairs are there to report?"

Lo replied, "I didn't investigate. Tell me, what kind of man would you say Hsieh Shang is?" Huan said, "Shang is a person who is superior to me."

Lo continued, "Would someone who is superior to you do any wrong? That's why I didn't ask a single question."

Huan marveled at his meaning, but did not reprimand him. (*CS* 92.33b-34a)

¹*Lo Han PC*: The governor of Ching Province, Yü Liang, had earlier (in 339) commissioned Lo Han to serve as his divisional administrator, and when Huan Wen came to govern the province (in 345), he was promoted to aide.

20. Wang Hsi-chih was friendly with both Wang Hsiu and Hsü Hsün, but after the two men had died (ca. 358), Hsi-chih's evaluation of them became more critical. K'ung Yen admonished him, saying, "Your Excellency used to go about in the company of Wang Hsiu and Hsü Hsün and you enjoyed their friendship. Now that they've passed away, if you don't exhibit a friendship which is 'respectful at their death,'¹ it won't be accepted by the people." Hsi-chih was very ashamed.

¹"Analects" I, 9: Be respectful of your parents at their death, and continue so for long afterward; and the virtue of the people will be restored to abundance.

21. When Hsieh Wan was defeated at Shou-ch'un (Anhui, in 359),¹ even though he was about to flee for his life, he still demanded his jade-studded stirrups (teng). His older brother Hsieh An, who was in the army, from first to last had never said anything whatever to Wan either of blame or praise. But on that day he made a point of saying, "Right now what need is there to trouble yourself over this?"² (TPYL 764)

¹For Hsieh Wan's defeat, see above, SSHY V, 55, n. 1.

²SSHY Comm.: Before Hsieh Wan's death (ca. 360), Hsieh An had not yet assumed public office but was living in lofty seclusion in the Eastern Mountains (Chekiang). Furthermore, how would he have been willing to enter so easily into the ranks of the army? This account in the Shih-shuo is badly mistaken.

22. Wang Ch'en said to Wang Hsün, "You too, in your own right, are really not bad in discussion. Why on earth should you compete with your younger brother Min?"¹

¹HCYC: Wang Min had outstanding talent, and both he and his older brother Wang Hsün were famous, although Min's reputation came out to the right (i.e., ahead) of Hsün's. For this reason their contemporaries made up a saying about them which went, "It's not that Wang Hsün isn't fine, but with Min for a younger brother, it's hard to be an elder brother."

23. When Yin Chi's illness became critical (in 397), when he looked at a person, he only saw half of his face.¹ His cousin, Yin Chung-k'an, who was "raising arms in Chin-yang,"² went to take his leave of Chi, and with tears falling, enjoined Chi to get over his ailment.
 Chi replied, "My illness will get better by itself. I'm only worried about what *you're* suffering from, that's all."³ (CS 83.16b)

¹One effect of the five-mineral powder, according to Yü Chia-hsi, was temporary impairment of vision; see "Han-shih san k'ao," Yü Chia-hsi lun-hsüeh tsa-chu, Peking, 1963, pp. 181-226.

²I.e., plotting a coup to remove the pernicious influence of Ssu-ma Tao-tzu and his faction at court. Cf. Ch'un-ch'iu, Ting 13 (Kung-yang chuan): Chao Yang of Chin raised arms in Chin-yang (Shansi) to drive away Hsün Yin and Shih Chi-she.

³CATC: When Yin Chung-k'an raised men-at-arms, Yin Chi did not accompany him. Chi felt, moreover, that he himself should remain at his own small post, and that he ought to stick to his job and nothing more. For him the "Chin-yang affair" was not something to get involved in. Every time Chung-k'an put pressure on him, Chi would always answer, "If I were to go forward, I wouldn't dare go with you; and if I were to draw back, I wouldn't dare go against you." Subsequently he died of anxiety.
 (According to Yin Chi's biography in CS 83.16ab--cf. also TCTC 109.3450-3451--Chi, after refusing angrily to participate in the

coup against Ssu-ma Tao-tzu, realized he would not survive the enmity of Chung-k'an and the others, and taking a five-mineral powder, resigned from his post. When Chung-k'an came to offer his sympathies, Chi replied, "My sickness will not involve more than my own death, but *your* sickness will bring about the ruin of our entire family. Take care of yourself and stop worrying about me!")

24. While the monk Shih Hui-yüan was living on Mt. Lu (Kiangsi),[1] even when he became old, he continued his expositions and discussions unabated. If among his disciples there were any who were indolent, Hui-yüan would say, "The evening glow of the mulberry and elm years of life has not much longer to shine. I only pray that the brilliance of the morning sun will grow brighter with the hours." Thereupon, with a sutra in his hand, he would mount to his seat and chant with a clear and ringing voice, his words and facial expression very intense, while the high-ranking disciples would all sit gravely with enhanced respect.

[1] *YCCC*: Lu Su (Chün-hsiao), originally surnamed K'uang, was the son of the King of Tung-yeh, a descendant of the Sage-king Yü of Hsia. At the end of Ch'in (ca. 209 B.C.) the rulers and elders of the Pai-yüeh (in southeast China), together with Wu Jui, came to the aid of Han (i.e., Liu Pang) in pacifying the realm, and the King of Tung-yeh died in battle. In the eighth year of Han (199 B.C.) Su was enfeoffed Baron of Yen-yang (Kiangsi), supported by the taxes of this district, and given the title Lord of [Yüeh]-lu.

Su and his older and younger brothers, seven men in all, were all fond of Taoist techniques, and accordingly lived [cheerfully] on the mountain overlooking Tung-t'ing Lake (Kiangsi). Therefore their contemporaries called it Mt. Lu. In the fifth year of the Yüan-feng era (106 B.C.) Emperor Wu made a tour of the south and sailed on the Yangtze River. He personally saw Su's spirit and enfeoffed him Grand Illustrious Duke (T'ai-ming kung), ordaining sacrifices to him there at each of the four seasons.

LSC: Mt. Lu is located in Chiang Province within Hsün-yang Commandery (Kiangsi). On the east it is surrounded by the P'eng Marshes (P'eng-tse), and on the west borders on the T'ung River (T'ung-ch'uan). There was once a Mister K'uang Su who came out from the borders of the Yin and Chou realms (the Yellow River Valley) to hide from the world and retire from his own age and live in seclusion at its base. Some say K'uang Su received his teaching from a transcendent being (*hsien-jen*) and wandered with him along its ranges, making his home on its cliffs and peaks. The mountain itself became his mansion. Thus contemporaries called it the hut (*lu*) of the divine immortal, and named it accordingly.

YSC: I (Shih Hui-yüan) have committed myself to this mountain for twenty-three years, twice walking through the Stone Gate (Shihmen), four times wandering over the Southern Range (Nan-ling), gazing eastward toward Censer Peak (Hsiang-lu-feng), peering northward toward Nine Rivers (Chiu-chiang). Rumor has it that there is a Stone Well (Shih-ching) and a Square Lake (Fang-hu) in which there are red scaly creatures (*ch'ih-lin*) which leap out. The rustics cannot describe them, but merely sigh in admiration over their wonders and say no more.

25. Huan Hsüan was fond of hunting, and every time he took to the fields his chariots and outriders were extremely numerous. Within the space of fifty or sixty li around, his flags and pennants shaded the swamplands. Charging with fine horses, he galloped and attacked as if he were flying. The twin flanks under his direction avoided neither hills nor valleys, and if any moving column was not closed, and a muntjac (chün) or a hare leaped through to escape, the assistants who were to blame would all be bound and tied up.

Huan Tao-kung was of the same clan as Huan Hsüan, and at the time (ca. 404) was serving as an aide in the Security Office. He was a man of considerable daring and forthright speech, and always girded himself on such occasions with a bright red wool rope attached at the middle of his waist.

Hsüan asked him, "What's this for?" He replied, "When Your Excellency hunts, you're fond of tying up your men and officers. If it should happen that my turn comes to be tied up, my hands can't bear coarse grass rope."

After this Hsüan moderated a little. (IWLC 24; TPYL 832)

26. Wang Hsü and his cousin, Wang Kuo-pao, worked together like lips and teeth, both of them manipulating positions of power and importance.[1] Kuo-pao's younger brother, Wang Ch'en, felt it to be unjust that they should act like this, and finally said to Wang Hsü, "While you're making this blazing fire, have you never given thought to 'the value of a jail warden'?"[2]

[1] CATC: While Wang Hsü was serving as administrator for the Prince of K'uai-chi (Ssu-ma Tao-tzu), by flattery and falsehood he came into his intimate favor [and thus alienated Wang Hsün and Wang Kung from the prince]. Wang Hsün and Wang Kung resented the fact that Kuo-pao and Hsü were subverting the government, and together with Yin Chung-k'an they set a date to rise up simultaneously and purge the court from within. When Kung arrived he beheaded Hsü [in the marketplace] to please the court nobles (397).

[Wang Kuo-pao PC: When Wang Kuo-pao was young, without cultivating the occupations of a gentleman, he made rapid progress in his generation]. The grand tutor, Hsieh An, was Kuo-pao's father-in-law. Hsieh hated him [as a person and always] rejected him without making use of him. [The Prince of Kuai-chi's wife was Kuo-pao's cousin (tsung-mei). Through this circumstance he got to have an early association with the prince and thus alienated An from the prince]. When An died (in 385) and the chancellor-prince was in control of the government, he transferred Kuo-pao [directly to personal attendant and] president of the Central Secretariat, [where he lived avariciously and wantonly and took] concubines by the hundreds.

[He became implicated in an incident and was relieved of his post. Even though Kuo-pao was honored by the chancellor-prince, he was not yet on intimate terms with Emperor Hsiao-wu (r. 373-396). When the emperor reviewed the ten thousand decisions, Kuo-pao presented himself to the emperor, who became extremely fond of him. When suddenly the emperor deceased (in 396), the government was carried on by the chief ministers. Kuo-pao's] cousin, Wang Hsü, had favor with the prince and spoke to him frequently on Kuo-pao's behalf. [The prince, for his part, resented Kuo-pao's goings and comings and never accepted him, but Hsü's pleading gradually carried the day, and Kuo-pao was transferred to be a vice-president, with simultaneous duties in the Board of Civil Office, and capital intendant, with the men-at-arms of the Eastern Palace (i.e., the crown prince's guard) for his bodyguard.

After Kuo-pao had attained his ambition] his power shook all those outside and inside the court. Wang Hsün, Wang Kung, and Yin Chung-k'an all enjoyed the confidence of Emperor Hsiao-wu, and were not intimate with the chancellor-prince. [Kuo-pao was profoundly afraid and resentful of them, while Chung-k'an and Wang Kung, for their part, resented his subversion of the government] and sent up a memorial to have him punished. [Kuo-pao was panic-stricken and, not knowing what to do, sought counsel of Wang Hsün.

Hsün said, "Yin and Wang never competed with you with any profound enmity in the past. It's only a matter of power and advantage, that's all. If you let go of your authority over the military, you'll surely avoid any great disaster." Kuo-pao said, "Wouldn't I become another Ts'ao Shuang?" (Ts'ao was executed in 249, after controlling the Wei court for nine years.) Hsün said, "What kind of talk is this? Have you committed the same crime as Ts'ao Shuang? Or are Yin and Wang the equals of Ssu-ma I?" (Ssu-ma I had ordered Ts'ao's execution.)] Ch'e Yin also urged him in the same vein.

[Kuo-pao became still more panic-stricken and resigned from his post]. Since the Prince of K'uai-chi was unable to resist the men-at-arms of the various court nobles, he accordingly acknowledged his crimes, and Kuo-pao was [arrested and] handed over to the director of punishments and permitted to commit suicide (397).

²*SC* (57.5b-6b): [When the Han chancellor, Chou Po (d. 169 B.C.), took up his post], someone sent up a notification to the emperor (Wen-ti, r. 179-157 B.C.) reporting that the chancellor was about to rebel. Emperor Wen sent him down to the director of punishments [where the officers were somewhat insulting. Po gave the jail warden a thousand pieces of gold, and the warden stated Po's innocence, using Po's son's wife, who was an imperial princess, as witness. The emperor thereupon pardoned Po and restored his noble rank and fief]. After Po had been released, he sighed and said, "I was once in command of an army of a million men, yet how was I to know the value of a jail warden?"

27. Huan Hsüan wanted to make Hsieh An's (d. 385) residence into a barracks. An's grandson, Hsieh Hun, said, "The goodness of the Earl of Shao¹ was such that kindness was even extended to the sweet pear tree (where he had held court). But the virtue of my late grandfather apparently wasn't enough even to preserve his residence of five *mou*." Huan Hsüan, ashamed, gave up his plan. (*CS* 79.11b)

¹The Earl of Shao (Shao-po) was the son by a concubine of King Wen, founder of Chou, and one of a triumvirate with the Duke of Chou during the infancy of King Ch'eng (r. 1115-1079 B.C.). His domain was the land west of the Chou capital (modern Sian). Song No. 16 of the "Book of Songs" states:

> Leafed out and shady is the sweet pear tree;
> Do not deface it, do not fell it,
> Where once the Earl of Shao was living.

HSWC (I, end): Formerly when the Way of Chou was at its height and the Earl of Shao was at court, the authorities requested him to summon the people (to his residence with their problems). The Earl of Shao said, "To burden the common people merely to accommodate one person was not the wish of our First Ruler, King Wen . . ." Whereupon, sitting in the open under a pear tree, he listened to their plaints. [The common people were very happy] . . . The poet, seeing the tree under which the Earl of Shao had rested, praised it in song, etc.

CHAPTER XI

Quick Perception

1. Yang Hsiu once served as Ts'ao Ts'ao's superintendent of records. At the time (208) he was supervising the construction of the gate of the chancellery and was just laying on the round and square rafters (*ts'ui-chüeh*). Ts'ao Ts'ao himself came out to look, and then had someone inscribe the doors with the character *huo*, "alive," and promptly departed.

As soon as Yang saw it he immediately ordered the gate to be torn down. After this was done, he said, "*Huo* in the middle of *men*, 'gate,' is the character *k'uo*, 'huge.' His Highness was evidently displeased that the gate was too large."[1] (*IWLC* 63; *TPYL* 183)

[1] *WSC*: Yang Hsiu once wrote a report on a certain matter. Anticipating that there would inevitably be further instructions back and forth, he had written in advance his replies in several pages. Attaching them in order, he went to Ts'ao's office. There he left orders with the caretaker, saying, "My original report will inevitably call forth instructions back and forth. Just reply to them in this order, that's all."

The wind came up and blew the papers, and the order became confused. Since the caretaker did not make any distinction between them, Hsiu's replies were all inappropriate. Ts'ao Ts'ao became angry and inquired back to the source. Hsiu was embarrassed and frightened, but replied with the facts, and thus what he had reported made a great deal of sense. [Although Ts'ao Ts'ao at first took it amiss], in the end it turned out to be correct. [Hsiu's ability and understanding were all of this sort].

(Passages in square brackets represent portions retained in the T'ang fragment but not carried in the Sung and later texts.)

2. Someone once offered Ts'ao Ts'ao a cup of curds (*lao*) to eat. Ts'ao tasted a little of it, then on the top of the lid wrote the character *ho*, "together," and showed it to the group, but no one in

the group could make out what he meant. When it came Yang Hsiu's turn, he proceded to taste some and said, "His Excellency is asking you *people (jen)* to taste *one (i) mouthful (k'ou)*. What are you waiting for?"[1]

[1] See the Glossary, under *ho*.

3. Ts'ao Ts'ao once passed beneath the memorial stele to the maid Ts'ao O (in K'uai-chi, Chekiang)[1] while Yang Hsiu was accompanying him. On the back of the stele they saw an inscription in eight characters: "*Huang-chüan yu-fu wai-sun chi-chiu*," literally, "Yellow pongee, youthful wife, maternal grandson, ground in a mortar."
Ts'ao Ts'ao asked Hsiu, "Do you understand it?"
He replied, "Yes."
Ts'ao Ts'ao said, "Don't tell me; wait while I think about it." After they had traveled on for thirty *li*, Ts'ao Ts'ao finally said, "I've got it!" He then had Hsiu record separately what he had understood it to mean. Hsiu wrote, "'Yellow pongee' is *colored silk (se-ssu)*, which, combined in one character, is *chüeh*, 'utterly.' 'Youthful wife' is young woman *(shao-nü)*, which, combined in one character, is *miao*, 'wonderful.' 'Maternal grandson' is a *daughter's son (nü-tzu)*, which, combined in one character, is *hao*, 'lovely.' 'Ground in a mortar' is to *suffer hardship (shou-hsin)*, which, combined in one character, is *tz'u*, 'words.'[2] The whole thing thus means: 'Utterly wonderful, lovely words.'"
Ts'ao Ts'ao had also recorded it in the same way that Hsiu had. Sighing, he said, "My ability is thirty *li* slower than yours!"[3] (*PTSC* 102; *TPYL* 93, 432, 589; *SWLC*, pieh 6)

[1] The complete text of the stele (*Ts'ao O pei*), by Han-tan Ch'un (fl. ca. 220), is preserved in *KWY* 19.
  KCTL: The filial daughter, Ts'ao O (d. 108) was a native of Shan-yin (Chekiang). Her father, Ts'ao Hsü (T'ang manuscript: Hsi), was skilled at beating time, singing, and dancing (*b'uâ-sâ) for the delight of the gods. In the second year of the Han Emperor An (r. 107-125), he went out to greet the river god, Lord Wu (i.e., the deified Wu Tzu-hsü, 6th cent. B.C.). As he made his way upstream against the waves, he was engulfed by the waters and drowned, and they could not recover the body. Ts'ao O was in her fourteenth year, and as she wept and longed for Hsü, she threw her father's clothes (*i*, following the T'ang text; the Sung text reads *chao*, "fingernails"; most others, *kua*, "a melon;" but clothing worn in life was normally used to recall a departed spirit) to ascertain the whereabouts of her father's body, saying, "If Father is here, the clothing will sink." Seventeen days thereafter the clothes suddenly sank, whereupon she threw herself into the river and died . . .
  Many years later the prefectural magistrate, Tu Shang (d. 166), in grief and pity for her loyalty, arranged a reburial for her and ordered his protégé, Han-tan Ch'un, to write a stele inscription for her.
  SSHY Comm.: Ts'ao O's stele was located in K'uai-chi Commandery (Chekiang), and neither Ts'ao Ts'ao nor Yang Hsiu had ever been south of the Yangtze River.
  IY: Ts'ai Yung (133-192), escaping from the troubles (of the Yellow Turban Revolt), took refuge in Wu, where he saw an inscrip-

tion which he deemed the work of a poet and not a mere forgery. Thereupon he inscribed eight characters on the side of the stele. Later Ts'ao Ts'ao saw them and was unable to make any sense out of them. When he asked his underlings, none of them understood what they meant either. A woman who was washing clothes by the bank of the Fen River said, "The one in the fourth carriage understands." On investigation, this turned out to be Ni Heng, who by the method of separating and combining parts of characters explained the meaning. Some say this washerwoman was Ts'ao O's ghost.

[2] Cf. *Shuo-wen*: *Tz'u* means "not to accept" (*pu-shou*) . . . When one "suffers hardship" (*shou-hsin*), it is proper to "decline" (*tz'u*) it. (But *tz'u*, meaning "word," is distinguished in *SW* from *tz'u*, "to decline.")

[3] Reading *chüeh* (*kâk/kau*) "aware," as *chiao* (*kâk/kau*), "by comparison," since these were interchangeable in the Six Dynasties (see No. 7, below).

4. While Ts'ao Ts'ao was campaigning against Yüan Shao, he was making an inventory of his armor and found he had an excess of thirty or forty *hu* of bamboo slips, all of them several inches long. Everyone said they were unusable and they were just giving orders to burn and dispose of them, when Ts'ao Ts'ao, [very reluctant to let them go], conceived of a way of using them, thinking they might be made into basket shields (*p'i-tun*), but as yet he had not revealed his intention. He sent a messenger to ask his superintendent of records, Yang Hsiu, what to do.

Yang answered him quick as an echo, in full agreement with Ts'ao's own idea. Everyone acknowledged Yang's discrimination and perceptiveness. (*PTSC* 121; *TPYL* 357, 962; *SLF* 24)

5. Wang Tun was leading his troops toward Chien-k'ang (in 324) and was about to arrive at the Great Pontoon Bridge (Ta-hang).[1] Emperor Ming (Ssu-ma Shao, r. 323-325) came out in person to Chung-t'ang.[2] Wen Ch'iao was serving as capital intendant, and the emperor ordered him to sever the Great Pontoon Bridge, but Ch'iao deliberately did not do so.[3] The emperor, greatly enraged, glared at him with wide eyes, and all his attendants were seized with terror. The emperor later summoned the nobles into his presence. When Ch'iao arrived he made no apology, but merely requested wine and roast meat.

A moment later Wang Tao arrived. With his feet bare, he fell to the ground and apologized, saying, "'The Majesty of Heaven is before his face'[4] and for this reason has made Wen Ch'iao incapable of apology." At this point Wen Ch'iao fell down and apologized, and the emperor finally was at ease. All the nobles joined in praising Wang's critical perceptiveness and his illustrious words.

[1] Spanning the Ch'in-huai River on the north-south axial road about five *li* south of the south central gate of Chien-k'ang.

[2] A military camp immediately outside the south central gate.

[3] *SSHY* Comm.: Both the *CYC* and the *TTCC* state that when Tun was about to arrive, Ch'iao burned the Vermilion Sparrow Bridge (Chu-ch'üeh ch'iao = the Great Pontoon Bridge) to block [the force of] his men-at-arms (so also *CS* 67.4a and *TCTC* 93.2925-6). To say that

he aroused the emperor's ire by *not* cutting the Great Pontoon Bridge is a gross misrepresentation. One text has: "The emperor himself urged Ch'iao to drink, but he would not drink, whereupon the emperor became angry." This gets closer to the facts.

⁴See *Tso-chuan*, Hsi 9 (Legge V, 154), where the Chou king sent a gift of sacrificial meat to Duke Huan of Ch'i (r. 685-643 B.C.) with the order that, because of his special merit, he should accept it without the usual obeisance. Duke Huan replied, "The majesty of Heaven is not a foot or a span from my face. How could I accept this order of the Son of Heaven and not fall down to do obeisance?"

Wang Tao's allusion to the *Tso-chuan* fits better if we assume, with the Commentary, that Wen Ch'iao had merely declined the royal toast.

6. While Ch'ih Yin was stationed at the northern headquarters as General Pacifying the North (in Ching-k'ou, northeast of Chien-k'ang, in 369), Huan Wen resented his occupying such a position of military power.¹ Ch'ih, who in his judgments of affairs was both simpleminded and dull, sent a memorandum to Huan in which he proposed that they join in encouraging the royal house to recover the imperial tombs (of Western Chin in Lo-yang).

Ch'ih's heir, Ch'ih Ch'ao,² had just gone out (of Huan's headquarters in Chien-k'ang), and was traveling along the road, when he heard a messenger (from his father) had arrived. He hastily seized the memorandum, and after he had finished reading it, tore it inch by inch into shreds. Turning around, he went back and wrote another memorandum (in his father's name) in which he stated that because of old age and sickness he could no longer endure the company of men and wished only to beg for a quiet place where he might take care of himself.³

When Huan Wen received the memorandum, he was greatly delighted, and the emperor immediately gave orders to have His Lordship transferred to supervise five commanderies and serve as grand warden of K'uai-chi (Chekiang). (*CS* 67.20b; *TPYL* 595)

¹*NHCC*: The people of Hsü Province (Kiangsu) are for the most part strong and ferocious and famous for their elite soldiers. For this reason Huan Wen always used to say, "In Ching-k'ou the wine is potable, the winnowing fans usable, and the soldiers deployable."

²He was Huan's aide at the time.

³*CYC*: The grand marshal (Huan Wen), about to make a punitive expedition against the Former Yen ruler Mu-jung Wei (r. 360-390), memorialized the throne seeking to compel the General Pacifying the North, Ch'ih Yin, together with Yüan Chen and others to take on the rigorous undertaking. [Yin] because he had [always] been sickly [was unable to endure military service, and himself memorialized the throne] requesting to retire. [The emperor granted his request and] ordered the grand marshal to take over [Yin's] commission, [making Yin General Crowning the Army].

SSHY Comm.: According to *CHS*, when Ch'ih Yin declined to go on this campaign, Huan Wen chided him for not accompanying him, so [I suspect] the *Shih-shuo*, in reporting that Yin was transferred and given K'uai-chi Commandery, is mistaken.

7. While Wang Hsün was serving as superintendent of records for Huan Wen, he used to go out during the spring months with Huan's eldest son, Hsi, and his brothers, riding on horseback into the suburbs. Those of the elegant gentlemen of the day who used to ride out with them moved forward together with their horses abreast. Wang Hsün alone was always in front by thirty or forty paces.¹ No one understood why until Hsi and his brothers, becoming tired, suddenly mounted a carriage and proceeded on wheels.² All (who had previously been abreast of them) thereafter appeared like attendants. It was only Wang Hsün who remained proud and aloof (*i̯ä̀k-i̯ä̀k) [as always] out in front. Such was the quickness of his perception.

¹*Chüeh shu-shih pu*; see above, No. 3, n. 3.

²Reading *hsiang*, "go toward," with the T'ang text, instead of *hui*, "turn back."

CHAPTER XII

Precocious Intelligence

1. Once when a guest was visiting Ch'en Shih overnight, Ch'en had his sons, Chi and Ch'en, cook some rice. The guest was having a discussion with Shih, and while the two boys were tending the fire they both neglected their work to listen on the sly. In the course of cooking they forgot to put in the wicker basket (*p'i*) for steaming, and the rice fell into the midst of the kettle.
   Ch'en Shih asked "That rice you're cooking--why isn't it steaming?"[1]
   Chi and Ch'en, kneeling upright, said, "Sir, you were talking with the guest and we were both listening on the sly, and in cooking we forgot to put in the wicker basket, and now it's all turned into gruel."
   Ch'en Shih said, "Did you understand anything we said?"
   They replied, "We noted it after a fashion." Whereupon the two boys both talked, each taking up the argument where the other left off, and in their telling nothing was omitted or wrong.
   Ch'en Shih said, "In that case just gruel is perfectly all right. Why do we have to have rice?" (*PTSC* 144; *TPYL* 859; *SWLC*, tu 16)

   [1]*Ho pu liu*. The T'ang fragment reads, *ho liu*, "What's holding it up?" *TPYL* 859 and *SWLC*, tu 16 are similar.

2. When Ho Yen was in his seventh year he was as bright and intelligent as a god. Ts'ao Ts'ao admired and loved him, and because Yen lived in the palace,[1] Ts'ao wanted to adopt him as his own son. Yen thereupon drew upon the ground, making a square, and kept himself inside it. When anyone asked the reason, he replied, "This is Mr. Ho's hut."
   As soon as Ts'ao Ts'ao knew of it he immediately sent him back [outside the palace]. (*TPYL* 385)

   [1]*WeiL*: Ho Yen's father died young, and while Ts'ao Ts'ao was serving as director of works he took Yen's mother into his household

297

[and cared for them both]. At the time (ca. 197), Ch'in I-lu's son, A-piao (SKWei 9.24a, comm., has "A-su" = Ch'in Lang) also followed his mother into the palace, and both boys were treated with favor like [Ts'ao's] own sons. [Su's (i.e., A-piao's) nature was conscientious and circumspect, while Yen cared for no man and dressed and ornamented himself like the "crown prince," Ts'ao P'ei. Therefore the "crown prince" especially hated him and never pronounced his name or surname], but always called him "False Son" (Chia-tzu).

[WSCC: Ho Yen's mother, Lady Yin*, was Ts'ao Ts'ao's honored concubine (fu-jen), therefore Yen grew up in the royal palace.]

(Passages in square brackets represent portions retained in the T'ang fragment but not carried in the Sung and later texts.)

3. When the Chin Emperor Ming (Ssu-ma Shao, r. 323-325) was only a few years old,[1] he was sitting on the knees of his father, Emperor Yüan (Ssu-ma Jui, r. 317-322). There was a man present who had come from Ch'ang-an (Shensi). Emperor Yüan was asking him news of Lo-yang (Honan), sobbing all the while and letting his tears flow. Emperor Ming asked, "Why does it make you cry?" Emperor Yüan then told him the whole story of the eastward crossing of the Yangtze River (307-312) and took the occasion to ask Emperor Ming, "In your opinion, how far away is Ch'ang-an compared with the sun?"

He replied, "The sun is farther away. Since I never heard of anyone coming here from the sun, we can know it for certain."

Emperor Yüan marveled at him. The next day he assembled all the ministers for a banquet to report this remark, and once more he asked the same question.

This time Emperor Ming replied, "The sun is nearer." Emperor Yüan turned pale [and asked abruptly], "But why did you change from what you said yesterday?"

He replied, "By just lifting your eyes you can see the sun, but [even if you lift your eyes] you can't see Ch'ang-an."[2] (CS 6.15b; IWLC 16)

[1]Shao was already eight in 307 when his father first crossed the Yangtze.

[2][HL: When Confucius was traveling in the east he observed two small boys arguing over when the sun is farther away and when nearer. One boy claimed it is farther away at midday, and the other claimed it is farther away when it first rises.

The one who claimed it is farther away (the text reads, "nearer") at midday, said, "When the sun first rises it's big as a chariot canopy, while at midday it's only as big as a bowl cover. This is because what's far away is small and what's near is big."

The one who claimed it is farther away when it first rises said, "When the sun (the text reads "moon") first rises, it's chilly and cool, but when it reaches the middle of the sky it's like touching boiling water. Isn't this because what's near is hot and what's far away is cool?"

SSHY Comm.: Is this exchange with Emperor Ming simply the argument of these two boys?]

4. The director of works, Ku Ho, was once engaging in "pure conversation" with other worthies of the time. Chang Hsüan-chih and Ku Fu

were, respectively, his daughter's and his son's sons.[1] Both were in their seventh year.[2] They were playing by the side of the dais, and at the time were listening to the conversation so intently that their spirits and senses seemed not to belong to them. As it grew dark, while they sat beneath the lamp, the two boys rehearsed together the words of "guest" and "host" without any omissions or mistakes.

Moving from his seat, and putting his mouth close to their ears, Ku said, "I never imagined that in our declining clan there would ever again be born such treasures as these!"

[1] Ku Fu's father was Ku Wei; Chang's mother's given name is not known.

[2] Cf. *SSHY* II, 51, above, where Chang is said to have been two years older than Ku.

5. When Han Po was seven or eight years old his family was wretchedly poor, and as it approached the time of great cold (middle or late January) he had only a short jacket which his mother, Lady Yin, had made herself. She had Po hold the ironing pan (*yü-tou*), saying to him, "Put on the jacket for now, and after a while I'll make you a pair of lined trousers."

Po then said, "This is already enough; I don't need the lined trousers." His mother asked the reason, and he replied, "The coals are inside the ironing pan, yet the handle is warm. Now, after putting on the jacket, I should be warm below as well. So I simply don't need anything more, that's all."

His mother marveled at him greatly, realizing that one day he would become an important instrument of state. (*CS* 75.34b)

6. When the Chin Emperor Hsiao-wu (Ssu-ma Yao, r. 373-396) was in his twelfth year,[1] although it was winter, he did not wear lined clothes in the daytime, but merely wore five or six unlined silk gowns one over the other. At night, on the other hand, he wrapped himself in successive layers of quilted coverlets. Hsieh An admonished him, saying, "Your Majesty's sage body should maintain a constant temperature. If in the daytime you are excessively cold and at night excessively warm, I'm afraid this is no suitable technique for preserving your health."

The emperor replied, "In the daytime I move around; at night I'm still."[2] Hsieh An came out sighing in admiration, and remarked, "The reasoning (*li*) of the Exalted One is not inferior to that of the preceding emperor" (his father, Ssu-ma Yü). (*IWLC* 70; *PSLT* 4; *SLF* 5; *TPYL* 708; *HTC* 4)

[1] The T'ang fragment and all the quotations in the T'ang and Sung encyclopedias read "thirteenth or fourteenth year." *SLF* 5 specifying that it was the time of his accession to the throne (A.D. 373). Ssu-ma Yao was born in 362.

[2] Cf. *Lao-tzu* 45: Bustle overcomes cold; stillness overcomes warmth.

7. When Huan Wen died (in 373), his son Hsüan was in his fifth year. At the time when he first removed his mourning clothes,[1] his uncle, Huan Ch'ung, accompanied him as they escorted the old civil and military officers on their way before bidding them farewell. As he did so

he pointed to them and said to Hsüan, "These are all your father's old officers and assistants." The instant he spoke, Hsüan burst into bitter weeping, poignantly moving all who were present.

Huan Ch'ung often eyed his own seat and said, "When Ling-pao (Hsüan's baby name) becomes a man, I should turn this seat over to him." Thus he nurtured and loved him even more than his own sons. (CS 99.1ab)

[1] I.e., with the end of the twenty-fifth month. See "Record of Rites" XXXIX, 1 (Legge, Li Ki II, 391).

CHAPTER XIII

Virile Vigor

1. When Generalissimo Wang Tun was young he used to have the reputation of being a country bumpkin (*t'ien-she*), and his speech also sounded like that of Ch'u. Emperor Wu (Ssu-ma Yen, r. 265-290) once invited the worthies of the time for a gathering and they were discussing artistic matters. Most of those present had some knowledge of the subject; Wang alone was totally uninvolved in the conversation, and his mood and expression were extraordinarily grim. Since he claimed for himself the ability to play the drums and pipes, the emperor [immediately] had someone fetch a drum and offered it to him. Right where he was sitting Wang shook out his sleeves and got up. Lifting the drumsticks he beat furiously with them, and the sound and rhythm were harmonious and rapid. His spirit and energy mounted with virility, as though no other persons were present. The entire company praised his martial vigor. (*CS* 98.14b; *PTSC* 130; *SLF*, hua 11)

2. Wang Tun in his own generation enjoyed a lofty and superior characterization, but he used to be excessively indulgent in matters of sex, and his physique was adversely affected by it. When his companions remonstrated with him, Tun said, "I simply wasn't aware of what was happening. If things are as you say, the solution is very easy."

So saying, he opened the postern gate [of the women's quarters] and drove out all the slave girls and concubines, thirty or forty in all, into the street, letting them go where they would. His contemporaries praised him for this.[1] (*CS* 98.15a)

[1]*TTCC*: Wang Tun's nature was unceremonious and simple, and his mouth never spoke about wealth [or status]. Such was his preservation of superiority!

(Cf. also *CS* 98.14b and Wang Tun's self-characterization in the next item, No. 3. Passages in square brackets represent portions retained in the T'ang fragment but not carried in the Sung and later texts.)

3. Wang Tun characterized himself as follows: "Lofty and transparent, heedless of petty details (*ṣiwo-ṣi̯uet); in his learning he comprehends the 'Tso Commentary.'"[1]

[1] CYC: When Wang Tun was young he was acclaimed to be lofty and forthright, comprehensive and transparent, with perspicacity and judgment.

4. After drinking, Wang Tun would always intone the song (by Ts'ao Ts'ao):[1]

> "The steed grown old, flat in his stall,
> Still wills to run ten thousand li;
> The brave knight in his evening years,
> Stouthearted, never will give up."

With his ju-i baton he would beat time on a spittoon (t'o-hu) until the mouth of the spittoon was completely in shards.[2] (CS 98.5b; PTSC 135, quoting YL)

[1] The full text of this yüeh-fu song, "Monument Mountain" (Chieh-shih shan), sung to the tune of "Marching out of the Hsia Gate" (Pu-ch'u Hsia-men hsing), can be found in the Sung-shu "Monograph on Music" (SS 21.17ab). Wang was singing from the fourth section:

> "The spirit tortoise, though long-lived,
> Still has a time that he must die.
> The leaping serpent, through the mists,
> At last becomes but dust and ashes.
>
> The steed grown old, etc. . . .
>
> Seasons of plenty or of want
> Rest not alone in Heaven's hand.
> Blessings of nurture and content
> May be attained for endless years.
>
> (Refrain)
> Lucky indeed that we have come!
> Oh let us sing to tell our aims!"

[2] The context in CS 98.5b implies that this song and the accompanying spittoon-smashing were expressions of Wang's resentment at not getting a post at court in 320.

5. The Chin Emperor Ming (Ssu-ma Shao, r. 323-325) wanted to build a moated terrace, but his father, Emperor Yüan (Ssu-ma Jui, r. 317-322), would not permit it. Emperor Ming, who was crown prince at the time, was fond of warfare and maintained a number of warriors.[1] These dug out the moat in a single night, so that it was completed by dawn. It is currently known as the Crown Prince's West Moat (T'ai-tzu hsi-ch'ih).[2] (TPYL 67, 98)

[1] Reading hao-wu yang-shih after both the T'ang and Sung texts.

[2] TYC: The West Moat was constructed by Sun Teng* (eldest son of Sun Ch'üan), who died while he was still crown prince.

SSHY Comm.: It [probably] is the same one which in the "History of Wu" (Wu-shih) is called the "West Garden" (Hsi-yüan). [In the intervening time the banks had broken down, and while the Chin emperor (Ming) was in the Eastern Palace as crown prince he had] merely repaired and restored it. [That is why it was commonly known as "the Crown Prince's West Moat"].

6. When Wang Tun was first contemplating a descent of the Yangtze River against the capital (in 321?) in order to reapportion and reconstitute the government, he first dispatched an aide to inform the court and to announce his intentions to the worthies of the time. Tsu T'i, who at the time had not yet taken up his post (as governor of Yü Province) in Shou-ch'un (Anhui),[1] with glaring eyes and stern voice said to the emissary, "You tell A-hei ("Blackie," Tun's baby name), 'How dare you be so insubordinate! Hurry up and make an about-face. If you don't do so on the instant, I'll lead three thousand men-at-arms to spear your feet with long spears and force you back upstream!'"

On hearing this, Wang desisted.

[1] Tsu T'i was appointed governor in the ninth month of 321 and died very soon thereafter, at least six months before Wang Tun's actual descent in the third month of 322; see *TCTC* 91.2889-2900. Before that he had been governor of Hsü Province (northern Kiangsu), stationed at Ching-k'ou, northeast of the capital.

7. Yü I had always had the ambition of recovering the Central Plain (North China). At the time his eldest brother, Yü Liang, was in a position of power and prestige, but as yet none of it had come into I's hands. When his older brother, Yü Ping, became chancellor (in 340), since Ping loathed military campaigns and dreaded disaster, his difference of opinion with Yü I on this score went on for some time. At last (in the fall of 343) he actually set forth. Completely pouring out the strength of Ching and Han (Hupei), and exhausting the total force of its ships and vehicles, he encamped his army at Hsiang-yang (northern Hupei). At a large gathering of his aides and officers he distributed their banners and armor, and as he personally handed out bows and arrows, he said, "Our progress will be as swift as the shooting of these arrows!"

Three times he rose up and repeated this statement, and as the hosts fixed their eyes on him, their martial spirit increased tenfold.[1] (*CS* 73.21a)

[1] *HCCC* (cf. also *CS* 73.17b): Yü I's style and deportment were excellent, and his ability generously admired. When he was young he had grand stratagems of broad scope. After he succeeded his elder brother, Liang (d. 340), in his post (as governor of Ching Province), he had the ambition of restoring order inside and outside the realm, and of sweeping away all evils.

At this time Tu I, Yin Hao, and others had flourishing reputations crowning the age, but Yü I never held them in the slightest honor. He often said, "These fellows should be kept on a high shelf until the realm is purged and settled, and only after that should we deliberate about how they should be employed." Such were his thoughts and mood. It was only with Huan Wen that he maintained friendly relations, and the two made a compact with each other that between them they would pacify the affairs of the whole world.

In the beginning Yü I set out on his own with the slaves (*nu*) under his command, together with chariots [oxen, donkeys,] and horses numbering in the ten thousands. He led a large army into Mien (northern Hupei), from which he planned to launch an attack against the Ti barbarians (i.e., Later Chao, 319-352), and accordingly encamped at Hsiang-yang.

Yü I PC: While Yü I was governor of Ching Province he always had great ambitions, and often remarked, "My family and status are awesome and honorable, and my older and younger brothers have all been generously favored. If I should not display my strength or put forth utter sincerity, how could I ever requite the state? Although Shu (i.e., Ch'eng-Han in Szechwan, 302-347) is protected by precipitous passes, and the Hu barbarians (i.e., Later Chao) are relying on brute strength, they are both lacking in moral principles, and are oppressive and cruel. We could easily take this opportunity to destroy them. At a time like this anyone who is unable to sweep away the two rebels and restore the Chin royal sway is no man!"

So saying, he issued a call to arms in three provinces, and completely exhausting the wealth of their treasuries, formed a host of 50,000, composed of a vast horde of raw recruits and trained soldiers, and led them directly toward Wei and Chao (Honan and Shansi). His army encamped at Hsiang-yang and its splendor dazzled the whole area north of the Han River.

8. After Huan Wen had pacified Shu (in 347), he gathered his aides and officers and set wine before them in the palace of Li Shih (the last ruler of Shu). All the local gentry of Pa and Shu (Szechwan) came in droves. Huan had always had a martial disposition and vigorous air, and moreover on this particular day his voice and intonation rang out heroically as he told how from antiquity to the present "success or failure have proceeded from men,"[1] and survival or perdition are bound up with human ability. His manner was rugged and flint-like (*luâi-lâk*) and the whole company sighed [uninterruptedly] in appreciation.

After the meeting dispersed everyone was still savoring its flavor with continued conversation. At the time Chou Fu of Hsün-yang (Anhui) said, "What a pity you fellows never saw the generalissimo, Wang Tun (d. 324)." [Fu had once served as Tun's aide.]

[1]See *SSHY* II, 69, above, and *Tso-chuan*, Hsi 16 (Legge V, 171).

9. Huan Wen was once reading (Huang-fu Mi's) "Lives of Eminent Gentlemen" (*HFMKSC*). When he came to the life of Ch'en Chung-tzu,[1] he threw the book away, saying, "Who could be so petty and perverse (*k'iei-k'ək*) as to live by himself?"

[1]*HFMKSC*: Ch'en Chung-tzu (fourth cent. B.C.) was a native of Ch'i (Shantung). His elder brother, Tai, was minister of Ch'i and lived on a salary of ten thousand *chung* of grain. Chung-tzu considered his elder brother's salary immoral, and accordingly fled to Ch'u (Hupei-Hunan) and lived at Wu-ling. [He said of himself, "Chung-tzu of Wu-ling, poor though he is, will never ask for immorally gotten food."]

Once he had gone without food for three days (and had lost both hearing and sight). Crawling on his belly, he managed to eat the

fruit of a plum tree growing by the well, and after three swallows
he could see again. He himself wove sandals and had his wife spin
hemp, so they might trade them for clothing and food.
   Once he returned to Ch'i to visit his mother, and someone presented his elder brother with a live goose. Chung-tzu knitted his
brows and asked, "What will you use this cackle-cackle (*ngiek-
ngiek) for?" Later his mother killed the goose, and Chung-tzu,
without realizing what he was doing, ate it. When his elder brother came in from outside, he asked, "Is this the flesh of that
cackle-cackle?" Chung-tzu immediately went outdoors, and gagging,
vomited it all up.
   The King of Ch'u, hearing of Chung-tzu's reputation, invited
him to serve as his minister, whereupon both husband and wife ran
away and lived by watering somebody's garden. [To the end of his
life he never compromised his integrity.]
   (The story of Chung-tzu appeared earlier in *Mencius* VI, 10;
Legge II, 284-287. Mencius, too, had only contempt for his pathological scruples and ended by observing, "Someone like Chung-tzu
would have to be an earthworm before he could really fulfill his
principles.")

10. Huan Shih-ch'ien was the eldest son by a concubine of the director of works, Huan Huo. His baby name was Chen-o, Suppressor of Evil.
In his seventeenth or eighteenth year,[1] before he had been recommended, the serving boys and slaves were already calling him Master
Chen-o (Chen-o lang). Since he used to live in Huan Wen's villa, he
accompanied Wen on his expedition (against Former Yen) at Fang-t'ou
(Honan, in 369). When his uncle, the General of Chariots and Horsemen, Huan Ch'ung, disappeared from the ranks, no one among those
present was able to volunteer to rescue him. Huan Wen said to Shih-
ch'ien, "Your uncle has fallen into the hands of the rebels. Did you
know it?"
   When Shih-ch'ien heard this, his martial spirit was aroused to the
highest pitch. Ordering Chu Pi to assist him, he whipped his horse
forward into the midst of a host of thirty or forty thousand, none of
whom resisted him. Riding directly in to where Ch'ung was, he brought
him back to safety. The three armies all praised him and conceded his
superiority.
   After that, in the area north of the Yellow River, people used his
name as a charm to stop malaria (nüeh).[2] (*CS* 74.5ab; *TPYL* 279)

[1] The T'ang fragment reads, "eighteenth or nineteenth."

[2] Both the quotation in *TPYL* 279 and the parallel account in *CS*
74.5ab supply the missing background. The latter records: "At the
time, to any who were suffering from malaria they would shout,
'Huan Shih-ch'ien is coming!' to frighten (the malarial demon),
and in most cases the afflicted person would recover, so much was
he feared."
   A similar case is recorded in *NS* 46.4b, involving Huan K'ang
(d. 483): "In all the villages through which Huan passed he indulged in acts of violence and destruction, so that people in
Chiang-nan (southern Kiangsu and Chekiang) were all afraid of him
and used his name to frighten little children (and make them behave). They would draw his picture in the temples, and those suffering from malaria would draw his picture and paste it on the

306   TALES OF THE WORLD

wall by their bed and in every case would be cured." The malarial demon was thought to be mean and cowardly, and hence afraid of heroic men; see above, SSHY II, 27.

11. While Ch'en K'uei was living on the western bank of the Yangtze,¹ all the people in the capital (Chien-k'ang) wanted to go to Niu-chu (across the river) to meet him. Since Ch'en's reasoning was excellent, people wanted to converse and match wits with him. But Ch'en would prop up his cheek with his *ju-i* baton and gaze toward Chicken-cage Mountain (Chi-lung shan, southeast of Chien-k'ang), and remark with a sigh, "Sun Ts'e's (d. 200) ambition and work are not being fulfilled."²

And thus no one in the entire company would get to converse with him.

¹*CYC*: Ch'en K'uei was Commandant of the West and at the same time grand warden of Huai-nan Commandery, stationed at Li-yang (northern Anhui).

²I.e., you people are coming north across the Yangtze in spite of Sun's last wish.

WL: (After Sun Ts'e had killed Hsü Kung) he was shot by one of Kung's retainers and wounded in the face. Holding up a mirror, Ts'e looked at himself and said to his attendants, "With a face like this how can I any longer establish my merit?" Whereupon he said to Chang Chao, "The Central States are at this moment in rebellion. Now with the hosts of Wu and Yüeh (Kiangsu and Chekiang) and the natural fastness of the Three Rivers (the Sung, the Tung, and the Lou, all flowing into Lake T'ai) we are in an adequate position to observe whether we will succeed or fail. You and the others take good care of my younger brother (Sun Ch'üan)."

So saying, he summoned Ch'üan and gave him the seal and ribbon, saying, "In matters like raising up the hosts of the land east of the Yangtze River or deciding the issue between two lines of battle, you're no match for me. But when it comes to putting responsibility on the worthy and employing the capable, so that each devotes his whole heart to his work, I'm no match for you. Be careful you don't go north across the Yangtze River!" When he had finished speaking, he died. He was only in his twenty-sixth year.

12. Once while Wang Hu-chih was among the company at Hsieh An's house, he chanted the lines (from the *Ch'u-tz'u*):

> "Coming he did not speak,
> And leaving took no leave.
> But mounting the whirlwind,
> Bore cloud banners aloft."¹

He remarked to the others, "When I come to that moment I feel as if there is no one else present in the room."

¹*Ch'u-tz'u* II, 6 (*Chiu-ko, Shao Ssu-ming*; Hawkes, *Songs of the South*, Oxford, 1959, p. 41).

13. When Huan Hsüan was descending the Yangtze River from the west (in 402) and had entered Shih-t'ou (west of Chien-k'ang), it was reported to him from the outside that the Prince of Liang, Ssu-ma

Chen-chih, had fled in revolt.¹ At the time Hsüan's mission had already been accomplished, and standing on the turret of his ship (p'ing-ch'eng), while bugles and drums started to play simultaneously, he kept chanting in a high voice (the lines of Juan Chi's poem):

> "Of flutes and pipes an echo still remains;
> The King of Liang, alas, oh where is he?"²

¹*CHS*: At first when Huan Hsüan usurped the throne, a certain person in the state named K'ung P'u, taking with him the Prince of Liang, Ssu-ma Chen-chih, fled to Shou-yang (emending "Hsün" to "Shou" after the T'ang fragment and *CS* 64.9a). After the loyalist banner had been restored (in 404) the prince returned to court and reached office as high as grand ordinary. Later (in 420) because of an offense he was executed by Liu Yü*.

²The lines are from one of Juan Chi's (210-263) numerous pieces entitled "Singing my Bosom Thoughts" (*Yung-huai shih*; see Ting Fu-pao, *Ch'üan san-kuo shih*, chap. 5, p. 219):

> By carriage we set out from the Wei capital (Ta-liang),
> And head southward, gazing toward the Piper's Terrace.
> Of flutes and pipes an echo still remains;
> The King of Liang, alas, oh where is he?
>
> The warriors eat husks and chaff,
> While worthies live amid the barren weeds.
> The strains of song and dance have not yet died away;
> Ch'in's men-at-arms already have arrived.
>
> The surrounding forests are no longer ours;
> Vermilion halls breed dust and grime.
> The army met defeat beneath Hua-yang,
> Their bodies now reduced to dust and ashes.

The allusions in Juan Chi's original poem to the "King of Liang" and the "Piper's Terrace" (Ch'ui-t'ai), which he had built near the Wei capital in Ta-liang (modern K'ai-feng), are to King Hui of Liang (r. 370-319 B.C.), made famous in the first chapter of *Mencius*. "The strains of song and dance" may refer to the festive meeting with the feudal lords recorded in *Chan-kuo ts'e* XXIII, Wei 2.17, concerning the "King of Liang, Wei Ying" (the personal name of King Hui). The "defeat beneath Hua-yang" (in Honan) by the Ch'in armies occurred later, in 273 B.C. (see *TCTC* 4.148). Huan Hsüan's use of the poem to celebrate the "fall" of Eastern Chin, and the flight of the Prince of Liang (also "Liang-wang"), was somewhat forced, to say the least.

CHAPTER XIV

Appearance and Behavior

1. When Ts'ao Ts'ao[1] was about to give audience to a Hsiung-nu envoy, since he himself felt that his own figure was insignificant and inadequate to impress a distant state with its virility, he had Ts'ui Yen[2] substitute for him on the throne, while Ts'ao himself, gripping his sword, stood at the head of the dais.

When the audience was ended he ordered a spy to ask the envoy, "What was the Prince of Wei like?"

The Hsiung-nu envoy replied, "The Prince of Wei was refined and prepossessing to an extraordinary degree. But the man at the head of the dais who was gripping his sword--this was the heroic and virile one."

When Ts'ao Ts'ao heard this, he had someone overtake and kill this envoy. (TPYL 389)

[1] WSCC: Ts'ao Ts'ao's physical appearance was short and small, but his spirit and intelligence shone forth heroically.

[2] WC: Ts'ui Yen's voice and appearance were lofty and vital. His eyes and brows were set far apart and transparent; his beard was four feet long. He was abundantly endowed with awesomeness and gravity.

2. Ho Yen was handsome in appearance and demeanor, and his face was extremely white. Emperor Wen of Wei (Ts'ao P'ei, r. 220-226)[1] suspected that he used powder. At the peak of the summer months he offered him some hot soup and dumplings (t'ang-ping). After Ho had eaten it he broke into a profuse sweat and with his scarlet robe[2] was wiping his face, but his complexion became whiter than ever.[3] (CHC 10, quoting WeiL; PTSC 128, 135; TPYL 21, 154, 379, 860, quoting YL)

[1] Emending the Sung text's "Emperor Ming" (Ts'ao Jui, r. 227-239) to "Emperor Wen," after WeiL and YL, since the latter would be chronologically more plausible.

²Scarlet clothes were traditionally worn by both emperor and courtiers during the first month of summer (the fourth lunar month). See "Record of Rites" VI, 36; Legge, *Li Ki* I, 269.

³*WeiL*: Ho Yen was by nature egocentric, and whether active or at rest was never without a powder puff in his hand. When he walked anywhere he looked back at his own shadow.
SSHY Comm.: According to this account, Ho Yen's seductive beauty was basically dependent on external ornament. Moreover, Yen had been reared within the palace and grew up with the emperor. Why, under those circumstances, would the emperor still have suspicions about his physical appearance and have to put him to the test before being sure?

3. Emperor Ming of Wei (Ts'ao Jui, r. 227-239) had the empress's younger brother, Mao Tseng, and Hsia-hou Hsüan sit together. Contemporaries referred to them as "bullrushes (*chien-chia* = Mao Tseng) growing beside a jade tree (Hsia-hou Hsüan)."[1] (*TYCT* 14; *IWLC* 22; *TPYL* 393)

[1]*WC*: Whenever Imperial Attendant Hsia-hou Hsüan sat together with Mao Tseng, Hsüan was extremely mortified over it, while Tseng's pleasure showed in his face. Emperor Ming resented this and had Hsüan demoted to be commander of the Plumed Forest Guards.

4. Contemporaries characterized Hsia-hou Hsüan as follows: "Transparently luminous (*lâng-lâng*) as though the sun and moon had entered his breast."
Li Feng[1] they characterized as: "Crumbling in ruins (*d'uâi-d'âng*), like a jade mountain about to collapse." (*IWLC* 22)

[1]*WeiL*: Emperor Ming had captured a man of Wu who had given himself up, and asked him, "In Chiang-tung (Kiangsu and Chekiang) what famous gentlemen have they heard of in the Central States?" The man responded with, "Li An-kuo." At this time Li Feng was a palace attendant and had changed his name to Li Hsüan.
The emperor asked, "And who is An-kuo?" The lords and ministers in attendance all immediately responded, "Li Feng." The emperor said, "Has Li Feng's reputation even reached as far as Wu and Yüeh?"

5. Hsi K'ang's body was seven feet, eight inches tall, and his manner and appearance conspicuously outstanding. Some who saw him sighed, saying, "Serene and sedate (*sieu-sieu siuk-siuk*), fresh and transparent (*sjang-lâng*), pure and exalted!" Others would say, "Soughing (*siuk-siuk*) like the wind beneath the pines, high and gently blowing."
Shan T'ao said, "As a person Hsi K'ang is majestically towering (*ngâm-ngâm*), like a solitary pine tree standing alone. But when he's drunk he leans crazily (*kuâi-ngâ*) like a jade mountain about to collapse."[1] (*MCYC*, shang; *TPYL* 389, 497)

[1]*Hsi K'ang PC*: K'ang was seven feet, eight inches tall, with an imposing facial expression. He treated his bodily frame like so much earth or wood (cf. No. 13, below) and never added any adornment or polish, yet had the grace of a dragon and the beauty of a phoenix, together with a natural simplicity and spontaneity (*tzu-*

jan). Just as he was, in the midst of a crowd of other figures, one would know unmistakably that he was a man of no ordinary capacity.

6. P'ei K'ai characterized Wang Jung[1] as follows: "His eyes flash (*lân-lân) like lightning beneath a cliff."

[1]*SSHY* Comm.: Wang Jung was short and small in stature, but his eyes were very clear and bright, and he could stare at the sun without being blinded.

7. P'an Yüeh had an extraordinarily handsome appearance and an attractive personality. When he was young he used to carry a crossbow and go out on the streets of Lo-yang, and all the women who met him would join hands to encircle him.

Tso Ssu, on the other hand, was extremely ugly.[1] He too walked about imitating Yüeh, whereupon a bevy of old crones joined in a line and spit at random at him. Ducking his head he hastened home.[2] (*CS* 55.17a; *TPYL* 755)

[1]*HWCC*: Tso Ssu's appearance was ugly and sickly, and he had no use for fine manners or ornaments.

[2]*YL*: P'an Yüeh's appearance was extremely handsome, and whenever he went abroad old crones would pelt him with fruit until they filled his carriage. Chang Tsai (d. ca. 304), on the other hand, was extremely ugly, and whenever *he* went abroad little boys would pelt him with tiles and rocks until they, too, filled his carriage.

SSHY Comm.: The two accounts disagree.

8. Wang Yen's face and appearance were symmetrical and beautiful, and he was subtle in conversing on the Mysterious (*hsüan*). He constantly gripped a sambar-tail chowry (*chu-wei*) with a white jade handle which was completely indistinguishable from his hand.

9. P'an Yüeh and Hsia-hou Chan both had handsome faces and enjoyed going about together. Contemporaries called them the "linked jade disks" (*lien-pi*).[1] (*CS* 55.1a)

[1]*PWKS*: Yüeh and Chan were sworn brothers and consequently liked to wander about together.

10. P'ei K'ai possessed outstanding beauty. One day unexpectedly he became ill. When his condition became critical (in 291) Emperor Hui (Ssu-ma Chung, r. 290-306) sent Wang Yen to visit him. At the time P'ei was lying with his face to the wall, but when he heard that Wang had arrived, having been sent by the emperor, with an effort he turned to look at him.

After Wang had come out, he said to the others, "His twin pupils flashed (*sĭɒm-sĭɒm*) like lightning beneath a cliff, and his energetic spirit moved vigorously. Within his body, of course, there's a slight indisposition."[1] (*TPYL* 366; *HTC* 4)

[1]*MSC* (cf. *CS* 35.16a): When P'ei K'ai's illness became critical, the emperor summoned and dispatched the palace attendant, Wang Yen, to visit him. K'ai turned his pupils to gaze at Yen and said,

"Have we never been acquainted?" After Yen had returned, he too sighed in admiration over the vigor of his spirit.

11. Someone once said to Wang Jung, "Hsi Shao stands out prominently like a wild crane in a flock of chickens."
Wang replied, "You never saw his father, Hsi K'ang, that's all."

12. P'ei K'ai possessed outstanding beauty and manners. Even after removing his official cap, with coarse clothing and undressed hair, he was always attractive. Contemporaries felt him to be a man of jade. One who saw him remarked, "Looking at P'ei K'ai is like walking on top of a jade mountain with the light reflected back at you." (CS 35.14a; TPYL 389)

13. Liu Ling's body was but six feet tall, and his appearance extremely homely and dissipated, yet detached and carefree (*i̯əu-i̯əu χuət-χuət), he treated his bodily frame like so much earth or wood.[1]

[1]Liu Ling's physical appearance was homely and mean, and his body only six feet tall. However, he indulged his fancy and let himself go. Carefree among others, he alone was in good spirits, the most self-possessed man of the entire age. He always considered the universe too confining.

14. The General of Spirited Cavalry, Wang Chi, was Wei Chieh's maternal uncle. Distinguished and forthright, he possessed an urbane charm. But whenever he saw Chieh he would always say with a sigh, "With such pearls and jade at my side I'm made aware of the foulness of my own body."[1] (CS 36.13a)

[1]Wei Chieh PC (Cf. CS 36.13ab): The General of Spirited Cavalry, Wang Chi, was once on an excursion with Chieh, and (the next day) said to the others, "Yesterday as I was sitting together with my nephew, it was as if a luminous pearl were at my side brilliantly shining on me."

15. Someone went to visit Grand Marshal Wang Yen. He happened to arrive when Wang Tun, Wang Jung, and Wang Tao were also present. Passing into another room, he saw Wang Yen's younger brothers, Wang Yü and Wang Ch'eng. Returning, he said to the others, "On today's trip wherever I cast my eyes I saw tinkling and dazzling (*li̯əm-lâng) pearls and jade."[1] (SWLC, hsin 3)

[1]Lin-lang chu-yü. All four characters contain the classifier for "jade" (yü), which is written as wang, the surname of each of the persons seen. Matching this graphic pun is the phonological one contained in the alliterative binome *li̯əm-lâng, which is onomatopoeia for the tinkling of gems.

16. When Chancellor Wang Tao saw Wei Chieh, he remarked, "You actually do have a frail body, just as they say. Even though you are affable and cheerful all day long, still it's 'as if you couldn't bear the weight of silken gauze.'"[1] (TPYL 386)

[1]Wei Chieh PC: Chieh had from childhood suffered from an emaciating illness.

(See Chang Heng's "Poetic Essay on the Western Capital," *Hsi-ching fu*, WH 2.24a:

> "At first the dancers entered languidly with
>   frail bodies,
> As if unable to bear the weight of silken gauze.")

17. Generalissimo Wang Tun said in praise of the grand marshal, Wang Yen, "When he's in a crowd of other men, he's like pearl or jade in the midst of tiles and stones." (*LSTC*; *IWLC* 22)

18. Yü Ai's height was not a full seven feet, yet the girdle at his waist measured ten double spans (*wei*). As if falling in ruins, he let himself go. (*CS* 50.7a)

19. When Wei Chieh was going down (in 312) to the capital (Chien-yeh)[1] from Yü-chang (Kiangsi), people had long since heard of his reputation, and onlookers were lined up along the road like a wall. Chieh had previously suffered from an emaciating illness and his body could not endure exertion. As a consequence he became sick and died, and his contemporaries claimed people had "stared Wei Chieh to death."[2] (*CS* 36.14ab; *TPYL* 739, 741)

[1] Omitting *chih*, "arrived," after *TPYL* 739 and 741.

[2] *Wei Chieh PC* (cf. *CS* 36.14a): In a crowd Wei Chieh truly possessed the regard due to an exceptional man. When he was still a young boy he was once riding a cart drawn by a white goat into the city of Lo-yang. Everyone in the marketplace asked, "Whose family's jade person is that?" Thereafter among the members of his family and associates in the province he was known as the "Jade Man."

SSHY Comm.: The *YCLJM* states: "Chieh arrived in Yü-chang on the sixth day of the fifth month of the sixth year of the Yung-chia era (June 26, 312). On the twentieth day of the sixth month (August 8) of the same year he died." This means that Chieh's stay in Yü-chang lasted only forty-five days. How could he have had time to go to the Lower Capital (*hsia-tu*) to die? Moreover, all accounts agree that Chieh died in Yü-chang, not in the Lower Capital.

(By omitting the word *chih*, "arrived," see above, n.1, it becomes unnecessary to assume he arrived in Chien-yeh.)

20. Chou I characterized Huan I as a "crag-crested, rock-strewn (*$\ast k\underset{\sim}{i}$əm-k'jię liek-lâk*), laughable man."
Some attribute the remark to Hsieh K'un. (*CS* 74.1a)

21. Chou I said of Wang Meng's father, Wang Na, "Aside from the fact that his physical appearance is imposing, within his genteel breast there's a personal magnetism (*kai*). If he were to preserve and use it, he could do all sorts of things."

22. When Tsu Yüeh saw Wei Yung, he remarked, "This man has the form of the base of a yak-tail standard (*mao*)."

23. Because of the Shih-t'ou incident[1] (in 328) the court had been thrown into a panic. Wen Ch'iao and Yü Liang took refuge with T'ao K'an and appealed for help. T'ao said to Wen, "When Emperor Ming

(Ssu-ma Shao, r. 323-325) made his last command, I was not included. Moreover, the blame for Su Chün's having started a revolt can be traced to the Yü family. If the Yü brothers (Liang, Ping, and I) were executed, it would still not be an adequate apology to make to the realm."[2]

At the time Yü Liang was in the stern of Wen's boat and heard what was said. Agitated and alarmed, he was without recourse. But on another day Wen urged him to go himself to see T'ao. Yü hesitated and could not bring himself to go.

Wen said, "The dogs of Hsi[3] are well known to me. You just go and see him. There's certain to be no cause for anxiety." Yü's manner and bearing had the aspect of a god, and the moment T'ao saw him he reversed his viewpoint, and they talked and enjoyed themselves the whole day. Love and respect had come to him all at once.

[1] The rebel Su Chün occupied the capital and took the young Emperor Ch'eng (Ssu-ma Yen*, r. 326-342) captive to the port of Shih-t'ou on the Yangtze in the summer of 328. See *TCTC* 94.2956.

CYC: When Su Chün reached Shih-t'ou from Ku-shu (upstream) and forcibly removed the emperor from the capital, Chün used the storehouse for a palace and had it guarded.

LKC (*Yao-cheng* section): At the end of the reign of Emperor Ming (ca. 325) there was a folk ditty (*yao*) which went:

> "Chick-chick lick!
> Pasture the horses beyond the mountain peak.
> When the Big Horse (Emperor Ming) dies,
> The Little Horse (Emperor Ch'eng) will starve."

Later Chün removed the emperor to Shih-t'ou, where the imperial diet was insufficient.

[2] HKCC: Emperor Ming's last command was that Yü Liang and Wang Tao should assist the young ruler, Emperor Ch'eng, to which end they were promoted to the rank of great minister. T'ao K'an and Tsu Yüeh were not included with them. K'an and Yüeh suspected that Liang was being remiss in regard to the last command.

CHS: At first Yü Liang wanted to summon Su Chün to court (to offer him a high post), but Pien K'un would not permit it. Then Wen Ch'iao and the grand wardens of the three Wu Commanderies (K'uai-chi, Wu-hsing, and Tan-yang) wanted to take up arms and defend the imperial house, but Liang would not permit it and issued an order instead which said, "Whoever takes up arms without authorization will be executed." This is why Chün succeeded in starting a revolt in the capital. (See also *TCTC* 93.2945-94.2967.)

[3] Emending *ch'i*, "mountain stream," to *Hsi* on the analogy of *NS* 47.10a, "What kind of a dog of Hsi is Hu Hsieh-chih (443-493) with his insatiable demands?" Hsi was a designation for the area of modern Kiangsi from which the T'ao family hailed, and its inhabitants were nicknamed "dogs of Hsi" by the easterners.

24. While Yü Liang was governor of Ching Province, stationed in Wu-ch'ang (between 334 and 340), one autumn evening when the air was fresh and the view clear, some assistants and clerks on Yü's staff, Yin Hao, Wang Hu-chih, and others, climbed the Southern Tower (Nan-lou) for a poetry session. Their songs and melodies were just getting

into full swing when they heard within the enclosed passage the sound of clogs making a great clatter. It turned out to be none other than Yü Liang himself, who on the spur of the moment had brought along ten or more of his associates for a walk. The earlier occupants were on the point of getting up and making way for him, but Yü said affably, "Gentlemen, stay awhile. The old chap's pleasure in this spot is by no means slight." So saying, he sat down on a folding chair (*hu-ch'uang*) and chanted poems and joked with the company. He remained seated throughout, enjoying himself hugely.

Later Wang Hsi-chih went down to the capital, and while talking with Chancellor Wang Tao, mentioned this incident. The chancellor said, "Yü Liang's manner and style on that occasion were certainly a bit on the decline."

Hsi-chih replied, "It's only the hills and streams that exist for him--nothing else."[1] (*CS* 73.10b; *IWLC* 70)

[1]*YLPW*: Those things which Yü Liang always loved and to which his heart was committed were constantly beyond the defilement of the world's dust. Even though from time to time he compromised his heart to accommodate to the world, he would retract his traces like the inchworm (*hu*) so that the square inch space of his heart remained profoundly tranquil, and he would continue as before in mystic contemplation (*hsüan-tui*) of hills and streams (*shan-shui*).

25. Wang T'ien possessed a handsome figure. Once when he went to visit his father, Wang Tao, the latter patted his shoulder and said, "My dear boy (A-nu), what a pity it would be if your ability didn't match your appearance!"

It was also said that Wang T'ien was in every respect like Wang Tao.[1]

[1]*YL*: Hsieh An once said, "When I was little, one day in the palace courtyard I chanced to see the chancellor, Wang Tao, and felt then as if a refreshing breeze had come to caress me."

26. When Wang Hsi-chih saw Tu I (d. before 335), he sighed in admiration, saying, "His face is like congealed ointment and his eyes like dotted lacquer; this is a man from among the gods and immortals."

Later when some contemporaries praised Wang Meng's (d. 347) appearance, Ts'ai Mo remarked, "It's a pity you people never saw Tu I, that's all."[1] (*CS* 93.5b; *TPYL* 389)

[1]*CTMSC*: During the Yung-ho era (345-354) Liu T'an and Hsieh Shang were discussing together personalities of the Central Court (Western Chin), and someone said, "Tu I was a pure standard lifted high, a model of excellence for those who came after. Moreover, his face was like congealed ointment and his eyes like dotted lacquer. In a rough way he might be compared with Wei Chieh." (Cf. *SSHY* IX, 42, above).

27. Liu T'an said of Huan Wen,[1] "His temples bristle like a rolled-up hedgehog's (*wei*) hide, and his eyebrows are as sharp as the corners of amethyst crystal. He's unquestionably a man in the same class with the dynastic founders, Sun Ch'üan[2] and Ssu-ma I."[3] (*CS* 98.17a)

[1]*SMTWCC*: Huan Wen was once praised by Wen Ch'iao, and was therefore given the name, Wen.

²*WuC*: The Han emissary, Liu Yüan*, said to those about him, "When I observe the brothers of the Sun family (Sun Ts'e and Sun Ch'üan), even though they possess ability and excellence, brilliance and perspicuity, and both of them have wealth and honor without end, it's only the younger brother, Ch'üan, the Filial and Incorrupt, whose form and appearance are majestically imposing, and whose bones and frame are extraordinary, signifying greatness and nobility."

³*CYC*: Ssu-ma I's heavenly bearing far surpassed others, and he possessed in epitome the qualities of all heroic warriors.

28. Wang Shao's manner and bearing resembled those of his father, Wang Tao. In his capacity as personal attendant he was once conferring titles on Huan Wen (in 363).¹ As Wang entered by the Great Gate dressed in his ceremonial robes, Huan, gazing across at him, said, "Ta-nu (Shao's baby name) surely and unmistakably has the plumes of a phoenix!"²

¹Huan was summoned to court in 363, on which occasion he was given the titles of personal attendant, grand marshal, governor-general of internal and external affairs, etc. See *TCTC* 101.3192.

²*CHS*: Wang Shao was handsome in his bearing and features, and maintained a dignified air.

29. Chih Tun characterized Wang Meng as follows: "Whenever he comes along adjusting his lapels, how light and airy (*χi̯ɒn-χi̯ɒn) his graceful soaring!"¹

¹*YL*: Wang Meng possessed an attractive bearing and appearance. Every time he viewed himself in a mirror he would say, "How on earth did Wang Na ever beget such a son?" His contemporaries considered it a perceptive remark.

30. Contemporaries characterized Wang Hsi-chih as follows: "Now drifting like a floating cloud; now rearing up like a startled dragon."¹ (*CS* 80.1a; *TPYL* 389)

¹This well-known characterization of Wang's calligraphy (see *CS* 80.1a) has somehow been misapplied to Wang himself.

31. Wang Meng was once sick and incommunicado to close friends and distant acquaintances alike. When Chih Tun came, the gatekeeper notified Wang in great agitation, "There's a strange-looking man at the gate. I didn't dare not notify you."
Wang replied, laughing, "It must be Chih Tun!"¹

¹*YL*: People were always wanting Juan Yü to accompany them to visit Chih Tun, but Juan would say, "I'd like to hear what he has to say, but I hate to look at his face."

SSHY Comm.: If this was so then Chih's appearance really must have been ugly and strange-looking.

32. There were some who felt that being compared to Hsieh Shang was no great honor. But the grand marshal, Huan Wen, said, "Gentlemen, don't underestimate him. Whenever Hsieh Shang stands on tiptoe beneath the north window playing the lute (*p'i-pa*), surely and unmis-

takably I start thinking of a Realized Man (*chen-jen*) from the edge of heaven."¹ (*IWLC* 44; *PTSC* 110; *CHC* 16; *PSLT* 18)

¹*CYC*: Hsieh Shang was a skilled musician.
YL: Chancellor Wang Tao once said, "When Hsieh Shang dangles his feet from the couch and props his head on his lute, I have thoughts of the edge of heaven."
(Kuo Mao-ch'ien, thirteenth cent., in the *YFSC* quotes the following account from the *YFKT*: "While Hsieh Shang was General Governing the West (354-356), he once put on a purple silk-gauze jacket and sat on a folding chair on the gate tower of the Fo-kuo Monastery overlooking the marketplace in Wu-ch'ang, and as he played the lute, composed the "Song of the Great Way," *Ta-tao ch'ü*. The people in the marketplace were unaware that it was someone of Three-Ducal rank.")

33. When Wang Meng was serving as a clerk in the Central Secretariat he went to visit Wang Ch'ia's office. At the time there was a layer of snow on the ground, and as Meng descended from his carriage outside the gate and walked into the office of the Imperial Secretariat [wearing his ceremonial robes],¹ Wang Ch'ia, who was gazing at him from a distance, sighed in admiration, saying, "This man no longer resembles someone living in the world!"

¹The bracketed expression is missing in the Sung edition.

34. While Ssu-ma Yü was serving as chancellor-prince (366-371), he went once with Hsieh An to visit Huan Wen. Wang Hsün was already in Huan's quarters, and Huan said to him, "You've always wanted to see the chancellor-prince; you may stay and observe from inside the curtain."
After the two guests had left, Huan asked Wang, "Well, after all, what do you think of him?" Wang replied, "The chancellor-prince has been taking responsibility for the government and is naturally majestic like a divine ruler.¹ But Your Excellency, too, is the object of all men's gaze. Otherwise how could the vice-president of the Court Secretariat (Hsieh An) have subordinated himself to you?"²

¹*HCYC*: The emperor (Ssu-ma Yü) was handsome in manner and demeanor, and his movements were dignified and circumspect.

²Hsieh had been Huan's sergeant-at-arms in 360.

35. During the reign of the Duke of Hai-hsi (Ssu-ma I**, r. 365-371), each morning as the courtiers gathered for the dawn audience, the audience hall would still be dark. It was only when the Prince of K'uai-chi, Ssu-ma Yü, came that all became radiantly light (*$\chi i\d{p}n$-$\chi i\d{p}n$), like dawn clouds rising. (*MCYC* 1; *TPYL* 389)

36. Hsieh Hsüan characterized his uncle, Hsieh An, as follows: "In his moments of leisure, without so much as even chanting aloud, but merely sitting composedly tweaking his nose and looking out of the corner of his eye, he naturally had the air of someone living in retirement among hills and lakes."

37. Hsieh An said, "When I look at Chih Tun's two eyes, they are intensely dark (*˙$i\v{a}m$-˙$i\v{a}m$), and gleaming black."

Sun Ch'o rejoined, "When I look at his stern angularity (*liəng-liəng), it reveals his forthrightness."

38. Once when Yü T'ung[1] and his younger brothers[2] were entering Wu Commandery (Soochow), they wanted to stay overnight in a way station. The younger brothers went up first and saw that a crowd of commoners (hsiao) had already filled the room and had not the slightest intention of vacating it for them. Yü T'ung said, "Let me try having a look." Accordingly, leaning on a staff, he took a small boy along with him. At his first entrance through the door all the guests looked up at his godlike bearing and withdrew at once.

[1] Liu Chün notes in the Commentary that in one account it was his uncle, Yü Liang.

[2] If it was Yü T'ung, no younger brothers are known; if Yü Liang, his younger brothers were I*, Ping, T'iao, and I.

39. Someone praised the splendor of Wang Kung's appearance with the words, "Sleek and shining (*$\hat{d}'\overset{\circ}{a}k$-$\hat{d}'\overset{\circ}{a}k$) as the willow in the months of spring." (IWLC 89)

CHAPTER XV

Self-renewal

1. When Chou Ch'u was young, his cruel and violent knight-errantry was a source of distress to his fellow villagers. Furthermore, in the stream which flowed through his native I-hsing Prefecture (Kiangsu) there was a scaly dragon (*chiao*), and in the hills a roving tiger,[1] both of which were terrorizing the local peasants. The people of I-hsing called the three of them the "Three Scourges," but Ch'u was the most terrible of them all. Someone suggested to Ch'u that he kill the tiger and behead the dragon, in reality hoping that of the "Three Scourges" only one would be left.

Ch'u promptly stabbed the tiger to death and proceeded to enter the stream to attack the dragon. But the dragon, now afloat, now submerged, traveled several tens of *li*, and Ch'u accompanied it for all of three days and three nights. His fellow villagers all thought he was already dead and were congratulating each other more than ever. But in the end Ch'u killed the dragon and emerged from the water. It was only after he heard that the villagers were congratulating each other that he finally understood what a source of distress he had been to the feelings of others, and he made up his mind to reform himself.

Accordingly he went into Wu Commandery (Soochow) and sought out the Lu brothers (Lu Chi and Lu Yün). Since Chi was not at home, he only saw Yün. He recounted the whole matter to him and added, "I've wanted to reform my ways, but the years have already slipped by, and till now I've never accomplished it."

Yün said, "The ancients honored the principle of hearing the Way in the morning and dying content in the evening.[2] How much more promising is your own future course! What's more, even though people are distressed that your ambition has never been established, why, indeed, should you worry that your good reputation won't become known?"

Ch'u thereupon exerted all his energies in a new direction, and in the end became a loyal minister and filial son.[3] (*CS* 58.1a; *IWLC* 96; *TPYL* 386; *SWLC*, hou 33)

¹The Commentary records the alternate reading, "white-faced tiger"; so also CS 58.1a.

KSCK: In I-hsing Commandery there was a tiger with a crooked foot, and by the Long Bridge of the River Isle (Ch'i-chu ch'ang-ch'iao) there was a green scaly dragon, both of whom consumed large numbers of people. West of the city wall lived Chou Ch'u. At the time they were called the "Three Scourges" of the commandery.

²See "Analects" IV, 8.

³There is a serious problem of anachronism in these events, since Chou, who was born in 236, was about twenty-five years older than either of the Lu brothers. In Chou's biography (CS 59.1b) it clearly states that he held office under the Wu kingdom. His reformation, therefore, must have occurred well before the fall of Wu in 280, while the Lus were still mere boys. Further evidence of the late provenance of this story is the fact that I-hsing was an Eastern Chin commandery. Before 317 it was called Wu-hsing.

2. When Tai Yüan was young he roved about as a knight-errant, undisciplined in the rules of proper behavior. He used to spend his time in the area between the Yangtze River and the Huai, attacking and robbing merchants and travelers. Lu Chi, having been on leave in his native Wu, was returning to Lo-yang (Honan), and his pieces of baggage were extremely numerous. Yüan sent some youths to rob and plunder them, while he himself remained on shore seated on a folding chair (hu-ch'uang), giving orders to his underlings and seeing that everything was done properly. Since Yüan's godlike demeanor was outstanding, even while stooping to such base conduct, his spirit and manner were still extraordinary.

Chi was in his cabin on board the boat and called out from a distance to Yüan, "With as much ability as *you* have, how can you still commit robbery?" Right then and there Yüan broke into tears and, throwing away his sword, gave his allegiance to Chi. As he spoke, his words were extraordinarily poignant. Chi came more and more to honor him, and after they had become fast friends wrote a letter of introduction¹ for him (to the Prince of Chao, Ssu-ma Lun). Later Yüan crossed the Yangtze River into Eastern Chin, where he held office as high as General Chastizing the West. (CS 69.12b; MCYC, hsia; TPYL 409)

¹The full text of Lu Chi's letter is found in Tai's biography (CS 69.12b-13a). In the Commentary Liu Chün quotes an abbreviated version from YYCS: I have heard that only after the ancient bow Fan-jo was mounted on a carriage did the virtue of (shooting the hawk on) a high wall ("Book of Changes," Hex, 40; Wilhelm I, 168) become manifest, and only after the pipes made from a lone bamboo were set in a row was the melody perfected which brought the gods down to earth (Chou-li III, Ta ssu-yüeh).

Your servant has observed the retired gentleman, Tai Yüan, polished in his integrity and established in his conduct, with the purity of "a well which has been cleansed" ("Book of Changes," Hex. 48; Wilhelm I, 199); content in poverty and happy in his determination, without any hankering after the winds or dust of the world. Truly he is the bequeathed treasure of the Southeast, the noble jadestone of the court. If he could commit himself to the crossroads of official life, he would surely be able to unite his tracks with those of the noble steeds Chi and Lu; or if he could make his honesty shine in the verandas and halls of the court, he would surely be able to send forth his radiance with the lustrous gems Yü and Fan. We people on an arid beach (the court) in the end must transport pearls (to make it moist); dwellers on a well-watered hill (recluses) are on their guard against contributing the jade (which keeps it watered) (see *Ta Tai Li-chi* VII, 64). But since either in light or darkness these gems reveal their form, they may be discerned even by those of ordinary intelligence.

(The account goes on to report that Ssu-ma Lun "immediately employed Yüan.")

CHAPTER XVI

Admiration and Emulation

1. When Chancellor Wang Tao was appointed director of works (in 321), Huan I, having put up his hair in two topknots and wearing a barkcloth skirt (*ch'ün*),[1] leaned on his staff and stole glances at him from the edge of the road. Sighing with admiration, he kept saying, "People say A-lung (Wang's baby name) is superb. There's no doubt about it, A-lung *is* superb!"

Without realizing it, he had reached the gate of the chancellery.

[1] I.e., dressed like a commoner, to avoid detection.

2. After Chancellor Wang Tao had crossed the Yangtze River (307), he said to himself, "Formerly on the banks of the Lo River (in Lo-yang) on many occasions I used to discuss the Way with P'ei Wei (d. 300), Juan Chan (d. 312), and the other worthies."

Yang Man said, "People have long since assumed this to be so. Why do you need to keep repeating it?"

Wang replied, "I don't mean that I need to do this, either. It's only that I long for those times, but they're irrevocable, that's all."

3. Whenever Wang Hsi-chih heard someone compare his own "Preface to the Lan-t'ing Collection" (*Lan-t'ing chi hsü*)[1] to Shih Ch'ung's "Preface to the Chin-ku Poems" (*Chin-ku shih hsü*),[2] or again, whenever someone matched him against Shih Ch'ung, he would look extremely pleased. (*CS* 80.7b)

[1] The text, which survives under several titles, was made famous by Wang's own calligraphic record, later copied and inscribed on stone, rubbings of which still exist. In the Commentary Liu Chün quotes an excerpt under the title *LHH* (cf. *CS* 80.6b-7b): "In the ninth year of the Yung-ho era (353), in the beginning of the third month of spring, we gathered at the Orchid Pavilion (Lan-t'ing) in

321

Shan-yin Prefecture of K'uai-chi Commandery to perform the rites of the spring purification (*hsi*). All the worthies had arrived and both young and old were gathered together. In this place were lofty hills and towering ranges, luxuriant forests and tall bamboos. In addition there were clear streams dashing and swirling, sparkling about us on the left and right, inviting us to float our wine cups on the winding waters. (Participants in this ancient rite would float their cups in turn down a winding stream, drinking a libation at whatever point the cup came to rest, and composing a poem on the spot.) Each person present took his turn. On this day the sky was bright and the air clear and mild; a breeze was gently blowing. Feasting our eyes and giving rein to our feelings—how truly enjoyable! Even though we lacked any accompaniment of silk or bamboo, of pipes or stringed instruments, for every cup there was a chanted poem—quite enough to express the hidden feelings of our hearts!

"Thus, I list here in order the persons present, recording what they wrote. Sun T'ung and the rest, twenty-six persons in all, composed poems as they appear below. Hsieh Sheng and the rest, fifteen persons in all, who found themselves unable to compose anything, paid the forfeit by drinking three dipperfuls (*tou*) of wine."

[2] For the complete text of this earlier preface, which served as Wang's model, see above, SSHY IX, 57, n. 1.

4. Wang Hu-chih had formerly been Yü Liang's secretarial aide. Later (in 334) Yü took on Yin Hao as his senior administrator. When Yin first arrived (in Wu-ch'ang), Yü Liang was on the point of dispatching Wang to the capital, but Wang himself petitioned to remain, saying, "This humble official has rarely seen a man of such abundant virtue. Yin Hao has only just arrived, and I still covet the chance to go about with him for a few days."

5. Whenever Ch'ih Ch'ao heard someone compare him to Fu Chien (ruler of Former Ch'in from 358-385), he was delighted.

6. Before Meng Ch'ang had achieved recognition, his family lived in Ching-k'ou (northeast of Chien-k'ang). Once he saw Wang Kung riding a high carriage and wearing a robe of crane's plumes. At the time there was a light snow on the ground. Stealing a glimpse of him through the fence, Ch'ang sighed in admiration, saying, "This is truly a man from among the gods and immortals!" (*PTSC* 129, 140, 152; *PSLT* 4; *TPYL* 774)

CHAPTER XVII

Grieving for the Departed

1. Wang Ts'an was fond of donkeys' brays. After he was buried (217), Emperor Wen of Wei (Ts'ao P'ei, r. 220-227) came to mourn at his grave. Looking back, he said to those who had come with him, "Wang was fond of donkeys' brays; each of you may now make a sound to escort him on his way."

   The attending guests accordingly, each in turn, made one donkey's bray. (*IWLC* 95; *PSLT* 29; *TPYL* 389, 901)

2. Once while Wang Jung was serving as president of the Imperial Secretariat (301-302), wearing his ceremonial robes and riding in a light one-horse carriage (*yao-ch'e*), he passed beneath Master Huang's Wineshop (*lu*).¹ Looking back, he remarked to the guests in the carriage behind him, "Long ago I used to drink and make merry in this wineshop with Hsi K'ang and Juan Chi, and in the outings in the Bamboo Grove I also took a humble part. But ever since Hsi K'ang's premature death (in 262) and Juan Chi's passing (263) I've been hemmed in by the times. Today as I look on this place, even though it's so near, it seems as far away as the hills and rivers."² (*CS* 43.13b; *TPYL* 828; *SWLC*, hsü 14)

   ¹*HSC*: A *lu* is a wineshop, so called because its walls are of earth, high on all four sides, like an earthen stove (*lu*).
   (See also *SSHY* IV, 90, and XXVI, 24, for other references to this place.)

   ²*CLCHL*: Such is the popular tradition. Yü Yüan-chih once asked his uncle, Yü Liang, about it. Liang replied, "I never heard of it while I was at the Central Court (in Lo-yang, before 311). This story has suddenly showed up here in Chiang-tso (i.e., in Eastern Chin, after 317), no doubt because some curiosity-monger just made it up, that's all."

3. Because Sun Ch'u possessed ability he seldom deferred to others,

except that he always respected Wang Chi. At the time of Chi's funeral (ca. 285) all the famous gentlemen were in attendance. Ch'u arrived late, and as he approached the corpse he wept so bitterly that all of the other guests were moved to tears. When his weeping was ended, addressing the spirit bed (*ling-ch'uang*) he said, "You always used to enjoy my imitation of a donkey's bray, so now I'll make one for you."

His rendition was so like the real sound that the guests all broke out laughing. Lifting his head, Sun said, "To think that (Heaven) lets you people live, while it has made this man die!"[1]

[1]*YL*: When Wang Chi was buried, Sun Ch'u mourned him with such extreme grief that all of the guests were moved to tears, but after Sun had imitated a donkey's bray they all broke out laughing. When Sun heard them he said, "Do you mean to say you people have not died, while (Heaven) has made Wang Chi die?" The guests were all incensed at this.

4. When Wang Jung lost his son (Wang Sui, d. ca. 275),[1] Shan Chien went to visit him. Wang's grief was such that he could not control himself. Chien said, "For a mere babe in arms, why go to such lengths?"

Wang said, "A sage forgets his feelings; the lowest beings aren't even capable of having feelings. But the place where feelings are most concentrated is precisely among people like ourselves."

Moved by his words, Chien grieved for him more than ever.[2] (*CS* 43.15a, of Wang Yen)

[1]Liu Chün notes in the Commentary that in one version it was Wang Yen whose son had died. This would agree with the account in *CS* 43.15a, where it is clearly stated Yen's son was an infant. Wang Sui, who died in his nineteenth year, could hardly class as a "babe in arms."

[2]*WYCS*: Wang Jung's son, Sui, was about to marry the daughter of P'ei Tun (a nephew of P'ei K'ai) but after Sui's premature death, Jung was excessive in his pain and grief and would not permit any other man to seek her hand, so that she lived to old age without anyone daring to marry her.

5. Someone mourned for Ho Ch'iao, saying, "How lofty and majestic (*ngâ-ngâ*), like the crashing of a pine tree from a height of ten thousand feet."

6. When Wei Chieh died in the sixth year of the Yung-chia era (312), Hsieh K'un wept for him so poignantly that it moved passersby on the road.[1]

Later, during the Hsien-ho era (326-335), Chancellor Wang Tao gave instructions, saying, "Wei Chieh should be reburied. This nobleman was looked up to by all the famous gentlemen of refined manners within the Four Seas. Let us perform a simple sacrifice to show our regard for an old friendship."[2]

[1]*YCLJM*: Wei Chieh died on the twentieth day of the sixth month of the sixth year (August 8, 312), and was buried in Nan-ch'ang (Kiangsi) east of the tomb of Hsü Shao (late second cent.). At the

time of Chieh's funeral Hsieh K'un poured out his sorrow in Wu-ch'ang (Hupei), and was so sorely grieved that he could not control himself. Someone asked him, "Why are you mourning and expressing your grief like this?"

Hsieh replied, "The pillar and beam have been broken. How can I not grieve?"

[2] (Wei) Chieh PC: During the Hsieh-ho era Chieh's remains were removed to Chiang-ning (= Chien-k'ang). Chancellor Wang Tao gave instructions, saying, "Tomorrow Wei Chieh should be reburied. . . . Let us perform the Three-victim Sacrifice (of an ox, a sheep, and a pig) to show our regard for an old friendship."

7. Ku Jung throughout his life had been a devotee of the seven-stringed zither (ch'in). When he was buried (322) a member of the family placed a zither on the spirit bed. As Chang Han went to mourn for him, he could not control his grief. Directly mounting the bed, he strummed the zither, and after performing several airs, stroked the instrument and said, "Ku Jung, do you still appreciate this?" So saying, he wept again profusely and then went out directly without grasping the hand of the bereaved son.[1] (CS 68.5ab; PTSC 85; SLF 11; TPYL 561, 577, 579)

[1] I.e., Ku P'i; see CS 68.5b. The custom of grasping the hand of the eldest surviving son, called the "bereaved son" (hsiao-tzu), or "funeral host" (sang-chu), seems to have been characteristic for this period. See also No. 15, below.

8. Yü Liang's son, Yü Hui, met his death during the troubles over Su Chün.[1] Chu-ko Hui's daughter, Wen-piao, was Yü Hui's wife. Since she had been left a widow, she was about to be remarried,[2] and Chu-ko Hui wrote a letter to Liang in which he mentioned it.

In Liang's reply he wrote, "Your worthy daughter is still young, and of course it is proper for her to remarry. But whenever I fondly recall my lost son, it is as if he had just died."

[1] I.e., during Su Chün's revolt of 327-328 against the Yü faction at court.

[2] I.e., to Chiang Pin. For his courtship, see below, SSHY XXVII, 10.

9. When Yü Liang died (340), Ho Ch'ung, who was present at the funeral, said, "As they bury the jade tree and lay it in the earth, it makes a man's feelings seem as if they could never come to an end!"[1] (CS 73.10b; PTSC 92; TPYL 556)

[1] SSC: At first when Yü Liang became ill (in 339), the practitioner (shu-shih), Tai Yang, said, "Some time ago after the Su Chün incident (328), while Yü Liang was at the White Stone Shrine (Pai-shih tz'u), he promised to make a thank offering of the ox which was hitched to his carriage. But since he never fulfilled that promise, he's being punished by the ghost of this shrine and can't be saved." The following year Liang died, as predicted.

LKC (Yao-cheng): When Yü Liang was first stationed at Wu-ch'ang (in 334), as he set out from Shih-t'ou (the port of Chien-k'ang), the commoners who watched from the shore sang:

"Lord Yü went up to Wu-ch'ang town,
His flags aflutter like flying birds.
Lord Yü to Yang-chou (Chien-k'ang) will return--
White horses draw his pennoned hearse."

Later, though repeatedly summoned, he did not come to the court. After a while he deceased, and only descended to the capital to be buried there.

10. When Wang Meng's illness became critical (in 347), he was lying beneath the lamp. Turning his sambar-tail chowry (*chu-wei*) around in his hand and looking at it, he sighed and said, "People like this have never reached forty!"[1]

When he died, Liu T'an was present at the preparation for burial and placed a chowry with a rhinoceros-horn handle (*hsi-ping*) in the coffin. As he did so he was completely overcome with grief.[2]

[1] Wang Meng died in his thirty-ninth year.

[2] (*Wang*) *Meng PC*: Liu T'an was on most friendly terms with Meng, and when Meng died T'an mourned him deeply. Even the love of brothers could not have surpassed theirs.

11. Following Chih Tun's mourning for the monk Fa-ch'ien*, his vitality and spirit became languid and spent, and his manner and bearing went more and more into a decline. He often remarked to others, "In antiquity Carpenter Shih discarded his hatchet after the death of the man from Ying,[1] and Po Ya broke the strings of his zither on the death of Chung Tzu-ch'i.[2] Making inference from my own experience and examining that of others, I know these were by no means empty tales. Since the one who understood me intuitively has passed away, now whenever I say anything no one appreciates it and 'my inmost heart is cramped and constricted.'[3] I might as well be dead!"

One year later, Chih Tun also passed away. (*KSC* 4; *Taishō* 50.349c; *CHC* 18; *TPYL* 409)

[1] *Chuang-tzu* (XXIV, 15b; Watson, p. 269): A man of Ying (Hupei) had some plaster smeared on his nose as thin as a fly's wing. He had Carpenter Shih slice it off with his hatchet. The plaster was completely removed, yet his nose was unharmed, and the man of Ying stood still without flinching. . . . (But after the death of the man of Ying) Carpenter Shih said, "It's true I could once do it, but now my 'material' is long since dead."

[2] *HSWC* IX: Po Ya (sixth cent. B.C.) used to play the zither while Chung Tzu-ch'i listened. Whenever in his playing his thoughts were on Mt. T'ai, Tzu-ch'i would say, "How well you play the zither-- lofty and majestic like Mt. T'ai!" Or in a quiet place when his thoughts were on flowing water, Tzu-ch'i would say, "How well you play the zither--rippling and purling like flowing water!"

But after Chung Tzu-ch'i died, Po Ya laid aside his zither and broke the strings, and to the end of his life never played it again, feeling that no one listening was worth playing for.

[3] "Songs," No. 147. The biography of Chih Tun (*KSC* 4; *Taishō* 50.349c) states that he composed an elegy for his friend entitled "Essay on Keen Awareness" (*Ch'ieh-wu chang*), which unfortunately does not survive.

12. When Ch'ih Ch'ao died (in 377), the attendants reported to his father, Ch'ih Yin, "The young master has died." Upon hearing it, Yin showed no grief, but simply said to the attendants, "You may notify me when the body is being prepared for burial."

Yin went to attend the preparation, where in one outburst of grief he was almost completely overcome.[1]

[1] *CHS*: Ch'ih Ch'ao, while only in his forty-second year, preceded his father, Ch'ih Yin, in death. Those persons with whom Ch'ao had friendly relations were all the most eminent and able men of the times, and on the day of his death there were over forty persons, both noble and lowly, who composed obituaries for him.

HCYC (cf. *CS* 67.21b-22a): Ch'ih Ch'ao's faction supported Huan Wen, and Ch'ao himself served as Huan's master strategist. Since his father, Yin, was loyal to the imperial house, Ch'ao did not let him know any of this. When Ch'ao was about to die, he took out a small box of letters and entrusted it to one of his retainers with the words, "I originally intended to burn this, but I'm afraid that since my father is getting on in years he will surely die of grief over my death. After I'm gone, if he is suffering seriously from loss of sleep or appetite, then present him with this box."

Yin later actually did suffer so acutely that he became ill, and the retainer accordingly did as Ch'ao had directed him and handed over Ch'ao's secret correspondence with Huan Wen. When Yin saw it, he immediately became very angry and said, "I only regret my little boy was so late a-dying!" After that he ceased to mourn.

13. When Tai K'uei saw the tomb of the dharma master Chih Tun (d. 366), he said, "The sound of his virtuous voice is not yet far removed, yet the trees encircling his tomb have already grown dense. May his spiritual principles go on and on, not ending with his life's destiny!"[1] (*IWLC* 40; *TPYL* 558)

[1] *CTC*: Chih Tun died in the first year of the T'ai-ho era (366) on Shih-ch'eng Mountain in Shan Prefecture (K'uai-chi Commandery), and was buried there.

FSMHSH: In the second year of the Ning-k'ang era (374) I (Wang Hsün) ordered my carriage and went to Shih-ch'eng Mountain in Shan Prefecture, which is the tomb of the dharma master. The high grave mound is thickly overgrown, and the slopes of the mound have become wild grass. The traces he left behind have not yet disappeared, though his person is already far removed. Whenever I fondly reminisce over the time when he was still alive in the days gone by, everything I encounter sends a pang of grief into my heart.

(*KSC* 4, *Taishō* 50.349c, locates Chih Tun's tomb on Wu Mountain in Yü-yao Prefecture, also in K'uai-chi Commandery, but the two sources cited above by Liu Chün, locating it on Shih-ch'eng Mountain, both being nearer in date to Tun's death than *KSC*, are to be preferred.)

14. Wang Hsien-chih was on friendly terms with Yang Sui. Sui was pure and incorruptible, unceremonious and noble. He became a secretary in the Central Secretariat but died young. Wang was deeply grieved and saddened by his death, and remarked to Wang Hsün, "This was a man who may be mourned by the whole family of the state."

15. Wang Hsün was on bad terms with Hsieh An.¹ Wang was in the east (K'uai-chi) when he learned of Hsieh's death (in 385), and, immediately coming out of retirement, went to the capital, where he visited his cousin, Wang Hsien-chih, and informed him that he was about to go to weep for Hsieh An. Hsien-chih had just gone to bed, but, hearing Hsün's voice, got up in alarm, saying, "It's just what I might have expected from you, Fa-hu!"

Wang thereupon proceeded to the Hsiehs' to weep. Commander Tiao Yüeh would not permit him to come forward, saying, "For as long as his Lordship was living, he never saw this guest." Wang for his part did not speak with him, but going directly forward, wept with intense grief, then withdrew without grasping Hsieh Yen's² hand.

> ¹CHS: Wang Hsün and his younger brother, Wang Min, were both married to women of the Hsieh family (Min to An's daughter; Hsün to his niece), but because of suspicion and jealousy had both been divorced. Since Hsieh An had annulled the marriage contract with Hsün, and moreover had separated his wife from him, the two clans had become mutually hostile.
>
> ²Hsieh Yen, as An's oldest surviving son, was serving as host (sang-chu).

16. Wang Hui-chih and his younger brother, Wang Hsien-chih, were both critically ill at the same time, but Hsien-chih died first (388). Hui-chih asked his attendants, "Why don't I hear any news at all? This must mean he's already dead." As he spoke he showed no hint of grief. Immediately ordering a sedan chair, he came to Hsien-chih's house to offer condolences, still without weeping at all. Since Hsien-chih had always been fond of the seven-stringed zither (ch'in), Hui-chih went directly in and sat on the spirit bed (ling-ch'uang). Taking Hsien-chih's zither, he started to play, but the strings were not in tune. Throwing it to the ground he cried out, "Tzu-ching! Tzu-ching! you and your zither are both gone forever!" Whereupon he gave himself up utterly to his grief for a long while. In a little more than a month he, too, was dead.¹ (CS 80.12a; TPYL 577)

> ¹YML: During the T'ai-yüan era (376-396) there came a Taoist master (shih) from afar—no one knew from whence—who said, "When a man's life is about to end, if there is someone living who is willing to substitute for him, the dying man may live. If he compels a man to substitute for him, it will not be for more than a short time."
>
> When people heard this they all discounted it as so much empty nonsense. Now the two brothers, Wang Hui-chih and Wang Hsien-chih, were especially close. When Hsien-chih's sickness was at the point of death, Hui-chih said to the master, "My ability is not as great as my brother's; our ranks also have been unequal. I request that my remaining years be substituted for my brother's."
>
> The master said, "In the case of a living man substituting for a dying one, it's only if his own life-span has years to spare that he would be able to fill the deficiency of the one who is dying. At present, since your worthy brother's life is about to end, and your own span also is on the point of exhaustion, what can you give him in substitution?"
>
> Hui-chih had been suffering earlier from a back ailment. When

Hsien-chih's illness became critical he had steadfastly forbidden any communication with Hui-chih (for fear of upsetting him), but when Hui-chih learned of his brother's death, suppressing his grief, he uttered not a single sound, but his back immediately ruptured and overflowed. Recalling the words of the master, he found them indeed to be true.

17. The night of Emperor Hsiao-wu's (Ssu-ma Yao, r. 373-396) funeral,[1] Wang Kung entered the mausoleum to pay his respects. He announced to his younger brothers, "Although the rafters have been renewed, still unmistakably the sorrow of the Song *Shu-li* remains."[2]

[1]*CHS*: When Emperor Hsiao-wu was buried, the Prince of K'uai-chi, Ssu-ma Tao-tzu, was holding the reins of government. He showed great favoritism to Wang Kuo-pao and entrusted him with critical decisions. Wang Kung attended the funeral, and on the occasion uttered these words.

[2]"Songs," No. 65. Cheng Hsüan's comment on this song interprets it as "a lamentation over the Chou capital (Lo-yang). A great officer of Chou is on campaign, and arriving at the capital, passes by the royal ancestral temple and finds the palace buildings all turned into fields of grain and millet. Lamenting the overthrow of the Chou royal house, he is agitated and cannot bear to go on, and so writes this song." The song begins:

> "Those ears of millet drooping down,
> Those growing sprouts of yellow grain--
> As I walk by them halting and havering,
> My inmost heart waves to and fro."

18. When Yang Fu died in his thirty-first year,[1] Huan Hsüan wrote a letter to Fu's cousin, Yang Hsin, in which he said, "Your worthy cousin was one to whom I could confide my feelings, and now he has died of a sudden illness. The sigh (of Confucius at the death of Tzu-lu), 'Heaven has cut me off!'[2]--how can I put it into words?"

[1]Cf. *SSHY* II, 104, above, where the Commentary, citing the "Yang Family Register" (*Yang SP*), states that he died in his *forty-sixth* year.

[2]*Kung-yang chuan*, Ai 14.

19. When Huan Hsüan was on the point of usurping the throne (404), he said to Pien Fan-chih, "Formerly Yang Fu consistently resisted this ambition of mine, but now for 'belly and heart'[1] I've lost Yang Fu, and for 'talons and teeth'[2] I've been deprived of So Yüan,[3] so now here I am pell-mell taking this reckless plunge. How can it possibly accord with the mind of Heaven?"

[1]See "Songs," No. 7:

> Gallant and brave the man of war,
> Belly and heart of his liege lord.

[2]See "Songs," No. 185:

> O Minister of War,
> Talons and teeth of our good king!

³*YML*: While So Yüan was in Li-yang (Anhui) he became ill. One year there came from the western border a young girl, named So-and-so, who claimed that she had been sent down from the gods to inquire of Yüan if she might be permitted to nurse and care for him. Yüan's nature was rigid and unbending, and, taking her for a malevolent and seductive spirit, he had her apprehended and committed to prison, and later executed in the marketplace.

Just before she died, the girl said, "Seventeen days from now Yüan will understand his mistake." On the appointed day Yüan died, as predicted.

CHAPTER XVIII

Living in Retirement

1. When Juan Chi whistled (*hsiao*), he could be heard several hundred paces away. In the Su-men Mountains (Honan) there appeared from nowhere a Realized Man (*chen-jen*) about whom the woodcutters were all relaying tales. Juan Chi went to see for himself and spied the man squatting with clasped knees by the edge of a cliff. Chi climbed the ridge to approach him and then squatted opposite him. Chi rehearsed for him briefly matters from antiquity to the present, beginning with an exposition of the Way of Mystical Quiescence (*hsüan-chi*) of the Yellow Emperor and Shen Nung, and ending with an investigation of the excellence of the Supreme Virtue (*sheng-te*) of the Three Ages (Hsia, Shang, and Chou). But when Chi asked his opinion about it he remained aloof and made no reply. Chi then went on to expound that which lies beyond Activism (*yu-wei chih wai*),[1] and the techniques of Resting the Spirit (*ch'i-shen*) and Conducting the Vital Force (*tao-ch'i*). But when Chi looked toward him for a reply, he was still exactly as before, fixedly staring without turning. Chi therefore turned toward him and made a long whistling sound. After a long while the man finally laughed and said, "Do it again." Chi whistled a second time, but as his interest was now exhausted, he withdrew. He had returned about half-way down the ridge when he heard above him a shrillness like an orchestra of many instruments, while forests and valleys reechoed with the sound. Turning back to look, he discovered it was the whistling of the man he had just visited.[2] (*CS* 49.3b)

[1]Following the Sung text; the others all read, "the doctrine of Activism" (*yu-wei chih chiao*), which sounds incongruous here. "Mysterious Quiescence," "Resting the Spirit," and "Conducting the Vital Force" are all Taoist terms.

[2]*WSCC*: Juan Chi often went riding alone wherever his fancy led him, not following the roads or byways, to the point where carriage tracks would go no farther, and always he would return weeping bitterly. Once while he was wandering in the Su-men Mountains

there was a recluse living there whose name no one knew, and whose
only possessions were a few *hu*-measures of bamboo fruit, a mortar
and pestle, and nothing more. When Juan Chi heard of him he went
to see him and began conversing on the Way of Non-action (*wu-wei*)
of high antiquity, and went on to discuss the moral principles (*i*)
of the Five Emperors and Three August Ones. The Master of Su-men
remained oblivious and never even looked his way. Chi then with a
shrill sound made a long whistling whose echoes reverberated
through the empty stillness. The Master of Su-men finally looked
pleased and laughed.

After Chi had gone down the hill, the Master gathered his
breath and whistled shrilly with a sound like that of the phoenix.
Chi had all his life been a connoisseur of music, and he borrowed
the theme of his discussion with the Master of Su-men to express
what was in his heart in a song, the words of which are:

> "The sun sets west of Mt. Pu-chou;
> The moon comes up from Cinnabar Pool.
> Essence of Yang is darkened and unseen;
> While Yin rays take *their* turn to win.
>
> His brilliance lasts but for a moment;
> Her dark will soon again be full.
> If wealth and honor stay but for a trice
> Must poverty and low estate be evermore?"

CLCHL: After Juan Chi returned (from the Su-men Mountains) he
proceeded to compose the "Discourse on Mr. Great Man" (*Ta-jen
hsien-sheng lun*; see CS 49.4a, partially translated in E. Balazs,
"Nihilistic Revolt," p. 238). What was said in this discourse all
represented the basic feelings in his breast and heart. The main
point was that Mr. Great Man was none other than Juan himself.

SSHY Comm.: Observing the mutual harmony of Juan's and the hermit's whistling, we find that it, too, comes close to (what
Chuang-tzu meant when he wrote), "merely by a meeting of the eyes,
the Way is communicated." (See *Chuang-tzu* XXI, 18a; Watson, p.
223.)

2. While Hsi K'ang was wandering among the mountains of Chi Commandery (Honan), he met the Taoist adept (*tao-shih*), Sun Teng,[1] and
thereafter continued his wanderings in his company. As K'ang was on
the eve of departing, Teng said, "As far as your ability is concerned,
it's high enough, but your way of preserving your own life is inadequate." (CS 49.12ab, 94.2ab)

[1]HKCH: In the summer Sun Teng wove garments out of grass, and in
the winter he covered himself with his unbound hair. He was fond
of reading the "Book of Changes" and playing a one-stringed zither.
All who saw him were attracted and delighted by him.

WSCC: Sun Teng was by nature free of both joy and anger. If
anyone doused him under water and then brought him out to look at
him, Teng would just laugh aloud. Whatever items of clothing or
food were provided him by households where he stayed he would
never decline, but when he left he would leave them behind.

WSC: During the Chia-p'ing era (249-253) some people of Chi
Prefecture had gone into the mountains, where they saw a man. The

place where he lived was an overhanging cliff rising a hundred *jen* (about 700 feet), where dense woods grew in shady luxuriance, yet his spirit and intelligence were extremely bright. He said of himself that his surname was Sun and his name, Teng, with the courtesy name, Kung-ho.

When he heard of him, Hsi K'ang followed him about for three years. K'ang asked for his prognosis concerning his own future, but Teng never answered. However, K'ang always sighed in respectful admiration over the fine subtlety contained in his godlike counsels. When K'ang was about to take his leave, he said to the man, "Sir, have you nothing, after all, to say?"

Teng finally answered, "Do you know anything about fire? When it is lit it gives light. Yet knowing when not to use the light is, after all, included in knowing when to use it. When a man is born he is endowed with ability. Yet knowing when not to use his ability is, after all, included in knowing when to use it. Thus, knowing when to use light is included in getting enough fuel to keep it burning, and knowing when to use ability is included in understanding things well enough to complete one's allotted years. Now your ability is abundant, but your understanding slight. You'll have difficulty avoiding trouble in today's world. Don't ask me anything more."

K'ang was unable to use his advice, and when he became involved in the Lü An affair (see *SSHY* VI, 2, n. 1) and was cast into prison, he composed a poem reproaching himself, as follows:

> "In the past I used to blush before Liu-hsia Hui,
> But now I am ashamed before Sun Teng."

(The complete poem is preserved in *WH* 23.8a, *Yu-fen shih*, "Songs of Frustration in Seclusion;" Liu-hsia Hui was an officer in Lu in the sixth century B.C. who was dismissed from office three times but never left the state.)

WYCS: Sun Teng was the one interviewed by Juan Chi. Hsi K'ang treated him as his teacher, with all the ceremony expected of a disciple. During the transition between Wei and Chin (ca. 260-265) it was easy to fall prey to jealousy and suspicion; both noble and base were engulfed together. For this reason Sun Teng was silent on some points.

3. When Shan T'ao was about to leave the selection bureau[1] (in 262) and wanted to recommend Hsi K'ang as his successor, K'ang wrote him a letter announcing the breaking off of their friendship.[2] (*CS* 49.12b)

[1] Shan T'ao left the Board of Civil Office to become cavalier attendant-in-ordinary shortly before Hsi K'ang's death in 262. See *TCTC* 78.2464/5.

[2] (*Hsi*) *K'ang PC*: Did K'ang not recognize that Shan was not simply according with his own feelings by offering a mere office? Indeed he recognized that Shan also wished to demonstrate his own unswerving integrity by stopping the mouth of the one who was being recommended, and that was all. So he replied to T'ao in a letter in which he said of himself that he could not endure to drift with the vulgar crowd, and criticized and belittled T'ang (the founder of Shang) and Wu (the founder of Chou). When the generalissimo (Ssu-ma Chao) got word of it, he resented him.

(The text of K'ang's letter is preserved in *WH* 43.1a-3a, and abridged in *CS* 49.12b-14a; translated by J. R. Hightower in Cyril Birch, ed., *Anthology of Chinese Literature*, New York, 1965, pp. 162-164.)

4. Li Hsin was Li Chung's fifth[1] son. Pure and incorruptible, he had far-reaching principles, but since in his youth he had been weak and sickly, he was unwilling to marry or take office. He resided in Linhai Commandery (Chekiang), living below his elder brother's (Li Shih*) grave. Since he had an eminent reputation, Chancellor Wang Tao wanted to summon him to court to honor him and therefore appointed him to an office in his own administration. When Hsin received the letter of notification he laughed and said, "Wang Tao is just using a title to borrow a man." (*MCYC* 1; *TPYL* 386)

[1] *TPYL* 386 reads "sixth."

5. Ho Chun, the fifth[1] younger brother of the General of Spirited Cavalry, Ho Ch'ung, because of lofty sentiments had fled the world, but Ho Ch'ung kept urging him to take office. Chun replied, "Why is my title of Fifth (Ti-wu)[2] necessarily lower in rank than yours of General of Spirited Cavalry (P'iao-chi)?" (*CS* 93.9a; *IWLC* 48; *TPYL* 238)

[1] Following the text as quoted in *IWLC* 48 and *TPYL* 238.

[2] A pun based on the fact that he was Ch'ung's fifth (*ti-wu*) younger brother and that Ti-wu was the surname of a famous minister of the Later Han Dynasty, Ti-wu Lun (ca. 10-90 A.D.; see *HHS* 71.1a-7a). The sentence could also read, "Why is my name, Ti-wu, necessarily inferior to yours?"

6. While Juan Yü was living in the Eastern Mountains (Chekiang), serene and without duties, he was always inwardly content within his breast. Someone asked Wang Hsi-chih about him, and Wang replied, "This gentleman comes near to (what Lao-tzu meant by) 'not being surprised by either favor or disgrace.'[1] In what respect did even the 'impassive intuition' (*ch'en-ming*) of the ancients[2] surpass this?" (*CS* 49.10a)

[1] *Lao-tzu* 13.

[2] I.e., of Yen Tsun (alias Chuang Tsun) of Shu (fl. ca. A.D. 1). *FY* (VI): Chuang Tsun of Shu was impassive and intuitive (*ch'en-ming*). He would not do anything which appeared improper, nor gain anything by improper means. Living long in seclusion, he never altered his integrity.

(Li Kuei's seventh-century comment explains *ch'en-ming* as "mystically quiescent, *hsüan-chi*, oblivious of the world and without overt acts, *wu-chi*.")

7. When K'ung Yü was young he had the ambition of living in refined retirement. It was only after he was forty years old that he answered the summons of the General Pacifying the East, Ssu-ma Jui (later Emperor Yüan, r. 317-322).[1] During the period before he had taken office he used to lie in bed and sing or play the flute, admonishing and instructing himself. He called himself Master K'ung (*K'ung-lang*).

He wandered away among the rocks on the mountains, and the common people claimed he possessed Taoist arts (*tao-shu*) and erected a temple to him while he was still living. To this day the Temple of Master K'ung (*K'ung-lang miao*) still stands. (CS 78.1b)

[1]*K'ung Yü PC*: During the great upheavals of the Yung-chia era (307-312) Yü entered the mountains of Lin-hai Commandery (eastern Chekiang), where he sought neither fame nor achievement. Emperor Yüan commanded him to serve as his aide.

CS 78.1b: Yü entered the mountains of Hsin-an (western Chekiang) where he changed his surname to Sun and lived by farming and study. His trustworthiness became renowned throughout the neighboring villages. Later he suddenly took his leave, and everyone said he was a god and erected a shrine to him. It was not until the Yung-chia era that Emperor Yüan, then serving as General Pacifying the East and stationed in Yang Province (Kiangsu-Anhui-Chekiang), commanded him to serve as his aide.

8. Liu Lin-chih of Nan-yang Commandery (Honan), a high-minded and forthright man, well versed in the histories and commentaries, was living in retirement in the Yang-ch'i Mountains (Hupei). At the time (379), Fu Chien was threatening the Yangtze River area,[1] and the governor of Ching Province (Hupei), Huan Ch'ung,[2] wishing to do his utmost for the welfare of the state, summoned Liu to be his senior administrator. He dispatched a messenger by ship to go and meet him and to make gifts and offerings in great profusion.

When Lin-chih heard the summons, he boarded the ship but did not accept any of the presents. Instead, all along the way he distributed them to poor and destitute people. By the time they arrived at (Ch'ung's headquarters in) Shang-ming (Hupei) they were all gone. As soon as he saw Ch'ung he took the occasion to state his own uselessness and then beat a hasty retreat.

He continued to live in the Yang-ch'i Mountains for many years. Both when he had clothing and food and when he had not, he always shared what he had with the villagers. When it happened that he himself was destitute, the villagers also did likewise with him. He was most thoroughly trusted by all his neighbors.[3] (*PTSC* 68)

[1]Fu Chien took Hsiang-yang (N. Hupei) in 379; see *TCTC* 104.3288.

[2]Huan was appointed governor of Ching Province in 377; see *TCTC* 104.3282.

[3]*TTCC*: When Lin-chih was young he valued honesty and simplicity, humble deference, and fewness of desires. He loved roaming among hills and swamps and was determined to maintain a free life of retirement from the world.

Huan Ch'ung once went to his home. At the time Lin-chih was picking mulberry leaves and said to Ch'ung, "Since Your Excellency has taken the trouble to honor me with your presence, you should first visit my father."

Ch'ung then went to visit his father, and his father summoned Lin-chih, and only after that did he finally come back, dressed in a coarse bark-cloth garment, and talked with Ch'ung. His father ordered Lin-chih personally to bring thick wine, meat, and vegetables and to wait on the guest. Ch'ung wanted to have one of his own men take his place, but the father refused, saying, "If you have an official do it, then it will go against this old rustic's wishes."

Ch'ung thereupon acquiesced happily and stayed until dusk before finally leaving. He took the occasion to invite Lin-chih to serve as his senior administrator, but the latter steadfastly declined.

The place where he lived in the Yang-ch'i Mountains was near the highway, and people and officials on their way back and forth would always stop at his house. Lin-chih would always wait on them personally, and, whatever gifts they offered, he would never accept any of them.

About 100 li from his home there lived a lone old woman who took sick and was about to die. She said to someone, "It's only Senior Administrator Liu who should bury me." Liu went in person to wait on her, and when she died he took care of her funeral. His acts of kindness and love were all of this sort. He died of old age.

9. Chai T'ang of Nan-yang (Honan) and Chou Shao of Ju-nan (Honan) were friends in their youth. They both lived in retirement at Hsün-yang (Kiangsi). After Yü Liang spoke to Chou about his duty to the present world, Chou proceeded to take office, but Chai clung to his determination more stubbornly than ever. Later Chou went to visit Chai, but the latter would not talk with him.[1]

[1] *HsünYC*: Earlier (in 334), when Yü Liang was appointed governor of Chiang Province (western Hupei and Kiangsi), he heard of Chai T'ang's reputation and, tying his girdle and putting on his sandals, set out to see him. Liang's manner toward him was extremely respectful. T'ang remarked, "Your Excellency is just revering a 'dried tree and rotten stump,' that's all."

Liang praised his ability as a conversationalist and memorialized the emperor to appoint him erudite of the State Academy, but he never took up the post. Yü Liang's superintendent of records said of him, "This gentleman is a reclining dragon and may not be disturbed." He died at home.

10. Meng Chia and his younger brother, Meng Lou, lived in Yang-hsin Prefecture of Wu-ch'ang Commandery (Hupei). Meng Chia moved about in official circles and had a flourishing reputation in the contemporary world, while Meng Lou had never come out from seclusion. People in the capital longed to see him, and accordingly sent a letter to Lou reporting that his elder brother was on the point of death.

In great agitation Lou arrived at the capital. Upon seeing him, the worthies of the time all sighed in veneration, all the while saying to each other, "Since Meng Lou is like this, it's all right if Meng Chia dies."[1]

[1] *MCSM*: When Meng Lou was young he was an admirer of antiquity and wore cotton clothes and ate vegetarian food and lingered beneath the mat door and bamboo hedge (of the hermit), cutting himself off from the affairs that most men love. Both near and distant kin admired his filial devotion. The generalissimo (Huan Wen) had the Prince of K'uai-chi (Ssu-ma Yü) summon him into his administration, but he claimed illness and did not come. The chancellery year after

year kept the position vacant, but he remained tranquilly unconcerned, and to the day of his death never compromised his determination, for which his contemporaries admired him.

11. While the monk K'ang Seng-yüan was living in Yü-chang (Kiangsi, ca. 340) several tens of *li* from the city walls, he built a *vihāra* (*ching-she*) beside a mountain range along the bank of a long stream. Fragrant trees were ranged in the cloistered courtyard; a clear brook gushed along beneath the eaves of the hall. Here he lived at leisure, studying and lecturing, refining his mind with the flavor of the Truth (*li*). Yü Liang and the others came often to see him and observed his daily practice and demeanor, finding his cultivated manner (*feng-liu*) becoming more and more refined. In addition to this his existence was comfortable and he possessed the means for self-contentment. His fame and reputation consequently became so flourishing that later, unable to endure it, he eventually emerged from seclusion. (*KSC* 4; *Taishō* 50.347a)

12. Since Tai K'uei was sharpening his integrity in retirement in the Eastern Mountains (Chekiang), and his elder brother, Tai Tun,[1] was desirous of establishing his merit as a "suppressor of evil" (*shih-o*),[2] the grand tutor, Hsieh An, said to Tun, "How vastly different you two brothers are in your ambition and work!"
Tun replied, "In the case of this petty official, I 'can't endure the misery of poverty,' while in the case of my younger brother, 'it doesn't alter his happiness.'"[3]

[1] Emending the "Tai Lu" of the text to agree with *CS* 79.13a.

[2] See "Songs," No. 253: "Give rest to the Four Quarters . . . Suppress robbers and tyrants."

[3] See "Analects" VI, 11: "Others cannot endure the misery of poverty; for Yen Hui it does not alter his happiness."

13. While Hsü Hsün was living in retirement in a secluded cave south of Yung-hsing Commandery (Chekiang), gifts from noblemen from all around would keep coming in. Someone said to Hsü, "I've heard that the man of Chi Mountain (the ancient recluse, Hsü Yu) did not, it seems, behave quite like this."
Hsü replied, "Food wrapped in husks and rushes and put in boxes and baskets is surely somewhat lighter than the treasure of the whole realm?"[1] (*MCYC*, chung)

[1] The sage-king Yao had offered the realm to Hsü Yu; see *Chuang-tzu* XXVIII, 10a (Watson, p. 309).

14. Fan Hsüan had never in his life entered the gate of any public office. Han Po was once riding with him and, misleading him, started to ride into the commandery headquarters.[1] Fan immediately jumped down from the rear of the carriage.[2]

[1] Probably in Yü-chang (Kiangsi), Fan Hsüan's home, where Han Po once served as grand warden.

[2] *HCYC*: When Fan Hsüan was young he esteemed living in retirement.

His home was in Yü-chang Commandery, where he established a reputation for purity and incorruptibility.

15. Every time Ch'ih Ch'ao heard of someone desiring to live in lofty retirement, he would always put up a subsidy for him of a million cash, and in addition would build a residence for him. While he was living in the Shan Mountains (Chekiang) he once constructed a house for Tai K'uei which was extremely refined and genteel. When Tai first went there to live[1] he wrote letters to all his intimate friends, saying, "Recently when I arrived in the Shan Mountains, it was like coming to an official mansion."

Ch'ih also offered to put up a subsidy of a million cash for Fu Yüan,[2] but Fu's retirement failed to meet his standards, so he did not carry through his bequest.[3] (CS 67.22b; IWLC 36; TPYL 510)

[1] The Sung text reads, "When Tai first went to his former residence (*chiu-chü*)." I have followed IWLC 36 and TPYL 510 in deleting the *chiu*, "former," from in front of *chü*, "residence," and have translated *chü* as a verb, "to live."

[2] The "Fu Ch'iung" of the Sung text is evidently an error; see above, SSHY VII, 25, and the FuSP.

[3] CS 67.22b: Ch'ih was by nature fond of hearing about people who lived in retirement. If any of them was able to decline the comforts of life and shake out his clothes (in farewell to the world), he would build a house for him and make vessels and clothing, and provide servants and boys, and lay out one hundred pieces of gold, sparing no expense.

16. Hsü Hsün was fond of wandering among mountains and streams and his physique was well suited to mountain climbing. His contemporaries used to say, "Hsü not only has superb feelings (*sheng-ch'ing*); he really has the equipment for traversing the superb (*chi-sheng*)."[1] (MCYC, chung; SWLC, ch'ien 14)

[1] A pun on the word *sheng*, "surpassing," "superb," which had a particular reference to famous mountains of outstanding beauty (*ming-sheng*).

17. Ch'ih Hui was on friendly terms with the Buddhist householder (*chü-shih*) Hsieh Fu and often praised him, saying, "Although Hsieh Fu's knowledge and experience don't surpass those of other men, for him those areas which may ensnare the mind have utterly disappeared."[1]

[1] HCYC: Hsieh Fu occupied himself with long fasts and offerings, entertaining monks and sharing their duties, teaching and giving alms without weariness. Because of his mother's old age he returned to Jo-yeh in the Southern Mountains (south of K'uai-chi). The governor (of K'uai-chi Principality), Ch'ih Yin, recommended that he be summoned to the capital for the post of erudite, but he did not take up his duties.

Earlier the moon had transgressed the constellation Shao-wei, also known as the Recluse, Ch'u-shih (part of Leo), which prognosticators interpreted to presage (the death of) a recluse. At the time, Tai K'uei was living in the Shan Mountains (in K'uai-chi

Commandery), and since he had excellent abilities and skills, and associated with noble and great men, he was more celebrated than Hsieh Fu. (At this news) his contemporaries became concerned for him, when suddenly Fu died. The people of K'uai-chi Commandery then teased the people of Wu (Soochow), saying, "The eminent gentleman of Wu (Tai had been a recluse in Wu for several months; see *CS* 94.33a) sought death in vain!" (Cf. *CS* 94.30ab)

CHAPTER XIX

Worthy Beauties

1. Ch'en Ying was a native of Tung-yang Commandery (southern Shantung). When he was young he cultivated virtuous conduct and was known and praised in his home village. In the great disorders at the end of the Ch'in (ca. 207 B.C.) the people of Tung-yang were on the point of making Ying their chief (*chu*), but his mother said to him, "It won't do. Ever since I've been a wife in your family we've rarely experienced anything but poverty and low station. To become wealthy and honorable all at once is unlucky. It would be better to be a man in the ranks under the command of somebody else. Then, if his affairs are successful, in a modest way you'll share in his benefits. And if they're unsuccessful, the calamity will have somebody else to fall on."[1] (*SC* 7.3b-4a)

   [1]Ch'en followed this advice and offered his services to the eventually unsuccessful Hsiang Yü.

2. Since the palace women of the Han Emperor Yüan (Liu Shih, r. 48-33 B.C.) were numerous, he ordered an artist to make portraits of them, so that whenever he wanted to call one, he could always summon her according to her portrait. The ordinary ones among them all bribed the artist, but Wang Ch'iang, whose face and figure were very beautiful, was resolved not to seek favors by unfair means, and as a result the artist disfigured her appearance in her portrait.
   Later the Hsiung-nu came on a peace mission, seeking a lovely lady from the Han emperor.[1] The emperor felt that Wang Ch'iang would fulfill the qualifications to go, but after having summoned her for an interview, was loathe to let her go. However, her name had already been sent on, and he did not wish to change in mid-course, so in the end she went. (*TPYL* 381)

   [1]*HS* (94.7ab): In the first year of the Ching-ning era (33 B.C.), the *shan-yü*, Hu-han-hsieh, came to court and said he wished to marry into the Han imperial family, so that he might become more

intimately associated with it. Emperor Yüan bestowed on him the
daughter of a good family from the rear palace named Wang Ch'iang.
The *shan-yü* was delighted and sent up a letter expressing his wish
to protect the borders. (Cf. also HS 9.14a; trans. H. H. Dubs,
History of the Former Han Dynasty, vol. II, Baltimore, 1944, p.
335.)

CT: When Wang Ch'iang was in her seventeenth year her manners
and appearance were exceedingly beautiful and she was known
throughout the empire for her chastity. But her father, Wang Jang,
would not promise her to any other important persons who sought
her hand, and in the end presented her to the Han Emperor Yüan.
The emperor was an impetuous and disorganized person (*ts'âu-ts'i)
who was unable to make distinctions between members of his harem,
and Wang Ch'iang's resentment over this was of long standing. It
happened that when the *shan-yü* sent his emissary, the emperor ordered his palace ladies to adorn themselves and come out for the
emissary to invite one of them. The emperor then announced
throughout the palace, "Anyone who would like to go to the *shan-
yü*, rise!"

Sighing deeply, Ch'iang shifted from her mat and rose. When the
emperor looked at her he was filled with surprise and remorse. But
by this time the emissary had also seen her, and the emperor had
no way of detaining her, so in the end he bestowed her upon the
shan-yü. The *shan-yü* was greatly pleased and presented her with
precious gifts.

Wang Ch'iang had a son, named Shih-wei. When the *shan-yü* died
Shih-wei succeeded to the throne. The usual custom with the
Hsiung-nu is that when the father dies, the son takes his mother
to wife. Wang Ch'iang asked Shih-wei, "Are you a Chinese or a
Hsiung-nu?"

Shih-wei answered, "I just want to be a Hsiung-nu." At this
Wang Ch'iang swallowed poison and took her own life.

(The story is pure fiction, since the *shan-yü*, Hu-han-hsieh,
died in 31 B.C., only two years after his marriage to Wang Ch'iang,
and was succeeded by the son of an earlier Hsiung-nu wife. See HS
94.10b.)

3. The Han Emperor Ch'eng (Liu Ao, r. 32-7 B.C.) doted upon Lady Flying Swallow, Chao Fei-yen. Fei-yen slandered Lady Pan Chieh-yü,
claiming she was invoking imprecations (against Lady Chao), whereupon
they interrogated her. In her defense she said, "I've heard that
'life and death are appointed by Fate, and wealth and honor depend on
Heaven.'[1] If even the cultivator of goodness doesn't find happiness,
what can the doer of evil hope for? If ghosts and spirits have any
understanding, they'll not accept the complaints of the evil and obsequious, and if they *haven't* any understanding, what advantage is
there in complaining to them? Of course I didn't do it."[2] (HS 97B.8b;
TPYL 144)

[1]"Analects" XII, 5.

[2]HS (97B.8a-10b): The emperor was going on an outing in the rear
park and wished to have Lady Pan ride with him in the palanquin
(*nien*). Chieh-yü declined his invitation.

(The scene is illustrated, not without humor, in Ku K'ai-chih's hand scroll, "Instructions of the Palace Preceptress," now in the British Museum.)

When Chao Fei-yen slandered Empress Hsü and Pan Chieh-yü, Chieh-yü countered with the defense (quoted in the anecdote above). The emperor took pity on her and presented her with one hundred catties of gold.

Fei-yen was arrogant and envious, and Chieh-yü, fearing her life would be endangered, requested to wait on the dowager empress Wang in the Palace of Eternal Trust (Ch'ang-hsin kung). When the emperor died (7 B.C.), Chieh-yü was granted full rights of burial in the imperial mausoleum, and was placed there upon her death.

4. When the Wei Emperor Wu (Ts'ao Ts'ao) died (in 220), his son, Emperor Wen (Ts'ao P'ei, r. 220-227), took over all his father's palace women to serve as his own attendants. When Emperor Wen was ill and near death (in 227), his mother, the dowager empress Pien,[1] came out of seclusion to visit the sick man. As the dowager empress entered the door she observed that the attendants were all the beloved favorites of former days. She asked, "When did you come here?"

They replied, "We came over at the time of recalling the spirit (of the late Emperor Wu)."[2]

For this reason the dowager empress went no farther, but sighing, said, "Not even dogs and rats would eat your leftovers.[3] Death is certainly what you deserve!"

When she went to (his burial in) the imperial mausoleum, she did not even perform the ritual mourning.

[1] *WeiS*: (When Empress Pien was born) there was a yellow vapor filling the room for several days, and her father, Marquis Ching, wondered at it and inquired of the fortune-teller Wang Yüeh*, who said, "This is an auspicious omen."

When she was in her twentieth year Ts'ao Ts'ao took her into his household in Chiao (Anhui). Her nature was simple and frugal, and she had no liking for flowery ornaments. She had the virtuous conduct befitting a mother.

[2] The departed spirit was recalled immediately after death by holding a garment formerly worn by the deceased.

[3] See *Tso-chuan*, Chuang 6 (Legge V, 79): The Marquis of Teng said, "(If I kill the Viscount of Ch'u,) people will not even eat my leftovers."

HS 98.16a: (When Wang Mang demanded the state seal from Empress Yüan in A.D. 9, she replied,) "Anyone who would take advantage of other people's misfortunes to seize their state, who no longer regards kindness or morality--not even dogs and pigs would eat his leftovers!"

5. Mother Chao (Chao I, d. 243) once gave her daughter in marriage. When the daughter was about to depart for her husband's home, Mother Chao admonished her, saying, "Be careful not to do any good."

The daughter said, "If I don't do good, then may I do evil?"

Her mother said, "If even good may not be done, how much less evil!"[1]

[1] *Huai-nan-tzu* (XVI, 274): There was once a man who was giving his

daughter in marriage who instructed her, "If you do good, good people will resent it." She replied, "Then I suppose I ought to do evil?" He said, "If even good may not be done, how much less evil!"

> SSHY Comm.: Empress Yang (consort of Ssu-ma Shih) said of this passage, "Although this advice is vulgar, it may be used to instruct people in the world."

6. Hsü Yün's wife was the daughter of Juan Kung and the younger sister of Juan K'an. She was extraordinarily homely. After the marriage ceremony was over, Yün had no intention of ever entering her apartment again. The members of her family were very upset over this. It happened once that Yün was having a guest come, and his wife had a female slave look to see who it was. She returned and reported, "It's Master Huan." Now "Master Huan" was Huan Fen.

The wife said, "Then there's nothing to worry about. Huan will surely urge him to come to my apartment."

As expected, Huan said to Hsü, "Since the Juan family gave you a homely daughter in marriage, they obviously did so with some purpose in mind. You would do well to look into it."

Accordingly, Hsü had a change of heart and entered his wife's apartment. But the moment he saw her he immediately wanted to leave again. His wife foresaw that if he went out this time there would be no further chance of his returning, so she seized his robe in an effort to detain him. Hsü took the occasion to say to his wife, "A wife should have four virtues.[1] How many of them do *you* have?"

His wife answered, "Where your bride is deficient is only in her appearance. But a *gentleman* should have a hundred deeds. How many have *you*?"

"I have them all."

"Of those hundred deeds, virtue is the first. If you love sensual beauty, but don't love virtue,[2] how can you say you have them all?"

Yün looked ashamed, and thereafter held her in respect and honor. (SKWei 9.35a, comm., quoting WSCC; SWLC, hou 12)

> [1]*Chou-li* (I, 48): The nine preceptresses (*chiu-pin*) have charge of the methods of womanly instruction in training the nine imperial concubines (*chiu-yü*) in womanly virtue, womanly speech, womanly appearance, and womanly work.
>
> (Cheng Hsüan's comment interprets these to mean, respectively, chastity and obedience, graciousness and cultivation, complaisance and loveliness, and the weaving of silk and linen.)

> [2]"Analects" IX, 16: I have not seen any who love virtue as they love sensual beauty.

7. While Hsü Yün was serving as a clerk in the Board of Civil Office most of his appointments were from his own village. The Wei Emperor Ming (Ts'ao Jui, r. 227-239) dispatched an officer of the Palace Guard to apprehend him. Yün's wife (Lady Juan) came out and warned her husband, saying, "An enlightened ruler may be forced to yield through reason, but it's difficult to appeal to him through his emotions."

After Yün arrived, the emperor closely interrogated him. Yün replied, "(Confucius said,) 'Recommend those who are known to you.'[1] Your servant's fellow villagers are the ones who are known to him.

Your Majesty may investigate and see for yourself if they are suited to their offices or not. If they're not suited to their offices, your servant will bear the blame for it."

After investigation, it was found that for every office he had secured the right man, so that in the end the emperor released him. And since Yün's clothing was worn and tattered, the emperor issued an order to supply him with new clothes.

When Yün was first apprehended, his entire household was weeping and wailing, but his bride, Lady Juan, said with complete self-composure, "Don't worry. After a while he'll return." Whereupon she cooked some millet gruel and waited for him. In a short time Yün arrived.[2] (SKWei 9.34b, comm., quoting WSCC; SWLC, hsü 4)

[1] "Analects" XIII, 2.

[2] WSCC: Earlier while Yün was serving in the Board of Civil Office, he selected and transferred the grand warden of a certain commandery. Emperor Ming suspected that the man he employed was not in the proper sequence and was about to punish him for it. Yün's wife, Lady Juan, came out barefooted and said, "An enlightened ruler, etc." Yün nodded assent and went in. When the emperor angrily upbraided him, Yün replied, "Although the term for the warden of Such-and-such Commandery was full, and his documents had arrived first, nevertheless the *year* (of appointment) is secondary; the *day* is primary."

The emperor, coming forward, took up the case and examined it, and finally became reconciled. When he dismissed Yün, observing that his clothes were worn out, he said, "You're an honest official."

(Cf. SKWei 9.34b, comm., quoting WSCC. It seems that two wardens' terms of office were up simultaneously, and both were eligible for transfer. Yün had merely transferred the one whose documents indicated an earlier *day* of appointment, disregarding the fact that in terms of the *year* both were eligible.)

8. When Hsü Yün was punished (in 254) by Prince Ching (Ssu-ma Shih), his servants went in to tell his wife (Lady Juan), who was just then at her weaving. Her spirit and facial expression showed no change. She only said, "I knew it was so, long ago."[1]

The servants wanted to hide Yün's sons (Ch'i and Meng), but his wife said, "Don't concern yourselves with the sons' affairs."

Later she moved to the neighborhood of Yün's tomb. Prince Ching dispatched Chung Hui to visit the boys. If the level of their ability came up to that of their father, he was to apprehend them. The sons consulted with their mother about it, and she said, "Even though you two are fine boys, your ability and endowment are not excessive. If you speak out frankly with him whatever is in your hearts and thoughts, you'll have nothing to worry about. It's not necessary to show extreme grief, either; stop at whatever point Hui stops. Beyond that you might ask a few questions about affairs at court." The sons followed her advice. After Hui returned he reported the circumstances (to Prince Ching), and in the end they were spared.

[1] WC: Earlier Hsü Yün had been on intimate terms with Hsia-hou Hsüan and Li Feng. There was a falsely fabricated edict making Hsüan generalissimo and Yün grand marshal, both with noble rank

and high authority. Without warning someone came riding before
dawn and handed the edict to Yün's gateman, announcing, "There's
an edict!" and then galloped away. Yün threw the document in the
fire and burned it without revealing its contents to Ssu-ma Shih.

  WeiL: The following year (254) Li Feng was arrested. Yün was
about to go for an interview with the generalissimo (Ssu-ma Shih),
and had already gone out the gate, but was vacillating and uncertain. When he was half way there he turned back to fetch his ceremonial trousers. When the generalissimo heard about it, he chided
him, saying, "Certainly I have arrested Li Feng. What are all you
gentlemen and great officers so nervous about?"

  It happened that the General Governing the North, Liu Ching,
had just died, so Yün was appointed in his place. The generalissimo sent a letter to Yün in which he said, "Although General
Governing the North is a post with few duties, you will be controlling an entire area. I will think of you beating the flowery
drum, establishing your vermilion credentials, putting your local
province in order. This is what might be called 'walking by day
dressed in embroidered silks.'" (A parody of a celebrated remark
by Hsiang Yü; see *SC* 7.17a.)

  It happened that some official memorialized the throne to the
effect that Yün had previously taken official food and monies and
grain and distributed them without authorization to various riffraff and to his own underlings. His death sentence was commuted to
banishment to the border. He died *en route*. (Cf. *SKWei* 9.34b,
comm., quoting *WeiL*.)

  WSCC: When Yün was appointed General Governing the North he was
happy, and said to his wife, "Now I know I've escaped!" His wife
replied, "Your ruin is obvious in this; what escape is there?" (Cf.
SKWei 9.35a, comm., quoting *WSCC*.)

  CCKT: Since Yün had correct (i.e., loyalist) feelings, and was
on bad terms with "Emperor Wen" (Ssu-ma Chao), the latter had him
killed in secret.

  (Liu Chün in the Commentary also mentions a letter of Lady Juan
to her husband, contained in the *FJC*, in which she describes the
origins of his troubles in terms which are "exceedingly bitter and
heartrending," but whose text he unfortunately finds "too long" to
record.)

9. Wang Kuang took to wife the daughter of Chu-ko Tan. When he entered
her room and they exchanged words for the first time, Wang blurted out
to his wife, "My bride's spirit and appearance are ignoble and low-
class, totally unlike her father!"

  His wife replied, "My great husband can't exactly compare with *his*
father (Wang Ling), either, yet he's pitting a mere woman against a
magnificent hero!"[1] (*CHC* 19; *TPYL* 382)

[1] A later commentator, who refers to himself as "Your servant"
(*ch'en*), writes: "Wang Kuang was a famous gentleman; how could he
have spoken lightly of his father-in-law? The story is untrue!"

10. When Wang Ching was young he lived in poverty and want, but after
he became an official his salary reached two thousand piculs. His
mother said to him, "You were originally the son of a poor family.
Now that your salary has reached two thousand piculs, don't you think
you might stop with this?"

Ching was unable to use her advice, and eventually became president of the Imperial Secretariat. But since he had assisted the Wei, he was deemed disloyal to the Chin, and was apprehended (in 260). Weeping profusely, he apologized to his mother, saying, "Because I failed to follow your advice, we've now come to today's extremity!"

Without the slightest expression of reproach, his mother said to him, "As a son you were filial, and as a minister you were loyal. With both filial devotion and loyalty, in what way have you betrayed me?"[1] (SKWei 9.35b).

[1] WCSY: During the troubles of Ts'ao Mao (whose unsuccessful attempt in 260 to check the rise of the Ssu-ma clan is told above, SSHY V, 8, n. 1) the palace attendants, Wang Ch'en* and Wang Yeh, hastened to inform Ssu-ma Chao, but Wang Ching, because he was a proper and honest man, did not leave the palace with them. Through Ch'en and Yeh he declared his intention, but later (Chao) had Ching executed, together with his mother.

CCKT: When Wang Ch'en* and Wang Yeh were about to leave (the palace), they called out to Ching, who did not follow them but said, "My dear friends, you go ahead."

HCCC: Earlier, when Ts'ao Mao was about to punish Ssu-ma Chao on his own, Ching had admonished him, saying, "Long ago when Duke Chao of Lu (sixth cent. B.C.) couldn't endure the Chi family, he was defeated and fled and lost his state, becoming the laughing-stock of the whole realm. Today the power has rested in the Ssu-ma family for a long time. It is not a matter of only one day's standing that everyone in court would give their lives for them, without any regard for principles either of rebellion or subservience. Moreover, the Palace Guard is an empty shell without an inch of armor. How could Your Majesty possibly make use of it? Yet, if suddenly you should do so, by attempting to rid yourself of evil, would you not only deepen it the more?"

Mao did not listen. Afterward, they killed both Ching and his mother. When he was about to die, he wept and apologized to his mother, but her facial expression did not change. Smiling, she said to him, "Who among men doesn't die? In the past the reason I restrained you was that I feared you wouldn't keep to your proper place. But now that we're both dying together, what is there to regret?" (Cf. SKWei 9.35b, comm., quoting WCSY)

KPCC: Wang Ching was a proper and honest man, but because he was disloyal to our dynasty (i.e., Chin), he was executed.

SSHY Comm.: According to what is recorded in CCKT and KPCC, Ching was really loyal and blameless toward the Wei. Yet the WCSY states on the one hand that he was "a proper and honest man," and on the other that "through Ch'en* and Yeh he declared his intention." What a contradiction! Therefore the words of the two accounts (CCKT and KPCC) get closer to the truth.

11. The first time Shan T'ao met Hsi K'ang and Juan Chi he became united with them in a friendship "stronger than metal and fragrant as orchids."[1] Shan's wife, Lady Han, realized that her husband's relationship with the two men was different from ordinary friendships, and asked him about it. Shan replied, "It's only these two gentlemen whom I may consider the friends of my mature years."

His wife said, "In antiquity Hsi Fu-chi's wife also personally observed Hu Yen and Chao Ts'ui.² I'd like to peep at these friends of yours. Is it all right?"

On another day the two men came, and his wife urged Shan to detain them overnight. After preparing wine and meat, that night she made a hole through the wall, and it was dawn before she remembered to return to her room.

When Shan came in he asked her, "What did you think of the two men?" His wife replied, "Your own ability is in no way comparable to theirs. It's only on the basis of your knowledge of men and your judgment that you should be their friend."

Shan said, "They, too, have always considered my judgment to be superior."³ (*TPYL* 409; *TPKC* 235)

¹"Book of Changes" (*Hsi-tz'u* A6; Wilhelm I, 329): When two men are of one mind, their keenness will cut metal; the words of those who are of one mind are fragrant as orchids.

²See *Tso-chuan*, Hsi 23 (Legge V, 187): The son of the Duke of Chin, Chung Erh, was passing through Ts'ao (Shantung). Duke Kung of Ts'ao heard that he had unseparated (?) ribs (*p'ien-hsieh*), and wanted to observe him naked in the bath. Hsi Fu-chi's wife said, "I observed the followers of the son of the Duke of Chin, Hu Yen and Chao Ts'ui, and they are both worthy of being ministers of state."

³*CYC*: Shan T'ao's cultivated tolerance was untrammeled and free, and his judgment vast and far-reaching. His mind remained beyond the realm of worldly affairs, yet he stooped and rose with the times. He once had a relationship with Juan Chi and Hsi K'ang which transcended words. But whereas all the other gentlemen encountered difficulties in the world, T'ao alone preserved his vast overflowing judgment.

WYCS: Lady Han possessed ability and understanding. Before Shan T'ao became an official he used to say to her in jest, "You can endure poverty, but when I reach one of the Three Ducal Offices, I don't know whether you can stand being a lady or not, that's all!"

12. The daughter born to Wang Tun's wife, Lady Chung (Chung Yen), was beautiful and chaste. Her elder brother, Wang Chi, was looking about for a good match for her, but had not yet found any. There was a certain son of a military family who had outstanding ability, and Wang, wishing to give his younger sister in marriage to him, consulted his mother about it. Lady Chung said, "If he really is someone with ability, his background may be overlooked. However, you must be sure to let me see him."

Wang Chi accordingly had the son of the military family mingle with a crowd of commoners, and let his mother watch them from behind the curtain. Afterward his mother said to Chi, "The one with such-and-such clothes and physique—isn't he the one you had picked?"

Wang Chi replied, "He's the one."

His mother said, "This boy's ability is adequate to raise him above the crowd. However, his background is humble, and if he doesn't have a long life, he'll never get to exercise his ability or usefulness. As I observed his physiognomy and bony structure (*hsing-ku*), it's evident he won't live to old age. You may not contract a marriage with him." Wang Chi followed her advice, and as it turned out, in a few years the son of the military family died. (*CS* 96.4a)

13. Chia Ch'ung's first wife, Li Wan, was the daughter of Li Feng. When Feng was executed (in 254), she was divorced and exiled to the border (Lak-lang, Korea). Later she was pardoned and allowed to return. But Ch'ung had by then already been remarried to Kuo Huai, the daughter of Kuo P'ei. Emperor Wu (Ssu-ma Yen, r. 265-290) made a special dispensation, permitting Ch'ung to have a left-hand and a right-hand wife. But Lady Li, who was living apart outside the capital, was unwilling to return to Ch'ung's house.[1] Lady Kuo said to Ch'ung, "I want to go over and have a look at this Li woman."

Ch'ung said, "She's a firm, unbending person with ability and spirit. It would be better if you didn't go." In spite of this, Lady Kuo decked herself out in her full regalia and went at the head of a large retinue of attendants and slaves. When she arrived and entered the door, Lady Li rose to greet her, and Kuo unconsciously found her legs giving way of their own accord, and presently she was kneeling down, repeatedly making obeisance. After she had returned and related the incident to Ch'ung, Ch'ung said, "What did I tell you?"[2] (CS 40.8b)

[1] CCKT: When Emperor Wu ascended the throne (265), Lady Li was pardoned and returned to Lo-yang, and her daughter, Chia Ch'üan, the consort of Prince Hsien of Ch'i (Ssu-ma Yu, d. 283) wanted to have Ch'ung send Lady Kuo away and take back her mother. Ch'ung would not agree to this, but built a villa for Lady Li outside Lo-yang and had no communication with her.

When Ch'ung's mother, Lady Liŭ, was about to die, Ch'ung asked her what she wanted to say, and she replied, "I instructed you to welcome Lady Li back, and you still weren't willing. What point is there in asking about anything else?"

[2] CCKT: Emperor Wu, in view of the fact that Li Feng had offended the house of Chin, and moreover because Lady Kuo was the mother of the consort of the crown prince, Ssu-ma Chung (later Emperor Hui, r. 290-306), and therefore had no reason to be divorced, accordingly sent down an edict requiring Chia to sever all relations (with Lady Li), and not permitting any communication with her.

WYCS: After Chia Ch'ung had divorced Lady Li, he was remarried to Kuo Huai, the daughter of Kuo P'ei, the grand warden of Ch'eng-yang. After the ban against Lady Li had been lifted, an imperial rescript permitted Ch'ung to have a left-hand and a right-hand wife. Ch'ung's mother also admonished him to welcome Lady Li back. Kuo Huai was furious. Baring her arms she scolded Ch'ung, saying, "In your merit as codifier of the laws and aider in founding the dynasty I have a part. How does Li get to share it with me?"

Ch'ung accordingly built a house in Yung-nien Village (a suburb of Lo-yang) to keep Lady Li safe. Kuo Huai only learned of it later. Whenever Ch'ung left the house she always sent someone to keep an eye on him. So, although the imperial rescript permitted him to have a left-hand and a right-hand wife, Ch'ung replied to it with humble protestations that he dared not fulfill this ritual obligation.

SSHY Comm.: Now the CCKT, on the one hand, states that Emperor Wu sent down a rescript not permitting Lady Li to return, but the WYCS and (Chia) Ch'ung PC, on the other hand, both state that the rescript permitted his having a left-hand and a right-hand wife, but that Ch'ung, out of fear of Lady Kuo, dared not welcome Li back. The accounts in these three sources are by no means unanimous, and it is not known which is correct.

However, there were other reasons for Lady Li's not returning, and the statement in the *Shih-shuo* that she herself was unwilling to return is mistaken. Moreover, Kuo Huai was stubborn and wolfish, how could she have made obeisance when she approached Li? It's all nonsense!

14. Chia Ch'ung's first wife, Lady Li, wrote a book of "Instructions for Daughters" (*Nü-hsün*), which gained currency in the world. Lady Li's daughter, Chia Ch'üan, became the consort of Prince Hsien of Ch'i (Ssu-ma Yu), and Chia Nan-feng, the daughter of Ch'ung's second wife, Lady Kuo (Kuo Huai), became the empress of Emperor Hui (Ssu-ma Chung, r. 291-306). When Ch'ung died (in 282) the daughters of Ladies Li and Kuo each wished to have her own mother buried with him. For years the matter remained undecided, until Empress Chia was deposed (300). Lady Li was then duly buried with Ch'ung, and the matter was finally settled. (*CS* 40.8b)

15. When Wang Chan was young he had never been engaged to be married, and on his own behalf he sought the hand of the daughter of Ho P'u. Since his father, Wang Ch'ang, considered him to be stupid, and there happened to be no marriageable person available, Ch'ang let him follow his fancy, and gave his consent.

After they were married, it turned out that the bride possessed both beautiful features and chaste virtue. After she gave birth to Wang Ch'eng*, she became the maternal model of the Wang family. Someone asked Chan, "How did you know what kind of person she was?"

He replied, "I once saw her at the well drawing water. In every movement and gesture she never departed from her normal manner, and never once did she cast an improper glance. It was by this that I knew." (*SWLC*, hou 14)

16. Wang Hun's wife, Chung Yen, a daughter of the Chung family, was the great-granddaughter of the grand tutor, Chung Yu, and in her own right possessed outstanding ability and womanly virtue.[1] Lady Chung and Lady Ho, as the wives respectively of the elder and younger Wang brothers, Wang Hun and Wang Chan, always treated each other with affectionate respect. Lady Chung did not, because of her noble origin, act condescendingly toward Lady Ho, nor did Lady Ho, because of her lowly origin, act obsequiously toward Lady Chung. Within the household of Wang Chan's son, Wang Ch'eng*, they followed the rules of Lady Ho, and within the household of Wang Hun they took as their model the etiquette of Lady Chung. (*CS* 96.4ab)

[1]*FJC*: Lady Chung possessed literary ability, and her poems, poetic essays, hymns, and obituaries have become current in the world.

17. Li Chung was the son of Li Ping and a famous gentleman of the central Hsia (the area of Lo-yang). At the time people compared him to Wang Yen. When Sun Hsiu* first wanted to establish his prestige and power (in 300), everyone said, "Yüeh Kuang is the people's[1] hope; he may not be killed. Someone less important than Li Chung, on the other hand, isn't worth killing." So he compelled Chung to take his own life.

Earlier, while Chung was at home, someone ran in through the gate, and, taking a memorandum from inside his topknot, showed it to Chung. As Chung read it, his face paled. Entering the inner quarters, he showed it to his daughter, who immediately cried out, "It's all over!" Chung, understanding her meaning, went out and proceeded to take his own life.[2]

This daughter was extremely high-minded and intelligent, and Chung always consulted her about every situation.

[1] Emending *shih*, "family," to the graphically similar *min*, "people."

[2] *SSHY* Comm.: The sources all state that Chung, realizing that the Prince of Chao, Ssu-ma Lun, was about to raise a revolt, became so sick over it that he eventually died. Yet this source claims that he committed suicide, which runs quite contrary to the facts. Moreover, Ssu-ma Lun and Sun Hsiu* were cruel and tyrannical men, who with every move inflicted death and execution. Since they wished to establish their authority and power, they would without question have killed Chung openly. Why should they have forced him to commit suicide?

18. When Chou Chün was serving as General Pacifying the East, he was once out hunting when a violent rainstorm came up, just as he was passing by the home of the Li family (Li Po-tsung) of Ju-nan Commandery (Honan). The Li family was wealthy and well provided, but, as it happened, none of the men were at home. There was a daughter named Lo-hsiu, who, hearing that there was a noble person outside, with the help of one female slave slaughtered pigs and goats and prepared food and drink for several tens of men. Everything was carried out to perfection, and Chou did not hear the sound of anyone. When he peeked in surreptitiously, all he saw was a lone girl, whose form and appearance were unusually beautiful. Chün took the occasion to seek her for a concubine, but her father and elder brothers would not give their consent.

Lo-hsiu said to them, "Since our household is 'ruined and in trouble' (*t'ien-ts'ui*),[1] why grudge a lone daughter? If we contract a marriage with a noble family, hereafter we might be greatly benefited."

Her father and brothers followed her advice, and subsequently she gave birth to Chou I and his younger brothers, Chou Sung and Chou Mo. When they were grown Lo-hsiu said to I and the others, "The only reason I compromised my integrity to become a concubine in your family was to provide for my own household. If you don't treat the members of my family as you would your own kin, I for my part don't care to live out my remaining years."

Chou I and the others all obeyed her command, and from this time onward, as long as Lady Li lived, her family received openly equal treatment with members of the Chou family.[2] (*CS* 96.7b-8a)

[1] "Songs," No. 264, stanza 5.

[2] Liu Chün notes in the Commentary that according to the *Chou SP*, Chou Chün "took to wife" (*ch'ü*) the daughter of Li Po-tsung. She was not his "concubine" (*ch'ieh*).

19. When T'ao K'an was young he had great ambitions, but his family was desperately poor, and he lived with his mother, Lady Chan. A

native of the same commandery (P'o-yang, in Kiangsi), Fan K'uei by name, had always been well known, and when he was recommended for the degree Filial and Incorrupt (*hsiao-lien*, in 303), he stopped at K'an's house for the night (on his way to the capital). At the time sleet and snow had been falling for days, and K'an's house was "bare as hanging stone chimes,"[1] yet K'uei's horses and servants were extremely numerous. K'an's mother, Lady Chan, said to K'an, "You just go and see to it that the guests stay. I'll think of something."

Since Lady Chan's hair reached all the way to the floor, she cut it off and made it into two switches, which she sold for several *hu* of rice. She then chopped the pillars of the room, removing half of each for firewood, and ripped up the straw bed mats to make fodder for the horses. As the day drew toward evening, she served an exquisite meal, and no one in the company had any lack. K'uei not only sighed in admiration over her ability and resourcefulness, but also thanked her profusely for her generous intentions.

The next morning, as K'uei was leaving, K'an escorted him on his way, not stopping until he had traveled a hundred *li* or more. K'uei said, "I think you'd better return, sir (*chün*)." But K'an still did not go back. Finally K'uei said, "You (*ch'ing*) may go now! When I get to Lo-yang, I'll say a good word on your behalf." At this K'an finally turned back.

When K'uei reached Lo-yang he proceeded to praise K'an to Yang Cho, Ku Jung, and the others, and thus he gained a great and excellent reputation.[2] (*CS* 96.6a; 66.6ab)

[1] See *Tso-chuan*, Hsi 26 (Legge V, 198).

[2] *CYC* (cf. *CS* 66.6a-7a): T'ao K'an's father, Tan, took to wife the daughter of the Chan family of Hsin-kan (Kiangsi), who gave birth to K'an. Lady Chan was modest and respectful and possessed wisdom and ingenuity. Because the T'ao family was poor and low in status, she spun and reeled silk to provide for K'an, and had him make friendships with persons superior to himself. When K'an was young he served as a petty official in Hsün-yang Commandery (Kiangsi). The candidate for the degree Filial and Incorrupt, Fan K'uei of P'o-yang Commandery, was once passing by and stopped overnight at K'an's house. At the time, it was snowing hard and there was no straw in K'an's house. Lady Chan removed the straw mats on which they slept and ripped them up to provide for him. She secretly cut her hair and sold it to supply the needs of the guests. When K'uei learned of it he sighed in admiration. As K'uei was leaving, K'an accompanied him on his way. K'uei asked, "Do you want to be an official?"

K'an replied, "I have an ambition to become grand warden of a commandery."

K'uei said, "I'll talk with people and see if it can be done." When he passed by Lu-chiang Commandery (near Hsün-yang) he praised K'an to Chang K'uei, who summoned him to fill a vacancy on his staff, and recommended K'an for the degree Filial and Incorrupt. He was appointed secretary.

At the time, [the senior secretary of] Yü-chang [Principality (Kiangsi), Yang Cho, was a fellow villager of K'an, and had been praised in the village evaluations. K'an went to visit him. Cho said, "The 'Book of Changes' states: 'The pure and steadfast is worthy to manage affairs' (Hex. 1; Wilhelm II, 9). T'ao K'an is

such a person." Riding with him in the same carriage, he went to
see the clerk of the Central Secretariat,] Ku Jung. [Jung admired
him greatly.] Someone chided Cho, saying, "What are you doing
riding in the same carriage with a commoner?"

Cho replied, "This is an impoverished man of ability."

(The garbled text has been restored by interpolations from CS
66.7a, which appear in square brackets.)

WYCS: After T'ao K'an's mother had cut off her hair to take
care of her guests, someone hearing of it sighed and said, "Unless
she were such a mother, she never would have borne such a son!" So
saying, he recommended K'an to Chang K'uei. Yang Cho also recommended him. Later, when Cho became grader for ten commanderies, he
recommended K'an for minor grader in P'o-yang Commandery, and
after that he began to gain high rank.

20. When T'ao K'an was young he served as a minor official in charge
of fish weirs (in Hsün-yang Commandery). He once sent a present of
salted fish (cha) in an earthenware crock (k'an) to his mother (Lady
Chan). His mother sealed the fish in the crock, and, handing it back
to the messenger, sent back a letter upbraiding K'an as follows:
"While you are serving as a minor official, if I receive official
property as a present, it is not only of no benefit; it even adds to
my unhappiness!"[1] (CS 96.5b; IWLC 72; PTSC 146; TPYL 758, 862)

[1](T'ao) K'an PC: K'an's mother, Lady Chan, was worthy and intelligent and full of proper instructions. While K'an was in Wu-ch'ang
(Hupei, 325-328), he used to eat and drink at his ease with his
underlings, but always observed a limit in his drinking. When
someone urged him to take a little more, K'an was reflective for a
long time, and finally said, "Long ago in my youth I was often
under the influence of liquor, and as a consequence my two parents
suffered want. It's for this reason I dare not overstep my limit."

When K'an was in mourning for his mother (d. ca. 307) and was
living beneath her tomb, two strangers arrived unannounced to
offer condolences, and then withdrew without weeping. Their bearing and dress were unusual and strange, and K'an realized they
were not ordinary men. He dispatched someone to follow and observe
them, but the man saw only a pair of cranes flying away into the
sky (cf. CS 66.8a).

YML: T'ao K'an caught a fish in a border area southwest of
Hsün-yang, and personally gave the pool the name "Gate of Cranes"
(Ho-men).

(The inclusion of these seemingly unrelated events in the commentary seems to imply that the two cranes--actually hsien, or
transcendent beings--were the fish which Lady Chan refused to accept.)

SSHY Comm.: While Meng Tsung (third cent.), director of works
for the Wu Kingdom, was keeper of Thunder Lake (Lei-ch'ih, in
Anhui), he sent a present of salted fish to his mother, who refused to accept it. It was not T'ao K'an who did so. I suspect
some later person fabricated this story on the basis of Meng's experience.

21. When Huan Wen subdued Shu (Szechwan, in 347), he took Lady Li,
the younger sister of the last ruler, Li Shih (r. 343-347), as a

concubine, and treated her with extreme favor, always keeping her in
an apartment behind his study. Huan's wife, the Princess of Nan-
k'ang, knew nothing about it at first, but after she had heard, she
came with several tens of female attendants, brandishing a naked
sword, to attack her. It happened that just then Lady Li was combing
her hair, and her tresses fell covering the floor, while the color of
her skin was like the luster of jade. She made no movement of her
facial expression, but said calmly, "My kingdom has been destroyed
and my family ruined. I had no wish to come here. If I could be
killed today it would only be what I have longed for from the beginning."

The princess withdrew in shame.[1] (*TPYL* 154; *MCYC*, shang)

[1]*TC*: After Huan Wen had pacified Shu, he took the daughter (*sic*)
of Li Shih as a concubine. The princess (Huan's wife), a ferocious
and jealous woman, knew nothing about it at first, but after she
knew she went with drawn sword to Lady Li's apartment, wishing to
cut off her head then and there. When she saw Lady Li, the latter
was at the window combing her hair. Staying her hand, she faced
the princess, her spirit and expression calm and sedate. When she
spoke, her words were extremely sad and poignant, whereupon the
princess, throwing away her sword, came forward to embrace her,
crying, "Dear child, even *I* feel affection for you as I see you;
how much more must that old rascal!" And from that time on she befriended her.

22. Yü Yu was the younger brother of Yü Hsi. When Hsi was executed
(in 272) they were on the point of killing Yu as well. Huan Nü-yu,
the wife of Yu's son, Yü Hsüan, was the daughter of Huan Wen's younger
brother, Huan Huo. Going to Huan Wen's home in her bare feet she
sought to be let in, but the gatekeeper barred the way and would not
admit her. In a shrill voice the girl cried out, "What kind of petty
person are you who won't even let me enter my own uncle's gate!" So
saying, she rushed in headlong. Amid wailing and tears she pleaded
with Huan, saying, "Yü Yu has always been dependent on others. With
one leg three inches short, how could he ever become a rebel?"

Huan replied, laughing, "Your husband (and his family) were really
and truly in danger!" Whereupon he pardoned Yü Yu's entire family.[1]
(*CS* 73.16b; *SWLC*, hou 11, 20)

[1]*CHS*: Huan Wen killed Yü Hsi's younger brother, Ch'ien (in 371).
Hsi, hearing of trouble, escaped (to Hai-ling, in Kiangsu). Hsi's
younger brother, Yu, was slated for execution, but his son's wife,
a daughter of the Huan family, pleaded with Huan Wen, and Yu was
pardoned.

23. Hsieh An's wife, Lady Liu, curtained off her female attendants
and had them come out in front and perform music and dancing. She let
Hsieh watch them momentarily and then lowered the curtains. When
Hsieh sought to have them opened again, Lady Liu said, "I fear it
might damage your abundant virtue."[1]

[1]*TPYL* 521 (quoting *TC*): Lady Liu, the wife of the grand tutor,
Hsieh An, would not permit him to have any favored concubines in
separate quarters, but his lordship was very fond of music and
female beauty, and, unable to maintain his chastity, wanted to set

up female entertainers and concubines. His nephews on both sides of the family secretly understood his feelings, and together admonished Lady Liu that she should make some accommodation, saying, "The songs, *Kuan-chü* ("Songs," No. 1) and *Chung-ssu* (No. 5), display the virtue of not being jealous."

Lady Liu, realizing they were criticizing her, asked, "And who wrote those songs?"

They replied, "The Duke of Chou."

Lady Liu retorted, "The Duke of Chou was a *man* and wrote them for himself, that's all. Now if it had been the *Duchess* of Chou, the tradition wouldn't have contained these words!"

24. Huan Ch'ung did not like to wear new clothes. Once after his bath his wife, Wang Nü-tsung, purposely sent some new clothes for his use. Ch'ung was highly incensed and insisted on having them taken away. His wife had them taken back to him once more with the relayed message, "If your clothes never go through the stage of being new, by what process will they ever become old?" Lord Huan laughed aloud and put them on. (*PTSC* 129; *SLF* 12; *TPYL* 395, 689)

25. Wang Hsi-chih's wife, Lady Ch'ih (Ch'ih Hsüan), said to her two younger brothers, Ch'ih Yin and Ch'ih T'an, "In the Wang household, whenever they see the two Hsiehs, Hsieh An and Hsieh Wan, they overturn the baskets and put their clogs on backward (in their haste to meet them). But when they see you two coming, everything is calm and peaceful. You may as well not trouble yourselves to visit anymore." (*MCYC*, shang; *SWLC*, hou 10)

26. Wang Ning-chih's wife, Lady Hsieh (Hsieh Tao-yün), after going to live in the Wang family, felt a great contempt for Ning-chih. On returning for a visit to the Hsieh household, her mood was most unhappy. Her uncle, Hsieh An, hoping to comfort and relieve her, said, "Master Wang is, after all, the son of Wang Hsi-chih, and as a person in his own right isn't at all bad. Why do you resent him so much?"

She replied, "In this one household, for uncles I have (you), A-ta, and the central commander (Hsieh Wan or Hsieh Chü), and for cousins and brothers I have Feng (Hsieh Shao), Hu (Hsieh Lang), O (Hsieh Hsüan) and Mo (Hsieh Yüan).[1] But who would ever have imagined that between heaven and earth there actually exists someone called Master Wang?" (*CS* 96.9b)

[1] The following chart shows the relationships:

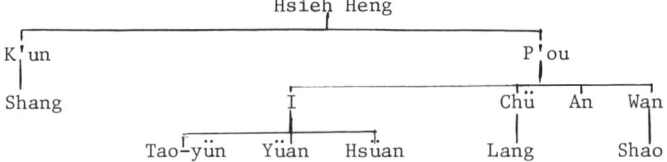

The identifications in parentheses are by no means certain; I have merely followed the *Hsieh SP* and *CS* 79.20a. Yang Yung, on grounds he does not explain, favors equating "A-ta" with the senior uncle, Hsieh Shang, and the "central commander" with Tao-yün's own father, Hsieh I. According to the *Hsieh SP*, both Hsieh Wan and Hsieh Chü held the title "central commander," but no source I have seen attributes it to Hsieh I.

Liu Chün's identifications in the Commentary seem garbled: first he combines "Feng" and "Hu" into a single name and identifies it with Hsieh Shao. Similarly, he combines "O" and "Mo," identifying it with Hsieh Yüan. He also cites "one text" which identifies Feng with Lang, O with Hsüan, Mo with Shao, and Hu with Yüan.

27. The armrest (*chi*) on which Han Po's mother, Lady Yin, used to lean was broken and falling apart. Her grandson on her daughter's side, Pien Fan-chih, seeing the armrest in such bad condition, was on the point of exchanging it, when Lady Yin replied, "If I didn't lean on this armrest, how would you ever get to see any antiques?"

28. Wang Ning-chih's wife, Hsieh Tao-yün, said to her younger brother, Hsieh Hsüan, "Why is it that [in your studies][1] you make no progress whatsoever? Is it that you occupy your mind with worldly matters, or are there limitations set by your heaven-appointed lot?" (*CS* 96.9b)

[1] The phrase in square brackets is interpolated from *CS* 96.9b.

29. When Ch'ih Ch'ao died (in 377), the elder and younger brothers of his wife, Chou Ma-t'ou, wanted to welcome their sister back to the Chou household, but to the very end she was unwilling to return home. She said, "Even though in life I can't share a common room with Master Ch'ih, in death may I not 'share a common grave'?"[1] (*TPYL* 517; *SWLC*, hou 11)

[1] See "Songs," No. 73:

> In life, though we have separate rooms,
> In death we'll share a common grave.

30. Hsieh Hsüan held his elder sister, Hsieh Tao-yün, in very high regard, while Chang Hsüan constantly sang the praises of his younger sister, and wanted to match her against the other. A certain Chi Ni went to visit both the Chang and the Hsieh families. When people asked him which was superior and which inferior, he replied, "Lady Wang's (i.e., Hsieh Tao-yun's) spirit and feelings are relaxed and sunny; she certainly has the manner and style of (the Seven Worthies) beneath the (Bamboo) Grove.[1] As for the wife of the Ku family (i.e., Chang Hsüan's sister), her pure heart gleams like jade; without a doubt she's the full flowering of wifely virtue." (*CS* 96.10b)

[1] See above, *SSHY* VIII, 29.

31. Wang Hui once went to visit Wang Hsi-chih's widow, Ch'ih Hsüan, and asked, "Haven't your eyes and ears suffered any impairment yet?"

She replied, "Hair turning white and teeth falling out belong in the category of the physical body. But when it comes to eyes and ears, they are related to the spirit and intelligence. How could I let myself be cut off from other people?"[1]

[1] *FJC*, "Memorial of Thanks" (*Hsieh-piao*): I (Ch'ih Hsüan) am ninety years old, and my solitary body survives alone. I desired to be favored with Your Majesty's pity, and You alone have vouchsafed to take care of me.

(Ch'ih Hsüan outlived her husband, Wang Hsi-chih (d. ca. 365), by about forty years.)

32. Han Po's mother, Lady Yin, accompanied her grandson, Han Hui-chih, to Heng-yang Commandery (Hunan). In Ho-lu Island they met Huan Hsüan. Pien Fan-chih,[1] who was her grandson on his mother's side, also came at the time to pay his respects. She said to him, "To think that I haven't died before seeing these two generations of upstarts (Huan Wen and Huan Hsüan) both become rebels!"

After they had been in Heng-yang several years, Hui-chih met disaster (in 404) at the hands of Hsüan's nephew, Huan Liang. Stroking his dead body, Lady Yin wept and said, "When your father (Han Po) quit his post long ago as grand warden of Yü-chang Commandery (Kiangsi), the letter summoning him to the capital arrived in the morning, and by evening he set out. You (have been meaning to) leave this commandery and town for several years, but because of (involvement with) certain persons, you've been unable to move, and now at last you've come upon disaster. What more is there to say?"

[1] Pien Fan-chih was deeply involved in Huan Hsüan's usurpation at the time.

CHAPTER XX

Technical Understanding

1. Hsün Hsü was skilled in the understanding of musical timbres and notes of the scale (*yin-sheng*). Contemporary critics claimed that his was an "intuitive understanding" (*an-chieh*). Accordingly, it was he who tuned the twelve pitch pipes (*lü-lü*), and corrected the court music (in 274). Whenever there was a New Year's ceremonial in the palace halls where music was performed, he personally tuned the *kungs* and *shangs* of the instruments so that none were out of tune.

Now Juan Hsien had a superb appreciation of music, and his contemporaries claimed that his was a "divine understanding" (*shen-chieh*). At each public gathering where music was performed,[1] in his heart he felt it to be out of tune, but since he had never uttered a single word about it directly to Hsü, the latter was mentally jealous of him, and had him sent out of the capital (Lo-yang) to serve as grand warden of Shih-p'ing Commandery (Shensi).

Later on there was an old peasant plowing in his field who found a jade foot rule (*ch'ih*) of the Chou period (trad. 1122-256 B.C.), which then became the standard measure for the whole realm. When Hsün tested it against the one he had used himself to determine the pitches of the bells, drums, metal and stone chimes, silk-stringed instruments, and bamboo pipes, he discovered that in all cases his was short by one grain of millet (*shu*), and thereafter he acknowledged the superiority of Juan's "divine knowledge."[2] (*CS* 22.18b; *PTSC* 105; *TPYL* 565)

[1] If *kung-hui*, translated "public gathering," were emended to the graphically similar *Kung-tseng* (Hsün Hsü's courtesy name), the sentence would read: "Every time Hsün performed music . . ."

[2] *CHL*: The use of bells and pitch pipes (*chung-lü*) as (tuning) instruments had been abandoned since the end of Chou (ca. 256 B.C.), but during the reigns of the Han Emperors Ch'eng (r. 32-7 B.C.) and Ai (r. 6-1 B.C.), the literati restored and regulated them. By the end of the Later Han (A.D. 220), however, they had again fallen

into desuetude. The Wei (220-265) had Tu K'uei, who understood the
notes for harmonizing the pitch pipes, remake them, but he was unable to check them against the "Canons" and "Rites," and merely
relied on the pitches of contemporary stringed instruments and
pipes and the lengths of contemporary "feet" and "inches" to
measure them, with the result that they were extremely at odds
with the standards in the "Rites."

It was at this point that the Chin Emperor Wu (Ssu-ma Yen, r.
265-299) ordered the director of the Central Secretariat, Hsün Hsü,
to determine the pitches of the bells and pipes according to the
measurements of the "Canons." After he had cast the pipes for the
pitches in metal, he searched earnestly after antique instruments,
and found several jade pitch pipes from the Chou era. Comparing
them with his own, he found no difference. Furthermore, in the
abandoned granaries of the various commanderies there were some
ancient metal bell measures from the Han era. When he sounded the
corresponding pitch pipes they all responded without being struck.
The sounds and pitches were in perfect agreement, and once more it
seemed as if all of them were complete.

CCKT: After the pitch pipes had been completed, Juan Hsien remarked, "The pitches of the pipes made by Hsün Hsü are too high. A
high pitch connotes grief. 'The music of a dying state is sad and
full of longing, and its people are in misery' ("Greater Preface
to the 'Book of Songs'"). Today if the pitches are not agreeable
and refined, I'm afraid they're not the centrally harmonious
pitches of a virtuous government. (The sharping) must be caused by
a difference in length between ancient and modern foot rules."

However, since the modern bell measures and stone chimes were
those made by Tu K'uei in the Wei era, and did not correspond with
Hsün Hsü's pitch pipes, and since the pitches and sounds (of the
latter) were pleasant and refined; since, moreover, for a long
time no one had been familiar with the instruments made by Tu
K'uei, his contemporaries did not consider it worthwhile to change
them. Hsü's nature was self-assured and haughty, and so on the
pretext of some incident he had Hsien demoted and transferred to
serve as grand warden of Shih-p'ing Commandery, where he became
ill and died. Later they found in the earth an ancient bronze
(*sic*) foot rule. Comparing its measurements with Hsü's modern foot
rule, they found the latter to be short by four degrees (*fen*). It
was only then that people realized Hsien had, after all, understood the pitches, but there was no one who could correct them.

KPCC: (In 273) when Hsün Hsü first put on a performance of the
dance "Great Symbol of True Virtue" (*Cheng-te ta-hsiang*), he considered the pitch pipes fashioned by Tu-K'uei of Wei to be out of
harmony when matched against the original pitches (*pen-yin*; *CS*
22.18b reads, *pa-yin*, "eight timbres") of the grand music master
(*t'ai-yüeh*). From the Later Han until Wei the foot rule was longer
than in antiquity by four degrees or more, and since Tu K'uei had
depended on (Later Han models), he had correspondingly missed the
correct pitch. So Hsün Hsü, basing himself on (Cheng Hsüan's commentary on) the "Rites of Chou" (Ch. VI), heaped up grains of millet to create his standard of measurement. After measuring the
ancient instruments, he found them in agreement with his own calculations, and consequently he made them the standard to be used
in the rites for the suburban sacrifice and in the ancestral hall.

XX TECHNICAL UNDERSTANDING   359

(It appears that Hsün Hsü's archaistic reform probably *did* agree with the antique prescription, but grated on the sensitive ears of Juan Hsien who was accustomed to the lower pitch of his own times.)

2. Hsün Hsü was once sitting with Emperor Wu of Chin (Ssu-ma Yen, r. 265-299) eating bamboo shoots along with cooked rice. He said to those seated with him, "This has been steamed over firewood which has seen heavy service (*lao-hsin*)."
Someone in the company[1] did not quite believe him, and secretly sending to inquire about it, found that they had indeed used old carriage axles (*ch'e-chiao*). (*CS* 39.11b-12a; *IWLC* 80; *TPYL* 850)

[1] *CS* 39.12a, *IWLC* 80, and *TPYL* 850 all identify the inquirer as Emperor Wu himself.

3. Someone made a geomantic assessment (*hsiang*) of the tomb of Yang Hu's father, Yang Tao, saying, "From its rear (or, "his descendants," *hou*) will come forth a ruler who will receive the mandate of Heaven."[1]
Hu was dismayed by his words and accordingly dug away the rear of the tomb to destroy their efficacy. The geomancer stood by watching him, and said, "Even so there will come forth one in the Three Ducal Offices with a broken arm."
Soon thereafter Hu fell from his horse and broke his arm. His rank, as predicted, eventually reached the ducal level.[2] (*CS* 34.12b; *TPYL* 558; *TPKC* 389)

[1] Cf. *CS* 34.12b: Moreover there was one skilled in making geomantic assessments of tombs who said that the place where Yang Hu's ancestral tombs were located had an aura (*ch'i*) of sovereigns and kings about it, and if one should dig it, there would be no descendants. Hu accordingly dug it, etc.

[2] Yang Hu became General of Chariots and Horsemen with all the privileges of the Ducal Offices. He tried hard to decline and his memorial of refusal is preserved both in his biography, *CS* 34.3a-4a, and in *WH* 37.10b-11a.
YML: Yang Hu was a skillful horseman and charioteer. He had a son who, in his fifth or sixth year, was well behaved, intelligent, and lovable. When he excavated the rear of the tomb, the child immediately died. Yang was at the time military governor stationed at Hsiang-yang (Hupei), and while he was turning his horse, he fell to the ground and broke his arm. At the time all officialdom acclaimed his loyalty and sincerity.

4. Wang Chi was skilled in understanding the nature of horses. Once he was riding a horse which was wearing mottled mud protectors (*chang-ni*). In front of him was a stream which the horse steadfastly refused to cross. Wang said, "It must be that he wants to spare the mud protectors."
After he had someone remove them, the horse went directly across.[1] (*CS* 42.6b; *PTSC* 126; *CHC* 22; *TPYL* 359, 773)

[1] *YL*: Wang Chi was by nature a lover of horses, and was also extremely discriminating about them. For this reason Tu Yü characterized Wang as having a "weakness for horses," and Ho Ch'iao as

having a "weakness for money." Emperor Wu (Ssu-ma Yen, r. 265-299) then asked Yü, "And what weakness do *you* have?"

Yü replied, "I've a weakness for the 'Tso Commentary.'"

5. While Ch'en Shu was serving as a civil officer under the generalissimo, Wang Tun, he was the recipient of much favor and honor. When he died (322), Kuo P'u[1] went to weep for him. With poignant grief he cried out, "Ssu-tsu! (Ch'en's courtesy name) Who knows if it wasn't a blessing?" Shortly afterwards the generalissimo started his rebellion, just as Kuo had said. (CS 72.11a; TPKC 76)

[1] Kuo P'u was Tun's secretarial aide at the time; see TCTC 92.2892.

6. Emperor Ming of Chin (Ssu-ma Shao, r. 323-325) understood how to make geomantic divinations (*chan*) concerning tombs and houses. On hearing that Kuo P'u was undertaking someone's burial, the emperor went in mufti to watch, and took the occasion to ask the head of the household, "Why are you burying him at the dragon's horn? This way you'll bring about the extermination of your entire clan."[1]

The head of the household replied, "Kuo P'u told us, 'This is a burial at the dragon's ear, and in less than three years there will come a Son of Heaven.'"

The emperor asked, "Does this mean the family will produce a Son of Heaven?"

He replied, "It's not that they'll *produce* a Son of Heaven. It's just that there could come a Son of Heaven asking questions, that's all." (CS 72.11ab; PTSC 20; TPYL 556)

[1] CNTHCS: To bury at the dragon's horn will bring sudden wealth and honor, but afterward will come the extermination of the entire family.

7. When Kuo P'u crossed the Yangtze River (between 307 and 312),[1] he lived in Chi-yang Prefecture (on the river, east of Chien-k'ang). [When his mother died, he placed her][2] grave not a full hundred paces from the water, and his contemporaries considered it too close. Kuo P'u replied, "In the future it will all become dry land."

At present the sandy shore has widened so that all around the graveyard for several tens of *li* are mulberry groves and rice paddies. One of his poems states:

> "The northern mountain, steep and forbidding,
> The mighty ocean, heaving and tossing.
> Mound upon mound, the triple graves;
> 'Tis only mother and elder brothers."

(CS 72.11a; TPYL 558)

[1] *Kuo P'u PC*: When Kuo P'u was young he was fond of classical studies and (Taoist) techniques, and he understood divination by tortoise-shell and by milfoil stalks. During the Yung-chia era (307-312) the whole realm was on the brink of chaos. P'u cast the milfoil stalks, and sighing, said, "The black-haired Chinese are about to share a common fate with other peoples!" Whereupon he joined ten or more families of relatives and close friends, and fleeing southward across the river, settled at Chi-yang.

[2] The part enclosed in square brackets is added from the quotation in TPYL 558.

8. Chancellor Wang Tao ordered Kuo P'u to try forming a hexagram to tell his fortune. When the hexagram was completed, Kuo, his mood and expression extremely distressed, announced, "Your Excellency has the dangerous portent, 'Thunderbolt' (Chen)."[1]

Wang asked, "Is there any possibility it may be minimized or suppressed (*hsiao-fu*)?"[2]

Kuo said, "Order your carriage and go out of the city toward the west several *li*. There you will find a cypress tree. Cut it off to the same length as yourself and put it on the bed in the place where you usually sleep, and the calamity may be minimized."

Wang followed his directions, and within the space of several days, as predicted, a thunderbolt shattered the cypress in pieces. Wang's sons and younger brothers all offered congratulations, and his cousin, Generalissimo Wang Tun, said, "You actually succeeded in transferring the evil to the tree!" (*CS* 72.3a; *PTSC* 152; *SLF* 3; *TPYL* 13)

[1] "Book of Changes," Hex. 51 ☳☳ (Wilhelm I, 210-213).

[2] In the case of the hexagram Chen, if both positive lines are "nines" and all four negative ones are "sixes," the maximum potentiality would be present for change to something less dangerous. See Wilhelm I, xxix-xxxiv.

WYCS: As for Kuo P'u's ability to minimize disaster and turn misfortune to blessing, or to bolster a dangerous situation and seize the victory, his contemporaries all agreed that neither Ching Fang nor Kuan Lu could equal him.

9. Huan Wen had a superintendent of records who was skilled at discriminating between wines. Whenever Huan had wine he would always have him taste it first. The good he would call the "Administrator of Ch'ing Province" (southern Shantung and northern Kiangsu), and the bad he would call the "Inspector general of P'ing-yüan Commandery" (Shantung). This was because in Ch'ing Province there was a Ch'i Commandery, and in P'ing-yüan Commandery there was a Ko Prefecture. By the "Administrator" he meant wine that went all the way to the navel (*ch'i*), and by the "Inspector general" he meant wine that stayed above the diaphragm (*ko*). (*PTSC* 148; *SLF* 17; *TPYL* 371, 845)

10. Ch'ih Yin believed in the Taoist religion[1] with zealous devotion. Once he was suffering from an ailment in his bowels, which various Taoist physicians were unable to cure. Hearing that the Buddhist monk Yü Fa-k'ai had a good reputation, he went to consult him. After he had come, Fa-k'ai took his pulse and said, "What Your Excellency is suffering from is caused by none other than an excess of zeal (*ching-chin*), that's all." Whereupon he mixed a dose of medicine with some hot water and gave it to him. No sooner had Ch'ih taken the medicine than immediately he had an enormous bowel movement in which he evacuated several wads of paper, each as big as a fist. When he opened them up to look, they turned out to be the Taoist paper charms (*fu*) he had ingested earlier.[2]

[1] He belonged to the "Heavenly Master" sect (*T'ien-shih tao*); see Ch'ih Ch'ao's biography, *CS* 67.20a.

[2] Liu Chün cites a "*Chin-shu*" (not Fang Hsüan-ling's; cf. *KSC* 4; *Taishō* 50.350c): Fa-k'ai was skilled in medical arts. Once he was

traveling and stayed overnight with a host whose wife was in labor, but whose child, even after several days, had not yet dropped. Fa-k'ai said, "This is a simple matter to cure," and killing a well-fattened sheep, he fed the woman ten or more slices of its flesh and administered acupuncture (*chen*). (The *KSC* version states that he made soup and fed it all to her.) In a moment the child moved downward, and emerged wrapped in the sheep's fatty membrane (*liao*; probably the caul, or amniotic sac). Such was his consummate skill.

(It is interesting to note that the Western term for the caul, "amnion," is similarly associated with the sheep--Grk. *amnós*, "lamb.")

11. Yin Hao had a subtle understanding of the "pulses" (*ching-mo*),[1] but in his middle years he completely repudiated it. There was a man who always assisted him in his work who once without warning began knocking his head on the floor until the blood ran. When Hao asked his reason, he replied, "There's a matter of life and death which I've never been able to talk about."

After Yin had pressed him a long while for an answer, he finally said, "My mother's getting on toward a hundred years old and has been suffering from ill health now for a long time. If only she might be favored with just one palpation of the pulse by you, sir, then there's a chance she'll live. For payment I'd go to death by dismemberment without regret." Moved by his extreme sincerity, Hao had the old lady brought in. He felt her pulse and prepared a prescription. As soon as she had taken a dose of the medicine in hot water she was immediately improved. After that Yin burned all his medical books (*ching-fang*).

[1]*LSChing* 47: *Ching-mo* is the means whereby the body conducts the blood and the pneuma (*ch'i*), regulates the Yin and Yang forces, moistens the muscles and bones, and benefits the organs and joints.

Ibid. 10: *Ching-mo* is the means whereby one can determine death or life, locate the hundred illnesses, and harmonize the empty and the solid.

(There were thought to be separate "pulses," located in different parts of the forearms, for each of the internal organs. The term, in any case, is not to be identified exclusively with the circulation of the blood. See Yabuuchi Kiyo, *Chūgoku kodai no kagaku*, Tokyo, 1964, pp. 122ff., and Ilza Veith, trans., *The Yellow Emperor's Classic of Internal Medicine*, Berkeley and Los Angeles, 1966, pp. 42-49.)

CHAPTER XXI

Skill and Art

1. The game of pellet chess (tan-ch'i)¹ began from within the palace during the Wei Kingdom (220-265), where they used powder boxes (lien) to play. Emperor Wen (Ts'ao P'ei, r. 220-227) was especially subtle at this game, and using the corner of his handkerchief to flip the playing pieces, never missed a shot. There was once a guest who claimed that he was a capable player, so the emperor had him try it. The guest, who was wearing a cornered cap made of a coarse hempen kerchief, lowered his head to flip the playing pieces, surpassing in subtlety even the emperor.² (IWLC 74; WHLSC 42; TPYL 755; TPKC 228; YYTT, hsü 4; HCWT 2)

¹TCFH: Emperor Ch'eng of Han (r. 32-7 B.C.) was fond of football (ch'iu-chü, a military game played with a wool-filled leather ball kicked back and forth over a net between standing poles; see Chuang Shen, Chung-kuo ku-tai ti t'i-yü yün-tung, "Ancient Athletic Sports of China," TLTC 7.2, 1953, 38-40). Liu Hsiang (79-8 B.C.) felt that since the game was strenuous for the body and exhaustive of a man's strength, it was not a suitable sport for someone of the highest dignity. So the emperor, following the form for football, invented the game of pellet chess. One who observes its rules will find they are the rules for football.

SSHY Comm.: According to this statement by Fu Hsüan (in the TCFH), the game of pellet chess had originated long before the Wei. Moreover, in the biography of Liang Chi (d. 159 A.D., HHS 64.11a), it states, "Chi was skilled at pellet chess and reach-five (ko-wu, a checkers-like game)." Yet here (in the SSHY) it claims the game originated in the Wei era, which is clearly mistaken.

²TPTL (Preface, not included in WH 52): Games and sports were what I (Ts'ao P'ei) enjoyed in my youth, but it was only pellet chess in which you might say I exhausted its subtleties. When I was young I once wrote a poetic essay about it. In the old days in the

capital (Lo-yang, ca. 200 A.D.) there were two subtle players: the Marquis of Ho-hsiang, Tung-fang Shih-an, and the young lord Chang (Chang Kung-tzu). I have always regretted I did not get to play against them.

PWC: The emperor (Ts'ao P'ei) was skilled at pellet chess and was able to play using the corner of his handkerchief. At the time there was a scholar (*shu-sheng*) who also was able by lowering his head to toss the playing pieces with the corner of the kerchief he was wearing on his head.

(There is a brief discussion of this game, which resembles our game of marbles, and apparently originated from a form of fortune-telling by chance configuration, in Joseph Needham, *Science and Civilisation*, IV.1, 327. See also T'ung Shou, *Tan-ch'i k'ao* ["An Investigation of Pellet Chess"], in *TLTC* 4.7, 1947. Tantalizing details may be gleaned from the encyclopedias, especially *IWLC* 74, but I will cite only the *CCHH*, quoted in *TPYL* 755: "After the reigns of the Later Han Emperors Ch'ung and Chih [r. 145-146] this game was discontinued, and during the Chien-an era [196-219] of Emperor Hsien, while Ts'ao Ts'ao was in control of the government, bans and prohibitions were stringently enforced. No implements used in gambling games were permitted to be housed illegally within the palace. So the ladies of the palace, using golden hairpins and jade combs, played on the lids of powder boxes, in a game which bore some resemblance to pellet chess.

"When Emperor Wen ascended the throne [in 220], following the model of what the palace ladies had been doing, he revived the playing of pellet chess accordingly. At that time all the courtiers and famous gentlemen vied with one another in skill, and this is why the emperor wrote in his letter to Wu Chih [*WH* 42.5b], 'Games of pellet chess were set up at intervals, and we ended up playing sixes, *liu-po*.'")

2. The storied observatory of the Cloud-traversing Terrace (Ling-yün t'ai)[1] was built with consummate skill. First they weighed all the timbers for balance, and afterward fitted them together so that there was not even an ounce or a grain (*tzu-chu*)[2] of discrepancy. Though the terrace was built high and imposing, it always swayed with the wind, but never had any tendency to topple over. But when Emperor Ming of Wei (Ts'ao Jui, r. 227-239) climbed the tower, he became fearful that its condition was dangerous, so in addition to the original structure they used large timbers to buttress it. The tower began immediately to fall into delapidation and ruin, and critics claimed it was because the balance had been upset. (*IWLC* 63; *CHC* 24; *TPYL* 177; *TPKC* 225)

[1] One of the buildings of the T'ai-chi Palace built by the Wei in their capital at Lo-yang in 221.

[2] *LYKTP*: The Cloud-traversing Terrace's upper walls were 130 feet (13 *chang*) square and 9 feet high. The tower was 40 feet square and 50 feet high. The central mast (*tung*) rose 135 feet 7.5 inches from the ground.

3. Wei Tan was a capable calligrapher, and once when Emperor Ming of Wei was erecting a hall and wanted to put up a sign, he had Wei climb a ladder to inscribe it. After Wei had come down again the hair of

his temples had turned snow-white. It was for this reason he enjoined his sons and grandsons never again to study calligraphy.[1] (*TPYL* 747, 765; *SSYW*)

[1]*STSS*: Wei Tan was skilled in the formal script (*k'ai-shu*), and the palaces and towers of the Wei were for the most part inscribed by him. When Emperor Ming erected the Sky-traversing Observatory (Ling-hsiao kuan), through an oversight the sign was nailed in place beforehand. Accordingly, they placed Tan in a basket, and by means of a windlass (*lu-lu*) and long rope hoisted him up so that he was near enough to inscribe it. He was 250 feet from the ground and thoroughly frightened. When it was all over he warned his sons and grandsons to have nothing more to do with this formal script, and wrote it down in his family instructions.

4. Chung Hui was the maternal uncle of Hsün Hsü, but the dispositions and tastes of the two men were incompatible. Hsün had a valuable sword which may have been worth a million gold pieces (*chin*)[1] which was always kept at the home of his mother, Hui's sister, Lady Chung.[2] Hui was a skillful calligrapher, and, imitating Hsün's handwriting, wrote a letter to Hsün's mother demanding the sword, and by this means spirited it away and never returned it. Hsün Hsü knew that it was Chung who had done it, but he had no means of getting it back, so he mulled over in his mind some way to get even with him.

Later the Chung brothers, Chung Hui and Chung Yü, at the cost of ten million gold pieces erected a house, which had barely been completed. It was extremely exquisite and ornate, and they had not yet been able to move into it. Hsün, who was a very skillful painter, went in secretly and painted the walls of the Chungs' gatehouse with a portrait of their late father, Chung Yu, his clothes, cap, and features just as they were while he was alive. When the two Chungs entered the gate they were greatly affected and upset, and as a result the house remained empty and abandoned.[3] (*PTSC* 122; *TPYL* 180, 343; *LTMHC* 5)

[1]Supplying *chin*, "gold pieces," from the quotation in *PTSC* in 122.

[2]According to *KSCK*, Hsü entrusted the sword to his wife, not his mother.

[3]*WCSY*: Chung Hui was skilled at imitating other people's handwriting. On his campaign against Shu (in 264), while he was at Chien-ko (Szechwan), he requisitioned Teng Ai's memorial to the generalissimo, Ssu-ma Chao, and rewrote it, so abbreviating his words as to make the terminology and tenor sound rude and insubordinate, full of self-praise and boastfulness. It was because of this that Ai was apprehended.

(According to *TCTC* 78.2480, it was Wei Kuan who falsified the memorial, not Chung Hui.)

KSCK: At the time some people said that Hsün Hsü's revenge against Chung Hui exceeded his own loss by several times ten-fold. But that they did all this to each other merely by means of painting and calligraphy was the ultimate in skill and subtlety.

5. Yang Ch'en was comprehensive in his learning and a master at calligraphy.[1] In addition he was an able horseman and archer and a good hand at encirclement chess (*wei-ch'i*). The Yangs in later years were

mostly expert calligraphers,² but in archery and chess and the other arts no one ever equaled Ch'en.

¹*WTC*: Yang Ch'en was by nature capable in the draft (*ts'ao*) script, and also skilled in the cursive (*hsing*) and clerical (*li*) styles. He was acclaimed by everyone of his day.

²Yang Ch'en's sons, K'ai and Ch'üan, his grandson, Sui, and his great-grandsons, Fu, Fu*, and Hsin all gained recognition as calligraphers. The last-named served on Liu I-ch'ing's staff and was, perhaps, the source of this information.

6. When Tai K'uei went to study with Fan Hsüan,¹ he observed everything that Fan did. If Fan was reading, he also would read. If Fan was copying a text, he also would copy a text. It was only his fondness for painting which Fan considered to be of no use, feeling that it was not proper to trouble his thoughts over such a thing. Tai thereupon painted for him² illustrations for Chang Heng's "Poetic Essay on the Southern Capital" (*Nan-tu fu*).³ After Fan had finished looking at them, he sighed in admiration and admitted that they greatly enhanced the text. It was only then that he began to appreciate the value of painting. (*LTMHC* 5; *TPYL* 605, 750)

¹*CHS*: Tai K'uei, undaunted by a distance of a thousand *li*, went to Yü-chang (Kiangsi) to visit Fan Hsüan. When Hsüan saw K'uei he marveled at him and gave him his elder brother's daughter to wife.

²Adding *wei*, "for him," after *LTMHC* 5 and *TPYL* 750.

³*WH* 4.1a-7b; trans. von Zach, *Die Chinesischen Anthologie*, I, 38-44. The "Southern Capital" was Nan-yang (S. Honan), the poet's native place. In the poetic essay the scenery, flora, and fauna are described in the tradition of Ssu-ma Hsiang-ju's *Shang-lin fu*.

7. Hsieh An once said, "There has never been anything like Ku K'ai-chih's paintings since the existence of living beings (*ts'ang-sheng*)."¹ (*CS* 92.35ab; *LTMHC* 5)

¹The quotation in *LTMHC* gives the alternate reading, "Paintings like yours have never before existed since the olden times of Ts'ang Chieh (legendary inventor of writing)."

HCYC: Ku K'ai-chih was especially fond of colored paintings (*tan-ch'ing*), in which his subtlety surpassed all his contemporaries. Once he sent a chest of paintings to Huan Hsüan, all of them his best work which he deeply treasured and was loath to part with. He had sealed it tightly shut with a label in front. Huan accordingly opened the rear of the chest and removed the paintings, and after properly resealing it, returned the chest to Ku. When the latter saw that the label was still intact as before but the paintings were nowhere to be seen, he promptly exclaimed, "My wonderful paintings, being imbued with magic, have become transmuted, and have departed like men ascending to be immortals!" (Cf. *CS* 92.35b-36a.)

8. In his middle years Tai K'uei painted the subject "Walking the Buddha Image" (*hsing-hsiang*)¹ with consummate subtlety. When Yü Ho saw his work he said to Tai, "The spirit and intelligence of the image are too vulgar, which springs from the fact that your own worldly passions haven't been ended yet."

Tai replied, "Only a Wu Kuang² would escape this charge of yours."
(*LTMHC* 5)

¹I.e., bearing the Buddha image in procession during the Buddha's birthday celebration in the first half of the fourth month. A description of the procession as it was done in Khotan, Central Asia, around A.D. 400, can be found in *KSFHC* of the pilgrim Fa-hsien (*Taishō* 51.857b). See also A. C. Soper, *Literary Evidence for Early Buddhist Art in China*, Ascona, Switz., 1949, pp. 109-110.

²*LHC*: Wu Kuang was a man of Hsia times (trad. 2205-1766 B.C.) whose ears were seven inches long. He loved to play the zither and lived on calamus (*ch'ang-p'u*) and the roots of leeks (*chiu*). When T'ang (r. 1766-1754) was about to punish Chieh (the last ruler of Hsia), he consulted with Kuang. Kuang replied, "It's no affair of mine."

T'ang said, "How about I Yin?" Wu Kuang replied, "He's strong and powerful and can bear disgrace, but I don't know anything else about him."

When T'ang had conquered all under heaven, he yielded the throne to Kuang, who replied, "I've heard that in a world which doesn't possess the Way, one shouldn't even step on its soil. How much less so when you're yielding the throne to me!" So saying, he mounted a rock on his back and drowned himself in the Lu River (Shantung).

(A fuller account appears in *Chuang-tzu* XXVIII, 16b-17a; Watson, pp. 320-321.)

9. When Ku K'ai-chih painted P'ei K'ai's portrait he added three hairs to his cheek. When someone asked his reason, Ku said, "P'ei K'ai was an outstanding and transparent person who possessed a knowledge of human capabilities. It's precisely these hairs which represent his knowledge of human capabilities."

Those who looked at the painting searched for this, and actually did feel that the added three hairs seemed somehow to make it possess spirit and intelligence to a far greater degree than at the time before they had been applied.¹ (*CS* 92.35b; *IWLC* 74; *LTMHC* 5)

¹*SSHY* Comm.: Ku K'ai-chih painted a series of portraits of ancient worthies and wrote eulogies for all of them.

10. Wang T'an-chih considered the game of encirclement chess (*wei-ch'i*) a kind of "sedentary retirement" (*tso-yin*), while the monk Chih Tun considered it "manual conversation" (*shou-t'an*).¹ (*SWLC*, ch'ien 42)

¹*PWC*: The Sage-king Yao (trad. r. 2357-2258 B.C.) invented encirclement chess as a means of instructing his son, Tan Chu.

YL: Wang T'an-chih considered encirclement chess a kind of "manual conversation." Therefore while he was observing mourning, when guests arrived after the *hsiang*-sacrifice (marking the end of the 13- or 25-month period) he openly met and played with them.

11. Ku K'ai-chih was fond of drawing people's portraits. He wanted to picture Yin Chung-k'an,¹ but the latter said, "My features are ugly; just don't bother."

Ku replied, "But Your Excellency, it's precisely on account of your eye[2] that I want to do it. I'll simply indicate the pupil with a bright dot, and then with 'flying white' (*fei-pai*) gently brush over it, making it like light clouds veiling the sun."[3] (*CS* 92.35b, trans. Chen, *Ku K'ai-chih*, p. 15; *IWLC* 74; *LTMHC* 5; *TPYL* 740)

[1] Ku was an aide on Yin's staff while the latter was governor of Ching Province (Hupei-Hunan) between 392 and 399.

[2] Liu Chün notes in the Commentary that Yin was "squint-eyed" (*miao-mu*; see also *SSHY* XXV, 61, below). *CS* 92.35b merely describes the defect as "eye-trouble" (*mu-ping*).

[3] Some texts read "moon" for "sun."

12. Ku K'ai-chih painted Hsieh K'un among crags and rocks. When someone asked why he did so, Ku said, "Hsieh once said, 'When it comes to (living in seclusion on) a single hill or (fishing in) a single stream, I rate myself superior to him (i.e., Yü Liang).[1] This fellow should be placed among hills and streams." (*CS* 92.35b, trans. Chen, *Ku K'ai-chih*, p. 15; *IWLC* 74; *LTMHC* 5)

[1] See above, *SSHY* IX, 17, where this remark of Hsieh K'un is recorded in context.

13. Ku K'ai-chih would paint a portrait and sometimes not dot the pupils of the eyes for several years. When someone asked his reason, Ku replied, "The beauty or ugliness of the four limbs basically bears no relation to the most subtle part of a painting. What conveys the spirit and portrays the likeness lies precisely in these dots."[1] (*CS* 92.35b; *IWLC* 74; *LTMHC* 5)

[1] The text of *CS* 92.35b reads *ch'üeh-shao*, "missing," for *kuan*, "relation," which suggests a different punctuation: "The beauty or ugliness of the four limbs is basically not missing. But in relation to the subtle part of a painting, what conveys the spirit and portrays the likeness, etc." See Chen, *Ku K'ai-chih*, p. 28, n. 42.

14. Ku K'ai-chih once said, "To paint 'The hand sweeps over the five-stringed lute'[1] is easy, but to paint 'The eye escorts the homing goose'[2] is hard." (*CS* 92.35b)

[1] The "five-stringed lute" (*wu-hsien*) is described in the "Monograph on Rites and Music" (*Yüeh-li chih*) of the *Hsin T'ang-shu* (21.13ab) as being "like the four-stringed lute (*p'i-pa*), but smaller. It originated from the Northern States. Formerly it was played with a wooden plectrum, and the musician P'ei Shen-fu (7th cent.) was the first to play it with the hand. Emperor T'ai-tsung (r. 627-649) was extremely pleased by this, and later players practiced plucking the four-stringed lute as well."

It is clear that the *p'i-pa* was already known in China when Liu Hsi compiled the glossary, *Shih Ming*, around A.D. 200, for it is listed with the musical instruments in section 22. See also Laurence Picken, "The Origin of the Short Lute," *Galpin Society Journal* 8.1 (1955). If the *wu-hsien* was introduced at the same time, there would be little doubt that this is the instrument mentioned in Hsi K'ang's poem.

[2] Both lines are from the fourth of Hsi K'ang's poems to his brother, *Tseng hsiu-ts'ai ju-chün*. (*WH* 24.6a)

CHAPTER XXII

Favors and Gifts

1. At the New Year's Assembly (in 317) Emperor Yüan (Ssu-ma Jui, r. 317-323) drew Chancellor Wang Tao by the hand to mount the imperial dais. Wang steadfastly declined, but the emperor drew him the more insistently. Finally Wang said, "If the sun were to shine with exactly the same brilliance as all other things, what would the ministers below have to look up to?"[1] (CS 65.4b-5a; IWLC 4; PTSC 11; TPYL 29, 98)

[1]CHS (cf. CS 65.4b-5a): When Emperor Yüan rose to the honorable (i.e., imperial) title and the hundred officials were ranged by his throne, he commanded Wang Tao to ascend to the imperial seat, but the latter steadfastly declined, until in the end the emperor desisted.

2. Huan Wen occasionally invited his aides and assistants into his private quarters to spend the night. Yüan Hung and Fu T'ao arrived one after the other. When the names were being announced at headquarters, Yüan Hung, in doubt about which one was intended since there was another aide named Yüan, asked the messenger to check back. The messenger replied, "The aide is the Yüan of the combination Yüan-Fu. Why should there be any doubt about it?"[1]

[1]It is clear from SSHY XXVI, 12, below, that Yüan Hung resented this constant association of his name with Fu T'ao's.

3. Wang Hsün and Ch'ih Ch'ao both had remarkable ability and were singled out for affection by the grand marshal, Huan Wen.[1] Hsün was superintendent of records and Ch'ao was secretarial aide. Ch'ao's face was heavily bewhiskered, while Hsün's figure was short and squat. At the time (ca. 363) the people of Ching Province (Hunan-Hupei) made up a ditty about them which went,

> "The bewhiskered aide-de-camp
> And the short records lad

Can make his lordship happy,
Or make his lordship mad."

(CS 67.20a; IWLC 19; TPYL 249, 374, 465)

[1]HCYC: Ch'ih Ch'ao possessed talent and ability, while Wang Hsün possessed great capacity and popular regard. Both were doted on by Huan Wen.

4. Hsü Hsün stopped at the capital (Chien-k'ang) for one month (between 345 and 346). Not a day passed that the capital intendant, Liu T'an, did not go to pay him a visit. Sighing, Liu said to Hsü, "If you don't leave in a little while, I'll become a worthless and insignificant capital intendant!"[1]

[1]YL: When Hsü Hsün came out of retirement to the capital, within the space of nine days Liu T'an visited him eleven times. He said, "If after all this you still don't leave, you'll make me into an official of insignificant virtue with a salary of only two thousand piculs (the scale for minor provincial officials.)"

5. Emperor Hsiao-wu (Ssu-ma Yao, r. 373-396) held an assembly in the Western Hall of the palace, at which Fu T'ao was present. When Fu returned home, he got down from his carriage and called his son, Fu Hsi, and said to him, "A hundred people were there at this eminent gathering, and as His Majesty took his seat, before he had had a chance to talk about anything else, he first asked, 'Where is Fu T'ao? Is he here?' This sort of thing is obviously not easily achieved. To have a man like this for a father--what do you think of it?" (CS 92.33a; PTSC 82; TPYL 539)

6. While Pien Fan-chih was capital intendant (402),[1] Yang Fu came back briefly from Nan-chou (i.e., Ku-shu, in Anhui). After going to Pien's house, he said, "My illness is acting up (chi-tung),[2] and I can't endure sitting up." Pien thereupon opened the bed curtains and smoothed out the bedding. Yang went directly up onto the large bed, and, getting inside the coverlet, rested his head on the pillow. Pien turned and sat keeping vigil by his side from morning until evening. When Yang left, Pien said to him, "I've treated you with the highest principles. Don't you ever betray me!" (TPYL 699)

[1]WCL: When Huan Hsüan was in control of the government, Pien Fan-chih was transferred to become capital intendant (in 402; see TCTC 112.3539). After Hsüan was defeated, Pien was captured and executed (in 405; see TCTC 114.3579).

[2]Yang Yung in his notes for this anecdote interprets this to be a reaction from Yang Fu's having taken a five-mineral powder.

CHAPTER XXIII

The Free and Unrestrained

1. Juan Chi of Ch'en-liu (Honan), Hsi K'ang of Chiao Principality (Anhui), and Shan T'ao of Ho-nei (Honan) were all three of comparable age, Hsi K'ang being the youngest. Joining this company later were Liu Ling of P'ei Principality (Kiangsu), Juan Hsien of Ch'en-liu, Hsiang Hsiu of Ho-nei, and Wang Jung of Lang-yeh (Shantung). The seven used to gather beneath a bamboo grove, letting their fancy free in merry revelry. For this reason the world called them the "Seven Worthies of the Bamboo Grove."[1] (CS 49.12a; PSLT 30; TPKC 235)

> [1] CYC: At the time (ca. 260) the fame of the manner (of the "Seven Worthies") was wafted everywhere within the seas. Even down to the present (ca. 350) people continue to intone it.
>
> (The problem of the real or fancied existence of a group known as the "Seven Worthies of the Bamboo Grove," flourishing at the end of the Wei Kingdom in a place identified as "Bamboo Grove," Chu-lin, and located by Li Tao-yüan [d. 527] in LTYSCC 9, Ch'ing-shui, in Shan-yang Prefecture, near Lo-yang, has been treated by many scholars. See especially D. Holzman, "Les sept sages de la forêt des bambous et la société de leur temps," T'oung Pao 44, 1956, 317-346, and Ho Ch'i-min, Chu-lin ch'i-hsien yen-chiu, "A Study of the Seven Worthies of the Bamboo Grove," Hong Kong, 1966. There is no doubt that the seven were contemporaries and that at least some were close friends, but the earliest known reference to them as a group seems to have been Yüan Hung's [328-376] lost MSC, and the principal sources about their "merry revelries" are Sun Sheng's [ca. 302-373] CYC and Tai K'uei's [d. 396] CLCHL. It seems quite clear that the nostalgic refugees of Eastern Chin reconstructed the supposed association in their effort to idealize the spirit of freedom and transcendence the "Seven" came to symbolize. The recent discovery in 1960 of a stamped brick representation of them from a tomb at Hsi-shan-ch'iao near Nanking, dating from the fourth century, is further evidence of their popularity in the

southern capital. See *Wen-wu* 8-9, Aug. 1960, 37-42, and A. C. Soper, "A New Chinese Tomb Discovery: The Earliest Representation of a Famous Literary Theme," *Artibus Asiae* XXIV, 2, 1961, 79-86.)

2. While Juan Chi was in mourning for his mother (ca. 255), he was once present at a party at the house of Prince Wen of Chin (Ssu-ma Chao) where he was helping himself to meat and wine. The commandant of the capital province, Ho Tseng, who was also present, said to Prince Wen, "Your Excellency is now ruling the realm with filial devotion, yet Juan Chi, during an important period of mourning, has appeared openly among Your Lordship's guests drinking wine and eating meat. You should banish him beyond the sea to set right the teaching on public morals."

Prince Wen replied, "Here is Juan Chi, emaciated and depressed like this, yet you're unable to grieve with him. What's the reason? Furthermore, 'when one is ill, to drink wine and eat meat' is definitely in accord with the mourning rites."[1]

Chi continued drinking and devouring his food without interruption, his spirit and expression completely self-possessed. (*CS* 33.9b-10a; *TPYL* 845)

[1]Cf. "Record of Rites," 30 (Legge, *Li Ki* II, 185).

KPCC: Ho Tseng once said to Juan Chi, "You're a man who indulges his passions and gives free rein to his nature who will destroy public morals. At present the loyal and worthy are holding the reins of government--those who make close comparison between reputation and reality. How do you imagine the likes of you can survive?" Later he spoke about him to Ssu-ma Chao, but Chi continued to drink and devour his food without interruption.

Therefore during the transition from Wei to Chin (ca. 250-265), if ever there was a case of letting the hair fall loose, or acting in an unrestrained or contemptuous manner, or turning the back on the dead and forgetting the living, while claiming on the contrary to be fulfilling the rites, Juan Chi was such a man.

WSCC: Juan Chi was by nature extremely filial. While he was in mourning, even though he did not follow the ordinary prescriptions, nevertheless he was so wasted away that he nearly lost his life. However, he was profoundly hated and envied by cultivated and worldly gentlemen like Ho Tseng and others. The generalissimo, Ssu-ma Chao, loved him for his unhibited greatness, and never did him any harm.

3. Liu Ling was once suffering from a hangover (*ping-chiu*), and, being extremely thirsty, asked his wife for some wine. His wife, who had poured out all the wine and smashed the vessels, pleaded with tears in her eyes, saying, "You're drinking far too much. It's no way to preserve your life. You'll have to stop it."

Ling said, "A very good idea. But I'm unable to stop by myself. It can only be done if I pray to the ghosts and spirits and take an oath that I'll stop it. So you may get ready the wine and meat for the sacrifice."

His wife said, "As you wish," and setting out wine and meat before the spirits, requested Ling to pray and take his oath. Ling knelt down and prayed,

> "Heaven produced Liu Ling
> And took 'wine' for his name.
> At one gulp he will down a gallon—
> Five dipperfuls to ease the hangover.
> As for his wife's complaint,
> Be careful not to listen."

Whereupon he drained the wine and ate up the meat, and before he knew it was already drunk again.[1] (CS 49.17b-18a; SLF 17; TPYL 436, 846)

[1] The Commentary cites CLCHL as the source of this anecdote.

4. When Liu Ch'ang drank with other people he would mingle with riffraff and persons not in his own class. When someone chided him for this, he replied, "If it's someone superior to me, I can't help drinking with him; and if it's someone inferior to me, I also can't help drinking with him. And if it's someone of my own group, again I can't help drinking with him."[1]

Thus he would drink with people all day long and get drunk with them.

[1] See SSHY XXIV, 2, below, for a parody of this remark.

CYC: As a person, Liu Ch'ang was uninhibited and free (t'ung-ta).

5. There was a vacancy in the office of the commandant of infantry,[1] in the commisary of which were stored several hundred *hu* of wine. It was for this reason that Juan Chi requested to become commandant of infantry.[2] (CS 49.2b; SLF 17; TPYL 845)

[1] The office was originally created during the Former Han to command the garrison guarding the Upper Grove (Shang-lin) hunting preserve near the imperial palace in Ch'ang-an. Later it seems to have become a sinecure.

[2] WSC: Juan Chi was free and unrestrained, with feelings of contempt for the world, and he took no delight in public office. Prince Wen of Chin (Ssu-ma Chao) was personally very fond of Chi and often chatted and joked with him, allowing him to do whatever he wished and never forcing him to take office. Chi once said casually, "In my early years I used to roam about Tung-p'ing Commandery (Shantung) and enjoy the local scenery there. I'd like to be able to become grand warden of Tung-p'ing." Prince Wen was delighted and granted his wish. Chi immediately mounted a donkey and rode directly to the commandery, where he demolished all the walls and screens of the administrative offices, making an open vista inside and out. Thereafter his administration was pure and serene. Ten days later he remounted his donkey and departed.

Later, hearing that in the commissary of the commandant of infantry there were three hundred *shih* (roughly equivalent to the *hu*) of wine, he cheerfully sought to become commandant. Then he entered the administrative offices and, together with Liu Ling, drank and made merry.

CLCHL: Juan Chi and Liu Ling drank together in the commissary of the commandant of infantry, where both died while drunk.

SSHY Comm.: This story is the fabrication of curiosity-mongers, since Juan Chi died in the Ching-yüan era (263), and Liu Ling was still alive in the T'ai-shih era (265-274).

6. On many occasions Liu Ling, under the influence of wine, would be completely free and uninhibited, sometimes taking off his clothes and sitting naked in his room. Once when some persons saw him and chided him for it, Ling retorted, "I take heaven and earth for my pillars and roof, and the rooms of my house for my pants and coat. What are you gentlemen doing in my pants?"[1] (TPYL 845)

[1] TTCC: Some guests went to visit Liu Ling at a time when he happened to be stark naked. Ling, laughing, said, "I take heaven and earth for my house and home, and my room and roof for my pants and coat. You gentlemen shouldn't be in my pants in the first place, so now what are you complaining about?" Such was his self-abandon.

7. Juan Chi's sister-in-law (sao)[1] was once returning to her parents' home, and Chi went to see her to say good-bye. When someone chided him for this,[2] Chi replied, "Were the rites established for people like me?" (CS 49.3ab; IWLC 29; PSLT 6; TPYL 489, 517)

[1] The wife of Chi's older brother, Hsi, and mother of Juan Hsien.

[2] See "Record of Rites" I, 24 (Legge, Li Ki I, 77), quoted in the Commentary: "Sister-in-law (sao) and brother-in-law (shu) are not to exchange inquiries directly with each other."

8. The wife of Juan Chi's neighbor was very pretty. She worked as a barmaid tending the vats (lu) and selling wine. Juan and Wang Jung frequently drank at her place, and after Juan became drunk he would sleep by this woman's side. Her husband at first was extraordinarily suspicious of him, but after careful investigation he ceased after a while to think anything amiss.[1] (CS 49.3b; TPYL 828)

[1] WYCS: The unmarried daughter of Juan Chi's neighbor possessed talent and beauty, but died before being given in marriage. Chi had no relation to her and never knew her while she was living, but went to weep, and departed after exhausting his grief. His freedom and nonrestriction were always of this sort.

9. When Juan Chi was about to bury his mother, he steamed a fat suckling pig, drank two dipperfuls of wine, and after that attended the last rites. He did nothing but cry, "It's all over (ch'iung-i)!"[1] and gave himself to continuous wailing. As a result of this he spit up blood and wasted away for a long time.[2] (CS 49.3a; TPYL 375, 556)

[1] For a discussion of this apparently local practice of mourners in the Lo-yang area, later imitated in the southern capital, of crying to some sort of melody the words, "It's all over (ch'iung-i)!" or "What shall I do (nai-ho)?", see T'ang Ch'ang-ju, Wei-Chin Nan-pei ch'ao shih lun-ts'ung ("Essays on the History of the Wei, Chin, and North-South Dynasties"), Peking, 1955, p. 358. Cf. also No. 42, below.

[2] TTCC (cf. CS 49.2b-3a): When Juan Chi's mother was about to die, Juan was playing encirclement chess (wei-ch'i) as if nothing were happening. His opponent begged him to stop, but Chi was unwilling and stayed on to determine the outcome of the stakes. After that, he drank three dipperfuls of wine, lifted up his voice in a continuous wailing, spit up several pints (sheng) of blood, and wasted away for a long time.

10. Juan Hsien and Juan Chi lived on the south side of the street, and all the other Juans lived on the north (sunny) side. The northern Juans were all wealthy, while the southern Juans were poor. On the seventh day of the seventh month the northern Juans put on a grand sunning of their wardrobes, which all consisted of silk gauzes and colored and plain brocades, while Juan Hsien, using a bamboo pole, hung out a large pair of plain cloth calf-nose underpants (tu-pi kun) in his central courtyard. When someone remarked about this, he replied, "I'm not yet able to be completely free of worldly matters, so I just do this, that's all!"[1] (CS 49.4b)

[1]*CLCHL*: All the Juans of the former generation had been Juist scholars, accustomed to occupying posts. It was only the single household of Juan Hsien, which favored Taoism and repudiated official life, which was wine-loving and impoverished. According to ancient custom, on the seventh day of the seventh month there was a law that every household should sun its clothing. In the courtyards of the (wealthy) Juans there was a dazzling display of colored and plain brocades. Juan Hsien, who at the time was a young lad with his hair in tufts, set up a long bamboo pole and hung out a pair of calf-nose underpants.

(Another example of the late summer sunning to avoid mildew after the rainy season is recorded in *SSHY* XXV, 31, below.)

11. When Juan Chi was in mourning for his mother, P'ei K'ai went to pay him a visit of condolence. Juan was drunk at the time and was sitting with disheveled hair, his legs sprawled apart, not weeping. When P'ei arrived he put down a mat for himself on the floor, and after his weeping and words of condolence were completed, he departed.

Someone asked P'ei, "Generally when one offers condolences, the host weeps and the guest simply pays his respects. Since Juan was not weeping, why did *you* weep?"

P'ei replied, "Juan is a man beyond the realm of ordinary morality (fang-wai) and therefore pays no homage to the rules of propriety. People like you and me are still within the realm of custom (su-chung),[1] so we live our lives after the pattern set by etiquette." His contemporaries sighed in admiration over the way both men had found their true center.[2] (CS 49.3a)

[1]Cf. *Chuang-tzu* VI, 13a (Watson, p. 86).

[2]*MSC*: When Juan Chi was in mourning for his parents he did not follow the ordinary rites. P'ei K'ai went to pay him a visit of condolence, and found Chi drunk, with his hair disheveled and his legs sprawled apart, ignoring his visitor as if no one were present. K'ai wept, giving full vent to his grief, and then departed without the slightest expression of disapproval on his face. Such was his equanimity toward both those who agreed with and those who differed from him.

CLCHL: When P'ei K'ai offered condolences, he would be accepting toward outsiders, while preserving his inner principles. He had a completely unprejudiced mind, yet at the same time vast defenses.

12. The Juans were all great drinkers. When Juan Hsien arrived at the home of any of the clan for a gathering, they no longer used ordinary

wine cups (*pei*) for drinking toasts. Instead they would use a large earthenware vat (*weng*) filled with wine, and sitting facing each other all around it, would take large drafts. One time a herd of pigs came to drink and went directly up to the vat, whereupon pigs and men all proceeded to drink together. (*CS* 49.5a; *PTSC* 148; *TPYL* 758, 845)

13. Juan Hun's style and manner were like his father's (Juan Chi), and he, too, wanted to be free (*ta*). But Juan Chi said, "Juan Hsien has already joined us. You can't do it too."[1] (*CS* 49.4a)

[1]*CLCHL*: The reason why Juan Chi restrained Hun was because the latter did not yet understand his own reasons for becoming "free." Later, Juan Hsien's older brother's son, Chien, also occupied himself with "untrammeled freedom" (*k'uang-ta*). When his father died, as Chien traveled to the funeral, he encountered a heavy snowstorm and suffered from cold and freezing. Eventually he reached the home of the magistrate of Ling-i Prefecture (Anhui). The magistrate had set out for the other guests some wine pots and meat broth. Chien helped himself to them, thereby incurring the "pure criticism" (*ch'ing-i*) of the moralists. As a result he was rejected and without office for nearly thirty years.

At this time, though the reputation of the "Worthies of the Bamboo Grove" was high, the teaching regarding the rites was still strict. It was not until the Yüan-k'ang era (291-299) that people finally reached the point of letting themselves go in violation of the rites. Yüeh Kuang criticized such people, saying, "In the Moral Teaching (*ming-chiao*) surely there are pleasurable places. Why go to such lengths?" (Cf. *SSHY* I, 23, above.)

Yüeh Kuang's words contain the gist of the matter! He meant that the spirit of those later imitators of the "Seven Worthies" was not genuinely transcendent, but that they were merely taking advantage of it for self-indulgence and nothing more.

14. P'ei Wei's wife was the daughter of Wang Jung. Wang Jung once went early in the morning to P'ei's house, and without announcement walked straight into the bedroom. P'ei got down from the south side of the bed, and Wang's daughter P'ei got down from the north, and, facing Wang, they performed the greetings of host and guest without showing the slightest expression of embarrassment.

15. Juan Hsien had previously shown favor to a Hsien-pei slave girl in the household of his paternal aunt (*ku*). At the time when Hsien was in mourning for the death of his mother, the aunt was on the point of moving to a distant place.[1] At first she said she would leave the slave girl behind, but after she had set out, it turned out she had taken her along. Juan Hsien borrowed a guest's donkey, and, still wearing the clothes of mourning for a parent, rode after her himself, returning with the two of them riding one behind the other on the same saddle. Juan explained, "A man's seed is not to be lost." She was Juan Fu's mother.[2] (*CS* 49.4b-5a)

[1]*CS* 49.4b states that she was "returning to her husband's home."

[2]*CLCHL*: After Hsien had pursued the slave girl, contemporary discussions about this were heard in profusion, but after the end of Wei (265) they were hushed up and relegated to back alleys. By the

middle of the Hsien-ning era (275-279), however, they began again to mount the king's highways.

Juan Fu PC: Hsien wrote a letter to his aunt, saying, "The Hu barbarian slave girl has now given birth to a Hu barbarian son." The aunt wrote back, saying, "In Wang Yen-shou's 'Poetic Essay on the Lu Palace of Numinous Light' (*Lu Ling-kuang tien fu*; WH 11.12a) it says, 'Hu barbarians huddle in the distance (*yao-chi*) on the upper beams.' You may give him the courtesy name, Yao-chi, Huddled in the Distance." This is how Juan Fu received the courtesy name, Yao-chi.

16. After Jen K'ai had lost his power and prestige (in 272)[1] he no longer exercised any self-restraint. Someone said to Ho Ch'iao, "Why do you sit by and watch Jen K'ai going to ruin without coming to his rescue?"

Ho replied, "Jen K'ai is like the North Hsia Gate of Lo-yang. Splitting and splintering (*lâp-lâ*), all by itself it's about to collapse. It isn't something which can be shored up with one piece of wood."

[1]*CCKT*: K'ai possessed cultivated judgment and statesmanship, and most of the ten thousand decisions, great and small, were in his hands. But he was on bad terms with Chia Ch'ung, who uncovered the fact that K'ai was manipulating the Board of Civil Office, and moreover had the authorities memorialize the throne reporting that he was using the imperial eating utensils, whereupon he was impeached and relieved of his post. After that Emperor Wu's (Ssu-ma Yen, r. 265-290) feelings toward him became more distant.

17. When Liu Pao was young he used to go fishing in a grassy marsh. He was skilled at singing and whistling, and all who heard him used to linger and listen. There was an old woman who recognized him for an unusual man, and who so thoroughly enjoyed his singing and whistling that she killed a pig and served it to him. Liu Pao consumed the pig to the end without saying a word of thanks. The old woman saw that he was still not satiated and served him another pig. He ate half of it and left half, which he returned to her.

Later he became a secretary in the Board of Civil Office, where the old woman's son was serving as a petty clerk. Liu Pao singled him out for special promotion, and the young man, not knowing the reason, asked his mother. His mother told him (about the pigs), whereupon he prepared beef and wine and went to visit Liu Pao.

Pao said, "Go away! Go away! There's no further need to repay me."

18. Juan Hsiu used to travel everywhere on foot with one hundred cash (*ch'ien*) dangling from the end of his staff. When he came to a wine shop he would drink and enjoy himself there alone. Even when the most noble and influential men of the day invited him, he refused to go to their houses. (*CS* 49.8a)

19. While Shan Chien was serving as governor-general of Ching Province (in 309) he was always going out to drink. People made up a song about him which went:

> "Lord Shan at times once he is drunk,
> Heads straight for Kao-yang Pool.

> At day's end, slumped, he rides back home,
> Feeling no pain (*mieng-tieng*), oblivious to all.
>
> At other times he'll ride a dashing steed,
> Donning askew his egret cap.
> He lifts his hand and asks Ko Ch'iang,
> 'Am I doing as well as the Ping-chou boys?'"

The Kao-yang Pool was located in Hsiang-yang (northern Hupei, Shan's headquarters as governor-general).[1] Ko Ch'iang was Shan Chien's beloved general, a native of Ping Province (Shansi). (*CS* 43.7b–8a; *SLF* 17; *TPYL* 687, 845)

[1] *HYC*: The Later Han personal attendant, Hsi Yü, following the method of rearing fish proposed by the ancient worthy Fan Li (i.e., planting fertile females in a pool during the first third of the second month—see Li Shan's seventh-century commentary on Chang Hsieh's "Seven Commands," *Ch'i-ming*, *WH* 35.9a), constructed a fish pool. Along the pool's edge ran a high dike on which were planted bamboos and tall mallotus trees (*ch'iu*), while lotus (*fu-jung*), water chestnuts (*ling*), and water lilies (*chih*) floated on the water. It was a well-known resort for outings and banquets. Shan Chien often visited this pool, and never returned without getting magnificently drunk, at which times he would cry out, "This is my Kao-yang Pool!" The little boys of Hsiang-yang used to sing about it.

20. Chang Han did as he pleased without restraint. His contemporaries nicknamed him the "Juan Chi of East of the Yangtze River." Someone once asked him, "Do you think it's all right to do as you please and live for the present moment without making a name for yourself that will live after your death?"

Chang replied, "Making a name for myself after death isn't as good as one cup of wine right now."[1] (*CS* 92.16a; *PTSC* 148; *SLF* 17; *TPYL* 845)

[1] *WSC*: Han let his nature go where it would, and asked for nothing of the world in which he lived. His contemporaries honored his untrammeled freedom (*k'uang-ta*).

21. Pi Cho used to say, "Holding a crab's claw in one hand and a cup of wine in the other, paddling and swimming about in a pool of wine—ah! with that I'd be content to spend my whole life!"[1] (*CS* 49.22b; *SLF* 17; *TPYL* 846)

[1] *CHS*: At the end of the T'ai-hsing era (321) Pi Cho became president of the Board of Civil Office, but was always drinking and neglecting his duties. The man in the neighboring house was once brewing some wine which became ripe, and Cho in his drunkenness went by night among his vats (*weng*) to get some to drink. The owner, supposing him to be a thief, seized and bound him before realizing it was the president of the Board of Civil Office. After he had released him, Cho invited the owner to join him in a drinking bout beside the vats, and left only after getting drunk.

22. When Ho Hsün was on his way up to Lo-yang from K'uai-chi (in 290) to take up his post as chamberlain of the imperial grandson Ssu-ma

Yü*, his boat passed through the Glorious Gate (Ch'ang-men) of Wu Commandery (Soochow). Ho was sitting in the boat playing a seven-stringed zither (*ch'in*). Chang Han had never made his acquaintance before, but when he first heard from his position in the Pavilion of Golden Glory (Chin-ch'ang t'ing) the notes of the zither sounding so clear and pure, he went down to the boat where Ho was playing, and thereby got to converse with him. In this way they struck up a great friendship and liking for each other. Chang asked, "Where are you bound for?"

Ho replied, "Up to Lo-yang to take up a post. I'm just on my way."

Chang said, "I have some business in the northern capital, too, so I'll travel with you on the way." Thereupon he and Ho set out together. Chang had not notified his family beforehand, and the family found out about it only after pursuing him with inquiries. (*CS* 92.15b)

23. When Tsu Ti fled southward across the Yangtze River (between 307 and 312), in both his public and private life he was simple and frugal, with no love of fine clothing or the other amenities. Once when Wang Tao, Yü Liang, and the other gentlemen came in a group to visit Tsu, they were startled to see furs and padded robes piled up in layers and jewels and ornaments laid out in profusion. Finding the situation peculiar, the gentlemen asked him about it.

Tsu replied, "Last night we made another raid at Nan-t'ang (a suburb south of Chien-k'ang)." At the time Tsu always had in his employ strong ruffians to beat the drums and carry out raiding and plundering operations. The people in authority, for their part, tolerated it and asked no questions.[1]

[1] *CYC*: Tsu Ti was by nature thoroughly generous and not bound by petty restraints. Furthermore his retainers and companions were for the most part bold and unscrupulous bravos, all of whom Ti treated like sons and younger brothers. During the Yung-chia era (307-312), while refugees were numbered in the ten thousands and the area of Yang Province (Kiangsu, Chekiang, and Anhui) was suffering severe famine, (Ti's) retainers raided and foraged, but Ti always afforded them complete protection. Contemporary discussions for this reason minimized (his activities), and therefore for a long time he was not subjected to criticism.

24. The master of court ceremonials, K'ung Ch'ün, was fond of drinking. Chancellor Wang Tao once said to him, "Why are you always drinking? Have you never seen how the cloths used to cover wine jars (*p'ou*) in the wineshops rot away after a few days or months?"

Ch'ün replied, "That's not true. Have you never seen how meat marinated in wine dregs keeps longer than usual?"

Ch'ün once wrote to his relatives and old friends, "From this year's harvest I received a mere seven hundred *hu* of glutinous rice (*shu-mi*), not even enough for fermentation purposes!" (*CS* 78.11b-12a; *PTSC* 148; *SLF* 17; *TPYL* 845; *SWLC*, hsü 15)

25. Someone criticized Chou I for talking and joking with relatives and friends in a crude manner, without restraint or dignity.[1]

Chou rejoined, "I'm like the ten-thousand-*li* Long River (the Yangtze). How could it avoid making at least one turn in a thousand *li*?" (Cf. *CS* 69.17b)

¹*TTCC*: Wang Tao and Chou I and the other courtiers went to the home of the president of the Board of Civil Office, Chi Chan, to watch some female entertainers. Chan had a beloved concubine who was skilled in performing the new (i.e., Central Asian) music. Chou I, from where he was in the audience, wanted to communicate with Chan's concubine, thus exposing his depravity, yet in his face there was no evidence of shame. One of the officers memorialized the throne to have him impeached, but an imperial rescript granted him a special pardon.

26. While Wen Ch'iao's rank was still low, he often played *chaupar* (*shu-p'u*) with the merchants on the Ch'in-huai River (south of Chien-k'ang) in Yang Province, but with them he was always a "noncompetitor." On one occasion he lost everything he had in a gambling defeat and was left without any means of getting back home. Since he was a good friend of Yü Liang, from the middle of the boat where he was he shouted out to Liang in a loud voice, "You'll have to bail me out!"
Liang immediately sent the requisite amount, and after that he got to return home. He went through this sort of thing repeatedly.¹ (*TPYL* 754)

¹*CHS*: Ch'iao was characterized as "outstandingly transparent," and was not bound by petty rules of conduct.

27. Wen Ch'iao took pleasure in intemperate remarks, whereas Pien K'un always kept himself within the bounds of propriety and law.¹ They once went to Yü Liang's house where they got into a large argument. Every time Wen opened his mouth, the language was vulgar and obscene, but Yü remarked calmly, "Wen Ch'iao never utters a vulgar word the whole day long."²

¹*Pien K'un PC*: Pien K'un had only to stand in court with a proper expression, and "the hundred officials would tremble in awe." All the noble and unattached young people held him in worshipful esteem.

²This was not spoken in sarcasm. As Liu Chün explains in the Commentary, Yü admired Wen's "freedom from inhibition (*ta*)."

28. Chou I's manner and moral power were originally cultivated and dignified, and he had a profound ability to adjust to dangerous and chaotic times. As the years passed, however, after he had crossed the Yangtze River, he became more and more a heavy drinker and would occasionally be sober only for three days at a time.¹ His contemporaries called him the "Three-day Vice-President."² (*CS* 69.17b-18a; *IWLC* 48; *PTSC* 59; *PSLT* 21; *TPYL* 211, 497, 845)

¹The Sung text reads, "drunk for three days," a *lectio facilior*. I have emended to agree with quotations in *IWLC* 48 and *TPYL* 211, 497.
CYC: At first Chou I gained a flourishing reputation throughout the realm for his cultivated and exemplary conduct, but later he frequently had lapses caused by drinking. Yü Liang said of him, "Marquis Chou's later years might be called the 'decline of the phoenix's moral power.'" (See "Analects" XVIII, 5.)
YL: It was only on the occasion of his wife's funeral that Chou I was sober for three days, and on the occasion of his paternal aunt's (*ku*) funeral he was also sober for three days, all of

which resulted in a large loss of prestige. Every time he was
drunk, the nobles always gathered to take care of him. (Also
emended to agree with *TPYL* 497.)

[2] Chou I was left vice-president of the Court Secretariat between
320 and his death in 322; (see *TCTC* 91.2877).

29. While Wei Yung was serving as Wen Ch'iao's senior administrator,
Wen was very friendly with him, and frequently on the spur of the
moment would bring wine and salted dried meat (*fu*) to Wei's house,
where they would sit opposite each other all day with legs sprawled
apart unceremoniously. When Wei went to Wen's place it was the same.

30. At the time of Su Chün's rebellion (327) all the members of the
Yü family[1] scattered and fled. Yü Ping, who at the time was serving
as grand warden of Wu Commandery (Soochow), made his escape alone;
all his underlings had deserted him. A lone runner of the commandery
office single-handedly took Ping in a small boat out through the
mouth of the Ch'ien-t'ang River (Chekiang), concealing him under some
coarse bamboo matting. At the time Su Chün was offering a reward and
had instituted a manhunt for Ping, and his orders for the search and
investigation of every place where he might be staying were extremely
urgent. The runner, leaving the boat moored at a market wharf, had
gone ashore for a drink, and came back drunk. Waving his oar in the
direction of the boat he said to one of the investigators, "Ya lookin'
for Yü Ping? He's right in here!"

Ping was filled with great fear and panic, but dared not move.
When the investigator saw how small the boat was, and how narrow its
capacity, he figured the runner was just raving drunk, and never gave
it another thought. Instead he personally escorted the boat to the
opposite shore of the Chih (i.e., the Che) River, where Ping took
refuge with the Wei family of Shan-yin Prefecture (Chekiang) and so
managed to escape.[2]

Later, after the rebellion had been put down (328), Ping wanted to
requite the runner and offered him whatever his heart desired. The
man said, "My origins being as humble as they are, I don't want
either fame or rank. Ever since I was young I've worked hard at menial jobs like wielding the whip as a charioteer, and I've always
felt that I wasn't able to drink to my heart's content. If I could
just have enough wine to last the rest of my life, I wouldn't need
another thing!"

Ping built a large house for him, purchased male and female slaves,
and made sure there were a hundred *hu* of wine on the premises to last
till the end of his life. Contemporaries said that the runner not
only had wisdom; he had "mastered the meaning of life (*ta-sheng*)."[3]
(*PTSC* 77)

[1] Su Chün attempted to break the supremacy of the Yü family faction
at court which had been established in 325 by Yü Liang, and was
continued after his death in 340 by his younger brothers, Ping and
I, until 345.

[2] *CHS*: While Yü Ping was grand warden of Wu Commandery, Su Chün began his rebellion and dispatched troops to punish Ping. Ping abandoned the commandery and fled to K'uai-chi (Chekiang)

[3] The title of section XIX of *Chuang-tzu*.

382 TALES OF THE WORLD

31. When Yin Hsien was appointed grand warden of Yü-chang Commandery (Kiangsi), on the eve of his departure to take up his post the people of the capital (Chien-k'ang)¹ took the occasion to entrust him with a hundred or more letters. After he reached Shih-t'ou (in Kiangsi)² he threw them all into the water. As he did so he muttered the following incantation:

>   "Let those that sink sink,
>   And those that float float;
>   But Yin Hsien never can
>   Become a mailman."

(CS 77.22a)

¹*Tu-hsia*. Accounts of the same story, quoted from the HCC ("Record of Hsüan-ch'eng Commandery," the area of Yü-chang) in TPYL 70, and from YL in TPYL 593, and PTSC 103, substitute *chün*, "the commandery" (i.e., Yü-chang) for *tu-hsia*. It seems clear, in any case, that it was persons living in Chien-k'ang who had connections in Yü-chang.

²Not the Shih-t'ou which served as the port of Chien-k'ang on the Yangtze, but Shih-t'ou Station (*i*) in Nan-ch'ang Prefecture (Kiangsi), where there was an island in the Kan River later known as "Throw-letters Island" (T'ou-shu chu), named after this event. See TSFYCY 84.

32. While Wang Meng and Hsieh Shang were serving together as officers under Wang Tao's administration¹ Wang Meng once remarked, "Officer Hsieh here can perform an unusual dance."²

Hsieh immediately got up and danced, his spirit and mood both utterly composed. Wang Tao watched him intently, then said to the other guests, "Makes a person think of Wang Jung (d. 305)!" (CS 79.1b)

¹*Wang Meng PC*: Chancellor Wang Tao called into service famous gentlemen and contemporary worthies to assist in the restoration of the dynasty. Of those who were added to the ranks of officeholders, he always invited the most outstanding and eminent, and thus it was he who summoned Wang Meng to be one of his officers.

²*CYC*: Hsieh Shang was by nature free and unrestrained, and a skillful musician.

YL: Hsieh Shang, after a few drinks, right in the midst of the trays and tables, would dance the myna-bird dance (*ch'ü-yü wu*) of the taverns in the Lo-yang market, and do it exceedingly well.

CS 79.1b: Wang Tao held Hsieh Shang in profound esteem, and, comparing him to Wang Jung, often called him "the younger An-feng." Wang summoned him to serve as an officer, and when Hsieh had barely arrived in the provincial headquarters, he paid Wang a visit. In view of the fact that Hsieh possessed superior talents, Wang said to him, "I hear you can perform the myna-bird dance so well that everybody is dumbfounded. Is it true?"

Hsieh replied, "Fine." And immediately donning a robe and headband, started to dance. Wang had everyone present clap his hands in time with the dance, while Hsieh bent downward and up in their midst as if no one else were present. Such was his spontaneity and freedom.

33. While Wang Meng and Liu T'an were both living south of the Vermilion Sparrow Pontoon,[1] there was a festive banquet at the home of Huan I*. Hsieh Shang was just returning from mourning at the grave of his elder brother, P'ou, to observe the rite of "returning to weep" (fan-k'u) on the third day after the burial.[2] They wanted to invite Shang to the banquet, so they first dispatched a messenger, but he had not yet consented. He had, however, already halted his carriage, and when they insistently repeated the invitation, he finally turned his carriage around. It was only after they had greeted him at the door, and, steadying his arm, had helped him down from the carriage, that he got to remove his mourning headband and replace it with a cap. The merrymaking and feasting were already in mid-progress before he finally realized he had not yet removed his coarse hempen robe of mourning.[3]

[1] I.e., on the fashionable Black Clothing Street (Wu-i Chieh), south of Chien-k'ang, along the Ch'in-huai River.

[2] The rite involved returning to weep in the ancestral temple three days after burial. See "Record of Rites" IV, 15 (Legge, *Li Ki* I, 170).

[3] *SMTWCC*: Hsieh Shang was by nature informal and spontaneous, not bound by petty rules of conduct. After his elder brother (P'ou) was buried, he was on his way back from the grave. Wang Meng and Liu T'an were both enjoying an outing at Hsin-t'ing (south of Chien-k'ang). Meng wanted to invite Hsieh Shang to join them. Earlier he had talked it over with T'an, saying, "I reckon that Hsieh Shang will simply not care one way or the other."

T'an replied, "In Hsieh Shang's personality without doubt there would be the disposition to come." Whereupon they sent somebody to invite him. Shang at first declined, but already had abandoned all intention of returning home. So when they invited him a second time, he immediately wheeled his carriage about. Such was his spontaneity.

34. When Huan Wen was young his family was poor. Once while playing *chaupar* he suffered a huge loss, and his creditor kept demanding payment with extreme insistence. Huan thought over some scheme whereby he might extricate himself, but did not know how to get out of his dilemma.

Yüan Tan of Ch'en Commandery (Honan) was a bold and forthright man of many capabilities, so Huan was on the point of seeking help from Tan. But at the time Tan was in mourning for a parent, and Huan, afraid of placing him in a compromising position, broached the problem to him in very tentative terms. Quick as an echo, Tan immediately consented, without the slightest reluctance or hesitation. Thereupon he changed his clothes and tucked his cloth mourning cap in his bosom and followed Huan out to gamble with his creditor.

Tan had a long-standing reputation as a skillful player. As the creditor approached the gaming board, he said, "Now, of course, you're not playing at being Yüan Tan, are you?" Whereupon they played together at one hundred thousand points a throw, and were soon up into the millions. As Tan threw his winning counters (*ma*) down, he would shout at the top of his lungs as though no other person were present. Reaching into his bosom for his cloth cap, he flung it at his opponent with the words, "Now, at last, do you recognize Yüan Tan?"[1] (CS 83.8a)

[1]KT: Huan Wen while playing *chaupar* lost several hundred *hu* of rice, and sought rescue from Yüan Tan. Tan, who was in mourning for a parent, immediately replied, "It'll be a great pleasure; I'll certainly do it! All you have to do is shout with a loud voice." So saying, he immediately removed his mourning clothes, and they went out the gate together. Realizing that he still had a cloth mourning cap on his head, he threw it away and put on a small cap.

After he had begun to play, Yüan's manner was to shout and throw off his clothes, and in throwing the dice he always made either a "black" (*lu*) or a "pheasant" (*chih*; the two best throws). The two of them (Yüan and Huan) shouted in unison, while the opponent, thrown into utter confusion, lost several million.

35. Wang Yün said, "Wine is just the thing to make every man naturally remote from the world."[1]

[1]HCYC: Wang Yün from youth onward was fond of wine, and in later years became even more so. While he was living in K'uai-chi (Chekiang) there were very few days that he was sober.

36. Liu T'an said, "Sun T'ung is a madman. Whenever he goes anywhere he enjoys himself for days on end, and sometimes on his return he'll get halfway home and then suddenly turn back."[1]

[1]CHS: When Sun T'ung was young he was free and unrestrained and not bound by convention. He settled in K'uai-chi (Chekiang), since by nature he was fond of hills and streams. When he sought to become magistrate of Yin Prefecture (near Ningpo), he neglected all petty duties and let his fancy free, roaming about for pleasure. There was not a famous hill or outstanding stream he had not viewed in his travels.

37. Yüan Tan had two younger sisters. One, Nü-huang, was married to Yin Hao, and the other, Nü-cheng, to Hsieh Shang. He once said to Huan Wen, "It's a pity I don't have still another sister to make a match with you!" (TPYL 517)

38. While Huan Ch'ung was governor of Ching Province (Hunan-Hupei, 377-383), Chang Hsüan, who was then serving as personal attendant at court, was sent on a mission to see him in Chiang-ling (Hupei). On his way, as he passed Yang-ch'i Village (200 *li* downriver from Wu-ch'ang), he suddenly caught sight of a man carrying a small basket half filled with fish. The man came directly over toward Chang's boat and said, "I have some fish here for which I'd like to borrow your utensils to cut them into slices."

Chang accordingly moored the boat and took him in. He asked the man's name, and the man said he was Liu Lin-chih. Since Chang had long heard of his reputation, he welcomed him with great delight. When Liu learned that Chang had been entrusted with a mission from the capital, he asked, "Are Hsieh An and Wang T'an-chih both well?"

Chang wanted very much to keep on talking with him, but Liu had not the slightest intention of staying. As soon as he had finished eating the sliced fish, he started to leave, saying, "Just now I got these fish, and observed that there'd probably be utensils for slicing them on board your boat, and it was only for this reason that I came." With that he left. Chang proceeded to follow him all the way to his house, where Liu set out some wine for him. It was of extraordinarily impure quality, but because Chang held Liu's person in high esteem, he had no recourse but to drink it down. While they were drinking, seated opposite each other, Liu was the first to rise, saying, "Right now it's time to cut the rushes (ti)[1]; I shouldn't let it go any longer." Chang, for his part, had no way of detaining him. (PTSC 145; TPYL 862)

[1] *Miscanthus sacchariflorus*, a reed growing on the banks of streams, used for making mats.

39. Wang Hui-chih once went to visit Ch'ih Hui. While Ch'ih was still in the inner part of the house, Wang noticed that he had a small wool rug (*t'âp-təng)[1] and said to himself, "Where on earth did A-ch'i (Ch'ih Hui) get this thing?" Whereupon he ordered his attendants to send it back to his own house. When Ch'ih came out and was looking about for it, Wang said, "Just now there was 'a big strong man who put it on his back and ran off with it.'"[2] Ch'ih showed no sign of offense. (TPYL 708)

[1] These rugs, evidently of Iranian origin (cf. Pers. *tābīdan*, "spun," "woven"), are listed among the products of northwestern India (T'ien-chu) in HHS 118.12a and were still valued as luxury items in T'ang times; see E. H. Schafer, *Golden Peaches*, p. 198. The term is folk-etymologized in SM 18 as follows: "The *t'a-teng* is placed on a small stool (*t'a*) in front of a larger bed, as a means of mounting (*teng*) the bed."

[2] See *Chuang-tzu* VI, 6a (Watson, p. 80).

40. When Hsieh An first came out of retirement and went west to Chien-k'ang (in 360), he lost his carriage and ox by gambling, and was returning home on foot leaning on his staff. On the road he ran into Liu T'an, who said to him, "An-shih, are you all right?" Whereupon Hsieh rode back with him.

41. Lo Yu of Hsiang-yang (northern Hupei) possessed great refinement, but when he was young most people called him a fool. Once he attended another person's sacrifice for the purpose of begging for some of the food. He went very early before the gate was open. The host went out to welcome the spirits, and catching sight of him, asked, "Since it's not time yet, what are you doing here?"

Lo replied, "I heard you were holding a sacrifice and wanted to beg for a meal, that's all." Whereupon he ensconced himself by the side of the gate. When dawn came, he took the food and withdrew, without the slightest expression of embarrassment.[1]

As a person he possessed an excellent memory. When he accompanied Huan Wen on the pacification of Shu (Ch'eng-tu, in 347), he made a tour of inspection of Shu's walls and pylons, observation towers and edifices; the width or narrowness of its streets and crossroads, the abundance or paucity of the fruit trees and bamboos planted along them, were all silently recorded in his memory. Later, when Huan Wen met (the future) Emperor Chien-wen (Ssu-ma Yü) at Li-chou (near Chien-k'ang, in 365), Yu was also present. While they talked together about the events that had taken place in Shu, there were also some things left out or forgotten, all of which Yu named in order, without a single mistake or lapse of memory. Huan Wen checked his account against the records of the walls and pylons of Shu, and everything was exactly as he had said. Everyone present acknowledged his prowess with sighs of admiration. Hsieh An exclaimed, "Lo Yu is not a whit inferior to Wei Shu!"[2]

Later Lo was appointed governor of Kuang Province (Kwangtung and Kwangsi). When he was about to go to his post, the governor of Ching Province, Huan Huo (gov. 365-377) spoke to him, inviting him to come that evening and stay overnight. Lo replied, "I already have a prior engagement, but my host is poor, and perhaps has spent money for wine and meat. Visiting with him is based on a very old friendship. Please let me accept your invitation some other day."

Huan Huo secretly dispatched someone to spy on him, and when evening came he actually did go to the home of an assistant clerk in the Ching provincial administration, and stayed there every bit as happily as if his host had been someone of supreme prominence.

While he was in I Province (Szechwan), he said to his sons, "I have a dinner service for five hundred people." Everyone in the family was greatly shocked that Lo, having been so incorrupt in the past, should now suddenly have come into possession of this sort of thing. On investigation it turned out to be two hundred and fifty double sets (*t'a*) of black lacquered nesting boxes (*lei*). (*MCYC* 1)

[1]*CYC*: Lo Yu used to enjoy attending other people's sacrifices, whither he would go to beg for their leftover food. Regardless of whether it was an army camp, public office, tavern, or shop, he never considered it a disgrace. Huan Wen once chided him, saying, "You're far too undignified in your conduct. If it's food you need, why don't you come to me and ask for it, instead of going to such lengths?" But Yu proudly disdained his offer, saying, "If I came to you to ask for food, today I might get some, but tomorrow it would already be gone." Huan laughed aloud at him.

He began his official career in Ching Province, and later served in Huan Wen's headquarters (between 345 and 365). Because his family was poor, he begged for a position with a better salary. But although Huan treated him well because of his ability and learning, he still considered him undisciplined and dissolute, incapable of governing other people, and though he promised him a position, he never employed him.

Later another man in the same headquarters received the wardenship of a commandery. Wen gave a banquet to bid him farewell, to which Yu arrived extraordinarily late. When Wen asked him about it, Yu replied, "By nature I'm a drinker of wine and a lover of its flavor. Yesterday I received your gracious invitation and set out first thing this morning, but on the way I met a ghost who made great sport of me, saying, 'I only see you seeing off someone else to take up a commandery. Why don't I ever see someone else seeing *you* off to take up a commandery?' At first I was afraid, but in the end I became ashamed, and went back home to resolve the problem, and now without realizing it I've committed the offense of being tardy."

Although Huan laughed at his wit, in his heart he was somewhat shamed by it, and later he made him grand warden of Hsiang-yang Commandery.

²See above, *SSHY* VIII, 17.

42. Whenever Huan I* listened to unaccompanied singing (*ch'ing-ko*),¹ he would always cry aloud, "Alas! What shall I do (*nai-ho*)?"

Hsieh An, hearing him, said, "Tzu-yeh, you're what might be called a man of deep feeling all the way through!"

¹*Ch'ing-ko* were sung by female entertainers and usually dealt with erotic themes.

43. Chang Chan was fond of planting pines and cypresses in front of his study. At the same time, whenever Yüan Shan-sung went out for an excursion, he was always fond of having his companions compose pallbearers' songs (*wan-ko*).¹ Contemporaries used to say, "Chang sets out corpses below his room, and Yüan performs burials along the road."² (*CS* 83.7b; *TPKC* 253)

¹*HCYC*: Yüan Shan-sung was a skilled musician. Among the old songs of the northerners (i.e., Western Chin, 265-316) was a piece called "Hardships of Wayfaring" (*Hsing-lu nan*), whose text was somewhat coarse and unpolished. Shan-sung liked it and made its lines more literary and its rhythm more graceful. Every time he was exhilarated with wine he would sing it, following his own adaptation, and everyone who heard him would be reduced to tears.

Earlier, Yang T'an had been a skillful singer, and Huan I* a capable performer of pallbearers' songs, and now Shan-sung followed in their succession with his rendition of "Hardships of Wayfaring." Contemporaries called them the "Three Incomparables" (*san-chüeh*).

²Pines and cypresses, symbolizing by their winter greenness resistance to death, were planted in graveyards.

YL: Chang Chan was fond of planting pines in front of his study, and raising myna-birds (*ch'ü-yü*). Yang Shan-sung, whenever he went out for an excursion, was fond of making his companions compose pallbearers' songs. Contemporaries, etc.

44. While Lo Yu was serving as a clerk in the administration of Ching Province (Hunan-Hupei), the governor, Huan Wen (gov. 345-365), gave a farewell party for Wang Ch'ia. Lo Yu, having come forward next to Huan and sat for a while, finally excused himself to leave. Huan said, "But just now you wanted to consult about something. Why are you leaving so soon?"

Lo replied, "I've heard that the meat of white sheep is delicious, and since all my life I've never gotten to eat any, I made bold to seek a front seat, that's all. I've got nothing to consult about. Now that I've already eaten my fill, there's no further need to stay." He showed not the slightest expression of embarrassment. (*TPYL* 863)

45. Chang Chan, after a few drinks, used to sing pallbearers' songs (*wan-ko*) with great pathos and poignancy. Huan Ch'ung said to him, "You're not one of T'ien Heng's¹ retainers; how have you suddenly reached such perfection?"

[1]T'ien Heng was a descendant of the royal house of Ch'i (Shantung) who committed suicide when the first emperor of Han (Kao-tsu, r. 202-195 B.C.) conquered the territory of Ch'i in 202; see TCTC 11.359.

CTFH: A man was singing at a burial and someone remarked, "That person is accompanying a burial with music; isn't it improper?" Master Chiao (Chiao Chou, third cent. A.D.) replied, "In the 'Book of Documents' (Shu I; Legge III, 41) it says, 'When Yao died (trad. 2258 B.C.), throughout the territory within the Four Seas the eight musical timbres (pa-yin) were hushed.' How can there be any such thing as accompanying a burial with music?"

The man said, "But at modern burials there are those who sing pallbearers' songs. Why?" Master Chiao replied, "I have heard that when the Han Emperor Kao summoned T'ien Heng, as T'ien reached Shih-hsiang Pavilion (near Lo-yang), he cut his own throat, bequeathing his head, which his retainers bore (wan) to the palace in Lo-yang. They dared not weep, yet could not contain their grief, so they sang songs, to give vent to the sounds of their grief. But theirs was the practice of a single time. Now when there is a burial in the neighboring household, the pestles for pounding grain are stilled and pallbearers wear gags in their mouths. Who accompanies burials with music?"

Chuang-tzu (not in the present Chuang-tzu text): The reason for the origin of the coffin-rope chanties (fu-ou) is surely to be found in the lagging of some and the overexertion of others.

(Ssu-ma Piao's late third century commentary for this passage explains: "The reason why there are chanties for pulling the coffin ropes is because people have a disparity in their exertion of strength; therefore the songs are to urge them along," i.e., keep them in step.)

Tso-chuan (Ai 11; Legge V, 825): Duke Ai of Lu (r. 494-467 B.C.) joined forces with Wu to attack Ch'i . . . The Ch'i general Kung-sun Hsia ordered his men to sing the song, "Sacrifice for the Dead" (Yü-pin).

(Tu Yü's [d. 284] commentary on this passage explains: "Yü-pin is a song escorting the dead to burial. It shows that all men must die.")

SC (57.1b): Chou Po (fl. 200-175 B.C.) used to play the vertical flute (hsiao) as a musical accompaniment for funerals.

SSHY Comm.: Thus the origin of pallbearers' songs is of long standing; they did not originate with T'ien Heng. Nevertheless, Chiao Chou, in citing texts on the rites, seems to have had a clear basis for his opinion. It is not something which dull rustics like me have been able to hear about in detail. Being in doubt, I shall merely pass on my doubts and await the clarification of someone more broadly learned than I.

46. Wang Hui-chih was once temporarily lodging in another man's vacant house, and ordered bamboos planted. Someone asked, "Since you're only living here temporarily, why bother?" Wang whistled and chanted poems a good while; then abruptly pointing to the bamboos, replied, "How could I live a single day without these gentlemen?"[1] (CS 80.11ab; PSLT 3; TPYL 392)

[1]CHS: Wang Hui-chih was conspicuously undisciplined and wanted to defy convention and be free. But his indulgence in the pleasures

of sight and sound was somewhat excessive, and contemporaries, while delighting in his ability, considered his conduct indecent.

47. While Wang Hui-chih was living in Shan-yin (Chekiang),¹ one night there was a heavy fall of snow. Waking from sleep, he opened the panels of his room, and, ordering wine, drank to the shining whiteness all about him. Then he got up and started to pace back and forth, humming Tso Ssu's (d. 306) poem, "Summons to a Retired Gentleman" (*Chao yin-shih*).² All at once he remembered Tai K'uei, who was living at the time in Shan (south of Shan-yin). On the spur of the moment he set out by night in a small boat to visit him. The whole night had passed before he finally arrived. When he reached Tai's gate he turned back without going in.

When someone asked his reason, Wang replied, "I originally went on the strength of an impulse, and when the impulse was spent I turned back. Why was it necessary to see Tai?" (*CS* 80.11b)

¹*CHS*: Wang Hui-chih indulged his natural inclinations and lived free and uninhibited. Giving up his official post, he returned east to live in Shan-yin.

²The text is preserved in *WH* 22.2a-3a. Liu Chün quotes the opening lines:

"Propped on a staff I go to summon the retired gentleman,
Where weed-grown paths connect the then and now.
In the cliff cave there is no edifice;
Amid the mountains, only his singing zither.
White snow remains on the shadeward ridge,
Vermilion blooms blaze in the sunward grove."

48. Wang Hui once said, "Wine is just the thing which naturally draws a man up and sets him in a transcendent place."

49. Wang Hui-chih once came out of retirement to the capital and his boat was still moored by the banks of the Blue-green Stream (Ch'ing-ch'i).¹ He had long known that Huan I* was skilled at playing the transverse flute (*ti*), but had never made his acquaintance. It happened that Huan was passing by along the shore while Wang was in the boat. One of the passengers, recognizing him, said, "It's Huan I*." Wang immediately had someone convey his greetings, saying, "I hear you're skilled at playing the flute. Would you try playing for me once?"

Huan was already distinguished and famous at the time, but since he, too, had long been aware of Wang's reputation, he immediately turned around and dismounted from his carriage, and, sitting informally on a folding stool (*hu-ch'uang*), played three tunes for him. When he had finished playing, he immediately remounted his carriage and departed. Guest and host never exchanged a single word.² (*CS* 81.10ab; *IWLC* 44; *PTSC* 111)

¹Following *CS* 81.10a. The Blue-green Stream was a tributary of the Ch'in-huai River, flowing southward to the east of Chien-k'ang.

²*HCYC*: The General of the Left, Huan I*, was a skillful musician. Once Emperor Hsiao-wu (Ssu-ma Yao, r. 373-396) was holding a banquet, with Hsieh An in attendance. The emperor ordered Huan I* to

play the transverse flute. I* showed no offense in his spirit or expression, but after playing one tune laid the flute aside and said, "Your servant is not as good on the twelve-stringed zither (cheng) as he is on the transverse flute. Still, he's good enough to accompany singing or piping. He has a slave who is a skillful flute player, and, moreover, slave and master are accustomed to playing together. Your servant requests to have him brought in."

The emperor appreciated his forthrightness and permitted the slave to be summoned. After the slave arrived, he played the flute while Huan I* strummed the zither and sang a song of resentment. By this means he expressed his remonstrance.

50. When Huan Hsüan was summoned to the capital (ca. 387) to serve as equestrian forerunner to the crown prince (Ssu-ma Te-tsung),[1] his boat was moored at Rush Island (Ti-chu, in the Ch'in-huai River). Wang Ch'en, slightly drunk after having taken a powder, went to visit Huan. Huan set out wine for him, but since he was unable to drink it cold (because of the powder), Huan unthinkingly said to his attendants, "Have them warm (wen) the wine and bring it back." After doing so, he burst into tears and cried out, choking with grief.[2] At that point Wang got up to leave, but Huan, wiping away his tears with his handkerchief, said to him, "What has my violation of my father's taboo name (Wen) got to do with you?" Wang sighed and said, "Ling-pao, you're really and truly free (ta)!"[3] (PTSC 94)

[1] (Huan) Hsüan PC: Huan Hsüan had earlier been appointed equestrian forerunner to the crown prince. At the time, in view of the fact that Hsüan's father, Huan Wen (d. 373), had a record of disloyalty, the court accordingly held Hsüan in check with a simple appointment.

[2] CATC: Huan Hsüan surpassed other men in both grief and joy. At the first sign of delight or sorrow he never failed to cry out or choke up.

[3] IY: When Huan Hsüan was born there was a light illuminating the room. Someone who was skilled at divination said, "Since a strange radiance appeared when this child was born, he should be given the courtesy name, Wei-t'ien-jen ('For Heaven and Man')." But his father, Huan Wen, objected to a three-character name, so the diviner once more suggested the name, Shen-ling-pao ("Divine Spirit Treasure"), still using three characters. Since it was difficult to repeat his former rejection, Huan eliminated the character Shen ("Divine"), and named the child Ling-pao ("Spirit Treasure").

YL: Huan Hsüan never observed memorial days, but only memorial occasions. His freedom from inhibition, and refusal to be bound by convention, were all of this sort.

51. Wang Kung[1] once asked Wang Ch'en, "How would Juan Chi (d. A.D. 263) compare with Ssu-ma Hsiang-ju (d. 117 B.C.)?"

Wang replied, "In Juan Chi's breast it was a rough and rugged terrain (*luậi-k'uậi); that's why he needed wine to irrigate it."[2] (SLF 17; TPYL 371, 845; SWLC, hsü 14)

[1] In both SLF 17 and SWLC, hsü 14, the questioner is identified as Wang Hsün (d. ca. 325), which would be an anachronism. Probably the similarity of courtesy names (Wang Kung = Hsiao-po; Wang Hsün = Shao-po) accounts for the confusion.

²As Liu Chun explains in the Commentary, Wang "meant that Juan was in all respects the same as Hsiang-ju, but differed from him only in his drinking." Both men were unconventional, both were poets and musicians, both had written on the theme of the "Great Man" (i.e., the liberated man). Ssu-ma Hsiang-ju's "Poetic Essay on the Great Man" (*Ta-jen fu*) is preserved in *CSKST, Han* 21.7a-8a, and Juan Chi's "Biography of Mr. Great Man" (*Ta-jen hsien-sheng chuan*) in ibid., *San-kuo* 46.5a-11a.

52. Wang Ch'en sighed and said, "If for three days I don't drink any wine, I feel my body and spirit are no longer intimate with each other."¹ (*CS* 75.15a; *TPYL* 845)

¹A parody of *SSHY* IV, 63, above.

53. Wang Kung said, "A famous gentleman (*ming-shih*)¹ doesn't necessarily have to possess remarkable talent. Merely let a man be perpetually idle and a heavy drinker, and whoever has read the poem, "Encountering Sorrow" (*Li-sao*),² can then be called a 'famous gentleman.'" (*MCYC*, hsia; *TPKC* 845)

¹The distinction made in this period between "famous" (*ming*) and "eminent" (*kao*) is explained by the Buddhist biographer Hui-chiao (fl. 530), in the postface to his "Lives of Eminent Monks" (*KSC* 14; *Taishō* 50.419a): "If men of real achievement conceal their brilliance, then they are eminent (*kao*) but not famous (*ming*); when men of slight virtue happen to be in accord with their times then they are famous but not eminent." See A. F. Wright, "Biography and Hagiography: Hui-chiao's *Lives of Eminent Monks*," *Zinbun Kagaku Kenkyusyo, Silver Jubilee Volume*, Kyoto, 1954, p. 408.

²The first of the "Songs of the South" (*Ch'u-tz'u*), attributed to Ch'ü Yüan (b. 343 B.C.); trans. David Hawkes, *Ch'u Tz'u*, pp. 22-34.

54. As Wang Hsin climbed Mt. Mao (in Kiangsu),¹ he wept bitterly, saying, "Wang Hsin of Lang-yeh (Shantung) will finally die because of his passions!"²

¹It was in a cave on the slopes of this mountain that three brothers, surnamed Mao, were supposed to have become "transcendents" (*hsien*) some time during the Han Dynasty. Later Hsü Mi reputedly founded the Mao-shan sect of religious Taoism here, whose doctrines, according to T'ao Hung-ching's *Chen-kao* ("Proclamation of Truth," first published in 489), stressed the elimination of the passions as a means of achieving *hsien*-hood.

²*LAC*: Earlier (in 397), when Wang Kung was about to champion the right (by eliminating Ssu-ma Tao-tzu's faction at court), he sent out instructions in the three commanderies of Wu (K'uai-chi and Wu-hsing of Chekiang, and Tan-yang of Kiangsu). Wang Hsin was in mourning, but was nevertheless appointed governor of Wu Principality (Soochow). After Wang Kuo-pao's death (in 397), Kung disbanded his troops and ordered Hsin to resume his mourning attire. In a great rage Hsin countered by occupying the principal city of Wu in revolt. Kung sent his sergeant-at-arms, Liu Lao-chih, to punish Hsin, who was defeated, but none knew his whereabouts.

CHAPTER XXIV

Rudeness and Contempt

1. The merit and moral power of Prince Wen of Chin (Ssu-ma Chao) were exceedingly great, and when he sat in any company his majesty and awesomeness were like those of a king. It was only Juan Chi, who, if he were present, would sit with legs sprawled apart, whistling and singing, drinking without restraint, completely self-assured.[1] (*IWLC* 19; *PSLT* 18; *TPYL* 392)

   [1] *HCCC*: When Ssu-ma Chao was promoted to the rank of prince, the director of instruction, Ho Tseng, and the court ministers all performed the most abject obeisance. It was only Wang Hsiang who made a long bow standing with his hands pressed together (*i*), but did not get down on his knees (*pai*).

2. When Wang Jung was a young man of twenty he went to visit Juan Chi. At the time Liu Ch'ang was also present. Juan said to Wang, "I happen to have two dipperfuls of excellent wine which I will drink with you. That fellow, Liu Ch'ang, will not be joining us." Thereupon the two men proceeded to exchange goblets (*shang*) and drink to each other's health, while Liu Ch'ang never got a single cupful (*pei*). Nevertheless in their conversation and jokes the three men acted quite as if nothing were out of the ordinary.

   When someone asked Juan about it, he replied, "If it's someone superior to Liu Ch'ang, I have no choice but to drink with him, or if it's someone inferior to Liu Ch'ang, it's improper not to drink with him. It's only Liu Ch'ang himself with whom it's quite all right not to drink at all."[1] (*CS* 43.10a)

   [1] Cf. *SSHY* XXIII, 4, above, of which this is a parody.
   CYC: When Wang Jung was in his fifteenth year he accompanied his father, Wang Hun*, to his office, where Juan Chi saw him and took a fancy to him. Every time Juan visited Hun* he would talk with him only a moment and always go on to Jung's room where he would stay a long while. He said to Hun*, "Jung is pure and superior--not in your class at all!"

Once Jung went to visit Juan Chi, where they drank together, but Liu Ch'ang, who was also present, did not join them. Ch'ang showed no annoyance whatever. Afterward Jung asked Juan, "Who was that person?"

Juan replied, "Liu Ch'ang."

Jung said, "If it's someone superior to Liu Ch'ang, of course you drink with him, etc."

CLCHL: Earlier Juan Chi and Wang Jung's father, Wang Hun*, were both clerks in the Imperial Secretariat. Every time Juan Chi came to see Hun*, even before he was comfortably seated, he would always say, "Talking with you is not as good as talking with Jung," and he would go to Jung's room and not return home until sunset. Chi (b. 210) was twenty years older than Jung (b. 234), but treated him exactly like someone of his own generation.

Liu Ch'ang was an unconventional gentleman whose nature was extraordinarily bibulous. Juan Chi would exchange toasts with Wang Jung all day while Liu Ch'ang never received a single cupful, yet the three were completely at ease. Among those who discussed personalities the preferences for Wang Jung were all of this sort.

3. Chung Hui was thoroughly equipped with ability and reasoning powers, but he had not previously been acquainted with Hsi K'ang. Chung wanted to go to visit K'ang in company with other worthy and outstanding gentlemen of the time. K'ang was at that moment engaged in forging metal beneath a tree with Hsiang Hsiu assisting him at the bellows. K'ang continued to pound with the hammer without interruption, as if no one else were present. Some time passed without his exchanging a single word, until Chung finally rose to go. K'ang said, "What had you heard that made you come, and what have you seen that now makes you leave?"

Chung replied, "I came after hearing what I heard, and I'm leaving after seeing what I've seen."[1] (CS 49.15a)

[1]WSC: Hsi K'ang was by nature extremely dexterous, and he was able to forge iron. By his home he had a luxuriant willow tree, which he irrigated by channeling water around it. In summer its shade was extremely clear and cool, and he remained under it continuously, enjoying himself without regard for others. He did the forging himself, and even though his family was poor, if someone came to the forge (for a piece of work), K'ang would never accept any payment for it. Only when relatives or friends of long standing arrived with chicken or wine would he stop to drink and eat, or engage in "pure conversation" with them.

WSCC: Chung Hui was on familiar terms with the generalissimo, Ssu-ma Shih, and his younger brother, Ssu-ma Chao. Having heard of Hsi K'ang's reputation, he went to visit him. Hui was a famous nobleman, and because of his talent and ability was honorable and prosperous. His carriage horses were sleek, and his clothing light, and guests and retainers clustered about him like clouds. At the moment of his visit K'ang was squatting with his legs apart working at his forge. When Hui arrived he gave him no greeting. Hui resented it deeply, and later, on the pretext of the Lü An affair (see above, SSHY VI, 2), he slandered K'ang, implicating him in it.

4. Hsi K'ang was on friendly terms with Lü An. Whenever one of them thought of the other, though he might be a thousand li away, he would

order his carriage and go to visit him. Later An came once at a time
when K'ang was not at home, and K'ang's older brother, Hsi, came out
the door to invite him in, but he would not enter. Instead, he wrote
the character *feng*, "phoenix," on the door and left.[1] Unaware of his
meaning, Hsi still took it for a compliment, but An had done it on
purpose. The character *feng* (is composed of two parts): *fan-niao*,
"ordinary bird."[2] (*CS* 49.14a)

[1]*CPKM*: When Juan Chi was in mourning, Hsi Hsi went to pay him a
visit of condolence. Now Chi was able to look with the whites of
his eyes, and he used the whites of his eyes when greeting worldly
gentlemen. When Hsi arrived, Chi did not perform the customary
weeping. Observing his white eyes, Hsi withdrew in dismay.
    Later, when Hsi's brother, K'ang, learned of it, he took a gift
of wine, and, tucking his zither under his arm, went to visit Chi,
after which they became good friends.

KPCC: Lü An once went to visit Hsi K'ang, and happened to pick
a time when the latter was away on a trip. K'ang's older brother,
Hsi, dusted off the mat and waited for him to come in. An never
turned his head, but sat alone in his carriage. K'ang's mother
then went out to invite him in, setting out wine and food. But An
asked for K'ang's son, Shao, and after talking and joking with him
for a long time, he departed. Such was his contempt for the honorable.

[2]*SW*: *Feng* (***b'i̯ŭm*), a divine bird; derived from *niao*, "bird,"
with *fan* (***b'i̯w̯ăm*), "ordinary," as phonetic.

5. When Lu Chi first came to Lo-yang from Wu (in 280), he consulted
Chang Hua about whom he should visit. Liu Pao was the first on the
list. After he had gone to his house, he found Liu was still observing mourning, but since Liu was by nature a lover of wine, when the
civilities were ended, the first thing he did, without talking about
anything else, was merely to ask, "In eastern Wu I hear there are
long-necked bottle gourds (*hu-lu*). You haven't by any chance brought
any seeds along with you, have you?"
    Liu Chi and his younger brother, Lu Yün, were extraordinarily disappointed, and regretted having gone to see him. (*TPYL* 979)

6. When Wang Ch'eng went out from Lo-yang (in 307) to become governor-general of Ching Province (Hupei),[1] his older brother, Grand Marshal
Wang Yen, and other worthies of the time who came to see him off overflowed the roads.
    In the courtyard at the time there was a large tree, in the upper
branches of which was a magpie's (*ch'üeh*) nest. Taking off his outer
garment and headcloth, Wang Ch'eng climbed directly up into the tree
to fetch the magpie fledglings. When his underclothes (*liang-i*)
caught on a branch of the tree, he proceeded to take them off as well.
After getting the fledglings, he climbed back down to play with them,
his spirit and expression completely self-possessed, as if no one
else were present.[2] (*CS* 43.18a)

[1]*CYC*: During the reign of Emperor Hui (Ssu-ma Chung, r. 290-306),
the grand marshal, Wang Yen, spoke to the officials in charge of
selection, urging that his younger brother, Ch'eng, be made governor (*sic*; cf. *TCTC* 86.2732) of Ching Province, and that his cousin,

Wang Tun, be made governor of Ch'ing Province (Shantung). Both Ch'eng and Tun visited the grand marshal to decline the posts, but the grand marshal said to them, "The royal house is on the verge of collapse. Therefore if you two occupy the areas of Ch'i (Shantung) and Ch'u (Hupei), externally we may establish our family hegemony, and internally we could save the imperial house. This is what is expected of you two, my younger brothers."

[2] *TTCC*: Wang Ch'eng was loose and undisciplined, not bound by convention. His contemporaries considered him "free" (*ta*).

7. Whenever the monk Kao-tso (Śrīmitra) was among the company at the home of the chancellor, Wang Tao, he would always recline at ease by the chancellor's side. But whenever he saw Pien K'un, he would change his expression to one of great dignity, saying, "There's a man of propriety and law."[1] (*KSC* 1; *Taishō* 50.327c)

[1] *KTC*: Wang Tao once went to visit His Reverence (Śrīmitra), who unfastened his girdle and reclined at ease with insightful conversation and spiritual understanding. But when he saw the president of the Imperial Secretariat, Pien K'un, he pulled in his lapels and adjusted his expression. Contemporaries admired the way he responded to each in the appropriate manner.
  KSC 1; *Taishō* 50.327c: When someone asked Śrīmitra why (he behaved informally with Wang Tao and formally with Pien K'un), he replied, "Wang Tao treats people in an urbane way, while Pien K'un approaches everyone according to rules and regulations. This is the only reason I do so."

8. At the same time that Huan Wen was serving as governor of Hsü Province (Kiangsu), Hsieh I** was grand warden of Chin-ling Commandery within the province. In the past they had generally been on friendly terms, but there had been nothing out of the ordinary. At the time that Huan was transferred to become governor of Ching Province (Hunan-Hupei, in 345), during the interval before he started westward, his attitude and manner became exceedingly cordial. Hsieh I** suspected nothing; it was only Lady Wang (Wang Sui §), the wife of his younger brother, Hsieh Chü, who realized his motives in doing so and often said, "Huan Wen's attitude is extraordinarily different from what it was. He must be planning to go west in company with Hsieh I**."

Without announcement Huan picked Hsieh as his sergeant-at-arms. After Hsieh had gone up the Yangtze to Ching Province, he still continued the relation they had had as commoners, and in Huan's presence would push back his headband and whistle and chant poems no differently from the way he had done in the old days. Huan often called him "My ultramundane (*fang-wai*) sergeant-at-arms."

Later, under the influence of wine, Hsieh became less and less careful about the morning and evening formalities.[1] Whenever Huan retired to his inner quarters Hsieh would always follow him in. Afterward on occasions when Hsieh was drunk, Huan would go to the apartment of his wife, the Princess of Nan-k'ang, to get away from him. His wife said, "If you didn't have that crazy sergeant-at-arms, how would I ever get to see you?" (*CS* 79.12a; *PTSC* 68; *TPYL* 248)

[1] *CS* 79.12a reads: formalities of the court (*ch'ao-t'ing* for *chao-hsi*).

9. Right in front of his older brother, Hsieh An, Hsieh Wan was about to get up and look for the urinal. At the time Juan Yü was among the company and remarked, "Households that have newly become prominent are frank, but without manners."[1]

[1] Members of the Juan family had been prominent civil officials since Later Han times (23-220 A.D.). The Hsiehs, on the other hand, began as military men and achieved status only under the Eastern Chin (317-420).

10. Hsieh Wan was the son-in-law of Wang Shu,[1] governor of Yang Province. On one occasion, wearing a white silk kerchief on his head, Hsieh rode in a small sedan chair (*chien-yü*) directly to the governor's reception hall to see Wang Shu, and said to him bluntly, "People say you're a fool, sir. It's true, sir; you really *are* a fool!"

Wang Shu replied, "It's not that people don't say this. It's just a case of delayed appointment to office, that's all."[2] (*CS* 79.19a)

[1] *Hsieh SP*: Wan married Wang Shu's daughter, Ch'üan.

[2] (*Wang*) *Shu PC*: When Shu was young he realized his powers in solitude, and withdrew from the world in quietness. No one as yet knew him. Hence the statement, "It's a case of delayed appointment to office."

11. While Wang Hui-chih was serving as Huan Ch'ung's cavalry aide, Huan asked him, "Which office are you in?" Wang replied, "I don't know which office, but since every now and then I see people leading horses in, it seems to be where they take care of horses."

Huan asked him on another occasion, "How many horses are there under your supervision?" Wang replied, "Since Confucius 'didn't ask about the horses,'[1] how should anyone know their number?"

On still another occasion Huan asked, "How many horses have died?" Wang replied, "'Not yet knowing about life, how can one know about death?'"[2] (*CS* 80.11a)

[1] "Analects" X, 12: When the stables burned down, the Master retired to the court and asked, "Were any people hurt?" He did not ask about the horses.

[2] Ibid. XI, 11.

12. Hsieh An once went out of retirement with his younger brother, Hsieh Wan, westward (from the Eastern Mountains to Chien-k'ang). As they were passing through Wu Commandery (Soochow), Hsieh Wan wanted them to go together to visit the grand warden, Wang T'ien, at his home. Hsieh An said, "I'm afraid he won't necessarily entertain us. You're just not important enough."

Wan continued insistently to demand that they go, but An was adamant in refusing to turn back. In the end Wan went alone. After he had sat for a while, Wang proceeded to retire into his inner quarters. Hsieh appeared extraordinarily pleased, supposing that his host was about to treat him generously. After a long while Wang finally came back out with his hair newly washed and spread it out to dry. Again he did not stop to sit down, but continued to rest on a folding stool (*hu-ch'uang*) in the central courtyard drying his hair in the sun. His spirit and manner were proud and contemptuous, and he had not the slightest intention of entertaining his visitor.

At this point Hsieh finally withdrew. Before he had reached the
boat he shouted out from a distance for Hsieh An. An said to him,
"A-li (Wang T'ien) just doesn't do that sort of thing." (CS 65.11ab)

13. While Wang Hui-chih was serving as Huan Ch'ung's aide, Huan said
to him, "You've been in my headquarters a long time now. It's time we
got together and put your affairs in order."
Wang at first made no answer, but merely looked high in the air
and pressed his hand-board (shou-pan) against his cheek. Finally he
said, "Ever since morning the Western Hills[1] certainly have had a
lively air about them!"[2] (CS 80.11a; PTSC 69, 128; TPYL 498, 692)

[1]Yang Yung in his edition of the SSHY suggests this may be an
oblique reference to the ancient recluses, Po I and Shu Ch'i (trad.
1122 B.C.), who retired to Mt. Shou-yang (in Kansu) singing the
song,

> "To climb those Western Hills,
> And pluck the brackens there!"   (SC 61.3a)

If this was indeed Wang's intention, he would be saying in effect,
"If you don't like my performance in office, I can always become a
recluse!" It seems more in keeping with Wang's character, however,
to take his remark merely as another ploy to change the subject.

[2]CS 80.11a: Wang Hui-chih was once accompanying Huan Ch'ung on a
journey when it happened that a violent rainstorm came up. Hui-
chih accordingly dismounted from his horse, and, pushing aside
(the curtains), got inside (Huan's) carriage, saying, "How does
Your Excellency get away with commandeering a whole carriage all
to himself?" (The story in our text follows immediately.)

14. When Hsieh Wan went on the northern expedition (against Former
Yen in 358)[1] he constantly demonstrated his superiority by whistling
and chanting poems, and never showed any consideration for his officers or men. His elder brother, Hsieh An, highly respected and loved
Wan, but sensing that Wan would surely be defeated, he accompanied
him on the expedition.[2] Very casually he said to Wan, "Since you're
the supreme commander, you should invite your generals to banquets
now and then to cheer their morale."
Wan followed his advice and forthwith called together all the
generals, but said nothing whatsoever to them, except to point toward
those seated about him with his ju-i baton and remark, "You gentlemen
are all stalwart foot soldiers (tsu)."[3] The generals were highly incensed and resented him all the more for this. Hsieh An, wishing to
make some profound demonstration of kindness and trust, went in person to every one, from the divisional commanders on down, to express
his earnest apologies on behalf of his brother.
After Hsieh Wan was defeated (in 359), the rank and file wanted to
use the occasion to get rid of him, but at the same time they said,
"We should spare him for Hsieh An's sake." Thus by good fortune he
escaped with his life. (CS 79.19b; PTSC 135; TPYL 392, 703)

[1]In the autumn of 358 Hsieh Wan was made western commandant and
governor-general of four northern provinces, and participated in
the campaign against Former Yen (348-370) in northern Anhui. But
in the winter of the following year he was disastrously routed

even before joining battle with the enemy, for which he was degraded to the rank of commoner. See *TCTC* 100.3168, 3176-7.

[2] Since Hsieh An did not emerge from seclusion in the Chekiang hills until 360, his participation in the campaign of 358 seems rather unlikely. See also *SSHY* X, 21, n. 2, above.

[3] Hu San-hsing (13th cent.) comments at *TCTC* 100.3176: "All who had personally exerted themselves in the ranks considered the terms *ping*, 'man-at-arms,' and *tsu*, 'foot soldier,' taboo words. Now these men had already become generals, yet Wan was calling them 'foot soldiers,' thereby intensifying their resentment."

15. Whenever Wang Hsien-chih and his younger brother Hui-chih went to visit their maternal uncle, Ch'ih Yin, they always wore leather shoes (*lü*), and in their greeting were most careful to observe the etiquette proper to maternal nephews. But after Yin's son, Ch'ih Ch'ao, died (in 377) they always wore wooden clogs (*chi*), and their deportment and manners were contemptuous and rude. When Ch'ih asked them to be seated, they would always say, "We're busy and haven't any time to sit."

Once, after they had left, Yin said with deep feeling, "If Ch'ao hadn't died, those rats wouldn't dare act like that!"[1] (*CS* 67.22a; *TPYL* 698)

[1] *SSHY* Comm.: Ch'ih Yin's son, Ch'ao, had a tremendous reputation, and in addition had received special patronage from Huan Wen. For this reason people paid respect to Ch'ih Yin on Ch'ao's account.

16. Wang Hui-chih was once traveling through Wu Commandery (Soochow), when he noticed that at the home of a certain gentleman and great officer there were some extremely fine bamboos. The owner already knew that Hui-chih would be going by and for this reason had watered and swept and put everything in order and was sitting in his reception hall waiting for him.

Wang went by in a small sedan chair (*chien-yü*) directly to a spot beneath the bamboos, where he intoned poems and whistled for a long while. The host, already disappointed, was still hopeful that on his way back they might make contact, but after a while Wang was on the point of going directly out the gate. His host would not tolerate it at all, but ordered his attendants to bolt the gate and not let him out. Through this means Wang gained a better appreciation of his host, and in the end remained to sit and enjoy himself thoroughly before leaving. (*CS* 80.11a)

17. Once when Wang Hsien-chih was passing through Wu Commandery on his way from K'uai-chi (Chekiang), he heard that Ku Pi-chiang had a famous garden there. Although he had previously never been acquainted with the owner, he went directly to his house. It happened that Ku was just then entertaining guests and friends with food and drink, but Wang wandered about at will through the garden, and, when he had finished, pointed around to indicate its good and bad features, just as if no one else were present.

Ku, suddenly losing his patience, said, "To be inconsiderate of one's host is impolite, but to presume on one's noble birth to be insolent toward others is downright immoral. Anyone who fails on both

counts isn't even fit to be classified as a northern boor (*ts'ang*)!"
And with that he drove Wang's attendants out the gate. Wang, alone in
the sedan chair, was turning this way and that (looking for his attendants). Ku, observing that the attendants after a long time had
still not returned, later ordered someone to escort Wang outside the
gate. Through it all Wang remained carefree and unconcerned.[1] (*CS*
80.13a; *IWLC* 65; *TPYL* 824)

[1] *CS* 80.13a: With that Ku drove Wang out the gate. Wang remained
contemptuous, not deigning to give it a thought.

CHAPTER XXV

Taunting and Teasing

1. While Chu-ko Chin was serving as governor of Yü Province (southern Honan), and was about to send his lieutenant-governor to the court (at Lo-yang), he said to him, "My little son knows how to converse; you may talk with him." The lieutenant-governor went several times to visit Chin's son, K'o, but K'o refused to see him. Later they met by chance at a gathering at the home of Chang Chao, where the lieutenant-governor cried out to K'o, "Tut! tut! young master!"

Hearing this, K'o teased him, saying, "Yü Province has risen in revolt! Why the 'tut! tut!'?"

The lieutenant-governor replied, "The governor is enlightened, and his subjects worthy. I haven't heard of any revolt."

K'o said, "In antiquity, even when the Sage-king Yao was on the throne, the Four Ill-Omened Ones (ssu-hsiung)[1] were among his subjects."

The lieutenant-governor retorted, "It wasn't only the Four Ill-Omened Ones. So was (Yao's idiot son) Tan Chu!" At this the whole company roared with laughter. (*IWLC* 25; *TPYL* 390)

[1] See *Tso-chuan*, Wen 18 (Legge V, 283). These were mythical monsters driven out by the Sage-king Yao. The four are usually listed as: (1) Hun Tun ("Chaos"), sometimes equated with Huan Tou, Yao's unworthy minister; (2) Ch'iung Ch'i ("Total Monstrosity"), sometimes equated with Kung Kung, Yao's "director of works"; (3) T'ao Wu ("Blockhead"), sometimes equated with Kun, the father of Yü; and (4) T'ao T'ieh ("Glutton"), sometimes equated with the San-miao, an ancient tribe in Ch'u (Huan-Hupei).

2. "Emperor Wen" of Chin (Ssu-ma Chao) was riding in the same carriage with the two Ch'ens (Ch'en Ch'ien and Ch'en T'ai). As he passed by Chung Hui's place, he called out to invite him to ride with them, then immediately drove the carriage off, leaving him behind. By the time Chung had come out, the carriage was already far away. After

Chung had caught up with them, the "Emperor" teased him, saying, "When I made an appointment with you to travel, why did you dilly-dally so? I kept looking for you, but you were far, far away (*yao-yao*)[1] and never came."

Chung Hui replied, "Martial (*chiao*),[2] virtuous (*i*),[3] and true (*shih*),[4] why should I have to keep company with the crowd (*ch'ün*)?"[5]

On another occasion the "Emperor" asked Hui, "What sort of man was Kao Yu?"[6]

Hui replied, "He didn't come up to the Sage-kings Yao and Shun at the top of the scale, nor did he compare with the Duke of Chou and Confucius at the bottom, but for all that, he was the most virtuous (*i*) knight of his entire age."[7]

[1] A homonym of the taboo name of Chung Hui's deceased father, Chung Yu.

[2] The taboo name of Ch'en Ch'en's father, Ch'en Chiao.

[3] The taboo name of Ssu-ma Chao's father, Ssu-ma I.

[4] A homonym of the taboo name of Ch'en T'ai's great-grandfather, Ch'en Shih.

[5] The taboo name of T'ai's father, Ch'en Ch'ün.

[6] Another allusion to Chung Yu. Kao Yu was a minister of the Sage-king Shun. See also No. 3, below.

[7] For further examples of this parlor game of punning on the taboo names of other people's fathers, a playful form of insult, see Nos. 3 and 33, below.

3. Chung Yü served as a palace attendant and possessed a quick wit. One time he was present at a banquet in the house of Prince Ching of Chin (Ssu-ma Shih). At the time Ch'en Ch'ün's son, T'ai, and Wu Chou's son, Kai, were with him among the company, and were both teasing Yü.

Prince Ching said, "What sort of man was Kao Yu?"[1]

Yü replied, "A virtuous (*i*)[2] knight of antiquity." Then, turning around, he said to Ch'en T'ai and Wu Kai, "A gentleman is 'all-embracing (*chou*)[3] and impartial'; he 'keeps company with all men (*ch'ün*), and joins no factions (*tang*).'"[4]

[1] See above, No. 2, n. 6, an indirect reference to Yü's father, Chung Yu.

[2] See above, No. 2, n. 3.

[3] The taboo name of Wu Kai's father, Wu Chou, and at the same time an allusion to "Analects" II, 14.

[4] See above, No. 2, n. 5, and "Analects" XV, 22.

4. Hsi K'ang, Juan Chi, Shan T'ao, and Liu Ling were in the Bamboo Grove drinking and were well in their cups when Wang Jung arrived later. Juan Chi said, "Here comes this vulgar fellow again to spoil our mood."[1]

Laughing, Wang replied, "Do you mean to say your mood is something that can be spoiled?" (*CS* 43.10a)

[1] *WSCC*: Contemporaries felt that Wang Jung was not yet able to transcend the vulgar.

5. (After the conquest of Wu in 280) Emperor Wu of Chin (Ssu-ma Yen, r. 265-290) asked the last Wu ruler, Sun Hao (r. 264-280), "I hear you southerners like to sing 'you-your' songs (erh-ju ko).¹ Could you sing one for us?"

Hao was just in the midst of drinking, and therefore raised his cup to pledge a toast to the emperor, singing,

> "Formerly your (ju) neighbor,
> Now your minister.
> To you (ju) a cup of wine;
> May you live a myriad springs!"

The emperor regretted having asked him. (TPYL 118, 571)

¹See *Mencius* VIIB, 31 (Legge II, 494): "If a man can fulfill his true nature (shih) by not accepting the terms of address 'you' or 'your' (erh-ju), there is no place he goes where he will not act morally."

Chiao Hsün's (18th cent.) commentary (*Cheng-i*) explains: "'You' and 'your' are general terms of address used by the honorable in speaking to the base, and by superiors to inferiors. When the base and inferior naturally and comfortably accept them, this is what is meant by their 'true nature.'"

6. When Sun Ch'u was young he wanted to become a recluse. Speaking of it once to Wang Chi, he intended to say, "I'll pillow my head on the rocks and rinse my mouth in the streams." Instead, he said by mistake, "I'll rinse my mouth with rocks and pillow my head on the streams."

Wang asked, "Are streams something you can pillow on, and rocks something you can rinse with?"

Sun replied, "My reason for pillowing on streams is to 'wash my ears,'¹ and my reason for rinsing with rocks is to 'sharpen my teeth' (li-ch'ih)."² (CS 56.16a; TPYL 368; TPKC 245)

¹*ISC*: When Hsü Yu was offered the throne by the Sage-king Yao, his friend, Ch'ao Fu, rebuked him, whereupon Yu crossed a clear cold stream to wash his ears and wipe his eyes, saying, "Just now by listening to covetous words, I betrayed my friend."

²"A fellow with sharp teeth" (li-ch'ih erh; see below, No. 54) seems to be someone eager to make a reputation.

7. (In Chang Min's poetic essay) "Ch'in Tzu-yü's Head Reproaches Him" (*T'ou tse Ch'in Tzu-yü*)¹ are the words:

> "You've never been the equal of
> Wen Yung of T'ai-yüan (Shansi),
> Or Hsün Yü of Ying-ch'uan (Honan),
> Or Chang Hua of Fan-yang (Hopei),
> Or Liu Hsü, the imperial clan officer,²
> Or Tsou Chan of I-yang (Honan),
> Or Cheng Hsü of Ho-nan (Honan).
>
> Among these gentlemen
> One (Wen Yung) stammers and stutters out of tune,
> Another (Hsün Yü), sick and ugly, rarely speaks.
> One (Chang Hua), lacking manners, is overstocked
>   with airs,³

XXV TAUNTING AND TEASING 403

Another (Liu Hsü), foulmouthed, is short on wit.
The mouth of one (Tsou Chan) seems stuffed
    with syrup,
The head of another (Cheng Hsü) looks like a
    kerchiefed drug pestle.
Still, since their writings are readable,
And their thoughts both clear and orderly,
They climbed on dragons, flew with phoenixes,
And all together mounted heaven's hall.

(*IWLC* 17; *JCSP* 4)

[1]*CMC* (*T'ou tse Tzu-yü wen*): Among my friends is one Mr. Ch'in. Although he is honored as the husband of my older sister, we have, since our youth, been on very familiar terms. Among our contemporaries who are also on intimate terms are Wen Yü of T'ai-yüan, Hsün Yü of Ying-ch'uan, Chang Hua of Fan-yang, and the gentlemen Liu Hsü and Tsou Chan of Nan-yang, and Chang Hsü of Honan, all of whom in succession climbed to positions at court, leaving this worthy alone to live in a "lowly alley." He frequently "offered his services for sale," but no one ever put up a "good price" ("Analects" IX, 13). With proud determination and self-composure, he was never discouraged or downcast, but carried on cheerfully. Moreover, he thought it strange that after his worthy friends had all gained positions they never (sought out their old friend in answer to) the "sounds of the woodcutters or of the crying birds" ("Songs," No. 165), and they severely violated the code of Wang Yang* and Kung Yü, one of whom dusted off his cap (waiting for the other to recommend him). Therefore, because of the beauty of Mr. Ch'in's facial appearance, I have written this essay about his head reproaching him, by way of teasing him. At the same time I have poked fun at his six friends in it. Though it may appear to be mere buffoonery, it really has a moral. The text is as follows:

  In the first year of the T'ai-shih era (265), Ch'in Tzu-yü's head reproached him, saying, "I've been your head now for ten thousand days and more.

'The Great Clod endowed me with vitality and
    fashioned me with form.' (*Chuang-tzu* VI, 5b)
I've grown you hair and skin,
And placed on you nose and ears,
Laid on eyebrows and beard, inserted molars
    and teeth.
Your pupils flash with light
And your two cheekbones stand out high.
Each time you go out or come in,
Or while you roam the marketplace and town,
Travelers on the road make way for you;
Those who are seated fall respectfully to
    their knees.
Some call you 'Lord,' or 'Sir,'
Others call out, 'General!'
Clasping their hands, they fall down prostrate,
Or, standing, wait in agitated woe.

The reason that they do so, of course, is the
    greatness of my form.

You wear no cap or crown on your head,
Dangle no gold or silver at your waist;
You use spangles for a hairpin,
A hair ornament for a hat.
Your thought and manner are both far from normal,
And you eat only grains and greens.
You bend and toil among the fields;
With dung and earth you're soiled and black.
The season ends; the years go by,
And never once do you repent.
You hate me for my physical appearance;
I despise you for your attitude.
If you go on like this you'll surely be involved
    in grief.

You treat me like a rival, and I look on you
    as a foe.
We're always unhappy; both of us are miserable.
Alas! the pain of it!

If you want to be sought out by others,
Then you should be like (the ancient ministers)
    Kao Yu and Hou Chi,
Or like Wu Hsien and I Chih,
Who guided and preserved the royal house and were
    enfeoffed in perpetuity.

Or if you want to make a name as eminent,
Then you should be like (the recluses) Hsü Yu
    and Tzu-tsang,
Or like Pien Sui and Wu Kuang.
Washing your ears to hide from office,
A fragrant memory for a thousand years.

Or if you want to be a wandering adviser,
Then you should be like Ch'en Chen and Ching T'ung,
Or like Lu Chia and Teng Yü,
Who turned disaster into blessing by using words
    with great facility.

Or if you want to move upward with rapidity,
Then you should be like Chia I seeking to be tested,
Or Chung Chün requesting to be sent.
They honed and whetted themselves sharp as
    spear points to do the business of the king.

Or if you want to be calm and tranquil,
You should be like Lao-tzu, who 'held fast the One,'
Or like Chuang-tzu, who let himself go free,
Untrammeled and beyond desire, his will
    transcending clouds and sun.

Or if you want to live secluded, then you should
    be like Jung Ch'i,
A leather thong around you for a girdle,
Or like the Old Fisherman beside the
    gurgling stream;
The one sojourning on sacred hills,

The other dangling bait in mighty streams.
These are the mere trifles by which men publicize
    themselves and make their names.

But as for you, you don't strive above after the
    Way or the Power,
Nor follow in the middle with the Confucians
    and Mohists.
Clodlike, in poverty and misery you've clung to
    this stupid delusion.

If one should search your feelings or observe
    your aims,
He'd find that in retirement you're no recluse;
In public life aspire to no high posts,
But vainly while away your days and wear
    your body out
Doing what any ordinary man delights in.
Is it not indeed a mistake?"

Whereupon Tzu-yü became bemused, deep in his thoughts, and said at last,

"In all you have instructed me, I humbly obey
    your will.
Since I received a nature which is bound and tied,
    eternally proper and correct,
Suppose I were endowed with Heaven's favor,
    according to your wish.

You wish to make me loyal?
Then I should be like (the suicides) Wu Tzu-hsü
    or Ch'ü Yüan.
You wish to make me faithful?
Then I should destroy my body to perfect my name.
You wish to make me resolute and true?
Then I should plunge in fire and water to preserve
    my purity.
These four things are what all men hate,
So I dare not think of doing them."

His head replied,

"What you call the 'Law of Heaven and Web of Earth'
Are but unyielding virtue taken to extremes.
If not climbing mountains or embracing trees (like
    the suicide-recluses, Pao Chiao and Chieh
    Chih-t'ui),
Then lifting skirts to jump over streams (like
    the suicides, Wu Kuang and Shen-t'u Ti).
I mean to tell you how to nourish life
And teach you how to roam in freedom,
But you, with the sensibility of a nit or louse,
Refuse to listen to my counsel.
Alas, how sad, that I should within a human frame
Yet have to be, of all things, just *your* head!
Compare yourself with others of your age,
And take a lesson from your peers.

>   You've never been the equal of
>   Wen Yung . . . (as in the text)
>
>   By licking piles (the doctor) got (five) carriages;
>   Diving into the deep (the boy) retrieved a pearl.
>   But how can they be compared to you,
>   Who foul your lips and tongue,
>   And douse your hands and feet in vain?
>   You live in a world full of affairs,
>   But are ashamed to seek after power,
>   And like the man who dug into the earth and carried
>   a large vat in his arms (to water his garden),
>   You find it hard to acquire wealth.
>
>   Alas, Tzu-yü!
>   How do you differ from a bear in his cage,
>   Or a tiger in his sunken pit,
>   Or a hungry crab among the rocks,
>   Or a rat within his hole?
>   Although the effort spent is great,
>   The profit gained is bitter indeed.
>   Better by far to crouch miserable and maimed,
>   Living till old age without expectations.
>   Even the deformed in body can still remain unbound.
>   Is not this your destiny? Why must you live
>   among the great?"

[2] *SSHY* Comm.: Liu Hsü, like Chang Hua, hailed from Fan-yang, and that is why he is called "the clan officer," to vary their epithets.

[3] *WSC*: As a person, Chang Hua was deficient in etiquette, and overstocked with airs.

SSHY Comm.: Making inference from this statement, these six lines refer in order to the above-named six persons, and the statement "whose mouth seems stuffed with syrup" refers to Tsou Chan. Chan's eloquence and beauty were outstanding and widely acclaimed, but whether or not there ever was this particular statement made about him is not known.

8. Wang Hun and his wife, Lady Chung (Chung Yen), were once sitting together when they saw their son, Wang Chi, passing through the courtyard. With a pleased expression, Hun said to his wife, "That you have borne me a son like this is enough to put my mind at ease."

Laughing, his wife replied, "If I'd gotten to marry your younger brother, Wang Lun, the sons I'd have borne would definitely not have been merely like this!" (*CS* 96.4a)

9. Hsün Yin and Lu Yün had previously not been acquainted with each other. When the two met at a gathering in the home of Chang Hua, Chang had them converse together. Since he considered them both to have unusual ability, he forbade them to use the ordinary words of greeting. Lu Yün therefore raised his hand and said, "Lu Shih-lung here, the 'Gentleman-Dragon among the Clouds' (*Yün-chien Shih-lung*).[1]

Hsün Yin responded, "Hsün Ming-ho here, the 'Crying Crane beneath the Sun' (*Jih-hsia Ming-ho*)."[2]

Lu continued, "Since you've opened up the blue clouds (*ch'ing-yün*),[3] and spied the white pheasant (*pai-chih*),[4] why don't you stretch your bow and fit your arrow to the string?"

Hsün replied, "I originally supposed it was a 'dragon in the clouds,' 'spirited and strong' (**g'jwi-g'jwi*),[5] but now it turns out to be only a 'deer on the mountain' (*shan-lu*),[6] an 'elaphure in the wild' (*yeh-mi*).[7] The quarry is weak and the crossbow strong, so I'm reluctant to shoot." At this Chang clapped his hands and laughed aloud. (*CS* 54.16ab; *IWLC* 25; *TPYL* 390; *TPKC* 253)

[1] See "Book of Changes," Hex. 1, Ch'ien (Wilhelm I, 8): Clouds follow the dragon.

[2] See ibid, Hex. 61, Chung-fu (Wilhelm I, 252): "A crying crane in the shade . . ." Hsün's name, Yin, "Hidden," is a homonym of *yin*, "shade." *Jih-hsia*, "Beneath the Sun," was an alternate name for the capital at Lo-yang, which was near Hsün's native place.

[3] "Blue clouds" was occasionally used as a metaphor for the recluse, who lived high in the mountains. Since Hsün's name, Yin, means "hidden," "living as a recluse," this might be taken in reference both to Lu Yün ("Clouds") and Hsün Yin.

[4] A rare bird of the south, formerly brought as tribute to the Chou kings. Lu Yün was a southerner, and a "rare bird" of a sort.

[5] See "Songs," No. 167: Four stallions spirited and strong . . .

[6] Lu Yün's surname was a homonym of *lu* (**luk*), "deer," and was written with classifier 170 (*fu*, "mound," "hill").

[7] See "Songs," No. 23: In the wild a dead deer lies . . .

10. Lu Wan once went to visit Chancellor Wang Tao, who fed him some curds (*lao*). After Lu had returned home he proceeded to get sick. The following morning he wrote Wang a note, saying, "Yesterday I ate a little too much curds and was in critical condition all night. Though I'm a native of Wu, I came very near to becoming a northern (*ts'ang*) ghost!" (*CS* 77.2b; *TPYL* 858)

11. When Emperor Yüan's (Ssu-ma Jui, r. 317-322) son Ssu-ma Yü was born (in 320), he made presentations all around to his ministers. In expressing his thanks, Yin Hsien said, "The birth of an imperial son is cause for the whole realm to rejoice together. But since your servant earned no merit in the matter, he doesn't presume to hope for such a generous gift."

Laughing, the emperor said, "In a matter of this kind how could I have let you earn any merit?" (*SWLC*, hou 5)

12. Chu-ko Hui and Chancellor Wang Tao were once arguing together about the order of precedence of their respective surnames. Wang said, "Why is it people don't say 'Ko and Wang,' but always 'Wang and Ko'?"

Chu-ko Hui retorted, "It's just like their saying 'donkeys and horses,' rather than 'horses and donkeys,' Does that mean donkeys are better than horses?" (*CS* 77.20ab; *TPYL* 362)

13. When Liu T'an saw Chancellor Wang Tao for the first time it was

at the height of the summer months. The chancellor, pressing his abdomen against a pellet chessboard,[1] remarked, "Ah! how cool (*ho nai ch'eng*)!"

After Liu had left, someone asked him, "Now that you've seen Wang Tao, what do you think of him?"

Liu replied, "I didn't observe any other special accomplishments, except merely to hear him talk in the Wu dialect, that's all."[2] (*SLF* 4; *TPYL* 21, 371, 755)

[1] The board for this game was about two feet square, raised slightly in the center, and made of polished stone. See above, *SSHY* XXI, 1.

[2] *YL*: Liu T'an said, "What's so special about the chancellor? All he can do is talk in the Wu dialect and spit a fine spittle."

14. Wang Tao was once drinking together with the other courtiers. Raising a colored glass (*liu-li*) bowl, he said to Chou I, "The belly of this bowl is extraordinarily empty, yet it's called a precious vessel. Why?"[1]

Chou replied, "This bowl is lustrous and luminous, genuinely clear and translucent. That's the only reason it's precious."

[1] *SSHY* Comm.: He said this to make fun of Chou for his lack of ability. See also No. 18, below.

15. Hsieh K'un said to Chou I, "You're like a sacred tree (*she-shu*). When seen from a distance, towering majestically, it brushes the blue sky. But when one comes in for a closer look, its roots turn out to be the lair of foxes, and underneath there's accumulated filth and nothing more."[1]

Chou replied, "The fact that its branches brush the sky is no indication that it's high, and the fact that foxes have fouled up its lower part is no indication that it's unclean. The pollution of 'accumulated filth' is what you yourself are harboring. Why bother to boast about yourself?"

[1] *SSHY* Comm.: He meant that Chou I was fond of lechery. (Cf. *Han-fei-tzu* XXXIV, 243: The most hateful things are rats in the sacred tree. Since it is a sacred tree, there is a clay shrine built under it, and rats use it for a place to live. Smoke them out and the tree will be burned; flush them out and the clay will dissolve.)

16. When Wang Yüeh was young he was affable and well-mannered, and his father, Chancellor Wang Tao, loved and doted on him with the utmost affection. They often played encirclement chess (*wei-ch'i*) together. Once, when the chancellor was on the point of making a move, Wang Yüeh pressed down his fingers and would not let him. Laughing, the chancellor said, "How do you get to do that? It seems we have a 'melon-creeper relationship' (*kua-ko*)[1] with each other!" (*CS* 65.10a)

[1] *Kua-ko* (literally, "melon vines and creeping beans") is glossed in the Commentary, which cites *TT*, as a metaphor for "distant and intimate relationships" (*su-ch'in*). Yang Yung's note on this passage suggests that winning the game might sever the intertwining relationship.

17. Emperor Ming (Ssu-ma Shao, r. 323-325) once asked Chou I, "What sort of person is Liu T'an?"

Chou replied, "Of course he's a gelded bull weighing a thousand catties (*chin*)." Wang Tao guffawed at his answer, so Chou continued, "Not as attractive, to be sure, as a curly-horned cow, pirouetting round and round."[1]

[1] Liu Chün points out in the Commentary that this last jibe was aimed at Wang Tao, who was something of a ladies' man.

18. Chancellor Wang Tao was once propping his head on Chou I's knees. Pointing to Chou's belly, he said, "What have you got in there?"

Chou replied, "In here is an empty cavern with nothing in it. However, there's room for several hundred of you fellows." (*CS* 69.18a; *SWLC*, hou 20)

19. Kan Pao was relating to Liu T'an the contents of his "Record of the Search for Spirits" (*Sou-shen chi*).[1] Liu said to him, "You're what might be called the Tung Hu[2] of the ghostly world." (*CS* 82.14a)

[1] The original work is lost. Present editions, one in eight *chüan* and one in twenty, based on compilations of quoted fragments, date from the Ming Dynasty. An early fragment was later found in Tunhuang.

KSCK (cf. *CS* 82.13b-14a): Kan Pao's father had a favorite concubine of whom his mother was extremely jealous. When they buried Pao's father, she took the occasion to push the girl into the tomb. After ten years his mother died also, and when they opened his father's tomb to place her in it, the concubine was found lying on the coffin. On close examination it appeared she was still warm, moist and breathing. They drove back home with her, and at the end of the day she revived, and told them how Pao's father had continually given her food and drink and had lain beside her, bestowing favor and affection just as when he was alive. Whatever fortunes and misfortunes befell the family, he always told her. On comparison with actual events, all were verified. After her restoration to normal health it was several more years before she died. It was on this account that Pao wrote the "Record of the Search for Spirits," in which are matters to arouse the feelings, like the above.

[2] *Ch'un-ch'iu chuan* (cf. *Tso-chuan*, Hsüan 2, Legge V, 290-291): Chao Ch'uan attacked Duke Ling of Chin in the peach garden. Chao Tun, who was fleeing, but had not yet left the territory of Chin, returned. The grand historian, Tung Hu, wrote: "Chao Tun murdered (*shih*) his lord."

Tun protested, "But that's not so!"

Tung replied, "You're an upright minister, but when you escaped you didn't leave your state, and after you returned you didn't punish the murderer. If it wasn't your crime, whose was it?"

Confucius said, "Tung Hu was a good historian of antiquity. His rule for writing was not to conceal. Chao Tun was a worthy great officer of antiquity. In accordance with Tung's rule he accepted the blame."

20. Hsü Tsao once went to Ku Ho's house. Until that moment Ku had been asleep within the bed curtains. On his arrival, Hsü went straight

over to the pillow at the corner of the bed to talk with him. Presently he invited Ku to go out walking with him. Ku thereupon ordered his servants to fetch new clothes from the table (chi),[1] and changed into them from those he was wearing.

Laughing, Hsü said, "Do you mean to say you have walking clothes, too?"

[1] Some texts read "pillow" (chen), for "low table" (chi).

21. K'ang Seng-yüan's eyes were deep-set and his nose high. Chancellor Wang Tao often teased him about it. Seng-yüan replied,

> "The nose is the face's mountain,[1]
> And the eyes its pools (yüan),[2]
> If the mountain's not high, it has no power,
> Or the pools not deep, they are not clear."

(KSC 4; Taishō 50.347a; TPYL 365-367)

[1] Kuan Lu PC (SKWei 29.20a, comm.): The nose is the mountain in the middle of the heavens. (See above, SSHY X, 6, n. 3.)

[2] A pun on K'ang's name-in-religion, Seng-yüan.

22. Ho Ch'ung used to go to the Wa-kuan Temple (in Chien-k'ang) where he performed rites and worshipped with fervent devotion. Juan Yü once said to him, "Your ambition is greater than all space and time (yü-chou), and your valor traverses the ages."

Ho asked, "And to what do I owe this sudden accolade from you today?"

Juan replied, "I'm aiming at becoming grand warden of a commandery of several thousand households, and still haven't been able to achieve it. But you're aiming at becoming a buddha. Don't you call that great?" (CS 79.9a)

23. (In 343) Yü I had started on a large-scale expedition against the Hu barbarians (Shih Hu of Later Chao, r. 334-349). But after he had formed his battle lines, he stopped short and stationed his men at Hsiang-yang (northern Hupei).[1]

Yin Hsien sent him a letter enclosing an "as-you-wish" baton (ju-i) with one corner broken off, to tease him.

Yü replied with another letter, stating, "I received what you sent. Although it's a damaged object, I still intend to repair and use it."

[1] CYC: Yü I led his hosts up the Mien River (a tributary of the Han) with the intention of punishing the northern barbarians (Ti). But after he had reached Hsiang-yang, the northern barbarians were still strong and it was not yet possible to fight a decisive battle. It happened that Emperor K'ang (Ssu-ma Yüeh*, r. 342-344) had deceased (ninth month, 344), and I's older brother, Ping, also died (eleventh month). Yü I, leaving his oldest son, Fang-chih, to guard Hsiang-yang, hastened back himself to Hsia-k'ou (up the Yangtze from Wu-ch'ang).

24. Huan Wen, taking advantage of a fall of snow, was about to go hunting, but before doing so he dropped by the houses of Wang Meng, Liu T'an, and the other conversationalists. When Liu T'an saw him

dressed so lightly and severely, he asked, "You old rascal (lao-tsei), what are you going to do in this outfit?"

Huan retorted, "If I didn't do this, then how in blazes could you fellows get to sit around and talk?"[1]

[1] YL: When Huan Wen was returning from a military campaign, the capital intendant, Liu T'an, went out several tens of *li* to meet him. Huan refused altogether to converse with him, except to state bluntly, "For the fact that you're able to wear long gowns and converse with 'pure talk,' whose is the credit, after all?"

Liu retorted, "For the vitality and duration of the virtue of the Chin, how can *you* take the credit?"

SSHY Comm.: The accounts differ slightly, so I have recorded the latter in detail.

25. Ch'u P'ou once asked Sun Sheng, "When will your history of the dynasty[1] be completed?"

Sun replied, "It should have been finished long ago, but in public life I've no leisure, so it's dragged on until now."

Ch'u said, "The ancients 'transmitted, but did not create.'[2] What's the necessity of being in the 'silkworm chamber' (*ts'an-shih*)?"[3]

[1] Sun wrote two histories, "Annals of the Wei" (WSCC) and "Annals of the Chin" (CYC), both of which are frequently quoted by Liu Chün, and which also served as sources for the official histories. According to Sun's biography (CS 82.12ab), the latter work included an account of Huan Wen's defeat at Fang-t'ou (Honan) in 369 in terms unacceptable to Huan, who threatened the family with reprisals if the manuscript were published unchanged. Since Sun stubbornly refused to change it, his sons surreptitiously introduced the necessary revisions, and thereafter two versions were current.

[2] "Analects" VII, 1. Ironically, Ssu-ma Ch'ien himself also claimed to follow this dictum. See SC 130.11b.

[3] HS (54.13a-14a): When Li Ling surrendered to the Hsiung-nu, Emperor Wu (r. 140-87 B.C.) was in a towering rage . . . Since the grand historian (Ssu-ma Ch'ien) had vigorously championed Ling's loyalty, the emperor supposed Ch'ien to be Ling's advocate-at-large, and sentenced him to punishment by castration (*fu-hsing*). Whereupon Ch'ien wrote his "Records of the Grand Historian" (SC), transmitting events from the time of T'ang Yao (trad. 2357-2258 B.C.) and Yü Shun (2255-2208) on down to the capture of the *lin*-unicorn (481 B.C.).

HS (62.18b-19a): Ch'ien wrote a letter to Jen An in which he said, ". . . After Li Ling had surrendered alive, I, too, was thrown into the silkworm chamber . . ."

Commentary of Su Lin (3rd cent.): The punishment of castration was performed in a secret chamber heated by fire. At the time it was like a silkworm chamber. In the old days in P'ing-yin (Honan) there was a Silkworm Chamber Prison.

(The origin of the term *ts'an-shih* is still obscure. See Dubs, *History of the Former Han Dynasty*, I, 322, n. 7.1. Chauncey Goodrich, in "Two Chapters in the Life of an Empress of the Later Han," II, HJAS 26, 1966, 202, suggests an interesting connection between punishments and textile-making.

26. While Hsieh An was living in the Eastern Mountains (Chekiang), orders from the court summoning him to the capital to take office came down frequently, but he never moved. Later (in 360) he came out of retirement to become Huan Wen's sergeant-at-arms (stationed in Wu-ch'ang, Hupei). As he was about to set out from Hsin-t'ing (a suburb of Chien-k'ang), the courtiers all came out to give him a farewell party.

Kao Sung, who was then serving as junior censor, also went to bid him farewell. Earlier Kao had had a few drinks and took advantage of the fact to act as if he were drunk. Teasing Hsieh, he said, "You often disregarded the will of the court and remained in lofty retirement in the Eastern Mountains. At the time, whenever anyone talked about it, they would always say, 'If Hsieh An is unwilling to come out of retirement, what's to be done about the people?' But now I'm wondering, what will the people do about *you*?" Hsieh laughed, but did not answer.[1] (CS 79.5a)

[1] *FJC*: Huan Hsüan once asked Hsieh Tao-yün, the wife of Wang Ning-chih, "Your uncle, the grand tutor (Hsieh An), lived as a recluse in the Eastern Mountains for over twenty years, but later failed to fulfill his determination to remain there. What were his reasons?"

Lady Hsieh answered, "My late uncle, the grand tutor, in his early conception of what is correct, took 'uselessness' for his cardinal principle, and considered public life versus retirement to be a contrast of inferior versus superior. It was not until his mature conception of what is correct that he considered them to be merely the difference between activity and quiescence."

27. At first while Hsieh An was living in the Eastern Mountains as a commoner, some of his older and younger brothers[1] had already become wealthy and honorable. Whenever there was a gathering of the various branches of the family it always created quite a stir among the populace.

An's wife, Lady Liu, teased him, saying, "Shouldn't a great man like you be like this too?"

Holding his nose,[2] Hsieh replied, "My only fear is that I shan't escape it, that's all." (CS 79.4b-5a; TPYL 367)

[1] I.e., Hsieh I, Hsieh Chü, and Hsieh Shih.

[2] There is an implied pun in this gesture, as popular notions equated *fu*, "wealthy" (*$p\underset{\wedge}{i}\partial u$), and *fu*, "rotten" (*$b'\underset{\wedge}{i}u$). See also *SSHY* IV, 49, above.

28. The monk Chih Tun through an intermediary once approached the monk Chu Ch'ien to purchase Yang Mountain (Chekiang)[1] from him. Chu Ch'ien sent back the answer, "I never heard of Ch'ao Fu or Hsü Yu[2] purchasing a mountain for their hermitage." (*KSC* 4; *Taishō* 50.348a; *IWLC* 36; *TPYL* 510)

[1] All versions have the graphically similar, but unknown, "Yin Mountain." I have emended the text to agree with *SSHY* II, 76, above, and the *KSC* account, where it is stated that it was actually only a small ridge on the side of Yang Mountain, located in Shan Prefecture, 200 *li* south of K'uai-chi, which Chih Tun had attempted to purchase for his hermitage. Ch'ien's reply in the *KSC*

account is prefaced with the words, "If you want to come, I'm always glad to give it to you. Who ever heard of Ch'ao Fu, etc." Chih Tun did spend the last year of his life (365-366) in retirement on Yang Mountain. See *SSHY* II, 76, and Zürcher, *Conquest*, pp. 120-122.

KISMC: When Chih Tun received Chu Ch'ien's reply, he was simply embarrassed and nothing more.

[2] Celebrated hermits of antiquity.

29. Wang Meng and Liu T'an never had any respect for Ts'ai Mo. The two men once went to Ts'ai's place to converse, and after a long while finally asked him, "How would you rate yourself in comparison with Wang Yen (d. 311)?"
Ts'ai replied, "I'm not the equal of Wang Yen."
Wang and Liu glanced at each other and smiled, then they asked, "In what respect aren't you his equal?"
Ts'ai replied, "Wang Yen was spared ever having guests like you."

30. When Chang Hsüan-chih was in his eighth year one of his front teeth was missing. An older person, knowing he was an unusual child, once made a point of teasing him about it and asked, "Why have you opened that dog hole in your mouth?"
Quick as a flash Chang answered, "Just to let people like you go in and out!"

31. On the seventh day of the seventh month Ho Lung went out in the sun and lay on his back. When people asked what he was doing, he replied, "I'm sunning my books."[1] (*IWLC* 4; *MCYC* 1; *SLF* 5; *TPYL* 31, 371, 393)

[1] Cf. *SSHY* XXIII, 10, above. Quotations of this passage in *IWLC* 4, *SLF* 5, and *TPYL* 31 all read: "Seeing the neighbors all sunning their clothes, Ho Lung lay on his back and exposed his belly, saying, 'I'm sunning my books.'"
MCYC 1 is even more specific: "Everybody was sunning his clothes and books. It was only Ho Lung who lay on his back in the courtyard facing the sun. When people asked about it, he replied, "I'm just sunning the books in my belly (where memory is stored), that's all."

32. Hsieh An originally had the determination to live as a recluse in the Eastern Mountains. But later stringent orders from the court kept coming, and, unable any longer to protect himself, he finally went to take up his post as Huan Wen's sergeant-at-arms (in 360). At the time someone made Huan a present of some medicinal herbs, among which was some *yüan-chih* ("far-reaching determination").[1] Huan took some and asked Hsieh, "This medicine is also called *hsiao-ts'ao* ("small grass"). How is it that the same thing has two names?"
Hsieh did not have time to answer before Ho Lung, who was present at the time, answered in a flash, "That's easy to explain. When you're living as a recluse it's 'far-reaching determination,' and when you're out in public life it's 'small grass.'"
Hsieh An appeared extremely embarrassed at this. But Huan Wen, glancing at him, laughed and said, "This statement[2] by Aide-de-camp Ho isn't bad at that, and, you'll have to admit, it's extremely apt." (*IWLC* 25; *TPYL* 466, 989; *SWLC*, ch'ien 33, pieh 20)

¹*PTKM* 6: *Yüan-chih* is bitter and nonpoisonous . . . It can increase wisdom and keenness of sight and hearing, helps one not to forget, fortifies one's determination and doubles one's strength . . . When ingested over a long period it lightens the body so that it will not grow old, improving the complexion and lengthening the years. The leaves are called *hsiao-ts'ao*, "small grass." It increases the semen and replenishes the *yin* force, and puts an end to loss through dream emissions.

²Emending *kuo*, "transgression," "lapsus," to *t'ung*, a measure term for statements, as in *TPYL* 989.

33. Yü Yüan-chih once went to visit Sun Sheng (Sun An-kuo). On the way he happened to catch sight of Sun's son, Fang, outside. Fang was still young, but he possessed a quick wit. By way of testing him, Yü asked, "Where's your father, Sun An-kuo?"

Quick as a flash, the boy replied, "At the house of *your* father, Yü Chih-kung (Yü I)."

Yü laughed aloud and said, "The Suns are pretty *prosperous* (*sheng*), to have a boy like you!"

Sun Fang snapped back, "It's not equal to the *luxuriant luxuriance* (**i̯ək-i̯ək*) of the Yüs!"

After Sun Fang had returned home he told everybody, "I certainly won, since I got to repeat his old man's name twice!"¹ (*CS* 82.13a)

¹*Sun Fang PC*: Sun Fang and his older brother, Ch'ien, were both outstanding, and were students together with Yü I's son, Yüan-chih. In his youth Yüan-chih had an excellent reputation, and therefore with a laugh he teased Sun Fang, saying, "The Suns have now become *prosperous* (*sheng*)" (Sheng being Fang's father's taboo name).

Fang immediately replied, "It's not equal to the luxuriant luxuriance, etc." (I--**i̯ək*--being Yüan-chih's father's taboo name).

Fang's wit in repartee was superb and his contemporaries all looked up to him. Prince Ching (Ssu-ma Shih), Ch'en T'ai, Chung Hui, and the other worthies all had exchanges with him, but could never surpass him.

34. Fan Wang was once at a gathering in the home of Emperor Chien-wen (Ssu-ma Yü, r. 371-372) and was on the point of being defeated in a conversation bout. Pulling Wang Meng by the hand, he begged, "You help me!"

Wang replied, "This isn't the kind of thing that can be helped even by the 'strength that uproots mountains'!"¹

¹An allusion to the swan song of Hsiang Yü (d. 202 B.C.) when he was surrounded by the Han forces at Kai-hsia (Shantung; see *SC* 7.30a):

"My strength uprooted mountains,
My might overarched the world . . ."

35. While Ho Lung was serving as Huan Wen's aide to the Commandant of the Southern Man barbarians (ca. 345), there was a gathering on the third day of the third month,¹ at which everyone composed poems. Whoever was unable to do so paid a forfeit by drinking three dipperfuls of wine.

At first Lung was unable to compose anything and paid the forfeit.

But after drinking the three dipperfuls, he seized a brush and wrote the words:

"The *chü-yü* leaps in the clear pool."

Huan Wen asked, "What on earth is a *chü-yü*?"
Lung replied, "The Man barbarians call 'fish' *chü-yü*.
Huan asked, "Who ever heard of using the Man language to compose poetry?"
Lung replied, "I came a thousand *li* to serve under Your Excellency's command, and only got to be an aide in the Man-barbarian headquarters (Hsiang-yang, Hupei), so how can I avoid using the Man language?" (*PSLT* 21; *TPYL* 390, 785; *TPKC* 246; *SWLC*, pieh 6)

[1] For the *hsi*, or rite of spring purification performed on the third day of the third month, see above, *SSHY* XVI, 3.

36. Yüan Ch'iao once went to visit Liu Hui. At the time Hui was in an inner room sleeping, and had not yet gotten up, so Yüan composed the following poem to tease him:

"The horn-graced pillow gleams on the patterned pad;
The broidered cover shines on the extended mat."[1]

Liu had married the daughter of the Chin Emperor Ming (Ssu-ma Shao, r. 323-325), the Princess of Lu-ling. When the princess saw the poem, she remarked with some pique, "That Yüan Ch'iao is a madman left over from a bygone age!"

[1] See "Songs," No. 124:

The horn-graced pillow gleams,
The broidered cover shines.
My fair one has departed hence;
With whom--alone till dawn?

TSH: Duke Hsien of Chin (r. 675-650 B.C.) was fond of aggressive warfare, and many of the people of his state had perished, so they composed (the above) song (as a protest).

37. Yin Jung responded to a poem of Sun Ch'o with the words,

"So now again I'll imitate a song . . ."

Liu T'an, laughing at the awkwardness of his wording, asked, "Just what is it you want to imitate?"
Yin replied, "I'll even imitate his 'slippity-slops' (**d'âp-lâp*). Why must it only be his 'tingally-lings' (**ts'i̯ang-lieng*)?"[1]

[1] I take this pair of contrasting rhyming binomes to refer respectively to crudities or refinements of Sun's style. Yang Yung's note, following a suggestion of Jao Tsung-i, takes **d'âp-lâp* to be a variant of *ṣai-lâp, an eighth-century transcription for the Sanskrit term *ṣāḍava*, the *rāga* or musical mode appropriate for morning chants. See Vajrabodhi's (fl. 720-741) *Chin-kang-ting yü-ch'ieh chung lüeh-ch'u nien-sung ching* (*Vajra-śekhara-yoga-tantra*) 4; *Taishō* 18.248a. Though the reasoning is ingenious, I find this interpretation unconvincing for the following reasons: (1) Even if we emend **d'âp* to *sâp, as Jao suggests, the phonetic proximity to *ṣāḍ-* is still unsatisfactory, and even if there was indeed a Chinese

transcription in existence in the fourth century for sādava, it is extremely unlikely that the method of chanting Tantric texts expounded in Vajrabodhi's abridgment of the *Vajra-śekhara-yoga-tantra* was known in China that early, or that a mere layman like Sun Ch'o, whose extant works reveal familiarity with only the most exoteric Sanskrit terms, would have known it. (2) On the other hand, the binome *d'âp-lâp (written with various graphs) means "sloppy," "slovenly," "shuffling," and need not be explained any further. As for *ts'i̯ang-lieng, Yang is himself aware that this is a binome and cites a passage from Sun Ch'o's "Poetic Essay on Roaming in the T'ien-t'ai Mountains" (*Yu T'ien-t'ai-shan fu*; WH 11.4ab):

> "Wearing the dense cover (*si̯əm-si̯əm) of coarse woolens,
> And rattling the *tingally-ling* (*lieng-lieng) of (the monk's) pewter staff . . ."

which may well have been Yin Jung's model.

Other allusions to Sun Ch'o's alleged vulgarity may be found in SSHY XXVI, 9, 15, 17, and 20, below.

38. After Huan Wen had deposed the Duke of Hai-hsi (Ssu-ma I**, r. 365-371)[1] and established Emperor Chien-wen (Ssu-ma Yü, r. 371-372), the deposed emperor's personal attendant, Hsieh An, had an interview with Huan, at which he prostrated himself before him. Huan was startled and said with a laugh, "An-shih, what are you doing, going to such lengths?"

Hsieh replied, "I've never seen a case where the ruler prostrated himself (*pai*)[2] in front, while his minister stood upright (*li*)[3] behind." (CS 98.26b)

[1] CYC: When the Duke of Hai-hsi was young he had "eunuch's sickness" (i.e., was impotent), and had members of the harem have illicit relations with his attendants to beget a son. Huan Wen, returning to Ku-shu from Kuang-ling, passed through the capital, and on orders from the dowager empress deposed him and made him Duke of Hai-hsi.

[2] Hsieh is playing on the similarity in sound between *fei* (*pi̯wɒi), "deposed," and *pai* (*pwai), "prostrate oneself."

[3] The parallel passage in CS 98.26b reads *i*, "bow with hands together," instead of *li*, "stand."

39. Ch'ih T'an once wrote a letter to Hsieh An in which he referred to Wang Hsiu in the following terms: "I hear there is a certain young man who is cherishing ideas of 'inquiring about (the size and weight of) the tripods (*wen-ting*).'[1] I don't know if this is a case of 'Duke Huan's (r. 685-643 B.C.) virtue declining,'[2] or of the 'later generation which is to be held in awe.'"[3]

[1] I.e., Wang Hsiu is challenging Hsieh An's title as chief conversationalist.

SC (40.8ab; cf. *Tso-chuan*, Hsüan 3; Legge V, 293): King Chuang of Ch'u (r. 613-591 B.C.) was reviewing his troops on the outskirts of Chou (Lo-yang). King Ting of Chou (r. 606-586) sent Wang-sun Man to welcome and entertain the King of Ch'u. When the King of Ch'u inquired about the size and weight of the tripods (the symbols of Chou authority over the feudal states), Man replied, "The strength of a state depends on the virtue of its ruler, not on the tripods."

King Chuang said, "You would be no better off with *nine* tripods (the original number cast by Yü for the 'Nine Provinces'). The mere beak of a broken hook of the Ch'u state would be enough to match nine tripods."

²*Tso-chuan*, Hsi 4; Legge V, 140: Duke Huan of Ch'i invaded Ch'u, charging them with failure to send tribute of *pao-mao* sedge to the Chou court.

³"Analects" IX, 23: The later generation is to be held in awe. How can one know if those who come after will not be the equals of those of the present day?

40. Chang Chen was the grandfather of Chang P'ing. One time he said to P'ing's father, "I'm no match for you."
Before P'ing's father had quite understood the reason for the remark, Chang Chen went on, "*You* have a fine son."
P'ing, who was only a few years of age at the time, pressing his hands together, said, "Grandpa, is it fair to use a son to poke fun at his father?" (*CS* 75.34a)

41. Hsi Tso-ch'ih (a native of Hsiang-yang in the south) and Sun Ch'o (whose family hailed from T'ai-yüan in the north) had not previously known each other. Both were present at a gathering of Huan Wen's staff (in Hsiang-yang, ca. 345). Huan said to Sun, "You may converse with my aide, Hsi Tso-ch'ih."
Sun began (quoting "Songs," No. 178):

"Stupid the southern boors of Ching
Who dare oppose a mighty state."

Hsi countered (quoting "Songs," No. 177):

"In punishing the northern hordes (Hsien-yün),
Our troops have come to T'ai-yüan town."

42. Huan Ssu was Wang Hun's nephew on his mother's side (*wai-sheng*), and in his physical features resembled his uncle, a fact which was exceedingly distasteful to him. His paternal uncle, Huan Wen, said, "You don't resemble him all the time, but only occasionally. A constant resemblance is a physical matter, whereas an occasional resemblance is spiritual."
Huan Ssu was more displeased than ever. (*TPYL* 396)

43. Wang Hui-chih once went to visit Hsieh Wan.¹ The monk Chih Tun was already present among the company and was looking about him with extreme haughtiness. Wang remarked, "If Chih Tun's beard and hair were both intact,² would his spirit and mood be even more impressive than they are now?"
Hsieh replied, "Lips and teeth are necessary to each other, and one can't do without either of them,³ but what have the beard and hair do with the spirit and intelligence?"
Chih Tun, his mood and expression showing extreme displeasure,

said, "My seven-foot body is this day at the service of you two worthies!" (*TPYL* 368)

¹In the quotation in *TPYL* 368, the host is Hsieh Hsüan.

²I.e., if he were not a monk.

³See *Kung-yang chuan*, Hsi 2: When the lips are missing, the teeth are cold.

44. When Ch'ih Yin was appointed to the northern headquarters (in Ching-k'ou) as governor-general of Hsü Province (369),¹ Wang Hui-chih went up to the Ch'ih family gate and called out, "'The strategy of adaptation to change is not his forte'!" He kept intoning it over and over without stopping.

Yin's son, Ch'ih Jung, said to his brother, Ch'ao, "Father was just appointed to his post today, and for Wang Hui-chih to talk like this is extraordinarily impudent, not to say absolutely intolerable."

Ch'ih Ch'ao replied, "What he's repeating is Ch'en Shou's (d. 297) criticism of Chu-ko Liang (d. 234).² When someone compares the head of your family to Chu-ko Liang, what more can you say?"

¹*NHCC*: Formerly the headquarters of the governor-general of Hsü Province was called "eastern," but after the Chin capital moved south (in 317), the governor of Hsü Province, Wang Shu*, was given the additional title, Commandant of the North, so the designation "northern headquarters" took its origin from this.

²*WYCS* (cf. *CS* 82.1b): Earlier, Ch'en Shou's father had been serving as Ma Shu's aide. When Chu-ko Liang executed Shu (in 228), he shaved Shou's father's head. Liang's son, Chan, also despised Shou, so when Shou was compiling the "Record of the Shu Kingdom" (*SKShu*), he made his criticism of Chu-ko Liang on the basis of his personal feelings.

SKShu (5.21b): Chu-ko Liang moved his hosts about year after year without success; it seems that the strategy of adaptation to change was not his forte.

45. Wang Hui-chih once went to visit Hsieh An. Hsieh asked him, "What is meant by a 'seven-word poem'?"¹

By way of reply, Hui-chih quoted the lines (from the *Ch'u-tz'u*):

> "Is it better to be spirited and proud like a colt
> of a thousand *li*,
> Or to drift aimlessly about like a duck in the
> midst of a pond?"²

¹*TFSC*: When Emperor Wu of Han (r. 140-87 B.C.) was on the Po-liang Terrace, he had all his ministers compose "seven-word poems" (i.e., with seven words to each line).

SSHY Comm.: The "seven-word" form took its origin from this.

(Yang Yung's note, citing the commentary of Liu P'an-sui, *SSHYCC*, observes that if the origin of the "seven-word" form actually dates from the second century B.C., Hsieh An's question about it would be meaningless. Similarly, if it did not originate until *after* the fourth century A.D., it could not even have been asked. It is therefore reasonable to conclude, if the evidence of this anecdote is reliable, that the "seven-word" form was known and self-consciously practiced by the mid-fourth century, though it did not reach its florescence until the fifth or sixth, from which, indeed, numerous examples survive. Classical prototypes from the *Ch'u-tz'u*, or other early sources, are plainly fortuitous, and stories about the origin drawn from *TFSC* or *SCC*, since they date from no earlier than the fifth century, are certainly suspect. The famous "seven-word chain verses," presumably composed on the Po-liang Terrace in 108 B.C., are attested only in the anonymous preface to the "Po-liang Poems" in the T'ang anthology, *Ku-wen yüan*, ch. 8).

[2]*Pu-chü* 18-19 (Hawkes, *Songs of the South*, p. 89). If the particles, *chih* and *hu*, are removed, the lines have seven syllables.

46. Wang T'an-chih and Fan Ch'i were once summoned simultaneously by Emperor Chien-wen (Ssu-ma Yü, r. 371-372). Fan was older but lower in rank, while Wang was younger but higher in rank. As they were about to go in, each more and more insistently urged the other to go first.

After this had gone on for some time, Wang finally ended up behind Fan, where he quipped, "Winnow it and toss it; the chaff and unripened kernels fall in front."

Fan retorted, "Sift it and wash it; the sand and gravel remain behind."[1] (*CS* 56.17a)

[1]Liu Chün notes in the Commentary that the same story is told of Sun Ch'o and Hsi Tso-ch'ih (so *CS* 56.17a).

47. When Liu Yüan-chih was young he was recognized by Yin Hao, who praised him to Yü Liang. Yü Liang was extremely pleased and proceeded to take him on as an assistant. After he had greeted him, he had him sit on a single couch (*tu-t'a*) while he conversed with him. That day Liu failed conspicuously to come up to expectations, and Yü, somewhat disappointed, finally named him "Yang Hu's crane."

Previously, Yang Hu (d. 278) had a crane which was skilled at dancing. One time Yang praised it to a guest, but after the guest arrived,[1] when Hu tried to drive it forward, it made a flurry of feathers (**d'ung-mung*) but would not dance. This is why Yü Liang compared Liu Yüan-chih to the crane. (*SLF* 18; *TPYL* 916)

[1]Adding *chih*, "to arrive," after *k'o*, "guest," to agree with the quotations in *SLF* 18 and *TPYL* 916.

48. Wei I had always possessed a magnanimous nature, but literary ability and scholarship were not among his accomplishments. On his first appointment to public office, as he was about to set out for his post, Yü Ts'un teased him, saying, "I'll make a 'three-point pact'[1] with you: for 'pure conversationalists,' death; for writers and essayists, mutilation; and for estimators of character, penalties to match their crimes."

Wei laughed good-humoredly, with no trace of resentment in his face.

[1]*HS* (1A.20a; trans. Dubs, *History*, I, 58): When the Duke of P'ei (Liu Pang, later Emperor Kao, r. 206-195 B.C.) entered Hsien-yang (the Ch'in capital, in Shensi, 207 B.C.), he summoned the fathers and elders, and said, "The empire has suffered under the oppressive laws of Ch'in for a long time now . . . Today I'll make a

pact of only three points with you fathers and elders: for murderers, death; for those who injure others and for robbers, penalties to match their crimes, and no more."

49. Ch'ih Ch'ao wrote a letter to Yüan Hung characterizing Tai K'uei and Hsieh Fu as follows: "Those whose manner is constant and responsible should have their reputations published abroad, and no others." Ch'ih considered Yüan himself to be inconstant, and therefore took this means to needle him.

50. Fan Ch'i wrote a letter to Ch'ih Ch'ao in which he said, "Wang Hsien-chih has no forgiveness or tolerance anywhere in his body. Lift up his skin, and underneath you will find no extra generosity."
  Ch'ih Ch'ao wrote back, "How can not having any extra generosity anywhere in his body compare with not being real anywhere in his body?"[1]
  Fan Ch'i was by nature specious and unreal, full of affectations. This is why Ch'ih Ch'ao ridiculed him.

[1]Cf. the characterization of Wang Shu by Hsieh An, *SSHY* VIII, 78, above.

51. The two Ch'ihs (Ch'ih Yin and Ch'ih T'an) were devotees of the Tao,[1] while the two Hos (Ho Ch'ung and Ho Chun) were devotees of the Buddha.[2] Both made large contributions of money to gain merit. Hsieh Wan remarked, "The two Ch'ihs pay court to the Tao, while the two Hos fawn on the Buddha." (*CS* 77.9a)

[1]*CHS*: Ch'ih Yin and his younger brother, T'an, were devotees of the Way of the Heavenly Master (T'ien-shih Tao).

[2]*CYC*: Ho Ch'ung by nature was fond of the Way of the Buddha; he worshipped at and repaired Buddhist monasteries, and supported monks by the hundreds. For a long while when he was governor of Yang Province (Kiangsu-Anhui-Chekiang) he drafted petty officials and commoners (for work on the monasteries), and rewarded them handsomely for their efforts. For this reason he was criticized by people far and near. Ch'ung's younger brother, Chun, was also extremely zealous, and did nothing but read sutras and build and repair monasteries.

52. While Wang T'an-chih was in the western provincial headquarters at Chiang-ning (seat of the governor of Yang Province),[1] he once held a debate with Chih Tun. Han Po, Sun Ch'o, and the others were all present. Chih Tun's argument frequently suffered minor reverses, whereupon Sun Ch'o remarked, "Today the dharma master is like a man wearing a tattered padded coat in a briar patch;[2] everywhere he touches he gets snagged." (*TPYL* 819)

[1]Although T'an-chih's father, Shu, was governor of Yang Province between 354 and his death in 368 (*TCTC* 99.3138), I can find no reference to T'an-chih's ever having held that post. Chih Tun lived in the capital between 338 and 342, and again from 362 to 365; see Zürcher, *Conquest*, pp. 117, 120.

[2]See *SC* 110.15a: Chung-hsing Yüeh obtained some Chinese brocaded padded coats and rode with them through grass and brambles. His

coat and trousers were all torn and tattered, demonstrating that they did not remain whole and in good condition like the felt and furs worn by the Hsiung-nu.

53. Fan Ch'i, observing that Ch'ih Ch'ao's worldly sentiments were not sufficiently bland (*tan*), made sport of him, saying, "Po I and Shu Ch'i, Ch'ao Fu and Hsü Yu,[1] all have had their reputations come down unbroken to the present day. Did they have to labor their spirits and toil their bodies like Shih K'uang 'adjusting the bridges of his zither,' or Hui-tzu 'leaning on his desk'?"[2]

Ch'ih had not yet answered, when Han Po interposed, "Why not (be like the cook, Pao Ting, and just) let your 'roving blade' (move freely in places that are) all empty?"[3]

[1] Ancient recluses.

[2] *Chuang-tzu* (II, 20b; Watson, p. 42): Chao Wen strumming his zither, Shih K'uang adjusting his bridges, Hui-tzu leaning on his desk--these three were nearly perfect in their wisdom, and they were all well-versed in their art. Therefore their reputations have come down to these latter years.

[3] Ibid. (III, 1b-3a; Watson, pp. 50-51): The cook, Pao Ting, was cutting up an ox for Prince Wen-hui . . . He explained, "After three years I no longer saw whole oxen . . . I've used this knife for nineteen years now, and have cut up a thousand oxen, yet the knife blade is still as sharp as when it came fresh from the whetstone."

Prince Wen-hui asked the reason, and Pao Ting replied, "Between those joints there is space, yet the knife blade has no thickness. Using what has no thickness to enter where there is space--swish! swish! for the roving blade there is sure to be more than enough room!"

54. (The future) Emperor Chien-wen (Ssu-ma Yü, r. 371-372) was once walking in the upper part of the palace. Wang Hsi-chih (d. ca. 365) and Sun Ch'o were behind him. Pointing at Emperor Chien-wen, Wang said to Sun, "Here's a man who chews on fame (*tan-ming k'o*)."[1]

Turning back, Emperor Chien-wen said, "Naturally there are in the realm fellows with sharp teeth (*li-ch'ih erh*)."

Later (in 379) when Wang Yün became governor of K'uai-chi Principality (Chekiang), Hsieh Hsüan came out of the capital as far as Ch'ü-o (southeast of Chien-k'ang) to give him a farewell party. Wang Yün's son, Wang Kung, who had just quit his post as privy councillor,[2] was also present. During the conversation Hsieh mentioned this incident, and as he did so cast a glance at Wang Kung, saying, "Your teeth, too, seem not to have been dull, eh?"

Wang replied, "They're not dull; I've had some experience of that." (*HTC* 4)

[1] The quotation in *HTC* 4 reads *tan-shih*, "chews on rocks" (to sharpen his teeth). See above, No. 6, for a similar expression.

[2] This would involve an anachronism, since Wang Kung was transferred from the post of curator of the Palace Library to clerk in the Central Secretariat, but did not take up his post because of the death of his father, Wang Yün, in 384; see *CS* 84.1b. It may

have been the earlier occasion of his declining the post of assistant archivist (ibid., 1ab) on the pretext of illness, but really because it was not a high enough office and therefore "not worth bothering over," that is meant. This might explain the reference to his "sharp teeth" (i.e., love of fame?).

55. One summer day Hsieh Hsüan was lying stretched out on his back, when his uncle, Hsieh An, arrived unexpectedly, early in the morning. Hsüan had no time to put on his clothes, but dashed out of the room barefooted before getting into his clogs and offering salutations. Hsieh An observed, "Your behavior might be called 'first rude, and afterward respectful,'[1] eh?" (TPYL 21; SWLC, hou 21)

[1] Chan-kuo ts'e (III): Su Ch'in was adviser to King Hui (-wen) of Ch'in, r. 337-311 B.C.), but his counsels were not used. With his coat of black sable in tatters and his hundred catties of gold exhausted, he returned to Lo-yang in abject poverty. His mother and father would not speak to him, nor did his wife so much as get down from her loom on his account. His sister-in-law would not even cook for him.

Later, as leader of the "vertical alliance" against Ch'in, when he passed by Lo-yang, his carriages and riders and baggage train formed a mighty host. Su Ch'in's brothers and wife and sister-in-law averted their eyes, not daring to look at him. Laughing, Ch'in said to his sister-in-law, "How is it you were first rude and afterward respectful?"

His sister-in-law apologized, saying, "Because I saw my elder brother's status is high and his money plentiful."

Ch'in sighed and said, "If when a person is wealthy and honorable his relatives hold him in awe, but when he's poor and lowly they treat him with contempt, how much worse would it be in the case of nonrelatives!"

56. While Ku K'ai-chih was serving as Yin Chung-k'an's assistant, when the latter was governor of Ching Province (392-399), he requested a leave of absence to return east (to K'uai-chi). At that time the regulations governing such cases did not provide for the use of cloth sails. Ku insistently demanded to have one, and after finally succeeding, set out on his journey down the Yangtze. When he had gotten as far as Broken Tomb Island (P'o-chung, in Hupei), he ran into a windstorm and suffered heavy damages. In a note to Yin Chung-k'an he wrote, "The place is named Broken Tomb, and it really was an escape by breaking out of the tomb! The traveler is safe and sound, and the cloth sail intact." (CS 92.35a; PTSC 138; SLF 16; TPYL 634, 771)

57. When Fu Lang first crossed the Yangtze River (in 383), Wang Su-chih, who was an enormously curious person, kept asking him about personalities in the Central States, and about local products and customs there, without stopping.

Fu Lang got very annoyed with him, and the next time when he started again to ask about the price of male and female slaves, Lang replied, "The diligent and attentive ones with some intelligence cost up to a hundred thousand cash, but the brainless ones who keep asking slavish and servile questions only bring a few thousand and no more."[1]

¹*PCJCS*: Wang Ch'en and his elder brother, Wang Kuo-pao, ordered their carriage and went to visit Fu Lang. The śramaṇa, Chu Fa-t'ai, asked Lang, "Have you seen the Wang brothers yet?"

Lang replied, "You don't mean the one with a dog's face and a human heart, and the other with a human face and a dog's heart, by any chance?" This was because Wang Ch'en was ugly but talented, and Wang Kuo-pao handsome but cruel.

Lang was once at a banquet with the other courtiers. At the time all the worthies were using spittoons (*t'o-hu*). Lang, wishing to do them one better, had a small boy kneel down and open his mouth, into which he spit, after which he had the boy go out holding it in his mouth.

He was also a good connoisseur of flavors. The Prince of K'uai-chi, Ssu-ma Tao-tzu, once set some exquisite delicacies before him. When he had finished eating them, Tao-tzu asked, "How does the food in Kuan-chung (Shensi) compare with this?"

Lang replied, "They're both good, except that the salt flavor in this is a trifle raw." Tao-tzu immediately checked with the cook and found it to be exactly as he said.

Someone killed a chicken and fed it to him. Lang said, "This chicken was accustomed to perching in a spot where he was always half-exposed." When they investigated the matter, this also was confirmed.

On another occasion he was eating a roast goose, and knew all the spots where the plumage had been either white or black. In every case they tested and recorded the correspondences and Lang never missed by the smallest fraction.

Lang wrote a book called "Master Fu" (*Fu-tzu*) in several tens of *chüan*, similar to the *Lao-tzu* and *Chuang-tzu*.

58. The reception hall of the Eastern Villa¹ was a room paneled with wooden boards. Hsieh Chung once went there to visit the grand tutor, Ssu-ma Tao-tzu, at a time when it was filled with guests. From the first Hsieh exchanged words with no one, but only stared up at the ceiling and said, "I see Your Highness has now 'Western-barbarianized' (*Hsi-Jung*) his room."²

¹The residence of Ssu-ma Tao-tzu; see above, *SSHY* II, 100, n. 2.

²See "Songs," No. 128:

> When I think of my lord,
> Warm and gentle as jade,
> There in his room of wooden boards,
> How it tangles the corners of my heart!

CSH: Duke Hsiang of Ch'in (r. 777-766 B.C.) made ready his men-at-arms and armor to punish the Western Barbarians (Hsi-Jung). His wife felt lonely for her lord and therefore composed this song.

SCMKC: The "room of wooden boards" was the duke's residence among the Western Barbarians.

59. Whenever Ku K'ai-chih chewed sugarcane (*kan-che*) he would always start at the tip and work toward the root. When anyone asked his reason, he would reply, "By slow degrees I enter¹ the realm of delight." (*CS* 92.35a; *IWLC* 87)

¹Emending the *chih*, "arrive at," to *ju*, "enter," after CS 92.35a and *IWLC* 87.

60. Emperor Hsiao-wu (Ssu-ma Yao, r. 373-396) entrusted Wang Hsün with the task of finding a husband for his daughter, the Princess of Chin-ling, saying, "Since persons in the massive boulder category, like Wang Tun (d. 324) and Huan Wen (d. 373), are no longer to be found, you may more or less use your discretion. But on the other hand, someone who likes to meddle in other people's affairs is definitely not what I want. Someone just like Liu T'an (d. ca. 346) or Wang Hsien-chih (d. 388) would be the best."
  Hsün recommended Hsieh Hun.¹
  Afterward, when Yüan Shan-sung wanted to contract a marriage with the Hsiehs, Wang Hsün said to him, "Don't you dare come near the 'forbidden meat slice' (*chin-lüan*)!"² (CS 79.11ab)

¹*HCYC* (cf. *CS* 79.11ab): Earlier, Emperor Hsiao-wu had consulted with Wang Hsün about a son-in-law for his daughter, the Princess of Chin-ling. Hsün recommended Hsieh Hun, saying, "The man's ability is not equal to Liu T'an's, but is not inferior to Wang Hsien-chih's." The emperor replied, "In that case, he'll do."

²*CS* 79.11b: When Emperor Yüan (Ssu-ma Jui, r. 317-322) was first stationed at Chien-yeh (in 307), both public and private resources were utterly exhausted, and whenever anyone obtained a suckling pig it was considered a rare delicacy. A slice from the upper part of the nape of the neck was especially prized and would always be presented to the emperor. None of his subordinates would ever dare to eat it. At the time it was known as the "forbidden meat slice."

61. Huan Hsüan was once playing "sequences" (*yü-tz'u*) with Yin Chung-k'an, and everyone was making sequences on the word, **lieu*, "ended." Ku K'ai-chih began:

  "Flames devour the level plain, and leave no
      trace unburned." (**li̯äu*)

Huan continued:

  "With white clothes wrap the coffin round, and by it
      plant the banners." (**d'i̯äu*)

Yin added:

  "Throw the fish into the deep; release the
      flying bird." (**tieu*)

Next they did sequences on the word, **ngjwiḙ*, "danger." Huan Hsüan began:

  "Poised on a spear point, rice is washed, and on a
      sword point steamed." (**tś'wiḙ*)

Yin continued:

  "An old man of a hundred years climbs up a
      withered branch." (**tśiḙ*)

Ku added:

  "Upon the windlass (*lu-lu*) o'er the well there lies
      an infant child." (**ńźi*)

One of Yin's aides who was present chimed in:

> "Blind man astride a sightless horse at midnight
> brinks the deep abyss." (*$\hat{d}'i\varrho$)

"Hear! Hear!" cried Yin, "You're getting too close to home!" This was because Yin Chung-k'an was squint-eyed (*miao-mu*).[1] (*CS* 92.35a, trans. S. H. Chen, *Biography*, pp. 13-14; *TPYL* 390, 740; *SWLC*, pieh 20)

[1] See above, *SSHY* XXI, 11.

CHS: Yin Chung-k'an's father had a chronic illness and was ailing for a long time. Yin had no leisure even to untie the girdle of his gown for several years, while he personally compounded the medicines, mixing them with boiling water. One time by accident he brushed away some tears with the hand with which he had been mixing medicine, and afterward became squinted in one eye.

62. Huan Hsüan once went out to practice archery. He had an aide named Liu and another aide named Chou who paired off to compete with each other. As the contest drew toward completion they lacked but one hit.

Liu said to Chou, "If you don't make a hit this time, I'll flog you."

Chou replied, "How has it come to the point of taking a flogging from you?"

Liu said, "If even a man as noble as Po-ch'in[1] didn't escape a flogging, how much less should you?"

Chou showed not the slightest sign of feeling insulted. Huan remarked to Yü Hung, "Aide-de-camp Liu should quit reading books, and Aide-de-camp Chou should apply himself a bit more to his studies." (*IWLC* 25)

[1] *SSTC* (4, *Tzu-ts'ai*): Po-ch'in, son of the Duke of Chou, and K'ang-shu, the duke's younger brother, went to see the Duke of Chou three times, and all three times they were flogged. K'ang-shu became frightened and said to Po-ch'in, "There's a certain Master Shang, a worthy man. I'll go with you to see him." Whereupon they went to see Master Shang and consulted him about the problem.

Master Shang said, "On the sunny slope of the Southern Mountain there's a tree called the *ch'iao* (tall)." The two boys went to look at it, and saw that the *ch'iao* was indeed tall, high and lofty and reaching upward. They returned to report to Master Shang, who told them, "The *ch'iao* is the father's way. Now, on the shady slope of the Southern Mountain is a tree called the *tzu* (the catalpa)." The two boys went again to look at it, and saw that the *tzu* was indeed lowly and respectful, drooping downward. They returned and reported to Master Shang, who told them, "The *tzu* (***tsi̯əg*) is the son's (***tsi̯əg*) way."

Next day the two boys went to see the Duke of Chou. As they entered the door they hastened forward. After mounting the dais, they knelt down. The duke patted their heads, comforted and fed them, saying, "Have you been to see the gentleman (i.e., Shang-tzu)?"

"Record of Rites" (VIII, 1; Legge, *Li Ki* I, 345): When King Ch'eng (trad. 1115-1091 B.C.) committed an offense, the Duke of Chou would flog Po-ch'in.

63. Huan Hsüan was discussing the *Lao-tzu* with the monk Tao-yao, while Wang Chen-chih, who was serving as Huan's supervisor of records, was also present. Huan said, "Supervisor Wang, here, may regard his own baby name, and think of its meaning."[1]

Wang had not yet answered, but began to guffaw loudly. Huan added, "Wang Ssu-tao is 'Thinking of the Way,' so he's able to laugh like a big boy."[2] (*IWLC* 25)

[1] Wang's baby name was Ssu-tao, "Thinking of the Way."

[2] See *Lao-tzu* 41: Gentlemen of the lowest order when they hear of the Way guffaw loudly at it. If they did not guffaw, it would not be fit to be the Way.

(Wang Chen-chih was the grandson of the great Taoist calligrapher, Wang Hsi-chih.)

64. When Tsu Kuang walked he always drew in his head. One time he went to visit Huan Hsüan, and as he first got down from his carriage, Huan said, "The sky is extremely clear and bright, but Aide-de-camp Tsu seems to be coming from the middle of the darkest corner of the room (*wu-lou*)."[1] (*TPYL* 364; *SWLC*, hou 18)

[1] I.e., the northwest corner, where the household god was kept. See "Songs," No. 256, stanza 7:

> Observe how you are in your house,
> So as not to be ashamed even in the *wu-lou*.

65. Huan Hsüan had always despised his cousin, Huan Hsiu.[1] While Hsiu was living at the capital he owned a fine peach tree, and Hsüan frequently went to his place to ask for peaches, but in the end he never got any good ones. Hsüan wrote a letter to Yin Chung-wen in which he made sport of Huan Hsiu, saying, "When the 'virtue of the ruler is prosperous and enlightened,'[2] the distant Su-shen tribes[3] send as tribute their thornwood (*hu*) arrows. But when this is not the case, then even things that grow between one's own fence and wall are unobtainable." (*IWLC* 86; *SWLC*, hou 25)

[1] See below, *SSHY* XXXVI, 8.
   HCYC: When Huan Hsiu was young he was despised by Huan Hsüan, who was always making sport of him in his remarks.

[2] See *Tso-chuan*, Hsüan 3 (Legge V, 293).

[3] The Su-shen tribes of Chou times occupied the area of Kirin in Manchuria and were thought to be the ancestors of the Jurchen and Manchus of later times.
   Kuo-yü (5; Lu 2): While Confucius was in Ch'en (Honan) a peregrine falcon (*shun*) perched in the courtyard of the Marquis of Ch'en and died, a thornwood arrow thrust through its body with a stone arrowhead a foot and eight inches in length . . . When they asked Confucius about it, he replied, "The falcon has come from a great distance. This is a Su-shen arrow. Long ago when King Wu (trad. 1122-1116) conquered the Shang, he opened up communications with the nine I tribes in the north and the hundred Man tribes in the south, and had each send tribute of its local products. Whereupon the Su-shen sent tribute of thornwood arrows . . . When the ancient kings distributed offices to those of different surname

from themselves, in order that they should not forget to be submissive, they distributed to Ch'en the tribute of the Su-shen. If you were to look for the Su-shen arrows in the ancient administrative seat, you might find some. They sent someone to look, and found them in a golden casket, just as they had been in the old days.

CHAPTER XXVI

Contempt and Insults

簡傲

1. The grand marshal, Wang Yen, once asked his son, Wang Hsüan, "Your uncle, Wang Ch'eng, is a famous gentleman. Why is it you don't admire or respect him?"
   Hsüan replied, "Who ever heard of a famous gentleman who spends the whole day talking nonsense?"

2. Yü Liang once said to Chou I, "Everyone compares you to Yüeh."
   Chou asked, "Which Yüeh? Are you referring to Yüeh I?"[1]
   "No," replied Yü, "just Yüeh Kuang."
   Chou said, "Why carve and paint the woman of Wu-yen[2] to make her come up to Hsi Shih?"[3] (CS 69.17b; IWLC 25)

   [1] SC (cf. 80.1a-7a, abbreviated): Yüeh I was a native of Chung-shan (Hopei), a worthy man, who served as a general under King Chao of Yen (r. 311-279 B.C.), and led the feudal lords in a punitive attack against Ch'i (Shantung). He died in the state of Chao (Shansi).

   [2] LNC: Chung-li Ch'un was a woman of Wu-yen in Ch'i (Shantung), whose ugliness was unparalleled. She had a yellow head and deep-set eyes, was tall and burly with large joints. Her nose tilted upward and she had a large adam's apple, with thick neck and thin hair, a bent waist and chicken breast. Her skin was like varnish. She had lived thirty years (some texts say "forty") without ever being tolerated or accepted by anyone, and though she had been offered in marriage, there were no takers. Finally she went in person to see King Hsüan of Ch'i (r. 455-405 B.C.), and begged to serve in the rear palace. As she did so she advised the king about the four perils (then threatening the Ch'i state). The king made her his legal consort.

   [3] WYCC: Kou Chien (r. 496-465 B.C.), King of Yüeh (Chekiang), found the daughter of a fuel-gatherer in the mountains, named Hsi Shih,

and presented her to the King of Wu, Fu Ch'ai (r. 495-473). (Hsi Shih became the paradigm of feminine beauty.)

3. The monk Chu Ch'ien said, "People call Yü Liang a famous gentleman—him with three *tou* or more of faggots and brambles in his breast!"[1]

[1] Yü Liang had participated in the suppression of Chu Ch'ien's brother, Wang Tun, in 324. Though he was not himself actively anticlerical, his brother, Yü Ping, pursued such a policy after Liang's death in 340; so much so, that Chu Ch'ien and other monks withdrew from the capital to the K'uai-chi area in Chekiang. See Zürcher, Conquest, p. 106.

4. Yü Liang's power and dignity were sufficient to overthrow Wang Tao.[1] While Yü was at Shih-t'ou* (i.e., Shih-shou, in Hupei, as governor of Ching Province between 334 and 339), Wang was once present at a party in Yeh-ch'eng (southwest of Chien-k'ang). A strong wind started to raise the dust, and Wang, whisking it away with his fan, said, "Yü Liang's dust is contaminating me!"[2] (CS 65.9a)

[1] Although Wang Tao continued to hold high posts until his death in 339, his power at court was overshadowed by Yü Liang after the rebellion of his cousin, Wang Tun (322-324). Yü's power derived primarily from his position as brother-in-law to Emperor Ming (Ssu-ma Shao, r. 323-325).

[2] SSHY Comm.: Wang Tao possessed cultivated tolerance and was impartial in extending help. While Yü Liang was stationed in Wu-ch'ang (334-339), a rumor was circulated (in 338; TCTC 96.3022) that Yü would come down (to the capital to depose Wang from the chancellorship). Through his understanding and magnanimity, Wang scotched it, and the noisy gossip died a natural death (see above, SSHY VI, 13). How could there have been any incident such as his fanning away the dust?

WYCS (Biography of Tai Yang): The grand warden of Tan-yang Commandery (Chien-k'ang), Wang Tao, inquired of Yang about the reason for his having been ill for the past seven years.

Yang replied, "Your Lordship was born in the year of the Monkey (*shen*; Wang Tao was born in 276, a *ping-shen* year), and you are a lord of this locality, yet in the direction west-southwest (*shen*) there is a large smelting operation (*yeh*), from which the light of the fire illumines the sky. This means metal (= west) and fire (= south) are fusing together, and fire and water are boiling together, and that is why they are harming each other."

Wang Tao then called in the magistrate of Yeh* Prefecture, I Hsün, and had his headquarters moved eastward [and thereafter administered the commandery from Tung-an, whereupon his illness began to improve. Tung-an is] the present Tung-yeh*. (Bracketed section added from KI.)

TYC: Yeh-ch'eng ("Smelting City") Prefecture in Tan-yang Commandery is three *li* from the palace. During the Wu Kingdom (220-280) it was the place where metals were smelted. After the pacification of Wu (in 280) it was still in operation. . . . Sun Ch'üan built Yeh-ch'eng as a place for smelting.

SSHY Comm.: After they had set up the large fortification at

Shih-t'ou (on the Yangtze west of Chien-k'ang), there was no room in the vicinity for the (original) small walled town (of Shih-t'ou, built in 212; see TCTC 66.2114). So at this time they moved the prefectural seat and vacated the city and simply relocated it in Yeh*. Yeh-ch'eng was probably the original administrative seat for Chin-ling (= Chien-k'ang). In the sixth year of the Han Emperor Kao (201 B.C.), when he ordered the building of walls for all prefectural towns, Mo-ling (= Chin-ling) should not have been the only exception.

5. When Wang Hsi-chih was young he suffered from a severe impediment in his speech. One time when he was at the home of the generalissimo, Wang Tun, Wang Tao and Yü Liang came in later, and Wang Hsi-chih immediately got up to leave. The generalissimo detained him, saying, "It's only the director of works from your own family and Yü Liang. What objection can you possibly have to them?"

6. Chancellor Wang Tao belittled Ts'ai Mo, saying, "When I used to go on outings with Wang Ch'eng (d. 320) and Juan Chan (d. 312?) by the shores of the Lo River (south of Lo-yang), where did anyone ever hear of any son of Ts'ai K'o?"[1] (CS 65.8b-9a)

[1] (Ts'ai) K'o PC: Ts'ai K'o was a collateral grandson of Ts'ai Yung. When he was young he was fond of study and possessed a cultivated superiority. His physical appearance was impressive and severe, and no one dared act informally in his presence. Liu Cheng possessed outstanding talent and his carriages and wardrobe were extravagantly ornate. He used to tell people, "Silk gauze (sha-hu) is only what people ordinarily wear; but whenever I happen upon Ts'ai K'o at any gathering, I feel uncomfortable all the rest of the day." Thus he was held in awe.

At this time Ch'en-liu (Honan) was a large commandery with many distinguished gentlemen in it. Wang Ch'eng was once passing through the commandery, and as he entered its territory he asked, "There are a lot of distinguished gentlemen from this commandery. Who are they?"

A petty officer answered, "Well, there's Chiang T'ung, and Ts'ai K'o."

At the time there was a large number of high-ranking personages from Ch'en-liu, so Ch'eng pursued his question further, asking, "Why have you only named these two?"

The petty officer replied, "Just now I thought Your Lordship was asking about *people*; I wasn't thinking about rank." Wang Ch'eng laughed and asked no more questions.

TC (cf. CS 65.8b-9a): Lady Ts'ao, the wife of Chancellor Wang Tao, was extremely jealous by nature, and hemmed the chancellor about with rigid restrictions, not permitting him to have any personal attendants, so that even the most unimportant menials had all to be selected by her. If from time to time any pretty ones appeared, she would always scold them unmercifully. Wang Tao was unable to endure this for long, and in the end secretly set up establishments where concubines lived in large numbers and their sons and daughters multiplied in droves.

Some time later, on the day of the New Year gathering, Lady Ts'ao was out on the Terrace of Blue-green Distance (Ch'ing-su t'ai), from which she saw in the distance two or three boys riding

on goats, all of them very well-bred and lovable, and as she
looked at them from a distance, she was drawn to them with deep
affection, and said to her slave girl, "Go out and inquire whose
sons they are."

The girl did not carry out her order, but answered instead,
"They're the sons of Number Four and Number Five." On hearing this,
Lady Ts'ao was filled with consternation, and in a towering rage
she ordered her carriage. Taking along twenty attendants and slave
girls, she herself seized a kitchen knife and set out in person to
hunt down and punish her quarry.

Wang for his part also hurriedly ordered his carriage, and with
flying reins charged out of the gate. Still chafing at the slowness of the ox, he clutched the carriage railing with his left
hand, and with his right brandished his sambar-tail chowry, using
the handle to assist the driver in whipping the ox. Eventually,
with great commotion and wild haste, he barely managed to arrive
ahead of his wife.

When Ts'ai Mo heard of it he laughed aloud and made a point of
going to visit Wang. "The court wishes to offer you the Nine Bestowals" (see above, SSHY IV, 67, n. 1), he announced. "Did you
know about it?"

Supposing him to be serious, Wang started to excuse himself
with humble protestations. Ts'ai went on, "I haven't heard about
the rest, except that among the Bestowals there's to be a short-shafted calf cart and a long-handled chowry."

Wang was miserably mortified by this, and later criticized
Ts'ai, saying, "In the old days, when I used to gather with Wang
Ch'eng and Juan Chan by the Lo River, I never heard in all the
realm that there was any son of Ts'ai K'o!" This he said because
of his pique over what Ts'ai had previously said in jest.

7. When Ch'u P'ou had newly crossed the Yangtze River (ca. 320), he
was once entering the east (Chekiang), and came to the Chin-ch'ang
Pavilion in Wu (Soochow).[1] Various prominent persons from the area of
Wu were gathered for a banquet in the pavilion. Although in the past
Ch'u P'ou had enjoyed an honorable reputation, at the time, since he
was traveling in haste, he was not recognized or singled out. They
instructed the waiters to give him a great deal of hot tea (ming-chih), but to put very few rice dumplings wrapped in bamboo leaves
(tsung) into the liquid. As soon as he finished drinking the tea they
would immediately add more, so that in the end he never got to eat
his fill.

After Ch'u had finished drinking (the tea), he nonchalantly raised
his hand and announced to the company, "My name is Ch'u P'ou." At
this the whole banquet broke up in alarm and everyone was thrown into
confusion.

[1]*CCTSH*: Once while I (Hsieh Hsin, fourth cent.) was looking for a
teacher, I was passing through Wu and came to the Glorious Gate
(Ch'ang-men), where suddenly I spied this pavilion flanking a
canal parallel to the river. The signboard on it read, "Chin-ch'ang" ("Metal Prosperity"). I asked an old man about it, and he
told me, "Long ago when Chu Mai-ch'en (second cent. B.C.) was
holding office under the Han, he was returning on his way to become governor of K'uai-chi Principality, and met his welcoming

officers, who were staying in an adjoining room in the inn here. (Not yet aware of his identity), they began competing with him for the best seats at table, until Mai-ch'en took out his (metal) seal and sash of office, whereupon all the officers prostrated themselves before him shamefacedly and took the lower seats. Because of this incident they built a pavilion here and called it 'Chin-shang' ('Metal-wound'). It's just that the original meaning of the words was lost (that the pavilion is now known by the homophonous name, 'Chin-ch'ang')."

8. While Wang Hsi-chih was in the south,[1] whenever Chancellor Wang Tao wrote him a letter he would always sigh in disappointment over his sons and nephews (*chih*). "Hu-t'un, Tiger-piglet (Wang P'eng-chih), and Hu-tu, Tiger-calf (Wang Piao-chih)," he wrote, "are turning out to be just like (their names)."

[1]Since this is the only place in *SSHY* where "the south" (*nan*) is used alone to designate a place, there is some ambiguity about the location. Kawakatsu et al. in their translation identify it with K'uai-chi, in Chekiang, but that area is usually referred to as "the east" in other anecdotes. Furthermore, Wang Hsi-chih did not become governor of K'uai-chi until 348, nine years after Wang Tao's death. Yang Yung in his notes on this passage attempts to identify it with Nan Commandery, in Hupei, noting that Wang Hsi-chih once served as governor of Chiang Province, for which Nan Commandery was sometimes the administrative seat. But in this case also the appointment followed Wang Tao's death by at least a year.

9. Once when Ch'u P'ou was descending southward (from the capital), Sun Ch'o saw him on board the boat, and in the course of their conversation they touched on Liu T'an's death (ca. 347). Sun wept profusely, and took the occasion to chant the words (from the "Songs"):

> "With this man's passing (*wang*),
> The state has suffered sorely."[1]

Ch'u, becoming very angry, replied, "In his whole life Liu T'an never had any relations with you, and yet now you're presenting this pose toward other people!"

Holding back his tears, Sun said to Ch'u, "You should remember me (too, when I'm gone)!" His contemporaries all laughed at him for being so talented, yet at the same time so vulgar by nature. (*CS* 75.34a)

[1]"Songs," No. 264, stanza 5. The original context requires the following reading:

> "People have fled away (*wang*);
> The state has suffered sorely."

10. (Ca. 346) the General Governing the West (stationed in Wu-ch'ang, Hupei), Hsieh Shang, wrote a letter to Yin Hao, who was then governor of Yang Province (Kiangsu-Chekiang), requesting the governorship of K'uai-chi Principality (Chekiang) on Liu T'an's behalf.[1]

Yin replied, "Liu T'an is the biggest of all the swashbucklers (*hsia*), who promotes the interests of those who agree with him and is vindictive against those who disagree. He's constantly talking about having you degraded drastically; yet, after all that, are you still running errands for him?"

[1] Hsieh Shang's cousin, Hsieh An, was Liu T'an's brother-in-law.

11. When Huan Wen invaded Lo-yang (in 356), he crossed to the north by way of the Huai and Ssu rivers.[1] Climbing to the turret of his ship (*p'ing-ch'eng lou*) with his subordinate officers, he looked out over the Central Plain, and with deep feeling said, "For causing the Sacred Land to be engulfed (by barbarians) and to lie waste for a hundred years, Wang Yen and those about him can't escape bearing the blame!"[2]

His aide-de-camp, Yüan Hung, answered him forthrightly, "Fate naturally brings its falls and rises; why was it necessarily the fault of Wang Yen and those about him?"

Coloring angrily, Huan Wen turned about and said to all who were present, "Have you gentlemen ever heard of Liu Piao (d. 208)? He owned a large ox weighing a thousand catties. It ate ten times as much fodder and beans as ordinary oxen, but when it came to bearing heavy burdens or traveling long distances, it wasn't even the equal of a sick calf. When Ts'ao Ts'ao invaded Ching Province (Hupei, in 203) he cooked the ox to feast his officers and men. At the time everyone expressed delight." Huan's intention was to make an analogy with Yüan Hung. Everyone present was frightened, and even Yüan himself turned pale. (*CS* 98.20b-21a)

[1] For a discussion of the water route to the north from the Yangtze Delta in ancient and medieval times, see Hibino Takeo, "*Suikeichū Gisuihen o yomu*" ("Notes on the 'I River Chapter' of the *Shui-ching chu*"), *Ritsumeikan bungaku* 180 (1960), 754-757. The Ssu River flowed southward through Shantung into the Huai, which, in turn, could be reached by lakes and canals from the Yangtze.

[2] *PWKS*: Although Wang Yen occupied an exalted office, he did not restrict himself with its duties. The contemporary age was so influenced by him that people felt ashamed to talk about the Moral Teaching (*ming-chiao*), and from clerks in the Imperial Secretariat on down, everybody admired the principle of folding the hands in silence, and took the neglect of duty for their ideal. Although all was still at peace within the Four Seas, those who understood the true state of affairs realized that they were on the verge of ruin.

CYC: When Wang Yen was about to be killed by Shih Lo (in 311), he said to those about him, "If our group had not revered frivolity and emptiness (*fu-hsü*), we never would have come to this."

12. Yüan Hung and Fu T'ao were serving together on Huan Wen's staff. Every time Huan had an outing or a banquet, he would always refer to them as "Yüan-Fu." Yüan felt extremely insulted by this, and often complained to Huan, saying, "Your Excellency's generous intentions are still not sufficient to bring glory to the officers of state. As long as I'm placed shoulder to shoulder with Fu T'ao, what disgrace is equal to this?" (*CS* 92.29a)

13. While Kao Jou was in retirement in the east (K'uai-chi) he was held in very great esteem by Hsieh Shang. But after he came out to

the capital (Chien-k'ang), he was not recognized by either Wang Meng or Liu T'an. Hsieh Shang said, "Recently I've seen Kao Jou writing memorials in large numbers, but so far he's gotten no results."

Liu T'an replied, "Naturally he can't live in an out-of-the-way place, and without any rank in his little corner (*kâk-ńẑi̯ak) write proposals and treatises for other people."

When Kao Jou heard of it, he said, "I had nothing to ask from him." Someone repeated his remark to Liu T'an, who said, "Indeed, I, too, have nothing to offer him." However, whenever he was going to an outing or a banquet, he would always write to his hosts, "You may invite the magistrate of An-ku." The magistrate of An-ku was Kao Jou.[1]

[1]*KJCH*: Kao Jou was married to the daughter of Hu-wu Fu-chih, who in her twentieth year had the perceptiveness of someone twice her age and was moreover pure and gracious in appearance, near to being a lady of the upper class. Jou's family estate was affluent, and after he had quit his post as aide to the director of works, and magistrate of An-ku Prefecture (Chekiang), he built a home by the Ch'üan Stream in Tung-shan Prefecture (Chekiang). Since his desire for an active life was slight, and moreover since he loved to amuse himself in company with his worthy wife, he had the intention of remaining there the rest of his life. But when the president of the Imperial Secretariat, Ho Ch'ung, selected him to be aide to the General Crowning the Army, he responded to the summons, albeit with the gravest reluctance. Bound together with tender affection, he and his wife were unable to part from each other, and the poems and letters they sent back and forth were limpidly beautiful and poignant.

14. Liu T'an, Chiang Pin, Wang Piao-chih, and Sun Ch'o were once seated together at a party. Chiang and Wang had mutually contemptuous expressions on their faces. Chiang made a threatening gesture with his hand toward Wang and shouted, "You rapacious clerk!" His tone and expression were both extremely harsh.

Liu T'an, looking around at Chiang, asked, "Is this real anger, and not just the *sound* of ugly words or the *sight* of boorish looks?"[1]

[1]*SSHY* Comm.: Liu T'an meant that it was not so much that Chiang's remark was ugly or boorish (for that could have been a pose), but that he actually *was* angry at Wang (an unpardonable breach of manners).

15. When Sun Ch'o composed the "Eulogy to Master Shang-ch'iu"[1] in his "Eulogies on the Immortals" (*Lieh-hsien tsan*), he wrote:

> "What he is herding--what are they?
> They seem almost to be not real pigs.
> If they should meet with wind or clouds,
> They'd soar like dragons in the air."[2]

The majority of his contemporaries thought it was a capably written piece of verse, but Wang Shu said to the others, "Recently I saw a composition by the son of the Sun family in which he asked, 'What are they?' Well, they were real pigs."

[1]*LHC*: Shang-ch'iu-tzu Chin was a native of Shang-i (Shensi) who was fond of blowing the thirty-six-pipe mouth organ (*yü*) while he

herded pigs. At age seventy he had neither married a wife nor
grown old. When people asked about the essentials of his way of
life he would say, "I only eat old thistles (*shu*) and calamus
(*ch'ang-p'u*) roots, and drink water. In this way I don't get hungry or old, that's all." When the noble and wealthy heard of it
and tried eating this diet, they could never last through a year
before quitting, and claimed there must be some secret formula.
The Commentary supplies the first stanza of the "Eulogy":

> "Shang-ch'iu stands above the crowd,
> Holding his staff, he blows the *yü*,
> Thirsty, he drinks from chilly springs,
> And hungry, eats the calamus."

[2] See "Book of Changes" Hex. 1 (Ch'ien) *Wên-yen-chuan* (Wilhelm II,
15): Clouds follow the dragon; winds follow the tiger.

16. (In 362) Huan Wen wanted to have the capital moved back to Loyang, in order to promote the work of enlarging and pacifying the empire. Sun Ch'o sent up a memorial warning against such a move in
which the argumentation was extremely reasonable.[1]

When Huan saw the memorial, he mentally accepted it, but at the
same time was angry with Sun for disagreeing with him. He sent someone to convey his thoughts to Sun, saying, "Why don't you reread your
own 'Poetic Essay on Fulfilling My Original Resolve' (*Sui-ch'u fu*),[2]
instead of forcing your way into other people's and the state's affairs?" (*CS* 56.17a-19b)

[1] The full text appears in Sun's biography, *CS* 56.17a-19b. The Commentary quotes the following excerpts (cf. *CS* 56.17b): "When Emperor Chung-tsung (Ssu-ma Jui, r. 317-322) took his dragon
flight . . . he depended in reality on the ten-thousand-*li* Long
River (the Yangtze) to mark his northern boundary and protect
him . . . Otherwise the barbarian horses would long since have
trampled the ground of Chien-k'ang, and the area east of the river
would have become the hunting ground of jackals and wolves." (The
second sentence is a paraphrase rather than a quotation of the *CS*
text.)

[2] The Commentary summarizes the contents as "setting forth the doctrine of 'stopping when one has enough' (*Lao-tzu* 44). See above,
SSHY II, 84, n. 1, for the preface of the essay.

17. Sun Ch'o and his older brother Sun T'ung once went to Hsieh An's
house to spend the night, and their conversation on this occasion was
extremely miscellaneous and trivial. Hsieh's wife, Lady Liu, was behind the wall listening and heard everything they said. The next day,
on returning (from escorting the Sun brothers home), Hsieh asked his
wife, "What did you think of last night's guests?"

Lady Liu replied, "In my late elder brother's home (Liu T'an, d.
ca. 347) there were never any guests like these." Hsieh appeared
deeply embarrassed. (*TPYL* 405)

18. (The future) Emperor Chien-wen (Ssu-ma Yü) was once conversing
with Hsü Hsün. Hsü said, "Let's discuss the problem of the conflict
between loyalty to ruler or parent," whereupon Emperor Chien-wen made
no further response. After Hsü had left, he said, "Hsü Hsün certainly
should not have gone so far as this!"[1]

¹*Ping Yüan PC* (cf. *SKWei* 11.20a, comm.): The Wei captain of the imperial guard (i.e., the 'Crown Prince,' Ts'ao P'ei, while Later Han was still ostensibly in power, ca. 210) was once holding a discussion with various worthies, and said, "Suppose now you have one medicinal pill which can cure one man's illness, and your ruler and your father are both sick. Should you give it to your ruler or to your father?"

Everyone spoke in clamorous confusion, some in favor of the father and some of the ruler. Ping Yüan (who was then the captain's senior administrator) stated categorically, "Father and son are one stock; there's no problem."

SSHY Comm.: The relation between ruler and parent has been like this since antiquity. I don't quite understand why Emperor Chien-wen disparaged Hsü's intentions.

19. After Hsieh Wan's defeat at Shou-ch'un (Anhui, in 359),¹ he wrote a letter to Wang Hsi-chih in which he said, "I'm ashamed to have betrayed your former kindness."

Pushing the letter aside, Wang said, "This was the self-admonition of the sage-kings, Yü and T'ang!"²

¹I.e., his rout by the Former Yen (307-370). See *TCTC* 100.3176-7.

²Founders respectively of Hsia (trad. 2205-1766) and Shang (1766-1122). See *Tso-chuan*, Chuang 11; Legge V, 88): Yü and T'ang blamed themselves, and their prospering was great because of it.

SSHY Comm.: Yü and T'ang blamed themselves, even with their sagelike moral power, and therefore they were able to prosper. But in this case Hsieh Wan went to his defeat for disregarding the rules of war. Even though he should still blame himself, what help was there in that? It was for this reason that Wang did not approve of Wan. (I have emended the text following Wang Li-ch'i's collation, changing *k'o*, "may," to *ho*, "what," and *wang* (for Wang Hsi-chih) to *pu*, "not.")

20. A transverse flute (*ti*) which Ts'ai Yung (d. 192) had once made from a bamboo rafter which had caught his eye,¹ Sun Ch'o allowed a female dancer to brandish about and break. On hearing of it, Wang Hsi-chih cried out in great indignation, "A priceless musical instrument which has been a family heirloom for three generations,² that blankety-blank idiot³ son of the Sun family has smashed and broken!"

¹"Preface to the Poetic Essay on the Long Flute," by Fu T'ao (*CTFHsü*): My colleague, Huan I*, has an old long flute. The old man who transmitted it to him said it was made by Ts'ai Yung. Long ago when Ts'ai was fleeing from the troubles (at the end of Later Han) to the area south of the Yangtze River, he spent the night in an inn at K'o-t'ing (near K'uai-chi), whose rafters were made of bamboo. Looking up and seeing the rafters, Ts'ai Yung said, "That's good bamboo," and selecting one, he made it into a flute, the sound of whose notes was uniquely beautiful. It has been handed down through successive generations to the present day.

²*San-tsu shou*. The Commentary gives the alternate reading, *t'ai*, "terrace," for the third character.

³*Hui-wa-tiao* (*χjwei-ngwa-tieu*), literally, "viper-tile-string-of-

cash." The Commentary gives an alternate reading, *wang-fan* (*'wâng-b'iwɒm), "emaciated-common," for the first two characters. The variants suggest either a corrupt text or some colloquial swearword for which no standard characters existed. The last character, *tiao*, in its alternate form, could conceivably be a scribal error for *tai*, "idiot," and I have so translated.

21. Wang T'an-chih did not get on at all with the monk Chih Tun. Wang called Chih a "specious sophist," and Chih characterized Wang with the words, "Wearing a greasy cap and tattered cloth single robe, with a copy of the 'Tso Commentary' tucked under his arm, chasing along behind Cheng Hsüan's (d. 200) carriage--I ask you, what sort of dust-and-filth bag is he, anyhow?"[1]

[1] *YL*: Chih Tun said, "Wang T'an-chih, wearing a greasy cap, with the 'Tso Commentary' tucked under his arm and chasing after Cheng Hsüan, considers himself his foremost disciple. But, to speak candidly, he never gets away from being a mere dust-and-filth bag."

22. Sun Ch'o composed an obituary for Wang Meng (d. 347), which went,

"I together with the Master--
A friendship not for power or gain.
Our hearts were pure as limpid water,[1]
As we shared this mystic flavor."

When Wang Meng's grandson, Wang Kung, saw it, he remarked, "The talented gentleman is immodest. Why would my late grandfather ever have had any dealings with this man?" (*TPYL* 596)

[1] See "Record of Rites" XXXIII, 23 (Legge, *Li Ki* II, 348), misquoted by Liu Chün in the Commentary under the influence of *Chuang-tzu* XX, 13ab (Watson, p. 215): "The friendship of gentlemen is tasteless as water; that of petty men is sweet as new wine."

23. Hsieh An once said to his sons and nephews, "It's only Hsieh Wan who alone in our family will have a thousand-year reputation."
Hsieh Hsüan said, "The feelings Wan carries in his bosom aren't yet sufficiently humble; how does he alone get to have such a reputation?"[1]

[1] For an example of Hsieh Wan's arrogance, see above, *SSHY* XXIV, 14.

24. With a knowing air Yü Ho said to Hsieh An, "P'ei Ch'i relates in his 'Forest of Conversations' (*YL*)[1] that Hsieh An said of P'ei Ch'i, 'P'ei's not a bad fellow; what need is there anymore to drink wine?' And in another passage P'ei says that Hsieh An characterized Chih Tun,[2] saying, 'He's like Chiu-fang Kao[3] and his judging of horses. Chiu-fang paid no attention to whether the horses were black or brown, but picked them for their spirit and endurance.'"
Hsieh An replied, "I never made either one of those statements. P'ei himself just made them up out of whole cloth, that's all!"
Yü's mood was considerably dampened by this, and accordingly he recited for Hsieh Wang Hsün's "Poetic Essay on Passing Beneath Master Huang's Wineshop" *Ching Huang-kung chiu-lu-hsia fu*.[4]
When he had finished reading it, Hsieh said absolutely nothing

either in praise or criticism of the work, but merely remarked, "So you're now a scholar of Mr. P'ei, eh?"[5]

From this time on the "Forest of Conversations" fell into disrepute. Any copies still in existence today were all made previous to this incident, and even these no longer include any conversations attributed to Hsieh An.

[1] HCYC: In the mid-Lung-ho era (362), P'ei Ch'i of Ho-tung (Shansi) gathered noteworthy conversations and repartee from the Han and Wei dynasties down to the present, and called them the "Forest of Conversations." His contemporaries for the most part liked their contents, and the style was flowing and smooth. Later it was alleged that the incidents involving Hsieh An were untrue, and moreover someone at a gathering at Hsieh's place recited the "Poetic Essay on Master Huang's Wineshop," composed by the director of instruction, Wang Hsün, which was included in it. In addition to harboring resentment against Wang (see n. 5 below), Hsieh An remarked to the reciter, "So now you're a scholar of Mr. P'ei, eh?" And from this point on everybody deprecated its contents.

Among Hsieh An's fellow villagers was a person who had quit his post as magistrate of Chung-su Prefecture (Kwangtung), who came to visit An. An asked him what he had gotten for his homecoming emolument. He replied, "Ling-nan (Kwangtung) is a poverty-stricken area. All I have is a batch of fifty thousand palm-leaf fans (*p'u-k'uei shan*). What's worse is that, since it's the wrong season, they're a glut on the market."

An thereupon picked one out from among them and carried it in his hand, and after that throughout the capital lords and commoners vied with each other in emulating him, wearing the fans on their persons. The market price went up several-fold, and within ten days to a month they were all sold out. Thus "whatever An liked grew feathers and fur," and "whatever he hated became boils and bruises." One word of criticism by Hsieh An would devalue perfect excellence for a thousand years, whereas in the case of something he approved of, it would shoot up a nonexistent value to a hundred pieces of gold. Can those in high position afford to be careless about their likes and dislikes, or of their granting and taking away of approval?

[2] CTC (cf. KSC 4; Taishō 50.348b): Chih Tun would always lift out the main ideas of a text without paying attention to the images or analogies used to illustrate them, and in analyzing or explaining paragraphs and sentences there would occasionally be omissions. His literal-minded disciples for the most part considered this dubious, but when Hsieh An heard of it he praised Chih, saying, "This is the way Chiu-fang Kao judged horses, etc."

[3] Lieh-tzu (VIII, 95; Graham, p. 170): Po Yüeh said to Duke Mu of Ch'in (r. 659-621 B.C.), "Among those with whom I carry firewood and bind vegetables is one Chiu-fang Kao. This man's knowledge of horses is not inferior to my own."

The duke sent him to look for a horse. When he returned he announced, "I've found one. It's a stallion and brown." But when the duke sent someone to fetch it, it turned out to be a mare and black. The duke said, "If he can't tell a male from a female in furry animals, how can he know anything about horses?"

Po Yüeh replied, "When someone like Kao looks at a horse, it's a heaven-given faculty. He gets the fine points and pays no attention to the coarser ones. He gets at the inside and pays no attention to the outside. He sees what he sees and doesn't see what he doesn't see. He looks for what he's looking for and leaves aside what he's not looking for. When someone like him judges a horse you have something more valuable than horses." As predicted, it turned out the horse had legs which would carry it a thousand *li*.

[4] See above, *SSHY* IV, 90; XVII, 2; (see also Hsiang Hsiu's "Poetic Essay on an Old Friendship" (*Ssu-chiu fu*; *WH* 16.8ab).

[5] Though Hsieh's ostensible objection to the *YL* was P'ei's presumed disregard for facts, it seems his real annoyance sprang from his feud with Wang Hsün, who had divorced Hsieh's niece; see above, *SSHY* XVII, 15, n. 1. As for the factual reliability of Wang Hsün's poetic essay, Yü Ho's own father, Yü Liang, had already cast doubt on it; see above, *SSHY* XVII, 2, n. 2.

25. Wang T'an-chih was not recognized by Chih Tun, and accordingly composed a treatise on "Why a Śramaṇa is not Capable of Becoming an Eminent Gentleman" (*Sha-men pu-te wei kao-shih lun*), the general outline of which maintained that an eminent gentleman always lives in a state of mental freedom, harmonious and joyful, while the śramaṇa, although claiming to be beyond earthly ties, is, on the contrary, more than ever in bondage to his doctrine and cannot be said to be fully self-possessed in his feelings and disposition.

26. Someone asked Ku K'ai-chih, "Why don't you ever chant poems in the manner of the scholars of Lo-yang (*Lo-sheng yung*)?"

Ku replied, "Why should I make a noise like an old slave woman?" (*CS* 92.36a)

27. Yin Chi and Yü Heng were both grandsons on their mothers' side[1] of Hsieh Shang. Yin was quick-witted from his youth, but Yü was never appreciated. One time they both went to visit Hsieh An. An stared intently at Yin Chi and then said, "A-ch'iao, you certainly resemble your grandfather, Hsieh Shang."

At this Yü muttered in a low voice, "How does it turn out that he resembles him?"

Hsieh An continued, "Ch'ao's cheeks are like Hsieh Shang's."

Yü said, "If his cheeks resemble Hsieh Shang's, is that enough to make him a great man?"

[1] *Hsieh SP*: Hsieh Shang's oldest daughter, Seng-yao, married Yü Ho (Heng's father), and his second daughter, Seng-shao, married Yin K'ang (Chi's father).

28. An old characterization of Han Po went, "Seize his elbow, and there's no character or bone (*feng-ku*)."[1]

[1] *SL*: Fan Ch'i said, "Han Po is like a fleshy (i.e., boned) duck."

29. After Fu Hung had rebelled against the Later Ch'in (384-417) and returned his allegiance to the Chin (in 384), the grand tutor, Hsieh An, often entertained him. Hung fancied himself to have ability, and

in most cases enjoyed getting the better of other people. On one occasion there was no one present who could break him, but it happened that Wang Hui-chih arrived, and the grand tutor had them converse together. Wang merely stared at him for a long time, then, turning, said to the grand tutor, "He, too, in the end is no different from the others." Fu withdrew in great embarrassment.

30. When the monk Chih Tun entered the east (K'uai-chi), he went to see Wang Hui-chih and his brothers.[1] After his return to Chien-k'ang someone asked him, "After seeing the Wangs, what do you think of them?"

Chih replied, "I saw a flock of white-necked crows (*pai-ching wu*)[2] and heard nothing but the sound of their loud caw-cawing."

[1] Beside Wang Hui-chih, Wang Hsi-chih had six other sons, four of whom are mentioned in other *SSHY* anecdotes: Ning-chih, Su-chih, Ts'ao-chih, and Hsien-chih.

[2] *Corvus torquatus*. These birds are usually seen alone or in pairs but join in noisy flocks in October and November. See Wilder, G. D., and Hubbard, H. W., *Birds of Northeastern China*, p. 127.

31. When Wang T'an-chih recommended Hsü Hsün to be appointed a clerk in the Board of Civil Office, Ch'ih T'an said, "The chancellor-prince (Ssu-ma Yü) is a lover of gossip (*hao-shih*), don't let Hsü Hsün get to sit at the head of the company."

32. Wang Ho-chih once said of Hsieh Yen, "He's as nervous and fidgety (*χwâk-χwâk*) as a falconer who's lost his falcon."

33. When Huan Hsüan saw someone who was not quick-witted, he would always say angrily, "I suppose if you got some pears from the Ai family,[1] you'd cook them before eating, wouldn't you?" (*SLF* 27; *TPYL* 969; *SWLC*, h u 26)

[1] The Commentary quotes an "old saying": "In Mo-ling (Chien-k'ang) there was a pear tree belonging to the Ai Chung family, whose fruit was extremely delicious and grew as large as *sheng*-measures, and which would dissolve as soon as they entered the mouth. It was said that stupid persons who did not discriminate between flavors, after getting these good pears, would cook them before eating."

CHAPTER XXVII

Guile and Chicanery

1. When Ts'ao Ts'ao was young he used to be fond of playing the knight-errant (*yu-hsia*)[1] with Yüan Shao. Observing that a certain man had just taken a wife, they took advantage of the situation to steal into the courtyard of the groom's house and during the night's festivities shouted out, "There's a kidnapper about!"

As the people inside the "blue-green hut" (*ch'ing-lu*)[2] all rushed out to look, Ts'ao Ts'ao entered, and drawing his sword seized the bride and made off with her. Reemerging together with Yüan Shao, they lost their way and landed in a bramble patch, from which Shao was unable to extricate himself. Ts'ao thereupon shouted again in a loud voice, "The kidnapper is here!"

In a desperate panic Shao wrenched himself free, and in this way they both escaped.[3] (*TPYL* 699)

[1] A full discussion of this form of swashbuckling may be found in James J. Y. Liu, *The Chinese Knight-Errant*, London and Chicago, 1967.

[2] *YYTT* 1: According to the wedding ritual of the Northern Dynasties (385-589), blue-green cloths were draped to form a room just inside and outside the gate, which was called the "blue-green hut." It was within this space that the bride and groom exchanged salutations and the groom welcomed his bride.

[3] *TMC* (cf. *SKWei* 1.2a, comm.): Ts'ao Ts'ao's baby name was A-man. When he was young he was fond of guile and chicanery, and roamed about freely without restraint.

SSTY (cf. *SKWei* 1.2ab, comm.): When Ts'ao Ts'ao was young he was fond of knight-errantry and lived dissolutely without cultivating his conduct. Once he entered without authorization into the home of the attendant, Chang Jang. When Chang pointed him out with his hand in the courtyard, Ts'ao vaulted over the wall and left. He possessed strength surpassing that of other men, and consequently no one could harm him.

2. Once while Ts'ao Ts'ao was on campaign he lost the way to a water supply and the three armies were all suffering from thirst. At this point he issued the order: "Ahead is a large grove of plum trees loaded with fruit. The sweet-sour juice may serve to quench your thirst."

When the officers and men heard this their mouths all began to water, and by this means they were able to reach a spring which lay ahead of them. (*PTSC* 14; *CHC* 9; *SLF* 26; *TPYL* 57, 295, 970; *SWLC*, hou 25)

3. Ts'ao Ts'ao used to say, "Whenever anyone wants to threaten me, I always feel a presentiment of it in my heart." Accordingly he said to one of his underlings with whom he was intimate, "Hide a dagger in your bosom and come stealthily to my side. I will, of course, say that I feel a presentiment in my heart and have you seized and punished. But, for your part, don't say a word about having been asked to do it, and nothing more will come of it. What's more, I'll reward you generously."

When the man was seized he was completely confident, supposing there was nothing to be afraid of, and as a result he was decapitated. Until the moment of his death this man was unaware of what was happening. But Ts'ao Ts'ao's subordinates thought it was all real, and those who were plotting rebellion suppressed their feelings.[1] (*PTSC* 20; *TPYL* 393; *SWLC*, hou 21)

[1] *TMC*: Once while Ts'ao Ts'ao was in the army the grain in the warehouse was insufficient. He said privately to the mess officer, "What shall we do?"

The mess officer replied, "We might use a reduced *hu*-measure to satisfy them."

Ts'ao said, "Good."

Later it was rumored in the ranks that Ts'ao was cheating the men, so Ts'ao pointed out his mess officer, and behind his back circulated the rumor:

> "Using a small *hu*-measure
> He robbed the army's treasure,"

whereupon he had him decapitated. As he did so he said to the mess officer, "As a special case I must borrow your death in order to mollify the hearts of the men." His sudden changes and treacheries were all of this sort.

4. Ts'ao Ts'ao used to say, "No one may make a false move toward me while I'm asleep, or I'll immediately knife him without even realizing what I've done. All you attendants had better be extremely cautious about this."

Some time later he was feigning sleep when a person who was in his favor stealthily placed a coverlet over him, whereupon Ts'ao immediately knifed her to death. From this time on, whenever Ts'ao Ts'ao was asleep, none of his attendants dared approach him. (*PTSC* 20; *TPYL* 393; *SWLC*, hou 21)

5. When Yüan Shao was young he once dispatched a man by night to thrust a two-edged sword (*chien*) at Ts'ao Ts'ao (through the bed curtains). The thrust was a little low and failed to hit the mark. Ts'ao calculated that the next one would surely be higher, and therefore lay face down on the bed. When the sword struck again, it was, as expected, too high.[1] (*TPYL* 393, 706)

[1] *SSHY* Comm.: It was only later on that Yüan and Ts'ao, because of the tripartite division of the empire, began to go separate ways. Before this there is no record of any alienation or rift between them. What reason would Yüan have had to thrust at him with a sword?

6. After the generalissimo, Wang Tun, had begun his rebellion (in 323),[1] he bivouacked his troops at Ku-shu (west of Chien-k'ang). The Chin Emperor Ming (Ssu-ma Shao, r. 323-325), even though he possessed valor and martial ability, was still suspicious and fearful of Wang's intentions. Accordingly, donning his armor and riding a Pa-tsung (Szechwan) horse, he took in his hand a present of a gold horsewhip, and secretly went to investigate the position and strength of Wang's troops.

Ten or more *li* before he reached Wang's camp, there was an old woman innkeeper who kept a rest station and eating place. As the emperor passed by he stopped to rest, and said to the old woman, "Wang Tun has raised an army to plot rebellion, and suspicion and harm will befall all loyal and good subjects. The court is frightened and alarmed, and the gods of soil and grain are in trouble. So I've been working morning and night to spy on him, and I'm afraid my person and movements might possibly be detected, or that something may go awry. In the event of my being pursued, would you be so good as to conceal me?" Whereupon he presented the old woman innkeeper with the horsewhip and departed.

He traveled on to Tun's camp, made a tour through it, and then went out. Some of the officers noticed him and remarked, "This is no ordinary man!" Wang Tun, who was lying asleep, felt a sudden presentiment in his heart, and awaking said, "This must be the brown-bearded Hsien-pei slave who's come here!" Whereupon he ordered some horsemen to pursue him.[2]

After a while the pursuing officers began to sense they had been traveling a little too far, and therefore asked the old woman, "You haven't by any chance seen a brown-bearded man riding a horse past here, have you?"

The old woman answered, "He left long ago. You couldn't possibly catch up with him." Whereupon the horsemen gave up the thought of further pursuit and turned back. (*CS* 6.17b; *CHC* 22; *TPYL* 359; *TPKC* 403)

[1] *TCTC* 92.2911 dates Wang's arrival at Ku-shu in the fourth month of 323; *CS* 6.17b places this incident in the sixth month of 324.

[2] *IY*: The emperor went in person to Ku-shu. At the time Wang Tun was taking a nap. Majestically awaking with a start, he said, "There's a brown-haired Hsien-pei slave who's come into camp! Why haven't you bound and captured him?"

The emperor's mother, Lady Hsün, was a native of the (Hsien-pei) state of Yen (Hopei), so his appearance was similar to hers.

7. When Wang Hsi-chih[1] was under ten years old,[2] his uncle, the generalissimo, Wang Tun, was extremely fond of him, and frequently had him sleep within his own bed curtains.
   One morning (in 322?) the generalissimo had gotten out of bed first before Hsi-chih had gotten up. A short while later Ch'ien Feng entered the room and the two men started to discuss business. Forgetting all about the fact that Hsi-chih was still inside the bed curtains, Wang Tun proceeded to talk about his plot to rebel.
   Hsi-chih woke up, and after he heard what they were discussing, he realized there was no prospect of escaping alive. Accordingly he gagged and vomited, soiling his face and bedclothes, then feigned a deep sleep.
   Wang Tun was already half through discussing his business before he remembered that Hsi-chih had not yet gotten up. Then with a shock of alarm he cried, "There's no help for it but to put him out of the way!" But when he opened the curtains and saw the vomit spread in all directions, he believed that Hsi-chih really was in a deep sleep, and thereby the boy's life was preserved. At the time people praised Wang Hsi-chih for his sagacity. (CS 76.3b, of Wang Yün-chih)

   [1]*SSHY* Comm.: All accounts attribute this incident to Wang Yün-chih (ca. 303-342, the son of Wang Shu*, Tun's first cousin; see CS 76.3b). I suspect that the attribution here to Wang Hsi-chih is an error.

   [2]Since the attribution to Wang Hsi-chih is probably false in any case, the given age, "under (*chien*) ten," should perhaps be emended to "just (*ts'ai*) ten," after Shen's text, as Yang Yung suggests. Hsi-chih, who was born in 309, would have been about eleven. Yün-chih, on the other hand, who was born about 303, would have been at least in his late teens. The circumstances as related in CS 76.3b, that he had retired early "on the excuse of being drunk," and Tun's mental acceptance of drunkenness as the cause of the deep sleep and vomiting, all tend to confirm the older age.

8. T'ao K'an, having come down from the upper reaches of the Yangtze River to the aid of the capital during the troubles over Su Chün (in 328), ordered the execution of Yü Liang, saying, "It's necessary to sacrifice Yü Liang in order to mollify Su Chün."
   If Yü had wanted to take refuge or hide somewhere it would have been impossible, or if he had wanted to meet T'ao K'an face to face, he was afraid he would be apprehended, and he was in a quandary whether to go forward or backward. Wen Ch'iao urged Yü to go and visit T'ao K'an, saying, "Just prostrate yourself (*pai*) before him from a distance, and nothing further will come of it; I guarantee it for you."
   Yü Liang followed Wen's advice and went to see T'ao. As soon as he arrived he prostrated himself. T'ao himself got to his feet and stopped him, saying, "For what reason is Yü Yüan-kuei prostrating himself before T'ao Shih-heng?"
   When Yü had finished he again made his way down to the lowest seat. Again T'ao himself demanded that he come up and sit with him. After he was seated, Yü finally confessed his faults and blamed himself and made his profound apologies. Quite unconsciously T'ao found himself becoming generous and forgiving.[1] (CS 73.4b)

¹Cf. the similar story in *SSHY* XIV, 23, above.

CYC: At this time (328) Emperor Ch'eng (Ssu-ma Yen*, r. 326-324) was still in swaddling clothes (actually he was seven), and the empress dowager, Empress Mu (consort of Emperor Ming, and Yü Liang's niece), was regent. The president of the Central Secretariat, Yü Liang, as eldest maternal uncle, was in charge of the government and wished to pattern his administration after an elegant model and to extend the imperial sway to the Four Seas. Su Chün, however, was massing his men-at-arms and approaching the suburbs of Chien-k'ang, and had become a rallying point for fugitives.

Liang attempted to summon Chün to court, but neither Wang Tao nor Pien K'un wanted to do it. Liang said, "Su Chün is a jackal and a wolf; in the end he's bound to make trouble and rebellion. As Ch'ao Ts'o (a Legalist adviser of the Han Emperors Wen and Ching, 179-143 B.C.) said, 'Penalize them and they'll rebel; don't penalize them and they'll also rebel.'" Accordingly (in the emperor's name) he issued an indulgent rescript offering Chün the post of grand director of agriculture.

Chün angrily replied, "Yü Liang just wants to entice me in order to kill me." Whereupon he took possession of the capital.

When the General Pacifying the South, Wen Ch'iao, learned of the rebellion, he wept aloud, and, boarding a boat, dispatched his aide, Wang Ch'ien-ch'i, to propose the General Chastizing the West, T'ao K'an, as chief of the alliance (*meng-chu*), and together they went to the aid of the capital.

At the time Yü Liang had been badly defeated and had taken refuge with Ch'iao. Everyone was blaming Liang and belittling him, but Ch'iao held him in greater esteem and respect than ever, and divided his men-at-arms to match and support him.

9. Wen Ch'iao had lost his wife. The family of his paternal great-aunt (*tsung-ku*), Lady Liu,¹ because of the disorders of the times, had broken up and scattered. There was only one daughter left, very beautiful and intelligent, and the aunt entrusted Wen Ch'iao with the task of finding her a suitable husband. Wen, who had secret designs on marrying the girl himself, replied, "A good son-in-law is hard to find. But how would someone be who was merely like me?"

His great-aunt said, "This old battered relic is only looking for some crude means of survival, something adequate to comfort me for my remaining years. How could I presume to hope for someone like you?"

Wen then withdrew, and after a few days announced to his great-aunt, "I've already found a matrimonial candidate. His family and status are, in a general way, all right. The son-in-law himself is a famous official, in no way inferior to myself." So saying, he deposited an engagement present of a jade mirror stand (*ching-t'ai*). His great-aunt was utterly delighted.

After the wedding and the exchange of bowing, the girl pushed aside the silk fan² with her hand, clapped her palms together, and laughed aloud, saying, "I suspected all along that it was you, you old rascal! It turned out just the way the diviner said it would!"

The jade mirror stand had come into Wen Ch'iao's possession while he was serving as Liu K'un's senior administrator, during the northern expedition against Liu Ts'ung (in 314).³ (*IWLC* 40; *PSLT* 4, 6; *TPYL* 541, 702, 717, 805; *PTSC* 134, 136; *CHC* 25; *SLF* 9)

[1]*SSHY* Comm.: In the *Wen SP* it states that Ch'iao first married the daughter of Li Heng of Kao-p'ing (Shantung), then married the daughter of Wang Hsü* of Lang-yeh (Shantung), and last of all married the daughter of Ho Sui of Lu-chiang (Anhui). Nowhere is there any report of his having married a Lady Liu, so the present account is mistaken.

(A later commentator, calling himself Ku-k'ou, perhaps T'ang in date, adds: "'Lady Liu' merely refers to Ch'iao's father's aunt [*ku*]. It does not imply that her daughter's surname was Liu. Liu Chün's note is not quite to the point." However, Lady Liu, being Wen Ch'iao's father's paternal aunt, must have had the maiden name of Wen, and Liu could indeed have been her married name as well as the maiden name of her daughter, so Liu Chün's objection remains unanswered.)

[2]*HWCH* 1: According to the wedding ritual in olden times, an attendant boy would screen the bride with a silk-gauze fan. Removal of the fan (at the moment when the bride and groom first saw each other) was called "retiring the fan" (*ch'üeh-shan*).

[3]*WYCS*: In the second year of the Chien-hsing era (314) Wen Ch'iao became Liu K'un's provisional left assistant sergeant-at-arms and governor-general of military affairs at the front in the expedition against Liu Ts'ung of Former Chao (r. 310-318).

10. Chu-ko Hui's daughter, Wen-piao, was the wife of Yü Hui (d. 328). After she became a widow she vowed that she would never again leave her home in marriage. Now this girl's nature was extremely proper and firm, and there was no prospect of ever getting her to set foot again in a wedding carriage. But since Chu-ko Hui had promised her in marriage to Chiang Pin, he moved the family to be near the Chiangs. At that time, tricking his daughter, he had announced, "It's time to move," whereupon all the members of the family left at once, leaving the daughter behind alone. When she woke up to what had happened, it was already too late for her to leave.

When Chiang Pin came that evening the girl cried and carried on at great length, but after several days she gradually subsided. Chiang Pin then came in after dark to spend the night, but still remained on the opposite bed. Later, observing that her mood was growing calmer, Pin at length feigned a nightmare, not awaking for a long while as his cries and gasps became more and more agitated. Finally the girl called for her slave girl and said, "Call to Mr. Chiang and wake him up!"

At this Chiang leaped up and came over to her, saying, "I myself am a man of the world. What have my nightmares to do with you that I should be called? But since we have this mutual relation, you can't very well avoid talking with me." The girl was silent and ashamed, and after this her feelings and attitude grew more and more affectionate.[1] (*TPYL* 541)

[1]*SSHY* Comm.: Chu-ko Hui's pure brilliance and Chiang Pin's generous savoir faire were such that surely they would never act contrary to the proper code laid down by the sages, nor practice the foul behavior of the Man and I barbarians. Liu I-ch'ing's words are too contemptuous.

11. When the monk Chih Min-tu was about to flee southward across the Yangtze River (between 326 and 342),[1] he had as his companion a northern (ts'ang) monk. Min-tu plotted with him, saying, "If we go to the land east of the river with nothing but the old theory, I'm afraid we'll never manage to eat." So together they concocted the "Theory of Mental Nonexistence" (hsin-wu i).[2]

As it turned out, this northern monk never succeeded in crossing the river, but Min-tu actually expounded on the theory in the south for many years.

Later another northern monk came south to whom the former monk had entrusted the following message: "Tell Min-tu for me that the 'Theory of Nonexistence' is completely unfounded. We concocted this scheme as an expedient to save ourselves from starvation and nothing more. Don't go on with it; otherwise you'll be betraying the Tathāgata."

[1] Cf. *KSC* 4 (*Taishō* 50.347a).

MTSMTM: Chih Min-tu was talented and knowledgeable, pure and outstanding.

MTT: Chih Min-tu, refined yet plain,
Who love what is, yet pluck the new,
Holding them both for all to see,
You can surpass all other men.

The world admires your matchlessness;
All vie to get your precious jewels;
The lone paulownia on I's sunward slope,
The floating chime stone by Ssu's banks.

[2] *SSHY* Comm.: The "old theory" stated: "When one possesses omniscience (*chung-chih*), and through it is able to illumine all things, then the myriad bonds come to an end, and this state is called Empty Nonexistence (*k'ung-wu*). Because it abides eternally and does not change, it is called Subtle Existence (*miao-yu*)."

The "new theory" of Nonexistence, on the other hand, states: "The substance (*t'i*) of omniscience is hollow, like the Great Void (*t'ai-hsü*). Though void, it is nevertheless able to know; though nonexistent, it is nevertheless able to respond. That which occupies the Ideal (*tsung*) and reaches the Ultimate (*chi*), is it not Nonexistence alone?" (Cf. W. Liebenthal, *Book of Chao*, Peking, 1948, pp. 151-52, and Zürcher, *Conquest*, pp. 99-102; 353, n. 88).

12. The ugliness of Wang T'an-chih's younger brother, Wang Ch'u-chih, was unsurpassed. Even by the time he was grown no one had offered to make any marriage contract with him.

Sun Ch'o had a daughter, A-heng, who was also mean and perverse. She, too, had no prospect of marriage. Accordingly, Sun went to visit Wang T'an-chih and asked to see Ch'u-chih.

After he had seen him, he proceeded to dissimulate, saying, "It turns out this man is perfectly all right, after all. He's not at all like what people have said about him. How could it have happened that until now no marriage has ever been arranged for him? Now I have a daughter, who, when all's said and done, isn't at all bad. But for an insignificant and impoverished gentleman (*han-shih*) like me it wouldn't be proper to make any arrangement with you. I wish you would have Ch'u-chih marry the girl."

Wang T'an-chih was delighted, and notified his father, Wang Shu, saying, "Sun Ch'o has just now come and out of the blue says he wants a wedding contract with Ch'u-chih."

Wang Shu was both surprised and pleased. It was only after the wedding had taken place and the girl's obstinacy and garrulousness were well on the way to surpassing Ch'u-chih's own that they realized how Sun Ch'o had taken them in.

13. Fan Wang as a person was fond of utilizing sagacious devices, but occasionally through excessive devising, he came to grief. It happened once that after being dismissed from office (in 369), he was living in Tung-yang Commandery (Chekiang). The grand marshal, Huan Wen, was then stationed in Nan-chou (at Ku-shu, in Anhui), so Fan went there intending to throw in his lot with him. At the time (ca. 372) Huan was just on the point of summoning the malcontented and the frustrated to arms with a view to overthrowing the court. Moreover, while Fan Wang was living in the capital he had from the beginning always had a fine reputation. Huan supposed that Fan had come so great a distance just to throw in his lot with himself, and his happiness knew no bounds.

When Fan entered the hall, Huan's whole body was stretched taut with anticipation, and he talked and laughed with great delight. Turning around he remarked to his secretary, Yüan Hung, "Lord Fan for the time being can serve as minister grand ordinary."

Fan had no sooner seated himself than Huan thanked him for his kindness in coming so great a distance. But although Fan had indeed intended to throw in his lot with Huan, he nevertheless became apprehensive that if he catered to the trend of the times he might lose his reputation, so in the end he replied, "Although I cherish this audience, it happens that my deceased son is secretly buried hereabouts, and it's for this reason that I've come to visit his grave." Huan was visibly disappointed. All his former humility and deference in one moment came to an abrupt end.[1] (CS 75.25b-26a)

[1]CHS: Earlier Huan had invited Fan Wang to be his senior administrator while Huan was general of the western expedition against Shu (in 347), and later he memorialized to have him made governor of Chiang Province (Kiangsi), but Fan did not accept either post. On returning to the capital he took the occasion to request to become grand warden of Tung-yang Commandery. Huan bitterly resented him for this.

Subsequently, Fan was serving as governor of Hsü Province (northern Kiangsu and Anhui). When Huan started on his northern expedition against Yen (in 369), he ordered Fan to proceed from Liang Principality (Kiangsu), but Fan missed the appointed time, and Huan, harboring a deep resentment, memorialized to have Fan reduced to commoner status.

Fan then lived in Wu (Soochow), and later came to Ku-shu to see Huan, who said to his underlings, "Since Fan Wang has finally come to see me, I ought to promote him to General Protecting the Army." But after several days Fan excused himself to return home. Huan said, "You've only just come; why are you leaving again so soon?"

Fan replied, "My little son of several years died, and since the past years have been a succession of turmoil, as an expedient

I buried him in this place and have come to pay my respects. Since my business is completed, I'm leaving, that's all." Huan was all the more angry at him for this and never paid any more attention to him.

14. When Hsieh Hsüan was young he was fond of wearing a fragrant sachet of purple silk gauze dangling over his hand. His uncle, the grand tutor, Hsieh An, disliked it, but did not want to hurt his feelings, so as a ruse he gambled with him, and, winning the sachet, immediately burned it. (*CS* 79.12b; *PTSC* 136; *TPYL* 389, 704)

CHAPTER XXVIII

Dismissal from Office

1. At the time of the Western Chin court (265-316), when he was a young man, Chu-ko Hung had a reputation for purity, and was held in honor by Wang Yen. Contemporary character estimates even compared him with Wang. Later he was slandered by members of the faction of his stepmother's family, who accused him of being "insane and seditious."
 On the eve of his banishment to a distant place, his friends, all followers of Wang Yen, went to visit him in prison to bid him farewell. Hung asked, "Why is the court banishing me?"
 Wang replied, "They say you're 'insane and seditious.'"
 Hung said, "If I'm seditious, then I should be killed; and if insane, why should I be banished?" (*TPYL* 739)

2. As Huan Wen entered Shu (western Szechwan, in 347)[1] and had come into the midst of the Three Gorges,[2] someone in the ranks captured a baby gibbon (*yüan*). Its dam, clinging to the bank and crying pitifully, followed for over a hundred *li* and would not go away. Finally she leaped onto the boat and on landing immediately expired. When they tore her open and looked into her abdomen they found her entrails all cut, inch by inch. When Huan Wen heard of it he was furious, and ordered the man dismissed.

[1] In the campaign against Li Shih; see above, *SSHY* VII, 20.

[2] See *SSHY* VII, 20, n. 4.
 ChingCC: The Four Gorges stretch along the Yang-tze for several hundred *li*. Along both banks continuous mountains rise with almost no breaks. Layered cliffs and heaped-up battlements darken the sky, obscuring the sun. Frequently there are gibbons high up on the cliff whose cries are long-drawn, shrill, and distant. A fisherman's song goes:

> "Of the Three Gorges of Pa-tung, the Wu Gorge
> is the crown;

One cry of the gibbon and tears have soaked
my gown.

3. After Yin Hao had been dismissed (in 353) and was living in Hsin-an (western Chekiang),[1] all day long he kept writing characters in the air. Officials and commoners of Yang Province (Kiangsu-Anhui-Chekiang), remembering his past favors while he was governor (346-350), followed him about secretly and observed him, discovering that he was writing only the four characters, to-to kuai-shih, "Tut! tut! what a strange business!" and nothing else. (CS 77.26a)

[1]CYC: Earlier (in 352), while Yin Hao had been stationed as general of the central army at Shou-yang (northern Anhui), the Ch'iang (Former Ch'in) general, Yao Hsiang, sent up a letter offering his allegiance and surrendering to the Chin. Later he committed some offense, and Hao secretly plotted to have him executed. It happened that just then (in 353) there was an incident in Kuan-chung (Ch'ang-an, capital of Former Ch'in); Fu Chien* (r. 351-355) died (actually not until 355; the "incident" was the rebellion of Chang Yü; see TCTC 99.3133). Yin led an army north without authorization, claiming that he was going to restore the imperial tombs of Western Chin (in Lo-yang). Yao Hsiang was sent ahead, but becoming fearful (of Yin's possible treachery), turned back. When Yin's army reached Shan-sang (in southern Honan), he heard that Hsiang was about to arrive, and abandoning his baggage, he fled hastily to defend Chiao (southern Honan). When Hsiang arrived, he occupied Shan-sang, burned the cargo left behind in Yin's boats, and proceeded to Shou-yang, where he plundered the refugees and returned to Huai-nan (in Anhui).

Most of Yin Hao's officers and men mutinied. The General of the Western Expedition, Huan Wen, accordingly sent up a memorial demanding Yin Hao's dismissal. The Generalissimo Controlling the Army (Ssu-ma Yü) petitioned that Yin be relieved of his command, his name stricken from the nobility, and that he become a commoner. Yin hastened back to Chien-k'ang to apologize for his offense, and afterward was sent to Hsin-an Prefecture in Tung-yang Commandery.

4. During a banquet at Huan Wen's place a certain aide-de-camp picked up (chi)[1] boiled shallots (hsieh) with his chopsticks to eat, but they did not immediately break apart.[2] Those who were eating with him, moreover, offered no assistance, and he kept holding them without letting go, so that the whole company roared with laughter.

Huan Wen said, "If people don't even assist each other while eating from the same platter, how much less would they do so in danger or distress?" Whereupon he ordered that (those who had not helped) be dismissed from office. (PTSC 145; TPYL 849, 977)

[1]All texts read I (PTSC 145 has I*, and states it was the aide's personal name). But in TPYL 849 and 977 it appears as chi, "to take an object up with chopsticks." I have therefore emended to chi.

[2]See "Record of Rites" XVII, 27 (Legge, Li Ki II, 79): In selecting boiled shallots, a gentleman severs the root from the tops.

5. After Yin Hao had been dismissed (353) he harbored resentment against the future Emperor Chien-wen (Ssu-ma Yü),[1] saying, "He lifted

me up and set me on a hundred-foot tower, and then shouldered the
ladder and made off with it."[2]

[1] Ssu-ma Yü, hoping to check the rise of Huan Wen at court in 351,
kept Yin Hao in power, and ultimately encouraged his disastrous
mission by not heeding those who advised stopping him; see *TCTC*
99.3120 and 3134-5.

[2] *HCYC*: Although Yin Hao had been dismissed and degraded, he maintained a calm spirit and submitted to fate, never ceasing to chant
poems with an elegant air. Even the members of his own family did
not see the grief he felt over being set adrift. His nephew, Han
Po, at first accompanied him to his place of exile, and after a
full year returned to the capital. Hao, who had always been fond
of him, escorted him as far as the river's edge and chanted a poem
of Ts'ao Shu (fl. ca. 300):

> "The rich and noble even strangers join,
> While poor and base the nearest kin forsake."

Whereupon his tears fell.
   SSHY Comm.: It was only this one incident in which his grief
was visible on the outside, so the stories about "writing in the
air" and "making off with the ladder" are not necessarily all
true.

6. After Teng Hsia had been dismissed from office (in 369) he went to
visit the imperial tombs (near Chien-k'ang). On his way he saw the
grand marshal, Huan Wen, who asked him, "Why have you grown so much
thinner?"
   Teng replied, "I feel ashamed before Meng Min; I can't help being
regretful over the broken pot."[1] (*TPYL* 378)

[1] *Kuo Lin-tsung PC*: Meng Min (second cent. A.D.) was simple and
straightforward. While sojourning in T'ai-yüan (Shansi) he lived
among common and vulgar people and did not yet have any reputation. Once he went to the marketplace to buy a pot. As he was
carrying it home on his shoulder it fell to the ground and broke,
but he continued on his way without looking back. Just then he
happened upon Kuo T'ai, who marveled as he saw him, and asked, "A
broken pot is a regrettable thing; why didn't you look back?"
   Meng answered, "The pot was already broken; what good would it
do to look at it?" Kuo admired his resoluteness, and because of
this incident realized his virtuous nature. Thinking to himself
that he would surely make an excellent gentleman, he urged him to
read. Meng then traveled about studying with different teachers
for ten years and eventually became famous. He was summoned to all
three Ducal Offices, but did not accept any of them. In Tung-hsia
(K'uai-chi) he was considered an excellent worthy.

7. After Huan Wen had deposed the grand minister, Ssu-ma Hsi, and his
son, Ssu-ma Tsung (in 371),[1] he proceeded to send up a memorial,
stating, "It is fitting to cut off one's closer sentiments in order
to preserve long-range plans. If we get rid of the grand minister and
his son, we may be spared later regrets."
   Emperor Chien-wen (Ssu-ma Yü, r. 371-372) responded to the
memorial in his own hand, "I have not the heart even to speak of the

matter, much less go beyond words." Huan Wen continued to send up further memorials whose language grew successively more insistent and stringent. Chien-wen finally replied, "If the House of Chin is to remain vital and enduring, then Your Excellency should obey this rescript. But if the great mandate has passed from Us, then We request to make way for a more worthy man."

When Huan Wen read the rescript his hands trembled and the sweat poured down his face. After that he desisted. The grand minister and his son were exiled to distant Hsin-an (western Chekiang). (*TPYL* 99, 387)

[1] Prince Wei of Wu-ling, Ssu-ma Hsi, and his son, Tsung, together with other members of the royal family and nobility, were accused of sedition by Huan Wen in 371.

SMHC: During the four or five years before his downfall, Ssu-ma Hsi was fond of singing pallbearers' songs (*wan-ko*), and while he himself swung a large handbell (*ling*), he would have those about him practice harmonizing with him. On one occasion during a banquet a female entertainer did an imitation of a person from Hsin-an singing and dancing to words of parting and separation, whose sounds were very sad. Later, as it turned out, Hsi was exiled to Hsin-an.

8. After Huan Hsüan's defeat (in 404), his personal attendant, Yin Chung-wen, returned to the capital to become consulting aide to the grand marshal, Liu Yü*. His mood appeared somehow to be no longer what it was in days gone by. In front of the reception hall of the grand marshal's headquarters there was an ancient locust tree (*huai*) with very luxuriant foliage. On the occasion of the first of the month Yin was in the reception hall with all the others and looked intently at the tree for a long while. Sighing, he said, "The locust tree is declining; it no longer has the will to live."[1] (*CS* 99.23a)

[1] *CATC*: With Huan Hsüan's defeat, Yin Chung-wen returned to the capital. In consideration for the fact that Yin had protected and accompanied the two Chin empresses, the consort of Emperor Mu (r. 345-361), née Ho, and the consort of Emperor An (r. 397-418), née Wang, and furthermore, feeling that his great faithfulness should be fully recognized, Liu Yü* took him on as senior administrator for the General Controlling the Army. Yin himself felt that his reputation was on a par with the untrammeled ones of the past, and that his status should have reached the apogee of honor. Latecomers like Hsieh Hun and his ilk were all persons he had despised in the past, yet now he was ranked shoulder to shoulder with them, which caused him continuous depression and loss of face. Later, as it turned out, he was exiled to Hsin-an.

9. Since Yin Chung-wen had in the past possessed both fame and prestige, he himself thought that he would surely become a pillar of state in the court administration (after Huan Hsüan's fall in 404), but instead he was unexpectedly made grand warden of Tung-yang, for which he felt an intense sense of injustice.[1] When he was on his way to the commandery, as he came to Fu-yang (near Hangchow), he sighed with deep feeling and said, "As I look on the form and aspect of these mountains and streams, they are about to produce another Sun Ts'e."[2] (*CS* 99.23a; *MCYC*, chung)

¹*CATC*: Yin Chung-wen was later made grand warden of Tung-yang, which made him more and more angry and resentful, until he finally plotted rebellion with Huan Yin (a cousin of Huan Hsüan), but subsequently surrendered and was executed. Chung-wen was once looking in a mirror and did not see his head. Then without warning disaster struck.

²*SSHY* Comm.: Sun Ts'e (elder brother and counselor of Sun Ch'üan, founder of the Wu Kingdom in 222) was a native of Fu-yang, and for this reason Yin sighed when he reached it.

CHAPTER XXIX

Stinginess and Meanness

1. Ho Ch'iao was by nature extremely stingy. In his household there were some excellent plums, but when his brother-in-law, Wang Chi, asked for some, he gave him no more than thirty or forty. Wang Chi, taking advantage of Ho's being on night duty at the palace, led some young men who could eat them, who went, axes in hand, into the orchard. After they had all eaten their fill, they chopped down the trees and sent a cartload of branches to Ho with the question, "Sir, how do these compare with your plums?" After Ho received their message he merely laughed and nothing more.[1] (CS 42.6ab differs considerably)

   [1]CCKT: Ho Ch'iao was ungenerous by nature. In managing his family wealth he sought to imitate princes and nobles, but was so extremely stingy that he was beginning to get a reputation for violating propriety.
   YL: Whenever Ho Ch'iao's younger brothers went into the orchard to eat plums, he would always count the leftover pits and charge them accordingly. It was for this reason that Ch'iao's wife's younger brother, Wang Chi, chopped them down.

2. Wang Jung was so stingy and mean that when his nephew got married he presented him with a single unlined gown, and afterward proceeded to send him a bill for it.[1] (CS 43.12b-13a; IWLC 40; TPYL 541, 691)

   [1]WYCS (cf. 43.12b): Wang Jung was by nature so extremely stingy that he could not even support himself. None of his possessions ever went outside the family. Everybody in the realm used to say that his was an "incurable sickness between the heart and the diaphragm." (See above, SSHY IV, 14, n. 4.)

3. Since the director of instruction, Wang Jung, was both noble and wealthy, he was unequaled in all Lo-yang for his estates and houses,

slaves, herdsmen, fertile fields, water mills (*shui-tui*)[1] and the like. His bonds of indebtedness were so numerous that he spent all his time with his wife spreading out the counting rods (*ch'ou*) under the lamp and calculating the sums.[2] (*CS* 43.12b; *TPYL* 472, 762)

[1] For a discussion of water mills, see Needham, *Science and Civilisation*, IV, 2, 390-403.

[2] *CCKT*: Wang Jung was by nature unceremonious and abrupt, and paid no attention to decorum or prestige. In his treatment of himself he was extremely frugal, yet his possessions were excessively abundant. Judges of character felt that the prestige he commanded for one of his position was not weighty.

WYCS: Wang Jung was fond of making money, and his orchards and fields were spread all over the realm. The aged couple were constantly using ivory counting rods day and night, reckoning up the family finances.

CYC: Wang Jung was worth a great deal in property and money, but always appeared to be in want. Some said he did so deliberately in order to make himself inconspicuous, but Tai K'uei characterized him as follows: "By being inconspicuous and silent in an age of danger and chaos, Wang Jung avoided pain and disaster. Since he was both intelligent and wise, he survived."

Someone remarked, "Do you mean to say that a great minister who takes his responsibilities to heart would act like that?"

K'uei replied, "Fortune is sometimes perilous, sometimes safe; the times now dark, now enlightened. According to what you say, then people like Ch'ü Yüan* (minister of Duke Ling of Wei, r. 543-493 B.C., who spent most of his life out of office) and Chi Cha (heir of King Shou-meng of Wu, r. 585-561 B.C., who refused his birthright) all turned their backs on their responsibilities. Observing great men from antiquity onward, would you say it was Wang Jung alone who acted this way?"

4. At Wang Jung's place there were some excellent plums which he frequently sold. But fearing lest other people might get possession of the pits, he always bored holes through their kernels. (*CS* 43.13a; *IWLC* 86; *PSLT* 30; *SWLC*, hou 25)

5. Wang Jung's daughter was given in marriage to P'ei Wei, to whom he had lent several tens of thousands of cash. When the daughter came home for a visit[1] Jung's expression was unhappy. But when she hastened to repay the money he immediately cheered up. (*CS* 43.12b; *IWLC* 40; *TPYL* 541)

[1] It was customary for a bride to return home to visit her parents on the anniversary of her wedding; see "Record of Rites" I, 24; Legge *Li Ki* I, 77.

6. While Wei Chan was stationed in Hsün-yang (as governor of Chiang Province, ca. 308-ca. 312), an old friend came to him for shelter (as a refugee from the north), but he provided no entertainment for him whatever, except only to give him one catty of the herb *wang-pu-liu-hsing*.[1] After the man had gotten his present, he immediately ordered his carriage.

When Wei's nephew, Li Ch'ung,[2] heard about it, he remarked, "My maternal uncle is so penny-pinching that he's even hard pressed over having to part with plants and trees." (TPYL 521, 991)

[1] *Vacaria vulgaris*, a medicinal herb in the dianthus family.
PTKM (VII): *Wang-pu-liu-hsing* grows on Mt. T'ai (Shantung) . . . it cures boils and gets rid of colds . . . If taken over a long period it produces lightness of body.

[2] Emending the "Li Kuei" (courtesy name, Hung-fan) of the text to Li Ch'ung (courtesy name, Hung-tu), after the Commentary.

7. Chancellor Wang Tao was economical and frugal by nature. His headquarters were full to overflowing with delicious fruits which he never distributed, so that by spring they had all spoiled. When the inspector-general reported it, Wang had him get rid of them, saying, "Be careful not to let my eldest son (Wang Yüeh) know about it!" (CS 65.1b)

8. During Su Chün's rebellion (328) Yü Liang fled southward for refuge and went to see T'ao K'an,[1] who had always held Yü in high esteem and honor. T'ao was by nature economical and frugal. When mealtime came, they were eating uncooked shallots (*hsieh*), and on this occasion Yü left the white bulbs uneaten. T'ao asked him, "What are you going to do with those?"

Yü replied, "Of course they can be planted." At this T'ao heaved a large sigh of admiration that Yü was not only a cultivated gentleman, but at the same time possessed a genuine talent for administration. (CS 73.5a; TPYL 977)

[1] See above, SSHY XXVII, 8.

9. Ch'ih Yin had amassed a huge fortune and possessed several million cash. His son, Ch'ih Ch'ao, was temperamentally altogether different. Once Ch'ao went at dawn to visit his father. According to the Ch'ih family regulations, the younger generation did not sit down in the presence of their elders, so Ch'ao stood up to talk. After a while the conversation touched on matters of finance and property. Ch'ih Yin said, "You just want to get your hands on my money, that's all." Whereupon he opened the treasure-house for one day, letting Ch'ao use its contents in any way he wished.

Yin at first thought that he would merely lose several hundred thousand cash or so. But Ch'ao proceeded in one day to distribute it among relatives and friends, so that when he had gotten all the way around, the treasure was almost completely exhausted. When Yin heard of it he was alarmed and dismayed, but could do absolutely nothing about it.[1] (CS 67.20a; TPYL 191, 836; SLF 10)

[1] *CHS* (cf. CS 67.20a): When Ch'ih Ch'ao was young he was exceptionally uninhibited and unrestrained, and had the capacity to transcend worldly considerations.

CHAPTER XXX

Extravagance and Ostentation

1. Every time Shih Ch'ung invited guests for banquet gatherings he always had beautiful girls serving the wine. If any guests failed to drain their cups, he would have an attendant decapitate the girls one after the other. Chancellor Wang Tao and his cousin, the generalissimo, Wang Tun, both went on one occasion to visit Shih Ch'ung. The chancellor had never been able to drink, but with every toast forced himself to do so until he was dead drunk. Each time it came the generalissimo's turn, however, he deliberately refused to drink, in order to observe what would happen. Even after they had already decapitated three girls his facial expression remained unchanged and he was still unwilling to drink. When the chancellor chided him for it, the generalissimo said, "If he wants to go ahead and kill somebody from another family, what business is it of yours?"[1] (CS 98.1a)

[1] WYCS: While Shih Ch'ung was governor of Ching Province (Hupei-Hunan) he plundered, robbed, and killed people in order to gain power and wealth.

WCHTYC: The chancellor had always been held in honor by the fathers. Wang K'ai once asked Wang Tun, "I hear your cousin (Wang Tao) is a fine man, and is, moreover, a connoisseur of music. I'm going to have some female musicians perform at my place, and you may bring him along."

Accordingly they went. As the girls were playing the flute, one of them had a slight lapse of memory. Wang K'ai, noticing it, had an attendant strike and kill her right in front of the steps, his facial expression remaining unchanged all the while.

When the chancellor returned home he said, "I'm afraid as long as this gentleman remains in the world, we're bound to have this kind of incident."

(In the KI the latter account is quoted in still greater detail, with some variations. In Wang Tao's biography in CS 98.1a Wang K'ai, not Shih Ch'ung, is also given as host of the banquet, and Wang Tao saves the life of one of the girls by drinking for both himself and Wang Tun. His final remark is, "If Tun's heart is so hard and unfeeling in this world, he'll come to no good end.")

2. In Shih Ch'ung's privy there were always ten or more female slaves lined up, all beautifully dressed and ornamented, holding onycha paste (*chia-chien fen*), aloeswood lotion (*ch'en-hsiang chih*) and the like, with no amenity lacking. In addition they would give each guest a new change of clothes and put it on him before letting him out. Most guests were too bashful to be able to use the privy, but when Generalissimo Wang Tun went, he removed his old clothes and put on the new, his spirit and expression completely self-assured. The slave girls said among themselves, "This guest is definitely capable of becoming a rebel!"[1] (*CS* 98.15a; *IWLC* 35)

[1] *YL*: While Liu Shih (219-309) was visiting Shih Ch'ung, he went to the privy and saw there red silk curtains (*chiang-sha chang*), a large bed, cushions, and rush mats (*yin-ju*), all very beautiful. Two female slaves were holding brocaded aromatic sachets (*hsiang-nang*). Shih turned around and retreated in haste, saying to Ch'ung, "Just now by mistake I entered your bedroom." Ch'ung replied, "It's just the privy."

3. Emperor Wu (Ssu-ma Yen, r. 265-290) once favored Wang Chi's house with a visit.[1] Wang tendered him a banquet for which he used all colored-glass (*liu-li*) utensils. Over a hundred female slaves, wearing silk gauze trousers and blouses, offered food and drinks with their hands. The steamed suckling pig was succulent and delicious with an extraordinary flavor. The emperor marveled at it and asked the reason. Wang replied, "They used human milk to feed the suckling pig."[2]

The emperor was deeply offended, and though the meal was not yet over, he left abruptly. It was something which even Wang K'ai and Shih Ch'ung would never have thought of doing. (*CS* 42.6b; *IWLC* 84, 85 (bis); *PTSC* 129; *TPYL* 371, 472, 756, 816)

[1] Wang Chi's wife was the emperor's daughter, the Princess of Ch'ang-shan.

[2] Wang Chi's biography (*CS* 42.6b) states that the suckling pig was *steamed* in human milk.

4. Wang K'ai used to warm the caldron by burning fried rice cakes (*i-pu*), while Shih Ch'ung would cook roasts over beeswax candles (*la-chu*). K'ai constructed a purple silk windbreak for walking (*pu-chang*), with dark blue-green silk gauze lining, forty *li* long. Ch'ung constructed a *brocaded* windbreak *fifty li* long, to do him one better. Shih used pungent fagara (*chiao*) to make plaster to plaster his room.[1] Wang promptly used red ocher (*ch'ih-shih chih*) to plaster his walls.[2] (*CS* 33.21a; *IWLC* 80, 85, 89; *PTSC* 2, 4, 5; *SLF* 10; *TPYL* 74, 472, 766, 815, 852, 870, 958; *SWLC*, hsü 18)

[1] Adding *ni-wu* after *TPYL* 958 and 472, on the analogy of *CS* 33.21a.

[2] *CCKT*: According to the old regulations the serpent eagle (*chen*) was not permitted to be brought north across the Yangtze River, because when even its feathers are placed in wine the drink becomes

lethal. While K'ai was serving as Commandant Standing by the Army (in the crown prince's guard), he secured a *chen* fledgling from Shih Ch'ung (who had secured it while he was governor of Ching Province; see *CS* 33.20b), and raised it. It became as large as a goose (e), its beak alone measuring over a *ch'ih* in length. It ate only snakes and vipers.

The governor of the capital province memorialized to have K'ai and Ch'ung apprehended, but an imperial rescript pardoned them both, and immediately ordered the bird burned in the streets of the capital. K'ai remained completely at ease in mood and expression throughout, without a trace of apprehension or fear.

5. Whenever Shih Ch'ung served bean congee (*tou-chou*) for a guest, the instant it was ordered it would be ready. And always, even in winter, he managed to have minced leek and duckweed pickles (*chiu-p'ing chi*). Moreover, even though his ox was not the equal of Wang K'ai's either in build or in strength, nevertheless whenever he went out with K'ai on an excursion, if it was extremely late when they started back, they would race to enter the gates of Lo-yang before they closed, and though Ch'ung's ox was thirty or forty paces behind, he would speed ahead like a flying bird. Though K'ai's ox ran with all his might, he could not keep up with him. K'ai constantly gripped his wrists in frustration over these three matters.

Finally he secretly bribed the steward of Ch'ung's household and his charioteer to find out how they did it. The steward said, "Beans take an extremely long time to boil, so I merely prepare some precooked bean powder (*shu-mo*) ahead of time. When guests arrive, I make plain (rice) congee, into which I throw the powder. As for the minced leek and duckweed pickles, I pound some leek roots in a mortar and mix them with wheat sprouts, that's all."

Next he inquired of the charioteer. The charioteer replied, "Your ox is basically not slow. It's just that the charioteer (running at his side) can't keep up and holds him back, that's all. When you're in a hurry, if he'd let go of the carriage shaft, then the ox will run."

K'ai followed their advice in everything, and in subsequent contests came out ahead. When Shih Ch'ung learned afterward what had happened, he had both informers killed.[1] (*CS* 33.21b-22a; *TPYL* 27, 841; *SLF*, hua 22)

[1]*CCKT*: Shih Ch'ung was by nature fond of knight-errantry. In his contests with Wang K'ai their mutual efforts to outdo each other were dizzying.

6. Wang K'ai had an ox called "Eight-hundred-*li* Brindled" (*Pa-pai-li po*),[1] whose hooves and horns he was constantly polishing. Wang Chi said to K'ai, "I'm not as good a marksman as you. Let's have a shooting match today and gamble for your ox; I'll match him with one hundred thousand cash."

Relying on his own superior skill, and confident moreover that there surely was no possibility of Wang Chi killing such a splendid beast, K'ai immediately consented, allowing Chi to shoot first. The instant Chi raised his bow he pierced the target, whereupon, seating himself on a folding stool, he shouted to his attendants, "Hurry up and fetch me the ox's heart!" In a very brief time the roasted heart was brought on. Chi ate one slice and immediately departed. (CS 42.6a)

¹SSHY Comm.: The "Book of Judging Oxen" (HsNC) came out of the tradition of Ning Ch'i and was transmitted to Po-li Hsi (both seventh cent. B.C.). During the Han period, Hsüeh Kung of Ho-hsi (early second cent. B.C.) got possession of the book and used it to judge oxen never missing in a hundred thousand cases. Because the ox originally carried heavy burdens and traveled long distances and had never been subjected to drawing covered or cabined carriages, (after ox-drawn passenger vehicles came into vogue in Han times) the text was accordingly no longer transmitted. Later, during the Wei Kingdom Kao-t'ang Lung revived its transmission and presented a copy to Ssu-ma I (179-251), and after him Wang K'ai got possession of the work.

(In the Sung text this passage appears to be quoted from the preface of a fourth or fifth century edition of the "Book of Oxen." Following Yang Yung's notes, I have made it all part of Liu Chün's own commentary.)

The SSHY Comm. (or another commentator, calling himself "Your Servant" ch'en), cites the HsNC: "If the 'hidden bow' (yin-hung) is attached to the nape of the neck, it is a thousand-li (ox)." He further cites the HsNC commentary (chu): "The 'hidden bow' refers to the twin tendons leading from the tailbones and attached to the nape of the neck, as was the case with the ox reared by Ning Ch'i." The Commentary concludes: "Wang K'ai's ox also had the 'hidden bow.'"

Ning Ch'i's "Book" (i.e., the HsNC): For convenience in whipping the head, it should be high, and the hundred parts of the body should be tightly knit. An ox with large hollows at the loins and wide-set ribs is difficult to feed. One with a dragon head and protruding eyes is fond of jumping. Furthermore, its horns should be slender, its body close-knit, its shape should be like a scroll.

(Oxen were employed for heavy hauling at least as early as Western Chou times--see "Songs," No. 227: "We loaded our handcarts/ We hitched our oxen to carriages." Ox-drawn carriages for human transport came into common use among the upper classes only after the beginning of Han, due to the general shortage of horses after the civil wars--see SC 23.1a. Model clay covered oxcarts have been recovered from Han tombs--see, e.g., Kaizuka Shigeki, ed., Chūgoku, Vol. I, Sekai bunkashi taikei, Tokyo, 1958, p. 242-- and fine examples abound for the Six Dynasties. See, e.g., Hsin Chung-kuo ti k'ao-ku shou-huo, ed. by the Archeological Institute of the Chinese Academy of Sciences, Peking, 1962, pl. XCVIII. Presumably with the new function of oxen as passenger carriers, the old criteria, which applied primarily to endurance, were no longer appropriate. Joseph Needham finds the yoke harness for oxen still in use in China, relatively unchanged since early antiquity. See Needham, Science and Civilisation, IV.2, 306, and fig. 537).

7. Wang K'ai once punished a man for not wearing anything but his underwear (jih). Because Wang was on duty in the palace, he placed

the man in a doubly sequestered inner chamber, connected by labyrinthine passageways, and would not permit anyone to let him out. After that the man went hungry for days, confused and not knowing which way to go. Later, after an intermediary (*yin-yüan*) offered to die in his stead, he finally got to come out.

8. In their competition for display Shih Ch'ung and Wang K'ai exhausted every refinement and elegance in ornamenting their carriages and clothing.[1] Since Emperor Wu (Ssu-ma Yen) was Wang K'ai's nephew, he frequently helped K'ai out, and on one occasion presented him with a coral (*shan-hu*) tree[2] two *ch'ih* or so in height. Its branches and twigs spread luxuriantly, and in all the world it would have been extremely hard to find its equal. K'ai showed it to Ch'ung, who after looking at it struck it with an iron *ju-i* baton, completely shattering it in one blow. Shocked and dismayed, supposing that Ch'ung had done it out of jealousy over his own treasure, K'ai's tone and expression became severe.

Ch'ung said, "It's not worth worrying about. I'll repay you today." Whereupon he ordered his attendants to bring out all his coral trees, every one of them three and four *ch'ih* in height, their branches and trunks surpassing anything in this world, and their luster and color overwhelming the eyes—six or seven trees in all, many more than there ever were in K'ai's place. K'ai stood there speechless and unstrung. (*CS* 33.21ab; *TPYC* 236)

[1] *HWCC*: Shih Ch'ung's wealth and possessions had accumulated to a magnitude of ten thousand gold pieces. His house and rooms, carriages and horses, were in presumptuous imitation of the imperial princes, and the delicacies of his cuisine always exhausted the treasures of sea and land. The hundreds of ladies in his rear apartments all trailed silks and embroideries, ear ornaments, gold, and kingfisher feathers, and the players in his string and pipe ensembles were all the choicest in the world. In constructing arbors or excavating ponds, he used to the utmost all human ingenuity. Even when vying for eminence with imperial relatives like Yang Hsiu (uncle of Empress-dowager Ching-hsien, the consort of Ssu-ma Shih) and Wang K'ai (brother-in-law of Ssu-ma Chao) and their ilk in their display of luxury and ostentation, Ch'ung was still at the forefront of the most extreme. Hsiu and the others were constantly mortified and envious, feeling they could never keep up with him.

[2] *NCIWC*: Coral grows in the country of Ta-Ch'in (the Roman Orient). There is an island in the midst of the Swelling Sea (*Chang-hai*, the old name for the Gulf of Tonkin, but here evidently the Mediterranean?), seven or eight hundred *li* distant from their country, called Coral-tree Island (*Shan-hu-shu chou*). On the sea floor there are large rocks where the water is over twenty *chang* deep. The coral grows on the surface of the rocks. When it first grows, it is white and soft like fungus. The men of the country board great ships carrying iron nets, which they first submerge beneath the water. After one year the coral grows through the interstices of the net, and its color is still yellow, with its branches and twigs interlocking to a height of three or four *ch'ih*. The trunks of the largest ones are a *ch'ih* or more in circumference. After

three years, when the color is pink (*ch'ih*), then by means of the iron net they wrench free their roots and draw the iron net into a ship, lifting the net back up with a windlass (*chiao-ch'e*). They then cut and carve the coral into any shape they wish. But if too much time passes before it is carved, then it becomes brittle and shatters into tiny pieces. The large ones are transported to the king's treasury, and the small ones are sold.

KC: The large pieces of coral are large enough to serve as carriages axles.

9. After Wang Chi had been cashiered,[1] he moved his residence to the foot of Pei-mang Mountain (just north of Lo-yang). At the time the population was numerous and land was dear. Since Chi was fond of shooting from horseback, he bought a plot of land for a riding course, and placed strings of cash all around the plot to mark the boundaries of the course. Contemporaries called it the "Golden Moat" (Chin-kou). (*CS* 42.6a; *IWLC* 66; *CHC* 18; *MCYC*, chung; *SLF* 10; *TPYL* 472, 836)

[1]*CCKT*: Wang Chi bore a grievance against his cousin, Wang Yu (emending the "T'ien" of the text, after *CS* 42.6a; because Wang Yu had claimed Chi was unable to care for his father). When Chi became intendant of Ho-nan (in Shansi), before he had taken up his post, he was traveling past Wang Yu's mansion, and a petty official in Yu's employ failed to step down immediately out of his path. Chi horsewhipped him right in front of his carriage. The authorities memorialized to have him relieved of his post. Evaluations of character considered Chi inferior to Yu. Later he sought to be transferred to Grand Master of the Horse, but Wang Yu had already been appointed to that post. Chi was accordingly dismissed to live outside the capital.

10. Shih Ch'ung once went with Wang Tun into the premises of the Grand Academy (*t'ai-hsüeh*).[1] On seeing images of Confucius' disciples, Yen Hui[2] and Yüan Hsien, Ch'ung sighed and said, "If we had 'mounted to Confucius' hall' together with them, why would there necessarily have been any distance between them and us?"

Wang replied, "I don't know about the others, but Tzu-kung[3] would have been pretty close to you."

Ch'ung replied with a straight face, "A gentleman ought to make both his person and his reputation great. Why go to such lengths as talking to people through a broken jug for a window?"[4] (*CS* 33.22a; *PTSC* 83; *TPYL* 388)

[1]Emending the text to agree with *CS* 33.22a. The Grand Academy, established in Former Han to train future officials in the Confucian classics, had fallen into decay at the end of Later Han, but was refurbished by the Wei in 224. It was, however, soon overshadowed by the more exclusive School for the Sons of State (*kuo-tzu hsüeh*) in 276, later known as *kuo-tzu chien*. See Zürcher, *Conquest*, p. 57.

[2]*KTCY* (cf. *SC* 67.2ab): Yen Hui was twenty-nine years younger than Confucius, yet his hair was white. He died prematurely in his thirty-second year.

[3]*SC* (67.7a, 11b): Tuan-mu Tz'u (Tzu-kung) was once minister of Lu

(Shantung) where he amassed a thousand gold pieces in his household. When Tzu-kung visited Yüan Hsien, the narrow lane was too small to accommodate his carriage.

⁴*Chuang-tzu* XXVIII, 14ab (Watson, pp. 315-316): Yüan Hsien lived in a hut with a mulberry doorpost and broken jugs for windows. (The full passage is quoted in the Commentary at *SSHY* II, 9, above).

11. The Prince of P'eng-ch'eng (Ssu-ma Ch'üan) owned a fast ox which he loved and cherished very dearly. The grand marshal, Wang Yen, in an archery contest with him, gambled for the ox and won it. The Prince of P'eng-ch'eng said, "If you want to ride with him yourself, then there's no argument, but if you want to eat him, I'll give you twenty fat ones to take his place. In that way you'll not be deprived of something to eat, and I'll get to keep what I love." Wang thereupon killed the ox and ate it.

12. When Wang Hsi-chih was young[1] he was once sitting in the last seat at a banquet at Chou I's place. He cut a slice of ox heart and ate it, and after that everyone revised his view of him.[2] (*CS* 80.1a)

[1] Wang's biography (*CS* 80.1a) states that he was "in his thirteenth year."

[2] Cf. No. 6, above.
 SSHY Comm.: Contemporary custom considered ox heart a delicacy, so Hsi-chih ate it first (*sic*).
 (The above comment by Liu Chün implies that the present text of *SSHY* may be defective. The account in *CS* 80.1a similarly reads: "Before any of the seated guests had eaten any, Chou I first cut a slice and fed it to Hsi-chih, and after that Hsi-chih's reputation was made.)

CHAPTER XXXI

Anger and Irascibility

1. Ts'ao Ts'ao owned a female entertainer whose voice was extraordinarily clear and high, but whose temper was vicious and ugly. At times he wanted to kill her, but was unwilling to part with her talent; or again he wanted to dismiss her, but could not bear the thought. In the end he selected a hundred singers and had them all trained at the same time. After a short time, just as he had hoped, there appeared one whose voice equaled the first one's, whereupon Ts'ao immediately had the one with the bad temper killed. (*TPYL* 586; *SWLC*, hou 16)

2. Wang Shu was by nature short-tempered. Once while he was attempting to eat an egg he speared it with his chopstick, but could not get hold of it. Immediately flying into a great rage, he lifted it up and hurled it to the ground. The egg rolled around on the ground and had not yet come to rest when he got down on the ground and stamped on it with the teeth of his clogs, but again failed to get hold of it. Thoroughly infuriated, he lay on the ground and seized it in his mouth. After biting it to pieces he immediately spewed it out.

When Wang Hsi-chih heard about it he laughed aloud, saying, "If the father, Wang Ch'eng*, had had a temper like this, even with his reputation there still wouldn't be the slightest thing about him worth discussing. How much less in the case of Wang Shu!"[1] (*CS* 75.5b)

   [1]*CHS*: Wang Shu was pure and noble, unceremonious and correct, and was accorded special recognition in his youth. It was only his shortness of temper which impeded him.

3. Wang Hu-chih once took the occasion of a snowfall to visit his cousin, Wang T'ien. Hu-chih's speech and manner were somewhat irritating and offensive to T'ien, who started to color and grow restless. Sensing that T'ien was offended, Hu-chih immediately moved his

couch near to him, and, taking him by the arm, said, "Is it worth it for you to quarrel with your old cousin?"

Thrusting aside his hand, T'ien replied, "Cold as a ghost's hand! What's the idea of forcing your way in here and grabbing a man by the arm!"

4. Huan Wen was once playing *chaupar* with Yüan Tan. One of Yüan's throws (*ch'ih*) did not suit him, and with a ferocious expression he threw all five dice (*mu*) away.

Wen Ch'iao remarked, "After seeing Yüan Tan 'transfer his anger,' I understand why Yen Hui was so esteemed."[1]

[1]"Analects" VI, 4: Duke Ai (r. 494-468 B.C.) asked which of the disciples was most fond of learning. Confucius replied, "There was Yen Hui--he was fond of learning. He did not transfer his anger or repeat his mistakes. Unfortunately his life was short and he died."

5. Hsieh I was by nature rough and impetuous. Once when something did not go to his liking he betook himself to berate Wang Shu, letting words fly with extreme abusiveness. Wang kept an impassive expression and turned his face to the wall, not daring to move for half a day. A long while after Hsieh had left, Wang turned his head and asked a petty official in attendance, "Has he left yet?"

He replied, "Yes, he's left." Whereupon Wang resumed his seat. Contemporaries sighed in admiration over the fact that (Wang), although his own temper was short, was still able on occasion to be tolerant.[1] (*CS* 75.5b)

[1]Wang's biography (*CS* 75.5b) notes that his practice was to "overcome anger with gentleness," especially after his assumption of greater responsibility at court.

6. Wang Hsien-chih once went to visit Hsieh An. It happened that Hsi Tso-ch'ih was already among the company. Hsieh was about to offer Wang a place on the same couch (*t'a*), but Wang hesitated and did not sit down, so Hsieh led him around and offered him the opposite couch.

After they had left, Hsieh said to his nephew, Hsieh Lang, "Hsien-chih truly and unmistakably stands pure and undefiled, but people have boasted about him so much, it's been just enough to make him lose his spontaneity."[1]

[1]*LCCCC*: Wang Hsien-chih was by nature extremely proper and haughty, and never had anything to do with those not in his class.

7. Wang Ch'en and Wang Kung were once both present at a banquet in the home of Ho Ch'eng. Kung was capital intendant at the time (389), while Ch'en had just been appointed governor of Ching Province (Hunan and Hupei).[1] When it came time for his departure, he urged Kung to drink a toast with him, but Kung would not drink. Ch'en forcibly compelled him, growing more and more insistent, until finally each wound the belt of his skirt around his hand (in a gesture of challenge). Nearly a thousand men from Kung's headquarters were all summoned into the room. Although Ch'en's attendants were few, he also ordered them to come forward, intending to fight it out to the death then and there. Ho Ch'eng, in desperation, got up and placed his seat between

the two, and only by this means got them to separate and go their ways. As the saying goes: "Associations based on power and profit-- these the ancients were ashamed of."[2]

[1]*LKC* (*Yao-cheng*): Earlier, when Huan Shih-min (a son of Huan Huo) was serving as governor of Ching Province (Hunan-Hupei), and was stationed at Shang-ming (Hupei, in 384), the people suddenly started to sing the ballad of Huang T'an, which goes: "While Huang T'an played the hero in Yang Province,/ Great Buddha (Ta-fo) came to Shang-ming." In a brief time Shih-min died (389), and Wang Ch'en became governor of Ching Province. 'Buddha's Greatness' (Fo-ta) was Wang Ch'en's baby name.

[2]See *HS* 32.11a.

8. When Huan Hsüan was a little boy he and his older and younger cousins used to raise geese and have them fight together. Every time Hsüan's goose lost it used to make him extremely angry, so that one night he went to the goose pen, seized his cousins' geese, and killed them all.

When morning came the members of the family were all startled and alarmed, claiming it was supernatural and uncanny. They reported it to Hsüan's uncle, Huan Ch'ung, who said, "There's no reason to think it uncanny. It's probably just one of Hsüan's pranks and nothing more." Upon inquiry, it turned out to be as he had said.

CHAPTER XXXII

Slander and Treachery

1. Wang Ch'eng's outward appearance was very relaxed and open, but inwardly he was really a headstrong knight-errant (*hsia*).[1] (*CS* 43.18a)

   [1] *TTCC* (cf. 43.18a, 19b): Liu Kun once said to Wang Ch'eng, "Even though your outward appearance is relaxed and open, inwardly you're really a headstrong knight-errant. If you live in the world with these attributes, it would be hard for anyone to accomplish your death."
   Ch'eng was silent and did not answer. Later he was actually killed by Wang Tun (in 312). When Liu Kun learned of it he said, "He simply chose death himself, that's all."

2. Yüan Yüeh was eloquent and capable in disquisitions on "short and long strategems,"[1] and in addition possessed a refined power of reasoning. When he first became Hsieh Hsüan's aide he was treated with considerable deference. Later he lost one of his parents, and after the mourning period was ended and he had returned to the capital (Chien-k'ang), the only thing he carried about with him was the "Intrigues of the Warring States" (*Chan-kuo ts'e*) and nothing else. Speaking about it with others, he would say, "In my youth I used to study the 'Analects' (*Lun-yü*) and *Lao-tzu*, and I'd also look occasionally into *Chuang-tzu* and the 'Book of Changes' (*I*).
   After coming to the capital he became advisor to the Prince of K'uai-chi, Ssu-ma Tao-tzu, by whom he was treated with the greatest intimacy. But after nearly subverting the very springs and pivot of government, he was suddenly executed (389).[2] (*CS* 75.17a)

   [1] One of the alternate titles of the *Chan-kuo ts'e* was "The Book of Short and Long Strategems" (*Tuan-ch'ang shu*). This semifictional work was produced in the second century B.C. and edited by Liu Hsiang (80-9 B.C.). There is a complete annotated translation by J. I. Crump, Jr., *Chan-kuo ts'e*, Oxford, 1970.

²*Yüan SP:* During the T'ai-yüan period (376-396) Yüan Yüeh was in the favor of the Prince of K'uai-chi, and often urged him to take sole possession of the power at court. The prince secretly accepted his counsel, but Wang Kung, hearing of this advice, spoke of it to Emperor Hsiao-wu (r. 373-396), who made Yüeh responsible for the other's offense, and had Yüeh executed in the marketplace. Afterward the sounds of agreement or difference among the various factions were broadcast throughout the court and into the provinces.

3. Emperor Hsiao-wu (Ssu-ma Yao, r. 373-396) was very intimate and deferential toward Wang Kuo-pao and Wang Ya.¹ Ya had recommended Wang Hsün to the emperor, and the emperor wanted to meet him. One evening as he was conversing with Kuo-pao and Ya, the emperor, who was slightly flushed with wine, gave the order to summon Hsün. But just before Hsün arrived, even after the voices of the servants relaying the announcement of his arrival had already been heard, Kuo-pao, realizing himself that his own ability fell below Hsün's, was afraid that he would be overthrown and that Hsün would wrest away his favor, so he said, "Wang Hsün is one of the most famous men of the present age; it wouldn't be fitting if Your Majesty saw him while flushed with wine. Naturally it would be better to summon him on some other occasion."

The emperor accepted his advice, believing in his heart that Kuo-pao had done it out of loyalty. As a result he never saw Hsün. (*CS* 75.13b)

¹*CATC*: Whenever the emperor set out wine for a banquet gathering, if he had invited Wang Ya but Ya had not yet arrived, the emperor would not raise his cup until he came. Contemporary judgments used to claim that both Wang Hsün and Wang Kung were fit to serve as tutors to the crown prince, but Ya, because of the high favor in which he stood, surpassed them both to become grand tutor and left vice-president of the Imperial Secretariat.

4. Wang Hsü frequently slandered Yin Chung-k'an to his cousin, Wang Kuo-pao. Yin deeply resented it and sought a plan of action from Wang Hsün. Hsün said to him, "Just go for frequent visits to Wang Hsü's place, and each time always ask that the room be cleared of other people. Then take the occasion to discuss irrelevant matters. In this way the two Wangs' friendship will become estranged."

Yin followed his advice. When Kuo-pao next saw Wang Hsü, he asked him, "The other day when you and Chung-k'an cleared the room of other people, what did you talk about?"

Hsü said, "Naturally it was just ordinary chitchat. There wasn't anything else to discuss."

Kuo-pao thought, however, that Hsü had some secret plot against himself, and, as predicted, their warm friendship grew daily more distant, and the slander thereby came to an end.¹

¹*SSHY* Comm.: When Kuo-pao found favor with the Prince of K'uai-chi (Ssu-ma Tao-tzu), it was through Wang Hsü that he gained his access. "Sharing a common hatred, they sought each other out, like merchants in the marketplace" (*Tso-chuan*, Chao 13; Legge V, 650). All their lives, until the day of their execution (in 397), they never became estranged. How could any interference by Chung-k'an have created a rift?

CHAPTER XXXIII

Blameworthiness and Remorse

1. Emperor Wen of Wei (Ts'ao P'ei, r. 220-226) was jealous of his younger brother, the Prince of Jen-ch'eng (Ts'ao Chang), for his valor and manliness.[1] Therefore on one occasion in the apartment of their mother, the Dowager Empress Pien, while they were playing encirclement chess (*wei-ch'i*), and were both eating jujubes (*tsao*), Emperor Wen inserted poison into the stems of some of the jujubes, then picked out the edible ones for himself and started to eat them. The prince, quite unaware of any treachery, proceeded to eat the rest at random. After the poison started to take effect, the empress looked for water to save his life, but the emperor had ordered the attendants in advance to destroy all the vessels for drawing and jars for storing water. The empress ran barefooted to the well but found nothing to draw with, and shortly thereafter the prince died.

Later the emperor wanted to do away with the Prince of Tung-o, Ts'ao Chih, but the dowager empress said, "You've already killed my Jen-ch'eng; you can't kill my Tung-o as well!"[2] (*IWLC* 87; *TPYL* 965)

[1]*WeiL*: The Prince of Jen-ch'eng was firm and valorous by nature and had a brown beard. During the northern expedition against Tai Commandery (Shansi), alone with the hundred or so men under his command he broke through the enemy lines and escaped. Hearing of it, Ts'ao Ts'ao remarked, "That brown-bearded boy of mine is really employable!"

[2]*WC*, *FCC* (cf. *SKWei* 29.12a): Emperor Wen asked Chou Hsüan (d. ca. 239) for an interpretation of his dream, saying, "I dreamed I was rubbing a coin on the whetstone, trying to obliterate its inscription, but it only grew more distinct than ever. What does that signify?"

Hsüan, looking very unhappy, did not reply. When the emperor kept asking insistently, he said, "In Your Majesty's family affairs, though you wish them to be such-and-such, the dowager empress will not consent. That's why even though you were trying to obliterate the inscription, it only grew more distinct, that's all."

The emperor had wanted to punish the crimes of his younger brother, Chih, but, under pressure from the dowager empress, only inflicted a demotion in rank.

2. Wang Hun's second wife was a daughter of the Yen family of Lang-yeh (Shantung). At the time he married her Wang was serving as governor of Hsü Province (northern Kiangsu and Anhui). In the marriage ceremony, after the bride's obeisance (pai) was concluded, Wang was on the point of making a responding obeisance, when the onlookers all said, "Lord Wang is the ruler of the province, while the bride is only one of the subjects of the province. There's probably no reason to make a responding obeisance." Whereupon Wang desisted.

His son by the first marriage, Wang Chi, felt that his father, by not making the responding obeisance, had not completed the ceremony, and was afraid they were not legally husband and wife, so he did not do obeisance before her either, and thereafter referred to her as "Concubine Yen" (Yen-ch'ieh). The Yen family felt it to be a disgrace, but since the groom's family was nobility, in the end they never dared sue for a divorce.[1]

[1] SSHY Comm.: The marriage ceremony is the greatest expression of the way of humanity. Why, merely because of a single non-obeisance, should the bride then become a concubine or maidservant? The words of the Shih-shuo at this point are quite mistaken.

3. When Lu Chi was defeated at Ho-ch'iao (Honan), he was slandered by Lu Chih and sentenced to death (in 303).[1] On the eve of his execution he sighed and said, "Would that I might hear once more the cry of the cranes at Hua-t'ing![2] But will I ever again get to do so?" (CS 54.15a)

[1] WYCS: When the Prince of Ch'eng-tu, Ssu-ma Ying, was campaigning against the Prince of Ch'ang-sha, Ssu-ma I*, he employed Lu Chi as governor-general of military affairs at the front.

(Lu) Chi PC: The senior administrator of Ssu-ma Ying, Lu Chih, differed from Chi's younger brother, Yün, in his likes and dislikes. Furthermore, the attendant, Meng Chiu, was seeking the position of magistrate of Han-tan Prefecture (northern Honan) from Ying (actually on behalf of Chiu's father; see TCTC 85.2687), and Ying transferred the case to Yün. Yün, who at the time was Ying's left-assistant sergeant-at-arms, said, "A man who has been mutilated (Chiu was a eunuch) may not be employed to rule over the people."

When he learned of this, Chiu harbored a grievance against Yün, and schemed with Chih, biding his time until a convenient day should arrive. So when Lu Chih suffered his disastrous defeat at the Seven-li Stream (Ch'i-li chien, near Lo-yang), Chiu slanderously charged that it had happened as a result of Chi's plotting a revolt. Ying accordingly had Ch'ien Hsiu decapitate Chi.

Previous to this, one evening Lu Chi had dreamed that a black shroud wrapped itself about his carriage, which his hands could not remove, even with the greatest effort, and he felt unhappy about it. The next morning Hsiu's men-at-arms arrived by stealth.

Removing his armor and putting on his gown and cap, Chi went out
to see Hsiu, his expression and manner both self-composed, and
thus he met his death. At the time he was in his forty-third year.
There was not a man among his officers who did not weep for him.
On that day heaven and earth were suffused together in mist and a
great wind snapped the trees in two. On the level ground snow fell
a foot deep. (It was the tenth month = November; see *TCTC* 85.2688.)

KPCC: When Lu Chi's father, Lu K'ang, executed Pu Ch'an (in
272), all the members of Ch'an's and his collaborator's families
were exterminated. Those who knew this blamed K'ang for it, so
when K'ang's sons, Lu Chi and Lu Yün, were killed, their families,
including the three clans (father's, mother's, and wives') were
wiped out without trace.

²*PWKS*: Hua-t'ing is an estate outside the suburbs of Yu-ch'üan
Prefecture in Wu Commandery (Soochow), where there are clear
springs and luxuriant forests. After the pacification of Wu (280),
Lu Chi and his younger brother, Yün, both roamed about here for
ten years or more.

YL: While Lu Chi was serving as governor-general of military
affairs north of the Yellow River, hearing the sound of the alarm
horn, he said to Sun Ch'eng (later executed with him), "Hearing
this is not as good as hearing the cry of the cranes at Hua-t'ing!"

SSHY Comm.: This is the reason why on the eve of his execution
there was this sigh. (The similarity to Li Ssu's remark to his son
as both went to their execution in Hsien-yang in 208 B.C. is surely
not fortuitous; see *SC* 87.20b.)

4. Liu K'un was skillful in rallying men to his cause, but inept at
governing them. Although in one day there might be several thousand
men who would throw in their lot with him, their dispersal and defec-
tion was also like this, so that in the end he never established anything permanent.¹ (*CS* 62.3b)

¹*TTCC*: While Liu K'un was serving as governor of Ping Province
(Shansi) he gathered together the local chieftains and entered into an alliance with them, leading them forth to battle, but internally he never governed his people. As a consequence he finally
lost his army, was deserted by his officers, and accomplished
nothing.

Ching Yin (fifth cent.), whose commentary on this passage is
included in the *SSHY* Comm., writes: "Liu K'un was governor of Ping
Province during the first years of the Yung-chia era (ca. 307). At
that time Chin-yang (the provincial capital, near T'ai-yüan) was a
deserted city with rebels and bandits attacking on all sides, yet
he was able to gather together officers and men and march in resistance against Liu Yüan (founder of Former Chao, r. 304-310),
and Shih Lo (founder of Later Chao, r. 329-333). In the space of
ten years, though defeated, he was still able to restore order. If
he was 'unable to govern,' would he have gotten to do this? During
days of cruelty and desolation, when there was no smoke from human
habitation for a thousand *li* around, how could there have been 'in
one day several thousand men who would throw in their lot with
him'? And if in one day several thousand men deserted him, again,
how would he have been able in the space of twelve years to face

such hardships? The *Shih-shuo*, mistakenly infatuated with the bizarre, is careless about facts and principles." (The last sentence is supplied from *KI*.)

5. When Wang Ch'eng first came down to the capital (Chien-k'ang, in 312), Chancellor Wang Tao said to the generalissimo, Wang Tun, "We can't let anymore Ch'iang barbarians come out east!"[1] Wang Ch'eng's face resembled that of a Ch'iang.

[1]*SSHY* Comm.: Wang Ch'eng was, to be sure, killed by Wang Tun (in 312), but how could the chancellor, with his reputation and virtue, have said a thing like this! (The Ch'iang were a proto-Tibetan pastoral people inhabiting the highlands of the west and northwest.)

6. When Generalissimo Wang Tun started his revolt (in the first month of 322), his cousin, Chancellor Wang Tao, and Tao's various relations of the same generation (*hsiung-ti*),[1] went to court to apologize for their deficiencies. Chou I was deeply worried over the Wangs, and when he first entered the court he wore a very worried expression. The chancellor called to Lord Chou and said, "The lives of all of us are in your hands!"[2]

Chou went directly past without answering. After he went in he argued vehemently to save their lives, and when they were pardoned, Chou was so pleased that he drank to celebrate. When it came time for him to emerge from the audience, the Wangs remained by the door. Chou said, "This year if we kill off all the rebel rascals, I ought to take that gold seal the size of a *tou*-measure[3] and tie it behind my elbow."

When Wang Tun reached Shih-t'ou (the port of Chien-k'ang) he asked the chancellor, "Should Lord Chou be given one of the Three Ducal Offices?"

The chancellor did not reply.

Tun asked again, "Should he be president of the Imperial Secretariat, then?"

Again there was no answer.

Thereupon Tun said, "In that case, we should just kill him and be done with it."

The chancellor still remained silent. It was only after Chou I had been killed (one or two months later) that the chancellor finally realized it was Chou who had saved his own life. With a sigh he said, "Even though I didn't kill Lord Chou myself, it was because of me that he died. Wherever he is in the nether world, I have betrayed this man!"[4] (*CS* 69.19b)

[1]According to the *JMP*, neither of Wang Tao's two younger brothers (he was the eldest) survived the downfall of Western Chin (316), so we should understand *hsiung-ti* in its broadest connotation. *TCTC* 92.2899 specifies Wang Sui**, Wang I*, Wang K'an*, Wang Pin, and "over twenty others."

[2]According to *CS* 69.19b, Liu Wei, the principal object of Wang Tun's revolt, had urged that the entire Wang clan be exterminated.

[3]The gold seal was Wang Tao's emblem of office as director of works and chancellor.

[4]*YYCS*: After Wang Tun had conquered the capital, his aide, Lü I, advised him, saying, "Chou I and Tai Yüan both have enough fame and

prestige to delude the masses. Lately their words have lacked all evidence of shame or fear. If you don't get rid of them, your campaigns will never come to an end." Tun instantly agreed with him, and forthwith killed Tai Yüan and Chou I.

Earlier, Lü I had served as a clerk in one of the secretariats, and since Tai Yüan was his superior officer, the latter had always maintained a superior air and treated Lü like a person of small capacity. This was the reason he peddled this advice regarding him.

7. Wang Tao (b. 276) and Wen Ch'iao (b. 288) went together to see Emperor Ming (Ssu-ma Shao, r. 323-325). The emperor asked Wen how his predecessors had gained possession of the realm. Wen did not answer for a moment, whereupon Wang said, "Wen Ch'iao is too young and not very familiar with what happened. Let me tell it for Your Majesty." Wang then proceeded to recount in detail the beginnings of Prince Hsüan's (Ssu-ma I, d. 251) founding of the dynasty, how he exterminated all the famous clans and established in favor those who sided with himself.[1] When he came to the last years of Prince Wen (Ssu-ma Chao, d. 265) and the incident of the murder of Duke Kao-kuei (Ts'ao Mao, r. 254-260),[2] Emperor Ming, on hearing this, pressed his face down against the couch and cried, "If it was as you say, how can Our mandate endure?"

[1] *SSHY* Comm.: This refers to when Prince Hsüan founded the dynasty by executing Ts'ao Shuang (in 249) and placing power in the hands of Chiang Chi (fl. ca. 250) and his party.

[2] See above, *SSHY* V, 8, n. 4.

8. In the midst of a large company Generalissimo Wang Tun once said, "Among the Chou clan there has never yet been anyone who became one of the Three Ducal Officers."

Someone answered, "It was only Chou I who already had a five-counter (*ma*) lead, but didn't make it."[1]

The generalissimo said, "When I first met Chou in Lo-yang (before 311), the moment we met we were immediately en rapport. But it happened that the world was in turmoil, and so he has come to this!" Whereupon he wept tears for him. (*CS* 69.19a)

[1] Emending *i*, "town," to the graphically similar *i**, "already," after Yang Yung's suggestion in his notes on this passage. The translation is tentative, but the remark is an obvious allusion to gambling.

TTCC (cf. *CS* 69.19a): One of Wang Tun's aides was once playing *chaupar* at Tun's place, and just as he was about to win (*ch'eng-tu*) and his counters (*ma*) were leading the game (following *CS* 69.19a), he was "killed." Whereupon he said to Tun, "The Chou family had had high prestige for successive generations, yet none of them has ever reached a rank as high as the Three Ducal Offices. When Chou I was on the brink of making it, but didn't bring it to fruition, there was some similarity to these counters of mine, eh?"

Weeping with deep feeling, Tun said, "When Chou I was a young lad I met him in the eastern palace (i.e., in the crown prince's guard at Lo-yang), and from the moment we met we opened our hearts to each other. And then when I offered him the Three Ducal Offices (see No. 6, above), how could I have been plotting any mischief? I was coerced by the royal laws. The depth of my sorrow--how can it ever be expressed in words?" (The black-hearted hypocrite!)

9. When Wen Ch'iao first accepted the commission of the director of works, Liu K'un, to persuade Emperor Yüan (r. 317-322) to ascend the throne,[1] his mother, Lady Ts'ui, steadfastly clung to him and held him back, so that Ch'iao finally parted from her only by tearing his robe. Even after he had won honor and nobility in the Eastern Chin court, estimates of his character in his home village in the north never exceeded what they had been before. Every time he was given a noble title the emperor always had to issue a special edict before he would accept it.[2] (CS 67.2a)

[1] See above, SSHY II, 35.

[2] YYCS (cf. CS 67.2ab and TCTC 90.2860): After Emperor Yüan had ascended the throne, he appointed Wen Ch'iao cavalier attendant-in-ordinary (in 218). But since his mother had died while he was pressed by campaigns against rebels, and since he had been unable to go north to her funeral, Ch'iao adamantly declined. The emperor then issued an edict stating, "Since Wen Ch'iao has not yet buried his mother, and, furthermore, since there is some difference of opinion on the subject at court, he adamantly refuses to take up his post. Let us therefore have a discussion by all present, and We shall decide upon a middle course." (The wording differs considerably in CS and TCTC.)

10. Yü Liang wanted to bring Chou Shao up out of retirement, but Shao only kept declining the more adamantly. Each time Yü went to visit Chou, Yü would enter by the south (i.e., front) gate while Chou made his exit by the rear gate. One time, however, Yü went directly by stealth and Chou had no time to escape. They conversed with each other the entire day. Yü asked Chou for something to eat, and Chou produced some vegetable fare, which Yü proceeded to force himself to eat with great gusto. They talked together about the affairs of the world, and agreed to support and encourage each other, and together help to bear the burdens of the world.

After Chou became an official, he reached the rank of general, with a salary of two thousand piculs of grain. But it never suited his fancy, and once in the middle of the night he cried out with deep feeling, "The great man has been bought by Yü Liang!" Whereupon he heaved a great sigh, and an abscess developed in his back, after which he died.[1]

[1] HsünYC: Chou Shao was a recluse on Lu Mountain of Hsün-yang Commandery (Kiangsi) together with Chai T'ang. When Yü Liang became governor of Chiang Province (Hupei-Kiangsi, in 334) he heard of the reputation of Chai and Chou. Tying on his girdle and donning his shoes, he went to visit them where they were. When they heard that Yü was arriving, they would, as time went on, avoid him more and more. So one time Yü went by stealth. It happened that Chou Shao was shooting birds with a crossbow in the woods, and Yü came there to talk to him.

After returning, he reported, "This man may be brought up out of retirement." Whereupon he appointed him Protector Governing the Man Barbarians and grand warden of Hsi-yang Commandery (Hupei).

YLC (Yü Liang's letter to Chou Shao): The inhabitants of the one commandery of Hsi-yang fall short of the truth. Except it be by one who treads the Way with truth and simplicity, how can its vagrants and fugitives be governed? I have consulted with persons at court and in the provinces, and everyone agrees you are the man. So today I have sent up a memorial requesting that you be given the post. Do not refuse.

11. Juan Yü was a follower of the Great Dharma (Mahayana Buddhism), in which his devotion and credulity went to extremes. When his eldest son, Juan Yung, was not yet twenty he was suddenly stricken by a severe illness. Since the boy was the one in whom all his love and honor were concentrated, Juan prayed on his behalf to the Three Treasures (the Buddha, the Dharma, and the Sangha), not slackening by day or by night, for he felt that if his utmost sincerity had any power to move, he would surely receive help. But in the end the child did not recover, whereupon Juan bound himself to an eternal hatred of the Buddha, and all the devotion of his present and past lifetimes was totally wiped out.[1]

[1]SSHY Comm.: Anyone with the wisdom and understanding of Juan Yü would surely not have this kind of weakness. If this account is not mistaken, how great was his delusion!

When King Wen's (d. 1135 B.C.) time was up, even his sage sons (King Wu and the Duke of Chou) could not hold back his years. When the Śākya clan was exterminated, there was no supernatural power which could avail to lengthen their lives (see the *Virūdhakarāja-sūtra, Fo-shuo Liu-li-wang ching*; *Taishō* No. 513, XIV, 783-785, in which King Virūḍhaka slaughters the Śākyas in retribution for acts committed in a former incarnation). Therefore one's karma has a definite limit, and its retribution cannot be altered. If a man makes a request by prayer, expecting it to be efficacious, he is denying experience and nullifying his own doctrine. Surely he is only a vulgar disciple and nothing more. How could one talk with him about divine wisdom?

12. Whenever Huan Wen came face to face with Emperor Chien-wen (Ssu-ma Yü, before he became emperor in 371) he could never say very much. But after he had deposed the Duke of Hai-hsi (Ssu-ma I**, r. 365-371),[1] it became necessary to explain his reasons, so he prepared in advance to say several hundred words, setting forth the pros and cons of deposing or establishing the emperor. But after he saw Chien-wen, the latter immediately burst into tears which coursed down his cheeks in several tens of streams. Mortified and ashamed, Huan Wen could not get to say a word. (CS 98.26b)

[1]See above, SSHY II, 59.

13. As he was reclining on his bed Huan Wen once said, "If I keep on like this doing nothing (*dz'iek-dz'iek*), I'll be the laughingstock of Emperors Wen and Ching (Ssu-ma Chao and Ssu-ma Shih)."[1] Then, after crouching and getting up from his seat, he continued, "Even if I can't let my fragrance be wafted down to later generations, does

that mean I'm incapable of leaving behind a stench for ten thousand years?" (CS 98.24b-25a)

   [1] Ssu-ma Chao and Ssu-ma Shih were the second and eldest sons respectively of Ssu-ma I, and the real founders of the Chin Dynasty. Ssu-ma Shih deposed the Wei ruler, Ts'ao Fang (r. 240-254) in 254, and Ssu-ma Chao killed his puppet successor, Ts'ao Mao (see above, No. 7) in 260. Chao's son, Yen, then accepted the abdication of Ts'ao Huan (r. 260-265), and mounted the throne as Emperor Wu of Chin (r. 265-290).

14. While Hsieh An was in the east (i.e., in K'uai-chi, before 360) he used to travel by boat with coolies (*hsiao-jen*) pulling the boat. Sometimes they would be slow, and sometimes fast, sometimes they would stop, and at other times linger, or again they would let the boat go untended hither and yon, jolting the passengers or crashing into the shore. At first Hsieh never uttered any complaints, and people thought he was always free of anger or joy.

But one time he was on his way back (by carriage) from escorting the body of his elder brother, Hsieh I (d. 358), to its burial. At sunset a driving rainstorm had come up, and the coolies were all drunk and incapable of performing their duties. At this point Hsieh, rising from the middle of the carriage, seized the carriage pole (*ch'e-chu*) with his own hands and lunged at the driver, his voice and expression both extremely harsh.

Even though water by nature is calm and gentle, when it enters a narrow gorge it dashes and plunges. If we should compare it to human emotions, we would certainly understand that in a harassed and narrow place there is no possibility of preserving one's composure.[1] (*SLF* 3; *TPYL* 10, without final paragraph)

   [1] The Commentary cites the familiar passage in *Mencius* (VIA, 2): "In the case of dashing water, channel it east and it will flow east, west and it will flow west. Strike it and make it leap, and you may force it past your forehead; pump it and conduct it, and you may bring it up a mountain. But is this the nature of water? Of course a man may be made to do what is not good. Human nature, too, is like this."

15. Emperor Chien-wen (Ssu-ma Yü) once saw some rice (*tao*) growing in a paddy, and, not recognizing what it was, asked, "What kind of grass is that?"

His attendants replied, "It's rice." After the emperor returned, he did not go out again for three days. As he explained, "How could anyone depend on the end product (*mo*) without recognizing the source (*pen*)?"[1] (*TPYL* 839)

   [1] The statement could also be translated: "How could anyone depend on secondary matters without recognizing the primary?"
   SSHY Comm.: Duke Wen of Chin (r. 635-628 B.C.) learned from outside states how to plant rice (emending the *ts'ai*, "vegetables," of the text to *mi*, "rice," after parallel passages in *Hsin-yü*, *Shuo-yüan*, etc.), and Tseng Ts'an (5th cent. B.C.) learned to stretch sheep's hide on a frame (emending *mu*, "to herd," to *chia*, "to stretch on a frame," after the same sources). Even in the unlikely event of the emperor not recognizing the rice, why should he have been so remorseful? The account is surely spurious.

16. Huan Ch'ung was hunting at Shang-ming (Hupei), when a letter from the east (Chien-k'ang) arrived relating the news of the great victory on the Huai River (the repulsion of Fu Chien's invasion in 383). Speaking to his attendants, he said, "The striplings of the Hsieh family (Hsieh Hsüan and Hsieh Shih) have roundly defeated the rebels." Whereupon he took sick and passed away.

Conversationalists considered this death to have been a more worthy act than his yielding of the governorship of Yang Province (Kiangsu-Anhui-Chekiang) to Hsieh An (in 375), or his going to Ching Province (Hunan-Hupei, in 377).[1]

[1] *HCYC*: Huan Ch'ung originally felt that generals and statesmen were suited to different tasks, and that their talents and functions were dissimilar. Estimating his own virtue and capacities to be inferior to Hsieh An's, he therefore divested himself of the governorship of Yang Province and yielded it to An, claiming that he himself was a little more experienced in military governorships. When he was serving as governor of Ching Province (377-383), he heard that Fu Chien himself had emerged in the area of the Huai and Fei rivers. Deeply concerned for the basic territory of Chin, he dispatched three thousand elite troops which had been under his command to the rescue. At the time Hsieh An had already dispatched the Chin armies to the Huai River, and desired moreover to give the outward appearance of idle leisure. Therefore he ordered Ch'ung's troops to return to Ching Province. In great alarm Ch'ung cried out, "Hsieh An may have the capacity to serve at court and in the ancestral temple, but is totally untrained in military strategy. I predicted that the rebels would surely destroy Hsiang-yang (Hsiang-yang fell in 379) and then concentrate their forces in the Huai and Fei river area. Now, when the great enemy has arrived, as I predicted, Hsieh is just amusing himself with conversation and making a show of leisure. He's dispatched a bunch of inexperienced striplings whose armies in reality are too few and too weak. Who knows what will happen to the realm? We might as well 'fasten our lapels on the left' (and fall under barbarian rule)!"

When unexpectedly he heard news of the great and glorious victory, he was overcome with shame and mortification and passed away.

17. After Huan Hsüan had newly taken revenge and destroyed Yin Chung-k'an (in 399/400),[1] he was once listening to an exposition of the "Analects." When he reached the passage, "Wealth and honor are what all men desire, but if they have not been obtained in accord with the Way, the good man will not remain in possession of them,"[2] his mood and expression became exceedingly morose.

[1] *LAC*: Yin Chung-k'an was drawn to Huan Hsüan because of human sentiment, but, suspecting that the court was about to put Hsüan in his own place as governor of Ching Province, he dispatched the monk Chu Seng-ch'ien to offer precious gifts to the favorites of the chancellor-prince (Ssu-ma Tao-tzu) and to the attendants of the intermediary nun (Miao-yin) in an effort to denigrate Hsüan. Knowing of his plot, Hsüan attacked and destroyed him.

[2] "Analects" IV, 5.

CHAPTER XXXIV

Crudities and Slips of the Tongue

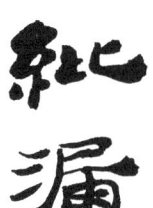

1. When Wang Tun had just married the Princess (of Wu-yang, Ssu-ma Hsiu-i), once as he was going to the privy he observed a lacquered box filled with dried jujubes (*kan-tsao*), originally intended to be used as nose-stoppers. Supposing that even in the privy they were also providing fruit, Wang proceeded to eat them all up.

When he came back the slave girls held out a golden washbasin filled with water and colored glass (*liu-li*) bowl filled with "bath beans" (*tsao-tou*). Tun proceeded to empty them into the water and drink them down, supposing them to be dried cooked rice. All the slave girls cupped their hands over their mouths and laughed at him. (*IWLC* 48, 87; *TPYL* 367, 391, 712, 760, 965; *PTSC* 135; *YYTT*, hsü 4; *TPKC* 263; *SWLC*, hsü 10)[1]

[1] *IWLC* 48 and *TPYL* 712 and 965 all add that the place was the home of Shih Ch'ung. *TPYL* 367 makes Shih Ch'ung the provider, but does not mention Wang Tun.

2. When Emperor Yüan (Ssu-ma Jui, r. 317-322) first gave audience to the director of works, Ho Hsün, their conversation touched upon events of the Wu Kingdom (222-280). The emperor asked, "When Sun Hao (last ruler of Wu, r. 264-280) was 'burning and sawing off heads,'[1] he cut off the head of a Ho. Who was it?" Ho Hsün had not yet gotten to answer before the emperor remembered it himself and blurted out, "Ah yes, it was Ho Shao."[2]

Ho Hsün said, weeping, "Your servant's father encountered a monarch without morals. Since 'the wound is great and the pain deep,'[3] I had no way of looking up to reply to Your Majesty's illustrious question." Emperor Yüan was so ashamed that for three days he did not go abroad. (*CS* 68, 16b; *TPYL* 763)

[1] *SKWu* 3.18b-19a: One of Sun Hao's beloved concubines sent someone to the marketplace of Chien-yeh to rob and plunder the money and possessions of the common people. The commandant in charge of the

marketplace, Ch'en Sheng, had formerly been a favored minister of Sun Hao, and, relying on the generous treatment he had received from Hao, bound the culprit according to the law.

The concubine complained about it to Hao, who in a great rage borrowed some pretext to burn and saw off Sheng's head (in 273), throwing his body beneath Lookout Mountain (Ssu-wang, west of Chien-yeh).

[2] *SSHY* Comm.: Shao was Hsün's father. *WuC*: Hao was cruel and rapacious, arrogant and proud, and Shao sent up a letter sharply admonishing him (the full text is found in *SKWu* 20.3b-6b). Hao deeply resented it. Those who were intimate with him, fearful of Shao's probity, slandered Shao, claiming he was detracting from affairs of state, whereupon he was publicly reprimanded, but later restored to his former post.

Shao suffered a stroke (*chung o-feng*) which left his mouth incapable of forming speech. Suspecting that he was feigning illness, Hao apprehended him and incarcerated him in a wine cellar. He examined him by flogging him with a thousand strokes, but to the end he never uttered a single word, so he killed him (in 275).

[3] See "Record of Rites" XXXIX, 1 (Legge, *Li Ki* II, 391): When the wound is great, its days are long; when the pain is deep, its healing slow.

3. When Ts'ai Mo crossed the Yangtze River (ca. 307-312), he saw a sand crab (*p'eng-ch'i*), and was greatly delighted, crying out, "(As it says in the *Erh-ya*),[1] 'the edible crab (*hsieh*) has eight legs plus two claws.'" Whereupon he gave the order to have it boiled. But only after he had eaten it and subsequently vomited it up and been miserably sick did he realize it was not an edible crab.

Later when he was speaking to Hsieh Shang about the incident, Hsieh said, "You didn't read the *Erh-ya* thoroughly enough, and were nearly killed by your ancestor's 'Essay on Exhortation to Learning' (*Ch'üan-hsüeh chang*)."[2] (*CS* 77.19b; *TPYL* 942)

[1] *Erh-ya* 16 (*Shih-yü*, "Explanation of Fishes"): "The smallest species of the *hua-che* crab is the *lao*." Kuo P'u's (276-324) gloss explains: "The *hua-che* is the same as the *p'eng-hua*. It resembles the edible crab (*hsieh*), but is smaller."

SSHY Comm.: Today's *p'eng-ch'i* is smaller than the *hsieh*, but larger than the *p'eng-hua*, and is what the *Erh-ya* means by *hua-che*. However, all three of these creatures have eight legs and two claws and are very much alike in appearance. It was because Ts'ai Mo had not been particular about the size, that he came to grief after eating it. That is why Hsieh said, "You didn't read the *Erh ya* thoroughly enough."

[2] *Ta-Tai Li-chi*, *Ch'üan-hsüeh p'ien* (VII, 64): The edible crab (*hsieh*), with its two claws and eight legs and no place to live except the holes of snakes and earthworms, scrambles about with all its might.

SSHY Comm.: It was for this reason that Ts'ai Mo's ancestor, Ts'ai Yung (132-192), wrote his essay, "Exhortation to Learning" (*Ch'üan-hsüeh chang*), taking his inspiration from this passage. (Fragments of Ts'ai's essay are gathered in *CHHW* 80.1b-2b.)

4. When Jen Chan was young he had an extremely good reputation. On the occasion of the death of Emperor Wu (Ssu-ma Yen, r. 265-290), when they chose one hundred and twenty pallbearers, all outstanding and accomplished young men of the time, Chan was among them. And when Wang Jung was choosing a husband for his daughter and from among the finest of all the pallbearers singled out four persons, Jen was still among those. As a boy and young man his spirit and intelligence were most lovable, and contemporaries used to say that even his shadow was good.

But from the moment he crossed the Yangtze River (ca. 307-312), he seemed to lose his ambition. Chancellor Wang Tao invited the worthies of the time who had been the first to cross the river all to come to Shih-t'ou (the port of Chien-k'ang), where he held a reception for Jen and treated him just as in the former days. But as soon as he saw him he felt there was a difference. After the banquet was ended and they were drinking toasts, Jen suddenly asked someone, "Is this early-picked tea (*tś'ia) or late-picked tea (*mieng)?"[1] Sensing that people were looking at him strangely, he hastened to explain himself, adding, "What I just asked was, are the drinks hot (*ńźiät) or cold (*lieng), that's all."

Once he followed a funeral procession as it passed beneath his lodgings, weeping tears of poignant sorrow. When Chancellor Wang heard about it he remarked, "The man's a sentimental idiot!" (*PTSC* 56; *TPYL* 490, 739, 867)

[1]*Erh-ya* 14 (*Shih-mu*, "Explanation of Trees"): "The *chia* is the 'bitter *t'u*' plant (of 'Songs,' No. 35, etc.)." Kuo-P'u's gloss elaborates: "The *chia* tree is small like the gardenia (*chih-tzu*), and produces leaves even in winter, which may be boiled to make a potable infusion. Nowadays we call the early picked leaves *ch'a* (*tś'ia) and those taken later, *ming* (*mieng), or *ch'uan*. The people of Shu (western Szechwan) call it *k'u-ch'a*, "bitter tea" (written with the same characters as *k'u-t'u*).

(Kuo P'u's identification of the *k'u-t'u* of *Erh-ya* 14 with *k'u-ch'a*, the contemporary Shu term for tea, *camellia sinensis*, can hardly be correct, since the earliest known textual reference to tea which leaves no room for doubt is found in the biography of Wei Chao, d. 273, in *SKWu* 20.10a, where it is stated he used tea as a substitute for wine. Tea was apparently indigenous to the Szechwan area sometime before this and gradually came into use as a common beverage in all of southern China by the end of the third century. It remained unknown in the north, except as an exotic item, until well into T'ang times, 618-906. The first attested use of the character *ch'a*--with one less stroke than *t'u*--occurred in Lu Yü's "Tea Classic," *Ch'a-ching*, in 780. See Paul Pelliot's review of C. A. S. Williams, *A Manual of Chinese Metaphor*, in *T'oung Pao* XXI, 1922, 435-436. Two facts seem to emerge from the present anecdote: first, that Jen Chan as a northerner had heard of tea, but did not really know what it was, and second, that in the fourth century the word for "tea" was pronounced *tś'ia, and not *d'uo; otherwise Jen's hasty effort to cover his faux pas with the quasi homophones, *ńźiät for tś'ia, and *lieng for *mieng, would hardly make sense.)

5. Hsieh Chü used to climb to the top of the room to fumigate rats. Since his son, Hsieh Lang, had no way of knowing that his father did

this kind of thing,¹ when he heard someone say that there was "some idiot" who used to do this, he made sport of him. At the time he himself repeated the story more than once. His uncle, Hsieh An, realizing that Lang didn't know it was his own father, waited until he was finished speaking, and then said to Lang, "People of the world have used this to cast aspersions on my middle brother;² they even say that I used to do it with him!"

Hsieh Lang was mortified and flushed with embarrassment. For a whole month he closed his study door and did not go abroad. Hsieh An's hypothetical citing of his own fault to awaken Lang is what might be called virtuous instruction.

¹Hsieh Chü died ca. 350, when Lang could not have been more than twelve.

²*Chung-lang* usually meant the "middle son" of three. Hsieh Chü was actually the second of the six sons of Hsieh P'ou, but as the Commentary notes: "He was probably called 'Middle Son' from the time when there were only three of them, and the name was never changed."

6. Yin Chung-k'an's father, Yin Shih, suffered from palpitation of the heart (*hsü-chi*).¹ Whenever he heard ants moving under his bed, he thought it was oxen fighting. Emperor Hsiao-wu (Ssu-ma Yao, r. 373-396), not knowing that it was Yin's father, once asked Chung-k'an, "Wasn't there a Yin who suffered from this kind of illness?"

Chung-k'an, weeping, rose from his seat and said, "Whether your servant 'advances or retreats, he has no place to go.'"² (*CS* 84.12a; *SLF* 30; *TPYL* 741, 947)

¹Yin Shih's ailment is differently named in the different sources. *CS* 84.12a calls it "excessive keenness of hearing" (*erh-ts'ung*); *HCYC*, cited in the Commentary, uses the term *shih-hsin ping*, literally, "missing heart-beat sickness." After 1600 the term *shih-hsin* meant acute depression or melancholia. See Nathan Sivin, *Chinese Alchemy*, Cambridge, Mass., 1968, p. 303.

²"Songs," No. 257, stanza 10, end.

7. While Yü Hsiao-fu was serving as personal attendant to Emperor Hsiao-wu (Ssu-ma Yao, r. 373-396), the emperor once asked him casually, "Since you've been serving here in the inner palace, I haven't so far heard whether you have anything to contribute."

Because Yü's home was wealthy¹ and near the ocean, he thought the emperor was expecting some token of his regard, so he replied, "The season's still too warm, and I haven't been able yet to send any sardines (*chih-yü*) or shrimps (*hsia*) and salted fish (*cha*). In a little while you should have a contribution!" The emperor clapped his hands and laughed aloud.² (*CS* 76.16b; *TPYL* 943; *SWLC*, hou 34)

¹The text reads: "Because Yü's home was in Fu-ch'un (near Hangchow)." But since neither his biography (*CS* 76.16b) nor any of the quotations contain the syllable *ch'un*, and since, moreover, the name of the town was changed in 371 to Fu-yang, to avoid the taboo name of Empress Cheng, and finally since there seems to be a connection between Yü's wealth (*fu*) and the expected gift, I have followed the emendation suggested by Yang Yung in his notes.

²In the CS 76.16b account, Yü, embarrassed by his faux pas, became so drunk he had to be lifted from the floor.

8. After Wang Ch'en died (in 392), in discussions at court someone said that his older brother, Wang Kuo-pao, ought to replace him as governor of Ching Province. Kuo-pao's superintendent of records sent him a sealed report by night which said, "The matter of the Ching provincial governorship has already been accomplished." Kuo-pao was enormously happy. That night he opened a side door and called in his staff. Although the conversation never touched on his becoming governor of Ching Province, nevertheless his mood and expression were extremely expansive.

In the morning he sent someone to make inquiries and found there was no such thing at all.¹ Immediately summoning his superintendent of records, he took him to task, saying, "Why did you make such a mess of my affairs?"

¹*CATC*: When Wang Ch'en died, the Prince of K'uai-chi (Ssu-ma Tao-tzu) wanted to have Wang Kuo-pao replace him. But Emperor Hsiao-wu intervened with a rescript, ordering that Yin Chung-k'an be appointed, whereupon he desisted.

CHAPTER XXXV

Blind Infatuations

1. The Wei Empress Chen was intelligent and beautiful. She had formerly been the wife of Yüan Hsi and had been greatly favored. When Ts'ao Ts'ao massacred the inhabitants of Yeh (southern Hopei, in 205), he gave the order immediately to summon Lady Chen, but his attendants reported, "The Commandant of the Five Offices (Ts'ao P'ei) has already taken her away."
Ts'ao Ts'ao said, "Then this year's crushing of the rebels was all for the sake of that rascal (nu)!"[1] (PTSC 26)

[1]WeiL: In the middle of the Chien-an era (ca. 200) Yüan Shao took the daughter of Chen Hui (SKWei 5.4b-5a gives his name as I) for his middle son, Hsi. Upon Shao's death (in 202) Hsi went out from Yeh to become governor of Yu Province (northern Hopei), while Lady Chen remained behind to care for her mother-in-law (ku, i.e., Yüan Shao's wife, Lady Liu*). At the time that the walls of Yeh were breached (205), Ts'ao P'ei, who was accompanying the campaign, entered Yüan Shao's house. Lady Chen, startled with fright, buried her head in her mother-in-law's lap. Ts'ao P'ei said to Shao's wife, Mme. Yüan, "Support Lady Chen and make her lift her head." Seeing that her beauty was out of the ordinary, he sighed over her in admiration. When Ts'ao Ts'ao heard of P'ei's feelings, he immediately welcomed her as a bride for him, and she lived with him illegally (her husband was still living until 207) for several years.
WCSY: When Ts'ao Ts'ao subjugated Yeh, Ts'ao P'ei went ahead of him into the mansion of Yüan Shang (Hsi's younger brother), where he saw a woman with disheveled hair and soiled face weeping, standing behind Yüan Shao's wife, Lady Liu*. On inquiry, P'ei learned that she was the wife of Yüan Hsi. He had someone hold aside her hair while he wiped her face with his sleeve. The beauty of her features was beyond compare. After he had gone, Lady Liu* said to Lady Chen, "You're not going to die after all." Thereupon

Ts'ao P'ei took her into his own household and she was highly favored.

WSCC: At the time that Ts'ao P'ei took Yüan Hsi's wife into his own household, K'ung Jung wrote a letter to Ts'ao Ts'ao, in which he said, "When King Wu (founder of Chou, r. 1122-1115) punished Chou Hsin (last ruler of Shang, r. 1154-1122), he bestowed (Chou Hsin's favorite concubine) Tan-chi upon the Duke of Chou." (Actually he beheaded her.)

Because of Jung's vast learning, Ts'ao really thought this was what the "Book of Ducuments" (Shu) and the traditions recorded. Later when he saw Jung and asked about it, Jung replied, "Reconstructing the past in terms of the present, I just imagined it was so."

2. Hsün Ts'an and his wife, Ts'ao P'ei-ts'ui, were extremely devoted to each other. During the winter months his wife became sick and was flushed with fever, whereupon Ts'an went out into the central courtyard, and after he himself had taken a chill, came back and pressed his cold body against hers. His wife died, and a short while afterward Ts'an also died. Because of this he was criticized by the world.

Hsün Ts'an had once said, "A woman's virtue is not worth praising; her beauty should be considered the most important thing."[1] On hearing of this, P'ei Wei exclaimed, "This is nothing but a matter of whimsy; it's not the statement of a man of complete virtue. Let's hope that men of later ages won't be led astray by this remark!"[2] (IWLC 32; MCYC, hsia; PSLT 6; TPYL 431)

[1] A parody of "Analects" I, 7.

[2] (Hsün) Ts'an PC: Ts'an always considered that the ability and intelligence of women was not worth discussing, and claimed that he himself considered their beauty the most important thing. The daughter of the General of Spirited Cavalry, Ts'ao Hung, was beautiful, so Ts'an asked her hand in marriage. Her face and clothing and the curtains of her apartment were extremely lovely, and Ts'an spent all his time in the bedchamber in dissipation and dalliance. After some years his wife took sick and died. Before she was buried Fu Chia went to pay Ts'an a visit of condolence. Ts'an was not weeping, but his very spirit was wounded. Chia asked him, "When a woman is well endowed with both ability and beauty, it's indeed difficult to lose her. But in the case of your marriage, since you dispensed with ability and kept only beauty, it shouldn't be such a difficult experience. Why such an extreme of grief?"

Ts'an replied, "Such a fine person would be difficult ever to find again. When I think back about the departed, though she couldn't be said to possess the unique beauty of an 'overthrower of cities,' still it isn't easy to experience her loss, and my pain and sorrow can know no end." Within the year he also was dead. At the time of death he was only in his twenty-ninth year.

Ts'an was unceremonious and aristocratic, and had no concourse with ordinary people. Those with whom he did associate were the outstanding and great of the entire age. On the evening of his burial there were no more than ten or so persons who attended the ceremony--all chosen from among famous gentlemen of his own age who had known him well. When they mourned him it moved even passersby on the road. Although Ts'an was mean and narrow-minded and had destroyed himself by his dissipation and dalliance, nevertheless those who understood him still regretted his loss as an able conversationalist.

SSHY Comm.: Ho Shao*, discussing Hsün Ts'an's character once said, "Confucius praised the conversation of the virtuous, but Hsün Ts'an was deficient in this. If we look back at what he said, there was more than enough; it was his understanding that was inadequate."

3. Chia Ch'ung's second wife, Lady Kuo (Kuo Huai), was cruel and jealous. She had a son named Li-min. On his first birthday[1] Ch'ung returned from outside when the wet nurse was carrying the child in her arms in the central courtyard. When the child saw Ch'ung he jumped up and down with delight, and Ch'ung went up to him and fondled him in the wet nurse's arms.

Seeing all this from a distance, Lady Kuo thought that Ch'ung was in love with the wet nurse, and immediately had her killed. The child missed her so sorely that he continued to cry, refusing to drink the milk of any other, until at length he died. After that Lady Kuo never had another son.[2] (CS 40.6b)

[1] CS 40.6b reads: "In his third year."

[2] CS 40.6b records that Lady Kuo did actually have another son, who suffered exactly the same fate, after which Ch'ung had no more heirs.

CCKT: Lady Kuo was the mother of Empress Chia (consort of Emperor Hui, r. 291-306). Being by nature high-minded and perceptive, and knowing that the empress had no son, Lady Kuo was extremely solicitous and affectionate toward the Crown Prince Min-huai (son of Lady Hsieh, later deposed and killed), and frequently encouraged him. On the eve of her death (between 282 and 300) she admonished Empress Chia to devote all her attention to the crown prince, and her words were very earnest. Said she, "Don't let either the lady-in-waiting, Chao Ts'an, or the mother of Chia Mi (Chia Wu, Chia Ch'ung's youngest daughter, wife of Han Shou; see No. 5, below) go in and out of the palace. These two will make a chaos of your affairs." But the empress was unable to utilize her advice, and in the end was executed with all her clan (in 300).

Liu Chün (or a later commentator calling himself "your servant" ch'en), states in the Commentary: "According to these words of Fu Ch'ang (author of the CCKT), Lady Kuo was a worthy and enlightened woman. If on that occasion she instructed Empress Chia to console and love the Crown Prince Min-huai, how could she on this occasion have given way to jealousy and cruelty, and herself have caused her own son's death? If it is, after all, a true account, then was it a difference between the affairs of others and her own, or a difference between her disposition in old age and in her prime?"

4. When Sun Hsiu** surrendered to the Chin (ca. 276), the Chin Emperor Wu (Ssu-ma Yen, r. 265-290) received him cordially and heaped him with favors, giving him his wife's younger cousin (i-mei),[1] Lady K'uai, in marriage. In their family life the two were very close.

Once in a fit of jealousy the wife reviled Hsiu**, calling him a "son of a badger" (ho-tzu).² Hsiu** felt greatly wronged by this and thereafter no longer entered her apartment. Very contrite and full of self-reproach, Lady K'uai sought rescue from the emperor. At the time there was a general amnesty, and all the grandees were just going out after the dawn audience. The emperor singled out Hsiu** and detained him, saying very affably, "The whole realm is clear and untrammeled. Might not Lady K'uai get to follow its example?"

Hsiu** removed his cap and made his apologies, and thereafter the couple lived as husband and wife as before.

[1] Lady K'uai, being a granddaughter of Yang Chün's paternal aunt, was a second cousin of Empress Yang, who was Yang Chün's daughter and the consort of Emperor Wu.

[2] The K'uai family hailed from Hsiang-yang (northern Hupei) and considered themselves northerners. Sun Hsiu** was from Wu in the southeast. Northerners spoke contemptuously of natives of Wu as ho-tzu, while natives of Wu reciprocated by calling northerners ts'ang-fu, "oafs," or "brutes."

5. Han Shou was handsome in appearance and features, and Chia Ch'ung summoned him for his aide. Every time Ch'ung held a meeting of his staff, his daughter, Chia Wu, watched through the blue-green chain-decorated doorway (ch'ing-so). When she saw Shou she liked him and constantly cherished thoughts of him in her heart, expressing them in the chanting of poems. Later one of her slave girls went to Shou's home where she related all this, and in addition spoke of the girl's radiant beauty. As he heard it, Shou was moved in his heart, and accordingly requested the slave girl to carry back a secret message.

On the appointed day he went to spend the night. Shou surpassed all others in nimbleness, and entered by leaping over the wall, so that no one in the household knew of his visit. After that Ch'ung became aware that his daughter was being rather lavish in applying make-up, and her elation was far beyond the normal. Later when he called together his aides, he noticed that Shou had about him the aura of an exotic perfume, one which had been sent as tribute from a foreign country. Once it was applied to a person it lasted for months without fading.¹ According to Ch'ung's calculation, Emperor Wu (Ssu-ma Yen, r. 265-290) had only bestowed this perfume on himself and on Ch'en Ch'ien; no other family possessed it. He suspected that Shou had been intimate with his daughter, yet the walls surrounding his house were double and solid, the main gates and side gates (ko) strong and impenetrable. How could he have gotten in? In the end he attributed it to robbers, and ordered someone to repair the walls. The messenger came back and reported, "Everything else is the same as usual, except only the northeast corner, where there seem to be human footprints. But the wall is too high to be leaped over by any man."

Ch'ung accordingly gathered his daughter's attendants and interrogated them closely, and they responded with the facts. Ch'ung kept the matter secret and gave his daughter to Shou in marriage. (CS 40.8b-9a; TPYL 392)

[1] TFSSCC: In the time of the Han Emperor Wu (r. 140-87 B.C.) the king of the country of the Yüeh-chih (Kushāna) in the Western Regions sent an emissary who presented four ounces (liang) of

perfume, the size of a sparrow's egg, black as the fruit of the mulberry. When it was burned as incense, the fragrance lasted three months without fading.

(Liu Chün hazards a guess in the Commentary that this was Han Shou's scent. The description fits loosely that of the vanilla-scented resin, storax--Chin. *su-ho*--described as "dark purple in color," and imported in pre-T'ang times from Rome and Parthia, later from the Sassanian Empire. See Schafer, *Golden Peaches*, p. 168.)

6. Wang Jung's wife always addressed Jung with the familiar pronoun "you" (*ch'ing*). Jung said to her, "For a wife to address her husband as 'you' is disrespectful according to the rules of etiquette. Hereafter don't call me that again."

His wife replied, "But I'm intimate with you and I love you, so I address you as 'you.'[1] If *I* didn't address you as 'you,' who else would address you as 'you'?" After that he always tolerated it. (*IWLC* 32, attrib. to Wang Hun and Chung Yen)

[1] Wives were apparently expected to use the more formal term *chün*, "my lord," but there is ample evidence that many did not. See, e.g., *SSHY* XIX, 6, above.

7. Chancellor Wang Tao had a favorite concubine, surnamed Lei, who used to interfere a good deal in matters of state and would accept bribes. Ts'ai Mo used to refer to her as "President Lei" (Lei Shang-shu). (*SWLC*, hou 16)

CHAPTER XXXVI

Hostility and Alienation

1. Sun Hsiu* already harbored a grudge against Shih Ch'ung for not letting him have Shih's concubine, Green Pearl (Lü-chu),[1] and in addition he hated P'an Yüeh, because in the past the latter had treated him uncivilly.[2]

Later, when Hsiu* became president of the Central Secretariat, Yüeh saw him in the department office and took the occasion to call out to him, "President Sun, do you remember our association of times gone by?"

Hsiu* replied (quoting the "Book of Songs"),

> "Within my midmost heart I've stored it;
> What day do I ever forget it?"[3]

It was then that Yüeh knew for certain that he would not escape alive.

Later (in 300), when they apprehended Shih Ch'ung and his nephew, Ou-yang Chien, on the same day they also apprehended Yüeh.[4] Shih was the first to be escorted to the marketplace for execution, and at the time did not know anything about the others. When P'an arrived later, Shih said to him, "An-jen, have you, too, come to this?"

P'an replied, "You might say,

> 'Till heads are white, we'll share a common fate.'"

In the "Preface to the Collected Poems of Chin-ku" (*Chin-ku shih hsü*)[5] P'an had written,

> "I cast my lot with my friend Shih;
> Till heads are white we'll share a common fate."

And now his prophecy was being fulfilled. (*CS* 55.16b-17a; *WH* 20.22b, Li Shan's commentary; *TPYL* 587; *SWLC*, pieh 32)

[1] *KPCC* (cf. *CS* 33.21ab): Shih Ch'ung had a female entertainer named Green Pearl who was both beautiful and expert on the transverse

flute (*ti*). Sun Hsiu* sent a messenger to ask for her. Ch'ung's villa was at the foot of Pei-mang Mountain (north of Lo-yang). At the time, he had mounted the Cool Observation Tower (Liang-kuan) and was looking out over the clear water. When the messenger reported his mission, Ch'ung brought out thirty or forty of his female slaves and concubines to show him, saying, "Help yourself to whichever one you choose."

The messenger said, "I was originally instructed to point out Green Pearl, but I don't know yet which one is she."

With sudden vehemence Ch'ung cried, "Green Pearl is the one I love; you can't have her!"

The messenger said, "My master is broadly acquainted with matters ancient and modern, and has searched and scrutinized far and near. I pray you to reconsider the matter." Ch'ung would not consent. Even after the messenger had gone out and returned, to the end he would not give in.

²*WYCS*: While P'an Yüeh's father, P'an Tz'u, was serving as grand warden of Lang-yeh (southern Shantung), Sun Hsiu* served under him as a minor clerk. On several occasions Yüeh kicked Hsiu* and did not treat him like a human being.

(Hu San-hsing's commentary at *TCTC* 83.2644 states that P'an Yüeh, not his father, was governor of Lang-yeh Principality, and "frequently flogged" Sun Hsiu* while the latter was in his employ.)

³"Songs," No. 228 (end).

⁴*CYC*: Earlier (in 296) while Ou-yang Chien was serving as grand warden of P'ing-i Commandery (Shensi), and the Prince of Chao, Ssu-ma Lun, was General Chastizing the West, Sun Hsiu*, acting as Lun's "belly and heart," was ravaging the region between the Passes (Shensi), and Chien frequently called him to account. For this reason there was bad feeling between them.

WYCS: Shih Ch'ung and P'an Yüeh were on very friendly terms with Chia Mi. When Mi was dismissed (in 300), Ch'ung was afraid that eventually his own life would be in danger, so he plotted with the Prince of Huai-nan (Ssu-ma Yün) to execute Ssu-ma Lun, but the affair leaked out and Ch'ung was arrested, and all his relatives, from those for whom a year's mourning was prescribed (uncles, first cousins, grandparents) on up, were beheaded.

Earlier Yüeh's mother had warned him to make contentment his way of life. When he was arrested, as he bade farewell to his mother, he cried out, "Mother, I've betrayed you!"

Ch'ung's home was north of the Yellow River. When those who came to arrest him arrived, he thought, "I'll only be exiled to Chiao (Annam) or Kuang (Kwangtung and Kwangsi), that's all." It was not until the van had carried him to the Eastern Marketplace (in Lo-yang) that he realized the gravity of the situation. With a sigh he said, "You fellows are doing this to profit from my family's wealth."

The one who had arrested Ch'ung replied, "If you knew that wealth would be your undoing, why didn't you dispose of it long ago?" Ch'ung was unable to reply.

⁵The lines are from the text, not the preface (see *WH* 20.22b). The immediate context goes:

"In spring's splendor who would not be loving?
It's only when the year is cold, good friends are rare.
I cast my lot with my friend Shih, etc."

YL: When P'an and Shih were executed together in the Eastern Marketplace, Shih said to P'an, "They're killing off all the heroes in the realm. What can you do now?" P'an replied, "When brave warriors choke the ditches and gulleys, the dammed-up waters will rise up to drown the others!"

2. When Liu Yü and his younger brother, Liu K'un, were young, they were hated by Wang K'ai. Once he invited the two of them to stay overnight, intending quietly to do away with them. He had a pit dug, and when the pit was finished, he awaited his chance to harm them.

Shih Ch'ung had been a long-time friend of Yü and K'un, and when he learned that they had gone to K'ai's to stay overnight, he knew there would be foul play, so he went that night to visit K'ai at his home, and asked, "Where are the two Lius?"

Trapped and unable to conceal the truth, K'ai replied, "In the back room, sleeping." Shih thereupon went directly in, and personally leading them out, departed with them in the same carriage. He said to them, "What business did you young people have going so recklessly to another person's house to stay overnight?"[1] (CS 33.21a)

[1] TTCC: Liu K'un and his older brother, Yü, were both well known and consorted freely with the families of the mighty and noble. Their contemporaries considered them great men.

3. While Generalissimo Wang Tun was holding Prince Min (Ssu-ma Ch'eng) prisoner (during Wang's rebellion, in 322), he dispatched his cousin, Wang I*, by night to bring the prince in a carriage to Wu-ch'ang (in Hupei) and kill him en route.[1] At the time the details were not fully known; even members of Prince Min's own family did not know all about it, and his sons, Wu-chi and his younger brother, were both in infancy.

Wang I*'s son Hu-chih, as he grew up became very intimate with Wu-chi. Once while they were playing together, Wu-chi went into the house to ask his mother, Lady Chao, to prepare a meal for Hu-chih. Amid tears, his mother replied, "When Wang Tun cruelly put your father to death, he borrowed the hand of Hu-chih's father, Wang I*, to do it. The reason why in all these years I've never told you is that the Wang family is powerful and you boys were still young, and I didn't want to have this noised abroad, just hoping that way to avoid trouble."

With a startled cry, Wu-chi drew his sword and rushed out. But Hu-chih had left and was already far away.

[1] CYC: Once as Ch'eng was passing through Wu-ch'ang, Wang Tun held a banquet in his honor, and when everyone was merry with wine, he said to Ch'eng, "Your Highness is sincere and honest and a fine gentleman, but no military genius." Ch'eng replied, "How do you know a lead sword can't make one cut?" (This statement was first made by Pan Ch'ao, a first-century general.)

When Tun was about to plot rebellion (in 322), he invited Ch'eng to serve as his sergeant-at-arms. Ch'eng said with a sigh,

"I'm as good as dead! The land is barren, the inhabitants few, my forces are left orphaned, and all reinforcements are cut off. To go to the aid of my sovereign in his distress would be the loyal thing to do, and to die for the king's business the right thing to do. If I die for loyalty and the right, what more could I ask?" Whereupon he circulated a summons to arms among all the commanderies, and joined the loyalist forces. Tun dispatched his maternal cousin, Wei I, to attack Ch'eng, and Wang I* sent a rebel force to meet him. Ch'eng died in the carriage.

Wang I* PC: Once while Wang Tao and Yü Liang were on a boating excursion at Shih-t'ou (the port of Chien-k'ang), it chanced that Wang I* came and joined them. That day a brisk wind was flying in the sails, and Wang I*, reclining on the ship's turret, was whistling a long tune, his spirit and manner most unrestrained.

Tao said to Liang, "Wang certainly has savoir faire."

Liang replied, "He's just easing his unrestrained feelings, that's all."

Wang's nature was haughty and overbearing, and whoever did not agree with him he would oppose. For this reason he was disliked by others.

4. When Ying Chan was appointed governor of Ching Province (Hunan-Hupei),[1] the son of Wang I*, Wang Ch'i-chih, and the son of the Prince of Chiao, Ssu-ma Wu-chi, arrived together at Hsin-t'ing (a suburb of Chien-k'ang) to bid him farewell. Since the guests who were present were exceedingly numerous, no one was aware that the two men were both present. One guest remarked, "When the Prince of Chiao, Ssu-ma Ch'eng, came to grief, it wasn't the intention of Wang Tun, but was just done by Wang I*, that's all."

On hearing this, Wu-chi seized a sword from an attending military aide, and there and then was about to cut off Ch'i-chih's head. Ch'i-chih ran and threw himself into the water. A boatman came to his rescue and drew him out, and thus he was able to escape.[2] (Cf. CS 37.26ab)

[1]This appears to be an error for Chiang Province (Hupei-Kiangsi), where Ying was appointed governor ca. 325.

[2]CHS (cf. CS 37.26ab): While Ch'u P'ou was governor of Chiang Province (342-343), Ssu-ma Wu-chi, who was present at a party, drew his sword to decapitate Wang Ch'i-chih. P'ou and Huan Ching both restrained him. The censors reported to the throne that Wu-chi had attempted without authorization to kill a man, but a rescript came back permitting him to ransom himself.

SSHY Comm.: The previous anecdote (No. 3) had already stated that Wu-chi's mother had informed him of his father's murder, yet the present anecdote states on the contrary that a guest recounted the event. Moreover, Wang I*'s murder of Ssu-ma Ch'eng was well known by everyone far and near. How could Wang Hu-chih and his younger brother have been ignorant of it? Ho Fa-sheng's words (in CHS) are all a factual record.

5. Wang Hsi-chih had always despised Wang Shu.[1] As Shu reached his later years his reputation grew more and more weighty, and Hsi-chih felt a greater sense of injustice than ever. While Shu was grand warden of K'uai-chi (Chekiang) he lost his mother, and remained at

Shan-yin (in K'uai-chi Commandery) to observe the mourning period. Hsi-chih replaced him as grand warden, and frequently stated that he would come out to Shan-yin to make a condolence call, but for days on end he never fulfilled his promise. Some time later he went to Shu's house and announced himself. After the host (Shu) had wept before the spirit tablet, Hsi-chih departed without coming forward, in order to insult him. Thereafter their mutual hostility and alienation were greatly aggravated.[2]

Later (in 354), when Wang Shu became governor of Yang Province (Kiangsu-Anhui-Chekiang), Wang Hsi-chih was still only grand warden of the commandery. When he first got news of Shu's appointment he dispatched an aide to the court requesting that K'uai-chi be detached from Yang Province to form Yüeh Province (eastern Kiangsu and Chekiang), but the messenger who carried his proposals failed in his mission, so that Hsi-chih became a great laughingstock of the worthies of the time. Shu secretly had a functionary enumerate all the illegal practices in Hsi-chih's commandery. Since they had previously been alienated, Shu's order was, in his own eyes, doing the appropriate thing. Hsi-chih promptly claimed illness and quit the commandery (355), and remained angry and embittered to the end of his life.[3] (CS 80.8b-9a)

[1] Wang Shu was still relatively unknown by the age of thirty, and many of his contemporaries considered him dull. Cf. SSHY IV, 22, and XXXI, 2, above.

[2] CS 80.8b-9a: Hsi-chih made one visit of condolence and never visited Wang Shu again. Whenever Shu heard the sound of the horn at the gate he thought Hsi-chih was coming to call on him, and would always sprinkle and sweep and wait for him. After this had gone on for several years and Hsi-chih never paid any attention to him, Shu became deeply resentful.

[3] CHS (cf. CS 80.8b-9a): Wang Hsi-chih and Wang Shu differed in their ambitions and aspirations, and the two were unequal in ability. While Shu was serving as grand warden of K'uai-chi he was observing mourning within the area of the commandery. Wang Hsi-chih later assumed the grand wardenship and extended a visit of condolence, but nothing more. Since he never called again, Shu became deeply resentful.

After the mourning period was ended, Shu was appointed governor of Yang Province. When he took up his post he made a tour through all the commanderies, but did not go past Hsi-chih's place. On the eve of his departure he bid him a single farewell and left.

Wang Hsi-chih had said earlier to his friends, "After Wang Shu has completed his mourning he would be just right as president of a secretariat, and in his old age he might get to be a vice-president. For him ever again to aspire to the grand wardenship of K'uai-chi is naturally out of the question."

But after Shu had manifestly received an appointment, he proceeded to make an investigation of K'uai-chi Commandery, searching out its assets and liabilities, and found that the one in charge (Hsi-chih) had been remiss in forwarding taxes. Hsi-chih was humiliated and embittered, and thereafter claimed illness and quit the commandery. Before the grave of his parents he made a vow (the full text is in CS 80.9a, where it is dated on a day equivalent to

April 7, 355) never again to hold office. In consideration of the bitterness of his vow, the court never reappointed him.

6. Wang Hsün in conversations with Wang Kung (had agreed that Wang Kuo-pao should be eliminated), but later he gradually changed his mind. Kung said to Hsün, "So then you're no longer predictable?"

Hsün replied, "Wang Ling* opposed the Han Empress Lü (r. 187-180 B.C.) in court, while Ch'en P'ing agreed with her and kept silent.¹ Let me just ask you--in the end how did it turn out?" (CS 65.12b-13a)

¹HS (40.18b-19a): Empress Lü wanted to make princes of all the Lüs and consulted the minister of the right, Wang Ling*, who deemed it not permissible. She then consulted the chancellor of the left, Ch'en P'ing, who said, "It is permissible." After Ling had gone out, he took P'ing to task, but P'ing said, "In opposing the empress to her face on court matters, I'm no match for you. But in preserving the gods of soil and grain and making the House of Liu secure, you're no match for me!"

CATC (cf. CS 65.12b-13a): Earlier Wang Kung went to the imperial tombs (for the burial of Emperor Hsiao-wu in 396), intending to decapitate Wang Kuo-pao. but after Wang Hsün had strongly remonstrated with him opposing it, he finally desisted. Later Kung said to Hsün, "The other day when I observed you, you were exactly like Hu Kuang (a minister of the Later Han in the second century A.D., whose tact enabled him to survive six reigns)." Hsün replied, "Wang Ling opposed Empress Lü in court, etc."

CS 65.12b: Hsün said, "Even though in the end Kuo-pao will cause trouble and rebellion, no important crime or insubordination on his part has yet become manifest. If we should move against him now, before the event, we are sure to cause large-scale disaffection at court and in the provinces. Furthermore, if we build up a powerful army and stealthily make our moves in the capital itself, who would believe it was not insubordination? If eventually Kuo-pao should not have reformed, and his evil ways are proclaimed throughout the realm, then if we should eliminate him in accord with the aspirations of the times, there would indeed be no troubles we could not surmount."

7. When Wang Kung died (in 398), they hung up his head by the Great Pontoon Bridge (Ta-hang, spanning the Ch'in-huai River south of Chien-k'ang). The grand tutor, Ssu-ma Tao-tzu, ordered his carriage to be driven out to the place where it was displayed. After gazing long and intently at the head, he said, "Why were you in such a hurry to kill me?"¹

¹HCYC (cf. CS 84.4ab): Wang Kung, profoundly dreading an impending disaster, wrote a protesting memorial and raised an army. Thereupon the court dispatched the general of the left, Hsieh Yen, to punish Kung. Defeated, Kung fled to Ch'ü-o (southeast of Chien-k'ang), where he was captured by the lakeshore patrol. (Kung, unaccustomed to riding, had developed blisters on his thighs, and, shifting to a boat, attempted to join Huan Hsüan's army which was approaching from the west down the Yangtze River. In one of the small lakes adjoining the river, Ch'ang-t'ang-hu, he was recognized and reported to the shore patrol. See TCTC 110.3478 and CS 84.4a.)

Earlier, Ssu-ma Tao-tzu had been friendly with Kung, and he wished to ride out of the capital now to rebuke him to his face. But when he heard of the threatened approach of the western army of Huan Hsüan, he gave the order to have him beheaded in Ni-t'ang (northwest of Chien-k'ang), and to have his head suspended by the Eastern Pontoon Bridge (Tung-hang).

8. When Huan Hsüan was on the point of usurping the throne (early in 404), his cousin, Huan Hsiu, wanted to take the opportunity of Hsüan's being at the home of Hsiu's mother, Yü Yao, to attack him. Mme. Yü said, "I pray you two, just let me pass my remaining years in peace. I've raised him (Hsüan) like a mother, and I can't bear to see you do this thing."[1]

[1]*CATC*: When Huan Hsiu was young he was insulted by his cousin, Hsüan, who was always rude to him when he spoke. Hsiu harbored a deep resentment over it and secretly plotted to take his life. Hsiu's mother said, "Ling-pao (Hsüan's baby name) looks on me as his own mother. How can you two bear to plot against your own flesh and bone?" Whereupon he desisted.

Biographical Notices, Glossary of Terms, and Official Titles, Abbreviations, and Bibliography

Biographical Notices

The following notices include all of the 626 persons who are mentioned in the anecdotes. (Names occurring only in the annotations may be found in the Index.) Each entry normally begins with the family and personal name of the subject with variant if any, followed in parentheses by the courtesy name and baby name if known. Next come the birth and death dates or approximate period of activity of the subject. (Unless otherwise specified, dates are A.D.)

This information is followed by an abbreviated reference citation to biographical information available in the appropriate dynastic histories. The acronyms which appear *after* the descriptive material refer to the lost biographical sources cited in Liu Chün's Commentary. (See the list of Abbreviations beginning on p. 665.)

At the conclusion of each entry there is a listing of all anecdotes, by chapter and number, in which the subject appears. An italicized number signifies the anecdote in which the Commentary contains the subject's biography. A number enclosed in parentheses indicates an anecdote in which the person appears by implication but is not actually named in the Chinese text; a question mark in parentheses indicates uncertainty about whether the person is involved in the anecdote.

CHAI T'ANG  (Tao-yüan  ; var. -shen 深). ca. 272-344. CS 94.19b-20a. A recluse who lived on Mt. Lu, near Hsün-yang (Kiangsi), whose family had originated in the north. While others suffered from brigands during the troubles following the barbarian invasions of 307-312, his unblemished reputation saved both him and his neighbors. *CYC.* XVIII, *9.*

CHAN, Lady 湛氏. d. ca. 307. *CS* 96.5-6a. The wife of T'ao Tan and mother of T'ao K'an, a native of Yü-chang Commandery (Kiangsi). *CYC.* XIX, *19.*

CHANG, Lady 張氏. late second to early third cent. The wife of Chen I 甄逸 and mother of Empress Chen of the Wei; maternal grandmother of the Wei Emperor Ming (r. 227-239). II, *13.*

CHANG, Lady* 張氏. late fourth cent. A younger sister of Chang Hsüan who married into the Ku 顧 family. XIX, *30.*

CHANG CHAN 張湛 (Ch'u-tu 處度). fl. ca. 370. The author of the earliest surviving commentary on the *Lieh-tzu*, and thought by some to be the compiler of the *Lieh-tzu* itself. He traced his ancestry indirectly to Wang Pi of the third century. *CTKPKM*; *Chang SP*. XXIII, *43, 45.*

CHANG CH'ANG 張暢, var. HUNG 鴻 (Wei-po 威伯). fl. late third cent. A native of Wu Commandery (Soochow). Though he lived through difficult times, he maintained his principles without compromise. *THC*. VIII, *20.*

CHANG CHAO 張昭 (Tzu-pu 子布). 156-236. *SKWu* 7.1a-6a. A native of P'eng-ch'eng (northern Kiangsu), he crossed the Yangtze during the turbulence at the close of Later Han (ca. 180); he served first under the Wu leader, Sun Ts'e (d. 200), and later under Sun Ch'üan (r. 222-252), rising to high honors. He is still remembered as a calligrapher, excelling in the clerical (*li*) style. *HCWC.* XXV, *1.*

CHANG CHEN 張鎮 (I-yüan 義遠). fl. ca. 300-325. The grandfather of Chang P'ing. A native of Wu, he was made grand warden of Ts'ang-wu Commandery (Kwangsi) ca. 302-303. For his service in subduing Wang Tun's elder brother, Wang Han, in 324, he was enfeoffed Marquis of Hsing-tao Prefecture (Kwangsi). *CTWP.* XXV, *40.*

CHANG HAN 張翰 (Chi-ying 季鷹). fl. first quarter, fourth cent. *CS* 92.15b-16a. A native of Wu Commandery (Soochow) who gained some reputation in his day as a poet. He served on the staff of the Prince of Ch'i, Ssu-ma Chiung, in Lo-yang during the latter's brief ascendancy as grand marshal in 301-302, but returned immediately thereafter to his native Wu. *WSC.* VII, *10;* XVII, *7;* XXIII, *20, 22.*

CHANG HSÜAN(-CHIH) 張玄(之) (Tsu-hsi 祖希). second half, fourth cent. A member of a prominent gentry family, his grandfather having been grand warden of Wu Commandery (Soochow), and his mother the daughter of the director of works, Ku Ho. He himself served successively as president of the Board of Civil Office, General

Governing the Army, grand warden of Wu-hsing, and governor of K'uai-chi Principality (both in Chekiang). He and his contemporary, Hsieh Hsüan (ca. 351-396), were known respectively as the "southern" and "northern" Hsüan. HCYC. II, 51; III, 25; V, 66; XII, 4; XIX, 30; XXIII, 38; XXV, 30.

CHANG HUA 張華 (Mao-hsien 茂先). 232-300. CS 36.15a-24b. Orphaned in his youth, he tended sheep for a living, but was befriended and educated by certain members of the gentry in his prefecture. After the Chin came to power in 265 he became grand ordinary, in charge of court ceremonial, but was dismissed when a beam in the ancestral temple broke. He had an enormous reputation for erudition, and compiled the early encyclopedia, Po-wu-chih 博物志, fragments of which still survive. He was killed during the War of the Eight Princes by the Prince of Chao, Ssu-ma Lun, in 300. WYCS. I, 12; II, 23; IV, 68; VIII, 19; IX, 8; XXIV, 5; XXV, 7, 9.

CHANG HUNG. See CHANG CH'ANG.

CHANG K'AI 張闓 (Ching-hsü 敬緒). ca. 265-328. CS 76.20a-21a. He served for a while as an aide in the entourage of Ssu-ma Jui before the latter's accession to the throne of Eastern Chin in 317. For his part in that event he was ennobled Marquis of Tan-yang, later becoming personal attendant and governor of Chin-ling Principality (Nanking). After arousing the jealousy of his rivals by saving the area from drought by irrigation, he was relieved of his post, though later restored. For his participation in the suppression of Su Chün in 328, he was named director of punishments and given other titles, but finding himself in ill health, he quit his post and died soon thereafter, in his sixty-fourth year. FMTS; CHS. X, 13.

CHANG MIN 張敏. late third cent. Author of the poem, "Ch'in Tzu-yü's Head Reproaches Him" (T'ou tse Ch'in Tzu-yü). He served under the Chin as aide to the General Pacifying the South, crown prince's chamberlain, and senior administrator to the grand warden of Chi-pei (northern Kiangsu). JCSP. (XXV, 7).

CHANG P'ING 張憑 (Chang-tsung 長宗). mid-fourth cent. CS 75.34ab. A man of short stature, who, after his recommendation for the degree, Filial and Incorrupt (hsiao-lien), by the warden of his native commandery in Wu (Soochow), passed his capital examinations with a high score and served as grand ordinary erudite under Ssu-ma Yü between 345 and 361, while the latter was Generalissimo Controlling the Army. Subsequently he became a clerk in the Board of Civil Office and central assistant censor. He was a talented writer and produced a commentary on the "Analects" much admired in its day. SMTWCC. IV, 53, 82; XXV, 40.

CHANG T'IEN-HSI 張天賜 (Ch'un-chia 純嘏; baby-name, Tu-huo 獨活). ca. 344-404. CS 86.32a-34b. Great-grandson of Chang Kuei 軌, who was governor of Liang Province (Kansu) at the time of the fall of Lo-yang in 311 and took advantage of his isolation to declare his independence. It was not until 354, however, when Kuei's grandson,

Chün 駿, assumed the royal title, that the state of Former Liang (354-376) was formally founded. T'ien-hsi, Chün's youngest son, ruled it from 364 to 376, when he was defeated by Fu Chien and taken captive to the Former Ch'in capital in Ch'ang-an (Shensi). Accompanying his new master on the ill-fated southern expedition of 383, he was again defeated, this time by Eastern Chin, and taken captive to Chien-k'ang, where he was given the titles of cavalier attendant-in-ordinary, and Duke of Hsi-p'ing. Later he was demoted to serve as grand warden of Lu-chiang Commandery (Anhui). In 404 the usurper, Huan Hsüan, used him briefly as Commandant Protecting the Ch'iang-barbarians and "governor of Liang Province." *LCC*; *CHS*. II, *94*, 99; VIII, 152.

CHAO, Lady 趙氏. late third to early fourth cent. The wife of Ssu-ma Ch'eng and mother of Ssu-ma Wu-chi. *Ssu-ma SP*. XXXVI, 3.

CHAO CHIH 趙至 (Ching-chen 景真). ca. 247-283. *CS* 92.9a-11b. The son of a military colonist near Lo-yang, he ran away from home to become a disciple of Hsi K'ang, later changing his name and fleeing to the northeast, where he served in the headquarters of the governor of Yu Province (northern Hopei and southern Manchuria). See T'ang Ch'ang-ju, "*Chin-shu* Chao Chih chuan chung so-chien-ti Ts'ao-Wei shih-chia chih-tu," *Wei-Chin Nan-pei-ch'ao shih lun-ts'ung*, Peking, 1955, pp. 30-36. *CCHs*. II, *15*.

CHAO FEI-YEN 趙飛燕 (d. A.D. 1). *HS* 97B.10b-18a. The daughter of a commoner and an accomplished singer and dancer. She was first the concubine of a local official near Ch'ang-an, and later, having been seen by Emperor Ch'eng (Liu Ao, r. 32-7 B.C.) on an incognito excursion, was taken into the palace, where she soon displaced Pan Chieh-yü as legal consort in 18 B.C. She and her younger sister both enjoyed lavish favors for over ten years, and at Emperor Ch'eng's death in 7 B.C. she became dowager empress. Reduced to the rank of commoner in 1 A.D., she took her own life. *HS, Wai-ch'i chuan*. XIX, *3*.

CHAO I 趙姬. d. 243. "Imperial Concubine Chao," also known as "Mother Chao" 趙母, a member of the Chao family of Ying-ch'uan (Honan). She was first the wife of Yü Wei 虞韙, and after his death was summoned, because of her reputation for scholarship and letters, to the palace of the Wu ruler, Sun Ch'üan (r. 239-252) at Chien-yeh (Nanking). She was the author of a lost commentary on Liu Hsiang's 劉向 (first cent., A.D.) "Lives of Virtuous Women" (*Lieh-nü chuan chieh* 烈女傳解, or *Chao-mu chu* 趙母注). *HFMLNC*. XIX, *5*.

CHAO MU 趙穆 (Chi-tzu 季子). d. ca. 320. He served as an aide in the administration of the Prince of Tung-hai, Ssu-ma Yüeh, around 307, and later, fleeing to Chien-yeh (Nanking), became tutor to Ssu-ma Shao (later Emperor Ming, r. 323-325). At the end of his life he was serving as grand warden of Wu Commandery (Soochow) with the noble title, Marquis of Nan-hsiang. *CWCHC*. VIII, *34*.

CHAO YÜEH 趙悅 (Yüeh-tzu 悅子). fl. late fourth cent. After serving in Huan Wen's administration during the latter's tenure as grand marshal (363-373) as work detail officer, he moved up to general of the Left Palace Guard. *TSMLSM*. VIII, *102*.

CH'E YIN 車胤 (Wu-tzu 武子). d. ca. 397. *CS* 83.14b-15b. Son of Ch'e Yü. A diligent student in his youth but without money for oil, he studied "by the light of fireflies." He began his official career in Huan Wen's administration of Ching Province (Hunan-Hupei), sometime between 345 and 361. In 375 he returned to court as a clerk in the Central Secretariat, and later became a personal attendant. Around 385 he was made a scholar of the Grand Academy and erudite in charge of the education of the sons of the nobility. Toward the end of his life he was consulted on matters pertaining to the suburban sacrifices and the "Hall of Light" (*ming-t'ang*), and antagonized the faction of Ssu-ma Tao-tzu and Wang Kuo-pao, who wanted to make changes in the court ritual. His final office was president of the Board of Civil Office. *HCYC*. II, 90; VII, 27.

CH'E YÜ 車育. fl. early fourth cent. The father of Ch'e Yin, he seems only to have served in minor capacities in his native commandery of Nan-p'ing (Hupei). *HCYC*. VII, 27.

CHEN, Empress 甄皇后. (183-221). *SKWei* 5.4b-9a. The fifth daughter of Chen I 逸. Her father died in her third year and she grew up with a somewhat studious turn of mind. Around the year 200 she married Yüan Hsi 袁熙, the second son of Yüan Shao. When Hsi became governor of Yu Province (northern Hopei) in 202 (*TCTC* 64.2044), she remained to care for her father's sister in Yeh (northern Honan). After Ts'ao Ts'ao's conquest of Chi Province (southern Hopei and northern Honan) in 205, he took her for his eldest son, P'ei (Emperor Wen, r. 220-227). Yüan Hsi fled to the Wu-huan in the northeast, where he was killed two years later (*TCTC* 65.2073). On P'ei's accession in 220, Mme. Chen became empress. She was the mother of Ts'ao Jui (Emperor Ming, r. 227-239), but incurring the emperor's anger when she protested the favors shown to the (later) Empress Kuo and the Lady Li, she was forced to commit suicide in 221. The tradition of her love for Ts'ao P'ei's younger brother, Chih, carried in Li Shan's note at the beginning of Ts'ao Chih's *Lo-shen fu* (*WH* 19.7b) is probably folklore. *WeiS*. II, *13*; XXXV, 1.

CH'EN CH'EN 陳諶 (Chi-fang 季方). fl. ca. 130-200. *HHS* 92.16a. Youngest son of Ch'en Shih. He and his father and brother, Ch'en Chi, were known as the "Three Gentlemen" (*san-chün*), and their portraits were painted and exhibited in a hundred cities "as an encouragement to public morals." The three were repeatedly summoned by the chancellor's office and showered with gifts from high officials. *HHHC*; *HNHHC*. I, 6, 7, 8, 10; IX, 6; XII, 1.

CH'EN CHI 陳紀 (Yüan-fang 元方). ca. 130-200. *HHS* 92.15a-16a. Eldest son of Ch'en Shih. The Han general Tung Cho (d. 192) consulted him about moving the capital to Ch'ang-an in 190, but obtained a negative reaction. He died as president of the Imperial Secretariat, having refused the title of grand marshal. A lost work in ten *chüan*, the *Ch'en-tzu*, is attributed to him. *HHHC*. I, *6*, *8*, *10*; II, 6; III, 3; V, 1; IX, 6; X, 3; XII, 1.

CH'EN CHIAO 陳矯 (Chi-pi 季弼). d. 237. *SKWei* 22.12b-14b. After fleeing across the Yangtze during the upheavals following the Yellow Turban Revolt of 184, Ch'en declined service under Sun Ts'e of Wu and returned to his native Kuang-ling (northern Kiangsu). Later his commandery was besieged by Sun Ch'üan, and he sought and received rescue of Ts'ao Ts'ao, who took him on as a staff officer. When Ts'ao died in 220, it was Ch'en who urged Ts'ao P'ei to cut short his mourning and mount the throne of the new dynasty of Wei. After distinguished service to the Wei court he ended his days with the title of director of instruction. XXV, 2.

CH'EN CH'IEN 陳騫 (Hsiu-yüan 休淵). 212-292. *CS* 35.1a-3a. A younger brother of Ch'en Pen, described as something of an opportunist. For his part in assisting the Chin Dynasty to power in 265 he was heaped with civil and military honors and the governor-generalship of several provinces. He died holding the rank of grand marshal. *CYC*. V, 7; XXV, 2; XXXV, 5.

CH'EN CH'ÜN 陳羣 (Chang-wen 長文). d. 236. *HHS* 92.16a; *SKWei* 22.3a-8a. The son of Ch'en Chi. He held many high posts under the Wei, including director of works, and is credited with the formulation of the system of laws governing the nine grades of officials for that dynasty. *WeiS*. I, 6, *8*; V, 3; IX, 5, 6; XXV, 3.

CH'EN CHUNG 陳忠 (Hsiao-hsien 孝先). late second to early third cent. The son of Ch'en Ch'en. When summoned to office in his provincial administration, he declined to serve. *Ch'en SP*. I, *8*.

CH'EN FAN 陳蕃 (Chung-chü 仲舉). ca. 95-168. *HHS* 96.1a-11b. He became grand tutor during the regency of the Empress Dowager Tou 竇 (147-167), and joined Tou Wu 竇武 in a struggle to purge the government of eunuch control, but was killed by his adversaries. He had been removed from the capital to Yü-chang (Kiangsi), "because his loyalty and uprightness irritated the imperial relatives." *JNHHC*; *HNHHC*. I, *1*; VIII, 1, 3; IX, 1.

CH'EN I 陳遺. fl. ca. 400-420. *NS* 73.7b. A native of Wu Commandery (Soochow) famed for his filial piety. I, 45.

CH'EN K'UEI 陳逵 (Lin-tao 林道). mid-fourth cent. He inherited the title of Duke of Kuang-ling, and began his career as a palace attendant, later serving as commandant of the Palace Guard. After that he served two commanderies in the provinces as grand warden. *Ch'en K'uei PC*; *CYC*. IX, *59*; XIII, 11.

CH'EN PEN 陳本 (Hsiu-yüan 休元). mid-third cent. *CS* 35.1a. A son of Ch'en Chiao, he served successively as a grand warden and director of punishments, though he had never read any treatises on law. His highest office was General Governing the North under Western Chin. *WCSY*; *WC*. V, 7.

CH'EN SHIH 陳寔 (Chung-kung 仲弓). 104-187. *HHS* 92.13a-15a. Repeatedly summoned to high office, he never assumed any post higher than magistrate of T'ai-ch'iu Prefecture (Honan). His reputation was so great, however, that 30,000 persons were said to have attended his funeral. *Ch'en Shih chuan.* I, 6, 7, 8; II, 6; III, 1, 2, 3; V, 1; IX, 6; X, 3; XII, 1.

CH'EN SHOU 陳壽 (Ch'eng-tso 承祚). 233-297. *CS* 82.1a-2b. A native of the Shu Kingdom who early in his career gained a reputation for resistence to overbearing superiors, and was accordingly frequently dismissed from office. Under eclipse after the fall of Shu in 263, he finally rose to prominence under the patronage of Chang Hua, and received the post of historian, in which capacity he compiled the dynastic histories of the Three Kingdoms, *San-kuo chih*. Later he was transferred to the post of censor, but left the court when his mother died. His final office was on the staff of the crown prince. *WYCS.* XXV, 44.

CH'EN SHU 陳述 (Ssu-tsu 嗣祖). d. 322. An officer on the staff of Wang Tun, he died of natural causes just prior to Tun's revolt in the spring of 322. *Ch'en SP.* XX, 5.

CH'EN T'AI 陳泰 (Hsüan-po 玄伯). d. 260. *SKWei* 22.8a-12a. A son of Ch'en Ch'ün noted for his bravery and decisiveness. He fought for the Wei Kingdom against Shu and was named General Chastizing the West, governor-general of Yung and Liang Provinces (Shensi), and finally, right vice-president of the Imperial Secretariat. When Ssu-ma Chao rejected his counsel to kill Chia Ch'ung to appease the people after the latter had ordered the death of Ts'ao Mao in 260, he committed suicide. *WC*; *KPCC*; *HCCC*; *WSCC.* V, 8; VIII, 108; IX, 5, 6; XXV, 2, 3.

CH'EN WEI 陳煒 (var. 煒). late second cent. He was Great Officer of the Center ca. 162, when K'ung Jung was a small boy. II, 3.

CH'EN YING 陳嬰. late fourth to early third cent. B.C. *SC* 7.3b-4a. An officer under Hsiang Liang 項梁, a rival of Liu Pang 劉邦, founder of the Han Dynasty (r. 206-195 B.C.). *SC.* XIX, 1.

CH'EN YING's Mother 陳嬰母. late fourth cent. B.C. *SC* 7.4a. XIX, 1.

CHENG A-CH'UN 鄭阿春. d. 326. *CS* 32.8b-10a. Eldest daughter of Cheng K'ai 愷 and orphaned at an early age. She was first married to a member of the T'ien 田 family, but after her husband's premature death, went to live with her maternal uncle, of the Wu 吳 family. After having been promised again in marriage to still another family, she came to the attention of Emperor Yüan (Ssu-ma Jui, r. 317-322), who took her into the palace in 317, five years after the death of his first wife, Empress Yü 虞. She was the mother of Emperor Chien-wen (Ssu-ma Yü, r. 371-372), and after the latter's accession in 371, received the posthumous title, Empress Dowager Wen-hsüan 文宣太后. *CHS.* V, 23.

CHENG CH'UNG 鄭沖 (Wen-ho 文和). d. 274. *CS* 33.5b-7b. A Confucian scholar and editor of a commentary on the "Analects" who began his career as grand warden of Ch'en-liu Commandery (Honan), and in 251 rose to become director of works for the Wei Kingdom. After the establishment of Chin in 265 he was rewarded for his part in the founding with the title of grand tutor. *WYCS.* III, 6; IV, 67.

CHENG HSÜ 鄭翃 (Ssu-yüan 思潚), second half, third cent. A contemporary of Chang Min from Lo-yang, he was an officer of the palace guard. *CCKT.* XXV, 7.

CHENG HSÜAN 鄭玄 (K'ang-ch'eng 康成). 127-200. *HHS* 65.11b-16b. One of the greatest commentators on the classics of all time, and the most illustrious of Ma Jung's disciples. After a tour of service at court he returned to writing commentaries and teaching, numbering K'ung Jung among his disciples. His reputation apparently spared him from the ravages of the Yellow Turban revolt in 184, but during the civil war between Ts'ao Ts'ao and Yüan Shao he was forced to move while ill and died in the summer of his seventy-fourth year. *HKKSC*; *Cheng Hsüan PC.* IV, 1, 2, 3; XXVI, 21.

CHI NI 濟尼. late fourth cent. Otherwise unknown. XIX, 30.

CHIA, Empress. See CHIA NAN-FENG.

CHIA CH'ÜAN 賈荃. d. after 300. Mentioned, *CS* 40.7b-8b. Elder daughter of Chia Ch'ung and Li Wan, she became the consort of the Prince of Ch'i, Ssu-ma Yu (d. 283). *CCKT.* XIX, 14.

CHIA CH'UNG 賈充 (Kung-lü 公閭). 217-282. *SKWei* 15.21a, comm.; *CS* 40.1a-7b. A son of Chia K'uei's old age who was left an orphan while still very young. For his services in helping to codify the Wei laws while still a clerk in the Central Secretariat, he was made a palace attendant. After accompanying the generalissimo Ssu-ma Shih in the suppression of Kuan-ch'iu Chien's uprising in 255, he became sergeant-at-arms for Shih's brother and successor, Ssu-ma Chao, and by his military exploits in the northwest greatly assisted in laying the foundations for Western Chin before Chao's death in 264. After Chin was founded in the following year, Chia was again employed in the gigantic task of codifying the laws, for which he was given the titles of General of Chariots and Horsemen and cavalier attendant-in-ordinary, eventually becoming president of the Imperial Secretariat. His eldest daughter, Ch'üan 荃, had been married to the Prince of Ch'i, Ssu-ma Yu (d. 283), and his younger daughter, Nan-feng 南風, was betrothed to the crown prince, Ssu-ma Chung (the future Emperor Hui, r. 290-306) around 272, after which Chia rose to be director of works, personal attendant, grand marshal and grand protector. Between 279 and 280 he directed the successful campaign against the Wu Kingdom and at his death in 282 received a state funeral. *CCKT.* III, 6; V, 8; XIX, 13, 14; XXXV, 3, 5.

CHIA LI-MIN 賈黎民. d. before 282, in infancy. Mentioned, *CS* 40.6b. A son of Chia Ch'ung by Kuo Huai, he died after his mother had his wet nurse killed in a fit of jealousy. *CCKT.* XXXV, 3.

CHIA NAN-FENG 賈南風 (baby name, Shih 峕). d. 300. *CS* 31.17a-20a. Daughter of Chia Ch'ung and Kuo Huai, and consort of the imbecile Emperor Hui (Ssu-ma Chung, r. 291-306). While Chung was crown

prince and a suitable match was being sought for him, members of
the Chia-Kuo clique succeeded in getting the empress's ear against
the better judgment of Emperor Wu (Ssu-ma Yen, r. 265-290). The
couple were engaged when Chung was in his thirteenth year and Nan-
feng in her fifteenth. In 272 she was declared legal consort, and
from that moment on she completely controlled her weak-minded husband who was terrified by her tantrums. She began in 291 by ordering the death of the chancellor, Yang Chün, father of the dowager empress, and all the members of their family. Childless herself, she intended to set up her nephew, Chia Mi 謐, in place of
the designated crown prince, Ssu-ma Min-huai 愍懷, whom she deposed in 299 and killed in the following year. This act triggered
a coup d'etat led by the Prince of Chao, Ssu-ma Lun, who killed
Empress Chia and all the members of her clan, thus beginning the
bloody civil wars known as the "War of the Eight Princes" (300-
306). *WYCC*. XIX, *14*.

CHIA NING 賈寧 (Chien-ning 建寧). early fourth cent. An illegitimate
son brought up in the consort family which produced Empress Chia
(d. 300). At first allied with Wang Tun's adopted son, Ying, after
the suppression of Tun's revolt in 324, he fled to Wu Commandery
(Soochow), where he was treated with contempt. Learning of the
disturbances at the capital over Su Chün's revolt in 327, he threw
in his lot with the latter, who employed him as his chief adviser.
He had the forethought to surrender to the loyalists before Su
Chün's final defeat in 328, and thus lived to serve as grand warden of Hsin-an Commandery (Chekiang) for some years thereafter.
CYC. VIII, *67*.

CHIA WU 賈午. d. 300. Mentioned, *CS* 40.8b-9a. Youngest daughter of
Chia Ch'ung and wife of Han Shou, whose son, Han Mi 謐, was adopted
into the Chia family after Ch'ung's death in 282 without male
heirs. She was instrumental in urging her aunt, Empress Chia, to
depose Crown Prince Min-huai in 299, but perished in Ssu-ma Lun's
purge of the Chia clan the following year. *KT*. XXXV, *5*.

CHIANG AI 江斅 (Chung-k'ai 仲凱; baby name, Lu-nu 盧奴). fl. ca.
400. *CS* 56.11a. A son of Chiang Pin who served as governor of
Lang-yeh Principality (northern Kiangsu), palace attendant, and
advisory aide to the General of Hardy Horsemen. His reputation was
made on unceremoniousness and modesty. *CATC*; *SS*. V, *63*.

CHIANG KUAN 江灌 (Tao-ch'ün 道羣). d. ca. 375. *CS* 83.13b-14a. A
cousin of Chiang Pin. While Ssu-ma Yü was Generalissimo Controlling the Army (345-352), he served as his administrator, later becoming a clerk in the Board of Civil Office, returning still later
as Yü's sergeant-at-arms. Being a very proper man, he alienated
some very influential people, including Huan Wen, and while the
latter held the supreme power at court, Chiang never held any important posts. In 373 he served briefly as Huan's consulting aide,
and after Huan's death in the same year, became an officer in the
Imperial Secretariat. He died before he could take up his post as
grand warden of Wu Commandery (Soochow). *CHS*. VIII, *84*, *135*.

CHIANG PIN 江虨 (Ssu-hsüan 思玄). d. ca. 370. CS 56.10b-11a. A champion go-player in his day. After serving in the administrations of Wen Ch'iao and Ch'ih Chien, he moved in 340 to Wu-ch'ang (Hupei), where he joined the staff of Yü Ping and later Yü I, who replaced Ping as governor of Ching Province (Hunan-Hupei) from 340 until his death in 345. After that, Chiang returned to the capital where he served in both the Imperial Secretariat and the Board of Civil Office, eventually becoming president of the latter. Around 350 he was serving as governor of K'uai-chi Principality (Chekiang), and later as vice-president of the Imperial Secretariat. While Ssu-ma Yü was chancellor-prince between 366 and 371, Chiang was a member of his staff. HKCC. V, 25, 42, 46; VIII, 127; IX, 56; X, 18; XXVI, 14; XXVII, 10.

CHIANG TUN 江惇 (Ssu-ch'üan 思悛). 305-353. CS 56.11b. Younger brother of Chiang Pin. Though he combined Confucianism and Taoist philosophy in the best hsüan-hsüeh tradition, he was definitely opposed to mere libertinism, as the title of his "Treatise Clarifying the Way and Praising Restraint" (T'ung-tao ch'ung-chien lun 通道崇檢論) suggests. During Su Chün's rebellion (327-328) he fled to Tung-yang Commandery (western Chekiang), where he remained a recluse, resisting all calls to office until his death. HKCC. VIII, 94, (127).

CH'IAO HSÜAN 喬玄 (Kung-tsu 公祖). fl. late second cent. A specialist in the "Record of Rites" and the Yen 嚴 edition of the "Spring and Autumn Annals." His highest office was president of the Imperial Secretariat. HsHS. VII, 1.

CH'IEN FENG 錢鳳 (Shih-i 世儀). d. 324. A native of Wu (Soochow) described as "treacherous, secretive and avaricious," he served as aide-de-camp to Wang Tun but was executed after Tun's defeat in 324. CYC. XXVII, 7.

CHIH CHAN 摯瞻 (Ching-yu 景游). d. ca. 317. A nephew of Chih Yü. Beginning his career as historian at the Western Chin court in Loyang after the barbarian invasions began, he joined Wang Tun's staff in Yang Province (Kiangsu-Anhui-Chekiang) around 309, and governed several commanderies of that province under Wang's supervision. But after antagonizing his patron he was sent to Sui Commandery (Hupei) where, foreseeing Wang's rebellious ambitions as early as 317, he resisted his influence in Ching Province (Hunan-Hupei) but was killed by Wang shortly afterwards. Chih-shih shih-pen. II, 42.

CHIH MIN-TU 支愍度. early fourth cent. KSC 4; Taishō 50.347a. A monk of northern origin who fled south between 326 and 342. He was known primarily as a cataloguer of Buddhist texts, though his "General Catalogue of Sūtras and Śāstras" (Ching-lun tu-lu) survives only in quotations in CSTCC. He is also credited with cofounding the "School of Mental Nonexistence" (Hsin-wu i), a kind of subjective idealism. MTSMTM; MTT. XXVII, 11.

CHIH TUN 支遁 (Tao-lin 道林). 314-366. KSC 4; Taishō 50.348b-349c. Probably the most admired and most influential of the cultivated clergy living in the area of Chien-k'ang (Kiangsu) and K'uai-chi (Chekiang) during the Eastern Chin. Originally from a northern gentry family named Kuan 關, he spent his youth in the K'uai-chi area studying the "Smaller Version" of the *Prajñāpāramitā-sūtra*, but was not ordained until his twenty-fifth year. Thereafter he divided his time between monasteries in the capital and K'uai-chi, lecturing and participating in "pure conversation" sessions with the great figures of the day. Among his lay disciples were Yin Hao, Hsieh An, Wang Hsi-chih, Ch'ih Ch'ao, and Sun Ch'o. He is credited with founding one of the "Six Schools" of early Chinese Buddhism, viz., the Chi-se ("The Emptiness of Matter-as-such"). See Fukunaga Mitsuji, "Shi Ton to sono shūi," *Bukkyo shigaku* V, 1956, 102-104, and Zürcher, *Conquest*, pp. 116-130. KISMC. II, 45, 63, 76, 87; III, 18; IV, 25, 30, 32, 35, 36, 37, 38, 39, 40, 41, 42, 43, 45, 51, 55; VI, 31; VIII, 83, 88, 92, 98, 110, 119, 123, 136; IX, 54, 60, 67, 70, 76, 85; XIV, 29, 31, 37; XVII, 11, 13; XXI, 10; XXV, 28, 43, 52; XXVI, 21, 24, 25, 30.

CHIH YÜ 摯虞 (Chung-chih 仲洽). d. 311. CS 51.11a-19b. A native of Ch'ang-an (Shensi), he studied in his youth with Huang-fu Mi and became a voluminous writer, the bulk of his works being commentaries and textual studies. He served successively as curator of the Imperial Library and lord grand ordinary. Accompanying the kidnapped Emperor Hui (r. 290-306) to his native Ch'ang-an in 304, Chih became separated from the imperial cortege and many of his manuscripts were scattered and lost. Later, during the barbarian attack on Lo-yang in 311, he died of starvation. WYCS. IV, 73.

CH'IH CH'AO 郗超 (Chia-pin 嘉賓; Ching-hsing 景興). 336-377. CS 67.20a-22b. Son of Ch'ih Yin and grandson of Ch'ih Chien. First an aide under Huan Wen, and later his senior administrator, he became the one chiefly responsible for encouraging Huan toward usurpation, which the latter nearly accomplished before his death in 373. Ch'ih was reared in the tradition of the Taoist sect of the Heavenly Master but became a devout Buddhist and lay disciple of the monk Chih Tun. His important manual for a layman, "Essentials of Religion" (*Feng-fa yao* 奉法要), is preserved in *Hung-ming-chi* 13; *Taishō* 52.86a-89b; translated, Zürcher, *Conquest*, pp. 164-176. CHS. II, 59, 75; VI, 27, 30, 32; VII, 22, 25; VIII, 117, 118, 126, 145; IX, 49, 62, 67, 79, 82; XI, 6; XVI, 5; XVII, 12; XVIII, 15; XIX, 29; XXII, 3; XXIV, 15; XXV, 44, 49, 50, 53; XXIX, 9.

CH'IH CHIEN 郗鑒 (Tao-hui 道徽). 269-339. CS 67.13a-19a. A descendant of the Han censor, Ch'ih Lü 慮; father of Ch'ih Yin and Ch'ih T'an, and father-in-law of Wang Hsi-chih. In spite of a poverty-stricken youth, he managed to educate himself, and when invited to join the staff of the ambitious princes Ssu-ma Lun and Ssu-ma Yüeh, he declined. Surviving the famine following invasions of the north by the Hsiung-nu in 309 and 311 through the generosity of admirers, he managed to escape southward, and under the Eastern Chin rose to the highest honors as director of works and grand marshal. Hsi Chien PC. I, 24; II, 38; VI, 19; IX, 14, 19; X, 14.

CH'IH HSÜAN 郗璿 (Tzu-fang 子房). ca. 315-405. The daughter of Ch'ih Chien and wife of Wang Hsi-chih. Wang SP. VI, 19; XIX, 25, 31.

CH'IH HUI 郗恢 (Tao-yin 道胤; baby name, A-ch'i 阿乞). d. 398. CS 67.23a-24b; KSC 1; Taishō 50.328c. A son of Ch'ih T'an and cousin of Ch'ih Ch'ao. He possessed a magnificent physique with an imposing beard, and from a position in the palace guard advanced rapidly, becoming governor of Yung Province (southern Shensi and northern Szechwan) in 392, where he had to deal with frequent border incidents with the neighboring state of Later Ch'in (384-417) and two years later with the invading armies of Northern Wei (384-535). In 397 he joined Wang Kung and Yin Chung-k'an against the clique of Ssu-ma Tao-tzu at court, and after Huan Hsüan's coup the following year, served as president of the Imperial Secretariat. Becoming involved in an internecine struggle among Hsüan's underlings, he was killed on orders from Yin Chung-k'an in the winter of 398. CHS. XVIII, 17; XXIII, 39.

CH'IH JUNG 郗融 (Ching-shan 景山; baby name, Ts'ang 倉). mid fourth cent. The second son of Ch'ih Yin, he died before assuming any office. Ch'ih SP. XXV, 44.

CH'IH LUNG 郗隆 (Hung-shih 弘治). d. 301. A man noted for his fair appraisals of others. After serving in the Board of Civil Office, he became governor of Yang Province (Kiangsu-Anhui-Chekiang). When the Prince of Ch'i, Ssu-ma Chiung, raised the standard of revolt against the Prince of Chao, Ssu-ma Lun, who attempted to usurp the throne in 301, Ch'ih Lung resisted the summons, for which he was killed. CCKT; YenCC. IX, 9.

CH'IH MAI 郗邁 (Ssu-yüan 思遠). fl. early fourth cent. Son of Ch'ih Chien's elder brother. He served as governor of Yen Province (southern Shantung), and General Protecting the Army. CHS. I, 24.

CH'IH T'AN 郗曇 (Ch'ung-hsi 重熙). 320-361. CS 67.22b. The second son of Ch'ih Chien, father of Ch'ih Hui, and uncle of Ch'ih Ch'ao. He began his career as a private secretary to Wang Tao, and in his thirtieth year (ca. 348) was transferred to the palace as an attendant. He later served as Ssu-ma Yü's sergeant-at-arms while the latter was General Controlling the Army (ca. 350-357), and also worked in the Board of Civil Office. He replaced Hsün Hsien as northern commander in 358, and became governor-general of five provinces with headquarters in Hsia-p'ei (northern Kiangsu). The following year, while engaged in the campaign against Yen in the north, he became ill and retreated, causing a serious rout of the Chin forces, for which he was degraded. He died shortly afterward. (Ch'ih) T'an PC. XIX, 25; XXV, 39, 51; XXVI, 31.

CH'IH TAO-MAO 郗道茂. second half, fourth cent. The daughter of Ch'ih T'an, she was married to Wang Hsien-chih and later divorced, the one act of which he repented on his deathbed. Wang SP. I, 39.

CH'IH YIN 郗愔 (Fang-hui 方回). 313-384. CS 67.19a-20b. Son of Ch'ih Chien and father of Ch'ih Ch'ao. A man of mild, noncompetitive disposition, who nearly died from the excesses of mourning his parents. He served as senior administrator, first for Ho Ch'ung while the latter was regent after the death of Emperor K'ang toward the end of 344, and later for Ch'u P'ou while P'ou was stationed in Ching-k'ou (Kiangsu). Related by marriage to Wang Hsi-chih, he was, like him, a devotee of the Heavenly Master sect of religious Taoism, and spent a good deal of time in retirement in K'uai-chi (Chekiang). In 369, while he was governing Hsü and Yen provinces (northern Anhui and Southern Shantung) Huan Wen asked him to accompany him on the campaign against the Former Yen state in the north, but Yin's son, Ch'ao, then serving as Huan's aide, intervened to have Yin made governor of K'uai-chi, where he spent the remainder of his life. He received the posthumous title of director of works. *Ch'ih Yin PC.* II, (59); IX, 24, *29*; XI, 6; XVII, 12; XIX, 25; XX, 10; XXIV, 15; XXV, 44, 51; XXIX, 9.

CHIN-LING, Princess of 晉陵公主. late fourth to early fifth cent. The daughter of Emperor Hsiao-wu (Ssu-ma Yao, r. 373-396) and wife of Hsieh Hun. *HCYC*. XXV, *60*.

CH'IN TZU-YÜ 秦子羽. second half, third cent. A nom de plume of Chang Min (?). XXV, 7.

CHING FANG 京房 (Chün-ming 君明). 77-37 B.C. *HS* 75.6a-11b; 88.10b-11a. His original surname was Li 李, and he belonged to the group of scholars who compiled the "Kung-yang Commentary" to the "Spring and Autumn Annals" (*Ch'un-ch'iu Kung-yang chuan*). He was noted both as a musician and as a fearless critic of contemporary morals. After offending some highly placed courtiers, he was slandered and condemned to public execution. *HS*. X, *2*.

CHOU CHEN 周鎮 (K'ang-shih 康時). early fourth cent. Son of Chou Chen* 震. His reputation was based on his frugality and incorruptibility. *YCLJM*; *CHS*. I, *27*.

CHOU CH'ENG 周乘 (Tzu-chü 子居). second cent. *HHS* 91.7b-14b. A contemporary of Ch'en Fan whose administrative ability was admired by the latter. He served for a while as grand warden of T'ai-shan (Shantung). *JNHHC*. I, 2; VIII, *1*.

CHOU CH'U 周處 (Tzu-yin 子隱). 236-297.   58.1a-3b. A native of the Wu Kingdom who gained a reputation even as a youth for his great physical strength, love of the chase, and loose morals. After ridding his village of a marauding tiger and water-monster, he realized he himself had been considered a third "scourge" and reformed his ways. After the fall of Wu in 280 he traveled to Lo-yang and was appointed successively to several grand-wardenships in the north, where he recovered his reputation and was known as a good administrator. Declining a promotion to cavalier attendant-in-ordinary at court, he accepted the governorship of Ch'u Principality (Hupei), where he saved his constituents from a demoralized situation. He died in 297 resisting the rebel Ch'i Wan-nien 齊萬年 and left behind two literary works: a gazetteer of Ch'u Principality and a history of the Wu Kingdom (*Wu-shu*). *Chou Ch'u PC*; *CYC*. XV, *1*.

CHOU CHÜN 周浚 (K'ai-lin 開林). second half, third cent.   61.1a-3a. Father of Chou I, Chou Sung, and Chou Mo. At first avoiding office, he eventually accepted a post as clerk in the Imperial Secretariat under the Wei government in Lo-yang, and later became governor of Yang Province (Kiangsu-Anhui). He participated in the Chin campaign against the Wu Kingdom in 280, for which he was rewarded by the first Chin emperor (Ssu-ma Yen, r. 265-299) by being made a personal attendant. In 291 he became governor-general of Yang Province and General Pacifying the East. *PWKS*. XIX, *18*.

CHOU FU 周馥 (Tsu-hsüan 祖宣). d. 311. *CS* 61.6b-9a. A second cousin of Chou I. He served as intendant of Ho-nan (Lo-yang) and, later, governor-general of military affairs in Yang Province (Kiangsu-Anhui-Chekiang) during the "War of the Eight Princes" (300-306). After suppressing the revolt of Ch'en Min 陳敏 in the Yangtze Delta area in 305, he was rewarded with noble rank. At the time of the Hsiung-nu invasions of the north in 310, he memorialized the throne to move the capital to Shou-ch'un (Anhui), thereby arousing the resentment of the Prince of Tung-hai, Ssu-ma Yüeh, who felt he should have been consulted. Yüeh sent an army against Fu which was defeated. But after Yüeh received reinforcements from the future founder of Eastern Chin, Ssu-ma Jui (Emperor Yüan, r. 317-322), Fu's army was routed and he died in flight of an illness in 311, ironically the year Lo-yang was lost. *TTCC*. VI, *9*.

CHOU FU* 周馥 (Chan-yin 湛隱). fl. mid-fourth cent. He once served as an aide under Wang Tun and was grand warden of Chin-shou (Szechwan) at the time of Huan Wen's pacification of Li Shih in 347. *CHS*. XIII, *8*.

CHOU HUI 周悝 (Hung-wu 弘武). fl. late third to early fourth cent. One of the "Twenty-four Friends" of Chia Mi 賈謐. *WYCS*. IX, *8*.

CHOU I 周顗 (Po-jen 伯仁). 269-322. *CS* 69.16a-20a. The eldest son of Chou Chün, and elder brother of Chou Sung and Chou Mo, he was described as handsome and quick-witted, very much of a bon vivant. At the age of twenty he inherited his father's title of marquis and went to the capital where he served in the Board of Civil Office, later joining the staff of the Prince of Tung-hai (Ssu-ma Yüeh) as senior administrator. In 311 he fled to Chien-yeh to join Ssu-ma Jui and the following year was sent to Ching Province (Hunan-Hupei), but, unable to cope with the rebellion of Tu T'ao 杜弢, fled for refuge to Wang Tun's headquarters in Wu-ch'ang (Hupei). When Ssu-ma Jui became emperor in 317, he returned to the capital where he was made president of the Board of Civil Office and vice-president of the Imperial Secretariat, but was soon impeached for drunkenness. In 318 his titles were restored, but incidents arising from his drunkenness increased, and he earned the sobriquet of "Three-day-sober vice-president." He died a bloody death after insulting the rebel Wang Tun in 322. *YYCS*; *CYC*. II, *30*, 31, 40; V, 23, 26, 27, 29, 30, 31, 33; VI, 21, 22; VII, 14; VIII, 47, 48; IX, 12, 14, 16, 19, 22; XIV, 20, 21; XIX, 18; XXIII, 25, 28; XXV, 14, 15, 17, 18; XXVI, 2; XXX, 12; XXXIII, 6, 8.

CHOU I* 周翼 (Tzu-ch'ing 子鄉). ca. 300-364. Son of Chou Yu 優 and Ch'ih Chien's sister. He served under the Eastern Chin as magistrate of Yen Prefecture (Chekiang) and governor of Ch'ing Province (southern Shantung). *Chou-SP*. I, *24*.

CHOU MA-T'OU 周馬頭. second half, fourth cent. Daughter of Chou Min 閔 and wife of Ch'ih Ch'ao. *Ch'ih SP*. XIX, *29*.

CHOU MO 周謨 (Shu-chih 叔治). fl. early fourth cent. *CS* 61.5b-6b. Second younger brother of Chou I (269-322). He had an undistinguished career at Chien-k'ang as capital intendant, personal attendant, and general of the Central Palace Guard. *TTCC*. V, *26*; VII, *14*; (XIX, *18*).

CHOU SHAO 周邵 (Tzu-nan 子南). d. ca. 335. A recluse who lived with Chai T'ang on Mt. Lu (Kiangsi), but who, after being persuaded by Yü Liang to enter official life, became Protector Governing the Man-barbarians and grand warden of Hsi-yang Commandery (southern Honan) around 334. *HsYC*. XVIII, *9*; XXXIII, *10*.

CHOU SUNG 周嵩 (Chung-chih 仲治). d. 324. *CS* 61.3a-5b. First younger brother of Chou I, he was described as "impatient, brusque, decisive, and forthright." After becoming junior censor he bitterly opposed the rise of Wang Tun, who later had him executed. The whole family was devoutly Buddhist, and even at his execution Sung is reported to have been intoning sutras. *TTCC*; *CYC*. V, *26*, *27*; VI, *21*; VII, *14*; (XIX, *18*).

CHU, Mme. 宋夫人. d. ca. 245. The second wife of Wang Jung* 王融 and stepmother of Wang Hsiang; mother of Wang Lan 覽. Many stories are told of her unfairness to Hsiang and of his filial devotion to her. *WHSC*; *CYC*; *HKCHTC*; *YYCS*. I, *14*.

CHU CH'IEN 竺潛 (Fa-shen 法深; alias Tao-ch'ien 道潛). 286-374. *KSC* 4; *Taishō* 50.347c-348b. A Buddhist monk from an unknown family, who is said in the *KSC* to have been the younger brother of Wang Tun. He first studied with the Confucian scholar Liu Yüan-chen 劉元真, then after reading the Lotus Sutra (*Saddharma-puṇḍarīka*) entered the sangha in his eighteenth year. During the troubles attending the fall of the Western Chin (307-312) he fled south and enjoyed the favor of emperors and courtiers at the Eastern Chin capital (Chien-k'ang), later retiring to the K'uai-chi area (Chekiang) where he died in his eighty-ninth year. *KISMC*. I, *30*; II, *48*; IV, *30*; V, *45*; XXV, *28*; XXVI, *3*.

CHU FA-T'AI 竺法汰. 320-387. *KSC* 5; *Taishō* 50.354b. A disciple of Fo-t'u-teng in the Later Chao capital at Yeh (Honan). After his master's death in 349 he wandered with his fellow disciple Tao-an, establishing Buddhist centers in other parts of China. In 365 he came with forty disciples to Chien-k'ang, where he remained at the Wa-kuan Monastery. He is counted the founder of the "Variant School of Fundamental Nonbeing" (*Pen-wu i-tsung*), but no clear statement of his ideas remains. Titles of some of his correspondence are preserved in *CSTCC* 12; *Taishō* 55.84c. *AFSC*. IV, *54*; VIII, *114*.

CHU PI 宋群. fl. late fourth cent. An officer under Huan Shih-ch'ien. XIII, *10*.

CHU TAN 朱誕 (Yung-ch'ang 永長). fl. late third cent. A native of Wu Commandery (Soochow). Although serving briefly in the Wu government, after the fall of Wu in 280 he returned to his native place and spent his remaining days a recluse. THC. VIII, 20.

CHU TAO-CH'IEN. See CHU CH'IEN.

CHU TAO-I 竺道壹 (alias Chu Te 德 and Tao-i tao-jen 道人). KSC 5; Taishō 50.357ab. A native of Wu and member of the locally prominent Lu 陸 family. He was a disciple of Chu Fa-t'ai and honored by lay followers like Wang Hsün and Wang Min. From 366 to 370 he lived in the Wa-kuan Monastery in Chien-k'ang, and after Fa-t'ai's death in 387 he returned to Wu Commandery (Soochow) where he lived in retirement on Hu-ch'iu 虎丘 Mountain, later becoming abbot of the Chia-hsiang Monastery in K'uai-chi (Chekiang). YYLLSH; MTSMTM. II, 93.

CHU TE 竺德 See CHU TAO-I.

CHU-KO, Lady 諸葛氏. mid-third cent. Daughter of Chu-ko Tan and wife of Wang Kuang. Apart from the incident recounted in SSHY, nothing further is known of this mettlesome female. XIX, 9.

CHU-KO CHIN 諸葛瑾 (Tzu-yü 子瑜). 174-241. SKWu 7.12b-16b. The older brother of Chu-ko Liang. During the civil wars at the close of Later Han he emigrated south of the Yangtze where he came to the attention of Sun Ch'üan, founder of the Wu Kingdom (r. 222-252). Sun employed him as his senior administrator and in 215 sent him on a diplomatic mission to Liu Pei, founder of the rival Kingdom of Shu (Szechwan) (r. 221-223). Though he talked in the presence of his younger brother, Liang, who was then acting as Liu's adviser, he maintained an impeccable loyalty to Wu and continued to do so even when the two states were at war. After the official founding of the Wu Kingdom in 222, Chin was given high military honors and ennobled a marquis. WuS. IX, 4; XXV, 1.

CHU-KO CHING 諸葛靚 (Chung-ssu 仲思). late third cent. CS 77.20a. The youngest son of Chu-ko Tan, father of Chu-ko Hui, and younger brother of the concubine of Ssu-ma Chao's younger brother, Chou 伷. After his father was executed by Ssu-ma Chao for rebellion against the Ssu-ma clan in 257, he fled for assylum to Wu, where he became General of the Right and grand marshal. After the conquest of Wu by Chin in 280, he returned to his home in Lang-yeh (Shantung) but remained in seclusion, refusing even to see his boyhood friend and relative by marriage, Ssu-ma Yen, who was then ruling as Emperor Wu (r. 265-290) and who personally summoned him to serve as personal attendant. CCKT. II, 21; V, 10.

CHU-KO FEI 諸葛妃. late third cent. The older sister of Chu-ko Ching, she became the favored concubine (fei) of Ssu-ma Chou 司馬伷, the uncle of Emperor Wu of Chin (Ssu-ma Yen, r. 265-290). CCKT. V, 10.

CHU-KO HENG 諸葛衡 (Chün-wen 峻文). fl. mid-fourth cent. He became grand warden of Ying-yang Commandery (Honan) and married the daughter of Teng Yu. *Chu-ko SP*. V, 25.

CHU-KO HUI 諸葛恢 (Tao-ming 道明). 284-345. *CS* 77.20a-21b. Son of Chu-ko Ching, and father-in-law of Yü Hui and later of Chiang Pin and Hsieh Shih. After fleeing south around 317 and serving the Eastern Chin court in minor posts, he rose to president of the Imperial Secretariat, personal attendant, and Great Officer of Brilliang Favor. *(Chu-ko) Hui PC*. V, 25; VII, 11; XVII, 8; XXV, 12; XXVII, 10.

CHU-KO HUNG 諸葛宏 (Mao-yüan 茂遠). fl. ca. 300. He served as Wang Yen's superintendent of records, but won the enmity of the conservatives at court and was banished to a distant post. *WYCS*. IV, 13; XXVIII, 1.

CHU-KO K'O 諸葛恪 (Yüan-hsün 元遜). 203-253. *SKWu* 19.1a-14b. The eldest son of Chu-ko Chin. Greatly honored by Sun Ch'üan (r. 222-252), he became one of Wu's leading military figures in the wars with Wei, but after a disastrous defeat in 253 at Shou-ch'un (Anhui), because of complaints of arrogance and mistreatment of his men, he was killed by his superior, Sun Chün 孫峻, with all the members of his family. *CPC*. XXV, 1.

CHU-KO LIANG 諸葛亮 (K'ung-ming 孔明). 181-234. *SKShu* 5.1a-17a. A gifted poet who spent his early years in study and retirement and was finally prevailed upon to join the fortunes of Liu Pei in 207. When Liu founded the Shu Kingdom in 221, Chu-ko became his chief counselor and commander of all major military operations, winning the reputation of the greatest strategist of all time. He died in a campaign against Wu. *ShuC*. V, 5; (VIII, 99); IX, 4; XXV, 44.

CHU-KO TAN 諸葛誕 (Kung-hsiu 公休). d. 258. *SKWei* 28.11b-16b. A cousin of Chu-ko Liang and Chu-ko Chin who remained in the Wei Kingdom. While serving on the Wei Board of Civil Office he made his reputation as a judge of men and rose quickly to eminence. Because of his friendship with the "idle talkers," Hsia-hou Hsüan and Teng Yang, he was dismissed by Emperor Ming (Ts'ao Jui, r. 227-339), but with the regency of Hsia-hou Hsüan's uncle, Ts'ao Shuang, in 240 the "idle talkers" came temporarily back into power, and Tan was appointed governor of Yang province (northern Kiangsu and Anhui) and charged with the suppression of "rebels" in the southeast. In the summer of 257, eight years after the downfall of Shuang's clique, the court, then dominated by Ssu-ma Chao and suspicious of Tan's loyalties, recalled him to the capital. Tan responded by killing the man sent to succeed him as governor and allying himself with Wu. Ssu-ma Chao went against him in person, and Tan was finally defeated and executed early in 258. *WC*. IX, 4; XIX, 9.

CHU-KO WEN-HSIUNG 諸葛文熊. fl. mid-fourth cent. Youngest daughter of Chu-ko Hui and wife of Hsieh Shih. *Hsieh SP*. V, 25.

CHU-KO WEN-PIAO 諸葛文彪. fl. mid-fourth cent. Eldest daugher of Chu-ko Hui, she was first married to Yü Hui, before the latter was eighteen. When Hui was killed by Su Chün in 328, she reluctantly consented to be remarried to Chiang Pin. *Yü SP.* V, *25*; XVII, 8; XXVII, 10.

CH'U P'OU 褚裒 (Chi-yeh 季野). 303-349. *CS* 93.6a-8b. The father-in-law of Emperor K'ang (Ssu-ma Yüeh, r. 343-344) and a member of the anti-Yü faction which was dominant between 345 and 346. Beginning his career on the staff of Yü Liang in 323, he rose slowly, but during Emperor K'ang's brief reign he was heaped with honors, and in 349 as governor of Yen Province (southern Shantung, northern Kiangsu and Anhui) he led a successful expedition against the Hsiung-nu state of Later Chao (319-351) in the north, but died soon after retaking the city of P'eng-ch'eng (northern Kiangsu). A very taciturn man, he was said to express approval or disapproval without talking. He is usually known by his posthumous title of grand tutor. *CYC.* I, *34*; II, 54; IV, 25; VI, 18; VII, 16; VIII, 66, 70; XXV, 25; XXVI, 7, 9.

CH'U SHUANG 褚爽 (Hung-mao 弘茂; baby name, Ch'i-sheng 期生). fl. late fourth cent. *CS* 93.13a. A grandson of Ch'u P'ou and father of Empress Ssu 思 (Ch'u Ling-yüan 靈媛, 384-436) who was the consort of the last Chin ruler, Emperor Kung (Ssu-ma Te-wen 德文, r. 419-420). He achieved considerable fame as an expert in the *Lao-tzu* and *Chuang-tzu* and was counted a friend by Yin Chung-k'an. He died at an early age while serving as grand warden of I-hsing Commandery (Kiangsu). *HCYC.* VII, *24*.

CH'U T'AO 褚陶 (Chi-ya 季雅). fl. late third cent. *CS* 92.12a. A native of Wu Commandery (Soochow), quiet and studious by nature. By his twelfth or thirteenth year he had already produced two noteworthy poetic essays, "Seagulls" (*Ou-niao fu* 鷗鳥賦) and "The Watermill" (*Shui-tui fu* 水碓賦), and he consistently refused calls to public office. After the surrender of Wu in 280 he took a position in the Imperial Secretariat in Lo-yang. At his death in his fifty-fifth year he held the title of central commander. *Ch'uSCC.* VIII, *19*.

CHUNG, Mme. 鍾太夫人. mid-third cent. The sister of Chung Hui and Chung Yü, and mother of Hsün Hsü. XXI, 4.

CHUNG HAO 鍾晧 (Chi-ming 季明). second cent. *HHS* 92.12a-13a. Though summoned "nine times" to assume various posts, he never took up any office. He was related by marriage to Li Ying, his older brother's wife being the latter's paternal aunt. Hao's nephew, Chin 瑾, was also the same age as Ying and married his younger sister. *HHHC.* I, *5*.

CHUNG HUI 鍾會 (Shih-chi 士季). 225-264. *SKWei* 28.26a-37a. Youngest son of Chung Yü and younger brother of Chung Yu. He was precocious like his elder brother and had memorized the Classics by the age of fifteen. A staunch champion of the "Moral Teaching" (*ming-chiao*) against the Taoistic revolt of Hsi K'ang and the others of the "Seven Worthies of the Bamboo Grove," he gained high favor with the Ssu-ma clique at court. Serving an apprenticeship in the Imperial and Central secretariats, he became private secretary to

Ssu-ma Chao, and later as General Governing the West he led a successful expedition against Shu in 264. But he was killed by his mutinous troops when he attempted a last-minute coup against his former patrons, the Ssu-ma clan, on the eve of the latter's founding of the Chin Dynasty (265-420). He is perhaps best known for his editing of a study of the relation between ability and human nature, the *Ssu-pen lun* 四本論 (see IV, 5). *WC*. II, 11, *12*; IV, 5; V, 6; VIII, 5, 6, 8; XIX, 8; XXI, 4; XXIV, 3; XXV, 2.

CHUNG YA 鍾雅 (Yen-chou 彥冑). d. 328-329. *CS* 70.22a-23b. The great-grandson of a younger brother of Chung Yu. Around 304 he served as an aide under the Prince of Tung-hai, Ssu-ma Yüeh, later becoming a clerk in the Imperial Secretariat. After the fall of Lo-yang in 311, he migrated to Chien-k'ang, where he first served as Chancellor Wang Tao's secretarial aide and later as governor of Lin-hai Principality (Chekiang). Soon afterward he returned to court as cavalier attendant and left assistant in the Imperial Secretariat. For a time he was junior administrator under Wang Tun, where he won recognition in the suppression of a local rebellion in Kuang-te Prefecture (Anhui). On the death of Emperor Ming in 325 he became junior censor. When Su Chün's revolt began in 327 he was sent out from the capital to stop him, but, finding himself outnumbered, retreated. The following year he became personal attendant to the boy-emperor Ch'eng (r. 326-342) and was with him when the emperor was abducted to Shih-t'ou in 328. He was killed early the following year in an effort to break the siege and bring the emperor to safety. (Chung) Yu *PC*. III, *11*; V, 34, 35.

CHUNG YEN-CHIH 鍾琰之. mid-third cent. *CS* 96.3b-4b. The great-granddaughter of Chung Yu, daughter of Chung Hui* 徽之, and wife of Wang Hun. She is described as well educated and beautiful, a prolific composer of poems, poetic essays, odes, and laments. *WangSP*. XIX, *12*, *16*; XXV, 8.

CHUNG YU 鍾繇 (Yüan-ch'ang 元常). d. 230. *SKWei* 13.1a-8b. A great-grandson of Chung Hao. During the power struggle following the death of Emperor Ling (r. 168-189) in the early summer of 189, when Tung Cho had set up a separate capital in Ch'ang-an, Yu was instrumental in restoring Emperor Hsien (r. 190-220) to Lo-yang in 196, for which he was made assistant censor, personal attendant, and vice-president of the Court Secretariat. Later, as commandant of the capital province he assisted Ts'ao Ts'ao against Yüan Shao and against other local warlords and Hsiung-nu uprisings. With the founding of Wei in 220 he became chancellor and later grand marshal, moving to grand tutor with the accession of Emperor Ming (r. 227-239). Toward the end of his life he strongly advocated reforming the penal code to substitute forced labor for death and mutilation, but was overruled. *WC*. II, 11, 12; XIX, 16; XXI, 4.

CHUNG YÜ 鍾毓 (Chih-shu 稚叔). d. 263. *SKWei* 13.8b-10a. Eldest son of Chung Yu. In his youth he was considered precocious and was already a junior attendant of the emperor in his fourteenth year. In 231 when Shu was threatening Wei's western border, and again in 244 when Ts'ao Shuang attacked Shu, he advised restraint, for which he gained prestige at court. After Shuang's downfall in 249, he became an assistant censor and personal attendant and director of punishments, in which last capacity he instituted a number of legal reforms. After the suppression of the insurrection of Kuan-ch'iu Chien 毋丘儉 and Wen Ch'in 文欽 in Shou-yang (Anhui) in 255, Yü was appointed governor of Ch'ing Province (Shantung), and later military governor of Ching Province (Hunan-Hupei) where he died in 263. He is known by his posthumous title, General of Chariots and Horsemen. WeiS. II, 11, 12; V, 6; XXI, 4; XXV, 3.

CH'UAN TSUNG 全琮 (Tzu-huang 子璜). d. 249. SKWu 15.4b-6b. A native of Ch'ien-t'ang (Hangchow), whose nature was generous to a fault. He participated in many campaigns of Wu against Shu, and at the end of his life was grand marshal. of Wu. HCWC. IX, 2.

FA-CH'IEN 法虔. d. ca. 365. Mentioned, KSC 4; Taishō 50.349c. A monk who was a fellow student and intimate friend of Chih Tun. CTC. XVII, 11.

FA-KANG 法岡 (var. 綱 ; also known by the title Tao-jen 道人). fl. ca. 397. CS 65.13b; KSC 1; Taishō 50.329a. A disciple of Saṃghadeva in Chien-k'ang. IV, 64.

FA-SHEN 法深. See CHU CH'IEN.

FAN CH'I 范啟 (Jung-ch'i 榮期). fl. mid-fourth cent. A noted conversationalist who also achieved some reputation as a writer in his day. He was a palace attendant at his death. CHS. IV, 86; XXV, 46, 50, 53.

FAN HSÜAN 范宣 (Hsüan-tzu 宣子, or Tzu-hsüan). fl. ca. 376-396. CS 91.15a-16a. An uncle by marriage of Tai K'uei. From his youth, which was clouded by poverty and menial work, he loved seclusion and reading, and most of his adult life seems to have been a continuous rejection of calls to public office. He made a living as a teacher and once taught the monk Hui-yüan. His personal outlook was strongly Confucian, and he resisted the contemporary vogue of philosophical Taoism. (Fan) Hsüan PC. I, 38; XVIII, 14; XXI, 6.

FAN K'UEI 范逵. late third to early fourth cent. A native of P'o-yang Commandery. CYC. XIX, 19.

FAN NING 范甯 (Wu-tzu 武子). 339-401. CS 75.26a-31a. Son of Fan Wang and father of the Buddhist apologist Fan T'ai 泰, as well as maternal uncle of Wang Ch'en and Wang Kuo-pao. The family was devoutly Buddhist, but like many other Buddhists in public life Fan Ning favored the Juist "Teaching of Names" (ming-chiao) and passionately opposed the "frivolity and libertinism" of the philosophical Taoists. His diatribe against Wang Pi and Ho Yen is included in his biography in CS. In both his early posts as magistrate of Yü-hang and Yü-chang (Kiangsi) he worked tirelessly to build schools and promote promising scholars. At court, as clerk in the Central Secretariat, he pushed for measures to restore the old rituals but became so unpopular he asked leave to return to the provinces. He wrote commentaries on the "Analects" and the

"Ku-liang Commentary on the Spring and Autumn Annals" (*Ch'un-ch'iu Ku-liang chuan*). *CHS*. II, 97; V, 66; VIII, 150.

FAN P'ANG 范滂 (Meng-po 孟博). 137-169. *HHS* 97.16b-19b. An extremely severe remover of corrupt officials who belonged to the anti-eunuch faction in the Later Han court. He was imprisoned in 166, released, and finally executed during the bloody revenge of the eunuchs in 169. *CFHC*. VIII, 3.

FAN TZU-CHAO 樊子昭. late second to early third cent. A merchant of Ju-nan Commandery (Honan) who gained a reputation for generosity and honesty. *CCWCL*. IX, 2.

FAN WANG 范汪 (Hsüan-p'ing 玄平). ca. 308-372. *CS* 75.23b-26a. The father of Fan Ning. After his own father's early death, Wang fled south across the Yangtze in his sixth year (ca. 313) and lived with his mother's family, a branch of the Yü clan. He suffered privations but managed to educate himself, and at the age of twenty came to Chien-k'ang just at the time of Su Chün's uprising against the Yüs (327). Fleeing westward, he joined his kinsman Yü Liang in Hsün-yang (Kiangsi), and after the rebellion was put down remained with Yü's staff in Wu-ch'ang (Hupei) over ten years. Later he became governor of the two provinces Hsü and Yen (southern Shantung and northern Anhui). Missing an appointment to meet Huan Wen on his northern expedition of 369, he was dismissed from office and remained in retirement until his death in 372. *Fan Wang PC*. XXV, 34; XXVII, 13.

FENG HUAI 馮懷 (Tsu-ssu 祖思). mid-fourth cent. He served as grand ordinary and General Protecting the Army, and was also a cosigner, along with Ho Ch'ung, Chu-ko Hui and others, of a memorial dated 340 directed against Yü Ping, who was then serving as regent, requesting that the Buddhist clergy be exempted from civil ceremonies. See *Hung-ming chi* 12; *Taishō* 52.79c-80a; transl., Zürcher, *Conquest*, pp. 161-162. *Feng SP*. IV, 32.

FENG PO 馮播 (Yu-sheng 友聲). fl. mid-third cent. Father of Feng Sun. *CHL*. VIII, 22.

FENG SUN 馮蓀 (Hui-ch'ing 惠卿). d. ca. 303. A son of Feng Po who was serving as personal attendant in 302, but was killed by the Prince of Ch'ang-sha (Ssu-ma I*) during the "War of the Eight Princes." *PWKS*. VIII, 22.

FO-T'U-TENG 佛圖澄. fl. 310-348. *KSC* 10; *Taishō* 50.383b-387a; *CS* 95.19a-25a. A Kuchean monk who arrived in Lo-yang in 310 during the barbarian invasions. After being introduced to the Hsiung-nu general, Shih Lo, who later ruled the Later Chao state from 319-333, he served as court chaplain and prognosticator, later serving Lo's nephew, Shih Hu (r. 335-349) in Yeh (northern Honan) in the same capacity, at which time he received the title, *Ta ho-shang* 大和尚. He trained a number of disciples, the most notable among whom was Shih Tao-an. See A. F. Wright, "Fo-t'u-teng, a Biography," *Harvard Journal of Asiatic Studies* XI (1948), 321-371. (*Fo-t'u-teng PC*. II, 45.

FU CHIA 傅嘏 (Lan-shih 蘭石; var. 碩). 205-255? SKWei 21.23a-28a. Though he began as a member of the coterie of Ho Yen, he was of a more conservative turn of mind and dissociated himself from the others before the downfall of Ts'ao Shuang in 249. Joining the faction of Ssu-ma Chao, he was made intendant of the Capital Commandery (Lo-yang) and president of the Board of Civil Office. He was author of one of the essays in Chung Hui's *Ssu-pen lun* 四本論 and maintained that natural ability (*ts'ai* 才) and human nature (*hsing* 性) are identical (*t'ung* 同). WC. IV, 9; VII, 3; VIII, 8.

FU CHIEN 符堅 (Yung-ku 永固; Wen-yü 文玉; baby name, Chien-t'ou 肩頭). 338-385. CS 113-114.30b. Also known as Emperor Hsüan-chao, temple name, Shih-tsu 世祖 (r. 358-385), of the Former Ch'in state (351-394), with its capital in Ch'ang-an (Shensi). Descended from a Ti (Proto-Tibetan) family of the Shensi area which had founded the Former Ch'in state, he came to the throne by force in 357 and by 370 had conquered all of north China. In a desperate bid to annex Eastern Chin and thus reunite the whole realm in 383, he was defeated by vastly inferior forces at the Fei River (Anhui) and died a broken man two years later, while his erstwhile empire was divided among his generals. See M. C. Rogers, *The Chronicle of Fu Chien*, Chinese Dynastic Histories Translations No. 10, Berkeley and Los Angeles, 1968. CPCS. II, 94, 99; VI, 37; VII, 22; XVI, 5; XVIII, 8.

FU CH'IEN 服虔 (Tzu-shen 子慎). d. ca. 190. HHS 109B.13ab. A commentator on the *Tso-chuan*. Before his death during the turmoil of the Yellow Turban Revolt he had been serving as grand warden of Chiuchiang Commandery (Kiangsi). HNC. IV, 2, 4.

FU HSI-(CHIH) 伏系之 (Ching-lu 敬魯). late fourth to early fifth cent. Mentioned, CS 92.33a. A son of Fu T'ao who also achieved some literary fame in his day. He served as personal attendant and Great Officer of Brilliant Favor. WCL. XXII, 5.

FU HUNG 符宏 (Yung-tao 永道). d. ca. 405. Mentioned, CS 114.22a. Fu Chien's (r. 358-385) eldest son and heir apparent, who fled with his wife and mother from Ch'ang-an to Chien-k'ang in 385, after the Later Ch'in ruler, Yao Ch'ang 姚萇 (r. 384-393), murdered his father. During Huan Hsüan's usurpation in 404 he was named governor of Liang Province (Kansu), though in exile. Sometime after Huan's downfall he was executed for involvement with rebels in the Hsiang River area (Hunan). HCYC. XXVI, 29.

FU LANG 符朗 (Yüan-ta 元達). d. 389. CS 114.30b-32a. The son of a first-cousin of Fu Chien, whom the latter hailed as "the thousand-*li* colt of our family." He was bookish, a gourmet, and a lover of landscape and "pure conversation." His forte was an ability to insult people with total urbanity. As Former Ch'in's governor of Ch'ing Province (southern Shantung), he surrendered to Hsieh Hsüan after the battle of the Fei River in 383 and went to live in the Eastern Chin capital, where he was lionized by everyone who considered himself a cultivated gentleman. Two of these, Wang Ch'en and Wang Kuo-pao. were, however, so effectively insulted by him that they arranged his execution in 389, when Ch'en was appointed governor of Ching Province (Hunan-Hupei). PCJCS. XXV, 57.

FU LIANG 傅亮 (Chi-yu 季友). 374-426. *NS* 15.19b-21b; *SS* 43.8a-13b. Second son of Fu Yüan. He served successively as president of the Imperial Secretariat and Left Great Officer of Brilliant Favor. In 426 he was executed for some unnamed offense against the Sung court. *WCL*. IV, 99; VII, 25.

FU T'AO 伏滔 (Hsüan-tu 玄度). ca. 317-396. *CS* 92.29b-33a. He began his career as an aide under Huan Wen, and after Huan's debacle at Fang-t'ou (Shantung) in 369 accompanied him on the punitive drive against the scapegoat general Yüan Chen 袁真 at Shou-ch'un (Anhui), on which occasion he composed his "Discourse on the Rectification of the Huai (River Area)" (*Cheng-Huai lun*), quoted at length in his biography. He later became grand historian and was noted for his literary skill. *CHS*. II, 72; XXII, 2, 5; XXVI, 12.

FU TI 傅迪 (Ch'ang-yu 長猷). d. 421. *SS* 43.8a; *NS* 15.19b. The eldest son of Fu Yüan. More conservative than his younger brother, Liang, he only reached the rank of president of the Five Armies before his death in 421. *SS*. VII, 25.

FU YÜAN 傅瑗 (Shu-yü 叔玉; baby name, Yüeh 約). fl. late fourth cent. The father of Fu Liang and Fu Ti. Living most of his life as a recluse, he eventually reached office as grand warden of An-ch'eng Commandery (Kiangsi). *FuSP*; *WCL*. VII, 25; XVIII, 15.

HAN, Lady 韓氏. mid-third cent. The wife of Shan T'ao; said to be talented and intelligent. Her husband teased her by saying he knew she could endure poverty but was not sure she could stand being a lady. *WYCS*. XIX, 11.

HAN HUI-CHIH 韓繪之 (Chi-lun 季倫). d. 404. Mentioned, *CS* 75.36b. The son of Han Po. After his installation as grand warden of Heng-yang Commandery (Hunan) sometime after 400, he became one of several victims of the abortive uprising of Huan Liang in the autumn of 404. *Han SP*. XIX, 32.

HAN PO 韓伯 (K'ang-po 康伯). fl. mid. and late fourth cent. *CS* 75.34b-36b. A nephew of Yin Hao and, like his uncle, a skilled conversationalist. He served successively as grand warden of Yü-chang (Kiangsi), capital intendant, president of the Board of Civil Office, and grand ordinary, but is best known as the author of the standard commentary on the *Hsi-tz'u* ("Appended Sayings") of the "Book of Changes." *HCYC*. I, 38, 47; II, 72, 79; IV, 27; V, 57; VII, 23; VIII, 90; IX, 63, 66, 81; XII, 5; XVIII, 14; XIX, 27, 32; XXV, 52, 53; XXVI, 28.

HAN SHOU 韓壽 (Te-chen 德真). d. 291. *SKWei* 24.2b, comm.; indirectly mentioned, *CS* 40.7a. The husband of Chia Ch'ung's daughter, Chia Wu, and father of Han Mi 謐. Mi changed his surname to Chia after Ch'ung's death in 282 and was adopted to replace Ch'ung's only sons, both dead in infancy. Han Shou became cavalier attendant-in-ordinary in 290 and intendant of Ho-nan (Lo-yang) but died the following year. *CCKT*; *KT*. XXXV, 5.

HO, Lady 郝氏 (also known as Mme. HO 郝夫人). second half, third cent.

Mentioned, *CS* 96.3b-4b. The daughter of Ho P'u, wife of Wang Chan, and mother of Wang Ch'eng* 承. Though originating from an obscure family, she brought a great deal of credit to her husband's family as a model of maternal grace. *Wang Ju-nan PC*. XIX, *15*, 16.

HO CH'ENG 何澄 (Tzu-hsüan 子玄; var. Chi-hsüan 季玄). d. ca. 404. *CS* 93.9ab. Third son of Ho Chun, and brother of Empress Chang, the consort of Emperor Mu (Ssu-ma Tan, r. 345-361). A favorite of Emperor Hsiao-wu (Ssu-ma Yao, r. 373-396), he became governor of Wu Principality (Soochow), and on the accession of Emperor An (Ssu-ma Te-tsung, r. 397-418) was named vice-president of the Imperial Secretariat. When Huan Hsüan usurped the throne early in 404, he claimed illness and retired, dying shortly thereafter. *CHS*. XXXI, *7*.

HO CH'IAO 和嶠 (Chang-yü 長輿). d. 292. *CS* 45.13a-14b. He became personal attendant to the Chin Emperor Wu (r. 265-289), and once aroused the resentment of Empress Chia by a candid statement concerning the dim-wittedness of the crown prince (later Emperor Hui, r. 290-306). However, on Emperor Hui's accession in 290 he was named grand tutor to the crown prince and cavalier attendant-in-ordinary. Like Wang Jung he was both wealthy and penurious. *CCKT*. I, 17; III, 5; V, *9*, 11, 12, 14, 27; VIII, 15; IX, 16, 18; XVIII, 5; XXIII, 16; XXIV, 1.

HO CHUN 何準 (Yu-tao 幼道). ca. 311-357). *CS* 93.9ab. The fifth younger brother of Ho Ch'ung and father of Empress Chang (d. 411), consort of Emperor Mu (Ssu-ma Tan, r. 345-361). Like his brother, he was an ardent patron of Buddhism and built many pagodas and temples, but unlike Ch'ung he never entered public life. At his death in 357 the posthumous title, Great Officer of Brilliant Favor, was dutifully declined by his son, Hui 惔. *CHS*. XVIII, *5*; XXV, 51.

HO CH'UNG 何充 (Tz'u-tao 次道). 262-346. *CS* 77.6a-9a. Related by marriage to both Yü Liang's and Wang Tao's families, he was also the brother-in-law of Emperor Ming (Ssu-ma Shao, r. 323-325) and could not avoid prominence at court. A devout Buddhist by religion and Confucianist by ideology, he found himself often opposed to the faction led by his brother-in-law, Yü Liang. His many titles and offices included General of Spirited Cavalry and president of the Central Secretariat. *CYC*. II, 54; III, *17*, 18; V, 28, 41; VIII, 59, 60, 67, 130; IX, 26, 27; XVII, 9; XVIII, 5; XXV, 22, 51.

HO HSÜN 賀循 (Yen-hsien 彥先). 260-319). *CS* 68.15a-21b. The son of Ho Shao. The family surname was originally Ch'ing 慶 but had been changed during the Han to the synonymous Ho to avoid the taboo of Emperor An's (r. 107-125) father, Liu Ch'ing. Hsün's father had lived in Shan-yin (Chekiang), but when he was killed by Sun Hao in 275 the family moved beyond the borders of the Wu Kingdom, returning after Wu was conquered by Western Chin in 280. Introduced at the Chin court in Lo-yang by his fellow countryman, Lu Chi, he served in the administration of the Prince of Chao (Ssu-ma Lun), but at the latter's attempted usurpation in 301 he claimed illness and retired. When Ssu-ma Jui founded the Eastern Chin in 317, Hsün was called to be governor of Tan-yang (Chien-k'ang) and later of Wu Commandery (Soochow), but again claimed "foot trouble" and did not assume his post. He eventually came to the capital on the emperor's urgent request, very weak and emaciated by illness, but died in 319. The title, director of works, by which he is usually known, was posthumously conferred. *Ho Hsün PC*. II, 34; X, *13*; XXIII, 22; XXIV, 2.

HO LUNG 郝隆 (Tso-chih 佐治). mid-fourth cent. A humorous man whose highest office seems to have been aide-de-camp on the staff of Huan Wen while the latter was commandant of the Southern Man Barbarians (ca. 360). *CHLSM*. XXV, *31*, 32, 35.

HO P'U 郝普 (Tao-k'uang 道匡). mid-third cent. The father-in-law of Wang Chan; a man of lowly origin whose highest rank was grand warden of Lo-yang Commandery. *Ho SP*; *Wang Chan PC*; (*Wang*) *Ju-nan PC*. XIX, *15*.

HO SHAO 賀邵 (Hsing-po 興伯). 227-275. *SKWu* 20.3b-7b. A native of K'uai-chi (Chekiang). In 258 he became cavalier attendant-in-ordinary to Sun Hsiu (r. 258-264) and shortly afterward was appointed grand warden of Wu Commandery (Soochow). He rose to become president of the Central Secretariat and grand tutor under Sun Hao (r. 264-280), whose reprobate behavior he rebuked in a long memorial recorded in his biography. Around 275 he suffered a stroke and resigned his post, having lost his powers of speech. Sun Hao, still smarting from the memorial, suspected his motives and confiscated all his property. Ho, standing by speechless, was himself killed and his family banished to Lin-hai by the sea. *WuC*. III, *4*; XXXIV, 2.

HO TSENG 何曾 (Ying-k'ao 穎考). 199-278. *CS* 33.7b-12b. A man of extreme integrity and filial devotion who served both the Wei and Western Chin courts with such exacting rectitude that he was feared by all. He was commandant of the capital province (Lo-yang) between ca. 250 and 255, later becoming director of instruction with a noble title. In 264 when Ssu-ma Chao became Prince of Chin, Tseng was one of his closest advisers, and after Chao's death the following year he urged Chao's son, Yen, to mount the Chin throne. Tseng became chancellor and later served as grand marshal with the title of duke. He died in his eightieth year and was buried with great pomp. *CCKT*. XXIII, *2*.

HO YEN 何晏 (P'ing-shu 平叔). ca. 190-249. *SKWei* 9.24ab, biography of Ts'ao Shuang, comm. A grandson of the Han general, Ho Chin 進, or of his younger brother, Miao 苗. His father died when he was small. His mother, Lady Yin, became a concubine of Ts'ao Ts'ao when he was around six, after which he was raised as a prince and married to Ts'ao's daughter (his own half sister, as some sources claim), the Princess of Chin-hsiang 金鄉. Though exceptionally gifted, he was somewhat given to dissipation, for which he was hated by Emperor Wen and kept out of office during the latter's reign (220-227). With the accession of Emperor Ming (r. 227-239) he became more active in affairs. When his friend Ts'ao Shuang became regent in 240, he was raised to cavalier attendant-in-ordinary, personal attendant, and president of the Board of Civil Office, in which last post he was able to place his personal friends, all devotees of "pure conversation" (ch'ing-t'an), into positions of power. He was killed by Ssu-ma I in 249 when Ts'ao Shuang's clique fell. WL. II, 14. 99; IV, 6, 7, 10; VII, 3; (VIII, 110); IX, 31; X, 6; XII, 2; XIV, 2.

HSI HSI 嵇喜 (Kung-mu 公穆). mid-third cent. The elder brother of Hsi K'ang, who ended his career as governor of Yang Province (Anhui-Kiangsu) for Western Chin. CPKM. XXIV, 4.

HSI K'ANG 嵇康 (Shu-yeh 叔夜). 223-262. SKWei 21.8a-9b, comm.; CS 49.11a-16b. He and Juan Chi share the places of highest regard in the group later known as the "Seven Worthies of the Bamboo Grove." A sensitive poet, musician, and active supporter of the Wei royal family, to which he was related by marriage, he was excluded from public office by the dominant Ssu-ma faction and devoted himself to Taoist pursuits and literature. Becoming innocently involved in a friend's personal problems, he was condemned to death, largely at the urging of Chung Hui, as a threat to public morality. The Wei Kingdom ended three years after his death. He is often referred to by his sinecure title, Chung-san ta-fu 中散大夫. WCHL; HKCH; (Hsi) K'ang PC; see also R. van Gulik, Hsi K'ang and His Poetical Essay on the Lute, Tokyo, 1941, and D. Holzman, La vie et la pensée de Hi K'ang, Leiden, 1957. I, 16, 43; II, 15, 18; III, 8; IV, 5, 21, 98; VI, 2; VIII, 29; IX, 31, 67; XIV, 5, (11); XVII, 2; XVIII, 2, 3; XIX, 11; XXIII, 1; XXIV, 3, 4; XXV, 4.

HSI SHAO 嵇紹 (Yen-tsu 延祖). 253-304. CS 89.2a-5b. Son of Hsi K'ang. Because of his father's execution by the Ssu-ma clan in 262, he remained for some time thereafter in total obscurity. After the founding of Chin in 265, upon the urging of Shan T'ao, he took office as curator of the palace library, later rising to various governorships, and finally cavalier attendant-in-ordinary and personal attendant. In this latter capacity he lost his life protecting Emperor Hui (r. 290-306) in 304 during the "War of the Eight Princes." WYCS. I, 43; III, 8; V, 17; VIII, 29, 36; XIV, 11.

HSI TSO-CH'IH 習鑿齒 (Yen-wei 彥威). d. 384. CS 82.16a-21b. A native of Hsiang-yang (Hupei), who became a personal friend and lay disciple of the monk Shih Tao-an. His principal claim to fame was his monumental "Annals of Han and Chin" (HCCC) in 54 chüan, now surviving only in occasional quotations found at the close of certain chapters of Ssu-ma Kuang's TCTC (ca. 1086) covering this period. His motive for writing was said to be opposition to Huan Wen's usurpatorial ambitions, through a theory of legitimacy based on continuity of the royal line, rather than ritual abdication. After serving as Huan Wen's superintendent of records in Wu-ch'ang (Hupei), and later as his lieutenant-governor for Ching Province (Hunan-Hupei), around the year 371, he offended his superior and was demoted to govern a remote commandery in the south. After developing some kind of foot ailment, he returned to his native Hsiang-yang some time before 379, when the Former Ch'in ruler, Fu

Chien (r. 357-385), took the city and carried both Hsi and his friend Tao-an to Ch'ang-an (Shensi). But here his illness became critical, and he returned to Hsiang-yang to die in 384. *CHS.* II, 72; IV, 80; XXV, 41, (46).

HSIA-HOU CHAN 夏侯湛 (Hsiao-jo 孝若). 243-291. *CS* 55.1a-9b. A close friend of the poet P'an Yüeh. He took his first degree around 270, and at the end of his life held the rank of clerk in the Central Secretariat. *WSC.* II, 65; IV, 71; XIV, 9.

HSIA-HOU HSÜAN 夏侯玄 (T'ai-ch'u 太初). 209-254. *SKWei* 9.26a-33b. Elder brother of the first wife of Ssu-ma Shih, Hsia-hou Hui 徽. He was also a cousin of the Wei regent, Ts'ao Shuang, after whose execution in 249 he made an abortive effort to restore the power of the Wei royal family and overthrow the chancellor, Ssu-ma I, but was apprehended and killed in 254 along with Li Feng, Chang I 張緝, and others. He was greatly admired in his day as a conversationalist. *WSCC; KPCC; SY; MSC.* V, 6, 7; VI, 3; VII, 3; VIII, 8; IX, 4; XIV, 3, 4.

HSIANG CH'UN 向純 (Ch'ang-t'i 長悌). d. 311. Eldest son of Hsiang Hsiu. He became personal attendant, but while fleeing with his brother T'i during the sack of Lo-yang in 311, was killed by bandits. *CLCHL; CCKT.* VIII, 29.

HSIANG HSIU 向秀 (Tzu-ch'i 子期). ca. 221-ca. 300. *CS* 49.16a-17b. Most famous as a member of the "Seven Worthies of the Bamboo Grove," and author of a lost commentary on the *Chuang-tzu* (quotations survive in Chang Chan's fourth-cent. commentary to *Lieh-tzu* and in the seventh-cent. *Ching-tien shih-wen* of Lu Te-ming), which strongly influenced the revival of philosophical Taoism during the third century. His "Poetic Essay on Recalling an Old Friendship," relating his friendship with Hsi K'ang and Lü An, is found in *WH* 16.7b-9a. After Hsi K'ang's execution in 262, however, he became disillusioned with detachment as a way of life, and entered government service, rising to become cavalier attendant-in-ordinary under the Chin. *Hsiang Hsiu PC.* II, 18; IV, 17, 32; VIII, 29; IX, 44; XXIII, 1; XXIV, 3.

HSIANG HSIUNG 向雄 (Mao-po 茂伯). d. 283. *CS* 48.1a-2a. A man of very rigid principles, he began as superintendant of records for Wang Ching while the latter was grand warden of Ho-nei (northern Honan). After Wang's death in 260, he served a succession of grand wardens in the same post, often coming into violent conflict with them. Later he was a palace attendant, and still later governor of Ch'in Province (Shensi). Returning to the capital, he served as junior censor, personal attendant, and finally capital intendant. After remonstrating vainly with Emperor Wu over the banishment of the Prince of Ch'i, Ssu-ma Yu, in 283, he died in a fit of indignation. *HCCC; SY.* V, 16.

HSIANG T'I 向悌 (Shu-hsün 叔遜). d. 311. Second son of Hsiang Hsiu. He became an assistant censor, but while fleeing from the sack of Lo-yang in 311 with his older brother Ch'un, he was killed by bandits. *CLCHL; CCKT.* VIII, 29.

HSIAO LUN 蕭倫 (Tsu-chou 祖冏). mid-fourth cent. A specialist in the three books on ritual (*Li-chi*, *Chou-li*, and *I-li*) who served as a palace attendant and erudite of the School for Sons of the State. *CPKM*; *LCCCC*. VIII, 75; IX, 69.

HSIEH AN 謝安 (An-shih 安石). 320-385. *CS* 79.4a-9a. Third son of Hsieh P'ou, brother-in-law of Liu T'an, and father-in-law of Wang Kuo-pao. His early years were spent in comfortable retirement in K'uai-chi (Chekiang). In 360, when he was already past forty, he finally accepted office as Huan Wen's sergeant-at-arms. Later he rose to become personal attendant, in which post he survived Huan's attempted usurpation in 373. He became governor-general of military affairs in five provinces, and at the climax of his career in 383 he thwarted the attempted invasion of Fu Chien, though the actual fighting was done by his younger brother and nephew. His last title was grand protector, and after his death he was given the posthumous title of grand tutor. *WTC*. I, 33, *34*, 36; II, 62, 70, 71, 75, 78, 90, 92; III, 23; IV, 24, 39, 48, 52, 55, 79, 82, 87, 94; V, 18, 55, (57), 60, 61, 62; VI, 27, 28, 29, 30, 33, 34, 35, 37; VII, 21, 24; VIII, 63, 76, 77, 78, 97, 101, 102, 116, 125, 129, 131, 133, 139, 140, 141, 143, 146, 147, 148; IX, 45, 46, 52, 55, 57, 59, 60, 62, 67, 69, 70, 73, 74, 75, 76, 77, 78, 82, 84, 85, 87; X, 21, 27; XII, 6; XIII, 12; XIV, 34, 36, 37; XVII, 15; XIX, 23, 25, 26; XXI, 7; XXIII, 38, 40, 41, 42; XXIV, 9, 12, 14; XXV, 26, 32, 39, 45, 55; XXVI, 17, 23, 27, 29; XXVII, 14; XXXI, 6; XXXIII, 14; XXXIV, 5.

HSIEH CHEN 謝甄 (Tzu-wei 子微). fl. late second cent. *HHS* 98.5ab. He was even more renowned than Kuo T'ai as a knower of men, but never rose above a minor post in Yü-chang Commandery (Kiangsi). He was killed after insulting the powerful general Ts'ao Ts'ao. *JNHHC*. VIII, *3*.

HSIEH CHÜ 謝據 (Hsüan-tao 玄道; baby name, Hu-tzu 虎子). ca. 318-350. The second son of Hsieh P'ou, between Hsieh I and Hsieh An. He was the husband of Wang Sui§ 綏 and the father of Hsieh Lang. XXIV, 8; XXXIV, *5*; (XIX, 26?).

HSIEH CHUNG 謝重 (Ching-chung 景重). late fourth to early fifth cent. *CS* 79.20ab. Son of Hsieh Lang and cousin of Hsieh Ling-yün. He served for awhile as Ssu-ma Tao'tzu's senior administrator. *HCYC*. II, *98*, 100, 101; XXV, 58.

HSIEH FENG 謝奉 (Hung-tao 弘道). fl. ca. 340-360. Son of Hsieh Feng*鳳. He served as General Pacifying the South and (concurrently?) governor of Kuang Province (Kwangtung-Kwangsi), later returning to Chien-k'ang for a brief term as president of the Board of Civil Office. After being dismissed, he retired to his native place in Chekiang about 360. *CPKM*. II, 83; VI, *33*; VIII, 85, 112; IX, 40.

HSIEH FU 謝敷 (Ch'ing-hsü 慶緒). late fourth cent. *CS* 94.31ab; *KSC* 4 (*Taishō* 50.350b), 5 (356c), and 7 (371b). He is usually designated "the Householder" (*chü-shih* 居士 = Sk. *gṛhapati*, a Buddhist layman). A native of K'uai-chi Commandery (Chekiang), he spent ten years in retirement among the T'ai-p'ing Mountains of that area. Among his close friends were several eminent monks and laymen, and his preface to the manual on breathing techniques, the Anāpānasmṛti-sūtra (An-pan shou-i ching 安般守意經), is preserved in CSTCC 6, Taishō 55.43c ff.; see also Zürcher, Conquest, p. 366, n. 283. HCYC. XVIII, 17; XXV, 49.

HSIEH HSÜAN 謝玄 (Yu-tu 幼度; baby name, O 遏, changed from 羯, to avoid a T'ang taboo). 343-388. CS 79.12b-18a. Third son of Hsieh I and a nephew of Hsieh An. Beginning his career in Huan Wen's headquarters while the latter was stationed in Wu-ch'ang (Hupei) ca. 363-365, he was later placed in charge of military operations in seven provinces (377). His finest hour was the defeat of the invading armies of Fu Chien at the Fei River (Anhui) in 383, for which he was rewarded with the governorship of K'uai-chi Principality (Chekiang). He is often known by his posthumous title, General of Chariots and Horsemen. Hsieh Ch'e-ch'i chia-chuan. II, 78, 92; IV, 41, 52, 58; V, (57); VI, 35, 38; VII, 22, 23; VIII, 146, 149; IX, 46, 71, 72; XIV, 36; XIX, 26, 28, 30; XXV, 54, 55; XXVI, 23; XXVII, 14; XXXII, 2; XXXIII, (16).

HSIEH HUN 謝混 (Shu-yüan 叔源; baby name, I-shou 益壽). d. 412. CS 79.11a-12a. Son of Hsieh Yen, grandson of Hsieh An, and a second cousin of Hsieh Ling-yün. He married the Princess of Chin-ling, a daughter of Emperor Hsiao-wu (Ssu-ma Yao, r. 373-396), and served the Eastern Chin as president of the Central Secretariat, vice-president of the Imperial Secretariat, and president of the Board of Civil Office. But since he belonged to the faction of Liu I* 劉毅 (d. 412), which attempted to oppose the rise of the grand marshal, Liu Yü*, who later founded the Sung, he was apprehended by the latter and permitted to commit suicide in 412. CATC. II, 105; VI, 42; X, 27; XXV, 60.

HSIEH I 謝奕 (Wu-i 無奕). d. 358. CS 79.12ab. Eldest son of Hsieh P'ou, elder brother of Hsieh An, and father of Hsieh Hsüan. He first served as Huan Wen's sergeant-at-arms and drinking companion before becoming magistrate of Yen Prefecture (Chekiang). In 357 he replaced his elder brother, Shang, as governor of Yü Province (northern Anhui) and General Pacifying the West, stationed at Wu-ch'ang (Hupei), but died a year later. CHS. I, 33; II, 71; IV, 41; (V, 57); IX, 59; XXIV, 8; XXXI, 5; XXXIII, 14.

HSIEH K'UN 謝鯤 (Yu-yü 幼輿). 280-322. CS 49.18b-21a. Father of Hsieh Shang. A very unconventional man who loved Lao-tzu and the "Book of Changes"; he spent most of his time with music and calligraphy, and in the company of the "Eight Free Spirits" (pa-ta): Hu-wu Fu-chih and the others. After fleeing southward around 311, he served as grand warden of Yü-chang (Kiangsi) while Wang Tun was stationed there as governor of Yang Province, and was called to be Tun's senior administrator when the latter became generalissimo in 317. CYC; Hsieh K'un PC. II, 46; IV, 20; VIII, 36, 51, 97; IX, 17; X, 12; XIV, 20; XVII, 6; XXI, 12; XXV, 15.

HSIEH LANG 謝朗 (Ch'ang-tu 長度; baby name, Hu-erh 胡兒). second half, fourth cent. CS 79.20a. Eldest son of Hsieh Chü, who died when Lang was very young, and nephew of Hsieh An. His highest office was grand warden of Tung-yang (Chekiang). *HCYC*. II, 71, 79; IV, 39; VIII, 139; IX, 46; XIX, 26; XXXI, 6; XXXIV, 5.

HSIEH LING-YÜN 謝靈運. 385-433. *SS* 67.1a-33b. Also known as the Duke of K'ang-lo 康樂; a son of Hsieh Huan and grandson of Hsieh Hsüan. Most famous as a nature poet and lay defender of Buddhism who introduced to the intellectual world the theory of "instantaneous illumination" (*tun-wu* 頓悟), developed by the monk Chu Tao-sheng 竺道生 (ca. 360-434). He also followed an official career, beginning about 405, as an aide on the staff of the grand marshal, Ssu-ma Te-wen 德文, and later (ca. 406-412) of Liu I* (d. 412), the unsuccessful opponent of the founder of Sung, Liu Yü*. Always haunted by his family's prominence under the Eastern Chin, Hsieh's loyalty to the new dynasty frequently faltered. Between brief assignments in the Sung court as curator of the Palace Library and personal attendant, he also served as grand warden of Yung-chia Commandery (Chekiang) and governor of Lin-ch'uan Principality (Kiangsi). But because of frequent sick leaves to the K'uai-chi area (Chekiang) and alleged maladministration, he was banished in 433 to Kuang Province (Kwangtung-Kwangsi), where, again charged with plotting a rebellion, he was sentenced to death. See J. D. Frodsham, *The Murmuring Stream: The Life and Works of The Chinese Nature Poet Hsieh Ling-yun*, 2 vols., Kuala Lumpur, 1968. *HCL*. II, *108*.

HSIEH P'IN 謝聘 (Hung-yüan 弘遠). fl. mid-fourth cent. The younger brother of Hsieh Feng. He served as personal attendant and director of punishments. *Hsieh SP*. IX, *40*.

HSIEH P'OU 謝裒 (Yu-ju 幼儒). early fourth cent. Chiefly famous as the father of Hsieh I, Hsieh Chü, Hsieh An, Hsieh Wan, Hsieh Shih, and Hsieh T'ieh, most of whom achieved high recognition in Eastern Chin. P'ou served as personal attendant, president of the Board of Civil Office, and governor of Wu Principality (Soochow). *YCLJM*. V, *25*; XXIII, 33.

HSIEH SHANG 謝尚 (Jen-tsu 仁祖; baby name, Chien-shih 墅石). 308-357. *CS* 79.1a-3b. Son of Hsieh K'un and cousin of Hsieh An. Considered a prodigy as a boy, he was much honored in his lifetime, serving successively as vice-president of the Imperial Secretariat, governor of Yü Province (Anhui, 350-354), and General Governing the West, stationed at Wu-ch'ang (Hupei). After Huan Wen had temporarily recaptured Lo-yang in 356, he nominated Shang to be its governor, but illness prevented his assuming the post and he died in the following year. He was a skillful musician, and is credited with reviving the "ancient music" south of the Yangtze. *CYC*. II, *46*, 47; IV, 22, 28, 88; V, 52, (58); VII, 18; VIII, 89, 103, 104, 124, 134; IX, 21, 26, 36, 50; X, 19; XIV, 32; XXIII, 32, 33, 37; XXVI, 10, 13, 27; XXXIV, 3.

HSIEH SHAO 謝韶 (Mu-tu 穆度; baby name, Feng 封). mid-fourth cent. Mentioned, *CS* 79.20a. A son of Hsieh Wan, he served as sergeant-at-arms to his kinsman, Hsieh Hsüan, but died in his thirty-third year. XIX, *26*.

HSIEH SHIH 謝石 (Shih-nu 石奴). 327-388. CS 79.20b-21b. Fifth son of Hsieh P'ou, younger brother of Hsieh An, and son-in-law of Chu-ko Hui. After distinguishing himself in the successful defense against the invasion of Fu Chien in 383, he became president of the Imperial Secretariat. Concerned over the decline of education in his home area, he memorialized to revive the Imperial Academy in order to provide teachers for provincial and commandery schools. HCYC; Hsieh SP. II, 90; V, 25, (57); (VI, 35).

HSIEH TAO-YÜN 謝道蘊 (var. 韞). second half, fourth cent. CS 96.9b-10b. Daughter of Hsieh I, elder sister of Hsieh Hsüan, and wife of Wang Ning-chih. She was a very prolific poet but nothing has survived of her work. FJC. II, 71; XIX, 26, 28, 30.

HSIEH WAN 謝萬 (Wan-shih 萬石). ca. 321-361. CS 79.18b-19b. A younger brother of Hsieh An and son-in-law of Wang Shu. He began his career on the staff of Ssu-ma Yü in 345. Later, when he became governor of Yü Province (southern Honan) with military oversight over four provinces, he took part in the border clashes with Former Yen (307-370) in 358. After alienating both officers and men through his arrogance and neglect, he crowned an ignoble military career with a disasterous rout at Shou-ch'un (Anhui) in 359, whereupon he was divested of all offices and titles. Thereafter he avidly espoused the cause of the recluse until his death a few years later. CCHS. II, 77, 82; IV, 56, 91; V, 55, (57); VI, 31; VIII, 88, 93, 122; IX, 49, 55, 60; X, 21; XIX, 25, 26(?); XXIV, 9, 10, 12, 14; XXV, 43, 51; XXVI, 19, 23.

HSIEH YEN 謝琰 (Yüan-tu 瑗度; baby name, Mo-pei 末婢). d. 400. CS 79.9b-11a. Hsieh An's youngest son, and the father of Hsieh Hun. He became personal attendant to Emperor Hsiao-wu (r. 373-396), and participated with his cousin, Hsüan, in the campaign against Fu Chien in 383, for which he was ennobled. At his father's death in 385 he retired from office, later serving briefly as governor of K'uai-chi Principality (Chekiang) and vice-president of the Imperial Secretariat. While Ssu-ma Tao-tzu was Prince of K'uai-chi, Yen was his sergeant-at-arms. After helping to suppress the uprising of Wang Kung in 398, he was transferred to serve as governor of Hsü Province (Anhui-Kiangsu), and joined Liu Lao-chih in quelling Sun En's rebellion in 400. Stationed in K'uai-chi, he failed to make adequate military preparations and was killed in battle by his own mutinous troops. XVII, 15; XXVI, 32.

HSIEH YÜAN 謝荊 (Shu-tu 叔度; baby name, Mo 末). late fourth cent. Mentioned, CS 79.20a. Second son of Hsieh I and older brother of Hsieh Hsüan. He was once grand warden of I-hsing (Kiangsu). XIX, 26.

HSIEH YÜEH-CHING 謝月鏡. early fifth cent. The daughter of Hsieh Chung and wife of Wang Yin-chih, son of Wang Kung. Hsieh SP. II, 100.

HSIN P'I 辛毗 (Tso-chih 佐治). d. 324. SKWei 25.1a-6a. With the founding of the Wei Kingdom in 220 he received noble rank and died in battle against Shu in 234 while assigned to cool the hot blood of the Wei commander, Ssu-ma I. His highest office was commandant of the Palace Guard. WC. V, 5.

HSING CH'IAO 邢喬 (Tseng-po 曾伯). fl. late third cent. He once served as commandant of the Capital Province. CCKT. VIII, 22.

HSÜ CH'I 許奇 (Tzu-t'ai 子泰). second half, third cent. SKWei 9.35b, comm. The eldest son of Hsü Yün, he won the respect of the founder of Western Chin, Ssu-ma Yen (Emperor Wu, r. 265-290), and served him first as assistant to the grand ordinary, in charge of court ceremonial, and later served his successor, Emperor Hui (r. 291-306), as commandant of the Capital Province. Since his father had met his death at the hands of Ssu-ma Yen's uncle, Ssu-ma Shih, in 254, it took a special act of indulgence to grant him access to the emperor's person. SY; CCKT. XIX, 8.

HSÜ CH'IEN 許虔 (Tzu-cheng 子政). fl. late second cent. HHS 98.9a. Elder brother of Hsü Shao. Noted for his strict probity in selecting officials for his commandery, his reputation was eventually eclipsed by his younger brother. He died at the age of thirty-four. JNHHC. VIII, 3.

HSÜ CHIH 徐穉 var. 稚 (Ju-tzu 孺子). 97-168. HHS 83.5b-7a. He lived in poverty throughout his life, doing his own farming and never responding to the numerous calls from high officials to enter government service. HCHHS. I, 1; II, 2.

HSÜ HSÜN 許詢 (Hsüan-tu 玄度). fl. ca. 358. A recluse-poet who lived in the Chekiang hills, whom Ssu-ma Yü (Emperor Chien-wen, r. 371-372) considered "more subtle" than any of his contemporaries, and who is credited by T'an Tao-luan (fifth cent.) in the HCYC (see SSHY IV, 85) as the first literary figure, along with Sun Ch'o, to employ Buddhist imagery and terminology in his poems. Strongly influenced by the monk Chih Tun, he steadfastly refused public office, but died relatively young. HCYC. II, 69, 73; IV, 38, 40, 55, 85; VIII, 95, 111, 119, 144; IX, 50, 54, 55, 61; X, 20; XVIII, 13, 16; XXII, 4; XXVI, 18, 31.

HSÜ HSÜN's mother 許詢母. fl. mid-fourth cent. The daughter of Hua I. Hsü SP. VIII, 95.

HSÜ LIU 許柳 (Chi-tsu 季祖). d. 328-329. A son of Hsü Meng and father of Hsü Yung. Married to the granddaughter of Tsu T'i, he became involved in Su Chün's rebellion in 327 through T'i's older brother Yüeh, who had him appointed capital intendant after Su's occupation of Chien-k'ang. When the rebellion was put down early in 329, he was executed. Hsü SP. III, 11.

HSÜ MENG 許猛 (Tzu-pao 子豹). second half, third cent. SKWei 9.35b, comm. Like his brother, Hsü Ch'i, he was an expert in ritual and in evaluating men. During the period 291-299 he was governor of Yu Province (northern Hopei). SY; CCKT. XIX, 8.

HSÜ NING 徐寧 (An-ch'i 安期). early fourth cent. CS 74.17b-18a. A native of Tung-hai Commandery (Chekiang) who became friendly with the general Huan I while the latter was traveling through Yü prefecture (Anhui) during Hsü's magistracy there. Huan recommended him to Yü Liang, who gave him a post as clerk in the Board of Civil Office. Later he became governor of Chiang Province (Hupei-Kiangsi). *HCCPS*. VIII, 65.

HSÜ SHAO 許邵 (Tzu-chiang 子將). ca. 153-198. *HHS* 98.7b-9a. Renowned as a knower of men, he is sometimes credited with the famous characterization of Ts'ao Ts'ao (otherwise attributed to Ch'iao Hsüan): "the hero of a rebellious age; the villain of an orderly one." He and his friends used to hold characterization sessions known as "first-of-the-month critiques" (*yüeh-tan p'ing* 月旦評), by which many a reputation was made or ruined. Fleeing southward during the disorders accompanying the Yellow Turban Revolt of 184, he served briefly under Sun Ts'e's administration of Yü-chang Commandery (Kiangsi) and died at the age of forty-five. *HNHHC*. VIII, 3.

HSÜ TSAO 許璪 (Ssu-wen 思文). fl. first half, fourth cent. After serving under Wang Tao while the latter was governor of Yang Province (Kiangsu-Anhui-Chekiang) between 318 and 339, he later became a clerk in the Board of Civil Office. His title of personal attendant may have been posthumous. *CPKM*; *Hsü SP*. VI, 16; XXV, 20.

HSÜ YUNG 許永 (Ssu-pi 思妣). d. 328-329. Son of Hsü Liu, he was executed with his father because of the latter's involvement in Su Chün's revolt. *Hsü SP*. III, 11.

HSÜ YÜN 許允 (Shih-tsung 士宗). d. 254. *SKWei* 9.34a-35b, comm. Brother-in-law of Juan K'an and a friend of Hsia-hou Hsüan and Li Feng, he became involved in their plot against the dictator Ssu-ma Shih and was arrested. He "died" on the way to exile in Lak-lang (North Korea) in 254. *WL*. XIX, 6, 7.

HSÜN CHING 荀靖 (Shu-tz'u 叔慈). late second to early third cent. *SKWei* 10.1a, comm. Third son of Hsün Shu, he lived most of his life as a recluse. *ISC*. I, 6; IX, 6.

HSÜN CHÜ-PO 荀巨伯. fl. ca. 147-167. Nothing is known of him beyond the incident in I, 9. *Hsün-shih chia-chuan*. I, 9.

HSÜN HSIEN 荀羨 (Ling-tse 令則). 321-358. *CS* 75.22b-23b. A son of Hsün Sung 崧. Caught in Su Chün's rebellion (328) in his seventh year, he showed early signs of physical bravery, but when eight years later his family engaged him to the Princess of Hsün-yang, a younger sister of Ssu-ma Yü (Emperor Chien-wen, r. 371-372), his courage left him completely and he went into hiding. After he was twenty and duly married to the princess, he moved freely in the highest circles, claiming among his friends Liu T'an, Wang Meng, and Yin Hao. When Ch'u P'ou became General Chastizing the North stationed in Ching-k'ou (Kiangsu) in 344, Hsün became his senior administrator. Later he himself, as commandant of the north and governor of Hsü and Yen provinces (southern Shantung and northern Kiangsu and Anhui), was stationed there, moving in 350 to Hsia-p'ei (northern Kiangsu), where in 356 he was engaged in border skirmishes with the non-Chinese Former Yen state (307-370). After his death in 358 he received the posthumous title, General of Spirited Horsemen. *CYC*. II, 74.

HSÜN HSÜ 荀勗 (Kung-tseng 公曾). d. 289. *CS* 39.10-16a. A great-grandson of Hsün Shuang and grandson on his mother's side of Chung Yu. He was first attached to the administration of the Wei regent, Ts'ao Shuang, and upon the latter's downfall in 249, presented himself to Ts'ao's rival, Ssu-ma Shih, who sent him into the provinces as magistrate of An-yang (northern Honan). Later he returned to court as an aide of the generalissimo Ssu-ma Chao. With the establishment of Western Chin in 265 he assisted in the codification of laws and was rewarded with noble rank and the presidency of the Central Secretariat. Because he had been instrumental in establishing Chia Ch'ung's daughter (Chia Nan-feng) as consort of Emperor Hui (Ssu-ma Chung, r. 290-306), his reputation suffered after her death in 300, but he is chiefly remembered for his legal code and his continuation of Hsün I's musical reforms. *YYCS*; *WYCS*. II, 99; V, 14; XX, 1, 2; XXI, 4.

HSÜN I 荀顗 (Ching-ch'ien 景倩). 205-274. *CS* 39.8a-10a. Sixth son of Hsün Yü 彧. Serving first as a personal attendant under the Wei, he narrowly escaped death during the purge of Ts'ao Shuang's clique in 249, whereupon he joined the forces of Ssu-ma Shih. He replaced his nephew, Ch'en T'ai, as vice-president of the Board of Civil Office in 260. On the eve of the founding of Western Chin in 265 he was made director of works and commissioned, along with Yang Hu, to codify the "Rituals of Chin." After the accession of Emperor Wu (Ssu-ma Yen, r. 265-290) he became a duke, and sometime later director of instruction and grand marshal. Toward the end of his life he addressed himself to revising the official musical pitches according to "ancient" standards. *CCKT*. II, 99; IX, 6.

HSÜN SHU 荀淑 (Chi-ho 季和). 83-149. *HHS* 92.1a-2a. A descendant in the eleventh generation from the philosopher Hsün-tzu (third cent. B.C.). During the regency of the Empress Dowager Liang 梁 (144-150) he was recommended for the degree, Honest and Upright (*fang-cheng*), but after criticizing the empress's brother, Liang Chi 冀, he was demoted to fill a vacancy as magistrate of Lang-ling (Honan). After his death, Li Yin, then president of one of the secretariats, mourned for him as for his own teacher. *HHHC*. I, 5, 6; IX, 6.

HSÜN SHUANG 荀爽 (Tz'u-ming 慈明). late second to early third cent. *SKWei* 10.1a, comm. Sixth son of Hsün Shu. Under the patronage of Tung Cho (d. 192) he rose from obscurity to become director of works within the space of 95 days. *ISC*. I, 6; II, 7; IX, 6.

HSÜN TS'AN 荀粲 (Feng-ch'ien 奉倩). ca. 212-240. *SKWei* 10.12ab, comm. Fifth son of Hsün Yü 彧. Being of an intellectual and an esthetic turn of mind, he preferred a life aloof from public affairs. He married the daughter of Ts'ao Hung 洪, a member of the ruling house, and was so extremely devoted to her that it is claimed he died of grief after her premature death when he was only in his twenty-ninth year. *Hsün Ts'an PC*. IV, 9; V, 59; VII, 3; XXXV, 2.

HSÜN YIN 荀隱 (Ming-ho 鳴鶴). late third cent. He served successively as crown prince's chamberlain and director of punishments, but died young. *HSCC.* XXV, 9.

HSÜN YÜ 荀彧 (Wen-jo 文若). 163-212. *HHS* 100.18b-25b; *SKWei* 10.1a-11b. Son of Hsün Kun 緄. After attaching himself to Ts'ao Ts'ao's headquarters in 189, he became the latter's trusted adviser, but incurred his enmity when he opposed Ts'ao's ennoblement as duke in 212 and was obliged to commit suicide. Since his grandfather, Hsün Shu, had died in 149, fourteen years before Yü was born, stories associating him with Shu are clearly anachronistic. *TL.* I, 6; IX, 6.

HSÜN YÜ* 荀寓 (Ching-po 景伯). second half, third cent. A grandson of Hsün Yü, he served the Western Chin court in some minor capacity. *Hsün SP*; *SY.* XXV, 7.

HU, Lady 胡氏. mid. fourth to early fifth cent. Mother of Lo Ch'i-sheng and Lo Tsun-sheng. I, 43.

HU WEI 胡威 (Po-hu 伯虎). d. 280. *CS* 90.3b-5a. Son of Hu Chih 質. Both father and son gained reputations for their frugality and incorruptibility. He was governor of Hsü Province (N. Kiangsu and Anhui) at his death. *CYC.* I, 27.

HU-WU FU-CHIH 胡毋輔之 (Yen-Kuo 彥國). ca. 264-ca. 312. *CS* 49.21a-22a. A heavy drinker and one of the "Eight Free Spirits" (*pa-ta*) of the end of the Western Chin (early fourth century). He served in several minor posts, and was ennobled for his participation in the suppression of the Prince of Ch'i (Ssu-ma Chiung) in 302. After the fall of Lo-yang and the death of his patron, Ssu-ma Yüeh, he fled south and died soon after arriving at his post as governor of Hsiang Province (Hunan). *YCLJM.* I, *23*; VIII, 53; IX, 15.

HUA HSIN 華歆 (Tzu-yü 子魚). 157-231. *SKWei* 13.10a-14b. After the death of the Later Han Emperor Ling in 189, he became personal attendant to Emperor Hsien (r. 190-220). He succeeded Hsün Yü in the service of Ts'ao Ts'ao and rose to be director of instruction under the Wei Emperor Wen (r. 220-226). His last title was cavalier attendant-in-ordinary. *WeiC.* I, *10*, 11, 12, 13; V, 3.

HUA I 華軼 (Yen-hsia 彥夏). d. 311. *CS* 61.15a-16b. He had served as cavalier attendant-in-ordinary at the Lo-yang court and as senior administrator for the Prince of Tung-hai (Ssu-ma Yüeh) when the latter was governor of Yen Province (southern Shantung). Around 310 he was named governor of Chiang Province (Kiangsi and Kiangsu) and gained a good name both among the older gentry families of that area and the new refugee families pouring in from the north to escape the barbarian invasions. In spite of the crisis and insecurity of the throne, he maintained a firm loyalty to the court in Lo-yang: when the local military governor, Ssu-ma Jui, who later founded the Eastern Chin state in Chien-k'ang (Nanking, 317-420), issued orders, he insisted on having confirmation from Lo-yang before complying. After Lo-yang fell in 311, Hua was summoned to serve as Jui's senior administrator but refused. During the civil strife which ensued he was killed with all the members of his family. *YYCS*. VII, 9.

HUAN CH'IEN 桓謙 (Ching-tsu 敬祖). d. 410. *CS* 74.15b-16b. The third son of Huan Ch'ung. He was governor of Wu Principality (Soochow) at the time of Sun En's depredations in 399 and fled to Wu-hsi, after which he was called to the capital to become president of the Board of Civil Office. At the time of Huan Hsüan's descent on the capital in 402, the court, hoping to separate him from his cousin, dispatched him westward to serve as governor-general of military affairs in the four provinces of Ching, I, Ning, and Liang (roughly Hupei and Szechwan). Later he was recalled to Chien-k'ang and made president of the Imperial Secretariat, personal attendant, and general of the Palace Guard. With his cousin's usurpation in 404, he became governor of Yang Province (Kiangsu-Anhui-Chekiang) and was enfeoffed Prince of Hsin-an, but because of rivalry with another member of the Huan family he took refuge in 408 with the Later Ch'in ruler, Yao Hsing (r. 394-416), in Ch'ang-an (Shensi). Yao used him in a campaign against Shu in the southwest but never quite trusted him, and he eventually was killed by one of Yao's generals in 410. *CHS*. IX, 88.

HUAN CH'UNG 桓沖 (Yu-tzu 幼子; var. Hsüan-shu 玄叔 and Hsüan-tzu 玄子; baby name, Mai-te 買德). 328-384. *CS* 74.10a-15a. A younger brother of Huan Wen, who, after achieving merit in his older brother's early campaigns, became governor-general of military affairs in seven commanderies of Ching Province (Hunan-Hupei). Later, after accompanying Wen on the 356 campaign in which Lo-yang was temporarily recovered, he was given noble rank and in 363 made governor of Chiang Province (Hupei-Kiangsi). After Huan Wen's death in 373, the Huan clan was eclipsed by that of Hsieh An, but on the death of Ch'ung's brother, Huo, in 377, Ch'ung succeeded him as governor of Ching Province. In 383, when Fu Chien was threatening the Eastern Chin domain, Ch'ung, then also governor of Chiang Province (Hupei-Kiangsi), sent troops to defend the capital, but because of his disagreement with Hsieh An over defense policy, was humiliated by Hsieh's victory at the Fei River (Anhui) and died the following year. He was granted the posthumous title of grand marshal. *Huan Ch'ung PC*. XII, 7; XIII, 10; XVIII, 8; XIX, 24; XXIII, 38, 45; XXIV, 11, 13; XXXI, 8; XXXIII, 16.

HUAN FAN 桓範 (Yün-ming 允明). d. 249. *SKWei* 9.22b-23a, comm. A member of the faction of the Wei prince, Ts'ao Shuang, he served as grand director of agriculture under the latter's regency (240-249). He perished in Ts'ao's downfall in 249. *WL*. XIX, 6.

HUAN HSI 桓熙 (Po-tao 伯道; baby name, Shih-t'ou 石頭). fl. late fourth cent. The eldest son of Huan Wen, he became governor of Yü Province (southern Honan). *CHS*. XI, 7.

HUAN HSIN 桓歆 (Shu-tao 叔道; baby name, Shih 式). second half, fourth cent. Third son of Huan Wen, he became president of one of the secretariats. *Huan SP*. III, 19.

HUAN HSIU 桓修 (Ch'eng-tsu 承祖; baby name, Yai 崖). d. 404. *CS* 74.16b-17b. A son of Huan Ch'ung by his second wife, Yü Yao, and the son-in-law of Emperor Chien-wen (Ssu-ma Yü, r. 371-372). He served under Huan Hsüan's brief usurpation in 404 as governor of two provinces but was killed by Liu Yü* in the same year. *HCYC*; Huan *SP*; *CATC*. XXV, 65; XXXVI, 8.

HUAN HSÜAN 桓玄 (Ching-tao 敬道; baby name, Ling-pao 靈寶). 369-404. *CS* 99.1a-21a. The youngest son, by a concubine, of Huan Wen, who on his deathbed in 373 made him his heir. He inherited the title, Duke of Nan Commandery (Hupei) three years later. In 391 he joined the staff of the crown prince at the capital. When Emperor Hsiao-wu died in 396, Hsüan was made grand warden of I-hsing (Kiangsu), but soon retired to his native Chiang-ling (Hupei), where he nursed the ambition to carry out his father's aborted hope of founding a new dynasty. Joining the party opposing the Prince of K'uai-chi, Ssu-ma Tao-tzu, he became, with the death of Wang Kung in 398, the new leader of the opposition and assumed the governorship of Chiang Province (Hupei-Kiangsi). In late 399 or early 400 he annexed Ching Province, forcing the suicide of its governor, Yin Chung-k'an, and in the spring of 402, on the pretext of suppressing the already defunct revolt of the Taoist magician Sun En, he descended the Yangtze River toward the capital, where he established himself as virtual dictator. On January 2, 404, he proclaimed himself emperor of the Ch'u Dynasty. After three months he was overthrown and killed by Liu Yü*, who founded the Sung Dynasty (420-479) sixteen years later. Huan Hsüan *PC*. I, 41, 42, 43; II, 101, 103, 104, 106, 107; IV, 65, 102, 103, 104; VIII, 156; IX, 86, 87, 88; X, 25, 27; XII, 7; XIII, 13; XVII, 18, 19; XIX, 32; XXIII, 50; XXV, 61, 62, 63, 64, 65; XXVI, 33; XXVIII, 8; XXXI, 8; XXXIII, 17; XXXVI, 8.

HUAN HUO 桓豁 (Lang-tzu 朗子). 320-377. *CS* 74.3b-5a. The second younger brother of Huan Wen, he accompanied the latter on his northern campaigns. During the reign of Emperor Chien-wen (371-372) he became a clerk in the Board of Civil Office and later palace attendant. Between 365 and 377, he served as governor of Ching Province (Hunan-Hupei) with the title General Chastizing the West. He is often referred to by his posthumous title, director of works. (Huan) Huo *PC*. XIII, 10; XXIII, 41.

HUAN I 桓彝 (Mao-lun 茂倫). 275-328. *CS* 74.1a-3a. The father of Huan Wen. He rose from poverty and obscurity to serve on the staff of the Prince of Ch'i (Ssu-ma Chiung) and later fled south to serve under the Eastern Chin, where he became a secretary in the Central Secretariat and in the Board of Civil Office. During Wang Tun's rebellion (322-324) he was cavalier attendant-in-ordinary and for his part in Wang Tun's suppression was given a noble title. In 328 while governor of Hsüan-ch'eng Principality (Anhui) he was killed attempting to resist the rebel Su Chün and was given the posthumous title, General Pacifying the South. He was also one of the "Eight Free Spirits" (*pa-ta*). Huan I *PC*. I, 30; VIII, 48, 65, 66; IX, 13; XIV, 20; XVI, 1.

HUAN I* 桓伊 (Shu-hsia 叔夏; baby name, Tzu-yeh 子野 or Yeh-wang 野王). d. ca. 392. *CS* 81.9b-11b. A distant relative of Huan Wen.

Because of his military prowess, he was stationed on the northern border as grand warden of Huai-nan (northern Anhui) and governor-general of military affairs in three provinces to guard against the threatened invasion by the Former Ch'in ruler, Fu Chien (r. 357-384). He shared honors with Hsieh Hsüan in Fu's defeat at the Fei River in 383, for which he received noble titles. In spite of these honors, he remained a modest man of cultivated taste and had a reputation as the greatest flautist of his generation, as well as being an accomplished player of the twelve-stringed zither, or *cheng*. During his governorship of the two provinces of Chiang and Yü (Hupei-Kiangsi-Anhui), he distinguished himself for his liberal and enlightened policies. *HCYC.* V, *55*; IX, *42*; XXIII, *33, 42, 49.*

HUAN LIANG 桓亮 (Ching-chen 景真). d. 404. The son of Huan Hsüan's older half brother, Chi 濟. When Hsüan was executed in the fall of 404, he gathered an army in Ch'ang-sha and declared himself governor of Hsiang Province (Hunan), killing ten or more of the key loyalists, including Han Hui-chih. He was then promptly killed himself by one of Liu I*'s generals. *HCYC.* XIX, *32.*

HUAN NÜ-YU 桓女幼. late fourth cent. Mentioned, *CS* 73.16b. Daughter of Huan Huo (or Huan Mi?) and wife of Yü (Shu-) hsüan. *Yü SP.* XIX, *22.*

HUAN PO-TZU 桓伯子, late fourth to early fifth cent. Huan Wen's second daughter and wife of Wang Yü. *Wang SP.* V, *58.*

HUAN SHIH-CH'IEN 桓石虔 (baby name, Chen-o 鎮惡). d. 388. *CS* 74.5a-6a. The eldest son of Huan Huo, by a concubine. He engaged in many campaigns against the Former Ch'in forces of Fu Chien (r. 358-385) and his various generals, for which he gained a great reputation for bravery. With the death of his uncle, Huan Ch'ung, in 384, he was appointed governor of Yü Province (southern Honan) to replace his kinsman, Huan I*, who then became governor of Chiang Province, in a shuffling maneuver by Hsieh An, designed to prevent disaffection in the Huan clan. He died in 388. *CHS.* XIII, *10.*

HUAN SSU 桓嗣 (Kung-tsu 恭祖; baby name, Pao-nu 豹奴). second half, fourth cent. *CS* 74.15ab. The oldest son of Huan Ch'ung by his first wife, Wang Nü-tsung. When his father was stationed at Wu-ch'ang (Hupei) as General Governing the West in the autumn of 377, Ssu was named governor of Chiang Province (Kiangsi and eastern Hupei), where his administration won praise for frugality and efficiency. Later he was stationed at Hsia-k'ou (west of Wu-ch'ang) as grand warden of two neighboring commanderies. He is usually known by his posthumous title, Southern Commander. *CHS.* XXV, *42.*

HUAN TAO-KUNG 桓道恭 (Tsu-yu 祖猷). d. 405. A younger first cousin of Huan I who served as grand warden of Huai-nan Commandery (Anhui) before becoming governor of Chiang-hsia Province (Hupei) under Huan Hsüan's short-lived Ch'u Dynasty (January to April 404). He was executed by the restored Chin government the following year. *Huan SP.* X, *25.*

HUAN WEN 桓溫 (Yüan-tzu 元子). 312-373. *CS* 98.16b-29b. Son of Huan I.

Rising rapidly from an obscure military family of Chiao Principality (Anhui), he served first as governor of Lang-yeh Principality (southern Shantung) and later exercised the dominant power at the Eastern Chin court as General Pacifying the West and governor of Ching Province from 345 to 363, when he became grand marshal. After that he was virtual dictator and was only prevented by his death in 373 from usurping the throne, after having deposed one emperor and set up a puppet in 371. Between 354 and 356 and again in 369 he temporarily recovered some of north China which was at the time occupied by non-Chinese dynasties, but could not persuade the court to return to the old Western Chin capital in Lo-yang. He is sometimes referred to by his posthumous title, Marquis of Hsüan-wu. *Huan Wen PC*. II, 55, 56, 58, 59, 60, 64, 85, 95, 101, 102; III, 16, 19, 20; IV, 22, 29, 80, 87, 92, 95, 96; V, 44, 50, 54, 55; VI, 25, 26, 27, 29, 33, 39; VII, 19, 20, (22), 27; VIII, 48, 73, 79, 101, 102, 103, 105, 115, 117; IX, 32, 35, 36, 37, 38, 41, 45, 52; X, 19; XI, 6, 7; XII, 5, 7; XIII, 8, 9, 10; XIV, 27, 28, 32, 34; XIX, 21, 32; XX, 9; XXII, 2; XXIII, 34, 37, 41, 44; XXIV, 8; XXV, 24, 26, 35, 38, 41, 42, 60; XXVI, 11, 12, 16; XXVII, 13; XXVIII, 2, 4, 6, 7; XXXI, 4; XXXIII, 12, 13.

HUAN YIN 桓胤 (Mao-tsu 茂祖). d. 407. *CS* 74.15b. A grandson of Huan Wen's younger brother, Ch'ung. He was president of the Central Secretariat when his cousin, Huan Hsüan, usurped the throne early in 404. Hsüan appointed him president of the Board of Civil Office, but with Hsüan's downfall a few months later, Yin gave himself up to the restoration government and was sent to a post in the provinces. Later he became the focus of a plot by Yin Chung-wen and others to make him successor to the lost throne of Huan Hsüan. When the plot was uncovered in 407, all his family and supporters were exterminated. *CHS*. IV, 100.

HUANG HSIEN 黃憲 (Shu-tu 叔度). second cent. *HHS* 83.4a-5b. He was considered by his contemporaries to be a reincarnation of Yen Hui (514-483 B.C.), the favorite disciple of Confucius. Like Hui, he came from a humble family, his father having been a cow-doctor, and like Hui, also, he aroused the profound admiration of his elders and superiors. He died at the age of 48 without ever having accepted office. *TL*. I, 2, 3.

HUANG-FU MI 皇甫謐 (Shih-an 士安; baby names, Ching 靜 and Hsüan-yen 玄晏). 215-282. *CS* 51.1a-10b. A native of the northwest frontier. In his younger days he is described as being "wild and profligate," but after reaching his twentieth year, on the remonstrances of an aunt, he settled down to diligent study and thereafter was "never seen without a book in his hand." Much of his life was passed in relative poverty. He suffered much in later years from what appears to have been arthritis, but he continued his studious life, spurning all calls to public office. He was subject to depressions and made at least one unsuccessful attempt at suicide. He is mostly rembered for his biographical collections: "Lives of Eminent Gentlemen" (*Kao-shih chuan* 高士傳), "Lives of Recluses" (*I-shih chuan* 逸士傳), and "Lives of Virtuous Women" (*Lieh-nü chuan* 烈女傳). *WYCS*. IV, 68.

JEN, Lady 任氏. late third cent. Wife of Wang I and mother of Wang Ch'eng. YCLJM. X, 10.

JEN CHAN 任瞻 (Yü-chang 育長). late third to early fourth cent. A man of great promise in his youth who, after crossing the Yangtze during the troubles of 307-312, seems to have lost his direction. He served successively as vice-president of a secretariat and governor-general of military affairs in a province, his last post being grand warden of T'ien-men (Chekiang). CPKM. XXXIV, 4.

JEN JANG 任讓, d. 328/329. A general under Su Chün's command during the latter's rebellion, he was executed after its suppression. CYC. III, 11.

JEN K'AI 任愷 (Yüan-p'ou 元褒). ca. 215-275. CS 45.15b-17b. The son of a high officer of Wei, he was married to a daughter of Emperor Ming (Ts'ao Jui, r. 227-239). With the founding of Chin in 265, he became a personal attendant of Emperor Wu (Ssu-ma Yen, r. 265-290), with the title of Marquis, and was high in the emperor's graces. Later, encountering the enmity of Chia Ch'ung, he became the victim of politically inspired slander, including the charge that he was using the imperial tableware (actually part of his wife's dowry), which ultimately brought him to disgrace and dismissal from the sensitive post of president of the Board of Civil Office in 272. Thereafter he seemed to disintegrate and lived a life of drunkenness and profligacy, sometimes spending 10,000 cash on a single meal. He died within three years. CCKT. XXIII, 16.

JEN YÜ 任頤. fl. ca. 317. A native of Lin-hai (Chekiang) and casual guest of Wang Tao. YL. III, 12.

JUAN, Mme. 阮夫人. mid-third cent. Daughter of Juan Kung and wife of Hsü Yün. XIX, 6, 7.

JUAN CHAN 阮瞻 (Ch'ien-li 千里). fl. 307-312. CS 49.5a-6a. Eldest son of Juan Hsien. A man of placid disposition and few attachments. He was noted for his ability to get the essence of a work without close study. He died in his thirtieth year, having reached only a minor post on the staff of the crown prince. MSC. VIII, 29, 139; IX, 20; XVI, 2; XXVI, 6.

JUAN CHI 阮籍 (Ssu-tsung 嗣宗). 210-263. SKWei 21.7b-8a, comm. CS 49.1a-4a. A gifted poet and musician, one of the "Seven Worthies of the Bamboo Grove," who managed to avoid involvement in the political intrigues of the transitional period between Wei and Chin by a façade of continual drunkenness. WSCC. I, 15; IV, 67; VIII, 29; XVII, 2; XVIII, 1; XIX, 11; XXIII, 1, 2, 5, 7, 8, 9, 10, 11, 13, 51; XXIV, 1, 2; XXV, 4.

JUAN CHI's sister-in-law 阮籍嫂. mid-third cent. The wife of Juan Chi's older brother Hsi and mother of Juan Hsien. XXIII, 7.

JUAN FU 阮孚 (Yao-chi 遙集). 278/9-326/7. CS 49.6a-7b. A grandson of Juan Chi's older brother and the son of Juan Hsien by a Hsien-pei slave girl. He made his way south during the barbarian invasions of 307-312 and, though employed in the Eastern Chin government, seems to have been given to drunkenness and sloth, and was often in want. He became personal attendant in 323, and for his part in repressing the revolt of Wang Tun was ennobled a marquis, and the following year made president of the Board of Civil Office. He died on the way to take up his post as governor of Kuang Province (Kwangtung-Kwangsi), whither he himself had requested to be sent to avoid trouble in the capital from the rising power of the consort family of Yü, who held the supremacy between 325 and 345. *CYC*; (*Juan*) *Fu PC*. IV, 76; VI, *15*; VIII, 29, 104; XXIII, 15.

JUAN HSIEN 阮咸 (Chung-jung 仲容). 234-305. *CS* 49.4b-5a. A son of Juan Chi's older brother, Hsi 熙, and, together with his famous uncle, a member of the "Seven Worthies of the Bamboo Grove." He was extremely unconventional by nature, always poor, and a great lover of wine, for which some blamed his death, though his biography states he died of "old age." When Shan T'ao recommended him to Emperor Wu (Ssu-ma Yen, r. 265-290) for a position on the sensitive Board of Civil Office, he was rejected, as indeed Shan fully expected he would be. He was a skillful musician, playing both the Central Asian lute (*p'i-pa* 琵琶) and an adaptation with round sound box, which has been named after him. *MSC*; *STCS*; *CYC*; *CLCHL*. VIII, *12*, 29; XX, 1; XXIII, 1, 10, 12, 15.

JUAN HSIU 阮脩 (Hsüan-tzu 宣子). ca. 270-312. *CS* 49.7b-8b. A nephew of Juan Chi of Bamboo Grove fame. He made his reputation as an iconoclast, his favorite topic of conversation being the nonexistence of ghosts. For at least part of his life he was unemployed and extremely impoverished. He was killed by bandits as he fled southward from the disorders around 312. *MSC*. IV, *18*; V, 21, 22; XXIII, 18.

JUAN HUN 阮渾 (Ch'ang-ch'eng 長成). late third cent. *SKWei* 21.8a, comm.; *CS* 49.4a. The second son of Juan Chi. An unpretentious and simple man, he never rose higher than a position on the staff of the crown prince, where he was assigned around 285, soon after which he died. *SY*. VIII, *29*; XXIII, 13.

JUAN K'AN 阮侃 (Te-ju 德如). mid-third cent. Youngest son of Juan Kung. Though he was an advocate of the "conformist" tradition (*ming-li*), he was counted among the friends of the very unconventional Hsi K'ang. His highest office was grand warden of Ho-nei Commandery (northern Honan). *CLCM*. XIX, 6.

JUAN KUNG 阮共 (Po-yen 伯彥). first half, third cent. Father of Juan K'an and Mme. Juan 阮夫人. He served as an officer in the Wei Palace Guard. *CLCM*. XIX, 6.

JUAN WU 阮武 (Wen-yeh 文業). ca. 200-265. A straightforward, uncomplicated man, honored in his day as a knower of men. When his kinsman, Juan Chi, was only a lad and still unknown, Juan Wu considered him of great promise and superior even to himself. At his death he left a manuscript in eighteen *chüan*, thereafter known as *Juan-tzu*, which has not survived. *TTHS*; *CLC*. VIII, *13*.

JUAN YU-O 阮幼娥. late third to early fourth cent. Daughter of Juan Fan 蒼 and wife of Liu Sui; mother-in-law of Yü I. *Liu SP*. VI, 24.

JUAN YÜ 阮裕 (Ssu-k'uang 思曠). ca. 300-360. *CS* 49.9b-11a. Son of Juan I 顗 and cousin of Juan Chi. He began as Wang Tun's superintendent of records, but during Tun's abortive rebellion (322-324) saved his life by remaining drunk at the right moments. In 326 he entered the Imperial Secretariat for a brief term before retiring to Shan Prefecture in K'uai-chi (Chekiang), where he refused all further summons from the court but accepted short residencies as grand warden in two commanderies adjacent to K'uai-chi merely as a means of subsistence. He was not bookish by nature but was capable of grasping the general meaning of a work without close study, for which he was greatly admired. *Juan Kuang-lu PC*. I, *32*; IV, 24; V, 53, 61; VIII, 55, 96; IX, 27, 30, 36; XVIII, 6; XXIV, 22; XXXIII, 11.

JUAN YUNG 阮墉 (Yen-lun 彥倫). d. ca. 340. Mentioned, *CS* 49.11a. The eldest son of Juan Yü. He served as superintendent of records in a provincial administration, but died at an early age. *Juan SP*. XXXIII, *11*.

KAN PAO 干寶 (Ling-sheng 令升). late third to early fourth cent. *CS* 82.13a-15a. A native of Wu who assisted the first Eastern Chin emperor to power in 317 and was given a post in the historian's office. Later he became magistrate of Shan-yin Prefecture (Chekiang) and afterward, through the intervention of Wang Tao, was named cavalier attendant-in-ordinary at court and supervised the compiling of the "Western Chin Annals" (*KPCC*). He is best known, however, for his collection of supernatural tales of departed spirits, *Sou-shen chi* 搜神記. He also wrote commentaries on the *Tso-chuan*, *Chou-li* and "Book of Changes." *CHS*. XXV, *9*.

K'ANG FA-CH'ANG 康法暢. fl. ca. 326-342. *KSC* 4; *Taishō* 50.347a. A monk of Sogdian (?) origin who emigrated to the Eastern Chin capital in Chien-k'ang together with Chih Min-tu and K'ang Seng-yüan around the third decade of the fourth century. He is credited with a work on judging character entitled *Jen-wu shih-i* 人物始義 in which he characterized himself modestly as follows: "His awareness is keen and spirited; his ability and rhetoric comprehend all arguments." *JWSI*. II, *52*.

K'ANG SENG-YÜAN 康僧淵. fl. ca. 300-350. *KSC* 4; *Taishō* 50.346c-347a. He was born in Ch'ang-an (Shensi), probably of Sogdian parents, and possessed the deep-set eyes and prominent nose of a Western barbarian, though he spoke Chinese like a native. He crossed the Yangtze during the Yung-chia period (307-312), or shortly thereafter, and was active in Chien-k'ang until about 340, when, because of anti-Buddhist sentiment at court, he withdrew to an idyllic retreat outside of Yü-chang (Kiangsi), where many prominent men of the day were said to have visited him. He specialized in both versions of the *Prajñāpāramitā-sūtra*. *SYCS*. IV, *47*; XVIII, 11; XXV, 21.

KAO JOU 高柔 (Shih-yüan 世遠). fl. ca. 344. Himself a member of a wealthy clan, he married a daughter of Hu-wu Fu-chih who was noted for her intelligence and beauty, and they lived together in comfortable seclusion in the Chekiang hills. For brief intervals he came reluctantly out of retirement to serve as an aide to the director of works, or as magistrate of An-ku Prefecture (Chekiang), and in 343 or 344 he finally responded to Ho Ch'ung's call to serve as his aide. KJCH. II, 84; XXVI, 13.

KAO SUNG 高崧 (Mao-yen 茂琰; baby name, A-ling 阿鄹). d. ca. 365. CS 71.14b-16a. A son of Kao Li 悝. He served as superintendent of records for Ho Ch'ung while the latter was governor of Yang Province (Kiangsu-Anhui-Chekiang) between 343 and 346. After getting the hsiu-ts'ai degree and becoming an erudite of the Grand Academy, he lost his father and fought a lawsuit over the disposition of the body, since his father had been dismissed for improper conduct in office. The court finally took pity on him and gave him a position in the Central Secretariat. During Ssu-ma Yü's regency (between 345 and 361) he served as his sergeant-at-arms, later becoming a clerk in the Board of Civil Office and finally personal attendant to Emperor Ai (Ssu-ma P'ei, r. 362-365). He became involved in some unnamed plot and died out of office. CHS. II, 82; XXV, 26.

KAO-TSO TAO-JEN 高坐道人 (Śrīmitra, Po Shih-li-mi-to-lo 帛尸黎密多羅). fl. ca. 310-340. CSTCC 13 (Taishō 55.98c-99a); KSC 1 (Taishō 50.327c-328a). A Central Asian monk, perhaps from Kuchā, who, according to his biographer, renounced a kingdom in favor of his younger brother to join the sangha. Arriving in China during the barbarian invasions of 307-311, he traveled to Chien-k'ang, where he was installed in the Chien-ch'u 建初 Monastery. There he instructed many disciples in Buddhist chant (fan-pai 梵唄) and enjoyed the respect and friendship of Wang Tao, Yü Liang, Chou I, and other important members of the Eastern Chin court. He is said never to have learned Chinese but spoke always through an interpreter. His name, Kao-tso, "High Seat," was derived from the name of a monastery built by his tomb in Shih-tzu Kang 石子岡, just south of Chien-k'ang. Kao-tso PC. II, 39; VIII, 48; XXIV, 7.

KO YÜ 葛旟 (Hsü-yü 虛旟). d. 302. A member of the staff of the Prince of Ch'i, Ssu-ma Chiung, who rose to power with him and was killed when Chiung fell in 302. CWKSM; CYC. V, 17.

KU FU 顧敷 (Tsu-ken 祖根). second half, fourth cent. A son of Ku Wei and grandson of Ku Ho. He served for a while as historian but died in his twenty-third year. KKCCC. II, 51; XII, 4.

KU HO 顧和 (Chün-hsiao 君孝). 288-351. CS 83.1a-4a. Great-grandson of Ku Jung* 容 and son of Ku Hsü 叙; a kinsman of Ku Jung 榮, who considered him the shining hope of the family. His father died in his second year (289), and he was reared by an uncle, Ku Chung 眾 (d. 346). While Wang Tao was director of instruction he took him on his staff, and in 323 he served briefly as the rebel Wang Tun's superintendent of records, later rejoining Wang Tao as lieutenant-governor of Yang Province (Kiangsu-Chekiang) while the latter was governor. He returned from there to the court and became senior administrator for Ch'ih Chien, who was then director of works, and in 335 was named junior censor. Toward the end of his life he was president of the Imperial Secretariat and cavalier attendant-in-ordinary. *Ku Ho PC.* II, *33*, 37, 51; VI, 16, 22; X, 15; XII, 4; XXV, 20.

KU HSIEN 顧顯 (Meng-chu 孟著). fl. ca. 320. A member of the distinguished Ku family of Wu Commandery (Soochow) and a nephew of Ku Jung. Though he died young, he had already achieved some reputation. *HKCC.* V, *29*.

KU I 顧夷 (Chün-ch'i 君齊). fl. second half, fourth cent. A native of Wu Commandery (Soochow), he apparently never assumed any public office. *Ku SP.* IV, *91*.

KU JUNG 顧榮 (Yen-hsien 彥先). 270-322. *CS* 68.1a-5b. A native of Wu, grandson of Ku Yung, chancellor of the Wu Kingdom under Sun Ch'üan, and son of Ku Mu 穆. He accompanied Lu Chi and his brother to Lo-yang after the conquest of Wu in 280, where he served in the office of the director of punishments and later as senior administrator for Ssu-ma Ch'ien 虔. Becoming involved in the attempted usurpation of Ssu-ma Lun in 300, he barely escaped execution with the latter's downfall in the following year. After the fall of Lo-yang in 311 he fled south and joined the staff of Ssu-ma Jui, founder of Eastern Chin, and rose to become General of Spirited Cavalry before his death. *WSC.* I, *25*; II, 29, 33; VII, 19, 20; XVII, 7; XIX, 19.

KU K'AI-CHIH 顧愷之 (Ch'ang-k'ang 長康). ca. 345(?)-406. *CS* 92.34b-36b. Son of Ku Yüeh-(chih) and famous as a poet, painter, calligrapher, and buffoon, about whom little is known beyond the numerous anecdotes collected in his biography, and the paintings attributed to him in the British Museum, Freer Gallery, etc. His first official post was as an aide in Huan Wen's administration of Ching Province (before 353), and later (ca. 392) he served Yin Chung-k'an in the same capacity. At the end of his life he was cavalier attendant-in-ordinary at court. *WCL*; see also S. H. Ch'en, *Biography of Ku K'ai-chih*, Chinese Dynastic Histories Translations, no. 2, Berkeley and Los Angeles, 1953. II, 85, *88*, 95, 98; IV, 98; XXI, 7, 9, 11, 12, 13, 14; XXV, 56, 59, 61; XXVI, 26.

KU PI-CHIANG 顧辟疆. second half, fourth cent. A member of a prominent family of Wu Commandery (Soochow) who had, after several posts locally, become aide-de-camp to the General Pacifying the North. *Ku SP.* XXIV, *17*.

KU SHAO 顧劭 (Hsiao-tse 孝則). fl. early third cent. *SKWu* 7.10ab. A native of Wu Commandery (Soochow), the eldest son of Ku Yung, and son-in-law of Sun Ts'e, elder brother of the founder of the Wu Kingdom (223-280). He served as grand warden of Yü-chang Commandery (Kiangsi) when he was twenty-seven, but died five years later. *HCWC.* VI, *1*; IX, 2, 3.

KU YUNG 顧雍 (Yüan-t'an 元歎). 168-243. *SKWu* 7.7a-9a. A native of Wu Commandery (Soochow), and considered Ts'ai Yung's most accomplished pupil in both the zither and calligraphy. Beginning his career as magistrate of a small prefecture, he served as deputy for Sun Ch'üan in K'uai-chi Commandery (Chekiang), and after Sun declared himself Emperor of Wu in 223, Ku became president of the Imperial Secretariat in the Wu government and was showered with noble titles. He died in 243 in his seventy-sixth year while occupying the post of chancellor. *CPC*; *WuC*. VI, 1.

KU YÜEH(-CHIH) 顧悅(之) (Chün-shu 君叔). b. 320. *CS* 77.27ab. Father of the painter, Ku K'ai-chih. He began his career as lieutenant-governor of Yang Province (Kiangsu-Anhui-Chekiang) under Yin Hao's administration. After Yin's disgrace in 353 and death three years later, some of his enemies at court tried to prevent his receiving posthumous honors, but Ku stoutly and successfully defended him. He later became left assistant of the Imperial Secretariat. *CHS*; *KYC*. II, 57.

K'UAI, Lady 蒯氏 (late third cent.). A daughter of the maternal aunt of Empress Yang, consort of Emperor Wu (Ssu-ma Yen, r. 265-290), whose family had settled in Hsiang-yang (northern Hupei). She was married to Sun Hsiu**, a descendant of the Wu royal family. *CYC*. XXXV, 4.

KUAN LU 管輅 (Kung-ming 公明, 209-256). *SKWei* 29.12b-25b. Described as homely and unceremonious, he seems to have been something of a bon vivant with a ready wit. In consequence, everybody loved him but never took him seriously. Since he made a specialty of telling fortunes by the "Book of Changes," he was frequently consulted for prognostications. *Kuan Lu PC*. X, 6.

KUAN NING 管寧 (Yu-an 幼安). 158-241. *SKWei* 11.20b-26a. Said to be a lineal descendant of Kuan Chung (d. 645 B.C.), the adviser to Duke Huan of Ch'i. He lost his father when he was sixteen and lived in poverty for a period with Ping Yüan and Hua Hsin. In 191 he fled the disorders attending the fall of Later Han, together with Ping Yüan, to what is now southwestern Manchuria, returning to the Shantung area in 226, but never accepting office. *FT*. I, 11.

K'UANG SHU 匡術. fl. mid-fourth cent. While serving as magistrate of Fou-ling Prefecture (Anhui), he somehow offended the court and fled to throw in his lot with the rebel Su Chün. When the rebellion was put down in 328, he was pardoned. *CYC*. V, 36, 38.

KUNG-SUN TU 公孫度 (Sheng-chi 升濟; var. Shu-chi 叔). d. 204. *SKWei* 8.12b-13b. Raised on the northeast frontier, he was appointed governor of Chi Province (northern Hopei). After a brief interlude in Tung Cho's army around 190, he returned as grand warden of Liao-tung Commandery (southwest Manchuria), where he instituted a semi-independent regime, with suzerainty over both the north Korean kingdom of Koguryo and the nomadic Wu-huan 烏丸 tribes to the north and west. He assumed the titles Marquis of Liao-tung and governor of P'ing Province (Manchuria), but died before realizing his royal ambitions. *WeiS*. VIII, 4.

K'UNG AN-KUO 孔安國 (An-huo 安國). d. 408. *CS* 78.3b-4a. (Not to be confused with the famous Han scholar of the same name.) He was the sixth son of K'ung Yü, much younger than his brothers. Orphaned at an early age, he lived in dire poverty until his probity won him the attention of Emperor Hsiao-wu (r. 373-396), whom he served with almost filial devotion as personal attendant. Later he rose to grand ordinary, governor of his native K'uai-chi Principality (Chekiang), and finally vice-president of the Imperial Secretariat. HCYC. I, 46.

K'UNG CH'EN 孔沈 (Te-tu 德度). mid-fourth cent. CS 78.12a. A son of K'ung Ch'ün, recognized in his day as one of the paragons representing each of the four leading clans of Eastern Chin (viz., K'ung, Wei 魏, Yü 虞, and Hsieh). Ho Ch'ung recommended him for Wang Tao's staff while the latter was director of instruction (323-339), and as literary tutor for the Prince of Lang-yeh, neither of which posts he accepted. K'ung SP. II, 44; VIII, 85.

K'UNG CHOU 孔伷 (var. 宙). d. 165. Father of K'ung Jung, who died when the latter was in his thirteenth year. He served as general commander of T'ai-shan Commandery (Shantung). HsüHS. II, 3.

K'UNG CH'UN-CHIH 孔淳之 (Yen-shen 彥深). 372-430. SS 93.9ab; NS 75.9a-10a. A recluse who loved wandering among the Chekiang hills, often disappearing for ten or more days at a time. He was a close friend of the Buddhist monk Shih Fa-ch'ung 釋法崇, who shared his love of mountains. Because of his surname, he was frequently called to various posts but always declined. SS. II, 108.

K'UNG CH'ÜN 孔群 (Ching-lin 敬林; var. Ching-hsiu 休). fl. mid-fourth cent. CS 78.11b-12a. A native of K'uai-chi Commandery (Chekiang) who narrowly escaped death during Su Chün's revolt (327-328). He held office as a junior censor. KCHHC. V, 36; XXIII, 24.

K'UNG JUNG 孔融 (Wen-chü 文舉). 153-208. HHS 100.4a-17b and SKWei 12.4a-6b (biography of Ts'ui Yen, comm.). A descendant of Confucius in the twentieth generation, one of the "Seven Masters of the Chien-an Era" and a patron of the commentator Cheng Hsüan. He was minister of Pei-hai Commandery (Shantung) during the Yellow Turban Revolt (184-215), and later served at court as great officer of the center. Charged with slandering the court to an ambassador from the Wu warlord Sun Ch'üan, he was executed with all the members of his family by Ts'ao Ts'ao in 208. HsüHS, K'ung Jung PC, WSCC, WCSY. II, 3, 4, 8.

K'UNG T'AN 孔坦 (Chün-p'ing 君平). 286-336. CS 78.4a-9b. Son of K'ung K'an and a nephew of K'ung Yü; noted in his day as a specialist in the "Spring and Autumn Annals" (Ch'un-ch'iu). After gaining some merit in the suppression of Su Chün under T'ao K'an in 328, he served for a while as grand warden of Wu Commandery (Soochow). Later he was transferred to the palace as personal attendant but, incurring the anger of the chancellor, Wang Tao, he was demoted to director of punishments, soon after which he became ill and died. WYCS. II, 43, 44; V, 37, 43.

K'UNG YEN 孔嚴 (P'eng-tsu 彭祖). d. 370. CS 78.9b-11b. A nephew of K'ung Yü. He was a studious man who in 346 was Yin Hao's lieutenant-governor of Yang Province (Kiangsu-Anhui-Chekiang) and in 362 became capital intendant. Later he served as president of the Board of Civil Office and was ennobled Marquis of Hsi-yang. Around 367 he left the capital to become grand warden of Wu-hsing Commandery (Chekiang), where he remained until his death in 370. CHS. IX, 40, 45; X, 20.

K'UNG YÜ 孔愉 (Ching-k'ang 敬康). 268-342. CS 78.1a-3a. At the close of Western Chin he is said to have used the alias Sun 孫. A native of K'uai-chi Commandery (Chekiang), he was instrumental in suppressing the rebel Hua I 華軼 around 320, for which he was ennobled by the Eastern Chin court. About a decade later he became vice-president of one of the secretariats and subsequently governor of K'uai-chi, where he attempted to revive the Han system of land tenure. He is usually known by the title, General of Chariots and Horsemen. K'ung Yü PC. V, 38; IX, 13; XVIII, 7.

KUO, Lady 郭氏. fl. ca. 300. The wife of Wang Yen, her nature is described as dull-witted, stubborn, and insatiably acquisitive. X, 8, 9, 10.

KUO HSIANG 郭象 (Tzu-hsüan 子玄). d. 312. CS 50.8a-9a. A brilliant conversationalist, especially on Lao-tzu and Chuang-tzu, but regarded by his contemporaries as "second to Wang Pi." He served in the administration of the Prince of Tung-hai, Ssu-ma Yüeh 越, and was highly regarded by his patron. His commentary on Chuang-tzu, thought to be based on that of Hsiang Hsiu, is still the most venerated though not necessarily the most faithful interpretation of that philosopher; see Fukunaga Mitsuji, "Kaku Zō no Sōshi kaishaku," Tetsugaku kenkyū 37.2-3 (1954). WSC. IV, 17, 19, 32; VIII, 26, 32.

KUO HUAI 郭槐 (Yü-huang 玉璜). d. ca. 282-300. CS 40.6b-8b. The daughter of Kuo P'ei and second wife of Chia Ch'ung. As mother of Empress Chia (d. 300), she was posthumously honored as Princess Hsüan of I-ch'eng 宜城宣君. She is depicted as a jealous, domineering woman who hired spies to follow her husband to make certain he never went near his first wife, Li Wan. ChiaSP. XIX, 13, 14; XXXV, 3.

KUO HUAI* 郭淮 (Po-chi 伯濟). d. 255. SKWei 26.13b-17a. After serving Ts'ao Ts'ao as a successful commander in the northwest, he welcomed the founding of Wei in 220 and was appointed governor of Yung Province (Shensi). After 249 he was made General Chastizing the West and governor-general of Yung and Liang provinces (Shensi-Kansu). Altogether he spent thirty years among the Hu (proto-Turkic?) and Ch'iang (proto-Tibetan) peoples of the northwestern border. Late in life he was honored with the title, General of Chariots and Horsemen and enfeoffed Marquis of Yang-ch'ü (Shansi). WCSY. V, 4.

KUO I 郭奕 (T'ai-yeh 泰業). d. 287. CS 45.18b-19b. He began his career in the Wei Kingdom around 260 as magistrate of Yeh-wang

Prefecture (Honan), and around 264 was in the service of the generalissimo, Ssu-ma Chao. After the change of dynasty in 265 he rose rapidly in rank, receiving a noble title, and was appointed governor of Yung Province (Shensi). About 285 he became president of the Board of Civil Office. *CCKT.* VIII, 9.

KUO P'EI 郭配. mid-third cent. *CS* 40.7b. Grand warden of Ch'eng-yang (northern Shantung); father of Kuo Huai. *WYCS.* XIX, 13.

KUO P'U 郭璞 (Ching-ch'un 景純). 276-324. *CS* 72.1a-13a. A man of unprepossessing manner, somewhat given to dissipation, who found his way into the administration of Wang Tun. Because of his refusal to rescind a prognostication of Tun's failure, he joined the large number of Tun's victims in 324. Kuo was interested in the occult as well as the more conventional fields of literature and philology. His best known works are the commentaries on the *Mu T'ien-tzu chuan* 穆天子傳, the *Shan-hai ching* 山海經, the *Erh-ya* 爾雅, and the *Ch'u-tz'u* 楚辭. His creative pieces include the "Poetic Essay on the Yangtze River" (*Chiang-fu* 江賦; *WH* 12.5b-14a), and "Poems on Wandering Immortals" (*Yu-hsien shih* 遊仙詩; *WH* 21.15a-17b). *WYCS*; *Kuo P'u PC.* IV, 76; XX, 5, 6, 7, 8.

KUO T'AI 郭泰 (Lin-tsung 林宗). 128-169. *HHS* 98.1a-2b. He is described as being unusually tall (eight *ch'ih*) and extremely punctilious in his social relations. Orphaned early and poverty-stricken, at twenty-one he traveled from Shansi to Honan to study, but "never altered his happy disposition." To him is attributed the origin of "pure conversation" (*ch'ing-t'an*), as he was skilled in characterization and noted for the caustic purity of his criticisms, which won him a leadership role in the battle of the literati against the consort families and eunuchs at the close of Later Han. *HSHS.* I, 3; III, 17; X, 3.

KUO YÜ 郭豫 (T'ai-ning 泰寧). fl. late third cent. *SKWei* 26.17a. The father-in-law of Wang Yen. He was aide to the chancellor when he died at an early age. *CCKT.* X, 8.

LEI, Lady 雷氏. early fourth cent. A concubine of Wang Tao and mother of his second and third sons, Wang T'ien and Wang Ch'ia. *YL.* XXXV, 7.

LI, Lady 李氏. fl. ca. 347. The younger sister of Li Shih of the Ch'eng-Han Kingdom in Shu (r. 343-347), who became the concubine of Huan Wen upon the latter's conquest of Shu in 347. *TC.* XIX, 21.

LI CHIH 李志 (Wen-tsu 溫祖). fl. mid-fourth cent. A grandson of Li Chung. He became attendant-in-ordinary without portfolio and minister of Nan-k'ang (Kiangsi). *CPKM*; *Li SP.* IX, 68.

LI CHUNG 李重 (Mao-tseng 茂曾). 253-300. *SKWei* 18.4b; *CS* 46.18a-22b. Asked at a very early age to serve as examiner for official candidates, he refused, but maintained a keen interest in administrative matters throughout his life. Texts of several memorials on such subjects as the nine categories of officials (*chiu-p'in* 九品), the limitation of slaveholding, prohibition against the sale of real property by peasants, etc., were incorporated in his biography. In 290 he became director of punishments and turned his interests toward judicial matters. Later, as a member of the Board of Civil Office, he attacked the problem of using wasted resources hidden among persons posing as "recluses." In 300 he became sergeant-at-arms for the Prince of Chao, Ssu-ma Lun, but chafing under the pressures placed on him by this ambitious man, he took sick and died. *CCKT*. IX, *46*; XIX, 17.

LI CH'UNG 李充 (Hung-tu 弘度). mid-fourth cent. *CS* 92.20a-22b. A calligrapher and specialist in public administration (*hsing-ming* 刑名), he opposed the "frivolous" tendencies of some Taoists and offered a Confucianized interpretation of *Lao-tzu* and *Chuang-tzu* in his commentary on the "Analects," his "Notes for Study" (*Hsüeh-chen* 學箴), quoted in his biography, and his "Interpretation of *Chuang-tzu*" (*Shih-Chuang lun* 釋莊論), fragments of which survive in other works. He served as recording secretary to the chancellor (Wang Tao) and was later sent to administer Shan Prefecture (Chekiang). At the end of his career he was grand historian. *CHS*. II, *80*; IX, 46; XXIX, 6.

LI FENG 李豐 (An-kuo 安國; alias Hsüan 宣). d. 254. *SKWei* 9.31a-33b. The son of an officer in the Wei Palace Guard whose reputation as a judge of character was widespread in his day. One of the contributors to Chung Hui's "Treatise on the Four Basic Relations Between Human Nature and Natural Ability," he upheld the position that the two are different. During the regency of Ts'ao Shuang (240-249), as a vice-president of the Imperial Secretariat, he mediated between Ts'ao and the generalissimo, Ssu-ma I, thus escaping death when Ts'ao fell in 249. Li's son, T'ao 韜, married Emperor Ming's daughter, the Princess of Ch'i, and Li himself became president of the Central Secretariat in 252. Because of his friendship with Hsia-hou Hsüan and other partisans of the Wei royal house against the Ssu-ma family, he was called to account early in 254 by Ssu-ma Shih, who, in a fit of rage, beat him to death with the handle of a sword, later killing Hsia-hou Hsüan, Li T'ao, and others as well. *WeiL*. XIV, *4*; XIX, 13.

LI HSI 李喜 (var. 憙 and 熹; Chi-ho 季和). mid-third cent. *CS* 41.4a-6b. After refusing to serve on the staff of Ssu-ma I 懿 in 249, he later became lieutenant-governor of Ping Province (Shansi). In 252 he accepted a summons to serve on the staff of Ssu-ma I's son, Shih, when the latter became generalissimo, and accompanied him in the campaign against Kuan-ch'iu Chien 毋丘儉 in 255. Still later he served as junior censor and successively as governor of Liang Province (Kansu) and Chi Province (N. Hopei), and commandant of the Capital Province (Honan). With the founding of Chin in 265 he became vice-president of the Imperial Secretariat and Great Officer of Brilliant Favor. After his death he was given the posthumous title, Grand Protector. *CCKT*. II, *16*.

LI HSIN 李廞 (Tsung-tzu 宗子). d. ca. 350. The fifth son of Li Chung. A very studious man, fond of calligraphy and music, who was bedridden most of his life because of ill health, and who declined all calls to public office. He fled southward about 312 with his elder brother, Shih*, but until his death, sometime between 345 and 354, he continued to avoid public life. *WTC.* XVIII, *4*.

LI KUEI 李軌 (Hung-fan 弘範). early fourth cent. His highest office was clerk in the Imperial Secretariat. *CHS.* XXIX, *6*.

LI LO-HSIU 李絡秀. late third to early fourth cent. *CS* 96.7b-8a. Daughter of Li Po-tsung, wife of Chou Chün, and mother of Chou I and his brothers. *Chou SP.* VII, *14*; XIX, *18*.

LI PING 李秉 (Hsüan-chou 玄冑). mid-third cent. *SKWei* 18.4ab. The father of Li Chung, and governor of Ch'in Province (Shensi) under the Wei Kingdom. *YCLJM.* XIX, *17*.

LI PO-TSUNG 李伯宗. mid-third cent. Father of Li Lo-hsiu, and maternal grandfather of Chou I. *Chou SP* XIX, *18*.

LI SHEN 李慎 (Man-ch'ang 曼長, var. Chen-ch'ang 真). fl. ca. 300. *CS* 44.6b. (The name Shun 順 in all texts avoids the taboo name of one of the sons of Emperor T'ai-tsung of T'ang, Li Shih-min 李世民). The second son of Li Yin, whose highest office was grand constable (*t'ai-p'u ch'ing* 太僕卿). *CCKT.* VIII, *22*.

LI SHIH 李勢 (Tzu-jen 子仁). d. 361. *CS* 121.12b-14b. The sixth and last of a line of Taoist rulers of the Ch'eng-Han Kingdom, with its capital in Ch'eng-tu (Szechwan), which had been founded in 302. Shih came to the throne in 343 and seems to have built his reputation on his penchant for killing people and taking their wives into his harem. After Huan Wen's successful advance up the Yangtze and seizure of Ch'eng-tu in 347, Shih surrendered and was taken to Chien-k'ang, where he was given a noble title and lived on another fourteen years. *HYKC.* VII, *20*; XIII, *8*; XIX, *21*.

LI SHIH* 李式 (Ching-tse 景則). 273-326. *CS* 46.22b. The eldest son of Li Chung, who combined the ideals of the literatus and recluse (*ju-yin* 儒隱). After fleeing southward, ca. 312, he became grand warden of Lin-hai (Chekiang) and later personal attendant at court. *WTC.* XVIII, *4*.

LI SHUN 李順. See LI SHEN.

LI WAN 李婉. d. before 300. Mentioned, *CS* 40.7b-8b. The daughter of Li Feng and first wife of Chia Ch'ung. When Feng was executed in 254, she was exiled to Lak-lang (North Korea), and Chia remarried Kuo Huai. In 265 she was pardoned and returned to Lo-yang, but was never reunited with her husband. While in exile she composed a book of instructions for her daughters in eight *chüan*, known alternately as "Instructions for Daughters" (*Nü-hsün* 女訓), or "Instructions of Mme. Li" (*Li fu-jen hsün*), or "Rules and Admonitions of Mme. Li" (*Li fu-jen tien-chieh* 典戒). *FJC*; *Chia SP*; *Chia Ch'ung PC.* XIX, *13*, *14*.

LI YANG 李陽 (Ching-tsu 景祖). fl. late third cent. He was governor of Yu Province (northern Hopei) sometime between 265 and 290. *CPKM*; *YL.* X, *8*.

LI YIN 李胤 (Hsüan-po 宣伯). d. 282. CS 44.5a-6b. A native of Liao-tung (Manchuria), he served as a clerk in the administration of the generalissimo, Ssu-ma Chao, around 260. After the establishment of Western Chin in 265, he was ennobled a marquis and soon moved to become president of the Board of Civil Office. In 275 he became personal attendant and later president of the Imperial Secretariat. The last five years before his death in 282 he held the rank of director of instruction. VIII, 22.

LI YING 李膺 (Yüan-li 元禮). 110-169. HHS 97.7a-12a. As commandant of the Capital Province, he was an implacable foe of eunuchs in government and eventually fell, together with Ch'en Fan and Tou Wu, in their struggle against eunuch control, being forced to commit suicide in 169. In addition to his prominent role at court, he also showed considerable prowess on the battlefield against the incursions of the Hsien-pei and Hsiung-nu on the northern frontier. HYHHS. I, 4, 5; II, 3; VIII, 2; IX, 1.

LIU, Lady 劉氏. late third to early fourth cent. A cousin of Wen Ch'iao's father, and mother of Ch'iao's third (?) wife. Wen SP. XXVII, 9.

LIU, Mme. 劉夫人. early and middle fourth cent. Daughter of Liu Tan 耽, younger sister of Liu T'an, and wife of Hsieh An. Hsieh SP. I, 36; VIII, 147; XIX, 23; XXVI, 17.

LIU AO 劉驁 (T'ai-sun 太孫). d. 7 B.C. HS 10. Emperor Ch'eng of the Former Han Dynasty (r. 32-7 B.C.). HS. XIX, 3.

LIU CH'ANG 劉昶 (Kung-jung 公榮). mid-third cent. A great drinker, whose highest office was governor of Yen Province (southern Shantung). CYC; Liu SP. XXIII, 4; XXIV, 2.

LIU CHAO 劉肇. late third cent. A contemporary of Wang Jung, he once served as grand warden of Nan Commandery (Hupei), and attempted to bribe Wang, who was then personal attendant. CYC. VI, 6.

LIU CH'AO 劉超 (Shih-yü 世踰). d. 328/329. CS 70.19b-22a. A seventh-generation descendant of one of the Later Han princes. Selected as personal attendant by Ssu-ma Jui (later Emperor Yüan, r. 317-322), he accompanied the latter south in 307, and served in the Palace Guard after Jui mounted the throne in 317. He was an extremely taciturn man, studious in his habits and rarely participating in social events. His frugality was proverbial and he consistently refused the emperor's gifts. When Su Chün sacked the capital in 328, he was made General of the Right Guard and accompanied the boy-Emperor Ch'eng (Ssu-ma Yen*, r. 326-342) on foot through rain and mud to the fortification at Shih-t'ou north of the capital when the latter was forcibly removed thither. There he lost his life in a vain attempt with Chung Ya to take the emperor to safety. CYC. III, 11.

LIU CH'E 劉徹. r. 140-87 B.C. SC 12; HS 6. Emperor Wu of Former Han, who brought the Chinese empire to its greatest size and splendor since the Ch'in unification. X, 1.

LIU CHEN 劉楨 (Kung-kan 公幹). d. 215/217. SKWei 21.3b-5a, comm. under Wang Ts'an. One of the "Seven Masters of the Chien-an Period" (196-219), along with K'ung Jung, Ch'en Lin 陳琳, Wang Ts'an, Hsü Kan 徐幹, Juan Yü* 阮瑀, and Ying Ch'ang 應瑒. Some of his poems are included in the WH (20.9ab; 23.19a-20b; 29.8b-9a). First attached to Ts'ao Ts'ao's staff while the latter was chancellor (208-213), he joined that of Ts'ao's heir, Ts'ao P'ei (Emperor Wen of Wei, r. 220-226), in 211, but offended P'ei's wife, Mme. Chen 甄夫人, at a drinking party by failing to prostrate himself when she entered and was sentenced to hard labor by Ts'ao Ts'ao, from which he was subsequently pardoned by Ts'ao P'ei. According to the Comm., he died of an illness in 215, but according to SKWei 21.5a, it was two years later. TL; WSC; WC. II, 10.

LIU CHIEN 劉簡 (Chung-yüeh 仲約). fl. ca. 360. A native of Nan-yang Commandery (Anhui), his highest office was aide to the grand marshal (Huan Wen). Liu SP. V, 50.

LIU CHIN 劉瑾 (Chung-chang 仲璋). fl. ca. 400. A grandson on his mother's side of Wang Hsi-chih. He served as president of the Board of Civil Office and grand ordinary minister. LCCH. IX, 87.

LIU CHING-NÜ 劉靜女. first half of fourth cent. Daughter of Liu Sui and wife of Yü I. Yü SP. VI, 24.

LIU CH'OU 劉疇 (Wang-ch'iao 王喬). d. 311. A skillful conversationalist on the subject of Names and Principles (ming-li). Beleaguered in a fort, ca. 307, he escaped death at the hands of his barbarian assailants by blowing a tune from the steppe on the reed horn (chia 笳) so mournfully that his would-be captors turned back in homesickness. But before he could flee southward across the Yangtze, he was killed by the governor of Yü Province (southern Honan), Yen Ting 閻鼎, who, after the fall of Lo-yang in 311, was attempting to reestablish the capital in Ch'ang-an (Shensi). TCCCC. VIII, 38, 61.

LIU CHUN 劉準 (Chün-p'ing 君平). late third cent. He served successively as grand warden of Ho-nei (northern Honan), personal attendant, vice-president of the Imperial Secretariat, and director of instruction. CCKT. V, 16.

LIU HSÜ 劉訏 (Wen-sheng 文生). second half, third cent. Imperial clan officer at the Western Chin court. CPKM. XXV, 7.

LIU HUI 劉恢 (Tao-sheng 道生). mid-fourth cent. Though thought to possess great promise in both civil and military affairs, he was only sergeant-at-arms to the General of Chariots and Horsemen when he died in his thirty-sixth year. SMTWCC. VIII, 73; XXV, 36.

LIU HUNG 劉宏 (Chung-chia 終嘏). fl. late third cent. First younger brother of Liu Ts'ui, son-in-law of Wang Jung, and grandfather of Liu T'an. He served as curator of the Palace Library and Great Officer of Brilliant Favor. CCKT. VIII, 22.

LIU I 劉毅 (Chung-hsiung 仲雄). ca. 210-285. CS 45.1a-12b. A descendant of the Han royal family, noted in his day for his stern incorruptibility and fearless attacks against wrongdoing. He became president of one of the secretariats and commandant of the Capital Province under the Chin. WYCS. I, 17.

LIU LAO-CHIH 劉牢之 (Tao-chien 道堅). d. 402. CS 84.6a-10a. In 376 he served as Hsieh Hsüan's aide while the latter was stationed in Kuang-ling Commandery (Kiangsu), and in 383 he distinguished himself in the defense against Fu Chien's invasion, for which he was rewarded with a noble title and the governorship of P'eng-ch'eng Principality (Kiangsu), his native place. During Wang Kung's coup of 397 he was Kung's sergeant-at-arms, but feeling himself slighted, defected to the forces of Ssu-ma Tao-tzu. After Kung's death in 398, Liu replaced him as governor-general in the eight provinces Kung had supervised. Huan Hsüan, still championing Wang Kung, demanded the death of Liu, but was unheeded by the court. Between 399 and 401 Liu had repeated encounters with the Taoist rebel, Sun En, in the Yangtze Delta area, and after Sun's defeat and death in 402, Liu's reputation was at its peak. It was then that he was sent to stop Huan Hsüan's descent on the capital, but, worried by fear of reprisals by rivals at court should he succeed, he defected to Hsüan, which signaled the collapse of the loyalist cause. Hsüan made him governor of K'uai-chi Principality, but by now Liu's overactive anxieties had found a new source in Huan himself, and he was on the point of counter-defecting, when his subordinates, losing all confidence in his stability, deserted him. Alone and in despair, he hanged himself. HCYC. IV, 104.

LIU K'UN 劉琨 (Yüeh-shih 越石). 271-318. CS 62.1a-13b. A member of the circle of "Twenty-four Friends" of Chia Mi, which included the eccentric aristocrat, Shih Ch'ung, and writers like Ou-yang Chien and the brothers Lu Chi and Lu Yün. After accompanying Emperor Hui (r. 290-306) to Ch'ang-an (Shensi) in 304, during the vicissitudes of the "War of the Eight Princes," he was ennobled and later (307) appointed governor of Ping Province (Shansi), remaining in the north after the fall of Lo-yang in 311 and supporting the restoration of Eastern Chin from behind the enemy lines. His memorial, sent through Wen Ch'iao, urging Ssu-ma Jui to mount the throne, is preserved in WH 37.15a-19a. In 317 he was killed by the Hsien-pei governor of the neighboring province of Chi (Hopei), Tuan P'i-ti 段匹磾. WYCS. II, 35, 36; VII, 9; VIII, 43; XXVII, 9; XXXIII, 4, 9; XXXVI, 2.

LIU LIN-CHIH 劉驎之 (Tzu-chi 子驥). fl. ca. 380. CS 94.22b-23b. A recluse of the Yang-ch'i Mts. (Hupei) who endeared himself to the local peasants by sharing everything with them, attending all their weddings and funerals, and turning down even the invitation of Huan Ch'ung to serve on his staff. TTCC. XVIII, 8; XXIII, 38.

LIU LING 劉伶 (Po-lun 伯倫). d. after 265. CS 49.17b-18b. One of the "Seven Worthies of the Bamboo Grove" about whose bibulous habits many legends gathered, but about whose person little is known. His only surviving piece of writing is the "Hymn to the Virtue of Wine" (Chiu-te sung 酒德頌). MSC; CLCHL. IV, 69; VIII, 29; XIV, 13; XXIII, 1, 3, 6; XXV, 4.

LIU MO 劉漠 (Ch'ung-chia 沖嘏). fl. late third cent. Second younger brother of Liu Ts'ui, son-in-law of Wang Jung, and friend of Wang Yen, who served as governor of Hsiang Province (northern Hupei?). *CHL*. VIII, 22.

LIU NA 劉訥 (Ling-yen 令言). fl. late third to early fourth cent. A native of P'eng-ch'eng (Anhui). Though his father had been magistrate of Lo-yang Prefecture (Honan) under the Wei Kingdom, he himself became commandant of the Capital Province (Honan) under the Chin. *Liu SP*; *WTC*. IX, 8.

LIU PA 劉寶 (Tao-chen 道真). late third cent. Uncle of Liu Sui, and protégé of Ssu-ma Chün, Prince of Fu-feng. *CPKM*. I, 22; VIII, 64; XXIII, 17; XXIV, 5.

LIU PEI 劉備 (Hsüan-te 玄德). 162-223. *SKShu* 2. A descendant of the Former Han Emperor Ching (Liu Ch'i, r. 156-141 B.C.). In 221 he founded the Shu (Han) Kingdom (221-263) in the southwest. He is known by various titles: "First Ruler" (*hsien-chu* 先主), King of Han-chung, and his posthumous title, Emperor Chao-lieh. At first, he ranged with Ts'ao Ts'ao against Yüan Shao and later became Ts'ao's implacable enemy. VII, 2.

LIU PIAO 劉表 (Ching-sheng 景升). d. 208. *SKWei* 6.34a-36b. One of the would-be independent generals of Later Han, who after 189 was governor of Ching Province (Hunan-Hupei) and made it a center of intellectual and literary activity. After an attack by Ts'ao Ts'ao in 203, his influence was greatly diminished, and he died a natural death in 208. *LCNM*. XXVI, 11.

LIU SHAO 劉劭 (Yen-tsu 彥祖). mid-fourth cent. A son of Liu Sung 松 and grandson of Liu Na, he gained some reputation as a scholar and calligrapher. Just before the fall of Lo-yang in 311 he fled alone on horseback to Yang Province (Kiangsu-Anhui-Chekiang), where he served the Eastern Chin court as Emperor Ch'eng's (r. 326-342) personal attendant and later as grand warden of Yü-chang (Kiangsi). *WTC*. II, 53.

LIU SHIH 劉奭. r. 48-33 B.C. *HS* 9. Emperor Yüan of Han. X, 2; XIX, 2.

LIU SHIH* 劉爽 (Wen-shih 文時). fl. mid-fourth cent. He began his career as consultant to the General of Chariots and Horsemen, later becoming minister of Ch'ang-sha (Hunan), and ending in the capital again as cavalier attendant-in-ordinary. *TSMLSM*; *Liu SP*. IX, 53.

LIU SUI 劉綏 (Wan-an 萬安). late third to early fourth cent. Son of Liu Pin 斌 (var. Fu 賦) and father-in-law of Yü I, his highest office seems to have been senior administrator to the General of Hardy Horsemen. *Liu SP*. VI, 24; VIII, 64; IX, 28.

LIU T'AN 劉惔 (Chen-ch'ang 真長). ca. 311-347. *CS* 75.32a-34a. A descendant of the Han royal family and brother-in-law of Hsieh An. After an extremely impoverished youth, he gained a reputation as a skilled conversationalist and became a frequent guest at gatherings in the villa of Ssu-ma Yü, who ruled later as Emperor Chien-wen between 371 and 372. His office at the time of his death in his thirty-sixth year was capital intendant. *Liu Yin PC.* I, *35*; II, 48, 54, 64, 66, 67, 69, 73; III, 18, 22; IV, 26, 33, 46, 53, 56, 83; V, 44, 51, 53, 54, 59; VII, 18, 19, 20; VIII, 22, 75, 77, 83, 86, 87, 88, 109, 110, 111, 116, 118, 121, 124, 130, 131, 135, 138, 146; IX, 29, 30, 36, 42, 43, 44, 48, 50, 56, 58, 73, 76, 77, 78, 84 XIV, 27; XVII, 10; XXII, 4; XXIII, 33, 36, 40; XXV, 13, 17, 19, 24, 29, 37; XXVI, 9, 10, 13, 14, (17).

LIU TS'UI 劉粹 (Ch'un-chia 純嘏). fl. late third cent. A son-in-law of Wang Jung, he once served as personal attendant. *CCKT.* VIII, *22*.

LIU TS'UNG 劉聰 (Hsüan-ming 玄明). d. 318. *CS* 102.1a-23b; *WS* 95.3b-6b. The fourth son of Liu Yüan 淵, the Hsiung-nu founder of Former Chao (304-329), who succeeded him as second ruler (310-318). *CYC.* XXVII, *9*.

LIU YÜ 劉輿 (Ch'ing-sun 慶孫). 265?-311? *CS* 62.14a-15b. The elder brother of Liu K'un and descendant of the Han imperial family. Beginning his career in the Imperial Secretariat, he managed to offend Sun Hsiu*, an important member of the faction of the Prince of Chao, Ssu-ma Lun, to whose son Liu's younger sister was married, and was dismissed. After Lun's death in 301, he joined forces with the Princes of Ch'i (Ssu-ma Chiung), Tung-hai (Ssu-ma Yüeh), and Fan-yang (Ssu-ma Hsiao 虓), becoming grand warden of Ying-ch'uan (Honan). When Ssu-ma Hsiao was defeated in 302, he fled north of the Yellow River to become grand warden of Wei Commandery (northern Honan), and after Hsiao's death he became Ssu-ma Yüeh's senior administrator. From there he rose rapidly to a position of great power and instituted a reign of terror in which many literati who dared oppose him lost their lives. He died from an infected finger in his forty-seventh year some time before the sack of Lo-yang in 311. *CYC.* VI, *10*; VIII, 28; XXXVI, 2.

LIU YÜ* 劉裕 (Te-yü 德輿). 356-422. *SS* 1-3. The founder of the Liu-Sung Dynasty (420-479), who reigned as Emperor Wu (420-422); also an uncle of Liu I-ch'ing, author of the *SSHY*. He first gained recognition under the Chin by his part in the suppression of Sun En's rebellion in 402 and later by restoring the dynasty after Huan Hsüan's interregnum in 404. Still later, in 410, he crushed the Southern Yen state in the north, recovered Lo-yang in 416, and in the following year destroyed Later Ch'in. Now virtual dictator in Chin, he had Emperor An (Ssu-ma Te-tsung, r. 397-418) killed, replacing him with a puppet, whose abdication he accepted two years later. XXVIII, 8.

LIU YÜAN-CHIH 劉爰之 (Tsun-tsu 遵祖). mid-fourth cent. He gained a reputation as a conversationalist while quite young, and after a term in the Central Secretariat became grand warden of Hsüan-ch'eng (Anhui). *HKCC.* XXV, *47*.

LO CH'I-SHENG 羅企生 (Tsung-po 宗伯). 364/5-399/400. *CS* 89.25b-26b. Advisory aide to Yin Chung-k'an in Wu-ch'ang, during the latter's governorship of Ching Province (Hunan-Hupei) at the end of the fourth century. When Huan Hsüan attacked in 399/400, Lo remained loyal to Yin and was killed. *CHS*. I, *43*.

LO HAN 羅含 (Chün-chang 君章). ca. 303-380. *CS* 92.33a-34b. Beginning in a minor post in his home province of Ching (Hunan-Hupei), he later served under Yü Liang's administration of the province (328-340) and still later as lieutenant-governor under Huan Wen (346-363). A treatise by him on reincarnation, the *Keng-sheng-lun* 更生論, composed about 370, is preserved in the Buddhist anthology, *Hung-ming chi* (*Taishō* 52.27bc), but apart from the subject of rebirth (which is treated without reference to karma), it contains no distinctively Buddhist ideas. See Zürcher, *Conquest*, pp. 16, 135-136. *Lo Fu-chün PC*. V, *56*; X, 19.

LO TSUN-SHENG 羅遵生. late fourth to early fifth cent. Mentioned, *CS* 89.25b-26a. Younger brother of Lo Ch'i-sheng, he was spared at the latter's death in 400. *CHS*. I, *43*.

LO YU 羅友 (Chai-jen 宅仁). mid-fourth cent. A native of Hsiang-yang (northern Hupei), and lover of wine and low-born company. After serving under Huan Wen, he became grand warden of his native commandery and was later transferred successively to the governorship of the two provinces of Kuang (Kwangtung-Kwangsi) and I (Szechwan). In these frontier posts he held the reins of government with a very light grip, which won him the goodwill of all his constituents. He died in I Province. *CYC*. XXIII, *41*, *44*.

LU CHI 陸機 (Shih-heng 士衡). 261-303. *CS* 54.1a-15b. A native of Wu Commandery (Soochow), whose grandfather had been chancellor, and whose father grand marshal, of the Wu Kingdom (223-280). Chi was of imposing stature and voice, and early showed prowess as a writer. He was twenty when Wu was conquered by Western Chin in 280, and for nearly a decade he remained in obscurity in his home village. In 289 he ventured north with his brother, Lu Yün, and at Lo-yang made the acquaintance of Chang Hua, who introduced him at court. He began as a libationer in the retinue of the grand tutor, Yang Chün, and narrowly escaped death when the Yang family was wiped out by Empress Chia in 291. He then attached himself successively to various of the imperial princes, and during the heat of the "War of the Eight Princes" (300-306), while commanding the forces of the Prince of Ch'eng-tu (Ssu-ma Ying), he was the victim of false charges of treachery and was executed with his two sons in 303. There are 109 pieces attributed to him in the *WH* alone, but he is best known for his "Poetic Essay on Writing" (*Wen-fu*), *WH* 17.1a-6b, of which there are at least three published translations in English: E. R. Hughes, *The Art of Letters*, New York, 1951, Achilles Fang, "Rhyme-prose on Literature," *HJAS* 14 (1951), pp. 527-566, and S. H. Chen, "Essay on Literature," in Birch and Keene, *Anthology of Chinese Literature*, vol. 1, New York, 1965, pp. 204-214. *CYC*; (*Lu*) *Chi PC*. II, *26*; IV, 84, 89; V, 18; VII, 19, 20, 39; XV, 1, 2; XXIV, 5; XXXIII, 3.

LU CHI* 陸績 (Kung-chi 公紀). late second to early third cent. *SKWu* 12.9b-10b. A younger contemporary of P'ang T'ung. A man of bold and martial manner, he retained a lifelong interest in astronomy and the "Book of Changes." He correctly predicted his own death, which occurred in his thirty-second year. *WSC*. IX, 2.

LU CHIH 盧志 (Tzu-tao 子道). d. ca. 311. *CS* 44.8a-10b. Youngest son of Lu T'ing. During the "War of the Eight Princes" (300-306), he was senior administrator in the government of Yeh Commandery (northern Honan) under the Prince of Ch'eng-tu, Ssu-ma Ying. When Lo-yang fell to Shih Lo in 311, he attempted to join Liu K'un in the north but was captured and killed. *SY*. V, *18*; XXXIII, 3.

LU HSÜN 陸遜 (Po-yen 伯言). 183-245. *SKWu* 13.1a-12a. A member of an important Wu family, he served as chancellor under Sun Ch'üan, founder of the Wu Kingdom (r. 222-252), and was married to Ch'üan's niece. He was the grandfather of Lu Chi and Lu Yün. *WuS*. V, *18*.

LU K'AI 陸凱 (Ching-feng 敬風). 198-269. *SKWu* 16.3a-10b. A first cousin, once-removed, of Lu Hsün, he had a distinguished military career in the Wu Kingdom, becoming general of the northern expedition in 235 and Generalissimo Governing the West, stationed in Ching Province (Hupei) in 242. It was at this point that he was ennobled a marquis. In 266 he was recalled to the capital to be chancellor of the left. Since his ruler, Sun Hao (r. 264-280), like most last rulers, is depicted in the records as cruel and tyrannical, Lu's biography is filled with his remonstrances. *WuL*. X, *5*.

LU K'ANG 陸抗 (Yu-chieh 幼節). 226-274. *SKWu* 13.12a-19a. Second son of Lu Hsün 遜 and grandson on his mother's side of Sun Ts'e, elder brother of the founder of Wu. He was the father of Lu Chi and Lu Yün. Because of his connection with the Wu royal family he rose rapidly to positions of trust and figured prominently in the wars against Wei. When Sun Hao mounted the throne in 264, Lu became generalissimo and governor of I Province (Szechwan). After exterminating the rebel Pu Ch'an 步闡 in 272, he was named grand marshal and governor of Ching Province (Hunan-Hupei), but died of an illness in the fall of 274. *WuL*. III, *4*; V, *18*.

LU LIANG 陸亮 (Ch'ang-hsing 長興). fl. late third cent. Under Chia Ch'ung's patronage he became president of the Board of Civil Office around 279, but was eventually dismissed for corruption. *CCKT*. III, 7.

LU MAI 陸邁 (Kung-kao 功高; var 公高). fl. early fourth cent. A native of Wu Commandery (Soochow), noted for his clear wit and lofty manner. His highest office was apparently clerk of the Board of Civil Office. *LP*. X, *16*.

LU T'ING 盧珽 (Tzu-hu 子笏). fl. ca. 265. Father of Lu Chih. He served as grand warden of T'ai-shan Commandery (Shantung) and later rose to be president of a secretariat. *WC*. V, *18*.

LU T'UI 陸退 (Li-min 黎民). fl. second half, fourth cent. A son-in-law of Chang P'ing and member of the Lu family of Wu Commandery

(Soochow). His highest office was Great Officer of Brilliant Favor. *Lu SP*. IV, *82*.

LU WAN 陸玩 (Shih-yao 士瑤). ca. 277-340. *CS* 77.2a-4b. A native of Wu (Soochow), who served as an aide to Ssu-ma Jui before the latter mounted the Eastern Chin throne in Chien-k'ang as Emperor Yüan in 317. A modest man with a dry sense of humor, he was well loved by his contemporaries. Since Wang Tun had forced him into his service, he was spared after Tun's revolt was crushed in 324 only by the intervention of Wen Ch'iao. He later became vice-president of the Board of Civil Office, and for helping suppress Su Chün's revolt in 328/329, he was ennobled. After the successive deaths of Wang Tao (339), Ch'ih Chien (339), and Yü Liang (340), he was elevated to become director of works. He died sometime later at the age of sixty-three, receiving the posthumous title of grand marshal. *Lu Wan PC*. III, *13*; V, *24*; X, *17*; XXV, *10*.

LU YÜ 盧毓 (Tzu-chia 子家). d. 257. *SKWei* 22.19b-22b. Beginning under the Wei as a clerk in the Board of Civil Office, he moved to palace attendant in 227, later to grand warden of two provincial commanderies, and back to personal attendant in 234, finally becoming president of the Board of Civil Office and commandant of the Capital Province. *WC*. V, *18*.

LU YÜN 陸雲 (Shih-lung 士龍). 262-303. *CS* 54.16a-21b. A noted poet, less famous than his elder brother, Lu Chi. After the fall of his native Wu in 280, he migrated to Lo-yang with his brother, where he held various posts under the patronage of the Prince of Ch'eng-tu, Ssu-ma Ying. When his brother fell victim to intrigue in 303, Yün also perished. *Lu Yün PC*. V, *18*; VIII, (*19*), *20*, *39*; XV, *1*; XXIV, *5*; XXV, *9*.

LÜ AN 呂安 (Chung-t'i 仲悌). d. 262. A person of similar temperament to that of Hsi K'ang who shared his aversion to the rise of the Ssu-ma family in the Wei Kingdom. In 262, when An's older brother, Sun 巽, guilty of adultery with An's wife, Lady Hsü 徐, tried to divert attention by accusing An of unfilial behavior toward his mother, Ssu-ma Chao promptly imprisoned An. Hsi K'ang, called in as a witness in An's defense, exposed the facts of the case, but both An and K'ang were executed for daring to withstand Ssu-ma Chao. *CYC*; *KPCC*. XXIV, *4*.

LÜ-CH'IU CH'UNG 閭丘沖 (Pin-ch'ing 賓卿). d. ca. 311. A man known in his time as a fair-minded judge of men. From a position as senior administrator to the grand tutor, he gradually rose to become Great Officer of Brilliant Favor, never receiving any spectacular recognition, though always known as a clear and perspicuous writer, without pride or pretense, a lover of music, and possessor of an unsullied reputation. He was killed by bandits outside the city of Lo-yang sometime before its fall in 311. *YenCC*. IX, *9*.

LÜ-CHU 綠珠 (d. 300). Mentioned, *CS* 33.21ab. A female entertainer (flautist) who became the concubine of Shih Ch'ung. After Ch'ung's death in 300 she committed suicide. *KPCC*. XXXVI, *1*.

MA JUNG 馬融 (Chi-ch'ang 季長). 79-166. *HHS* 90A.1a-15b. The dean of the Han commentators, who is said to have had over one thousand "disciples" or protégés who carried on his philological tradition, the greatest of whom was Cheng Hsüan. Besides commentaries on the Classics, Ma also made annotations for *Lao-tzu*, *Huai-nan-tzu*, and the *Li-sao*. *MJTH*. IV, *1*.

MAN FEN 滿奮 (Wu-ch'iu 武秋). late third cent. *SKWei* 26.5b-6a, comm. Grandson of Man Ch'ung 寵 (d. 242) and, like the other members of the family, large of frame. Beginning his career in the Board of Civil Office, he became governor of Chi Province (N. Hopei), and around 295 was made president of the Court Secretariat and commandant of the Capital Province. Sometime thereafter he was killed by Miao Yüan 眊願 (not, as claimed in the Comm., by Hsün I 荀顗, who died in 274; see Li Shan's seventh-cent. commentary to Shen Yüeh's 沈約 [441-513], "Reprimand of Wang Yüan," *Tsou-t'an Wang Yüan* 奏彈王源). *WH* 40.8a. *HCCCC*; *CCKT*. II, *20*; IX, 9.

MAO HSÜAN 毛玄 (Po-ch'eng 伯成). late fourth cent.(?) He must have died young, as his highest rank was marching aide to the General Chastizing the West. *CHLSM*. II, *96*.

MAO TSENG 毛曾. fl. 227-237. *SKWei* 5.12a-13a. The younger brother of Empress Mao, consort of the Wei Emperor Ming (Ts'ao Jui, r. 227-239). On Emperor Ming's accession, members of the empress's family were immediately catapulted to positions of honor, and Tseng became an officer in the Palace Guard, later promoted to cavalier attendant-in-ordinary and commander. The family was evidently of humble origin, and Tseng's deportment is characterized as rude and arrogant. *WC*. XIV, *3*.

MEI I 梅頤 (Chung-chen 仲真). mid-fourth cent. A studious man who spent much of his youth in retirement; he once served as grand warden of Yü-chang (Kiangsi). *CCKT*; *YCLJM*. V, *39*.

MENG CH'ANG 孟昶 (Yen-yüan 彥遠). d. 410. He won recognition in his youth from Wang Kung, and was appointed capital intendant for his participation in Kung's coup against Ssu-ma Tao-tzu in 397. Like Yang Fu 羊孚 and many other idealistic men of the time, he welcomed Huan Hsüan as a liberator, as did his superior, Liu Lao-chih. But after Hsüan's usurpation in 404, he joined Liu Yü* to overthrow him, and in 408 moved from president of the Board of Civil Office to vice-president of the Imperial Secretariat. Later, faced with certain defeat while engaged in suppressing the sequel of Sun En's revolt in Yang Province (Kiangsi-Chekiang) in 410, he took poison and died. *CATC*. IV, *104*; XVI, 6.

MENG CHIA 孟嘉 (Wan-nien 萬年). mid-fourth cent. *CS* 98.29b-30b. A son-in-law of T'ao K'an and native of Wu-ch'ang (Hupei). he served in Yü Liang's administration of Chiang Province (Hupei-Kiangsi) sometime after 334 when the latter was appointed governor-general of military affairs with headquarters in Wu-ch'ang. Subsequently he became lieutenant-governor of the same province, and after Huan Wen assumed the governor-generalship in Wu-ch'ang in 345, Meng served as his aide. Later he was summoned to the capital by Emperor Mu (Ssu-ma Tan, r. 345-361), but declined, spending his later years in retirement in the area of K'uai-chi (Chekiang). He died at the age of 51 or 53. *(Meng) Chia PC.* VII, *16*; XVIII, *10*.

MENG LOU 孟陋 (Shao-ku 少孤). fl. ca. 365-370. CS 94.18ab. A younger brother of Meng Chia who never held office and was known as "Meng the Recluse." While mourning his mother he refrained from wine and meat for over ten years. He wrote commentaries on all three of the Classics devoted to rites (*Li-chi, Chou-li, I-li*) and on the "Analects," none of which have survived. *MCSM.* XVIII, *10*.

MENG MIN 孟敏 (Shu-ta 叔達). second cent. A younger contemporary of Kuo T'ai. *Kuo Lin-tsung PC.* XXVIII, *6*.

MU HSI 繆襲 (Hsi-po 熙伯). 186-245. *SKWei* 21.21a, biog. under Liu Shao, comm. The son of Mu Fei 斐, he served "four successive Wei rulers" (Ts'ao Ts'ao, Ts'ao P'ei, Ts'ao Jui, and Ts'ao Fang) as censor, and Ts'ao Jui as personal attendant. He died in 245 with the rank of Great Officer of Brilliant Favor, having enjoyed some reputation as a writer. One of his funeral songs (*wan-ko* 挽歌) is included in *WH* 28.16a. *WCHL* and *WCC.* II, *13*.

NAN-K'ANG, Princess of 南康公主. mid-fourth cent. Daughter of Emperor Ming (Ssu-ma Shao, r. 323-325) and Empress Yü, and legal wife of Huan Wen. *HCYC.* XIX, *21*; (XXIV, *8*).

NI HENG 禰衡 (Cheng-p'ing 正平). 171-196. *HHS* 110B. As a youth he gained a reputation for his quick wit and equally quick temper, and for his skill as a writer. Of his voluminous literary output, only a few pieces survive, the most celebrated being the "Poetic Essay on the Parrot" (*Ying-wu fu* 鸚鵡賦, *WH* 13.13a-15a). When Ts'ao Ts'ao moved the Later Han capital to Hsü 許 (in Honan) in 195, Heng fled to Ching Province (Hupei-Hunan), but returned to Hsü the following year, where he was recommended to Ts'ao Ts'ao by his friend K'ung Jung. After alienating Ts'ao by his insolence, he was sent off to the governor of Ching Province (Hunan-Hupei), Liu Piao 劉表 (d. 208), who soon dismissed him for the same reason, sending him to the grand warden of Chiang-hsia (Hupei), Huang Tsu 黃祖 (d. 208), who, unable to bear his insults, finally killed him. *WSC*; *TL*; cf. also *TCTC* 62.1993. II, *8*.

OU-YANG CHIEN 歐陽建 (Chien-shih 堅石). ca. 265-300. *CS* 33.23ab. A nephew of Shih Ch'ung who served successively as magistrate of Shan-yang Prefecture (Honan) and clerk of the Imperial Secretariat, then grand warden of P'ing-i (Shensi). Since he had offended Sun Hsiu*, a minion of the Prince of Chao, Ssu-ma Lun, he perished in the purges preparatory to Lun's usurpation in 300. *CYC.* IV, *21*; XXXVI, *1*.

PAN CHIEH-YÜ 班婕妤. d. shortly after 7 B.C. *HS* 97B.8a-10b. Chieh-yü is merely a title for palace ladies in favor, not her given name, which is unknown. While serving as a lady-in-waiting during the reign of Emperor Ch'eng (Liu Ao, r. 32-7 B.C.), she at first displaced Empress Hsü, but later (18 B.C.) was herself displaced by Chao Fei-yen. *HS*; *Wai-ch'i chuan.* XIX, *3*.

PAN KU 班固 (Meng-chien 孟堅). d. A.D. 92. *HHS* 70A.6a-70B.22a. The author of the *HS*, which had been begun by his father, Pan Piao 彪. He also edited the encyclopedic work, *Po-hu t'ung* 白虎通 and composed the celebrated "Poetic Essays on the Western and Eastern Capitals" (*Hsi-tu, Tung-tu fu*; *WH* 1-2) and was considered an encyclopedic genius in his day. IV, 99.

P'AN NI 潘尼 (Cheng-shu 正叔). ca. 250-310. *CS* 55.17a-26a. A cousin of P'an Yüeh, and like him, famous as a poet (see *WH* 24.16b-18b; 26.11b-12a). His "Discourse on Calming Oneself" (*An-shen lun* 安身論) is quoted at length in his biography. Around 283 he took the *hsiu-ts'ai* degree and was named grand ordinary erudite, later being sent to Kao-lu Prefecture (Shensi) as magistrate. In 291 he became attendant to the crown prince, but when Ssu-ma Lun attempted to usurp the throne in 300 he claimed illness and withdrew from court, joining the loyalist forces of Ssu-ma Chiung in the following year. During the next three years he rose successively to cavalier attendant-in-ordinary, personal attendant, curator of the Palace Library, and in 305 he became president of the Central Secretariat. Around 310, as he fled with his family from the barbarian incursions of Lo-yang, he was intercepted by bandits and died of an illness in their encampment. *WSC*. III, 5.

P'AN T'AO 潘滔 (Yang-chung 陽仲). d. 311. He served as equestrian forerunner on the staff of the crown prince around 300, and in 306 as cavalier attendant-in-ordinary. In 311, while serving as intendant of Honan, stationed in Lo-yang, he was killed in Shih Lo's sack of the city. *CYC*. VII, 6; VIII, 28.

P'AN YÜEH 潘岳 (An-jen 安仁). 247-300. *CS* 55.9b-17a. Famous both for his writings, many of which are preserved in the *WH*, and for his physical beauty. Beginning as a secretary in the administration of Chia Ch'ung while the latter was grand marshal (ca. 278), he moved on to cavalier attendant and historian. He was chief among the literary group known as the "Twenty-four Friends," patronized by Chia Ch'ung's adopted son, Mi 賈謐 (d. 300). When Yang Chün was executed by Empress Chia in 291, P'an was at the time serving on Yang's staff and narrowly escaped death. In 300 Sun Hsiu*, an enemy since childhood, became president of the Central Secretariat where P'an was working. Through a slanderous charge that P'an was involved in the revolt of the Prince of Ch'i, Ssu-ma Chiung, Sun arranged to have him executed in the same year. *CYC*. II, 107; IV, 70, 71, 84, 89; VIII, 139; XIV, 7, 9; XXXVI, 1.

P'ANG T'UNG 龐統 (Shih-yüan 士元). 177-214. *SKShu* 7.1a-4a. A nephew of P'ang Te-kung 德公, who characterized him as a "phoenix fledgling" (*feng-ch'u* 鳳雛). Liu Pei, in his efforts to enlarge the Shu Kingdom, made him commander of the northern expedition, but he was killed in the attack on Lo-yang in 214. *Shu C*; *HYC*; *HYKC*. II, 9; IX, 2, 3.

P'EI CH'I 裴啟 (var. Jung 榮) (Jung-ch'i 榮期). fl. second half, fourth cent. His father, P'ei Chih 稚, was magistrate of Feng-ch'eng. Even from his youth he enjoyed describing personalities, and his "Forest of Conversations" (*Yü-lin* 語林), compiled in 362, represents an earlier anecdotal collection which supplied much of the material used in the *SSHY*. The book enjoyed great popularity until Hsieh An blackballed it, claiming it had misquoted him. *P'ei-shih chia-chuan*; *HCYC*. IV, *90*; XXVI, 24.

P'EI CH'IEN 裴潛 (Wen-hsing 文行). d. 244. *SKWei* 23.16b-18a. During the disorders caused by the Yellow Turban Revolt in 184, he took refuge with Liu Piao, governor of Ching Province (Hunan-Hupei). Later Ts'ao Ts'ao entrusted him with minor posts, eventually granting him noble rank. When Ts'ao P'ei ascended the Wei throne in 220, Ch'ien was named cavalier attendant-in-ordinary, and on the accession of Ts'ao Jui in 227 he became grand marshal and president of the Imperial Secretariat. *WC*. VII, *2*.

P'EI CH'O 裴綽 (Chi-shu 季舒). fl. mid-third cent. *SKWei* 23.19a, comm.; *CS* 35.18b. The fourth son of P'ei Hui. He served as a palace attendant, but died young. *WCML*. IX, *6*.

P'EI HSIA 裴遐 (Shu-tao 叔道). fl. ca. 300. *SKWei* 23.19a, comm. Grandson of P'ei Hui and nephew of P'ei K'ai, and son-in-law of Wang Yen. He favored the conservative "Moral Teaching" (*ming-chiao*), and the clarity of his arguments was compared to the notes of the zither. *CCKT*; *TTCC*. IV, *19*; VI, 9; IX, 6, 33.

P'EI HSIU 裴秀 (Chi-yen 季彥). 224-271. *SKWei* 23.18b, comm.; *CS* 35.3a-7a. The son of P'ei Ch'ien and father of P'ei Wei. His reputation was made when he redrew the ancient maps of the empire according to a more accurate scale, containing all the contemporary administrative divisions. After the founding of Western Chin in 265, he was granted a noble title and reached the rank of director of works. *YYCS*. VIII, *7*.

P'EI HUI 裴徽 (Wen-chi 文季). fl. 230-249. *SKWei* 23.18b, comm. The father of P'ei K'ai and onetime governor of Chi Province (Hopei). *YCLJM*. IV, *8*, 9; IX, 6.

P'EI K'AI 裴楷 (Shu-tse 叔則). 237-291. *CS* 35.13b-16b. Third son of P'ei Hui, cousin of P'ei Hsiu, and brother-in-law of Wang Jung. He gained a reputation for an elegant manner and appearance and was known to contemporaries as the "Man of Jade." Known chiefly as an expert in the *Lao-tzu* and "Book of Changes," he eventually reached the rank of president of the Central Secretariat and personal attendant. *CCKT*. I, *18*, 20; II, 19; III, 5; V, 13; VI, 7; VIII, 5, 6, 8, 14, 24, 38; IX, 6; XIV, 6, 10, 12; XXI, 9; XXIII, 11.

P'EI K'ANG 裴康 (Chung-yü 仲豫). fl. mid-third cent. *SKWei* 23.19a, comm. The second son of P'ei Hui. He became a commander of the Palace Guard, and was noted for his "vast tolerance." *CPKM*; *CCKT*. IX, *6*.

P'EI MO 裴邈 (Ching-sheng 景聲). fl. ca. 305. *SKWei* 23.18b, comm. A cousin of P'ei Wei, who admired Mo's talents and enjoyed conversing with him. He held several minor posts on the administrative staff of the grand tutor, Ssu-ma Yüeh, and though military matters were never within his competency, he was praised for his "frugality and gravity." *CCKT*. VI, *11*; VIII, 28; IX, 6.

P'EI TSAN 裴瓚 (Kuo-pao 國寶). fl. second half, third cent. SKWei 23.19a, comm. A son of P'ei K'ai. He held a post in the Central Secretariat when he died at an early age. CCKT. IX, 6.

P'EI WEI 裴頠 (I-min 逸民). 267-300. SKWei 23.18b, comm., CS 35.7a-13b. Youngest son of P'ei Hsiu, and son-in-law of Wang Jung. In 291, for his merit in crushing the revolt of the empress's father, Yang Chün, he was ennobled a marquis, and henceforth devoted himself to the restoration of what he felt to be the neglected virtues of antiquity. His treatise, "In Praise of Actuality" (Ch'ung-yu lun 崇有論), quoted in extenso in his biography, appeared in 297, and was a scathing attack on the supporters of "Nonactuality" (wu 無), led by Wang Yen. After becoming vice-president of the Imperial Secretariat, he became involved in the "War of the Eight Princes" (300-306) and was killed by the Prince of Chao (Ssu-ma Lun) in 300. CHTCCC; HCCCC. II, 23; IV, 11, 12; VI, 12; VIII, 18; IX, 6, 7, 34; XVI, 2; XXIII, 14; XXIX, 5; XXXV, 2.

PI CHO 畢卓 (Mao-shih 茂世). d. ca. 329. CS 49.22ab. In his youth he belonged to the circle of Hu-wu Fu-chih and other libertines known as the "Eight Free Spirits" (pa-ta), who shocked Lo-yang society at the end of the third century. After crossing the Yangtze with the Eastern Chin court, he became president of the Board of Civil Office in 322, and died about seven years later. CHS. XXIII, 21.

PIEN, "Empress" 卞皇后. 160-240. SKWei 5.2a-9a. The legal consort of Ts'ao Ts'ao and mother of Ts'ao P'ei and Ts'ao Chih, who displaced Lady Ting 丁夫人 in 196. She had originally been a dancing girl whom Ts'ao Ts'ao encountered while he was still in Chiao (Shantung) in 179. WeiS. XIX, 4; XXXIII, 1.

PIEN FAN-CHIH 卞範之 (Ching-tsu 敬祖; baby name, Chü 鞠). d. 405. CS 99.21a. The grandson, on his mother's side, of Yin Hao's sister. He was Huan Hsüan's senior administrator in 402 and composed the imperial rescript making Hsüan emperor in January 404. During the three months of Huan Hsüan's usurpation he served as capital intendant and personal attendant, and, faithful to the end, was executed with Huan in March 404. WCL. XVII, 19; XIX, 27, 32; XXII, 6.

PIEN JANG 邊讓 (Wen-li 文禮). d. ca. 210. HHS 110B, 10a-14b. An illustrious writer of poetic essays (fu), the text of one of which, "On the Magnificent Terrace" (Chang-hua fu), is quoted in his biography. He was also admired for his ready wit as a conversationalist. After resigning as grand warden of Chiu-chiang (Kiangsi) in about 192, he returned to his native village in Ch'en-liu, where a neighbor slandered him to Ts'ao Ts'ao, who had him killed sometime between 196 and 220. WSC. II, 1.

PIEN K'UN 卞壺 (Wang-chih 望之). 281-328. CS 70.11a-18a. A member of Yü Liang's faction at the Eastern Chin court. He was serving as historian during the period 307-312 while Lo-yang was being threatened by barbarian invaders, and took refuge with his brother-in-law, P'ei Tun 裴遁, who was then governor of Hsü Province (Anhui). After the establishment of Eastern Chin in 317 he served first as clerk in the Board of Civil Office and after 323 became junior censor, then president of the Imperial Secretariat. For participating in the suppression of Wang Tun's rebellion in 324, he was made a duke. Conservative ideologically, he bitterly opposed the "libertinism" of the so-called "Eight Free Spirits" (*pa-ta*). He was captured and killed while attempting to crush the rebellion of Su Chün against the Yü faction in 328. *Pien K'un PC*; *TTCC*. (II, 48); VIII, 50, *54*; IX, 24; XXIII, 27; XXIV, 7.

PING YUAN 邴原 (Ken-chü 根矩). d. 211. *SKWei* 11.17a-20a. Orphaned at ten, he received an education through the kindness of a teacher. At the outbreak of the Yellow Turban Revolt in his area in 184, he fled by sea to the hills of Kiangsu, but when the area was overrun, fled again to the northeast (Manchuria), where he aroused the fears of the local satrap, Kung-sun Tu. Again escaping to his home village (in Shantung), he took service under Ts'ao Ts'ao, and lost his life in one of the campaigns against Wu in 211. *Ping Yüan PC*. VIII, *4*.

SAMGHADEVA. See SENG-CHIA-T'I-P'O.

SENG-CHIA-T'I-P'O 僧伽提婆 (Samghadeva). late fourth cent. *KSC* 1; *Taishō* 50.328c-329b. A Kashmiri monk of the Sarvāstivāda, or "Realistic," School of Indian Buddhism, who arrived in Ch'ang-an (Shensi) around 381 and introduced the Abhidharma, or theoretical literature, of this school. In 383, in collaboration with Chu Fo-nien 竺佛念, he translated the monumental *Jñānaprasthāna-abhidharma-śāstra* (*A-p'i-t'an pa-chien-tu lun*; *Taishō* 26, no. 1543). After the fall of Former Ch'in in 385, he migrated to Lo-yang (Honan) and from there to Hui-yüan's community on Mt. Lu (Kiangsi) in 391, where he made a retranslation of the *Abhidharma-hṛdaya śāstra* (*A-p'i-t'an hsin lun*; *Taishō* 28, no. 1550) at Hui-yüan's request. His earlier translation of the same work, done at Ch'ang-an in 384, no longer survives. He arrived in Chien-k'ang in 397 and remained there until his death. *CCH*. IV, *64*.

SENG-I 僧意. fl. ca. 350. A monk residing in the Wa-kuan Monastery of Chien-k'ang, who was friendly with Wang Hsiu. IV, 57.

SHAN CHIEN 山簡 (Chi-lun 季倫). 253-312. *CS* 43.6b-8b. The son of Shan T'ao. He was governor of Ch'ing Province (Shantung) and later personal attendant. In 306 he became president of the Board of Civil Office, and in the following year governor of Yung Province (Shensi) and General Governing the West, but was soon recalled to Lo-yang to be vice-president of the Imperial Secretariat. In 309 he was named General Chastizing the South and governor-general of military affairs in the four southern provinces of Ching, Hsiang, Chiao and Kuang, stationed in Hsiang-yang (northern Hupei), where he distinguished himself primarily as a drinker. When Lo-yang fell in 311, Chien moved to Hsia-k'ou (Hupei). He died the following year. *YYCS*. VIII, *29*; XVII, 4; XXIII, 19.

SHAN HSIA 山遐 (Yen-lin 彥林). fl. ca. 317-343. *CS* 43.8b. Son of Shan Chien and grandson of Shan T'ao. In the early days of Eastern Chin, as the magistrate of Yü-yao Prefecture (Chekiang), he collided with some rapacious members of the powerful clan of Yü 虞 and was eventually impeached. Later, around 343, as grand warden of Tung-yang (Chekiang), he instituted a very severe administration, complaints about which reached the ears of Emperor K'ang (r. 343-344), who issued a rebuke. He died in office not long thereafter. *TungYC*. III, *21*.

SHAN KAI 山諧 (Po-lun 伯倫). late third cent. *CS* 43.6a. Eldest son of Shan T'ao, his highest office was general of the Left Palace Guard. *CCKT*. V, *15*.

SHAN T'AO 山濤 (Chü-yüan 巨源). 205-283. *CS* 43.1a-6a. Related on his mother's side to the Chin royal family of Ssu-ma, he found it difficult to maintain his early association with the pro-Taoist Wei loyalists like Hsi K'ang, with whom he is usually listed among the "Seven Worthies of the Bamboo Grove." After Ts'ao Shuang's fall in 249, he capitulated to the anti-Taoist, pro-Ssu-ma camp, accepting office under their patronage. After the formal establishment of Chin in 265, he was named concurrently vice-president of the Imperial Secretariat and president of the Board of Civil Office, an office which he held between 272 and 279. At his death in 283, he was director of instruction. *YYCS*. II, 78; III, *5*, 7, 8; V, *15*; VII, *4*, *5*; VIII, 8, 10, 12, 17, 21, 29; XIV, 5; XVIII, 3; XIX, 11; XXIII, 1; XXV, 4.

SHAN YÜN 山允 (Shu-chen 叔真). late third cent. *CS* 43.6b. Third son of Shan T'ao, described as "puny and ricketty" but "exceptionally intelligent." (V, *15*).

SHEN CH'UNG 沈充 (Shih-chü 士居). d. 324. *CS* 98.15a-16a. A native of Wu-hsing (Chekiang) and partisan of Wang Tun, in whose administration he began as an aide. He led one of Tun's divisions in the rebellion of 324 and was soundly defeated by loyalist forces under Su Chün. Fleeing to his home in Wu-hsing, he fell into the hands of one of his former generals, Wu Ju 吳儒, who killed him but who was killed in turn by Ch'ung's son, Ching 勁, together with his whole family. *CYC*. VI, 18; X, *16*.

SHIH CH'UNG 石崇 (Chi-lun 季倫; baby name, Ch'i-nu 齊奴). 249-300. *CS* 33.18b-23a. One of the "Twenty-four Friends" of Chia Mi 賈謐 and a favorite of the Chin Emperor Wu (Ssu-ma Yen, r. 265-290). He was an extremely wealthy and ostentatious man, whose rivalry in extravagance with Wang K'ai was proverbial. Because of his association with Chia Mi, he fell in the purge of the Chia clan by Ssuma Lun in 300. *CKSH*. IX, *57*; XVI, 3; XXX, 1, 2, 3, 4, 5, 8, 10; XXXVI, 1, 2.

SHIH HU 石虎 (Chi-lung 季龍). d. 349. *CS* 106-107. A Hsiung-nu of the Chieh 羯 tribe of Shang-tang (Shansi), nephew of Shih Lo, who, after killing off the latter's sons, succeeded him as third ruler of Later Chao (r. 335-349), moving the capital from Hsiang Principality (Hopei) to Yeh (northern Honan). *ChaoS*. II, *45*.

SHIH HUI-YÜAN 釋慧遠. 334-416/7. *CSTCC* 15, *Taishō* 55.109bff.; *KSC* 6, *Taishō* 50.357cff.; trans. Zürcher, *Conquest*, pp. 240-253. A learned disciple of Tao-an, he came south in 379 and established a religious community on Mt. Lu in Kiangsi in 402, the prototype of the Pure Land Sect. His able synthesis of philosophical Taoism with the current interpretations of the Mahayana Buddhism of the *Prajñāpāramitā-sūtras* won him such high regard that even the ambitious usurper, Huan Hsüan, bowed to his arguments that the Buddhist clergy should be exempt from civil responsibilities. See W. Liebenthal, "Shih Hui-yüan's Buddhism as Set Forth in His Writings," *JAOS* 70 (1950), 243-259; Kimura Eiichi, ed., *E-on kenkyū* (2 vols.), Kyoto, 1960. *YFSM*. IV, *61*; X, *24*.

SHIH LO 石勒 (Shih-lung 世龍). 274-333. *CS* 104-105. A Hsiung-nu of the Chieh tribe of Shang-tang (Shansi), who originally served under the Former Chao rulers Liu Yüan 劉淵 (r. 304-310) and Liu Ts'ung 聰 (r. 310-317). He later set up the rival state of Later Chao (319-351) in Hsiang Principality (Hopei), ruling from 319 to 333. *Shih Lo chuan*. (II, *45*); VII, *7*.

SHIH TAO-AN 釋道安. 312-385. *CSTCC* 15, *Taishō* 55.108a-109b; *KSC* 5, *Taishō* 50.351c-354a. This homely but brilliant man, who came originally from an impoverished gentry family in north China and became a monk at age twelve or thirteen, was perhaps the single person most responsible for the spread of Mahayana Buddhism in China, especially the *Prajñāpāramitā-sūtras*, through his school of "Fundamental Nonbeing" (*Pen-wu*), during the middle decades of the fourth century. A pupil of the Kuchean missionary, Fo-t'u-teng, at the Later Chao capital in Yeh (southern Hopei), he continued throughout his life to be an avid scholar, and devoted his later years to teaching a large group of disciples and to the study and exposition of the sutras. Between 349 and 365 he traveled about the area of Shansi, Hopei, and Honan. Fleeing southward in 365 from the invading armies of Former Yen (349-370), he established a Buddhist center in Hsiang-yang (northern Hupei), but when Hsiang-yang fell to Fu Chien in 379, he was taken to the Former Ch'in capital at Ch'ang-an (Shensi), where he remained until his death in 385. His disciples, including Shih Hui-yüan, dispersed to other parts of Eastern Chin, where they were influential in stimulating interest in the *Prajñāpāramitā* literature. *Tao-an ho-shang chuan*. See also Arthur E. Link, "Biography of Tao-an," *T'oung-pao* 46 (1958), 1-48; Ui Hakuju, *Shaku Dōan kenkyū*, Tokyo, 1956; T'ang Yung-t'ung, *Han-Wei*, pp. 187-228, 242-251; Zürcher, *Conquest*, pp. 185-204. VI, *32*.

SHU HSI 束皙 (Kuang-wei 廣微). fl. late third cent. *CS* 51.19b-26b. The family name had been changed from Shu 疏 during the rebellion of the Red Eyebrows around 23 A.D. He was greatly admired as a scholar and writer and is responsible for some of the annals and monographic essays in the present *CS*. The texts of two of his essays, "Apology for Living in Seclusion" (*Hsüan-chü shih* 玄居釋) and "Encouragement to Agriculture" (*Ch'üan-nung* 勸農) occupy most of his biography. He was serving as historian in 281 when the "Bamboo Annals" (*Chu-shu chi-nien* 竹書紀年) were discovered in an old Chou tomb in Chi Commandery (Honan) and was assigned the thankless task of assembling the dislocated bamboo slips in their proper order. *WSC*. VI, *41*.

SO YÜAN 索元 (T'ien-pao 天保). d. 403? A member of an Iranian (Saka?) family which had settled in Tun-huang several generations earlier. He served the Chin government as grand warden of Li-yang (northern Anhui), but his role as advisor to Huan Hsüan before the latter's usurpation in 404 is not clear. *So SP*. XVII, 19.

ŚRĪMITRA. See KAO-TSO TAO-JEN.

SSU-MA CHAO 司馬昭 (Tzu-shang 子上). 211-265. *CS* 2.7b-20a. Second son of Ssu-ma I, younger brother of Ssu-ma Shih, and father of Ssu-ma Yen, first ruler of the Chin Dynasty (265-420). He is usually referred to by his posthumous titles, T'ai-tsu, or Prince Wen. Because of his service to the Wei Kingdom, he was enfeoffed Prince of Chin in 254, and as generalissimo during the last decade of Wei he held the reins of power. After killing the fourth Wei ruler, Ts'ao Mao (Kao-kuei hsiang-kung, r. 254-260), in 260, he prepared to mount the throne himself but was prevented by death in 265. *WeiS*; *CFCC*. I, 15, 43; II, 17, 18; III, 6; IV, 67; V, 8; VI, 2; VIII, 5; IX, 5; XXIII, 2; XXIV, 1; XXV, 2; XXXIII, 7, 13.

SSU-MA CH'ENG 司馬承 (Yüan-ching 元敬). 264-322. *CS* 37.23a-36a. The son of Ssu-ma Hsün 遜 (d. 266), Prince of Chiao, from whom he inherited the title. After he was appointed governor of Hsiang Province (Hunan-Kwangtung-Kwangsi) by Emperor Yüan (Ssu-ma Jui, r. 317-322) in 321, he was invited by Wang Tun to help direct his planned revolt. Ch'eng resisted, bringing swift retaliation from Tun through the hand of Wang I*. He is sometimes referred to by his posthumous title, Prince Min. *CYC*. XXXVI, 3, 4.

SSU-MA CHEN-CHIH 司馬珍之 (Ching-tu 景度). d. ca. 420. *CS* 64.9a. Grandson of the Prince of Liang 梁, Ssu-ma Feng 逢 (d. ca. 385), whose title he inherited. His loyalty in refusing to serve the usurper Huan Hsüan in 404 gave him great prestige in the restoration, but Liu Yü*, founder of the Sung Dynasty (420-479), fearing trouble from the Chin princes, had him put to death on the eve of his own accession to the Sung throne in 420. *HCYC*. XIII, 13.

SSU-MA CHIUNG 司馬冏 (Ching-chih 景治). d. 302. *CS* 59.18a-24a. Son of Ssu-ma Yu, from whom he inherited the title, Prince of Ch'i. After the accession of Emperor Hui in 290 he became cavalier attendant-in-ordinary and General of the Left Army. During the "War of the Eight Princes" Chiung successfully put down the attempted usurpation of the Prince of Chao, Ssu-ma Lun, in 301, and was rewarded with the title of grand marshal, after which he became extremely influential at court and nearly fell heir to the throne. But because of charges of dissipation and his indiscriminate use of mediocre men, he was killed by the Prince of Ch'angsha, Ssu-ma I*, in 302. *YYCS*. V, 17; VII, 10.

SSU-MA CH'ÜAN 司馬權 (Tzu-yü 子輿). d. 276. *CS* 37.12ab. A younger brother of Ssu-ma I. He was enfeoffed Prince of P'eng-ch'eng (northern Kiangsu) upon the accession of Emperor Wu (Ssu-ma Yen, r. 265-290), and later took up his residence in the capital at Lo-yang. *CFCS*. XXX, 11.

SSU-MA CHUNG 司馬衷 (Cheng-tu 正度). 259-306. CS 4. The second son of Ssu-ma Yen, founder of Chin, who, though an imbecile, was named crown prince in 267 and ascended the throne as Emperor Hui in 290. His consort, the daughter of Chia Ch'ung, was named empress, and because of her husband's mental incompetence wielded the real power during his reign. Her extravagant abuses, which included murdering the dowager Empress Yang in 291 and the crown prince in 300, soon brought about her downfall, and in the ensuing vacuum the various princes began to compete for supremacy, the so-called "War of the Eight Princes" (300-306). During this troubled period, the emperor was a mere captive of the varying contenders, and was eventually poisoned, allegedly by Ssu-ma Yüeh 越, in 306. V, 9; IX, 32; X, 7; XIV, 10; XIX, 14.

SSU-MA CHÜN 司馬駿 (Tzu-tsang 子臧). 232-286. CS 38.6a-7a. Canonized Prince Wu 武王, the seventh son of Ssu-ma I 懿 (the fourth by Mme. Fu 伏; Liu Chün, quoting YYCS, has "seventeenth" by mistake), renowned as a studious and filial man. After a succession of noble titles and military posts under the Wei, with the Chin takeover in 265 he became Generalissimo Governing the West, stationed in Ch'ang-an. In 275 he crushed an uprising among the proto-Tibetan Ch'iang tribes in the northwest, for which he was brought to the capital in Lo-yang and named Prince of Fu-feng (Ch'ang-an). In 280 he became General of Spirited Cavalry but died "in distress" over the unchecked rise of the Prince of Ch'i, Ssu-ma Yu in 286. YYCS. I, 22.

SSU-MA HSI 司馬晞 (Tao-shu 道叔; var. -sheng 升). 316-381. CS 64.8a-9a. Fourth son of Emperor Yüan (Ssu-ma Jui, r. 317-322) and brother of Emperor Ming (Ssu-ma Shao, r. 323-325); also known as Prince Wei of Wu-ling. He became personal attendant on the accession of Emperor K'ang (Ssu-ma Yüeh*, r. 343-344), and received the title of grand minister (t'ai-tsai 太宰) around 345. Though not a studious type, he was considered a capable general. Huan Wen was profoundly jealous of him, and soon after the enthronement of his half brother, Ssu-ma Yü (Emperor Chien-wen, r. 371-372) accused him of rebellious ambitions and got him exiled to Hsin-an (western Chekiang), where he died in 381. SMHC. VI, 25; XXVIII, 7.

SSU-MA HSIU-I 司馬脩褘. late third to early fourth cent. A daughter of Emperor Wu (Ssu-ma Yen, r. 265-290) who was married to Wang Tun. She is also known as the Princess of Wu-yang 舞陽公主. XXXIV, 1.

SSU-MA HUI 司馬徽 (Te-ts'ao 德操). d. 208. A man who was renowned in his day as a knower of men, but who lived most of his life in poverty and obscurity in Ching Province (Hupei). After Ts'ao Ts'ao conquered the province in 208, he "wanted to make large use of him, but as it happened, Hui took sick and died." Ssu-ma Hui PC. II, 9.

SSU-MA I 司馬懿 (Chung-ta 仲達). 179-251. CS 1. Father of Ssu-ma Chao, and grandfather of the founder of Chin, Ssu-ma Yen (Emperor Wu, r. 265-290). After gaining influence in the Wei Kingdom through his successful campaigns against Shu in the southwest, he achieved the chancellorship by murdering his predecessor, Ts'ao Shuang, in 249, but died only two years later. He is often referred to by his posthumous titles, "Emperor Hsüan" and "Kao-tsu." (II, 16); V, 4, 5; XIV, 27; XXXIII, 7.

SSU-MA I* 司馬乂 (Shih-tu 士度). 277-304. CS 59.25a-28a. Sixth son of Ssu-ma Yen (seventeenth, according to PWKS), enfeoffed Prince of Ch'ang-sha in 289. During the "War of the Eight Princes" (300-306), I* killed the original leader of the loyalists, Ssu-ma Chiung, in 302, and two years later was killed by order of Ssu-ma Ying in a struggle over the capital. PWKS; CPKM. II, 25.

SSU-MA I** 司馬奕 (Yen-ling 延齡). 342-386. CS 8.15a-19b. Also known as Prince of Tung-hai, Duke of Hai-hsi, and Emperor Fei ("Deposed," r. 365-371). He was the son of Emperor Ch'eng (Ssu-ma Yen*, r. 326-342) and son-in-law of Yü Ping. He succeeded his older brother, Ssu-ma P'ei (Emperor Ai, r. 362-365), but fell victim to the ambition of the would-be usurper, Huan Wen, who deposed him in 371 on an unsubstantiated charge that the emperor was impotent and that his three sons who were in line for the succession had actually been fathered by palace favorites. CYC. II, 59, (101); IX, 41; XIV, 35; XXV, 38; XXXIII, 12.

SSU-MA JUI 司馬睿 (Ching-wen 景文). 276-322. CS 6.7a-15a. A great-grandson of Ssu-ma I 懿, and eldest son of Ssu-ma Chin 覲 (d. 304). He was named Prince of Lang-yeh in 290 and cavalier attendant-in-ordinary in 292. During the "War of the Eight Princes" (300-306) he fought with his uncle, the Prince of Tung-an (Ssu-ma Yu 繇) against the Prince of Ch'eng-tu (Ssu-ma Ying), narrowly escaping death when Yu was killed in 304. Later he was stationed in Hsia-p'ei 下邳 (N. Anhui) as governor-general of military affairs in Hsü Province (N. Kiangsu and Anhui) and shortly thereafter of Yang Province (Kiangsu-Chekiang). In 307, on the advice of Wang Tao, he set up loyalist headquarters in Chien-yeh (Nanking), becoming chancellor in 315, ascending the throne as Emperor Yüan of Eastern Chin in 317. He died early in 322 during the rebellion of Wang Tun. He is also known by his temple name, Chung-tsung. CFCS. II, 29; V, 23, 45; VIII, 46; IX, 13; X, 11, 13; XII, 3; XIII, 5; XVIII, 7; XXII, 7; XXV, 11; XXIV, 2.

SSU-MA LUN 司馬倫 (Tzu-i 子彝). d. 301. CS 59.9b-18a. The ninth son of Ssu-ma I, by Mme. Po 柏. He was named Prince of Lang-yeh on the accession of Emperor Wu in 265, and later (ca. 277) Prince of Chao. After deposing and murdering Empress Chia in 300, he usurped the throne in the following year, but was quickly eliminated by the Prince of Ch'i, Ssu-ma Chiung. CFCS. I, 18; V, 19; IX, 46; (XV, 2).

SSU-MA NAN-TI 司馬南弟. mid-fourth cent. The daughter of Emperor Ming (Ssu-ma Shao, r. 323-325), named Princess of Lu-ling in 323, the wife of Liu Hui. CYC. XXV, 36.

SSU-MA P'EI 司馬丕 (Ch'ien-ling 千齡). 340-365. CS 8.11a-15a. Eldest son of Emperor Ch'eng (Ssu-ma Yen*, r. 326-342) and originally declared crown prince by him. Since he was only an infant at his father's death, he was temporarily set aside by Yü Ping in favor of his uncle, Ssu-ma Yüeh* (Emperor K'ang, r. 343-344), and did not come to the throne until 362. Since he died shortly thereafter, he is known to posterity as the Lamented Emperor (Ai-ti, r. 362-365). A devotee of Taoism, he tried a diet which avoided the five cereals, which, in conjunction with his experiments with elixirs, greatly hastened his demise. CHS. V, 41, (65).

SSU-MA P'I 司馬毗. early fourth cent. The legal heir of the Prince of Tung-hai, Ssu-ma Yüeh. VIII, 34.

SSU-MA SHAO 司馬紹 (Tao-ch'i 道畿). 299-325. CS 6.15b-22b. The eldest son of Emperor Yüan (Ssu-ma Jui, r. 317-322) by a concubine, née Hsün 荀, declared crown prince in 317, despite his father's wish to replace him with the son of Empress Cheng, Ssu-ma Yü, who later ruled as Emperor Chien-wen, 371-372. When Wang Tun first revolted in 322, fearing Shao's considerable ability, he attempted to set him aside, but after Shao's accession as Emperor Ming (r. 323-324), he himself crushed Wang's second and last revolt in 324. He is sometimes referred to by his posthumous title, Su-tsung 肅宗. CHS. V, 23, 30, 32, 37, 45; VII, 13; IX, 14, 17, 19, 22; XI, 5; XII, 3; XIII, 5; XIV, 23; XX, 6; XXV, 17; XXVII, 6; XXXIII, 7.

SSU-MA SHIH 司馬師 (Tzu-yüan 子元). 208-255. CS 2.1a-7b. The eldest son of Ssu-ma I 懿 and elder brother of Ssu-ma Chao. He became cavalier attendant-in-ordinary around 238, and generalissimo early in 252, replacing his father as the chief holder of power in the Wei state. After deposing the third Wei ruler, Ts'ao Fang 曹芳, in 254, he undertook in 255 personally to crush the uprising of Kuan-ch'iu Chien 毋丘儉 and Wen Ch'in in the southeast, but died of a malignant tumor in the same year. He received the posthumous title, Prince Ching 景王. WS. II, 16; XIX, 8; XXV, 3; XXXIII, 13.

SSU-MA TAO-TZU 司馬道子 (Tao-tzu 道子). 364-402. CS 64.13b-22b. Fifth son of Emperor Chien-wen (Ssu-ma Yü, r. 371-372), and brother of Emperor Hsiao-wu (Ssu-ma Yao, r. 373-396); also known as Prince Hsiao-wen. Inheriting his father's title, Prince of K'uai-chi, he also held titles as director of instruction, governor of Yang Province (Kiangsu-Anhui-Chekiang), and grand tutor, with the posthumous title of chancellor. Because of his position, his faction, which included Wang Kuo-pao and Tao-tzu's own son, Yüan-hsien, dominated the Eastern Chin court from 385 until 402, when it was finally crushed by Wang Kung and Huan Hsüan, Tao-tzu himself perishing in the holocaust. His reputation was one of prodigality and corruption, mingled with a curious piety and lavish patronage of Buddhism. *Hsiao-wen wang chuan.* II, 98, 100, 101; IV, 58; V, 65; VIII, 154; (XXV, 58); XXXII, 2; XXXVI, 7.

SSU-MA TE-TSUNG 司馬德宗 (Te-tsung 德宗). 382-418. CS 10.1a-14b. The eldest son of Emperor Hsiao-wu (Ssu-ma Yao, r. 373-396), he was named crown prince in 387, and later ruled as Emperor An from 397 until his death at the hands of Liu Yü* two years before the fall of Chin. (XXIII, 50).

SSU-MA TSUNG 司馬綜. late fourth cent. Mentioned, CS 64.8b-9a. The eldest son and heir of Ssu-ma Hsi. Involved with his father in a plot against the throne in 371, he was exiled to Hsin-an (western Chekiang). *CMHC*. XXVIII, 7.

SSU-MA T'UNG 司馬彤 (Tzu-cheng 子徼). d. 301? *CS* 38.8b-11b. A son of Ssu-ma I by Mme. Chang 張. He was named Prince of Liang on the accession of Emperor Wu in 265, and after his half brother, Lun, usurped the throne in 301 he became grand minister and a pillar of state in Lun's government. He was subsequently killed during the uprising of the other princes against Lun. *CFCS*. I, *18*.

SSU-MA WU-CHI 司馬無忌 (Kung-shou 公壽). d. 350. *CS* 37.26ab. Also known as Prince Lieh, heir of Prince Min of Chiao, Ssu-ma Ch'eng. After serving as a palace a tendant between 326 and 334, he joined the administration of Ch'u P'ou while the latter was governor of Chiang Province (Hupei-Kiangsi). Early during the rebellion of Wang Tun (322) Tun had killed Wu-chi's father, Ssu-ma Ch'eng, then governor of Hsiang Province (Hunan), through the agency of Wang I*, and the shadow of this memory darkened Wu-chi's life. In 343 he became cavalier attendant-in-ordinary, and later grand warden of Nan (Hupei) and Ho-tung (northern Hunan) commanderies. He accompanied Huan Wen on his campaign against Shu (Szechwan) in 347 and died three years later. *Ssu-ma Wu-chi PC*. VII, 27; XXXVI, *3*, 4.

SSU-MA YAO 司馬曜 (Ch'ang-ming 昌明). 362-396. *CS* 9.6a-18b. Third son of Emperor Chien-wen (Ssu-ma Yü, r. 371-372), he succeeded the latter as Emperor Hsiao-wu (r. 373-396). He was a gifted and intelligent ruler, but toward the end of his reign somewhat given to debauchery. Eventually falling victim to palace intrigues, he was smothered to death by a disgruntled harem favorite whom he had teased about her age. He is sometimes referred to by his temple name, Lieh-tsung. *WCC*. I, 46; II, *89*, 90, 94, 101; V, 64, 65; VI, 40; VII, 28; XII, 6; XVII, 17; XXII, 5; XXV, 60; XXXII, 3; XXXIV, 6, 7.

SSU-MA YEN 司馬炎 (An-shih 安世). 236-290. *CS* 3. Son of Ssu-ma Chao, he accepted the abdication of the last Wei ruler and ruled as Emperor Wu of Chin from 265 to 290. Ennobled around 251, his rise at the Wei court was rapid. With his father's enfeoffment as Prince of Chin in 264, he was named legal heir, and on his father's death the following year, he succeeded to his principality, waiting only the suitable time to complete the formality of founding a new dynasty. In 280, after the conquest of Wu, he was for a while ruler of all China. He is also known by his posthumous title, Shih-tsu. *ChinSP*. I, *17*; II, 19, 20, 78; V, 9, 10, 11, 14, 15, 16; VII, 4; VIII, 17; IX, 32; X, 7; XII, 1; XIX, 13; XX, 2; XXV, 5; XXX, 3, 8; XXXIV, 4; XXXV, 4, 5.

SSU-MA YEN* 司馬衍 (Shih-ken 世根). 321-342. *CS* 7.1a-12b. Eldest son of Emperor Ming (r. 323-325), he was declared crown prince in 325, when he was only four years old. His father died shortly afterward and he ascended the throne as Emperor Ch'eng (r. 326-342), while his mother, Empress Yü, served as regent, and his uncle, Yü Liang, headed the dominant faction at court until Liang's death in 340. The emperor had barely come of age when he too died. *CSP*. II, 53; III, *11*; V, 34, 39, 41, (53).

SSU-MA YING 司馬穎 (Chang-tu 章度, var. Shu-tu 叔度). 279-306. CS 59.28a-32a. Sixteenth (PWKS has nineteenth) son of Ssu-ma Yen, and son-in-law of Yüeh Kuang. He was enfeoffed Prince of Ch'eng-tu and stationed in Yeh (S. Hopei). During the Prince of Chao's (Ssu-ma Lun) brief usurpation in 300, Ying rallied to the loyalist forces led by the Prince of Ch'i (Ssu-ma Chiung) to suppress him, and the "War of the Eight Princes" (300-306) began. From then until he was finally captured by imperial order and strangled in 306, he was involved in continual intrigue and fighting between the princely contenders for the throne. He was also known at various times by his titles, Imperial Younger Brother, chancellor, and generalissimo. CPWKS. II, *25*.

SSU-MA YU 司馬攸 (Ta-yu 大猷). 248-283. CS 38.11b-16b. The second son of Ssu-ma Chao, and younger brother of Emperor Wu (Ssu-ma Yen, r. 265-290); named Prince of Ch'i in 265 and placed in charge of all military operations for the Chin empire. A man of refined sensibilities and some literary ability, he was favored, both by popular regard and his brother's consent, for the succession, since the crown prince, Ssu-ma Chung, was obviously an imbecile. However, through the machinations of Hsün Hsü and others, who feared for their own favored positions at court should the succession go to Yu, the emperor's judgment, weakened by illness, was swayed late in 282 or early 283 to banish Yu to the family estate in Honei (Honan), while Chung's succession was confirmed. Deeply hurt, Ssu-ma Yu became seriously ill and died a few months later. CYC. IX, *32*; XIX, 14.

SSU-MA YÜ 司馬昱 (Tao-wan 道萬). 320-372. CS 8.1a-6a. The youngest son of Emperor Yüan (Ssu-ma Jui, r. 317-322) by the concubine, Lady Cheng 鄭. Though his candidacy to succeed Emperor K'ang in 344 was supported by the Yü faction at court, various intrigues prevented him from coming to the throne until 371/372, as Emperor Chien-wen, when he was over fifty, and then only as the puppet of Huan Wen. His previous titles had been Prince of Lang-yeh (until 326, and again from 365 to 371), Prince of K'uai-chi (326-365), Generalissimo Controlling the Army (345-357), director of instruction (357-366), and chancellor (366-371). He had a reputation for inward tranquillity and was a devoted patron of "pure conversation" and Buddhism. HCYC. I, *37*; II, 39, 48, 56, 57, 59, 60, 61, 89, 101; III, 20, 21; IV, 29, 40, 44, 51, 53, 56, 80, 85, 87; V, 23, 49, 65; VI, 25; VIII, 75, 89, 91, 106, 111, 113, 118, 138, 144; IX, 31, 34, 36, 37, 39, 40, 49, 65; (XII, 6); XIV, 34, 35; XXIII, 41; XXV, 11, 34, 38, 46, 54; XXVI, 18, 31; XXVIII, 5; XXXIII, 12, 15.

SSU-MA YÜ* 司馬遹 (Hsi-tsu 熙祖). d. 300. CS 53.1a-8a. The eldest son of Emperor Hui (Ssu-ma Chung, r. 290-306) by a concubine, and a favorite of his grandfather, Ssu-ma Yen (r. 265-290). He became crown prince with his father's accession in 290, but incurred the jealousy of Empress Chia, who deposed him as crown prince in 299 and executed him the following year, triggering the "War of the Eight Princes" (300-306). He is usually referred to by his posthumous title, Crown Prince Min-huai (Min-huai t'ai-tzu). (XXIII, 22).

SSU-MA YÜEH 司馬越 (Yüan-ch'ao 元超). d. 311. CS 59.36a-40a. Usually referred to as the Prince of Tung-hai, the second son of Ssu-ma T'ai. He began as a member of the crown prince's staff and served as an officer in the Palace Guard. He was a personal attendant during the regency of Yang Chün in 290, winning merit in Empress Chia's removal of the Yang consort-family the following year, whereupon he became a marquis, cavalier attendant-in-ordinary, vice-president of the Imperial Secretariat, and eventually Prince of Tung-hai. In 300 he was made president of the Central Secretariat. He was invited by Emperor Hui (r. 290-306) to assume control of the government as president of the Imperial Secretariat in 303, and remained the chief figure at court until he had suppressed the last of the insurgent princes in 306. The following year, when Emperor Huai (Ssu-ma Chih 熾, r. 307-313) ascended the throne, he continued, with occasional interludes, to wield supreme power as grand tutor and director of works. He died in the fall of Lo-yang. CPWKS. VI, *10*; VIII, 28, 33, 34.

SSU-MA YÜEH* 司馬岳 (Shih-t'ung 世同). 321-344. CS 7.12b-15b. The son of Emperor Ming (Ssu-ma Shao, r. 323-325), and younger brother of Emperor Ch'eng (Ssu-ma Yen*, r. 326-342) by the same mother. He ascended the throne in his twenty-second year in precedence over his elder brother, at the urging of Yü Ping, who was then the dominant figure at court, but died only two years later. He is known as Emperor K'ang, r. 342-344. CHS. V, *41*.

SU CHÜN 蘇峻 (Tzu-kao 子高). d. 328. CS 100.20b-24b. He gained a reputation for valor among the immigrants from the north in the Eastern Chin court around 317 and was made governor of Huai-ling Principality with noble rank in 323. After crushing Wang Tun's revolt in 324, he felt sufficiently powerful to take on the Yü faction, then dominant at court, and raised an armed coup in 327. After occupying the capital in 328, he was eventually killed the same year. WYCS; CYC. V, 25, *34*, 36, 37; VI, 17, 23; X, 16; XIV, 23; XVII, 8; XXIII, 30; XXVII, 8; XXIX, 8.

SU SHAO 蘇紹 (Shih-ssu 世嗣). 247-300. SKWei 16.5a, comm. The son of Su Yü. He served as tutor to the Chin Prince of Wu (Ssu-ma Yen 炎) and held several noble titles under the Chin. He bore a double relationship to Shih Ch'ung, being both the husband of Ch'ung's elder sister and uncle of his wife. CKSH. IX, 57.

SU TSE 蘇則 (Wen-shih 文師). d. 223. SKWei 16.2b-5a. The father of Su Yü. His early career was spent in the service of the Later Han government of frontier towns, where he attracted the attention of Ts'ao Ts'ao and served as guide for his army during the latter's suppression of the Taoist rebel Chang Lu 張魯 in Han-chung (southern Shensi) in 215. With the founding of Wei in 220, he came to Lo-yang and served as personal attendant to Emperor Wen (Ts'ao P'ei, r. 220-226). WeiS. IX, 57.

SU YÜ 蘇愉 (Hsiu-yü 休豫). fl. mid-third cent. The second son of Su Tse. He became grand ordinary and Great Officer of Brilliant Favor under the Western Chin, and was once praised for his loyalty and wisdom by Shan T'ao. CPKM; STCS. IX, 57.

SUN A-HENG 孫阿恒. second half, fourth cent. The daughter of Sun Ch'o and wife of Wang Ch'u-chih, whose ugliness and ill-temper, according to reports, surpassed even her husband's. *Wang SP*. XXVII, *12*.

SUN CH'IEN 孫潛 (Ch'i-yu 齊由). d. ca. 397. *CS* 82.12b. Eldest son of Sun Sheng and elder brother of Sun Fang. In 397, when Yin Chung-k'an, then grand warden of Yü-chang (Kiangsi), joined Wang Kung's attack on Wang Kuo-pao, he put pressure on Ch'ien to join his staff as advisory aide. Ch'ien adamantly held out against it, but died shortly afterward. *CPKM*. II, (40), *50*.

SUN CH'O 孫綽 (Hsing-kung 興公). fl. 330-365. *CS* 56.16a-19b. In his day he was considered the "Crown of literary men" and was much in demand as the composer of obituaries and eulogies. A devout Buddhist layman and disciple of Chih Tun, he attempted to harmonize Buddhism and the contemplative life with Confucianism and an active political career. See H. Wilhelm, "Sun Ch'o's *Yü-tao-lun*," *Sino-Indian Studies* V (1957), 261-271, and Richard Mather, "The Mystical Ascent of the T'ien-t'ai Mountains: Sun Ch'o's *Yu T'ien-t'ai-shan fu*, *Monumenta Serica*, XX (1961), 226-245. *CHS*; *SCFH*. II, *84*; IV, 30, 36, 78, 81, 84, 86, 89, 91, 93; V, 48; VI, 28; VIII, 85, 107, 119; IX, 36, 54, 61, 65; XIV, 37; XXV, 37, 41, (46), 52, 54; XXVI, 9, 14, 15, 16, 17, 22; XXVII, 12.

SUN CH'U 孫楚 (Tzu-ching 子荊). d. 282. *CS* 56.12a-16a. Grandfather of Sun Ch'o and Sun T'ung. After a life of seclusion in his native T'ai-yüan Commandery (Shansi), in 264, when he was over forty, he became an aide in the headquarters of the Wei emissary to Wu, Shih Pao 石苞, and on Shih's behalf composed a letter to the newly enthroned Wu ruler, Sun Hao (r. 264-280), which is preserved in *WH* 43.5a-8b. After the founding of Chin in 265, he joined the staff of his old friend, the Prince of Fu-feng (Ssu-ma Chün), and in 290 became grand warden of P'ing-i (Shensi), where he died two years later. *WSC*; *CYC*. II, *24*; IV, 72; XVII, 3; XXV, 6.

SUN CH'ÜAN 孫權 (Chung-mou 仲謀). 182-252. *SKWu* 2.1a-32b. The younger brother of Sun Ts'e, whom he succeeded in 200 as Marquis of Wu. In 229 he established the Kingdom of Wu (229-280), with its capital at Chien-yeh (Nanking), reigning from 229 to 252, with the posthumous title, Emperor Ta. *WuC*. XIV, *27*.

SUN EN 孫恩 (Ling-hsiu 靈秀). d. 402. *CS* 100.24b-27b. A nephew of the Taoist magician, Sun T'ai 泰. After T'ai's execution in 393, En raised an army in the coastal area of modern Chekiang to avenge him, killing Wang Ning-chih, the governor of K'uai-chi Principality, and overrunning the eastern part of Yang Province in 399, threatening the capital itself. After creating great havoc, he was eventually put down and killed in 402 by the armies of Liu Yü* and Liu Lao-chih. *CATC*. I, *45*.

SUN FANG 孫放 (Ch'i-chuang 齊莊). b. ca. 327. *CS* 82.12b-13a. Second son of Sun Sheng, renowned in his day as a precocious child. As an adult he became minister of Ch'ang-sha (Hunan). *Sun Fang PC*. II, 49, *50*; XXV, 33.

SUN HAO 孫皓 (Yüan-tsung 元宗, alias P'eng-tsu 彭祖). 242-284. SKWu 3.12a-29b. The last ruler of the Wu Kingdom (r. 264-280), known after his surrender to Chin in 280 as Marquis Returned to Obedience (Kuei-ming hou 歸命侯). He was the son of Sun Ho 和 and a grandson of the founder of Wu, Sun Ch'üan. WuL. II, 21; III, 4; X, 5; XXV, 5; XXXIV, 2.

SUN HSIU 孫休 (Tzu-lieh 子烈). 235-264. SKWu 3.5a-11b. The sixth son of Sun Ch'üan, he became the third ruler of the Wu Kingdom, known as Emperor Ching (r. 258-264). Studious and conscientious by nature, he is said to have neglected his books only during the pheasant season. HCWC; TLWS. X, 4.

SUN HSIU* 孫秀 (Chün-chung 俊忠). d. 301. He first served in a minor capacity under Ssu-ma Lun while the latter was prince of Sun's native Lang-yeh (Shantung). When Lun became Prince of Chao (Shansi), Hsiu* moved his family and continued in the prince's administration, high in his favor. Late in 300, when Lun attempted to usurp the throne, Hsiu* was president of the Central Secretariat and made all the major decisions. But when Lun fell in the spring of 301, Sun was executed by the Prince of Ch'i, Ssu-ma Chiung. CCKT; CYC. XIX, 17; XXXVI, 1.

SUN HSIU** 孫秀 (Yen-ts'ai 彥才). late third cent. A native of Wu Commandery (Soochow) and member of the Wu royal family. Feared by the last ruler, Sun Hao (r. 264-280), he fled for refuge to the Western Chin court at Lo-yang about 276, after which he was made governor of Chiao Province (Annam). TYKSL. XXXV, 4.

SUN SHENG 孫盛 (An-kuo 安國). ca. 302-373. CS 82.11a-12b. A grandson of Sun Ch'u, and first cousin of Sun T'ung and Sun Ch'o. He was the author of two lost histories frequently quoted in the SSHY Commentary, viz., the Wei-shih ch'un-ch'iu (WSCC), and the Chin yang-ch'iu (CYC), and in his own day gained a reputation for his skill as a conversationalist, his views tending toward the Juist "Teaching of Names" (ming-chiao). A quotation from his essay, "The Symbols of the 'Changes' Are More Subtle than the Visible Shapes of Nature" (I-hsiang miao-yü hsien-hsing), may be found at IV, 56, comm. After fleeing southward from T'ai-yüan (Shansi) in 312, he served successively on the staffs of T'ao K'an, Yü Liang, and Huan Wen, ending as curator of the Palace Library. (CHS). II, 49, IV, 25, 31, 56; XXV, 25, 33.

SUN TENG 孫登 (Kung-ho 公和). fl. 260-265. CS 94.1b-2b. A recluse who lived in a cave in the hills north of Chi Commandery (Honan), he was admired by both Hsi K'ang and Juan Chi. KCH; WSCC; WYCS. XVIII, 2.

SUN T'ENG 孫騰 (Po-hai 伯海; baby name, Seng-nu 僧奴). fl. late fourth cent. A son of Sun T'ung and nephew of Sun Ch'o. After a broad education he held a succession of offices culminating in director of punishments. CPKM. IX, 69.

SUN TS'E 孫策 (Po-fu 伯符). 175-200. SKWu 1.7b-17a. The eldest son of Sun Chien 堅 (d. 193), and elder brother of the founder of the Wu Kingdom, Sun Ch'üan (r. 222-252). Inheriting his father's estate in his nineteenth year (193), he began laying the groundwork for his brother's later rise. *WuL.* XIII, *11*; XXVIII, 9.

SUN T'UNG 孫統 (Ch'eng-kung 承公). fl. mid-fourth cent. *CS* 56.16a. Grandson of Sun Ch'u, and elder brother of Sun Ch'o. He fled south with his brother and his cousin, Sun Sheng, sometime between 307 and 312. Of a somewhat undisciplined nature, he preferred literature and country excursions in the K'uai-chi hills to public office, but did once serve as magistrate of Yü-yao Prefecture (Chekiang). *CHS.* VIII, 75; IX, *59*; XXIII, 36; (XXVI, 17).

SUNG WEI 宋禕. fl. ca. 324. A skilled flute (*ti*)-player, she had learned her art as an apprentice of Lü-chu, the celebrated concubine of Shih Ch'ung (d. 300). Later she entered the harem of Emperor Ming (Ssu-ma Shao, r. 323-325), but when the emperor's illness became serious, she was let go. The first to take her as a concubine was Juan Fu (d. 326). Earlier she had apparently been in the possession of Wang Tun (d. 324), and her final master was Hsieh Shang (d. 357). *IWLC* 44, under *ti.* IX, 21.

TAI K'UEI 戴逵 (An-tao 安道). d. 396. *CS* 94.31b-33b. A painter-musician who lived most of his days a recluse in the K'uai-chi area (Chekiang), with occasional visits to the capital, never accepting calls to public office. His "Treatise on Libertinism being Contrary to the Way" (*Fang-ta wei fei-tao lun* 放達為非道論) is quoted *in extenso* in his biography and shows him to have been thoroughly Confucian in outlook, though scornful of what he considered the superficiality of the contemporary literati. He was himself a Buddhist, and another treatise, "On the Resolution of Doubtful Points" (*Shih-i lun* 釋疑論), together with some of the correspondence on the subject with the monk Hui-yüan is preserved in the Buddhist anthology, *Kuang hung-ming chi* 18, *Taishō* 52.221c-224a. In these writings he still maintains the essentially Confucian view that one's lot in life is a matter of destiny, unaffected by good or evil karma. *CATC.* VI, *34*; VII, 17; XVII, 13; XVIII, 12, 15; XXI, 6, 8; XXIII, 47; XXV, 49.

TAI LU 戴逯. See TAI TUN.

TAI TUN 戴逯 (An-ch'iu 安邱). fl. 356-378. *CS* 94.33b. The elder brother of Tai K'uei, who, unlike K'uei, led an active public life, accompanying Huan Wen on his northern campaign of 356, and serving as grand warden of P'ei Commandery (southern Shantung) during Fu Chien's attempt to conquer it in 378. His highest office was grand director of agriculture. *Tai SP.* XVIII, *12*.

TAI YÜAN 戴淵, var. YEN 儼 (Jo-ssu 若思). ca. 260-322. *CS* 69.12b-14a. In his youth he was swashbuckling and undisciplined, and spent his time raiding the boats plying back and forth on the canals of his native commandery of Kuang-ling (Kiangsu). It was Lu Chi, a victim of one of Tai's raids while on his way north in 289 (see *SSHY* XV, 2), who is credited with starting him on a creditable career. Thereafter he served under several of the Western Chin princes, and with the establishment of Eastern Chin in 317 he became governor-general of military affairs in six provinces. After failing to halt Wang Tun at Shih-t'ou (the port of Chien-k'ang) in 322. he was executed by the latter together with Chou I. *YYCS*. VIII, *54*; XV, 2.

T'AI-SHU KUANG 太叔廣 (Chi-ssu 季思). d. 304. When the court instated Ssu-ma Ying, Prince of Ch'eng-tu, as next in line for the throne in 304, T'ai-shu was working in Ying's administration in Yeh (northern Honan). Ying sent him as his personal envoy to the capital in Lo-yang, but T'ai-shu, whose family lived in the capital, fearing reprisals against them from Ying's rivals at court, committed suicide instead. *WYCS*. IV, *73*.

TAO-CH'IEN 道潛. See CHU CH'IEN.

TAO-I. See CHU TAO-I.

TAO-YAO 道曜. fl. ca. 400. A Buddhist monk who was friendly with Huan Hsüan. XXV, 63.

T'AO FAN 陶範 (Tao-tse 道則; baby name, Hu-nu 胡奴). fl. ca. 376. *CS* 66.20b. Ninth (some say tenth) son of T'ao K'an, and the only one of K'an's seventeen sons to achieve fame. In 376 he was made Great Officer of Brilliant Favor. *T'ao K'an PC*; *CHS*. IV, 97; V, *52*.

T'AO K'AN 陶侃 (Shih-hsing 士行). 259-334. *CS* 66.6a-18b. Originally a native of what is now Hupei, he lost his father and lived in poverty with his mother. After the Wu Kingdom fell in 280, he moved to Lu-chiang (Anhui), where he held several minor posts before going north to Lo-yang, where he came under the patronage of Chang Hua. In 311 he returned south to become grand warden of Wu-ch'ang (Hupei). After the establishment of Eastern Chin in 317 he was dispatched south to become governor-general of military affairs in Chiao Province (Annam), and later governor of the three southern provinces of Hsiang, Kuang, and Ching (Hunan-Hupei and Kwangtung-Kwangsi) with the title, Duke of Ch'ang-sha. He figured prominently in putting down the rebellions both of Wang Tun in 324 and of Su Chün in 328, for which he was made personal attendant and grand marshal in 329. *T'ao-shih hsü*; *WYCS*. II, *47*; III, 11, 16; IV, 97; V, 39; XIV, 23; XIX, 19, 20; XXVII, 8.

TENG AI 鄧艾 (Shih-tsai 士載). 197-264. *SKWei* 28.16b-25b. He lost his father while very young, and fled as a refugee with his mother to Ju-nan Commandery (Honan) during Ts'ao Ts'ao's campaign in the south in 208. He worked for a time as a hired hand for a local farmer, then moved to Ying-ch'uan (Honan), where he began his schooling, but because of an impediment in his speech was unable at first to get official employment. Later he came to the attention of Ssu-ma I, who took him on his staff about 240. He moved to the Imperial Secretariat, where he supervised grain supplies for the army and instituted numerous irrigation and canal projects to increase production and transport. In 249 he accompanied an expedition against the Shu Kingdom in the southwest for which he received noble rank. In 256, after a successful campaign in the northwest, he was heaped with further honors and named General

Governing the West, and governor-general in charge of military affairs in Lung-yu (Shensi and Kansu). He accompanied Chung Hui on the campaign against Shu of 263, but, unjustly implicated in Chung's attempted rebellion the following year, he was executed with all his sons. His wife and grandchildren were banished to Central Asia. *WC*. II, *17*.

TENG HSIA 鄧遐 (Ying-yüan 應遠). d. ca. 370. *CS* 81.24a. Sometime grand warden of Ching-ling (Hupei) and officer under Huan Wen noted for his bravery. After the latter's defeat at Fang-t'ou (southern Honan), in the campaign against Former Yen in 369, he was dismissed because Huan "was ashamed and angry and afraid of him." He died soon thereafter. *TSMLSM*. XXVIII, 6.

TENG YANG 鄧颺 (Hsüan-mao 玄茂). d. 249. *SKWei* 9.21a, comm. (citing *WeiL*). He served as a clerk in the Central Secretariat during the reign of Emperor Ming (Ts'ao Jui, r. 227-239), but through some factional involvement was dismissed. Later, about 240, he joined the loyalist forces around Ts'ao Shuang against the Ssu-ma clan and was named grand warden of Yung-ch'uan Commandery (Honan), later rising to personal attendant and president of the Board of Civil Office. Described as avaricious by nature, he was not above receiving bribes from office-seekers. Ho Yen's meteoric rise was blamed on him, and when Ts'ao Shuang fell in 249, both Teng and Ho perished with him. *WeiL*. VII, *3*; X, 6.

TENG YU 鄧攸 (Po-tao 伯道). d. 326. *CS* 90.12a-14b. Orphaned while very young, he lived in reduced circumstances with his younger brother, but eventually came to the attention of the courtier Chia Hun 賈混, who gave him his daughter in marriage. Thereafter he moved in and out of the employ of the various Chin princes during the perilous years of the "War of the Eight Princes (301-306). Later he was appointed grand warden of Ho-tung Commandery (Shansi), but was captured when Shih Lo overran the area around 311. After some harrowing experiences he escaped and fled with his family through bandit-infested territory to Chien-k'ang, south of the Yangtze, but at the cost of having to abandon his only son in order to save the orphaned son of his brother. He held several important posts in the Eastern Chin government and helped suppress the rebellion of Wang Tun in 322. His final office was vice-president of the Imperial Secretariat. *CYC*; *TTCC*; *WYCS*; *CHS*. I, *28*; V, *25*; VIII, *34*, *140*; IX, *18*.

TIAO HSIEH 刁協 (Hsüan-liang 玄亮). d. 322. *CS* 69.8a-11b. After fleeing south around 307, he became vice-president of the Imperial Secretariat with the founding of Eastern Chin in Chien-k'ang in 317, and later president, in which capacity he assisted in drawing up a law code for the new dynasty. He strongly resisted the power of Wang Tao's faction at court, and enjoyed Emperor Yüan's confidence in the latter's fight against the rebel, Wang Tun, but was killed as he fled from the capital during Tun's first assault in 322. *YYCS*. V, *23*, *27*; VIII, *54*.

TIAO YÜEH 刁約. late fourth cent. A retainer in Hsieh An's household. XVII, 15.

TING T'AN 丁潭 (Shih-k'ang 世康). ca. 300-380. *CS* 78.12a-14b. A native of K'uai-chi Commandery (Chekiang), who in 320 became Wang Tao's sergeant-at-arms. Later he served as grand warden of Tung-yang Commandery (Chekiang), where he won praise for his incorruptible administration. When Emperor Ch'eng (Ssu-ma Yen*, r. 326-342) mounted the throne in 326 he was made cavalier attendant-in-ordinary, and throughout the ordeal of Su Chün's revolt in 327 never left the emperor's side, for which he was rewarded with noble rank after the revolt was suppressed in 328. He was named Great Officer of Brilliant Favor in 343 and remained in high honor until his death many years later in his eightieth year. *KCHHC*. IX, 13.

TS'AI HUNG 蔡洪 (Shu-k'ai 叔開). late third cent. Beginning his career in the Wu Kingdom, he was recommended by his local governor around 285 to go up to Lo-yang for the Chin capital examinations for the degree of *hsiu-ts'ai*. His highest post was magistrate of Sung-tzu Prefecture (Anhui). (*Ts'ai*) *Hung chi-lu*; *WYCS*. II, *22*; VIII, 20.

TS'AI K'O 蔡克 (Tzu-ni 子尼). d. 306. *CS* 77.11b-12b. The father of Ts'ai Mo, and an indirect descendant of Ts'ai Yung. A man of upright and somewhat forbidding character, he became an officer on the staff of the Prince of Ch'eng-tu (Ssu-ma Ying), ca. 302. Later joining the staff of Ssu-ma T'eng 騰 in Ho-pei, he was killed in the fall of Yeh (northern Hopei) in 306. *CCKT*; (*Ts'ai*) *K'o PC*. XXVI, *6*.

TS'AI MO 蔡謨 (Tao-ming 道明). 281-356. *CS* 77.11b-19b. The son of Ts'ai K'o, he began his career in the administration of the Prince of Tung-hai, Ssu-ma Yüeh, fleeing south sometime between 307 and 312, where he became a clerk on the staff of Wang Tun, while the latter was grand warden of I-hsing Commandery (Kiangsi). Later he was personal attendant in the palace, and in 327 fought against Su Chün in his capacity as governor of Wu Commandery (Soochow). He participated in a northern campaign under Yü Liang in 333, but returned after a disagreement with him. He remained, however, a partisan of the Yü faction at court, in opposition to Wang Tao. In 339 he was named General Chastizing the North, governor-general of military affairs in three provinces, and governor of Hsü Province (northern Kiangsu). In 342 he attained his highest office, director of instruction, but in 350, accused of having neglected his duties for three years, he was degraded to become a commoner and spent his remaining days in study and teaching. He was an outspoken foe of Buddhism throughout his life and had a reputation for being an extremely proper man. *Ts'ai Ssu-t'u PC*. V, *40*; VIII, 39, 63; XIV, 26; XXV, 29; XXVI, 6; XXXIV, 3; XXXV, 7.

TS'AI HSI 蔡系 (Tzu-shu 子叔). mid-fourth cent. The second son of Ts'ai Mo. He had some reputation as a writer, and became senior administrator to the General Controlling the Army, Ssu-ma Yü (between 345 and 361). *CHS*. VI, *31*; IX, 66(?).

TS'AI YUNG 蔡邕 (Po-chieh 伯喈). 132-192. *HHS* 90B.1a-23b. A poet, calligrapher, and musician noted for his filial devotion to an ailing mother. He penned the characters for the stone-inscribed version of the Classics cut during the reign of Emperor Ling (r. 168-189). During the troubles following the Yellow Turban Revolt of 184 he wandered for awhile as a refugee, then was appointed by Tung Cho to an alarming succession of offices in a brief space of time, ending with left commandant in 190, when he accompanied the hapless Emperor Hsien (r. 190-219) to Ch'ang-an (Shensi). Because of an unguarded remark regretting the assassination of Tung Cho in 192, Ts'ai was thrown into prison, where he died shortly afterward. *HSHS.* IX, *1;* XXVI, 20.

TS'AO CHANG 曹彰 (Tzu-wen 子文). d. 223. *SKWei* 9.1a-2b. The second son of Ts'ao Ts'ao by "Empress" Pien. He had a brown beard and possessed great physical bravery, with little taste for books. When the Wu-huan peoples of Tai Commandery (northern Shansi) rebelled in 218, Chang led the expedition against them, and with vastly inferior numbers inflicted a crushing defeat. After his father's death and the founding of Wei in 220, he was rewarded with a large dukedom and in 222 was named Prince of Jen-ch'eng. The following year, after coming to court and being denied an interview with his brother, Emperor Wen (Ts'ao P'ei, r. 220-226), he died under mysterious circumstances. Some said that he was poisoned. *WSCC; WL.* XXXIII, *1.*

TS'AO CHIH 曹植 (Tzu-chien 子建). 192-232. *SKWei* 19.3a-20b. Third son of Ts'ao Ts'ao, and younger brother, by the same mother, of Ts'ao P'ei, first ruler of Wei (Emperor Wen, r. 220-226). He was a gifted poet, well loved by his father, who more than once wished to make him his heir. When P'ei ascended the throne in 220, Chih was made Marquis of Chüan-cheng (Shantung) and three years later transferred to become Prince of Yung-ch'iu (Honan); still later (329) he was made Prince of Tung-o (Shantung), and after his death canonized as Prince of Ch'en. The frequent shifts made him anxious and unhappy, though the claim that all his poetry is a record of his political frustrations is exaggerated. See H. Frankel, "Fifteen Poems of Ts'ao Chih," *JAOS* 84 (1964), 1-14. *WC.* IV, *66;* V, 2; XXXIII, 1.

TS'AO JUI 曹叡 (Yüan-chung 元仲). 204-239. *SKWei* 3. Eldest son of Ts'ao P'ei (Emperor Wen of Wei, r. 220-227) by Empress Chen. After his mother's deposition and suicide in 221, he was temporarily set aside but succeeded his father as Emperor Ming (r. 227-239). *WMC.* II, *13;* V, 5; XIV, 3; XIX, 7; XXI, 2, 3.

TS'AO MAO 曹髦 (Yen-shih 彥士). 241-260. *SKWei* 4.14a-25b. A grandson of Ts'ao P'ei, he ruled from 254 to 260 and is known by his posthumous title, Duke Kao-kuei. After Ssu-ma Shih had dethroned the Prince of Ch'i, Ts'ao Fang (r. 240-254), the court established Mao but the latter, aware that all power was in the hands of the Ssuma family, personally staged a coup intended to do away with Shih's younger brother and successor, Ssu-ma Chao. Mao was killed during the fighting in the palace grounds by the crown prince's chamberlain, Ch'eng Chi 成濟, under orders from the commander of the Palace Guard, Chia Ch'ung. *WC; HCCC; WSCC; KPCC.* V, *8;* XXXIII, 7.

TS'AO MAO-CHIH 曹茂之 (Yung-shih 永世; baby name, Yü 晔). fl. mid-fourth cent. His highest office was clerk in the Imperial Secretariat. *Ts'ao SP*. IX, *68*.

TS'AO O 曹娥. d. 108. A filial girl of Shang-yü Prefecture (Chekiang) who drowned herself after the death of her father and to whom a monument was erected. *KCTL*. XI, *3*.

TS'AO P'EI 曹丕 (Tzu-huan 子桓). 187-226. *SKWei* 2. The eldest son of Ts'ao Ts'ao and first ruler of the Wei Kingdom as Emperor Wen (r. 220-226). Though not so gifted or well known as a writer as his younger brother, Ts'ao Chih, he produced a voluminous corpus of poems and essays. See, e.g., *WH* 22.4a; 27.13a; 29.9a; 42.5a-8a; and 52.4a-5b (the *Tien-lun* 典論, or "Treatise on Writings," an early attempt at literary criticism). II, *10*, *11*; IV, *66*; V, 2, 3; XIV, 2; XVII, 1; XIX, 4; XXI, 1; XXXIII, 1; XXXV, 1.

TS'AO P'EI-TS'UI 曹佩翠. d. ca. 240. The daughter of a cousin of Ts'ao Ts'ao who was married to Hsün Ts'an. His extreme devotion to her and frank admiration for feminine beauty shocked his contemporaries. (*Hsün*) *Ts'an PC*. XXXV, 2.

TS'AO P'I 曹毗 (Fu-tso 輔佐). mid-fourth cent. *CS* 92.18a-20a. A descendant of the Wei royal family, he won a considerable reputation in his day as a poet, especially for his "Songs to the Nymph, Orchid Fragrance" (*Lan-hsiang ko-shih* 蘭香歌詩), which unhappily do not survive. Like Yü Ch'an, he also wrote a "Poetic Essay on the Yang Capital" (*Yang-tu fu* 揚都賦), but his contemporaries deemed it inferior to Yü's. Ts'ao became an erudite of the Grand Academy and held various minor posts, ending with Great Officer of Brilliant Favor. The text of a complaint he once wrote concerning his unused talents, entitled "To the Literati" (*Tui-ju* 對儒), is preserved in his biography. *CHS*. IV, *93*.

TS'AO SHU 曹淑 (Mme, Ts'ao). late third and early fourth cent. Daughter of Ts'ao Shao 邵, wife of Wang Tao, and mother of Wang Yüeh. She had a reputation for extreme jealousy. *Wang SP*; *TC*. I, 29.

TS'AO TS'AO 曹操 (Meng-te 孟德; baby name, A-man 阿瞞). 155-220. *SKWei* 1. Often referred to as "Emperor Wu of Wei." His father, Ts'ao Sung 嵩, was the adopted son of the chief eunuch under the later Han Emperor Ling (r. 168-189). Fond of bold exploits even from his youth, he was at the same time well educated and a sensitive poet. His reputation was made in the campaign to suppress the Yellow Turban Revolt in 184, and his power increased after his victory over the rival general, Tung Cho, in 190. From 196 onward he was the virtual controller of the declining fortunes of the Later Han Dynasty with the titles generalissimo and chancellor. After his death, his son, P'ei, became the first ruler of the Wei Kingdom (220-265). II, 8; V, 2; VII, 1, 2; (X, 18); XI, 1, 2, 3, 4; XII, 2; (XIII, 4); XIV, 1; XIX, 4; XXVI, 11; XXVIII, 1, 2, 3, 4, 5; XXXI, 1; XXXV, 1.

TSO SSU 左思 (T'ai-ch'ung 太沖). d. 306. *CS* 92.7b-9a. Since his mother died while he was very young, his father was over-indulgent and his early education was slighted. Later, however, he became an omnivorous reader, and, because of an unprepossessing appearance and an impediment in his speech, he kept little company with his fellows, spending all his time in study and writing. He served as a libationer in Chang Hua's administration and later as a secretary for the notorious Chia Mi 賈謐, nephew of Empress Chia. When in 300 the Chia clan was wiped out by the Prince of Chao, Ssu-ma Lun, Tso Ssu retired from public life altogether. It was about 272, when his sister, Tso Fen 芬, entered the harem of Emperor Wu and the family moved to Lo-yang, that he conceived the plan for his "Poetic Essays on the Three Capitals" (San-tu fu 三都賦), on the writing of which he is said to have spent ten years. (Tso) Ssu PC. IV, 68; XIV, 7; (XXIII, 47).

TSOU CHAN 鄒湛 (Jun-fu 潤甫). second half, third cent. He achieved some fame as a writer and served as a personal attendant in the palace at Lo-yang. CCKT. XXV, 7.

TSU KUANG 祖廣 (Yüan-tu 淵度). fl. ca. 400. His highest office was senior administrator to the General Protecting the Army. Tsu SP. XXV, 64.

TSU NA 祖納 (Shih-yen 士言). late third cent., early fourth cent. CS 62.20a-22b. Elder brother of Tsu T'i and Tsu Yüeh by a different mother. After an impoverished youth, through his reputation as a conversationalist he was made tutor to the crown prince and a member of the staff of the director of punishments under Western Chin. Narrowly escaping death during the War of the Eight Princes (301-306), he later fled south with the fall of Western Chin and became an adviser to the Eastern Chin Emperor Yüan (r. 317-322), where he won a reputation as a chess player and was honored with the title, Great Officer of Brilliant Favor. WYCC. I, 26.

TSU T'I 祖逖 (Shih-chih 士稚). 266-321). CS 62.16a-20a. An adventurous type, not given to the amenities, who was still totally illiterate at fourteen. By applying himself assiduously to his books he won the degree Filial and Incorrupt (hsiao-lien) by his twenty-fourth year and not long thereafter the highest degree (hsiu-ts'ai). He served with Liu K'un in the administration of the Capital Province at Lo-yang. After leading a large contingent of his family south sometime around 311/312, he was appointed governor of Hsü Province (Anhui) and later Yü Province (southern Honan) by the Eastern Chin Emperor Yüan (Ssu-ma Jui, r. 317-322). Commissioned to recover the north in 319, he fought several successful battles against the Hsiung-nu generals, Shih Hu and Shih Lo, and in the autumn of 320 was promoted to General Governing the West, but died the following year a disillusioned man, having learned of the rebellious ambitions of Wang Tun. YYCS; CYC. VIII, 43; XIII, 6; XXIII, 23.

TSU YÜEH 祖約 (Shih-shao 士少). d. 330. CS 100.18a-20b. A younger own brother of Tsu T'i and half-brother of Tsu Na. He emigrated south of the Yangtze around 311/312 with his brother, T'i, and there served in minor capacities. Through his brother's influence he became personal attendant to Emperor Yüan (Ssu-ma Jui, r. 317-322), and after T'i's death in 221 succeeded him as governor of Yü Province (Anhui). For his merit in helping to suppress the rebellion of Wang Tun in 324 he was ennobled a marquis. He joined the rebellion of Su Chün against the Yü clan in 327 and was immediately made personal attendant, grand marshal, and president of the Imperial Secretariat in the latter's rebel government, but when the rebellion was crushed the following year Yüeh fled north to take refuge with the Hsiung-nu ruler, Shih Lo (r. 319-333), of Later Chao. Since the Tsu clan had previously been large landholders in Yu Province (Hopei), Shih was reluctant to trust him and in 330, on advice from an underling, put him to death with over one hundred members of his clan. *Tsu Yüeh PC*. VI, 15; VIII, 57, 88, 132; XIV, 22.

TS'UI, Lady 崔氏. d. 318. The daughter of Ts'ui Ts'an 參 and wife of Wen Tan 溫憺. When her son, Wen Ch'iao, went south in 317 to urge Ssu-ma Jui to ascend the throne of Eastern Chin, she was left behind and died within a year, guilt-feelings for which Ch'iao could never overcome. *Wen SP*. XXXIII, 9.

TS'UI LIEH 崔烈 (Wei-k'ao 威考). d. 194. *HHS* 82.20b-21b. His grandfather, father, and uncle were all known in their day as experts in the "Spring and Autumn Annals." After Lieh had purchased the rank of director of instruction under Emperor Ling (r. 168-189) for five million cash, he became known as T'ung-ch'ou ("Copper Stench"). Imprisoned by Tung Cho in 190, he perished four years later in the power struggle between Tung and Ts'ao Ts'ao. *WCC*. IV, 4.

TS'UI PAO 崔豹 (Cheng-hsiung 正熊). late third cent. His highest office was assistant to the grand tutor. *CPKM*. II, 28.

TS'UI YEN 崔琰 (Chi-kuei 季珪). ca. 154-216. *SKWei* 12.1a-7a. A man of impressive physical appearance who had been among the students of Cheng Hsüan but fled during the upheavals of the Yellow Turban Revolt in 184; after wandering four years he returned to Lo-yang to serve under Yüan Shao. When Ts'ao Ts'ao killed Yüan in 202, he took Ts'ui into his own administration as lieutenant-governor of Chi Province (southern Hopei), but when Ts'ao Ts'ao became "Prince of Wei" in 216, he suspected Ts'ui of disloyalty and ordered him to commit suicide. *WeiC*. XIV, 1.

TSUNG CH'ENG 宗承 (Shih-lin 世林). d. ca. 230. A contemporary of Ts'ao Ts'ao who maintained a relative aloofness from the chaotic events of the closing years of Later Han. After reluctantly accepting a post as grand warden of Han-chung (southern Shensi), he accompanied Ts'ao to Yeh (northern Honan) after the latter's pacification of Chi Province (Hopei) in 204, and remained there until the end of the dynasty, treated with respect, but held at low rank. *CKHHC*. V, 2.

TU I 杜乂 (Hung-chih 弘治). d. before 335. *CS* 93.5b-6a. The grandson of Tu Yü, and father of the consort of Emperor Ch'eng (Ssu-ma Yen*, r. 326-342). He died young, while the empress was still a baby, but had a fine reputation both for the delicacy of his physical beauty and the refinement of his manners. He was capital intendant when he died. *CYC*. VIII, *68*, 70; IX, 42; XIV, 26.

TU YÜ 杜預 (Yüan-k'ai 元凱). 222-284. *SKWei* 16.18b-19a, comm.; 34.14a-22a. Despised by some for the low company he kept in his youth, he was married to a younger sister of Ssu-ma Chao, which eased his way after the founding of Chin in 265. After assisting Chia Ch'ung and the others in drawing up a law code for the new dynasty, he was sent west on a series of campaigns against the proto-Tibetan border tribes who were harrassing Chin's western flank. During this period, he was the author of several recommendations to the court on grain storage and transport and price control. In 278 he was appointed General Governing the South, stationed in Hsiang-yang (Hupei), from which base he aided in the eventual crushing of Wu in 280, and remained there as governor-general until his death in 284, having instituted several important hydraulic projects. Though prominent in important military campaigns, he never mounted a horse and could not pierce a target. He had an almost obsessive interest in the *Tso-chuan* and his commentary on this work remained standard for centuries. *WYCS*. V, *12*, 13.

TU YÜ* 杜育 (Fang-shu 方叔). d. 311. He was considered something of a prodigy in his boyhood, and when fully grown possessed a fine manner and bearing, as well as literary talent, but his rank never rose above libationer. He died during the sack of Lo-yang in 311. *CCKT*. IX, *8*.

TUNG AI 董艾 (Shu-chih 叔智). d. 302. A member of the staff of the Prince of Ch'i, Ssu-ma Chiung, said to be jealous of a good reputation but uninterested in keeping the gentleman's code. He left a provincial post to join Chiung in suppressing the Prince of Chao, Ssu-ma Lun, in 301, for which he received a military commission, but perished with Chiung's downfall in 302. *CYC*; *PWKS*. V, *17*.

TUNG YANG 董養 (Chung-tao 仲道). fl. 265-311. *CS* 94.10b. He served under the Western Chin regime at Lo-yang, but "never sought wealth or notoriety." Following the downfall of Empress Yang in 291, he composed a "Treatise on Primordial Moral Influence" (*Yüan-hua lun* 元化論) in protest. Finding portents of impending disaster in Lo-yang after 307, he migrated with his wife to Shu (Szechwan) and was never heard from again. *WYCS*. VIII, *36*.

TUNG-FANG SHUO 東方朔 (Man-ch'ien 曼倩). fl. ca. 100-73 B.C. *SC* 126.7a-10a; *HS* 65.1a-23a. A courtier under Emperor Wu of Han (r. 140-87 B.C.) whose brash self-confidence and ready wit won him special favor with the emperor. Most of the stories clustering about his name appear to be legendary. *HS*; *Tung-fang Shuo PC*; *LHC*. X, *1*.

TUNG-WU HOU-MU 東武侯母. late second cent. B.C. *SC* 126.6b-7a. The wet nurse of Emperor Wu of Han (Liu Ch'e, r. 140-87 B.C.). Because of her favored position, members of her family rose rapidly from low to higher status, and ultimately created such a scandal in the capital that the emperor was about to banish her, but relented. *SC*. X, *1*.

T'UNG CH'IN-I 童秦姬. mid. and late fourth cent. Daughter of T'ung Kuei 僧, and mother of Wu T'an-chih and Wu Yin-chih. *Wu SP*. I, 47.

WANG, Lady 王氏. late third cent. Eldest daughter of Wang Jung and wife of P'ei Wei. *PSCC*. XXIII, 14; XXIX, 5.

WANG, Lady* 王氏. late third to early fourth cent. The sister of Wang K'an and wife of Juan Hsien's brother. VIII, 139.

WANG CHAN 王湛 (Ch'u-ch'ung 處仲). 249-295. *CS* 75.1a-2a. Son of Wang Ch'ang, younger brother of Wang Hun, father of Wang Ch'eng*, and uncle of Wang Chi. He was a large man, with prominent forehead and nose, which gave many persons, including the members of his own family, the impression that he was mentally defective. After his father's death in 259, when he was only ten, he remained for many years in obscurity by his father's grave. Only in 276 did he finally take office on the staff of the crown prince, and eventually rose to become governor of the Principality of Ju-nan (Honan). *TTCC*. VIII, 17. (74); IX, 23; XIX, 15, 16.

WANG CH'ANG 王昶 (Wen-shu 文舒). d. 259. *SKWei* 27.5b-11b. The father of Wang Chan, Wang Lun, and Wang Hun. He began his career on the staff of Ts'ao P'ei during the last years of Later Han, and on P'ei's accession to the Wei throne in 220 was named cavalier attendant and put in charge of developing the agricultural and forest land in the vicinity of the capital. Later he served as governor of Yen Province (southern Shantung), and with the accession of Emperor Ming (Ts'ao Jui, r. 227-239) received noble rank. He presented the emperor a "Treatise on Government" (*Chih-lun* 治論), in which he sought to restore the pre-Ch'in legal system, and a lengthy work on military tactics. The text of his family instructions to his sons and nephews is also carried *in extenso* in his biography. After Ssu-ma I's coup in 249 he again presented a five-point program: (1) recovery of education on the old model and elimination of the new (Neo-Taoist) vogue of frivolity, (2) the use of examinations to test candidates for office, (3) rewards for long and meritorious performance in office, (4) reduction of official salaries to a modest level, and (5) elimination of waste and luxury. Since he had fought successfully in campaigns against both Shu and Wu, and was instrumental in quelling the rebellion of Kuan-ch'iu Chien, he ended his days with the title of director of works. *WC*. VIII, 17; XIX, 15.

WANG CH'ANG* 王敞 (Mao-p'ing 茂平). ca. 282-304. *CS* 65.10a. The second younger brother of Wang Tao, he died before he had taken up the post of libationer to which he was called when he was in his twenty-second year. *Wang SP*. IX, 18.

WANG CHEN-CHIH 王楨之 (Kung-kan 公幹; baby name, Ssu-tao 思道). fl. ca. 400. *CS* 80.12a. A son of Wang Hui-chih, and nephew of Wang Hsien-chih. He served successively as personal attendant, and senior administrator for the grand marshal, Huan Hsüan. *Wang SP*. IX, 86; XXV, 63.

WANG CH'EN 王忱 (Yüan-ta 元達; baby name, Fo-ta 佛大). d. 392. *CS*

75.14b-16a. Fourth son of Wang T'an-chih, and younger brother of Wang Kuo-pao. He served successively as governor of Ching Province (Hunan-Hupei), governor-general of military affairs in three provinces, and General Establishing Valor. An admirer of the eccentric coterie which flourished at the close of Western Chin known as the "Eight Free Spirits" (pa-ta), he shocked the more sober society of the late fourth century by riding to visit his sick father-in-law drunk and unclothed, sometimes remaining drunk for months at a time. CATC. I, 44; III, 24; V, 66; VII, 26, 28; VIII, 150, 153, 154; X, 22, 26; XXIII, 50, 51, 52; XXXI, 7.

WANG CH'ENG 王澄 (P'ing-tzu 平子). 269-312. CS 43.17a-20a. A son of Wang I's 乂 third wife, Lady Jen, and third younger brother of Wang Yen. He was very fond of drinking and is included in some listings of the so-called "Eight Free Spirits" (pa-ta), along with Hu-wu Fu-chih, Hsieh K'un, and others. He joined the staff of the Prince of Ch'eng-tu (Ssu-ma Ying, and after the execution of Lu Chi and his brother in 303, persuaded the prince to punish the person who had falsely accused them. After Ssu-ma Ying's death in 306, he moved to the staff of the Prince of Lung-hai (Ssu-ma Yüeh), later becoming governor of Ching Province (Hunan-Hupei), where his administration was rather lax and troubled by revolts. In 312, on his way to join Ssu-ma Jui (later the Eastern Chin Emperor Yüan, r. 317-322), in Chien-k'ang, he stopped to visit Wang Tun, then governor of Chiang Province (Hupei-Kiangsi), whom he insulted and by whom he was killed. CCKT. I, 23; V, 31; VII, 12; VIII, 27, 31, 45, 46, 51, 52; IX, 6, 11, 15; X, 10; XIV, 15; XXIV, 6; XXVI, 1; XXXII, 1; XXXIII, 5.

WANG CH'ENG* 王承 (An-ch'i 安期). ca. 275-320. CS 75.2a-3a. Son of Wang Chan and father of Wang Shu; a man of calm disposition and few words. In 301, during the "War of the Eight Princes" he fled from Lo-yang, but later was among those who welcomed back the abducted Emperor Hui (r. 290-306), for which he was ennobled Marquis of Lan-t'ien. He served awhile as secretarial aide to the Prince of Tung-hai, Ssu-ma Yüeh, later becoming grand warden of Tung-hai Commandery (Shantung), where his liberal administration became proverbial. About the time of Lo-yang's fall in 311, serenely facing dangers from invaders and bandits, he fled south to join the staff of Ssu-ma Jui (later Emperor Yüan, r. 317-322) in Chien-yeh (Nanking). According to his biographer in CS, he was even more prominent in the early days of Eastern Chin than were Wang Tao, Wei Chieh, Chou I, or Yü Liang. MSC. III, 9, 10; VIII, 34, 62, (74); IX, 10, 20, 23; XIX, 15, 16; XXVI, 6.

WANG CHI 王濟 (Wu-tzu 武子). ca. 240-ca. 285. CS 42.5a-7a. Second son and heir of Wang Hun 渾 (Hsüan-ch'ung) of the T'ai-yüan Wangs. At the age of twenty he married the Princess of Ch'ang-shan, a daughter of Emperor Wu (Ssu-ma Yen, r. 265-290), and for this reason held high rank at court (General of Spirited Horsemen and personal attendant) and was for a time on intimate terms with the emperor. Later, however, after an attempt to forestall the banishment of the emperor's younger brother, the Prince of Ch'i (Ssu-ma Yu), he was degraded, but still later restored to his former titles. CCKT. II, 24, 26; III, 5; IV, 72; V, 11; VIII, 17; XIV, 14; XVIII, 3; XIX, 12; XX, 4; XXV, 6, 8; XXIX, 1; XXX, 3, 6, 9; XXXIII, 2.

WANG CH'I-CHIH 王耆之 (Hsiu-tsai 修載). fl. mid-fourth cent. The third son of Wang I*, a cousin of Wang Tao. He served in the Central Secretariat and as grand warden of P'o-yang Commandery (Kiangsi). *Wang SP.* VIII, 122; XXXVI, 4.

WANG CH'IA 王洽 (Ching-ho 敬和). 323-358. *CS* 65.11b. The third and most renowned of Wang Tao's sons, and father of Wang Hsün and Wang Min. He was much admired by Emperor Mu (Ssu-ma Tan, r. 345-361), who wished to make him president of the Central Secretariat, but Wang steadfastly refused and died in his thirty-sixth year holding the title, Leader of the Palace Guard. He was a devout Buddhist and some of his correspondence with the monk Chih Tun is preserved in the Buddhist anthology, *Kuang hung-ming chi* 28, *Taishō* 52.323a. *CHS.* VIII, 114, 141; IX, 83; XIV, 33; XXIII, 44.

WANG CH'IANG 王嬙 (Chao-chün 昭君; alias Ming-chün 明君). fl. second half, first cent. B.C. *HS* 9.14a and 94B.7ab. The daughter of Wang Jang 穰, a concubine of the Former Han Emperor Yüan (Liu Shih, r. 48-33 B.C.) and later wife of the Hsiung-nu chieftain, Hu-han-hsieh 呼韓邪 (r. 58-31 B.C.). *HS; Hsiung-nu chuan.* XIX, 2.

WANG CHING 王經 (Yen-wei 彥緯). d. 260. *SKWei* 9.35b-36a. He became president of the Wei Imperial Secretariat around 257. In 260, when the ruler, Ts'ao Mao (r. 254-260), made his abortive coup against Ssu-ma Chao's control of the court, Wang, who opposed the move as futile, remained by his ruler's side after all others had deserted him. Mao was killed, and both Wang and his mother executed. *SY.* XIX, 10.

WANG CHING's mother 王經母. d. 260. Executed with her son; otherwise unknown. XIX, 10.

WANG CH'U-CHIH 王處之 (Wen-chiang 文將; baby name, A-chih 阿智). second half, fourth cent. Son of Wang Shu, younger brother of Wang T'an-chih, and son-in-law of Sun Ch'o. Said to be very unprepossessing in appearance and disagreeable in temperament, he seems never to have held any office. *Wang SP.* XXVII, 12.

WANG CH'ÜAN 王荃. mid-fourth cent. The daughter of Wang Shu and wife of Hsieh Wan. *Hsieh SP.* (XXIV, 10).

WANG FA-HUI 王法慧. 360-380. *CS* 32.12ab. A daughter of Wang Yün and consort of Emperor Hsiao-wu (Ssu-ma Yao, r. 373-396). She seems to have been an alcoholic, and the emperor, who was himself not noted for sobriety, once called in her father to reprimand her. Wang Yün promptly resigned from office, and the empress "made some slight reformation" but died at the age of twenty-one. *CHS.* V, 65.

WANG HAN 王含 (Ch'u-hung 處弘). d. 324. Elder brother of Wang Tun, he served for awhile as governor of Hsü Province (northern Kiangsu and Anhui) and later in the palace as Great Officer of Brilliant Favor. He fled from the capital to join his brother's revolt against the faction of Liu K'uei 劉隗 and Tiao Hsieh in 322, but during Tun's push toward Chien-k'ang in 324 he was defeated and drowned in the Yangtze River. *Wang Han PC.* II, 37; V, 28; VII, 15.

WANG HO-CHIH 王和之 (Hsing-tao 興道). late fourth cent. A son of Wang Hu-chih, he served as grand warden of Yung-chia Commandery (Chekiang), and later as palace attendant. YCC. XXVI, 32.

WANG HSI 王熙 (Shu-ho 叔和; baby name, Ch'i 齊). fl. ca. 400. Second younger brother of Wang Kung. He married the Princess of P'o-yang, daughter of Emperor Hsiao-wu (Ssu-ma Yao, r. 373-396), and served as Equestrian Forerunner to the crown prince before his early death. CHS. VI, 42.

WANG HSI-CHIH 王羲之 (I-shao 逸少). 309-ca. 365. CS 80.1a-10b. Son of Wang K'uang 曠 and nephew of Wang Tao. Famous for his draft style, he became one of China's greatest calligraphers. He served as an aide and later senior administrator to Yü Liang, eventually becoming governor of Chiang Province (Hupei-Kiangsi) and General of the Right Army (yu-chün), by which title he is usually known. In his later years he served as governor of K'uai-chi Principality, where, around 353, he hosted the famous poetry gathering at Lan-t'ing, immortalized by his own calligraphy. But when Wang Shu, whom he despised, was named his superior in 354, he resigned in protest and never held office again. His family was affiliated with the Heavenly Master sect of religious Taoism, but he himself was strongly attracted to the Buddhist monk Chih Tun. WTC. II, 62, 69, 70; IV, 36; V, 25, 61; VI, 19, 28(?); VIII, 55, 72, 77, 80, 88, 92, 96, 100, 108, 120, 132, 141; IX, 28, 29, 30, 47, 55, 62, (75), 85, 87; X, 20; XIV, 24, 26, 30; XVI, 3, 4; XVIII, 6; XIX, 25, 26, 31; XXV, 54; XXVI, 5, 8, 19; XXVII, 7; XXX, 12; XXXI, 2; XXXVI, 5;

WANG HSIANG 王祥 (Hsiu-cheng 休徵). 185-269. CS 33.1a-4a. One of China's most famous paragons of filial piety, about whom many legends clustered. During the turmoil at the end of the Han he fled with his stepmother to her old home in An-chiang (Anhui), where he remained in obscurity, caring for her old age for thirty years, finally emerging when he was over sixty to become lieutenant-governor of Hsü Province (northern Kiangsu and Anhui). His last title under the Wei was grand protector. After the Chin came to power in 265, he was enfeoffed a duke. CCKT; YYCS. I, 14, 19; IX, 6.

WANG HSIEN-CHIH 王獻之 (Tzu-ching 子敬). 344-388. CS 80.12a-14a. The seventh son of Wang Hsi-chih. He divorced his first wife, Ch'ih Tao-mao 郗道茂, daughter of Ch'ih T'an, and in ca. 374 remarried Ssu-ma Tao-fu 司馬道福, the Princess of Yü-yao 餘姚 (also known as Princess Min of Hsin-an 新安), third daughter of Emperor Chien-wen (Ssu-ma Yü, r. 371-372). Their own daughter, Shen-ai 神愛 (384-412) became the consort of Emperor An (Ssu-ma Te-tsung, r. 397-418) in 396 and is known as Empress Hsi. A trifle undisciplined in nature, he never matched his father's reputation as a calligrapher, but is still famous for his draft and clerkly styles. He was president of the Central Secretariat when he died. Wang SP; (Wang) Hsien-chih PC. I, 39; II, 86, 91; V, 59, 62; VI, 36, 37; VIII, 145, 146, 148, 151; IX, 70, 74, 75, 77, 79, 80, 82; XVII, 14, 15, 16; XXIV, 15, 17; XXV, 50, 60; (XXVI, 30); XXXI, 6.

WANG HSIN 王歆 (Po-yü 伯輿). d. 397? The son of Wang Hui and grandson of Wang Tao. He served as senior administrator for the director of instruction, and during Wang Kung's coup against Ssu-ma Tao-tzu in 397 joined Wang's cause, but later, rebelling against him, was presumably killed. *Wang SP*; *LAC*. XXIII, *54*.

WANG HSIU 王脩 (Ching-jen 敬仁; baby name, Kou-tzu 苟子, var. Hsün-tzu 荀子). ca. 335-358. *CS* 93.11a. Eldest son of Wang Meng. Though he died in his twenty-third year, he achieved considerable recognition both as a conversationalist and as a calligrapher. At the tender age of eleven or twelve he had already written a treatise which the very critical Liu T'an deigned to praise as "subtle." The monk Chih Tun once characterized him as a "man of transcendent awareness" (i.e., direct intuition). *WTC*. IV, *38*, 57, 83; VIII, 76, 123, 134, 137; IX, 48; X, 20; XXV, 39.

WANG HSÜ 王緒 (Chung-yeh 仲業). d. 397. The son of Wang I, and cousin of Wang Kuo-pao and Wang Ch'en. He served as administrator for the Prince of K'uai-chi, Ssu-ma Tao-tzu, and through flattery insinuated himself deeply into his favor. When Wang Kung and Yin Chung-k'an made their coup against Tao-tzu's clique in 397, Tao-tzu reluctantly agreed to execute Wang Hsü and Wang Kuo-pao to palliate the disaffected members of the court. *Wang SP*; *CATC*. X, *26*; XXXII, 4.

WANG HSÜAN 王玄 (Mei-tzu 眉子). d. 313. *CS* 43.17a. A son of Wang Yen. He had an abrupt, unrestrained manner and conspicuous ability, and began his career as an aide on the staff of the Prince of Tung-hai, Ssu-ma Yüeh. He was serving as grand warden of Ch'en-liu Commandery (Honan) during the fateful Yung-chia era (307-312), but because of his harsh administration was thoroughly unpopular. After attempting to join Tsu T'i's expedition against Shih Lo in 313, he was killed while defending himself against bandits. *CCKT*. VII, *12*; VIII, 35, 36; IX, 6; XXVI, 1.

WANG HSÜAN-CHIH 王玄之. d. ca. 340? *CS* 80.10b. The eldest son of Wang Hsi-chih, who apparently died young. (VIII, 151?)

WANG HSÜN 王珣 (Yüan-lin 元琳; baby names, Fa-hu 法護 and A-chao 阿苶). 350-401. *CS* 65.12a-13b. Eldest son of Wang Ch'ia, elder brother of Wang Min, and grandson of Wang Tao. After joining the staff of Huan Wen in 363, he accompanied him during the expedition against Yüan Chen 袁真 in 369, and was on intimate terms with Emperor Hsiao-wu (Ssu-ma Yao, r. 373-396), siding with the faction at court opposed to Ssu-ma Tao-tzu. His titles included Marquis of Tung-t'ing, personal attendant, General Aiding the State, vice-president and later president of the Imperial Secretariat. His close association with Buddhist monks, as well as his own and his brother's baby names, show a strong family affiliation with Buddhism. *Wang Ssu-t'u chuan*. II, *102*; III, 25, 26; IV, 64, 90, 92, 95, 96; VI, 39; VII, 28; VIII, 147; IX, 41, 83; X, 22; XI, 7; XIV, 34; XVII, 14, 15; XXII, 3; XXV, 60; XXVI, 24; XXXII, 3, 4; XXXVI, 6.

588   TALES OF THE WORLD

WANG HU-CHIH 王胡之 (Hsiu-ling 脩齡). d. ca. 364. CS 76.6b-7a. Son of Wang I*. Though he suffered all his life from epilepsy (feng-hsüan chi 風眩疾), he began his career as grand warden of Wu-hsing Commandery (Chekiang), and moved from there to become capital intendant. In 364 he was optimistically appointed governor of Ssu Province (Honan), and assigned the unrealistic task of integrating the long lost northern territories with that of Eastern Chin, but his illness became fatal at last and prevented his setting out from Chien-k'ang. Wang Hu-chih PC. II, 81; V, 52; VII, 27; VIII, 82, 125, 129, 131; IX, 47, 60, 85; XIII, 12; XIV, 24; XVI, 4; XXXI, 3; XXXVI, 3.

WANG HUI 王翬 (Ching-wen 敬文; baby name, Hsiao-nu 小奴). mid-fourth cent. CS 65.15ab. Sixth and youngest son of Wang Tao. He was modest and retiring by nature, and while serving as governor of Wu Principality (Soochow) distributed his private stock of grain to famine sufferers in the area. He was later governor of K'uai-chi Principality (Chekiang), and just before his death cavalier attendant-in-ordinary. (Wang) Shao (Wang) Hui PC. VI, 26, 38; XXIII, 48.

WANG HUI* 王徽 (Yu-jen 幼仁; baby name, Ching-ch'an 荊產). d. ca. 312. CS 43.20a. Second son of Wang Ch'eng 澄. He served as a clerk in the Imperial Secretariat and sergeant-at-arms under the General of the Right Army (his cousin, Wang Hsi-chih). Wang SP. II, 67; VIII, 52.

WANG HUI** 王惠 (Ling-ming 令明). 385-426. SS 58.1a-2a. A great-grandson of Wang Tao. With the founding of the Sung Dynasty in 420, he replaced Ts'ai K'uo 蔡廓 as president of the Board of Civil Office, by which title he is generally known. SS. XIX, 31.

WANG HUI-CHIH 王徽之 (Tzu-yu 子猷). d. 388. CS 80.11a-12a. The fifth son of Wang Hsi-chih. He had a reputation as an eccentric and undisciplined character, who never took seriously the few minor official posts he occupied, and who loved poetry and the company of bamboo trees which he cultivated in his mountain retreat at Shan-yin (Chekiang). He was very fond of his younger brother, Hsien-chih, and died only a short time after him. CPKM. VI, 36; VIII, 132, 136, 151; IX, 74, 80; XVII, 16; XXIII, 39, 46, 47, 49; XXIV, 11, 13, 15, 16; XXV, 43, 44, 45; XXVI, 29, 30.

WANG HUN 王渾 (Hsüan-ch'ung 玄冲). 223-297. CS 42.1a-5a. Son of Wang Ch'ang and father of Wang Chi. He began service as an attendant in the Wei palace, and with the founding of Western Chin in 265 was transferred to become governor of Hsü Province (southern Shantung and Anhui) and later of Yang Province (Kiangsu-Anhui-Chekiang). Pursuing an active military career, he was prominent in the suppression of Wu in 280, for which he was again transferred to Loyang and made vice-president of the Imperial Secretariat and cavalier attendant-in-ordinary. On the accession of Emperor Hui (Ssu-ma Chung, r. 290-306), he became personal attendant and director of instruction. YYCS. VIII, 17; XIX, 12, 16; XXV, 8; XXXIII, 2.

WANG HUN* 王渾 (Ch'ang-yüan 長源). mid-third cent. SKWei 24.3b, under

Ts'ui Lin 崔林, comm. Son of Wang Hsiung 雄, older brother of Wang I 乂, and father of Wang Jung 戎. He was president of one of the secretariats and governor of Liang Province (Kansu) under the Wei. SY. I, 21.

WANG HUN** 王混 (Feng-cheng 奉正). mid-fourth cent. CS 65.11a. A son of Wang T'ien who was adopted by his childless uncle, Wang Yüeh, as his heir and thus inherited his grandfather's (Wang Tao) noble title. He crowned an undistinguished career by becoming capital intendant. Wang SP. XXV, 42.

WANG I 王乂 (Shu-yüan 叔元). late third cent. SKWei 24.3b (mentioned, biog. of Ts'ui Lin 崔林, comm.). Son of Wang Hsiung 雄, younger brother of Wang Hun* 渾, and father of Wang Yen and Wang Ch'eng by Lady Jen 任. During the insurrection of the Wei generals Chung Hui and Teng Ai, after the conquest of the Shu Kingdom in 263, he was called to Ch'ang-an to assist Ssu-ma Chao, and later named governor of Yu Province (Hopei), with the title General Pacifying the North. Wang I PC. I, 26; VII, 5.

WANG I* 王廙 (Shih-chiang 世將). 276-322. CS 76.4b-7a. A cousin of Wang Tun and Wang Tao, brother-in-law of Emperor Yüan (Ssu-ma Jui, r. 317-322), father of Wang Hu-chih, and uncle of Wang Hsi-chih. He was famous in his time both as a painter and calligrapher, and was teacher both to Emperor Ming (Ssu-ma Shao, r. 323-325) and Wang Hsi-chih; see LTMHC 2; Acker, T'ang and Pre-T'ang, p. 161. He became involved in Wang Tun's rebellion in 322 and served under him as General Pacifying the South and governor of Ching Province (Hunan-Hupei), where he had served earlier, but after a harsh and unpopular administration had been recalled in 318. He died of natural causes shortly after arrival at his post. Wang I* PC. XXXVI, 3, 4.

WANG JUNG 王戎 (Chün-ch'ung 濬冲). 234-305. CS 43.9a-13b. The youngest member of the "Seven Worthies of the Bamboo Grove," who later made peace with the Ssu-ma faction and became Ssu-ma Chao's assistant. With the establishment of the Chin in 265 he became governor of Ching Province (Hunan-Hupei); in 290 he moved to president of the Imperial Secretariat and later became director of instruction (ca. 303), receiving a fief as Marquis of An-feng 安豐. Though enormously wealthy, he gained a reputation for extreme parsimony. CCKT. I, 16, 17, 19, 20, 21; II, 23; VI, 4, 5, 6; VIII, 5, 6, 10, 13, 14, 15, 22, 24, 29; IX, 6; XIV, 6, 11, 15; XVII, 2, 4; XXIII, 1, 8, 14, 32; XXIV, 2; XXV, 4; XXIX, 2, 3, 4, 5; XXXIV, 4; XXXV, 6.

WANG K'AI 王愷 (Chün-fu 君夫). fl. late third cent. CS 93.4a. The younger brother of the wife of Ssu-ma Chao. For his merit in the suppression of Yang Chün in 291 he was enfeoffed Duke of Shan-tu Prefecture (Hupei) and named cavalier attendant-in-ordinary. Later, involved in some plot, he was stripped of his titles, but subsequently had them restored. He and Shih Ch'ung lay claim to fame as the most ostentatiously extravagant personalities in the whole Six Dynasties period. CCKT. XXX, 3, 4, 5, 6, 7, 8; XXXVI, 2.

WANG K'AN 王諶 (Shih-chou 世冑). d. ca. 311. He served as an assistant in the Imperial Secretariat, where he made a reputation for conscientiousness and restraint. He was killed during Shih Lo's sack of Lo-yang in 311 and given the posthumous title of grand marshal. *CCKT.* VIII, *139.*

WANG KUANG 王廣 (Kung-yüan 公淵). ca. 210-251. *SKWei* 28.4b, comm. Son of Wang Ling and one of the four contributors to Chung Hui's "Treatise on the Four Basic Relations between Natural Ability and Human Nature" (*Ssu-pen lun*), Wang's position being that the two are "separate" (*li* 離). In view of the fact that he expressed strong criticism of Ts'ao Shuang and Ho Yen, and advised his father to join forces with Ssu-ma I, we may conclude he was not of Ts'ao Shuang's faction. He was, however, killed by Ssu-ma I after his father's suicide in 251; see *TCTC* 75.2384 and 2389. *WSCC*; *WC.* XIX, *9.*

WANG KUNG 王恭 (Hsiao-po 孝伯; baby name, A-ning 阿寧). d. 398. *CS* 84.1a-5a. A grandson of Wang Meng, and second son of Wang Yün. He became the brother-in-law of Emperor Hsiao-wu (Ssu-ma Yao, r. 373-396), which partly accounted for his being named capital intendant in 385 and later president of the Central Secretariat. Later he held several military commands and governorships in the provinces. After the Ssu-ma Tao-tzu forces had accomplished the murder of Emperor Hsiao-wu in 396, Wang Kung joined with Huan Hsüan and Yin Chung-k'an in an attempted coup against them. They forced the execution of Tao-tzu's favorite, Wang Kuo-pao, in 397, and elected Kung leader of the opposition. But Kung was defeated and killed by loyalist forces the following year, together with all the members of his family. A devout Buddhist, he chanted sutras at his execution. *LAC*; (*Wang*) *Kung PC.* I, *44*; II, 86, 100; IV, 101, 102; V, 63, 64; VI, 41, 42; VII, 26; VIII, 143, 153, 154; IX, 73, 76, 78, 84, 85; XIV, 39; XVI, 6; XVII, 17; XXIII, 51, 53; XXV, 54; XXVI, 22; XXXI, 7; XXXVI, 6, 7.

WANG KUO-PAO 王國寶 (Kuo-pao 國寶). d. 397. *CS* 75.12b-14b. The third son of Wang T'an-chih, and son-in-law of Hsieh An. His character is depicted in dark tones in the histories. Through his family connections with the favorite concubine of Ssu-ma Tao-tzu, he gained the latter's trust and was appointed president of the Central Secretariat. But his maternal uncle, Fan Ning, advised the emperor to remove him, and he was saved only by the intervention of the influential nun, Miao-yin 妙音. With the death of his younger brother, Wang Ch'en, in 392, he went into temporary hiding, but was reinstated and soon rose to become president of the Imperial Secretariat. When Wang Kung named Kuo-pao as one of the targets of his coup in 397, the terrified Ssu-ma Tao-tzu ordered Kuo-pao killed, but the agent lost his nerve. After a last-minute attempt to resist Wang Kung's forces, Kuo-pao was placed in the hands of the director of punishments and allowed to commit suicide. He is said to have owned entertainers and concubines "by the hundreds," and a villa full of curios and treasures from all over the world. *Wang Kuo-pao PC.* X, *26*; XXXII, 3, 4; XXXIV, 8.

WANG LANG 王朗 (Ching-hsing 景興). d. 228. *SKWei* 13.15a-22a. Grand warden of K'uai-chi (Chekiang) under the Later Han, he resisted Sun Ts'e's advance south of the Yangtze in 198, was defeated, and eventually entered the service of Ts'ao Ts'ao. He became director of instruction for the Wei Kingdom between 220 and 226, and the last year of his life was enfeoffed Marquis of Lan-ling. The texts of numerous memorials are included in his biography and he wrote many commentaries on the Classics, now lost. The *Sui-shu* bibliography lists a collection of his works in 54 *chüan* (*SuiS* 35.4a). *WeiS*. I, *12*, 13.

WANG LIEH 王烈 (Yang-hsiu 陽秀). fl. 220-265. The father of Wang K'an, father-in-law of Juan Hsien, and uncle of P'an Yüeh. He served as a censor under the Wei. *CCKT*. VIII, *139*.

WANG LIN-CHIH 王臨之 (Chung-ch'an 仲產; baby name, A-lin 阿林). mid-fourth cent. *CS* 76.14a. Second son of Wang Piao-chih, he served as grand warden of Tung-yang Commandery (Chekiang). *Wang SP*. IV, 62; VIII, *120*.

WANG LING 王淩 (Yen-yün 彥雲). 172-251. *SKWei* 28.1a-4b. Father of Wang Kuang and brother-in-law of Kuo Huai*. Appointed director of works and grand marshal in 249, after the downfall of Ts'ao Shuang, he was dispatched south in 251 as General Chastizing the East against the Wu forces. While on campaign he secretly plotted to restore the declining fortunes of the Wei royal house by setting up the Prince of Ch'u, Ts'ao Piao 彪 in a rival capital at Hsü-ch'ang (Honan). Ts'ao Piao was eventually pardoned, but Ling, already eighty years old and with his reputation ruined, was permitted to take his own life. His family were all made commoners. *WeiL*. V, *4*; XIX, 9.

WANG LUN 王淪 (T'ai-ch'ung 太沖). second half, third cent. The second son of Wang Ch'ang. He was by nature straightforward and unceremonious, and an admirer of *Lao-tzu* and *Chuang-tzu*. He is credited with two works: "Outline of the Principles of *Lao-tzu*" (*Lao-tzu li-lüeh*), and the "Chou Annals" (*Chou-chi*). He served as aide-de-camp to the generalissimo (Ssu-ma Shih?), but died in his twenty-fifth year. *Wang SP*. XXV, *8*.

WANG MENG 王濛 (Chung-tsu 仲祖). 309-347. *CS* 93.9b-11a. Son of Wang Na and father of the consort of Emperor Ai (Ssu-ma P'ei, r. 362-365). A man of affable manner and quick wit, he managed to live simply and without ostentation, and never rose above the rank of senior administrator in the service of Wang Tao. When his daughter became empress in 362, he was honored with the posthumous title, Great Officer of Brilliant Favor. *Wang Chang-shih PC*. II, 54, *66*, 68; III, 18, 21; IV, 22, 42, 53, 55, 56, 83; V, 49, 51, 54, 65; VII, 17, 18; VIII, 40, 76, 81, 83, 84, 86, 87, 92, 94, 98, 109, 110, 115, 121, 127, 133; IX, 30, 36, 42, 43, 44, 47, 48, 73, 76, 77, 78, 84; XIV, 21, 26, 29, 31, 33; XVII, 10; XXIII, 32, 33; XXV, 24, 29, 34; XXVI, 13, 22.

WANG MI 王謐 (Chih-yüan 稚遠). 360-407. *CS* 65.14ab. A son of Wang Shao and grandson of Wang Tao. He inherited the title Marquis of Wu-kang from his uncle, Wang Hsieh 協, who had died childless. At the time of Huan Hsüan's descent on the capital in 402, Mi was personal attendant to Emperor An (Ssu-ma Te-tsung, r. 397-418) and was sent to negotiate with Hsüan, who was greatly taken by him and offered him high honors in his own regime, elevating him eventually to president of the Board of Civil Office and director of instruction. Early in 404, when Hsüan usurped the throne, Mi was given still further honors. Because of his earlier friendship with Liu Yü*, Mi managed to survive Huan Hsüan's downfall three months later, and even became governor of Yang Province (Kiangsu-Anhui-Chekiang). But his involvement with Huan Hsüan clouded his last years with suspicion. CHS. IX, 83.

WANG MI* 王彌 (Seng-chen 僧珍). fl. ca. 397. KSC 1, Taishō 50.329a. A lay follower of Saṃghadeva in Chien-k'ang, wrongly identified in both the SSHY and CS 65.13b with Wang Min. CCH. IV, 64.

WANG MIN 王珉 (Chi-yen 季琰; baby name, Seng-mi 僧彌). 361-388. CS 13b-14a. A grandson of Wang Tao and younger brother of Wang Hsün. Like other members of his family he was a devout Buddhist and some of his eulogies of monks appear in the KSC. After a succession of court offices, including personal attendant, he replaced Wang Hsien-chih as president of the Central Secretariat and was thereafter known as the "Lesser Wang President" (hsiao-Wang-ling 小王令). (Wang) Min PC; HCYC. III, 24, 25; VI, 38; VIII, 152; X, 22.

WANG MU-CHIH 王穆之. d. 364. CS 32.8a. Daughter of Wang Meng and consort of Emperor Ai (Ssu-ma P'ei, r. 362-365), whom she had married while he was Prince of Lang-yeh. She died childless in 364. CHS. V, 65.

WANG NA 王訥 (Wen-k'ai 文開). late second to early third cent. The father of Wang Meng. He apparently fled southward during the Yung-chia era (307-312), but never served in any office higher than magistrate of Hsin-kan Prefecture (Kiangsi). Wang SP. (VIII, 40); XIV, 21.

WANG NA-CHIH 王訥之 (Yung-yen 永言). second half, fourth cent. A son of Wang Lin-chih. He served successively as left assistant in the Imperial Secretariat and central assistant censor. Wang SP. IV, 62.

WANG NING-CHIH 王凝之 (Shu-p'ing 叔平). d. 399. CS 80.10b. Second son of Wang Hsi-chih and husband of Hsieh Tao-yün. He served as governor of Chiang Province (Hupei-Kiangsi) and later of K'uai-chi Principality (Chekiang). Since he was a devotee of the religious Taoist sect of the Heavenly Master, when the Taoist magician-rebel Sun En threatened K'uai-chi in 399, he relied on exorcism to rid the principality of danger, and as a consequence lost his life. CATC; Wang SP. II, 71; (VIII, 151?); XIX, 26, 28; (XXVI, 30).

WANG NÜ-TSUNG 王女宗. mid-fourth cent. A granddaughter of Wang Tao, daughter of Wang T'ien, and wife of Huan Ch'ung. Huan SP. XIX, 24; (XXV, 42).

WANG P'ENG-CHIH 王彭之 (An-shou 安壽; baby name, Hu-t'un 虎㹠). first half, fourth cent. CS 76.8b. The eldest son of Wang Pin, and hence a first cousin once removed of Wang Tao. P'eng-chih's highest office was palace attendant. Wang SP. XXVI, 8.

WANG PI 王弼 (Fu-ssu 輔嗣). 226-249. *SKWei* 28.37a-38a, comm. His synthesis of Confucian and philosophical Taoist thought, epitomized in his commentaries on *Lao-tzu* and the "Book of Changes," has colored all subsequent interpretations of these works. Because of his involvement with the clique of Ts'ao Shuang, he was executed in 249 in his twenty-fourth year. (*Wang*) *Pi PC*. I, 99; IV, 6, 7, 8, 10; (VIII, 98, 110).

WANG PIAO-CHIH 王彪之 (Shu-hu 叔虎; baby name, Hu-tu 虎犢). 305-377. *CS* 76.8b-14a. The fourth son of Wang Pin, and the only one to gain a reputation. His beard and temples turned white in his twentieth year, which helped give him an air of wisdom. As director of punishments and later as president of the Board of Civil Office, he often served as confidant of Ssu-ma Yü (Emperor Chien-wen, r. 371-372). He served as governor of K'uai-chi Principality, cavalier attendant-in-ordinary, and, at Emperor Chien-wen's death in 372, it was largely his influence which prevented Huan Wen from usurping the throne. At his death in 377 he was heaped with posthumous honors. *Wang SP*. XXVI, 8, 14.

WANG PIN 王彬 (Shih-ju 世儒). ca. 275-333. *CS* 76.7a-8b. He fled south with his elder brother, Wang I*, around 312 and eventually became personal attendant at the Eastern Chin court. He courageously opposed the ambitions of his cousin, Wang Tun, refusing to be intimidated by the latter's threats of reprisal, which were never carried out. During Tun's rebellion (322-324) he was serving as governor of Chiang Province (Hupei-Kiangsi). After the destruction caused by Su Chün's revolt in 328, Pin was the architect for the new palace buildings, for which he was made a marquis and vice-president of the Imperial Secretariat. *Wang Pin PC*. VII, 15; XIX, 28.

WANG SENG-SHOU 王僧首. fl. ca. 400. Daughter of Wang Na-chih and wife of Yang Fu* 輔. *Yang SP*. IV, 62.

WANG SHAO 王劭 (Ching-lun 敬倫; baby name, Ta-nu 大奴). mid-fourth cent. *CS* 65.15a. The fifth son of Wang Tao, a man of handsome features and elegant manner, who won the admiration even of Huan Wen. He became president of the Board of Civil Office and vice-president of the Imperial Secretariat. (*Wang*) *Shao* (*Wang*) *Hui PC*. VI, 26; XIV, 28.

WANG SHU 王述 (Huai-tsu 懷祖). 303-368. *CS* 75.3a-6b. Son of Wang Ch'eng* 承, father of Wang T'an-chih, and father-in-law of Hsieh Wan. After an impoverished youth, he attained considerable eminence in later life, including the governor-generalship of Yang and Hsü provinces (Kiangsu-Anhui-Chekiang), cavalier attendant-in-ordinary, and president of the Imperial Secretariat. He is usually known by his hereditary title, Marquis of Lan-t'ien. *Wang Shu PC*. IV, 22; V, 47; VIII, 62, 74, 78, 91, 143; IX, 23, 47, 64; XXIV, 10; XXVI, 15; XXVII, 12; XXXI, 2, 5; XXXVI, 5.

WANG SHU* 王舒 (Ch'u-ming 處明). ca. 266-330. *CS* 76.12-3b. A cousin of Wang Tao and a close friend from his boyhood. He lived as a recluse until he was over forty, then around 306 joined Wang Tun's administration of Ch'ing Province (Shantung). The family crossed the Yangtze sometime between 307 and 312, and in 322 Tun again requested to have him appointed governor of Ching Province (Hunan-Hupei), but with Tun's fiasco in 324, Shu* refused to give sanctuary to Tun's brother, Han, and his son, Ying, but forced them both into the Yangtze River, where they drowned. The following year Shu* became governor of K'uai-chi Principality (Chekiang), and during Su Chün's rebellion in 327 he assumed the governorship of the very important Yang Province (Kiangsu-Anhui-Chekiang). After the suppression of Su Chün he was made a marquis. *Wang Shu* chuan.* VII, *15*; VIII, *46*; (IX, *83?*).

WANG SHUANG 王爽 (Chi-ming 季明; baby name, Shu 暗). d. 398. *CS* 93.12b-13a. Younger brother of Wang Kung. He was serving as personal attendant to Emperor Hsiao-wu (Ssu-ma Yao, r. 373-396) when the emperor was assassinated and in that capacity prevented Wang Kuo-pao from entering to investigate. He also managed to offend Kuo-pao's patron, Ssu-ma Tao-tzu, by reprimanding him for being too familiar while under the influence of liquor. When Wang Kung was killed in 398, Shuang also perished. *CHS.* IV, *104*; V, *64*, *65*; VI, *42*.

WANG SU-CHIH 王肅之 (Yu-kung 幼恭). second half, fourth cent. The fourth son of the famous calligrapher, Wang Hsi-chih. *Wang SP.* XXV, *57*; (XXVI, *30*).

WANG SUI 王綏 (Wan-tzu 萬子). ca. 257-275. *CS* 43.13b. The son of Wang Jung. Though excessively corpulent, he was thought to have much promise when he died in only his nineteenth year as a minor officer on the staff of the grand marshal. *CCKT*; "*CS.*" VIII, *29*; IX, *6*; XVII, *4*.

WANG SUI* 王綏 (Yen-yu 彥猷). d. 404. *CS* 75.15b-16a. Third son of Wang Yü, and first cousin of Huan Hsüan, who made him president of the Central Secretariat during his brief usurpation in 404. After Hsüan's fall three months later, he served briefly as governor of Ching Province (Hunan-Hupei), but died with his father and brothers in the purge of Huan supporters by Liu Yü* in the same year. *CHS.* I, *42*.

WANG SUI§ 王綏 . mid-fourth cent. Daughter of Wang T'ao 韜 and wife of Hsieh Chü, Hsieh An's elder brother. Her maternal protectiveness of her only son, Hsieh Lang, prompted Hsieh An to compare her to the worthies recorded in Liu Hsiang's (80-9 B.C.) "Lives of Virtuous Women" (*Lieh-nü chuan*). *Hsieh SP.* IV, *39*; XXIV, *8*.

WANG SUI** 王遂 (Ch'u-chung 處重). late third to early fourth cent. Younger brother of Wang Shu*. He became a vice-president of the Imperial Secretariat. *Wang Sui** PC.* VIII, *46*.

WANG T'AN-CHIH 王坦之 (Wen-tu 文度). 330-375. *CS* 75.6b-11b. Son of Wang Shu, from whom he inherited the title Marquis of Lan-t'ien, and father of Wang Yü, Wang Ch'en, and Wang Kuo-pao. He led an active political life at court, serving successively as personal attendant and president of the Central Secretariat. He aided Hsieh An in the restoration of Chin power following the attempted usurpation of Huan Wen in 373, and later served as governor of Hsü and Yen provinces (southern Shantung and northern Kiangsu and Anhui) and Commandant Governing the North, with headquarters in Kuangling (Kiangsu). Conservative in ideology, he bitterly opposed the libertinism of certain Taoist elements, whom he excoriated in a "Discourse Repudiating Chuang-tzu" (Fei-Chuang lun 非莊論). Although he personally hated the urbane monk Chih Tun, he was not anti-Buddhist, and once composed an essay on "Retribution," and at his death left his entire estate in Chien-k'ang to the An-lo Monastery. *Wang Chung-lang chuan*. II, 72, 79, (99); IV, 35; V, 46, 47; VI, 27, 29, 30; (VII, 26); VIII, 126, 128, 149; IX, 10, 52, 53, 63, 64, 72, 83; XXI, 10; XXIII, 38; XXV, 46, 52; XXVI, 21, 25, 31; XXVII, 12.

WANG TAO 王導 (Mao-hung 茂弘). 276-339. *CS* 65.1a-10a. Son of Wang Ts'ai 裁, and a cousin of Wang Tun. Fleeing southward in 307 with the Prince of Lang-yeh, Ssu-ma Jui, to Chien-yeh, he became his principal adviser, and took the leading role in founding the Eastern Chin in 317, at which time he was named chancellor. The following year he was named governor of Yang Province (Kiangsu-Anhui-Chekiang). He became personal attendant, director of works, and president of the Central Secretariat in 321, president of the Imperial Secretariat in 322, and served as director of instruction between 323 and his death in 339, although after his cousin Tun's abortive revolt of 322-324, his prestige at court was eclipsed by Yü Liang. See H. Meyer, *Wang Tao*, Berlin, 1973. *Wang Ch'eng-hsiang PC*. I, 27, 29; II, 31, 33, 36, 37, 40, 102; III, 12, 13, 14, 15; IV, 21, 22; V, 23, 24, 36, 37, 39, 40, 42, 45; VI, 8, 13, 14, 16, 19, 22; VII, 11; VIII, 37, 40, 46, 54, 57, 58, 59, 60, 61, 62; IX, 6, 13, 16, 18, 20, 23, 26, 28, 43; X, 11, 14, 15; XI, 5; XIV, 15, 16, 24, 25, 28; XVI, 1, 2; XVII, 6; XX, 8; XXII, 1; XXIII, 24, 32; XXIV, 7; XXV, 10, 12, 13, 14, 16, 17, 18, 21; XXVI, 4, 5, 6, 8; XXIX, 7; XXX, 1; XXXIII, 5, 6, 7; XXXIV, 4; XXXV, 7.

WANG T'IEN 王恬 (Ching-yu 敬豫; baby name, Ch'ih-hu 螭虎). early and mid-fourth cent. *CS* 65.11ab. Second son of Wang Tao by Lady Lei, definitely less in his father's favor than his older half brother, Yüeh. He was fond of fighting and hated study, and gained a reputation for arrogance and rudeness, but managed nevertheless to become the "number one" chess player of the Eastern Chin empire, and a master of the clerical style (*li-shu*) of calligraphy. He served as governor of K'uai-chi Principality (Chekiang) and cavalier attendant-in-ordinary, and was posthumously awarded the title, General of the Central Army. *WTC*. I, 29; VIII, 106; XIV, 25; XXIV, 12; XXXI, 3.

WANG TS'AN 王粲 (Chung-hsüan 仲宣). 177-217. *SKWei* 21.1a-9b. The descendant of an eminent Han family whose short stature and homely features kept him from public acclaim. But the scholar, Ts'ai Yung, recognizing his talents, offered to give him his entire library. During the turmoil at the end of Han he fled to the south, accompanying Ts'ao Ts'ao on his campaign against Wu in 216, but died the following year. He is best known as one of the "seven poets of the Chien-an Period" (*Chien-an ch'i-tzu*, 196-220), along with K'ung Jung, Ch'en Lin, Liu Chen, and others. *WeiC*. XVII, 1.

WANG TS'AO-CHIH 王操之 (Tzu-chung 子重). fl. late fourth cent. *CS* 80.12a. The sixth son of Wang Hsi-chih, he served successively as Curator of the Palace Library, personal attendant, president of the Board of Civil Office, and grand warden of Yü-chang (Kiangsi). *Wang SP*. IX, 74; (XXVI, 30).

WANG TUN 王敦 (Ch'u-chung 處仲; baby name, A-hei 阿黑). 266-324. *CS* 98.1a-15a. Son of Wang Chi 基 and cousin of Wang Tao. By some accounts he was also the elder brother of the monk Chu Ch'ien. Married to a daughter of Emperor Wu (Ssu-ma Yen, r. 265-290), he held great influence in the Western Chin court. After becoming governor of Yang Province (Kiangsu-Anhui-Chekiang) in 309, and his appointment by the future Eastern Chin Emperor Yüan (Ssu-ma Jui, r. 317-322) in 315 as Generalissimo Governing the East and governor of Chiang Province (Kiangsi-Hupei), with responsibility for military affairs in all six southern provinces, he was a power to reckon with in Eastern Chin as well. In 317, after the new government was established in Chien-k'ang, he moved to the strategically important post of governor of Ching Province (Hunan-Hupei) with headquarters in Wu-ch'ang (Hupei), controlling the upper Yangtze. From here he moved against the capital to check the rise of an opposing faction in two abortive rebellions in 322 and 324, after which he died of an illness in utter disgrace. (*Wang*) *Tun PC*. II, 37, 42; IV, *20*; V, 28, 31, 32, 33; VII, 13, 15; VIII, 43, 46, 49, 51, 55, 58, 79; IX, 6, 12, 15, 21; X, 12; XI, 5; XIII, 1, 2, 3, 4, 6, 8; XIV, 17; XX, 5, 8; XXV, 60; XXVI, 5; XXVII, 6, 7; XXX, 1, 2, 10; XXXIII, 5, 6, 8; XXXIV, 1; XXXVI, 3, 4.

WANG WEI-CHIH 王徽之 (Wen-shao 文助; baby name, Seng-en 僧恩). fl. mid-fourth cent. *CS* 75.11b. The second son of Wang Shu. He married the Princess of Hsün-yang, and served as a clerk in the Central Secretariat until his death in his thirtieth year. *WSSC*. IX, *64*.

WANG YA 王雅 (Mao-ta 茂達). 334-400. *CS* 83.16b-18a; mentioned, *KSC* 13, biog. of Hui-shou 慧受, *Taishō* 50.410b. He rose rapidly through assistant in the Imperial Secretariat to director of punishments, then personal attendant to Emperor Hsiao-wu (Ssu-ma Yao, r. 373-396), where he was treated with great favor. Though he served concurrently as capital intendant, commander of the Crown Prince's Guard, and junior tutor to the crown prince, he remained in the emperor's inner circle of advisers, and lived with great ostentation, his carriages and mounts numbering in the hundreds. After the emperor's death in 396, he was moved to left vice-president of the Imperial Secretariat, in which post he died four years later. (*Wang*) *Ya PC*; *CATC*. XXXII, *3*.

WANG YEN 王衍 (I-fu 夷甫). 256-311. *CS* 43.13b-17a. Son of Wang I and first cousin of Wang Jung. A precocious youth and refined conversationalist who championed the primacy of the concept of "Non-actuality" (*wu*), he avoided public office as long as he could, but eventually entered the staff of the crown prince, and after numerous escapes during the vicissitudes of the "War of the Eight Princes" (301-306), became intendant of the Capital Commandery, then president of the Board of Civil Office, president of the Central Secretariat, and finally president of the Imperial Secretariat, director of works, and director of instruction (the equivalent of chancellor), but, according to his biography, all his efforts were directed at self-preservation rather than the common good. When the Hsiung-nu armies threatened the capital in 311 he became grand marshal, but was soon defeated and captured by Shih Lo, who had him killed. His last words were allegedly a recantation of his "devotion to vanity." *YYCS*; *CCKT*. II, *23*; IV, 11, 12, 13, 18, 19; V, 20; VI, 8, 9, 11, 12; VII, 4, 5, 16; VIII, 21, 24, 25, 27, 31, 32, 37, 46; IX, 6, 8, 9, 10, 15, 20; X, 8, 9; XIV, 8, 10, 15, 17; XIX, 17; XXIV, 6; XXV, 29; XXVI, 1, 11; XXVIII, 1; XXX, 11.

WANG YIN-TZU 王愔子. early fifth cent. Son of Wang Kung and son-in-law of Hsieh Chung. *Hsieh SP*. II, *100*.

WANG YING 王應 (An-ch'i 安期). d. 324. *CS* 98.9b-9a. Originally the son of Wang Tun's older brother, Han, he was adopted by Tun, who had no male heir. He was given a high command in Tun's abortive revolt of 324, and after Tun's defeat and death he took refuge with his cousin Wang Shu*, who promptly had him drowned. *CYC*. VII, *15*; VIII, *49*; *96*.

WANG YING* 王穎 (Mao-ying 茂英). ca. 280-300. *CS* 65.10a. The next younger brother of Wang Tao, who died in his twentieth year, having reached the rank of consultant (*i-lang* 議郎), an office usually held by young men holding the first degree (*hsiao-lien* 孝廉). *Wang SP*. IX, *18*.

WANG YING-YEN 王英彥 (var. Yen-ying 彥英). fl. late fourth cent. Daughter of Wang Lin-chih and wife of Yin Chung-k'an. *Yin SP*. IV, *62*.

WANG YÜ 王愉 (Mao-ho 茂和; baby name, Chü 駒). d. 404. *CS* 75.12ab. Second son of Wang T'an-chih, half brother of Wang Kuo-pao and Wang Ch'en, and son-in-law of Huan Wen. He began his career as sergeant-at-arms to the General Aiding the State, and at the time of the execution of his half brother, Kuo-pao, in 397, he requested to be relieved of office, but was pardoned and sent to be governor of Chiang Province (Hupei-Kiangsi). Almost immediately he was captured by the forces of Huan Hsüan and Yin Chung-k'an, who were descending on the capital from Chiang-ling to aid Wang Kung in punishing Ssu-ma Tao-tzu. Wang Yü then served for a short while as governor of K'uai-chi Principality (Chekiang), and later as Huan Hsüan's vice-president of the Imperial Secretariat during the latter's brief usurpation in 404. After Huan's fall three months later, Yü was killed with other members of his family by Liu Yü*. *HKCC*. I, *42*; (V, *58*).

WANG YÜ* 王詡 (Chi-yin 季胤). fl. late third cent. The second younger brother of Wang Yen. His highest office was magistrate of Hsiu-wu Prefecture (Honan). *Wang SP*; *CKSH*. XIV, *15*.

WANG YÜEH 王悦 (Ch'ang-yü 長豫; also known as Ta-lang 大郎). d. before 339. CS 65.10a-11a. The eldest and favorite son of Wang Tao and Mme. Ts'ao, he died before his father, having only reached the rank of clerk in the Central Secretariat. He earned a reputation for filial devotion and frugality. CHS. I, 29; VIII, 96; XXV, 16; XXIX, 7.

WANG YÜN 王蘊 (Shu-jen 叔仁; baby name, A-hsing 阿興). 330-384. CS 93.11b-13a. The son of Wang Meng and father of Wang Kung and Wang Shuang and Empress Ting (Wang Fa-hui), the consort of Emperor Hsiao-wu (Ssu-ma Yao, r. 373-396). While serving in the Board of Civil Office he gained a reputation for fairness in the appointment of officials. Later as grand warden of Wu-hsing Commandery (Chekiang) in a time of famine, he proved unselfish and generous to a fault and was dismissed for "misuse of government grain." After his daughter was established as empress in 373, he was offered a marquisate, which he refused, but finally in 379 accepted the governorship of Hsü Province (Kiangsu-Anhui), and later the vice-presidency of the Imperial Secretariat and other high honors. After requesting to be removed from the palace and its gruesome intrigues, he ended with the governorship of K'uai-chi Principality (Chekiang), where he passed his last years, rarely sober but always affable and open. VII, 26; VIII, 137; XXIII, 35; XXV, 54.

WEI CHAN 衛展 (Tao-shu 道舒). fl. ca. 306-320. CS 36.14b-15a. A first cousin, once removed, of Wei Kuan. As governor of Chiang Province (Kiangsi-Hupei) during the troubled years 307-312, he provided assistance to many refugees from the north. After the establishment of Eastern Chin in 317 he was made director of punishments, in which capacity he wrote a celebrated memorial on corporal punishment, part of which is preserved in the "Monograph of Punishments and Law" (Hsing-fa chih, CS 30.26b-27b). YCLJM. XXIX, 6.

WEI CHIEH 衛玠 (Shu-pao 叔寶). CS 36.13a-15a. The second son of Wei Heng 恒 and grandson of Wei Kuan. He married the daughter of Yüeh Kuang, and served in the Western Chin court as Equestrian Forerunner to the crown prince. His health was always poor, and though extremely emaciated, he possessed such fine features and complexion that he was known as the "Jade Man." His prowess as a "pure conversationalist" was often compared to that of Ho Yen and Wang Pi. Fleeing south in 311, he finally reached Yü-chang (Kiangsi) early in the following year, but died only forty-five days after his arrival. Popular tradition states that he had been "stared to death" by the admiring townsfolk. CCKT; (Wei) Chieh PC. II, 32; IV, 14, 18, 20; VII, 8; VIII, 45, 51; IX, 42; XIV, 14, 16, 19; XVII, 6.

WEI I 衛顗 (Ch'ang-ch'i 長齊). fl. mid-fourth cent. A member of the upper gentry of K'uai-chi Commandery (Chekiang) who served as magistrate of Shan-yin Prefecture. Wei SP. VIII, 85; XXV, 48.

WEI KUAN 衛瓘 (Po-yü 伯玉). 220-291. CS 36.1a-3a. He was personal attendant to the last Wei ruler, Ts'ao Huan (r. 260-265), and served under Chung Hui in the campaign against Shu in 263. When the latter attempted rebellion, Wei led the mutiny against him, for which he was granted high military titles and noble rank. He continued his rise under the Western Chin (265-316), becoming president of the Imperial Secretariat and personal attendant in 275, and director of works and grand protector in 280. Involved in the dispute over Emperor Wu's heir, he was killed in 291 under the instigation of Empress Chia, who never forgave him for trying to remove her consort, Emperor Hui (Ssu-ma Chung, r. 291-306), from the succession because of his mental incompetence. *CCKT*. VII, *8*; VIII, *23*; X, *7*.

WEI SHU 魏舒 (Yang-yüan 陽元). 209-290. *CS* 41.1a-4a. A large man, unpretentious and unconventional, with an enormous capacity for wine and superb skill as an archer. He outlived three wives, himself living into his eighty-second year. Under the Wei he was governor of Chi Province (Hopei) and later personal attendant. With the founding of Chin in 265, he was transferred to president of the Board of Civil Office, but was soon dismissed for involvement in some unnamed incident. In 280 he was reinstated as a vice-president, and when Shen T'ao died in 283, he replaced him as director of instruction. In 286, however, he resigned because of failing health and died four years later. *WYCS*. VIII, *17*; XXIII, *41*.

WEI TAN 韋誕 (Chung-chiang 仲將). fl. ca. 200-230. *SKWei* 21.21b-22a, comm., citing *WCHL*. A noted calligrapher who contributed to the perfecting of the modern formal script (*k'ai-shu* 楷書). He wrote inscriptions for most of the Wei palace buildings. *WCHL*. V, *62*; XXI, *3*.

WEI T'I 魏愓. fl. late fourth cent. Younger brother of Wei Yin who became a palace attendant. *Wei SP*. VIII, *112*.

WEI YIN 魏隱 (An-shih 安時). fl. late fourth cent. A native of K'uai-chi Commandery (Chekiang) who became a junior censor. *Wei SP*. VIII, *112*.

WEI YUNG 衛永 (Chün-ch'ang 君長). fl. mid-fourth cent. He seems to have risen no higher than senior administrator to the General of the Left Army. *Wei SP*. VIII, *107*; IX, *69*; XIV, *22*; XXIII, *29*.

WEN CHI 溫畿 (Yüan-fu 元甫). dl. ca. 311. He was governor of Hsiang Province (Hunan) at the time of his death, which must have occurred before the fall of Western Chin (316). *CCKT*. VIII, *38*.

WEN CH'IAO 溫嶠 (T'ai-chen 太真). 288-329. *CS* 67.1a-13a. When he was still a young man, during the Hsiung-nu incursions of the north between 307 and 311, he won a reputation for his courageous resistance under the command of his kinsman, Liu K'un. In 317 he was sent south on behalf of Liu to join the restoration government of Ssu-ma Jui (Emperor Yüan, r. 317-322). There he served as governor of Chiang Province (Kiangsi and Hupei) and General Pacifying the South, and for aiding in the suppression of Wang Tun in 324 and Su Chün in 328 earned the title, Generalissimo of Spirited Cavalry. He was married at least three times: first to the daughter of

Li Huan 李桓, then to the daughter of Wang Hsü 王詡, and thirdly to the daughter of Ho Sui 何邃. *YYCS*. II, *35*, 36; IV, 77; V, 32; VI, 17; IX, 25; XI, 5; XIV, 23; XXIII, 26, 27, 29; XXVII, 8, 9; XXXI, 4; XXXIII, 7, 9.

WEN YÜ 溫顒. second half, third cent. A contemporary of Chang Min who hailed from T'ai-yüan (Shansi). XXV, 7.

WU CHAN 吳展 (Shih-chi 士季). late third cent. He served as governor of Kuang Province (Kwangtung-Kwangsi) for the Wu Kingdom (221-280), and grand warden of Wu Commandery (Soochow). After the surrender of Wu in 280 he returned to his native village (in Kiangsu) to spend his remaining years in total seclusion. *THC*. VIII, *20*.

WU CHOU 武周 (Po-nan 伯南). first half, third cent. He held the title Great Officer of Brilliant Favor under the Wei. *WC*. XXV, *3*.

WU KAI 武陔 (Yüan-hsia 元夏). fl. mid-third cent. *CS* 45.14b-15a. He began his official career as grand warden of Hsia-p'ei Commandery (Anhui) around 227, and later served on the staff of Ssu-ma Shih while the latter was generalissimo. He rose to become commandant of the Capital Province and was ennobled a marquis. In 265, with the founding of Western Chin, because of his reputation as a judge of men, he became president of the Board of Civil Office and Great Officer of Brilliant Favor. *YYCS*. VIII, *14*; IX, 5; XXV, 3.

WU T'AN-CHIH 吳坦之 (Ch'u-ching 處靖; baby name, Tao-chu 道助). late fourth cent. Son of Wu Chien 堅 and T'ung Ch'in-i 童秦姬, and elder brother of Wu Yin-chih. He was only a work-detail officer on the staff of the Western Commandant, Yüan Chen 袁真, when his mother died, from the shock of which he did not survive. *Wu SP*. I, *47*.

WU YIN-CHIH 吳隱之 (Ch'u-mo 處默; baby name, Fu-tzu 附子). d. 413. *CS* 90.14b-17a. Son of Wu Chien 堅 and T'ung Ch'in-i, and younger brother of Wu T'an-chih. Beginning his career on the staffs of military men, he rose to grand warden of Chin-ling (Kiangsu), and thence to the capital and the crown prince's guard. In every office he occupied he always distributed his salary among relatives and lived himself in the severest austerity. In 402 Huan Hsüan sent him south to govern Kuang Province (Kwangtung-Kwangsi) and clean up the corruption left by venal predecessors who had grown fat on the pearl trade there. After an exemplary term, in which he maintained his frugal habits even in this lush environment, he was captured by the rebel forces of Lu Hsün 盧循 in 410, as they overran Kuang Province. Because of his former association with Huan Hsüan, he narrowly escaped death, but was released by the rebels and returned to Chien-k'ang, where he became president of one of the secretariats and grand ordinary, still maintaining his austerity as before. Claiming old age, he resigned in 412 and died the following year. *HTC*; *CATC*; *CHS*. I, *47*.

YANG ___, son of 楊氏子. early fourth cent. An unidentified boy mentioned at II, 43, whose family originated in Liang 梁 Principality (Kaifeng). He was not related to the other Yangs 楊 mentioned in the *SSHY*, all of whom hailed from Hung-nung (Honan).

YANG CH'EN 羊忱, (alias T'ao 陶). (Ch'ang-ho 長和). ca. 255-311. A calligrapher of some reputation in his day who was for a while governor of Yang Province (Kiangsu-Anhui-Chekiang) and later personal attendant at the Western Chin court in Lo-yang. He died during the barbarian invasion of Lo-yang in 311. A man of great probity, he had earlier fled from the capital rather than serve in the administration of the would-be usurper, Ssu-ma Lun, in 300. WTC. V, 19, 25; VIII, 11; XXI, 5.

YANG CHI 楊濟 (Wen-t'ung 文通). d. 291. CS 40.17b-18a. A younger brother of Yang Chün, and uncle of Empress Yang, consort of Ssu-ma Yen (Emperor Wu, r. 265-290). Because of this connection, and because he once saved Emperor Wu's life on a hunting expedition, he enjoyed great favor and was named grand tutor to the crown prince. When Empress Yang, as dowager empress, fell victim to the jealous power of Empress Chia in 291, however, the entire Yang family was wiped out. PWKS. V, 12.

YANG CH'IAO 楊喬 (Kuo-yen 國彥). fl. ca. 300. The eldest son of Yang Chun, he held office as high as grand warden. HCCCC; CCKT. IX, 7.

YANG CHO 羊 (var. 楊) 晫). late third to early fourth cent. Mentioned, CS 66.6a. Grader for ten commanderies in the Anhui area at the turn of the fourth century. CYC. XIX, 19.

YANG CHUN 楊濬 (Shih-li 始立). fl. ca. 300. A member of the Yang family of Hung-nung (Shansi), which had been powerful until the downfall of Empress Yang in 291. Chun was appointed governor of Chi Province (southern Hopei) around 299. Realizing the danger of too intimate an involvement in the feuds of the "Eight Princes" (300-306), he spent his term as governor drinking and going on excursions, and died of natural causes in his twenty-eighth year. SY; HCCCC. VIII, 58; IX, 7.

YANG CH'ÜAN 羊權 (Tao-yü 道輿). late fourth to early fifth cent. Son of Yang Ch'en and collateral descendant of Yang Ping. He became left assistant in the Imperial Secretariat. Yang SP. II, 65.

YANG FU 羊孚 (Tzu-tao 子道). ca. 358 or 373-403. Eldest son of Yang Sui and elder brother of Yang Fu*. After a term as erudite of the Grand Academy, he became lieutenant-governor of Yen Province (southern Shantung and northern Kiangsu). In 402 when the grand marshal, Huan Hsüan, descended on the capital from Chiang-ling (Hupei), ostensibly to crush Sun En's rebellion, but actually to usurp the throne, Yang joined his staff as secretarial aide. According to the Yang SP (II, 104), he died before Huan (i.e., before 404) in his forty-sixth year. SSHY (XVII, 18) on the other hand, stressing his premature death, places it in his thirty-first year. Yang SP. II, 104, 105; IV, 62, 100, 104; VI, 42; XVII, 18, 19; XXII, 6.

YANG FU* 羊輔 (Yu-jen 幼仁). fl. ca. 400. Younger brother of Yang Fu 孚. He served as work-detail officer in the Palace Guard. Yang SP. IV. 62.

YANG HSIN 羊欣 (Ching-yüan 敬元). 370-442. A cousin of Yang Fu and grandson of Yang Ch'üan. He was quiet and retiring by nature, fond of calligraphy, which he studied as a boy with Wang Hsien-chih, and deeply interested in the Taoist cult of immortality. During the disturbed period between 397 and 400 he went into retirement, but emerged briefly to serve Huan Hsüan before the latter's downfall, early in 404. After the founding of Sung in 420 he served as senior administrator to Liu I-ch'ing, author of the *SSHY*. The last twelve years of his life were spent as grand warden of the Hsin-an Commandery (Chekiang). *Sung-shu*. XVII, *18*.

YANG HSIU 楊脩 (Te-tsu 德祖). ca. 178-220. *HHS* 84.24a-25a. While Ts'ao Ts'ao was serving as chancellor (208-213) under the Later Han Emperor Hsien (r. 190-220), he appointed Yang Hsiu his superintendent of records. Later accused of disorderly conduct, Yang was executed by Ts'ao, leaving behind a voluminous literary estate, none of which has survived. *WSC*. XI, *1, 2, 3, 4*.

YANG HSIU* 羊琇 (Chih-shu 稚舒). ca. 236-283. *CS* 93.2a-3a. A cousin of Yang Hui 徽 (214-278), the second wife of Ssu-ma Shih, and a close friend of Ssu-ma Yen, founder of Chin. He aided in the campaign against Shu in 263, and after the founding of Chin in 265 achieved high honors, including Central Protector of the Army and cavalier attendant-in-ordinary. For protesting the banishment of the Prince of Ch'i, Ssu-ma Yu, in 283, he was degraded, and shortly afterward took sick and died. *CCKT*. V, *13*.

YANG HU 羊祜 (Shu-tzu 叔子). 221-278. *CS* 34.1a-12b. A grandson on his mother's side of Ts'ai Yung, and younger brother of the consort of Ssu-ma Shih. His family had produced officials for nine generations without a blemish on the record, and Hu himself, being a very impressive person, had an enormous reputation in his own day. After serving as vice-president of the Imperial Secretariat and governor-general of military affairs in Ching Province (Hunan-Hupei), he died in the pacification of the Wu Kingdom in 278. Even the inhabitants of Wu were said to have mourned his loss with intense grief. *CCKT*. II, *86*; III, *6*; VII, *5*; VIII, *9, 11*; IX, *51*; XX, *3*; XXV, *47*.

YANG LANG 楊朗 (Shih-yen 世彥). fl. early fourth cent. The son of Yang Chun. His highest office seems to have been governor of Yung Province (northern Hupei). *CPKM*; *Yang SP*; *WYCS*. VII, *13*; VIII, *58, 63*.

YANG K'AI 羊楷 (Tao-mao 道茂). fl. early fourth cent. A son-in-law of Chu-ko Hui, who served as a clerk in the Imperial Secretariat. *Yang SP*. V, *25*.

YANG KU 羊固 (Tao-an 道安). fl. early fourth cent. A noted calligrapher in the draft (*ts'ao*) and semi-cursive (*hsing*) styles, he crossed the Yangtze in the migrations of 307-312 and later became a palace attendant. *MTTKLSM*; *WTC*. VI, *20*.

YANG KUANG 楊廣 (Te-tu 德度). late fourth or early fifth cent. Son of Yang Liang 亮 and older brother of Yang Ch'üan-ch'i 佺期. *LAC*. I, *41*.

YANG MAN 羊曼 (Yen-tsu 延祖). 274-328. CS 49.23b-24b. A son of Yang Chien 監, and grandson of Yang Hu's older brother. After fleeing southward between 307 and 312, he served first as aide to Ssu-ma Jui (Emperor Yüan, r. 317-322) and later was superintendent of records for the chancellor, Wang Tao. While grand warden of Chin-ling Commandery (Kiangsu), he became involved in some scandal which caused his dismissal. He was somewhat bibulous and dissolute by nature, and was included along with Juan Fu, Juan Fang, Ch'ih Chien, Hu-wu Fu-chih, Pien K'un, Ts'ai Mo, and Liu Sui in a group known as the "Eight Elders" (pa-po), as well as the more notorious "Eight Free Spirits." While Wang Tun was plotting rebellion in 322, Yang was on his staff but managed to escape involvement by remaining drunk most of the time. After Tun's suppression in 324, Yang replaced Juan Fu as capital intendant. During Su Chün's attack on the capital in 328, he led the defense of the Yün-lung Gate and was killed at his post. Yang Man PC. VI, 20; XVI, 2.

YANG MAO 楊髦 (Shih-yen 士彦). d. 311. A younger son of Yang Chun who perished in the sack of Lo-yang in 311. HCCCC; CCKT. IX, 7.

YANG PING 羊秉 (Ch'ang-ta 長達). d. before 291. The eldest son of Yang Yu, elder brother of Yang Ch'en, and an antecedent of Yang Ch'üan. He died without heirs in his thirty-second year, having reached only the rank of aide to the General Controlling the Army. Yang Ping hsü. II, 65.

YANG SUI 羊綏 (Chung-yen 仲彦). fl. mid-fourth cent. The son of Yang K'ai and grandson of Chu-ko Hui on his mother's side. The highest office he held was clerk in the Imperial Secretariat. Yang SP. V, 60; VI, 42; XVII, 14.

YANG TAO 羊衜. d. 232. The father of Yang Hu. He was grand warden of Shang-tang Commandery (Shansi) when he died, in Hu's twelfth year. (XX, 3.)

YANG YU 羊㻱 (K'an-fu 堪甫). fl. mid-fourth cent. Father of Yang Ping and Yang Ch'en, and a cousin of Yang Hu. Yang SP. VIII, 11.

YEN YIN 嚴隱 (Chung-pi 仲弼). fl. late third cent. A native of Wu Commandery (Soochow) who served as magistrate of Wan-ling Prefecture (Anhui) until the fall of Wu in 280, at which time he resigned his post. THC. VIII, 20.

YIN, Mme. 殷夫人. first half, fourth cent. The younger sister of Yin Hao, and mother of Han Po. HTC. I, 47; XII, 5; XIX, 27, 32.

YIN CHI 殷覬. var. I 顗 (Po-t'ung 伯通, var. -tao 道; baby name, A-ch'ao 阿巢). d. 397. CS 83.16ab. A son of Yin K'ang 康 and older brother of Yin Chung-wen. Hsieh Shang was his maternal grandfather. He was named Commandant of the Southern Barbarians, stationed in Chiang-ling (Hupei), around 385, and in 397 was approached by his cousin, Yin Chung-k'an, who was then governor of Ching Province, to join in the coup against Ssu-ma Tao-tzu at court. Because of his refusal, Chi became a marked man and promptly resigned his post. He died shortly thereafter, apparently from an overdose of drugs. *CATC.* I, *41*; X, 23; XXVI, 27.

YIN CHUNG-K'AN 殷仲堪. d. 399/400. *CS* 84.11a-18a. Son of Yin Shih and cousin of Yin Chung-wen, and son-in-law of Wang Lin-chih. He belonged to the faction at the Eastern Chin court which attempted to curb the influence of Ssu-ma Tao-tzu. Appointed governor of the strategic Ching Province (Hunan-Hupei) in 392, he was subsequently attacked by the ambitious governor of the neighboring province of Chiang (Hupei-Kiangsi), Huan Hsüan, in late 399 or early 400 and forced to commit suicide. Like the Wang family of Lang-yeh, he was, at least in his youth, an adherent of the religious sect of Taoism known as the Way of the Heavenly Master (T'ien-shih Tao). *CATC.* I, *40*, 42, 43; II, 103; III, 25; IV, 60, 61, 62, 63, 65; VI, 41; VII, 28; VIII, 156; IX, 81; X, 23; XXI, 11; XXV, 56, 61; XXXII, 4; XXXIII, 17; XXXIV, 6.

YIN CHUNG-WEN 殷仲文 (Chung-wen 仲文). d. 407. *CS* 99.21b-23b. Son of Yin K'ang 康, younger brother of Yin Chi, and a cousin of Yin Chung-k'an. He began as an aide to the Prince of K'uai-chi, Ssu-ma Tao-tzu, from whom he received very deferential treatment. But since he was married to Huan Hsüan's elder sister, after 398, when Huan and Yin's cousin, Chung-k'an, openly opposed Tao-tzu and his faction, Tao-tzu's favor cooled and he was demoted to be grand warden of Hsin-an Commandery (western Chekiang). When Huan Hsüan executed Ssu-ma Tao-tzu in 402, Chung-wen joined Huan as consulting aide and actually drafted the document urging him to accept the Nine Bestowals, preparatory to mounting the throne. With Huan's usurpation early in 404, Chung-wen became personal attendant and was generously rewarded. A few months later when Huan was overthrown, he managed by an adroit memorial to clear his own name, but after three years again became involved in an attempt to restore Huan Hsüan's lost dynasty, and was executed with all the members of his clan by Liu Yü*. His (hostile) biographer in *HCYC*, composed during the Liu-Sung period, observes: "He was by nature avaricious and stingy, much given to accepting bribes, and though his family for generations had been wealthy, he seemed never to have enough." *HCYC.* II, *106*; IV, 99; VIII, 156; IX, 45, 88; XXV, 65; XXVIII, 8, 9.

YIN HAO 殷浩 (Yüan-yüan 淵源; vary. Shen-yüan 深源). 306-356. *CS* 77.22a-26a. Son of Yin Hsien and uncle of Han Po, famous in his day as a conversationalist. He began his career as secretarial aide in Yü Liang's headquarters at Wu-ch'ang (Hupei) around 334, and moved on to senior administrator in the chancellor's office. After a period of ten years in seclusion following his mother's death, he eventually agreed to serve as governor of Yang Province (Kiangsu-Anhui-Chekiang) in 346, becoming generalissimo of the central army in 350. In an attempt to anticipate, and thus thwart, the ambitions of Huan Wen, he made an abortive move to recover the north in 352-353 but was soundly defeated, for which Huan managed to get him dismissed and exiled to western Chekiang. There he spent his last years immersed in the study of Buddhist scriptures. *Yin Hao PC*; *CHS.* II, 80; III, *22*; IV, 22, 23, 26, 27, 28, 31, 33,

34, 43, 46, 47, 48, 50, 51, 56, 59, 74; V, 53; VII, 18; VIII, 80, 81, 82, 90, 93, 99, 100, 113, 115, 117, 121; IX, 30, 33, 34, 35, 38, 39, 51, XIV, 24; XVI, 4; XX, 11; XXIII, 37; XXV, 47; XXVI, 10; XXVIII, 3, 5.

YIN HSIEN 殷羨 (Hung-ch'iao 洪喬). late third to early fourth cent. CS 77.22a. The father of Yin Hao. His last office was grand warden of Yü-chang (Kiangsi), after which he received the title, Great Officer of Brilliant Favor. *Yin SP*. XXIII, *31*; XXV, 11, 23.

YIN JUNG 殷融 (Hung-yüan 洪遠). fl. first half, fourth cent. Uncle of Yin Hao. He began his career in Yü Liang's administration, later becoming capital intendant and president of the Board of Civil Office. His highest office was lord grand ordinary. *CHS*. IV, *74*; IX, 36, 69; XXV, 37.

YIN SHIH 殷師 (Tzu-huan 子桓; baby name, Shih-tzu 師子). mid-fourth cent. The father of Yin Chung-k'an. He served as consulting aide to the General of Spirited Cavalry and grand warden of Chin-ling (Nanking). Most of his adult life he suffered an ailment (*shih-hsin* 失心) which caused palpitations of the heart and excessive sensitivity to sounds. It was while mixing medicine for this that his son, Chung-k'an, is said to have impaired the sight of one eye. *Yin SP*; *HCYC*. XXXIV, *6*.

YIN YÜN 殷允 (Tzu-ssu 子思). fl. mid-fourth cent. The younger brother of Yin Chung-wen and cousin of Yin Chung-k'an. He was a modest and retiring person with a bookish turn of mind. After serving in Huan Wen's headquarters in Wu-ch'ang (Hupei) while the latter was Generalissimo Governing the West (348-354), he eventually became president of the Board of Civil Office. *CHS*. VIII, *145*.

YING CHAN 應詹 (Ssu-yüan 思遠). 274-326. *CS* 70.1a-6a. Orphaned and sickly in his youth, he nevertheless won a reputation early for sterling character and literary talent. He moved successively through the employ of several of the warring Chin princes, adroitly avoiding death, and after the establishment of Eastern Chin in 317 served as governor of I Province (Szechwan) from 324 until his death two years later. He received the posthumous titles, governor of Chiang Province (Kiangsi and Hupei) and General Governing the South. *WYCS*. XXXVI, *4*.

YÜ AI 庾敳 (Tzu-sung 子嵩). 262-311. *CS* 50.7a-8b. He is described as rotund in form and jovial in disposition and is listed as one of the "Eight Free Spirits" (*pa-ta*), whose bizarre antics in the closing years of the Western Chin drew sharp criticism from conservatives like P'ei Wei. He perished in the fall of Lo-yang in 311. *CYC*. IV, *15*, 75; V, 20; VI, 10; VIII, 15, 26, 33, 38, 41, 42, 44; IX, 11, 15, 58; XIV, 18.

YÜ CH'AN 庾闡 (Chung-ch'u 仲初). ca. 287-340. *CS* 92.16a-18a. A poet of considerable popularity in his day, though almost nothing of his work survives. Although he was of the same clan as Yü Liang, the relationship is unclear. After losing his mother in the fall of Lo-yang in 311, when he was about twenty-four, he refrained, so it is said, from combing his hair, bathing, marriage, wine, and meat for twenty years. He served in the Eastern Chin court as cavalier attendant and grand historian. There is no doubt that much of his popularity as a poet is based on respect for his filial devotion and the high moral tone of his work, though Hsieh An considered him merely imitative; see *SSHY* IV, 79. His most celebrated piece seems to have been a description of Chien-k'ang, called "Poetic Essay on the Yang Capital" (*Yang-tu fu* 楊都賦; see IV, 77). *CHS*. II, 59; IV, 77, 79.

YÜ CHIEN 虞謇 (Tao-chih 道真). mid-fourth cent. Younger brother of Yü Ts'un, he apparently made some reputation as a *go* player, but reached office no higher than work-detail officer in his home commandery of K'uai-chi (Chekiang). *FWCP*. III, 17.

YÜ CH'IEN 庾倩 (Shao-yen 少彥; baby name, Ni 倪). d. 371. Fifth son of Yü Ping and elder brother of the consort of Emperor Fei (Ssu-ma I**, r. 365-371). He had reached office only as high as senior administrator for the grand minister when he was falsely accused of treason and executed in 371 on orders from Huan Wen, who feared the Yü and Yin clans would oppose his imperial ambitions. *HKCC*. VIII, 72.

YÜ CH'IU 虞球 (Ho-lin 和琳). fl. mid-fourth cent. A member of one of the principal families of K'uai-chi Commandery (Chekiang), whose only office seems to have been palace attendant. *Yü SP*. VIII, 85.

YÜ FA-K'AI 于法開. ca. 310-370. *KSC* 4, *Taishō* 50.350ab). A disciple of Yü Fa-lan 于法蘭 (fl. ca. 315-330), who had founded the Yüan-hua Monastery in the Shan Mts. near K'uai-chi (Chekiang) and had died in Indochina on an unsuccessful pilgrimage to India. Fa-k'ai specialized in the "Larger" *Prajñāpāramitā-sūtra* (*Fang-kuang ching*) and the *Saddharma-puṇḍarīka* (*Fa-hua ching*), but made his real reputation as a physician. In 361, summoned to the bedside of Emperor Mu (Ssu-ma Tan 聃, r. 345-361), he realized the emperor was dying and refused to see him a second time, for which he nearly lost his life. He became abbot of the Yüan-hua Monastery after his master's death, and between 325 and 335 the monastery became a center for a strong rivalry with Chih Tun's "School of the Emptiness of Matter-as-Such" (*Chi-se tsung*). Fa-k'ai's school came to be known by the term, "Illusion of Conscious Impressions" (*Shih-han*). See Zürcher, *Conquest*, pp. 140-143; T'ang, *Han Wei*, pp. 263-265; Liebenthal, *Book of Chao*, pp. 162-164. *MTSMTM*. IV, 45; XX, 10.

YÜ FEI 虞騑 (Ssu-hsing 思行). fl. ca. 320. *CS* 76.17a. He served with Huan I as a clerk in the Board of Civil Office and later as grand warden of Wu-hsing Commandery (Chekiang). He was Great Officer of Brilliant Favor when he died. *YKLC*. IX, 13.

YÜ HENG 庾恒 (Ching-tse 敬則). late fourth cent. The son of Yü Ho and Hsieh Seng-yao 謝僧要, Hsieh Shang's eldest daughter. He reached vice-president of the Imperial Secretariat. *Yü SP*; *Hsieh SP*. XXVI, 27.

YÜ HO 庾龢 (Tao-chi 道季). ca. 329-366. CS 73.11a-12a. Third son of Yü Liang and husband of Hsieh Shang's eldest daughter. Around 360 he became capital intendant, and in 366 General Leading the Army, but died soon afterward. HKCC. II, 79; IX, 63, 68, 82; XXI, 8; XXVI, 24.

YÜ HSI 庾希 (Shih-yen 始彥). d. 372. CS 73.16a-17a. The eldest son of Yü Ping. The Yü faction had lost power after Yü I's death in 345, giving way to the rising fortunes of Huan Wen, but the latter was intensely wary of a comeback after the accession of Emperor Fei (Ssu-ma I**, r. 366-371), whose empress was Yü Hsi's sister and who had placed the various members of her family in high posts. Hsi was dismissed as governor of Hsü and Yen provinces (Anhui and southern Shantung) early in 366, when the Hsien-pei armies overran his territory. His brothers Ch'ien and Jou 柔 were killed in 371 on the charge of plotting rebellion. Another brother, Yün 藴, committed suicide the same year. Still another, Yu 友, being related by marriage to the Huans, was spared; see SSHY XIX, 22. Hsi fled with his brother Mo 邈 and Mo's son Yu* 攸 to the swampy area of the Chekiang coast, where they rallied their forces. Acting on secret orders from his brother-in-law, the newly deposed Emperor Fei, Hsi raised a revolt at Ching-k'ou (Kiangsu) in the summer of 372, but was quickly crushed and executed with the remaining members of his family. CHS. VI, 26; XIX, 22.

YÜ HSI* 庾羲 (Shu-ho 叔和; baby name, Tao-en 道恩). fl. ca. 345. CS 73.10b-11a. The third son of Yü Liang. When he was appointed governor of Wu Principality (Soochow), moved by the poverty and suffering of his constituents, he sent a strongly worded memorial to Emperor Mu (Ssu-ma Tan, r. 345-361), whose wasteful extravagance he deeply deplored, together with some poems in like vein. He died shortly after assuming the governorship. HKCC. V, 48.

YÜ HSIAO-FU 虞嘯父. d. ca. 405. CS 76.16b-17a. While he was personal attendant to Emperor Hsiao-wu (Ssu-ma Yao, r. 373-396), he was highly favored. Later, in 397, while governor of Wu Principality (Soochow) he became involved in the rebellion of Wang Hsin, and was stripped of office and made a commoner. Entering the administration of Wang Hsüan in 401, he rose to become governor of K'uai-chi Principality (Chekiang) before his death in 405. CHS. XXXIV, 7.

YÜ HSÜAN 庾宣. See YÜ SHU-HSÜAN.

YÜ HUI 庾會 (Hui-tsung 會宗; baby name, A-kung 阿恭). 310-328. Yü Liang's eldest son, killed in his nineteenth year by Su Chün during the latter's purge of the Yü family in 328. YÜ SP. V, 25; VI, 17; XVII, 8.

YÜ HUNG 庾鴻 (Po-luan 伯鸞). late fourth to early fifth cent. A son of Yü K'ai 楷 and grandson of Yü Hsi*. CTKPKM; YÜ SP. XXV, 62.

YÜ I 庾翼 (Chih-kung 稚恭). 305-345. CS 73.17b-22a. Fourth younger brother of Yü Liang, distinguished as the "Lesser Yü." In 327, when he was twenty-one, after being defeated by the rebel Su Chün, he was transferred to the staff of the grand marshal, T'ao K'an, and later moved through several important military posts, ultimately replacing his brother, Yü Liang, at the latter's death in 340, as governor of Ching Province (Hunan-Hupei) and General Chastizing the West, with headquarters in Wu-ch'ang (Hupei). When Emperor K'ang ascended the throne in 343, Yü requested to lead a punitive expedition against Shih Hu (r. 334-349), ruler of Later Chao, who was then threatening the western frontier. Failing to get clearance, he set out on his own, but on reaching Hsia-k'ou (northern Hupei), he desisted. His wish to be replaced as governor of Ching Province by his son, Yüan-chih, was denied by the court, and when he died in 345 his place was taken by the ambitious general, Huan Wen. *Yü I PC*. II, *53*; VI, 24; VII, 19; VIII, 69, 73; XIII, 7; (XIV, 23); XXV, 23, 33.

YÜ LIANG 庾亮 (Yüan-kuei 元規). 289-340. *CS* 73.1a-10b. A cousin of Yü Ai, and the eldest brother of Empress Mu, consort of Emperor Ming (Ssu-ma Shao, r. 323-325), during whose reign he was Curator of the Palace Library and after whose death he became president of the Central Secretariat and the real holder of power at court, until his appointment as General Chastizing the West and governor of the three provinces of Yü (northern Anhui), Chiang (Kiangsi and Anhui), and Ching (Hunan-Hupei) after the suppression of Su Chün's uprising against the Yü family in 328. Thenceforward until his death in 340, he continued to exert a strong influence from his strategic position at Wu-ch'ang (Hupei). *CYC*. I, *31*; II, 30, 41, 49, 50, 52; III, 14; IV, 22, 75, 77, 78, 79; V, 25, 35, 37, 45; VI, 13, 17, 18, 23; VII, 11, 16; VIII, 33, 35, 38, 41, 42, 65, 68, 69, 72, 107; IX, 15, 17, 23, 70; XIII, 7; XIV, 23, 24, (38); XVI, 4; XVII, 8, 9; XVIII, 9, 11; XXIII, 26, 27; XXV, 47; XXVI, 2, 3, 4, 5; XXVII, 8; XXXIII, 10.

YÜ PING 庾冰 (Chi-chien 季堅). 296-344. *CS* 73.13a-16a. Second younger brother of Yü Liang, and elder brother of Empress Mu, consort of Emperor Ming (Ssu-ma Shao, r. 323-325). He was also the father of Empress Yü, the consort of the Deposed Emperor, Ssu-ma I** (r. 365-371). The Yü faction's dominance lasted from about 325 to 345, culminating in the rule of their puppet, Emperor K'ang (Ssu-ma Yüeh*, r. 342-344), after which their implacable enemy and partisan of Buddhism, Ho Ch'ung, managed to remove them from power. Yü Ping was himself strongly anti-Buddhist and played a prominent role in the controversy over the autonomy of the sangha in 340, while he was regent for the boy-emperor Ch'eng (Ssu-ma Yen*, r. 326-342). After the death of his rival, Wang Tao, in 339, Ping became the most powerful figure at court and is credited with instigating a series of repressive measures there until he replaced his brother, Liang, as governor of Chiang Province (Hupei and Kiangsi) in 340, where he remained until his death. *CYC*. V, *41*, 43; XIII, 7; (XIV, 2, 3); XXIII, 30.

YÜ SAN-SHOU 庾三壽. fl. ca. 300. The daughter of Yü Tsung, wife of Wang Na, and mother of Wang Meng. *Wang SP*. VIII, *40*.

YÜ (SHU-) HSÜAN 庾(叔)宣. later fourth cent. Eldest son of Yü Yu and the husband of Huan Nü-yu, daughter of Huan Wen's younger brother, Huo. *Yü SP*. XIX, 22.

YÜ TSUNG 庾琮 (Tzu-kung 子躬). fl. ca. 300. Elder brother of Yü Ai and father-in-law of Wang Na. He never rose higher than a minor office in the administration of the grand marshal. *YYCS*. VIII, 30, 40.

YÜ TS'UN 虞存 (Tao-ch'ang 道長). mid-fourth cent. A native of K'uai-chi Commandery (Chekiang), who served as Ho Ch'ung's superintendent of records while the latter was governing the commandery. He later became a senior administrator for the Palace Guard and a clerk in the Board of Civil Office. *YTLH*. III, 17; VIII, 85; XXV, 48.

YÜ T'UNG 庾統 (Ch'ang-jen 長仁; baby name, Ch'ih-yü 赤玉). first half, fourth cent. The son of Yü Liang's younger brother, I. He served as grand warden of Hsün-yang Commandery (Kiangsi), but died in his twenty-ninth year. *Yü SP*. VIII, 69, 89; XIV, 38.

YÜ YAO 庾姚. late fourth to early fifth cent. The daughter of Yü Mieh 蔑 and second wife of Huan Ch'ung; mother of Huan Hsiu. *Huan SP*. XXXVI, 8.

YÜ YU 庾友 (Hui-yen 惠彥; alias Hung-chih 弘之; baby name, Yü-t'ai 玉臺). fl. ca. 370. Third son of Yü Ping, he escaped Huan Wen's purge of the Yü clan in 371-372 through his connection as father-in-law of Huan's niece. He served successively as clerk in the Central Secretariat and grand warden of Tung-yang Commandery (Chekiang). *Yü SP*. XIX, 22.

YÜ YÜAN-CHIH 庾袁之 (Chung-chen 仲真; baby name, Yüan-k'o 園客). ca. 325-360. *CS* 73.21b-22a. The second son of Yü I and said to have inherited his father's manner. When Huan Wen replaced Yü I as governor of Ching Province (Hunan-Hupei) in 345, Yüan-chih was transferred to become grand warden of Yü-chang Commandery (Kiangsi). He died in his thirty-sixth year. *Yü SP*; *CHS*. VII, 19; XXV, 33.

YÜAN CH'IAO 袁喬 (Yen-shu 彥叔; baby name, Yang 羊). 312-347. *CS* 83.5b-7a. Son of Yüan Kuei 瓌. He began as assistant historian, later rising to clerk of the Imperial Secretariat. When Huan Wen was stationed at Ching-k'ou (Kiangsu) in 344, Yüan became his sergeant-at-arms. In 346 he accompanied Huan on his suppression of the secessionist Ch'eng-Han (Szechwan) ruler, Li Shih (r. 343-347), and is credited with much of the strategy of that campaign. Huan was on the point of making him governor of I Province (western Szechwan) when he died. He was noted for his scholarship and produced commentaries on the "Analects" and "Songs." *Yüan-shih chia-chuan*. II, 90; IV, 78; IX, 36, 65; XXV, 36.

YÜAN CHUN 袁準 (Hsiao-ni 孝尼). fl. 265-274. *CS* 83.8a. An extremely diffident and retiring man, he never held any but minor posts, spending all of his time in literary pursuits. A fragment of his "Treatise on Natural Ability and Human Nature" (*Ts'ai-hsing lun*), quoted in *IWLC* 21.6ab, reveals his interest in contemporary intellectual problems. *Yüan-shih chi*; *YenCC*. IV, *67*; V, *2*.

YÜAN HSI 袁熙 (Hsien-i 顯奕). d. 205. Mentioned, *SKWei* 6.21b. The second son of Yüan Shao and first husband of Empress Chen. He was appointed governor of Yu Province (northern Hopei) by the Later Han court in 202, but after Ts'ao Ts'ao's conquest of Yeh in 205, in which he lost his wife to Ts'ao P'ei, he was attacked by one of his own generals who had capitulated to Ts'ao, and with his younger brother, Shang 尚, fled to the Wu-huan tribes in Liao-hsi (southwestern Manchuria). In 207 he and his brother were captured and killed by the grand warden of Liao-tung, and their heads sent to Ts'ao Ts'ao, who had placed a heavy reward on them. *WeiL*. XXXV, *1*.

YÜAN HUNG 袁宏 (Yen-po 彦伯; baby name, Hu 虎). 328-376. *CS* 92.22b-29b. A writer of considerable reputation in his day, author of the still extant Later Han history, *Hou-Han chi* 後漢紀, and of the lost collection of biographies, *Ming-shih chuan* (*MSC*), as well as numerous poems of rhymed history (*yung-shih shih* 詠史詩), and poetic essays, e.g., *Tung-cheng fu* 東征賦 and *Pei-cheng fu* 北征賦, describing the founding and attempted expansion of Eastern Chin. Beginning as an aide under Hsieh Shang in Yü Province (Anhui) between 350 and 354, he served a term under Hsieh Feng as sergeant-at-arms while the latter was stationed in Kwangtung, and accompanied Huan Wen on his northern expedition of 354-356 as secretarial aide. Later he was in the Board of Civil Office, and at the end of his career was grand warden of Tung-yang (Chekiang). *HCYC*. II, *83*, 90; IV, 88, 92, 94, 96, 97; VIII, 34, 145; IX, 79; XXII, 2; XXV, 49; XXVI, 11, 12; XXVII, 13.

YÜAN K'O-CHIH 袁恪之 (Yüan-tsu 元祖). fl. ca. 405. He became personal attendant around 405. *Yüan SP*. IX, *81*.

YÜAN KUNG 袁公, fl. ca. 140. The magistrate of Yeh Prefecture (southern Hopei) at the above date. III, 3.

YÜAN LANG 袁閬 (Feng-kao 奉高). second cent. *HHS* 83.4b-5a; 86.5b. (The Yüan Hung 閎 [Hsia-fu 夏甫] of the text is an error.) He had been a friend of Huang Hsien in his boyhood and introduced him to Ch'en Fan. After being summoned to serve in the grand marshal's headquarters, he died without every having accepted office. *JNHHC*. I, *3*; II, 1, 7.

YÜAN NÜ-CHENG 袁女正. first half, fourth cent. Youngest sister of Yüan Tan and wife of Hsieh Shang. *Yüan SP*. XXIII, *37*.

YÜAN NÜ-HUANG 袁女皇. first half, fourth cent. The first younger sister of Yüan Tan and wife of Yin Hao. *Yüan SP*. XXIII, *37*.

YÜAN PAO 袁豹 (Shih-wei 士蔚). d. 413. *CS* 83.9a. Around 400 he was assistant historian and subsequently served as senior administrator to the grand marshal, and later capital intendant. *WCL*. IV, *99*.

YÜAN SHAN-SUNG 袁山松 (var. Yüan Sung 崧). d. 401. *CS* 83.7b. The son of Yüan Fang-p'ing 方平. He wrote a history of the Later Han Dynasty, some of whose monographs are incoporated in the official HHS. His hobby was collecting and rewriting old tunes, especially funeral songs, which he sang with great effect, especially when slightly under the influence of drink. He was grand warden of Wu Principality (Soochow) while it was overrun by Sun En in 401, and died defending Hu-tu Prefecture (near Shanghai). HCYC. I, 45; XXIII, 43; XXV, 60.

YÜAN SHAO 袁紹 (Pen-sh'u 本初). d. 202. HHS 104A.1a-25a; SKWei 6.14b-25b. An illegitimate son of Yüan Feng 逢, later adopted by his uncle, Yüan Ch'eng 成. At the peak of a brilliant military career, he led the campaign against Tung Cho in 190, but later, falling out with his erstwhile ally, Ts'ao Ts'ao, he was decisively crushed by the latter in 200, and died two years later. XI, 4; XXVII, 1, 5.

YÜAN TAN 袁耽 (Yen-tao 彥道). ca. 315-339. CS 83.8ab. An unconventional person whose reputation seems largely based on his prowess as a gambler. During the suppression of Su Chün's revolt in 328 he served as Wang Tao's aide and was rewarded with a fief and the grand wardenship of Li-yang Commandery (Anhui). In 335, because of misleading information he had sent on to court about some northern barbarian "invaders" in his commandery, he was cashiered, but later reinstated as an officer in Wang Tao's administration with heavy responsibilities. He apparently died before Wang Tao (d. 339). YSCC. XXIII, 34, 37; XXXI, 4.

YÜAN YÜEH (-CHIH) 袁悅(之)(Yüan-li 元禮). d. 389. 75.17a. He served a while as Hsieh Hsüan's aide and later, returning to the capital, made a close study of the "Intrigues of the Warring States" (Chan-kuo ts'e) and attempted applying its wily principles by advising the Prince of K'uai-chi, Ssu-ma Tao-tzu, with whom Yüan had very close connections, to assume dictatorial powers. However, Emperor Hsiao-wu (Ssu-ma Yao, r. 373-396), on being warned by Wang Kung, had Yüan executed in 389. Yüan SP. VIII, 153; XXXII, 2.

YÜEH, Lady 樂氏. late third cent. The daughter of Yüeh Kuang and wife of Ssu-ma Ying. II, 25.

YÜEH KUANG 樂廣 (Yen-fu 彥輔). 252-304. CS 43.21b-24a. Father-in-law both of Ssu-ma Ying and Wei Chieh. He was of a tolerant and irenic disposition, but considered more brilliant as a conversationalist than as a writer, preferring a rational, common-sense approach to learned or literary ones. He succeeded Wang Jung as president of the Imperial Secretariat, but because of his daughter's marriage to the Prince of Ch'eng-tu (Ssu-ma Ying), his loyalty was questioned by Ssu-ma I* 乂 after Ying's movement against the latter in 303, for which, it is said, he died of mortification early in the following year. YYCS. I, 23; II, 23, 25, 99?; IV, 14, 16, 70; VIII, 23, 25, 31; IX, 7, 8, 10, 46; XXVI, 2.

Glossary of Terms and Official Titles

a-che 阿堵. this. Six Dynasties colloquialism; equivalent to modern *che* 這.

a-che wu 阿堵物. these objects, this stuff.

A-nu 阿奴. "slavey"; pet name for younger brothers.

a-p'i-t'an 阿毗曇 (*'â-b'ji-d'âm). abhidharma, "on the Teaching"; a generic term for exegetical Buddhist works.

advisory aide (*tzu-i ts'an-chün* 諮議參軍). the principal aide in a military headquarters.

aide-de-camp (*ts'an-chün* 參軍). a subordinate official in a military headquarters.

an-chieh 闇解. intuitive understanding, not mediated by intelligence.

an-ku 闇故. scribal error for *tou-pien* 闘變?

an-tang 闇當. scribal error for *tou-pien* 闘變?

*b'iwɒng 平. plain.

bodhisattva (**b'uo-d'iei-sât-ɣwa* 菩提薩華). a being destined for enlightenment who postpones his own nirvana to save others. See *san-sheng*.

*b'uâ-sâ 䟺跋. to dance with mincing steps; cognate with **b'uət-suət*.

*b'uət-suət 勃窣. confined, cramped, to walk with mincing steps.

candana (*tśiän-d'ân 旃檀). white sandalwood (*santalum album*), the aromatic heartwood of a small parasitic tree of India and Southeast Asia.

capital intendant (*yin* 尹). the civilian administrator of the capital.

cavalier attendant (*san-chi shih-lang* 散騎侍郎). a palace appointment with unspecified duties.

cavalier attendant-in-ordinary (*san-chi ch'ang-shih* 散騎常侍). an honorary palace appointment for distinguished men.

cavalry aide (*chi-ping ts'an-chün* 騎兵參軍). a subordinate military office attached to the cavalry.

censor (*yü-shih* 御史). a court officer charged with surveillance over court affairs.

census aide (*hu-ts'ao ts'an-chün* 戶曹參軍). a military official in charge of records of the local populace.

cha 臘, the year-end sacrifice.

cha 鮓 or 鰶, salted fish.

cha 樝. haws, the small yellowish red fruit of the *chaenomeles japonica*.

ch'a 茶 (*tś'ia). tea (*camellia sinensis*). Sometimes distinguished as "early-picked" leaves, as opposed to *ming* 茗, "late-picked," perhaps the original Shu 蜀 term for tea.

ch'a 唼. to moisten the lips.

chan 占. to divine.

chan-hsiang 占相. divination by observing the physiognomy.

chancellor (*ch'eng-hsiang* 丞相). the actual chief of state, responsible directly to the emperor.

chang 丈. a measure of length; ten *ch'ih* 尺.

chang 璋. a jade scepter held during audience with the ruler.

chang 麞. the musk deer (*moschus chinloo*), a small hornless deer. The male is tusked and possesses a scent gland prized for perfumes.

chang 障. to screen.

chang 章. an essay, or section of a literary work.

chang-ni 障泥. mud protectors, saddle cloths hanging from each side of a horse.

chang-ts'ao 章草 . a variety of draft script.

ch'ang-hsing 長星 . a comet; sometimes also *hui-hsing* 彗星 .

ch'ang-ming 昌明 . utterly brilliant.

ch'ang-p'u 菖蒲 . calamus reeds.

ch'ang-t'an 常談 . usual talk.

chao 爪 . fingernails.

chao-hsi 朝夕 . morning and evening.

Chao-yang 朝陽 . the Eastern Slope (= Lo-yang).

ch'ao-t'ing 朝廷 . the (imperial) court.

ch'ao-wu 超悟 . transcendent perceptiveness, the ability to understand without the intervention of reason.

chaupar (*t'i̯u-b'uo 樗蒲). an Indian gambling game similar to backgammon, played on a board, with flat elongated dice pointed at the ends. From Sanskrit *catuspata*, "four cloths," or *catuspatha*, "crossroads."

che-chien 折簡 . a half-summons, served in less serious offenses.

ch'e 徹 . to penetrate, be thorough.

ch'e-chiao 車腳 . carriage footings, i.e., axles.

ch'e-chu 車柱 . carriage pole, the central mast supporting the canopy.

chen 鴆 . the serpent eagle (*haematornis cheela*), a large, black-crested predator ranging the hills between Hainan and Burma, living chiefly on snakes and therefore believed to be poisonous. See Schafer, *Vermilion Bird*, p. 245.

chen 枕 . pillow--in Six Dynasties usually wood or ceramic.

Chen 震 . "Thunderbolt." Hex. 51 of the "Book of Changes."

chen 針 or 鍼 . needle; acupuncture, the practice of inserting needles at key points in the body to clear blockages in the circulation of the pneuma (*ch'i* 氣).

chen 貞 . true, chaste, uncompromising.

chen-jen 真人 . Realized or Perfected Man--a Taoist term.

ch'en 臣 . servant, vassal; (in direct address) your servant.

ch'en-hsiang chih 沈香汁 . aloeswood lotion, made by soaking decayed branches of aloeswood in water. See Schafer, *Golden Peaches*, p. 113.

ch'en-ming 沈冥. literally, "submerged and dark"; impassive and intuitive.

cheng 箏 . the twelve-stringed zither, tuned to the pentatonic scale with movable bridges and plucked with the fingers.

cheng-meng 正夢 . regular dreams, not caused by unusual circumstances.

cheng tzu yu shan-ho chih i 正自有山河之異 .

ch'eng 渹 or 瀞 (**tsiɒng*). See *ho nai ch'eng*.

ch'eng 丞 . assistant.

ch'eng 酲 . a hangover; recovery from drunkenness.

ch'eng 誠 . sincerity; inner accord with the Tao which results in supernatural powers.

ch'eng-tu 成都 . to win--a gambling term.

chi 極 . the Ultimate.

chi 掎 . to pick up with chopsticks.

chi 迹 . footsteps, traces; overt acts.

chi 几. a low table; armrest.

chi 屐 . wooden clogs, similar to Japanese *geta*.

chi 齏 . minced pickles, finely chopped vegetables marinated in vinegar.

chi-chiu 齏臼 . minced or ground in a mortar.

chi-heng 璣衡 . the *hsüan-chi* 璿璣 and *yü-heng* 玉衡, ancient astronomical instruments mentioned in the "Book of Documents" (II, 5), whose nature and function are speculative; by metonymy, the dome of heaven.

Chi-se 即色 . "Matter-as-such" (*rūpam eva*), the name of the "school" of early Chinese Buddhism associated with Chih Tun 支遁 .

chi-sheng 濟勝 . to traverse the superb, i.e., climb mountains.

chi-tung 疾動 . to have an illness act up.

ch'i 溪 . mountain stream.

ch'i 齊 . equal.

ch'i 臍 . navel.

ch'i 氣. pneuma, the vital force circulating through the body or any aura emanating from it; seasonal forces, the ether appropriate to each season.

ch'i-chüeh 七覺. *sapta bodhyaṅgāni*, the seven degrees of enlightenment: (1) *smṛti*, mindfulness, (2) *dharma-pravicaya*, selection of consciousness data, (3) *vīrya*, zealous progress, (4) *prīti*, exhilaration, (5) *praśrabdhi*, a feeling of lightness, (6) *samādhi*, concentration, (7) *upekṣa*, indifference to distractions.

ch'i-shen 棲神. Resting the Spirit--a Taoist longevity technique.

chia 笳. "bugle"; a horn with a reed mouthpiece, used by northern nomadic people.

chia 架. a frame; to stretch on a frame.

chia 檟. the mallotus tree (*mallotus japonicus*), sometimes mistakenly identified with the tea plant.

chia 袷. a lined garment for informal wear.

chia-chien fen 甲煎粉. onycha paste, an aromatic unguent used for lipstick, made from the plate or lid of the onycha, a snail-like mollusk, mixed with the ashes of certain herbs and fruit flowers and impregnated with beeswax. See Schafer, *Golden Peaches*, p. 175.

Chia-p'ing 嘉平. Auspicious Leveling--the Hsia Dynasty name for the year-end sacrifice.

chia-tzu 假子. false son.

ch'ia 帢. a cap without corners designed in the third century; later apparently identified with the *chüeh-chin* 角巾, or cornered cap.

chiang-sha chang 絳紗帳. deep red silk-gauze curtains.

chiang-wu t'ung 將無同. "Aren't they the same?"

Ch'iang 羌. a proto-Tibetan pastoral people who had inhabited west and northwest China since Han times; one branch founded the Later Ch'in state in Shensi (384-417).

chiao 獢. martial.

chiao 蛟. a scaly dragon or water monster which devoured humans.

chiao 椒. fagara (*xanthoxylum piperitum*), a pungent spice similar to pepper.

chiao-ch'e 絞車. a windlass or capstan.

chiao-li 交禮. the exchange of bows, or ceremony of exchange, during a wedding.

ch'iao 喬 . lofty; the name of a tall tree.

chieh-hsi 解禊 . See *hsi* 禊 .

chieh-i 解義 . "explanatary interpretation," a type of commentary.

ch'ieh 妾 . concubine; a self-deprecatory term used by wives in addressing their husbands.

Chien 蹇 . "Obstruction." Hex. 39 of the "Book of Changes."

chien 劍 . a long two-edged sword.

chien 簡 . uncomplicated, unceremonious; rude.

chien 減 . to reduce; less than, under.

chien-chi 見機 . seeing the springs of action, clairvoyant.

chien-chia 蒹葭 . bullrushes.

Chien-P'i 蹇否 . Trouble and "Stagnation" (the second is Hex. 12 of the "Book of Changes").

chien-pu 筧布 . sheer cloth, a very costly fabric produced in the Szechwan area; a whole bolt could be contained in a bamboo tube (*t'ung-chung* 筒中). Alternately known as *huang-jun* 黃潤 , "yellow luster."

chien-yü 肩輿 . a single-passenger sedan chair, borne on the shoulders of two bearers.

ch'ien 錢 . cash, round metal currency with a square hole in the center usually estimated at one-tenth of a *liang* 兩 , or "ounce."

Ch'ien 乾 . "the Creative." Hex. 1 of the "Book of Changes."

Ch'ien* 謙 . "Modesty." Hex. 15 of the "Book of Changes."

chih 芡 . the water-lily (*eurale ferox*).

chih 質 . plain, unadorned; the opposite of *wen* 文 , cultivated.

chih 雉 . "pheasant," the second highest throw in the game of *chaupar*, in which two dice land with white sides up, marked with pheasants, and three with black sides up; worth fourteen points.

chih 至 . to arrive.

chih 姪 . nephew, son of a brother; a self-deprecatory term used by young men addressing older men.

chih 之 (a particle).

chih-i 至義 . ultimate principle.

chih-jen 至人 . the Perfect Man; = the Buddha.

chih-li 至理 . the Ultimate Truth. See also *li* 理.

chih pu-chih 旨不至 . "meanings do not reach."

chih-tsu 至足 . perfect contentment.

chih-tzu 梔子 . the gardenia (*gardenia jasminoides*).

chih-yü 鱕魚 . sardines (*sardinella zunasi*).

ch'ih 赤 . flesh-colored, pink.

ch'ih 齒 . front teeth; the "throws" of the game *chaupar*.

ch'ih 尺 . a measure of length; a "foot," ten *ts'un* 寸 , or "inches." In Later Han it was 23.5 centimeters, in Wei 24.1, and in Chin 24.5.

ch'ih-hsiao 鶌鶋 . a small bird, perhaps an oriole, which makes both raucous and mellifluous cries; tradition considered it a transformed owl.

ch'ih-lin 赤鱗 . light-red scaly creatures.

ch'ih-shih chih 赤石脂 . red bole. See *wu-shih san*.

chin 巾 . a kerchief or headcloth, worn on informal occasions.

chin 金 . gold piece, a coin weighing one catty (*chin* 斤).

chin 斤 . a catty, or 16 *liang* 兩 ; roughly equivalent to 1 1/3 lbs.

chin-chi 錦罽 . brocaded wool fabric.

chin-lüan 禁臠 . a forbidden slice of meat; the choicest cut from the nape of the neck, reserved for the emperor.

ch'in 琴 , the seven-stringed zither.

ch'in-ch'in 親親 . to be intimate with the intimate; to make the intimate intimate.

ch'in-su 親疏 . to be intimate with the distant; to make the distant intimate.

ching-fang 經方 . books of medical prescriptions and cures.

Ching-ming 淨名 . "Pure Reputation"; = Vimalakīrti.

ching-mo 經脈 . the pulses (of the pneuma emanating from various organs of the body); diagnosis by taking the pulses.

ching-she 精舍. a *vihāra*, or Buddhist retreat.

ching-t'ai 鏡臺. a mirror stand.

ch'ing 卿. you (familiar address). See also *chün* 君; *ju* 汝.

ch'ing 頃. one hundred *mou* 畝, roughly fifteen acres.

ch'ing-Fo 請佛. "inviting the Buddha," the ceremony of bathing an image of the infant Buddha on his birthday, the eighth day of the fourth lunar month.

ch'ing-i 清議. "pure criticism," censure of court personalities by persons in provincial areas.

ch'ing-ko 清歌. unaccompanied singing by female entertainers.

ch'ing-lu 青廬. the "blue-green hut." A temporary enclosure built of bamboo poles and draped with blue-green cloths before and behind the main gate of the bridegroom's house during wedding festivities.

ch'ing-so 青璅. a doorway decorated with a blue-green chain design.

Ch'ing-ssu 清祀. Pure Sacrifice, the Shang Dynasty name for the year-end sacrifice.

ch'ing-t'an 清談. "pure conversation." Beginning in Later Han as a discussion of personalities (see *ch'ing-i*), it moved in the third century toward philosophical subjects, especially Non-actuality (*wu* 無) and the "Three Mysteries" (*san-hsüan* 三玄, i.e., *Lao-tzu*, *Chuang-tzu*, and the "Book of Changes").

ch'ing-yen 清言. (= *ch'ing-t'an*).

ch'ing-yün 青雲. blue clouds.

chiu 舅. maternal uncle, mother's younger brother; term of address for father-in-law, sometimes also for wife's elder brother.

chiu 韭. leeks (*allium odorum*).

chiu-chü 舊居. former residence.

chiu-hsi 九錫. See Nine Bestowals.

chiu-pin 九嬪. the nine preceptresses of the imperial harem (*Chou-li*).

chiu-p'ing chi 韭萍齏. minced leek and duckweed pickles.

chiu-yü 九御. the nine imperial concubines (*Chou-li*).

ch'iu 楸. the mallotus tree. See also *chia* 檟.

ch'iu-chü 蹴鞠. football, a military game played with a wool-filled leather ball.

ch'iung-i 窮矣. "It's all over!" A cry of mourners in the Lo-yang area.

cho 濁. turgid (with nasal passages blocked?); a characteristic of northern speech.

cho-ting 琢釘. throwing spikes, a boy's game similar to mumblety-peg.

Chou-pei 周髀. the gnomon of Chou; an eight-foot pole used to measure the shadow of the sun at noon on the summer and winter solstices.

ch'ou-suan 籌算. counting rods, varying in length from six *ts'un* 寸 to one *ch'ih* 尺, made of bamboo or ivory, and used for calculation--the predecessor of the abacus. See Needham, *Science and Civilisation* III, pp. 70-72.

chu 筑. bamboo zither, a five-stringed zither played with a bamboo plectrum.

chu 主. lord, chief of an alliance; the "host" or proposer of a topic at a "pure conversation" session.

chu 住. *sthiti*, state or stage on the way toward enlightenment.

chu-shih 柱石. plinth stone.

chu-wei 麈尾. sambar-tail chowry, or fly whisk, made from the tail of a large, dark brown, long-tailed deer (*cervus unicolor*) inhabiting the mountains of Southeast Asia.

ch'u 出. a bout (of "pure conversation"), consisting of one clarification (*t'ung* 通) of the topic, and one objection or rebuttal (*nan* 難); interchangeable with *fan* 番.

ch'u-shih 處士. retired gentleman, gentry-recluse. Also the name of a constellation; see Shao-wei 少微.

ch'uan 荈. "late-picked" tea leaves.

ch'uang 牀. a raised dais for sitting, a couch; a bed for sleeping, usually curtained.

Chun 屯. "Difficulty at the Beginning." Hex. 3 of the "Book of Changes."

ch'un-keng 蓴羹. water-lily soup, a southern delicacy made from stems of the edible water plant *brasenia purpurea*.

chung 重. heavy; to give weight to.

chung 鍾. a grain measure equal to four *tou* 斗.

chung-chih 種智. omniscience (*sarvajñā*).

Chung-fu 中孚. "Inner Truth." Hex. 61 of the "Book of Changes."

chung-lang 中郎. middle son.

chung-lü 鐘律. bells and pitch pipes; (synechdoche for music).

chung-ming yün-lu ch'e 中鳴雲露車. "internally sounding cloud-dew chariot," a military chariot equipped with a tower for observation and drums and gongs to sound advances and retreats.

chung o-feng 中惡風. to suffer a stroke or cerebral hemorrhage.

chung-wai 中外. cousin, son of a maternal aunt.

ch'ung-ho 沖和. agreeable moderation.

chü 橘. the tangerine (*citrus reticulata*).

chü-mu yu Chiang-Ho chih i 舉目有江河之異.

chü-shih 居士. *gṛhapati*, a householder or Buddhist layman of means who supports the sangha.

chü-yü 姁隅 (*tsi̯u-ngi̯u). a Man 蠻 dialect term for "fish" in the Hupei area.

ch'ü 娶. to take a wife.

ch'ü-yü 鴝鵒. the myna (*aethiopsar cristellatus*), a medium-sized black bird with a tuft at the base of the bill which mimics other bird-calls and may be taught to mimic human speech.

ch'ü-yü wu 鴝鵒舞, the myna-bird dance, whose movements apparently resembled those of the bird.

ch'üan-hui 荃蕙. names of two fragrant plants.

chüeh 覺. to be aware, awake; *bodhi*, enlightenment. Sometimes interchangeable with the homophone 較 (both *kåk/kau), "by comparison."

chüeh-chin 角巾. a cornered cap made of coarse white linen worn by recluses. By Chin times it seems to have been identified with the *ch'ia* 恰 and was worn by scholars of the Grand Academy.

chüeh-ming 絕冥. Absolute Mystery, the reality beyond mundane experience.

chüeh shu-shih pu 覺數十步. "by about thirty or forty paces."

ch'üeh 鵲. the magpie (*pica pica sericea*), a long-tailed black and white bird common in north China.

ch'üeh-shan 卻扇. "to retire the fan," the moment of the wedding ritual when the silk-gauze fan separating bride and groom was removed for their first mutual recognition.

ch'üeh-shao 缺少. to lack, be missing.

chün 峻. lofty.

chün 麕. the muntjack (*muntiacus muntjak vaginalis*), a small horned deer of south China and Indo-China.

chün 君. you, sir (deferential address). See also *ch'ing* 卿 ; *ju* 汝.

chün 儁. paragon.

chün-tzu 君子. a lord's son; a gentleman--the opposite of a *hsiao-jen* 小人.

ch'ün 裙. skirt or apron.

ch'ün 羣. crowd.

clerk (*li* 吏 or *lang* 郎). any of a number of minor officials doing clerical work in an administrative office.

Commandant of Infantry (*pu-ping hsiao-wei* 步兵校尉). by Chin times a title without duties.

Commandant of Southern Barbarians (*nan-Man hsiao-wei* 南蠻校尉). the title of the governor-general of military operations in Ching Province (Hunan-Hupei).

Commandant of the Capital Province (*ssu-li hsiao-wei* 司隸校尉). the title of the governor-general of the Lo-yang area.

Commander (*chung-lang chiang* 中郎將). an officer of the Palace Guard.

Commander of the Plumed Forest Guards (*yü-lin chien* 羽林監). an officer of the Palace Guard.

commandery (*chün* 郡). the largest administratiave unit within a province (*chou* 州).

crown prince's equestrian forerunner (*t'ai-tzu hsien-ma* 太子洗馬). a member of the crown prince's staff in charge of his education.

curator of the palace library (*mi-shu ch'eng* 秘書丞). an officer in charge of palace documents, directly responsible to the president of the Central Secretariat--often a member of the royal family.

dāna, almsgiving. See *liu-tu*.

*d'âi-śi̯əu 大獸. a large animal. A pun for **t'âi-śi̯əu* 太守, grand warden.

d'am 淡 . limpid.

d'âp-lâp 榻臘 . sloppy, slovenly, shuffling.

dharma master. See *fa-shih*.

dharmakāya (*fa-shen* 法身). the Absolute; one of the three "bodies" of the Buddha, the substratum out of which the other two (i.e., sambhoga-kāya, the enjoyment body of the paradises, and nirmāna-kāya, the earthly body of Śākyamuni) are manifested.

dhūta (*d'əu-t'â* 頭陀). ascetic exercises.

dhyāna, meditation. See *liu-tu*.

d'iäu 旐 . a banner used to decorate coffins in a funeral procession.

d'ie̯ 池 . a pool or abyss; a moat.

d'ieng-d'ieng 亭亭 . brightness (of the moon); loftiness (of mountains).

director of instruction (*ssu-t'u* 司徒). one of the Three Ducal Offices (*san-kung*) reserved for persons winning special recognition at the head of the government; *ssu-t'u* was at some periods equivalent to chancellor (*ch'eng-hsiang* 丞相).

director of punishments (*t'ing-wei* 廷尉). the judge charged with trying offenders against the state.

director of the Central Secretariat (*chung-shu chien* 中書監). an office parallel to president of the Central Secretariat (*chung-shu-ling* 令).

director of works (*ssu-k'ung* 司空). one of the Three Ducal Offices. See *san-kung*.

divisional administrator (*pu ts'ung-shih* 部從事). the officer in a provincial administration responsible for liaison with the commanderies within the province.

d'âk-d'âk 濯濯 . sleek and shining.

d'uâi-d'âng 頹唐 . crumbling in ruins, dilapidated.

d'ung-mung 軬氄 . with a flurry of feathers.

dz'iek-dz'iek 寂寂 . doing nothing, living in quietude.

dz'uâi-nguei 崔嵬 . tall and towering.

e 鵝 . the domestic goose.

erh-ju ko 爾汝歌 . "you-your" songs; playfully insulting songs using the condescending forms of the second personal pronoun.

erh-shun 耳順 . (the age of) ears being obedient, i.e., sixty ("Analects" II, 4).

erh-ts'ung 耳聰 . (the state of) ears being (too) sensitive, a malady associated with palpitation of the heart (*hsü-chi* 虛悸).

erudite of the Grand Academy (*t'ai-hsüeh po-shih* 太學博士). a professor in the state academy who trained the sons of noble families in the Classics.

fa-shih 法師. dharma master, a title generally applied to eminent monks, but especially to the one whose function was the explication of difficult points in a Buddhist lecture.

fan 番. a bout (of "pure conversation"). See *ch'u*.

fan 凡 . generally; ordinary.

fan-k'u 反哭 . returning (to the ancestral temple) to weep; an act performed three days after the burial of a close relative.

fan-niao 凡鳥 . ordinary bird. See *feng* 鳳 .

fang-pien 方便 . *upāya*; expedient means, skill in adapting Buddhist teaching to the capacity of the hearer.

fang-wai 方外. beyond the (eight) directions; transcendental, beyond ordinary moral standards.

fei 廢 (*piwɐi*). to depose.

fei-pai 飛白 . "flying white," a calligraphic technique with dry brush, leaving uninked streaks on the paper.

fen 分 . portion, lot; the hundredth part of a *ch'ih*

fen 粉 . face powder.

feng 封 . the imperial sacrifice to Heaven performed on Mt. T'ai.

feng 鳳 (***b'iŭm*). a fabulous bird, the phoenix (explained in *SW* as composed of 凡 ***b'iwăm*, "ordinary," as phonetic and 鳥 "bird" as classifier).

feng-chü 峯岠 . mountain-top majesty.

feng-chüeh 風角 . divination by the direction of the wind.

feng-ku 風骨 . character and bone; style.

feng-liu 風流. "mannered flow," cultivated style, urbanity; a favored life style of the upper classes during the Six Dynasties.

feng-yün 風韻 . style, tone.

field work officer (*t'ien-ts'ao chung-lang* 田曹中郎). an aide in the headquarters of the grand marshal responsible for supervising work in the fields.

Filial and Incorrupt (*hsiao-lien* 孝廉). the third degree on the road to an official career, achieved during the Six Dynasties by recommendation from prominent persons of one's native commandery.

Fo-hsing 佛性. buddha-nature, the potential buddha within human nature.

fu 賦. poetic essay, a literary form in rhymed sections with prose introduction and interludes.

fu 符. a charm or talisman, often in the form of scraps of paper with cryptic characters, worn about the person or ingested for protective purposes by sectarian Taoists.

fu 阜. mound, hill (classifier 170).

fu 浮. floating, frivolous.

fu 綍. coffin ropes.

fu 脯. salted dried meat, used as an accompaniment for wine.

fu 富 (*$pi̯əu$*), wealthy. A pun for 腐 *$b'i̯u$*, rotten.

fu-hsing 腐刑. punishment by castration.

fu-hsü 浮虛. frivolity and emptiness; a pejorative description of "pure conversation."

fu-jen 夫人. an honored concubine of an emperor; Madame, a respectful title for the wife of a prominent man.

fu-jung 芙蓉. lotus (*nelumbo nucifera*).

fu-kuei 簠簋. a bamboo vessel used in Chou times for sacrificial grain.

fu-ou 綍謳. coffin-rope chanties, sung by pallbearers to keep in step.

general (*chiang-chün* 將軍). a military title applied both to officers in the field and to nonmilitary figures at court.

General Chastizing the South (*cheng-nan chiang-chün* 征南將軍). the title of generals sent on specific assignments south of the capital. There were corresponding appointments for each of the directions.

General Controlling the Army (*fu-chün chiang-chün* 撫軍將軍). a special post reserved for members of the imperial family.

General Governing the West (*chen-hsi chiang-chün* 鎮西將軍). the title of generals stationed in Ching Province (Hunan-Hupei), the most influential of the four directions, because of its strategic location on the upper Yangtze.

General Leading the Army (*ling-chün chiang-chün* 領軍將軍). a court title without military duties.

General of Chariots and Horsemen (*ch'e-chi chiang-chün* 車騎將軍). a court title of great honor, just below General of Spirited Cavalry.

General of Spirited Cavalry (*p'iao-chi chiang-chün* 驃騎將軍). a court title of great honor, just below Generalissimo.

General of the Central Guard (*chung-chün chiang-chün* 中軍將軍). an officer of the Palace Guard.

General Pacifying the South (*p'ing-nan chiang-chün* 平南將軍). the title of generals specifically sent to quell uprisings in one of the four directions.

General Protecting the Army (*hu-chün chiang-chün* 護軍將軍). a court title.

Generalissimo (*ta chiang-chün* 大將軍). a high military title comparable in honor to the Three Ducal Offices (*san-kung*).

*$g'jwi$-$g'jwi$ 騤騤. spirited and strong.

governor (*tz'u-shih* 刺史). literally, "goader and commissioner"; the civil administrator of a province (*chou* 州); also *nei-shih* 內史 ("internal commissioner"), the civil administrator of a principality (*kuo* 國).

governor-general (*tu-tu* 都督). a military command, usually embracing operations in several provinces.

grader (*chung-cheng* 中正). an officer charged with ranking officials within a province or commandery on a ninefold graded scale (*chiu-p'in* 九品).

grand astrologer (*t'ai-shih* 太史). an officer charged with observing and recording natural portents as well as human events; hence the alternate translation, "grand historian."

grand marshal (*t'ai-wei* 太尉). one of the Three Ducal Offices (*san-kung*)--in some periods named *ssu-ma* 司馬 ; he was commander-in-chief of all military operations in the realm.

grand ordinary (*t'ai-ch'ang* 太常). an officer in charge of court ceremonial, especially the imperial sacrifices.

grand protector (*t'ai-pao* 太保). an honorary court title, just below grand tutor (*t'ai-fu* 太傅).

grand tutor (*t'ai-fu* 太傅). a high court title with no duties attached.

grand warden (*t'ai-shou* 太守). the administrator of a commandery (*chün* 郡).

Great Officer of Brilliant Favor (*kuang-lu ta-fu* 光祿大夫). a sort of majordomo in the palace.

*γap-iäp 洽渫. mud-roiled.

*γuâi-wâng 回遑. to vacillate, pace to and fro.

han 酣. slightly tipsy; a spree.

han-feng 寒風. See *kuang-mo*.

han-shih 寒士. an insignificant or impoverished gentleman of an unimportant family (*han-men* 寒門).

han-shih san 寒食散. cold-food powder. See *wu-shih san*.

hao 浩. vast.

hao-shih 好事. to be fond of gossip or of meddling in other people's affairs.

hao-wu yang-shih 好武養士. "loving valor and supporting warriors."

historian (*chu-tso lang* 著作郎). the person charged with collecting and editing the documents which eventually went into the official history of a dynasty.

ho 合. to join, be combined; as a scribal pun: composed of *jen* 人, "man," *i* 一, "one," and *k'ou* 口, "mouth."

ho 臛. meat broth.

ho 何. what, how, why?

ho-liu 何留. "what is detaining (it)?"

ho nai ch'eng 何乃𠎶. "How cool!" (local dialect of Wu area).

ho pu-liu 何不餾. "Why is it not steaming?"

ho-shang 和尚 (*γuâ-ziang). "Your Reverence," "Reverend"; a respectful term of address for Buddhist monks, perhaps derived through the Khotanese *vādhyā from Sanskrit *upādhyāya*, "teacher."

ho-tzu 貉子. "son of a badger," a contemptuous epithet used by northerners in referring to natives of Wu.

hou 後. rear; descendants.

hou-ch'i 候氣. to observe the seasonal forces by arranging twelve ash-filled pitch pipes (*lü-lü* 律呂), corresponding to each of the twelve months, in a radiating circle within a hermetically sealed room, and noting when the seasonal force of each month disturbs the ashes within the corresponding pipe.

hsi 禊 or *chieh-hsi* 解禊. a spring purification ceremony held on the third day of the third lunar month beside a winding stream (*ch'ü-shui* 曲水), in which celebrants floated cups of wine downstream and composed extempore poems when the cups came to rest on the bank.

Hsi 傒. the area of Kiukiang in Kiangsi, whose inhabitants used to be nicknamed "dogs of Hsi" (*Hsi-kou* 傒狗) by the people of Wu.

Hsi-Jung 西戎. "Western barbarians," an old term for the inhabitants of Shensi and Kansu.

hsi-ping 犀柄. rhinoceros-horn handle (of a sambar-tail chowry).

hsia 俠. knight-errant, swashbuckler. See *yu-hsia* 遊俠.

hsia 蝦. shrimps.

hsia 下. second syllable of *t'ien-hsia* 天下, the realm.

hsia-tu 下都. the lower capital (i.e., Chien-k'ang); to descend (the Yangtze) to the capital.

hsiang 象. the "Images," interpretations of the hexagrams of the "Book of Changes" as a whole.

hsiang 相. to characterize, give a succinct resumé of a man's character; to divine through geomancy or physiognomy; a minister of state, specifically, chancellor.

hsiang 向. to go toward.

hsiang 祥. a sacrifice marking the end of thirteen or twenty-five months' mourning.

hsiang 想. thoughts, imagination.

hsiang-nang 香囊. an aromatic sachet, often worn at the wrist.

hsiang-wang 相王. chancellor-prince, the title of a member of the royal family serving as chancellor.

hsiao 小. See *hsiao-jen* 小人.

hsiao 簫. the vertical flute, bamboo cut on an angle at the top joint for blowing with holes for stopping.

hsiao 嘯. to whistle. The method seems to have been by inserting two fingers in the mouth; see the tomb engraving of the "Seven Worthies of the Bamboo Grove" in *Wen-wu* 1965.8, where Juan Chi is so represented.

hsiao 鴞. See *ch'ih-hsiao*.

hsiao-fu 消伏. to minimize or suppress--from *hsiao-hsi fei-fu* 消息飛伏,--diminution or increase, soaring visibly or lying hidden.

hsiao-jen 小人. a commoner; a petty person--the opposite of a *chün-tzu* 君子.

hsiao-lien 孝廉. See Filial and Incorrupt.

hsiao-ts'ao 小草. See *yüan-chih*.

hsiao-tzu 小子. "little boy," a patronizing form of address to juniors.

hsiao-tzu 孝子. filial son; specifically, a son mourning a deceased parent.

hsiao-yao 逍遙. free roaming, freedom gained by transcending the world (*Chuang-tzu* I).

hsieh 寫. to pour forth, express; to write.

hsieh 蟹. the edible crab (*brachyura brachyura*), rather large, with serrated shell and thick mandibles.

hsieh 薤. shallots (*allium bakeri*).

hsien 仙. a transcendent being, an "immortal"; the highest level of existence in Taoist thought, in which the adept transcends time and space.

hsien-hou 先後. those before and behind, attendants ("Songs" 237).

Hsien-pei 鮮卑. a semi-agricultural people living on China's northeastern frontier from about the third century A.D., who founded the Yen and Northern Wei states in north China (third to sixth centuries); their language was proto-Altaic and their physical features somewhat fairer than the Chinese.

hsien-tsai hsin 現在心. (insight into) present thoughts; = āsravakṣaya-jñāna. See *san-ming*.

Hsien-yün 獫狁. a nomadic people who occasionally threatened the northern frontier during the Chou period.

hsin-mao 辛卯. (cyclical combination.)

hsin-nei 心內. within the mind.

hsin-wu i 心無義. the theory of Mental Nonexistence (one of the "Six Schools" of early Chinese Buddhism), attributed to Chih Min-tu 支愍度--a kind of idealism.

hsing 性 . human nature; a person's endowment at birth.

hsing-hsiang 行像 . walking the (Buddha) image in procession during the celebration of the Buddha's birthday in the fourth lunar month.

hsing-ku 形骨 . the bony structure of the body, a key to divination by physiognomy.

hsing-san 行散 . walking (to circulate through the system) a five-mineral powder. See *wu-shih san*.

hsing-shu 行書 . cursive script.

hsiu 休 . to rest; happiness, good fortune.

hsiu-shou 袖手 . to put one's hands into one's sleeves; probably a scribal error for *shen-wang* 神王 .

hsiu-ts'ai 秀才 . Outstanding Talent, the highest degree to which promising young men were recommended on the way to an official career.

Hsiung-nu 匈奴 . a nomadic, horse-breeding people living on China's northern and northwestern frontier from the second century B.C., who founded the Former and Later Chao states in north China during the fourth century A.D.

hsiung-po 兄伯 . eldest brother.

hsiung-ti 兄弟 . brothers; male relatives of the same generation.

Hsü 須 (*the name of a star*).

hsü 壻 . son-in-law.

hsü 許 . a mansion; (*as a verbal complement*), more or less, somewhat; (*as a final particle*), the equivalent of *hu* 乎 .

hsü-chi 虛悸 . palpitation of the heart. See also *shih-hsin ping*.

hsü-fu 胥附 . to bring the distant near ("Songs" 237).

hsü-sheng 虛勝 . the Empty and Transcendent.

hsü-tan 虛誕 . nihilism and libertinism.

hsüan 玄 . the Mysterious, the mystical world beyond sense experience epitomized in the "Three Mysteries" (*san-hsüan* 三玄 , i.e., *Lao-tzu*, *Chuang-tzu*, and the "Book of Changes").

hsüan-chi 玄寂 . Mysterious Quiescence, a primitive form of Taoism supposedly practiced by the Yellow Emperor and Shen-nung.

hsüan-chi 璿璣 . See *chi-heng*.

hsüan-feng 玄風 . the vogue of the Mysterious; (= *hsüan-hsüeh*).

hsüan-hsü 玄虛 . the Mysterious and Empty.

hsüan-hsüeh 玄學 . the Mysterious Learning, a blend of "New Text" Confucianism and philosophical Taoism popular in the third and fourth centuries.

hsüan-miao 玄妙. the Mysterious and Subtle.

hsüan-sheng 玄勝. the Mysterious and Transcendent.

hsüan-tui 玄對 . mystic contemplation (*said of viewing landscapes*).

hsüan-yen 玄言 . conversation about the Mysterious; = "pure conversation."

hsüan-yüan 玄遠 . the Mysterious and Remote, mystical aloofness from public life.

hsün 薰 . a fragrant plant.

hu 楛 . the thornwood, a tree growing in present Manchuria which yields a reddish, straight-grained wood prized for making arrow shafts.

Hu 胡 . a generic term for non-Chinese peoples of the north and west, including the Hsiung-nu, Yüeh-chih, Central Asians, and Indians.

hu 蠖. the inchworm, the larva of the moth *hemirophila atrilineata*, which moves by alternately looping and stretching forward--an image of alternate retirement and activity.

hu 斛 . a measure of volume, equivalent to ten *tou* 斗 .

hu 笏 . a long narrow tablet, signifying official rank, held upright before the body during an audience with the emperor.

hu 乎. (interrogative and exclamatory final particle.)

hu-ch'uang 胡床. a folding chair, or campstool, introduced into China during the Six Dynasties by nomadic peoples from the northwest. See C. P. Fitzgerald, *Barbarian Beds*, London, 1965, and review by Donald Holzman in *T'oung Pao* 50 (1967), pp. 279-292.

hu-lien 瑚璉 . a sacrificial vessel used for offering millet in ancient times.

hu-lu 壺盧 . the bottle gourd.

hua-che 蝐蠌 . a small species of crab apparently identical with the *p'eng-ch'i*.

huai 槐. the locust tree (*sophora japonica*).

huan-chung 環中. the center of the circle; = *tao-shu*.

huang-chung 黃鐘. "yellow bell," the standard pitch from which all the others are derived. See *lü-lü*.

huang-chüan 黃絹. yellow pongee; = *se-ssu* 色絲, colored silk--a scribal pun for *chüeh* 絕, "utterly,"

huang-ch'üeh 黃雀. the brown sparrow (*passer rutilans*).

huang-jun 黃潤. "yellow sheen." See *chien-pu*.

hui 諱. taboo name, or personal name--normally not used outside the family.

hui 回. to turn back.

hui 會. (pronounced *k'uai* in K'uai-chi 會稽).

hui 徽. See *wei* 微.

hui-wa-tiao 虺瓦弔 (*χjwei-ngwa-tieu*). literally, "viper-tile-string-of-cash," an expletive; the last character, sometimes written 吊, may be a corruption of *tai* 呆, "idiot." See also *wang-fan-tiao*.

hun-t'ien 渾天. literally, "whole heaven," the celestial sphere; one of three ancient theories of the universe, in which the earth is conceived as a smaller sphere within a larger celestial sphere.

huo 活. alive (*phonetic in k'uo* 闊).

I 椅 (a *personal name*?)

I* 倚 (*variant of preceding entry.*)

i 懿. virtuous.

i 義. moral principle, social obligation (a Confucian concept); meaning, interpretation.

i 一. one.

i 邑. town.

I 易 (**iäk*). to change; the "Book of Changes" (= *Chou-i* 周易); (**ie*), easy, simple.

i 姨. aunt, mother's sister; wife's sister; term of address for a concubine.

i 驛. station.

i 衣. clothing.

i 揖. to bow with hands clasped or pressed together.

i 詣. to go to a destination; by extension, to get directly to the point.

i 異. different, other.

i-ch'i 奕棊. "chess," a general term for board games. See also *chaupar*; *tan-ch'i*; *wei-ch'i*.

i-fu 倚伏. literally, "leaning and depending," the mutual dependence of prosperity and calamity (*Lao-tzu* 58).

i hsiung-ti 姨兄弟. sons of a maternal aunt--cousins; husbands of sisters--brothers-in-law.

i-lang 議郎. consultant, a subordinate office usually held by young men with the first two degrees.

i-li 義理. Meanings and Principles. See also *li-i*.

i-pu 餌餔. fried rice cakes.

i-shu 醫術. medical arts, especially the new techniques brought by Buddhist monks from India.

i tzu-mei 姨姊妹. (*the female counterpart of i hsiung-ti*.)

*$i\ddot{a}k$-$i\ddot{a}k$ 奕奕. proud and aloof.

*˙$i\ddot{a}m$-˙$i\ddot{a}m$ 厭厭. with tranquil contentment; apathetic; dark (of the moon).

*˙$i\ddot{a}m$-˙$i\ddot{a}m$ 黯黯. intensely black, dark.

*$iang$-$pu\hat{a}$ 揚波. tossing waves.

*$iang$-$iang$ 洋洋. rippling and purling.

*˙$iang$-$t\acute{s}iang$ 鞅常. numerous, abundant.

*$ipng$-$t\hat{a}$ 英多. heroes aplenty.

*$i\partial k$-$i\partial k$ 翼翼. luxuriant; reverent.

*˙$i\partial m$-˙$i\partial m$ 愔愔. amiable and relaxed.

*$i\partial u$-$i\partial u$ χu∂t-χu∂t 悠悠忽忽. detached and carefree.

   imperial clan officer (*tsung-cheng ch'ing* 宗正卿, or *shih-ch'ing* 士卿). the person responsible for ranking the imperial relatives in order of proximity to the emperor.

   Imperial Secretariat (*shang-shu* 尚書). the central deliberative body at court, subdivided into the Board of Civil Office (*li-pu* 吏部), The Board of Punishments (*hsing-pu* 刑部), the Board of Works (*kung-pu* 工部), etc.

inspector-general (*tu-yu* 都郵). an officer of a commandery who makes periodic rounds of inspection among the prefectures.

jen 人. a human being.

jen 仞. a measure of height equivalent to eight *ch'ih*.

jih 衵. underwear.

Jih-hsia 日下. Beneath the Sun (= Lo-yang).

ju 入. to enter

ju 汝. you (condescending term of address). See also *ch'ing* 卿; *chün* 君.

ju-i 如意. literally, "as you wish," a baton about a foot or 18 inches in length, slightly curled at one end--perhaps originally a back scratcher.

ju-lai 如來. See *tathāgata*.

jun 潤. luster.

jung 融. intelligent; glossed as *t'iao-ch'ang* 條暢 in the Commentary.

junior grader (*hsiao chung-cheng* 小中正). See grader.

junior tutor to the crown prince (*t'ai-tzu shao-fu* 太子少傅). a member of the crown prince's retinue assisting with his studies.

kai 概. originally an instrument for leveling grain measures; by derivation, moderation, a sense of proportion; personal magnetism, charisma.

k'ai-fa 楷法. the method of writing formal script (*k'ai-shu* 楷書), as opposed to clerical script (*li-shu* 隸書), cursive script (*hsing-shu* 行書), or draft script (*ts'ao-shu* 草書). All but *li-shu*, a squarish adaptation introduced during the Han of the standardized seal script (*hsiao-chuan* 小篆) of the third century B.C., were innovations of the third and fourth centuries A.D.

k'ai-mei 開美. to bring out the excellence (of others).

*kåk-ńźiak 角䚢. a corner.

kan 感. stimulus; correlative with *ying* 應, response. By concentrating one's inner sincerity (*ching-ch'eng* 精誠), one may stimulate the universe to respond with a special sign.

kan-che 甘蔗. sugarcane.

kan-tsao 乾棗. dried jujubes. See *tsao*.

k'an 柑. an earthenware crock holding about five sheng 升.

kao 高. eminent, as opposed to ming 名, famous.

kao-shan 高山. high mountain.

Ken 艮. "Mountain." Hex, 52 of the "Book of Changes."

keng-chieh 耿介. resolute integrity.

keng-pei 羹杯. soup ladle or cup.

*k'iei-k'ək 溪刺. petty and perverse.

k'iəm-k'jie liek-lâk 嶮崎歷落. crag-crested and rock-strewn.

k'jie-k'iu 崎嶇. in agitated woe, upset.

ko 合. a measure equal to about three cubic inches, or one tenth of a sheng 升.

ko 膈. diaphragm.

ko 閤. side gate--one of the smaller gates on either side of the main gate.

ko-hsia 閤下. below the side gate.

ko-wu 格五. "reach-five," a game similar to checkers.

k'o 客. "guest," the interlocutor in a "pure conversation."

k'o 可. may; it's all right.

kou 狗. cub, puppy.

k'ou 口. mouth, mouthful.

ksānti. patient endurance. See liu-tu.

ku 姑. paternal aunt, father's sister; term of address for one's husband's mother; general term of address for older women.

ku 鼓. drums (there are many varieties).

ku-ts'ai 菰菜. wild rice (zizania latifolia), an edible grain growing along the shallows of waterways in the Yangtze Delta.

ku-yao 鼓夭. "portent of tolling."

ku ying jang tu hsü 故應讓杜許.

kua 瓜. melon.

kua-jen 寡人. "We," a self-deprecatory term affected by the feudal lords of the Chou period, occasionally used by holders of high military commands in the Six Dynasties.

kua-ko 瓜葛. a "melon-creeper" relationship, an intimate relation.

Kuai 夬. "Resoluteness." Hex. 43 of the "Book of Changes."

kuai 乖. turn aside, deviate.

*kuâi-ngâ 傀俄. leaning crazily; cognate with many binomes meaning "towering," "lofty," etc.

K'uai* 鄶 (special form for first character in K'uai-chi 會稽).

kuan 關. point of contact, relation.

kuan 管. pipe, a vertical pitch pipe without holes, general term for wind instruments.

*kuân 官. office; pun on *kuân 棺, coffin.

kuang-mo 廣莫. "Broad and Boundless"; an old designation for the north wind.

k'uang 曠. untrammeled.

k'uang-ta 曠達. untrammeled freedom.

kuei 晷. the shadow cast by a gnomon. See *Chou-pei*.

kuei 桂. (a) *osmanthus fragrans*, a treelike shrub with fragrant blossoms which grows in all parts of China (no examples in *SSHY*); (b) *cassia cinnamomum*, the cassia tree, whose bark is used for cinnamon, which grows only south of the Yangtze River.

kuei 珪. a ceremonial jade scepter, pointed at one end, held by courtiers in the Chou period during audience with the ruler.

**k'uət-k'uət* 窟窟. digging by slow degrees (?)

kun 幝. underpants, a loincloth.

K'un 坤. "the Receptive." Hex. 2 of the "Book of Changes."

kung-ch'e 公車. literally, "public carriages"; the gate of the palace to which petitioners came.

kung-fu 公府. "Your Lordship," the term of address for those in the Three Ducal Offices.

kung-hui 公會. a public gathering.

kung-shang 宮商. the first two notes of the pentatonic scale, corresponding roughly to *fa* and *sol* of the solfège system.

k'ung-ch'üeh 孔雀 . the peacock (*pavo cristatus*).

k'ung-wu 空無 . "Empty Nonexistence."

kuo 過 . to exceed; a transgression, lapsus.

kuo-ch'ü hsin 過去心 . (insight into) past thoughts;
= *pūrvanivāsānusmṛti-jñāna*. See *san-ming*.

kuo-tzu hsüeh 國子學 . a school for the sons of noblemen established in Lo-yang in 276; later known as *kuo-tzu chien* 監 .

k'uo 闊 . vast, commodious.

la 臘 . a generic term for the year-end sacrifice.

la-chu 蠟燭 . beeswax candles.

*lâ-lâ 羅羅 . loosely spreading.

lai-chiu 來久 . for a long time now.

*lâk-tâk 樂託 . wild and unbridled.

**lâk-lâk miuk-miuk* 洛洛穆穆 . lackadaisical and easygoing.

**lân-dź'ia* 蘭闍 . *rañjanī*, "good cheer," a Buddhist greeting.

*lân-lân 爛爛 . flashing.

lang 郎 . "Master" (term of address for young boys).

*lâng-lâng 琅琅 (onomatapoeia for the clear tones of stone chimes).

*lâng-lâng 朗朗 . transparently luminous.

*lâng-pwai 狼狽 . to be disconcerted, thrown into confusion.

lang-yü 朗豫 . transparently tranquil.

lao 蟧 . a species of small crab, evidently related to the *hua-che* and identical with the *p'eng-hua*.

lao 酪 . See *yang-lao*.

lao-hsin 勞薪 . firewood which has seen heavy duty.

lao-sheng 老生 . an old scholar.

lao-tsei 老賊 . "you old rascal" (a familiar term of address).

*lâp-lâ 拉攦 . splitting and splintering.

lei 櫑 . lacquered boxes for eating, partitioned internally, and made to fit together in pairs.

lei 誄. obituary, a poetic lament for the dead.

li 梨. pear.

li 李. plum.

li 離. separate, unrelated.

li 里. a measure of distance, roughly one-third of an English mile; a village.

li 理. a principle, or topic of conversation; reason, rationality; Truth, the underlying principle governing all existence (especially after the fourth century).

li 立. to stand upright.

li-chih 理致. the effect of (one's) reasoning.

li-ch'ih 礪齒. to sharpen the teeth.

li-ch'ih erh 利齒兒. a fellow with sharp teeth, i.e., a person eager to make a reputation.

li-chung 理中. the heart of Truth.

li-hui 理會. convergence with Truth, the point where Truth is understood.

li-i 理義. Principles and Meanings. See also *i-li*.

li-k'u 理窟. a storage cave of Truth.

li-shu 隸書. clerical script. See *k'ai-fa*.

li-yüan 理源. the source of Truth.

*liäm 廉. modest.

**liän-dz'iän* 連錢. mottled, speckled.

liang 兩. an ounce; 1/16 of a *chin* 斤.

liang 亮. brightness.

liang-i 涼衣. cool clothing, i.e., underclothes.

liao 膋. the caul, or amniotic sac, which sometimes covers the head of a newly born infant.

*liäu 燎. to burn.

libationer (*chi-chiu* 祭酒). a title of distinction awarded to senior personal attendants of the emperor.

lien 奩. a cosmetic case, or powder box, usually of lacquered wood and cylindrical in shape.

lien-pi 連璧. linked jade discs.

lien-t'a 連榻. adjoining couches, low daises placed together for greater intimacy in conversation. See also *tu-t'a*.

*lieng 冷. cold.

*lieu 了. to end.

*lieu-lieu 了了. quick and perceptive, clever.

*liəm-lâng 琳瑯. dazzling, scintillating; also onomatapoeia for the tinkling of gems.

*liəng-liəng 稜稜. angularity, austerity.

lieutenant-governor (*pieh-chia* 別駕). "riding a separate carriage," a special assistant to the governor of a province.

lin 麟. "unicorn," a mythical animal (possibly an extinct species of an actual animal) whose rare appearances were deemed auspicious.

lin-lang chu-yü 琳瑯珠玉.

ling 菱. the water-chestnut plant (*trapa natans*).

ling 鈴. a handbell, with handle and internal clapper.

ling-chih 靈芝. the magic mushroom; originally, perhaps, any of several types of fungus growing in mountainous areas, thought to have levitational properties. Some have sought to identify it with *fomes japonicus*, a shelflike fungus growing from decayed tree trunks.

ling-ch'uang 靈牀. spirit bed, a raised dais on which the coffin was placed in the reception hall of the home of the deceased before burial.

ling-shang 令上. a transcendent level of existence.

ling-shih 令史. a petty clerk.

ling-ta 令達. transcendently free.

liu 餾. to steam (rice). See *ho-liu*; *ho pu-liu*.

liu-li 琉璃 (*liəu-ljie). *vaiḍurya*, or colored glass.

liu-po 六博. "sixes," a gambling game played on a board with dice.

liu-tu 六度. the Six Perfections (*pāramitā*) or means of reaching Nirvana: (1) *dāna*, almsgiving, (2) *śīla*, keeping the commandments,

(3) *kṣānti*, patient endurance, (4) *vīrya*, zealous progress, (5) *dhyāna*, meditation, (6) *prajñā*, gnosis, or transcendental insight.

liu-t'ung 六通 . the Six Supernatural Faculties (*abhijñā*): (1) *divya-cakṣuḥ*, divine sight, (2) *divya-śrota*, divine hearing, (3) *rddhi-sākṣātkriya*, intuitive powers (of being where one wishes), (4) *paracitta-jñāna*, knowing the minds of others, (5) *pūrvanivāsānus-mṛti-jñāna*, knowing past existences, (6) *āsravakṣaya-jñāna*, knowing that defilements have ceased.

lo-han 羅漢 (*lâ-χân). *arhat*, a worthy, a perfected saint (Theravāda).

Lo-sheng yung 洛生詠. the manner of intoning poems of the Lo-yang scholars--an effort by the refugee court at Chien-k'ang in the fourth century to preserve the court speech of Western Chin.

lord grand ordinary (*t'ai-ch'ang ching* 太常卿). an officer in charge of court ceremonies.

lou-chin 漏盡. *āsravakṣaya* (*-jñāna*), knowledge that defilements have ceased. See *liu-t'ung*.

Lu 陸. a surname; homophonous with *lu* 鹿 , deer (both *luk).

lu 簏. a round bamboo basket used for storage.

lu 墟. a wineshop; specifically, the thick earth walls in which vats of fermenting wine were stored.

lu 盧 . "black," the highest throw in the game of *chaupar*, in which all five dice land black side up; worth sixteen points.

lu-lu 轆轤. a windlass used for hoisting buckets from wells.

lu-yü kuai 鱸魚膾. sliced perch.

**luậi-k'uậi* 礨塊. rough and rugged; gnarled and knotty.

*luậi-lâk 磊落 . rugged, flintlike.

*luậi-luâ 磊砢. rugged, gnarled.

lü 履 . leather shoes or sandals; "Treading," Hex. 10 of the "Book of Changes."

lü-lü 律呂. the six male and six female pitches of the twelve-tone gamut formed by cutting bamboo pipes successively by 2/3 and 4/3 lengths alternately.

ma 馬. literally, "horse"; a counter for keeping score in gambling games.

magistrate (*ling* 令). the administrator of a prefecture (*hsien* 縣).

mao 旄. a yak-tail standard carried by armies.

mao-shan 毛扇, or *yü-shan* 羽扇. a feather fan made from the whole wing of a bird.

master of court ceremonials (*hung-lu ch'ing* 鴻臚卿). literally, "lord transmitter of greatness"; a court officer in charge of special entertainments.

mei 美. excellent, beautiful.

men-sheng 門生. retainers or protégés, usually promising young men recommended by the gentry of their home districts to the sponsorship of prominent figures at court.

meng-chu 盟主. chief of the blood oath, the leader of a coalition of factions.

meng-ch'en 蒙塵. "covered with dust."

mi 米. uncooked rice.

mi 麋. the elaphure (*alces machlis*), a large dark reddish-brown deer of northern China.

mi-mi 靡靡. slowly, lasciviously.

*miäng-tieng 茗𤗉. tipsy, "feeling no pain."

miao-mu 眇目. squint-eyed, with one eye closed or clouded by some infirmity.

miao-yu 妙有. Subtle Existence, the potentially existent within Non-existence.

min 民. people.

ming 冥. dark, a twilight state of mystical intuition; to be intuitively one with the Tao.

ming 名. given name; reputation.

ming 茗 (*miäng, or *mieng*). tea leaves—a local Wu term, later distinguished as "late-picked" leaves.

ming-chiao 名教. literally, "Doctrine of Names"; the Moral Teaching, a mixture of Confucian, Legalist, and Dialectic principles favored by persons active in public life, and generally opposed to the Taoist principle of Naturalness (*tzu-jan* 自然).

ming-chih 茗汁. tea as a drink; hot water with an infusion of tea leaves.

ming-k'o 茗柯. a branch of the tea plant.

ming-kuang chin 明光錦. bright luminary brocade, a fabric depicting heavenly bodies.

ming-li 名理. Names and Principles; the art of matching names with their corresponding realities—a favorite topic of "pure conversation."

ming-sheng 名勝. famous mountains.

ming-shih 名士. a famous gentleman, a man of worldly sophistication—as opposed to *kao-shih* 高士, an *eminent* gentleman who transcends the world.

*mi̯wɒng 明. luminous, enlightened.

*mjwe̯i-mjwe̯i 霢霂. indefatigable.

mo 末. end branches, secondary considerations—as opposed to *pen* 本, root.

mo 脈. the pulses.

Mo-hsia 末下 (an old name for Chien-k'ang).

mou 畝. an area equivalent to about one-sixth of an acre.

mu 木. "wood," the dice of the game *chaupar*, five in number, flat and elongated, with pointed ends, black on one side and white on the other; a calf was painted on two of the black surfaces and a pheasant on two of the white ones.

mu 牧. to herd; a herdsman.

mu-ping 目病. eye-trouble.

nai 柰. the Chinese apple (*pirus malus*).

nai-ho 柰何. "What shall I do?" A cry of mourners in the Lo-yang area.

nan 難. to raise objections, or rebut the arguments of the "host" (*chu* 主) in a "pure conversation."

nan 南. south.

*ngâ-ngâ 峨峨. lofty and majestic.

*ngâm-ngâm 巖巖. towering, cliff-like.

*ngiek-ngiek 鶂鶂. "cackle-cackle"; the domestic goose.

*ngjwei-ngjwei 巍巍. lofty and majestic.

*ngjwie̯ 危. danger.

ni-wu 泥屋. to plaster a room.

nien 輦. a palanquin, holding more than one passenger, lifted on lateral poles by human carriers.

Nine Bestowals (*chiu-hsi* 九錫). originally a special recognition by the Son of Heaven for outstanding merit; in the Six Dynasties period usually offered to successful usurpers by the abdicating ruler. They consisted of: (1) chariots and horsemen, (2) ceremonial robes, (3) musical instruments, (4) the privilege of having a vermilion gate, (5) a raised dais, (6) a post in the Palace Guard, (7) bows and arrows, (8) axes and halberds, and (9) special wine for sacrifice to one's ancestors.

nu 奴. a male slave.

Nü 女 (the name of a star).

nüeh 瘧. malaria or other undulating fevers; a homophone of *nüeh* 虐, cruel.

*nźi 兒. a small boy.

*nźiät 熱. hot.

officer (*yüan* 掾). a general term for subordinates in commandery or prefectural offices.

pa-chi 八及. the Eight Attainers (second cent. A.D.): (1) Chai Ch'ao 翟超, (2) Chang Chien 張儉, (3) Ch'en Hsiang 陳翔, (4) K'ung Yü 孔昱, (5) Liu Piao 劉表, (6) T'an Fu 檀敷, (7) Ts'en Chih 岑晊, (8) Yüan K'ang 苑康.

pa-chün 八俊. the Eight Heroes (second cent. A.D.): (1) Chao Tien 趙典, (2) Chu Yü 朱寓, (3) Hsün Yü 荀昱, (4) Li Ying 李膺, (5) Liu Yu 劉祐, (6) Tu Mi 杜密, (7) Wang Ch'ang 王暢, (8) Wei Lang 魏朗.

pa-po 八伯. the Eight Elders (ca. 317-330): (1) Ch'ih Chien 郗鑒, (2) Hu-wu Fu-chih 胡毋輔之, (3) Juan Fang 阮放, (4) Juan Fu 阮孚, (5) Liu Sui 劉綏, (6) Pien K'un 卞壼, (7) Ts'ai Mo 蔡謨, (8) Yang Man 羊曼.

pa-ta 八達. the "Eight Free Spirits," a group of libertines who flourished in the late third and early fourth centuries: (1) Hsieh K'un 謝鯤, (2) Hu-wu Fu-chih 胡毋輔之, (3) Huan I 桓彝, (4) Juan Fang 阮放, (5) Juan Fu 阮孚, (6) Kuang I 光逸, (7) Pi Cho 畢卓, (8) Yang Man 羊曼.

pa-yin 八音. the eight musical timbres: (1) metal (bells and gongs), (2) stone (chimes), (3) earth (ocarina), (4) hide (drums), (5) silk (strings), (6) wood (clappers), (7) gourd (mouth organs), (8) bamboo (flutes).

pai 白. "white," the fourth highest throw in the game *chaupar*, in which all five dice land white side up; worth eight points.

pai 拜 (**pwai*). to do obeisance, to kneel and bow so that the forehead touches the hands stretched on the ground in front; a pun for **p̯i̯wɐi* 廢, to depose.

pai-chih 白雉. white pheasant.

pai-ching wu 白頸烏. the white-necked crow (*corvus torquatus*), smaller than the jungle crow (*corvus levaillantii*), but more raucous.

pai-shih ying 白石英. milky quartz. See *wu-shih san*.

pai-yen erh 白眼兒. "white-eyed boy," a person glaring in wide-eyed rage.

palace attendant (*huang-men shih-lang* 黃門侍郎). a post often assigned to young men of noble families before they were entrusted with administrative responsibilities.

pan 板. congratulatory wooden placards sent out on auspicious occasions, responses to which were written on the reverse side.

pao-mao 苞茅. sedge, a fragrant herb produced in the south, used for straining wine.

paricitra (**puâ-lji-tśi̯ĕt* 波利質). "everywhere fragrant," a mythical tree growing in one of the Buddhist paradises which sends its fragrance upwind; the Chinese translated name is *pien-hsiang* 遍香.

parinirvāna (**b'uân-niər-γuân* 般泥洹). perfect extinction, entrance into Nirvana at death; specifically, the death of Śākyamuni.

pei 桮. wine cup.

pei 婢. female slave.

pen 本. root; primary considerations. See *mo* 末.

pen-tsou 奔走. headlong runner ("Songs" 237).

pen-yin 本音. original pitches.

p'eng-ch'i 彭蜞. the sand crab (*graspus graspus*), a small crab with hairless mandibles and squarish shell which lives in holes in the sand and is inedible.

p'eng-hsing 彭星. tangle-star, perhaps a tailless comet, described as looking like cotton wool.

p'eng-hua 彭蝟. a species of small crab. See *lao* 螃.

personal attendant (shih-chung 侍中). one of five distinguished persons selected in any given time to attend the emperor.

pi-chih 辟支 (*pi̯äk-tśi̯e). pratyeka-buddha, one who is self-enlightened. See also yüan-chüeh.

pi-wu 必無. "definitely does not have."

p'i 匹. a bolt of cloth four chang 丈 in length.

p'i 皮. skin, hide.

p'i 箄. a bamboo basket lowered into a kettle for steaming rice.

P'i 否. "Stagnation." Hex. 12 of the "Book of Changes."

p'i-pa 琵琶. the lute, a four-stringed instrument with shallow pear-shaped sounding box and fretted neck, played with a wide plectrum, imported from Central Asia through the northwest during the second century A.D.

p'i-tun 梐楯. basket shields, made of radiating splints between which shorter pieces of bamboo were woven to produce a round shield.

*p'iän-p'iän 翩翩. fluttering and flapping.

p'iao-chi 驃騎. (General of) Spirited Cavalry.

picul. See shih 石.

pien-hsiang 遍香. "everywhere fragrant." See paricitra.

pien-i 變易. to transform.

*pi̯ĕn-pi̯ĕn 彬彬. perfectly balanced (between plainness and refinement).

p'ien-hsieh 駢脅. with ribs joined together.

ping 兵. weapons; men-at-arms, soldiers.

ping 餅. round flat cakes made of wheat or rice flour, dumplings.

ping-shen 丙申 (cyclical combination).

ping-chiu 病酒. to suffer from a hangover. See also ch'eng 酲.

p'ing 萍. duckweed (spirodela polyhiza), a floating, edible water plant.

p'ing-ch'eng lou 平乘樓. a mounting-tower or turret on ships of war.

p'ing-feng 屏風. a screen or windbreak; a windowpane (?).

p'ing-hun 平婚. marriage between families of equal status--emended from shih-hun 世婚.

GLOSSARY 647

*p'jwei-p'jwei 霏霏. flurrying (of snow).

po 伯. elder, elder brother; term of address for male elders and husbands.

Po 剝. "Ruin," Hex. 23 of the "Book of Changes."

po-i 博奕. a generic term for gambling games.

p'ou 瓿. a wine jar.

prajñā. gnosis, transcendental insight. See liu-tu.

prefecture (hsien 縣). a subdivision of a commandery (chün 郡).

president of the Board of Civil Office (li-pu shang-shu 吏部尚書). chief of the division of the Imperial Secretariat charged with selecting and appointing persons recommended for office in the court administration.

president of the Central Secretariat (chung-shu ling 中書令). the person who had general oversight of the palace library and all state documents.

president of the Imperial Secretariat (shang-shu ling 尚書令). the presiding officer over the highest body of the court administration to which the subdivisions were responsible.

principality (kuo 國). the equivalent of a commandery (chün 郡), whose titular head would be a prince of the royal blood, but whose civil administrator was a governor (nei-shih 內史).

province (chou 州). the largest administrative subdivision of the empire, administered by a governor (tz'u-shih 刺史), who was directly responsible to the court.

pu 不 (a negative adverb); sometimes used for P'i 否 --Hex. 12 of the "Book of Changes."

pu-chang 步障. a windbreak made of a cloth mounted on poles stretched along a walkway for privacy.

Pu-chou 不周. "Non-surrounding"; an old designation of the northwest wind.

pu-i 布衣. a "man in plain clothing," a commoner of the gentry class who has not yet been appointed to office.

pu-i 不易. unchanging.

pu-lou 培塿. a small mound.

pu-pi wu 不必無. does not necessarily lack.

pu-sheng 不生. is not living.

pu-shou 不受. does not accept. See *tz'u*.

pu-t'an 不談 does not talk.

p'u-k'uei shan 蒲葵扇. a palm-leaf fan made from the *livistonia chinensis*, which grows in the Kwangtung area.

*puât-jiu 鉢釪. *pātra*, the almsbowl of a Buddhist monk--a Sanskrit-Chinese hybrid.

"pure conversation." See *ch'ing-t'an*.

rūpa (*se* 色). matter; specifically, visible sense data.

*sai-lâp 灑臘. *sāḍava*--an Indian raga, or musical mode.

san-chüeh 三絕. the "Three Incomparables"; famed singers of pallbearers' songs: Huan I* 桓伊, Yang T'an 羊曇, and Yüan Shan-sung 袁山松.

san-chün 三君. the "Three Gentlemen"; martyrs in the struggle against the palace eunuchs, 168 A.D.: Ch'en Fan 陳蕃, Liu Shu 劉淑, and Tou Wu 竇武.

san-fu 三府. the Three Ducal Offices. See also *san-kung*.

san-hsüeh 三學. those in the first three, or learning, stages of the four stages of Buddhist discipleship: (1) *śrotāpanna*, stream-winners, (2) *sakṛdāgāmin*, once-returners, (3) *anāgāmin*, non-returners. The fourth stage is arhatship; see *wu-hsüeh*.

san-kung 三公. the Three Ducal Offices at the apex of the court administration: (1) director of instruction (*ssu-t'u* 司徒), (2) director of works (*ssu-k'ung* 司空), and (3) grand marshal (*t'ai-wei* 太尉).

san-ming 三明. the Three Insights (*vidyā*) gained through enlightenment: (1) *āsravakṣaya-jñāna*, knowing that defilements have ceased (= *hsien-tsai hsin* 現在心), (2) *pūrvanivāsānusmṛti-jñāna*, knowing past existences (= *kuo-ch'ü hsin* 過去心), and (3) *cyutyupapāda-jñāna*, knowing future existences (= *wei-lai hsin* 未來心).

san-pao 三寶 (*triratna*). the Three Treasures: the Buddha (*Fo* 佛), the Dharma, or Teaching (*fa* 法), and the Sangha, or monastic community (*seng* 僧).

san-sheng 三乘 (*triyāna*). the Three Vehicles (transporting beings to Nirvana): (1) *śrāvaka-yāna*, hearers or disciples (sometimes called Hinayana, the "Lesser Vehicle"), (2) *pratyeka-buddha-yāna*, the self-enlightened, and (3) *bodhisattva-yāna*, saviors of others (sometimes called Mahayana, the "Greater Vehicle").

san-tsu shou 三祖壽. (a family heirloom) three generations old.

sang-chu 喪主. the funeral host; in the case of the death of younger members of the family or women, always the head of the household; if the head died, the eldest surviving son.

sao 嫂. wife of an elder brother, a term of address for older women.

sao 騷. "elegy," the predominant form of poetry in the *Ch'u-tz'u* 楚辭.

*sâp 靸. smashed.

se 瑟. the twenty-five-stringed zither.

se-ssu 色絲. colored silk. See *huang-chüan* 黃絹.

secretarial aide (*chi-shih ts'an-chün* 記室參軍). the principal drafter of documents in a military headquarters.

senior administrator (*chang-shih* 長史). the chief subordinate officer in any of several administrative units.

sergeant-at-arms (*ssu-ma* 司馬). a subordinate office in a military headquarters, just below senior administrator (*chang-shih* 長史) in peacetime but above him in wartime.

sha-hu 紗縠. silk gauze.

sha-lo 紗羅. silk gauze woven with intersecting diagonal strands.

shan 山. mountain.

shan-hu 珊瑚 (*san-ɣuo; cf. Persian *sanga*, "stone"). coral; the best examples were imported from the Mediterranean. See Schafer, *Golden Peaches*, p. 246.

shan-lu 山鹿. a deer on the mountain.

shan-shui 山水. mountains and streams, landscape.

shan-yü 單于. the title of Hsiung-nu chieftains.

shang 觴. goblet; larger than a *pei* 桮.

shang-chang 上章. to offer a petition to the Celestial Ruler (T'ien-ti 天帝), usually requesting healing or extension of life; a practice of the Heavenly Master Sect of Taoism.

shang-ch'ing 上清. the Upper Purity, or middle level of heaven. See also *t'ai-ch'ing*; *yü-ch'ing*.

shang-jen 上人. "Your Reverence," a term of address to monks.

Shao-wei 少微 (the name of a constellation).

she 社. a sacred mound of earth dedicated to the soil gods of a particular locality.

she-jen 舍人. chamberlain, a member of the crown prince's household staff.

she-shu 社樹. a tree on or beside a sacred mound.

shen 申. the ninth of the Twelve Branches in the sexagenary cycle; the direction west-south-west of the twelve directions.

shen-chieh 神解. divine understanding, imparted by superior intelligence. See also *an-chieh*.

shen-ming 神明. intelligence; the gods.

shen-t'ung 身通 (ṛddhi-sākṣātkriya). intuitive powers. See *liu-t'ung*.

shen-wang 神王. exhilarated in spirit.

sheng 升. the tenth part of a *tou*.

sheng 笙. a mouth organ made of thirteen bamboo pipes of different lengths, each with a metal reed, fitted into a gourd (later wood) wind chamber. Each pipe has a hole near the base for stopping with the fingers. When blown the instrument produces continuous chords, usually open fifths or clusters. The origin appears to have been in Southeast Asia.

sheng 甥. a male cousin, son of a paternal aunt or maternal uncle; nephew, son of a sister; brother-in-law, wife's brother or sister's husband.

sheng 盛. prosperous, flourishing.

sheng 聖. a sage--the highest ideal in Confucianism.

sheng 勝. to overcome; surpassing, superb.

sheng-ch'ing 勝情. superb feelings, superior sensitivity.

sheng-te 盛德. abundant virtue.

sheng-lü 聲律. sounds and pitches; music.

sheng-wen 聲聞 (śrāvaka). a hearer, a disciple of the Buddha.

shih 氏. family (often occurs after maiden name of married women).

shih 士. a gentleman, a member of the landholding or official class.

shih 式. the divining board--a circular template (representing heaven) superimposed on a square base (representing earth), turning on a central axis and marked with cyclical and astrological signs. Divination was based on where it came to rest after spinning.

shih 弑. to murder a superior.

shih 石. a rock; a picul (or *tan*), a measure equivalent to ten *tou*, or 3.16 cubic *ch'ih* 尺.

shih 碩. boulder.

Shih 詩. the "Book of Songs," an anthology of the period 1000 to 600 B.C.; as a generic term, lyric poetry of four or five words to the line with rhymes falling generally at the end of the even-numbered lines.

shih 師. a Taoist master of the Heavenly Master Sect. See also *tao-shih*.

shih 實. true, real.

shih-chung ju 石鐘乳. stalactite. See *wu-shih san*.

shih-erh ju 十二入. the Twelve Entrances (*āyatana*), i.e., the six senses and their corresponding objects: the eyes (*caksuh*) and visible sights (*rūpa*); the ears (*śrota*) and sounds (*śabda*); the nose (*ghrāṇa*) and smells (*gandha*); the tongue (*jihva*) and tastes (*rasa*); the body (*kāya*) and tangible objects (*spraṣṭavya*); the mind (*manaḥ*) and mental data (*dharma*).

shih-hsin ping 失心病. palpitation of the heart. See also *hsü-chi*.

shih-hun 世婚. See *p'ing-hun*.

shih-o 式遏. to suppress evil ("Songs" 253).

shih-shu 事數. enumerations of items of Buddhist technical terminology.

shih-wu 士伍. a military colonist. See T'ang Ch'ang-ju, *Wei-Chin nan-pei-ch'ao shih lun-ts'ung*, pp. 30-36.

Shih-yü 釋魚. "Explanation of Fishes" (section of *Erh-ya* 爾雅).

shou-kuo 首過. to confess one's transgressions--a practice of the Heavenly Master sect of Taoism.

shou-hsin 受辛. to suffer hardship. See *tz'u*.

shou-pan 手版. a hand tablet, an emblem of office similar to the *hu* 笏.

shou-t'an 手談. manual conversation (said of the game *wei-ch'i*).

shu 朮. a variety of thistle which grows in mountainous areas.

shu 叔. uncle, father's younger brother; brother-in-law.

shu 黍. millet; a wine pot holding three *sheng* 升.

shu-mi 秫米. glutinous rice used for making wine.

shu-mo 熟末. precooked bean powder.

shu-sheng 書生. a scholar.

shu-shih 術士. a practitioner of magic spells, divination, healing, and exorcism; the successor to the *fang-shih* 方士 of Han times whose role seems to have overlapped with both that of the orthodox Taoist priesthood (*tao-shih* 道士) and of the "mediums" (*wu* 巫) associated with "unorthodox" local cults.

shu-shu 數術. divination techniques.

shui-tui 水碓. a water mill, a water-powered wheel with either vertical or horizontal axle which operates a trip-hammer for hulling grain. See Needham, *Science and Civilisation* IV.2, pp. 390-396.

shun 隼. the eastern perigrine falcon (*falco perigrinus calidus*), a rare migrant in northeastern China which breeds on the steppes of northern Asia.

shuo 槊. a long spear eighteen *ch'ih* 尺 in length.

*si̯ang-lâng 爽朗. fresh and transparent.

*si̯ɒm-si̯ɒm 閃閃. flashing.

*si̯əm-si̯əm 森森. thick as a forest, in dense profusion.

*sieu-sâk 蕭索. lonely, bored.

*sieu-si̯e 蕭灑. lighthearted and carefree.

*sieu-sieu si̯uk-si̯uk 蕭蕭肅肅. serene and sedate.

śīla. Keeping the (Buddhist) commandments. See *liu-tu*.

*si̯uk-si̯uk 肅肅. sedate and dignified; onomatapoeia for the soughing of the wind.

*si̯uk-si̯uk 謖謖. brisk and bracing.

*si̯wo-si̯uĕt 疏率. heedless of petty details.

śramaṇa (**ṣa-muən* 沙門). a Buddhist monk.

ssu 寺. a Buddhist monastery.

ssu-meng 思夢. yearning dreams.

ssu-ta 似達. seemingly free (not derogatory).

ssu-ti 四諦. *catvāri ārya-satyāni*, the Four (Noble) Truths of Buddhism: (1) life is suffering (*duḥkha*), (2) suffering is caused by the massing together of or attachment to the data of consciousness (*samudaya*), (3) suffering ceases with the cessation of these data (*nirodha*), (4) there is a way to cessation (*mārga*).

ssu-yu 四友. the Four Friends (of Wang Tun 王敦): (1) Hu-wu Fu-chih 胡毋輔之, (2) Wang Ch'eng 王澄, (3) Wang Yen 王衍, (4) Yü Ai 庾敱.

stupa. (*in early transcriptions not distinguished from* Buddha—*b'iuət-d'uo* 佛圖), a reliquary shrine or Buddha hall.

su-ch'in 疏親. distant and intimate; to make the intimate distant.

su-chung 俗中. within the realm of custom, bound by worldly morality.

su-ho 蘇和. storax (*styrax officinalis*), a vanilla-scented resin, dark purple in color; imported in Han times from Parthia and during the Six Dynasties from the Sassanids. See Schafer, *Golden Peaches*, pp. 168-169.

su-ming 宿命. (insight into) previous existences. See *liu-t'ung*.

Su-shen 肅慎. an ancient tribe or federation living in the area of modern Kirin (Manchuria) during the Chou period.

subordinate (*ts'ung-shih* 從事). a relatively low supervisory office within civil and military administrations.

sui-chin 碎金. splintered gold; normally an image for elegant style.

sung 頌. a hymn or liturgical song for ceremonial occasions.

śūnyatā (*k'ung* 空). emptiness of self-being or independent existence—a basic Mahayana concept.

superintendent of records (*chu-pu* 主簿). the executive officer of any of several administrative units, most importantly of a commandery, where he was the right arm of the grand warden (*t'ai-shou* 太守).

ta 達. to be thoroughly free; said of one who comprehends the unity of the mundane and ultramundane. See also *k'uang*; *t'ung* 通.

ta-cha 大蜡. Great Year-end Sacrifice—the name used in Chou times.

Ta-chuang 大壯. "Power of the Great." Hex. 34 of the "Book of Changes."

ta-fa 大法. "Great Teaching"; gloss for *abhidharma*, the exegetical literature of Buddhism.

ta-sheng 達生. to master the meaning of life.

t'a 榙. a set of two lacquered boxes which fit together. See also *lei* 櫑.

t'a 榻. a low couch for sitting, smaller than a *ch'uang* 牀.

t'a-hsin 他心. *paracitta-jñāna*. (insight into) the minds of others. See *liu-t'ung*.

t'ai 臺. a terrace.

t'ai-ch'ing 太清. the Grand Purity, the highest of the three levels of heaven. See also *shang-ch'ing*; *yü-ch'ing*.

t'ai-hsü 太虛. the Great Void, a Taoist concept comparable to Non-actuality (*wu* 無).

t'ai-hsüeh 太學. the Grand Academy, a school for the study of the Classics established in Han times. See also *kuo-tzu hsüeh*.

t'ai-p'u 太僕. grand master of the horse, an officer in charge of the imperial stables and carriages.

t'ai-shou 太守. grand warden, administrator of a commandery (*chün* 郡).

T'ai-wei 太微. a celestial enclosure (*yüan* 垣) which includes parts of the constellations Virgo, Leo, and Coma Berenices.

t'ai-yüeh 太樂. grand music master, an office established in Chou times to standardize the court music.

tan 淡. bland, flavorless; without strong emotional overtones.

tan-ch'i 彈棋. pellet chess, a game played with a stone playing board and marbles. See Needham, *Science and Civilisation* IV.1, p. 327.

tan-chiao 單絞. an unlined robe of yellow-green silk.

tan-ch'ing 丹青. red and blue; colored painting.

tan-ming k'o 啖名客. a man who chews, or devours, fame; one who lives for his reputation.

tan-shih 啖石. to chew on rocks (to sharpen the teeth).

t'an-t'an chih hsü 談談之許.

tang 黨. a faction or clique.

t'ang-ping 湯餅. hot soup with dumplings.

t'ang 塘. a dike or embankment.

tao 稻. the rice plant.

tao 道. the Way.

tao-ch'i 導氣. conducting the pneuma or vital force, a Taoist longevity technique employing calisthenics.

tao-shih 道士. Taoist master, a priest of the Heavenly Master sect.

tao-shu 道術. Taoist arts; techniques of longevity, healing, exorcism, etc.

tao-shu 道樞. the axis of the Way. See also *huan-chung*.

*t'âp-təng 氍毹, a small wool rug of Iranian origin. Cf. Persian *tābīdan*, "woven"; folk etymology in the *Shih-ming* 釋名 explains it as "something placed on a stool, *t'a* 榻, for mounting, *teng* 登, a bed."

tathāgata (*ju-lai* 如來). "Thus Come" or "Thus Gone," an epithet of the Buddha.

te 德. moral power.

te-i 得一. to obtain one; to attain the One (*Lao-tzu* 39).

teng 鐙. stirrups.

Ti 氐. a proto-Tibetan people settled in the northwestern part of China since Han times.

Ti 狄. "Northern Barbarians," a term vaguely inclusive of Hsiung-nu 匈奴, Hsien-pei 鮮卑, and others.

ti 荻. rushes (*miscanthus sacchariflorus*), such as are used for mats.

ti 笛. the transverse flut--a bamboo pipe blown through a hole on the side, with five stopped holes and a thin membrane over a non-stopped hole which gives a reedy timbre.

ti 地. *bhūmi*, a stage in the progress of a bodhisattva.

ti-lu 的盧. White Forehead; a horse with white extending from forehead to mouth, considered inauspicious. See also *yü-yen*.

ti-wu 第五. fifth.

t'i 體. body, to embody, to realize; substance, reality.

t'i-wai 體外. beyond the body, the metaphysical world.

t'ien 天. heaven, nature.

t'ien-chen 天真. natural simplicity.

t'ien-erh 天耳. *divya-śrota*, divine hearing. See *liu-t'ung*.

t'ien-hsia 天下. all-under-heaven, the realm.

t'ien-jan 天然. the naturally-so (not artificial).

t'ien-she 田舍. literally, "a hut in the paddy-fields"; a peasant.

t'ien-shih tao 天師道. the Heavenly Master sect of Taoism. See also *wu-tou-mi tao*.

t'ien-ts'ui 殘瘁. ruined and in trouble ("Songs" 264).

t'ien-yen 天眼. *divya-cakṣuḥ*, divine sight. See *liu-t'ung*.

*tiep-sap 輒戢. startled, frightened; cognate with **tsiap-siap* 懾悑.

*tieu 鳥. a bird.

Tiger-swift Commander (*hu-pen chung-lang chiang* 虎賁中郎將). an officer of the Palace Guard.

ting 鼎. a three-footed bronze ritual vessel; "Tripod"--Hex. 50 of the "Book of Changes."

to-to kuai-shih 咄咄怪事.

t'o 唾. to spit.

t'o-hu 唾壺. a spittoon; in the fourth century usually of gray glazed stoneware with bulbous base and wide flaring rim.

tou 斗. a "dipperful," a somewhat variable liquid measure; specimens from the Chin period measure around 2.45 liters. See Tzu Ch'i, "Ku-tai liang-ch'i hsiao-k'ao," *Wen-wu* 1964.7.

tou-chiang 鬭將. scribal error for *tou-pien* 鬭變.

tou-chou 豆粥. bean congee.

tou-pien 鬭變. a brawl, a private quarrel.

*ts'â-ngâ 嵯峨. crag-crested.

*ts'â-ngât 嵯薛. craggy.

*ts'â-t'â 磋跎. to stumble; to slip by (of time).

ts'ai 裁. to trim; barely, just.

ts'ai 才. natural ability, talent.

ts'ai 菜. vegetables.

ts'an-chua 摻撾 or *ts'an-chui* 搥. "three beats," a drum rhythm, perhaps in triple time.

ts'an-shih 蠶室. the "silkworm chamber," a prison where castrations were performed.

Ts'ang Chieh 蒼頡. the legendary inventor of writing.

ts'ang-fu 傖父. "old boor," a contemptuous term for northerners used by the people of Wú in the third and fourth centuries.

ts'ang-sheng 蒼生. teeming living beings; humanity.

tsao 棗. the jujube plum (*zizyphus vulgaris*), a large tree common in north China which produces a red pulpy fruit about the size and shape of olives.

tsao-tou 澡豆. "bath beans," small pellets made from ground dried peas (*pisum sativum*), mixed with fragrant herbs and used as a bath soap. See E. H. Schafer, "The Development of Bathing Customs in Ancient and Medieval China," *Journal of the American Oriental Society* 76.2 (1956), p. 64.

ts'ao-shu 草書. draft script. See also *k'ai-fa*.

*tṣ'ăt-tṣ'ăt 察察. pristine purity, unsullied whiteness; perhaps with an overtone of "petty investigation."

*ts'âu-ts'i 造次. impetuous and disorganized; in a hurry.

ts'en-mou 岑牟. a high-peaked hat for ceremonial occasions.

*tsɛng-tsɛng 錚錚. onomatopoeia for the clanging of bells or gongs.

*tsiän-tsi̭uk 煎蹙. miserable and maimed.

*ts'iang-lieng 鎗鈴. "ting-a-ling"; onomatopoeia for refined sounds.

*tsi̭ap-lji̭e 倭蘿. a cap decorated with white egret plumes worn in the Wu area.

*tśi̭e 枝. branch.

tso-yin 坐隱. sedentary retirement; said of the game *wei-ch'i*.

tsu 卒. underling; runner for administrative offices; a foot soldier.

ts'u-po 蔟箔. a spinning frame for silkworms.

ts'ui-chüeh 㮇桷. round- and square-sectioned rafters.

*tsuk-tsuk 鏃鏃. avant-garde, out in front.

ts'un 寸. "inch"; one tenth of a *ch'ih* 尺.

tsung 宗. the ideal; a synonym of *li* 理.

tsung 粽. rice dumplings wrapped in bamboo leaves.

tsung-ku 從姑. a great-aunt, sister of father's paternal uncle.

tsung-mei 從妹. a female cousin, daughter of a paternal uncle younger than oneself.

*ts'ung-ts'ung 怱怱. nervous, agitated, intelligent.

*tś'wie 炊. to steam (rice).

tu 犢. "calf," the third highest throw in the game *chaupar*, in which two of the dice land black calf-side up, the other three being white; worth ten points.

tu 杜. to dissemble.

tu-chiang 都講. a discussant; one whose function is to raise points for clarification during expositions of the Classics in the Grand Academy, or objections to be answered in a Buddhist lecture.

tu-hsia 都下. the capital.

tu-pi kun 犢鼻褌. calf-nose drawers--a loincloth draped in two loops.

tu-t'a 獨榻. a single couch for seating one person. See also *lien-t'a*.

t'u 荼 (*d'uo). a bitter edible plant later confused with the tea plant (*tś'ia 茶).

tuan 端. a bolt of cloth varying from sixteen to sixty *ch'ih* 尺 in length. See also *p'i* 匹.

T'uan 彖. the "Judgments," laconic decisions based on the hexagrams of the "Book of Changes" taken as a whole.

*tuət-nguət 突兀. lofty and towering.

*tuət-tsia 咄嗟. immediately.

tun-wu 頓悟. sudden enlightenment; an intuitive flash, not preceded by any gradual accumulation of knowledge.

tung 棟. a pillar; the central mast of a tower or pagoda.

t'ung 通. comprehensive understanding; freedom from customary inhibitions; in a "pure conversation," a clarification of a topic.

t'ung 同. identical, the same.

tzu 梓. the catalpa tree (*catalpa bungei*).

tzu 子. a son.

tzu-chu 錙銖. ancient weights, calculated at 600 and 100 grains of millet respectively.

tzu-shih ying 紫石英. amethyst. See *wu-shih san*.

tzu-jan 自然. the Self-so; naturalness--the Taoist principle of following one's own nature and not conforming to imposed standards.

tz'u 辭. to decline--explained in *SW* as composed of *shou* 受. "to accept." and *hsin* 辛. "hardship"; an expression, a word; specifically the "elegies" of the *Ch'u-tz'u* 楚辭.

vaiḍurya (*lieu-ljie 琉璃). colored glass.

vice-president (*p'u-yeh* 僕射). one of two (left and right) assistants to the president of the Imperial Secretariat (*shang-shu ling* 尚書令).

vihāra (*ching-she* 精舍). a Buddhist retreat for meditation and study.

vīrya (*ching-chin* 精進). zealous progress. See *liu-tu*.

wai-sheng 外甥. a nephew, son of a sister.

wai-sun 外孫. maternal grandson (= *nü-tzu* 女子, "daughter's son," a scribal pun for *hao* 好, "lovely,"

wan 挽. to draw a coffin or hearse with ropes.

wan-ko 挽歌. pallbearers' songs.

wang 望. hope, expectation.

wang 亡. to perish; to flee.

wang 王. king (a common surname); to rule as king, to be exhilarated.

wang-fan-tiao 尪凡弔 (**wâng-b'iwɒm-tieu*). "emaciated common string-of-cash," an expletive (alternate reading for *hui-wa-tiao* 瓴瓦弔).

wang-pu-liu-hsing 王不留行. "even a king does not stay its progress," a medicinal herb (*vacaria vulgaris*) in the dianthus family used for boils and the common cold.

*wâng-ziang 汪翔. vast and limitless.

wei 猬. the hedgehog (*erinaceus koreanus*).

wei 微. scribal error for *hui* 徽.

wei 圍. a double span, the distance between the tips of the small fingers when the thumbs are touching.

wei-ch'i 圍棊. encirclement chess, or *go*, played on a board marked into grids, with small flat round playing pieces of black and white stone to distinguish the two sides; the object of the game is completely to encircle the opponent's pieces, the two players alternately placing their pieces at intersections of the grids.

wei-chiu 未久. not yet a long time.

wei-lai hsin 未來心. *cyutyupapāda-jñāna*, (insight into) future existences. See *san-ming*.

wei-hsia 未下. "not yet putting down"; scribal error for Mo-hsia 末下.

wei-yen 微言. "subtle words," a term originally applied to Confucius' teaching (*HS* 30.1a), and during the Six Dynasties to "pure conversation."

wen 文. patterned, cultivated--as opposed to *chih* 質, "plain"; literature, civilization.

wen 溫. warm, to warm; also the taboo name of Huan Wen

wen-ting 問鼎. to inquire about the tripods, i.e., to test the moral strength of a dynasty.

weng 甕. a large earthenware vat for storing wine.

wo 我. I, the self; *ātman*, the pseudo-personality according to Buddhism.

wo-lung 臥龍. a reclining dragon.

work-detail officer (*kung-ts'ao shih* 功曹史). the personnel officer of a commandery (*chün* 郡).

wu 五. five.

wu 無. (a) the Non-actual, the substratum from which all actual things evolve; (b) Nonbeing (*abhava*), nonexistence in time and space (= Nirvana); (c) Nothing, the uncaused and uncausing opposite of Something (*yu* 有).

wu-chi 無跡. without traces, i.e., without overt action in the world.

wu-hsien 五絃. the five-stringed lute, a variety of the *p'i-pa* 琵琶, a Central Asian instrument introduced into China during the second century A.D.

wu-hsüeh 無學. those in the nonlearning stage of Buddhist discipleship, i.e., *arhats*, or perfected saints. See *san-hsüeh*.

Wu-huan 烏桓. a tribal federation northeast of China in the second and third centuries B.C., remnants of which still survived in the fourth cent. A.D.

wu-ken 五根. the five roots of sensation (*indriya*): (1) the eyes (*kaṣuḥ*), (2) the ears (*śrota*), (3) the nose (*ghrāṇa*), (4) the tongue (*jihva*), (5) the body (*kāya*).

wu-li 五力. the Five Powers (*bala*) of a Buddha: (1) faith (*śraddha*), (2) zealous progress (*vīrya*), (3) mindfulness (*smṛti*), (4) concentration (*samādhi*), (5) transcendental insight (*prajñā*).

wu-lou 屋漏. the dark of the room, i.e., the northwest corner, where the household god was kept.

wu-pi fa 無比法. the "Matchless Teaching"; gloss for *abhidharma*, the exegetical literature of Buddhism. See also *ta-fa*.

wu-shih san 五石散. a five-mineral powder (also called *han-shih san* 寒食散, "cold-food powder," since it was taken only with cold food). An elixir claimed to possess both therapeutic and tranquilizing properties, much in vogue during the third and fourth centuries. The pulverized ingredients were: (1) stalactite (*shih-chung ju* 石鐘乳), (2) sulphur (*shih-liu huang* 石琉黃), (3) milky quartz (*pai-shih ying* 白石英), (4) amethyst (*tzu-shih ying* 紫石英), and (5) red bole (*ch'ih-shih chih* 赤石脂), a clay containing silicon, aluminum and ferous oxide. Some accounts also include cinnabar (*tan-sha* 丹砂 = HgS).

wu-tou-mi tao 五斗米道. the "Five-Pecks-of-Rice sect" of Taoism, founded by Chang Tao-ling 張道陵 in Han-chung 漢中 (Szechwan) in the late second century A.D. Later known as the "Heavenly Master sect (*t'ien-shih tao* 天師道).

wu-wei 無為. non-contrived, non-purposive action--a Taoist concept.

wu-yin 五陰. the Five Components (*skandha*) making up the pseudo-personality in Buddhism: (1) the physical body (*rūpa*), (2) sensations (*vedanā*), (3) concepts (*saṁjñā*), (4) mental acts (*saṁskāra*), (5) consciousness (*vijñāna*).

*χiɒn-χiɒn 軒軒. light and airy; radiantly beaming.

*χwâk-χwâk 霍霍. nervous and fidgety.

Ya 雅. the "Court Songs"--the second and third sections of the "Book of Songs."

ya-hou hui 牙後惠. "ultramolar favors," favors in the form of verbal recommendations.

ya-liang 雅量. cultivated tolerance, the ability to face any crisis with equanimity.

yang 陽. sunny side; positive or "masculine" force.

Yang 炗 (name of a star).

yang-lao 羊酪. goat curd, a yogurt-like culture made from goat's milk, introduced into north China by pastoral-nomadic peoples on the border.

yang-mei 楊梅. arbutus berries (*myrica rubra*).

yang-sheng 養生. to nourish life--a Taoist technique involving diet, calisthenics, certain sexual practices, the ingestion of herbs and mineral elixirs, as well as ridding the mind of worldly ambitions.

yao 妖. insubstantial; seductive.

yao 謠. a folk saying or ditty circulated by children and considered to be clairvoyant or prophetic. See also *yen*; *yü* 語.

Yao 爻. the "Interpretations"--meanings given to the individual lines of the hexagrams in the "Book of Changes."

yao-ch'e 軺車. a light one-horse carriage.

yao-chi 遙集. to huddle in the distance.

yao-miao 要妙. the Essential and Subtle.

yao-yao 遙遙. far, far away.

yeh 冶. to smelt metal; also Yeh-ch'eng 冶城, a smelting center west of Chien-k'ang.

yeh-chan 野戰. battle in the wilds, guerilla warfare.

yeh-mi 野麋. an elaphure in the wild.

yen 諺. a folk ditty or maxim. See also *yao* 謠.

yen-hsing 雁行. walking in goose formation, i.e., beside and a little behind--as prescribed for younger members of each generation when walking with the elder in "Record of Rites" V, 52.

yen-shih 鹽豉. salted legume, a leguminous vegetable marinated in brine and used in the south for seasoning.

yin 陰. shady side; negative or "feminine" force.

yin 隱. hidden, retired.

yin 因. causes.

yin-hung 隱虹. the "hidden bow"--the neck tendons of an ox which in exceptional cases were thought to connect directly with the tail.

yin-ju 茵蓐. cushions and mats made of rushes.

yin-sheng 音聲. musical timbres and notes of the scale.

yin-yüan 因緣. the Buddhist principle of Dependent Origination (*pratītya-samutpāda*), sometimes represented as a cycle of twelve preconditions, beginning with nescience (*avidyā*) and ending with old age and death (*jāra-maraṇa*); an intermediary, someone on whom one depends.

ying 癭. goiter.

Ying-huo 熒惑. the planet Mars.

yu 蕕. *caryopteris divaricata*, a foul-smelling plant.

yu 柚. the pomelo (*citrus aurantium*), a citrus fruit somewhat less juicy than the grapefruit.

yu 有. (a) the Actual; manifest objects and experiences in the world (evolved from the Non-actual, *wu* 無); (b) Being (*bhava*), existence in time and space (= *saṁsāra*); (c) Something (the opposite of Nothing, *wu*).

yu 又. again, further.

yu-fu 幼婦. youthful wife; = *shao-nü* 少女, a scribal pun for *miao* 妙, "wonderful."

yu-hsia 游俠. a knight-errant, a free-lance warrior who rescues the oppressed and helpless; during the Six Dynasties the *hsia* seem to have been mere swashbuckling buccaneers.

yu-hun 幽婚. posthumous marriage; marriage to a ghost.

yu-ming 幽冥. the "secluded and dark," the nether world.

yu-tao chün-tzu 有道君子. Gentleman with Principles, a Later Han designation for candidates aspiring to office.

yu-wei chih wai 有為之外. beyond activism. See also *wu-wei*.

yung 永. eternal, permanent.

yung-shih shih 詠史詩. chanted history poems; historic events in compressed, eliptical verse--a mnemonic device.

yü 語. a saying. See also *yao* 謠; *yen*.

yü 竽. a large mouth organ, similar to the *sheng*, with 36 pipes, the longest of which is four *ch'ih* and two *ts'un* in length. A perfectly preserved Han example was recently unearthed in the first tomb of Ma-wang-tui 馬王堆, near Ch'ang-sha.

yü-ch'ing 玉清. the lowest of the three levels of heaven. See also *shang-ch'ing*; *t'ai-ch'ing*.

yü-chou 宇宙. space and time; the universe.

yü-heng 玉衡. See *chi-heng*.

yü-tou 熨斗. an ironing pan; a dipper-shaped flatiron filled with embers.

yü-tz'u 語次. "word-sequences," a parlor game modeled after the "linked-verse game" (*lien-chü* 連句) of the Han period, in which each participant contributes a seven-word line on a prescribed topic which is at the same time the rhyme to be used at the end of the line.

yü-wu 禦侮. guarding against insults ("Songs" 237).

yü-yen 榆雁. Elm Goose; a horse with a white forehead. See *ti-lu*.

yüan 源. a source.

yüan 淵. a deep pool; an abyss.

yüan 猨. the gibbon (*hylobates concolor*), a long-armed, tailless ape inhabiting mountainous areas of central and south China.

yüan 垣. celestial enclosure, an area of the night sky enclosing certain constellations.

yüan-chih 遠志. "far-reaching determination," a medicinal herb (*polygala japonica*); also known as "small grass" (*hsiao-ts'ao* 小草).

yüan-ch'u 鵷鶵. a mythical bird which rests only on the paulownia tree and eats only the fruit of the *lien* 楝 bamboo.

yüan-chüeh 緣覺. *pratyeka-buddha*, one who is self-enlightened in a buddha-less age. See also *pi-chih*; *san-sheng*.

yüeh-fu 樂府. the Board of Music established in Han times to collect folk songs; poems composed on themes of original *yüeh-fu* poems, or written in imitation of them.

yün-ching 雲津. the cloudy ford (the Milky Way).

yün-mu 雲母. "mother-of-cloud," mica. Used for both window panes and screens, and pulverized for consumption as a drug or to coat fancy stationery.

Abbreviations

Unless marked by an asterisk, all titles are of works cited in Liu Chün's Commentary.

AFSC	*An fa-shih chuan* 安法師傳, anon. (concerns Shih Tao-an 釋道安. 312-385)
APTH	*A-p'i-t'an hsü* 阿毗曇叙. by Shih Hui-yüan 釋慧遠 (334-416)
CATC	*Chin An-ti chi* 晉安帝紀 by Wang Shao-chih 王韶之 (fifth cent.; covers period 397-418)
CC	*Chia-chieh* 家誡, by Li Ping 李秉 (third cent.)
CCH	*Ch'u-ching hsü* 出經叙, anon. (fifth or sixth cent.)
CCHH	*Ch'i-ching hou-hsü* 棊經後序, anon.
CCHs	*Chao Chih hsü* 趙至叙, by Hsi Shao 嵇紹 (253-304)
CCKIY	*Ch'un-ch'iu k'ao-i yu* 春秋考異郵, by Sung Chün 宋均 (third cent.)
CCKT	*Chin chu-kung tsan* 晉諸公贊. by Fu Ch'ang 傅暢 (early fourth cent.)
CCMSC	*Chung-ch'ao ming-shih chuan* 中朝名士傳. See *MSC*
CCTSH	*Chin-ch'ang t'ing shih hsü* 金昌亭詩序, by Hsieh Hsin 謝歆 or Hsieh Shao 韶 (fourth cent.?)
*CCW	*Ch'üan Chin wen* 全晉文. See *CSKST*
CCWCL	*Wan-chi lun* 萬機論, by Chiang Chi 蔣濟 (fl. ca. 250)
CFCC	*Chin-chi* 晉紀, by Chu Feng 朱鳳 (fourth cent.)

665

CFCS	*Chin-shu* 晉書, by Chu Feng 朱鳳
CFHC	*Han-chi* 漢紀, by Chang Fan 張璠 (fourth cent.; covers period A.D. 25-220)
CFSC	*Chih Fa-shih chuan* 支法師傳, by Ch'ih Ch'ao 郗超 ? (336-377)
*CHC	*Ch'u-hsüeh chi* 初學記, edited by Hsü Chien 徐堅 et al. (ca. 700)
ChaoS	*Chao-shu* 志書, by T'ien Jung 田融 (fourth cent.; concerns Later Chao, 319-351)
ChiCC	*Chi-chou chi* 冀州記, by Hsün Ch'o 荀綽 (early fourth cent.)
ChingCC	*Ching-chou chi* 荊州記, by Sheng Hung-chih 盛弘之 (fifth cent.)
*CHHW	*Ch'üan Hou-Han wen* 全後漢文. See *CSKST
CHL	*Chin hou-lüeh* 晉後略, by Hsün Ch'o (early fourth cent.; covers period 265-317)
CHLSM	*Cheng-hsi liao-shu ming* 征西寮屬名, anon. (concerns staff of Huan Wen 桓溫, ca. 345-363)
CHS	*(Chin) chung-hsing shu* (晉)中興書, by Ho Fa-sheng 何法盛 (fifth cent.; covers period 317-420)
CHTCCC	*Chin Hui-ti ch'i-chü chu* 晉惠帝起居注, anon. (covers period 290-306)
Ch'uSCC	*Ch'u-shih chia-chuan* 褚氏家傳, by Ch'u Chi 褚觀 et al. (fifth cent.?)
CIHS	*Hsin-shu* 新書, by Chia I 賈誼 (201-169 B.C.)
CKCH	*Chin ku cheng-hsi ta-chiang-chün chang-shih Meng Fu-chün chuan* 晉故征西大將軍長史孟府君傳, by T'ao Ch'ien 陶潛 (365-427; concerns Meng Chia 孟嘉, fourth cent.)
CKHHC	*Ch'u-kuo hsien-hsien chuan* 楚國先賢傳, by Chang Fang 張方 (late third cent.)
CKSH	*Chin-ku shih hsü* 金谷詩敘, by Shih Ch'ung 石崇 (249-300)
CKT	*Chan-kuo ts'e* 戰國策, edited by Liu Hsiang 劉向 (80-9 B.C.)
CLC	*Ch'en-liu chih* 陳留志, by Chiang Ch'ang 江敞 (fourth cent.)
CLCHL	*Chu-lin ch'i-hsien lun* 竹林七賢論, by Tai K'uei 戴逵 (d. 396)
CLMSC	*Chu-lin ming-shih chuan* 竹林名士傳. See *MSC*
CMC	*Chang Min chi* 張敏集, by Chang Min 張敏 (third cent.)
CNTHCS	*Ch'ing-niao-tzu hsiang-chung shu* 青鳥子相冢書, anon.
CPC	*Chiang-piao chuan* 江表傳, anon. (concerns period 317-420)
CPCS	*Ch'in-shu* 秦書, by Ch'e P'in 車頻 (fourth cent.; concerns Former Ch'in, 351-395)
CPKM	*Chin pai-kuan ming* 晉百官名, anon. (fifth cent.)

CPSC	*Chou-pei (suan-ching)* 周髀（算經）, anon. (ca. A.D. 200)	
*CS	*Chin-shu* 晉書, edited by Fang Hsüan-ling 房玄齡 et al. (644)	
CSC	*(Cheng) shih-chu* （鄭）詩注, by Cheng Hsüan 鄭玄 (127-200)	
*CSCC	*Chin-shu chiao-chu* 晉書斠注, edited by Wang Shih-chien (1859)	
CSH	*Ch'in-shih hsü* 秦詩序, by Mao Ch'ang 毛萇 (ca. 130 B.C.)	
CShuo	*Chiu-shuo* 舊說, anon.	
*CSKST	*Ch'üan shang-ku san-tai Ch'in-Han san-kuo liu-ch'ao wen* 全上古三代秦漢三國六朝文, edited by Yen K'o-chün 嚴可均 (1893)	
*CSKW	*Ch'üan san-kuo wen* 全三國文. See *CSKST	
CSMSC	*Cheng-shih ming-shih chuan* 正始名士傳. See MSC	
CSP	*Chin-shih p'u* 晉世譜, anon. (fifth cent.)	
CSSP	*Chih-shih shih-pen* 摯氏世本, anon.	
*CSTCC	*Ch'u san-tsang chi-chi* 出三藏記集, by Seng-yu 僧佑 (ca. 510-518)	
CT	*Ch'in-ts'ao* 琴操, by Ts'ai Yung 蔡邕 (132-192)	
CTC	*Chih Tun chuan* 支遁傳, anon. (cf. CFSC	
*CTCC	*Chu-tzu chi-ch'eng* 諸子集成 (8 vols.), Shanghai, 1954	
*CTCKC	*Ching-ting Chien-k'ang chih* 景定建康志, by Chou Ying-ho 周應合 (1260)	
CTFH	*Chiao-tzu fa-hsün* 譙子法訓, by Chiao Chou 譙周 (third cent.)	
CTFHsü	*Ch'ang-ti fu hsü* 長笛賦序, by Fu T'ao 伏滔 (ca. 317-396)	
CTHC	*Ch'ien-t'ang (hsien) chi* 錢唐（縣）記, by Liu Pao 劉寶 (late third cent.)	
CTKPKM	*Chin tung-kung pai-kuan ming* 晉東宮百官名, anon.	
CTMSC	*Chiang-tso ming-shih chuan* 江左名士傳, by Liu I-ch'ing (403-444)	
*CTSW	*Ching-tien shih-wen* 經典釋文, by Lu Te-ming 陸德明 (d. ca. 630)	
CTWP	*Chang Ts'ang-wu pei* 張蒼梧碑, anon. (ca. 325)	
CWCC	*Chin wen-chang chi* 晉文章記, by Ku K'ai-chih 顧愷之 (ca. 345-406)	
CWCHC	*Chao Wu-chün hsing-chuang* 趙吳郡行狀, anon. (concerns Chao Mu 趙穆, d. ca. 320)	
CWKSM	*Ch'i-wang kuan-shu ming* 齊王官屬名, anon. (concerns Ssu-ma Chiung 司馬冏, d. 302)	
CWMC	*Chu Wei-mo ching* 註維摩經, by Seng-chao 僧肇 (ca. 406)	
CYC	*Chin yang-ch'iu* 晉陽秋, by Sun Sheng 孫盛 (ca. 302-373)	

FCC	*Fang-ch'i chuan* 方伎傳 (section of *WC*)	
FJC	*Fu-jen chi* 婦人集, anon.	
FMTS	*Fu-min t'ang sung* 富民塘頌, by Ko Jung 葛洪 (ca. 250-330)	
FSMHSH	*Fa-shih mu-hsia-shih hsü* 法師墓下詩序, by Wang Hsün 王珣 (350-401)	
FSTI	*Feng-su t'ung-i* 風俗通義, by Ying Shao 應劭 (late second cent.)	
FT	*Fu-tzu* 傅子, by Fu Hsüan 傅玄 (d. 278)	
FTT	*Fa-t'ai tsan* 法汰贊, by Sun Ch'o 孫綽 (fl. 330-365)	
FWCP	*Ch'i-p'in* 棊品, by Fan Wang 范汪 (ca. 308-372)	
FY	*Fa-yen* 法言, by Yang Hsiung 楊雄 (53 B.C.-A.D. 18)	
*FYCL	*Fa-yüan chu-lin* 法苑珠林, by Shih Tao-shih 釋道世 (668)	
HCC	*Hsüan-ch'eng chi* 宣城記, anon. (concerns Hsüan-ch'eng Commandery)	
HCCC	*Han-Chin ch'un-ch'iu* 漢晉春秋, by Hsi Tso-ch'ih 習鑿齒 (d. 384)	
HCCPS	*Hsü-Chiang-chou pen-shih* 徐江州本事, anon.	
HCHHS	*Hou-Han shu* 後漢書, by Hsieh Ch'eng 謝承 (third cent.)	
HCHS	*Han-shu* 漢書, by Hsieh Ch'en 謝沈 (fourth cent.; covers period A.D. 25-220)	
HCL	*Hsin-chi lu* 新集錄, by Ch'iu Yüan-chih 丘淵之 (fifth cent.)	
*HCTC	*Hsi-ching tsa-chi* 西京雜記, by Wu Chün 吳均 (sixth cent.)	
HCWC	*Wu-chi* 吳紀, by Huan Chi 環濟 (third cent.)	
HCYC	*Hsü Chin yang-ch'iu* 續晉陽秋, by T'an Tao-luan 檀道鸞 (fifth cent.)	
HFMKSC	*Kao-shih chuan* 高士傳, by Huang-fu Mi 皇甫謐 (215-282)	
HFMLNC	*Lieh-nü chuan* 列女傳, by Huang-fu Mi	
HHC	*Huan Hsüan chi* 桓玄集, by Huan Hsüan 桓玄 (369-404)	
HHCS	*Hsi-ho chiu-shih* 西河舊事, anon.	
HHHC	*Hsien-hsien hsing-chuang* 先賢行狀, anon.	
HHPC	*Hsiang Hsiu pen-chuan* 向秀本傳, anon. (early fourth cent.)	
*HHS	*Hou-Han shu* 後漢書, edited by Fan Yeh 范曄 (398-445)	
*HKC	*Hsi K'ang chi* 嵇康集, edited by Lu Hsün 魯迅 (1913)	
HKCC	*Chin-chi* 晉紀, by Hsü Kuang 徐廣 (fifth cent.)	
HKCH	*Hsi K'ang chi hsü* 嵇康集序, anon.	
HKCHTC	*Hsiao-tzu chuan* 孝子傳, by Hsiao Kuang-chi 蕭廣濟 (fourth cent.)	
HKKSC	*Kao-shih chuan* 高士傳, by Hsi K'ang 嵇康 (223-262)	
HKLC	*Li-chi* 歷紀, by Hsü Kuang 徐廣 (fifth cent.)	

HL	*Hsin-lun* 新論, by Huan T'an 桓譚 (first cent. A.D.)
HMC	*Hsiang-ma ching* 相馬經, attrib. to Sun Yang 孫陽 (sixth cent. B.C.)
HNC	*Han-nan chi* 漢南紀, by Chang Ying 張瑩 (third cent.?)
HNHHC	*Hai-nei hsien-hsien chuan* 海內先賢傳, anon. (third cent.)
HS	*Han-shu* 漢書, by Pan Ku 班固 (A.D. 32-92)
HsCCC	*Hsieh Ch'e-ch'i chuan* 謝車騎傳, anon. (concerns Hsieh Hsüan 謝玄, ca. 351-396)
HSC	*Han-shu chu* 漢書注, by Wei Chao 韋昭 (third cent.)
HSCC	*Hsün-shih chia-chuan* 荀氏家傳, anon. (late third cent.)
HsHS	*Hsü Han-shu* 續漢書, by Ssu-ma Piao 司馬彪 (240-305)
HsHsC	*Hsü Hsün chi* 許詢集, by Hsü Hsün 許詢 (d. ca. 358)
HsNC	*Hsiang-niu ching* 相牛經, attrib. to Ning Ch'i 寧戚 (685-643 B.C.); edited by Wang Liang 王良 (first cent. A.D.?) and/or Kao-t'ang Lung 高堂隆 (early third cent.)
HsS	*Hsiang-shu* 相書, anon.
HSSL	*Han-shih-san lun* 寒食散論, by Ch'in Ch'eng-tsu 秦承祖 (fl. 443-453)
HsünYC	*Hsün-yang chi* 潯陽記, by Chang Seng-chien 張僧鑒 (fourth cent.)
HSWC	*Han-shih wai-chuan* 韓詩外傳, by Han Ying 韓嬰 (fl. 179-ca. 120 B.C.)
HT	*Hua-tsan* 畫贊, by Ku K'ai-chih 顧愷之 (ca. 345-406)
HTC	*Hsiao-tzu chuan* 孝子傳, by Cheng Ch'i-chih 鄭緝之 (fifth cent.)
HTCC	*Hsi Tso-ch'ih chi* 習鑿齒集, by Hsi Tso-ch'ih 習鑿齒 (d. 384)
HTCCC	*Hui-ti ch'i-chü chu* 惠帝起居注, by Lu Chi 陸機 (261-303)
HWC	*Huan Wen chi* 桓溫集, by Huan Wen 桓溫 (312-373)
HWCC	*Hsü wen-chang chih* 續文章志, by Fu Liang 傅亮 (374-426)
*HWCH	*Hsia-wai chün-hsiao* 霞外攟屑, by P'ing Pu-ch'ing 平步青 (seventeenth cent.)
HWKS	*Han-Wu ku-shih* 漢武故事, attrib. to Pan Ku 班固 (A.D. 32-92), prob. by Wang Chien 王儉 (fifth cent.)
HYC	*Hsiang-yang chi* 襄陽記, by Ch'ang Chü 常璩 (fourth cent.)
HYHHS	*Hou-Han shu* 後漢書, by Hsüeh Ying 薛瑩 (d. 280-290)
HYI	*Hsiao-yao i* 逍遙義, by Hsiang Hsiu 向秀 (ca. 221-300) and/or Kuo Hsiang 郭象 (d. 312)
HYKC	*Hua-yang kuo-chih* 華陽國志, by Ch'ang Chü 常璩 (fourth cent.)
HYL	*Hsiao-yao lun* 逍遙論, by Chih Tun 支遁 (314-366)

ICTT	*I-ch'ien tso-tu* 易乾鑿度, by Cheng Hsüan 鄭玄 (127-200)	
IH	*I-hsü* 易序, by Cheng Hsüan	
IHMYHHL	*I-hsiang miao-yü hsien-hsing lun* 易象妙於見形論, by Sun Sheng 孫盛 (ca. 302-373)	
*IS	*I-shih* 繹史, compiled by Ma Su 馬驌 (seventeenth cent.)	
ISC	*I-shih chuan* 逸士傳, by Huang-fu Mi 皇甫謐 (215-282)	
*IWLC	*I-wen lei-chü* 藝文類聚, edited by Ou-yang Hsün 歐陽詢 (557-641)	
IY	*I-yüan* 異苑, by Liu Ching-shu 劉敬叔 (fifth cent.)	
JCCCW	*Ch'üan-chin wen* 勸進文, by Juan Chi 阮籍 (210-263)	
*JCSP	*Jung-chai sui-pi* 容齋隨筆, compiled by Hung Mai 洪邁 (1123-1202)	
*JMP	*Shih-shuo jen-ming p'u* 世說人名譜, by Wang Tsao 汪藻 (thirteenth cent.)	
JNHHC	*Ju-nan hsien-hsien chuan* 汝南先賢傳, by Chou Fei 周斐 (fourth cent.)	
JWSI	*Jen-wu shih-i* 人物始義, by K'ang Fa-ch'ang 康法暢 (fl. 326-342)	
KC	*Kuang-chih* 廣志, by Kuo I-kung 郭義恭 (fourth cent.)	
KCCC	*K'uai-chi chün chi* 會稽郡記, anon.	
KCHHC	*K'uai-chi hou-hsien chi* 會稽後賢記, by Chung Li-hsiu 鍾離岫 (fourth cent.?)	
KCTL	*K'uai-chi tien-lu* 會稽典錄, by Yü Yü 虞預 (fourth cent.)	
KCTTC	*K'uai-chi t'u-ti chih* 會稽土地志, by Chu Yü 朱育 ? (third cent.)	
KHCTC	*Chuang-tzu chu* 莊子注, by Kuo Hsiang 郭象 (d. 312)	
*KI	*Shih-shuo hsin-yü k'ao-i* 世說新語考異, by Wang Tsao 汪藻 (thirteenth cent.)	
KISMC	*Kao-i sha-men chuan* 高逸沙門傳, by Chu Fa-chi 竺法濟 (fourth cent.)	
KJCH	*Kao Jou chi hsü* 高柔集敘, by Sun T'ung 孫統 (fourth cent.)	
KKCCC	*Chia-chuan* 家傳, by Ku K'ai-chih 顧愷之 (ca. 345-406; = KYC?)	
KLC	*Kuan Lu chuan* 管輅傳, anon. (late third cent.)	
KPCC	*Chin-chi* 晉紀, by Kan Pao 干寶 (fourth cent.)	
*KSC	*Kao-seng chuan* 高僧傳, by Hui-chiao 慧皎 (ca. 350)	
KSCK	*K'ung-shih chih-kuai* 孔氏志怪, by K'ung Shen 孔慎 (fourth cent.?)	
*KSFHC	*Kao-seng Fa-hsien chuan* 高僧法顯傳, anon. (fifth cent.)	
KSK	*Ku-shih k'ao* 古史考, by Chiao Chou 譙周 (third cent.)	
KT	*Kuo-tzu* 郭子, by Kuo Ch'eng-chih 郭澄之 (fourth cent.)	

KTC	Kao-tso chuan 高坐傳 (similar to KSC 1.327c; concerns Śrīmitra, 310-340)	
KTCY	K'ung-tzu chia-yü 孔子家語, edited by Wang Su 王肅 (d. 256)	
KTT	K'ung Ts'ung-tzu 孔叢子, by K'ung Fu 孔鮒 (fl. ca. 200 B.C.)	
*KWY	Ku-wen yüan 古文苑, anon. (seventh cent.?)	
KYC	Ku Yüeh chuan 顧悅傳, by Ku K'ai-chih 顧愷之. See KKCCC	
LAC	Lung-an chi 隆安記, by Chou Chih 周祗 (early fifth cent.; covers period 397-401)	
LCC	Liang-chou chi 涼州記, by Chang Tzu 張資 (fourth cent.?)	
LCCCC	Chin-chi 晉紀, by Liu Ch'ien-chih 劉謙之 (fifth cent.)	
LCCH	Liu Chin chi hsü 劉瑾集敘, anon. (early fifth cent.)	
LCI	Li-chi i 禮記義, by Chang Liang 張亮 (third or fourth cent.)	
LCNM	Liu Chen-nan ming 劉鎮南銘, anon. (concerns Liu Piao 劉表, d. 208)	
LHC	Lieh-hsien chuan 列仙傳, by Liu Hsiang 劉向 (80-9 B.C.)	
LHH	Lin-ho hsü 臨河敘, by Wang Hsi-chih 王羲之 (ca. 309-365)	
LiSCC	Li-shih chia-chuan 李氏家傳, anon.	
LKC	Ling-kuei chih 靈鬼志, by Hsün*** 荀氏 (fourth cent.?)	
LNC	Lieh-nü chuan 列女傳, by Liu Hsiang 劉向 (80-9 B.C.)	
LP	Lu-pei 陸碑, anon. (concerns Lu Mai 陸邁, early fourth cent.)	
LSC	Lu-shan chi 廬山記, by Shih Hui-yüan 釋慧遠 (334-416)	
LSCC	Lü-shih ch'un-ch'iu 呂氏春秋, sponsored by Lü Pu-wei 呂不韋 (d. 253 B.C.)	
*LSChing	Ling-shu ching 靈樞經, attrib. to the Yellow Emperor (actually eighth cent. A.D.)	
*LSTC	Lei-shu ts'an-chüan 類書殘卷, anon. (sixth cent.)	
LTL	Liu T'an lei 劉恢誄, by Sun Ch'o 孫綽 (fl. 330-365)	
*LTMHC	Li-tai ming-hua chi 歷代名畫記, by Chang Yen-yüan 張彥遠 (847)	
*LTYSCC	Shui-ching chu 水經注, by Li Tao-yüan 酈道元 (d. 527)	
*LYCLC	Lo-yang ch'ieh-lan chi 洛陽伽藍記, by Yang Hsien-chih 楊衒之 (early sixth cent.)	
LYKTP	Lo-yang kung-tien pu 洛陽宮殿簿, anon.	
MaoSC	Mao-shih chu 毛詩注, by Mao Ch'ang 毛萇 (fl. ca. 130 B.C.)	
MCSM	Meng Ch'u-shih ming 孟處士銘, by Yüan Hung 袁宏 (328-376)	
MJTH	Tzu-hsü 自敘, by Ma Jung 馬融 (A.D. 79-166)	
MKC	Miao-kuan chang 妙觀章, by Chih Tun 支遁 (314-366)	

MSC	*Ming-shih chuan* 名士傳, by Yüan Hung 袁宏 (328-376). See also *CCMSC*, *CLMSC*, and *CSMSC*
MT	*Mou-tzu* 牟子 (*Li-huo lun* 理惑論, attrib. to Mou-tzu, late second cent. A.D.; some parts perhaps fifth cent.)
MTSMTM	*Ming-te sha-men t'i-mu* 名德沙門題目, by Sun Ch'o 孫綽 (fl. 330-365)
MTT	*Min-tu tsan* 愍度贊, by Sun Ch'o (concerns Chih Min-tu early fourth cent.)
MTTKLSM	*Ming-ti tung-kung liao-shu ming* 明帝東宮僚屬名, anon. (covers period 317-325)
NCIWC	*Nan-chou i-wu chih* 南州異物志, by Wan Chen 萬震 (third cent.)
NHCC	*Nan Hsü-chou chi* 南徐州記, anon.
*NS	*Nan-shih* 南史, edited by Li Yen-shou 李延壽 (ca. 629)
-PC	——— *pieh-chuan* 別傳 ("Separate Biography of ———")
PCJCS	*Ch'in-shu* 秦書, by P'ei Ching-jen 裴景仁 (fifth cent.)
PCNC	*Pi-ch'iu-ni chuan* 比丘尼傳, by Shih Pao-ch'ang 釋寶唱 (early sixth cent.)
PenT	*Pen-ts'ao* 本草, anon. (perhaps third cent. A.D.). See also *PTKM* and *SNS*
PH	*P'u-hsü* 譜敘, by Hua Ch'iao 華嶠 (fl. 270-300)
PSCC	*P'ei-shih chia-chuan* 裴氏家傳, anon. (early fifth cent.?)
*PSLT	*Po-shih liu-t'ieh* 白氏六帖, compiled by Po Chü-i 白居易 (772-846)
PT	*P'ei-tzu* 裴子 (= *YL*?)
*PTKM	*Pen-ts'ao kang-mu* 本草綱目, edited by Li Shih-chen 李時珍 (1596)
*PTSC	*Pei-t'ang shu-ch'ao* 北堂書鈔, compiled by Yü Shih-nan 虞世南 (558-638)
PWC	*Po-wu chih* 博物志, by Chang Hua 張華 (232-300)
PWKS	*Pa-wang ku-shih* 八王故事, by Lu Lin 盧綝 (fourth cent.; covers period 300-306)
PYC	*P'an Yüeh chi* 潘岳集, by P'an Yüeh 潘岳 (247-300)
SC	*Shih-chi* 史記, by Ssu-ma Ch'ien 司馬遷 (145-90? B.C.)
SCC	*San-Ch'in chi* 三秦記, by Hsin*** 辛氏 (fifth cent.?)
SCFH	*Sui-ch'u fu hsü* 遂初賦敘, by Sun Ch'o 孫綽 (fl. 330-365)
SCH	*San-chiang hsü* 三將敘, by Yen Yu 嚴尤 (first cent. B.C.)
SCMKC	*Shih-ching, Mao-kung chu* 詩經毛公注 (= *MaoSC*)
ShuC	*Shu-chih* 蜀志, by Ch'en Shou 陳壽 (233-297). See *SKShu*
SKCS	*Shan-kung ch'i-shih* 山公啟事, by Shan T'ao 山濤 (205-283). See *STCS*

SKShu	*San-kuo chih, Shu-chih* 三國志蜀志, by Ch'en Shou 陳壽 (233-297)	
SKWei	*San-kuo chih, Wei-chih* 魏志, by Ch'en Shou	
SKWu	*San-kuo chih, Wu-chih* 吳志, by Ch'en Shou	
SL	*Shuo-lin* 說林, anon.	
*SLF	*Shih-lei fu* 事類賦, by Wu Shu 吳淑 (947-1002)	
SM	*Shih-ming* 釋名, attrib. to Liu Hsi 劉熙 (written ca. A.D. 200)	
SMHC	*Ssu-ma Hsi chuan* 司馬晞傳, anon. (late fourth cent.)	
SMTWCC	*Wen-chang chih* 文章志, sponsored by Sung Ming-ti 宋明帝 (Liu Yü** 劉彧, r. 465-472)	
SNS	*Shen-nung shu* 神農書, anon. (early antecedent of *PenT* and *PTKM*)	
-SP	── *shih-p'u* 氏譜 ("Genealogy of the ── Family")	
*SPTK	*Ssu-pu ts'ung-k'an* 四部叢刊 (collectanea; first series, 1936)	
*SS	*Sung-shu* 宋書, edited by Shen Yüeh 沈約 (441-513)	
SSC	*Sou-shen chi* 搜神記, by Kan Pao 干寶 (fourth cent.)	
*SSHY	*Shih-shuo hsin-yü* 世說新語, by Liu I-ch'ing 劉義慶 (403-444)	
*SSHYCC	*Shih-shuo hsin-yü chiao-chien* 校箋, by Liu P'an-sui 劉盼遂	
SSTC	*Shang-shu ta-chuan* 尚書大傳, attrib. to Fu Sheng 伏勝 (second cent. B.C.)	
SSTY	*Tsa-yü* 雜語, by Sun Sheng 孫盛 (= *I-t'ung tsa-yü* 異同雜語)	
ST	*Shih-tzu* 尸子, attrib. to Shih Chiao 尸佼 (fourth cent. B.C.)	
STCS	*Shan T'ao ch'i-shih* 山濤啟事 (= *SKCS*)	
STPF	*Sun-tzu ping-fa* 孫子兵法, by Sun Wu 孫武 (ca. 400-320 B.C.)	
STSS	*Ssu-t'i shu-shih* 四體書勢, by Wei Heng 衛恒 (d. 291)	
*SuiS	*Sui-shu* 隋書, edited by Wei Cheng 魏徵 (580-643) et al.	
SunCC	*Sun Ch'o chi* 孫綽集, by Sun Ch'o 孫綽 (fl. 330-365)	
SungS	*Sung-shu* 宋書 (author not identified; not *SS*)	
SW	*Shuo-wen chieh-tzu* 說文解字, by Hsü Shen 許慎 (ca. A.D. 100)	
*SWLC	*Shih-wen lei-chü* 事文類聚, compiled by Chu Mu 祝穆 (1246)	
SY	*Shuo Yüan* 說苑, by Liu Hsiang 劉向 (80-9 B.C.)	
SYCS	*Chin-shu* 晉書, by Shen Yüeh 沈約 (441-513)	
TC	*Tu-chi* 妒記, by Yü T'ung-chih 虞通之 (fifth cent.)	
TCCCC	*Chin-chi* 晉紀, by Ts'ao Chia-chih 曹嘉之 (fourth cent.?)	
TCFH	*Tan-ch'i fu hsü* 彈棊賦叙, by Fu Hsüan 傅玄 (217-278)	

674 TALES OF THE WORLD

*TCTC	*Tzu-chih t'ung-chien* 資治通鑒, by Ssu-ma Kuang 司馬光 (1084)	
TFSC	*Tung-fang Shuo chuan* 東方朔傳, anon.	
TFSSCC	*Shih-chou chi* 十州記, attrib. to Tung-fang Shuo 東方朔 (fl. 100-73 B.C.; actually fourth cent. A.D.)	
THC	*Ts'ai Hung chi* 蔡洪集, by Ts'ai Hung 蔡洪 (late third cent.)	
THL	*Tao-hsien lun* 道賢論, by Sun Ch'o 孫綽 (fl. 330-365)	
TJHCS	*Chin-shu* 晉書, by Tsang Jung-hsü 臧榮緒 (late fifth cent.)	
TKHC	*Tung-kuan Han-chi* 東觀漢記, by Liu Chen 劉珍 (first cent. A.D.)	
TKHTC	*Hsiao-tzu chuan* 孝子傳, by Tsung Kung 宗躬 (fifth cent.)	
TKTC	*T'ai-k'ang ti-chi* 太康地記 (= *Chin t'ai-kang san-nien ti-chi* 晉太康三年地記), anon. (A.D. 282)	
TL	*Tien-lüeh* 典略, by Yü Huan 魚豢 (third cent.)	
TLWS	*T'iao-lieh Wu-shih* 條列吳事, anon. (covers period 229-280)	
TMC	*Ts'ao Man chuan* 曹瞞傳, anon. (concerns Ts'ao Ts'ao 曹操, 155-220)	
*TPKC	*T'ai-p'ing kuang-chi* 太平廣記, compiled by Li Fang 李昉 (893)	
TPTL	*Tien-lun* 典論, by Ts'ao P'ei 曹丕 (187-226)	
*TPYL	*T'ai-p'ing yü-lan* 太平御覽, compiled by Li Fang (893)	
TSC	*T'a-ssu chi* 塔寺記, by Shih T'an-tsung 釋曇宗 (fifth cent.)	
*TSFYCY	*Tu-shih fang-yü chi-yao* 讀史方輿紀要, by Ku Tsu-yü 顧祖禹 (seventeenth cent.)	
TSH	*T'ang-shih hsü* 唐詩序, by Mao Ch'ang 毛萇 (fl. ca. 130 B.C.)	
TSMLSM	*Ta-ssu-ma liao-shu ming* 大司馬僚屬名, by Fu T'ao 伏滔 (ca. 317-396; concerns Huan Wen's 桓溫 staff, 363-373)	
TT	*Tu-tuan* 獨斷, by Ts'ai Yung 蔡邕 (132-192; a glossary to *Li-chi* 禮記)	
TTCC	*Chin-chi* 晉紀, by Teng Ts'an 鄧粲 (fourth cent.)	
TTHS	*Hsin-shu* 新書, by Tu Tu 杜篤 (late third cent.?)	
TungYC	*Tung-yang chi* 東陽記, anon. (concerns Tung-yang Commandery)	
TWSC	*Ti-wang shih-chi* 帝王世紀, by Huang-fu Mi 皇甫謐 (215-282)	
TYC	*Tan-yang chi* 丹陽記, by Shan Ch'ien-chih 山謙之 (fifth cent.; concerns Tan-yang Commandery)	
TYCCC	*T'ai-yüan ch'i-chü chu* 泰元起居注, anon. (concerns period 376-396)	
*TYCT	*Tiao-yü chi-ts'an* 琱玉集殘, anon. (sixth cent.)	
TYKSL	*T'ai-yüan Kuo-shih lu* 太原郭氏錄, anon.	

WC	*Wei-chih* 魏志, by Ch'en Shou 陳壽 (233-297; = *SKWei*)
WCC	*Wen-chang chih* 文章志, by Chih Yü 摯虞 (late third cent.)
WCH	*Wen-chang hsü* 文章敘 (= *WCL*?)
WCHL	*Wen-chang hsü-lu* 文章敘錄 (= *WCL*?)
WCHTYC	*Wang Ch'eng-hsiang te-yin chi* 王丞相德音記, anon. (concerns Wang Tao 王導, 276-339)
WCL	*Wen-chang lu* 文章錄, by Ch'iu Yüan-chih 丘淵之 (fifth cent.). See also *WCH* and *WCHL*
WCML	*Wang-ch'ao mu-lu* 王朝目錄, anon. (covers period 265-317)
WCSY	*(Wei-Chin) shih-yü* (魏晋)世語, by Kuo Pan 郭頒 (late third cent.)
WCTI	*Wu-ching t'ung-i* 五經通義, attrib. to Liu Hsiang (80-9 B.C.)
WCWS	*Wei-shu* 魏書, by Wang Ch'en 王沈 (late third/early fourth cent.)
WCYI	*Wu-ching yao-i* 五經要義, by Lei Tz'u-tsung 雷次宗 (386-448)
WeiL	*Wei-lüeh* 魏略, by Yü Huan 魚豢 (third cent.)
WeiS	*Wei-shu* 魏書, anon. (*not SKWei*)
*WH	*Wen-hsüan* 文選, compiled by Hsiao T'ung 蕭統 (501-531)
WHC	*Wu-hsing chi* 吳興記, by Shan Ch'ien-chih 山謙之 (fifth cent.; concerns Wu-hsing Commandery)
*WHLSC	*Wen-hsüan, Li Shan chu* 文選李善注, by Li Shan 李善 (seventh cent.)
WHSC	*Wang Hsiang shih-chia* 王祥世家, anon. (concerns Wang Hsiang, 185-269)
WHsC	*Wang Hsiu chi* 王脩集, by Wang Hsiu 王脩 (ca. 335-358)
WKT	*Wei-kuo t'ung* 魏國統, by Liang Tso 梁祚 (fifth cent.)
WMC	*Wei-mo chuan* 魏末傳, anon. (concerns period 220-265)
WSC	*Wen-shih chuan* 文士傳, by Chang Yin 張隱 (fourth cent.)
WSCC	*Wei-shih ch'un-ch'iu* 魏氏春秋, by Sun Sheng 孫盛 (ca. 302-373)
WSSC	*Wang-shih shih-chia* 王氏世家, anon. (concerns Wangs of T'ai-yüan)
WTC	*Wen-tzu chih* 文字志, anon.
WTYHC	*Ying-hsiung chi* 英雄記, by Wang Ts'an 王粲 (177-217)
WuC	*Wu-chih* 吳志 (= *SKWu*; combines *WuS* and *Hsü Wu-shu* 續吳書, by Wei Chao 韋昭, third cent.)
WuL	*Wu-lu* 吳錄, by Chang Po 張勃 (third cent.)
WuS	*Wu-shu* 吳書, by Hsiang Chün 項峻 (third cent.). See *WuC*
WWIL	*Wei-Wu i-ling* 魏武遺令, by Ts'ao Ts'ao 曹操 (155-220)

WYCC	*Wu-Yüeh ch'un-ch'iu* 吳越春秋, by Chao Yeh 趙曄 (second cent.)
WYCS	*Chin-shu* 晉書, by Wang Yin 王隱 (fourth cent.)
YangCC	*Yang-chou chi* 揚州記, anon.
YCC	*Yung-chia chi* 永嘉記, by Cheng Chi-chih 鄭緝之 (fifth cent.; concerns Yung-chia Commandery)
YCCC	*Yü-chang chiu-chih* 豫章舊志, anon. (concerns Yü-chang Commandery)
YCL	*Yü-chia lun* 庾家論, anon. (fourth cent.)
YCLJM	*Yung-chia liu-jen ming* 永嘉流人名, anon. (concerns period 307-312)
YehCC	*Yeh-chung chi* 鄴中記, by Lu Hui 陸翽 (fourth cent.; concerns Later Chao. 329-352)
YenCC	*Yen-chou chi* 兗州記, by Hsün Ch'o 荀綽 (fourth cent.)
*YFSC	*Yüeh-fu shih-chi* 樂府詩集, by Kuo Mao-ch'ien 郭茂倩 (thirteenth cent.)
YFSM	*Yüan Fa-shih ming* 遠法師銘, by Chang Yeh 張野 (350-418?)
YHC	*Yüan Hung chi* 袁宏集, by Yüan Hung 袁宏 (328-376)
YHHC	*(Hou)-Han chi* (後)漢紀, by Yüan Hung
YHLH	*Yüan-hua lun hsü* 元化論序, by Hsieh K'un 謝鯤 (280-322; preface to the *Yüan-hua lun* of Tung Yang 童養, 265-311)
YHSW	*Shih-wei* 士緯, by Yao Hsin 姚信 (third cent.)
YHYH	*Yin Hsien yen-hsing* 殷羨言行, anon. (concerns Yin Hsien, fl. early fourth cent.)
YKLC	*Yü Kuang-lu chuan* 虞光祿傳, anon. (concerns Yü Fei 虞騑, fl. ca. 320)
YL	*Yü-lin* 語林, by P'ei Ch'i 裴啟 (362)
YLC	*Yü Liang chi* 庾亮集, by Yü Liang 庾亮 (289-340)
YLCTTM	*Yü Liang ch'i ts'an-tso ming* 庾亮啟參佐名, anon. (concerns staff of Yü Liang, ca. 325-340)
YLL	*Yü Liang lei* 庾亮誄, by Sun Ch'o 孫綽 (fl. 330-365)
YLLSM	*Yü Liang liao-shu ming* 庾亮僚屬名, anon. (concerns staff of Yü Liang, ca. 325-340)
YLPW	*Yü Liang pei-wen* 庾亮碑文, by Sun Ch'o 孫綽 (fl. 330-365)
YML	*Yu-ming lu* 幽明錄, by Liu I-ch'ing 劉義慶 (403-444)
YPH	*Yang Ping (chi) hsü* 羊秉(集)叙, by Hsia-hou Chan (243-291)
YSC	*Yu-shan chi* 遊山記, by Shih Hui-yüan 釋慧遠 (334-416)
YSCC	*Yüan-shih chia-chuan* 袁氏家傳, anon. (concerns Yüan Tan 袁耽, ca. 315-339)
*YSCH	*Yen-shih chia-hsün* 顏氏家訓, by Yen Chih-t'ui 顏之推 (531-595)

YSSC	*Yüan-shih shih-chi* 袁氏世紀, anon.
YTLH	*Yü Ts'un lei hsü* 虞存誄敘, by Sun T'ung 孫統 (fourth cent.)
YYCS	*Chin-shu* 晉書, by Yü Yü 虞預 (fourth cent.)
YYLC	*Yü Yü Liang chien* 與庾亮牋, by Sun Ch'o 孫綽 (fl. 330-365)
YYLLSH	*Yu Yen-ling-lai shih hsü* 遊嚴陵瀨詩敘, by Wang Hsün 王珣 (350-401)
*YYTT	*Yu-yang tsa-tsu* 酉陽雜俎, by Tuan Ch'eng-shih 段成式 (ninth cent.)

Bibliography

A. Texts of the SSHY

1. *Shih-shuo hsin-shu* 世說新書. Originally in 10 *chüan*—the "T'ang fragment." Part of an eighth-century manuscript brought to Japan perhaps as early as the ninth century and including most of *chüan* 6 (Chapters X-XIII), with Liu Chün's unabridged commentary.
   A photolithographic reproduction was published by Lo Chen-yü 羅振玉 in 1916, bearing the title, *T'ang-hsieh-pen Shih-shuo hsin-shu ts'an-chüan* 唐寫本世說新書殘卷. A still later photographic reproduction in halftone, under the title, *Tōshōhon Sesetsu shinsho* 唐鈔本世說新書, edited by Kanda Kiichirō 神田喜一郎 and Nishikawa Yasushi 西川寧, appeared as No. 176 in the series *Shoseki meihin sōkan* 書跡名品叢刊, Tokyo, 1972.
   Lo's edition is reproduced in the Peking reprint of 1956 and some other modern editions.

2. *Shih-shuo hsin-yü* 世說新語, in 3 *chüan*. Published by Yen Shu 晏殊 (991-1055), with Liu Chün's commentary drastically abridged. Not extant.

3. *Shih-shuo hsin-yü*. Published by Tung Fen 董弅 in 1138, based on a collation of Yen's text with one in the possession of Wang Chu 王洙. The blocks were destroyed by fire some time before 1188. Not extant.

4. *Shih-shuo hsin-yü*. Published by Lu Yu 陸游 (1125-1209) through the Ch'uan-shih lou 傳是樓 in 1188, exactly duplicating Tung's text. Not extant.

5. *Shih-shuo hsin-yü*. Published by Wang Tsao 汪藻 (thirteenth cent.), including a preface by Wang himself, *Shih-shuo hsü-lu* 世說敘錄; an appendix of alternate readings, *K'ao-i* 考異, based on an early commentary by Ching Yin 敬胤 (probably fifth cent.); and genealogical tables, *Jen-ming p'u* 人名譜, of the principal families mentioned in the text.

A photolithographic reproduction of an original of this edition preserved in Japan in the Maeda 前田 Collection, known alternately as the Sonkei Kaku 尊敬閣 or Kanazawa Bunkō 金澤文庫 edition, was published in Tokyo in 1929.

This text is again reproduced in the Peking edition of 1956 and other modern editions.

6. *Shih-shuo hsin-yü*. Published by Liu Ying-teng 劉應登 (Sung), an annotated text surviving only in quotations in Ling Ying-ch'u's and Wang Shih-chen's Ming editions.

7. *Shih-shuo hsin-yü*. Published by Yüan Chiung 袁褧 in 1535 through the Chia-ch'ü t'ang 嘉趣堂, based on Lu Yu's edition.

8. *Shih-shuo hsin-yü*. Published by Ling Ying-ch'u 凌瀛初 (Ming), incorporating annotations by Liu Ying-teng (Sung).

9. *Shih-shuo hsin-yü pu* 補 in 20 chüan. First published by Wang Shih-chen 王世貞 (1526-1590) in 1556. An abridgement of an amplified text by Ho Liang-chün 何良俊 (Ming), which incorporated reconstructions of P'ei Ch'i's 裴啟 *Yü-lin* 語林 (A.D. 362) culled from quotations in Liu Chün's Commentary and elsewhere. It includes a commentary by Chang Wen-chu 張文柱 (Ming).

Two Japanese editions, published in 1694 and 1779, incorporate the punctuation and annotations of Li Chih 李贄 (1527-1602) and bear the title, *Li Cho-wu p'i-tien Shih-shuo hsin-yü pu* 李卓吾批點⋯⋯補. These are the basis of all premodern Japanese editions.

10. *Shih-shuo hsin-yü*. Published by Chiang Huang-t'ing 蔣篁亭 sometime between 1723 and 1730, based on a collation of Lu Yu's and Yüan Chiung's texts. Not extant; the basis of the following text.

11. *Shih-shuo hsin-yü*. Published by Shen Yen 沈巖 in 1730 through the Han-fen lou 涵芬樓 in Shanghai, based on Chiang's text.

It is photolithographically reproduced in the *SPTK* edition of 1929 and includes Shen's collations, *Shih-shuo hsin-yü chiao-yü* 校語.

12. *Sesetsu shōsatsu* 世說鈔撮. Published by the priest Kenjō 顯常, Edo, 1763, based on Wang Shih-chen's supplemented text.

13. *Sesetsu onshaku* 世說音釋. Published by Onda Chūjin 恩田仲任, Edo, 1816; based on Wang Shih-chen's text, with glosses.

14. *Sesetsu sembon* 世說箋本. Published by Hata Shigen 秦士鉉, Edo, 1826, based on Wang Shih-chen's text and incorporating comments by Liu Ying-teng (Sung), Li Chih (Ming), and others.

15. *Shih-shuo hsin-yü*. Published by Wang Hsien-ch'ien 王先謙 in 1891 through the Ssu-hsien chiang-she 思賢講舍 of Shanghai. It includes Wang's own collations, *Chiao-k'an hsiao-shih* 校勘小識 and supplement, *pu* 補, plus Yeh Te-hui's 葉德輝 (late nineteenth cent.) listing of "unauthorized passages," *SSHY i-wen* 佚文, culled from various quotations, and his bibliography of works cited in Liu Chün's Commentary, *Shih-shuo hsin-yü chu yin-yung shu-mu* 注引用書目.

16. *Shih-shuo hsin-yü chiao-chien* 校箋. Published serially by Liu P'an-sui 劉盼遂 in *Wen-tzu t'ung-meng* 文字同盟 11-13 (1927), and *Kuo-hsüeh lun-ts'ung* 國學論叢 1-4 (1928).

17. *Shih-shuo hsin-yü chiao-chien* 校箋. Published by Yang Yung 楊勇, Hong Kong, 1969. A definitive modern edition, utilizing Wang Li-ch'i's emendations (see below, under Special Studies), with others suggested by Yang himself.

18. *Shih-shuo hsin-yü pu-cheng* 補正. Published by Wang Shu-min 王叔岷, Taipei, 1975.

B. Translations

1. *Sesetsu shingo* 世說新語. Translated by Okada Seinoshi 岡田正之識 for the series *Kambun sōsho* 漢文叢書 (Tsukamoto Tessan 塚本哲三, general editor), Tokyo, 1925. A *kambun* translation of Wang Shih-chen's (supplemented) text, with interpretations and laconic comments based on *Sesetsu sembon*.

2. *Sesetsu shingo*. Translated by Omura Umeo 大村梅雄. In *Chūgoku koten bungaku zenshū* 中國古典文學全集, No. 32 in the series *Rekidai zuihitsu shū* 歷代隨筆集, Tokyo, 1959. An incomplete translation of the pre-Ming (unsupplemented) text into modern Japanese with brief annotation.

3. *Sesetsu shingo*. Translated by Kawakatsu Yoshio 川勝義雄, Fukunaga Mitsuji 福永光司, Murakami Yoshimi 村上嘉實, and Yoshikawa Tadao 吉川忠夫. In *Chūgoku koshōsetsushū* 中國古小說集 (*Sekai bungaku taikei* 世界文學大系 71, Yoshikawa Kōjirō, general editor), Tokyo, 1964. A complete, annotated translation into modern Japanese, with appendices of biographical notes and official titles.

4. *Sesetsu shingo*. Translated by Mori Mikisaburō 森三樹三郎. In *Chūgoku koten bungaku taikei* 中國古典文學大系 9, Tokyo, 1969.

5. *Anthologie chinoise des 5e et 6e siècles: le Che-chouo-sin-yu par Lieou (Tsuen) Hiao-piao*. Translated by Bruno Belpaire. Editions Universitaires, Paris, 1974. A complete translation into French with laconic annotation.

C. Special Studies

Chan Hsiu-hui 詹秀惠. *Shih-shuo hsin-yü yü-fa t'an-chiu* 語法探究. Taipei, 1972.

Chang Shun-hui 張舜徽. "Shih-shuo hsin-yü chu shih-li" 注釋例. In *Kuang-chiao ch'ou-lüeh* 廣校讎畧. Peking, 1963. Pp. 192-212.

Chao Kang 趙岡. "Shih-shuo hsin-yü Liu-chu i-li k'ao" 劉注義例考. In *Kuo-wen yüeh-k'an* 國文月刊 28 (1949), 20-26.

Ch'en Chih 陳直. "Tu Shih-shuo hsin-yü cha-chi" 讀世說新語札記. In *Chung-hua wen-shih lun-ts'ung* 中華文史論叢 5, Peking, 1964, 364.

Ch'en Yin-k'o 陳寅恪. "Shu Shih-shuo hsin-yü wen-hsüeh lei 'Chung Hui chuan Ssu-pen lun shih-pi' t'iao hou" 書世說新語文學類「鍾會撰四本論始畢條後. In *Chung-shan ta-hsüeh hsüeh pao* 中山大學學報 56 (1956), 70-73.

Ch'eng Tu-yüan 程篤原. "Shih-shuo hsin-yü chien cheng" 箋證. In *Kuo-li Wu-Han ta-hsüeh wen-che chi-k'an* 國立武漢大學文哲季刊, 7.2 (1942), 1-26; 7.3 (1943), 1-18.

Chi Yung 紀庸. "Shih-shuo hsin-yü chih wen-chang" 文章. In *Kuo-wen yüeh-k'an* 國文月刊 64 (1959), 22-26.

Chou I-liang 周一良. "*Shih-shuo hsin-yü* cha-chi" 札記. In *Wei-Chin nan-pei-ch'ao lun-chi* 魏晉南北朝論集, Peking, 1963. Pp. 397-401.

Chu Chien-hsin 朱建新. "*Shih-shuo hsin-yü* chih yen-chiu" 研究. In *Chen-chih hsüeh-pao* 貞知學報 1.1 (1942).

Eichhorn, Werner, "Zur chinesischen Kulturgeschichte des 3. und 4. Jahrhunderts." In *Zeitschrift der Deutschen Morgenländischen Gesellschaft* 19 (1937), 451-483.

Furuta Keiichi 古田敬一. *Sesetsu shingo itsubon* 佚文 *Chūbun kenkyū sōkan* 中文研究叢刊 2. Hiroshima, 1955.

———. *Sesetsu shingo kōkanbyō* 校勘表 *Chūbun kenkyū sōkan* 5. Hiroshima, 1957.

———. "Ruisho nado shoin *Sesetsu shingo* ni tsuite" 類書等所引世說新語について. In *Hiroshima Daigaku bungakubu kiyō* 廣島大學文學部紀要 3 (1953), 145-166.

Ho Ch'ang-ch'ün 賀昌羣. "*Shih-shuo hsin-yü* cha-chi" 札記. In *Kuo-li chung-yang t'u-shu-kuan kuan-k'an* 1 (1947), 1-7. On the term *chu-wei* 麈尾.

Hsü Chen-o 徐震堮. "*Shih-shuo hsin-yü* li ti Chin-Sung k'ou-yü shih-i" 裏的晉宋口語釋義. In *Hua-tung shih-ta hsüeh-pao* 華東師大學報 (1957), 50-61.

Hsü Shih-ying 許世瑛. "Ts'ung *Shih-shuo hsin yü* k'an Wei-Chin jen hsi-su ti i-pan" 從……看魏晉人習俗的一斑. In *Hsin she-hui yüeh-k'an* 1.7 (1948), 8-10.

———. "T'an-t'an *Shih-shuo hsin-yü* chung 'chien'-tzu ti t'e-shu yung-fa ho pei-tung-ti chi-chung chü-hsing" 談談……中見字的特殊用法和被動的幾種句型. In *Ta-lu tsa-chih* 大陸雜誌 25.10 (1961), 297-303.

———. "T'an-t'an *Shih-shuo hsin-yü* chung 'hsiang'-tzu ti t'e-shu yung-fa" 「相」字的特殊用法. Ibid. 27.9 (1963), 273-282.

———. "*Shih-shuo hsin-yü* chung ti-i shen ch'eng-tai-tz'u yen-chiu" 第一身稱代辭研究. In *Tan-chiang hsüeh-pao* 淡江學報 2 (1963), 1-24.

———. "*Shih-shuo hsin-yü* chung ti-erh shen ch'eng-tai-tz'u yen-chiu" 第二身. In *Bulletin of the Institute of History and Philology, Academia Sinica* 36 (1965), 185-235.

Hung, William 洪業, ed. *Index to Shih-Shuo Hsin-Yü and to the Titles Quoted in the Commentary*. Harvard-Yenching Institute Sinological Index Series 12. Peiping, 1933.

I Hsiao-nung 易笑儂. "*Shih-shuo hsin-yü* chung chih wen-chang" 文章. In *Chien-she* 建設 9.10 (1961), 34-39.

Kawakatsu Yoshio 川勝義雄. "Edo jidai ni okeru *Sesetsu* kenkyū no ichimen" 江戸時代における……研究の一面. In *Tōhōgaku* 東方學 20 (1960), 104-118. On a manuscript commentary on the *Shih-shuo hsin-yü* by the eighteenth-century priest Kōhō 高峰, preserved in the Kenninji, Kyoto.

———. "*Sesetsu shingo* no hensan o megutte" 編纂をめぐって. In *Tōhō gakuhō* 東方學報 41 (1970), 217-234.

Kōzen Hiroshi 興膳宏. "Sesetsu shingo no gunzō" 群豪. In Sekai bungaku taikei 71 (1965), monthly supplement 85, 2-4.

Li Hsing-chien 李行健. "Shih-shuo hsin-yü chung fu-tz'u 'tou' ho 'liao' yung-fa ti pi-chiao" 副詞"都"和"了"用法的比較. In Yü-yen hsüeh lun-ts'ung 語言學論叢 2 (1958), 73-83.

Liu P'an-sui 劉盼遂. "T'ang-hsieh pen Shih-shuo hsin-shu pa-wei" 唐寫本……書跋尾. In Ch'ing-hua hsüeh-pao 清華學報 2.2 (1925), 589-592.

Mather, Richard B. "Chinese Letters and Scholarship in the Third and Fourth Centuries: the Wen-hsüeh P'ien of the SSHY." In Journal of the American Oriental Society 84.4 (1964), 348-391.

―――――. "Some Examples of 'Pure Conversation' in the SSHY." In Transactions of the International Conference of Orientalists in Japan 9 (1964), 58-70.

―――――. "The Fine Art of Conversation: the Yen-yü P'ien of the SSHY." In Journal of the American Oriental Society 91.2 (1971), 222-275.

Morino Shigeo 森野繁夫. "Toku Sesetsu shingo sakki: Bungaku hen" 讀……札記文學篇. In Chūgoku chūsei bungaku kenkyū 中国中世文学研究 2 (1962), 38-47.

―――――. "Sesetsu shingo kōi no kachi" 考異の價値. Ibid. 3 (1963), 22-32.

Murakami Yoshimi 村上嘉實. "Sesetsu shingo no kishi-teki seikaku" 機智的性格. In Shirin 史林 29.3 (1945), 30-48.

―――――. "Sesetsu shingo ni arawaretaru kosei" に現れたる個性. In Haneda hakase shōju kinen tōyōshi ronsō 羽田博士頌壽記念東洋史論叢. Kyoto, 1950. Pp. 949-969.

Obi Kōichi 小尾郊一. "'Kei'-ji ni tsuite: Sesetsu shingo nōto yori" 「聲」字について……ノート. In Chūgoku chūsei bungaku kenkyū 3 (1963), 1-7.

Okamura Shigeru 岡村繁. "Sesetsu shoken wagen yōten kō" 所見話言用典考. In Hiroshima daigaku bungakubu kiyō 5 (1954), 208-240.

Ōyane Bunjirō 大矢根文次郎. "Sesetsu to kyokasei" 教化性. In Tōyō bungaku kenkyū 東洋文学研究 8 (1960), 59-71.

―――――. "Sesetsu no genkyo to sono sesshu kaishū ni tsuite" 原據とその截取改修について. Ibid. 9 (1961), 35-56.

Shen Chia-pen 沈家本 (Ch'ing). Shih-shuo chu so-yin shu-mu 注所引書目. Originally in Ku shu-mu ssu-chung 古書目四種. Reprinted, Peking, 1963.

Shen Chien-chih 沈劍知. "Shih-shuo hsin-yü chiao-chien" 校箋. In Hsüeh-hai 學海 1.1, 2, 3, 6 (1955); 2.1 (1956).

Takahashi Kiyoshi 高橋清. Sesetsu shingo sakuin 索引 Chūbun kenkyū sōkan 6. Hiroshima, 1959.

Tōyō bungaku kenkyū, Sesetsu rinkōkai 東洋文学研究世説輪講會. "Sesetsu shingo yakkai: Kangōhen 24" 世說新語譯解. 簡傲篇第二十四. In Tōyō bungaku kenkyū 14 (1966), 37-48.

———. "*Sesetsu shingo* yakkai: *Haichōhen* 25 排調篇." Ibid. 15 (1967), 65-79.

Utsunomiya Kiyoyoshi 宇都宮清吉. "*Sesetsu shingo* no jidai" 時代. In *Tōhō gakuhō* 10.2 (1939). Revised for *Kandai shakai-keizaishi kenkyū* 漢代社會經濟史研究. Tokyo, 1955. Pp. 473-521.

Wang Chih-ch'ang 汪之昌. "*Shih-shuo hsin-yü* chu yin ch'ün-shu mu-lu" 注引羣書目錄. In *Ch'ing-hsüeh-chai chi* 青學齋集. a Ch'ing work. Republished, 1930.

Wang Li-ch'i 王利器. "*Shih-shuo hsin-yü* chiao-k'an chi" 校勘記. Attached to second volume of the Peking edition, 1956.

Yang, V. T. "About *Shih-shuo hsin-yü*." In *Journal of Oriental Studies* 2.2 (1955), 309-315.

Yoshikawa Kōjirō 吉川幸次郎. "*Sesetsu shingo* no bunshō 文章. In *Tōhō gakuhō* 10.2 (1939), 199-255. Trans. Glen W. Baxter, *Harvard Journal of Asiatic Studies* 18 (1955), 124ff.

D. Background Studies

Acker, W. R. B. *Some T'ang and Pre-T'ang Texts on Chinese Painting*. Leiden, 1954.

Archaeological Institute, Chinese Academy of Sciences, eds. *Hsin Chung-kuo-ti k'ao-ku shou-huo* 新中國的考古收穫. Peking, 1962.

Balazs, Etienne, "Entre revolte nihiliste et évasion mystique." In *Etudes Asiatiques* 2 (1948), 27-55. Trans. in *Chinese Civilization and Bureaucracy*, New Haven, 1964. Pp. 226-254.

———. "La crise sociale et la philosophie politique à la fin des Han." In *T'oung Pao* 39 (1949), 83-131; trans. ibid., pp. 187-225.

Birch, Cyril, ed. *Anthology of Chinese Literature*, Vol. I. New York, 1965.

Chang Fu 張溥 (fl. ca. 1630-40). *Han-Wei liu-ch'ao pai-san chia chi* 漢魏六朝百三家集. Edition of 1879.

Chao I 趙翼 (1727-1814). *Nien-erh-shih cha-chi* 廿二史劄記. 2 vols. Reprinted, Peking, 1963.

Chen, Shih-hsiang. *Biography of Ku K'ai-chih*. Chinese Dynastic Histories Translations No. 2. Berkeley and Los Angeles, 1953.

Ch'en, Kenneth, "Anti-Buddhist Propaganda during the Nan-ch'ao." In *HJAS* 15 (1952), 166-192.

———. "Neo-Taoism and the Prajña School." In *Chinese Culture* 1.2 (1957), 33-46.

Ch'en Yin-k'o 陳寅恪. "*Hsiao-yao-yu* Hsiang-Kuo i chi Chih Tun i t'an-yüan" 逍遙遊向郭義及支道義探源. In *Ch'ing-hua hsüeh-pao* 12 (1937), 309-314.

———. *T'ao Yüan-ming chih ssu-hsiang yü ch'ing-t'an chih kuan-hsi* 陶淵明之思想與清談之關係. Chungking, 1945.

———. "Tung-Chin nan-ch'ao chih Wu-yü" 東晉南朝之吳語. In *Bulletin of the Institute of History and Philology, Academia Sinica* 7.1 (1947), 1-4.

Chou Fu-ch'eng 周輔成. "Wei-Chin nan-pei-ch'ao shih-ch'i wei-wu-lun ssu-hsiang ti fa-chan"魏晉南北朝時期唯物論思想的發展. In *Li-shih chiao-hsüeh* 歷史教學, Feb. 1957, pp. 2-3.

Chou I-liang 周一良. *Wei-Chin nan-pei-ch'ao lun-chi* 魏晉南北朝論集. Peking, 1963.

Demiéville, Paul. "La pénétration du Bouddhisme dans la tradition philosophique chinoise." In *Cahiers d'histoire mondiale* 3.1 (1956), 19-38.

Dubs, Homer H., trans. *History of the Former Han Dynasty*. 3 vols. Baltimore, 1938-1955.

Duyvendak, J.J.L., trans. *The Book of Lord Shang*. London, 1928.

Egerod, S., and Glahn, E., eds. *Studia Serica Bernhard Karlgren Dedicata*. Copenhagen, 1959.

Eichhorn, Werner. "Description of the Rebellion of Sun En." In *Mitteilungen des Instituts für Orientforschung* 2.1 (1954), 325-352.

──────. "Nachträgliche Bemerkungen zum Aufstandes des Sun En." Ibid. 2.3 (1954), 463-476.

Fan Ning 范寧. "Lun Wei-Chin shih-tai chih-shih fen-tzu ti ssu-hsiang fen-hua chi ch'i she-hui ken-yüan"論魏晉時代知識分子的思想分化及其社會根源. In *Li-shih yen-chiu* 1955.4, 113-131.

Fan Shou-k'ang 范壽康. *Wei-Chin chih ch'ing-t'an* 魏晉之清談. Shanghai, 1936.

Fitzgerald, C. P. *Barbarian Beds*. London, 1965. See also review by D. Holzman, "A propos de l'origine de la chaise en Chine," in *T'oung Pao* 53.4-5 (1957), 279-292.

Frodsham, J. D. "The Origins of Chinese Nature Poetry." In *Asia Major* (n.s.) 8.1 (1960), 68-104.

──────, and Ch'eng Hsi, trans. *An Anthology of Chinese Verse: Han Wei Chin and the Northern and Southern Dynasties*. Oxford, 1967.

──────. *The Murmuring Stream: the Life and Works of the Chinese Nature Poet Hsieh Ling-yün (385-433), Duke of K'ang-lo*. 2 vols. Kuala Lumpur, 1968.

Fu Mao-mien 傅懋勉. "Lun Chin-tai ti yin-i ssu-hsiang ho yin-i shih-jen"論晉代的隱逸思想和隱逸詩人. In *Wen-shih-che* 文史哲 4 (1958), 20-24.

Fukunaga Mitsuji 福永光司. "Kaku Zō no Sōji kaishaku" 郭象の莊子解釋. In *Tetsugaku kenkyū* 哲學研究 37.2 (1954) 46-62; 37.2 (1954) 167-177.

──────. "Shi Ton to sono shūi: Tō-Shin no Rō-Sō shisō" 支遁とその周圍. 東晉の老莊思想. In *Bukkyō shigaku* 佛教史學 5.2 (1956), 12-34.

──────. "Chi Chō no Bukkyō shisō: Tō-Shin Bukkyō no ichi seikaku" 郗超の佛教思想・東晉佛教の一性格. In *Tsukamoto hakase shōju kinen Bukkyōshigaku ronshū* 塚本博士頌壽紀念佛教史學論叢. Kyoto, 1961. Pp. 631-646.

Fung, Yu-lan. *A History of Chinese Philosophy*. 2 vols. trans. Derk Bodde, Princeton, 1952-1953.

Goodrich, Chauncey. "Two Chapters in the Life of an Empress of the Later Han, II." *Harvard Journal of Asiatic Studies* 26 (1966), 187-210.

Graham, A. C. "Kung-sun Lung's Essay on Meanings and Things." *Journal of Oriental Studies* 2 (1955), 282-301.

———. "Two Dialogues in the *Kung-sun Lung-tzu*: 'White Horse' and 'Left and Right.'" *Asia Major* 11.2 (1965), 128-150.

Griffith, S. B. *Sun-tzu, the Art of War*. Oxford, 1963.

Hawkes, David. *Ch'u-tz'u, The Songs of the South*. Oxford, 1959.

Hibino Takeo 日比野丈夫. "*Suikeichū Gisuihen* o yomu" 水經注沂水篇を讀む. In *Ritsumeikan bungaku* 立命館文学 180 (1960), 754-757.

Ho, Ch'ang-ch'ün 賀昌羣. *Wei-Chin ch'ing-t'an ssu-hsiang ch'u-lun* 魏晉清談思想初論. Shanghai, 1947.

Ho Ch'i-min 何啟民. *Chu-lin ch'i-hsien yen-chiu* 竹林七賢研究. Taipei, 1966.

Ho Peng-yoke (Ho Ping-yü). *The Astronomical Chapters of the Chin-shu*. Paris, 1966.

Ho Tzu-ch'üan 何茲全. *Wei-Chin nan-pei-ch'ao shih-lüeh* 魏晉南北朝史略. Shanghai, 1958.

Holzman, Donald, "Les sept sages de la forêt des bambous et la société de leur temps." In *T'oung Pao* 44 (1956), 317-346.

———. "Gen Ki to Kei Kō to no Dōka shisō" 阮籍と秘康との道家思想. In *Tōhō Shūkyō* 東方宗教 10 (1956), 1-20.

———. *La vie et la pensée de Hi K'ang*. Leiden, 1957.

———. "Une conception chinoise du héros." In *Diogène* 36 (1961), 37-55. On Juan Chi's 阮籍 *Ta-jen hsien-sheng chuan* 大人先生傳.

Hou Wai-lu 侯外廬. "Wei-Chin ssu-hsiang chih li-shih pei-ching yü chieh-chi ken-yüan" 魏晉思想之歷史背景與階級根源. In *Hsin chien-she* 新建設 2.5 (1950), 4-9.

——— et al. *Chung-kuo ssu-hsiang t'ung-shih* 中國思想通史. 5 vols. Second ed., Peking, 1962.

Hsü Shih-ying 許世瑛. "Shih 'a-nu'" 釋「阿奴」. In *Kuo-wen yüeh-k'an* 75 (1949), 31-32.

———. "Chin-shih nan-pei-jen hsiang-ch'ing" 晉時南北人相輕. In *Ta-lu tsa-chih* 1.6 (1950) 17.

———. "Chin-shih pei-chien-che ch'eng tsun-kuei-che yüeh 'kuan'" 晉時卑賤者稱尊貴者曰「官」. Ibid. 1.7 (1950), 3.

———. "Chin-shih hsia-chi kuan-li tzu-ch'eng yüeh 'min'" 晉時下級官吏自稱曰「民」. Ibid. 1.8 (1950), 6.

———. "Wei-Chin jen hsin-mu chung 'ts'ang'-tzu ti i-i" 魏晉人心目中「傖」字的意義. In *K'un-lun* 崑崙 4.1 (1960), 6.

———. "Wang Hsi-chih fu-tzu ho T'ien-shih-tao ti kuan-hsi" 王羲之父子和天師道的關係. Ibid. 4.2 (1960), 5-6.

Hughes, E. R. *Two Chinese Poets: Vignettes of Han Life*. Princeton, 1960.

Hurvitz, Leon. "'Render unto Caesar' in Early Chinese Buddhism." In *Sino-Indian Studies* 5.3-4 (1957), 2-36.

Jen Chi-yü 任繼愈. "Wei-Chin ch'ing-t'an ti shih-chih ho ying-hsiang" 魏晉清談的實質和影響. In *Li-shih chiao-hsüeh*, Oct. 1956, pp. 9-11.

Kaizuka Shigeki, ed. *Silver Jubilee Volume of the Zinbun Kagaku Kenkyusyo*. Kyoto University. Kyoto, 1954.

———. *Chūgoku* 中國. 4 vols. Sekai bunkashi taikei 世界文化史大系. Tokyo, 1958.

Kao Ming 高明 ed. *Liang Chin nan-pei-ch'ao wen-hui* 兩晉南北朝文彙. Hong Kong, 1960.

Kawakatsu Yoshio 川勝義雄. "Gi-Shin nanchō no monsei kori" 魏晉南北朝の門生故吏. In *Tōhō gakuhō* 28 (1958), 175-218.

———. "Ryū-Sō seiken no seiritsu to kanmon bujin" 劉宋政權の成立と寒門武人. Ibid. 36 (1961), 215-233.

———, ed. *Chūgoku chūseishi kenkyū* 中國中世史研究. Tokyo, 1970.

Kimura Eiichi 木村英一. ed. *E-on kenkyū* 慧遠研究. 2 vols. Kyoto, 1960.

Ku Chieh-kang 顧頡剛. "Liu-ch'ao men-fa" 六朝門閥. In *Kuo-li Wu-Han ta-hsüeh wen-che chi-k'an* 5.4 (1936), 829-876.

Lamotte, Etienne. *L'enseignment de Vimalakīrti*. Louvain, 1962.

Legge, James, trans. *The Chinese Classics*. 5 vols. Oxford and Hong Kong, 1868-1893.

———, trans. *The Li Ki*. 2 vols. Sacred Books of the East, Vols. 27-28. Oxford, 1885.

Liebenthal, Walter. *The Book of Chao (Chao-lun)*. **Monumen**ta Serica, Monograph XIII. Peking, 1948.

———. "Chinese Buddhism during the Fourth and Fifth Centuries." In *Monumenta Nipponica* 11.1 (1955), 44-83.

Link, Arthur E. "The Biography of Tao-an." In *T'oung Pao* 46 (1958), 1-48.

———. "The Taoist Antecedents of Tao-an's Prajñā Ontology." In *History of Religions* 9.2-3 (1969-1970), 181-215.

Liu, James J. Y. *The Chinese Knight-Errant*. London and Chicago, 1967.

Liu Ta-chieh 劉大杰. *Wei-Chin ssu-hsiang lun* 魏晉思想論. Shanghai, 1939.

Lu Hsün 魯迅. *Chung-kuo hsiao-shuo shih lüeh* 中國小說史略. Revised edition of 1930; reprinted, Peking, 1958.

———. ed. *Hsi K'ang chi* 嵇康集. Peking, 1956.

———. "Wei-Chin feng-tu chi wen-chang yü yao chi chiu chih kuan-hsi" 魏晉風度及文章與藥及酒之關係. In *Erh-i chi* 而已集, Vol. III of Collected Works. Peking, 1961. Pp. 379-395.

Lü Ssu-mien 呂思勉. *Liang-Chin nan-pei-ch'ao shih* 兩晉南北朝史. 2 vols. Hong Kong, 1948.

Margouliès, G. *Le "Fou" dans le Wen Siuen*. Paris, 1926.

Maspero, Henri. *Le Taoïsme et les religions chinoises*. Paris, 1971. Based on *Mélanges posthumes sur les religions et l'histoire de la Chine*, Paris, 1950.

Masutomi Junosuke 益富壽之助. "Shōsōin yakubutsu o chūshin to suru kodai sekiyaku no kenkyū" 正倉院藥物を中心とする古代石藥の研究. In *Shōsōin no kōbutsu* 正倉院之鑛物, Vol. I. Kyoto, 1958. Pp. 21-22.

Mather, Richard B. "The Landscape Buddhism of the Fifth Century Poet Hsieh Ling-yün." In *Journal of Asian Studies* 18 (1958/9), 67-79.

⸻. "The Mystical Ascent of the T'ien-t'ai Mountains: Sun Ch'o's *Yu T'ien-t'ai-shan fu*." In *Monumenta Serica* 20 (1961), 226-245.

⸻. "Vimalakīrti and Gentry Buddhism." In *History of Religions* 8.1 (1968), 60-73.

⸻. "A Note on the Dialects of Lo-yang and Nanking during the Six Dynasties." In Tse-chung Chow, ed., *Wen-lin*. Madison, 1968.

⸻. "The Controversy over Conformity and Naturalness during the Six Dynasties." In *History of Religions* 9.2-3 (1969-1970), 160-180.

Matsumoto Gamei 松本雅明. "Kō-Kan no tohi shisō" 後漢の逃避思想. In *Tōhō gakuhō* 12.3 (1941), 381-412.

Meng Ssu-ming 蒙思明. "Liu-ch'ao shih-tsu hsing-ch'eng ti ching-kuo" 六朝世族形成的經過. In *Wen-shih tsa-chih* 文史雜誌 1.9 (1941), 1-22.

Meyer, Hektor. *Wang Tao--Gründungdminster der Ost-Chin*. Berlin, 1973.

Miyakawa Hisayuki 宮川尚志. "Rikuchō jidaijin no Bukkyō shinkō" 六朝時代人の佛教信仰. In *Bukkyōshigaku* 4.2 (1955), 1-17.

⸻. *Rikuchōshi kenkyū: seiji shakai hen* 六朝史研究·政治社會篇. Tokyo, 1956.

⸻. *Rikuchōshi kenkyū: shūkyō hen* 宗教篇. Kyoto, 1964.

⸻. "Son On Ro Jun no ran ni tsuite" 孫恩盧循の亂について. In *Tōyōshi kenkyū* 東洋史研究 30.2-3 (1971), 1-30.

Miyazaki Ichisada 宮崎市定. *Kyūhin kanjin hō no kenkyū* 九品官人法の研究. Kyoto, 1956.

⸻. "Seidan" 清談. In *Shirin* 31 (1946), 1-17.

Murakami Yoshimi 村上嘉實. *Chugoku no sennin: "Hōbokushi" no shisō* 中國の仙人 抱朴子の思想. Kyoto, 1956.

⸻. "Initsu" 隱逸. In *Shirin* 29.6 (1956), 461-479.

⸻. "Seidan to Bukkyō" 清談と佛教. In *Tsukamoto hakase shōju kinen Bukkyōshigaku ronshū* 塚本博士頌壽紀念佛教史學論叢. Kyoto, 1961. Pp. 818-831.

Needham, Joseph. *Science and Civilisation in China*. Vols. I-IV.3. Cambridge, 1954-1971.

Obi Kōichi 小尾郊一. "Rikuchō bungaku ni arawareta sansui kan" 六朝文学に現われた山水觀. In *Chūgoku bungakuhō* 8 (1958), 79-94.

_____. *Chūgoku bungaku ni arawareta shizen to shizen kan* 中国文学に現われた自然と自然観. Tokyo, 1962.

Ōchō E'nichi 横超慧日. "Chūgoku nanbokuchō jidai no Bukkyō gakufū" 中国南北朝時代の佛教学風について. In *Nihon Bukkyō gakkai nenpō* 日本佛教学会年報 17 (1952), 1-26.

Okamura Shigeru 岡村繁. "Kō-Kan makki no heiron-teki kifū ni tsuite" 後漢末期の評論的気風について. In *Nagoya daigaku bungakubu kenkyū ronshū* 名古屋大学文学部研究論集. Nagoya, 1960. Pp. 67-112.

_____. "Gi-Shin nanbokuchō ni okeru heiron-teki kifū no kenkyū" 魏晋南北朝における評論的気風の研究. In *Kakko kenkyū oyobi josei kenkyū hōkoku shūroku* 各個研究および助成研究報告集録. Tokyo, 1953. P. 301.

Okazaki Fumio 岡崎文夫. *Gi-Shin nanbokuchō tsūshi* 魏晋南北朝通史. Tokyo, 1932. Reprinted, 1954.

Petrov, A. A. *Wang Pi: His Place in the History of Chinese Philosophy* (in Russian). Monograph 13, Institute of Oriental Studies, Moscow Academy of Science, 1936. English review and summary by Arthur Wright in *Harvard Journal of Asiatic Studies* 10 (1947), 75-80.

Picken, Laurence. "The Origin of the Short Lute." *Galpin Society Journal* 8.1 (1955).

Rogers, Michael C. *The Chronicle of Fu Chien*. Chinese Dynastic Histories Translations 10. Berkeley and Los Angeles, 1968.

_____. "The Myth of the Fei River." In *T'oung Pao* 54 (1968), 50-72.

Rosenfield, John M. *The Dynastic Arts of the Kushans*. Berkeley and Los Angeles, 1967.

Schafer, Edward H. "The Pearl Fisheries of Ho-p'u." *Journal of the American Oriental Society* 72 (1952), 155-168.

_____. *The Golden Peaches of Samarkand*. Berkeley and Los Angeles, 1963.

_____. *The Vermilion Bird*. Berkeley and Los Angeles, 1967.

Schlegel, Gustave. *Uranographie Chinoise*. The Hague, 1875.

Shryock, J. K., trans. *The Study of Human Abilities: the Jen-wu Chih of Liu Shao*. New Haven, 1937. Reprinted, 1966.

Shou P'u-hsüan 壽普暄. "Yu *Ching-Lien shih-wen* shih-t'an *Chuang-tzu* Ku-pen" 由經典釋文試探莊子古本. In *Yen-ching hsüeh pao* 28 (1940), 89-96.

Shu Shih-ch'eng 束世澂. "Wei-Chin ch'ing-t'an lüeh-lun" 魏晋清談略論. In *Li-shih chiao-hsüeh*, Dec. 1957, pp. 10-15.

Soper, Alexander C. *Literary Evidence for Early Buddhist Art in China*. Ascona, 1959.

_____. "A New Chinese Tomb Discovery: The Earliest Representation of a Famous Literary Theme." *Artibus Asiae* 24.2 (1961), 79-86.

Stein, Rolf A. "Remarques sur les mouvements du Taoïsme politico-religieux au IIe siècle ap. J.-C." In *T'oung Pao* 50 (1963), 1-78.

T'ang Ch'ang-ju 唐長孺. *Wei-Chin nan-pei-ch'ao shih lun-ts'ung* 魏晋南北朝史論叢. Peking, 1955. Reprinted, 1962.

———. *Wei-Chin nan-pei-ch'ao shih lun-tsung hsü-p'ien* 續篇. Peking, 1959.

T'ang Yung-t'ung 湯用彤. *Han-Wei liang-Chin nan-pei-ch'ao Fo-chiao-shih* 漢魏兩晉南北朝佛教史. 2 vols. Shanghai, 1938. Reprinted with postface, Peking, 1955.

———. *Wei-Chin hsüan-hsüeh lun-kao* 魏晉玄學論稿. Peking, 1957.

———. "Tu Liu Shao *Jen-wu chih*" 讀劉邵人物志. In *T'u-shu chi-k'an* (n.s.) 2 (1940), 4-18.

———. "Wang Pi chih *Chou-i Lun-yü* hsin-i" 王弼之周易論語新義. In *T'u-shu chi-k'an* (n.s.) 4 (1943), 28-40. Trans. by Walter Liebenthal as "Wang Pi's New Interpretation of the *I-ching* and *Lun-yü*" in *Harvard Journal of Asiatic Studies* 10 (1947), 124-161.

——— and Jen Chi-yü 任繼愈. *Wei-Chin hsüan-hsüeh chung ti she-hui ssu-hsiang lüeh-lun* 魏晉玄學中的社會政治思想略論. Shanghai, 1956. Based on an earlier article in *Li-shih yen-chiu* 1954.3, pp. 63-93.

Ting Fu-pao 丁福保. *Ch'üan Han san-kuo Chin nan-pei-ch'ao shih* 全漢三國晉南北朝詩. Shanghai, 1916. Reprinted, Taipei, 1962.

Tökei, Ferenc. *Genre Theory in China in the 3rd-6th Centuries*. Budapest, 1971.

Tsukamoto hakase shōju kinen Bukkyōshigaku ronshū 塚本博士頌壽記念佛教史學論集. Kyoto, 1961.

Tsukamoto Zenryū 塚本善隆. *Chūgoku Bukkyō tsūshi* 中国佛教通史, Vol. I. Tokyo, 1968.

Tuckerman, Bryant. *Planetary, Lunar, and Solar Positions. . .at Five Day and Ten Day Intervals*. Vol. II: *A.D. 2 to A.D. 1649*. Philadelphia, 1964.

T'ung Shou 童壽. "Tan-ch'i K'ao" 彈棊考. *Ta-lu tsa-chih* 4.7 (1952), 241-242.

Tzu Ch'i 紫溪. "Ku-tai liang-ch'i hsiao-k'ao" 古代量器小考. In *Wen-wu* 文物 7 (1964), 39-54.

Utsunomiya Kiyoyoshi 宇都宮清吉. *Kandai shakai-keizaishi kenkyū* 漢代社会經濟史研究. Tokyo, 1955.

Van Gulik, R. H. *Hsi K'ang and His Poetical Essay on the Lute*. Tokyo, 1941. Reprinted, 1968.

Veith, Ilza. *The Yellow Emperor's Classic of Internal Medicine*. Berkeley and Los Angeles, 1966.

Von Zach, E., trans. *Die Chinesische Anthologie*. 2 vols. Cambridge, Mass., 1958.

Waley, Arthur. *170 Chinese Poems*. New York, 1938.

———. *The Secret History of the Mongols*. London, 1963.

Wan Sheng-nan 萬繩楠. "Wei-Chin nan-pei-ch'ao shih-tai ti ssu-hsiang ti chu-liu shih shen-ma?" 魏晉南北朝思想的主流是什麼. In *Shih-hsüeh yüeh-k'an* 史學月刊 Aug. 1957, pp. 8-12.

Wang Yi-t'ung 王伊同. "Pu *Wei-chih* Ho Yen chuan" 補魏志何晏傳. In *Shih-hsüeh nien-pao* 史學年報 3.1 (1939), 49-62.

Wang Yi-t'ung 王伊同. *Wu-ch'ao men-ti* 五朝門第 (English title: "The social, political and economic aspects of the influential clans of the Southern Dynasties"). 2 vols. Nanking, 1943.

Watson, Burton, trans. *The Complete Works of Chuang-tzu*. New York, 1968.

―――――. *Chinese Lyricism: Shih Poetry from the Second to the Twelfth Century*. New York, 1971.

―――――. *Chinese Rhymeprose: Poems in the Fu Form from the Han and Six Dynasties Periods*. New York, 1971.

Wilhelm, Helmut. "Sun Ch'o's *Yü-tao-lun*." In *Sino-Indian Studies* 5 (1957), 261-271.

―――――. "Shih Ch'ung and his *Chin-ku-yüan*." In *Monumenta Serica* 18 (1959), 315-327.

Wilhelm, Richard, trans. (Engl. edition, trans. C. F. Baynes). *The I Ching or Book of Changes*. 2 vols. London, 1951.

Williams, J. *Observations of Comets from B.C. 611 to A.D. 1640, Extracted from the Chinese Annals*. London, 1871.

Wright, Arthur F., "Fo-t'u-teng," in *HJAS* 11 (1948), 322-370.

―――――. "Biography and Hagiography: Hui-chiao's Lives of Eminent Monks." *Zinbun Kagaku Kenkyusyo Silver Jubilee Volume*. Kyoto, 1954.

―――――. *Buddhism in Chinese History*. Stanford, 1959.

Yang Lien-sheng 楊聯陞. "Tung-Han ti hao-tsu" 東漢的豪族. In *Ch'ing-hua hsüeh-pao* 11.4 (1936), 1007-1063.

―――――. *Studies in Chinese Institutional History*. Cambridge, 1960.

―――――. *Excursions in Sinology*. Cambridge, 1969.

Yang Yün-ju 楊筠如. *Chiu-p'in chung-cheng yü liu-ch'ao men-fa* 九品中正與六朝門閥. Shanghai, 1920.

Yoshikawa Kōjirō 吉川幸次郎. "Rikuchō joji shōki 六朝助字小記. In *Chūgoku sambun ron* 中国散文論. Tokyo, 1945. Pp. 92-141.

Yoshikawa Tadao 吉川忠夫. "Rikuchō shi-daifu no seishin seikatsu" 六朝士大夫の精神生活. In *Sekai rekishi: kodai* 世界歴史：古代 (Iwanami kōza). Tokyo, 1970.

―――――. *Ō Gishi: rikuchō kizoku no shakai* 王羲之：六朝貴族の社会. Tokyo, 1972.

Yü Chia-hsi 余嘉錫. *Yü Chia-hsi lun-hsüeh tsa-chu* 余嘉錫論學雜著. Peking, 1963.

―――――. "Han-shih-san k'ao" 寒石散考. Ibid., pp. 181-226.

―――――. "Shih Ts'ang-Ch'u" 釋傖楚. Ibid., pp. 227-234.

Yü Ying-shih 余英時. "Han-Chin chih chi shih chih hsin tzu-chüeh yü hsin ssu-ch'ao" 漢晉之際士之新自覺與新思潮. In *Hsin-ya hsüeh-pao* 新亞學報 4.1 (1959), 25-144.

Zürcher, Erik. *The Buddhist Conquest of China*. 2 vols. Leiden, 1959.

Index

Index 引得

The following list includes only those personal names which appear in the footnotes. For occurrences of personal names in the anecdotes proper, the reader should consult the Biographical Notices. Certain place names which are frequently mentioned, such as Lo-yang, Chien-k'ang, and K'uai-chi, have been excluded, as have the names of provinces and dynasties and most of the sources listed in the Abbreviations. Characters for romanized terms may be found in the Glossary.

"Abhidharma" (*a-p'i-t'an*), 125
Abhidharmahṛdaya-śāstra. *See under* Buddhist scriptures
activism vs. quietism, 97, 224, 331, 412
Actuality. *See* yu 有
"Administrator of Ch'ing Province" (青州從事), 361
Ai, Duke of Lu (魯哀公), 212, 388, 466
Ai, Emperor of Chin (晉哀帝), 114, 191
Ai, Emperor of Han (漢哀帝), 104–105, 357
Ai Chung 哀仲, 440
Āmra Grove, 55
An, Emperor of Han (漢安帝), 49, 293
An-ling 安陵 (prefecture), 188
An-lu 安陸 (prefecture), 188
An-shih 安石 (island), 174
"Analects" (*Lun-yü* 論語), 4, 5, 16, 17, 18, 20, 33, 39, 41, 53, 55, 58, 60, 62, 65, 78, 96, 111, 140, 146, 168, 174, 198, 204, 218, 221, 239, 260, 276, 283, 287, 319, 337, 341, 343, 344, 380, 396, 401, 403, 411, 417, 466, 468, 478, 485
aromatics. *See* cosmetics and aromatics
Avarice Spring. *See* T'an-shui

Bamboo Grove. *See* "Seven Worthies of the Bamboo Grove"
Being. *See* yu
Black Clothing Street (*Wu-i chieh* 烏衣街), 184, 383
Blue-green Distance, Terrace of (Ch'ing-su t'ai 青疎臺), 430
"Book of Changes." *See* "Changes, Book of"
"Book of Documents." *See* "Documents, Book of"
"Book of Filial Piety." *See* Hsiao-ching
"Book of Music." *See* "Music, Book of"

696   TALES OF THE WORLD

"Book of Rites." See "Rites, Book of"
"Book of Songs." See "Songs, Book of"
Broken Tomb (P'o-chung 破冢 ; island), 422
Bronze Sparrow Terrace (T'ung-ch'üeh t'ai 銅雀臺), 70, 126
Buddhism: "Abhidharma," 125; anti-clericalism, 439; ascetic exercises (dhūta), 50; Buddha, birthday of, 74, 367; Buddha, invitation of (ch'ing-fo), 74; Buddha, walking image of (hsing-hsiang), 366-367; buddha-nature (fo-hsing), 115; Buddhist poetry, 137; Dependent Origination (pratītya-samutpāda), 112, 123; devotion of Chou Sung, 164; devotion of Ho family, 420; devotion of Juan Yü, 476; dispersion of Tao-an's disciples, 238; enlightenment, 111, 115; enumerated terms (shih-shu), 123; feasts and offerings, 338; Karma, 476; lectures for laymen, 108-109, 112, 113, 115, 125, 237-238, 288; mantras (chou), 50; nirvana, 55; origin in China, 104-105; Six Faculties (liu-t'ung), 119-120; Six Perfections (pāramitā), 112, 117-118; "Six Schools," 111; sutras, 104-105, 123 (see also Buddhist scriptures); Three Insights (san-ming), 119-120; Three Treasures (san-pao), 476; Three Vehicles (san-sheng), 112, 119.
Buddhist scriptures: Abhidharmahṛdaya-śāstra (A-p'i-t'an hsin-ching 阿毗曇心經), 125; Dhammapada (Fa-chü-ching 法句經), 108; Jñānaprasthāna-abhidharma-śāstra (A-p'i-t'an pa-chien-tu lun 阿毗曇八犍度論), 125; Mahānibbāna-sutta (Ta pan-nieh-p'an ching 大般涅槃經), 51; Mahāparinirvāṇa-sūtra (Fo-shuo ta pan-ni-yüan ching 佛說大般泥洹經), 51, 115; Prajñāpāramitā-sūtras (see separate entry); Saddharmapuṇḍarīka-sūtra (Fa-hua ching 法華經), 112; Satyasiddhi-śāstra (Ch'eng-shih lun 成實論), 108, 116; "Sutra in Forty-two Sections," 104-105; Ta chih-tu lun 大智度論 , 55, 120; Ta pi-ch'iu san-ch'ien wei-i ching 大比丘三千威儀經), 86; Vajraśekhara-yoga-tantra (Chin-kang-ting yü-ch'ieh-chung lüeh-ch'u nien-sung ching 金剛頂瑜珈中略出念誦經), 415-416; Vimalakīrti-nirdeśa (Wei-mo-chieh ching 維摩詰經), 56, 74, 111, 113, 117-118; Virūdhaka-rāja-sūtra (Fo-shuo Liu-li-wang ching 佛說琉璃王經), 476

calligraphy: clerical script (li-shu), 269; copying texts, 366; draft script (chang-ts'ao), 269; formal script (k'ai-shu), 365; imitations of others' writing, 365; Tai K'uei, 192; Wang Hsi-chih, 269, 315; Wang Hsien-chih, 269; Wei Tan's inscription on Ling-hsiao Observatory, 364-365; Yang 羊 family and tradition of, 365-366
candana (sandalwood), 108
Carpenter Shih (匠石), 326
Celestial (Heavenly) Master, 361, 420
Celestial Ruler, 19
"celestial sphere" (hun-t'ien), 92
Censer Peak (Hsiang-lu feng 香鑪峯), 288
Central Asiatics. See Hu
Central Peak. See Sung (mountain)
Ch'a-ching 茶經 (text), 481
Chai T'ang 摧湯 , 475
Chan-kuo ts'e 戰國策 (Tuan-ch'ang shu 短長書), 307, 422, 468
Chang-an 章安 (prefecture), 185
Chang An-shih 張安世 , 42
Chang Chao 張昭 , 306
Chang Chien 張儉 , 248
Chang Chün 張駿 , 73
Chang-hai 張海 (Swelling Sea = Mediterranean), 462-463
Chang Heng 張衡 , 128, 312
Chang Hsieh 張協 , 378
Chang Hua 張華 , 136

Chang Hung 張泓, 281
Chang Jang 張讓, 441-442
Chang K'uei 張逵, 352
Chang Kung-tsu 張恭祖, 93
Chang Kung-tzu 張公子, 364
Chang Liang 張良, 42, 47, 200-201, 214
Chang Mao 張茂 (Wei-k'ang 偉康), 253
Chang Tsai 張載 (Meng-yang 孟陽), 128, 310
Chang Yü 張遇, 451
Ch'ang-an 長安 (prefecture), 5, 8, 47, 61, 123, 264, 271, 274, 298, 373, 451
Ch'ang-fu. See Long Mountain
Ch'ang Gate. See Glorious Gate
Ch'ang-hsin kung 長信宮 (palace), 342
Ch'ang-i, Prince of (昌邑王), 77
Ch'ang-kuang, Princess of (長廣公主), 155
Ch'ang-shan. See Long Mountain
Ch'ang-shan, Princess of (常山主), 155, 459
Ch'ang-t'ang Lake (長塘湖), 494
Ch'ang-ti fu hsü 長笛賦敘 (preface), 436
"Changes, Book of" (易; Chou-i 周易): interpretations of, 121-122, 123-124, 215, 277-280, 361; lectures sponsored by Huan Wen, 107; quoted, 28, 85, 135-136, 137, 167, 215, 223, 232, 233, 240, 267, 269, 283, 319, 347, 351, 407, 435, 468
    separate hexagrams: Hex. 1 (Ch'ien), 75, 107-108, 122; Hex. 2 (K'un), 75, 107-108, 122; Hex. 3 (Chun), 75; Hex. 10 (Lü), 279; Hex. 12 (P'i), 75; Hex. 15 (Ch'ien*), 279; Hex. 23 (Po), 75; Hex. 29 (K'an), 122; Hex. 34 (Ta-chuang), 279; Hex. 39 (Chien), 75; Hex. 43 (Kuai), 43; Hex. 50 (Ting), 279; Hex. 51 (Chen), 361; Hex. 52 (Ken), 279; Hex. 57 (Sun), 122; Hex. 61 (Chung-fu), 49, 124
Chao, Duke of Lu (魯昭公), 346
Chao, Emperor of Han (漢昭帝), 77
Chao, King of Ch'in (秦昭王), 267
Chao, King of Yen (燕昭王), 428
Chao, Prince of. See Ssu-ma Lun

Chao Ch'uan 趙穿, 409
Chao Hsiang-tzu 趙襄子, 155
Chao I 趙翼 (Yang-ho 陽和; alias of Chao Chih), 37
Chao Kao 趙高, 275
Chao Kuang-han 趙廣漢, 87
Chao Mu 趙穆, 222
Chao Tien. See "Eight Heroes"
Chao Ts'an 趙槧, 486
Chao Ts'ui 趙衰, 347
Chao Tun 趙盾 (Hsüan-tzu 宣子), 167, 409
Chao Wen-tzu 趙文子, 219
Chao Yang 趙鞅, 287
Chao-yin shih 招隱詩 (poem), 389
Ch'ao Fu 巢父, 25, 31, 40, 63, 402, 412-413, 421
Ch'ao Ts'o 晁錯, 445
Chaupar. See gambling
Che 浙 (river), 186
Ch'e Yin 車胤, 290
Chen Ch'ang 甄暢, 35-36
Chen Chiang 甄姜, 35
Chen Hsiang 甄象, 35
Chen Hui 甄會. See Chen I
Chen I 甄逸 (var., Hui 會), 35, 484
Chen Jung 甄榮, 35
Chen-kao 真誥 (text), 391
Chen Tao 甄道, 35
Chen Te 甄德, 155
Chen T'o 甄脫, 35
Chen Yao 甄堯, 35
Chen Yen 甄儼, 35
Chen Yü 甄豫, 35
Ch'en 陳 (commandery), 383
Ch'en, Marquis of (陳侯), 426
Ch'en Chen 陳軫, 404
Ch'en Chih-shu 陳穉淑, 5
Ch'en Chung-tzu 陳仲子 (Tzu-chung 子終), 69, 304
Ch'en Ch'ün 陳羣, 401
Ch'en Fan 陳蕃, 210, 211, 248
Ch'en Heng 陳恒 (alias T'ien Ch'ang 田常), 44
Ch'en-liu 陳留 (commandery), 26, 202, 222, 371, 430
Ch'en P'ing 陳平, 494
Ch'en Sheng 陳聲, 479-480
Ch'en Shih 陳寔, 3, 401
Ch'en Tai 陳戴, 304
Ch'en T'ai 陳泰, 414
Cheng, Empress (鄭后; A-ch'un 阿春), 482
Cheng, Lady (鄭氏; wife of Yang Chih), 62

Cheng-fu 箏賦 (poetic essay), 142
Cheng Hsüan 鄭玄, 78, 98, 106, 119, 276, 329, 343, 358, 437
Cheng-i 正義 (commentary), 402
Cheng-lu t'ing. See General Chastizing Caitiffs, Pavilion of
Cheng-shih 正始 (era), 11, 95, 103, 137, 226, 235, 250
Cheng T'ai 鄭太, 8
Cheng-te ta-hsiang. See "Great Symbol of True Virtue"
Ch'eng, Emperor of Chin. See Ssu-ma Yen*
Ch'eng, Emperor of Han (漢成帝), 61, 104-105, 357, 363
Ch'eng, King of Chou (周成王), 57, 279, 290, 425
Ch'eng Chi 成濟, 152
Ch'eng-shih lun. See under Buddhist scriptures
Ch'eng-yang 城陽 (commandery), 348
chess. See games
Chi 汲 (commandery), 332
Chi 季 (family), 346
Chi 箕 (mountain), 25, 40, 337
Chi* 稽 (mountain), 10
Chi 驥 (steed), 320
Chi Cha 季札, 42, 456
Chi Ch'ü Yüan wen 祭屈原文 (text), 74
Chi-se lun 即色論 (text), 110-111
Chi-yang 暨陽 (prefecture), 189, 360
Ch'i 齊 (commandery), 361
Ch'i 祁 (prefecture), 256
Ch'i-chu ch'ang-ch'iao 淇水長橋 (bridge), 319
Ch'i-fa 七發 (text), 133
Ch'i Hsi 祁奚, 29-30
Ch'i-li ch'iao. See Seven-li Bridge
Ch'i-li chien. See Seven-li Stream
Ch'i-ming 七命 (text), 378
Ch'i Wu 祁午, 29-30
Ch'i-wu lun 齊物論 (section of *Chuang-tzu*), 124
Chia, Empress (賈后; Chia Nan-feng 南風), 182, 281, 486
Chia, Ch'ung 賈充, 79, 84, 281, 377
Chia Ch'üan 賈荃, 348

Chia-feng shih 家風詩 (poems), 130
Chia I 賈誼, 132, 139, 404
Chia K'uei 賈逵, 94
Chia Mi 賈謐, 128, 486, 490
Chia Piao 賈彪, 81
Chia-p'ing 嘉平 (era), 332
Chia Wu 賈午, 486
Chiang Chi 蔣濟, 249, 474
Chiang-hsia 江夏 (commandery), 46, 286
Chiang-k'ou 江口, 170
Chiang-ling 江陵 (prefecture), 20, 69, 76, 82, 144, 209, 226, 384
Chiang-ning 江寧 (prefecture), 325, 420
Chiang Pin 江彬, 325
Chiang T'ung 江統, 430
Ch'iang 羌 (people), 148, 262, 451, 473. See also Ch'iang, Western
Ch'iang, Western (西羌), 41, 42
Chiao 譙 (principality), 10, 342, 371, 451
Chiao Hsün 焦循, 402
Chiao Po 焦伯, 152
Chicken-cage Mountain (Chi-lung shan 雞籠山), 306
Chieh 介 (ancient state), 63
Chieh 桀 (ancient tyrant), 270, 367
Chieh Chih-t'ui 介之推, 405
Chieh Hu 解狐, 29-30
Chieh-ku 嶰谷 (valley), 39
Chieh-shih shan 碣石山 (song), 302
Chieh Yü 接輿 (Lu T'ung 陸通, "Madman of Ch'u"), 39, 65, 66
Ch'ieh-wu chang 切悟章 (essay), 326
Chien 蹇 (Hex. 39), 75
Chien, Duke of Ch'i (齊簡公), 44
Chien-an 建安 (era), 30, 34, 137, 364, 484
Chien-chang 建章 (palace), 42
Chien-hsing 建興 (era), 51, 446
Chien-ko 劍閣 (prefecture), 365
Chien-p'ing 建平 (commandery), 225
Chien-tzu 簡子 ("Man of K'uang"), 168
Chien-wen, Emperor of Chin. See Ssu-ma Yü

Chien-wen shih-i 簡文諡議 (proposal), 137
Chien Wu 肩吾, 66
Ch'ien Hsiu 牽秀, 471-472
Ch'ien-t'ang 錢塘 (prefecture), 186
Ch'ien-t'ang 錢塘 (river), 381
Ch'ien-t'ang Inn (錢唐亭), 185-186
Chih 銍 (prefecture), 10
Chih 淛 (river; modern Che 浙), 381
Chih, Emperor of Han (漢質帝), 364
Chih Ch'ien 支謙, 111
chih-li. See Ultimate Principle
Chih-lo. See under *Chuang-tzu*
Chih Po 智伯, 155
Chih Tun 支遁, 190
Chih-tzu 痣子, 67
Chih-wu lun 指物論 (essay), 99
Chih Yü 摯虞, 128
Chih-yüan ssu. See Jetavana Temple
Ch'ih Chien 郗鑒, 286
Ch'ih T'an 郗曇, 262
Chin, Duke of (晉公), 347
Chin-ch'ang Pavilion. See Pavilion of Golden Glory
Chin-ch'ang t'ing. See Pavilion of Golden Glory
Chin-ch'eng 金城, 57
Chin-hsiang 金鄉 (prefecture), 13
Chin-hua tien. See Hall of Golden Splendor
Chin-ku 金谷 (creek), 264
Chin ku cheng-hsi ta-chiang-chün chang-shih Meng Fu-chün chuan 晉故征西大將軍長史孟府君傳 (biography), 204
Chin-ku shih hsü 金谷詩序 (preface), 321, 489-491
Chin-ling 金陵 (commandery), 75, 164, 395, 430
Chin-shang 金傷 ("Metal-wound"), 432
Chin-yang 晉陽 (prefecture), 43, 287, 472
Chin yang-ch'iu 晉陽秋 (text), 411
Ch'in, Earl of (秦伯), 67, 99
Ch'in Ching 秦景, 104
Ch'in-fu 琴賦 (poetic essay), 142, 238

Ch'in-huai 秦淮 (river), 90, 184, 294, 380, 383, 494
Ch'in I-lu 秦宜祿, 298
Ch'in Lang 秦郎 (A-piao 阿豹; var., A-su 蘇), 298
Chinese language (Han, or Ch'in 秦), 50, 117
Ching, Duke of Ch'i (齊景公), 33, 44
Ching, Duke of Chin (晉景公), 45, 98
Ching, Emperor of Han (漢景帝), 271, 445
Ching, Marquis (敬侯), 342
Ching-ch'u 景初 (era), 36
Ching Fang 京房, 361
Ching-hsien, Empress-dowager (景獻太后; née Yang 羊), 462
Ching Huang-kung chiu-lu-hsia fu 經黃公酒壚下賦 (poetic essay), 138, 437-438
Ching-k'ou 京口, 57, 65, 171, 186, 189, 246, 295, 303, 322, 418
Ching Lü 景廬, 104
Ching-ning 竟寧 (era), 340
Ching Tan 井丹 (Ta-ch'un 大春), 270
Ching Tan* 景丹, 44
Ching T'ung 闓通, 404
Ching Yin 敬胤 (comm. on *SSHY*), quoted, 472
Ching-yüan 景元 (era), 373
ch'ing-fo, 74
Ch'ing Mountain (青山), 142
ch'ing-t'an. See "pure conversation"
ch'ing-yen. See "pure conversation"
Chiu, Prince (公子糾), 260
Chiu-che pan 九折坂 (slope), 58
Chiu-fang Kao 九方皋, 437-439
chiu-hsi. See Nine Bestowals
Chiu-ko 九歌 (section of *Ch'u-tz'u*), 306
Chiu-te sung 酒德頌 (ode), 128-130
ch'iu-chü, 363
Ch'iu-hsing fu 秋興賦 (poetic essay), 79
Ch'iu-shui. See under *Chuang-tzu*
Ch'iung-ch'i. See Four Ill-omened Ones
Ch'iung-lai 邛郲 (commandery), 58

Cho 涿 (commandery), 93
Cho Mao 卓茂, 65
cho-ting, 27
Cho Wang-sun 卓王孫, 271
Cho Wen-chün 卓文君, 271
Chou 紂. *See* Chou Hsin
Chou 周 (family), 474
Chou, Duchess of (周姥), 354
Chou, Duke of (周公; Chi Tan 姬旦), 29, 30, 49, 57, 82, 127, 279, 290, 354, 401, 425, 476
Chou*, Duke of (周公; fl. 841 B.C.), 275
Chou Feng 周豐, 212
Chou Hsin 紂辛, 41, 88, 260, 263, 270, 485
Chou Hsüan 周宣, 470
Chou I 周顗, 14, 50
Chou-i. See "Changes, Book of"
Chou-li. See "Rites of Chou"
Chou Liang-kung 周亮工, 27
Chou Po 周勃, 290, 388
Chou-shih 周詩 (poems), 130
Chou Yü 周瑜, 249
Chu 洙 (river), 180
Chu Ch'ien 竺潛 (Fa-shen 法深), 89
Chu Fa-t'ai 竺法汰, 423
Chu Lan 朱覽, 9
Chu Po 朱博, 49-50
Chu-ko Chan 諸葛瞻, 418
Chu-ko Liang 諸葛亮, 190, 235
Chu-ko Tan 諸葛誕, 154
Chu-ko Yao 諸葛瑤, 229
Chu-lin 竹林, 371
Chu Mai-ch'en 朱買臣, 431-432
Chu Mu 朱穆, 210
Chu Seng-ch'ien 竺僧虔, 478
chu-wei. See sambar-tail chowry
Chu Yü. *See* "Eight Heroes"
Ch'u, Viscount of (楚子), 342
Ch'u Ho-tzu 褚䂮子, 57
Ch'u P'ou 褚裒, 68, 492
Ch'u-tz'u 楚辭, 306, 391, 418-419
Chuan Hsü 顓頊, 6
Chuang, Duke of Ch'i (齊莊公), 44, 168
Chuang, Duke of Ch'u (楚莊公), 243, 416-417
Chuang-hsiang, King of Ch'in (秦莊襄王), 33
Chuang Tsun. *See* Yen Tsun
Chuang-tzu 莊子 (Chuang Chou 莊周): *Ch'i-wu lun* 齊物論, 124; *Chih-lo* 至樂, 100; *Ch'iu-shui* 秋水, 100; commentary of Hsiang Hsiu/Kuo Hsiang, 100, 109-110, 116, 219; *Hsiao-yao yu* 逍遙遊, 109-110, 111; *Ma-t'i* 馬蹄, 100; *Ta-sheng* 達生, 381; *Yü-fu* 漁父, 120-121; quoted, 6, 32-33, 40, 52, 54-55, 60-61, 62, 66, 67, 69, 79, 83, 88, 90, 95, 96, 98, 99, 100-101, 106, 116, 117, 122-123, 133, 135, 137, 176, 192, 215, 218, 219, 221, 231, 241, 259, 272-273, 285, 326, 332, 337, 375, 385, 388, 403, 404, 421, 423, 437, 464, 468
Chun 屯 (Hex. 3), 75
Ch'un-ch'iu. See "Spring and Autumn Annals"
Chung Chün 終軍, 404
Chung Erh 重耳, 347
Chung-fu 中孚 (Hex. 61), 49, 124
Chung-fu 仲父. *See* Kuan Chung
Chung-hsing Yüeh 中行說, 420
Chung Hui 鍾會, 11, 96, 122, 180, 414
Chung Hung 鍾嶸, 136
Chung I 鍾儀 (Yün, Duke of 鄖公), 45-46
Chung-li Ch'un 鍾離春, 428
Chung-mou 中牟 (prefecture), 85
Chung-ni. *See* Confucius
Chung-shan 中山, 428
Chung-ssu 螽斯 (song), 354
Chung-su 中宿 (prefecture), 438
Chung-t'ang 中堂 (encampment), 294
Chung-tsung. *See* Ssu-ma Jui
Chung-tu 中都 (prefecture), 43
Chung-tzu. *See* Ch'en Chung-tzu
Chung Tzu-ch'i 鍾子期, 56, 326
Chung Yen 鍾琰, 488
Chung Yu 鍾蹂, 401
Ch'ung, Emperor of Han (漢沖帝), 364
Ch'ung-ch'iu 崇丘 (song), 130
Ch'ung Tsung 充宗, 276
Ch'ung-yu lun 崇有論 (essay), 97
Chü-lu 鉅鹿 (commandery), 278
Chü-t'ang Gorge. *See* Yangtze Gorges
chü-yü 姁䰽 (fish), 415
Ch'ü-fou 曲阜, 127
Ch'ü-li 曲禮 (section of "Record of Rites"), 12

INDEX   701

Ch'ü-o 曲阿 (Lake of Crooked Banks), 67, 421, 494
Ch'ü Yüan 屈原, 65, 74, 139, 391, 405
Ch'ü Yüan* 瀘瑗 (Po-yü 伯玉), 456
Chüan-ch'eng 鄄城 (prefecture), 126
Ch'üan-ch'uan 甽川 (Ch'üan Stream), 69, 434
Ch'üan-hsüeh chang 勸學章 (essay), 480
Ch'üan-hsüeh p'ien 勸學篇 (section of *Ta-Tai Li-chi*), 480
Ch'üan-Jung. See "Dog Barbarians"
Ch'üan Stream. See Ch'üan-ch'uan
Ch'üeh Chih 郤至, 255
Cinnabar Pool (Tan-yüan 丹淵), 332
Cloud Dragon Gate (Yün-lung men 雲龍門), 152
Cloud-traversing Terrace (Pavilion). See Ling-yün t'ai (ko)
cold-food powder. See five-mineral powder
comets (*ch'ang-hsing, p'eng-hsing*), 194
Commander Wang. See Chung-lang
"Concubine Yen" (顧姜), 471
Confucianism (Juism; see also *ming-chiao*), 198, 245; in Juan family, 375; relation to Mohism, 405; relation to Taoism, 40, 96-97, 101, 234
Confucius (K'ung Ch'iu 孔丘; Chung-ni 仲尼), 4, 26, 33, 39, 53, 54-55, 60, 78, 79, 82, 91, 95, 96, 101, 107, 139, 167, 168-169, 179-180, 197-198, 226, 260, 263, 276, 280, 298, 329, 343, 396, 401, 409, 426, 463, 466, 486
congratulatory placards (*pan* 板), 74, 144
Cool Observation Tower (Liang-kuan 涼觀), 490
Coral-tree Island (Shan-hu shu chou 珊瑚樹洲), 462
coral trees (*shan-hu shu* 珊瑚樹), 462-463
cosmetics and aromatics, 308-309, 449, 459, 479, 488
Crooked Banks, Lake of. See Ch'ü-o
Cypress Beam Terrace (Po-liang t'ai 柏梁臺), 56, 418-419

dancing: female dancer smashes flute, 436; Great Symbol of True Virtue dance (Cheng-te ta-hsiang), 358; myna-bird dance (*ch'ü-yü wu*), 382; Ts'ao Hsü dances for the gods
Dependent Origination. See under Buddhism
Deposed Emperor of Chin. See Ssu-ma I**
Dhammapada. See under Buddhist scriptures
Dharmarakṣa (Fa-hu 法護), 108
divination: and "Book of Changes," 277-280; divining board (*shih*), 92-93; geomancy, 359, 360; milfoil, 279-360; naming children, 390; physiognomy, 278, 347; stars, 278; techniques (*shu-shu*), 115; tortoise shell, 360; wind (*feng-chüeh*), 92, 278. See also "Changes, Book of"
divining board, 92-93
"Documents, Book of" (*Shu* 書), 38, 42, 49-50, 56, 64, 83, 89, 168, 172, 199, 277, 388, 485
"Dog Barbarians" (Ch'üan-Jung 犬戎), 275
Double Ninth Festival, 205
Dragon Gate. See Lung-men
drinking. See wine
Duke of Chou. See Chou, Duke of

Eastern Mountains (Tung-shan 東山 Prefecture), 63, 72, 174, 189, 191, 207, 231, 236, 287, 334, 337, 396, 412, 413, 434
Eastern Pontoon Bridge (東桁 = Great Pontoon Bridge?), 495
Eastern Villa (Tung-fu 東府), 75-76, 423
"Eight Attainers" (*pa-chi* 八及), 248
"eight dragons," 6
"Eight Free Spirits" (*pa-ta* 八達), 245, 254
"Eight Heroes" (*pa-chün* 八俊): Chao Tien 趙典; Chu Yü 朱寓; Hsün Yü 荀昱; Li Ying 李膺; Liu Yu 劉祐; Tu Mi 杜密; Wang Ch'ang* 王暢; Wei Lang 魏郎, 248-249
"Eight-hundred-*li* Brindled" (Pa-pai-li po 八百里駁; Wang K'ai's ox), 460

"Eight Paragons" (*pa-yüan* 八元), 248, 279
"Eight P'eis" (八裴), 250
"Eight Princes, War of" (八王之亂), 199, 201, 206
"Eight Victors" (*pa-k'ai* 八凱), 248, 279
"Eight Wangs" (八王), 250
elixir of immortality, 66
Emptiness (*k'ung* 空 = śūnyatā), 111, 114. See also Great Void
Empty and Transcendent (*hsü-sheng* 虛勝), 96, 262
Empty Nonexistence (*k'ung-wu* 空無), 447
encirclement chess. See games
erh-ju ko. See "you-your" songs
Erh-ya 爾雅 (dictionary), 47, 480, 481
Essential and Subtle (*yao-miao* 要妙), 224
"Eulogy to Master Shang-ch'iu" (商丘子贊; in *Lieh-hsien tsan*, 434-435

Fa-hsien 法顯, 51, 367
Fa-hu 法護. See Wang Hsün
Fa-hua ching. See under Buddhist scriptures
Fa-shen 法深. See Chu Ch'ien
Fa-sheng 法勝 (Dharmajina?), 125
Fa-wei 法威, 115
"famous gentlemen" (*ming-shih* 名士), 391, 428, 429
Fan 璠 (gem), 320
Fan Ch'i 范啟, 439
Fan-jo 繁弱 (ancient bow), 319
Fan Li 范蠡, 378
Fan P'ang 范滂, 3, 211
Fan Tseng 范增, 217
Fan Wen-tzu 范文子, 46
Fan-yang 范陽 (commandery), 159, 402
Fan Ying 樊英, 124
Fang-chang. See Three Isles of the Transcendents
Fang-feng 防風, 148
Fang-shan. See Square Mountain
fang-shih. See under Taoism
Fang-t'ou 枋頭 (battleground), 59, 141, 305
Fei River (淝水), battle of, 73, 175, 193, 207, 418
Fen 汾 (river in K'uai-chi), 294
feng 封 (sacrifice), 66

Feng 灃 (river), 208
Feng-chieh 奉節 (mod. prefecture), 58
feng-liu 風流 ("urbanity"), 45, 69, 177, 233, 245, 259, 337
Feng T'ing 馮亭, 38
Feng To 馮紞, 257
"Filial Piety, Book of." See *Hsiao-ching*
First Emperor of Ch'in (秦始皇帝), 65-66, 197
"Five Ch'ens" (五陳), 250
Five Classics (五經), 135, 218
"Five Hsüns" (五荀), 250
five-mineral powder (*wu-shih san* 五石散; *han-shih san* 寒食散): 36, 370, 390; impairment of vision after taking, 287-288; walking after taking (*hsing-san*), 19-20, 75, 143, 246
"Five-Pecks-of-Rice sect," 64
Five Sacred Peaks, 25
Five Sovereigns (五帝), 148
Flowery Grove Park (Hua-lin yüan 華林園), 60, 194
Fo-kuo Monastery (佛國寺), 316
Fo-shuo Liu-li-wang ching. See under Buddhist scriptures
Fo-shuo ta pan-ni-yüan ching. See under Buddhist scriptures
folding chairs (*hu-ch'uang* 胡床), 314, 316, 319, 389, 396
"Forest of Conversations." See *Yü-lin*
Foundry City. See Yeh-ch'eng
"Four Friends" (四友): of Confucius, 263; of Wang Tun, 253; of Wen, King of Chou, 263
Four Ill-omened Ones (*ssu-hsiung* 四凶): Ch'iung Ch'i 窮奇, or Kung Kung 共工; Hun Tun 渾敦, or Huan Tou 驩兜; T'ao T'ieh 饕餮, or San Miao 三苗; T'ao Wu 檮杌, or Kun 鯀, 400
"free" (達), 12-13, 100, 183, 235, 236-237, 371-391 *passim*, 395. See also "unimpeded"; "untrammeled"
"Free Wandering" (*hsiao-yao* 逍遙), 12-13. See also *Chuang-tzu*, *Hsiao-yao yu*
"frivolity" (*fu-hsü* 浮虛), 88, 433. See also nihilism and libertinism

INDEX   703

Fu Ch'ai 夫差 (King of Wu 吳), 429
Fu Ch'ang 傅暢 (author of *CCKT*), 486
Fu Chia 傅嘏, 94-95, 485
Fu Chien 苻堅, 90-91, 175, 192-193, 478
Fu Chien* 傅健, 451
Fu Chih 傅祗, 182
Fu Ch'iung 傅瓊 (Fu Yüan 瑗), 338
Fu-ch'un. *See* Fu-yang
Fu-feng 扶風 (principality), 93
Fu Hsi 伏羲, 65
Fu Hsien 傅咸, 56
Fu Hsüan 傅玄, 363
Fu I 傅毅, 104
Fu Mi 傅宓, 225
Fu-niao fu 服鳥賦 (poetic essay), 132
Fu Sheng 伏生, 49
Fu-shih chu 服氏注 (subcommentary), 93
Fu T'ao 伏滔, 139-140, 141, 436
Fu T'ao chi 伏滔集 (collected works), 65
Fu-tzu 苻子 (text), 423
Fu-yang 富陽 (prefecture; before 271 = Fu-ch'un 富春), 453, 482
Fu-yen 傅儼, 31
Fu Yüeh 傅說, 30-31
funerals, 323-330 *passim*; "bereaved son" (*hsiao-tzu*), 325; "funeral host" (*sang-chu*), 325, 328; funeral processions, 326, 481; geomancy before burial, 359-360; Liu Lin-chih undertakes old woman's burial, 336; pallbearers for Chin Emperor Wu, 481; pallbearers' songs (*wan-ko*), 387-388, 453; select attendance at Hsün Ts'an's funeral, 485-486; and singing, 388; "spirit bed" (*ling-ch'uang*), 324, 325, 328. *See also* mourning.

gambling: 88, 206-207, 385, 449; archery contests, 460-461, 464; *chaupar* (*shu-p'u*), 88, 175, 380, 384-385, 466, 474-475; *po-i*, 88; "sixes" (*liu-po*), 364
games: encirclement chess or *go* (*wei-ch'i*), 88, 171, 179, 183, 192, 365, 367, 374, 408, 470;

football (*ch'iu-chü*), 363; *i-ch'i*, 27; pellet chess (*tan-ch'i*), 363-364, 408; "reach-five" (*ko-wu*), 363; "sequences" (*yü-tz'u*), 64, 424-425; throwing spikes (*cho-ting*), 27. *See also* gambling
Gandhāra, 55
"Gate of Cranes" (Ho-men 鶴門; a pool), 352
General Chastizing Caitiffs, Pavilion of (Cheng-lu t'ing 征虜亭), 191
geomancy, 359, 360
ghostly liaison. *See* marriage, posthumous
ghosts and spirits (*kuei-shen* 鬼神), 159-161, 162, 385, 386
Glorious Gate (Ch'ang-men 昌門), 285, 379, 431
go. *See* games, encirclement chess
goat curd (*yang-lao*), 44, 73, 292-293, 407
"Golden Moat" (Chin-kou 金溝), 463
Grand Academy (*t'ai-hsüeh* 太學), 37, 180-181, 463
Grand Ultimate, Hall of (T'ai-chi Palace, 太極殿), 176, 364
Great Buddha (Ta-fo 大佛; = Wang Ch'en), 467
Great Gate (Ta-men 大門), 315
Great Pontoon Bridge (Ta-hang 大桁; also Vermilion Sparrow Bridge, Chu-ch'üeh ch'iao 朱雀橋), 184, 294-295, 383, 494
Great Symbol of True Virtue Dance (*Cheng-te ta-hsiang* 正德大象), 358
Great Void (*t'ai-hsü* 太虛), 447. *See also* Emptiness
"Greater Preface to the 'Book of Songs'" (*Shih ta-hsü* 詩大序), 358

Hai-hsi, Duke of. *See* Ssu-ma I**
Hall of Golden Splendor (Chin-hua tien 金華殿), 61
Han 漢 (river), 70, 304
Han-Chin ch'un-ch'iu 漢晉春秋 (text), 135
Han-fei-tzu 韓非子 (text), 34, 42, 173, 408
Han Hu 韓虎, 62
Han-ku 函谷 (pass), 118

704 TALES OF THE WORLD

Han Po 韓伯, 452
han-shih san. See five-mineral powder
Han Shou 韓壽, 486
Han-shu. See "History of the Han Dynasty"
Han-tan 邯鄲 (prefecture), 471
Han-tan Ch'un 邯鄲淳, 37, 293
Hangchow Bore, 186
Hao 鎬 (ancient capital), 275
Hao 濠 (river), 60
Heng-t'ang 橫塘, 168
Heng-yang 衡陽 (commandery), 135, 356
"History of the Han Dynasty" (Han-shu 漢書), 42, 143, 200
Ho, Empress (何后; consort of Mu, Emperor of Chin), 453
Ho Chia 郗嘉, 167
Ho Ch'iao 和嶠, 359
Ho-ch'iao 河橋 (place), 471
Ho-ching 河津 (place), 5
Ho Ch'ung 何充, 90, 206, 434
Ho Fa-sheng 何法盛 (author of CHS), 163, 492
Ho-hsiang, Marquis of (合鄉侯), 364
Ho-lu Island (闔廬洲), 356
Ho-lü 闔閭 (King of Wu 吳), 210
Ho-men. See "Gate of Cranes"
Ho-nan 河南 (prefecture), 264, 402, 463
Ho-nei 河內 (commandery), 83, 157, 371
Ho Shao* 何劭, 486
Ho Sui 何邃, 446
Ho Tseng 何曾, 392
Ho-tung 河東 (commandery), 438
ho-tzu 貉子 ("son of a badger"), 487. See also southerners
Ho Yen 何晏, 11, 20, 103, 122, 137, 140, 219, 226, 237, 245, 257, 260
Hou Chi 后稷, 63, 404
Hou T'u 后土 (Kou Lung 句龍), 161-162
Hsi* 窶 (surname), 10
Hsi, dogs of (傒狗; epithet), 313
hsi 禊. See spring purification rites
Hsi, Duke of Lu (魯僖公), 63
Hsi-ching fu 西京賦 (poetic essay), 128, 312
Hsi Fu-chi 僖負羈, 346-347

Hsi-hao 西豪 (village), 6
Hsi-ho 西河, 180
Hsi Hsi 郗憘, 191
Hsi-Jung. See Jung, Western
Hsi-Jung chuan 西戎傳 (section of WeiL), 104
Hsi K'ang 嵇康, 83, 100, 102-103, 139, 140, 154, 262, 368
Hsi-ling Gorge. See Yangtze Gorges
Hsi-men Pao 西門豹, 173
Hsi-shan ch'iao 西善橋 (modern suburb of Nanking), 371-372
Hsi Shao 嵇紹, 154
Hsi Shih 西施, 428-429
Hsi Tso-ch'ih 習鑿齒, 419
Hsi-yang 西陽 (commandery)
Hsi Yü 習郁, 378
Hsia-hou Hsüan 夏侯玄, 97, 140, 214, 344-345
Hsia-k'ou 夏口, 410
Hsia-kuei 下邽 (prefecture), 8
Hsia Shih 夏施, 88
Hsia-ts'ai 下蔡, 175
Hsiang, Duke of Ch'in (秦襄公), 423
Hsiang, King of Chou (周襄王), 49
Hsiang-ch'eng 項城, 148
Hsiang Hsiu 向秀, 112, 140, 268, 439. See also under Chuang-tzu
Hsiang Liang 項梁, 149
Hsiang-niu ching 相牛經 ("Judging Oxen, Book of"), 461
Hsiang pu-chin i 緣不盡意 (essay), 132
hsiang-sacrifice, 367
Hsiang-yang 襄陽 (commandery), 156, 193, 238, 303-304, 359, 387, 410, 415, 417, 478
Hsiang Yü 項羽, 200, 217, 340, 345, 414
Hsiao, Duke of Ch'in (秦孝公), 64
Hsiao-ch'eng, King of Chao (趙孝成王), 38
Hsiao-chi 孝己, 28-29
Hsiao-ching 孝經 ("Book of Filial Piety"), 12, 19, 30, 71, 158, 162, 279
hsiao-ts'ao (herb), 413-414
Hsiao Tzu-liang 蕭子良, 126
Hsiao-wen, King of Ch'in (秦孝文王), 33

INDEX 705

Hsiao-wu, Emperor of Chin. *See* Ssu-ma Yao
Hsiao-yao yu. See under *Chuang-tzu*
Hsiao-yao yu-hsüan lun 逍遙遊玄論 (essay), 110
Hsieh 偰 (ancient minister), 63
Hsieh 謝 (family), 175, 412, 478
Hsieh, Lady 謝氏 (mother of Crown Prince Min-huai), 486
Hsieh An 謝安 (grand tutor), 76, 175, 207, 289, 389, 420, 433
Hsieh An* 謝安 (fl. ca. 300; General Chastizing Caitiffs), 191
Hsieh Chan 謝瞻, 76, 143
Hsieh Ch'e-chi chia-chuan 謝車騎家傳 (biography), 67
Hsieh Chü 謝據, 412
Hsieh Chüeh 謝瑒, 76
Hsieh Heng 謝衡, 354
Hsieh Hsüan 謝玄, 418
Hsieh Hsün 謝詢, 76
Hsieh Hui 謝晦, 76
Hsieh Hun 謝混, 136, 137, 453
Hsieh I 謝奕, 354-355, 412
Hsieh K'un 謝鯤, 12, 140, 325, 354
Hsieh-piao 謝表 ("Memorial of Thanks"), 355
Hsieh P'ou 謝裒, 354
Hsieh Seng-shou 謝僧韶, 439
Hsieh Seng-yao 謝僧要, 439
Hsieh Shang 謝尚, 175, 244, 260, 314, 354
Hsieh Sheng 謝勝, 322
Hsieh Shih 謝石, 412
Hsieh Tao-yün 謝道韞, 412
Hsieh Tun 謝遁, 76
Hsieh Wan 謝萬, 175
Hsieh Yen 謝琰, 193, 494
Hsien, Duke of Chin (晉獻公), 28, 36, 415
Hsien, Emperor of Han (漢獻帝), 364
Hsien-an 咸安 (era), 60
Hsien-ho 咸和 (era), 324-325
Hsien-jen lun 賢人論 (var., *Hsien-ch'üan lun* 賢全論; essay), 135
Hsien-men 羨門 (ancient adept), 103
Hsien-ning 咸寧 (era), 198, 377
Hsien-pei 鮮卑 (people), 6, 189, 262, 376-377, 443

Hsien Taoism, 20
Hsien-yang 咸陽 (= Ch'ang-an), 419, 472
Hsien-yün 獫狁 (people), 417
Hsin-an 新安 (commandery), 229, 285, 335
Hsin-kan 新淦 (prefecture), 351
Hsin T'ang-shu 新唐書 (text), 368
Hsin-t'ing 新亭 (suburb of Chien-k'ang), 45, 190, 383, 412, 492
hsin-wu i 心無義 ("Theory of Mental Nonexistence"), 447
Hsin-yeh 新野 (prefecture), 238
Hsin-yü 新語 (text), 477
Hsing-lu nan 行路難 (song), 387
Hsing-ning 興寧 (era), 259
hsing-san. See under five-mineral powder
Hsiu-ch'u 休屠, 105
Hsiung-nu 匈奴 (people), 6, 13, 15, 48, 53, 105, 199, 214, 308, 340-341, 411, 421
Hsü, Empress (許皇后; consort of Ch'eng, Emperor of Han), 342
Hsü, Lady (徐氏; wife of Lü An), 180
Hsü Chang 許章, 251
Hsü-ch'ang 許昌 (prefecture), 221
Hsü Ching 許靖, 249
Hsü Hsün 許詢, 190, 251
Hsü Kung 許貢, 306
Hsü Mi 許謐, 391
Hsü Shao 許劭, 249, 324
Hsü Shen 許慎 (author of *SW*), 4
Hsü Shu 許庶, 250
Hsü Yu 許由, 25, 31, 40, 54, 63, 402, 404, 412, 413, 421
Hsü Yün 許允, 150
hsüan. See Mysterious
Hsüan, Emperor of Han (漢宣帝), 77
Hsüan, King of Ch'i (齊宣王), 428
Hsüan, King of Chou (周宣王), 29
Hsüan, Prince of Chin. See Ssu-ma I
Hsüan-ch'eng 宣城 (commandery), 285
hsüan-feng. See Mysterious Learning
hsüan-hsü. See Mysterious and Empty
hsüan-hsüeh. See Mysterious Learning

hsüan-miao. See Mysterious and Subtle
Hsüan-wu 宣武 (review grounds), 181, 198
hsüan-yüan. See Mysterious and Remote
Hsüeh, Mme. (薛夫人), 8
Hsüeh Kung 薛公, 461
Hsüeh Kung-tsu 薛莹祖, 5
Hsüeh-tsan 雪讚 (poem), 143
Hsün, Lady (荀氏; mother of Ming, Emperor of Chin), 443
Hsün Chien 荀儉, 6, 29
Hsün Ching 荀靖, 29
Hsün Fu 荀夢, 6
Hsün Hsü 荀勗, 83, 153-154, 257
Hsün I 荀顗, 10, 152, 153-154
Hsün K'ai 荀闓 (Tao-ming 道明), 202
Hsün Kun 荀緄, 6, 29
Hsün Lin-fu 荀林父, 168
Hsün Shu 荀淑, 4
Hsün Su 荀肅, 6
Hsün Tao 荀燾, 6, 29
Hsün Ts'an 荀粲, 237
Hsün-tzu 荀子 (Hsün Ch'ing 荀卿), 65
Hsün Wang 荀汪, 6, 29
Hsün-yang 尋陽 (commandery), 288, 304, 307, 336, 351, 456, 475
Hsün Yin 荀寅, 287
Hsün Yü. See "Eight Heroes"
Hu 胡 (Indians, Central Asiatics; sometimes also Hsiung-nu, Hsien-pei), 6, 15, 86, 88, 148
Hu Chih 胡質, 14
hu-ch'uang. See folding chairs
Hu-han-hsieh 呼韓邪 (Hsiung-nu chieftain), 340-341
Hu Hsieh-chih 胡諧之, 313
Hu Kuang 胡廣, 494
Hu San-hsing 胡三省 (commentator), 398, 490
Hu-tu 滹瀆, 22
Hu-wu Fu-chih 胡母輔之, 434
Hu Yen 狐偃, 347
Hua 華 (mountain), 198
Hua-hsia 華夏 (China), 259
Hua-lin yüan. See Flowery Grove Park
Hua Shih 華士, 180
Hua-shu 華黍 (song), 130
Hua T'an 華譚, 42
Hua-t'ing 華亭 (estate), 471-472

Hua Tzu-yü 華子魚, 65
Hua-yang 華陽, 307
Hua-yang, Lady (華陽夫人), 33
Huai 淮 (river), 41, 192-193, 207, 319, 433, 478
Huai, Emperor of Chin. See Ssu-ma Chih
Huai-nan 淮南 (commandery), 306, 451
Huai-nan, Prince of. See Ssu-ma Yün
Huai-nan-tzu 淮南子 (Liu An 劉安), 42, 70, 343-344
Huan 緩 (ancient physician), 99
Huan, Duke of Ch'i (齊桓公), 46, 47-48, 53, 235, 260, 275, 283, 286, 295, 416-417
Huan Ching 桓景, 492
Huan Hsüan 桓玄, 76, 209, 366, 370, 453-454, 494-495
Huan Huo 桓豁, 467
Huan I 桓彝, 17, 132, 141, 260
Huan I* 桓伊, 436
Huan K'ang 桓康, 305
Huan Shih-min 桓石民, 467
Huan Tou. See Four Ill-omened Ones
Huan Wen 桓溫, 144, 204-205, 303, 327, 336, 411
Huan Yin 桓胤, 454
Huang Chiung 黃瓊, 3
Huang-ch'u 黃初 (era), 34, 148
Huang-fu Mi 皇甫謐, 128, 304
Huang-kung chiu-lu. See Master Huang's Wineshop
Huang T'an 黃憲, 467
Huang-ti. See Yellow Emperor
Hui, Emperor of Chin. See Ssu-ma Chung
Hui-chiao 慧皎 (author of KSC), 391
Hui Shih 惠施 (Hui-tzu 惠子), 60, 117, 122-123, 421
Hui-wen, King of Chao (趙惠文王), 267
Hui-wen, King of Ch'in (秦惠文王), 422
human nature. See Natural Ability and Human Nature
Hun Tun. See Four Ill-omened Ones
Hung-fan 洪範 (section of "Book of Documents"), 49
Hung-nung 弘農 (commandery), 52
Huo Ch'ü-ping 霍去病, 77
Huo Kuang 霍光, 76-77

I 易. See "Changes, Book of"
I 嶧 (mountain), 447
I 夷 (people), 426. See also I, Eastern
I 沂 (river), 9, 433
I, Eastern (Tung-I 東夷; people), 41
I-ch'ang 宜昌 (modern prefecture), 58
I Chi 伊籍, 43
I-ch'i 伊耆 (legendary ruler), 7
i-ch'i 奕棋, 27
I Chih 伊陟, 404
I-chou 益州, 127
I-fu 意賦 (poetic essay), 132-133
I-hsi 義熙 (era), 137
I-hsiang miao-yü hsien-hsing 易象妙於見形 (essay), 121
I-hsing 義興 (commandery), 76, 318-319
I Hsün 奕遜, 429
I-k'ao 邑考 (eldest son of Wen, King of Chou), 153
I-li 儀禮 (text), 276
I-ts'un 伊存 (Kushān ambassador), 104
I-yang 義陽 (commandery), 402
I Yin 伊尹, 76-77, 367
immortality cult, 20
India, northern (T'ien-chu), 104
Inherited Splendor, Gate of (Ch'eng-hua men 承華門), 166
"Inspector-general of P'ing-yüan Commandery" (平原督郵), 361
"Intrigues of the Warring States." See Chan-kuo ts'e
"invitation of the Buddha," 74

Jao Tsung-i 饒宗頤 (contemporary scholar), 86, 415
Jen An 任安, 411
Jen Fang 任昉, 126
Jetavana Temple (Chih-yüan ssu 祇洹寺), 237
Jih-hsia Ming-ho 日下鳴鶴 (Hsü Yin), 406
Jñānaprasthāna-abhidharma-śāstra. See under Buddhist scriptures
Jo-yeh 若邪 (prefecture), 338
Ju-nan 汝南 (commandery), 4, 11, 26, 29, 45, 210, 248, 249, 251, 336, 350
Ju-Tao lun 儒道論 (essay), 40
Juan Chan 阮瞻, 12, 101, 140, 222

Juan Chi 阮籍, 12, 97, 140, 307, 333, 394
Juan Chien 阮簡, 376
Juan Fu 阮孚, 223
Juan Hsi 阮熙, 374
Juan Hsien 阮咸, 140, 374
Juan Yü 阮裕, 315
"Judging Oxen, Book of." See Hsiang-niu ching
Juism. See Confucisnism
Jung, Western (西戎; "Western Barbarians"), 42, 275. See also "Dog Barbarians"
Jung Ch'i 榮期 (Ch'i-ch'i 汲期), 404
Jurchen (people), 426

Kai-hsia 陔下, 414
Kan 贛 (river), 382
Kan-ch'üan 甘泉 (palace), 105
Kan Lo 甘羅, 51-52
Kan Mao 甘茂, 52
Kan Pao 干寶, 133
K'ang, Duke of Ch'in (秦康公), 36
K'ang, Emperor of Chin (晉康帝), 57
K'ang-shu 康叔 (younger brother of Duke of Chou), 425
Kao, Emperor of Han. See Liu Pang
Kao-p'ing 高平 (commandery), 9, 251, 446
Kao-shih chuan. See "Lives of Eminent Gentlemen"
Kao-t'ang Lung 高堂隆, 461
Kao-tso 高座 (tomb), 50
Kao-yang 高陽, 6
Kao-yang Pool (高陽池), 377-378
Kao Yao 皋陶 (Kao Yu 繇), 83, 91, 401, 404
Kao Yu. See Kao Yao
Kao Yu* 高誘 (commentator), 4, 42
Keng 耿 (ancient capital), 44
Khotan, 367
Ko 高 (prefecture), 361
Ko Ch'iang 葛彊, 378
Ko Hung 葛洪, 136
Ko Lu 葛盧, 63
ko-wu 格五, 363
K'o-t'ing 柯亭 (inn), 436
Kou Chien 勾踐 (King of Yüeh 越), 428-429
Kou Lung 勾龍. See Hou T'u
Kou-shih 緱氏 (prefecture), 36
Ku 顧 (family), 82

Ku Ho 顧和, 47
Ku Jung 顧榮, 201, 352
Ku K'ai-chih 顧愷之, 58
Ku-k'ou 谷口 (commentator on SSHY), 446
Ku P'i 顧邳, 325
Ku-shih 古詩. See Ku-shih shih-chiu shou
Ku-shih shih-chiu shou 古詩十九首, 143
Ku-shu 姑孰 (Nan-chou 南州), 49, 73, 76, 77, 141, 229, 237, 370, 443, 448
Ku Wei 顧隗, 299
Ku-wen yüan 古文苑 (anthology), 419
Kuai 夬 (Hex. 43), 43
K'uai-chi, Prince of. See Ssu-ma Tao-tzu; Ssu-ma Yü
Kuan Chung 管仲, 46, 48, 53, 65, 235, 260, 283
Kuan-chung 關中 (area), 12, 147, 149, 423, 451
Kuan-chü 關雎 (song), 354
Kuan Lu 管輅, 361
Kuan Ning 管寧, 7
Kuan Yu-an 管幼安, 65
Kuang-ling 廣陵 (commandery), 151
Kuang-ling san (song), 180
Kuang-wu, Emperor of Han (漢光武帝), 44, 47, 270
K'uang 匡 (ancient state), 168-169
k'uang 曠. See "untrammeled"
K'uang Su. See Lu Su
kuei 桂 (cassia cinnamomum), 6
Kuei 巋 (mountain), 121
K'uei 夔 (ancient musician), 56
Kumārajīva, 111
Kun 鯀. See Four Ill-omened Ones
K'un-lun 崑崙 (mountains), 39, 41, 70; Hanging Orchards, of, 136
K'un-yeh 昆邪 (Hsiung-nu chieftain), 105
Kung, Duke of Ts'ao (曹共公), 347
Kung Kung 共工, 161. See also Four Ill-omened Ones
Kung Sheng 龔勝, 139
Kung-shu Pan 公輸般, 106
Kung-sun Hsia 公孫夏, 388
Kung-sun Lung-tzu 公孫龍子, 99, 105
Kung-sun Shu 公孫述, 47

Kung-yang chuan 公羊傳 (commentary), 30, 287, 329, 418
Kung Yü 貢禹, 403
K'ung An-kuo* 孔安國 (Han literatus), 78
K'ung Ch'ang 孔萇, 214
K'ung Ch'iu. See Confucius
K'ung Jung 孔融, 485
K'ung-lang miao 孔郎廟 (shrine), 335
K'ung P'u 孔璞, 307
K'ung T'an 孔坦, 226
K'ung-tzu chia-yü 孔子家語 (text), 33
Kuo, Mistress (郭舍人), 274-275
Kuo Hsiang 郭象, 40. See also under Chuang-tzu
Kuo Mao-ch'ien 郭茂倩 (author of YFSC), 316
Kuo Pan 郭頒 (author of WCSY), 150
Kuo P'u 郭璞, 137, 189, 480, 481
Kuo T'ai 郭泰, 452
kuo-tzu hsüeh 國子學 (later, kuo-tzu chien 監), 463
Kuo-yü 國語 (text), 117, 426-427
Kushāna. See Yüeh-chih, Greater

Lai Village (瀨鄉), 69
Lak-lang 樂浪 (in Korea), 348
Lan-t'ai Stone Chamber (蘭臺石室), 104
Lan-t'ing chi hsü 蘭亭集序 (preface), 321
landscape (shan-shui 山水): Hsieh K'un and, 254, 368; Hsü Hsün and, 338; Yü Liang and, 314
Lang-yeh 琅邪 (commandery), 57, 174, 234, 261, 371, 391, 446, 471, 490
lao 酪. See goat curd
Lao Lai-tzu 老萊子, 65
Lao-tzu 老子 (Li Po-yang 李伯陽), 4, 11, 26, 34, 40, 67, 69, 83, 88, 95-102 passim, 137, 218, 219, 220, 231, 232, 259, 262, 299, 334, 404, 423, 426, 435, 468. See also Tao-te ching
lectures for laymen. See under Buddhism
legal code of Chin, 83
Legalism, 64
Lei-ch'ih. See Thunder Lake
Li, King of Chou (周厲王), 275

Li, Lady (李氏; mother of Wen, Duke of Chin), 36
Li, Prince of Huai-nan. See Liu Ch'ang
Li Chao 李昭, 152
Li Chi 麗寄, 204
Li-chi. See "Rites, Record of"
Li-chou 漆洲, 386
Li Ch'ung 李充 (Hung-tu 弘度), 457
Li Feng 李豐 (An-kuo 安國; alias Li Hsüan 宣), 95, 150, 309, 344-345
Li Heng 李暅, 446
Li Hsien 李蘭, 32
Li Hsiung 李雄, 53
Li Hsüan. See Li Feng
Li Hsün 李尋, 49
li-i 理義. See Principles and Meanings
Li Kuei 李軌 (Hung-fan 弘範), 100, 457
Li Ling 李陵, 411
Li Ping 李冰, 9
Li Po-yang. See Lao-tzu
Li-sao 離騷 (section of Ch'u-tz'u), 74, 391
Li Shan 李善 (commentator), 40, 42, 74, 101, 126, 378, 489
Li Shih 李勢 (last ruler of Ch'eng-Han 成漢), 58, 450
Li Shih-ch'i 麗食其, 200-201
Li Ssu 李斯, 64, 472
Li T'e 李特, 206
Li-yang 歷陽 (prefecture), 138, 306, 330
Li Ying 李膺, 4. See also under "Eight Heroes"
Liang 梁 (principality), 52, 448
Liang, King of (梁王; Wei Ying 魏嬰, var., 罃; also known as Hui, King of Liang, 梁惠王), 307
Liang, Chi 梁冀, 363
Liang Lei 梁蕾, 270
Liang-li 梁里 (creek), 46
Liang Sung 梁松, 270
Liang-tu fu 兩都賦 (poetic essay), 128, 134, 135
Liao-tung 遼東 (commandery), 38, 211
libertinism. See nihilism and libertinism
Lieh-hsien tsan 列仙贊 (poems), 434

Lieh-nü chuan 列女傳 (text), 113
Lieh-tzu 列子, 19, 52, 63, 99, 192, 438-439
Lien P'o 廉頗, 197, 267
Lien Shu 連叔, 66
Lin-chiang, Prince of. See Liu Jung
Lin-ch'iung 臨邛 (prefecture), 271
Lin-ch'uan 臨川 (commandery), 14, 20, 262
Lin-erh 臨兒 (Lumbinī), 104
Lin-hai 臨海 (commandery), 86, 285, 334-335
Lin Hsiang-ju 藺相如, 197, 267
Lin-i 臨沂 (prefecture), 201
Ling, Duke of Chin (晉靈公), 167, 409
Ling, Duke of Wei (衛靈公), 456
Ling-hsiao kuan 陵霄觀 (Sky-traversing Observatory), 365
Ling-i 浚儀 (prefecture), 376
Ling Lun 伶倫, 39
Ling-nan 嶺南, 23
Ling-yün t'ai (ko) (陵雲臺 [閣]; Cloud-traversing Terrace [Pavilion]), 152, 177, 280
Liu, Lady (劉氏; wife of Chen Yen), 35-36
Liu*, Lady (劉氏; Yüan, Mme., 袁夫人, wife of Yüan Shao), 484
Liǔ, Lady (柳氏; mother of Chia Ch'ung), 348
Liu Ch'ang 劉長 (Li, Prince of Huai-nan, 淮南厲王), 155
Liu Cheng 劉整, 430
Liu Chi 劉璣, 18
Liu Chien-chih 劉簡之, 79
Liu Ch'ien-chih 劉謙之, 79
Liu Ching 劉靜, 345
Liu Fang 劉放, 156
Liu Han 劉漢. See Liu Mo
Liu Hsia 劉夏, 18
Liu Hsia* 劉遐, 57
Liu-hsia Hui 柳下惠, 333
Liu Hsiang 劉向, 104-105, 113, 363, 468
Liu Hua 劉華, 249
Liu I 劉毅 (third cent.), 158, 182, 258
Liu Jung 劉榮 (Lin-chiang, Prince of, 臨江王), 70
Liu K'uei 劉愧, 49
Liu K'uei* 劉逵, 128

710 TALES OF THE WORLD

Liu Lao-chih 劉牢之, 391
Liu Ling 劉伶, 140, 268, 373
Liu Mo 劉漠 (miswritten Liu Han 漢), 97
Liu Pang 劉邦 (P'ei, Duke of, 沛公; later, Kao, Emperor of Han, 漢高帝), 47, 155, 200-201, 214, 217, 286, 288, 388, 419, 430
Liu Pao 劉寶, 251
Liu Pei 劉備 (founder of Shu 蜀 Kingdom), 77, 190, 235, 250
Liu Piao 劉表, 31-32
Liu Shih 劉寔, 18, 255, 459
Liu Shu. See "Three Gentlemen"
Liu T'an 劉惔, 244, 314
Liu Tsung 劉琮, 32
Liu Wei 劉疇, 166, 473
Liu Wu 劉武 (Hsiao, Prince of Liang 梁孝王), 271
Liu Yao 劉曜, 48
Liu Yu. See "Eight Heroes"
Liu Yü* 劉裕 (Wu, Emperor of Sung, 宋武帝), 307
Liu Yüan 劉淵 (founder of Former Chao 趙), 199, 472
Liu Yüan* 劉琨 (emissary of Shu Kingdom), 315
"Lives of Eminent Gentlemen" (Kao-shih chuan 高士傳); by Hsi K'ang, 270-271; by Huang-fu Mi, 304
Lo 洛 (river), 42, 430
Lo-an 樂安 (principality), 282
Lo-yang scholars, chanting poems in manner of (Lo-sheng yung 洛生詠): Hsieh An, 190-191; Ku K'ai-chih's refusal, 439
Lokakṣema (translator), 108
Long Mountain (Ch'ang-fu 長阜; = Ch'ang-shan 長山?), 69, 70
Lookout Mountain (Ssu-wang 四望), 480
Lou 婁. See Three Rivers of Wu
Lou Hu 樓護, 281
Lu 陸 (family), 82
Lu 廬 (mountain), 125, 288
Lu 廬 (river), 367
Lu 騄 (steed), 320
Lu Chi 陸機, 137
Lu Chia 陸賈, 404
Lu-chiang 廬江 (commandery), 9, 164-165, 351, 446
Lu Chih* 廬植, 161
Lu Chung-lien 魯仲連, 65
Lu Ch'ung 盧充, 159-161
Lu Jung 路戎, 166
Lu K'ang 陸抗, 472
Lu-ling 廬陵 (commandery), 204
Lu Ling-kuang tien fu 魯靈光殿賦 (poetic essay), 377
Lu Na 陸納, 71
Lu Su 盧俗 (Chün-hsiao 君孝; alias K'uang Su 匡俗; Lord of Yüeh-lu 越廬君; Grand Illustrious Duke, T'ai-ming kung 太明公), 288
Lu Te-ming 陸德明, 101
Lu T'ung. See Chieh Yü
Lu Tzu-han 盧子幹, 93
Lu Yü 陸羽, 481
Lumbinī. See Lin-erh
Lun-heng 論衡 (text), 162
Lun-yü. See "Analects"
Lun-yü chi-chieh 論語集解 (commentary), 260
Lung 龍 (mountain), 205
Lung-an 隆安 (era), 125, 144
Lung-ho 隆和 (era), 438
Lung-men 龍門 (Dragon Gate), 5, 56
Lü, Empress (呂后; consort of Kao, Emperor of Han), 494
Lü An 呂安, 100, 180-181, 262, 333, 393
Lü Ch'ien 呂虔, 9
Lü Hsün 呂遜, 180
Lü I 呂漪, 473
Lü Pu-wei 呂不韋, 33
Ma, Empress of (Later) Han (漢馬后), 93
Ma Shu 馬騶, 418
Ma-t'i. See under Chuang-tzu
Ma Yüan 馬援, 47
magicians. See under Taoism
Mahānibbāna-sutta. See under Buddhist scriptures
Mahāparinirvāṇa-sūtra. See under Buddhist scriptures
malaria (nüeh 瘧), 44, 305-306
Man 蠻 (language), 63, 415
Man 蠻 (people), 63, 415, 426, 476
Man Fen 滿奮, 261
Manchus (people), 426
Mañjuśrī (bodhisattva), 56, 110, 111
mantras (chou 咒), 50

"manual conversation" (*shou-t'an* 手談), 367
Mao 茅 (mountain), 391
Mao An-chih 毛安之, 176
Mao Ch'ang 毛萇, 118
Mao-shan sect, 391
marriage: arrangement of, 349, 384, 424, 445-446, 481; clandestine affairs, 487; concubines, 15, 350, 353, 471, 488, 489, 490; divorce, 19, 328, 348-349; engagement and wedding presents, 445, 455; left and right wives, 348; matches, suitability of, 163-164, 175, 347, 447-448; posthumous (*yu-hun*), 159-161; relations between husband and wife, 163-164, 486-487, 488; wedding ceremony, 441, 445, 471; and widows, 355, 446; wife's reunion with parents on anniversary of, 456
Mars (Ying-huo 熒惑), 59-60
Master Huang's Wineshop (Huang-kung chiu-lu 黃公酒壚), 138, 323, 437-438
"Matter-as-such, School of" (Chi-se tsung 即色宗), 111
Māyā (mother of Buddha), 104
meanings (*chih* 旨), 99
Meanings and Principles (*i-li* 義理), 218. See also Principles and Meanings
medical arts (*i-shu* 醫術), 115: acupuncture (*chen*), 99, 362; Buddhist vs. Taoist physicians, 361; cerebral hemorrhage (*chung o-feng*), 480; excessive keenness of hearing (*erh-ts'ung*), 482; incurable sickness "between heart and diaphragm," 98-99, 455; palpitation of the heart (*hsü-chi*; *shih-hsin ping*), 482; "pulses" (*ching-mo*), 361-362; Yü Fa-k'ai as obstetrician, 361-362. See also medicines
medicines: herbs, 413-414, 456-457; ingestion of paper charms (*fu*), 361; drugs compounded with boiling water, 425; laxative prescribed, 361. See also five-mineral powder
Mediterranean. See Chang-hai

Mei 郿 (fort), 149
Mei Ch'eng 枚乘, 133
Mei T'ao 梅陶, 170
"Memorial of Thanks." See Hsieh-piao
Mencius (孟子), 5, 33, 42, 65, 85, 134, 305, 307, 402, 477
Meng 蒙 (mountain), 127
Meng, Mr. (孟氏; commentator), 100
Meng-ching 孟津, 41
Meng Chiu 孟玖, 471
Meng Min 孟敏, 452
Meng Tsung 孟宗, 352
Meng Yüan-chi 孟元基, 38
"Mental Nonexistence, Theory of." See *hsin-wu i*
Miao-yin 妙音 (nun), 209, 478
Mien 冕 (music master), 60
Mien 沔 (river), 304, 410
military colonists (*shih-wu* 士伍), 37
Min 崏 (mountain), 124
Min-ch'ih 澠池, 38
Min-huai, Crown Prince (愍懷太子), 486
Min Tzu-ch'ien 閔子騫 (disciple of Confucius), 35-36
Ming, Emperor of Chin. See Ssu-ma Shao
Ming, Emperor of Han (漢明帝), 93, 104-105
Ming, Emperor of Wei. See Ts'ao Jui
ming-chiao 名教 ("Moral Teaching"), 5, 12, 376, 433
ming-li. See Names and Principles
Ming-shih chuan 名士傳 (text), 140, 222
Ming-tan lun 明膽論 (essay), 262
Mo-hsia 末下 (= Chien-yeh 建業), 44
Mo-ling 秣陵 (= Chien-yeh), 77, 430, 440
Mo-tzu 墨子 (Mo Ti 墨翟), 106, 173. See also Mohism
Mo-yeh 莫邪, 210
Mohism, 405
Mokṣala (translator), 108
"Moral Teaching." See *ming-chiao*
mourning, 214, 235, 241, 352, 367, 372, 374, 375, 376-377, 383-384, 492-493; crying "It's all over!" (*ch'iung-i*), 374; *hsiang*-sacrifice, 367; mourning

attire, 383-384; "returning to weep" (*fan-k'u*), 383; weeping before the spirit tablet, 493. *See also* funerals
Mu, Duke of Ch'in (秦穆公), 36, 438
Mu, Emperor of Chin (晉穆帝), 57, 235, 263
Mu, Empress of Chin (晉穆后; Yü Wen-chün 庾文君), 228, 445
Mu-jung Ch'ui 慕容垂, 59
Mu-jung Chün 慕容雋, 175, 238
Mu-jung Wei 慕容暐, 295
music: Central Asian, 379; controversy over pitches, 357-359; dispelling melancholy, 61; "eight timbres" (*pa-yin*), 217, 388; female performers, 170, 353-354, 380, 458, 465, 489; flautists, 255, 489-490; human voice superior to instruments, 205; lute song (*Ta-tao ch'ü*), 316; "Monograph on Music" (*Sung-shu, Yüeh-chih*), 302; "Music, Book of" (*Yüeh*), 92, 168; poetic essays on, 142, 238; string and pipe ensembles, 462; zither melodies, 180, 181. *See also* dancing; singing
  musical instruments: *cheng*, 142, 389-390; *chia*, 307; *ch'in*, 142, 158, 192, 217, 238, 264, 325, 328, 332, 279; *hsiao*, 307, 388; *ku*, 30-31, 307; *kuan*, 307; *p'i-pa*, 315-316, 368; *se*, 217, 264, 267; *sheng*, 264; *ti*, 255, 389-390, 436, 458-459, 489-490; *wu-hsien*, 368; *yü*, 434-435;
"Music, Book of" (*Yüeh* 樂), 92, 168
Mysterious, the (*hsüan* 玄), 100, 102, 122, 123, 241, 278, 310. *See also* Mysterious and Empty; Mysterious Learning; etc.
Mysterious and Empty (*hsüan-hsü* 玄虛), 172
Mysterious and Remote (*hsüan-yüan* 玄遠), 96, 139, 235, 281
Mysterious and Subtle (*hsüan-miao* 玄妙), 97
Mysterious and Transcendent (*hsüan-sheng* 玄勝), 259
Mysterious Learning (*hsüan-hsüeh* 玄學; *hsüan-feng* 風), 100, 106

Mystical Quiescence (*hsüan-chi* 玄寂), 331, 334
Names and Principles (*ming-li* 名理), 42, 96, 102, 114, 219
Nan 南 (commandery), 31, 124, 244, 182, 202, 209, 249, 432
Nan-ch'ang 南昌 (prefecture), 324, 382
Nan-chou. *See* Ku-shu
Nan-kai 南陔 (song), 130
Nan-p'ing 南平 (commandery), 208-209
Nan-t'ang 南塘 (southern bank, Ch'in-huai River), 90, 379
Nan-tu fu 南都賦 (poetic essay), 366
Nan-yang 南陽 (commandery), 146, 210, 252, 335, 336, 366
Nara (Japan), 56
natural, the. *See tzu-jan*
Natural Ability and Human Nature (*ts'ai-hsing* 才性), 94, 96, 110, 118. *See also* Ssu-pen lun
"naturally-so," the (*t'ien-jan* 天然), 116
Nature. *See tzu-jan*
New Year's Assembly (*cheng-hui* 正會), 87, 357, 369, 430
Ni Heng 禰衡, 294
Ni-t'ang 倪塘 (suburb), 495
nihilism and libertinism (*hsü-tan* 虛誕), 98, 245
Nine Bestowals (*chiu-hsi* 九錫), 76, 127, 152, 431
Nine Springs (九泉; the underworld), 247, 267
Nine Rivers (Chiu-chiang 九江), 288
Nine Turns, Slope of. *See* Chiu-che pan
Ning Ch'i 寧戚, 461
Ning-k'ang 寧康 (era), 71, 176, 327
Ning Yüeh 寧越, 85
Nirvāna, 55
Niu-chu 牛渚, 138, 306
Non-actuality (*wu* 無), 96-98, 122. *See also* Non-being; Nothing
Non-being (*wu* 無; *abhava*, Non-existence), 118, 447. *See also* Non-actuality; Nothing
North Fortress Mountain (Pei-ku shan 北固山), 65-66

INDEX   713

North Hsia Gate (北夏門), 377
northerners, epithet for,
  (ts'ang-fu 傖父, "boor,"
  "brute"), 186, 256, 399, 407,
  447, 487
Northerners and Southerners,
  erudition of, 105-106. See also
  northerners; southerners
Nothing (wu 無), 96, 116. See
  also Non-actuality; Non-being
Nothingness (hsü-wu 虛無), 98.
  See also Empty Nonexistence
nudity, 12, 374
Nü-hsün 女訓 (text), 349

O-mei 峨嵋 (mountain), 40
"Old Fisherman" (Yü-fu 漁父),
  and Ch'ü Yüan, 139; and Confucius, 65, 79, 404; Chap. of
  Chuang-tzu, 120-121
"Old Man of Ch'u" (Ch'u-lao 楚
  老), 139
Orchid Pavilion (Lan-t'ing 蘭亭),
  321-322
Ou-yang Chien 歐陽堅, 103
Overturned Boat Mountain (Fu-chou
  shan 覆舟山), 174
oxen and ox carts, 461

pa-chün. See "Eight Heroes"
Pa-hsien lun 八賢論 (essay), 138-
  139
Pa-tsung 巴賨, 443
Pa-tung 巴東 (commandery), 450
Pai-hua 白華 (song), 130
Pai-lou t'ing. See White Tower
  Pavilion
Pai-ma lun 白馬論 (essay), 105
Pai-yüeh 百越 (people), 288
painting: 365-368 passim;
  "flying-white" (fei-pai) tech-
  nique, 368; by Hsün Hsü, 365;
  by Ku K'ai-chih, 366, 367-368;
  by Tai K'uei, 366
pallbearers' songs, 387-388, 453
pan 柩, 74, 144
Pan Ch'ao 班超, 491
Pan Ku 班固, 47, 50, 61, 128,
  134, 135, 143
Pan Piao 班彪, 47
P'an Keng 盤庚 (ancient ruler),
  44
P'an Tsung 潘綜, 22
P'an Tz'u 潘妣, 490
P'an Yüeh 潘岳, 83, 137, 265

P'ang Te-kung 龐德公, 65
P'ang T'ung 龐統, 65
Pao Chi-li 鮑李禮, 21
Pao Chiao 鮑焦, 405
Pao-p'u tzu 抱樸子 (text), 20, 74
Pao Ssu 褒姒 (ancient beauty),
  275
Pao Ting 庖丁 (cook), 421
parinirvāṇa (Buddha's death
  scene), 51, 55
Pavilion of Golden Glory (Chin-
  chang t'ing 金昌亭), 379, 431-
  432
pearl industry, 24
pears from Ai family (哀家梨),
  440
Pei-cheng fu 北征賦 (poetic es-
  say), 139-140
Pei-hai 北海 (commandery), 7
Pei-mang 北邙 (mountain), 242,
  463, 490
Pei-men 北門 (song), 67-68
P'ei 沛 (principality), 37, 171,
  371
P'ei Hsia 裴遐, 46
P'ei Hsiu 裴秀, 83
P'ei Hui 裴徽, 278
P'ei K'ai 裴楷, 11, 140, 219, 324
P'ei-kung. See P'ei Wei
P'ei Shen-fu 裴神符 (T'ang musi-
  cian), 368
P'ei Sung-chih 裴松之 (commen-
  tator), 27, 154
P'ei Swamp (沛澤), 25
P'ei Tsan 裴瓚, 182
P'ei Tun 裴盾, 324
P'ei Wei 裴頠 (P'ei-kung 裴公),
  211, 214, 251
Pen T'ai 賁泰, 45
P'eng-ch'eng 彭城 (principality),
  262
P'eng-lai. See under Three Isles
  of the Transcendents
P'eng Marshes (P'eng-tse 彭澤),
  288
physiognomy, divination by, 278,
  347
Pi Kan 比干, 260
P'i 否 (Hex. 12), 75
Pien Ho 卞和, Jewel of, 34, 41,
  267
Pien K'un 卞壼, 313, 445
Pien Sui 卞隨, 404
Pien Tan 卞眈, 71
Ping-fu 餅賦 (poetic essay), 195

Ping Yüan 邴原, 7, 436
P'ing, Duke of Ch'i (齊平王), 44
P'ing, Duke of Chin (晉平王), 168
P'ing-i 馮翊 (commandery), 490
P'ing-Lo piao 平洛表 (memorial), 236
P'ing-yang 平陽 (Hsiung-nu capital), 48
P'ing-yin 平陰, 411
P'ing-yü 平輿 (prefecture), 210
P'ing-yüan 平原 (principality), 38
Piper's Terrace (Ch'ui-t'ai 吹臺), 307
Po 剝 (Hex. 23), 75
Po 亳 (ancient capital), 44
Po-ch'eng 伯成 (Tzu-kao 子高), 31-33
Po Ch'i 白起 (Lord of Wu-an 武安), 36-38
Po-ch'in 伯禽 (son of Duke of Chou), 425
Po-chou 柏舟 (song), 94
Po-hu t'ung-i 白虎通義 (text), 143
Po I 伯夷, 24, 31, 33, 62, 397, 421
po-i, 88
Po-li Hsi 百里奚, 14, 461
Po-liang t'ai. *See* Cypress Beam Terrace
Po Ya 伯牙 (ancient musician), 56, 326
Po Yüeh 伯樂, 438-439
P'o-kang 破岡 (suburb of Chien-k'ang), 192, 283
P'o-yang 鄱陽 (commandery), 351-352
Prajñāpāramitā-sūtras: Fang-kuang ching 放光經 ("Larger Version," *Ta-p'in* 大品), 108, 111, 114; *Kuang-tsan ching* 光讚經 (another version of same), 108, 111; *Tao-hsing po-jo ching* 道行般若經 ("Smaller Version," *Hsiao-p'in* 小品), 108, 114, 115, 117-118
Principles and Meanings (*li-i* 理義), 66, 109, 271. *See also* Meanings and Principles
Pu Ch'an 步闡, 472
Pu-chou 不周 (mountain), 332
Pu-ch'u Hsia-men hsing 步出夏門行 (tune), 302

Pu-chü 卜居 (section of *Ch'u-tz'u*), 419
Pu-kuang Ward (步廣里), 222
Pu yü ku-chun hsiang-wen i 不與古君相聞議 (proposal), 157-158
P'u 濮 (river), 60-61
"pure conversation" (*ch'ing-t'an* 清談; *ch'ing-yen* 清言), 11, 56, 63-64, 89
  individual bouts: Chih Tun and Wang Meng, 114; Fu Chia and Hsün Ts'an, 96; Ho Yen and Wang Pi, 95; Hsieh An and Wang Meng, 231; Hsieh An's exposition of *Yü-fu*, 120; Hsieh Lang and Chih Tun, 113; Hsü Hsün and Wang Hsiu, 112-113; Huan Hsüan and Yin Chung-k'an, 126; Huan Wen chides Liu T'an, 410-411; castigates Wang Yen, 433; Kuan Lu and P'ei Hsiu, 278; Kuo Hsiang and P'ei Hsia, 102; Liu T'an and Chang P'ing, 119; Seng-i and Wang Hsiu, 122; Ssu-ma Yü and Hsü Hsün, 435-436; T'ai-shu Kuang and Chih Yü, 131; Wang Chan on "Book of Changes," 215; Wang Yen and P'ei Wei, 102; Yang Fu and Yin Chung-k'an, 124; Yin Hao, and Hsieh Shang, 106-107; and Liu T'an, 106, 110; and Sun Sheng, 109, 121-122; and Wang Tao, 103; and Yin Jung, 131-132
  reputations as conversationalists: Ho Ch'ung, 256; Hsi K'ang, 393; Kuo Hsiang, 221; Liu T'an, 232, 239, 262; P'ei Wei, 216; Shan T'ao, 198-199, 218; Wang Ch'eng*, 251-252; Wang Meng, 241-242, 262; Wei Chieh, 224, 226; Yin Hao, 232-233, 238, 258, 259; Yüeh Kuang, 219

quietism. *See* activism vs. quietism

Recluse, the. *See* Shao-wei
"Record of Rites." *See* "Rites, Record of"
"Record of the Shu Kingdom" (*Shu-chih* 蜀志), 418
"Records of the Grand Historian" (*Shih-chi* 史記), 42, 411

Red Eyebrows (Ch'ih-mei 赤眉), 65
Red Ti. See Ti
"Rites, Book of" (Li 禮), 92, 168, 179, 222, 358. See also I-li; "Rites of Chou"; "Rites, Record of"
"Rites of Chou" (Chou-li 周禮), 93, 98, 319, 343, 358
"Rites, Record of" (Li-chi 禮記), 7, 12, 30, 47, 52, 61, 64, 78, 90, 91, 93, 131, 134, 158, 169, 179, 212, 219, 230, 241, 300, 309, 372, 374, 383, 425, 437, 451, 456, 480
Rush Island (Ti-chu 荻渚), 390

sacrifices (tz'u 祠), 385-386; cha (year-end sacrifice), 7-8; feng (sacrifice on Mt. T'ai), 66; hsiang (end of mourning), 367; Three-victim, 325
ṣāḍava (Indian rāga), 415-416
Saddharmapuṇḍarīka-sūtra. See under Buddhist scriptures
sage and emotions (topic), 122, 324
Sāla trees, 51, 55
salted legumes (yen-shih 鹽豉), 44
sambar-tail chowry (chu-wei 麈尾), 55-56, 99, 103, 109, 310, 326
san-chün. See "Three Gentlemen"
San Miao. See Four Ill-omened Ones
San-tu fu 三都賦 (poetic essay), 127-128, 134, 135
Sanskrit (Hu 胡) language, 50
Satyasiddhi-śāstra. See under Buddhist scriptures
Second Emperor of Ch'in (秦二世), 64, 275
"sedentary retirement" (tso-yin 坐隱), 367
Self-so, the. See tzu-jan
"sequences." See under games
Seven-li Bridge (Ch'i-li ch'iao 七里橋), 155
Seven-li Stream (Ch'i-li chien 七里澗), 471
"seven-word poems" (七言詩), 418-419
"Seven Worthies of the Bamboo Grove" (Chu-lin ch'i-hsien 竹林七賢), 10, 112, 220, 234, 254, 268, 323, 355, 371-376 passim, 401
seventh day (of seventh month), 375, 413
Sha-lü 沙律 (Indian sage), 104
Sha-men pu-te wei kao-shih lun 沙門不得為高士論 (essay), 439
Shan 剡 (prefecture), 13, 17, 66, 68, 115, 327, 338, 389, 412
Shan-ling 山陵 (mausoleum), 23
Shan-sang 山桑 (prefecture), 451
Shan T'ao 山濤, 140, 268
Shan-yang 山陽 (prefecture), 37, 189, 371
Shan-yin 山陰 (prefecture), 71, 239, 293, 322, 381, 389, 493
Shan Yün 山允, 157
Shang 商. See Tzu-hsia
Shang, Lord of. See Wei Yang
Shang, Master (Shang-tzu 商子), 425
Shang Ch'en 商臣 (Ch'u prince), 200
Shang-ch'iu, Master. See Shang-ch'iu-tzu Chin
Shang-ch'iu-tzu Chin 商丘子胥 (transcendent being), 434-435
Shang-chün shu 商君書 (text), 64
Shang Jung 商容, 3, 4
Shang-lin 上林 (preserve), 373
Shang-lin fu 上林賦 (poetic essay), 77, 366
Shang-ming 上明 (prefecture), 335, 467, 478
Shang-shu ta-chuan 尚書大傳 (text), 50
Shang-tang 上黨 (commandery), 38, 39
Shang-yü 上虞 (prefecture), 10, 231
Shao, Duke of (召公; fl. 841 B.C.), 275
Shao, Earl of (召伯), 290-291
Shao-cheng Mao 少正卯, 91, 180
Shao Hao 少昊 (legendary ruler), 65
Shao Hu 召忽, 260
Shao-nan 召南 (section of "Book of Songs"), 65
Shao ssu-ming 少司命 (section of Ch'u-tzu), 306
Shao-wei 少微 (the Recluse--Ch'u-shih 處士 --a constellation), 338

Shen Ch'ung 沈充, 253
Shen-ling-pao 神靈寶 (Huan Hsüan), 390
Shen Nung 神農 (legendary ruler), 65, 331
Shen Sheng 申生, 28
Shen-t'u Ti 申徒狄, 405
Sheng wu ai-lo lun 聲無哀樂論 (essay), 102
Shih 詩. See "Songs, Book of"
Shih-ch'eng 石城 (mountain), 327
Shih-chi. See "Records of the Grand Historian"
Shih Chi-she 士吉射, 287
Shih Chien 石鑒, 83
Shih Chung-ho 史仲和, 37
Shih Ch'ung 石崇, 252
Shih-hsiang Pavilion (尸鄉亭), 388
Shih Hsien 石顯, 276
Shih Hu 石虎 (ruler of Later Chao), 53, 410
Shih K'uang 師曠 (ancient musician), 176
Shih-lin 士林 (section of *WuL*), 243
Shih Lo 石勒 (founder of Later Chao), 15, 199, 214, 433, 472
Shih-mu 釋木 ("Explanation of Trees"; section of *Erh-ya*), 481
Shih-p'in 詩品 (text), 136
Shih-p'ing 始平 (commandery), 265, 357
Shih-shou 石首. See Shih-t'ou*
Shih-shuo jen-ming p'u 世說人名譜 (genealogies), 63, 195
Shih Tao-an 釋道安, 238
Shih-t'ou 石頭 (fortification; port of Chien-k'ang), 57, 85-86, 87, 166, 167, 169, 203, 229, 282, 306, 312-313, 325, 430, 473, 481, 492
Shih-t'ou* 石頭 (= Shih-shou 石首; in Hupei), 429
Shih-t'ou Station (石頭驛; in Kiangsi), 382
Shih-tzu-kang 石子岡, 50
Shih-wei 世達 (son of Wang Ch'iang 王墻), 341
Shih-wei 式微 (song), 94
Shih Yü 史魚, 37
Shih-yü 釋魚 ("Explanation of Fishes"; section of *Erh-ya*), 480
Shōsōin (treasury), 56

Shou-ch'un 壽春 (prefecture), 68, 236, 262, 287, 303, 436
Shou-meng, King of Wu (吳壽夢王), 456
Shou-yang 首陽 (mountain), 397
Shou-yang 壽陽 (prefecture), 59, 193, 307, 451
Shu 書. See "Documents, Book of"
Shu Ao 叔敖, 65
Shu Ch'i 叔齊, 24, 31, 33, 397, 421
Shu-li 黍離 (song), 48, 329
Shu Tiao 豎刁, 53, 375
Shu-tu fu 蜀都賦 (poetic essay), 42, 118, 127-128
Shun 舜 (Yü Shun 虞舜), 25, 29, 42, 56, 63, 65, 83, 88, 148, 165, 228, 401, 411
Shun, Emperor of Han (漢順帝), 124
Shuo-fu 說郛 (collectanea), 140
Shuo-wen 說文 (dictionary), 294
Shuo-yüan 說苑 (text), 477
"silkworm chamber" (*ts'an-shih* 蠶室), 411
singing, 205, 293, 377, 387, 388, 465; pallbearers' songs (*wan-ko*), 387-388, 453; unaccompanied (*ch'ing-ko*), 387
Six Faculties (*liu-t'ung* 六通), 119-120
Six Perfections (*liu-tu* 六度), 112, 117-118
"Six Schools" of early Buddhism, 111
Sky-traversing Observatory. See Ling-hsiao kuan
slaves (male, *nu*; female, *pei*), 14, 70, 304, 381, 390, 455-456, 459, 490; literate, 94, 256; price of in north, 422
Something. See *yu* 有
"Songs, Book of" (*Shih* 詩), 26, 30, 36, 48, 54, 57-58, 65, 66, 67-68, 72, 73, 77, 118-119, 168, 216, 217, 218, 277, 278-279, 290-291, 326, 329, 337, 350, 354, 355, 403, 407, 415, 417, 423, 426, 432, 481, 482, 489-490
Sou-shen chi 搜神記 (text), 409
Southern Mountains (Nan-shan 南山), 338, 425
Southern Range (Nan-ling 南嶺), 288

Southern Tower (Nan-lou 南樓), 313-314
southerners, epithet for: *ho-tzu* 貉子 ("son of a badger"), 487; and "you-your" songs (*erh-ju ko* 爾汝歌), 402
spittoons (*t'o-hu* 唾壺), 302, 423
spontaneity. See *tzu-jan*
"Spring and Autumn Annals" (*Ch'un-ch'iu* 春秋), 29, 65, 93, 229, 281, 287
spring purification rites (*hsi* 禊; *chieh-hsi* 禊), 42, 160, 321-322, 414-415
Square Lake (Fang-hu 方湖), 288
Square Mountain (Fang-shan 方山), 174, 284
Ssu 泗 (river), 180, 433, 447
Ssu-chiu fu 思舊賦 (poetic essay), 439
Ssu-ma 司馬 (historian), 245
Ssu-ma Chao 司馬昭 (Wen, Prince of Chin 晉文王), 9, 11, 83, 150, 154, 333, 345, 346, 365, 373, 393, 462
Ssu-ma Ch'eng 司馬承 (Prince Min, 愍王), 209
Ssu-ma Chi-chu 司馬季主 (diviner of Ch'u), 139
Ssu-ma Ch'ien 司馬遷 (Grand Historian), 62, 411
Ssu-ma Ch'ien* 司馬虔, 13
Ssu-ma Chih 司馬熾 (Huai, Emperor of Chin, 晉懷帝), 48
Ssu-ma Chou 司馬伷, 152, 154
Ssu-ma Chung 司馬衷 (Hui, Emperor of Chin, 晉惠帝), 154, 156, 199, 222, 348, 394, 486
Ssu-ma Ch'ung 司馬冲, 165
Ssu-ma Hsiang-ju 司馬相如 (poet), 77, 136, 366
Ssu-ma I 司馬懿 (Hsüan, Prince of Chin, 晉宣王), 53, 83, 290, 401, 461
Ssu-ma I* 司馬乂 (Prince of Ch'ang-sha, 長沙王), 471
Ssu-ma I** 司馬奕 (Hai-hsi, Duke of, 海西公; Deposed Emperor of Chin, 晉廢帝), 54, 76-77
Ssu-ma Jui 司馬睿 (Yüan, Emperor of Chin, 晉元帝; Chung-tsung 中宗), 46, 47-48, 50, 87, 165, 190, 424, 435

Ssu-ma Lun 司馬倫 (Chao, Prince of, 趙王), 13, 350, 490
Ssu-ma Piao 司馬彪 (commentator), 100, 388
Ssu-ma Shao 司馬紹 (Ming, Emperor of Chin, 晉明帝), 87, 169, 233, 285, 313, 429, 445
Ssu-ma Shih 司馬師 (Ching, Prince of Chin, 晉景王; Generalissimo), 83, 95, 150, 393, 414, 462
Ssu-ma Tao-tzu 司馬道子 (K'uai-chi, Prince of, 會稽王; chancellor-prince, grand tutor), 20, 73, 175, 208, 246, 287, 289-290
Ssu-ma Wei 司馬瑋 (Ch'u, Prince of, 楚王), 182
Ssu-ma Yao 司馬曜 (Hsiao-wu, Emperor of Chin, 晉孝武帝), 77, 175, 176, 239, 246, 289-290, 389, 469, 494
Ssu-ma Yen 司馬炎 (Wu, Emperor of Chin, 晉武帝), 15, 56, 84-85, 182, 213, 358, 360, 377, 477
Ssu-ma Yen* 司馬衍 (Ch'eng, Emperor of Chin, 晉成帝), 50, 53, 87, 170, 226, 313, 445
Ssu-ma Yen** 司馬晏 (Wu, Prince of, 吳王), 265
Ssu-ma Ying 司馬穎 (Ch'eng-tu, Prince of, 成都王), 242, 471
Ssu-ma Yu 司馬攸 (Ch'i, Prince of, 齊王), 153, 155, 156, 348
Ssu-ma Yü 司馬昱 (Chien-wen, Emperor of Chin, 晉簡文帝; General Controlling the Army; Prince of K'uai-chi; chancellor-prince), 57, 76-77, 90, 235, 259, 262, 336
Ssu-ma Yüeh 司馬越 (Tung-hai, Prince of, 東海王), 200
Ssu-ma Yüeh* 司馬岳 (K'ang, Emperor of Chin, 晉康帝), 410
Ssu-ma Yün 司馬允 (Huai-nan, Prince of, 淮南王), 490
Ssu-pen lun 四本論 ("Treatise on the Four Basic Relations between Natural Ability and Human Nature"), 94, 110, 123
stimulus-response (*kan* 感), 123
Stone Gate (Shih-men 石門): in Kwangtung, 24; on Mt. Lu, 288
Stone Well (Shih-ching 石井), 288

stupa, 51
Su Ch'in 蘇秦, 422
Su Chün 蘇峻, 86, 167, 168-169, 229, 325
Su Lin 蘇林 (commentator), 411
Su-men 蘇門 (mountains), 331-332
Su Shao 蘇紹 (Wu, Duke of Shih-p'ing, 始平武公), 265
Su-shen 肅慎 (ancient people), 426-427
Su Shih 蘇碩, 169
Subtle Existence (miao-yu 妙有), 447. See also yu 有
sudden enlightenment, 111
Śuddhodana (father of Buddha), 104
sugarcane (kan-che 甘蔗), 423
Sui 隨 (principality), 51
Sui 隨, Pearl of, 41-42
Sui Chi 隨季, 184
Sui-ch'u fu 遂初賦 (poetic essay), 69, 435
Sun Ch'eng 孫承, 472
Sun Ch'ien 孫潛, 414
Sun Ch'o 孫綽, 137, 419
Sun Ch'üan 孫權 (founder, Wu Kingdom), 27, 77, 250, 306, 429, 454
Sun En 孫恩, 64, 145
Sun Sheng 孫盛, 27-28, 154, 157, 205, 268, 371
Sun Shu-ao 孫叔敖, 16-17
Sun Teng 孫登 (recluse), 139, 332-333
Sun Teng* 孫登 (son of Sun Ch'üan), 302
Sun Ts'e 孫策, 315
Sun T'ung 孫統, 322
Sun Tzu 孫資, 156
Sun-tzu 孫子 (Ping-fa 兵法; military text), 199
Sun Wu 孫武 (author of Sun-tzu), 198-199
Sung 嵩 (mountain), 25
Sung 松 (river). See Three Rivers of Wu
Sung-shu 宋書, "Monograph on Music" (Yüeh-chih 樂志), 302
"Sutra in Forty-two Sections." See under Buddhist scriptures
Swelling Sea. See Chang-hai

ta 達. See "free"
Ta-cha 大蜡 (Great Year-end Sacrifice), 7
Ta chih-tu lun. See under Buddhist scriptures
Ta Ch'in 大秦 (Roman Orient), 462
Ta-hsia 大夏 (Bactria?), 39
Ta-hsia Gate (大夏門), 156
Ta-hsien hsü I 大賢須易 ("Great Worthies Need the 'Changes'"; text), 132
Ta-jen fu 大人賦 (poetic essay), 391
Ta-jen hsien-sheng lun 大人先生論 (essay), 332, 391
Ta-liang 大梁 (ancient capital), 307
Ta pi-ch'iu san-ch'ien wei-i ching. See under Buddhist scriptures
Ta ssu-yüeh 大司樂 (section of Chou-li), 319
Ta Tai Li-chi 大戴禮記 (text), 320, 480
Ta-tao ch'ü 大道曲 (song), 316
Tai, Prince of Chou (周王子帶), 49
Tai Ao 戴奧, 98
Tai K'uei 戴逵, 129, 371, 456
Tai Liang 戴良, 4
Tai Yang 戴洋 (practitioner), 325, 429
Tai Yüan 戴淵, 473-474
T'ai, Lake (太湖), 201, 306
T'ai, Mt. (泰山), 6, 66, 229, 326, 457
T'ai-an 太安 (era), 191
T'ai-chi Palace. See Grand Ultimate, Hall of
T'ai-chia 太甲 (ancient ruler), 77
T'ai-ch'iu 太丘 (prefecture), 81-82
T'ai-ho 太和 (era), 96, 327
T'ai-hsing 太興 (era), 378
T'ai-hsüan ching 太玄經 (text), 134
T'ai-kung Wang 太公望, 180
T'ai-p'ing yin 太平引 (song), 181
T'ai-shih 太始 (era), 373, 403
T'ai-tsung, Emperor of T'ang (唐太宗), 368
T'ai-wei 太微 (celestial enclosure), 59-60
T'ai-yüan 太原 (commandery), 43, 106, 234, 256, 261, 402, 417, 452, 472

T'ai-yüan 太元 (era), 176-177, 194, 328, 469
Tan-chi 妲己 (concubine of Chou Hsin), 485
tan-ch'i 彈棋 (game), 363-364, 408
Tan Chu 丹朱 (son of Yao, 367, 400
Tan-t'u 丹徒, 57
Tan-yang 丹陽 (commandery), 17, 23, 63, 77, 90, 205, 235, 285, 313, 391, 429
T'an-shui 貪水 (Avarice Spring), 23-24
Tang-yin 蕩陰 (commandery), 22, 154
T'ang 湯 (founder, Shang Dynasty), 77, 333, 367, 436
T'ang Yao. See Yao
Tao. See Way, the
Tao-an. See Shih Tao-an
Tao-hsing po-jo ching. See *Prajñāpāramitā-sūtras*
Tao-piao 道標 (monk), 125
Tao-te ching 道德經, 124. See also *Lao-tzu*
Tao-te lun 道德論 (essay), 96, 97
T'ao-chi. See *Fu T'ao chi*
T'ao Ch'ien 陶潛, 204
T'ao Hung-ching 陶弘景, 391
T'ao K'an 陶侃, 169, 225
T'ao-lin 桃林, 198-199
T'ao Tan 陶丹, 351
T'ao T'ieh. See Four Ill-omened Ones
T'ao Wu. See Four Ill-omened Ones
Taoism: Celestial (Heavenly) Master sect (*t'ien-shih tao*), 361, 420; Celestial Ruler (T'ien-ti), 19; Conducting the Vital Force (*tao-ch'i*), 331; confession (*shou-kuo*), 19; devotion of Ch'ih family, 361, 420; devotion of Wang Ning-chih, 64; elixirs of immortality, 66; "Five-Pecks-of-Rice" sect (*wu-tou-mi tao*), 64; immortality cult (Hsien Taoism), 20; Kingdom of Shu-Han (Ch'eng-Han), 206; magicians, (*fang-shih*), 66; Mao-shan sect, 391; masters (*shih*; *tao-shih*), 328-329, 332; Mystical Quiescence (*hsüan-chi*), 331, 334; "non-action" (*wu-wei*), 40, 332; paper charms (*fu*), 361; petitions (*shang-chang*), 19; practitioners (*shu-shih*), 325; Realized Men (*chen-jen*), 316, 331; Resting the Spirit (*ch'i-shen*), 331; Sun En's Rebellion, 64, 145; Taoist poetry, 137; Taoist techniques (*tao-shu*), 288, 335, 360; transcendent beings (*hsien*), 66, 70, 288, 391

tea, 481
Teng, Marquis of (鄧侯), 342
Teng Ai 鄧艾, 3, 365
Teng Sui 鄧綏, 15-16
Teng Yang 鄧颺, 11, 219
Teng Yu 鄧攸, 222
Teng Yü 鄧禹, 65, 404
Terrace of Blue-green Distance. See Blue-green Distance, Terrace of
third day (of third month). See spring purification rites
Thousand-*li* Lake (Ch'ien-li 千里), 44
"Three-day Vice-president" (Chou I), 380-381
"Three Gentlemen" (*san-chün* 三君): Ch'en Fan 陳蕃, Liu Shu 劉淑, and Tou Wu 竇武, 248
Three Gorges. See Yangtze Gorges
"Three Incomparables" (*san-chüeh* 三絕): Huan I* 桓伊, Yang T'an 羊曇, and Yüan Shan-sung 袁山松, 387
Three Insights (*san-ming* 三明), 119-120
Three Isles of the Transcendents (*san-shan* 三山): Fang-chang 方丈, P'eng-lai 蓬萊, and Ying-chou 瀛洲, 65-66
Three Rivers of Wu (吳三江): Lou 婁, Sung 松, and Tung 東, 201, 306
"Three Scourges" (*san-heng* 三橫), 318-319
Three Treasures. See under Buddhism
Three Vehicles. See under Buddhism
Three-victim sacrifice, 325
"Three-word Aide" (Juan Hsiu), 101

"Throw-letters Island" (T'ou-shu chu 投書渚), 382
Thunder Lake (Lei-ch'ih 雷池), 352
Ti 氐 ("proto-Tibetans"), 90, 192, 207, 262
Ti 狄 ("northern barbarians"), 73, 168, 304, 410; Red Ti (赤狄), 168
Ti-ch'üan 秋泉, 222
Ti-wu I 第五猗, 51-52
Ti-wu Lun 第五倫, 334
Ti-wu Yüan-hsien 第五元先, 93
T'ien Ch'ang. See Ch'en Heng
T'ien-chu 天竺 (northern India), 104
T'ien Heng 田橫, 387-388
T'ien Kuang 田光, 65
t'ien-shih tao. See Taoism
T'ien-t'ai shan fu 天台山賦 (poetic essay), 137, 416
T'ien-ti. See Taoism
Ting, King of Chou (周定王), 416
Ting Mi 丁謐, 278
Tonkin, Gulf of, 462
Tou Wu. See "Three Gentlemen"
T'ou-shu chu. See "Throw-letters Island"
T'ou tse Tzu-yü wen 頭責子羽文 (text), 403
transcendent beings (*hsien*). See under Taoism
Truth (*li* 理), 242, 256, 266; convergence with (*li-hui*), 224; entrance into, 223; flavor of, 337; heart of (*li-chung*), 113, 242; in Buddhist sutras, 104; intuitively identified with, 136; source of (*li-yüan*), 103; storage cave of (*li-k'u*), 119; understanding of, 227, 237, 262. See also Ultimate Principle
Tsai Wo 宰我 (disciple of Confucius), 276
ts'ai-hsing 才性. See Natural Ability and Human Nature
Ts'ai Mo 蔡謨 (Tao-ming 道明), 202, 228
Ts'ai Yung 蔡邕, 4, 37, 293-294, 430, 480
Ts'ang Chieh 蒼頡 (inventor of writing), 366
ts'ang-fu. See northerners

Ts'ao, Lady (曹夫人; wife of Wang Tao), 226, 228, 430-431
Ts'ao Chiu 曹咎, 149
Ts'ao Fang 曹芳 (Wei ruler), 12, 151, 477
Ts'ao Hsü 曹盱 (var., Hsi 胯), 293
Ts'ao Huan 曹奐 (last ruler of Wei), 127, 477
Ts'ao Hung 曹洪, 485
Ts'ao Jui 曹叡 (Ming, Emperor of Wei, 魏明帝), 156, 309
Ts'ao Mao 曹髦 (Kao-kuei hsiang-kung 高貴鄉公), 346, 477
Ts'ao O pei 曹娥碑 (stele), 293
Ts'ao P'ei 曹丕 (Wen, Emperor of Wei, 魏文帝), 35, 148, 298, 363, 436
Ts'ao Piao 曹彪, 148
Ts'ao Shu 曹據, 452
Ts'ao Shuang 曹爽, 11, 83, 95, 280, 290, 474
Ts'ao Ts'ao 曹操 (Wu, "Emperor" of Wei, 魏武帝), 286, 364
Tseng hsiu-ts'ai ju-chün 贈秀才入軍 (poem), 368
Tseng Ts'an 曾參 (Tseng-tzu 曾子; disciple of Confucius), 35-36, 179-180, 477
Tso-chuan 左傳 ("Tso Commentary"), 5, 22, 30, 40, 42, 45, 46, 49, 62, 63, 67, 73, 83, 93-94, 98, 117, 161, 163, 167-168, 176, 183, 184, 200, 222, 226, 247, 248, 254, 281, 295, 302, 304, 342, 347, 351, 360, 388, 409, 416, 417, 426, 436, 437, 469
Tso Ssu 左思, 42, 118, 389
Tso-t'ang 作唐 (prefecture), 209
Tsou Yang 鄒陽, 271
Tsu-i 祖乙 (Shang ruler), 44
Tsu Yüeh 祖約, 313
Ts'ui Chuan 崔譔, 100
Ts'ui Shao-fu 崔少府, 159-161
Ts'ui Shu 崔杼, 44, 168
Ts'ui Sui 崔隨, 261
Ts'ung-cheng shih 從征詩 (poem), 60
Tu I 杜乂, 303
Tu K'uei 杜夔, 358
Tu Mi. See "Eight Heroes"
Tu Shang 度尚, 293
Tu T'ao 杜弢, 225

Tu Yü 杜預 (commentator), 67, 94, 359, 388
T'u-shan 塗山, 48
Tuan-ch'ang shu. See Chan-kuo ts'e
Tuan-mu Tz'u. See Tzu-kung
Tun-huang 敦煌 (commandery), 56, 409
Tung 東 (commandery), 93, 276
Tung 東 (river). See Three Rivers of Wu
Tung-an 東安 (prefecture; = Tung Yeh*), 429
Tung-an Temple (東安寺), 114
Tung An-yü 董安于, 173
Tung-cheng fu 東征賦 (poetic essay), 141
Tung-ching fu 東京賦 (poetic essay), 128
Tung Cho 董卓, 8
Tung Chung-shu 董仲舒, 28
Tung Chung-ta 董仲達, 10
Tung-fang Shih-an 東方世安, 364
Tung-fang Shuo 東方朔, 65, 123
Tung Fu-ch'i 董待起, 28
Tung-hai 東海 (commandery), 85, 229
Tung-hsia 東夏 (= K'uai-chi 會稽), 452
Tung Hu 董狐, 167, 409
Tung-o 東阿 (principality), 126
Tung-p'ing 東平 (commandery), 180, 429
Tung-shan Prefecture. See Eastern Mountains
Tung-t'ing 洞庭 (lake), 288
Tung-yang 東陽 (commandery), 70, 90, 117, 123, 173, 189, 285, 340, 448, 451, 453-454
Tung-yeh 東野 (ancient state), 288
Tung-yeh* 東冶 (prefecture; = Tung-an), 429
t'ung 通. See "unimpeded"
T'ung-ch'üeh t'ai. See Bronze Sparrow Terrace
T'ung River (通川), 288
Turkestan, 6
Tzu-ch'an 子產, 62
Tzu-chang 子張 (Chuan-sun Shih 顓孫師; disciple of Confucius), 263
Tzu-ch'u 子楚. See Chuang-hsiang, King of Ch'in

Tzu-chung 子終. See Ch'en Chung-tzu
Tzu-hsia 子夏 (disciple of Confucius), 179-180
tzu-jan 自然: natural, the, 205; Nature, 116; Self-so, the, 133; spontaneity, 309-310, 466
Tzu-kao 子高. See Po-ch'eng
Tzu-kung 子貢 (Tuan-mu Tz'u 端木賜; disciple of Confucius), 33, 78, 96, 263, 463-464
Tzu-lu 子路 (Chung Yu 仲由; disciple of Confucius), 168-169, 260, 329
Tzu-shang 子上, 200
Tzu-ssu. See Yüan Hsien
Tzu-ts'ai 梓材 (section of Shang-shu ta-chuan), 425
Tzu-tsang 子臧, 404
Tzu-wen 子文, 65
Tzu-yüan. See Yen Hui

Ultimate Principle (chih-li 至理), 99
"unimpeded" (t'ung 通), 12-13, 235, 371-391 passim. See also "free"; "untrammeled"
"untrammeled" (k'uang 曠), 88, 100, 371-391 passim, 404. See also "free"; "unimpeded"

Vajrabodhi (translator), 415-416
Vajraśekhara-yoga-tantra. See under Buddhist scriptures
Vermilion Sparrow Bridge. See Great Pontoon Bridge
Vimalakīrti, 56, 111
Vimalakīrti-nirdeśa. See under Buddhist scriptures
Virūḍhaka, King, 476
Virūḍhakarāja-sūtra. See under Buddhist scriptures
vision, theories of, 116-117

Wa-kuan Temple (瓦官寺), 108, 123, 205, 238, 260, 410
"Walking the Buddha Image," 366-367
Wan-ling 宛陵 (prefecture), 262
Wang, Dowager Empress (王太后; consort of Yüan, Emperor of Han), 342
Wang, Empress (王后; consort of An, Emperor of Chin), 453

Wang Ch'ang 王昶 (d. 259), 9
Wang Ch'ang*. See "Eight Heroes"
Wang Ch'en 王忱 (d. 392), 423
Wang Ch'en* 王沈 (third cent.), 151-152, 346
Wang Ch'eng 王澄 (P'ing-tzu 平子), 63, 254
Wang Ch'eng* 王承 (An-ch'i 安期), 17, 140, 234, 262
Wang Chi 王濟, 42
Wang Ch'iao 王喬, 103
Wang Ch'ien-ch'i 王愆期, 445
Wang Ching 王經, 151-152
Wang Chung-lang 王中郎 (Commander Wang), 75
Wang Ch'ung 王充, 162
Wang Ch'üan 王奎, 396
Wang Han 王含, 285
Wang Hsi 王熙, 113
Wang Hsi-chih 王羲之, 114, 260, 426, 440
Wang Hsiang 王祥, 392
Wang Hsien-chih 王獻之, 440
Wang Hsü 王詡, 264, 446
Wang Hsüan-chih 王玄之, 245
Wang Hsün 王珣 (Fa-hu 法護), 238, 245, 327, 390
Wang Hui-chih 王徽之, 19
Wang Hun 王渾 (father of Wang Chi), 488
Wang Hun* 王渾 (father of Wang Jung), 392-393
Wang Hun** 王混 (son of Wang T'ien), 71
Wang I* 王廙, 51, 170, 209, 473
Wang I-fu hua-tsan 王夷甫畫讚 (poem), 223
Wang Jang 王穰, 341
Wang Jung 王戎, 101, 140, 155, 200, 221, 251, 268
Wang Jung* 王融, 8
Wang K'ai 王愷, 175, 458
Wang K'an* 王侃, 473
Wang Kuang 王廣, 95
Wang Kung 王恭, 20, 26, 290, 391, 469
Wang Kung-chung 王公仲, 10
Wang Kuo-pao 王國寶, 76, 175, 177, 208, 329, 391, 423
Wang Ling* 王陵, 494
Wang Mang 王莽, 175, 342
Wang Min 王珉, 238, 244, 328
Wang-ming lun 王命論 (essay), 47
Wang Na 王訥, 315

Wang Ning-chih 王凝之, 245, 412, 440
Wang Pao 王裒, 136
Wang Pi 王弼, 11, 40, 55, 103, 106, 113, 122, 137, 140, 226, 235, 237, 245, 278
Wang Piao-chih 王彪之, 76, 172, 176
Wang Pin 王彬, 473
wang-pu-liu-hsing (herb), 456-457
Wang-shih p'u 王氏譜 (genealogy), 63
Wang Shu 王述 (Huai-tsu 懷祖), 420
Wang Shu* 王舒 (Ch'u-ming 處明), 75, 418
Wang Shuo 王朔, 123
Wang Ssu 王思, 243
Wang Su 王肅, 255
Wang Su-chih 王肅之, 440
Wang Sui* 王綏 (d. 404), 175
Wang Sui** 王璲 (brother of Wang Shu*), 473
Wang-sun Man 王孫滿, 416-417
Wang T'an-chih 王坦之, 75
Wang Tao 王導 (chancellor, 丞相), 50, 64, 190, 204, 206, 208, 262, 286, 313, 316, 445, 492
Wang T'ien 王恬, 171, 206
Wang Ts'ao-chih 王操之, 440
Wang Tsun 王尊 (loyal minister), 58
Wang Tsun* 王尊 (erudite), 104
Wang Tun 王敦 (generalissimo), 50, 101, 164, 170, 209, 225, 229, 254, 285, 395, 429
Wang Yang 王陽 (first cent. B.C.), 58
Wang Yeh 王業, 151-152
Wang Yen 王衍 (grand marshal), 140, 223, 324
Wang Yen-shou 王延壽 (poet), 377
Wang Yin 王隱, 134, 157
Wang Ying 王應 (An-ch'i 安期), 229
Wang Yü 王愉, 175
Wang Yüeh 王悅 (son of Wang Tao), 208
Wang Yüeh* 王越 (fortune teller), 342
Wang Yün 王蘊, 242
Wang Yün-chih 王允之, 444
water-lily soup (ch'un-keng 蓴羹), 44

INDEX   723

Way, the (Tao 道), 257, 265, 405, 476, 478; guffawing at, 426; in agreement with, 274; Hsi K'ang's ability did injury to, 257; Ho Ch'ung pays court to, 420; non-verbal communication of, 332; possessing, 276; Wang Tao's discussion of, 321; Yü Ai's resemblance to, 265
Wei 魏 (family of Shan-yin), 381
Wei 渭 (river), 149
Wei, Duke of Chou (周威公), 85
Wei, Viscount of (微子), 260
wei-ch'i. See games, encirclement chess
Wei Chieh 衛玠, 140, 314
Wei Ch'üan 衛權, 128
Wei Hsiao 魏囂, 47
Wei I 魏人, 492
Wei Kuan 衛瓘, 365
Wei Lang. See "Eight Heroes"
Wei-mo-chieh ching. See under Buddhist scriptures
Wei-shih ch'un-ch'iu 魏氏春秋 (text), 411
Wei-t'ien-jen 為天人 (Huan Hsüan), 390
Wei Ts'ao 衛璪, 46
Wei Yang 衛鞅 (Shang, Lord of, 商君), 64
Wei-yang 渭陽 (district), 35-36
Wei-yang 未央 (palace), 61, 123
Wei Ying. See Liang, King of
Wen 溫 (prefecture), 157, 255
Wen, Duke of Chin (晉文公), 36, 47-48, 286, 477
Wen, Emperor of Han (漢文帝), 155, 194, 290, 445
Wen, Emperor of Wei. See Ts'ao P'ei
Wen, King of Chou (周文王), 29, 41, 63-64, 85, 127, 153, 180, 263, 280, 290-291, 476
Wen Ch'iao 溫嶠, 77, 166, 214, 314
Wen-hui, Prince (文惠君), 421
Wen-yen chuan 文言傳 (section of "Book of Changes"), 435
Wen Ying 文穎 (commentator), 194
"West Garden." See West Moat
West Moat, Crown Prince's (T'ai-tzu hsi ch'ih 太子西池; = "West Garden," 西苑), 302
"Western barbarians." See Jung, Western

Western Hills (Hsi-shan 西山), 397
Western Temple (Hsi-ssu 西寺), 112
whistling (hsiao 嘯), 50, 144, 189; Hsieh I**, 395; Hsieh K'un, 235; Hsieh Wan, 397; Juan Chi, 331-332, 392; Liu Pao, 377; Wang Hui-chih, 388, 398; Wang I*, 492
White Horse Temple (Pai-ma ssu 白馬寺; in Chien-k'ang), 109
White Rock Mountain (Pai-shih shan 白石山), 68, 237
White Stone Shrine (Pai-shih tz'u 白石祠), 325
White Tower Pavilion (Pai-lou t'ing 白樓亭), 239
wine, 371-399 passim; Chang Han's "one cup right now," 378; Chou I's three-day sobriety, 380-381; Juan Chi and barmaid, 374; Juan Chi becomes commandant of infantry, 373; Juan family drinks with pigs, 375-376; Juan Hsiu drinks alone, 377; K'ung Ch'ün marinates his insides, 379; Liu Ch'ang drinks with everybody, 373; Liu Ling's "Hymn to Wine," 128-130; Liu Ling swears off, 372-373; Pi Cho swimming in a pool of, 378; Pi Cho stealing from neighbor's vat, 378; Shan Chien at Kao-yang Pool, 377-378; Wang Ch'en's three days without, 391
wool rugs, 385
wu 無. See Non-actuality; Non-being; Nothing
Wu 吳 (commandery), 22, 72, 82, 91, 169, 201, 229, 253, 285, 317, 318, 339, 379, 396, 398, 448, 472
Wu 巫 (gorge). See Yangtze Gorges
Wu 烏 (mountain), 327
Wu, Duke of Shih-p'ing. See Su Shao
Wu, Emperor of Chin. See Ssu-ma Yen
Wu, Emperor of Han (漢武帝), 56, 65-66, 77, 105, 123, 288, 411, 418-419, 487
Wu, "Emperor" of Wei. See Ts'ao Ts'ao

724 TALES OF THE WORLD

Wu, King of Chou (周武王), 29, 41, 45, 153, 198-199, 333, 426, 476, 485
Wu, Lord. See Wu Tzu-hsü
Wu, speech of (吳聲), 78, 408
Wu-an 武安, 38
Wu-an, Lord of. See Po Ch'i
Wu-ch'ang 武昌 (commandery), 20, 49, 54, 58, 70, 88, 102, 171, 184, 188, 204, 225, 236, 283, 313, 316, 325-326, 336, 352, 384, 410, 412, 429, 432, 491
Wu-ch'eng 烏程 (prefecture), 174
Wu Ch'i 吳起 (author of Wu-tzu 吳子, military text), 198-199
Wu Chih 吳質, 364
Wu Chou 武周, 219
Wu-chung 吳中. See Wu (commandery)
Wu Fen 吳奮, 157-158
Wu Hsien 巫咸, 404
Wu-hsing 吳興 (commandery), 14, 68, 77, 90, 169, 186, 193, 285, 313, 319, 391. See also I-hsing
Wu-i. See Black Clothing Street
Wu Ju 吳儒, 285
Wu Jui 吳芮, 288
Wu-kuan 武關 (pass), 8
Wu Kuang 務光, 404, 405
Wu-ling 於陵, 69, 304
Wu-shih 吳史 (text), 302
wu-shih san. See five-mineral powder
Wu-ting 武丁 (Shang ruler), 28, 31
wu-tou-mi tao. See under Taoism
Wu-tzu 吳子 (text), 199
Wu Tzu-hsü 伍子胥 (Lord Wu, 伍君神), 293, 405
Wu-yen 無鹽, 428

Yang, Empress (羊皇后; consort of Ssu-ma Shih), 343
Yang-ch'eng 陽城, 25, 38
Yang Chi 羊綸, 213
Yang-ch'i 陽岐 (mountains), 335-336
Yang-ch'i Village (陽岐村), 384
Yang Ch'iao 楊喬, 228
Yang Chih 羊祉, 62
Yang Cho 羊晫, 351-352
Yang Chun 楊準, 228
Yang Ch'üan 羊權, 366
Yang Ch'üan-ch'i 楊佺期, 20, 144

Yang Chün 楊駿 (d. 291), 182
Yang Chün* 楊俊 (early fourth cent.), 228
Yang Fu 羊孚 (Tzu-tao 子道), 366
Yang Fu* 羊輔 (Yu-jen 幼仁), 366
Yang Hsin 羊欣, 366
Yang-hsin 陽新 (prefecture), 336
Yang Hsiu 羊琇, 462
Yang Hsiung 揚雄 (poet), 49, 134, 136
Yang K'ai 羊楷, 366
Yang Liang 羊亮, 213
Yang Lin 楊琳 (d. 291), 228
Yang Lin* 羊廞 (late fourth cent.), 244
Yang Mao 楊髦, 228
Yang Mountain (岬山), 66, 412-413
Yang Ping 羊秉, 213
Yang-she Hsi 羊舌肸 (Shu-hsiang 叔向), 225
Yang Shen 楊紳, 228
Yang-sheng lun 養生論 (essay), 102
Yang Shih 羊式, 213
Yang Sui 羊綏, 366
Yang Tao, Empress (楊悼后; second consort of Wu, Emperor of Chin), 222
Yang-tu fu 楊都賦 (poetic essay), 133-134
Yang Yu 羊鱻, 62
Yangtze Gorges (san-hsia 三峽): Chü-t'ang 瞿塘, Wu 巫, and Hsi-ling 西陵, 58, 206, 450
Yao 堯 (T'ang Yao 唐堯), 25, 29, 32, 40, 63, 88, 148, 165, 228, 367, 388, 400, 401, 402, 411
Yao 崤 (mountains), 118
Yao-cheng 謠徵 (section of LKC), 169, 313, 325, 467
Yao Hsiang 姚襄, 451
Yao-tien 堯典 (section of "Book of Documents"), 172
Yeh 鄴 (prefecture), 37, 70, 82, 126, 484
Yeh* 冶 (prefecture), 429-430
Yeh-ch'eng 冶城 (fortification), 63, 429-430
Yeh-wang 野王 (prefecture), 212
Yellow Emperor (Huang-ti 黃帝), 39, 331
Yellow Turbans (Huang-chin 黃巾), 65, 89, 211, 250, 293
Yen 顏 (family of Lang-yeh), 471

INDEX 725

Yen chin-i lun 言盡意論 (essay), 102
Yen Hui 顏回 (Tzu-yüan 子淵; disciple of Confucius), 4, 53, 95, 213, 263
Yen-ling 延陵, 179
yen-shih. See salted legumes
Yen Ting 閻鼎, 228
Yen Tsun 嚴尊 (alias Chuang Tsun 莊尊), 334
Yen-yang 鄢陽, 288
Yen Yen-chih 顏延之, 74
Yen Ying 晏嬰, 52, 65
Yin 鄞 (prefecture), 384
Yin 印 (error for Yang 岬). See Yang Mountain
Yin, Empress (陰后; Yin Li-hua 陰麗華, consort of Kuang-wu, Emperor of Han), 270
Yin, Lady (殷夫人; mother of Han Po), 299
Yin*, Lady (尹夫人; mother of Ho Yen), 298
Yin Chi-fu 尹吉甫, 28
Yin Chiu 陰就 (Hsin-yang, Marquis of, 新陽侯), 270
Yin Chung-k'an 殷仲堪, 70, 76, 144, 208, 290
Yin Hao 殷浩, 303
Yin Hsien 殷羨, 19
Yin Islet (印渚), 68
Yin K'ang 殷康, 439
Yin Po-ch'i 尹伯奇, 28
Yin Po-kuei 尹伯郜, 29
Yin Tao-hu 殷道護, 21
Ying 郢 (ancient capital), 106, 326
Ying 潁 (river), 25
Ying-chou. See Three Isles of the Transcendents
Ying-ch'uan 潁川 (commandery), 3, 5, 28, 29, 31, 45, 210, 248, 402
Ying-huo. See Mars
Ying-yang 滎陽, 200
"you-your" songs (*erh-ju ko* 爾汝歌), 402
yu 有: Actuality (evolved from *wu*), 96-97; Being, Existence (*bhava*; correlative with *wu*), 118; Something (opposite of *wu*), 116. See also Subtle Existence
Yu, King of Chou (周幽王), 275

Yu-ch'üan 由拳 (prefecture), 472
Yu-fen shih 幽憤詩 (poem), 333
Yu-i 由儀 (song), 130
Yu-keng 由庚 (song), 130
Yu-li 羑里, 263
Yu T'ien-t'ai-shan fu. See *T'ien-t'ai-shan fu*
Yung-chia 永嘉 (era), 13, 15, 46, 222, 226, 228, 312, 324, 335, 360, 379, 472
Yung-ch'iu 雍丘 (principality), 126
Yung-ho 永和 (era), 260, 314, 321
Yung-hsing 永興 (commandery), 337
Yung-huai shih 詠懷詩 (poems), 307
Yung-nien Village (永年里), 348
Yung-shih shih 詠史詩 (poems), 138
Yü 瑜 (gem), 320
Yü 禹 (founder of Hsia Dynasty), 33, 41, 42, 45, 63-64, 88, 148, 288, 400, 417, 436; "Yü's walk" (*Yü-pu* 禹步), 64
Yü 庾 (family), 57, 229, 313
Yü Ai 庾敳, 140
Yü Ch'an 庾闡, 59
Yü-chang 豫章 (commandery), 3, 19, 20, 21, 46, 74, 77, 166, 169, 170, 179, 225, 226, 282-283, 312, 337-338, 351, 356, 366, 382
Yü-chia lun 庾家論 (essay), 229
Yü Ch'ien 庾倩, 189, 353
Yü Fang-chih 庾方之, 410
Yü Ho 庾龢, 439
Yü Hsi* 庾羲, 206
Yü Huan 魚豢 (author of *WeiL*), 105
Yü I 庾翼 (Chih-kung 稚恭), 205, 317, 381
Yü I* 庾懌, 56, 317
Yü Jang 豫讓, 155
Yü Jou 庾柔, 189
Yü-kung lei 庾公誄 (obituary), 134, 173
Yü Liang 庾亮, 90, 225, 228-229, 286, 317, 323, 492
Yü-lin 語林 (text), 138, 437-438
Yü Mo 庾邈, 189
Yü-pin 虞殯 (song), 388
Yü Ping 庾冰, 90, 189, 317, 410, 429
Yü-shan fu 羽扇賦 (poetic essay), 56

Yü Shun. *See* Shun
Yü T'iao 庾絛, 317
Yü Tsung 庾琮, 229
Yü tz'u-shih Chou Chün shu 與刺史周俊書 (letter), 218
Yü-yang Drum-roll (*Yü-yang ts'an-chua* 漁陽參撾), 30-31
Yü-yao 餘姚 (prefecture), 327
Yü Yu 庾友, 189
Yü Yuan-chih 庾爰之, 323
Yü Yün 庾蘊, 189
Yüan, Emperor of Chin. *See* Ssu-ma Jui
Yüan, Emperor of Han (漢元帝), 175
Yüan, Empress (元皇后; = Wang, Dowager Empress), 342
Yüan, Mme. (= Liu*, Lady; wife of Yüan Shao), 484
Yüan Chen 袁真, 59, 295
yüan-chih (medicine), 413-414
Yüan-feng 元封 (era), 288
Yüan Hsien 原憲 (Tzu-ssu 子思; disciple of Confucius), 31-33, 158, 463-464
Yüan Huan 袁渙, 237

Yüan Hung 袁宏, 5, 76, 371
Yüan K'ang 苑康, 6
Yüan-k'ang 元康 (era), 222, 264, 376
Yüan Lang 袁閬, 4
Yüan Shang 袁尚, 484
Yüan Shao 袁紹, 484
Yüan-shou 元壽 (era), 104
Yüan Yang 袁羊 (Ch'iao 喬), 71
Yüeh, Lady (樂氏; wife of Yang Yu), 62
Yüeh Chao 樂肇, 43
Yüeh-chih, Greater (大月氏; = Kushāna), 104
Yüeh I 樂毅, 428
Yüeh K'ai 樂凱, 43
Yüeh Kuang 樂廣, 46, 97-98, 140, 376
Yüeh-li chih 樂禮志 (section of *Hsin T'ang-shu*), 368
Yüeh Mo 樂謨, 43
Yün, Duke of (鄆公). *See* Chung I
Yün-chien Shih-lung 雲間士龍 (Lu Yün 陸雲), 406
Yün-kang 雲岡 (caves), 51, 56